The Matarese Circle
The Parsifal Mosaic

Robert Ludlum

Published in 1993 by Diamond Books,
an imprint of HarperCollins*Publishers*,
77–85 Fulham Palace Road
Hammersmith, London W6 8JB

This Diamond Books omnibus edition first published 1993
9 8 7 6 5 4 3 2 1

The Matarese Circle © Robert Ludlum 1979
The Parsifal Mosaic © Robert Ludlum 1982

ISBN 1 85813 263 0 (UK)
ISBN Diamond Books 0261 661612 (international edition)

Phototypeset in Ehrhardt by Intype, London

Printed in France by Maury-Eurolivres

The Author asserts the moral right to
be identified as the author of this work

Contents

The Matarese Circle

For Jonathan,
with much love and deep respect

Book I

1

WE THREE KINGS OF ORIENT ARE,
BEARING GIFTS WE TRAVERSE AFAR . . .

The band of carollers huddled at the corner, stamping their feet and swinging their arms, their young voices penetrating the cold night air between the harsh sounds of automobile horns and police whistles and the metallic strains of Christmas music blaring from speakers above garishly lighted store fronts. The snowfall was dense, snarling traffic, causing the hordes of last-minute shoppers to shield their eyes and somehow manage to side-step suddenly lurching automobiles as well as mounds of slush and each other. Tyres spun on the wet streets; buses inched in maddening starts and stops, and the bells of uniformed Santas kept up their incessant if futile clanging.

FIELD AND FOUNTAIN,
MOOR AND MOW-AN-TEN . . .

A dark Cadillac sedan turned the corner and crept past the carollers. The lead singer, dressed in a costume that was somebody's idea of Dickens' Bob Cratchit, approached the right rear window, his gloved hand outstretched, his face contorted in song next to the glass.

FOLLOWING YA-HON-DER STAR . . .

The angry driver blew his horn and waved the begging caroller away, but the middle-aged passenger in the back seat reached into his overcoat pocket and pulled out several bills. He pressed a button; the rear window glided down and the grey-haired man thrust the money into the outstretched hand.

"God bless you, sir!" shouted the caroller. "The Boys Club of East Fiftieth Street thanks you. Merry Christmas, sir!"

The words would have been more effective had there not been a stench of whisky emanating from the mouth that yelled them.

"Merry Christmas," said the passenger, pressing the window button to shut off further communication.

There was a momentary break in the traffic. The Cadillac shot forward only to be forced to an abrupt, sliding stop thirty feet down the street. The driver gripped the steering wheel; it was a gesture that took the place of cursing out loud.

"Take it easy, Major," said the grey-haired passenger, his tone of voice at once sympathetic and commanding. "Getting upset won't solve anything; it won't get us where we're going any faster."

"You're right, General," answered the driver with a respect he did not feel. Normally, the respect was there, but not tonight, not on this particular trip. The general's self-indulgence aside, he had one hell of a nerve requesting his aide to be available for duty on Christmas Eve. For driving a rented, *civilian* car to New York so the general could play games. The major could think of a dozen acceptable reasons for being on duty tonight, but this was not one of them.

A whore house. Stripped of its verbal frills, that's what it was. The Chairman of the Joint Chiefs of Staff was going to a *whore house* on Christmas Eve! And because games were played, the general's most confidential aide had to be there to pick up the mess when the games were over. Pick it up, put it together, nurse it through the next morning at some obscure motel, and make goddamn sure no one found out what the games were or who the mess was. And by noon tomorrow the Chairman would resume his ramrod bearing, issue his orders, and the evening and the mess would be forgotten.

The major had made these trips many times during the past three years – since the day after the general had assumed his awesome position – but the trips always followed periods of intense activity at the Pentagon, or moments of national crisis, when the general had shown his professional mettle. But never on such a night as this. Never on Christmas Eve, for Christ's sake! If the general were anyone else but Anthony Blackburn, the major might have objected on the grounds that even a subordinate officer's family had certain holiday priorities.

But the major would never offer the slightest objection about anything where the general was concerned. "Mad Anthony" Blackburn had carried a broken young lieutenant out of a North Vietnamese prison camp, away from torture and starvation, and brought him through the jungles back to UN lines. That was years ago; the lieutenant was a major now, the senior aide to the Chairman of the Joint Chiefs of Staff.

Military men often spoke bromidically of certain officers they'd follow to hell and back. Well, the major had been to hell and back with Mad Anthony Blackburn and he'd return to hell in a shot with a snap of the general's fingers.

They reached Park Avenue and turned north. The traffic was less snarled than the crosstown route, as befitted the better section of the city. Fifteen more blocks to go; the brownstone was on Seventy-first Street between Park and Lexington.

The senior aide to the Chairman of the Joint Chiefs of Staff would park the Cadillac in a prearranged space in front of the building and watch the general get out of the car and walk up the steps to the bolted entrance door. He would not say anything, but a feeling of sadness would sweep over the major as he waited.

Until a slender woman – dressed in a dark silk gown with a diamond choker at her throat – reopened the door in three and a half or four hours and flicked the front lights. It would be the major's signal to come up and collect his passenger.

*

10

"Hello, Tony." The woman swept across the dimly lit hallway and kissed the general's cheek. "How are you, darling?" she said, fingering her diamond choker as she leaned towards him.

"Tense," replied Blackburn, slipping his arms out of his civilian overcoat, held by a uniformed maid. He looked at the girl; she was new and lovely.

The woman saw his glance. "She's not ready for you, darling," she commented, taking his arm. "Perhaps in a month or two. Come along now, we'll see what we can do about that tension. We've got everything you need. The best hashish from Ankara, absinthe from the finest still in Marseilles, and precisely what the doctor ordered from our own special catalogue. Incidentally, how's your wife?"

"Tense," said the general quietly. "She sends you her best."

"Do give her my love, darling."

They walked through an archway into a large room with soft, multi-coloured lights that came from unseen sources; circles of blue and magenta and amber revolving slowly across the ceiling and the walls. The woman spoke again.

"There's a girl I want to have join you and your regular. Her background is simply tailor-made, darling. I couldn't believe it when I interviewed her; it's incredible. I just got her from Athens. You'll adore her."

Anthony Blackburn lay naked on the king-sized bed, tiny spotlights shooting down from the mirrored ceiling of blue glass. Aromatic layers of hashish smoke were suspended in the still air of the dark room; three glasses of clear absinthe stood on the bedside table. The general's body was covered with streaks and circles of waterpaint, fingermarks everywhere, phallic arrows pointing to his groin, his testicles and erect penis coated in red, his breasts black, matching the matted hair of his chest, the nipples blue and joined by a straight fingerline of flesh-white. He moaned and whipped his head back and forth in sexual oblivion as his companions did their work.

The two naked women alternately massaged and spread the thick globules of paint on the writhing body. As one revolved her breasts about his moaning, moving face the other cupped his genitalia, groaning sensually with each stroke, uttering false, muted screams of climax as the general approached orgasm – halted by the professional who knew her business.

The auburn-haired girl by his face kept whispering breathless, incomprehensible phrases in Greek. She removed herself briefly to reach for a glass on the table; she held Blackburn's head and poured the thick liquid between his lips. She smiled at her companion, who winked back, Blackburn's red-coated organ in her hand.

Then the Greek girl slid off the bed, gesturing towards the bathroom door. Her associate nodded, extending her left hand up towards the general's head, inserting her fingers into his lips to cover for her companion's brief indisposition. The auburn-haired woman walked across the black carpet and went into the bathroom. The room resounded with the groans of the general's writhing euphoria.

Thirty seconds later, the Greek girl emerged, but she was no longer naked. She was dressed now in a dark tweed coat with a hood that covered her hair. She stood

11

momentarily in the shadows, then stepped to the nearest window and gently pulled back the heavy drapes.

The sound of shattering glass filled the room and a rush of wind billowed the curtains. The figure of a broad-shouldered, stocky man loomed in the window; he had kicked in the panes, and now leaped through the frame, his head encased in a ski-mask, a gun in his hand.

The girl on the bed whipped around and screamed in terror as the killer levelled his weapon and pulled the trigger. The explosion was muted by a silencer; the girl slumped over the obscenely painted body of Anthony Blackburn. The man approached the bed; the general raised his head, trying to focus through the mists of narcotics, his eyes floating, guttural sounds coming from his throat. The killer fired again. And again; and again, the bullets entering Blackburn's neck and chest and groin, the eruptions of blood mingling with the glistening colours of the paint.

The man nodded to the girl from Athens; she rushed to the door, opened it and said in Greek, "She'll be downstairs in the room with revolving lights. She's in a long red dress, with diamonds around her neck."

The man nodded again and they rushed out into the corridor.

The major's thoughts were interrupted by the unexpected sounds that seemed to come from somewhere inside the brownstone. He listened, his breath suspended.

They were shrieks of some kind . . . yelling . . . *screams*. People were screaming!

He looked up at the house; the heavy door flew open as two figures ran outside and down the steps, a man and a woman. Then he saw it and a massive pain shot through his stomach: the man was shoving a gun into his belt.

Oh, my God!

The major thrust his hand under the seat for his Army automatic, pulled it out and leapt from the car. He raced up the steps and inside the hallway. Beyond, through the arch, the screams mounted; people were running, several up the staircase, others down.

He ran into the large room with the insanely revolving coloured lights. On the floor he could see the figure of the slender woman with the diamonds around her neck. Her forehead was a mass of blood; she'd been shot.

Oh, Christ!

"*Where is he?*" he shouted.

"Upstairs!" came the scream from a girl huddled in the corner.

The major turned in panic and raced back to the ornate staircase, taking the steps three at a time, passing a telephone on a small table on the landing; its image stuck in his mind. He knew the room; it was always the same room. He turned in the narrow corridor, reached the door and lunged through it.

Oh, Jesus! It was beyond anything in his imagination, beyond any of the previous games, beyond any mess he had seen before. The naked Blackburn covered with blood and painted obscenities, the dead girl slumped over him, her face on his genitals. It was a sight from hell, if hell could be so terrible.

The major would never know where he found the self-control, but find it he did. He slammed the door shut and stood in the corridor, his automatic raised. He grabbed a woman who raced by towards the staircase, and shouted.

"Do as I say, or I'll kill you! There's a telephone over there. Dial the number I tell you! Say the words I tell you, the *exact words*!" He shoved the girl viciously towards the hallway phone.

The President of the United States walked grimly through the door into the Oval Office and over to his desk. Already there, and standing together, were the Secretary of State and the Director of the Central Intelligence Agency.

"I know the facts," said the President harshly in his familiar drawl, "and they turn my stomach. Now tell me what you're doing about them?"

The Director of the CIA stepped forward. "New York Homicide is co-operating. We're fortunate in so far as the general's aide remained by the door and threatened to kill anyone who tried to get past him. Our people arrived, and were at the scene first. They cleaned up as best they could."

"That's cosmetics, goddamn it!" said the President. "I suppose they're necessary, but that's not what I'm interested in. What are your ideas? Was it one of those weird, kinky New York murders, or was it something else?"

"In my judgement," answered the Director, "it was something else. I said as much to Paul here last night. It was a thoroughly analysed, pre-arranged assassination. Brilliantly executed. Even to the killing of the establishment's owner, who was the only one who could shed any light."

"Who's responsible?"

"I'd say KGB. The bullets fired were from a Russian Graz-Burya automatic, a favourite weapon of theirs."

"I *must* object, Mr President," said the Secretary of State. "I can't subscribe to Jim's conclusion; that gun may be unusual, but it *can* be purchased in Europe. I was with the Ambassador for an hour this morning. He was as shaken as we were. He not only disclaimed any *possible* Russian involvement, but correctly pointed out that General Blackburn was far more acceptable to the Soviets than any who might immediately succeed him."

"The KGB," interrupted the Director, "is often at odds with the Kremlin's diplomatic corps."

"As the Company is with ours?" asked the Secretary.

"No more than your own Consular Operations, Paul," replied the Director.

"Goddamn it!" said the President. "I don't need that crap from you two. Give me facts. You first, Jim. Since you're so sure of yourself, what have you come up with?"

"A great deal." The Director opened the file folder in his hand, took out a sheet of paper and placed it in front of the President. "We went back fifteen years and put everything we learned about last night into the computers. We cross-checked the concepts of method, location, egress, timing and teamwork. We matched it all with every known KGB assassination during the period. We've come up with three profiles. Three of the most elusive and successful killers in Soviet intelligence. In each case, of course, the man operates under normal covert procedures, but they're all assassins. We've listed them in order of expertise."

The President studied the three names:

Taleniekov, Vasili. Last reported post: South-west Soviet Sectors.
Krylovich, Nikolai. Last reported post: Moscow, VKR.
Zhukovski, Georgi. Last reported post: East Berlin, Embassy Attaché.

The Secretary of State was agitated; he could not remain silent. "Mr President, this kind of speculation – based at best on the widest variables – can only lead to confrontation. It's not the time for it."

"Now, wait a minute, Paul," said the President. "I asked for facts, and I don't give a damn whether the time's right or not right for a confrontation. The Chairman of the Joint Chiefs of Staff was killed. He may have been a sick son of a bitch in private life, but he was a hell of a good soldier. If it was a Soviet assassination, I want to know it." The chief executive put the paper down on the desk, his eyes still on the Secretary. "Besides," he added, "until more is known there won't be any confrontations. I'm certain Jim has kept this at the highest level of security."

"Of course," said the Director of the CIA.

There was a rapid knock on the Oval Office door. The President's senior communications aide entered without waiting for a response.

"Sir, the Premier of Soviet Russia is on the Red telephone. We've confirmed the transmission."

"Thank you," said the President, reaching for a phone with very thick wires behind his chair. "Mr Premier? This is the President."

The Russian's words were spoken rapidly, briskly, and at the first pause, an interpreter translated. As was customary, the Soviet interpreter stopped and another voice – that of the interpreter's American counterpart – said simply, "Correct, Mr President."

The four-way conversation continued.

"Mr President," said the Premier, "I mourn the death – the murder – of General Anthony Blackburn. He was a fine soldier who loathed war, as you and I loathe war. He was respected here, his strength and perception of global problems a beneficial influence on our own military leaders. He will be sorely missed."

"Thank you, Mr Premier. We, too, mourn his death. His murder. We are at a loss to explain it."

"That is the reason for my call, Mr President. You must know beyond doubt that General Blackburn's death – his murder – would never be desired by the responsible leadership of the Soviet Socialist Republic. The contemplation of it would be an anathema. I trust I make myself clear, Mr President."

"I think so, Mr Premier, and I thank you again. But if I may, are you alluding to the outside possibility of irresponsible leadership?"

"No more than those in your Senate who would bomb the Ukraine. Such idiots are dismissed, as they should be."

"Then I'm not sure I grasp the subtlety of your phrasing, Mr Premier."

"I shall be clearer. Your Central Intelligence Agency has produced three names it believes may be involved with the death of General Blackburn. They are not, Mr President. You have my solemn word. They are *responsible* men, held in absolute control by their superiors. In point of fact, one man, Zhukovski, was hospitalized a week ago. Another, Krylovich, has been stationed at the Manchurian border for the past eleven months. And the respected Taleniekov is, to all intents and purposes, retired. He is currently in Moscow."

The President paused and stared at the Director of the CIA. "Thank you for the clarification, Mr Premier, and for the accuracy of your information. I realize it wasn't easy for you to make this call. Soviet intelligence is to be commended."

"As is your own. There are fewer secrets these days; some say that is good. I weighed the values, and had to reach you. We were not involved, Mr President."

"I believe you. I wonder who it was."

"I'm troubled, Mr President. I think we should both know the answer to that."

2

"Dimitri Yurievich!" roared the buxom woman good-naturedly as she approached the bed, a breakfast tray in her hand. "It's the first morning of your holiday. The snow is on the ground, the sun is melting it, and before you shake the vodka from your head, the forests will be green again!"

The man buried his face in the pillow, then rolled over and opened his eyes, blinking at the sheer whiteness of the room. Outside the large windows of the *dacha*, the branches of the trees were sagging under the weight of their blinding white blankets.

Yurievich smiled at his wife, his fingers touching the hairs of his beard, grown more grey than brown. "I think I burned myself last night," he said.

"You would have!" laughed the woman. "Fortunately, my peasant instincts were inherited by our son. He sees fire and doesn't waste time analysing the components, but puts it out!"

"I remember him leaping at me."

"He certainly did." Yurievich's wife put the tray on the bed, pushing her husband's legs away to make room for herself. She sat down and reached for his forehead. "You're warm, but you'll survive, my Cossack."

"Give me a cigarette."

"Not before fruit juice. You're a very important man; the cupboards are filled with cans of fruit juice. Our lieutenant says they're probably there to put out the cigarettes that burn your beard."

"The mentality of soldiers will never improve. We scientists understand that. The cans of juice are there to be mixed with vodka." Dimitri Yurievich smiled again, not a little forlornly. "A cigarette, my love? I'll even let you light it."

"You are impossible!" She picked up a pack of cigarettes from the bedside table, shook one out and put it between her husband's lips. "Be careful not to breathe when I strike the match. We'd both explode, and I'll be buried in dishonour as the killer of the Soviet's most prominent nuclear physicist."

"My work lives after me; let me be interred with smoke." Yurievich inhaled as his wife held the match. "Our son is faring well this morning?"

"He's fine. He was up early oiling the rifles. His guests will be here in an hour or so. The hunt begins around noon."

"Oh, Lord, I forgot about that," said Yurievich, pushing himself up on the pillow into a sitting position. "Do I really have to go?"

"You and he are teamed together. Don't you remember telling everyone at dinner that father and son would bring home the prize game?"

Dimitri winced. "It was my conscience speaking. All those years in the laboratories while he grew up somehow behind my back."

His wife smiled. "It will be good for you to get out in the cold air. Now finish your cigarette, eat your breakfast and get dressed."

"You know something?" said Yurievich, taking his wife's hand. "I'm just beginning to grasp it. This is a holiday. I can't remember our last one."

"I'm not sure there ever was one. You work harder than any man I've known."

Yurievich shrugged. "It was good of the army to grant our son leave."

"He requested it. He wanted to be with you."

"That was good of him, too. I love him, but I hardly know him."

"He's a fine officer, everyone says. You can be proud, my husband."

"Oh I am, indeed, my wife. It's just that I don't know what to say to him. We have so little in common. The vodka made things easier last night."

"You haven't seen each other in nearly two years."

"I've had my work, everyone knows that."

"You're a scientist." His wife squeezed Dimitri's hand. "But not today. Not for the next three weeks. No laboratories, no blackboards, no all-night sessions with eager young professors and students who want to tell everybody they've worked with the great Yurievich." She took the cigarette from between his lips and crushed it out. "Now, eat your breakfast and get dressed. A winter hunt will do you a world of good."

"My dear woman," protested Dimitri, laughing, "it will probably be the death of me. I haven't fired a rifle in over twenty years!"

Lieutenant Nikolai Yurievich trudged through the deep snow towards the old building that was once the *dacha's* stables. He turned and looked back at the huge three-storey main house. It glistened in the morning sunlight, a small alabaster palace set in an alabaster glen carved out of snow-laden forest. It was from another, far more graceful era that had disappeared, its like never to return again.

Moscow thought a great deal of his father. Everyone wanted to know about the great Yurievich, this brilliant, irascible man whose mere name frightened the leaders of the Western world. It was said that Dimitri Yurievich carried the formulae for a dozen nuclear tactical weapons in his head; that left alone in a munitions depot with an adjacent laboratory he could fashion a bomb that would destroy greater London, all of Washington and most of Peking.

That was the great Yurievich, a man immune from criticism or discipline, in spite of words and actions which were at times intemperate. Not in terms of his

16

devotion to the state; that was never in question. Dimitri Yurievich was the fifth child of impoverished peasants from Kourov. Without the state he would be behind a mule on some aristocrat's land. No, he was a Communist to his boots, but like all brilliant men he had no patience with bureaucracies. He had been outspoken about interference and he had never been taken to task for it.

Which was why so many wanted to know him. On the assumption, Nikolai suspected, that even knowing the great Yurievich would somehow transfer a touch of his immunity to them.

The lieutenant knew that was the case today and it was an uncomfortable feeling. The "guests" who were now on their way to his father's *dacha* had practically invited themselves. One was the commander of Nikolai's battalion in Vilnius, the other a man Nikolai did not even know. A friend of the commander's from Moscow, someone the commander said could do a young lieutenant a good turn when it came to assignments. Nikolai did not care for such enticements; he was his own man first, his father's son second. He would make his own way; it was very important to him that he do so. But he could not refuse this particular commander, for if there was any man in the Soviet army who deserved a touch of "immunity", it was Colonel Janek Drigorin.

Drigorin had spoken out against the corruption that was rife in the Select Officer Corps. The resort clubs on the Black Sea paid for with misappropriated funds, the stockhouses filled with contraband, the women brought in on military aircraft against all regulations.

He was cut off by Moscow, sent to Vilnius to rot in mediocrity. Whereas Nikolai Yurievich was a twenty-one-year-old lieutenant exercising major responsibility in a minor post, Drigorin was a major military talent relegated to oblivion in a minor command. If such a man wished to spend a day with his father, Nikolai could not protest. And, after all, the colonel was a delightful person; he wondered what the other man was like.

Nikolai reached the stables and opened the large door that led to the corridor of stalls. The hinges had been oiled; the old entrance swung back without a sound. He walked down past the immaculately kept enclosures that once had held the best of breeds and tried to imagine what that Russia had been like. He could almost hear the whinnies of fiery-eyed stallions, the impatient scuffing of hooves, the snorting of hunters eager to break out for the fields.

That Russia must have been something. If you weren't behind a mule.

He came to the end of the long corridor, where there was another wide door. He opened it and walked out into the snow again. In the distance, something caught his eye; it seemed out of place. *They* seemed out of place.

Veering from the corner of a grain bin towards the edge of the forest, there were tracks in the snow. Footprints, perhaps. Yet the two servants assigned by Moscow to the *dacha* had not left the main house. And the gamekeepers were in their barracks down the road.

On the other hand, thought Nikolai, the warmth of the morning sun could have melted the rims of any impressions in the snow; and the blinding light played tricks on the eyes. They were no doubt the tracks of some foraging animal. The lieutenant smiled to himself at the thought of an animal from the forest looking for grain here, at this cared-for relic that was the grand *dacha's* stables. The animals had not changed, but Russia had.

Nikolai looked at his watch; it was time to go back to the house. The guests would be arriving shortly.

Everything was going so well, Nikolai could hardly believe it. There was nothing uncomfortable at all, thanks in large measure to his father and the man from Moscow. Colonel Drigorin at first seemed ill-at-ease – the commander who had imposed himself on the well-known or well-connected subordinate – but Dimitri Yurievich would have none of it. He welcomed his son's superior as an anxious – if celebrated – father, interested only in furthering his son's position. Nikolai could not help but be amused; his father was so obvious. Vodka was delivered with the fruit juice and coffee, and Nikolai kept a sharp eye out for dangling cigarettes.

The surprise and delight was the colonel's friend from Moscow, a man named Brunov, a high-ranking party functionary in Military-Industrial Planning. Not only did Brunov and his father have mutual friends, it was soon apparent that they shared an irreverent attitude towards much of Moscow's bureaucracy – which encompassed, naturally, many of those mutual friends. The laughter was not long coming, each rebel trying to outdo the other with biting comments about this commissar-with-an-echo-chamber-for-a-head and that economist-who-could-not-keep-a-rouble-in-his-pocket.

"We are wicked, Brunov!" roared Nikolai's father, his eyes alive with laughter.

"Too true, Yurievich!" agreed the man from Moscow. "It's a pity we're so accurate."

"But be careful, we're with soldiers. They'll report us!"

"Then I shall withhold their payrolls and you'll design a back-firing bomb."

Dimitri Yurievich's laughter subsided for a brief moment. "I wish there were no need for the functioning kind."

"And I that such large payrolls were not demanded."

"Enough," said Yurievich. "The gamekeepers say the hunting here is superb. My son has promised to look out for me, and I promised to shoot the biggest game. Come now, whatever you lack we have here. Boots, furs . . . vodka."

"Not while firing, Father."

"By God, you *have* taught him something," said Yurievich, smiling at the colonel. "Incidentally, gentlemen, I won't hear of your leaving today. You'll stay the night, of course. Moscow is generous; there are roasts and fresh vegetables from Lenin-knows-where . . ."

"And flasks of vodka, I trust."

"Not flasks, Brunov. *Casks!* I see it in your eyes. We'll both be on holiday. You'll stay."

"I'll stay," said the man from Moscow.

The gunshots rang through the forest, vibrating in the ears. Nor were they lost on the winter birds; screeches and the snapping of wings formed a rolling coda to the echoes. Nikolai could hear excited voices as well, but they were too far away to be understandable. He turned to his father.

"We should hear the whistle within sixty seconds if they hit something," he said, his rifle angled down at the snow.

"It's an outrage!" replied Yurievich in mock anger. "The gamekeepers swore to me – on the side, mind you – that all the game was in this section of the woods. Near the lake. There was *nothing* over there! It's why I insisted they go there."

"You're an old scoundrel," said the son, studying his father's weapon. "Your safety's released. Why?"

"I thought I heard a rustle back there. I wanted to be ready."

"With respect, my father, please put it back on. Wait until your sight matches the sound you hear before you release it."

"With respect, my soldier, then there'd be too much to do at once." Yurievich saw the concern in his son's eyes. "On second thoughts, you're probably right. I'd fall and cause a detonation. That's something I know about."

"Thank you," said the lieutenant, suddenly turning. His father was right; there was something rustling behind them. A crack of a limb, the snap of a branch. He released the safety on his weapon.

"What is it?" asked Dimitri Yurievich, excitement in his eyes.

"Sh," whispered Nikolai, peering into the shaggy corridors of white surrounding them.

He saw nothing. He snapped the safety into its locked position.

"You heard it, too, then?" asked Dimitri. "It wasn't just this pair of fifty-five-year-old ears."

"The snow's heavy," suggested the son. "Branches break under its weight. That's what we heard."

"Well, one thing we *didn't* hear," said Yurievich, "was a whistle. They didn't hit a damn thing!"

Three more distant gunshots rang out.

"They've seen *something*," said the lieutenant. "Perhaps now we'll hear their whistle . . ."

Suddenly they heard it. A sound. But it was not a whistle. It was, instead, a panicked, elongated scream, faint but distinct. Distinctly a terrible scream. It was followed by another, more hysterical, stretched out until the echoes enlarged it into waves of something horrible.

"My *God*, what *happened*?" Yurievich grabbed his son's arm.

"I don't. . . ."

The reply was cut off by a third scream, searing and terrible. There were no words, only swallowed protests, shrieks of pain.

"Stay *here!*" yelled the lieutenant to his father. "I'll go to them."

"I'll follow," said Yurievich. "Go quickly, but be careful!"

Nikolai raced through the snow towards the source of the screams. They filled the woods now, less shrill, but more painful for the loss of power. The soldier used his rifle to crash his path through the heavy branches, bending, breaking, kicking up sprays of snow. His legs ached, the cold air swelled in his lungs, his sight was obscured by tears of fatigue.

He heard the roars first, and then he saw what he most feared, what no hunter ever wanted to see.

An enormous, wild black bear, his terrifying face a mass of blood, was wreaking his vengeance on those who'd caused his wounds, clawing, ripping, slashing at his enemy.

Nikolai raised his rifle and fired until there were no more shells in the chamber.

The giant bear fell. The soldier raced to the two men; he lost what breath he had as he looked at them.

The man from Moscow was dead, his throat torn, his bloodied head barely attached to his body. Drigorin was only just alive, and if he did not die in seconds, Nikolai knew he would reload his weapon and finish what the animal had not done. The colonel had no face; it was not there. In its place a sight that burned itself into the soldier's mind.

How? How could it have happened?

And then the lieutenant's eyes strayed to Drigorin's right arm and the shock was beyond anything he could imagine.

It was half severed from his elbow, the method of surgery clear: heavy calibre bullets.

The colonel's firing arm had been shot off!

Nikolai ran to Brunov's corpse; he reached down and rolled it over.

Brunov's arm was intact, but his left hand had been blown apart, only the gnarled, bloody outline of a palm left, the fingers strips of bone. His *left hand*. Nikolai Yurievich remembered the morning; the coffee and fruit juice and vodka and cigarettes.

The man from Moscow was left-handed.

Brunov and Drigorin had been rendered defenceless by someone with a gun, someone who knew what was in their path.

Nikolai stood up cautiously, the soldier in him primed, seeking an unseen enemy. And this was an enemy he wanted to find and kill with all his heart. His mind raced back to the footprints he had seen behind the stables. They were not those of a scavenging animal – though an animal's they were – they were the tracks of a killer so obscene there was nothing in the *Lubyanka* he did not deserve.

Who *was* it? Above all, *why?*

The lieutenant saw a flash of light. Sunlight off a weapon.

He made a move to his right, then abruptly spun to his left and lunged to the ground, rolling behind the trunk of an oak tree. He removed the empty magazine from his weapon, replacing it with a fresh one. He squinted his eyes up at the source of the light. It came from high in a pine tree.

A figure was straddling two limbs fifty feet above the ground, a rifle with a telescopic sight in his hands. The killer wore a white snow parka with a white fur hood, his face obscured behind wide black sunglasses.

Nikolai thought he would vomit in rage and revulsion. The man was smiling, and the lieutenant knew he was smiling down at him.

Furiously, he raised his rifle. An explosion of snow blinded him, accompanied by the loud report of a high-powered rifle. A second gunshot followed; the bullet thumped into the wood above his head. He pulled back into the protection of the trunk.

Another gunshot, this one in the near distance, not from the killer in the pine tree.

"Nikolai!"

His mind burst. There was nothing left but rage. The voice that screamed his name was his father's.

"Nikolai!"

Another shot. The soldier sprang up from the ground, firing his rifle into the tree and raced across the snow.

An icelike incision was made in his chest. He heard nothing and felt nothing until he knew his face was cold.

The Premier of Soviet Russia placed his hands on the long table beneath the window that looked out over the Kremlin. He leaned over and studied the photographs, the flesh of his large peasant face sagging with exhaustion, his eyes filled with anger and shock.

"Horrible," he whispered. "That men should die like this is horrible. At least, Yurievich was spared – not his life, but such an end as this."

Across the room, seated around another table, were two men and a woman, their faces stern, watching the Premier. In front of each was a brown file folder, and it was apparent that each was anxious to proceed with the conference. But with the Premier one did not push nor intrude on his thoughts; his temper could be unleashed by such displays of impatience. The Premier was a man whose mind raced faster than anyone's in that room, but his deliberations were nevertheless slow, the complexities considered. He was a survivor in a world where only the most astute – and subtle – survived.

Fear was a weapon he used with extraordinary skill.

He stood up, pushing the photographs away in disgust, and strode back to the conference table.

"All nuclear stations are on alert, our submarines approaching firing positions," he said. "I want this information transmitted to all embassies. Use codes Washington has broken."

One of the men at the table leaned forward. He was a diplomat, older than the Premier, and obviously an associate of long standing, an ally who could speak somewhat more freely than the other two. "You risk a reaction I'm not sure is wise. We're not that certain. The American ambassador was profoundly shocked. I know him; he wasn't lying."

"Then he wasn't informed," said the second man curtly. "Speaking for the VKR, we *are* certain. The bullets and shell casings were identified: seven-millimetre – grooved for implosion. Bore markings, unmistakable. They were fired from a Browning Magnum, Grade Four. What more do you need?"

"A great deal more than that. Such a weapon is not so difficult to obtain, and I doubt an American assassin would leave his business card!"

"He might if it was the weapon he was most familiar with. We've found a pattern." The VKR man turned to the middle-aged woman, whose face was chiselled granite. "Explain, if you will, Comrade Director."

The woman opened her file folder and scanned the top page before speaking. She turned to the second page and addressed the Premier, her eyes avoiding the diplomat. "As you know there were two assassins, presumably both male. One had to be a marksman of extreme skill and co-ordination, the other someone who undoubtedly possessed the same qualifications, but who was also an expert in electronic surveillance. There was evidence in the stables — bracket scrapings, suction imprints, footprints indicating unobstructed vantage points — that lead us to believe all conversations in the *dacha* were intercepted."

"You describe CIA expertise, comrade," interrupted the Premier.

"Or Consular Operations, sir," replied the woman. "It's important to bear that in mind."

"Oh, yes," agreed the Premier. "The State Department's small band of 'negotiators'."

"Why not the Chinese Tao-pans?" offered the diplomat earnestly. "They're among the most effective killers on earth. The Chinese had more to fear from Yurievich than anyone else."

"Physiognomy rules them out," countered the man from VKR. "If one was caught, even after cyanide, Peking knows it would be destroyed."

"Get back to this pattern you've found," interrupted the Premier.

The woman continued. "We fed everything through KGB computers, concentrating on American intelligence personnel we know who have penetrated Russia, who speak the language fluently, and are known killers. We have arrived at four names. Here they are, Mr Premier. Three from the Central Intelligence Agency, one from the Department of State's Consular Operations." She handed the page to the VKR man, who in turn rose and gave it to the Premier.

He looked at the names.

Scofield, Brandon Alan. State Department, Consular Operations. Known to have been responsible for assassinations in Prague, Athens, Paris, Munich. Suspected of having operated in Moscow itself. Involved in over twenty defections.

Randolph, David. Central Intelligence Agency. Cover is Import Traffic Manager, Dynamax Corporation, West Berlin Branch. All phases of sabotage. Known to have been instrumental in hydro-electrical explosions in Kazan and Tagil.

Saltzman, George Robert. Central Intelligence Agency. Operated as pouch courier and assassin in Vientiane under AID cover for six years. Oriental expert. Currently — since five weeks ago — in the Tashkent sector. Cover: Australian immigrant, sales manager: Perth Radar Corporation.

Bergstrom, Edward. Central Intelligence Agency . . .

"Mr Premier," interrupted the man from VKR. "My associate meant to explain that the names are in order of priority. In our opinion, the entrapment and execution of Dimitri Yurievich bears all the earmarks of the first man on that list."

"This is Scofield?"

"Yes, Mr Premier. He disappeared a month ago in Marseilles. He's done more damage, compromised more operations, than any agent the United States has fielded since the war."

"Really?"

"Yes, sir." The VKR man paused, then spoke hesitantly, as if he did not want to go on, but knew he must. "His wife was killed ten years ago. In East Berlin. He's been a maniac ever since."

"*East* Berlin?"

"It was a trap. KGB."

The telephone rang on the Premier's desk; he crossed rapidly and picked it up.

It was the President of the United States. The interpreters were on the line; they went to work.

"We grieve the death – the terrible murder – of a very great scientist, Mr Premier. As well as the horror that befell his friends."

"Your words are appreciated, Mr President, but as you know, those deaths and that horror were premeditated. I'm grateful for your sympathies, but I can't help but wonder if perhaps you are not somewhat relieved that the Soviet Union has lost its foremost nuclear physicist."

"I am not, sir. His brilliance transcended our borders and differences. He was a man for all peoples."

"Yet he chose to be a part of *one* people, did he not? I tell you frankly, my concern does not transcend our differences. Rather, it forces me to look to my flanks."

"Then, if you'll forgive me, Mr Premier, you're looking for phantoms."

"Perhaps we've found them, Mr President. We have evidence that is extremely disturbing to me. So much so that I have . . ."

"Forgive me once again," interrupted the President of the United States. "Your evidence has prompted my calling you, in spite of my natural reluctance to do so. The KGB has made a great error. Four errors, to be precise."

"*Four* . . ."

"Yes, Mr Premier. Specifically the names Scofield, Randolph, Saltzman and Bergstrom. None was involved, Mr Premier."

"You astonish me, Mr President."

"No more than you astonished me the other week. There are fewer secrets these days, remember?"

"Words are inexpensive; the evidence is strong."

"Then it's been so calculated. Let me clarify. Two of the three men from Central Intelligence are no longer in sanction. Randolph and Bergstrom are currently at their desks in Washington. Mr Saltzman was hospitalized in Tashkent; the diagnosis is cancer." The President paused.

"That leaves one name, doesn't it?" said the Premier. "Your man from the infamous Consular Operations. So bland in diplomatic circles, but infamous to us."

"This is the most painful aspect of my clarification. It's inconceivable that Mr Scofield could have been involved. More so than any of the others, frankly. I tell you this because it no longer matters."

"Words cost little . . ."

"Mr *Premier*, I must be explicit. For the past several years a covert, in-depth dossier has been maintained on Dr Yurievich, information added almost daily, certainly every month. In certain judgements, it was time to reach Dimitri Yurievich with viable options."

"*What?*"

"Yes, Mr Premier. Defection. The two men who travelled to the *dacha* to make contact with Mr Yurievich did so in our interests. Their source-control was Scofield. It was his operation."

The Premier of Soviet Russia stared across the room at the pile of photographs on the table. He spoke softly. "Thank you for your frankness."

"Look to other flanks."

"I shall."

"We both must."

3

The late-afternoon sun was a fireball, its rays bouncing off the waters of the canal in blinding oscillation. The crowds walking west on Amsterdam's Kalverstraat squinted as they hurried along the pavement, grateful for the February sun and gusts of wind that came off the myriad waterways that stemmed from the Amstel River. Too often February brought the mists and rain, dampness everywhere; it was not the case today and the citizens of the North Sea's most vital port city seemed exhilarated by the clear, biting air warmed from above.

One man, however, was not exhilarated. Neither was he a citizen nor on the streets. His name was Brandon Alan Scofield, attaché-at-large, Consular Operations, United States Department of State. He stood at a window four storeys above the canal and the Kalverstraat, peering through binoculars down at the crowds, specifically at the area of the pavement where a glass telephone booth reflected the harsh flashes of sunlight. The light made him squint, but there was no gratitude felt, no energy evident on Scofield's pallid face, a face whose sharp features were drawn and taut beneath a vaguely combed cover of light brown hair, fringed at the edge with strands of grey.

He kept refocusing the binoculars, cursing the light and the swift movements below. His eyes were tired, the hollows beneath dark and stretched, the results of too little sleep for too many reasons Scofield did not care to think about. There was a job to do and he was a professional; his concentration could not waver.

There were two other men in the room. A balding technician sat at a table with a dismantled telephone, wires connecting it to a tape machine, the receiver off the hook. Somewhere under the streets in a telephone complex, arrangements had been made; they were the only co-operation that would be given by the Amsterdam police, a debt called in by the attaché-at-large from the American State Department. The third person in the room was younger than the other two, in his early thirties and with no lack of energy on his face, no exhaustion in his eyes. If his features were taut, it was the tautness of enthralment; he was a young man eager for the kill. His weapon was a fast-film motion picture camera mounted on a tripod, a telescopic lens attached. He would have preferred a different weapon.

Down in the street, a figure appeared in the tinted circles of Scofield's binoculars. The figure hesitated by the telephone booth and in that brief moment was jostled by the crowds off to the side of the pavement, in front of the flashing glass, blocking the glare with his body, a target surrounded by a halo of sunlight. It would be more comfortable for everyone concerned if the target could be zeroed where he was standing now. A high-powered rifle calibrated for seventy yards could do it; the man in the window could squeeze the trigger. He had done so often before. But comfort was not the issue. A lesson had to be taught, another lesson learned, and such instruction depended on the confluence of vital factors. Those teaching and those being taught had to understand their respective roles. Otherwise an execution was meaningless.

The figure below was an elderly man, in his middle to late sixties. He was dressed in rumpled clothing, a thick overcoat pulled up around his neck to ward off the chill, a battered hat pulled down over his forehead. There was a stubble of a beard on his frightened face; he was a man-on-the-run and for the American watching him through the binoculars, there was nothing so terrible, or haunting as an old man-on-the-run. Except, perhaps, an old woman. He had seen both. Far more often than he cared to think about.

Scofield glanced at his watch. "Go ahead," he said to the technician at the table. Then he turned to the younger man who stood beside him. "You ready?"

"Yes," was the curt reply. "I've got the son of a bitch centred. Washington was right; you proved it."

"I'm not sure what I've proved yet. I wish I was. When he's in the booth, get his lips."

"Right."

The technician dialled the pre-arranged numbers and punched the buttons of the tape machine. He rose quickly from his chair and handed Scofield a semi-circular headset with a mouthpiece and single earphone. "It's ringing," he said.

"I know. He's staring through the glass. He's not sure he wants to hear it. That bothers me."

"*Move*, you son of a bitch!" said the young man with the camera.

"He will," said the older, light-haired Scofield, the binoculars and headset held firmly in his hands. "He's frightened. Each half-second is a long time for him and I don't know why . . . There he goes; he's opening the door. Everybody quiet." Scofield continued to stare through the binoculars, listened, and then spoke quietly into the mouthpiece. "*Dobri dyen, priyatyel. . . .*"

The conversation, spoken entirely in Russian, lasted for eighteen seconds.

"*Da svidaniya,*" said Scofield, adding "*zafira nochyu. Na mostye.*" He continued to hold the headset to his ear and watched the frightened man below. The target disappeared into the crowds; the camera's motor stopped, and the attaché-at-large put down the binoculars, handing the headset to the technician. "Were you able to get it all?" he asked.

"Clear enough for a voice print," said the balding operator, checking his dials.

"You?" Scofield turned to the young man by the camera.

"If I understood the language better, even l could read his lips."

"Good. Others will; they'll understand it very well." Scofield reached into his pocket, took out a small leather notebook, and began writing. "I want you to take the tape and the film to the embassy. Get the film developed right away and have duplicates made of both. I want miniatures; here are the specifications."

"Sorry, Bray," said the technician, glancing at Scofield as he wound a coil of telephone wire. "I'm not allowed within five blocks of the territory; you know that."

"I'm talking to Harry," replied Scofield, angling his head towards the younger man. He tore out the page from his notebook. "When the reductions are made, have them inserted in a single watertight flatcase. I want it coated, good enough for a week in the water."

"Bray," said the young man, taking the page of paper. "I picked up about every third word you said on the phone."

"You're improving," interrupted Scofield, walking back to the window and the binoculars. "When you get to every other one, we'll recommend an upgrade."

"That man wanted to meet tonight," continued Harry. "You turned him down."

"That's right," said Scofield, raising the binoculars to his eyes, focusing out the window.

"Our instructions were to take him as soon as we could. The cipher plain text was clear about that. No time lost."

"Time's relative, isn't it? When the old man heard the telephone ring, every second was an agonizing minute for him. For us, an hour can be a day. In Washington, for Christ's sake, a day is normally measured by a calendar year."

"That's no answer," pressed Harry, looking at the note. "We can get this stuff reduced and packed in forty-five minutes. We could make the contact tonight. Why don't we?"

"The weather's rotten," said Scofield, the binoculars at his eyes.

"The weather's perfect. Not a cloud in the sky."

"That's what I mean. It's rotten. A clear night means a lot of people strolling around the canals; in bad weather, they don't. Tomorrow's forecast is for rain."

"That doesn't make sense. In ten seconds we block a bridge, he's over the side and dead in the water."

"Tell that clown to shut up, Bray!" shouted the technician at the table.

"You heard the man," said Scofield, focusing on the spires of the buildings outside. "You just lost the upgrade. Your outrageous statement that we intend to commit bodily harm tarnishes our friends in the Company."

The younger man grimaced. The rebuke was deserved. "Sorry. It still doesn't make sense. The cipher was a priority alert; we should take him tonight."

Scofield lowered the binoculars and looked at Harry. "I'll tell you what *does* make sense," he said quietly, with an edge to his voice. "Somewhat more than those silly goddamned phrases someone found on the back of a cereal box. That man down there was terrified. He hasn't slept in days. He's strung out to the breaking point, and I want to know why."

"There could be a dozen reasons," countered the younger man. "He's old. Inexperienced. Maybe he thinks we're on to him, that he's about to be caught. What difference does it make?"

"A man's life, that's all."

"Come on, Bray, not from *you*. He's Soviet poison; a double agent."

"I want to be sure."

"And I want to get out of here," broke in the technician, handing Scofield a reel of tape and picking up his machine. "Tell the clown we never met."

"Thanks, Mr No-name. I owe you."

The CIA man left, nodding at Bray, avoiding any contact with his associate.

"There was no one here but us chickens, Harry," said Scofield after the door was shut. "You do understand that."

"He's a nasty bastard . . ."

"Who could tap the White House toilets, if he hasn't already," said Bray, tossing the reel of tape to the younger man. "Get our unsolicited indictments over to the embassy. Take out the film and leave the camera here."

Harry would not be put off; he caught the reel of tape, but made no move towards the camera. "I'm in this, too. That cipher applied to me as well as you. I want to have answers in case I'm asked questions; in case something happens between tonight and tomorrow."

"If Washington's right, nothing will happen. I told you. I want to be sure."

"What more do you *need?* The target thinks he just made contact with KGB-Amsterdam! You engineered it. You proved it!"

Scofield studied the younger man for a moment, then turned away and walked back to the window. "You know something, Harry? All the training you get, all the words you hear, all the experiences you go through, never take the place of the first rule." Bray picked up the binoculars, brought them to his eyes, and focused on a faraway point above the skyline. "Teach yourself to think like the enemy thinks. Not how you'd like him to think, but how he *really* thinks. It's not easy; you can kid yourself because that *is* easy."

Exasperated, the younger man spoke angrily. "For God's sake, what's that got to do with anything? We've got our proof!"

"Do we? As you say, our defector's made contact with his own. He's a pigeon who's found his own particular route to Mother Russia. He's safe; he's out of the cold."

"That's what he thinks, yes!"

"Then why isn't he a happy man?" asked Bray Scofield, angling the binoculars down at the canal.

The mist and the rain fulfilled Amsterdam's promise of winter. The night sky was an impenetrable blanket, the edges mottled by the shimmering lights of the city. There were no strollers on the bridge, no boats on the canal below; pockets of fog swirled overhead – evidence that the North Sea winds travelled south unencumbered. It was three o'clock in the morning. For some there would be no daybreak.

Scofield leaned against the iron railing at the west entrance of the ancient stone bridge. In his left hand was a small transistorized radio – not for verbal communication, only for receiving signals. His right hand was in his raincoat pocket, his extended fingers touching the barrel of a .22 calibre automatic, not much larger than a starter's pistol, with a report nowhere near as loud. At close range it was a very feasible weapon. It fired rapidly, with an accuracy sufficient for a distance measured in inches, and could barely be heard above the noises of the night. And usually not at all in a crowded street in daylight.

Two hundred yards away, Bray's young associate was concealed in a doorway on the Sarphatistraat. The target would pass him on the way to the bridge; there was no other route. When the old Russian did so, Harry would press a button on his transmitter: the signal. The execution was in progress; the victim was walking his last hundred yards – to the midpoint of the bridge, where his own personal hangman would greet him, insert a watertight packet in the victim's overcoat and carry out the appointed task.

In a day or so that packet would find its way to KGB-Amsterdam. A tape would be listened to, a film observed closely. And another lesson would be taught.

And, naturally, go unheeded, as all lessons went unheeded – as they always went unheeded. Therein lay the futility, thought Scofield. The never-ending futility that numbed the senses with each repetition.

What difference does it make? A perceptive question asked by an eager if not very perceptive young colleague.

None, Harry. None at all. Not any longer.

But on this particular night, the needles of doubt kept pricking Bray's conscience. Not his morality; long ago morality was replaced by the practical. If it worked, it was moral, if it did not, it wasn't practical, and *thus* was immoral. What bothered him tonight had its basis in that utilitarian philosophy. Was the execution practical? Was the lesson about to be taught the best lesson, the most feasible option? Was it worth the risks and the fallout that came with the death of an old man who'd spent his adult life in space engineering?

On the surface the answer would appear to be yes. Six years ago the Soviet engineer had defected in Paris during an international space exposition. He had sought and been granted asylum; he had been welcomed by the space fraternity in Houston, given a job, a house and protection. However, he was not considered an outstanding prize. The Russians had actually joked about his ideological deviation, implying that his talents might be more appreciated by the less demanding capitalistic laboratories than by theirs. He rapidly became a forgotten man.

Until eight months ago when it was discovered that Soviet tracking stations were gridding into American satellites with alarming frequency, reducing the value of photographic checks through sophisticated ground camouflage. It was as if the Russians knew in advance the great majority of orbital trajectories.

They did. And a trace was made; it led to the forgotten man in Houston. What followed was relatively simple. A technical conference that dealt exclusively with one forgotten man's small area of expertise was called in Amsterdam; he was flown over on government aircraft and the rest was up to a specialist in these matters. Brandon Scofield, attaché-at-large, Consular Operations.

Scofield had long since broken KGB-Amsterdam's codes and methods of contact.

He put them in motion and was mildly surprised at the target's reaction; it was the basis of his profound concern now. The old man showed no relief at the summons. After six years of a balancing act, the target had every right to expect termination with honours, the gratitude of his government, and the last years of his life spent in comfort. Expect, hell! Bray had indicated as much in their ciphered conversations.

But the old Russian was not a happy man. And there were no overriding personal relationships evident in Houston. Scofield had requested the Four-Zero dossier on the target, a file so complete it detailed the projected hours of bowel movements. There was nothing in Houston; the man was a mole – apparently in both senses of the word. And that, too, bothered Bray. A mole in espionage did not assume the characteristics of the social equivalent.

Something was wrong. Yet the evidence was there, the proof of duplicity confirmed. The lesson had to be taught.

A short, sharp whine came from the transmitter in his hand. It was repeated three seconds later; Scofield acknowledged receipt with the press of a button. He put the radio in his pocket and waited.

Less than a minute passed; he saw the figure of the old man coming through the blanket of fog and rain, a streetlight beyond creating an eerie silhouette. The target's gait was hesitant but somehow painfully determined, as if he were about to keep a rendezvous both desired and loathed. It did *not* make sense.

Bray glanced to his right. As he expected, there was no one in the street, no one anywhere to be seen in this deserted section of the city at three o'clock in the morning. He turned to his left and started up the ramp towards the midpoint of the bridge, the old Russian on the opposite side. He kept in the shadows; it was easy to do as the first three lights above the left railing had been shorted out.

The rain pounded the ancient cobblestones. Across the bridge proper, the old man stood facing the water below, his hands on the railing. Scofield stepped off the walkway and approached from behind, the sound of the downpour obscuring his footsteps. In his left raincoat pocket, his hand now gripped a round, flat case two inches in diameter and less than an inch thick. It was coated in waterproof plastic, the sides possessing a chemical that when immersed in liquid for thirty seconds became an instant adhesive; under such conditions it would remain where it was placed until cut free. In the case was the evidence: a reel of film and a reel of magnetic tape. Both could be studied by KGB-Amsterdam.

"*Plakhaya noch, stary priyatyel,*" said Bray to the Russian's back, while taking the automatic from his pocket.

The old man turned, startled. "Why did you contact me?" he asked in Russian. "Has anything happened?. He saw the gun and stopped. Then he went on, an odd calm in his voice suddenly replacing the fear. "I see it has, and I'm no longer of value. Go ahead, comrade. You'll do me an enormous favour."

Scofield stared at the old man; at the penetrating eyes that were no longer frightened. He had seen that look before. Bray answered in English.

"You've spent an active six years. Unfortunately, you haven't done us any favours at all. You weren't as grateful as we thought you might be."

The Russian nodded, "American," he said. "I wondered. A hastily called conference in Amsterdam on problems as easily analysed in Houston. My being allowed out of the country, albeit covertly, and guarded – that protection something less than complete once here. But you had all the codes, you said all the right words. And your Russian is flawless, *priyatyel*."

"That's my job. What was yours?"

"You know the answer. It's why you're here."

"I want to know why."

The old man smiled grimly. "Oh, no. You'll get nothing but what you've learned. You see, I meant what I said. You'll do me a favour. You're my *listok*."

"Solution to what?"

"Sorry."

Bray raised the automatic; its small barrel glistened in the rain. The Russian looked at it and breathed deeply. The fear returned to his eyes, but he did not waver or say a word. Suddenly, deliberately, Scofield thrust the gun up beneath the old man's left eye, steel and flesh making contact. The Russian trembled but remained silent.

Bray felt sick.

What difference does it make?

None, Harry. Not at all. Not any longer.

A lesson had to be taught.

Scofield lowered the gun. "Get out of here," he said.

"What? . . ."

"You heard me. Get out of here. The KGB operates out of the diamond exchange on the Tolstraat. Its cover is a firm of Hasidim, *Diamant Bruusteen*. Beat it."

"I don't understand," said the Russian, barely audible. "Is this another trick?"

"*Goddamn it!*" yelled Bray, trembling. "Get out of here!"

Momentarily, the old man staggered, then grabbed the railing to steady himself. He backed away awkwardly, then started running through the rain.

"*Scofield!*" The shout came from Harry. He was at the west entrance of the bridge, directly in the path of the Russian. "Scofield. For God's *sake!*"

"Let him go!" screamed Bray.

He was either too late or his words were lost in the pounding rain; he did not know which. He heard three muted, sharp reports and watched in disgust as the old man held his head and fell against the railing.

Harry was a professional. He supported the body, fired a last shot into the neck, and with an upward motion, edged the corpse over the railing into the canal below.

What difference does it make?

None at all. Not any longer.

Scofield turned away and walked towards the east side of the bridge. He put the automatic in his pocket; it seemed heavy.

He could hear racing footsteps drawing nearer through the rain. He was terribly tired and did not want to hear them. Any more than he wanted to hear Harry's abrasive voice.

"Bray, what the hell *happened* back there? He nearly got away!"

"But he didn't," said Scofield, walking faster. "You made sure of that."

"You're damn right I did! For Christ's sake, what's *wrong* with you?" The younger man was on Bray's left; his eyes dropped to Scofield's hand. He could see the edge of the watertight case. "*Jesus!* You never planted it!"

"What?" Then Bray realized what Harry was talking about. He raised his head, looked at the small round receptacle, then threw it past the younger man over the railing.

"What are you *doing*?"

"Go to hell," said Scofield quietly.

Harry stopped, Bray did not. In seconds, Harry caught up and grabbed the edge of Scofield's raincoat. "Christ Almighty! You *let* him get away!"

"Take your hands off me."

"*No*, damn it! You can't . . ."

It was as far as Harry got. Bray shot his right hand up, his fingers clasping the younger man's exposed thumb, and yanked it counterclockwise.

Harry screamed, his thumb was broken.

"Go to hell," repeated Scofield. He continued walking off the bridge.

The safe-house was near the Rozengracht, the meeting to take place on the second floor. The sitting room was warmed by a fire, which also served to destroy any notes that might be taken. A State Department official had flown in from Washington; he wanted to question Scofield at the scene, as it were, in the event there were circumstances that only the scene could provide. It was important to understand what had happened, especially with someone like Brandon Scofield. He was the best there was, the coldest they had; he was an extraordinary asset to the American intelligence community, a veteran of twenty-two years of the most complicated "negotiations" one could imagine. He had to be handled with care . . . at the source. Not ordered back on the strength of a departmental complaint filed by a subordinate. He was a specialist, and something had happened.

Bray understood this and the arrangements amused him. Harry was taken out of Amsterdam the next morning in such a way that there was no chance of Scofield's seeing him. Among the few at the embassy that had to be aware of the incident, Bray was treated as though no incident had taken place. He was told to take a few days off; a man was flying in from Washington to discuss a problem in Prague. That's what the cipher said. Wasn't Prague an old hunting ground of his?

Cover, of course. And not a very good one. Scofield knew that his every move in Amsterdam was now being watched, probably by teams of Company men. And if he had walked to the diamond exchange on the Tolstraat, he undoubtedly would have been shot.

He was admitted into the safe-house by a nondescript maid of indeterminate age, a servant convinced that the old house belonged to the retired couple who lived there and paid her. He said he had an appointment with the owner and his attorney. The maid nodded and showed him up the stairs to the first-floor sitting room.

The old gentleman was there but not the man from State. When the maid closed the door, the owner spoke.

"I'll wait a few minutes and then go back up to my apartment. If you need anything, press the button on the telephone; it rings upstairs."

"Thanks," said Scofield, looking at the Dutchman, reminded of another old man on a bridge. "My associate should be along shortly. We won't need anything."

The man nodded and left. Bray wandered about the room, absently fingering the books on the shelves. It occurred to him that he wasn't even trying to read the titles; actually he didn't see them. And then it struck him that he didn't feel anything, neither cold nor heat, not even anger or resignation. He didn't feel *anything*. He was somewhere in a cloud of vapour, numbed, all senses dormant. He wondered what he would say to the man who had flown thirty-five hundred miles to see him.

He did not care.

He heard footsteps on the stairs beyond the door. The maid had obviously been dismissed by a man who knew his way in this house. The door opened and the man from State walked in.

Scofield knew him. He was from Planning and Development, a strategist for covert operations. He was around Bray's age, but thinner, a bit shorter, and given to old-school-tie exuberance which he did not feel but which he hoped concealed his ambition. It did not.

"Bray, how *are* you, old buddy?" he said in a half-shout, extending an exuberant hand for a more exuberant grip. "My God, it must be damn near two years! Have I got a couple of stories to tell *you!*"

"Really?"

"*Have I!*" An exuberant statement, no question implied. "I went up to Cambridge for my twentieth and naturally ran into friends of yours right and left. Well, old buddy, I got pissed and couldn't remember what lies I told *who* about you! Christ Almighty, I had you an import analyst in Malaya, a language expert in New Guinea, an under-secretary in Canberra. It was hysterical. I mean, I couldn't *remember* I was so pissed."

"Why would anyone ask about me, Charlie?"

"Well, they knew we were both at State; we were friends, everybody knew that."

"Cut it out. We were never friends. I suspect you dislike me almost as much as I dislike you. And I've never seen you drunk in your life."

The man from State stood motionless; the exuberant smile slowly disappeared from his lips. "You want to play it rough?"

"I want to play it as it is."

"What happened?"

"Where? When? At Harvard?"

"You know what I'm talking about. The other night. What happened the other night?"

"You tell me. You set it in motion, you spun the first wheels."

"We uncovered a dangerous security leak. A pattern of active espionage going back years that reduced the effectiveness of space surveillance to the point where we now know it's been a mockery. We wanted it confirmed; you confirmed it. You knew what had to be done and you walked away."

"I walked away," agreed Scofield.

"And when confronted with the fact by an associate, you did bodily injury to him. To your *own man!*"

"I certainly did. If I were you I'd get rid of him. Transfer him to Chile; you can't fuck up a hell of a lot more down there."

"*What?*"

"On the other hand, you won't do that. He's too much like you, Charlie. He'll never learn. Watch out. He'll take your job one day."

"Are you drunk?"

"No, I'm sorry to say. I thought about it, but I've got a little acidity in my stomach. Of course, if I'd known they were sending you, I might have fought the good fight and tried. For old times' sake, naturally."

"If you're not drunk, you're off your trolley."

"The track veered; those wheels you spun couldn't take the curve."

"Cut the horseshit!"

"What a dated phrase, Charlie. These days we say bullshit, although I prefer lizardshit . . ."

"That's enough! Your action – or should I say inaction – compromised a vital aspect of counter-espionage."

"Now, *you* cut the horseshit!" roared Bray, taking an ominous step towards the man from State. "I've heard all I want to hear from you! I didn't compromise anything. *You* did! You and the rest of those bastards back there. You found an ersatz leak in your Goddamned sieve and so you had to plug it up with a corpse. Then you could go to the Forty Committee and tell *those* bastards how efficient you were!"

"What are you talking about?"

"The old man *was* a defector. He was reached, but he *was* a *defector.*"

"What do you mean 'reached'?" asked the man from State defensively.

"I'm not sure; I wish I did. Somewhere in that Four-Zero dossier something was left out. Maybe a wife that never died, but was in hiding. Or grandchildren no one bothered to list. I don't know but it's there. Hostages, Charlie! That's why he did what he did. And I was his *listok.*"

"What's that mean?"

"For Christ's sake, learn the language. You're supposed to be an expert."

"Don't pull that language crap on me, I *am* an expert. There's no evidence to support an extortion theory, no family reported or referred to by the target at any time. He was a dedicated agent for Soviet intelligence."

"*Evidence?* Oh, come on, Charlie, even you know better than that. If he was good enough to pull off a defection, he was smart enough to bury what had to be buried. My guess is that the key was timing, and the timing blew up. His secret – or secrets – were found out. He was reached; it's all through his dossier. He lived abnormally, even for an abnormal existence."

"We rejected that approach," said the man from State emphatically. "He was an eccentric."

Scofield stopped and stared. "You rejected? . . . An eccentric? Goddamn you, you *did* know. You could have *used* that, fed him anything you liked. But no, you wanted a quick solution so the men upstairs would see how good you were. You could have *used* him, not killed him! But you didn't know how, so you kept quiet and called out the hangmen."

"That's preposterous. There's no way you could prove he'd been reached."

"Prove it? I don't have to prove it, I know it."

"How?"

"I saw it in his eyes, you son of a bitch."

The man from State paused, then spoke softly. "You're tired, Bray. You need a rest."

"With a pension?" asked Scofield. "Or with a casket?"

4

Taleniekov walked out of the restaurant into a cold blast of wind that disturbed the snow, swirling it up from the pavement with such force that it became a momentary haze, diffusing the light of the streetlamp above. It was going to be another freezing night. The weather report on Radio Moscow had the temperature dropping below minus eight Celsius.

Yet it had stopped snowing early that morning; the runways at Sheremetyevo Airport were cleared and that was all that concerned Vasili Taleniekov at the moment. Air France, Flight 85, had left for Paris ten minutes ago. Aboard that plane was a Jew who was scheduled to leave two hours later on Aeroflot for Athens.

He would not have left for Athens if he had shown up at the Aeroflot terminal. Instead, he would have been asked to step into a room. Greeting him would have been a team from the *Vodennaya Kontra Rozvedka*, and the absurdity would have begun.

It was stupid, thought Taleniekov, as he turned right, pulling the lapels of his overcoat up around his neck and the brim of his *addyel* lower on his head; it *was* freezing; it would soon snow again. Stupid in the sense that the VKR would have accomplished nothing but provide a wealth of embarrassment. It would have fooled no one, least of all those it was trying to impress.

A dissident recanting his dissidency! What comic literature did the young fanatics in the VKR read? Where were the older and wiser heads when fools came up with such schemes?

When Vasili had heard of the plan, he had laughed, actually *laughed*. The objective was to mount a brief but strong campaign against Zionist accusations, to show people in the West that not all Jews thought alike in Soviet Russia.

The Jewish writer had become something of a minor cause in the American press – the New York press, to be specific. He had been among those who had spoken to a visiting senator in search of votes eight thousand miles away from a constituency. But race notwithstanding, he simply was not a good writer, and, in fact, something of an embarrassment to his co-religionists.

Not only was the writer the wrong choice for such an exercise, but for reasons intrinsic to another operation it was imperative that he be permitted to leave Russia.

He was a blind trade-off for the senator in New York. The senator had been led to believe it was his acquaintanceship with an attaché at the consulate that had caused Soviet emigration to issue a visa; the senator would make capital out of the incident and a small hook would exist where one had not existed before. Enough hooks and an awkward relationship would suddenly exist between the senator and "acquaintances" within the Soviet power structure; it could be useful. The Jew had to leave Moscow tonight. In three days the senator had scheduled a welcoming news conference at Kennedy Airport.

But the young aggressive thinkers at the VKR were adamant. The writer would be detained, brought to the *Lubyanka*—where the VKR had its headquarters replete with laboratories – and the process of transformation would commence. No one outside the VKR was to be told of the operation; success depended upon sudden disappearance, total secrecy. Chemicals would have been administered until the subject was ready for a different sort of news conference. One in which he revealed that Israeli terrorists had threatened him with reprisals against relatives in Tel Aviv if he did not follow their instructions and cry publicly to be able to leave Russia.

The scheme was preposterous and Vasili had said as much to his contact at the VKR, but was told confidentially that not even the extraordinary Taleniekov could interfere with Group Nine, *Vodennaya Kontra Rozvedka*. And what in the name of all the discredited Tzars was Group Nine?

It was the *new* Group Nine, his friend had explained. It was the successor to the infamous Section Nine, KGB, *Smert Shpionam*. That division of Soviet intelligence devoted exclusively to the breaking of men's minds and wills through extortion, torture and that most terrible of methods – killing loved ones in front of loved ones.

Killing was nothing strange to Vasili Taleniekov, but that kind of killing turned his stomach. The *threat* of such killing was often useful, but not the act itself. The State did not require it, and only sadists demanded it. If there was truly a successor to *Smert Shpionam*, then he would let it know with whom it had to contend within the larger sphere of KGB. Specifically, one "extraordinary Taleniekov". They would learn not to contradict a man who had spent twenty-five years roaming all of Europe in the cause of the State.

Twenty-five years. It had been a quarter of a century since a twenty-one-year-old student with a gift for languages had been taken out of his classes at the Leningrad University and sent to Moscow for three years of intensive training. It was training the likes of which the son of introspective Socialist teachers could barely believe. He had been plucked out of a quiet home where books and music and endless discussions of philosophy were the staple diet, and set down in a world of conspiracy and violence, where ciphers, codes and physical abuse were the main ingredients. Where all forms of surveillance and sabotage, espionage and the taking of life – not murder; murder was a term that had no application – were the subjects studied.

He might have failed had it not been for an incident that changed his life and gave him the motive to excel. It had been provided by animals . . . American animals.

He had been sent to East Berlin on a training exercise, an observer of undercover tactics at the height of the Cold War. He had formed a relationship with a young woman, a German girl who fervently believed in the cause of the Marxist state, and who had been recruited by the KGB. Her position was so minor her name was not even on a payroll; she was an unimportant organizer of demonstrations, paid with loose Reichsmarks from an expense drawer. She was quite simply a university student far more passionate in her beliefs than knowledgeable, a wild-eyed radical who considered herself a kind of Joan of Arc. But Vasili had loved her, loved her mad abandon, her impetuous grasping at life that was balanced by an ability to laugh.

They had lived together for several weeks and they were glorious weeks, filled with the excitement and anticipation of young love. And then one day she was sent across Checkpoint Kasimir. It was such an unimportant thing, a street-corner protest on the Kurfürstendamm. A child leading other children, mouthing words they barely understood, espousing commitments they were ill-prepared to accept. An unimportant ritual. Insignificant.

But not to the animals of the American Army of Occupation, G2 Branch, who set other animals upon her.

Her body was sent back in a hearse, her face bruised almost beyond recognition, the rest of her clawed to the point where the flesh was torn, the blood splotches of dried red dust. And the doctors had confirmed the worst. She had been repeatedly raped and sodomized, her pelvic area pounded by abuse.

Attached to the body – the note held in place by a nail driven into her arm – were the words: *Up your commie ass. Just like hers.*

Animals!

American animals who bought their way to victory without a shell having fallen on their soil, whose might was measured by unfettered industry that made enormous profits from the carnage of foreign lands, whose soldiers peddled cans of food to hungry children to gratify other appetites. All armies had animals, but the Americans were most offensive; they proclaimed such innocent righteousness. Forever the proverb was right: beware the sanctimonious, beneath there is boiling dirt.

Taleniekov had returned to Moscow, the memory of the girl's obscene death burned into his mind. Whatever he had been, he became something else. According to many, he became the best there was, and by his own lights none could possibly wish to be better than he did. With all its faults – and there were many – the Marxist eventuality was the true democratic future. He had seen the enemy and he was filth. But that enemy had resources beyond imagination, wealth beyond belief; so it was necessary to be better than he was in things that could not be purchased. One had to learn to think as he did. Then out-think him. Vasili had understood this; he became the master of strategy and counter-strategy, the springer of unexpected traps, the deliverer of unanticipated shock – death in the morning sunlight on a crowded street corner.

Death in the Unter den Linden at five o'clock in the afternoon. At that hour when the traffic was at its maximum.

He had brought that about, too. He had avenged the murder of a laughing child-woman years later, when as the director of KGB operations, East Berlin, he had drawn the wife of an American killer across the checkpoint. She had been run down cleanly, professionally, with a minimum of conscious pain; it was a far more merciful death than that delivered by animals four years earlier.

He had nodded in appreciation at the news of that death, yet there was no joy. He knew what that man was going through, and deserved as it was, there was no elation. For Taleniekov also knew that man would not rest until he found his own vengeance.

He did. Three years later in Prague.

A brother.

Where was the hated Scofield these days? wondered Vasili. It was close to a quarter of a century for him, too. They each had served their causes well, that much could be said for both of them. But Scofield was more fortunate; things were less complicated in Washington, one's enemies within more defined. The despised Scofield did not have to put up with such amateurish maniacs as Group Nine, VKR. The American State Department had its share of madmen, but sterner controls were exercised, Vasili had to admit that. In a few years, if Scofield survived in Europe, he would retire to some remote place and grow chickens or oranges or drink himself into oblivion. He did not have to be concerned about surviving in Washington, just in Europe.

Taleniekov had to worry about surviving in Moscow.

Things . . . *things* had changed in a quarter of a century. And he had changed; tonight was an example, but not the first. He had covertly thwarted the objectives of a fellow intelligence unit. He would not have done so five years ago – perhaps even two years ago. He would have confronted the strategists of that unit, stating that he understood the necessity for their secrecy, but having learned of their plans, strenuously objected on professional grounds. He was an expert, and in his expert judgement, the operation was not only miscalculated but less vital than another with which it interfered.

He did not take such action these days. He had not done so during the past two years as director of the South-west Sectors. He had made his own decisions, caring little for the reactions of damn fools who knew far less than he did. Increasingly, those reactions caused minor furores back in Moscow, still he did what he believed was right. Ultimately, those minor furores became major grievances and he was recalled to the Kremlin and a desk where stratagems were remote, dealing with progressive abstractions such as shadowy hooks into an American politician.

Taleniekov had fallen, he knew that. It was only a question of time. How much time had he left? Would he be given a small *ferma* north of Grasnov and be told to grow his crops and keep his own council? Or would the maniacs interfere with that course of action too? Would they claim the "extraordinary Taleniekov" was, indeed, too dangerous?

As he made his way along the street, Vasili felt so tired, so weary. Even the loathing he felt for the American killer who had murdered his brother was muted in the twilight of his feelings. He had so little feeling left.

The sudden snowstorm reached blizzard proportions, the winds gale force, causing eruptions of huge white sprays through the expanse of Red Square. Lenin's Tomb would be covered by morning. Taleniekov let the freezing particles massage his face as he trudged against the wind towards his flat. KGB had been considerate; his rooms were ten minutes from his office in Dzerzhinsky Square, three blocks away from the Kremlin. It was either consideration, or something less benevolent but infinitely more practical: his flat was ten minutes from the centres of crisis, three minutes in a fast automobile.

He walked into the entranceway of his building, stamping his feet as he pulled the heavy door shut, cutting off the harsh sound of the wind. As he always did, he checked his mail slot in the wall and, as always, there was nothing. It was a futile ritual that had become a meaningless habit for so many years, in so many mail slots, in so many different buildings.

The only personal mail he ever received was in foreign countries – under strange names – when he was in deep cover. And then the correspondence was in code and cipher, its meaning in no way related to the words on paper. Yet sometimes those words were very nice, often warm and friendly, and he would pretend for a few minutes that they were the real words, their meaning meant. But only for a few minutes; it did no good to pretend. Unless one was analysing an enemy.

He started up the narrow staircase, annoyed by the dim light of the low-wattage bulbs. He was quite sure the planners in Moscow's *Elektrichiskaya* did not live in such buildings.

Then he heard the creak. It was not the result of structural stress; it had nothing to do with the sub-freezing cold or the winds outside. It was the sound of a human being shifting his weight on a floorboard. His ears were the ears of a trained craftsman, distances judged quickly. The sound did not come from the landing above, but from higher up the staircase. His flat was on the next floor; someone was waiting for him to approach. Someone wanted him inside his rooms perhaps, egress awkward, a trap being set.

Vasili continued his climb, the rhythm of his footsteps unbroken. The years had trained him to keep such items as keys and cigarettes and coins in his left-hand pockets, freeing his right to reach quickly for a weapon, or to be used as a weapon itself. He came to the landing and turned; his door was only feet away, the upper staircase down the dimly lit corridor, around the bend of the railing.

There was the creak again, faint, barely heard, mixed with the sound of the distant wind outside. Whoever was on the staircase had moved back, and that told him two things: the intruder would wait until he was definitely inside the flat, and whoever it was was either careless or inexperienced or both. One did not move when this close to a quarry; the air was a conductor of motion.

In his left hand was his key; his right had unfastened the buttons of his overcoat and was now gripped around the handle of his automatic, strapped in an open holster across his chest. He inserted the key, opened the door, then yanked it shut, stepping back rapidly, silently into the shadows of the staircase. He stayed against the wall, his gun levelled in front of him over the railing.

The sound of footsteps preceded the rushing figure as it raced to the door. In the figure's left hand was an object; he could not see it now, it was hidden by the heavily clothed body. Nor were there seconds to wait. If the object was an explosive, it would be on a timer-release. The figure had raised his right hand to knock on the door.

"Press yourself into the door! Your *left hand in front* of you! Between your stomach and the wood! *Now!*"

"Please!" The figure spun half-way around; Taleniekov was on him, throwing him against the panel. He was a young man, a boy really, barely in his teens, thought Vasili. He was tall for his age, but his age was obvious from his face; it was callow, no trace of beard, the eyes wide and clear and frightened.

"Move back slowly," said Taleniekov harshly. "Raise your left hand. *Slowly.*"

The boy moved back, his left hand seen; it was clenched into a fist.

"I didn't do anything wrong, sir. I swear it!" The young man's whisper cracked in fear.

"Who are you?"

"Andrei Danilovich, sir. I live in the Cheryomushki."

"You're a long way from home," said Vasili, estimating that the housing development referred to by the boy was nearly forty-five minutes south of Red Square. "The weather's terrible and someone your age could be picked up by the *militsianyer.*

"I had to come here, sir," answered the young man quickly. "A man's been shot; he's hurt very badly. I think he's going to die. I am to give this to you." The boy opened his left hand; in it was a brass emblem. An army insignia denoting the rank of general. Its design had not been used in over thirty years. "The old man said to say the name Krupsky, Aleksie Krupsky. He made me say it several times so I wouldn't forget it. It's not the name he uses down at the Cheryomushki, but it's the one he said to give you. He said I must bring you to him. He's dying, sir!"

At the sound of the name, Taleniekov's mind raced back in time. Aleksie Krupsky! It was a name he had not heard in years, a name few people in Moscow wanted to hear. Krupsky was once the greatest teacher in the KGB, a man of infinite talent for killing and survival – as well he might be. He was the last of the notorious *istrebiteli*, that highly specialized group of *exterminators* that had been an élite outcrop of the old NKVD, its roots in the barely remembered OGPU.

But Aleksie Krupsky had disappeared – as so many had disappeared – at least a dozen years ago. There had been rumours linking him to the deaths of Beria and Zhukov, some even mentioning Stalin himself. Once in a fit of rage – or fear – Khrushchev had stood up in the Praesidium and called Krupsky and his associates a band of maniacal killers. That was not true; there was never any mania in the work of the *istrebiteli*, it was too methodical. Regardless, suddenly one day Aleksie Krupsky was no longer seen at the *Lubyanka*.

Yet there were other rumours. Those that spoke of documents prepared by Krupsky, hidden in some remote place, that were his guarantees to a personal old age. It was said these documents incriminated various leaders of the Kremlin in scores of killings – reported, unreported and disguised. So it was presumed that Aleksie Krupsky was living out his life somewhere north of Grasnov, on a *ferma*, perhaps, growing crops and keeping his own council.

He had been the finest teacher Vasili ever had; without the old master's patient instructions, Taleniekov would have been killed years ago. "Where is he?" asked Vasili.

"We brought him down to our flat. He kept pounding on the floor – our ceiling. We ran up and found him."

"We?"

"My sister and I. He's a good old man. He's been good to my sister and me. Our parents are dead. And I think he will soon be dead, too. Please hurry, sir!"

The old man on the bed was not the Aleksie Krupsky Taleniekov remembered. The close-cropped hair and the clean-shaven face that once displayed such strength were no more. The skin was pale and stretched, wrinkled beneath the white beard, and the long white hair was a bird's nest of tiny thin strings – matted, separated, revealing splotches of greyish flesh that was Krupsky's gaunt skull. The man was dying and could barely speak. He lowered the covers briefly and lifted a blood-soaked cloth away from the perforated flesh of a bullet wound.

Virtually no time was spent on greetings; the respect and affection in each man's eyes were sufficient.

"I widened my pupils into the death-stare," said Krupsky, smiling weakly. "He thought I was dead. He had done his job and ran."

"Who was it?"

"An assassin. Sent by the Corsicans."

"The Corsicans? What are you talking about? What Corsicans?"

"The Matarese. They know I know . . . what they are doing, what they are about to do. I am the only one left who would recognize them, who would dare speak of them. I stopped the contacts once, but I had neither the courage – nor the ambition – to expose them."

"I can't understand you."

"I will try to explain." Krupsky paused, gathering strength. "A short while ago, a general named Blackburn was killed in America."

"Yes, I know. The Chairman of the Joint Chiefs. We were not involved, Aleksie."

"Are you aware that *you* were the one the Americans believed the most likely assassin?"

"No one told me. It's ridiculous."

"No one tells you much any more, do they, my old student?"

"I don't fool myself, old friend. I've given. I don't know how much more I have to give. Grasnov is not far distant, perhaps."

"If it is permitted," interrupted Krupsky.

"I think it will be."

"No matter . . . Last month, the scientist, Yurievich. He was murdered while on holiday up in a Provasoto *dacha*, along with Colonel Drigorin and the man, Brunov, from Industrial Planning."

"I heard about it," said Taleniekov. "I gather it was horrible."

"Did you read the report?"

"What report?"

"The one compiled by VKR . . ."

40

"Madmen and fools," interjected Taleniekov softly.

"Not always," corrected Krupsky. "In this case they have specific facts, accurate as far as they go."

"What are these supposedly accurate facts?"

Krupsky, breathing with difficulty, swallowed and continued. "Shell casings, seven-millimetre, American. Bore markings from a Browning Magnum, Grade Four."

"A brutal gun," said Taleniekov, nodding. "Very reliable. And the last weapon that would be used by someone sent from Washington."

"Also a fact that could be overlooked in the barrage of charges and counter-charges." The old man paused, staring at his long-ago student. "The gun used to kill General Blackburn was a Graz-Burya."

Vasili raised his eyebrows. "A prized weapon when obtainable." He paused and added quietly, "I favour mine."

"Exactly. As the Magnum, Grade Four, is a favoured weapon of another."

Taleniekov stiffened. "Oh?"

"Yes, Vasili. VKR came up with several names it thinks could be responsible for Yurievich's death. The leading contender was a man you despise: 'Beowulf Agate'."

Taleniekov spoke in a monotone. "Brandon Scofield, Consular Operations. Code name, Prague – Beowulf Agate."

"Yes."

"Was he?"

"No." The old man struggled to raise his head on the pillow. "No more than you were involved with Blackburn's death. Don't you see? They know everything; even of operatives whose skills are proven but whose minds are tired. Who, perhaps, need a significant kill. Such men as you are diversions; there will be others. They shape events; they no longer serve them. They are testing the highest levels of power before they make their move."

"Who? Who are *they?*"

"The Matarese. The Corsican fever . . ."

"What does that *mean?*"

"It spreads. It has changed, far more deadly in its new form." The old *istrebiteli* fell back on the pillow; talking was not easy for him.

"You must be clearer, Aleksie. I can see nothing. What is this Corsican fever, this . . . Matarese?"

Krupsky's eyes were wide, now staring at the ceiling; he whispered. "No one speaks; no one dares to speak. Our own Praesidium; England's Foreign Office, its MI6 board room; the French Société Diable d'État. And the Americans. Oh, never forget the Americans! The well-dressed men of the State Department, the cowards in CIA . . . No one speaks. We are all touched. We are stained by the Matarese."

"*Stained?* How? What are you trying to say? What in heaven's name is the Matarese?"

The old man turned his head slowly; his lips trembled, his breathing was more difficult. "Some say it goes back as far as Sarajevo. Others swear it claims Dollfuss,

Bernadotte . . . even Trotsky on its list. We know about Stalin; we contracted for his death."

"Stalin? It's true then what was said?"

"Oh, yes. Beria, too; we paid." The *istrebitel*'s eyes seemed now to float out of focus. "In 'forty-five . . . the world thought Roosevelt succumbed to a massive stroke." Krupsky shook his head slowly, saliva at the corners of his mouth. "There were financial interests who believed his policies with the Soviet Union were economically disastrous. They could not permit any further decisions on his part. They paid, and an injection was administered."

Taleniekov was stunned. "Are you telling me that Roosevelt was *killed*? By this *Matarese*?"

"Assassinated, Vasili Vasilievich Taleniekov. That is the word, and that is one of the truths no one will speak of. So many . . . for so many years. None dare talk of the contracts, the payments. The admissions would be catastrophic . . . for governments everywhere."

"But *why*? Why was it used, this Matarese?"

"Because it was there. And available. And it removed the client from the scene."

"It's preposterous! Assassins have been *caught*. There's been no such name ever mentioned!"

"You should know better than that, Vasili Vasilievich. You've used the same technique yourself; no different from the Matarese."

"What do you mean?"

"You both kill . . . and programme killers." The old man acknowledged Taleniekov's nod. "The Matarese was dormant for years. Then it came back, but it was not the same. Killings took place without clients, without payments. Senseless butchery without a pattern. Men of value kidnapped and slain; aircraft stolen or blown up in mid-air, governments paralysed – payments demanded or wholesale slaughter the result. The incidents have become more refined, more professional."

"You're describing the work of terrorists, Aleksie. Terrorism has no central apparatus."

Once again the old *istrebitel* struggled to raise his head. "It does *now*. It has for the past several years. Baader-Meinhof, the Red Brigades, the Palestinians, the African maniacs – they all gravitate to the Matarese. It kills with impunity; it selects the subjects and leaves arrows that bring men and nations to the brink of disaster. It is throwing the two superpowers into chaos before it makes its boldest move. And that is to assume control of one or the other. Ultimately, both."

"How can you be certain?"

"A man was caught, a blemish on his chest, a soldier of the Matarese. Chemicals were administered, everyone ordered from the room but my source. I had warned him."

"*You?*"

"Hear me out. There is a timetable, but to speak of it would be to acknowledge the past; none dare do that! Moscow by assassination, Washington by purchase – murder if necessary. Two months, three at the outside; everything is in motion now. Action and reaction has been tested at the highest levels, unknown men positioned at the centres of power. Soon it will happen, and when it does, we are consumed. We are destroyed, subjects of the Matarese."

"Where is this man?"

"Dead. The chemicals wore off; there was a cyanide pellet sewn into his skin. He tore his own flesh and reached it."

"Assassinations? Purchase and murder? You must be more specific."

Krupsky's breath came shorter as he fell back on the pillow. But strangely, his voice grew firmer. "There is no time – I do not *have* the time. My source is the most reliable in Moscow – in all the Soviet."

"Forgive me, dear Aleksie, you were the best, but you do not exist any more. Everyone knows that."

"You must reach Beowulf Agate," said the old *istrebitel*, as though Vasili had not spoken. "You and he must find them. Stop them. Before one of us is taken, the other's destruction guaranteed. You and the man Scofield. You are the best now, and the best are needed."

Taleniekov looked impassively at the dying Krupsky. "That is something no one can ask me to do. If Beowulf Agate were in my vision, I would kill him. As he would kill me, if he were capable."

"You are *insignificant!*" The old man's breath was exhausted; he had to breathe slowly, in desperation, to get the air back in his lungs. "You have no time for yourselves, can't you understand that? They are in our clandestine services, in the most powerful circles of both governments. They used the two of you once; they will use you again, and *again*. They use only the best and they will kill only the best! You are their diversions, men and men like you!"

"Where is the proof?"

"In the pattern," whispered Krupsky. "I've studied it. I know it well."

"What pattern?"

"The Graz-Burya shells in New York; the seven-millimetre casings of a Browning Magnum in Provasoto. Within hours Moscow and Washington were at each other's throats. This is the way of the Matarese. It never kills without leaving evidence – often the killers themselves – but it is never the right evidence, never the true killers."

"Men have been caught who pulled triggers, Aleksie."

"For the wrong reasons, Vasili Vasilievich. Those reasons provided by the Matarese . . . Now, it takes us to the edge of chaos and overthrow."

"But *why?*"

Krupsky turned his head, his eyes in focus, pleading. "I don't *know*. The pattern is there but not the *reasons* for it. That is what frightens me. One must go back to understand. The roots of the Matarese are in Corsica. The madman of Corsica; it started with him. The Corsican fever. Guillaume de Matarese. He was the high priest."

"When?" asked Taleniekov. "How long ago?"

"During the early years of the century. Before the first decade was over . . . Guillaume de Matarese and his council. The high priest and his ministers. They've come back. They must be stopped. You and the man, Scofield! Their last ploy was with you!"

"Who are they?" asked Vasili, disregarding the statement. "Where are they?"

"No one knows." The old man's voice was failing now. He was failing. "The Corsican fever. It spreads."

"Aleksie, *listen* to me," said Taleniekov, disturbed by a possibility that could not be overlooked: the fantasies of a dying man could not be taken seriously. "Who is this reliable source of yours? Who is the man so knowledgeable in Moscow – in all the Soviet? How did you get the information you've given me? About the killing of Blackburn, the VKR report on Yurievich? Above all, this unknown man who speaks of timetables?"

Through the personal haze of his approaching death, Krupsky understood. A faint smile appeared on his thin, pale lips. "Every few days," he said, struggling to be heard, "a driver comes to see me, perhaps take me for a ride in the countryside. Sometimes to meet quietly with another. It's the State's kindness to a pensioned old soldier whose name was appropriated. I am kept informed."

"I don't understand, Aleksie."

"The Premier of Soviet Russia is my son."

Taleniekov felt a wave of cold rush through him. The revelation explained so much. The Premier had survived and won over so many others; he had emerged the victor as the barriers to power had been removed. One by one – selectively. Krupsky had to be taken seriously; the old *istrebitel* had possessed the information – the ammunition – to eliminate all who stood in the way of his son's march to premiership of Soviet Russia.

"Would he see me?"

"Never. At the first mention of the Matarese, he would have you shot. Try to understand, he would have no choice. But he knows I am right. He agrees, but will never acknowledge it; he cannot afford to. He simply wonders whether it is he or the American President who will be in the gunsight."

"I understand."

"Leave me now," said the dying Krupsky. "Do what you must do, Taleniekov. I have no more breath. Reach Beowulf Agate, find the Matarese. It must be stopped. The Corsican fever can spread no farther."

"The Corsican fever? . . . In *Corsica?*"

"The answer may be there. Many, many years ago. I don't know."

5

A coronary inefficiency had made it necessary for Robert Winthrop to use a wheelchair, but in no way did it impair the awareness of his mind, nor did he dwell on the infirmity. He had spent his life in the service of his government; there was never any lack of problems he considered more important than himself.

Guests at his Georgetown home soon forgot the wheelchair. The slender figure with the graceful gestures and the intensely interested face reminded them of the man he was: an energetic aristocrat who had used his private fortune to free himself from the marketplace and pursue a life of public advocacy. Instead of an infirm elder statesman with thinning grey hair and the still perfectly clipped moustache, one thought of Yalta and Potsdam and an aggressive younger man from the State Department forever leaning over Roosevelt's chair or Truman's shoulder to clarify this point or suggest that objection.

There were many in Washington – and in London and Moscow as well – who thought the world would be a better place had Robert Winthrop been made Secretary of State by Eisenhower but the political winds had shifted and he was not a feasible choice. And later, Winthrop could not be considered; he had become involved in another area of government that required his full concentration. He had been quietly retained as Senior Consultant, Diplomatic Relations, Department of State.

Twenty-six years ago Robert Winthrop had organized a select division within State called Consular Operations. And after sixteen years of commitment he had resigned – some said because he was appalled at what his creation had become, while others claimed he was only too aware of the necessary directions it had taken, but could not bring himself to make certain decisions. Nevertheless, during the ten years since his departure, he had been consistently sought out for advice and counsel. As he was tonight.

Consular Operations had a new director. A career intelligence officer named Daniel Congdon had been shifted from a ranking position at the National Security Agency to the clandestine chair at State. He had replaced Winthrop's successor and was finely attuned to the harsh decisions required by *Cons Op*. But he was new; he had questions. He also had a problem with a man named Scofield and was not sure how to handle it. He knew only that he wanted Brandon Alan Scofield terminated, removed from the State Department for good. His actions in Amsterdam could not be tolerated; they revealed a dangerous and unstable man. How much more dangerous would he be removed from the control of Consular Operations? It was a serious question; the attaché knew more about the State Department's clandestine networks than any other man alive. And since Scofield had initially been brought to Washington years ago by Ambassador Robert Winthrop, Congdon went to the source.

Winthrop had readily agreed to make himself available to Congdon but not in an impersonal office or an operations room. Over the years, the Ambassador had learned that men involved with clandestine operations instinctively reflected their surroundings. Short, cryptic sentences took the place of freer, rambling conversations wherein a great deal more could be revealed and learned. Therefore, he had invited the new director over for dinner.

The meal was finished, nothing of substance discussed. Congdon understood: the Ambassador was probing the surface before delving deeper. But now the moment had come.

"Let's go into the library, shall we?" said Winthrop, wheeling himself away from the table.

45

Once inside the book-lined room, the Ambassador wasted no time. "So you want to talk about Brandon."

"Very much so," replied the new director of *Cons Op*.

"How do we thank such men for what they've done?" asked Winthrop. "For what they've lost? The field extracts a terrible price."

"They wouldn't be there if they didn't want to be," said Congdon in polite counterpoint. "If, for some reason, they didn't need it. But once having been out there and survived, there's another question. What do we do with them? They're walking explosives."

"What are you trying to say?"

"I'm not sure, Mr Winthrop. I want to know more about him. Who is he? What is he? Where did he come from?"

"The child being the father of the man?"

"Something like that. I've read his file – a number of times, in fact – but I've yet to speak to anyone who really knows him."

"I'm not sure you'll find such a person. Brandon . . ." The elder statesman paused briefly and smiled. "Incidentally, he's called Bray, for reasons I've never understood. It's the last thing he does. Bray, I mean."

"That's one of the things I have learned," interrupted the director, returning Winthrop's smile as he sat down in a leather armchair. "When he was a child he had a younger sister who couldn't say Brandon; she called him Bray. The name just stuck with him."

"That must have been added to his file after I left. Indeed, I imagine a great deal has been added to that file. But as for his friends, or lack of them . . . he's simply a private person, quite a bit more so since his wife died."

Congdon spoke quietly. "She was killed, wasn't she?"

"Yes."

"In fact, she was killed in East Berlin ten years ago next month. Isn't that right?"

"Yes."

"And ten years ago next month you resigned the directorship of Consular Operations. The highly specialized unit you built."

Winthrop turned, his eyes levelled at the new director. "What I conceived and what finally emerged were two quite different entities. Consular Operations was designed as a humanitarian instrument, to facilitate the defection of thousands from a political system they found intolerable. As time went on – and circumstances seemed to warrant – the objectives were narrowed. The thousands became hundreds and, as other voices were heard, the hundreds were reduced to dozens. We were no longer interested in the scores of men and women who daily appealed to us, but instead listened to those select few whose talents and information were considered far more important than those of ordinary people. The unit concentrated on a handful of scientists and soldiers and intelligence specialists. As it does today. That's not what we began with."

"But as you pointed our, sir," said Congdon, "the circumstances warranted the change."

Winthrop nodded. "Don't mistake me, I'm not naïve. I dealt with the Russians at Yalta, Potsdam, Casablanca. I witnessed their brutality in Hungary in 'fifty-six, and I saw the horrors of Czechoslovakia and Greece. I think I know what the Soviets are capable of as well as any strategist in covert services. And for years I permitted those more aggressive voices to speak with authority. I understood the necessity. Did you think I didn't?"

"Of course not. I simply meant . . ." Congdon hesitated.

"You simply made a connection between the murder of Scofield's wife and my resignation," said the statesman kindly.

"Yes, sir, I did. I'm sorry, I didn't mean to pry. It's just that the circumstances . . ."

" 'Warranted a change'," completed Winthrop. "That's what happened, you know. I recruited Scofield; I'm sure that's in his file. I suspect that's why you're here tonight."

"Then the connection . . . ?" Congdon's words trailed off.

"Accurate. I felt responsible."

"But surely there were other incidents, other men . . . and women."

"Not the same, Mr Congdon. Do you know why Scofield's wife was selected to be the target that afternoon in East Berlin?"

"I assume it was a trap meant for Scofield himself. Only she showed up and he didn't. It happens."

"A trap meant for Scofield? In *East* Berlin?"

"He had contacts in the Soviet sector. He made frequent penetrations, set up his own calls. I imagine they wanted to catch him with contact sheets. Her body was searched, her purse taken. It's not unusual."

"Your assumption being that he'd use his wife in the operation?" asked Winthrop.

Congdon nodded. "Again, not unusual, sir."

"Not unusual? I'm afraid in Scofield's case it was impossible. She was part of his cover at the embassy, but never remotely connected to his covert activities. No, Mr Congdon, you're wrong. The Russians knew they could never spring a trap on Bray Scofield in East Berlin. He was too good, too efficient . . . too elusive. So they tricked his wife into crossing the checkpoint and killed her for another purpose."

"I beg your pardon?"

"An enraged man is a careless man. That's what the Soviets wanted to accomplish. But they, as you, misunderstood their subject. With his rage came a reaffirmation to sting the enemy in every way he could. If he was brutally professional before his wife's death, he was viciously so afterwards."

"I'm still not sure I understand."

"Try, Mr Congdon," said Winthrop. "Twenty-two years ago I ran across a government major at Harvard University. A young man with a talent for languages and a certain authority about him that indicated a bright future. He was recruited through my office, sent to the Maxwell School in Syracuse, then brought to Washington to become part of Consular Operations. It was a fine beginning for a possibly brilliant career in the State Department." Winthrop paused, his eyes straying as if lost in a personal reverie. "I never expected him to stay in *Cons Op*; strangely enough I thought of it as a springboard for him. To the diplomatic corps, to the ambassadorial level, perhaps. His gifts cried out to be used at international conference tables . . ."

"But something happened," continued the statesman, glancing absently back at the new director. "As *Cons Op* was changing, so was Brandon Scofield. The more vital those highly specialized defections were considered, the more quickly the violence escalated. On both sides. Very early, Scofield requested commando training; he spent five months in Central America going through the most rigorous survival techniques – offensive and defensive. He mastered scores of codes and ciphers; he was as proficient as any cryptographer in NSA. Then he returned to Europe and became *the* expert."

"He understood the requirements of his work," said Congdon, impressed. "Very commendable, I'd say."

"Oh yes, very," agreed Winthrop. "Because, you see, it had happened; he'd reached his plateau. There was no turning back, no changing. He could never be accepted around a conference table; his presence would be rejected in the strongest diplomatic terms because his reputation was established. The bright young government major I'd recruited for the State Department was now a killer. No matter the justification, he was a professional killer."

Congdon shifted his position in the chair. "Many would say he was a soldier in the field, the battleground extensive, dangerous . . . never-ending. He had to survive, Mr Winthrop."

"He had to and he did," concurred the old gentleman. "Scofield was able to change, to adapt to the new rules. But I wasn't. When his wife was killed, I knew I didn't belong. I saw what I had done: taken a gifted student for one purpose and seen that purpose warped. Just as the benign concept of Consular Operations had been warped – by circumstances that warranted those changes we spoke of. I had to face my own limitations. I couldn't continue any longer."

"But you did ask to be kept informed of Scofield's activities for several years. That's in the file, sir. May I ask why?"

Winthrop frowned, as if wondering himself. "I'm not sure. An understandable interest in him – even fascination, I suppose. Or punishment, perhaps; that's not out of the question. Sometimes the reports would stay in my safe for days before I read them. And, of course, after Prague I no longer wanted them sent to me. I'm sure that's in the file."

"Yes, it is. By Prague, I assume you refer to the courier incident."

"Yes," answered Winthrop softly. " 'Incident' is such an impersonal word, isn't it? It fits the Scofield in that report. The professional killer, motivated by the need to survive – as a soldier survives, turned into a cold-blooded killer, motivated solely by vengeance. The change was complete."

Again the new director of *Cons Op* shifted his position, crossing his legs uncomfortably. "It was established that the courier in Prague was the brother of the KGB agent who ordered the death of Scofield's wife."

"He was the brother, not the man who issued that order. He was a youngster, no more than a low-level messenger."

"He might have become something else."

"Then where does it end, Mr Congdon?"

"I can't answer that, Mr Winthrop. But I can understand Scofield's doing what he did. I'm not sure I wouldn't have done the same."

"With no sense of righteousness," said the ageing statesman, "I'm not sure I would have. Nor am I convinced that young man in Cambridge twenty-two years ago would have done so. Am I getting through to you, as is so often asked these days?"

"Painfully, sir. But in my defence – and in defence of the current Scofield – we didn't create the world we operate in. I think that's a fair thing to say."

"Painfully, fair, Mr Congdon. But you perpetuate it." Winthrop wheeled his chair to his desk and reached for a box of cigars. He offered the box to the director, who shook his head. "I don't like them, either, but ever since Jack Kennedy we're all expected to keep our supply of Havanas. Do you disapprove?"

"No. As I recall, the Canadian supplier was one of President Kennedy's more accurate sources of information about Cuba."

"Have you been around that long?"

"I joined the National Security Agency when he was a senator . . . Did you know that Scofield has recently begun to drink steadily?"

"I know nothing about the current Scofield, as you called him."

"His file indicates the use of alcohol, but no evidence of excess."

"I would think not; it would interfere with his work."

"It may be interfering now."

"*May* be? It either is or it isn't. I don't think that's such a difficult thing to establish. If he's drinking a great deal, that's excess; it would have to interfere. I'm sorry to hear it, but I can't say I'm surprised."

"Oh?" Congdon leaned forward in the chair. It was apparent that he thought he was about to be given the information he was seeking. "When you knew him as well as you did, were there signs of potential instability?"

"None at all."

"But you just said you weren't surprised."

"I'm not. I wouldn't be surprised at any thinking man turning to alcohol after so many years of living so unnaturally. Scofield is – or was – a thinking man, and God knows he's lived unnaturally. If I'm surprised, it's only that it's taken so long to reach him, affect him. What got him through the nights?"

"Men condition themselves. As you put it, he adapted. Extremely successfully."

"But still unnaturally," maintained Winthrop. "What are you going to do with him?"

"He's being recalled. I want him out of the field."

"Good. Give him a desk and an attractive secretary and have him analyse theoretical problems. Isn't that the usual way?"

Congdon hesitated before replying. "Mr Winthrop, I think I want him separated from the State Department."

The creator of *Cons Op* arched his eyebrows. "Really? Twenty-two years is insufficient for an adequate pension."

"That's not a problem; generous settlements are made. It's common practice these days."

"Then what does he do with his life? What is he? Forty-five . . . -six?"

"Forty-six."

"Hardly ready for one of these, is he?" said the statesman, fingering the wheel of his chair. "May I ask why you've come to that conclusion?"

"I don't want him around personnel involved with covert activities. According to our latest information, he's displayed hostile reactions to basic policy. He could be a negative influence."

Winthrop smiled. "Someone must have pulled a beaut. Bray never did have much patience with fools."

"I said *basic* policy, sir. Personalities are not the issue."

"Personalities, Mr Congdon, unfortunately are *intrinsic* to basic policy. They form it. But that's probably beside the point . . . at this point. Why come to me? You've obviously made your decision. What can I add?"

"Your judgement. How will he take it? Can he be trusted? He knows more about our operations, our contacts, our tactics, than any man in Europe."

Winthrop's eyes became suddenly cold. "And what is your alternative, Mr Congdon?" he asked icily.

The new director flushed; he understood the implication. "Surveillance. Controls. Telephone and mail intercepts. I'm being honest with you, sir."

"Are you?" Winthrop now glared at the man in front of him. "Or are you looking for a word from me – or a question – that you can use for another solution?"

"I don't know what you mean."

"I think you do. I've heard how it's done, incidentally, and it appals me. Word is sent to Prague, or Berlin, or Marseilles that a man's no longer in sanction. He's finished, out. But he's restless, drinks a lot. Contacts' names might be revealed by this man, whole networks exposed. In essence, the word spreads: your lives are threatened. So it's agreed that another man, or perhaps two or three, get on planes from Prague or Berlin or Marseilles. They converge on Washington with but one objective: the silencing of that man who's finished. Everyone's more relaxed, and the American intelligence community – which has remained outside the *incident* – breathes easier. Yes, Mr Congdon, it appals me."

The director of *Cons Op* remained motionless in the chair. His reply was delivered in a quiet monotone. "To the best of my knowledge, Mr Winthrop, that solution has been exaggerated far out of proportion to its practice. Again, I'll be completely honest with you. In fifteen years I've heard of its being exercised only twice, and in both . . . incidents . . . the agents out of sanction were beyond being salvaged. They had sold out to the Soviets; they *were* delivering names."

"Is Scofield beyond salvage? That's the correct phrase, isn't it?"

"If you mean do I think he's sold out, of course not. It's the last thing he'd do. I really came here to learn more about him, I'm sincere about that. How is he going to react when I tell him he's terminated?"

Winthrop paused, his relief conveyed, then frowned again. "I don't know because I don't know the current Scofield. It's drastic; what's he going to do? Isn't there a half-way measure?"

"If I thought there was one acceptable to us both, I'd leap at it."

"If I were you I'd try to find one."

"It can't be on the premises," said Congdon firmly. "I'm convinced of that."

"Then may I suggest something?"

50

"Please do."

"Send him as far away as you can. Some place where he'll find a peaceful oblivion. Suggest it yourself; he'll understand."

"He will?"

"Yes. Bray doesn't fool himself, at least he never did. It was one of his finer gifts. He'll understand because I think *I* do. I think you've described a dying man."

"There's no medical evidence to support that."

"Oh, for God's sake!" said Robert Winthrop.

Scofield walked across the hotel room and turned off the television set. He had not seen an American news broadcast in several years – since he was last brought back for an inter-operations briefing – and he was not sure he wanted to see one again for the next several years. It wasn't that he thought all news should be delivered in the ponderous tones of a funeral, but the giggles and leers that accompanied descriptions of fire and rape struck him as odd. At any moment he expected the anchormen would throw spitballs at one another and dip the blond tresses of the vacuous arts' critic into a prop inkwell.

He looked at his watch; it was twenty past seven. He knew it because his watch read twenty past midnight; he was still on Amsterdam time. His appointment at the State Department was for eight o'clock.

P.M. That was standard for specialists of his rank, but what was not standard was the State Department itself. Attachés-at-large for Consular Operations invariably held strategy conferences in safe-houses, usually in the Maryland countryside, or perhaps in hotel suites in downtown Washington.

Never at the State Department. Not for specialists expected to return to the field. But then Bray knew he was not scheduled to return to the field. He had been brought back for only one purpose. Termination.

Twenty-two years and he was out. An infinitesimal speck of time into which was compressed everything he knew – everything he had learned, absorbed and taught. He kept waiting for his own reaction, but there was none. It was as though he were a spectator, watching the images of someone else on a white wall, the inevitable conclusion drawing near, but not drawing him into the events as they took place. He was only mildly curious. How would it be done?

The walls of Under-Secretary of State Daniel Congdon's office were white. There was a certain comfort in that, thought Scofield. as he half-listened to Congdon's droning narrative. He could see the images. Face after face, dozens of them, coming into focus and fading rapidly. Faces of people remembered and unremembered, staring, thinking, weeping, laughing, dying . . . death.

His wife. Five o'clock in the afternoon. Unter den Linden.

Men and women running, stopping. In sunlight, in shadows.

But where was he? He was not there.

He was a spectator.

Then suddenly he wasn't. He could not be sure he heard the words correctly.

What had this coldly efficient under-secretary said? *Bern, Switzerland?*

"I beg your pardon?"

"The funds will be deposited in your name, proportionate allocations made annually."

"In addition to whatever pension I'm entitled to?"

"Yes, Mr Scofield. And regarding that, your service record's been predated. You'll get the maximum."

"That's very generous." It *was*. Calculating rapidly, Bray estimated that his income would be over $50,000 a year.

"Merely practical. These funds are to take the place of any profits you might realize from the sale of books or articles based on your activities in Consular Operations."

"I see," said Bray slowly. "There's been a lot of that recently, hasn't there? Marchetti, Agee, Snepp."

"Exactly."

Scofield could not help himself; the bastards *never* learned. "Are you saying that if you'd banked funds for them they wouldn't have written what they did?"

"Motives vary, but we don't rule out the possibility."

"Rule it out," said Bray curtly. "I know two of those men."

"Are you rejecting the money?"

"Hell, no. I'll take it. When I decide to write a book, you'll be the first to know."

"I wouldn't advise it, Mr Scofield. Such breaches of security are prohibited. You'd be prosecuted; years in prison inevitable."

"And if you lost in the courts, there just *might follow* certain extralegal penalties. A shot in the head while driving in traffic, for example."

"The laws are clear," said the under-secretary. "I can't imagine that."

"I can. Look in my Four-Zero file. I trained with a man in Honduras. I killed him in Madrid. He was from Indianapolis and his name was . . ."

"I'm *not interested* in past activities," interrupted Congdon harshly. "I just want us to understand each other."

"We do. You can relax. I'm not . . . breaching any security. I haven't the stomach for it. Also, I'm not that brave."

"Look, Scofield," said the under-secretary, leaning back in his chair, his expression pleasant. "I know it sounds trite, but there comes a time for all of us to leave the more active areas of our work. I want to be honest with you."

Bray smiled, a touch grimly. "I'm always nervous when someone says that."

"What?"

"That he wants to be honest with you. As if honesty was the last thing you should expect."

"I *am* being honest."

"So am I. If you're looking for an argument, you won't get it from me. I'll quietly fade away."

"But we don't want you to do that," said Congdon, leaning forward, his elbows on the desk.

"Oh?"

"Of course not. A man with your background is extraordinarily valuable to us.

Crises will continue to arise; we'd like to be able to call upon your expertise."

Scofield studied the man. "But not in-territory." A statement. "Not in-strategy."

"No. Not officially. Naturally, we'll want to know where you're living, what trips you make."

"I'll bet you will," said Bray softly. "But for the record, I'm terminated."

"Yes. However, we'd like it kept out of the record. A Four-Zero entry."

Scofield did not move. He had the feeling that he was in the field, arranging a very sensitive exchange. "Wait a minute, let me understand you. You want me officially terminated, but no one's supposed to know it. And although I'm officially finished, you want to maintain contact on a permanent basis."

"Your knowledge is invaluable to us, you know that. And I think we're paying for it."

"Why the Four-Zero then?"

"I'd have thought you'd appreciate it. Without official responsibilities you retain a certain status. You're still part of us."

"I'd like to know why this way."

"I'll be . . ." Congdon stopped, a slightly embarrassed smile on his face. "We really *don't* want to lose you."

"Then why terminate me?"

The smile left the under-secretary's face. "I'll call it as I see it. You can confirm it with an old friend of yours if you like. Robert Winthrop. I told him the same thing."

"Winthrop? He goes back a long time. What did you tell him?"

"That I don't want you around here. And I'm willing to pay out of budget and predate records to get you out. I listened to your words; you were taped by Charles Englehart in Amsterdam."

Bray whistled softly. "Old Crimson Charlie. I should have known it."

"I thought you did. I thought you were sending us a personal message. Nevertheless, we got it. We have a lot to do here and your kind of obstinacy, your cynicism, isn't needed."

"Now, we're getting somewhere."

"But everything else is true. We *do* need your expertise. We have to be able to reach you any time. You have to be able to reach *us*."

Bray nodded. "And the Four-Zero means that my separation is top-secret. The field doesn't know I'm terminated."

"Precisely."

"All right," said Scofield, reaching into his pocket for a cigarette. "I think you're going to a lot of unnecessary trouble to keep a string on me, but, as you said, you're paying for it. A simple field directive could accomplish the same thing: issue clearance until rescinded. Special category."

"Too many questions would be asked. It's easier this way."

"Really?" Bray lit the cigarette, his eyes amused. "All right."

"Good." Congdon shifted his weight in the chair. "I'm glad we understand each other. You've earned everything we've given you and I'm sure you'll continue to earn it . . . I was looking at your file this morning; you enjoy the water. God knows your record's filled with hundreds of contacts made in boats at night. Why not try it in the daylight? You've got the money. Why not go to someplace like the Caribbean and enjoy your life? I envy you."

Bray got up from his chair; the meeting was over. "Thanks, I may do that. I like warm climates." He extended his hand; Congdon rose and took it. While they shook hands, Scofield continued, "You know that Four-Zero business would make me nervous if you hadn't called me in here."

"What do you mean?" Their hands were clasped, but the movement stopped.

"Well, our own field personnel won't know I'm terminated, but the Soviets will. They won't bother me now. When someone like me is taken out-of-strategy, everything changes. Contacts, codes, ciphers, sterile locations; nothing remains the same. They know the rules; they'll leave me alone. Thanks very much."

"I'm not sure I understand you," said the undersecretary.

"Oh, come on, I said I'm grateful. We both know KGB-Washington keeps its cameras trained on this place twenty-four hours a day. No specialist who's to remain in sanction is *ever* brought here. As of an hour ago they know I'm out. Thanks again, Mr Congdon. It was considerate of you."

The Under-Secretary of State, Consular Operations, watched as Scofield walked across the office and let himself out the door.

It was over. Everything. He would never have to hurry back to an antiseptic hotel room to see what covert message had arrived. No longer would it be necessary to arrange for three changes of vehicle to get from point *A* to point *B*. The lie to Congdon notwithstanding, the Soviets probably did know he had been terminated by now. If they didn't they would soon. After a few months of inactivity the KGB would accept the fact that he was no longer of value. The rules were constant; tactics and codes *were* altered. The Soviets would leave him alone; they would not kill him.

But the lie to Congdon had been necessary, if only to see the expression on his face. We'd like it kept out of the record. *Four-Zero entry!* The man was so transparent! He really believed he had created the climate for the execution of his own man, a man he considered dangerous. That a supposedly active agent would be killed by the Soviets for the sake of a kill. Then – pointing to official separation – the Department of State would disclaim any responsibility.

The bastards *never* changed, but they knew so little. An execution for its own sake was pointless, the fallout often too hazardous. One killed for a purpose: to learn something by removing a vital link in a chain, or to stop something from happening. Or to teach a specific lesson. But always for a reason.

Except in instances like Prague, and even that could be considered a lesson. *A brother for a wife.*

But it was over. There were no strategies to create, no decisions to make that resulted in a defection or a turn-back, of someone living or not living. It was *over*.

Perhaps now even the hotel rooms would come to an end. And the stinking beds in rundown rooming houses in the worst sections of a hundred cities. He was so sick of them; he despised them all. With the exception of a single brief period – too brief, too *terribly brief* – he had not lived in a place he could call his own for twenty-two years.

But that terribly brief period, twenty-seven months in a lifetime, was enough to see him through the agonies of a thousand nightmares. The memories never left him; they would sustain him until the day he died.

It had been only a small flat in West Berlin, but it was the home of dreams and love and laughter he had never thought he'd be capable of knowing. His beautiful Karine, his adorable Karine. She of the wide, curious eyes and the laughter that came from deep inside her, and moments of quiet when she touched him. He was hers and she was his and . . .

Death in the Unter den Linden.

Oh, *God*! A telephone call and a password. Her husband needed her. *Desperately.* See a guard, cross the checkpoint. *Hurry!*

And a KGB pig had no doubt laughed. Until Prague. There was no laughter in that man after Prague.

Scofield could feel the sting in his eyes. The few sudden tears had made contact with the night wind. He brushed them aside with his glove and crossed the street.

On the other side was the lighted front of a travel agency, the posters in the window displaying idealized, unreal bodies soaking up the sun. The Washington amateur, Congdon, had a point; the Caribbean was a good idea. No self-respecting intelligence service sent agents to the islands in the Caribbean – for fear of winning. Another Cuba and the Kremlin might opt for a Section Eleven. Down in the islands, the Soviets would *know* he was out-of-strategy. He had wanted to spend some time in the Grenadines; why not now? In the morning he would . . .

The figure was reflected in the glass – tiny, obscure, in the background across the wide avenue, barely noticeable. In fact, Bray would *not* have noticed had the man not walked around the spill of a streetlamp. Whoever it was wanted the protection of the shadows in the street, whoever it was was following him. And he was good. There were no abrupt movements, no sudden jumping away from the light. The walk was casual, unobtrusive. He wondered if it was anyone he had trained.

Scofield appreciated professionalism; he would commend the man and wish him a lesser subject for surveillance next time. The State Department was not wasting a moment. Congdon wanted the reports to begin at once. Bray smiled; he would give the under-secretary his initial report. Not the one he wanted, but one he should have.

The amusement began, a short-lived pavane between professionals. Scofield walked away from the shop window, gathering speed until he reached the corner, where the circles of light from the four opposing streetlamps overlapped each other. He turned abruptly left, as if to head back to the other side of the street, then half-way through the intersection stopped. He paused in the middle of the traffic lane and looked up at the street sign – a man confused, not sure of where he was. Then he turned and walked rapidly back to the corner, his pace quickening until he was practically running when he reached the kerb. He continued down the pavement to the first unlighted shopfront, then he spun into the darkness of the doorway and waited.

Through the right-angled glass he had a clear view of the corner. The man following him would have to come into the overlapping circles of light now; they could not be avoided. A quarry was getting away! There was no time to look for shadows.

It happened. The overcoated figure came dashing across the avenue. His face came into the light.

His face came into the light.

Scofield froze. His eyes ached; blood rushed to his head. His whole body trembled, and what remained of his mind tried desperately to control the rage and the anguish that welled up and swept through him. The man at the corner was not from the State Department, the face under the light did not belong to anyone remotely connected to American intelligence.

It belonged to the KGB. To KGB-East Berlin.

It was a face on one of the half-dozen photographs he had studied – studied until he knew every blemish, every strand of hair – in Berlin ten years ago.

Death on the Unter den Linden. His beautiful Karine, his adorable Karine. Trapped by a team across the checkpoint, a unit set up by the filthiest killer in the Soviet. V. Taleniekov. Animal.

This was one of those men. That unit. One of Taleniekov's hangmen.

Here! In Washington! Within minutes of his termination at State!

So KGB had found out. And someone in Moscow had decided to bring a stunning conclusion to the finish of Beowulf Agate. Only one man could think with such dramatic precision. V. Taleniekov. Animal.

As Bray stared through the glass, he knew what he was going to do, what he had to do. He would send a last message to Moscow; it would be a fitting capstone, a final gesture to mark the end of one life and the beginning of another – whatever it might be.

He would trap the killer from KGB. He would kill him.

Scofield stepped out of the doorway and ran down the sidewalk, racing in a zigzag pattern across the deserted street. He could hear running footsteps behind him.

6

Aeroflot's night flight from Moscow approached the Sea of Azov north-east of Crimea. It would arrive in Sevastopol by one o'clock in the morning, something over an hour. The aircraft was crowded, the passengers by and large jubilant, on winter holiday leaves from their offices and factories. A scattering of military personnel – soldiers and sailors – were less exuberant; for them the Black Sea was not a vacation, but a return to work at the naval and air bases. They'd had their leaves in Moscow.

In one of the rear seats sat a man with a dark leather violin case held firmly between his knees. His clothes were rumpled, undistinguished, somehow in conflict with the strong face and the sharp, clear eyes that seemed to belong above other apparel. His papers identified him as Pyotr Rydukov, musician. His flight pass explained curtly that he was on the way to join the Sevastopol Symphony Orchestra as a violinist.

Both items were false. The man was Vasili Taleniekov, master strategist, Soviet Intelligence.

Former master strategist. Former director of KGB operations – East Berlin, Warsaw, Prague, Riga and the South-west Sectors, which consisted of Sevastopol, the Bosphorus, the Sea of Marmara and the Dardanelles. It was this last post that dictated the papers that put him on board the Sevastopol plane. It was the beginning of his flight from Russia.

There were scores of escape routes out of the Soviet Union, and in his professional capacity he had exposed them as he had found them. Ruthlessly, more often than not killing the agents of the West who kept them open, enticing malcontents to betray Russia with lies and promises of money. Always money. He had never wavered in his opposition to the liars and the proselytizers of greed; no escape route was too insignificant to warrant his attention.

Except one. A minor network-route through the Bosphorus and the Sea of Marmara into the Dardanelles. He had uncovered it several months ago, during his last weeks as director, KGB South-west Soviet Sectors. During the days when he found himself in continuous confrontation with hot-headed fools at the military bases and asinine edicts from Moscow itself.

At the time, he was not sure why he held back exposure; for a while he had convinced himself that by leaving it open and watching it closely, it could lead to a larger network. Yet in the back of his mind, he knew that was not true.

His time was coming; he was making too many enemies in too many places. There could be those who felt that a quiet retirement north of Grasnov was not for a man who held the secrets of the KGB in his head. Now he possessed another secret, more frightening than anything conceived of by Soviet intelligence. The Matarese. And that secret was driving him out of Russia.

It had happened so fast, thought Taleniekov, sipping the hot tea provided by the steward. *Everything* had happened so fast. The bedside – deathbed – talk with old Aleksie Krupsky and the astonishing things the dying man had said. Assassins sent forth to kill the elite of the nation – both nations. Pitting the Soviet and the United States against one another, until it controlled one or the other. A Premier and a President, one or both to be in a gunsight. Who were they? *What* were they, this fever that had begun in the first decades of the century in Corsica? The Corsican fever. The Matarese.

But it existed; it was functioning – alive and deadly. He knew that now. He had spoken its name, and for speaking it, a plan had been put in motion that called for his arrest; the sentence of execution would follow shortly.

Krupsky had told him that going to the Premier was out of the question so he had sought out four once-powerful leaders of the Kremlin, now generously retired, which meant that none dared touch them. With each he had spoken of the strange phenomenon called the Matarese, repeated the words whispered by the dying *istrebitel.*

One man obviously knew nothing; he was as stunned as Taleniekov had been. Two *said* nothing, but the acknowledgement was in their eyes, and in their frightened voices when they protested. Neither would be a party to the spreading of such insanity; each had ordered Vasili from his house.

The last man, a Georgian, was the oldest – older than the dead Krupsky – and in spite of an upright posture had little time left to enjoy a straight spine. He was ninety-six, his mind alert but given swiftly to an old man's fear. At the mention of the name Matarese, his thin, veined hands had trembled, then tiny muscular spasms seemed to spread across his ancient, withered face. His throat became suddenly dry; his voice cracked, his words barely audible.

It was a name from long ago in the past, the old Georgian had whispered, a name no one should hear. He had survived the early purges, survived the mad Stalin, the insidious Beria, but no one could survive the Matarese. In the name of all things sacred to Russia, the terrified man pleaded, walk *away* from the Matarese!

"We were fools, but we were not the only ones. Powerful men everywhere were seduced by the sweet convenience of having enemies and obstacles eliminated. The guarantee was absolute: the eliminations would never be traced to those who required them. Agreements were made through parties four and five times removed, dealing in fictitious purchases, unaware of what they were buying. Krupsky saw the danger; he knew. He warned us in 'forty-eight never to make contact again."

"Why did he do that?" Vasili had asked. "If the guarantee was proven true. I speak professionally."

"Because the Matarese added a condition: the council of the Matarese demanded the right of approval. That's what I was told."

"The prerogative of killers-for-hire, I'd think," Taleniekov had interjected. "Some targets simply aren't feasible."

"Such approval was never sought in the past. Krupsky did not think it was based on feasibility."

"On what, then?"

"Ultimate extortion."

"How were the contacts made with this council?"

"I never knew. Neither did Aleksie."

"*Someone* had to make them."

"If they are alive, they will not speak. Krupsky was right about that."

"He called it the Corsican fever. He said the answers might be in Corsica."

"It's possible. It's where it began, with the maniac of Corsica. Guillaume de Matarese."

"You still have influence with the party leaders, sir. Will you help me? Krupsky told me this Matarese must be . . ."

"*No!*" the old man had screamed, interrupting. "Leave me in peace! I've said more than I should, admitted more than I had a right to. But only to warn you, to *stop* you! The Matarese can do no good for Russia! Turn your back on it!"

"You've misunderstood me. It is *I* who want to stop *it*. *Them*. This Matarese council. I gave my word to Aleksie that . . ."

"But you've had no words with *me!*" the withered, once-powerful leader had shouted, his voice childlike in its panic. "I will deny you ever came here, deny anything you say! You are a stranger, and I do not know you!"

Vasili had left, disturbed, perplexed. He had returned to his flat expecting to spend the night analysing the enigma that was the Matarese, trying to decide what to do next. As usual he had glanced at the mail slot in the wall; he had actually taken a step away before he realized there *was* something inside.

It was a note from his contact at the VKR, written in one of the eliptical codes they had arranged between them. The words were innocuous: an agreement to have a late dinner at 11.30 and signed with a girl's first name. The very blandness of the note concealed its meaning. There was a problem of magnitude; the use of *eleven* meant emergency. No time was to be lost making contact; his friend would be waiting for him at the usual place.

He had been there. At a *piva kafe* near the Lomonossov State University. It was a raucous drinking establishment in tune with the new student permissiveness. They had moved to the rear of the hall; his contact had wasted no seconds getting to the point.

"Make plans, Vasili, you're on their list. I don't understand it but that's the word."

"Because of the Jew?"

"Yes, and it doesn't make sense! When that idiotic news conference was held in New York, we division men laughed. We called it 'Taleniekov's surprise'. Even a section chief from Group Nine said he admired what you did; that you taught a lesson to impetuous potato-heads. Then yesterday everything changed. What you did was no longer a joke, but rather a serious interference with basic policy."

"Yesterday?" Vasili had asked his friend.

"Late afternoon. Past four o'clock. That bitch director marched through the offices like a gorilla in season. She smelled a gang rape and she loved it. She told each division man to be at her office at five o'clock. When we got there and listened, it was unbelievable. It was as if you were personally responsible for every setback we've sustained for the past two years. Those maniacs from Group Nine were there, but not the section chief."

"How long have I got?"

"Three or four days at the outside. Incriminating evidence against you is being compiled. But silently, no one is to say anything."

"Yesterday . . ."

"What happened, Vasili? This isn't a VKR operation. It's something else."

It *was* something else and Taleniekov had recognized it instantly. The yesterday in question had been the day he had seen the two former Kremlin officials who had ordered him from their homes. The something else was the Matarese.

"One day I'll tell you, my friend," Vasili had answered. "Trust me."

"Of course. You're the best we have. The best we've ever had."

"Right now I need thirty-six, perhaps forty-eight hours. Do I have them?"

"I think so. They want your head, but they'll be careful. They'll document as much as they can."

"I'm sure they will. One needs words to read over the corpse. Thank you. You'll hear from me."

Vasili had not returned to his flat, but instead to his office. He had sat in the darkness for hours, arriving at his extraordinary decision. Hours before it would have been unthinkable, but not now. If the Matarese could corrupt the highest levels of the KGB, it could do the same in Washington. If the mere mentioning of its name called for the death of a master strategist of his rank – and there was no mistaking it: death was the objective – then the power it possessed was unthinkable. If, in truth, it was responsible for the murders of Blackburn and Yurievich, then Krupsky was right. There was a timetable. The Matarese were closing in, the Premier or President moving into the gunsight.

He had to reach a man he loathed. He had to reach Brandon Alan Scofield, American killer.

In the morning, Taleniekov had put several wheels in motion, one after the other. With his customary – if curtailed – freedom of decision, he let it be known quietly that he was travelling under cover to the Baltic Sea for a conference. He then scoured the rolls of the Musicians' Protective and found the name of a violinist who had retired five years ago to the Ural Mountains; he would do. Lastly, he had put the computers to work looking for a clue to the whereabouts of Brandon Scofield. The American had disappeared in Marseilles, but an incident had taken place in Amsterdam that bore the unmistakable mark of Scofield's expertise. Vasili had sent a cipher to an agent in Brussels, a man he could trust for he had saved his life on more than one occasion.

Approach Scofield, white status. Amsterdam. Contact must be made. Imperative. Stay with him. Apprise situation South-west Sector codes.

Everything had happened so rapidly, and Taleniekov was grateful for the years that made it possible for him to arrive at swift decisions. Sevastopol was less than an hour away. In Sevastopol – and beyond – those years of hard experience would be put to the test.

He took a room at a small hotel on the boulevard Chersonesus and called a number at the KGB headquarters that was not attached to a recorder; he had installed it himself.

VKR-Moscow had not as yet put out an alarm for him, that much could be ascertained from headquarters' warm greeting. An old friend had returned; it gave Vasili the latitude he needed.

"To be frank," he said to the night duty officer, a former associate, "we have our on-going problem with VKR. They've interfered again. You may get a teletype inquiry. You haven't heard from me, all right?"

"That's no problem as long as you don't show up here; you called on the right telephone. Are you staying in cover?"

"Yes. I won't burden you with my whereabouts. We're involved with a courier probe, convoys of trucks heading for Odessa, then south to the mountains. It's a CIA network."

"That's easier than fishing boats through the Bosphorus. By the way, does Amsterdam fit into your blueprints?"

Taleniekov was startled. He had not expected so quick a reply from his man there. "It could. What have you got?"

"It came in two hours ago; it took that long to break. Our cryptographer – the man you brought from Riga – recognized an old code of yours. We were going to send it on to Moscow with the morning's dispatches."

"Don't do that," said Vasili. "Read it to me."

"Wait a minute." Papers were shuffled. "Here it is. 'Beowulf removed from orbit. Storm clouds Washington. On strength of imperative will pursue and deliver white contact. Cable instructions capitol depot.' That's it."

"It's enough," said Taleniekov.

"Sounds impressive, Vasili. A white contact? You've struck a high-level defection, I gather. Good for you. Is it tied in with your probe?"

"I think so," lied Taleniekov. "But don't say anything. Keep VKR out."

"With pleasure. You want us to cable for you?"

"No," replied Vasili, "I can do it. It's routine. I'll call you this evening. Say nine-thirty; that should be time enough. Tell my old friend from Riga I said hello. No one else, however. And thank you."

"When your probe's over, let's have dinner. It's good to have you back in Sevastopol."

"It's good to be back. We'll talk." Taleniekov hung up, concentrating on the message from Amsterdam. Scofield had been recalled to Washington, but the circumstances were abnormal. Beowulf Agate had run into a severe State Department storm. That fact alone was enough to propel the agent from Brussels into a transatlantic pursuit, debts notwithstanding. A white status contact was a momentary truce; a truce generally meant that someone was about to do something drastic. And if there existed even the remote possibility that the legendary Scofield might defect, any risk was worth the candle. The man who brought in Beowulf Agate would have all of Soviet Intelligence at his feet.

But defection was not possible for Scofield . . . any more than it was for him. The enemy was the enemy; that would never change.

Vasili picked up the phone again. There was an all-night number in the Lazarev district of the waterfront used by Greek and Iranian businessmen to send out cables to their home offices. By saying the right words, priority would be given over the existing traffic; within several hours his cable would reach "capitol depot". It was a hotel on Nebraska Avenue in Washington, D.C.

He would meet Scofield on neutral ground, some place where neither could take advantage of the location. Within the departure gates of an airline where the security measures were the harshest – West Berlin or Tel Aviv, it did not matter; distance was inconsequential. But they had to meet, and Scofield had to be convinced of the necessity of that meeting. The cipher to Washington instructed the man from Brussels to convey the following to Beowulf Agate.

We have traded in blood very dear to both of us. In truth, I more than you but you could not know it. Now there is another who would hold us responsible for international slaughter on a scale to which neither of us can subscribe. I operate outside of authority and alone. We must exchange views – as loathsome as it may be to both of us. Choose a neutral location, within an airport security compound. Suggest El Al, Tel Aviv or German domestic carrier, West Berlin. This courier will know how to reply.

My name is known to you.

It was nearly four o'clock in the morning before he closed his eyes. He had not slept in nearly three days, and when sleep came, it was deep and long. He had gone to bed before there was any evidence of the sun in the eastern sky; he awoke an hour after it had descended in the west. That was good. His mind and his body had needed the rest, and one travelled at night to the place he was going in Sevastopol.

There were three hours before the duty officer arrived at KGB; it was simpler not to involve anyone else at headquarters. The fewer who knew he was in the city, the better. Of course, the cryptographer knew, he had deduced the connection from the cipher out of Amsterdam, but the man would say nothing. Taleniekov had trained him, taken a bright young man from the austerity of Riga to the freer life in Sevastopol.

The time could be well spent, thought Vasili. He would eat, then make arrangements for passage in the hold of a Greek freighter that would cut straight across the sea, then follow the southern coast through the Bosphorus, and on to the Dardanelles. If any of the Greek or Iranian units in the pay of the CIA or SAVAK recognized him – and it was possible – he would be entirely professional. As the previous director of the KGB sector, he had not exposed the escape route for personal reasons. However, if a musician named Pyotr Rydukov did not make a telephone call to Sevastopol within two days after departure, exposure was guaranteed, KGB reprisals to follow. It would be a shame; other privileged men might wish to use the route later, their talents and information worth having.

Taleniekov put on the undistinguished, ill-fitting overcoat and his battered hat. A slouch and a pair of steel-rimmed spectacles were added. He checked his appearance in the mirror; it was satisfactory. He picked up the leather violin case; it completed his disguise, for no musician left his instrument in a strange hotel room. He went out the door, down the staircase – never an elevator – and out into the Sevastopol streets. He would walk to the waterfront; he knew where to go and what to say.

Fog rolled in from the sea, curling through the beams of the floodlights on the pier. There was activity everywhere as the hold of the freighter was loaded. Men shouted as giant cranes swung cables cradling enormous boxcars of merchandise over the side of the ship. The loading crews were Russian, supervised by Greeks. Soldiers and *militsianyeri* milled about, weapons slung casually over their shoulder, ineffectual patrols more interested in watching the machinery than in looking for irregularities.

If they wanted to know, mused Vasili as he approached the officer at the entrance gate, he could tell them. The irregularities were in the huge containers being lifted over the hull of the ship. Men and women packed in shredded cardboard, tubes from mouths to airspaces where necessary, instructions having been given to empty bladders and bowels several hours ago; there would be no relief until well past midnight when they were at sea.

The officer at the gate was a young lieutenant, bored with his work, irritation in his face. He scowled at the slouching, bespectacled old man before him.

"What do you want? The pier is off-limits unless you have a pass." He pointed to the violin case. "What's that?"

"My livelihood, Lieutenant. I'm with the Sevastopol Symphony."

"I wasn't aware of any concerts scheduled for the docks."

"Your name, please?" said Vasili casually.

"What?"

Taleniekov stood up to his full height, the slouch gradually but clearly disappearing. "I asked you your name, Lieutenant."

"What for?" The officer was somewhat less hostile. Vasili removed the spectacles and looked sternly into his bewildered eyes.

"For a commendation or a reprimand."

"What are you talking about? Who are you?"

"KGB–Sevastopol. This is part of our waterfront inspection programme."

The young lieutenant was politely hesitant; he was not a fool. "I'm afraid I wasn't told, sir. I'll have to ask for your identification."

"If you didn't, it would be the first reprimand," said Taleniekov, reaching into his pocket for his KGB card. "The second would come if you speak of my appearance here tonight. The name, please."

The lieutenant told him, then added, "Do you people suspect trouble down here?" He studied the plastic card and returned it.

"Trouble?" Taleniekov smiled, his eyes humorous and conspiratorial. "The only trouble, Lieutenant, is that I'm being deprived of a warm dinner in the company of a lady. I think the new directors in Sevastopol feel compelled to earn their roubles. You men are doing a good job; they know that but don't care to admit it."

Relieved, the young officer smiled back. "Thank you, sir. We do our best in a monotonous job."

"But don't say anything about my being here; they're serious about that. Two officers of the guard were reported last week." Vasili smiled again. "In the directors' secrecy lies their true security. Their jobs."

The lieutenant grinned. "I understand. Have you a weapon in that case?"

"No. Actually, it's a very good violin. I wish I could play it."

Both men nodded knowingly. Taleniekov continued on to the pier, into the mêlée of machinery, dock workers and supervisors. He was looking for a specific supervisor, a Greek from Kaválla named Zaimis. Which was to say he was looking for a man whose heritage was Greek and whose mother's name was Zaimis, but whose citizenship was American.

Karras Zaimis was a CIA agent, formerly station chief in Salonika, now field expediter of the escape route. Vasili knew the agent's face from several photographs he had removed from the KGB files. He peered through the bodies and the fog and the floodlights; he could not spot the man.

Taleniekov threaded his way past rushing fork-lifts and crews of complaining labourers towards the huge cargo warehouse. Inside the enormous enclosure, the light was dim, the wire-meshed floodlights too high in the ceiling to do much good. Beams of flashlights crisscrossed the containers; men were checking numbers. Vasili wondered briefly how much talent was in those boxcars. How much information was being taken out of Russia. Actually, not a great deal of either, he reminded himself. This was a minor escape route; more comfortable accommodation was provided for serious talent and significant bearers of intelligence data.

His slouch controlling his walk and his spectacles awkwardly in place, he excused himself past a Greek supervisor arguing with a Russian foreman. He wandered towards the rear of the warehouse, past stacks of cartons and aisles blocked with freight dollies, studying the faces of those holding flashlights. He was becoming annoyed; he did not have the time to waste. Where was Zaimis? There had been *no* change of status; the freighter *was* the carrier, the agent *still* the conduit. He had read every report sent from Sevastopol; there had been no mention of the escape route whatsoever. Where *was* he?

Suddenly Taleniekov felt a shock of pain as the barrel of a gun was shoved viciously into his right kidney. Strong fingers gripped the loose cloth of his overcoat, crunching the flesh of his lower rib cage; he was propelled into a deserted aisle. Words were whispered harshly in English.

"I won't bother speaking Greek, or trying to get through to you in Russian. I'm told your English is as good as anyone's in Washington."

"Conceivably better than most," said Vasili through his teeth. "Zaimis?"

"Never heard of him. We thought you were out of Sevastopol."

"I am. Where is Zaimis? I must speak with Zaimis."

The American disregarded the question. "You've got balls, I'll say that for you. There's no one from KGB within ten blocks of here."

"Are you sure about that?"

"Very. We've got a flock of night owls out there. They see in the dark. They saw you. A violin case, *Christ!*"

"Do they look to the water?"

"Seagulls do that."

"You're very well organized, all you birds."

"And you're less bright than everyone says. What did you think you were doing? A little personal reconnaissance?"

Vasili felt the grip lessen on his ribs, then heard the muted sound of an object pulled out of rubber. A vial of serum. A *needle*. "Don't!" he said firmly. "Don't do that! Why do you think I'm here alone? I want to get out."

"That's just where you're going. My guess would be an interrogation hospital somewhere in Virginia for about three years."

"*No.* You don't understand. I have to make contact with someone. But not *that* way."

"Tell it to the nice doctors. They'll listen to everything you say."

"There's no time!" There *was* no time. Taleniekov could feel the man's weight shift; in seconds a needle would puncture his clothes and enter his flesh. It could not happen this way! He could not deal with Scofield officially!

None dare talk. The admissions would be catastrophic . . . for governments every-where. The Matarese.

If he could be destroyed in Moscow, the Americans would not think twice about silencing him.

Vasili raised his right shoulder – a gesture of pain from the gun barrel in his kidney. The gun was abruptly pressed farther into his back – a reaction to the gesture. In that split instant, the pressure point of the hand holding the gun was on the heel of the palm, not the index finger; but only for the briefest of instants. Taleniekov's movement was timed for it.

He spun to his left, his arm arching up, crashing down over the American's elbow, vicing it into his hip until the forearm cracked. He jabbed the fingers of his right hand into the man's throat, bruising the windpipe. The gun fell to the floor, its clatter obscured by the din of the warehouse. Vasili picked it up and shoved the CIA agent against a boxcar container. In his pain, the American held the hypodermic needle limply in his left hand; it, too, dropped to the floor. His eyes were glazed, but not beyond cognizance.

"Now, you *listen* to me," said Taleniekov, his face against Zaimis' face. "I've known about 'Operation Dardanelles' for nearly seven months. You deal in mediocre traffic; you're not significant. But that's not the reason I didn't blow you apart. I thought one day you might be of use to me. That time has come. You can accept it or not."

"Taleniekov defect?" said Zaimis, holding his throat. "No way. You're Soviet poison. A double entry, but no defector."

"You're right. I do not defect. And if that unthinkable option ever entered my mind, I'd contact the British, or the French before you. I said I wanted to get out of Russia, not betray it."

"You're lying," said the American, his hand slipping down to the lapel of his heavy cloth jacket. "You can go to anywhere you want."

"Not at the moment, I'm afraid. There are complications."

"What did you do, turn capitalist? Make off with a couple of pouches?"

"Come on, Zaimis. Which of us doesn't have his small box of resources? Often legitimate; funnelled monies can be delayed. Where's yours? I doubt Athens, and Rome is too unstable. I'd guess Berlin or London. Mine's quite ordinary: certificates of deposit, Chase Manhattan, New York City."

The CIA man's expression remained passive, his thumb curled beneath his jacket's lapel. "So you got caught," he said absently.

"We're wasting time!" Vasili barked. "Get me to the Dardanelles. I'll make my own way from there. If you don't, if a telephone call is not received here in Sevastopol when expected, your operation is finished. You'll be . . ."

Zaimis' hand shot up towards his mouth; Taleniekov grabbed the agent's fingers and twisted them violently outward. Stuck to the American's thumb was a small tablet.

"You damn *fool*! What do you think you're doing?"

Zaimis winced, the pain excruciating. "I'd rather go this way than in the *Lubyanka*."

"You *ass*! If anyone goes to the *Lubyanka*, it will be *me*! Because there are maniacs

65

just like you sitting at their desks in Moscow. And *fools* – just like you – who would prefer a tablet rather than listen to the truth! You want to die, I'll accommodate you. But first get me to the Dardanelles!"

The agent, breathing with difficulty, stared at Taleniekov. Vasili released his hand, removing the tablet from Zaimis' thumb.

"You're for real, aren't you?" Zaimis said.

"I'm for real. Will you help me?"

"I haven't got anything to lose," said the agent. "You'll be on our carrier."

"Don't forget. Word must get back here from the Dardanelles. If it doesn't, you're finished."

Zaimis paused, then nodded. "Check. We trade off."

"We trade off," agreed Taleniekov. "Now, can you get me to a telephone?"

The cinderblock cubicle in the warehouse had two phones – installed by Russians and no doubt electronically monitored by SAVAK and the CIA for intercepts, thought Vasili. They would be sterile; he could talk. The American agent picked up his when Taleniekov finished dialling. The instant the call was answered, Vasili spoke.

"Is this you, my old comrade?"

It was and it was not. It was not the section chief he had spoken with earlier; instead, it was the cryptographer Taleniekov had trained years ago in Riga and brought to Sevastopol. The man's voice was low, anxious.

"Our mutual friend was called to the code room; it was arranged. I said I'd wait for your call. I have to see you right away. Where are you?"

Zaimis reached over, his bruised fingers gripping the mouthpiece of Vasili's phone. Taleniekov shook his head; in spite of the fact that he trusted the cryptographer, he had no intention of answering the question.

"That's of no consequence. Did the cable come from 'depot'?"

"A great deal more than that, old friend."

"But it *came*?" pressed Vasili.

"Yes. But it's not in any cipher I've ever heard of. Nothing you and I ever used before. Neither during our years in Riga nor here."

"Read it to me."

"There's something else," insisted the code man, his tone now intense. "They're after you *openly*. I recycled the teletype to Moscow for in-house confirmation and burnt the original. It will be back in less than two hours. I can't *believe it*. I *won't* believe it!"

"Calm down. What was it?"

"There's an alert out for you from the Baltic to the Manchurian borders."

"VKR?" asked Vasili, alarmed but controlled; he had expected Group Nine to act swiftly but not quite this swiftly.

"*Not* just VKR. *KGB* – and every intelligence station we *have*! As well as all military units. *Everywhere*. This isn't *you* they speak of, it couldn't be. I will not believe it!"

"What do they say?"

"That you've betrayed the State. You're to be taken, but there's to be no *detention*, no interrogation *at all*. You're to be . . . executed . . . without delay."

"I see," said Taleniekov. And he did see; he expected it. It was not the VKR. It was powerful men who'd heard he had spoken a name that no one should hear. *Matarese*. "I've betrayed no one. Believe that."

"I do. I know you."

"Read me the cable from 'depot'."

"Very well. Have you a pencil? It makes no sense."

Vasili reached into his pocket for his pen; there was paper on the table. "Go ahead."

The man spoke slowly, clearly. "As follows: 'Invitation Kasimir. Schrankenwarten five goals' . . ." The cryptographer stopped: Taleniekov could hear voices in the distance over the line. "I can't go on. People are coming," he said.

"I *must* have the rest of that cable!"

"Thirty minutes. *Amar Magazin*. I'll be there." The line went down.

Vasili slammed his fist on the table, then replaced the phone as Zaimis did the same. "I *must have it*," he repeated in English.

"What's the Amar Magazin – the Lobster Shop?" asked the CIA man.

"A fish restaurant on Kerenski Street, about seven blocks from headquarters. No one who knows Sevastopol goes there; the food is terrible. But it fits what he was trying to tell me."

"What's that?"

"Whenever the cryptographer wanted me to screen certain incoming material before others saw it, he would suggest we meet at the *Amar*."

"He didn't just come to your office and talk?"

Taleniekov glanced over at the American. "You know better than that, Karras Zaimis. You people perfected electronic surveillance. We merely stole it."

The agent looked hard at Vasili. "They want you very dead, don't they?"

"It's a gargantuan error."

"It always is," said Zaimis, frowning. "You trust him?"

"You heard him. When do you sail?"

"Eleven-thirty. Two hours. Roughly the same time that confirmation's due back from Moscow."

"I'll be here."

"I know you will," said the agent. "Because I'm going with you."

"You *what?*"

"I've got protection out there in the city. Of course, I'll want my gun back. *And* yours. We'll see how much you want to get through the Bosphorus."

"Why should you do this?"

"I have an idea you may reconsider that unthinkable option of yours. I want to bring you in."

Vasili shook his head slowly. "Nothing ever changes. It will not happen. I can still expose you and you don't know how. And by exposing you, I blow apart your Black Sea network. It would take years to re-establish. Time is always the issue, isn't it?"

"We'll see. You want to get to the Dardanelles?"

"Of course."

"Give me the gun," said the American.

The restaurant was filled, the waiters' aprons as dirty as the sawdust on the floor. Taleniekov sat alone by the right rear wall, Zaimis two tables away in the company of a Greek merchant seaman whose face was creased with loathing for his surroundings. Vasili sipped iced vodka which helped disguise the taste of the fifth-rate caviar.

The cryptographer came through the door, spotted Taleniekov, and weaved his way awkwardly between waiters and patrons to the table. His eyes behind the thick lenses of his glasses conveyed at once joy and fear and a hundred unspoken questions.

"It's all so incredible," he said, sitting down. "What have they *done* to you?"

"It's what they're doing to themselves," replied Vasili. "They don't want to listen, they don't want to hear what has to be said, what has to be stopped. It's all I can tell you."

"But to call for your *execution*. It's inconceivable!"

"Don't worry, old friend. I'll be back – and, as they say – rehabilitated with honours." Taleniekov smiled and touched the man's arm. "Never forget. There are good and decent men in Moscow, more committed to their country than to their own fears and ambitions. They'll always be there, and those are the men that I will reach. They'll welcome me and thank me for what I've done. Believe that . . . Now, we're dealing in minutes. Where is the cable?"

The cryptographer opened his hand. The paper was neatly folded, creased into his palm. "I wanted to be able to throw it away, if I had to. I know the words." He handed the cipher to Vasili.

A dread came over Taleniekov as he read the message from Washington.

Invitation Kasimir. Schrankenwarten five goals, Unter den Linden. Przeclvac zero. Prague. Repeat text. Zero. Repeat again at will. Zero.

Beowulf Agate

When he had finished reading, the former master strategist of KGB whispered, "Nothing ever changes."

"What is it?" asked the cryptographer. "I didn't understand it. It's no code we've ever used."

"There's no way that you could understand," answered Vasili, anger and sadness in his voice. "It's a combination of two codes. Ours and theirs. Ours from the days in East Berlin, theirs from Prague. This cable was not sent by the man from Brussels. It was sent by a killer who won't stop killing."

It happened so fast there were only seconds to react, and the Greek seaman moved first. His weathered face had been turned towards the incoming customers. He spat out the words.

"Watch it! The goats are filthy!"

Taleniekov looked up; the cryptographer spun in his chair. Twenty feet away, in an aisle peopled by waiters, were two men who had not come in for a meal; their expressions were set, their eyes darting about the room. They were scanning the tables but not for friends.

"Oh, my *God*!" whispered the cryptographer turning back to Vasili. "They found the phone and tapped it. I was afraid of that."

"Followed you, yes," said Taleniekov, glancing over at Zaimis, who was half out of his chair, the *idiot*. "They know we're friends; you're being watched. But they didn't find the phone. If they were certain that I was here, they'd break in with a dozen soldiers. They're district VKR. I know them. Calmly now, take off your hat and slide out of your chair. Head towards the back hallway, to the men's room. There's a rear exit, remember?"

"Yes, yes, I remember," spluttered the man nervously. He got up, his shoulders hunched, and started for the narrow corridor several tables away.

But he was an academic, not a field man, and Vasili cursed himself for trying to instruct him. One of the two VKR men spotted him and came forward, pushing aside the waiters in the aisle.

Then he saw Taleniekov and his hand whipped into the open space of his jacket towards an unseen weapon. As he did so, the Greek seaman lurched up from his chair, weaving unsteadily, waving his arms like a man with too much vodka in him. He slammed against the VKR man, who tried to push him away. The Greek feigned drunken indignation and pushed back with such force that the Russian went sprawling over a table, sending dishes and food crashing to the floor.

Vasili sprang up and raced past his old friend from Riga, pulling him towards the narrow hallway; then he saw the American. Zaimis was on his feet, his gun in his hand. *Idiot*.

"Put that *away*!" shouted Taleniekov. "Don't expose . . ."

It was too late. A gunshot exploded through the sounds of chaos, escalating it instantly into pandemonium. The CIA man brought both his hands to his chest as he fell, the shirt beneath his jacket suddenly drenched with blood.

Vasili grabbed the cryptographer by the shoulder, yanking him through the narrow archway. There was a second gunshot; the code man arched spastically, his legs together, an eruption of flesh at his throat. He had been shot through the back of the neck.

Taleniekov lunged to the floor of the hallway, stunned at what followed. He heard a third gunshot, a shrill scream after it, penetrating the cacophony of screams surrounding it. And then the Greek seaman crashed through the archway, an automatic in his hand.

"Is there a way out back here?" he roared in broken English. "We have to run. The first goat got away. Others will come!"

Taleniekov scrambled to his feet and gestured for the Greek to follow him. Together they raced through a door into a kitchen filled with the terrified cooks and waiters, and out into an alley. They turned left and ran through a maze of dark connecting pavements between the old buildings until they reached the back streets of Sevastopol.

They kept running for over a mile. Vasili knew every inch of the city, but it was the Greek who kept shouting the turns they must make. As they entered a dimly lit side street, the seaman grabbed Taleniekov's arm; the man was out of breath.

"We can rest here for a minute," he said, gasping for air. "They won't find us."

"It's not a place we think of first in a search," agreed Vasili, looking at the row of neat apartment buildings.

"Always hide out in a well-kept neighbourhood," said the seaman. "The residents veer away from controversy; they'd inform on you in a minute. Everybody knows it so they don't look in such places."

"You say we can stay 'for a minute'," said Taleniekov. "I'm not sure where we'll go after that. I need time to think."

"You rule out the ship then?" asked the Greek, nodding, still breathless. "I thought so."

"Yes. Zaimis had papers on him. Worse, he had my gun. The VKR will be swarming over the piers within the hour."

The Greek studied Vasili in the dim light. "So the great Taleniekov flees Russia. He can remain only as a corpse."

"Not from Russia, only from frightened men. But I do have to leave – for a while. I've got to figure out how."

"There is a way," said the merchant seaman simply. "We'll head over the north-west coast, then south into the mountains. You'll be in Greece in three days."

"How?"

"There's a convoy of trucks that goes first to Odessa . . ."

Taleniekov sat on the hard bench in the back of the truck, the early light of dawn seeping through the billowing canvas flaps that covered the sides. In a while, he and the others would have to crawl beneath the floorboards, remaining motionless and silent on a concealed ledge between the axles, while they passed through the next checkpoint. But for an hour or so they could stretch and breathe air that did not reek of burned oil and grease.

He reached into his pocket and took out the cipher from Washington, the cable that had already cost three lives.

Invitation Kasimir. Schrankenwarten five goals, Unter den Linden. Przseclvac zero. Prague. Repeat text. Zero. Repeat again at will. Zero.

Beowulf Agate

Two codes. One meaning.

With his pen, Vasili wrote out that meaning beneath the cipher. *Come and take me, as you took someone else across a checkpoint at five o'clock on the Unter den Linden. I've broken and killed your courier, as another courier was killed in Prague. Repeat: Come to me. I'll kill you.*

Scofield

Beyond the American killer's brutal decision, the most electrifying aspect of Scofield's cable was the fact that he was no longer in the service of his country. He had been separated from the intelligence community. And considering what he had done and the pathological forces that drove him to do it, the separation was undoubtedly savage. For no government professional would murder a courier in the circumstances of this extraordinary Soviet contact. And if Scofield was nothing else, he was a professional.

The storm clouds over Washington had been catastrophic for Beowulf Agate. They had destroyed him.

As the storm over Moscow had destroyed a master strategist named Taleniekov.

It was strange, bordering on the macabre. Two enemies who loathed each other had been chosen by the Matarese as the first of its lethal decoys – plays and diversions, as old Krupsky had called them. Yet only one of those enemies knew it; the other did not. He was concerned solely with ripping scars open, letting the blood between them flow again.

Vasili put the paper back into his pocket, and breathed deeply. The coming days would be filled with move and counter-move, two experts stalking each other until the inevitable confrontation.

My name is Taleniekov. We will kill each other or we will talk.

7

Under-Secretary of State Daniel Congdon shot up from the chair, the telephone in his hand. Since his early days at NSA he had learned that one way of controlling an outburst was to physically move during a moment of crisis. And control was the key to everything in his profession; at least, the appearance of it. He listened as this particular crisis was defined by an angry Secretary of State.

Goddamn it, *he* was controlled.

"I've just met privately with the Soviet ambassador and we both agree the incident must not be made public. The important thing now is to bring Scofield in."

"Are you *certain* it was Scofield, sir? I can't believe it!"

"Let's say that until he denies it with irrefutable proof that he was a thousand miles away during the past forty-eight hours we must assume it *had* to be Scofield. No one else in clandestine operations would have committed such an act. It's unthinkable."

Unthinkable? *Incredible.* The body of a dead Russian delivered through the gates of the Soviet Embassy in the back seat of a Yellow Cab at 8.30 in the morning at the height of Washington's rush-hour traffic. And a driver who knew absolutely nothing except that he had picked up *two* drunks, not one – although one was in worse shape than the other. What the hell had happened to the other guy? The one who sounded like a Russkie and wore a hat and dark glasses and said the sunlight was too bright after a whole night of *Wodka*. Where was he? And was the fellow in the back seat all right? He looked like a mess.

"Who was the man, Mr Secretary?"

"He was a Soviet intelligence officer stationed in Brussels. The ambassador was frank; the KGB had no knowledge he was in Washington."

"A possible defection?"

"There's no evidence whatsoever to support that."

"Then what ties him to Scofield? Beyond the method of dispatch and delivery."

The Secretary of State paused, then replied carefully. "You must understand, Mr Congdon, the ambassador and I have a unique relationship that goes back several decades. We are often more candid with each other than diplomatic. Always with the understanding that neither speaks for the record."

"I understand, sir," said Congdon, realizing that the answer about to be given could never be referred to officially.

"The intelligence officer in question was a member of a KGB unit in East Berlin roughly ten years ago. I assume in the light of your recent decisions that you're familiar with Scofield's file."

"His wife?" Congdon sat down. "The man was one of those who killed Scofield's *wife?*"

"The ambassador made no reference to Scofield's wife; he merely mentioned the fact that the dead man had been part of a relatively autonomous section of the KGB in East Berlin ten years ago."

"That section was controlled by a strategist named Taleniekov. He gave the orders."

"Yes," said the Secretary of State. "We discussed Mr Taleniekov and the subsequent incident several years later in Prague at some length. We looked for the connection you've just considered. It may exist."

"How is that, sir?"

"Vasili Taleniekov disappeared two days ago."

"*Disappeared?*"

"Yes, Mr Congdon. Think about it. Taleniekov learned that he was to be officially retired, mounted a simple but effective cover, and disappeared."

"Scofield's been terminated . . ." Congdon spoke softly, as much to himself as into the telephone.

"Exactly," agreed the Secretary of State. "The parallel is our immediate concern. Two retired specialists now bent on doing what they could not do – or pursue – officially. Kill each other. They have contacts everywhere, men who are loyal to them for any number of reasons. Their personal vendetta could create untold problems for both governments during these precious months of conciliation. This cannot happen."

The director of *Cons Op* frowned; there was something wrong in the Secretary's conclusions. "I spoke with Scofield myself three nights ago. He didn't appear consumed with anger or revenge or anything like that. He was a tired field agent who'd lived . . . abnormally . . . for a long time. For years. He told me he just wanted to fade away, and I believed him. I discussed Scofield with Robert Winthrop, by the way, and he felt the same way about him. He said . . ."

"Winthrop knows *nothing*," interrupted the Secretary of State with unexpected harshness. "Robert Winthrop is a brilliant man, but he's never understood the meaning of confrontation except in its most rarefied forms. Bear in mind, Mr Congdon, Scofield killed that intelligence officer from Brussels."

"Perhaps there were circumstances we're not aware of."

"Really?" Again the Secretary of State paused, and when he spoke, the meaning behind his words was unmistakable. "If there *are* such circumstances, I submit we have a far more potentially dangerous situation than any personal feud might engineer. Scofield and Taleniekov know more about the field operations of both intelligence services than any two men alive. They must not be permitted to make contact. Either as enemies intent on killing one another, or for those circumstances we know nothing about. Do I make myself clear, Mr Congdon? As director of Consular Operations, it is your responsibility. How you *execute* that responsibility is no concern of mine. You may have a man beyond salvage. That's for you to decide."

Daniel Congdon remained motionless as he heard the click on the other end of the line. In all his years of service he had never received such an ill-disguised if oblique order. The language could be debated, not the command. He replaced the phone in its cradle and reached for another on the left side of his desk. He pressed a button and dialled three digits.

"Internal Security," said the male voice answering.

"This is Under-Secretary Congdon. Pick up Brandon Scofield. You have the information. Bring him in at once."

"One minute, sir," replied the man politely. "I think a level-two surveillance entry on Scofield came in a couple of days ago. Let me check the computer. All the data's there."

"A couple of days ago?"

"Yes, sir. It's on the screen now. Scofield checked out of his hotel at approximately eleven p.m. on the sixteenth."

"The sixteenth? Today's the nineteenth."

"Yes, sir. There was no time lapse as far as the entry was concerned. The management informed us within the hour."

"Where is he?"

"He left two forwarding addresses, but no dates. A sister's residence in Minneapolis and a hotel in Charlotte Amalie, St Thomas, US Virgin Islands."

"Have they been verified?"

"As to accuracy, yes, sir. A sister does live in Minneapolis and the hotel in St Thomas is holding a pre-paid reservation for Scofield effective the seventeenth. The money was wired from Washington."

"Then he's there."

"Not as of noon today, sir. A routine call was made; he hasn't arrived."

"What about the sister?" interrupted Congdon.

"Again a routine call. She confirmed the fact that Scofield called her and said he'd stop by, but he didn't say when. She added that it wasn't unusual; it was normal for him to be casual about visits. She expected him sometime during the week."

The director of *Cons Op* felt the urge to get up again, but he suppressed it. "Are you telling me you don't really know where he is?"

"Well, Mr Congdon, an S-level-two operates on reports received, not continuous visual contact. We'll shift to level-one right away. Minneapolis won't be any problem; the Virgin Islands could be, though."

"Why?"

"We have no reliable sources there, sir. Nobody does."

Daniel Congdon got up from his chair. "Let me try to understand you. You say Scofield's on level-two surveillance, yet my instructions were clear; his whereabouts were to be known at all times. Why *wasn't* a level-one put on him? Why wasn't continuous visual contact maintained?"

The man from Internal Security answered haltingly. "That wouldn't be my decision, sir, but I think I can understand it. If a level-one was put on Scofield, he'd spot it and . . . well, sheer perversity would make him mislead us."

"What the hell do you think he's just *done*? Find him! Report your progress hourly to this office!" Congdon sat down angrily, replacing the phone with such force that it jarred the bell. He stared at the instrument, picked it up, and dialled again.

"Overseas Communications, Miss Andros," said the woman's voice.

"Miss Andros, this is Under-Secretary Congdon. Please send a cipher specialist to my office immediately. Classification code *A* maximum security and priority."

"An emergency, sir?"

"Yes, Miss Andros, an emergency. The cable will be sent in thirty minutes. Clear all traffic to Amsterdam, Marseilles . . . and Prague."

Scofield heard the footsteps in the hallway and got out of the chair. He walked to the door and peered through the tiny round disc in the centre. The figure of a man passed by; he did not stop at the door across the way, the entrance to the suite of rooms used by Taleniekov's courier. Bray went back to the chair and sat down. He leaned his head against the rim, staring at the ceiling.

It had been three days since the race in the streets, three nights since he'd taken the messenger from Taleniekov – messenger three nights ago, killer on the Unter den Linden ten years before. It had been a strange night, an odd race, a finish that might have been otherwise

The man could have lived; the decision to kill him had gradually lost its urgency for Bray, as so much had lost urgency, so few convictions were left. The courier had brought it upon himself. The Soviet had gone into panic and pulled out a four-inch, razor-sharp blade from the recesses of the hotel chair and attacked. His death was due to Scofield's reaction; it was not the premeditated murder planned in the street.

Nothing ever changed much. The KGB courier had been used by Taleniekov. The man was convinced that Beowulf Agate was coming over, and the Russian who brought him in would be given the brassiest medal in Moscow along with all the perks that went with it.

"You've been tricked," Bray had told the courier while studying the cable in the hotel suite on Nebraska Avenue.

"Impossible!" the Soviet had yelled. "This is Taleniekov!"

"It certainly is. And he chooses a man from the Unter den Linden to make contact, a man whose face he knows I'll never forget. The odds were that I'd lose control and kill you. In *Washington*. I'm exposed, vulnerable . . . And you've been taken."

"*You're wrong!* It's a white contact!"

"So was East Berlin, you son of a bitch!"

"What are you going to do?"

"Earn some of my severance pay. You're coming in."

"No!"

"Yes."

The man had lunged at Scofield.

Three days had passed since that moment of violence, three mornings since Scofield had deposited the package at the embassy and sent the cipher to Sevastopol. Still no one had come to the door across the hall; and that was not normal. The suite was leased by a brokerage house in Bern, Switzerland, to be available for its "executives". Standard procedure for international businessmen, and also a transparent cover for a Soviet drop.

Bray had forced the issue. The cipher and the courier's dead body *had* to provoke *someone* into checking the suite of rooms. Yet no one had; it did not make sense.

Unless part of Taleniekov's cable was true: he was acting alone. If that were the case, there was only one explanation: the Soviet killer had been terminated, and before retiring to an isolated life somewhere in the vicinity of Grasnov, he had decided to settle an outstanding debt.

He had sworn to do so after Prague; the message had been clear: *You're mine, Beowulf Agate. Someday, somewhere. I'll see you take your last breath.*

A brother for a wife. The husband for the brother. It was vengeance rooted in loathing and that loathing never left. There'd be no peace for either of them until the end came for one. It was better to know that now, thought Bray, rather than find out on a crowded street or a deserted stretch of beach, with a knife in the side or a bullet in the head, fired from a dune of wild grass.

The courier's death was an accident, Taleniekov's would not be. There *would* be no peace until they met, and then death would come – one way or the other. It was a question now of drawing the Russian out; he had made the first move. He was the stalker, the role established.

The strategy was classic: tracks clearly defined for the stalker to follow, and at the chosen moment – least expected – the tracks would not be there, the stalker bewildered, exposed the trap sprung.

Like Bray, Taleniekov could travel anywhere he wished, with or without official sanction. Over the years, both had learned too many methods; a plethora of false papers was out there for purchase, hundreds of men everywhere ready to provide concealment or transportation, cover or weapons – any and all. There were only two basic requirements: identities and money.

Neither he nor Taleniekov lacked either. Both came with the profession, the identities quite naturally, the money less so – more often than not the result of having been hung up by bureaucratic delays in the forwarding of payments demanded. Every specialist worth his rank had his own personal sources of funds. Payments exaggerated, monies diverted and deposited in stable territories. The objective was neither theft nor wealth, merely survival. A man in the field had to be burned only once or twice to learn the necessity of economic back-ups.

Bray had accounts under various names in Paris, Munich, London, Geneva and Lisbon. One avoided Rome and the Communist bloc; the Italian Treasury was madness, and banking in the Eastern satellites too corrupt.

Scofield rarely thought about the monies that were his for the spending; in the back of his mind he supposed he would give them back one day. Had the predatory Congdon not flirted with his own temptations and made the official termination so complicated, Bray might have walked in the next morning and handed him the bankbooks.

Not now. The Under-Secretary's actions ruled it out. One did not hand over several hundred thousand dollars to a man who tried – however timorously – to orchestrate one s elimination while remaining outside the act itself. It was a very professional concept. Scofield recalled that years ago it had been brought to its zenith by the killers of the Matarese. But they were assassins for hire; there'd been no one like them in centuries, since the days of Hasan ibn as-Sabbāh. There would be no one like them ever again, and someone like Daniel Congdon was a pale joke in comparison.

Congdon. Scofield laughed and reached into his pocket for his cigarettes. The new director of Consular Operations was not a fool and only a fool would under-estimate him, but he had the upper-Washington mentality so prevalent in the management of clandestine services. He did not really understand what being in the field did to a man; he might mouth the phrases – twisted psychological terms reeking of depression and self-pity – but he did not see the simple line of action and reaction. Few did, or wanted to, because to recognize it meant admitting knowledge of abnormality in a subordinate whose function the department – or the Company – could do without. Quite simply, pathological behaviour was a perfectly normal way of life for a field man, and no particular emphasis was given to it. The man in the field accepted the fact that he was a criminal before any crimes had been committed. Therefore, at the first hint of activity he took measures to protect himself before anything happened; it was second nature.

Bray had done just that. While the messenger from Taleniekov had been seated across the room in the hotel on Nebraska Avenue, Scofield had made several calls. The first was to his sister in Minneapolis: he was flying out to the Mid-west in a couple of hours and would see her in a day or so. The second was to a friend in Maryland who was a deep-sea fisherman with a roomful of stuffed victims and trophies on the walls: where was a good, small place in the Caribbean that would take him on short notice? The friend had a friend in Charlotte Amalie; he owned a hotel and always kept two or three rooms open for just such emergencies. The fisherman from Maryland would call him for Bray.

So, for all intents and purposes, as of the night of the sixteenth, he was en route to the Mid-west . . . or the Caribbean. Both over fifteen hundred miles from

Washington – where he remained unobserved, never leaving the hotel room across the hall from the Soviet drop.

How often had he hammered the lesson into younger, less experienced field agents? Too many times to count. A man standing motionless in a crowd was difficult to spot, and a man who gave the appearance of running, but still remained motionless even more so.

So simple.

But Taleniekov was not simple and every hour escalated the complexity. All possible explanations had to be examined. The most obvious was that the Russian had activated a dormant drop known to him and his messenger; instructions could be sent quietly to Bern, the suite of rooms leased by cable. It would take weeks before the information was filtered back to Moscow – one drop among thousands everywhere.

If so – and it was perhaps the only explanation – Taleniekov was not merely acting alone, he was acting in conflict with KGB interests. His vendetta superseded his allegiance to his government, if the term had meaning any longer; it had little for Scofield. It was the only explanation. Otherwise the suite of rooms across the hall would be swarming with Soviets. They might wait twenty-four or thirty-six hours to check out FBI observation, but no more than that; there were too many ways to elude the bureau's surveillance.

Bray had the gut instinct that he was right, an instinct developed over the years to the point where he trusted it implicitly. Now he had to put himself into Taleniekov's place, think like Vasili Taleniekov would think. It was his protection against a knife in the side or a bullet from a high-powered rifle. It was the way to bring it all to an end, and not have to go through each day wondering what the shadows held. Or the crowds.

The KGB man had no choice; it was his move and it had to be in Washington. One started with the physical connection, and it was the dormant drop across the hall. In a matter of days – perhaps hours now – Taleniekov would fly into Dulles Airport and the hunt would begin.

But the Russian was no idiot; he would not walk into a trap. Instead, another would come, someone who knew nothing, who had been paid to be an unknowing decoy. An unsuspecting passenger whose friendship was carefully cultivated on a transatlantic flight; or one of dozens of blind contacts Taleniekov had used in Washington. Men and women who had no idea that the European they did well-paid favours for was a strategist for KGB. Among them would be the decoy, or decoys, and the birds. Decoys knew nothing; they were bait. Birds watched, sending out alarms when the bait was being taken. Birds and decoys; they would be Taleniekov's weapons.

Someone would come to the hotel on Nebraska Avenue. Whoever it was would have no instructions beyond getting into those rooms; no telephone number, no name that meant anything. And nearby, the birds would be gliding around, watching, waiting for the quarry to go after the bait.

When the quarry was spotted the birds must reach the hunter. Which meant that the hunter was also nearby.

This would be Taleniekov's strategy, for no other was available; it was also the strategy that Scofield would use. Three or four – five people at the outside – readily available for such employment. Simply mounted: phone calls placed at the airport, a meeting at a downtown restaurant. An inexpensive exercise considering the personal value of the quarry.

Sounds came from beyond the door. Voices. Bray got out of the chair and walked quickly to the tiny glass circle in the panel.

Across the hall a well-dressed woman was talking with the bell captain who carried her overnight bag. Not a suitcase, not luggage from a transatlantic flight, but a small overnight case. The decoy had arrived, the birds not far away. Taleniekov had landed; it had started.

The woman and the bell captain disappeared into the suite of rooms.

Scofield walked to the telephone. It was the moment to begin the counter-exercise. He needed time; two or three days were not out of the question. The waiting game had begun.

He called the deep-sea fisherman on the Maryland shore, making sure to dial direct. He capped the mouthpiece with his right hand, filtering his voice through his barely separated fingers. The greeting was swift, the caller in a hurry. "I'm in the Keys and can't reach that damned hotel in Charlotte Amalie. Call it for me, will you? Tell them I'm on a charter out of Tavernier and will be there in a couple of days."

"Sure, Bray. On a real vacation, aren't you?"

"More than you know. And thanks."

The next call needed no such artifice. It was to a Frenchwoman he had lived with briefly in Paris several years ago. She had been one of the most effective undercover personnel at Interpol until her cover was blown; she worked now for a CIA proprietary company based in Washington. There was no sexual attraction between them any longer but they were friends. No questions were asked when obscure requests were made.

He gave her the name of the hotel on Nebraska Avenue.

"Call in fifteen minutes and ring suite two-eleven. A woman will answer. Ask for me."

"Will she be furious, darling?"

"She won't know who I am. But someone else will."

Taleniekov leaned against the brick of the dark alleyway across from the hotel. For several moments he let his body sag and rolled his neck back and forth, trying to ease the tension, reduce the exhaustion. He had been travelling for nearly three days, flying for over eighteen hours, driving into cities and villages, finding those men who would provide him with false documents that would get him through three immigration stations. From Salonika to Athens, Athens to London, London to New York. Finally a late-afternoon shuttle-flight to Washington after visits to three banks in lower Manhattan.

He had made it; his people in place. An expensive whore he'd brought from New York and three others from Washington, two men and an older woman. All but one were well-spoken *nichevo*, what the Americans called *hustlers*. Each had performed services in the past for the generous "businessman" from The Hague, who had a proclivity for checking up on his associates and a penchant for confidence, both of which he paid for in large sums.

They were primed for their evening's employment. The whore was in the suite of rooms that was the Bern–Washington depot; within minutes Scofield would know it. But Beowulf Agate was no amateur; he would receive the news – from a desk clerk or switchboard operator – and send another to question the girl.

Whoever it was would be seen by one or all of Taleniekov's birds. The two men and the older woman. He had provided each with a miniaturized walkie-talkie no larger than a hand-held recorder; he had purchased four at the Mitsubi complex on Fifth Avenue. They could reach him instantly, unobtrusively. Except for the whore. No risk could be taken that such a device would be found on her. She was expendable.

One of the two men sat in a booth in the dimly lit cocktail lounge with small candle lanterns on each table. Beside him was an open attaché case, papers pulled out and placed under candlelight, a salesman summarizing the events of a business trip. The other man was in the dining room, the table set for two, the reservation made by a highly-placed aide at the White House. The host was delayed: several apologetic calls were received by the maître d'hôtel. The guest would be treated as befitted one receiving such apologies from 1600 Pennsylvania Avenue. Above any suspicion whatsoever.

But it was the older woman Taleniekov counted on most; she was paid well above the others and with good reason. She was not a *nichevo*, no hustler at all. She was a killer.

His unexpected weapon. A gracious, articulate woman of distinction who had no compunction about firing a weapon into a target across the room, or plunging a knife into the stomach of a dinner companion. Who could, at a moment's notice, change her appearance from the dignified to the harridan – and all shades in between. Vasili had paid her thousands over the past half-dozen years, several times having flown her to Europe for chores that suited her extraordinary talents. She had not failed him; she would not fail him tonight. He had reached her soon after landing at Kennedy Airport; she had had a full day to prepare for the evening. It was sufficient.

Taleniekov pushed himself away from the brick wall, shaking his fingers, breathing deeply, forcing thoughts of sleep from his mind. He had covered his flanks; now he could only wait. *If* Scofield wanted to keep the appointment – in the American's judgement, fatal to one of them. And why wouldn't he? It was better to get it over with than be obsessed with every patch of darkness or each crowded street in sunlight, wondering who might be concealed . . . taking aim, unsheathing a knife. No, it was far more desirable to conclude the hunt; that would be Beowulf Agate's opinion. And yet, how *wrong* he was! If there was only some way to reach him, *tell* him! There was the *Matarese!* There were people to see, to appeal to, to convince! Together they could do it; there were decent men in Moscow *and* Washington, men who would *not* be afraid.

But there was no way to reach Brandon Scofield on neutral ground, for no ground would be neutral to Beowulf Agate. At the first sight of his enemy, the

American would instantly use every weapon he had mustered to blow that enemy away. Vasili understood, for if he were Scofield, he would do the same. So it was a question of waiting, circling, knowing that each thought the other was the quarry which would expose himself first; each manoeuvring to cause his adversary to make that mistake.

The terrible irony was that the only significant mistake would come about if Scofield won. Taleniekov could not let that happen. Wherever Scofield was, he had to be taken, immobilized, *forced to listen*.

Which was why the waiting was so important now. And the master strategist of East Berlin and Riga and Sevastopol was an expert in patience.

"The waiting paid off, Mr Congdon," said the excited voice over the phone. "Scofield's on a charter out of Tavernier in the Florida Keys. We estimate he'll arrive in the Virgin Islands the day after tomorrow."

"What's the source of your information?" asked the Director of Consular Operations apprehensively, clearing the sleep from his throat, squinting at the clock on his bedside table. It was 3.00 in the morning.

"The hotel in Charlotte Amalie."

"What's the source of *their* information?"

"They received an overseas call asking that the reservation be held. That he'd be there in two days."

"Who made the call? Where did it come from?"

There was a pause on the other end of the State Department line. "We assume Scofield. From the Keys."

"Don't assume. Find out."

"We're confirming everything, of course. Our man in Key West is on his way to Tavernier now. He'll check out all the charter logs."

"Check out that phone call. Let me know." Congdon hung up and raised himself on the pillow. He looked over at his wife on the twin bed next to him. She had pulled the sheet over her head. The years had taught her to sleep through the all-night calls. He thought about the one he had just received. It was too simple, too believable. Scofield was covering himself in the haze of casual, spur-of-the-moment travelling; an exhausted man getting away for a while. But there was the contradiction: Scofield was not a man ever exhausted to the point of being casual about anything. He deliberately obscured his movements . . . which meant he *had* killed the intelligence officer from Brussels.

KGB. Brussels. Taleniekov.

East Berlin.

Taleniekov and the man from Brussels had worked together in East Berlin. In a 'relatively autonomous section of KGB' – which meant East Berlin . . . and beyond.

In Washington? Had that "relatively autonomous" unit from East Berlin sent men to Washington? It was not unreasonable. The word "autonomous" had two meanings. Not only was it designed to absolve superiors from certain acts of their subordinates but it signified freedom of movement. A CIA agent in Lisbon might track a man to Athens. Why not? He was familiar with an operation. Conversely, a KGB agent in London would follow an espionage suspect to New York. Given general clearance, it was in his line of duty. Taleniekov had operated in Washington; there was speculation that he had made a dozen trips or more to the United States within the past decade.

Taleniekov and the man from Brussels; *that* was the connection they had to examine. Congdon sat forward and reached for the telephone, then stopped. Timing was everything now. The cables had been received in Amsterdam, Marseilles and Prague nearly twelve hours ago. According to reliable informants, they had stunned the recipients. Covert sources in all three cities had reacted to the news of Scofield's "unsalvageable" behaviour with some panic. Names could be revealed, men and women tortured, killed, whole networks exposed; no time was to be lost eliminating Beowulf Agate. Word had been relayed by early evening that two men had already been chosen. In Prague and Marseilles; they were in the air now, on their way to Washington, no delays anticipated regarding passports or immigration procedures. A third would be leaving Amsterdam before morning; it was morning now in Amsterdam.

By noon, an execution team totally dissociated from the United States government would be in Washington. Each man had the same telephone number to call, an untraceable phone in the Baltimore ghetto. Whatever information had been gathered on Scofield would be relayed by the person at that number. And only one man could give that information to Baltimore. The man responsible: the director of Consular Operations. No one else in the United States government had the number.

Could one final connection be made? wondered Congdon. There was so little time and it would take extraordinary cooperation. Could that cooperation be requested, even approached? Nothing like it had ever happened. But it *could* be made, a location might be uncovered, a dual execution guaranteed.

He had been about to call the Secretary of State to suggest a very unusual, early-morning meeting with the Soviet ambassador. But too much time would be consumed with diplomatic complications, neither side wishing to acknowledge the objective of violence. There was a better way; it was dangerous but infinitely more direct.

Congdon got out of bed quietly, went downstairs and entered the small study that was his office at home. He went to his desk which was bolted into the floor, the lower right-hand drawers concealing a safe with a combination lock. He turned on the lamp, opened the panel and twisted the dial. The lock clicked; the steel plate sprang open. He reached inside and took out an index card with a telephone number written on it.

The number was one he never thought he would call. The area code was 902 – Nova Scotia – and it never went unanswered; it was the number for a computer complex, the central clearing house for all Soviet intelligence operations in North America. By calling it, he exposed information that should not be revealed; the complex in Nova Scotia was not supposedly known by US intelligence, but time and the extraordinary circumstances overrode security. There was a man in Nova Scotia who would understand; he would not be concerned about appearances. He had called for too many sentences of death. He was the highest-ranking KGB officer outside Russia.

Congdon reached for the telephone.

"Cabot Strait Exporters," said the male voice in Nova Scotia. "Night dispatcher."

"This is Daniel Congdon, Under-Secretary of State, Consular Operations, United States Government. I request that you put a trace on this call to verify that I'm telephoning from a private residence in Herndon Falls, Virginia. While you're doing that, please activate electronic scanners for evidence of taps on the line. You won't find any. I'll wait as long as you wish, but I must speak with Voltage One, *Vol't Odin*, I think you call him."

His words were greeted by silence from Nova Scotia. It did not take much imagination to visualize a stunned operator pushing emergency buttons. Finally, the voice replied.

"There seems to be interference. Please repeat your message."

Congdon did so.

Again, silence. Then. "If you'll hold on, the supervisor will speak with you. However, we think you've reached the wrong party here in Cape Breton."

"You're not in Cape Breton. You're in Saint Peter's Bay, Prince Edward Island."

"Hold on, please."

The wait took nearly three minutes. Congdon sat down; it was working.

Voltage One got on the line. "Please wait for a moment or two," said the Russian. There followed the hollow sound of a connection still intact but suspended; electronic devices were in operation. The Soviet returned. "This call, indeed, originates from a residential telephone in the town of Herndon Falls, Virginia. The scanners pick up no evidence of interference but, of course, that could be meaningless."

"I don't know what other proof to give you . . ."

"You mistake me, Mr Under-Secretary. The fact that you possess this number is not in itself earthshaking; the fact that you have the audacity to use it and ask for me by my code name, perhaps is. I have the proof I need. What is this business between us?"

Congdon told him in as few words as possible. "You want Taleniekov. We want Scofield. The contact ground is Washington. I'm convinced of it. The key to the location is your man from Brussels."

"If I recall, his body was delivered to the embassy several days ago."

"Yes."

"You've connected it with Scofield?"

"Your own ambassador did. He pointed out that the man was part of a KGB section in East Berlin in 1968. Taleniekov's unit. There was an incident involving Scofield's wife."

"I see," said the Russian. "So Beowulf Agate still kills for revenge."

"That's a bit much, isn't it? May I remind you that it would appear Taleniekov is coming after Scofield, not the other way around."

"Be specific, Mr Under-Secretary. Since we agree in principle, what do you want from us?"

"It's in your computers, or in a file somewhere. It probably goes back a number of years, but it's there; it would be in ours. We believe that at one time or another the man from Brussels and Taleniekov operated in Washington. We need to know the address of the hole. It's the only connection we have between Scofield and Taleniekov. We think that's where they'll meet."

"I see," repeated the Soviet. "And presuming there is such an address, or addresses, what would be the position of your government?"

Congdon was prepared for the question.

"No position at all," he replied in a monotone. "The information will be relayed to others, men very much concerned about Beowulf Agate's recent behaviour. Outside of myself, no one in my government will be involved."

"A ciphered cable, identical in substance, was sent to three counter-revolutionary cells in Europe. To Prague, Marseilles and Amsterdam. Such cells can provide killers."

"I commend you on your interception," said the Director of *Cons Op*.

"You do the same with us every day. No compliments are called for."

"You made no move to interfere?"

"Of course not, Mr Under-Secretary. Would you?"

"No."

"It's eleven o'clock in Moscow. I'll call you back within the hour."

Congdon hung up and leaned back in the chair. He desperately wanted a drink, but would not give in to the need. For the first time in a long career he was dealing directly with faceless enemies in Moscow. There could be no hint of irresponsibility; he was alone and in that solitary contact with his protection. He closed his eyes and pictured blank walls of white concrete in his mind's eye.

Twenty-two minutes later the phone rang. He sprang forward and picked it up.

"There is a small, exclusive hotel on Nebraska Avenue . . ."

8

Scofield let the cold water run in the basin, leaned against the sink, and looked into the mirror. His eyes were bloodshot from lack of sleep, the stubble of his beard pronounced. He had not shaved in nearly three days, the periods of rest were cumulatively not much more than three hours. It was shortly past four in the morning and no time to consider sleeping or shaving.

Across the hall, Taleniekov's well-dressed decoy was getting no more sleep than he was; the telephone calls were coming every fifteen minutes now.

Mr Brandon Scofield, please.
I don't know any Scofield! Stop calling me! Who are you?
A friend of Mr Scofield's. It's urgent that I speak with him.

He's not here! I don't know him. Stop it! You're driving me crazy. I'll tell the hotel not to ring this phone any more!

I wouldn't do that, if I were you. Your friend would not approve. You wouldn't be paid.

Stop it!

Bray's former lover from Paris was doing her job well. She had asked only one question when he had made the request that she keep up the calls.

"Are you in trouble, darling?"

"Yes."

"Then I'll do as you ask. Tell me what you can, so I'll know what to say."

"Don't talk over twenty seconds. I don't know who controls the switchboard."

"You *are* in trouble."

Within an hour, or less, the woman across the hall would go into panic and flee the hotel. Whatever she had been promised was not worth the macabre phone calls, the escalating sense of danger. The decoy would be removed; the hunter stymied.

Taleniekov would then be forced to send in his birds and the process would start over again. Only the phone calls would come less frequently, perhaps every hour, just when sleep was settling in. Eventually, the birds would fly away, there being limits as to how long they could stay in the air. The hunter's resources were extensive, but not *that* extensive. He was operating in foreign territory; how many decoys and birds were available to him? He could not go on indefinitely calling blind contacts, setting up hastily summoned meetings, issuing instructions and money.

No, he could not do that. Frustration and exhaustion would converge and the hunter would be alone, at the end of his resources. Finally, he would show himself. He had no choice; he could not leave the drop unattended. It was the only trap he had, the only connection between himself and the quarry.

Sooner or later Taleniekov would walk down the hotel corridor and stop at the door of suite 211. When he did, it would be the last sight he'd see.

The Soviet killer was good, but he was going to lose his life to the man he called Beowulf Agate, thought Scofield. He turned off the faucet and plunged his face into the cold water.

He pulled up his head; there were sounds of movement in the corridor. He walked to the tiny circular peephole. Across the way, a matronly-looking hotel maid was unlocking the door. Draped over her right forearm were several towels and sheets. A maid at four o'clock in the morning? Bray silently acknowledged Taleniekov's imagination; he had hired an all-night maid to be his late-night eyes inside. It was an able move, but flawed. Such an individual was too limited, too easily removed; she could be called away by the front desk. A guest had had an accident, a burning cigarette, an overturned pitcher of water. Too limited. And with a greater flaw.

In the morning she would go off duty. And when she did, she would be summoned by a guest across the hall.

Scofield was about to go back to his cold basin when he heard the commotion; he looked once more through the glass circle.

The well-dressed woman had walked out of the room, her overnight case in her hand. The maid stood in the door passively as the decoy's words were heard plainly.

"Tell him to go to hell!" shouted the woman. "He's a fucking nut, dear. This whole goddamn place is filled with nuts!"

The maid watched in silence as the woman walked rapidly down the corridor. Then she closed the door, remaining inside.

The matronly-looking maid had been paid well; she would be paid better in the morning by a guest across the hall. The negotiations would begin quickly the second she stepped out of the suite. Who was the man paying her? Where was he?

The string was drawing tighter, everything was patience now. And staying awake.

Taleniekov walked the streets, aware that his legs were close to buckling, struggling to stay alert and avoid colliding with the crowds on the sidewalk. He played mental games to keep his concentration alive, counting footsteps and cracks in the pavement and blocks between telephone booths. The radios could not be used any longer; the citizen-bands were filled with babble. He cursed the fact that there had not been time to purchase more sophisticated equipment. But he never thought it could possibly go on so *long*! Madness!

It was twenty minutes past eleven in the morning, the city of Washington vibrating, people rushing, automobiles and buses clogging the streets . . . and still the insane telephone calls kept coming to the suite at the Hotel on Nebraska Avenue.

Brandon Scofield, please. It's urgent that I speak with him . . .

Insanity!

What was Scofield *doing*? Where *was* he? Where were his intermediaries?

Only the old woman remained in the hotel. The whore had revolted, the two men long since exhausted, their presence merely embarrassing, accomplishing nothing. The woman stayed in the suite, getting what rest she could between the maddening telephone calls, relaying every word spoken by the caller. A female with a pronounced "foreign' accent, probably French, never staying on the line more than ten or twelve seconds, unable to be drawn out and very abrupt. She was either a professional, or being instructed by a professional; there could be no tracing the number or the location of the calls.

Vasili approached the phone booth fifty yards north of the hotel's entrance on the opposite side of the street. It was the fourth call he had made from this particular booth, and he had memorized the graffiti and the odd numbers scratched on the grey metal of the edge. He walked in, pulled the glass door shut, and inserted a coin; the tone hummed in his ear and he reached for the dial.

Prague!

His eyes were playing tricks on him! Across Nebraska Avenue a man got out of a taxi and stood on the pavement looking down the street towards the hotel. He knew that *man*!

At least, he knew the face. And it *was* Prague!

The man had a history of violence, both political and non-political. His police record was filled with assaults, theft and unproven homicides, his years in prison nearer ten than five. He had worked against the state more for profit than for ideology; he had been well paid by the Americans. His firing arm was good, his knife better.

That he was in Washington and less than fifty yards from this particular hotel could only mean he had a connection with Scofield. Yet there was no sense in the connection! Beowulf Agate had scores of men and women he could call upon for help in dozens of cities, but he would not call on someone from Europe *now*, and he certainly would not call on *this* man; the streak of sadism was conceivably unmanageable. Why was he here? Who had summoned him?

Who *sent* him? And were there others?

But it was the *why* that burned into Taleniekov's brain. It was profoundly disturbing. Beyond the fact that the Bern-Washington depot had been revealed — undoubtedly, unwittingly by Scofield himself — someone knowing it had reached Prague for a walking gun known to have performed extensively for the Americans.

Why? Who was the target?

Beowulf Agate?

Oh, God! There *was* a method; it had been used before by Washington . . . and strangely enough there was a vague similarity to the ways of the Matarese. *Storm clouds over Washington* . . . Scofield had run into a storm so severe that he had not only not been terminated, but conceivably his execution had been ordered.

Vasili had to be sure; the man from Prague might himself be a ploy, a brilliant ploy, designed to trap a Russian, not kill an American.

His hand was still suspended in front of the dial. He pressed down on the coin return lever and thought for a moment, wondering if he could take the risk. Then he saw the man across the street check his watch and turn towards the entrance of a coffee shop; he was going to meet someone. There *were* others, and Vasili knew that he could not afford *not* to take the risk. He had to find out; there was no way to know how much time was left. It might only be minutes.

There was a *pradavyet* at the embassy, a diplomatic assistant whose left foot had been blown off during a counter-insurgency operation in Riga a number of years ago. He was a KGB veteran and he and Taleniekov had once been friends. It perhaps was not the moment to test that former friendship, but Vasili had no choice. He knew the number of the embassy; it had not changed in years. He reinserted the coin and dialled.

"It's been a long time since that terrible night in Riga, old friend," said Taleniekov after having been connected to the *pradavyet's* office. He added quickly, "I heard that our former cryptographer was killed in Sevastopol. A tragedy."

"That would depend on the circumstances," was the swift, professional reply. The layers of memory had been peeled away rapidly, calmly, voice and words associated; not a beat had been lost. "Those circumstances have not been clarified. Would you remain on the line, please. I have another call."

Vasili stared at the telephone. If the wait was over thirty seconds, he'd have his answer; the former friendship would not survive. There were ways for even the Soviets to trace a call in the national capital of the United States. He turned his wrist and kept his eyes on the thin, jumping hand of his watch. *Twenty-eight, twenty-nine, thirty, thirty-one . . . thirty-two.* He reached up to break the connection when he heard the voice.

"*Taleniekov?* It *is* you?"

Vasili recognized the echoing sound of an activated jamming device placed over the mouthpiece of a telephone. It operated on the principle of electronic spillage; any intercepts would be clogged with static. "Yes, old friend. I nearly hung up on you."

"Riga was not that long ago. What *happened?* The stories we get are crazy."

"I'm no traitor."

"No one over here thinks you are. We assume you stepped on some large Muscovite feet. But can you return?"

"Someday, yes."

"I can't believe the charges. Yet you're *here!*"

"Because I must be. For Russia's sake, for all our sakes. *Trust* me. I need information quickly. If anyone at the embassy has it, you would."

"What is it?"

"I've just seen a man from Prague, someone the Americans used for his more violent talents. We kept an extensive file on him; I assume we still keep it. Do you know anything . . ."

"Beowulf Agate," interrupted the diplomat quietly. "It's Scofield, isn't it? That's what drives you still."

"Tell me what you know!"

"Leave it alone, Taleniekov. Leave *him* alone. Leave him to his own people; he's finished."

"My God, I'm *right,*" said Vasili, his eyes on the coffee shop across Nebraska Avenue.

"I don't know what you think you're right about, but I know three cables were intercepted. To Prague, Marseilles and Amsterdam."

"They've sent a team," broke in Taleniekov.

"Stay away. You have your revenge, the sweetest imaginable. After a lifetime, he's taken by his own."

"It can't happen! There are things you *don't know.*"

"It can happen regardless of what I know. We can't stop it."

Suddenly, Vasili's attention was drawn to a pedestrian about to cross the intersection not ten yards from the telephone booth. There was something about the man, the set expression of his face, the eyes that darted from side to side behind the lightly tinted glasses – bewildered, perhaps, but not lost, studying his surroundings. And the man's clothes, loose-fitting, inexpensive tweeds, thick and made to last . . . they were French. The glasses were *French*, the man's face itself *Gallic*. He looked across the street towards the marquee of the hotel, and hastened his step.

Marseilles had arrived.

"Come in to us." The diplomat was speaking. "Whatever happened cannot be irreparable in light of your extraordinary contributions." The former comrade from Riga was being persuasive. Too persuasive. It was not in character between professionals. "The fact that you came in voluntarily will be in your favour. Heaven knows, you'll have our support. We'll ascribe your flight to a temporary aberration, a highly emotional state. After all, Scofield killed your brother."

"I killed his wife."

"A wife is not blood. These things are understandable. Do the right thing. Come in, Taleniekov."

The excessive persuasion was now illogical. One did not voluntarily turn oneself in until the evidence of exoneration was more concrete. Not with an order for summary execution on one's head. Perhaps, after all, the former friendship could not stand the strain. "You'll protect me?" he asked the *pradavyet*.

"Of course."

A lie. No such protection could be promised. Something *was* wrong.

Across the street, the man wearing tinted glasses approached the coffee shop. He slowed his pace, then stopped and went up to the window as if studying a menu affixed to the glass. He reached into his pocket, took out a cigarette and lit it. From inside, barely seen in the sunlight, there was a flicker of a match. The Frenchman went inside. Prague and Marseilles had made contact.

"Thank you for your advice," said Vasili into the phone. "I'll think it over and call you back."

"It would be best if you didn't delay," answered the diplomat, urgency replacing sympathetic persuasion. "Your situation would not be improved by any involvement with Scofield. You should not be seen down there."

Seen down there? Taleniekov reacted to the words as though a gun had been fired in front of his face. In his old friend's knowledge was the betrayal! Seen down *where*? His colleague from Riga knew! The hotel on Nebraska Avenue. Scofield had not exposed the Bern depot – unwittingly or otherwise. *KGB had!* Soviet intelligence was a participant in Beowulf Agate's execution. *Why?*

The Matarese? There was no time to think, only act . . . The hotel! Scofield was not sitting alone by a phone in some out-of-the-way place, waiting to hear from intermediaries. He was in the *hotel*. No one would have to leave the premises to report to Beowulf Agate, no bird could be followed to the target. The target had executed a brilliant manoeuvre; he was in the direct range of fire, but unseen, observing but unobservable.

"You really *must* listen to me, Vasili." The *pradavyet's* words came faster now; he obviously sensed indecision. If his former colleague from Riga had to be killed, it could be done any number of ways within the embassy. That was infinitely preferable to a comrade's corpse being found in an American hotel, somehow tied to the murder of an American intelligence officer by foreign agents. Which meant the KGB had revealed the location of the depot to the Americans, but had not known the precise schedule of the execution at the time.

They knew it now. Someone in the State Department had told them, the message clear. His countrymen had to stay away from the hotel – as did the Americans. None could be involved. Vasili had to buy minutes, for minutes might be all he had left. Diversion.

"I'm listening." Taleniekov's voice was choked with sincerity, an exhausted man coming to his senses. "You're right. I've nothing to gain now, only everything to lose. I put myself in your hands. If I can find a taxi in this insane traffic, I'll be at the embassy in thirty minutes. Watch for me. I need you."

88

Vasili broke the connection, and inserted another coin. He dialled the hotel's number; no second could be wasted.

"He's *here*?" said the old woman incredulously, in response to Taleniekov's statement.

"My guess would be nearby. It would explain the timing, the phone calls, his knowing when someone was in the suite. He could hear sounds through the walls, open a door when he heard someone in the corridor. Are you still in your uniform?"

"Yes. I'm too tired to take it off."

"Check the surrounding rooms."

"Good heavens, do you know what you're asking? What if he . . ."

"I know what I'm paying; there's more if you do it. Do it! There's not a moment to be lost! I'll call you back in five minutes."

"How will I *know* him?"

"He won't let you into the room."

Bray sat shirtless between the open window and the door and let the cold air send shivers through his body. He had brought the temperature of the room down to fifty degrees, the chill was necessary to keep him awake. A cold tired man was far more alert than a warm one.

There was the tiny, blunt sound of metal slapping against metal, then the twisting of a knob. Outside in the hallway a door was being opened. Scofield got up from the chair, crossed to the window and closed it. He then walked quickly to another window, his minute lookout on a narrow world that soon would be the site of his reverse trap. It *had* to be soon; he was not sure how much longer he could go on.

Across the way, the pleasant-looking elderly maid had come out of the suite, towels and sheets still draped over her arm. From the expression on her face, she was perplexed but resigned. Undoubtedly, from her point of view, an unheard-of sum of money had been offered by a foreigner who only wished her to remain in a grand suite of rooms and stay awake to receive a series of very strange telephone calls.

And someone else had stayed awake to make those calls. Someone Bray owed a great deal to; he would repay her one day. But right now he concentrated on Taleniekov's bird. She was leaving; she was not capable of staying in the air any longer.

She had abandoned the drop. It was only a question of time now and very little time at that. The hunter would be forced to examine his trap. And be caught in it.

Scofield walked over to his open suitcase on the luggage rack and took out a fresh shirt. Starched, not soft; a crisp, starched shirt was like a cold room, a benign irritant; it kept one alert.

He put it on, and crossed to the bedside table where he had placed his gun, a Browning Magnum, Grade Four, with a custom-made silencer drilled to his specifications.

Bray spun around at an unexpected sound. There was a knocking, a hesitant tapping at his door. Why? He had paid for total isolation. The front desk had made it clear to those few employees who might have reason to enter room 213 that the sign on the knob was to be respected.

Do Not Disturb.

Yet someone was now disregarding that order, bypassing a guest's request that had been reinforced with several hundred dollars. Whoever it was was either deaf or illiterate or . . .

It was the maid. Taleniekov's bird, still in the air. Scofield peered through the tiny circle of glass that magnified the aged features of the face only inches away. The tired eyes, encased in wrinkled flesh swollen by lack of sleep, looked to the left, then to the right, then dropped to the lower part of the door. The old woman had to be aware of the *Do Not Disturb* sign, but it had no meaning for her. Beyond the contradictory behaviour, there was something odd about the face . . . but Bray had no time to study it further. In these new circumstances, the negotiations had to begin quickly. He shoved the gun into his shirt, the stiff cloth keeping the bulge to a minimum.

"Yes?" he asked.

"Maid service, sir," was the reply, spoken in an indeterminate brogue, more guttural than definable. "The management has asked that all rooms be checked for supplies, sir."

It was a poor lie, the bird too flawed to think of a better one.

"Come in," said Scofield, reaching for the latch.

"There's no answer in suite two–eleven," said the switchboard operator, annoyed by the persistence of the caller.

"Try it *again*," replied Taleniekov, his eyes on the entrance of the coffee shop across the street. "They may have stepped out for a moment, but they'll be right back. I *know* it. Keep ringing, I'll stay on the line."

"As you wish, sir," snapped the operator.

Madness! Nine minutes had passed since the old woman had begun the search, nine minutes to check four doors in the hallway. Even assuming all the rooms were occupied, and a maid had to give explanations to the occupants, nine minutes was far longer than she needed. A fourth conversation would be brief and blunt. *Go away. I am not to be disturbed.* Unless . . .

A match flared in the sunlight, its reflection sharp in the dark glass of the coffee shop window. Vasili blinked and stared; from one of the unseen tables inside there was a corresponding signal, extinguished quickly.

Amsterdam had arrived; the execution team was complete. Taleniekov studied the figure walking towards the small restaurant. He was tall and dressed in a black overcoat, a grey silk muffler around his throat. His hat, too, was grey, and obscured his profile, the features unable to be seen clearly.

The ringing on the telephone was now abrasive. Long sudden bursts resulting from a furious operator punching a switchboard button. There was no answer and Vasili began to think the unthinkable: Beowulf Agate had intercepted his bait. If so, the American was in greater danger than he could imagine. Three men had flown in from Europe to be his executioners, and – no less lethal – a gentle-appearing old woman whom he might try to compromise would kill him the instant she felt cornered. He would never know where the shot came from, nor that she even had a weapon.

"I'm sorry, sir!" said the operator angrily. "There's still no pick-up in suite two-eleven. I suggest you call again." She did not wait for a reply; the switchboard line was disconnected.

The *switchboard*? *The operator*?

It was a desperate tactic, one he would never condone except as a last-extremity measure; the risk of exposure was too great. But it *was* the last extremity and if there were alternatives he was too exhausted to think of them. Again, he knew only that he had to act, each decision an instinctive reflex, the shaping of those instincts trusted. He reached into his pocket for his money and removed five one-hundred-dollar bills. Then he took out his passport case, and extracted a letter he had written on an English-language typewriter five days ago in Moscow. The letterhead was that of a brokerage house in Bern, Switzerland; it identified the bearer as one of the firm's partners. One never knew.

He walked out of the telephone booth and entered the flow of pedestrians until he was directly opposite the entrance of the hotel. He waited for a break in the traffic, then walked rapidly across Nebraska Avenue.

Two minutes later a solicitous day manager introduced a Monsieur Blanchard to the operator of the hotel switchboard. This same manager – as impressed with Monsieur Blanchard's credentials as he was with the two hundred dollars the Swiss financier had casually insisted he take for his troubles – dutifully provided a relief operator while the woman talked alone with the generous Monsieur Blanchard.

"I ask you to forgive a worried man's rudeness over the telephone," said Talenie-kov, as he pressed three one-hundred-dollar bills into her nervous hand. "The ways of international finance can be appalling in these times. It is a bloodless war, a constant struggle to prevent unscrupulous men from taking advantage of honest brokers and legitimate institutions. My company has just such a problem. There's someone in this hotel . . ."

A minute later, Vasili was reading a master list of telephone charges, recorded by a mindless computer. He concentrated on the calls made from the second floor; there were two corridors, suites 211 and 212 opposite three double rooms in the west wing, four single rooms on the other side. He studied all charges billed to telephones 211 through 215. Names would mean nothing; local calls were not identified by number; long distance charges were the only items that might provide information. Beowulf Agate had to build a cover and it would not be in Washington. He had killed a man in Washington.

The hotel was, as Taleniekov knew, an expensive one. This was further confirmed by the range of calls made by guests who thought nothing of picking up a telephone and calling London as easily as a nearby restaurant. He scanned the sheets, concentrating on the *O.O.T.* areas listed.

212 . . . London, UK chgs: $26.50
214 . . . Des Moines, Ia. chgs: $4.75
214 . . . Cedar Rapids, Ia. chgs: $6.20

213 . . . Minneapolis, Minn. chgs: $7.10
215 . . . New Orleans, La. chgs: $11.55
214 . . . Denver, Colo. chgs: $6.75
213 . . . Easton, Md. chgs: $8.05
215. . . .Athens, Ga. chgs: $3.15
212 . . . Munich, Germ. chgs: $41.10
213 . . . Easton, Md. chgs: $4.30
212 . . . Stockholm, Swed. chgs: $38.25

Where was the pattern? Suite 212 had made frequent calls to Europe, but that was too obvious, too dangerous. Scofield would not place such traceable calls. Room 214 was centred in the Mid-west, Room 215 in the South. There *was* something but he could not pinpoint it. *Something* that triggered a memory.

Then he saw it ad the memory was activated, clarified. The one room without a pattern. Room 213. Two calls to Easton, Maryland, one to Minneapolis, Minnesota. Vasili could see the words in the dossier as if he were reading them. Brandon Scofield had a sister in Minneapolis, Minnesota.

Taleniekov memorized both numbers in case it was necessary to use them, if there was *time* to use them, to confirm them. He turned to the operator. "I don't know what to say. You've been most helpful but I don't think there's anything here that will help."

The switchboard operator had entered into the minor conspiracy, and was enjoying her prominence with the impressive Swiss. "If you'll note, Monsieur Blanchard, suite two-twelve placed a number of overseas calls."

"Yes, I see that. Unfortunately, no one in those cities would have anything to do with the present crisis. Strange, though. Room two-thirteen telephoned Easton, Maryland and Minneapolis. An odd coincidence, but I have friends in both places. However, nothing relevant . . ." Vasili let his words drift off, inviting comment.

"Just between the two of us, Monsieur Blanchard, I don't think the gentleman in room two-thirteen is all there, if you know what I mean."

"Oh?"

The woman explained. The DND on 213 was a standing order; no one was to disturb the man's privacy. Even room service was instructed to leave the tray tables in the hallway, and maid service was to be suspended until specifically requested. To the best of the operator's knowledge, there had been no such request in three days. Who could live like that?

"Of course, we get people like him all the time. Men who reserve a room so they can stay drunk for hours on end, or get away from their wives or meet other women. But three days without maid service, I think is *sick*."

"It's hardly fastidious."

"You see it more and more," said the woman confidentially. "Especially in the government, everyone's so harried. But when you think our taxes are *paying* for it — I don't mean *yours*, Monsieur . . ."

"He's in the government?" interrupted Taleniekov.

"Oh, we think so. The night manager wasn't supposed to say anything to *anybody*, but we've been here for years, if you know what I mean."

"Old friends, of course. What happened?"

"Well, a man came by last evening – actually it was this morning, around five a.m. – and showed the manager a photograph."

"A picture of the man in two-thirteen?"

The operator glanced around briefly; the door of the office was open, but she could not be overheard. "Yes. Apparently he's *really* sick. An alcoholic or something, a psychiatric case. No one's to say anything; they don't want to alarm him. A doctor will be coming for him some time today."

"Some time today? And, of course, the man who showed the photograph identified himself as someone from the government, didn't he? I mean, that's how you learned the guest upstairs was *in* the government?"

"When you've spent as many years in Washington as we have, Monsieur Blanchard, you don't have to ask for identification. It's all over their faces."

"Yes, I imagine it is. Thank you very much. You've been a great help."

Vasili left the room quickly and rushed out into the lobby. He had his confirmation. He had found Beowulf Agate.

But others had found him, too. Scofield's executioners were only a few hundred feet away, preparing to close in on the condemned man.

To break into the American's room to warn him would be to invite an exchange of gunfire; one or both would die. To reach him on the telephone would provoke only disbelief; where was the credibility in such an alarm delivered by an enemy one loathed about a *new* enemy one did not know existed.

There had to be a way and it had to be found quickly. If there were only time to send another with something on his person that would explain the truth to Scofield. Something Beowulf Agate would accept..

There was no time. Vasili saw the man in the black overcoat walk through the entrance of the hotel.

9

Scofield knew the instant the maid walked through the door what disturbed him about the elderly face. It was the eyes. There was an intelligence behind them beyond that of a plain-spoken domestic who spent her nights cleaning up the soil of pampered hotel guests. She was frightened – or perhaps merely curious – but whichever, neither was born of a blunt mind.

An actress, perhaps?

"Forgive my disturbin' you, sir," said the woman, noticing his unshaven face and the cold room and heading for the open bathroom door. "I'll not be a minute."

An actress. The brogue was an affectation, no roots in Ireland or the Highlands. Too, the walk was light; she did not have the leg muscles of an old woman used to the drudgery of carrying linens and bending over beds. And the hands were white and soft, not those of someone used to abrasive cleansers.

Bray found himself pitying her even while faulting Taleniekov's choice again. A maid would have been better – the fears were different.

"You've a fresh supply of towels, sir," said the old woman, coming out of the bathroom and heading for the door. "I'll be on my way. Sorry for disturbin' you."

Scofield stopped her with a small gesture. An authentic maid changing towels in a hotel would not have noticed.

"Sir?" asked the woman, her eyes alert.

"Tell me, what part of Ireland do you come from? I can't place the dialect. County Wicklow, I think."

"Yes, sir."

"The south country?"

"Yes, sir; very good, sir," she said rapidly, her left hand on the doorknob.

"Would you mind leaving me an extra towel? Just put it on the bed."

"Oh?" The old woman turned, the perplexed expression again on her face. "Yes, sir, of course." She started towards the bed.

Bray went to the door and pushed the bolt into place. He spoke as he did so, but gently; there was nothing to be gained by alarming Taleniekov's frightened bird. "I'd like to talk to you. You see, I watched you last night, at four o'clock this morning to be precise . . ."

A rush of air, the scratching of fabric. Sounds he was familiar with. *Behind him in the room.*

He spun, but not in time. He heard the muted spit and felt a razor- like cut across the skin of his neck. An eruption of blood spread over his left shoulder. He lunged to his right; a second shot followed, the bullet embedding itself in the wall above him. He swung his arm in a violent arc, sending a lamp off a table towards the *impossible* sight six feet away, in the centre of the room.

The old woman had dropped the towels and in her hand was a gun. Gone was her soft, gentle bewilderment, in its place the calm, determined face of an experienced killer. *He should have known!*

He dived to the floor, his fingers gripping the base of the table; he spun again to his right, then twisted to his left, lifting the table by its leg like a small battering ram. He rose, crashing forward; two more shots were fired, splintering the wood inches above his head.

He rammed the woman, hammering her back into the wall with such force that a stream of saliva accompanied the expulsion of breath from the snarling lips.

"*Bastard!*" The scream was swallowed as the gun clattered to the floor. Scofield dropped the table, slamming it down on her feet as he reached for the weapon.

He held it, stood up and grabbed the bent-over woman by the hair, yanking her away from the wall. The red wig beneath the ruffled maid's cap came off in his hand, throwing him off balance. From somewhere beneath the uniform, the grey-haired killer had pulled a knife – a thin stiletto. Bray had seen such weapons before; they were as deadly as any gun, the blades coated with succinylcholine. Paralysis began in seconds, death seconds later. A scrape or a superficial puncture was all the attacker needed to inflict.

She was on him, the thin knife plunging straight forward, the most difficult thrust to parry, used by the most experienced. He leaped backwards, crashing the gun down on the woman's forearm. She withdrew it quickly in pain, but no suspension of purpose.

"Don't *do* it!" he shouted, levelling the gun directly at her head. "Four shots were fired; two shells left! I'll kill you!"

The old woman stopped and lowered the knife. She stood motionless, speechless, breathing heavily, staring at him in a kind of ethereal disbelief. It occurred to Scofield that she had never been in this position before; she had always won.

Taleniekov's bird was a vicious hawk in the guise of a small, grey dove. That protective coloration was her irresistible insurance. It had never failed her.

"Who are you? KGB?" asked Bray, reaching for the towel on the bed, holding it against the wound on his neck.

"What?" she whispered, her eyes barely in focus.

"You work for Taleniekov. Where is he?"

"I'm paid by a man who uses many names," she replied, the lethal knife still held limply in her hand. Her fury was gone, replaced by fear and exhaustion. "I don't know who he is. I don't know where he is."

"He knew where to find you. You're something. Where did you learn? When?"

"When?" she repeated in her bloodless whisper. "When you were a child. Where? Out of Belsen and Dachau . . . to other camps, other fronts. All of us."

"*Christ* . . ." uttered Scofield softly. *Allofus.* They were legion. Girls taken from the camps, sent to the war fronts, to barracks everywhere, to airfields. Surviving as whores, dishonoured by their own, unwanted, ostracized. They became the scavengers of Europe. Taleniekov *did* know where to find his flocks.

"Why do you work for him? He's no better than those who sent you to the camps."

"I have to. He'll kill me. Now you say you will."

"Thirty seconds ago, I would have. You didn't give me a choice; you can now. I'll take care of you. You stay in contact with this man. How?"

"He calls. In the suite across the hall."

"How often?"

"Every ten or fifteen minutes. He'll call again soon."

"Let's go," said Bray cautiously. "Move to your right and drop the knife on the bed."

"Then you'll *shoot*," whispered the old woman.

"If I was going to, I'd do it now," said Scofield. He *needed* her, needed her confidence. "There'd be no reason to wait, would there? Let's get over to that phone. Whatever he was paying, I'll double."

"I don't think I can walk. I think you broke my foot."

"I'll help you." Bray lowered the towel and took a step towards her. He held out his hand. "Take my arm."

The old woman placed her left foot in front of her painfully. Then suddenly, like an enraged old lioness, she lunged forward, her face again contorted, her eyes wild.

The blade came rushing towards Scofield's stomach.

*

Taleniekov followed the man from Amsterdam into the elevator. There was one other couple in the car. Young, rich, pampered Americans; fashionably dressed lovers or newly-weds, aware only of themselves and their hungers. They had been drinking, the stale odour of wine hanging about them.

The Hollander in the black overcoat removed his grey Homburg, as Vasili, his face briefly turned away, stood next to him against the panelled wall of the small enclosure. The doors closed. The girl laughed softly; her companion pressed the button for the fifth floor. The man from Amsterdam stepped forward and touched number two.

As he moved back, he glanced to his left, his eyes making contact with Taleniekov's. The man froze, the shock total, the recognition absolute. And in that shock, that recognition, Vasili saw another truth: the execution trap was meant for him as well. The team had a priority, and it was Beowulf Agate, but if a KGB agent known as Taleniekov appeared on the scene he was to be taken out as ruthlessly as Scofield.

The man from Amsterdam swung his hat in front of his chest, plunging his right hand into his pocket. Vasili rushed him, pinning him against the wall, his left hand gripping the wrist in the pocket, slipping down, separating hand from weapon, groping for the thumb, twisting it back until the bone cracked and the man bleated. He sank to his knees.

The girl screamed. Taleniekov spoke in a loud voice. He addressed the couple.

"You will not be harmed. I repeat, you will not be harmed if you do as I say. Make no noise, and take us to your room."

The Hollander lurched to the right; Vasili slammed his knee into the man's face, vicing the head against the wall. He took his gun from his pocket and held it up, pointing at the ceiling.

"I will not use this. I *will not* use this unless you disobey. You're no part of our dispute and I don't want you harmed. But you must do as I say."

"*Jesus!* Jesus *Christ* . . . !" The young man's lips trembled.

"Take out your key," ordered Taleniekov almost amiably. "When the doors open walk casually in front of us to your room. You will be perfectly safe if you do as I say. If you don't, if you cry out, or try to raise an alarm, I shall have to shoot. I won't kill you; instead, I'll fire into your spines. You'll be paralysed for life."

"Oh, *Christ, please* . . . !" The young man's trembling spread throughout his head, neck and shoulders.

"*Please*, mister! We'll do whatever you say!" The girl at least was lucid; she took the key from her lover's pocket.

"Get up!" said Vasili to the man from Amsterdam. He reached into the killer's overcoat pocket and removed the Hollander's weapon.

The elevator doors opened. The couple walked out stiffly, passing an elderly man reading a newspaper, and turned right down the corridor. Taleniekov, his Graz-Burya concealed at his side, gripped the cloth of Amsterdam's overcoat, propelling him forward.

"One sound, Dutchman," he whispered. "And you'll not make another. I'll blow your back away; you won't have time to scream."

Inside the double room, Vasili shoved the Hollander into a chair, held his gun on him, and issued orders once again to the frightened couple. "Get inside that clothes closet. *Quickly!*"

Tears were streaming down the young man's pampered face; the girl pushed him into their dark, temporary cell. Taleniekov propped a chair underneath the knob and kicked it until it was wedged firmly between the metal and the rug. He turned to the Hollander.

"You have exactly five seconds to explain how it's to be done," he said, raising the automatic diagonally across the executioner's face.

"You'll have to be clearer," came the professional reply.

"By all means," Vasili slashed the barrel of the Graz-Burya downward, ripping the flesh of the assassin's face. Blood spread; the man raised his hands. Taleniekov bent over the chair and cracked both wrists in rapid succession. "Don't touch! We've just begun. Drink it! Soon you'll have no lips. Then no teeth, no chin, no cheekbones! Finally, I'll take your eyes. Have you ever seen a man like that? The face is a terrible source of pain, puncturing the eyes unendurable." Vasili struck again, now arching upwards, catching the man's nostrils in the swing.

"No . . . *No!* I followed *orders!*"

"Where have I heard that before?" Taleniekov raised the weapon; again the hands were raised and again they were repulsed with blows. "What *are* those orders, Dutchman? There are three of you and the five seconds have passed! We must be serious now." He tapped the barrel of the Graz-Burya harshly over the Hollander's left eye, then the right. "No more time!" He pulled the weapon back, then shoved it knifelike into Amsterdam's throat.

"*Stop!*" screamed the man, his air cut off, the word garbled. "I'll tell you . . . He betrays us, he takes money for our names. He's sold out to our enemies!"

"No judgements. The *orders!*"

"He's never seen me. I'm to draw him out."

"*How?*"

"*You.* I've come to warn him. You're on your way."

"He'd reject you. Kill you! A transparent device. How did you know the room?"

"We have a photograph."

"*Of him.* Not of me."

"Both of you, actually. But I show him only his. The night manager identified him."

"Who gave you this photograph?"

"Friends from Prague, operating in Washington, with ties to the Soviet. Former friends of Beowulf Agate who know what he's done."

Taleniekov stared at the man from Amsterdam. He was telling the truth, because the explanation was based on partial truth. Scofield would look for flaws, but he would not reject Amsterdam's words; he could not afford that luxury. He would take the Dutchman as hostage, and then position himself. Waiting, watching, unseen. Vasili pressed the barrel of the Graz-Burya into the Hollander's right eye.

"Marseilles and Prague. Where are they? Where will they be?"

"Other than the main elevators there are only two exits from the floors. The staircase and the service lift. One will be stationed in each."

"Which are where?"

"Prague on the staircase, Marseilles on the service lift."

"What's the schedule? By minutes."

"It's floating. I approach the door at ten past twelve."

Taleniekov glanced at the ersatz antique clock on the hotel room desk. It was eleven minutes past twelve. "They're in position now."

"I don't know. I can't see my watch, the blood's in my eyes."

"What's the termination? If you lie, I'll know it. You'll die in a way you've never dreamed of. Describe it!"

"Zero–lock is five minutes past the half hour. If Beowulf has not appeared in either location, the room is to be stormed. Frankly, I don't trust Prague. I think he'd throw Marseilles and myself in first to take the initial fire. He's a maniac."

Vasili stood up. "Your judgement exceeds your talents."

"I've told you everything! Don't strike me again. For God's sake, let me wipe my eyes. I can't *see*."

"Wipe them. I want you to see clearly. Get up!" The Hollander rose, his hands covering his face, brushing away the rivulets of blood, the Graz–Burya jammed into his neck.

Taleniekov stood motionless for a moment, looking at the telephone across the room. He was about to speak with an enemy he had hated for a decade, about to hear his voice.

He would try to save that enemy's life.

Scofield spun away as the lethal blade sliced into his shirt, blunted by the steel of his gun concealed under the starched cloth only minutes ago. The old woman was insane, suicidal! He would have to kill her and he did not *want to* kill her!

The *gun*.

He said four shells had been fired, two were left. *She* knew differently!

She was coming at him again, the knife criss-crossing in slashing diagonals; anything in its path would have to be touched, scraped – under normal circumstances a meaningless scratch, but not with this blade. He aimed the gun at her head and squeezed the trigger; there was nothing but the click of the firing pin.

He lashed his right foot, catching her between her breast and her armpit, staggering her for an instant, but only an instant. She was wild, clutching the knife as if it were her passport to life; if she touched him, she was free. She crouched, swinging her left arm in front of her, covering the blade that worked furiously in her right. He jumped back, looking for something, *anything* he could use to parry her lunges.

Why had she delayed before? Why had she suddenly stopped and spoken with him, telling him *things* that would make him think? Then he knew. The old hawk was not only vicious, but wise; she knew when she had to restore dissipated strength, knew she could do it only by engaging her enemy, lulling him, waiting for the unguarded instant . . . one *touch* of the coated blade.

She lunged again, the knife arcing up from the floor towards his legs. He kicked; she whipped the blade back, then slashed laterally, missing the kneecap by centimetres. As her arm swung left with the slash, he caught her shoulder with his right foot and hammered her backwards.

She fell; he grabbed the nearest upright object – a floor lamp with a heavy brass base – hurling it down at her as he kicked again at the hand that held the stiletto.

Her wrist was bent; the point of the blade pierced the fabric of her maid's uniform, entering the flesh above her left breast.

What followed was a sight he did not care to remember. The old woman's eyes grew wide and thyroid, her lips stretched into a macabre, horrible grin that was no smile. She began to writhe on the floor, her body convulsed and trembling. She rolled into a foetal position, pulling her thin legs into her stomach, the agony complete. Prolonged, muffled screams came from her throat as she rolled again, clawing the rug; mucus disgorged from her convoluted mouth, a swollen tongue blocking passage.

Suddenly there was a horrible gasp and a final expulsion of breath. Her body jerked off the floor spastically; it became rigid. Her eyes were open wide, staring at nothing, her lips parted in death. The process had taken less than sixty seconds.

Bray leaned over and lifted the hand, separating the bony fingers. He removed the knife, stood up and walked to the bureau where there was a book of matches. He struck one and held it under the blade. There was an eruption of flame, spitting so high that it singed his hair, the heat so intense it burned his face. He dropped the stiletto, stamping the fire out under his foot.

The phone rang.

"This is Taleniekov," said the Russian into the silence of the telephone. It had been picked up but there was no voice on the line. "I submit that your position is not lessened by acknowledging our contact."

"Acknowledged," was the one-word reply.

"You reject my cable, my white flag, and were I you, I would do the same. But you're wrong and I would be wrong! I swore I'd kill you, Beowulf Agate, and perhaps one day I will, but not now and not *this* way. I am no schoolboy who proclaims victory before going on to the rugby field. It's not a logical way of doing things in our business. I think that's a reasonable statement."

"You read my cipher," was the answer, delivered in a monotone. "You killed my wife. Come and get me. I'm ready for you."

"*Stop it! We* both killed. You took a *brother* . . . and before that, an innocent young girl who knew only slogans! No threat to the animals who raped her and killed her!"

"What?"

"There's no time! There are men who want to kill you, but I'm not one of them! I've caught one, however; he's with me now . . ."

You sent another," interrupted Scofield. "She's dead. The knife went into her, not me. The cut didn't have to be very deep."

"You had to have provoked her; it *was not* planned! But we waste seconds and you don't have them. Listen to the man I put on the phone. He's from Amsterdam. His face is damaged and he can't see very well, but he can speak." Vasili pressed the telephone against the Hollander's bloody lips and shoved the Graz-Burya into his neck. "Tell him, Dutchman!"

"Cables were sent . . ." The injured man whispered, choking on fear and blood. "Amsterdam, Marseilles, Prague. Beowulf Agate was beyond salvage. We could all be killed if he lived. The cables made the usual statements: they were alerts, urging us to take precautions, but we knew what they meant. Don't take precautions, take out the problem, eliminate Beowulf ourselves . . . None of this is new to you, Herr Scofield. You have given such orders; you know they must be carried out."

Taleniekov yanked the phone away while keeping the barrel of his weapon pressed against Amsterdam's neck. "You heard it. The trap you set for me is being used to ambush *you*. By your own people."

Silence. Beowulf Agate said nothing. Vasili's patience was running out. "Don't you *understand*? They've exchanged information, it's the only way they could have found the depot — what you call a 'drop'. Moscow *provided* it, can't you *see* that? Each of us is being used as the reason to execute the other, to kill us *both*. My people are more direct than yours. The order for my death has been sent to every Soviet station, civilian and military. Your State Department does it somewhat differently, the analysts take no responsibility for such unconstitutional decisions. They simply send warnings to those who care little for abstractions, but deeply for their lives."

Silence. Taleniekov exploded.

"What more do you *want*? Amsterdam was to draw you out; you would have had no choice. You would have tried to position yourself in one of two exits: the service area or the staircase. At this moment, Marseilles is by the service elevator, Prague on the staircase. The man from Prague is one you know well, Beowulf. You've employed his gun and his knife on many occasions. He's waiting for you. In less than fifteen minutes, if you do not appear in either place, they will take you in your room. What more *do* you want?"

Scofield answered at last. "I want to know why you're telling me this."

"Reread my cipher to you! This isn't the first time you and I have been used. An incredible thing is happening and it goes beyond you and me. A few men know about it. In Washington *and* Moscow. But they say nothing; no one can say anything. The admissions are catastrophic."

"What admissions?"

"The hiring of assassins. On both sides. It goes back years, *decades*."

"How does it concern me? I don't care about you."

"Dimitri Yurievich."

"What about him?"

"They said you killed him."

"You're lying, Taleniekov. I thought you'd be better at it. Yurievich was leaning, he was a probable. The civilian killed was my contact, under *my* source-control. It was a KGB operation. Better a dead physicist than a defected one. I repeat, come and get me."

"You're *wrong*! . . . Later! There's no time to argue. You want proof? Then listen! I trust your ear is more skilled than your mind!" The Russian quickly shoved the Graz-Burya into his belt and held the mouthpiece up in the air. With his left hand he gripped the throat of the man from Amsterdam, his thumb centring on the rings of trachea cartilage. He pressed; his hand was a vice, his fingers talons crushing fibre and bone as the vice closed. The Hollander twisted violently, his arms and hands thrashing, trying to break Vasili's grip, the effort useless. His cry of pain was an unbroken scream that diminished into a wail of agony. The man from Amsterdam fell to the floor unconscious. Taleniekov spoke again into the telephone. "Is there human bait alive who would permit what I've just done?"

"Was he given an alternative?"

"You're a *fool*, Scofield! Get yourself killed!" Vasili shook his head in desperation; It was a reaction to his own loss of control. "*No* . . . No, you mustn't. You can't understand, and I must try to grasp that, so you must try to understand me. I loathe everything you are, everything you stand for. But right now, we can do what few others can do. Make men listen, make them speak out. If for no other reason than they fear us, fear what we know. The fear is on *both* sides . . ."

"I don't know what you're talking about," interrupted Scofield. "You're mounting a nice KGB strategy; they'll probably give you a large *dacha* in Grasnov, but no sale. I repeat, come and get me."

"*Enough!*" shouted Taleniekov, looking at the clock on the desk. "You have eleven minutes! You know where your final proof is. You can find it in a service lift or on the staircase. Unless you care to learn it as you die in your room. If you create a disturbance, you'll draw a crowd. That's more to their liking, but I don't have to tell you that; you may recognize Prague, you won't Marseilles. You can't call the police, or risk the chance that the management will, we both know that. Go find your proof, Scofield! See if this enemy is lying. You'll get as far as your first turn in the corridor! If you live – which is unlikely – I'm on the fifth floor. Room five-zero-five. I've done what I can!" Vasili slammed down the phone, the gesture equal parts artifice and anger. Anything to jar the American, anything to make him think.

Taleniekov needed every second now. He had told Beowulf Agate that he had done what he could, but it was not true. He knelt down and tore off the black overcoat from Amsterdam's unconscious body.

Bray replaced the phone, his mind was working. If he'd only had sleep, or if he had not gone through the totally unexpected violence of the old woman's attack, or if Taleniekov had not told him so much of the truth, things would be clearer. But it had all happened and, as he had done so often in the past, he had to shift into a state of blind acceptance and think in terms of immediate purpose.

It was not the first time he had been the target of factions distinct from each other. One got used to it when dealing with opposing partisans from the same broad-based camps, although killing was rarely the objective. What was unusual was the timing, the converging of separate assaults. Yet it was so understandable, so *clear*.

Under-Secretary of State Daniel Congdon had really done it! The seemingly bloodless desk-man had found the courage of his own convictions. More specifically, he had found Taleniekov and Taleniekov's moves towards Beowulf Agate. What better reasoning existed for breaking the rules and eliminating a terminated specialist he considered dangerous? What better motive for reaching the Soviets, who could only favour the dispatch of both men?

So clear. So well orchestrated he or Taleniekov might have conceived the strategy. Denials and astonishment would go hand in hand, statesmen in Washington and Moscow decrying the violence of *former* intelligence officers – from another era. An era when personal anir.iosities often superseded national interests. *Christ, he* could hear the pronouncement, couched in sanctimonious platitudes made by men like Congdon who concealed filthy decisions under respectable titles.

The infuriating thing was that the reality supported the platitudes, the words were validated by Taleniekov's hunt for revenge. *I swore I'd kill you, Beowulf Agate, and perhaps one day I will.*

That day was today, the *perhaps* without meaning for the Russian. Taleniekov wanted Beowulf Agate for himself; he would brook no interference from killers recruited and programmed by desk-men in Washington and Moscow. *I will see you take your last breath* . . . Those were Taleniekov's words six years ago; he meant them then and he meant them now.

Certainly he would save his enemy from the guns of Marseilles and Prague. His enemy was worthy of a better gun, *his* gun. And no ploy was too unreasonable, no words too extreme, to bring his enemy into that gunsight.

He was tired of it all, thought Scofield, taking his hand away from the phone. Tired of the tension of move and counter-move. In the final analysis, who cared? The crisis was that of a non-event. Who gave a goddamn for two ageing *specialists*, dedicated to the proposition that each's counterpart should die?

Bray closed his eyes, pressing his lids together, aware that there was moisture in his sockets. Tears of fatigue, mind and body spent; it was no time to acknowledge exhaustion. Because he *cared*. If he had to die – and it was always an around-the-corner possibility – he was not going to be taken by guns from Marseilles, Prague *or* Moscow. He was better than that; he had always *been* better.

According to Taleniekov he had eleven minutes; two had passed since the Russian had made the statement. The trap was his room and if the man from Prague was the one Taleniekov had described, the attack would be made quickly, with a minimum of risk. Gas-filled pellets would precede any use of weapons, the fumes immobilizing anyone in the room. It was a tactic favoured by the killer from Prague; he took few gambles.

The immediate objective, therefore, was to get out of the trap. Walking in the corridor was not feasible, perhaps not even opening the door. Since it was Amsterdam's function to draw him out, and he had not been drawn, Prague and Marseilles would close in. If there was no one in the hallway – as the absence of sound indicated – they had nothing to lose. Their schedule would not be postponed, but it could be accelerated.

No one in the hallway . . . *someone* in the hallway. People milling around, excited, creating a diversion. Most of the time a crowd was to the killers' advantage, not the target's, especially if the target was identifiable and one or more of the killers were not. On the other hand, a target who knew precisely when and where the attack was to be made, could use a crowd to cover his run from ground-zero. An escape based on confusion and a change of appearance. The change did not have to be much, just

102

enough to cause indecision; indiscriminate gunfire during an execution had to be avoided.

Eight minutes. Or less. Everything was preparation. He would have his essential belongings, for when he began running, he'd have to keep running; how long and how far there was no way to tell, nor could he think about that now. He had to get out of the trap and elude three men who wanted him dead, one more dangerous than the other two for he was not sent by Washington or Moscow. He had come himself.

Bray crossed rapidly to the dead woman on the floor, dragged her to the bathroom, rolled the corpse inside, and closed the door. He picked up the heavy-based lamp and smashed it down on the knob; the lock was jammed, the door could be opened only by breaking it down.

His clothes could be left behind. There were no laundry marks or overt evidence connecting them immediately to Brandon Scofield; fingerprints would do that, but lifting and processing them would take time. He would be far away by then – if he got out of the hotel alive. His attaché case was something else; it contained too many tools of his profession. He closed it, spun the combination lock, and threw it on the bed. He put on his jacket and went back to the telephone. He picked it up and dialled the operator.

"This is room two-thirteen," he said in a whisper, effortlessly made to sound weak. "I don't want to alarm you, but I know the symptoms. I've had a stroke. I need help . . ."

He let the phone crash against the table and drop to the floor.

10

Taleniekov put on the black overcoat and reached down for the grey scarf, still draped around Amsterdam's neck. He yanked it off, wound it around his throat and picked up the grey hat which had fallen beside the chair. It was too large; he creased the crown so it covered his head less awkwardly, and started for the door, passing the closet. He spoke firmly to the couple within.

"Remain where you are and make no sound! I shall be outside in the corridor. If I hear noise, I'll come back and you'll be the worse for it."

In the hall, he ran towards the main elevators, and then beyond them, to the plain dark elevator at the end of the corridor. Against the wall was a tray table used by room service. He removed his Graz-Burya from his belt, shoved it in his overcoat pocket and pushed the button with his left hand. The red light went on above the door; the elevator was on the second floor. Marseilles was in position, waiting for Beowulf Agate.

The light went off and seconds later the number *three* shone brightly, then number *four*. Vasili turned around, his back to the sliding panel.

The door opened, but there were no words of recognition, no surprise expressed at the sight of the black overcoat or the grey hat. Taleniekov spun around, his finger on the trigger of his gun.

There was no one inside the elevator. He stepped in and pressed the button for the second floor.

"Sir? Sir? My God, it's the crazy one in two-thirteen!" The excited voice of the operator floated up piercingly from the telephone on the rug. "Send up a couple of boys! See what they can do! I'll call an ambulance. He's had an attack or something."

The words were cut off; the chaos had begun.

Scofield stood by the door, unlatched it and waited. No more than forty seconds passed when he heard the racing footsteps and the shouts in the corridor. The door burst open; the bell captain ran in, followed by a younger, larger man, a bellboy.

"Thank Christ it wasn't locked! *Where* . . . ?"

Bray kicked the door shut, revealing himself to the two men. In his hand was his automatic. "No one's going to get hurt," he said calmly. "Just do exactly as I tell you. You," Bray ordered the younger man, "take off your jacket and your cap. And you," he continued, speaking to the bell captain, "get on the phone and tell the operator to send up the manager. You're scared; you don't want to touch anything, there may have been trouble up here. You think I'm dead."

The older man stuttered, his eyes riveted on the gun, then ran to the phone. The performance was convincing, he was frightened out of his wits. He delivered the message almost verbatim.

Bray took the maroon and gold-striped jacket held out for him by the large subordinate. He removed his coat and put it on, bunching his own under his arm. "The *cap*," demanded Scofield. It was given.

The bell captain finished, his eyes staring wildly at Bray, his last plea screamed: "For Christ's sake, *hurry!* Get someone up here!"

Scofield gestured with his weapon. "Stand by the door next to me," he said to the frantic man, then addressed the younger. "There's a closet over there beyond the bed. Get inside. *Now!*"

The large, dense bellboy hesitated, looked at Bray's face, and retreated quickly into the closet. Scofield, his weapon pointed at the bell captain, took the necessary steps towards the closet and kicked the door shut. He spoke while picking up the heavy-based lamp by its stem. "Get over to your right! Do you understand? Answer me!"

"Yeah," was the muffled reply from inside.

"Knock on the door!"

The tap came from the extreme left, the young man's right. Bray crashed the base of the lamp down on the knob; it broke off. Then he raised his gun, its silencer attached, and fired one shot into the right side of the door. "That was a bullet!" he said. "No matter what you hear, keep your mouth shut or there'll be another. I'm right outside this door!"

"Oh, my *God* . . . !"

The man would stay silent through an earthquake. Scofield went back to the bell captain, picking up the attaché case on the way. "Where's the staircase?"

"Down the hall to the elevators, turn right. It's at the end of the corridor."

"The service elevator?"

"Same thing, the other way, the other end. Turn left at."

"Listen to me," interrupted Bray, "and remember what I tell you. In a few seconds we'll hear the manager and probably others coming down the hall. When I open the door, you step outside and shout – and I mean scream your fucking head off – then start running down the corridor with me."

"*Christ!* What am I supposed to say?"

"That you want to get out of here," answered Bray. "Say it any way you like. I don't think it'll be difficult for you."

"Where are we *going?* I got a wife and four kids!"

"That's nice. Why don't you go home?"

"*What?*"

"What's the quickest way to the lobby?"

"Christ, *I* don't know!"

"Elevators can take a long time."

"The staircase? The *staircase!*" The panicked bell captain found triumph in his deduction.

"Use the staircase," said Scofield, his ear at the door.

The voices were muffled, but intense. He could hear the words *police* and *ambulance*, and then *emergency*. There were three or four people.

Bray yanked the door back and pushed the bell captain out into the corridor. "*Now*," he said.

Taleniekov turned away as the service elevator opened on the second floor. Again the black overcoat and the distinctive grey hat evoked no sounds of recognition, and again he spun, his hand gripping the Graz-Burya in his pocket. Marseilles was nowhere in sight. There were tray tables of half-eaten food and the odour of coffee – remnants of late breakfasts piling up outside the elevator door – but no Marseilles.

A pair of hinged metal doors opened into the second-floor corridor, round windows in the centre of each panel. Vasili approached and peered through the right circle.

There he was. The figure in the heavy tweed suit was edging his way along the wall towards the corner of the intersecting hallway that led to room 213. Taleniekov looked at his watch; it was 12.31. Four minutes until the attack; a lifetime if Scofield kept his head about him. A diversion was needed; fire was the surest. A telephone call, a flaming pillow case stuffed with cloth and paper thrown into the hallway. He wondered if Beowulf Agate had thought of it.

Scofield had thought of *something*. Down the hall the light above one of the two main elevators went on; the door opened, and three men rushed out talking frantically. One was the manager, now close to panic; another man carried a black bag: a doctor. The third was burly, his face set, the hair close-cropped . . . the hotel's private police officer.

They raced past the startled Marseilles – who turned abruptly away – and proceeded down the long corridor that led to Scofield's room. The Frenchman reached into his pocket and took out a gun.

At the other end of the hallway, below a red *Exit* sign, a heavy door with a crash bar was pulled back. The figure of Prague stepped out, nodding at Marseilles. In his right hand was a long-barrelled, heavy-calibre automatic, in his left what looked like . . . it was . . . a *grenade*. The thumb was curved, pressing on the lever; the firing pin was out!

And if he had one grenade he had more than one. Prague was an arsenal. He would take whoever was in the area, as long as he took Beowulf Agate. A grenade hurled into a dead-end corridor, a swift race into the carnage before the smoke had cleared to put bullets into the heads of those surviving, making sure Scofield was the first. No matter what the American had thought of, he was cornered. There was no way out through the gauntlet.

Unless Prague could be stopped where he was, the grenade exploding beneath him. Vasili pulled the Graz-Burya from his pocket and pushed the swinging door in front of him.

He was about to shout when he heard the scream. screams from a man in panic.

"*Get out of here!* For Christ's sake, I've got to get *out of here!*"

What followed was madness. Two men in hotel uniforms came running out of the corridor, one turning right, crashing into Prague, who propelled him away, beating him with the barrel of his gun. Prague shouted at Marseilles, ordering him down the corridor.

Marseilles was no fool – any more than Amsterdam was; he saw the grenade in Prague's hand. The two men screamed at each other.

The elevator door closed.

It *closed*. The light went *off*. It had been on *Hold*!

Beowulf Agate had made his escape.

Taleniekov spun back behind the metal doors; in the confusion he had not been spotted. But Prague and Marseilles had seen the elevator; it obviously prodded the immediate recollection of a second man in a dark red jacket, running straight ahead, without panic, knowing what he was doing . . . and *carrying something under his left arm*. Like Vasili, the two executioners watched the lighted numbers above the elevator door, expecting, as Taleniekov expected, the letter *L* to light up, signifying the lobby. It did not.

The light reached *three*. It stopped.

What was Scofield *doing*? He could be running in the streets in seconds, finding safety in the crowds, heading for any of a hundred sanctuaries. He was staying at the killing ground! Again, *madness*!

Then Vasili understood. Beowulf Agate was coming after *him*.

He looked through the circular service window. Prague was talking wildly. Marseilles nodded, holding his finger on the left elevator button, as Prague ran back towards the staircase and disappeared beyond the door.

Taleniekov had to know what had been said. It could save seconds – if he could learn in seconds. He put the Graz-Burya in his pocket, burst through the swinging door, the grey silk scarf bunched high around his neck, the grey hat firmly down on his head, his face obscured. He shouted.

"Qu'est-ce que vous avez trouvé, par hasard?"

In Marseilles' excitement, the swiftness and the deception had their effect. The black overcoat, the grey blur of silk and fur and the French spoken with a Dutchman's guttural inflections; they were enough to confuse the image of a man he had met only once, briefly in a coffee shop. He was stunned; he ran towards Taleniekov, shouting in his native tongue, the words so rushed they were barely clear.

"What are you doing *here?* All hell has broken loose! Men are yelling in Beowulf's room; they break down doors! He got *away.* Prague has."

Marseilles stopped. He saw the face in front of him and his stunned expression turned into one of shock. Vasili's hand shot out, gripping the weapon in the Frenchman's hand, twisting it with such force that Marseilles screamed aloud. The gun was pried out of his fingers. Taleniekov slammed the man against the wall, hammering his knee into the Frenchman's groin, his left hand tearing at Marseilles' right ear.

"Prague has *what?* You have one second to tell me!" He crashed his knee up into the Frenchman's testicles. "*Now!*"

"We work our way to the roof . . ." Marseilles choked the answer, spitting it out between clenched teeth, his hand sprung back in pain. "Floor by floor . . . to the roof."

"Why?" My God! thought Vasili. They knew about the *roof.* There was a metal air duct connecting the hotel to the adjacent building. Did they know? He rammed his knee again and repeated.

"*Why?*"

"Prague believes Scofield thinks you have men in the streets . . . at the hotel doors. He'll wait until the police come . . . the confusion. He did something in the room! In the name of God, *stop!*"

Vasili smashed the handle of the Frenchman's gun into Marseilles' skull behind his left temple. The assassin collapsed, as the wound spat blood. Taleniekov propelled the unconscious, falling body along the wall, letting it drop, so that it fell across the intersecting corridor. Whoever came out of room 213 would be greeted by another unexpected sight. The panic would mount, precious minutes obtained.

The elevator on the left had responded to the Frenchman's call. Vasili raced inside and pressed the button for the third floor. The doors closed, as far down the hallway two excited men ran out of room 213. One was the hotel manager; he saw the fallen Frenchman in the centre of a blood-soaked carpet. He screamed.

Scofield took off the jacket and the cap, bunching them in a corner, and put on his coat. The elevator stopped at the third floor; he tensed at the sight of a portly maid who walked in carrying towels over her arm. She nodded; he stared at her. The doors closed and they proceeded to the fourth, where the maid got off. Bray reached over quickly and again pressed the button for the sixth floor; there were none above it.

If it were possible, one part of the insanity was going to be over with. He was not going to run away only to start running again, wondering where the next trap would be sprung. Taleniekov was in the hotel and that was all he had to know.

Room five–zero–five. Taleniekov had given the number over the phone; he had said he would be waiting. Bray tried to think back, tried to recall a cipher or a code that matched the digits, but there were none he could remember, and he doubted the KGB man would pinpoint his location.

Five–Zero–Five.

Five – *Death* – Five?

I'm waiting for you on the fifth floor. One of us will die.

Was it as simple as that? Was Taleniekov reduced to a challenge? Was his ego so inflamed or his exhaustion so complete, that there was nothing left but spelling out the duelling ground?

For Christ's sake, let's get it over with! I'm coming, Taleniekov! You may be good, but you're no match for the man you call Beowulf Agate!

Ego. So necessary. So tiring.

The elevator reached the sixth floor. Bray held his breath as two well-dressed men entered. They were talking business, last year's figures being the bothersome topic. Both glanced briefly, disapprovingly, at him; he understood. The beard, his bloodshot eyes. He clutched his attaché case and avoided their looks. The door started to close and Bray stepped forward, his hand inside his jacket.

"Sorry," he muttered. "My floor."

There was no one in the long corridor directly ahead, four storeys above 211 and 213. Far down on the right were two doors with circular windows. The service elevator. One panel had just swung shut; it still trembled. Scofield pulled his automatic partially out of his belt, then held it in place when he heard the rattle of dishes beyond the swinging doors. A service tray was being taken away; a man concealing himself with intent to kill did not make noise.

Down on the left, towards the staircase, a cleaning woman had finished a room. She pulled the door shut and wearily began to roll her cart towards the next.

Five–zero–five.

Five–death–five.

If there was a meeting ground, he was above it, on the high ground. But it was a high ground from which he could not see and time was running out. He thought briefly of approaching the cleaning woman, using her as a point somehow, but his appearance ruled it out. His appearance ruled out a great many things; shaving had been a luxury he could not afford, relieving himself precious moments given up, away from the sounds of the trap. The little things became so ominous, so all-important during the waiting games. And he was so tired.

Using the service elevator had to be ruled out; it was an enclosure too easily immobilized, isolated. The staircase was not much better, but he had an advantage; except for a roof – if there was an exit for the roof – it did not go higher. The sight-lines favoured the one above. Birds of prey swooped, they rarely attacked from below.

Sharks did, however.

Diversion. Any kind of diversion. Sharks were known to lunge up at inanimate objects, floating debris.

Bray walked rapidly towards the heavy door to the staircase, stopping briefly at the cleaning woman's cart. He removed four glass ashtrays, stuffing them into his pockets, and wedged the attache case between his arm and chest.

As quietly as he could, he pressed on the crash bar; the heavy steel door opened. He started down the steps, staying close to the wall, listening to the sound of his enemy.

It was there. Several storeys below he could hear rapid footsteps slapping against the concrete stairs. They stopped and Scofield stood motionless. What followed confused him. There was a slicing sound, a series of quick movements – abrasive, metallic. What was it?

He looked back up the steps at the metal door lie had just walked through, and he knew. The staircase was essentially a fire exit; the crash bars opened from the inside, not from the staircase, thus inhibiting thieves. The person below was using a thin sheet of metal, or plastic, stabbing the crack around the lock, pulling up and down to catch the rounded latch and open the door. The method was universal; most fire exits could be manipulated this way, if they were functional. They would be functional in this hotel.

The abrasive slicing stopped; the door had been opened.

Silence.

The door slammed shut. Scofield moved to the edge of the steps and looked below; he saw nothing but angled railings, squared at the corners, descending into darkness. Silently, he lowered one foot at a time and reached the next landing. He was on the fifth floor.

Five-zero-five. A meaningless number; a meaningless verbal complication.

Taleniekov's strategy was clear now. And logical. Bray would have used it himself. Once the chaos had begun, the Russian waited in the lobby, watching the elevators for a sign of his enemy, and when he did not appear, the assumption had to be that Beowulf was cut off, roving, probing for a way out.

Only after Taleniekov was certain that his enemy was not running into the streets, could he begin the final hunt from the staircase, lurching into the hallways, his weapon levelled for his moving target.

But the Russian could not start the kill from the top, he had to begin from the staircase in the lobby. He was forced to give up the high ground, as deadly a disadvantage on the staircase as it was in the hill country. Scofield put down his attache case and took out two of the glass ashtrays from his pocket. The waiting was about over; it would happen any second now.

The door below crashed open. Bray hurled the first ashtray down between the railings; the smashing of glass echoed throughout the descending walls of concrete and steel.

Footsteps lurching. The thud of a heavy body lunging, making contact with a wall. Scofield sprang towards the open space; he threw down the second ashtray. The glass shattered directly beneath; the figure below darted past the edge of the railing. Bray fired his gun; his enemy screamed: twisting in the air, hurling himself out of the sight-line.

Scofield took three steps down, pressing himself against the wall. He saw a thrashing leg and fired again. There was the singing sound of a bullet ricocheting off steel, embedding itself in cement. He had missed; he had wounded the Russian, but not lamed him.

There was suddenly another sound. Sirens. Distant. Outside. Drawing closer. And shouting, muted by the heavy exit doors; orders were being screamed in corridors and hallways.

Options were being cut off, the chance of escape diminishing with each new sound. It had to end now. There was nothing left but a final exchange. A hundred lessons from the past were summarized in one: *draw fire first, make the gun expose itself which means exposing part of you. A superficial wound means nothing if it saves your life.*

The seconds ticked off; there was no alternative.

Bray took out the two remaining ashtrays from his pocket and hurled them over the open space above the railing. He stepped down, and at the first sound of shattering glass, swung out his left arm and shoulder, jabbing the air, arcing in a half-circle, part of him in the Russian's direct line of fire. But not his weapon; it was ready for his own attack.

Two deafening explosions filled the vertical tunnel.

The gun was blown out of his hand! Out of his *right hand*! He watched helplessly as the weapon sprang out of his fingers, specks of blood spreading over his palm, the high-pitched ring of still-ricocheting bullet bouncing from steel to steel.

He had been disarmed by a misplaced shot. Killed by an echo. The Browning automatic clattered down the staircase. He dived for it, yet even as he did so he knew it was too late. The killer below came into view, struggling to his feet, the large barrel of his gun rising, directed at Scofield's head.

It was not Taleniekov, not the face in a thousand photographs, the face he had hated for a decade! It was the man from Prague, a man he had used so often in the cause of free-thinking people. That man was going to kill him now.

Two thoughts came rapidly, one upon the other. Final summations, as it were. His death would come quickly; he was grateful for that. And, at the last, he had deprived Taleniekov of his trophy.

"We all do our jobs," said the man from Prague, his three fingers tightening on the handle of the gun. "You taught me that, Beowulf."

"You'll never get out of here."

"You forget your own lessons. 'Drop your weapons, leave with the crowds.' I'll get out. But you won't. If you did, too many would die."

"*Padazdit!*" The voice thundered from above, no crash of a door preceding it, the man who roared having intruded swiftly, silently. The executioner from Prague spun to his left, ducking, swinging his powerful gun up the stairs at Vasili Taleniekov.

The Russian fired one shot, drilling a hole in Prague's forehead. The Czech fell across Scofield as Bray lunged for his gun, grabbing it off the step, rolling furiously down around the bend in the staircase. He fired wildly up at the KGB man; he would not permit Taleniekov to save him from Prague only to preserve his trophy.

I'll see you take your last breath . . .

Not here! Not now! Not while I can move!

And then he could not move. The impact came and Scofield only knew that his

110

head seemed to have split wide open. His eyes were filled with blinding streaks of jagged white light, somehow mingling with sounds of chaos. Sirens, screams, voices yelling from distant chasms far below.

In his rolling dive to get out of Taleniekov's line of fire, he had crashed his skull into the sharp steel edge of the corner railing post. A misplaced bullet, an echo, an inanimate shaft of structural steel. They would lead to his death.

The image was blurred but unmistakable. The figure of the powerfully built Russian came running down the staircase. Bray tried to raise the gun still in his hand; he could not. It was being crushed under a heavy boot; the weapon was being prised out of his hand.

"Do it," whispered Scofield. "For Christ's sake, do it now! You've won by an accident. It's the only way you could."

"I've won *nothing*! I want no such victory. Come! Move! The police are here; they'll be swarming up the staircase any moment."

Bray could feel the strong arms lifting him up, pulling his arm around a thick neck, a shoulder shoved into his side for support. "What the hell are you *doing?*" He was not sure the words were his; he could not think through the pain.

"You're hurt. The wound in your neck has opened; it's not bad. But your head is cut, I don't know how severely."

"What?"

"There is a way out. This was my depot for two years. I know every inch of the building. Come! *Help* me. Move your legs! The *roof*."

"My case . . ."

"I've got it."

They were in a large, pitch-black metal enclosure, steady blasts of cold air causing the corrugated sides to rattle, the near-freezing temperature producing audible vibrations. They crawled along the ribbed floor in darkness.

"This is the main air duct," explained Taleniekov, his voice low, aware of the magnified echo. "The unit serves the hotel and the adjacent office building. Both are comparatively small structures, owned by the same company."

Scofield had begun to find his mind again, the sheer movement forcing him to send impulses to his arms and legs. The Russian had torn a silk scarf apart, wrapping one half around Bray's head, the other around his throat. The bleeding had not stopped, but it was contained. He had found part of his mind, but there was still no clarity in what was happening.

"You saved my life. I want to know *why!*"

"Keep your voice down!" whispered the KGB man. "And keep moving."

"I want an answer!"

"I gave it to you."

"You weren't convincing."

"You and I, we live only with lies. We see nothing else."

"From you I expect nothing else."

"In a few minutes you can make your determination. I give you that."

"What do you mean?"

"We'll reach the end of the duct; there is a transom ten or twelve feet from the floor. In a rooftop storage area. Once down I can get us out on the street, but every second counts. Should there be people in the vicinity of the transom, they must be frightened away. Gunshots will do it; fire above their heads."

"*What?*"

"Yes. I'll give you your gun back."

"You killed my wife."

"You killed my brother. Before that your Army of Occupation returned the corpse of a young girl – a child – I loved very much. What came back was not pleasant."

"I don't know anything about that."

"Now you do. Make your determination."

The metal-webbed transom was perhaps four feet wide. Below was a huge, dimly lit room that served as a miniature warehouse filled with crates and boxes of supplies. There was no one in sight. Taleniekov handed Scofield the automatic, and began forcing the metal screen from its brackets with his shoulder. It sprung loose and fell crashing to the cement floor. The Russian waited several moments for a response to the noise; there was none.

He turned his body around and, legs first, began sliding out of the duct. His shoulders and head passed over the rim, his fingers gripping the edge; he was finding his balance, prepared for the drop to the floor.

The strange sound came faintly at first, then louder. *Step . . . scrape. Step . . . scrape. Step . . . scrape. Step.* Taleniekov froze, his body suspended between transom and floor.

"Good morning, Comrade," said the voice softly in Russian. "My walk has improved since Riga, no? They gave me a new foot."

Bray pulled back into the shadows of the duct. Below, beside a large crate was a man with a cane. A cripple whose right leg was no leg at all, but instead a limb of stiff, straight wood beneath the trousers. The man continued as he took a gun from his pocket.

"I knew you too well, old friend. You were a great teacher. You gave me an hour to study your depot. There were several means of escape, but this is the one you would choose. I'm sorry, my teacher. We cannot afford you any longer." He raised his gun.

Scofield fired.

They raced into the alley across the street from the hotel on Nebraska Avenue. Both leaned against the brick wall, breathing heavily, their eyes on the activity beyond. Three patrol cars, their lights revolving on their roofs, blocked the entrance of the hotel, hemming in an ambulance. Two stretchers were carried out, the bodies underneath covered with canvas; another emerged, Taleniekov could see the bloodied head of Prague. Uniformed police held back curious pedestrians, as their superiors rushed back and forth, barking into hand-held radios, issuing orders to unseen recipients.

A net was being formed around the hotel, all exits covered, all windows observed, weapons drawn against the unexpected.

"When you feel strong enough," said Taleniekov, speaking between swallows of

112

air, "we'll slip into the crowds and walk several blocks away where it will be safer to find a taxi. However, I'll be honest with you. I don't know where to go."

"I do," said Scofield, pushing himself away from the wall. "We'd better get going while there's confusion out there. Pretty soon they'll start an area search. They'll look for anyone wounded; there was a lot of gunfire."

"One moment." The Russian faced Bray. "Three days ago I was on a truck in the hills outside Sevastopol. I knew then what I would say to you if we met. I say it now. We will either kill each other, Beowulf Agate, or we will talk."

Scofield stared at Taleniekov. "We may do both," he said. "Let's go."

11

The cabin was in the backwoods of Maryland, on the banks of the Patuxent River, fields on three sides, water below. It was isolated, no other houses within a mile in any direction, accessible only by a primitive dirt road over which no taxi would venture. None was asked to do so.

Instead, Bray telephoned a man at the Iranian embassy, an unregistered SAVAK agent into hard drugs and exchange students whose exposure would be embarrassing to a benevolent Shah. A rented car was left for them in a metered parking lot on K Street, the keys under the floor mat.

The cabin belonged to a professor of political science at Georgetown, a closet homosexual Scofield had befriended years ago when he had torn up a fragment of a dossier that had nothing to do with the man's ability to evaluate classified data for the State Department. Bray had used the cabin a number of times during his recalls to Washington, always when he wished to be beyond reach of the desk-men, usually with a woman. A phone call to the professor was all that it took; no questions were asked, the location of the house key was given. This afternoon it was nailed beneath the second shingle from the right on the front roof. Bray got it by using a ladder propped against a near-by tree.

Inside, the decor was properly rustic; heavy beams and spartan furniture relieved by a profusion of quilted cushions, white walls and red-checked curtains. Flanking the stone fireplace were floor-to-ceiling bookcases, filled to capacity, the varied bindings lending additional colour and warmth.

"He is an educated man," said Taleniekov, his eyes scanning the titles.

"Very," replied Bray, lighting a gas-fed Franklin stove. "There are matches on the mantel, the kindling stacked and ready to light."

"How convenient," said the KGB man, taking a wooden match from a small glass on the mantel, kneeling down and striking it.

"It's part of the rent. Whoever uses the cabin cleans the fireplace and stacks it."

"Part of the rent? What are the other arrangements?"

"There's only one. Say nothing. About the place or the owner."

"Again, convenient." Taleniekov pulled his hand back as the fire leaped up from the dry wood.

"Very," repeated Scofield, adjusting the heater, satisfied it was functioning. He stood up and faced the Russian. "I don't want to discuss anything until I've had some sleep. You may not agree, but that's the way it's going to be."

"I have no objection. I'm not sure I'm capable of being lucid right now, and I must be when we talk. If it's possible, I've had less sleep than you."

"Two hours ago we could have killed each other," said Bray, standing motionless. "Neither of us did."

"Quite the reverse," agreed the KGB man, returning Scofield's gaze. "We prevented others from doing it."

"Which cancels any obligation between us."

"No such obligations exist, of course. However, I submit you may find a larger one when we talk."

"You could be right, but I doubt it. You may have to live with Moscow, but I don't have to live with what happened here in Washington today. I can do something about it. Maybe that's the difference between us."

"For both our sakes – for all our sakes – I fervently hope you're right."

"I am. I'm also going to get some sleep." Scofield pointed to a couch against the wall. "That pulls out into a bed; there are blankets in the closet over there. I'll use the bedroom." He started for the door, then stopped and turned to the Russian. "Incidentally, the door will be locked, and I'm a very light sleeper."

"A condition that afflicts us both, I'm sure," said Taleniekov. "You have nothing to fear from me."

"I never did," Bray said.

Scofield heard faint, sharp crackling sounds and spun under the sheets, his hand gripping the Browning automatic by his knees. He raised it between the covers as his feet shot out over the side of the bed; he was prepared to crouch and fire.

There was no one in the room. Moonlight streamed through the north window, shafts of colourless white light separated by the thick panes into single streaks of suspended, eerie illumination. For a moment he was not sure where he was, so complete had been his exhaustion, so deep his sleep. He knew by the time his feet touched the floor; his enemy was in the next room. A very strange enemy who had saved his life, and whose life he had saved minutes later.

Bray looked at the luminous dial of his watch. It was quarter past four in the morning. He had slept nearly thirteen hours, the heavy weight of his arms and legs, the adhesive moisture in his eyes, and the dryness of his throat evidence of having moved very little during that time. He sat for a while on the side of the bed, breathing the cold air deeply, putting the gun down and shaking his hands, slapping his fingers together. He looked over at the locked door of the bedroom.

Taleniekov was up and had started a fire, the sharp crackling was now the unmistakable sound of burning wood. Scofield decided to put off seeing the Russian for a few more minutes. His face itched, the growth of his beard so uncomfortable it had caused the beginning of a rash on his neck. There was always shaving equipment in the bathroom; he would afford himself the luxury of a shave and change the bandages he had placed on his neck and skull fourteen hours ago. It would postpone for a bit longer his talk with the former – defected? – KGB man. Whatever it concerned, Bray wanted no part of it, yet the unexpected events and decisions of the past twenty-four hours told him he was already involved. The bullet graze on his neck stung, the pain in his head a numbing throb.

It was 4.37 when he unlocked the door and opened it. Taleniekov was standing in front of the fire, sipping from a cup in his hand.

"I apologize if the fire awakened you," the Russian said. "Or the sound of the front door – if you heard it."

"The heater went out," said Scofield, looking down at the flameless gas Franklin that was the cabin's source of heat.

"I think the propane tank is empty."

"Is that why you went outside?"

"No, I went outside to relieve myself; there's no toilet here."

"I forgot."

"Did you hear me leave? Or return?"

"Is that coffee?"

"Yes," answered Taleniekov. "A bad habit I picked up from the West. Your tea has no character. The pot's on the burner." The KGB man gestured beyond a room divider where stove, sink and refrigerator were lined up against the wall. "I'm surprised you did not smell the aroma of freshly made coffee."

"I thought I did," lied Scofield, crossing to the stove and the pot. "But it was weak."

"And now we've both made our childish points."

"Childishly," added Bray, pouring coffee. "You keep saying you have something to tell me. Go ahead."

"First, I shall ask you a question. Have you ever heard of an organization called the Matarese?"

Scofield paused, remembering; he nodded. "Political killers for hire, run by a council in Corsica. It started well over a half-century ago and died out in the late 'forties, after the war. What about it?"

"It never died out. It went farther underground – became dormant, if you like – but it returned in a far more dangerous form. It's been operating since the early 'sixties. It operates now. It has infiltrated the most sensitive and powerful areas of both our governments. Its objective is the control over both our countries. The Matarese was responsible for the murders of General Blackburn here and Dimitri Yurievich in my country."

Bray sipped his coffee, studying the Russian's face over the rim of the cup. "How do you know that? Why do you believe it?"

"An old man who saw more in his lifetime than you and I combined made the identification. He was not wrong; he was one of the few who admitted – or will ever admit – having dealt with the Matarese."

"*Saw? Was?* Past tenses."

"He died. He called for me while he was dying; he wanted me to know. He had access to information neither you nor I would be given under any circumstances."

"Who was he?"

"Aleksie Krupsky. The name is meaningless, I realize, so I'll explain."

"Meaningless?" interrupted Scofield, crossing to an armchair in front of the fire, and sitting down. "Not entirely: Krupsky, the white cat of *Krivoi Rog*. *Istrebitel*. The last of the exterminators from Section Nine, KGB. The original Nine, of course."

"You do your school work well, but then, as they say, you're a Harvard man."

"That kind of school work can be helpful. Krupsky was banished twenty years ago. He became a non-person. If he were alive, I figured he was vegetating in Grasnov, not a consultant being fed information by people in the Kremlin. I don't believe your story."

"Believe it now," said Taleniekov, sitting down opposite Bray. "Because it was not 'people' in the Kremlin, just one man. His son. For thirty years one of the highest-ranking survivors of the Politburo. For the past six, Premier of Soviet Russia."

Scofield put his cup down on the floor and again studied the KGB man's face. It was the face of a practised liar, a professional liar, but not a liar by nature. He was not lying now. "Krupsky's son the Premier? That's . . . a shock."

"As it was to me, but not so shocking when you think about it. Guided at every turn, protected by his father's extensive collection of . . . shall we say memorabilia. Hypothetically, it could have happened here. Suppose your late John Edgar Hoover had a politically ambitious son. Who could have stood in his way? Hoover's secret files would have paved any road, even the floors leading to the Oval Office. The landscape is different, but the trees are the same genus. They haven't varied much since the senators gave Rome to Caligula."

"What did Krupsky tell you?"

"The past first. There were things I could not believe, until I spoke of them to several retired leaders of the Politburo. One frightened old man confirmed them, the others caused a plan to be mounted that called for my execution."

"Your . . . ?"

"Yes. Vasili Vasilievich Taleniekov, master strategist, KGB. An irascible man who may have seen his best years, but whose knowledge could be called upon for several decades perhaps – from a farm in Grasnov. We are a practical people; that would have been the practical solution. In spite of the minor doubts we all have, I believed that; I knew it was my future. But not after I mentioned the Matarese. Abruptly, everything changed. I, who have served my country well, was suddenly the enemy."

"What specifically did Krupsky say? What – in your judgement – was confirmed?"

Taleniekov recounted the dying *istrebitel's* words, admissions that traced scores of assassinations to the Matarese, including Stalin, Beria and Roosevelt. How the Corsican organization had been used by all the major governments, both within their borders and outside of them. None was exempt from the stain. Soviet Russia, England, France, Germany, Italy . . . the United States; the leaders of each, at one time or another, had made contracts with the Matarese.

116

"That's all been speculated upon before," said Bray. "Quietly, I grant you, but nothing concrete ever came out of the investigations."

"Because no one of substance ever dared testify. In Krupsky's words, the revelations would be catastrophic for governments everywhere. Now, there are new tactics being employed, all for the purpose of creating instability in the power centres."

"What are they?"

"Acts of terrorism. Bombings, kidnappings, the hijacking of aircraft; ultimatums issued by bands of fanatics, wholesale slaughter promised if they are not met. They grow in numbers every month and the vast majority are funded by the Matarese."

"How?"

"I can only surmise. The Matarese council studies the objectives of the parties involved, sends in the experts, and provides covert financing. Fanatics do not labour over the sources of funds, only their availability. I submit that you and I have used such men and women more often than we can count."

"For distinctly accountable purposes," said Bray, picking up his cup from the floor. "What about Blackburn and Yurievich? What did the Matarese accomplish by killing them?"

"Krupsky believed it was to test the leaders, to see if their own men could control each government's reactions. I'm not so sure now. I think perhaps there was something else. Frankly, because of what you've told me."

"What's that?"

"Yurievich. You said he was your operation. Is that true?"

Bray frowned. "True, but not that simple. Yurievich was grey; he wasn't going to defect in any normal sense. He was a scientist, convinced both sides had gone too far. He didn't trust the maniacs. It was a probe; we weren't sure where we were going."

"Are you aware that General Blackburn, who was nearly destroyed by the war in Korea, did what no Chairman of the Joint Chiefs has ever done in your history? He met secretly with your potential enemies. In Sweden, in the city of Skellefte on the Gulf of Bothnia, travelling under cover as a tourist. It was our judgement that he would go to any lengths to avoid the repetition of pointless slaughter. He abhorred conventional warfare, and he did not believe nuclear weapons would ever be used." The Russian stopped and leaned forward. "Two men who believed deeply, passionately, in the rejection of human sacrifice, who sought accommodation – both killed by the Matarese. So perhaps testing was only a part of the exercise. There could well have been another: to eliminate powerful men who believed in stability."

At first Scofield did not reply; the information about Blackburn was astonishing. "In the testing then, they pointed at me with Yurievich . . ."

"And at me with Blackburn," completed Taleniekov. "A Browning Magnum, Grade Four, was used to kill Yurievich; a Graz-Burya for Blackburn."

"And both of us set up for execution."

"Exactly," said the Soviet. "Because above all men in either country's intelligence service, we cannot be permitted to live. That will never change because we cannot change. Krupsky was right: we are diversions; we will be used and killed. We are too dangerous."

"Why do they think so?"

"They've studied us. They know we could no more accept the Matarese than we do the maniacs within our own branches. We are dead men, Scofield."

"Speak for yourself!" Bray was suddenly angry. "I'm out, terminated, *finished*! I don't give a Goddamn what happens out there! Don't you make judgements about me!"

"They've already been made. By others."

"Because *you* say so?" Scofield got up, putting the coffee down, his hand not far from the Browning in his belt.

"Because I *believed* the man who told me. It's why I'm *here*, why I *saved* your life and did not take it myself."

"I have to wonder about that, don't I?"

"What?"

"Everything timed, even to your knowing where Prague was on the staircase."

"I killed a man who had you under his gun!"

"*Prague?* A minor sacrifice. I'm a terminated encyclopaedia. I have no proof my government reached Moscow, only possible conclusions based on what *you* told me. Maybe I'm missing the obvious, maybe the great Taleniekov is eating a little temporary crow to bring in Beowulf Agate."

"*Damn* you, Scofield!" roared the KGB man, springing up from the chair. "I should have let you die! Hear me clearly. What you suggest is unthinkable and the KGB knows it. My feelings run too deep. I'd never bring you in. I'd kill you first."

Bray stared at the Russian, the honesty of Taleniekov's statement so clear. "I believe you," said Scofield, nodding, his anger diminishing in weariness. "But it doesn't change anything. I don't care. I really don't give a Goddamn . . . I'm not even sure I want to kill you any more. I just want to be left alone." Bray turned away. "Take the keys to the car and get out of here. Consider yourself . . . alive."

"Thank you for your generosity, Beowulf, but I'm afraid it's too late."

"What?" Scofield turned back to the Soviet.

"I did not finish. A man was caught, chemicals administered. There is a timetable, two months, three at the outside. The words were: 'Moscow by assassination; Washington by purchase – murder, if necessary.' When it happens, neither you nor I will survive. They'll track us to the ends of the earth."

"Wait a minute," said Bray, furious. "Are you telling me that your people *have* a man!"

"Had," interrupted Taleniekov. "Cyanide was implanted under his skin; he reached it."

"But he was *heard*. He was taped, recorded. His words were there!"

"Heard. Not taped, not recorded. And only by one man – who was warned by his father not to permit anyone else to listen."

"The *Premier?*"

"Yes."

"Then he knows!"

"Yes, he knows. And all he can do is try to protect himself – nothing particularly new in his position – but he can't speak of it. For to speak of it, as Krupsky said, is to acknowledge the past. This is the age of conspiracy, Scofield. Who cares to bring up past contracts? In my country there are a number of unexplained corpses; you're not so different over here. The Kennedys, Martin Luther King; perhaps most stunning, Franklin Roosevelt. We could all be at each other's throats – more precisely on the nuclear buttons – if our combined pasts were revealed. What would you do, if you were the Premier?"

"Protect myself," said Bray softly. "Oh, my God . . . "

"Now do you see?"

"I don't want to. I *really* don't *want* to. I'm out!"

"I submit that you cannot be. Nor I. The proof was yesterday on Nebraska Avenue. We're marked; they want us. They convinced others to have us killed – for the wrong reasons – but they were behind the strategy. Can you doubt it?"

"I wish I could. The manipulators are always easiest to manipulate, con-men the biggest suckers. Jesus!" Scofield walked to the stove to pour himself more coffee. Suddenly, he was struck by something not said, unclear. "I don't understand. From what little's known about the Matarese, it started as a cult and evolved into a business. It accepted contracts – or *supposedly* accepted contracts – on the basis of feasibility and price. It killed for money; it was never interested in power, *per se*. Why is it interested now?"

"I don't know," said the KGB man. "Neither did Krupsky. He was dying and not very lucid, but he said the answer might be in Corsica."

"Corsica? Why?"

"It's where it all began."

"Not where it is. *If* it is. The word was that the Matarese moved out of Corsica in the mid-'thirties. Contracts were negotiated as far away as London, New York . . . even Berlin. Centres of international traffic."

"Then perhaps clues to an answer is more appropriate. The council of the Matarese was formed in Corsica, only one name ever revealed. Guillaume de Matarese. Who were the others? Where did they go? Who are they *now?*"

"There's a quicker way of finding out than going to Corsica. If the Matarese is even a whisper in Washington, there's one person who can track it down. He's the one I was going to call anyway. I wanted my life straightened out."

"Who is he?"

"Robert Winthrop," said Bray.

"The creator of Consular Operations." The Russian nodded. "A good man who had no stomach for what he built."

"The *Cons Op* you're referring to isn't the one he began. He's still the only man I've heard of who can call up the White House and see the President in twenty minutes. Very little goes on that he doesn't know about. Or can't find out about." Scofield glanced over at the fire, remembering. "It's strange. In a way he's responsible for everything I am, and he doesn't approve of me. But I think he'll listen."

The nearest telephone booth was three miles down the highway beyond the dirt road to the cabin. It was ten past eight when Bray stepped in, shielding his eyes from the glare of the morning sun, and pulled the glass door shut. He had found Winthrop's private number in his attaché case; he had not called it in years. He dialled, hoping it was still the same.

It was. The cultivated voice on the line brought back many memories. Possibilities missed, many others taken.

"Scofield! Where *are* you?"

"I'm afraid I can't tell you that. Please try to understand."

"I understand you're in a great deal of trouble, and nothing will be served by running *away*. Congdon called. The man killed in the hotel was shot with a Russian gun . . ."

"I know. The Russian who killed him saved my life. That man was *sent* by Congdon, so were the other two. They were my execution team. From Prague, Marseilles and Amsterdam."

"Oh, my *God* . . ." The elder statesman was silent for a moment and Bray did not interrupt that silence. "Do you know what you're saying?" asked Winthrop.

"Yes, sir. You know me well enough to know I *wouldn't* say it unless I were sure. I'm not mistaken. I spoke to the man from Prague before he died."

"He *confirmed* it?"

"In oblique words, yes. But then, that's how those cables are sent; the words are always oblique."

Again there was a moment of silence before the old man spoke. "I can't believe it, Bray. For a reason you couldn't know. Congdon came to see me a week ago. He was concerned how you'd take retirement. He had the usual worries: a highly knowledgeable agent terminated against his will with too much time on his hands, perhaps too much to drink. He's a cold fellow, that Congdon, and I'm afraid he angered me. After all you've been through to have so little trust . . . I rather sardonically mentioned what you've just described – not that I ever dreamed he would consider such a thing, just that I was appalled at his attitude. So I *can't* believe it. Don't you see? He'd know I'd recognize it. He wouldn't take that risk."

"Then someone gave him the order, sir. That's what we have to talk about. Those three men knew where to find me, and there was only one way they could've learned. It was a KGB drop and they were *Cons Op* personnel. Moscow gave it to Congdon; he relayed it."

"Congdon reached the *Soviets*? That's not plausible. Even if he tried, why would they co–operate? Why would they reveal a drop?"

"Their own man was part of the negotiation; they wanted him killed. He was trying to contact me. We'd exchanged cables."

"Taleniekov?"

It was Scofield's moment to pause. He answered quietly. "Yes, sir."

"A *white* contact?"

"Yes. I misread it, but that's what it was. I'm convinced now."

"*You* . . . and Taleniekov? *Extraordinary*."

"The circumstances are extraordinary. Do you remember an organization from the 'forties that went by the name of the Matarese . . . ?"

They agreed to meet at nine o'clock that evening, a mile north of the Missouri Avenue exit of Rock Creek Park on the eastern side. There was an indented stretch of pavement off the road where automobiles could park and strollers could enter the various paths that overlooked a scenic ravine. Winthrop intended to cancel the day's appointments and concentrate on learning whatever there was to learn about Bray's astonishing – if fragmentary – information.

"He'll convene the Forty Committee, if he has to," said Scofield to Taleniekov on the way back to the cabin.

"Can he do that?" asked the Russian.

"The President can," answered Bray.

The two men talked little during the day, the strain of proximity uncomfortable for each. Taleniekov read from the extensive bookshelves, glancing at Scofield now and then, the look in his eyes a mixture of remembered fury and curiosity.

Bray felt the glances; he refused to acknowledge them. He listened to the radio for news reports about the carnage at the hotel on Nebraska Avenue, and the death of a Russian attache in the adjacent building. They were played down, de-emphasized, no mention made of the dead embassy official. It was suggested that the hotel killings were foreign in origin – that much was allowed – and no doubt criminally orientated, probably related to upper levels of the narcotics trade. The suppressants had been applied; the Department of State had moved swiftly, with sure-footed censorship.

And with each progressively fading report Scofield felt progressively trapped. He was becoming intrinsic to something he wanted no part of; his new life was not around the corner any longer. He began to wonder where it was, or if it would be. He was being inexorably drawn into an enigma called the Matarese.

At four o'clock he went for a walk in the fields and along the banks of the Patuxent. As he left the cabin, he made sure the Russian saw him slip the Browning automatic into his holster. The KGB man did see; he placed his Graz-Burya on the table next to the chair.

At five o'clock, Taleniekov made an observation. "I think we should position ourselves a good hour before the appointment."

"I trust Winthrop," replied Bray curtly.

"With good reason, I'm sure. But can you trust those he'll be contacting?"

"He won't tell anyone he's meeting us. He wants to talk to you at length. He'll have questions. Names, past positions, military ranks."

"I'll try to provide answers where they are relative to the Matarese. I will not be compromised in other areas."

"Bully for you."

"Nevertheless, I still think . . ."

"We'll leave in fifteen minutes," interrupted Scofield. "There's a diner on the way; we'll eat separately."

At 7.35, Bray drove the rented car into the south end of the parking area on the border of Rock Creek Park. He and the KGB man made four penetrations into the woods, sweeping in arcs off the paths, checking the trees and the rocks and the ravine below for signs of intruders. The night was bitterly cold; there were no strollers, no one anywhere. They met at a pre-arranged spot on the edge of the small gorge. Taleniekov spoke first.

"I saw nothing; the area is secure."

Scofield looked at his watch in the darkness. "It's nearly eight-thirty. I'll wait by the car; you stay up here at this end. I'll meet with him first and then signal you."

"How? It's several hundred yards."

"I'll strike a match."

"Very appropriate."

"What?"

"Nothing. It's unimportant."

At two minutes to nine, Winthrop's limousine came out of the Rock Creek exit, drove into the parking area, and stopped within twenty feet of the rented car. The sight of the chauffeur disturbed Bray, but only momentarily. Scofield recognized the huge man instantly; he had been with Robert Winthrop for over two decades. Rumours about a chequered Marine Corps career cut short by several courts martial followed the chauffeur, but Winthrop never discussed him other than to call him "my friend Stanley". No one ever pressed.

Bray walked out of the shadows towards the limousine. Stanley opened the door and was on the pavement in one motion, his right hand in his pocket, in his left a flashlight. He turned it on. Scofield shut his eyes. It went off in seconds.

"Hello, Stanley," said Bray.

"It's been a long time, Mr Scofield," replied the chauffeur. "Nice to see you."

"Thanks. Good to see you."

"The ambassador's waiting," continued the driver, reaching down and snapping the lock release. "The door's open now."

"Fine. By the way, in a couple of minutes I'm going to get out of the car and strike a match. It's the signal for a man to come and join us. He's up at the other end; he'll walk out of one of the paths."

"I gotcha. The ambassador said there'd be two of you. OK."

"What I'm trying to say is, if you still smoke those thin cigars of yours, wait till I get out before you light up. I'd like a few moments alone with Mr Winthrop."

"You've got a hell of a memory," said Stanley, tapping his jacket pocket with the flashlight. "I was about to have one."

Bray got into the back seat of the car and faced the man who was responsible for his life. Winthrop had grown old, so old, but in the dim light his eyes were still electric, still filled with concern. They shook hands, the elder statesman prolonging the grip.

"I've thought about you often," he said softly, his eyes searching Scofield's, then noting the bandages and wincing. "I have mixed feelings, but I don't think I have to tell you that."

"No, sir, you don't."

"So many things changed, didn't they, Bray? The ideals, the opportunities to do so much for so many. We were crusaders, really. At the beginning." The old man released Scofield's hand and smiled. "Do you remember? You came up with a processing plan that was to be cross-collateralized with lend-lease. Debts in occupied territories for multiple immigration. A brilliant concept in economic diplomacy, I've always said that. Human lives for monies that were never going to be repaid anyway."

"It would have been rejected."

"Probably, but in the arena of world opinion it would have pushed the Soviets to

122

the wall. I recall your words. You said 'if we're supposed to be a capitalistic government, don't walk away from it. Use it, define it. American citizens paid for half the Russian Army. Stress the psychological obligation. Get something, get *people.*' Those were your words."

"That was a graduate student expounding on naive theoretical geopolitics."

"There's often a great deal of truth in such naïveté. You know, I can still see that graduate student. I wonder about him . . ."

"There's no time now, sir," interrupted Scofield. "Taleniekov's waiting. Incidentally, we checked the area; it's clear."

The old man's eyes blinked. "Did you think it would be otherwise?"

"I was worried about a tap on your phone."

"No need for that," said Winthrop. "Such devices have to be listed somewhere, recorded somewhere. I wouldn't care to be the person who did such a thing. Too many private conversations take place on my telephone. It's my best protection."

"Did you learn anything?"

"About the Matarese? No . . . and *yes.* No, in the sense that even the most rarefied intelligence data contained no mention of it whatsoever, hasn't for the past forty-three years. The President assured me of this and I trust him. He was appalled; he leapt at the possibility and put men on the alert. He was furious, and frightened, I think."

"What's the 'yes'?"

The old man chose his words carefully. "It's obscure but it's there. Before I decided to call the President, I reached five men who for years – decades – have been involved in the most sensitive areas of intelligence and diplomacy. Of the five, three remembered the Matarese and were shocked. They offered to do whatever they could to help, the spectre of the Matarese's return was quite terrifying to them . . . Yet the other two – men, who if anything, are far more knowledgeable than their colleagues – claimed *never* to have heard of it. Their reactions made no sense; they *had* to have heard of it. Just as I had – my information minimal but certainly not forgotten. When I said as much, when I pressed them, both behaved rather strangely, and considering our past associations, not without insult. Each treated me as though I were some kind of aged patrician, given to senile fantasies. Really, it was astonishing."

"Who were they?"

"Again, odd . . ."

A flash of light in the distance; Scofield's eyes were drawn to it. And another . . . and *another.* Matches were being struck in rapid succession.

Taleniekov.

The KGB man was cupping matches and lighting one after another furiously. It was a warning. Taleniekov was warning him that something had happened – *was happening.* Suddenly the distant flame was constant, but broken by a hand held in front of the flame – in rapid sequences, more light, less light. Basic Morse. Dots and dashes.

Three dots repeated twice. *S.* A long spill, repeated once. A single dash. *T.S.T.*

"What's the matter?" asked Winthrop.

"Just a second," replied Scofield.

Three dots, broken, then followed by a dash. The letters *S* and *T* were being repeated. *S. T.*

Surveillance. Terminal.

The flame moved to the left, towards the road bordering the woods of the parking area, and was extinguished. The Soviet agent was repositioning himself. Bray turned back to the old man.

"How certain are you about your telephone?"

"Very. It's never been tapped. I have ways of knowing."

"They may not be extensive enough." Scofield touched the window button; the glass rolled down and he called to the chauffeur standing in front of the limousine. "Stan, come here!" The driver did so. "When you drove through the park, did you check to see if anyone followed you?"

"Sure did, and no way. I keep an eye on the rear view mirror. I always do, especially when we're meeting someone at night . . . Did you see the light up there? Was it your man?"

"Yes. He was telling me someone else was here."

"Impossible," said Winthrop emphatically. "If there is, it's no concern of ours. This is, after all, a public park."

"I don't want to alarm you, sir, but Taleniekov's experienced. There are no headlights, no cars in the road. Whoever's out there doesn't want us to know it, and it's not a night for a casual walk. I'm afraid it does concern us." Bray opened the door. "Stan, I'm going to grab my briefcase from my car. When I get back, drive out of here. Stop briefly at the north end of the lot by the road."

"What about the Russian?" asked Winthrop.

"That's why we're stopping. He'll know enough to jump in. He'd better."

"*Wait* a minute," said Stanley, no deference in his voice. "If there's any trouble, I'm not stopping for anyone. I've only got one job. To get *him* out of here. Not you or anybody else."

"We don't have time to argue. Start the engine." Bray ran to the rented car, the keys in his hand. He unlocked the door, removed his attache case from the front seat, and started back towards the limousine.

He never reached it. A beam of powerful light pierced through the darkness, aimed at Robert Winthrop's huge automobile. Stanley was behind the wheel, gunning the motor, prepared to bolt out of the area. Whoever held the light was not going to allow that to happen. He wanted that car . . . and whoever was in that car.

The limousine's wheels spun, screeching on the pavement, as the huge car surged forward. A staccato spray of gunfire erupted; windows shattered, bullets crunched into metal. The limousine wove back and forth in abrupt half-circles, seemingly out of control.

Two loud reports came from the woods beyond; the searchlight exploded, a scream of pain followed. Winthrop's car straightened out briefly, then lurched into a sharp left turn. Caught in the headlights were two men, weapons drawn, a third on the ground.

Bray's gun was in his hand; he dropped to the pavement and fired. One of the two men fell as the limousine completed the turn and roared out of the parking lot into the south-bound road.

Scofield rolled to his right; two shots were fired, the bullets singing off the pavement where he had been seconds ago. Bray got to his feet and ran in the darkness towards the railing that fronted the ravine.

He lunged over the top rail, his attache case slamming into the wood post, the sound distinct. The next gunshot was expected; it came as he hugged the earth and the rocks.

Lights. Headlights! Two beams shooting overhead, accompanied by the sound of a racing car. The smashing of glass came hard upon tyres screeching to a sudden stop. A shout – unclear, hysterical . . . cut off by a loud explosion – preceded silence.

The engine had stalled, the headlights still on, revealing curls of smoke and two immobile bodies on the ground, a third on his knees, looking around in panic. The man heard something; he spun and raised his gun.

A weapon was fired from the woods. It was final; the would-be killer fell.

"*Scofield!*" Taleniekov shouted.

"Over here!" Bray lunged up over the railing and ran towards the source of the Russian's voice. Taleniekov walked out of the woods; he was no more than ten feet from the stalled automobile. Both men approached the car warily; the driver's window had been shattered, blown apart by a single shot from the KGB man's automatic. The head beyond the fragmented glass was bloodied but recognizable. The right hand was wrapped in a tight bandage – still wrapped from an injured thumb broken on a bridge in Amsterdam at three o'clock in the morning by an angry, tired older man.

It was the aggressive young agent, Harry, who had killed so needlessly in the rain that night.

"Good *God!*" said Scofield.

"You know him?" asked Taleniekov, a curious note in his voice.

"His name was Harry. He worked for me in Amsterdam."

The Russian was silent for a moment, then spoke. "He was *with* you in Amsterdam, but he did not work for you, and his name was not 'Harry'. That young man is a Soviet intelligence officer, trained since the age of nine at the American Compound in Novograd. He was a VKR agent."

Bray studied Taleniekov's face, then looked back through the shattered window at Harry. "Congratulations. Things fall into place more clearly now."

"They don't for me, I'm afraid," said the KGB man. "Believe me when I tell you that it is most unlikely that any order out of Moscow would include a direct attack on Robert Winthrop. We're not fools. He's above reprisals – a voice and a skill to be preserved, not struck down. And certainly not for such – personnel – as you and me."

"What do you mean?"

"This was an execution team, as surely as those men at the hotel. You and I were not to be isolated, not to be taken separately. The kill was inclusive. Winthrop was to be executed as well, and for all we know he may have been. I submit that the order did not come from Moscow."

"It didn't come from the State Department. I'm damn sure of that."

"Agreed. Neither Washington nor Moscow, but a source capable of issuing orders in the name of one, or the other, or both."

"The Matarese?" said Scofield.

The Russian nodded. "The Matarese."

Bray held his breath, trying to think, to absorb it all. "If Winthrop's still alive, he'll be caged, tapped, held under a microscope. I won't be able to get near him. They'd kill me on sight."

"Again, I agree. Are there others you trust that can be reached?"

"It's crazy," said Scofield, shivering in the cold – and at the thought that now struck him. "There should be, but I don't know who they are. Whoever I went to would have to turn me over, the laws are clear about that. Police warrants aside, there's a little matter of national security. The case against me will be built quickly, legally. Suspected of treason, internal espionage, delivering information to the enemy. No one will touch me."

"Surely there are people who will *listen* to you."

"Listen to what? What do I tell them? What have I got? *You?* You'd be thrown into a maximum security hospital before you could say your name. The words of a dying *istrebitel?* A Communist killer? Where's the verification, even the logic? Goddamn it, we're cut off. All we've got are shadows!"

Taleniekov took a step forward, his conviction in his voice. "Perhaps old Krupsky was right; perhaps the answer is in Corsica, after all."

"Oh, Christ . . ."

"Hear me out. You say we have only shadows. If so, if we *had* more, traced even a few names, constructed a fabric of probability – built our own case if you will. Then could you go to someone, force him to listen to you?"

"From a distance," answered Bray slowly. "Only from a distance. Beyond reach."

"Naturally."

"The case would have to be more than probable, it'd have to get goddamned conclusive."

"I, too, could move men in Moscow if I had such proof. It was my hope that over here an inquiry might be made with less evidence. You're notorious for your never-ending Senate inquiries. I merely assumed it could be done, that you could bring it about."

"Not now. Not me."

"Corsica, then?"

"I don't know. I'd have to think about it. There's still Winthrop."

"You said yourself you could not reach him. If you tried to get near him, they'd kill you."

"People have tried before. I'll protect myself. I've got to find out what happened. He saw it for himself; if he's alive and I can talk to him, he'll know what to do."

"And if he's *not* alive, or you cannot reach him?"

Scofield looked at the dead men on the pavement. "Maybe the only thing that's left. Corsica."

The KGB man shook his head. "I look at odds more thoroughly than you, Beowulf. I won't wait. I won't risk that 'hospital' you speak of. I'll go to Corsica now."

126

"If you do, start on the south-east coast, north of Porto Vecchio."

"Why?"

"It's where it all began. It's Matarese country."

Taleniekov nodded. "Again, the school work. Thank you. Perhaps we'll meet in Corsica."

"Can you get out of the country?" asked Bray.

"Getting in, getting out . . . easily managed. These are not obstacles. What about yourself? If you decide to join me."

"I can buy my way to London, to Paris. I've got accounts there. If I do, count on three days, four at the outside. There are small inns up in the hills. I'll find you . . ."

Scofield stopped. Both men turned swiftly at the sound of an approaching automobile. A sedan swung casually off the road into the parking area. In the front seat was a couple, the man's arm draped over the woman's shoulder. The headlights shone directly on the immobile bodies on the pavement, the spill illuminating the shattered window of the stalled car and the bloody head inside.

The driver whipped his arm off the woman's shoulder, pushing her down on the seat, and gripped the steering wheel with both hands. He spun it violently to the right and sped back into the road, the roar of the motor echoing throughout the woods and the open space.

"They'll reach the police," said Bray. "Let's get out of here."

"I submit it would be best not to use that car," replied the KGB man.

"Why not?"

"Winthrop's chauffeur. You may trust him. I'm not sure I do."

"That's crazy! He was damn near killed!"

Taleniekov gestured at the dead men on the pavement. "These were marksmen, Russian or American, it makes no difference, they were experts – the Matarese would employ no less. The windshield of that limousine was at least five feet wide, the driver behind it an easy target for a novice. Why wasn't he shot? Why wasn't that car stopped? We look for traps, Beowulf. We were led into one and we didn't see it. Perhaps even by Winthrop himself."

Bray felt sick; he had no answer. "We'll separate. It's better for both of us."

"Corsica, perhaps?"

"Maybe. You'll know if I get there. Three, four days at the outside. If I go."

"Very well."

"Taleniekov?"

"Yes?"

"Thanks for using the matches."

"Under the circumstances, I believe you would have done the same for me."

"Under the circumstances . . . yes, I would."

"Has it struck you? We did not kill each other, Beowulf Agate. We talked."

"We talked."

A lone siren was carried on the cold night wind. Others would be heard soon; patrol cars would converge on the killing ground. Both men turned away from each other and ran, Scofield down the dark patch into the woods beyond the rented car, Taleniekov towards the railing that fronted the ravine in Rock Creek Park.

Book II

12

The thick-beamed fishing boat ploughed through the chopping swells like a heavy awkward animal dimly aware that the waters were unfriendly. Waves slapped against the bow and the sides, sending cascading sprays over the gunwhales, the tails of salt whipped by the early-morning winds into the faces of men handling the nets.

One man, however, was not involved with the drudgery of the catch. He pulled at no rope and manipulated no hook, nor did he join in the cursing and laughter that were by-products of making a living from the sea. Instead, he sat alone on the deck, a thermos of coffee in one hand, a cupped cigarette in the other. It was understood that should French or Italian patrol boats approach, he would become a fisherman, but if none did he was to be left by himself. No one objected to this strange man without a name, for each member of the crew was 10,000 lire richer for his presence. The boat had picked him up on a pier in San Vincenzo. The vessel's schedule had called for a dawn departure from the Italian coast, but the stranger had suggested that if the coast of Corsica were seen by dawn, captain and crew would have a far better catch for their labours. Rank had its privileges; the captain received 15,000 lire. They had sailed out of San Vincenzo before midnight.

Scofield twisted the top back on to the thermos and threw his cigarette over the side. He stood up and stretched, peering through the mists at the coastline. They had made good time. According to the captain they would be in sight of Solenzara within minutes; and within an hour they would drop off their esteemed passenger between Sainte Lucie and Porto Vecchio. No problems were anticipated; there were scores of deserted inlets on the rocky shoreline for a temporarily disabled fishing boat

Bray yanked on the cord looped around the handle of his attache case and strapped to his wrist; it was firm – and wet. The string-burn on his wrist was irritated by the salt water, but it would heal quickly, actually aided by the salt. The precaution might seem unwarranted, but the appearance of it was as valuable as the attachment. One could doze, and *Corsos* were known to be quick to relieve travellers of valuables – especially travellers who journeyed without identification, but with money.

"*Signore!*" The captain approached, his wide smile revealing an absence of eye teeth. "*Ecco.* Solenzara! *Trenta minuti. Nord di* Porto Vecchio!"

"*Grazie.*"

"*Prego!*"

In a half hour he'd be on land, in Corsica, in the hills where the Matarese was born. That it had been born was not disputed, that it had provided assassins-for-hire until the mid-'thirties was accepted as a firm probability. But so very little was known about it that no one really knew how much of its story was myth and how much based in reality. The legend was both encouraged and scorned at the same time; it was basically an enigma because no one understood its origins. Only that a madman named Guillaume de Matarese had summoned a council – from where was never recorded – and gave birth to a band of assassins, based, some said, on the killer-society of Hasan ibn as-Sabbāh in the eleventh century.

Yet this smacked of cult-orientation, thus feeding the myth and diminishing the reality. No court testimony was ever given, no assassin ever caught who could be traced to an organization called the Matarese; if there were confessions, none was ever made public. Still the rumours persisted. Stories were circulated in high places; articles appeared in responsible newspapers, only to be denied editorial substance in later editions. Several independent studies were begun; if any was completed, no one knew about it. And through it all, governments made no comment. Ever. They were silent.

And for a young intelligence officer studying the history of assassination years ago, it was this silence that lent a certain credibility to the Matarese.

Just as another silence, suddenly imposed three days ago, convinced him that the rendezvous in Corsica was no proposal made in the heat of violence, but the only thing that *was* left. The Matarese remained an enigma, but it was no myth. It was a reality. A powerful man had gone to other powerful men and spoken in alarm; it was not to be tolerated.

Robert Winthrop had disappeared.

Bray had run from Rock Creek Park three nights before and made his way to a motel on the outskirts of Fredericksburg. For six hours he had travelled up and down the highway calling Winthrop from a series of telephone booths, never the same one twice, hitching rides on the pretext of a disabled car to put distance between them. He had talked to Winthrop's wife, alarming her he was sure, but saying nothing of substance, only that he had to speak with the ambassador. Until it was dawn, and there was no answer on the phone, just interminable rings spaced farther and farther apart – or so it seemed – and no one at all on the line.

There had been nowhere to turn, no one to go to; the networks were spreading out for him. If they found him, his termination would be complete; he understood that. If he were permitted to live, it would be within the four walls of a cell, or worse, as a vegetable. But he did not think he would be permitted to live. Taleniekov had been right; they were both marked.

If there was an answer, it was four thousand miles away in the Mediterranean. In his attaché case were a dozen false passports, five bank books under assumed names, and a list of men and women who could find him all manner of transportation. He had left Fredericksburg at dawn two days ago, had stopped at banks in London and Paris, and late last night had reached a fishing pier in San Vincenzo.

And now he was within minutes of setting foot on Corsica. The long stretches of immobility in the air and over the water had given him time to think, or at least the time to organize his thoughts. He had to start with the incontrovertible; there were two established facts.

130

Guillaume de Matarese had existed and there'd been a group of men who had called themselves the Council of the Matarese, dedicated to the insane theories of its sponsor. The world moved forward by constant, violent changes of power. Shock and sudden death were intrinsic to the evolution of history. Someone had to provide the means. Governments everywhere would pay for political murder. Assassination – carried out under the most controlled methods, untraceable to those contracting for it – could become a global resource with riches and influence beyond imagination. This was the theory of Guillaume de Matarese.

Among the international intelligence community, a minority maintained that the Matarese had been responsible for scores of political killings from the second decade of the century through the mid-'thirties, from Sarajevo to Mexico City, from Tokyo to Berlin and points in between. In their view, the collapse of the Matarese was attributed to the explosion of World War II, with its growth of covert services where such murders were legitimized, or the council's absorption by the Sicilian Mafia, now entrenched everywhere, but centralized in the United States.

But this positive judgement was decidedly a minority viewpoint. The vast majority of professionals agreed with Interpol, Britain's MI6, and the American Central Intelligence Agency, who claimed that the power of the Matarese was exaggerated. It undoubtedly had killed a number of minor political figures in the maze of passionately ineffective French and Italian politics, but there was no hard evidence of anything beyond this. It was essentially a collection of paranoiacs led by a wealthy eccentric who was as misinformed about philosophy as he was about governments accepting his outrageous contracts. If it were anything else, these professionals claimed further, why had not *they* ever been contacted?

Because, Bray had believed years ago, as he believed now, *you were – we were – the last people on earth the Matarese wanted to do business with. From the beginning we were the competition – in one form or another.*

"*Quindici minuti!*" bellowed the captain from the open wheelhouse. "*Andare entro costa!*"

"*Grazie.*"

"*Prego!*"

The Matarese. *Was* it possible? A group of men selecting and controlling global assassinations, providing structure to terrorism, spawning chaos everywhere?

For Bray the answer was now yes. The words of a dying *istrebitel*, the sentence of death imposed by the Soviets on Vasili Taleniekov, his own execution team recruited from Marseilles, Amsterdam and Prague . . . all were a prelude to the disappearance of Robert Winthrop. All were tied to this modern Council of the Matarese. It was the unseen, unknown mover.

Who were they, these hidden men who had the resources to reach into the highest places of governments as readily as they financed wild-eyed terrorists and selected celebrated men for murder? The larger question was why. *Why?* For what purpose or purposes did they exist?

The *who* was the riddle that had to be unravelled first and whoever they were, there had to be a connection between them and those fanatics initially summoned by Guillaume de Matarese; where else could they have come from, how else could they have known? Those early men had come to the hills of Porto Vecchio; they had names. The past was the only point of departure he had.

There'd been another, he reflected, but the flare of a match in the woods of Rock Creek Park had erased it. Robert Winthrop had been about to name two powerful men in Washington who had vehemently denied any knowledge of the Matarese. In their denials was their complicity; they *had* to have heard of the Matarese – one way or the other. But Winthrop had not said those names; the violence had intervened. Now he would never say them.

Names past could lead to names present; in this case, they had to. Men left their works, their imprints on their times . . . their money. All could be traced and led somewhere. If there were keys to unlock the vaults that held the answers to the Matarese, they would be found in the hills of Porto Vecchio. He had to find them . . . as his enemy, Vasili Taleniekov had to find them. Neither would survive unless they did. There'd be no farm in Grasnov for the Russian, no new life for Beowulf Agate, until they found the answers and delivered them to those elusive men of conscience Taleniekov had spoken of three nights ago in Washington.

"*Attualmente!*" roared the captain, spinning the wheel. "*Lo accesso roccio!*" He turned, grinning at his passenger through the wind-blown spray. "*Cinque minuti, signore! La terra di Corsica!*"

"*Grazie.*"

"*Prego.*"

Corsica.

Taleniekov raced up the rocky hill in the moonlight, ducking into the patches of tall grass to obscure his movements, but not the path he was breaking. He did not want those following him to give up the hunt, merely to be slowed down, separated if possible; if he could trap one, that would be ideal.

Old Krupsky had been right about Corsica, Scofield accurate about hills north of Porto Vecchio. There were secrets here; it had taken him less than two days to learn that. Men now chased him through the hills in the darkness to prevent him from learning anything further.

Four nights ago Corsica had been a wildly speculative source, an alternative to capture, Porto Vecchio merely a town on the south-east coast of the island, the hills beyond unknown.

The hills were still unknown; the people who lived in them were distant, strange and uncommunicative, their Oltramontanan dialect difficult to understand, but the speculation had been removed. The mere mention of the Matarese was enough to cloud eyes that were hostile to begin with; pressing for even the most innocuous information was enough to end conversations barely begun. It was as if the name itself were part of a tribal rite of which no one spoke outside the enclaves in the hills, and never in the presence of strangers. Vasili had begun to understand within hours after he had entered the rock-dotted countryside; it had been dramatically confirmed the first night.

Four days ago he would not have believed it; now he knew it was so. The Matarese was more than legend, more than a mystic symbol to primitive hill people; it was a form of religion. It *had* to be; men were prepared to die to keep its secret.

Four days and the world had changed for him. He was no longer dealing with knowledgeable men, sophisticated equipment at their disposal. There were no computer tapes whirling inside glass panels at the touch of a button, no green letters rat-tat-tatting across black screens, delivering immediate information necessary for the next decision. He was probing the past among people of the past.

Which was why he wanted so desperately to trap one of the men following him up the hill in the darkness. He judged there were three of them; the crest of the hill was long and wide and dense with ragged trees and jagged rocks. They would have to separate in order to cover the various descents that led to further hills and the flatlands that preceded the mountain forests. If he could take one man and have several hours to work on his mind and body, he could learn a great deal. He had no compunction about doing so. The night before a wooden bed had been blown apart in the darkness as a Corsican stood silhouetted in the door frame, a Lupo shotgun in his hand. Taleniekov was presumed to have been in that bed . . . Just one man – *that* man – thought Vasili, suppressing his anger, as he ran into a small cluster of wild fir trees just beneath the crown of the hill. He could rest for a few moments.

Far below he could see the weak beams of flashlights. *One, two . . . three.* Three men and they *were* separating. The one on the extreme left was covering his area; it would take that man ten minutes of climbing to reach the cluster of wild fir. Taleniekov hoped it was the man with the Lupo. He leaned against a tree, breathing heavily, and let his body go limp.

It had happened so fast, the excursion into this primitive world. Yet there was a symmetry of a kind. He had begun running at night along the wooded banks of a ravine in Washington's Rock Creek Park and here he was in an isolated, tree-lined sanctuary high in the hills of Corsica. At night. The journey had been swift; he had known precisely what to do and when to do it.

Two days ago he had been in Rome's Leonardo da Vinci Airport, where he had negotiated for a private flight to Bonifacio, due west, on the southern tip of Corsica. He had reached Bonifacio by seven in the evening and a taxi had driven him north along the coast to Porto Vecchio and up to an inn in the hill country. He had sat down to a heavy Corsican meal, engaging the curious owner in off-hand conversation.

"I am a scholar of sorts," he had said. "I seek information about a *padrone* of many years ago. A Guillaume de Matarese."

"I do not understand," the innkeeper had replied. "You say a scholar of sorts. It would seem to me that one either is or is not, *signore*. Are you with some great university?"

"A private foundation, actually." Taleniekov had answered slowly, even hesitantly, thus opening a door with obvious reluctance. "But universities have access to our studies."

"*Una fondazione?*"

"*Una organizzazione accademica.* My section deals with little-known history in Sardinia and Corsica during the late nineteenth and early twentieth centuries. Apparently there was this *padrone* . . . Guillaume de Matarese. . . .who controlled much of the land in these hills north of Porto Vecchio."

"He owned most of it, *signore*. He was good to the people who lived on his lands. If that is control it is *benevolo*, no?"

"Naturally. And we would like to grant him a place in Corsica's history. I'm not sure I know where to begin."

"Perhaps . . ." The innkeeper had leaned back in the chair, his eyes levelled, his voice strangely non-committal. "The ruins of the Villa Matarese. It is a clear night, *signore*. They are quite beautiful in the moonlight. I could find someone to take you. Unless, of course, you are too exhausted from your journey."

"Not at all. It was a quick flight. From Milan."

He had been taken farther up into the hills, to the skeletal remains of a once-sprawling estate, the remnants of the great house itself covering nearly an acre of land. Jagged walls and broken chimneys were the only structures still standing. On the ground, the brick borders of an enormous circular drive could be discerned beneath the overgrowth as it swung in front of flat tiered relics that once had been marble steps. On both sides of the great house, stone paths sliced through the tall grass, dotted by broken trellises; remembrances of lushly cultivated gardens long since destroyed.

The entire ruins stood eerily on the hill in silhouette, heightened by the backwash of moonlight. Guillaume de Matarese had built a monument to himself and the power of the edifice had lost nothing in its destruction by time and the elements. Instead, the skeleton had a force of its own, giving rise to images that perhaps could not be fulfilled when whole. Villa Matarese had a mystic quality about it and that mysticism had been intrinsic to the dramatic lesson that had followed.

Vasili had heard the voices behind him, the young boy who'd escorted him was nowhere to be seen. There had been two men and those opening words of dubious greeting had been the beginning of an interrogation that had lasted over an hour. It would have been a simple matter to subdue both Corsicans and reverse the proceedings, but Taleniekov knew he could learn more through passive resistance; unschooled interrogators imparted more than they dragged forth when they dealt with trained subjects. He had stayed with his story of the *organizzazione accademica*; at the end, he had been advised bluntly.

"Go back where you came from, *signore*. There is no knowledge here that would serve you; we know nothing. Disease swept through these mountains years ago; none is left who might help you."

"There must be older people in the hills. Perhaps if I wandered about and made a few inquiries."

"We are older people, *signore*, and we cannot answer your inquiries. Go back. We are ignorant men in these parts, shepherds by trade and ownership. We are not comfortable when strangers intrude on our simple ways. Go back."

"I shall take your advice under consideration . . ."

"Do not take such trouble, *signore*. Just leave us," had been the reply.

In the morning, Vasili had walked back up into the hills, to the Villa Matarese and beyond, stopping at numerous thatched farmhouses, asking his questions, noting the dark Corsican eyes that had glared before the non-answers had been delivered, aware that he was being followed.

He had been told nothing, of course, but in the progressively hardened reactions to his presence he had learned something of consequence. Men were not only following him, they had been preceding him, alerting families in the hills that a stranger was coming. He was to be treated indifferently, no traveller to be brought in front of a fire or given tea; he was to be sent away, told nothing.

That night – last night, thought Taleniekov, as he watched the weaving beam of the flashlight on the left slowly ascend the hill – the innkeeper had approached his table.

"I am afraid, *signore*, that I cannot permit you to stay here any longer. I have rented the room."

Vasili had glanced up, no hesitation now in his speech. "A pity. I need only an armchair or a cot, if you could spare one. I shall be leaving first thing in the morning. I've found what I came for."

"And what is that, *signore?*"

"You'll know soon enough, my friend. Others will come after me, with the proper equipment and land records. There'll be a very thorough, very scholarly investigation. What happened here is fascinating. I speak academically, of course."

"Of course . . . Perhaps one more night."

Six hours later a man had burst into his room and fired two shots from the thick barrels of a deadly sawed-off shotgun called the Lupo – the "wolf". Taleniekov had been waiting; he had watched from behind a partially open closet door as the wooden bed exploded, the firm stuffing beneath the covers blown into the dark wall.

The sound had been shattering, an explosion echoing throughout the small country inn, yet no one had come running to see what had happened. Instead, the man with the Lupo had stood in the door frame and had spoken quietly in Oltramontanan, as if uttering an oath.

"*Perro nostro circulo*," he had said; then he had raced away.

It had meant nothing, yet Vasili knew then that it meant everything. Words delivered as an incantation after taking a life . . . *For our circle*.

Taleniekov had gathered his things together and fled from the inn. He had made his way towards the single dirt road that led up from Porto Vecchio and had positioned himself in the underbrush twenty feet from the edge. Several hundred yards below, he had seen the glow of a cigarette. The road was being guarded; he had waited. He had to.

If Scofield was coming he would use that road; it had been the dawn of the fourth day. The American had said that if Corsica was all that was left, he'd be there in three or four days.

By three in the afternoon there had been no sign of him, and an hour later Vasili knew he could wait no longer. Men had sped *down* the road towards the burgeoning port resort. Their mission had been clear: the intruder had eluded the roadblock. Find him, kill him.

Search parties had begun fanning through the woods; two Corsicans slashing the overgrowth with mountain machetes had come within thirty feet of him; soon the patrols would become more concentrated, the search more thorough. He could not wait for Scofield; there was no guarantee that Beowulf Agate had even escaped from the net being spread for him in his own country, much less was on his way to Corsica.

Vasili had spent the hours until sundown creating his own assaults on those who would trap him. Like a swamp fox, his trail appeared one moment heading in this direction, his appearance sighted over *there*; broken branches and trampled reeds were proof that he was cornered in a stretch of marshland that fronted on unclimbable rock wall, and as men closed in, his figure could be seen racing through a field a mile to the west. He was a yellowjack on the wind, visually stinging in a dozen different places at once.

When darkness had come, Taleniekov began the strategy that led him to where he was at the moment, hidden in a cluster of fir trees below the crown of a high hill, waiting for a man carrying a flashlight to approach. The plan was simple, carried out in three stages, each phase logically evolved from the previous. First came the diversion, drawing off the largest number of the attack pack as possible; then the exposure to the few left behind, pulling them farther away from the many; finally the separation of those few and the trapping of one. The third phase was about to be concluded as the fires raged a mile and a half below to the east.

He had made his way through the woods, descending in the direction of Porto Vecchio, travelling on the right side of the dirt road. He had gathered together dried branches and leaves, breaking several Graz-Burya shells, sprinkling the powder inside the pile of debris. He had ignited his pyre in the forest, waited until it had erupted and he had heard the shouts of the converging Corsicans. He had raced northward, across the road, into a denser, drier section of the wooded hill and repeated the action, lighting a larger pile of dried foliage next to a dead chestnut tree. It had spread like a fire-bomb, the flames leaping upward through the tree, promising to leap again, laterally into the surrounding forest. He had run once more to the north and had set his last and largest fire, choosing a beech tree long since destroyed by insects. Within a half hour the hills were blazing in three distinct areas, the hunters racing from one to another, containment and the search vying for priority.

He had crossed diagonally back to the south-west, climbing through the woods to the road that fronted the inn. He had emerged within sight of the window through which he had escaped the night before. He had walked out on the road, seeing several men with rifles – one weapon short-barrelled and thick: a Lupo – standing, talking anxiously among themselves. The rearguard, confused by the chaos below, unsure whether they should remain where they were, as instructed by superiors, or go to the aid of their island brothers.

The irony of coincidence had not been lost on Vasili as he had struck the match. The striking of a match had started it all so many days ago on Washington's Nebraska Avenue; it was the sign of a trap. It signified another in the hills of Corsica.

"*Ecco!*"

"*Leggiero!*"

"*E l'uomo lui! L'uomo!*"

The chase had begun; it was now coming to an end. The man with the flashlight was within a stone's throw from him; he would climb up into the cluster of wild fir before the next thirty seconds elapsed. Below, on the slope of the hill, the flashlight in the centre was several hundred yards to the south, its beam criss-crossing the ground in front of the Corsican holding it. Far down to the right, the third flashlight, which only seconds before had been sweeping frantically back and forth in semi-circles, was now oddly stationary, its beam angled down to a single spot. The position of the light and its abrupt immobility bothered Taleniekov, but there was no time to evaluate either fact. The approaching Corsican had reached the first tree in Vasili's natural sanctuary.

The man swung the beam of light into the cluster of trunks and hanging limbs. Taleniekov had broken a number of branches, stripping more than a few so that any light would catch the white wood. The Corsican stepped forward, following the trail; Vasili stepped to his left, concealed by a tree. The hunter passed within eighteen inches, his rifle at the ready. Taleniekov watched the Corsican's feet in the wash of light; when the left foot moved forward a beat would be lost for a right-handed marksman, the brief imbalance impossible to recover.

The foot left the ground and Vasili lunged, lashing his arm around the man's neck, his fingers surging in for the trigger enclosure, ripping the rifle out of the Corsican's hand. The beam of the flashlight shot up into the trees. Taleniekov crashed his right knee into his victim's kidney, dragging him backward, down on to the ground. He scissored the man's waist with his legs, forcing the Corsican's neck into a painful arch, the man's ear next to his lips.

"You and I will spend the next hour together," he whispered in Italian. "When the time's up, you'll have told me what I want to know, or you won't speak again. I'll use your own knife. Your face will be so disfigured no one will recognize you. Now get up slowly. If you raise your voice, you're dead!"

Gradually, Vasili released the pressure on the man's waist and neck. Both men started to rise, Taleniekov's fingers gripped around the man's throat.

There was a sudden *crack* from above, the sound echoing throughout the trees. A foot had stepped on a fallen branch. Vasili spun around, peering up into the dense foliage. What he saw caused him to lose his breath.

A man was silhouetted between two trees, the silhouette familiar, last seen in the door frame of a country inn. And as that last time, the thick barrels of a Lupo were levelled straight ahead. But now they were levelled at him.

In the rush of thought, Taleniekov understood that not all professionals were trained in Moscow and Washington. The frenetically waving beam of light at the base of the hill, suddenly still, motionless. A flashlight strapped to a sapling or a resilient limb, pulled back and set in motion to give the illusion of movement, its owner racing in darkness up a familiar incline.

"You were very clever last night, *signore*," said the man with the Lupo. "But there is nowhere to hide here."

"The *Matarese!*" screamed Vasili at the top of his lungs. "*Perro nostro circulo!*" he roared. He lunged to his left. The double-barrelled explosion of the Lupo filled the hills.

13

Scofield jumped over the side of the skiff and waded through the waves toward the shoreline. There was no beach, only boulders joined together, forming a three-dimensional wall of jagged stone. He reached a promontory of flat, slippery rock and braced himself against the waters, balancing the attaché case in his left hand, his canvas duffelbag in his right.

He rolled on to the sandy, vine-covered ground until the surface was level enough to stand. Then he ran into the tangled brush that concealed him from any wandering patrols above on the broken cliffs. The captain had warned him that the police were inconsistent; some could be bought, others not.

He knelt down, took a penknife from his pocket, and cut the webbed strap off his wrist, freeing the case. Then he opened the duffelbag and took out dry corduroy trousers, a pair of ankle boots, a dark sweater, a cap and a coarse woollen jacket, all bought in Paris, all labels torn off. They were sufficiently rough in appearances to be accepted as native garb.

He changed, rolled up the wet clothes and stuffed them into the duffelbag along with the attaché case. then started the long, winding climb to the road above. He had been to Corsica twice before – Porto Vecchio once – both trips basically concerned with an obnoxious, constantly sweating owner of fishing boats in Bastia who operated out of Murato and was on State's payroll as one more "observer" of Soviet Ligurian Sea operations. The brief sojourn south to Porto Vecchio had been in connection with the feasibility of covertly financing resort projects in the Tyrrhenian; he never knew what happened. While in Porto Vecchio he had rented a car and driven up into the hills. He had seen the ruins of Villa Matarese in the broiling afternoon sun and had stopped for a glass of beer at a roadside *taverna*, but the excursion had faded quickly from his mind. It never occurred to him that he would ever return. The legend of the Matarese was no more alive than the ruins of the villa. Not then.

He reached the road and pulled the cap down, the cloth covering the bruise on his upper forehead where he had collided with an iron post in a stairwell. A staircase where his life might have ended but for an enemy who had saved it.

Taleniekov. Had he reached Corsica? Was he somewhere in the hills of Porto Vecchio? It would not take long to find out. A stranger asking questions about a legend would be easily tracked down. On the other hand, the Russian would be cautious; if it had occurred to them to go back to the source of the legend, it might well occur to others to do the same.

Bray looked at his watch; it was nearly eleven-thirty. He took out a map, estimating his position as two and a half miles south of Sainte Lucie; the most direct line to the hills – to the Matarese hills, he reflected – was due west. But there was something to find before he entered those hills. A base of operations. A place where he could conceal his things with the reasonable expectation that they would be there when he came back. That ruled out any normal stop a traveller might make. He could not master the Oltramontanan dialect in a few hours; he'd be marked as a stranger and strangers were marks. He would have to make camp in the woods, near water if possible, and preferably within walking distance of a store or inn where he could get food.

He had to assume he would be in Porto Vecchio for several days. No other assumption was feasible; anything could happen once he found Taleniekov – *if* he found him – but for the moment the necessities had to be considered before any plan was formulated. All the little things.

There was a path – too narrow for any car to travel, a shepherd's route perhaps – that veered off the road into a gently rising series of fields; it headed west. He shifted the canvas duffelbag to his left hand and entered it, pushing aside low-hanging branches until he was in the tall grass.

By 12.45 he had walked no more than five or six miles inland, but he had purposely travelled in a zig-zag pattern that afforded him the widest views of the area. He found what he was looking for, a section of forest that rose abruptly above a stream, thick branches of Corsican pine sweeping down to the ground on the banks. A man and his belongings would be safe behind those walls of green. A mile or so to the south-west there was a road that led farther up into the hills. From what he could remember he was fairly certain this was the road he had taken to the ruins of Villa Matarese; there had been only one. Again, if memory served, he recalled driving past a number of isolated farmhouses on the way to the ruins on the hill and the inn where he had stopped for native beer during that hot afternoon. Only the inn came first, near that road on the hill, where a narrower road swung off it. To the *right* on the way up, on the *left* returning to Porto Vecchio. Bray checked his map again; it showed the hill road, and the branch to the right. He knew where he was.

He waded across the stream, and climbed the opposite bank to the cascading pines. He crawled underneath, opened his duffelbag and took out a small shovel, amused that two packets of toilet paper fell out with the instrument. The little things, he thought, as he started to dig into the soft earth.

It was nearly four o'clock. He had set up his camp beneath the screen of green branches, his duffelbag buried, the bandage on his neck changed, his face and hands washed in the stream. Too, he had rested, staring up at the filtered sunlight strained through the webbing of pine needles. His mind wandered, an indulgence he tried to reject but could not. Sleep would not come; thoughts did.

He was under a tree on the banks of a stream in Corsica, a journey that had begun on a bridge at night in Amsterdam. And now he could never go back unless he and Taleniekov found what they were looking for in the hills of Porto Vecchio.

It would not be so difficult to disappear. He had arranged many such disappearances in the past with less money and less expertise than he had now. There were so many places – the Melanesians, the Fijis, New Zealand, across to Tasmania, the vast expanses of Australia, Malaysia, or any of a dozen Sunda islands – he had sent men to such places, stayed cautiously in touch with a few over the years. Lives had been rebuilt, past histories beyond the reach of present associates, new friends, new occupations, even families.

He could do the same, thought Bray. Maybe he would; he had the papers and the money. He could pay his way to Polynesia or the Cook Islands, buy a boat for charter, probably make a decent living. It could be a good life, an anonymous existence, an end to the deadly games.

Then he saw the face of Robert Winthrop, the electric eyes searching his, and heard the anxiety in the old man's voice as he spoke of the Matarese.

He heard something else, too. Less distant, immediate, above in the sky. Birds were swooping down in frantic circles, their screeches echoing harshly, angrily over the fields and throughout the woods. Intruders had disturbed their fiefdom. He could hear men running, hear their shouts.

Had he been *spotted*? He rose quickly to his knees, taking his Browning from his jacket pocket, and peered through a spray of pine needles.

Below, a hundred yards to the left, two men had hacked their way with machetes down the overgrown bank to the edge of the stream. They stood for a moment, pistols in their belts, glancing swiftly in every direction, as if unsure of their next moves. Slowly Bray let out his breath; they were not after him; he had not been seen. Instead, the two men had been hunting – an animal that had attacked their goats, perhaps, or a wild dog. Not him. Not a stranger wandering in the hills.

Then he heard the words and knew he was only partially right. The shout did not come from either Corsican holding a machete; it came from over the bank of the stream, from the field beyond.

"*Il uomo. Eccolo! Il campo!*"

It was no animal being pursued, but a man. A man was running from other men, and to judge from the fury of his pursuers, that man was running for his life. Taleniekov? Was it Taleniekov? And if it was, why? Had the Russian learned something so quickly? Something that the Corsicans in Porto Vecchio would kill for?

Scofield watched as the two men below took the guns from their belts and ran up the bank out of sight into the bordering field. He crawled back to the trunk of the tree and tried to gather his thoughts. Instinct convinced him that *Il uomo, eccolo!* was Taleniekov. If so, there were several options. He could head for the road and walk up into the hills, an Italian crewman with a fishing boat in for repairs and time on his hands; he could stay where he was until nightfall, then thread his way under cover of darkness, hoping to get near enough to hear men's conversations; or he could leave now and follow the hunt.

The last was the least attractive – but likely to be the most productive. He chose it.

It was 5.35 when Bray first saw him, running along the crest of a hill, shots fired at his weaving, racing figure in the glare of the setting sun. Taleniekov, as expected, was doing the unexpected. He was not trying to escape; rather he was using the chase to sow confusion and through that confusion learn something. The tactic was sound; the best way to uncover vital information was to make the enemy protect it.

But what had he so far learned that would justify the risk? How long would he – or could he – keep up the pace and the concentration to elude his enemy? . . . The answers were as clear as the questions: isolate, trap and break. Within the territory.

Scofield studied the terrain as best he could from his prone position in the field. The early-evening breezes made his task easier; the grass bent with each gentle sweep of wind, his view clearer for it. He tried to analyse the choices open to

Taleniekov, where best to intercept him. The KGB man was running due north; another mile or so and he would reach the base of the mountains where he would stop. Nothing could be achieved by going up into them. He would double back, heading south-west to avoid being hemmed in by the roads. And somewhere he would create a diversion, one significant enough to escalate the confusion into a moment of chaos, the trap to follow shortly.

Intercepting Taleniekov might have to wait until that moment, thought Bray, but he preferred that it did not; there would be too much activity compressed into a short period of time. Mistakes were made that way. It would be better to reach the Russian beforehand. That way, they could develop the strategy together. Crouching, Scofield made his way south-west through the tall grass.

The sun fell behind the distant mountains; the shadows lengthened until they became long shafts of ink, spilling over the hills, enveloping whole fields that moments ago had been drenched in orange sunlight. Darkness came and still there was no sign, no sound of Taleniekov. Bray moved swiftly within the logical perimeters of the Russian's logical area of movement, his eyes adjusting to the darkness, his ears picking up every noise foreign to the fields and the woods. *Still* no Taleniekov.

Had the KGB man taken the risk of using either dirt road for faster mobility? If he had, it was foolhardy, unless he had conceived of a tactic better employed in the lower hills. The entire countryside was now alive with search parties ranging in size from two to six men, all armed, knives, guns and mountain machetes hanging from their clothing, their flashlight beams crisscrossing each other like intersecting lasers. Scofield raced farther west to higher ground, the myriad beams of light his protection against the roving, angry Corsicans; he knew when to stop, when to run.

He ran, cutting between two teams of converging men, halting abruptly at the sight of a whining animal, its fur thick, its eyes wide and staring. He was about to use his knife when he realized it was a shepherd's dog, its nostrils uninterested in human scent. The realization did not prevent him from losing his breath; he stroked the dog, reassuring it, then ducked beneath a flashlight beam that shot out of the woods, and scrambled farther up the sloping field.

He reached a boulder half buried in the ground and threw himself behind it. He got up slowly, his hands on the rock, prepared to spring away and run again. He looked over the top, down at the scene below, the flashlight beams breaking up the darkness, defining the whereabouts of the search parties. He was able to make out the crude wooden structure that was the inn he had stopped at years ago. In front of it was the primitive dirt road he had crossed several hours before to reach the higher ground. A hundred yards to the right of the inn was the wider, winding road that descended out of the hills down into Porto Vecchio.

The Corsicans were spread over the fields. Here and there Bray could hear the barking of dogs amid angry human shouts and the slashing of machetes. It was an eerie sight, no figures seen, just beams of light, shooting in all directions; invisible puppets dancing on illuminated strings in the darkness.

Suddenly, there was another light, yellow not white. *Fire.* An abrupt explosion of flames in the distance, to the right of the road that led to Porto Vecchio.

Taleniekov's diversion. It had its effect.

Men ran, shouting, the beams of light converging on the road, racing towards the spreading fire. Scofield held his place, wondering – clinically, professionally – how the KGB man would use his diversion. What would he do next? What method would he use to spring his trap on one man?

The beginning of the answer came three minutes later. A second, larger eruption of flames surged skyward about a quarter of a mile to the *left* of the road to Porto Vecchio. A single diversion was now two, dividing the Corsicans, confusing the search; fire was lethal in the hills.

He could see the puppets now, their strings of light fusing with the glow of the spreading flames.

Another fire appeared, this one massive, an entire tree bursting into a ball of yellowish white as though detonated by napalm. It was three hundred or four hundred yards *farther* left, a third diversion greater than the previous two. Chaos spread as rapidly as the flames, both in danger of leaping out of control. Taleniekov was covering all his bases; if a trap was not feasible he could escape in the confusion.

But if the Russian's mind was working as his might, thought Bray, the trap would be sprung in moments. He crawled around the boulder and started down the expanse of descending field, keeping his shoulders close to the ground, propelling himself as an animal, hands and feet working in concert.

There was a sudden flash far below on the road. It lasted no more than a second, a tiny eruption of light. A match had been struck. It appeared senseless until Bray saw a flashlight beam shoot out from the right, followed instantly by two others. The three beams converged in the direction of the briefly held match; seconds later they separated at the base of the hill that bordered the road below.

Scofield knew what the tactic was now. Four nights ago a match had been struck in Rock Creek Park to expose a trap; it was struck now to execute one. By the same man. Taleniekov had succeeded in throwing the Corsicans' search into chaotic paralysis; he was now drawing off the few left behind. The final chase had started; the Russian would take one of those men.

Bray took the automatic from the holster strapped beneath his jacket and reached into his pocket for his silencer. Snapping it into place, he unlatched the safety and began running diagonally to his left, below the crest of the hill. Somewhere within those acres of grassland and forest the trap would be sprung. It was a question of finding out precisely where, if possible immobilizing one of the pursuers, thus favouring the odds for the trap's success. Better still, taking one of the Corsicans; two sources of information were better than one.

He ran in spurts, staying close to the ground, his eyes on the three flashlight beams below. Each was covering a section of the hill, and in the spills he could see weapons clearly; at the first sign of the hunted, shots would be fired . . .

Scofield stopped. Something was wrong; it was the beam of light on the right, the one perhaps two hundred yards directly beneath him. It was waving back and forth too rapidly, without focus. And there was no reflection – not even a dull reflection – of light bouncing off metal – even dull metal. There was no weapon.

There was no hand holding that flashlight! It had been secured firmly to a thick branch or a limb; a feint, a false placement given false motion to cover another movement. Bray lay on the ground, concealed by the grass and the darkness, watching, listening for signs of a man running.

It happened so fast, so unexpectedly, that Scofield nearly fired his gun in instinctive defence. The figure of a large Corsican was suddenly beside him, above him, the crunch of a racing foot not eighteen inches from his head. He rolled to his left, out of the running man's path.

He inhaled deeply, trying to throw off the shock and the fear, then rose cautiously and followed as best he could the trail of the racing Corsican. The man was heading directly north along the hill, below the ridge, as Bray had intended doing, relying on beams of light and sound – or the sudden absence of both – to find Taleniekov. The Corsican was familiar with the terrain. Scofield quickened his pace, passing the centre beam of light still far below, and by passing it knowing that Taleniekov had fixed on the third man. The flashlight – barely seen – on the extreme north side of the hill.

Bray hurried faster; instinct told him to keep the Corsican in his sight. But the man was nowhere to be seen, no silhouette on the skyline, no sounds of running feet. All was silent, too silent. Scofield dropped to the ground and joined that silence, peering about in the darkness, his finger around the trigger of his automatic. It would happen any second. But how? *Where?*

About a hundred and fifty yards ahead, diagonally down to the right, the third beam of light appeared to go off and on in a series of short, irregular flashes. No . . . It was not being turned off and on rapidly; the light was being *blocked*. *Trees*. Whoever held the flashlight was walking into a cluster of trees growing on the side of the hill.

Suddenly, the beam of light shot upward, dancing briefly in the higher regions of the thinning trunks, then plummeted down, the glow stationary, dulled by the foliage on the ground. That was it! The trap had been sprung, but Taleniekov did not know a Corsican was waiting for a sign of that trap.

Bray got to his feet and ran as fast as he could, his boots making harsh contact with the profusion of rocks on the hillside. He had only seconds, there was so much ground to cover, and too much darkness; he could not tell where the trees began. If there was only an outline to fire at, the sound of a voice . . . *Voice*. He was about to shout, to warn the Russian, when he heard a voice. The words were in that strange Italian spoken by the southern Corsicans; the sound floated up in the night breezes.

Thirty feet below him! He saw the man standing between two trees, his body outlined in the spill of the muted, immobile beam of light that glowed up from the ground; the Corsican held a shotgun in his hands. Scofield pivoted to his right and sprang towards the armed man, his automatic levelled.

"The *Matarese!*" The name was screamed by Taleniekov, as was the enigmatic phrase that followed. "*Perro nostro circulo!*"

Bray fired into the back of the Corsican, the three rapid spits overwhelmed by an explosion from the shotgun. The man fell forward. Scofield dug his feet into the body, crouching, expecting an attack. What he saw prohibited it; the Corsican trapped by Taleniekov had been blown apart by his would-be rescuer.

"*Taleniekov?*"

"You! Is it *you*, Scofield?"

"Put that light out!" cried Bray. The Russian lunged for the flashlight on the ground, snapping it off. "There's a man on the hill; he's not moving. He's waiting to be called."

"If he comes, we must kill him. If we don't call, he'll go for help. He'll bring others back with him."

"I'm not sure his friends can spare the time," replied Scofield, watching the beam of light in the darkness. "You've got them pretty well tied up . . . There he goes! He's running down the hill."

"Come!" said the Russian, getting up, approaching Bray. "I know a dozen places to hide. I've got a great deal to tell you."

"You must have."

"I do. It's here!"

"What is?"

"I'm not sure . . . the answer, perhaps. Part of it anyway. You've seen for yourself. They're hunting me; they'd kill me on sight. I've intruded."

"*Ferma!*" The sudden command was shouted from beyond Scofield on the hill. Bray spun on the ground; the Russian raised his gun. "*Basta!*" The second command was accompanied by the snarling of an animal, a dog straining on a leash. "I have a two-barrelled rifle in my hands, *signori*," continued the voice . . . the unmistakable voice of a woman, speaking now in English. "As the one fired moments ago, it is a Lupo, and I know how to use it better than the man at your feet. But I do not wish to. Hold your guns to your sides, *signori*. Do not drop them; you may need them."

"Who are you?" asked Scofield, squinting his eyes at the woman above. From what he could barely see in the night light, she was dressed in trousers and a field jacket. The dog snarled again.

"I look for the scholar."

"The *what?*"

"I am he," said Taleniekov. "From the *organizzazione accademica*. This man is my associate."

"What the hell are you . . . ?" Bray looked over at the KGB man.

"*Basta!*" said the Russian quietly. "Why do you look for me, yet do not kill me?"

"Word goes everywhere. You ask questions about the *padrone* of *padroni*."

"I do. Guillaume de Matarese. No one wants to give me answers."

"One does," replied the woman. "An old woman in the mountains. She wants to speak with the *erudito*, the scholar. She has things to tell him."

"But you know what's happened here," said Taleniekov, probing. "Men are hunting me; they would kill me. You're willing to risk your own life to bring me – bring us – to her?"

"Yes. It is a long journey, and a hard one. Five or six hours up into the mountains."

"Please answer me. Why are you taking this risk?"

"She is my grandmother. Everyone in the hills despises her; she cannot live down here. But I love her."

144

"Who is she?"

"She is called the whore of Villa Matarese."

14

They travelled swiftly through the hills to the base of the mountains and up into winding trails cut out of the mountain forests. The dog had sniffed both men as the woman had placed her hand on each's shoulder; it was set free and preceded them along the overgrown paths, sure in its knowledge of the way, awaiting them at every turn.

Scofield thought it was the same dog he had come across so suddenly, so frighteningly, in the fields. He said as much to the woman.

"*Probabilmente, signore.* We were there for many hours. I was looking for you and I let him roam, but he was always near in case I needed him."

"Would he have attacked me?"

"Only if you raised your hand to him. Or to me."

It was past midnight when they reached a flat stretch of grassland that fronted what appeared to be a series of imposing, wooded hills. The low-flying clouds had thinned out; moonlight washed over the field, highlighting the peaks in the distance, lending grandeur to this section of the mountain range. Bray could see that Taleniekov's shirt beneath the open jacket was as drenched with sweat as his own; and the night was cool.

"We can rest for a while now, *signori,*" said the woman, pointing to a dark area several hundred feet ahead, in the direction the dog had raced. "Over there is a cave of stone in the hill. It is not very deep, but it is shelter."

"Your dog knows it," added the KGB man.

"He expects me to build a fire," laughed the girl. "When it is raining, he takes sticks in his mouth and brings them inside to me. He is fond of the fire."

The cave was dug out of dark rock, no more than ten feet deep, but at least six in height. They entered.

"Shall I light a fire?" Taleniekov asked, stroking the dog.

"If you wish. Ucello will like you for it. I am too tired."

"*Uccello?*" asked Scofield. " 'Bird'?"

"He flies over the ground, *signore.*"

"You speak English very well," said Bray, as the Russian piled sticks together within a circle of stones obviously used for previous fires. "Where did you learn?"

"I went to the convent school in Vescovato. Those of us who wished to enter the government programmes studied French and English."

Taleniekov struck a match beneath the kindling; the fire caught instantly, the flames crackling the wood, throwing warmth and light through the cave. "You're very good at that sort of thing," said Scofield to the KGB man.

"Thank you. It's a minor talent."

"It wasn't minor a few hours ago." Bray turned back to the woman, who had removed her cap and was shaking free her long dark hair. For an instant he stopped breathing and stared at her. Was it the hair? Or the wide, clear brown eyes that were the colour of a deer's eyes, or the high cheekbones or the chiselled nose above the generous lips that seemed so ready to laugh? Was it any of these things, or was he simply tired and grateful for the sight of an attractive, capable woman? He did not know; he knew only that this Corsican girl of the hills reminded him of Katrine, his wife whose death had been ordered by the man three feet away from him in that Corsican cave. He suppressed his thoughts and breathed again. "And did you," he asked, "enter the government programmes?"

"As far as they would take me."

"Where was that?"

"To the *scuola media* in Bonifacio. The rest I managed with the help of others. Monies supplied by the *fondos*."

"I don't understand."

"I am a graduate of the University of Bologna, *signore*. I am a *Comunista*. I say it proudly."

"Bravo . . ." said Taleniekov softly.

"One day we shall set things right throughout all Italy," continued the girl, her eyes bright. "We shall end the chaos, the Christian stupidity."

"I'm sure you will," agreed the Russian.

"But never as Moscow's puppets, that we will never be. We are *independents*. We do not listen to vicious bears who would devour us and create a worldwide fascist state. Never!"

"Bravo," said Bray.

The conversation trailed off, the young woman reluctant to answer further questions about herself. She told them her name was Antonia, but beyond that said little. When Taleniekov asked why she, a political activist from Bologna, had returned to this isolated region of Corsica, she replied only that it was to be with her grandmother for a while.

"Tell us about her," said Scofield.

"She will tell you what she wants you to know," said the girl, getting up. "I have told you what she instructed me to say."

"'The whore of Villa Matarese,'" repeated Bray.

"Yes. They are not words I would choose. Or ever use. Come, we have another two hours to walk."

They reached a flat crown of a mountain and looked down a gentle slope to a valley below. It was no more than a hundred and fifty yards from mountain crest to valley floor, perhaps a mile across the basin. The moon had grown progressively brighter; they could see a small farmhouse in the centre of the pasture, a barn at the end of a short roadway. They could hear the sound of rushing water; a stream flowed out of the mountain near where they stood, tumbling down the slope between a row of rocks, passing within fifty feet of the small house.

"It's very beautiful," said Taleniekov.

"It is the only world she has known for over half a century," replied Antonia.

"Were you brought up here?" asked Scofield. "Was this your home?"

"No," said the girl, without elaborating. "Come, we will see her. She has been waiting."

"At this hour of the night?" Taleniekov was surprised.

"There is no day or night for my grandmother. She said to bring you to her as soon as we arrived. We have arrived."

There *was* no day or night for the old woman sitting in the chair by the wood-burning stove, not in the accepted sense of sunlight and darkness. She was blind, her eyes two vacant orbs of pastel blue, staring at sounds and at the images of remembered memories. Her features were sharp and angular beneath the covering of wrinkled flesh; the face had once been that of an extraordinarily beautiful woman.

Her voice was soft, with a hollow whispering quality that forced the listener to watch her thin white lips. If there was no essential brilliance about her, neither was there hesitancy nor indecision. She spoke rapidly, a simple mind secure in its own knowledge. She had things to say and death was in her house, a reality that seemed to quicken her thoughts and perceptions. She spoke in Italian, but it was an idiom from an earlier era.

She began by asking both Taleniekov and Scofield to answer – each in his own words – why he was so interested in Guillaume de Matarese. Vasili replied first, repeating his story of an academic foundation in Milan, his department concentrating on Corsican history. He kept it simple, thus allowing Scofield to elaborate in any way he wished. It was standard procedure when two or more intelligence officers were detained and questioned together. Neither had to be primed for the exercise; the fluid lie was second nature to them both.

Bray listened to the Russian and corroborated the basic information, adding details on dates and finances he believed pertinent to Guillaume de Matarese. When he finished, he felt not only confident about his response, but superior to the KGB man; he had done his "school work" better than Taleniekov.

Yet the old woman just sat there, nodding her head in silence, brushing away a lock of white hair that had fallen to the side of her gaunt face. Finally, she spoke.

"You're both lying. The second gentleman is less convincing. He tries to impress me with facts any child in the hills of Porto Vecchio might learn."

"Perhaps in Porto Vecchio," protested Scofield gently, "but not necessarily in Milan."

"Yes. I see what you mean. But then neither of you is from Milan."

"Quite true," interrupted Vasili. "We merely work in Milan. I myself was born in Poland . . . northern Poland. I'm sure you detect my imperfect speech."

"I detect nothing of the sort. Only your lies. However, don't be concerned, it doesn't matter."

Taleniekov and Scofield looked at each other, then over at Antonia, who sat curled up in exhaustion on a pillow in front of the window.

"What doesn't matter?" Bray asked. "We *are* concerned. We want you to speak freely."

"I will," said the blind woman. "For your lies are not those of self-seeking men. Dangerous men, perhaps, but not men moved by profit. You do not look for the *padrone* for your own personal gain."

Scofield could not help himself; he leaned forward. "How do you know?"

The old woman's vacant yet powerful pale blue eyes held his; it was hard to accept the fact that she could not see. "It is in your voices," she said. "You are afraid."

"Have we reason to be?" asked Taleniekov.

"That would depend on what you believe, wouldn't it?"

"We believe a terrible thing has happened," said Bray. "But we know very little. That's as honestly as I can put it."

"What *do* you know, *signori?*"

Again Scofield and Taleniekov exchanged glances; the Russian nodded first. Bray realized that Antonia was watching them closely. He spoke as obviously to her as to the old woman. "Before we answer you, I think it would be better if your grand-daughter left us alone."

"No!" said the girl so harshly that Uccello snapped up his head.

"Listen to me," continued Scofield. "It's one thing to bring us here, two strangers your grandmother wanted to meet. It's something else again to be involved with us. My . . . associate . . . and I have experience in these matters. It's for your own good."

"Leave us, Antonia." The blind woman turned in the chair. "I have nothing to fear from these men and you must be tired. Take Uccello with you; rest in the barn."

"All right," said the girl, getting up, "but Uccello will remain here." Suddenly, from beneath the pillow, she took out the Lupo and levelled it in front of her. "You both have guns. Throw them on the floor. I don't think you would leave here without them."

"That's ridiculous!" cried Bray, as the dog got to its feet growling.

"Do as the lady says," snapped Taleniekov, shoving his Graz-Burya across the floor.

Scofield took out his Browning, checked the safety and threw the weapon on the rug in front of Antonia. She bent down and picked up both automatics, the Lupo held firmly in her hand. "When you've finished, open the door and call out to me. I will summon Uccello. If he does not come, you won't see your guns again. Except looking down the barrels." She let herself out quickly; the dog emitted a growl and returned to the floor.

"My granddaughter is high-spirited," said the old woman, settling back in her chair. "The blood of Guillaume, though several times removed, is still apparent."

"She's his granddaughter?" asked Taleniekov.

"His great-grandchild, born to my daughter's child quite late in *her* life. But that first daughter was the result of the *padrone* bedding his young whore."

'The whore of Villa Matarese,'" said Bray. "You told her to tell us that was what you were called."

The old woman smiled, brushing aside a lock of white hair. For an instant she was in that other world, and vanity had not deserted her. "Many years ago. We will go back to those days, but before we do, your answers, please. What *do* you know? What brings you here?"

"My associate will speak first," said Taleniekov. "He is more learned in these matters than I am, although I came to him with what I believed to be startling new information."

"Your name, please," interrupted the blind woman. "Your true name and where you come from."

The Russian glanced at the American; in the look between them was the understanding that no purpose would be served by further lies. On the contrary, that purpose might be thwarted by them. This simple but strangely eloquent old woman had listened to the voices of liars for the better part of a century – in darkness; she was not to be fooled.

"My name is Vasili Vasilivich Taleniekov. Formerly external affairs strategist, KGB, Soviet Intelligence."

"And you?" The woman shifted her blind eyes to Scofield.

"Brandon Scofield. Retired intelligence officer, Euro–Mediterranean Sectors, Consular Operations, United States Department of State."

"I see." The old courtesan brought her thin hands and delicate fingers up to her face, a gesture of quiet reflection. "I am not a learned woman, and live an isolated life, but I am not without news of the outside world. I often listen to my radio for hours at a time. The broadcasts from Rome come in quite clearly, as do those from Genoa, and frequently Nice. I pretend no knowledge, for I have none, but your coming to Corsica together would appear strange."

"It is, *madame*," said Taleniekov.

"Very," agreed Scofield.

"It signifies the gravity of the situation."

"Then let your associate begin, *signore*."

Bray sat forward in the chair, his arms on his knees, his eyes on the blind eyes in front of him. "At some point between the years 1911 and 1913, Guillaume de Matarese summoned a group of men to his estate in Porto Vecchio. Who they were and where they came from has never been established. But they gave themselves a name."

"The date was 4 April 1911," interrupted the old woman. "They did not give themselves a name, the *padrone* chose it. They were to be known as the Council of the Matarese . . . Go on, please."

"You were *there*?"

"Please continue."

The moment was unsettling; they were talking about an event that had been the object of speculation for decades, with no records of dates or identities, no witnesses. Now – delivered in a brief few seconds – they were told the correct year, the exact month, the precise day.

"*Signore* . . . ?"

149

"Sorry. During the next thirty years or so, this Matarese and his 'council' were the subject of controversy."

Scofield told the story rapidly, without embellishment, keeping his words in the simplest Italian he knew so there'd be no misunderstanding. He admitted that the majority of experts who had studied the Matarese legend had concluded it was more myth than reality.

"What do *you* believe, *signore?* That is what I asked you at the start."

"I'm not sure what I believe, but I know a very great man disappeared four days ago. I think he was killed because he spoke to other powerful men about the Matarese."

"I see." The old woman nodded. "Four days ago. Yet I thought you said thirty years . . . from that first meeting in 1911. What happened then, *signore?* There are many years to be accounted for."

"According to what we know – or what we think we know – after Matarese died the council continued to operate out of Corsica for a number of years, then moved away, negotiating contracts in Berlin, London, Paris, New York and God knows where else. Its activities began to fade at the start of the Second World War. After the war it disappeared; nothing was heard from it again."

A trace of a smile was on the old woman's lips. "So from nowhere it comes back, is that what you are saying?"

"Yes. My associate can tell you why we believe it." Bray looked at Taleniekov.

"Within recent weeks," said the Russian, "two men of peace from both our countries were brutally assassinated, each government led to believe the other was responsible. Confrontation was avoided by a swift exchange between our leaders, but they were dangerous moments. A dear friend sent for me; he was dying and there were things he wanted me to know. He had very little time and his mind wandered, but what he told me compelled me to seek out others for help, for guidance."

"What did he tell you?"

"That the Council of the Matarese was very much with us. That, in fact, it never disappeared but instead went underground, where it continued to grow silently and spread its influence. That it was responsible for hundreds of acts of terrorism and scores of assassinations during recent years for which the world condemned others. Among them the two men I just mentioned. But the Matarese no longer killed for money; instead, it killed for its own purposes."

"Which were?" asked the old woman in that strange, echoing voice.

"He did not know. He knew only that the Matarese was a spreading disease that had to be stamped out, but he could not tell me how, or whom to go to. No one who ever had dealings with the council will speak of it."

"He offered you nothing, then?"

"The last thing he said to me before I left him was that the answer might be in Corsica. Naturally, I was not convinced of that until subsequent events left no alternative. For either me or my associate, agent Scofield."

"I understand your associate's reason: a great man disappeared four days ago because he spoke of the Matarese. What was yours, *signore?*"

"I, too, spoke of the Matarese. To those men from whom I sought guidance, and

I was a man of credentials in my country. The order was put out for my execution."

The old woman was silent and, again, there was that slight smile on her wrinkled lips. "The *padrone* returns," she whispered.

"I think you must explain that," said Taleniekov. "We've been frank with you."

"Did your dear friend die?" she asked instead, her blind eyes questioning.

"The next day. He was given a soldier's funeral and he was entitled to it. He lived a life of violence without fear. Yet at the end, the Matarese frightened him profoundly."

"The *padrone* frightened him," said the old woman.

"My friend did not know Guillaume de Matarese."

"He knew his disciples. It was enough; they were him. He was their Christ, and as Christ, he died for them."

"The *padrone* was their god?" asked Bray.

"And their prophet, *signore*. They believed him."

"Believed what?"

"That they would inherit the earth. That was his vengeance."

15

The old woman's vacant eyes stared at the wall as she spoke in her half whisper.

He found me in the convent at Bonifacio and negotiated a favourable price with the Mother Superior. "Render unto Caesar," he said, and she complied for she agreed that I was not given to God. I was frivolous and did not take to my lessons and looked at myself in dark windows for they showed me my face and my body. I was to be given to man, and the padrone *was the man of all men.*

I was ten and seven years of age and a world beyond my imagination was revealed to me. Carriages with silver wheels and golden horses with flowing manes took me above the great cliffs and into the villages and the fine shops where I could purchase whatever struck me. There was nothing I could not have, and I wanted everything, for I came from a poor shepherd's family – a God-fearing father and mother who praised Christ when I was taken into the convent and never saw me again.

And always at my side was the padrone. *He was the lion and I was his cherished cub. He would take me around the countryside, to all the great houses and introduce me as his* protetta, *laughing when he used the word. Everyone understood and joined in the laughter. His wife had died, you see, and he had passed his seventieth year. He wanted people to know – his two sons above all, I think – that he had the body and the strength of youth, that he could lie with a young woman and satisfy her as few men could.*

Tutors were hired to teach me the graces of his court: music and proper speech, even history and mathematics, as well as the French language which was the fashion of the time for ladies of bearing. It was a wondrous life. We sailed often across the sea, on to

Rome, then would train north to Switzerland and across into France and to Paris. The padrone made these trips every five or six months. His business holdings were in those places, you see. His two sons were his directors, reporting to him everything they did.

For three years I was the happiest girl in the world for the world was given me by the padrone. And then that world fell apart. In a single week it came crashing down and Guillaume de Matarese went mad.

Men travelled from Zurich and Paris, from as far away as the great exchange in London, to tell him. It was a time of great banking investments and speculation. They said that during the four months that had passed, his sons had done terrible things, made unwise decisions, and most terrible of all had entered into dishonest agreements, committing vast sums of money to dishonourable men who operated outside the laws of banking and the courts. The governments of France and England had seized the companies and stopped all trade, all access to funds. Except for the accounts he held in Genoa and Rome, Guillaume de Matarese had nothing.

He summoned his two sons by wireless, ordering them home to Porto Vecchio to give him an accounting of what they had done. The news that came back to him, however, was like a thunderbolt striking him down in a great storm; he was never the same again.

Word was sent through the authorities in Paris and London that both the sons were dead, one by his own hand, the other killed – it was said – by a man he had ruined. There was nothing left for the padrone; his world had crumbled around him. He locked himself in his library for days on end, never coming out, taking trays of food behind the closed door, speaking to no one. He did not lie with me for he had no interest in matters of the flesh. He was destroying himself dying by his own hand as surely as if he had taken a knife to his stomach.

Then one day a man came from Paris and insisted on breaking into the padrone's privacy. He was a journalist who had studied the fall of the Matarese companies, and he brought with him an incredible story. If the padrone was driving himself into madness before he heard it, afterwards he was beyond hope.

The destruction of his world was deliberately brought about by bankers working with their governments. His two sons had been tricked into signing illegal documents, and blackmailed – held up to ruin – over matters of the flesh. Finally, they had been murdered, the false stories of their deaths acceptable, for the "official" evidence of their terrible crimes was complete.

It was beyond reason. Why had these things been done to the great padrone? His companies stolen from him and destroyed; his sons killed. Who would want such things to be done?

The man from Paris gave part of the answer. "One mad Corsican was enough for Europe for five hundred years, was the phrase he had heard. The padrone understood. In England, Edward was dead but he had brought about the French and English treaties of finance, opening the way for the great companies to come together, fortunes made in India and Africa and the Suez. The padrone, however, was Corsican. Beyond making profit from them, he had no use for the French, less so for the English. He not only refused to join the companies and the banks but he opposed them at every turn, instructing his sons to outmanoeuvre their competitors. The Matarese fortune blocked powerful men from carrying out their designs."

For the padrone it was all a great game. For the French and English companies, his playing was a great crime to be answered with greater crimes. The companies and their banks controlled their governments. Courts of law and the police, politicians and statesmen, even kings and presidents – all were lackeys and servants to the 'men who possessed vast sums of money. It would never change. This was the beginning of his final madness. He would find a way to destroy the corruptors and the corrupted. He would throw governments everywhere into chaos, for it was the political leaders who were the betrayers of trust. Without the cooperation of government officials his sons would be alive, his world as it was. And with governments in chaos, the companies and the banks would lose their protectors.

"They look for a mad Corsican!" he screamed. "They will not find him, yet he will be there."

We made a last trip to Rome – not as before, in finery and in carriages with silver wheels, but as a humble man and woman staying in cheap lodgings in the Via Due Macelli. The padrone spent days prowling the Borsa Valori, reading the histories of the great families who had come to ruin.

We returned to Corsica. He composed five letters to five men known to be alive in five countries, inviting them to journey in secrecy to Porto Vecchio on matters of the utmost urgency, matters pertaining to their own personal histories.

He was the once-great Guillaume de Matarese. None refused.

The preparations were magnificent, Villa Matarese made more beautiful than it had ever been. The gardens were sculptured and bursting with colour, the lawns greener than a brown cat's eyes, the great house and the stables washed in white, the horses curried until they glistened. It was a fairyland again, the padrone running everywhere at once, checking all things, demanding perfection. His great vitality had returned, but it was not the vitality we had known before. There was a cruelty in him now. "Make them remember, my child," he roared at me in the bedroom. "Make them remember what once was theirs!"

For he came back to my bed, but his spirit was not the same. There was only brute strength in the performance of his manhood; there was no joy.

If all of us – in the house and the stables and in the fields – knew then what we soon would learn, we would have killed him in the forest. I, who had been given everything by the great padrone, who worshipped him as both father and lover, would have plunged in the knife myself.

The great day came, the ships sailed in at dawn from Lido di Ostia, and the carriages were sent down to Porto Vecchio to bring up the honoured guests to Villa Matarese. It was a glorious day, music in the gardens, enormous tables heaped with delicacies, and much wine. The finest wines from all Europe, stored for decades in the padrone's cellars.

The honoured guests were given their own suites, each with a balcony and a magnificent view, and – not the least – each guest was provided with his own young whore for an afternoon's pleasure. Like the wines they were the finest, not of Europe, but of southern Corsica. Five of the most beautiful virgins to be found in the hills.

Night came and the grandest banquet ever seen at Villa Matarese was held in the great hall. When it was over, the servants placed bottles of brandy in front of the guests and were told to remain in the kitchens. The musicians were ordered to take their instruments into the gardens and continue playing. We girls were asked to go to the upper house to await our masters.

We were flushed with wine, the girls and I, but there was a difference between myself and them. I was the protetta *of Guillaume de Matarese and I knew a great event was taking place. He was my* padrone, *my lover, and I wished to be a part of it. In addition to which I'd spent three years with tutors, and although hardly a learned woman, I was given to better things than the giddy talk of ignorant girls from the hills.*

I crept away from the others and concealed myself behind a railing on the balcony above the great hall. I watched and listened for hours, it seems, understanding very little then of what my padrone *was saying, only that he was most persuasive, his voice at times barely heard, at others shouting as though he were possessed by the fever.*

He spoke of generations past when men ruled empires given them by God and by their own endeavours. How they ruled them with iron might because they were able to protect themselves from those who would steal their kingdoms and the fruits of their labours. However, those days were gone and the great families, the great empire builders – such as those in that room – were now being stripped by thieves and corrupt governments that harboured thieves. They – those in that room – had to look to other methods to regain what was rightfully theirs.

They had to kill – cautiously, judiciously, with skill and daring – and divide the thieves and their corrupt protectors. They were never to kill themselves, for they were the decision-makers, the men who selected victims – wherever possible victims chosen by others among the corrupted. Those in that room were to be known as the Council of the Matarese, and word was to go forth in the circles of power that there was a group of unknown, silent men who understood the necessity of sudden change and violence, who were unafraid to provide the means, and who would guarantee beyond living doubt that those performing the acts could never be traced to those purchasing them.

He went on to speak of things I could not understand: of killers trained by great pharaohs and Arabian princes centuries ago. How men could be trained to do terrible things beyond their wills, even beyond their knowledge. How others needed only the proper encouragement for they sought the assassin's martyrdom. These were to be the methods of the Matarese, but in the beginning there would be disbelief in the circles of power, so examples had to be made.

During the next few years selected men were to be assassinated. They would be chosen carefully, killed in ways that would breed mistrust, pitting political faction against political faction, corrupt government against corrupt government. There would be chaos and bloodshed and the message would be clear: the Matarese existed.

The padrone *distributed to each guest pages on which he had written down his thoughts. These writings were to be the council's source of strength and direction, but they were never to be shown to eyes other than their own. These pages were the Last Will and Testament of Guillaume de Matarese . . . and those in that room were his inheritors.*

Inheritors? asked the guests. They were compassionate, but direct. In spite of the villa's beauty and the servants and the musicians and the feast they had enjoyed, they knew he had been ruined – as each of them had been ruined. Who among them had anything left but his wine cellars and his land and rents from tenants to keep but a semblance of his former life intact? A grand banquet once in a great while, but little else.

The padrone *did not answer them at first. Instead, he demanded to know from each guest whether that man accepted the things he had said, if that man was prepared to become a* consigliere *of the Matarese.*

They replied yes, each more vehement than the last, pledging himself to the padrone's *goals, for great evil had been done to each of them and they wanted revenge. It was apparent that Guillaume de Matarese appeared to each at that moment a saint.*

Each, except one, a deeply religious Spaniard who spoke of the word of God and of His commandments. He accused the padrone *of madness, called him an abomination in the eyes of God.*

"Am I an abomination in your eye, sir?" asked the padrone.

"You are, sir," replied the man.

Whereupon the first of the most terrible things happened. The padrone *took a pistol from his belt, aimed it at the man, and fired. The guests sprang up from their chairs and stared in silence at the dead Spaniard.*

"He could not be permitted to leave this room alive," said the padrone.

As if nothing had happened, the guests returned to their chairs, all eyes on this mightiest of men who could kill with such deliberateness, perhaps afraid for their own lives, it was difficult to tell. The padrone *went on.*

"All in this room are my inheritors," he said. "For you are the Council of the Matarese and you and yours will do what I can no longer do. I am too old and death is near — nearer than you believe. You will carry out what I tell you, you will divide the corruptors and the corrupted, you will spread chaos and, through the strength of your achievements, you will inherit far more than I leave you. You will inherit the earth. You will have your own again."

"What do you — can you — leave us?" asked a guest.

"A fortune in Genoa and a fortune in Rome. The accounts have been transferred in the manner described in a document, one copy of which has been placed in each of your rooms. Therein also will you find the conditions under which you will receive the monies. These accounts were never known to exist; they will provide millions for you to begin your work."

The guests were stunned until one had a question.

" 'Your' work? Is it not our work?"

"It will always be ours, but I shall not be here. For I leave you something more precious than all the gold in the Transvaal. The complete secrecy of your identities. I speak to each of you. Your presence here this day will never be revealed to anyone on earth. No name, no description, no likeness of your face, no pattern of your speech can ever be traced to you. Neither will it ever be forced from the senile wanderings of an old man's mind."

Several of the guests protested — mildly to be sure — but with reason. There were many people at Villa Matarese that day. The servants, the grooms, the musicians, the girls . . .

The padrone *held up his hand. It was as steady as his eyes were glaring. "I will show you the way. You must never step back from violence. You must accept it as surely as the air you breathe, for it is necessary to life. Necessary to your lives, to the work you must do."*

He dropped his hand and the peaceful, elegant world of Villa Matarese erupted in gunfire and screams of death everywhere. It came first from the kitchen. Deafening blasts of shotguns, glass shattering, metal crashing, servants slain as they tried to escape through the doors into the great hall, their faces and chests covered with blood. Then from the

155

gardens; the music abruptly stopped, replaced by supplications to God, all answered by the thunder of the guns. And then – most horribly – the high-pitched screams of terror from the upper house where the young ignorant girls from the hills were being slaughtered. Children who only hours ago had been virgins, defiled by men they had never seen before on the orders of Guillaume de Matarese, now butchered by new commands.

I pressed myself back into the wall in the darkness of the balcony, not knowing what to do, trembling, frightened beyond any fear I could imagine. And then the gunfire stopped, the silence that followed more terrible than the screams, for it was the evidence of death.

Suddenly I could hear running – three or four men, I could not tell – but I knew they were the killers. They were rushing down staircases and through doors, and I thought, Oh, God in heaven, they are looking for me. But they were not. They were racing to a place where all would gather together; it seemed to be the north veranda, I could not be sure, all was happening so fast. Below in the great hall, the four guests were in shock, frozen to their chairs, the padrone holding them in their places by the strength of his glaring eyes.

There came what I thought would be the final sounds of gunfire until my own death. Three shots – only three – between terrible screams. And then I understood. The killers had themselves been killed by a lone man given those orders.

The silence came back. Death was everywhere – in the shadows and dancing on the walls in the flickering candlelight of the great hall. The padrone spoke to his guests.

"It is over," he said. "Or nearly over. All but you at this table are dead save one man you will never see again. It is he who will drive you in a shrouded carriage to Bonifacio where you may mingle with the night revellers and take the crowded morning steamer to Naples. You have fifteen minutes to gather your things and meet on the front steps. There are none to carry your luggage, I'm afraid."

A guest found his voice, or part of it. "And you, padrone?" he whispered.

"At the last, I give you my life as your final lesson. Remember me! I am the way. Go forth and become my disciples! Rip out the corruptors and the corrupted!" He was raving mad, his shouts echoing throughout the great house of death. "Entrare!" he roared.

A small child, a shepherd boy from the hills, walked through the large doors of the north veranda. He held a pistol in his two hands; it was heavy and he was slight. He approached the master.

The padrone raised his eyes to the heavens, his voice to God. "Do as you were told!" he shouted. "For an innocent child shall light your path!"

The shepherd boy raised the heavy pistol and fired it into the head of Guillaume de Matarese.

The old woman had finished, her unblinking eyes filled with tears.

"I must rest," she said.

Taleniekov, rigid in his chair, spoke softly. "We have questions, madame. Surely you know that."

"Later," said Scofield.

156

16

Light broke over the surrounding mountains as pockets of mist floated up from the fields outside the farmhouse. Taleniekov found tea, and with the old woman's permission, boiled water on the wood-burning stove.

Scofield sipped from his cup, watching the rippling stream from the window. It was time to talk again; there were too many discrepancies between what the blind woman had told them and the facts as they were assumed to be. But there was a primary question: why had she told them at all? The answer to that might make clear whether any part of her narrative should be believed.

Bray turned from the window and looked at the old woman in the chair by the stove. Taleniekov had given her tea and she drank it delicately, as though remembering those lessons in the social graces given a girl of "ten and seven years of age" decades ago. The Russian was kneeling by the dog, stroking its fur again, reminding it they were friends. He glanced up, as Scofield walked towards the old woman.

"We've told you our names, *signora*," said Bray, speaking in Italian. "What is yours?"

"Sophia Pastorine. If one goes back to look, I'm sure it can be found in the records of the convent at Bonifacio. That is why you ask, is it not? To be able to check?"

"Yes," answered Scofield. "If we think it's necessary, and have the opportunity."

"You will find my name. The *padrone* may even be listed as my benefactor, to whom I was ward – as an intended bride for one of his sons, perhaps. I never knew."

"Then we must believe you," said Taleniekov, getting to his feet and crossing to the chair in front of Sophia Pastorine. "You would not be so foolish as to direct us to such a source if it were not true. Records that have been meddled with are easily detected these days."

The old woman smiled, a smile with its roots in sadness. "I have no understanding of such matters, but I can understand if you have doubts." She put down her cup of tea on the ledge of the stove. "There are none in my memories. I have spoken the truth."

"Then my first question is as important as any we may ask you," said Bray, sitting down. "Why did you tell us this story?"

"Because it had to be told and no one else could do so. Only I survived."

"There was a man," interrupted Scofield. "And a shepherd boy."

"They were not in the great hall to hear what I heard."

"Have you told it before?" asked Taleniekov.

"Never," replied the blind woman.

"Why not?"

"Who was I to tell it to? I have few visitors, and those that come are from down in the hills, bringing me the few supplies I need. To tell them would be to bring them death, for surely they would tell others."

"Then the story *is* known," pressed the KGB man.

"Not what I've told you."

"But there's a secret down there! They tried to send me away, and when I would not go they tried to kill me."

"My granddaughter did not tell me that." She seemed truly surprised.

"I don't think she had time to," said Bray.

The old woman did not seem to be listening, her focus still on the Russian. "What did you say to the people in the hills?"

"I asked questions."

"You must have done more than that."

Taleniekov frowned, remembering. "I tried to provoke the innkeeper. I told him I would bring back others, scholars with historical records to study further the question of Guillaume de Matarese."

The woman nodded. "When you leave here, do not go back the way you came. Nor can you take my child's granddaughter with you. You must promise me that. If they find you, they will not let you live."

"We know that," said Bray. "We want to know why."

"All the lands of Guillaume de Matarese were willed to the people of the hills. The tenants became the heirs of a thousand fields and pastures, streams and forests. It was so recorded in the courts of Bonifacio and great celebrations were held everywhere. But there was a price, and there were other courts that would take away the lands if that price were known." The blind Sophia stopped, as if weighing another price, one of betrayal, perhaps.

"*Please*. Signora Pastorine," said Taleniekov, leaning forward in the chair.

"Yes," she answered quietly. "It must be told . . ."

Everything was to be done quickly for fear of unwanted intruders happening upon the great house of Villa Matarese and the death that was everywhere. The guests gathered their papers and fled to their rooms. I remained in the shadows of the balcony, my body filled with pain, the silent vomit of fear all around me. How long I stayed there, I could not tell, but soon I heard the running feet of the guests racing down the staircase to their appointed meeting place. Then there was the sound of carriage wheels and the neighing of horses; minutes later the carriage sped away, hooves clattering on the hard stone along with the rapid cracking of a whip, all fading away quickly.

I started to crawl towards the balcony door, not able to think, my eyes filled with bolts of lightning, my head trembling so I could barely find my way. I pressed my hands on the wall, wishing there were brackets I could hold on to, when I heard a shout and threw myself to the floor again. It was a terrible shout for it came from a child, and yet it was cold and demanding.

"Attualmente! E presto detto!"

The shepherd boy was screaming at someone from the north veranda. If all was senseless up to that moment, the child's shouts intensified the madness beyond any understanding. For he was a child . . . and a killer.

Somehow I rose to my feet and ran through the door to the top of the staircase. I was about to run down, wanting only to get away, into the air and the fields and the protection of darkness, when I heard other shouts and saw the figures of running men through the windows. They were carrying torches, and in seconds crashed through the doors.

158

I could not run down for I would be seen, so I ran above to the upper house, my panic such that I no longer knew what I was doing. Only running . . . running. And, as if guided by an unseen hand that wanted me to live, I burst into the sewing room and saw the dead. There they were, sprawled everywhere in blood, mouths stretched in such terror that I could still hear their screams.

The screams I heard were not real, but the shouts of men on the staircase were; it was the end for me. There was nothing left, I was to be caught. I would be killed.

And then, as surely as an unseen hand had led me to that room, it forced me to do a most terrible thing — I joined the dead.

I put my hands in the blood of my sisters, and rubbed it over my face and clothes, I fell on top of my sisters and waited.

The men came into the sewing room, some crossing themselves, others whispering prayers, but none deterred from the work they had to do. The next hours were a nightmare only the devil could conceive of.

The bodies of my sisters and I were carried down the staircase and hurled through the doors, beyond the marble steps into the drive. Wagons had been brought from the stables, and by now many were filled with bodies. Again, my sisters and I were thrown into the back of a cart, crowded with dead, like so much refuse.

The stench of waste and blood was so overpowering I had to sink my teeth into my own flesh to keep from screaming. Through the corpses above me and over the railings, I could hear men shouting orders. Nothing could be stolen from the Villa Matarese; anyone found doing so would join the bodies inside. For there were to be many bodies left inside, charred flesh and bones to be found at a later time.

The wagons began to move, smoothly at first, then we reached the fields, and the horses were whipped unmercifully. The wagons raced through the grass and over the rocks at immense speeds, as if every second was a second our living guards wished to leave behind in hell. There was death below me, death above me, and I prayed to Almighty God to take me also. But I could not cry out, for although I wanted to die, I was afraid of the pain of dying. The unseen hand held me by the throat. But mercy was granted me. I fell into unconsciousness: how long I do not know, but I think it was a very long time.

I awakened; the wagons had come to a stop and I peered through the bodies and the slats in the side. There was moonlight and we were far up in the wooded hills, but not in the mountains. Nothing was familiar to me. We were far, far away from Villa Matarese, but where I could not tell you then and cannot tell you now.

The last of the nightmare began. Our bodies were pulled off the wagons and thrown into a common grave, each corpse held by two men so that they could hurl it into the deepest part. I fell in pain, my teeth sinking into my fingers to keep my mind from crossing into madness. I opened my eyes and the vomit came again at what I saw. All around me dead faces, limp arms, gaping mouths. Stabbed, bleeding carcasses that only hours ago had been human beings.

The grave was enormous, wide and deep — and strangely, it seemed to me in my silent hysteria, shaped in the form of a circle.

Beyond the edge I could hear the voices of our grave-diggers. Some were weeping, while others cried out to Christ for mercy. Several were demanding that the blessed sacraments be given to the dead, that for the sake of all their souls, a priest be brought to the place of death and intercede with God. But other men said no, they were not the killers, merely those chosen to put the slain to rest. God would understand.

"*Basta!*" *they said. It could not be done. It was the price they paid for the good of generations yet to be born. The hills were theirs; the fields and streams and forests belonged to them! There was no turning back now. They had made their pact with the* padrone, *and he had made it clear to the elders: only the government's knowledge of a* conspirazione *could take the lands away from them. The* padrone *was the most learned of men, he knew the courts and the laws; his ignorant tenants did not. They were to do exactly as he had instructed the elders or the high courts would take the lands from them.*

There could be no priests from Porto Vecchio or Sainte Lucie or anywhere else. No chance taken that word would go out of the hills. Those who had other thoughts could join the dead; their secret was never to leave the hills. The lands were theirs!

It was enough. The men fell silent, picked up their shovels, and began throwing dirt over the bodies. I thought then that surely I would die, my mouth and nostrils smothered under the earth. Yet I think all of us trapped with death find ways to elude its touch, ways we could never dream of before we are caught. It happened for me.

As each layer of earth filled the circular grave and was trampled upon, I moved my hand in the darkness, clawing the dirt above me so that I could breathe. At the very end I had nothing but the smallest passage of air but it was enough; there was space around my head, enough for God's air to invade. The unseen hand had guided mine and I lived.

It was hours later, I believe, when I began to burrow my way to the surface, a . . . blind . . . unknowing animal seeking life. When my hand reached through to nothing but cold moist air, I wept without control, and a part of my brain went into panic, frightened that my weeping would be heard.

God was merciful, everyone had left. I crawled out of the earth, and I walked out of that forest of death into a field and saw the early sunlight rising over the mountains. I was alive, but there was no life for me. I could not go back to the hills for surely I would be killed, yet to go elsewhere, to arrive at some strange place and simply be, was not possible for a young woman in this island country. There was no one I could turn to, having spent three years a willing captive of my padrone. *Yet I could not simply die in that field with God's sunlight spreading over the sky. It told me to live, you see.*

I tried to think what I might do, where I might go. Beyond the hills, on the ocean coasts, were other great houses that belonged to other padroni, *friends of Guillaume. I wondered what would happen were I to appear at one of them and plead for shelter and mercy. Then I saw the error of such thinking. Those men were not my* padrone; *they were men with wives and families, and I was the whore of Villa Matarese. While Guillaume was alive, my presence was to be tolerated, even enjoyed, for the great man would have it no other way. But with him dead, I was dead.*

Then I remembered. There was a man who tended the stables of an estate in Nonza. He had been kind to me during those times we visited and I rode his employer's mounts. He had smiled often and guided me as to my proper deportment in the saddle, for he saw that I was not born to the hunt. Indeed, I admitted it and we had laughed together. And each time I had seen the look in his eyes. I was used to glances of desire, but his eyes held more than that. There was gentleness and understanding, perhaps even respect — not for what I was, but for what I did not pretend to be.

I looked at the early sun and knew that Nonza was on my left, probably beyond the mountains. I set out for those stables and that man.

He became my husband, and although I bore the child of Guillaume de Matarese, he accepted her as his own, giving us both love and protection through the days of his life. Those years and our lives during those years are no concern of yours, they do not pertain to the padrone. *It is enough to say that no harm came to us. For years we lived far north in Vescovato, away from the danger of the hill people, never daring to mention their secret. The dead could not be brought back, you see, and the killer and his killer son — the man and the shepherd boy — had fled Corsica.*

I have told you the truth, all of it. If you still have doubts, I cannot put them to rest.
Again she had finished.

Taleniekov got up and walked slowly to the stove and the pot of tea. "*Peru nostro circolo,*" he said, looking at Scofield. "Almost seventy years have passed and still they would kill for their grave."

"*Perdon?*" The old woman did not understand English, so the KGB man repeated his statement in Italian. Sophia nodded. "The secret goes from father to son. These are the two generations that have been born since the land was theirs. It is not so long. They are still afraid."

"There aren't any laws that could take it from them," said Bray. "I doubt there ever were. Men might have been sent to prison for withholding information about the massacre; but in those days, who would prosecute? They buried the dead, that was their conspiracy."

"There was a greater conspiracy. They did not permit the blessed sacraments."

"That's another court. I don't know anything about it." Scofield glanced at the Russian, then brought his eyes back to the blind eyes in front of him. "Why did you come back?"

"I was able to. And I was old when we found this valley."

"That's not an answer."

"The people of the hills believe a lie. They think the *padrone* spared me, sent me away before the guns began. To others I am a source of fear and hatred. It is whispered that I was spared by God to be a remembrance of their sin, yet blinded by God so as never to reveal their grave in the forests. I am the blind whore of Villa Matarese, permitted to live because they are afraid to take the life of God's reminder."

Taleniekov spoke from the other side of the stove. "But you said a while ago that they would not hesitate to kill you if you told the story. Perhaps if they were even aware that you *knew* it. Yet now you tell it to us, and imply that you want us to bring it out of Corsica. Why?"

"Did not a man in your own country call for you and tell you things he wanted you to know?" The Russian began to reply; Sophia Pastorine interrupted. "Yes, *signore.* As with that man, the end of my life draws near; with each breath I know it. Death, it seems, invites those of us who know some part of the Matarese to speak of it. I'm not sure I can tell you why, but for me, there was a sign. My granddaughter travelled down to the hills and came back with news of a scholar seeking information about the *padrone.* You were my sign. I sent her back to find you."

"Does she know?" asked Bray. "Have you ever told her? She could have brought the story out."

"Never! She is known in the hills, but she is not *of* the hills! She would be hunted down wherever she went. She would be killed. I asked for your word, *signori*, and you must give it to me. You must have nothing further to do with her!"

"You have it," agreed Taleniekov. "She's not in this room because of us."

"What did you hope to accomplish by speaking to my associate?" asked Bray.

"What his friend hoped for, I think. To make men look beneath the waves, to the dark waters below. It is there that the power to move the sea is found."

"The Council of the Matarese," said the KGB man, staring at the blind eyes.

"Yes . . . I told you. I listen to the broadcasts from Rome and Milan and Nice. It is happening everywhere. The prophecies of Guillaume de Matarese are coming true. It does not take an educated person to see that. For years I listened to the broadcasts and wondered. Could it be so? Was it possible they survive still? Then one night many days ago I heard the words and it was as though time had no meaning. I was suddenly back in the shadows of the balcony in the great hall, the gunfire and the screams of horror echoing in my ears. I was *there*, with my eyes before God took them from me, watching the terrible scene below. And I was remembering what the *padrone* had said moments before: 'You and *yours* will do what I can no longer do.' " The old woman stopped, her blind eyes swimming, then began again, her sentences rushed in fear.

"It *was* true! They *had* survived – not the council as it was then, but as it is today. 'You and yours.' The *yours* had survived! Led by the one man whose voice was crueller than the wind." Sophia Pastorine abruptly stopped again, her frail, delicate hands grasping for the wooden arm of her chair. She stood up and with her left hand reached for her cane by the edge of the stove.

"The list. You must have it, *signori*! I took it out of a blood-soaked gown almost seventy years ago after crawling out of the grave in the mountains. It had stayed next to my body through the terror. I had carried it with me so I would not forget their names and their titles, to make my *padrone* proud of me." The old woman tapped the cane in front of her as she walked across the room to a primitive shelf on the wall. Her right hand felt the edge, her fingers hesitantly dancing among the various jars until she found the one she wanted. She removed the clay top, reached inside, and pulled out a scrap of soiled paper, yellow with age. She turned. "It is yours. Names from the past. This is the list of honoured guests who journeyed in secrecy to Villa Matarese on the fourth of April, in the year nineteen hundred and eleven. If by giving it to you I do a terrible thing, may God have mercy on my soul."

Scofield and Taleniekov were on their feet. "You haven't," said Bray. "You've done the right thing."

"The only thing," added Vasili. He touched her hand. "May I?" She released the faded scrap of paper; the Russian studied. "It's the key," he said to Scofield. "It's also quite beyond anything we might have expected."

"Why?" asked Bray.

"Two of these names will startle you. To say the least, they are prominent. Here." Taleniekov crossed to Scofield, holding the paper delicately between two fingers so as not to damage it further. Bray took it in the palm of his hand.

"I don't believe it," said Scofield, reading the names. "I'd like to get this analysed to make sure it wasn't written five days ago."

"It wasn't," said the KGB man.

"I know. And that scares the hell out of me."

"*Perdoni?*" Sophia Pastorine stood by the shelf. Bray answered her in Italian.

"We recognize two of these names. They are well-known men . . ."

"But they are not the men!" broke in the old woman, stabbing her cane on the floor. "None of them! They are only the inheritors! They are controlled by *another*. He is the man!"

"What are you talking about? Who?"

The dog growled. Neither Scofield nor Taleniekov paid any attention; an angry voice had been raised. The animal got on its feet, now snarling, the two men – their concentration on Sophia – still ignoring it. But the old woman did not. She held up her hand, a gesture for silence. She spoke, her anger replaced by alarm.

"Open the door. Call out for my granddaughter. *Quickly!*"

"What is it?" asked the Russian.

"Men are coming. They're passing through the thickets, Uccello hears them."

Bray walked rapidly to the door. "How far away are they?"

"On the other side of the ridge, nearly here. Hurry!"

Scofield opened the door and called out. "You! Antonia, come here. Quickly!"

The dog's snarls were now emitted through bared teeth. Its head thrust forward, its legs stretched and taut, prepared to defend or attack. Leaving the door open, Bray crossed to a counter and picked up a lettuce leaf. He tore it in half and placed the yellow scrap of paper between the two sections, and folded them together. "I'll put this in my pocket," he said to the KGB man.

"I've memorized the names and the countries," replied Taleniekov. "But then, I'm sure you have, too."

The girl ran through the door, breathless, her field jacket only partially buttoned, the Lupo in her hand, the bulges of the automatics in her side pockets. "What's the matter?"

Scofield turned from the counter. "Your . . . grandmother said men were coming. The dog heard them."

"On the other side of the hill," interrupted the old woman. "Nine hundred paces perhaps, no more."

"Why would they *do* that?" asked the girl. "Why would they come?"

"Did they see you, my child? Did they see Uccello?"

"They must have. But I said nothing. I did not interfere with them. They had no reason to think . . ."

"But they saw you the day before," said Sophia Pastorine, interrupting again.

"Yes. I bought the things you wanted."

"Then why would you come back?" The old woman spoke rhetorically. "That is what they tried to understand, and they did. They are men of the hills; they look down at the grass and the dirt and see that three people travelled over the ground, not one. You must leave. All of you!"

"I will not do that, grandmother!" cried Antonia. "They won't harm us. I'll say I may have been followed, but I know nothing."

The old woman stared straight ahead. "You have what you came for, *signori*. Take it. Take her. Leave!"

Bray turned to the girl. "We owe her that," he said. He grabbed the shotgun out of her hands. She tried to fight back but Taleniekov pinned her arms and removed the Browning and the Graz–Burya automatics from her pockets. "You saw what happened down there," continued Scofield. "Do as she says."

The dog raced to the open door and barked viciously. Far in the distance, voices were carried on the morning breezes; men were shouting to others behind them.

"Go!" said Sophia Pastorine.

"Come on." Bray propelled Antonia in front of him. "We'll be back after they've left. We haven't finished."

"A moment, *signori*!" shouted the blind woman. "I think we have finished. The names you possess may be helpful to you, but they are only the inheritors. Look for the one whose voice is crueller than the wind. I heard it! Find him. The shepherd boy. It is he!"

17

They ran along the edge of the pasture on the border of the woods and climbed to the top of the ridge.

The shadows of the eastern slope kept them from being seen. There had been only a few seconds when they might have been spotted; they were prepared for that but it did not happen. The men on the opposite ridge were distracted by a barking dog, deciding whether or not to use their rifles on it. They did not, for the dog was retrieved by a whistle before such a decision could be made. Uccello was beside Antonia now in the grass, his breath coming as rapidly as hers.

There were four men on the opposite ridge – as there were four names on the scrap of yellow paper in his pocket, thought Scofield. He wished finding them, trapping *them*, were as easy as trapping and picking off the four men who now descended into the valley. But the four men on the list were just the beginning.

There was a shepherd boy to find. "A voice crueller than the wind" . . . a *child's* voice recognized decades later as one and the same . . . coming over the air waves from the throat of what had to be a very, very old man.

I heard the words and it was as though time had no meaning . . .

What were those *words*? Who was that *man*? The true descendant of Guillaume de Matarese . . . an old man who uttered a phrase that peeled away seventy years from the memory of a blind woman in the mountains of Corsica. In what *language*? It had to be French or Italian; she understood no other.

They had to speak with her again; they had to understand far more. They had *not* finished with Sophia Pastorine.

Bray watched as the four Corsicans approached the farmhouse, two covering the sides, two walking up to the door, all with weapons drawn. The men by the door paused for an instant; then the one on the left raised his boot and rammed it into the wood, crashing the door inward.

Silence.

Two shouts were heard, questions asked harshly. The men outside ran around opposite corners of the farmhouse and went inside. There was more shouting . . . and the unmistakable sound of flesh striking flesh.

Antonia started to get up, fury on her face. Taleniekov pulled her down by the shoulder of her field jacket. The muscles in her throat were pronounced; she was about to scream – Scofield had no choice. He clamped his hand over her mouth, forcing his fingers into her cheeks; the scream was reduced to a series of coughs.

"Be quiet!" whispered Bray. "If they hear you, they'll use her to get you down there!"

"It would be far worse for her," said Vasili, "and for you. You would hear her pain, and they would take you."

Antonia's eyes blinked; she nodded. Scofield relieved his grip, but did not release it. She whispered through his hand. "They hit her! A blind woman and they hit her!"

"They're frightened," said Taleniekov. "More than you can imagine. Without their land, they have nothing."

The girl's fingers gripped Bray's wrist. "What do you mean?"

"Not now!" commanded Scofield. "There's something wrong. They're staying in there too long."

"They've found something, perhaps," agreed the KGB man.

"Or she's telling them something, Oh, *Christ*, she can't!"

"What are you thinking?" asked Taleniekov.

"She said we'd finished. We *haven't*. But she's going to make sure of it! They'll see our footprints on the floor; we walked over wet ground; she can't deny we were there. With her hearing, she knows which way we went. She'll send them in another direction."

"That's fine," said the Russian.

"Goddamn it, they'll *kill* her!"

Taleniekov snapped his head back towards the farmhouse below. "You're right," he said. "If they believe her – and they will – they can't let her live. She's the source; she'll tell them that, too, if only to convince them. Her life for the shepherd boy. So we can find the shepherd boy!"

"But we don't *know* enough! Come on, let's go!" Scofield got to his feet, yanking the automatic from his belt. The dog snarled; the girl rose and Taleniekov pushed her down to the ground again.

They were not in time. Three gunshots followed one upon the other.

Antonia screamed; Bray lunged, holding her, cradling her. "*Please*, please!" he whispered. He saw the Russian pull a knife from somewhere inside his coat. "No! It's all right!"

Taleniekov palmed the knife and knelt down, his eyes on the farmhouse below. "They're running outside. You were right; they're heading for the south slope."

"*Kill them!*" The girl's words were muffled by Scofield's hand.

"To what purpose now?" said the KGB man. "She did what she wished to do, what she felt she had to do."

The dog would not follow them; commands from Antonia had no effect. It raced down into the farmhouse and would not come out; its whimpering carried up to the ridge.

"Goodbye, Uccello," said the girl, sobbing. "I will come back for you. Before *God*, I will come back!"

They walked out of the mountains, circling north-west beyond the hills of Porto Vecchio, then south to Sainte Lucie, following the stream until they reached the massive pine under which Bray had buried his attaché case and duffelbag. They travelled cautiously, using the woods as much as possible, separating and walking in sequence across open stretches so no one would see them together.

Scofield pulled the shovel from beneath a pile of branches, dug up his belongings, and they started out again, retracing the stream north towards Sainte Lucie. Conversation was kept to a minimum; they wasted no time putting distance between themselves and the hills.

The long silences and brief separations served a practical purpose, thought Bray, watching the girl as she pressed forward, bewildered, following their commands without thinking, tears intermittently appearing in her eyes. The constant movement occupied her view; she had to come to some sort of acceptance of her "grandmother's" death. No words from relative strangers could help her; she needed the loneliness of her own thoughts. Scofield suspected that in spite of her handling of the Lupo, Antonia was not a child of violence. She was no child to begin with; in the daylight he could see that she would not see thirty again, but beyond that, she came from a world of radical academics, not revolution. He doubted she would know what to do at the barricades.

"We must stop *running!*" she cried suddenly. "You may do what you like, but I am returning to Porto Vecchio. I'll see them *hanged!*"

"There's a great deal you don't know," said Taleniekov.

"She was killed! That is all I *have* to know!"

"It's not that simple," said Bray. "The truth is she killed herself."

"*They* killed her!"

"She forced them to." Scofield took her hand, gripping it firmly. "Try to understand me. We can't let you go back; your grandmother knew that. What happened during the past forty-eight hours has got to fade away just as fast as possible. There'll be a certain amount of panic up in those hills; they'll send men trying to find us, but in several weeks when nothing happens, they'll cool off. They'll live with their own fears but they'll be quiet. It's the only thing they can do. Your grandmother understood that. She counted on it."

"But *why?*"

"Because we have other things to do," said the Russian. "She understood that, too. It's why she sent you back to find us."

166

"What are these things?" asked Antonia, then answered for herself. "She said you had names. She spoke of a shepherd boy."

"But you must speak of neither," ordered Taleniekov. "Not if you wish her death to mean anything. We cannot let you interfere."

Scofield caught the sound in the KGB man's voice and for an instant found himself reaching for his gun. In that split second, the memory of Berlin ten years ago was prodded to the surface. Taleniekov had already made a decision: if the Russian had the slightest doubt, he would kill this girl.

"She won't interfere," said Bray, without knowing why he gave such a guarantee, but delivering it firmly. "Let's go. We'll make one stop; I'll see a man in Murato. Then if we can reach Bastia, I can get us out."

"To *where, signore*? You cannot order me . . ."

"Be quiet," said Bray. "Don't press your luck."

"No, don't," added the KGB man, glancing at Scofield. "We must talk. As before, we should travel separately, divide our work, set up schedules and points of contact. We have much to discuss."

"By my guess, there are ninety miles between here and Bastia. There'll be plenty of time to talk." Scofield reached down for his attaché case; the girl snapped her hand out of his, angrily moving away; the Russian leaned over for the duffelbag.

"I suggest we talk alone," he said to Bray. "She's not an asset, Beowulf."

"You disappoint me." Scofield took the duffelbag from the KGB man. "Hasn't anyone ever taught you to convert a liability into an asset?"

Antonia had lived in Vescovato, on the Golo River, twenty-odd miles south of Bastia. Her immediate contribution was to get them there without being seen. It was important that she make decisions, if only to take her mind off the fact that she was following orders she disagreed with. She did so rapidly, choosing primitive back roads and mountain trails she knew as a child and as a girl growing up in the province.

"The nuns brought us here for a picnic," she said, looking down at a dammed-up stream. "We built fires and ate sausage, and took turns going into the woods to smoke cigarettes."

They went on.

"This hill has a fine wind in the morning," she said. "My father made marvellous kites and we would fly them here on Sundays. After Mass, of course."

"We?" asked Bray. "Do you have brothers and sisters?"

"One of each. They're older than I am and still live in Vescovato. They have families and I do not see them often; there's not much to talk about between us."

"They didn't go to the upper schools then?" said Taleniekov.

"They thought such pursuits were foolish. They're good people but prefer a simple life. If we need help, they will offer it."

"It would be better not to seek it," said the Russian. "Or them."

"They are my family, *signore*. Why should I avoid them?"

"Because it may be necessary."

"That's no answer. You kept me from Porto Vecchio and the justice that should be done; you can't give me orders any longer."

The KGB man looked at Scofield, his intent in his eyes. Bray expected the Russian to draw his weapon. He wondered briefly what his own reaction would be; he could not tell. But the moment passed, and Scofield understood something he had not fully understood before. Vasili Taleniekov did not wish to kill, but the professional in him was in strong conflict with the man. The Russian was pleading with him. He wanted to know how to convert a liability into an asset. Scofield wished he knew.

"Take it easy," said Bray. "Nobody wants to tell you what to do except where your own safety's concerned. We said that before and it's ten times more valid now."

"I think it is something else. You wish me to stay silent. *Silent* over the killing of a blind, old woman!"

"Your safety depends on it, we told you that. She understood."

"She's dead!"

"But you want to live," insisted Scofield calmly. "If the hill people find you, you won't. And if it's known that you've talked to others, they'll be in danger, too. Can't you see that?"

"Then what am I to *do*?"

"Just what we're doing. Disappear. Get out of Corsica." The girl started to object; Bray cut her off. "And *trust us*. You *must* trust us. Your grandmother did. She did so we could live and find some people who are involved in terrible things that go beyond Corsica."

"You are not talking to a child. What do you mean, 'terrible things'?"

Bray glanced at Taleniekov, accepting his disapproval, but by nodding, overriding it. "There are men — we don't know how many — whose lives are committed to killing other men, who spread mistrust and suspicion by choosing victims and financing murder. There's no pattern except violence, *political* violence, pitting faction against faction, government against government . . . people against people." Scofield paused, seeing the concentration in Antonia's face. "You said you were a political activist, a Communist. Fine. Good. So's my associate here; he was trained in Moscow. I'm an American, trained in Washington. We're enemies; we've fought each other a long time. The details aren't important, but the fact that we're working together now is. The men we're trying to find are much more dangerous than any difference between us, between our governments. Because these men can escalate those differences into something nobody wants; they can blow up the globe."

"Thank you for telling me," said Antonia pensively. Then she frowned. "But how could she know of such things?"

"She was there when it all began," answered Bray simply. "Nearly seventy years ago at Villa Matarese."

The words emerged slowly as Antonia whispered. " 'The whore of Villa Matarese' . . . The *padrone*, Guillaume?"

"He was as powerful as any man in England or France, an obstacle to the cartels and the combines. He stood in their way and won too often, so they destroyed him. They used their governments to bring about his collapse; they killed his sons. He went crazy . . . but in his madness – and with the resources he had left – he put in motion a long-range plan to get revenge. He called together other men who'd been destroyed the same way he had; they became the Council of the Matarese. For years their speciality was assassination; years later they were presumed to have died. Now they've come back, more deadly than they ever were." Scofield paused; he had told her enough. "That's as plainly as I can explain it and I hope you understand. You want the men who killed your grandmother to pay for it. I'd like to think that one day they will, but I've also got to tell you that they don't much matter."

Antonia was silent for a few moments, her intelligent brown eyes riveted on Bray. "You're quite clear, Signore Scofield. If they don't matter, then I don't matter, either. Is that what you're saying?"

"I guess I am."

"And my socialist comrade," she added, glancing at Taleniekov, "would as soon remove my insignificant presence as not."

"I look at an objective," answered Vasili, "and I do my best to analyse the problems inherent in reaching it."

"Yes, of course."

"Then do I turn around and walk into the woods, expecting the gunshot that will end my life?"

"That's your decision," said Taleniekov.

"I have a choice then? You would take my word that I'll say nothing?"

"No," replied the KGB man. "I would not."

Bray studied Taleniekov's face, his right hand inches from the Browning automatic in his belt. The Russian was leading up to something, testing the girl as he did so.

"Then what is the choice?" continued Antonia. "To let one or the other of your governments put me away, until you have found the men you seek?"

"I'm afraid that's not possible," said Taleniekov. "We're acting outside our governments; we do not have their approval. To put it frankly, they seek us as intensely as we seek the men we spoke of."

The girl reacted to the Russian's startling information as though struck. "You're hunted by your own people?" she asked.

Taleniekov nodded.

"I see. I understand clearly now. You will not accept my word and you cannot imprison me. Therefore I am a threat to you – far more than I imagined. So I have *no* choice, do I?"

"You may have," replied the KGB man. "My associate mentioned it."

"What was that?"

"Trust us. Help us get to Bastia and trust us. Something may come of it." Taleniekov turned to Scofield and spoke one word. "Conduit."

"We'll see," said Bray, removing his hand from his belt. They were thinking along the same lines.

The State Department contact in Murato was not happy; he did not want the complication he was faced with. As an owner of fishing boats in Bastia he wrote

169

reports on Soviet naval manoeuvres for the Americans. Washington paid him well and Washington had cabled *alerts* to stations everywhere that Brandon Alan Scofield, former specialist in Consular Operations, was to be considered a defector. Under such a classification the rules were clear: take into custody, if possible, but if custody was out of the question, employ all feasible measures for dispatch.

Silvio Montefiori wondered briefly if such a course of action was worth a try. But he was a practical man and in spite of the temptation he rejected the idea. Scofield had the proverbial knife to Montefiori's mouth, yet there was some honey on the blade. If Silvio refused the American's request, his activities would be exposed to the *Soviets*. Yet if Silvio acceded to Scofield's wishes, the defector promised him ten thousand dollars. And ten thousand dollars even with the poor rate of exchange – was probably more than any bonus he might receive for Scofield's death.

Also, he would be alive to spend the money.

Montefiori reached the warehouse, opened the door and walked through the dark, deserted cavern until he stood next to the rear wall, as instructed. He could not see the American – there was too little light – but he knew Scofield was there. It was a matter of waiting while birds circled and signals were somehow relayed.

He took a thin, crooked cigar from his handkerchief pocket, fumbled through his trousers for a box of matches, extracted one and struck it. As he held the flame to the tip of the cigar, he was annoyed to see that his hand trembled.

"You're sweating, Montefiori." The voice came from the shadows on the left. "The match shows up the sweat all over your face. The last time I saw you, you were sweating. I was in charge of the pouch then, and asked you certain questions."

"Brandon!" exclaimed Silvio, his greeting effusive, if nervous. "My dear good friend! How fine it is to see you again . . . if I could see you."

The tall American walked out of the shadows into the dim light. Montefiori expected to see a gun in his hand, but, of course, it was not there. Scofield never did the expected.

"How are you, Silvio?" said the defector.

"Well, my dear good friend!" Montefiori knew better than to reach for a handshake. "Everything's arranged. I take a great risk, pay my crew ten times their wages, but nothing is too much for a friend I admire so. You and the *provocateur* need only to go to the end of Pier Seven in Bastia at one o'clock this morning. My best trawler will get you to Livorno by daybreak."

"Is that its usual run?"

"Naturally not. The usual port is Piombino. I pay for the extra fuel gladly, with no thought of my loss."

"That's generous of you."

"And why not? You have always been fair with me."

"And why not? You've always delivered." Scofield reached into his pocket and took out a roll of bills. "But I'm afraid there'll be some changes. To begin with, I need two boats; one is to sail out of Bastia to the south, the other north, both staying within a thousand yards of the coastline. Each will be met by a speedboat which will be scuttled. I'll board one, the Russian the other, I'll give you the signals. Once on board, he and I will both head for open water, where the two courses will be charted, the destinations known only to the captains and ourselves."

"So many complications, my friend! They are not necessary, you have my word!"

"And I'll treasure it, Silvio, but while it's locked in my heart, do as I say."

"Naturally!" said Montefiori, swallowing. "But you must realize how this will add to my costs."

"Then they should be covered, shouldn't they?"

"It gladdens me you understand."

"Oh, I do, Silvio." The American peeled off a number of very large bills. "For starters, I want you to know that your activities on behalf of Washington will never be revealed by me; that in itself is a considerable payment, if you place any value on your life. And I want you to have this. It's five thousand dollars." Scofield held out the money.

"My dearest fellow, you said *ten* thousand! It was on your *word* that I prepared my very expensive arrangements!" Perspiration oozed from Montefiori's pores. Not only was his relationship with the Department of State in untenable jeopardy, but this pig of a traitor was about to steal him blind!

"I haven't finished, Silvio. You're much too anxious. I know I said ten thousand and you'll have it. That leaves five thousand due you, without figuring in your additional expenses. Is that right?"

"Quite right," said the Corsican. "The expenses are murderous."

"So much is these days," agreed Bray. "Let's say . . . fifteen per cent above the original price, is that satisfactory?"

"With others I might argue, but never with you."

"Then we'll settle for an additional fifteen hundred, OK? That leaves a total of six thousand, five hundred coming to you."

"That is a troublesome phrase. It implies a future delivery and my expenses are current. They cannot be put off."

"Come on, old friend. Certainly someone of your reputation can be trusted for a few days."

"A few days, Brandon? Again, so vague. A 'few days' and you could be in Singapore. Or Moscow. Can you be more specific?"

"Sure. The money will be in one of your trawlers, I haven't decided which yet. It'll be under the forward bulkhead, to the right of the centre strut, and hidden in a hollow piece of stained wood attached to the ribbing. You'll find it easily."

"Mother of God, so will others!"

"Why? No one will be looking unless you make an announcement."

"It's far too risky! There's not a crewman on board who would hesitate to kill his mother in front of his priest for such an amount! Really, my dear friend, come to your senses!"

"Not to worry, Silvio. Meet your boats in the harbour. If you don't find the wood, look for a man with his hand blown off; he'll have the money."

"It will be trapped?" asked Montefiori incredulously, the sweat drenching his shirt collar.

"A set-screw on the side; you've done it before. Just remove it and the charge is deactivated."

"I'll hire my brother . . ." Silvio was depressed; the American was not a nice person. It was as if Scofield had been reading his thoughts. With the money on board, it would be counter-productive to have either boat sunk; the State Department might not pay in full. And by the time both were back in Bastia, the despicable Scofield could be sailing down the Volga. Or the Nile. "You won't reconsider, my dear good friend?"

"I'm afraid I can't. And I won't tell anybody how much Washington thinks of you, either. Don't fret, Silvio, the money will be there. You see, we may be in touch again. Very soon."

"Do not hurry, Brandon. And please, say nothing further. I do not care to know anything. Such burdens! What are the signals for tonight?"

"Simple. Two flashes of light, repeated several times, or until the trawlers stop."

"Two flashes, repeated . . . Distressed speedboats seeking help. I cannot be responsible for accidents at sea. *Ciao*, my old *friend* . . ." Montefiori blotted his neck with his handkerchief, turned in the dim light of the warehouse, and started across the concrete floor.

"Silvio?"

Montefiori stopped.

"Yes?"

"Change your shirt."

They had watched her closely for nearly two days now, both men silently acknowledging that a judgement had to be made. She would either be their conduit or she would have to die. There was no middle ground, no security prison or isolated compound to which she could be sent. She would be their conduit or an act of sheer, cold necessity would take place.

They needed someone to relay messages between them. They could not communicate directly; it was too dangerous. There had to be a third party, stationed in one spot, under cover, familiar with whatever basic codes they mounted – above all secretive and accurate. Was Antonia capable of being that person? And if she was, would she accept the risks that went with the job? So they studied her as if thrown into a crash-analysis of an impending exchange between enemies on neutral ground.

She was quick and had surface courage, qualities they had seen in the hills. She was also alert, conscious of danger. Yet she remained an enigma; her core eluded them. She was defensive, guarded, quiet for long periods, her eyes darting in all directions at once as though she expected a whip to crack across her back, or a hand to grab her throat from the shadows behind. But there were no whips, no shadows in the sunlight.

Antonia was a very strange woman and it occurred to both professionals that she was hiding something. Whatever it was – if it was – she was not about to reveal it. The moments of rest provided nothing; she kept to herself – intensely to herself – and refused to be drawn out.

But she did what they had asked her to do. She got them to Bastia without incident, even to the point of knowing where to flag down a broken-down bus that carried labourers from the outskirts into the port city. Taleniekov sat with Antonia in the front while Scofield remained at the rear, watching the other passengers.

They emerged on the crowded streets, Bray still behind them, still watching, still alert for a break in the pattern of surrounding indifference. A face suddenly rigid, a pair of eyes zeroing in on the erect, middle-aged man walking with the dark-haired woman thirty paces ahead. There was only indifference.

He had told the girl to head for a bar on the waterfront, a rundown hole where no one dared intrude on a fellow drinker. Even most *Corsi* avoided the place; it served the dregs of the piers.

Once inside, they separated again, Taleniekov joining Bray at a table in the corner, Antonia ten feet away at another table, the chair next to her angled against the edge, reserved. It did nothing to inhibit the drunken advances of the customers. These, too, were part of her testing; it was important to know how she handled herself.

"What do you think?" asked Taleniekov.

"I'm not sure," said Scofield. "She's elusive. I can't find her."

"Perhaps you're looking too hard. She's been through an emotional upheaval, you can't expect her to act with even the semblance of normalcy. I think she can do the job. We'd know soon enough if she can't; we can protect ourselves with prearranged cipher. And quite frankly, who else do we turn to? Is there a man at any station anywhere you could trust? Or I could trust? Even what you call drones outside the stations; who would not be curious? Who could resist the pressures of Washington or Moscow?"

"It's the emotional upheaval that bothers me," Bray said. "I think it happened long before we found her. She said she was down in Porto Vecchio to get away for a while. Get away from what?"

"There could be a dozen explanations. Unemployment is rampant throughout Italy. She could be without work. Or an unfaithful lover, an affair gone sour. Such things are not relevant to what we would be asking her to do."

"Those aren't the things I saw. Besides, why should we trust her, and even if we took the chance, why would she accept?"

"She was there when that old woman was killed," said the Russian. "It may be enough."

Scofield nodded. "It's a start, but only if she's convinced there's a specific connection between what we're doing and what she saw."

"We made that clear. She heard the old woman's words; she repeated them."

"While she was still confused, still in shock. She's got to be convinced."

"Then convince her."

"Me?"

"She trusts you more than she does her 'socialist comrade', that's obvious."

Scofield lifted his glass. "Were you going to kill her?"

"No. That decision would have had to come from you. It still does. I was uncomfortable seeing your hand so close to your belt."

"So was I." Bray put down the glass and glanced over at the girl. Berlin was never far away – Taleniekov understood that – but Scofield's mind and his eyes were not playing tricks with his memories now; he was not in a cave on the side of a hill watching a woman toss her hair free in the light of a fire. There was no similarity between his wife and Antonia any longer. He could kill her if he had to. "She'll go with me, then," he said to the Russian. "I'll know in forty-eight hours. Our first communication will be direct; the next two through her in prearranged code so we can check the accuracy . . . If we want her and she says she'll do it."

"And if we do not, or she does not?"

"That'll be my decision, won't it." Bray made a statement; he did not ask a question. Then he took out the leaf of lettuce from his jacket pocket and opened it. The yellowed scrap of paper was intact, the names blurred but legible. Without looking down, Taleniekov repeated them.

" 'Count Alberto Scozzi, Rome. Sir John Waverly, London. Prince Andrei Voroshin, St Petersburg' – the name Russia is added, and, of course, the city is now Leningrad. 'Señor Manuel Ortiz Ortega, Madrid. Josus' – which is presumed to be Joshua – 'Appleton, State of Massachusetts, America.' The Spaniard was killed by the *padrone* at Villa Matarese, so he was never part of the council. The remaining four have long since died, but two of their descendants are very prominent, very available. David Waverly and Joshua Appleton the fourth. Britain's Foreign Secretary and the senator from Massachusetts. I say we go for immediate confrontation."

"I don't," said Bray, looking down at the paper and the childlike writing of the letters. "Because we do know who they are, and we don't know anything about the others. Who are their descendants? Where are they? If there're more surprises, let's try to find them first. The Matarese isn't restricted to two men, and these two in particular may have nothing to do with it."

"Why do you say that?"

"Everything I know about both of them would seem to deny anything like the Matarese. Waverly had what they call in England a 'good war'; a young commando, highly decorated. Then a hell of a record in the Foreign Office. He's always been a tactical compromiser, not an inciter; it doesn't fit . . . Appleton's a Boston Brahmin who bolted the class lines and became a liberal reformer for three terms in the Senate. Protector of the working man as well as the intellectual community. He's a shining knight on a solid, political horse that most of America thinks will take him to the White House next year."

"What better residence for a *consigliere* of the Matarese?"

"It's too jarring, too pat. I think he's genuine."

"The art of conviction – in both instances, perhaps. But you're right; they won't vanish. So we start in Leningrad and Rome, trace what we can."

" 'You and *yours* will do what I can no longer do.' Those were the words Matarese used seventy years ago. I wonder if it's that simple."

"Meaning the 'yours' could be selected, not born?" asked Taleniekov. "Not direct descendants?"

"Yes."

"It's possible." but these were all once-powerful families. The Waverlys and the Appletons still are. There are certain traditions in such families, the blood is always uppermost. Start with the families. They were to inherit the earth; those were his words, too. The old woman said it was his vengeance.

Scofield nodded. "I know. She also said they were only the survivors, that they were controlled by another . . . that we should look for someone else."

" 'With a voice crueller than the wind,' " interrupted the Russian. " 'It is he,' she said."

"The shepherd boy," added Bray, staring at the scrap of yellow paper. After all these years, who is he? What is he?"

"Start with the families," repeated Taleniekov. "If he's to be found, it is through them."

"Can you get back into Russia? To Leningrad?"

"Easily. Through Helsinki. It will be a strange return for me. I spent three years at the university in Leningrad. It's where they found me."

"I don't think anyone'll throw you a welcome-home party." Scofield folded the scrap of yellow paper into the leaf of lettuce and put it in his pocket. He took out a small notebook. "When you're in Helsinki, stay at the Tavastian Hotel until you hear from me. I'll tell you who to see there. Give me a name."

"Rydukov, Pyotr," replied the KGB man without hesitating.

"Who's that?"

"A violinist in the Sevastopol Symphony Orchestra. I'll have his papers somewhat altered."

"I hope no one asks you to play."

"Severe arthritis has caused indisposition."

"Let's work out our codes," said Bray, glancing at Antonia, who was smoking a cigarette and talking to a young Bastian soldier standing next to her. She was handling herself well; she laughed politely but coolly, putting a gentle distance between herself and the impertinent young man. In truth, there was more than a hint of elegance in her behaviour, out of place in the waterfront café, but welcome to the eyes. His eyes, reflected Scofield, without thinking further.

"What do you think will happen?" asked Taleniekov, watching Bray.

"I'll know in forty-eight hours," Scofield said.

18

The trawler approached the Italian coastline. The winter seas had been turbulent, the cross-currents angry and the boat slow; it had taken them nearly seventeen hours to make the trip from Bastia. It would be dark soon, and a small lifeboat would be lowered over the side to take Scofield and Antonia ashore.

Besides getting them to Italy where the hunt for the family of Count Alberto Scozzi would begin, the tediously slow journey served another purpose for Bray. He had the time and the seclusion to try to learn more about Antonia Gravet – for that unexpectedly was her last name, her father having been a French artillery sergeant stationed in Corsica during the Second World War.

"So you see," she had told him, the curve of a smile on her lips, "my French lessons were very inexpensive. It was only necessary to anger *papa*, who was never comfortable with my mother's Cismontan Italian."

Except for those moments when her mind wandered back to Porto Vecchio, a change had come over her. She began to laugh, her brown eyes matching the laughter, bright, infectious, at times nearly manic, as if the act of laughing itself were a release she needed. It was almost impossible for Scofield to realize that the girl sitting next to him, dressed in khaki trousers and a torn field jacket, was the same woman who had been so sullen and unresponsive. Or who had shouted orders in the hills and handled the Lupo so effectively. They had several minutes left before going into the lifeboat, so he asked her about it. The Lupo, not the sudden laughter.

"I went through a phase; we all do, I think. A time when drastic social change seems only possible through violent activism. Those maniacs from the *Brigate Rosse* knew how to play upon our dramatics."

"The Brigades? You were with the *Red Brigades*? Good God!"

She nodded. "I spent several weeks at a *Brigatisti* camp in Medicina, learning how to fire weapons, and scale walls and hide contraband – none of which I did particularly well, incidentally – until one morning when a young student, a boy, really, was killed in what the leaders called a 'training accident'. A *training accident*, such a *military* sound, but they were not soldiers. Only brutes and bullies, let loose with knives and guns. He died in my arms, the blood flowing from his wound . . . his eyes so frightened and bewildered. I hardly knew him but when he died, I couldn't stand it. Guns and knives and clubs were not the way; that night I left and returned to Bologna."

"So what you saw in Porto Vecchio did not settle that question, have we settled ours?"

"What question?"

"Where I'm going. You and the Russian said I was to trust you, do as you were doing, leave Corsica and say nothing. Well, *signore*, we've left Corsica and I've trusted you. I didn't run away."

"Why didn't you?"

Antonia paused briefly. "Fear, and you know it. You're not normal men. You speak courteously, but you move too quickly for courteous men. The two don't go together. I think underneath you are what the crazy people in the *Brigate Rosse* would like to be. You frighten me."

"That stopped you?"

"The Russian wanted to kill me. He watched me closely; he would have shot me the instant he thought I was running."

"Actually, he didn't want to kill you and he wouldn't have. He was just sending a message."

"I don't understand."

"You don't have to, you were perfectly safe."

"Am I safe now? Will you take my word that I will say nothing and let me go?"

"Where to?"

"Bologna. I can always get work there."

"Doing what?"

"Nothing very impressive. I'm hired as a researcher at the university. I look up boring statistics for the *professori* who write their boring books and articles."

"A researcher?" Bray smiled to himself. "You must be very accurate."

"What is it to be accurate? Facts are facts. Will you let me go back to Bologna?"

"Your work isn't steady then?"

"It is work I *like*," replied Antonia. "I work when I wish to, leaving me time for other things."

"You're actually a self-employed freelancer with your own business," said Scofield, enjoying himself. "That's the essence of capitalism, isn't it?"

"And you're maddening! You ask questions but you don't answer mine!"

"Sorry. Occupational hazard. What was your question?"

"Will you let me go? Will you accept my word; will you trust me? Or must I wait for that moment when you cannot be watching and run?"

"I wouldn't do that, if I were you," replied Bray courteously. "Look, you're an honest person. I don't meet many. A minute ago you said you didn't run away before because you were afraid to, not because you trusted us. That's being honest. You brought us up to Bastia. Be honest with me now. Knowing what you know – seeing what you saw in Porto Vecchio – how good is your word?"

At midships, the lifeboat was being hoisted over the railing by four crewmen; Antonia watched it as she spoke. "You're being unfair. You know what I saw, and you know what you told me. When I think about it, I want to cry out and . . ." She did not finish; instead she turned back to him, her voice weary. "How good is my word? I don't know. So what's left for me? Will it be you and not the Russian who fires the bullet?"

"I may offer you a job."

"I don't want work from you."

"We'll see," said Bray.

"*Signore, presto, presto! La scialuppa!*"

The lifeboat was in the water. Scofield reached for the duffelbag at his side and got to his feet. He held out his hand for Antonia Gravet. "Come on. I've had easier people to deal with."

The statement was true. He could kill this woman if he had to. Still, he would try not to have to.

Where was the new life for Beowulf Agate now? God, *he hated this one*.

Bray hired a taxi in Fiumicino, the driver at first reluctant to accept a fare to Rome, changing his mind instantly at the sight of the money in Scofield's hand. They stopped for a quick meal and still reached the inner city before eight o'clock. The streets were crowded, the shops doing a brisk evening's business.

"Pull up in that parking space," said Bray to the driver. They were in front of a clothing store. "Wait here," he added, including Antonia in the command. "I'll guess your size." He opened the door.

"What are you doing?" asked the girl.

"A transition," replied Scofield in English. "You can't walk into a decent shop dressed like that."

Five minutes later he returned carrying a box containing denim slacks, a white blouse and a woollen sweater. "Put these on," he said.

"You're mad!"

"Modesty becomes you, but we're in a hurry. The stores'll close in an hour. I've got things to wear; you don't." He turned to the driver, whose eyes were riveted on the rear view mirror. "You understand English better than I thought," he said in Italian. "Drive around. I'll tell you where to go." He opened his duffelbag and pulled out a tweed jacket.

Antonia changed in the back seat of the taxi, glancing frequently at Scofield. As she slipped the khakis off and the denims on, her long legs caught the light of the streets. Bray looked out the window, conscious of being affected by what he saw in the corner of his eye. He had not had a woman in a very long time; he would not have this one. It was entirely possible that he might have to kill her.

She pulled the sweater over her blouse; the loose-fitting wool did not conceal the swell of her breasts and Scofield made it a point to focus his eyes on hers. "That's better. Phase one complete."

"You're very generous, but these would not have been my choice."

"You can throw them away in an hour. If anyone asks you, you're off a charter boat in Ladispoli." He addressed the driver again. "Go to the Via de Condotti. I'll pay you there; we won't need you any longer."

The shop on the Via de Condotti was expensive, catering to the idle and the rich, and it was obvious that Antonia Gravet had never been in one like it. Obvious to Bray; he doubted to anyone else. For she had innate taste – born, not cultivated. She might have been bursting at the sight of the wealth of garments displayed, but she was the essence of control. It was the elegance Bray had seen in the filthy waterfront café in Bastia.

"Do you like it?" she asked, coming out of a fitting room in a subdued, dark silk dress, a wide-brimmed white hat and a pair of high-heeled white shoes.

"Very nice," said Scofield, meaning it, and her, and everything he saw.

"I feel like a traitor to all the things I've believed for so long," she added, whispering. "These prices could feed ten families for a month! Let's go somewhere else."

"We don't have time. Take them and get some kind of coat and anything else you need."

"You *are* mad."

"I'm in a hurry."

From a booth on the Via Sistina, he called a *pensione* in the Piazza Navona where he stayed frequently when in Rome. The landlord and his wife knew nothing at all about Scofield – they were not curious about any of their transient tenants – except that Bray tipped generously whenever they accommodated him. The owner was happy to do so tonight.

The Piazza Navona was crowded; it was always crowded, thus making it an ideal location for a man in his profession. The Bernini statues and fountains were magnets for citizens and tourists alike, the profusion of outdoor cafés places of

178

assignation, planned and spontaneous; Scofield's had always been planned. A table in a crowded square was a good vantage point for spotting surveillance. It was not necessary to be concerned about such things now.

Now it was only necessary to get some sleep, let the mind clear itself. Tomorrow a decision would have to be made. The life or the death of the woman at his side whom he guided through Navona to an old stone building and the door of the *pensione*.

The ceiling of their room was high, the windows enormous, opening on to the square three storeys below. Bray pushed the overstuffed sofa against the door and pointed to the bed across the room.

"Neither of us slept very much on that damned boat. Get some rest."

Antonia opened one of the boxes from the shop in the Via de Condotti and took out the fine silk dress. "Why did you buy me these expensive clothes?"

"Tomorrow we're going to a couple of places where you'll need them."

"Why are we going to these places? They must surely be extravagant."

"Not really. There are some people I have to see, and I want you with me."

"I wanted to thank you. I've never had such beautiful clothes."

"You're welcome." Bray went over to the bed and removed the spread; he returned to the sofa. "Why did you leave Bologna and go to Corsica?"

"More questions," she said quietly.

"I'm just curious, that's all."

"I told you. I wanted to get away for a while. Is that not a good enough reason?"

"It's not much of an explanation."

"It's the one I prefer to give." She studied the dress in her hands.

Scofield slapped the spread over the sofa. "Why Corsica?"

"You saw that valley. It is remote, peaceful. A good place to think."

"It's certainly remote; that makes it a good place to hide out. Were you hiding from someone – or something?"

"Why do you say things like that?"

"I have to know. Were you hiding?"

"Not from anything you would understand."

"Try me."

"*Stop* it!" Antonia held the dress out for him. "Take your clothes. Take anything you want from me, I can't stop you! But leave me *alone*."

Bray approached her. For the first time, he saw fear in her eyes. "I think you'd better tell me. All that talk about Bologna . . . it was a lie. You wouldn't go back there even if you could. Why?"

She stared at him for a moment, her brown eyes glistening. When she began, she turned away, and walked to the window overlooking the Piazza Navona. "You might as well know, it doesn't matter any longer . . . You're wrong. I can go back; they expect me back. And if I do not return, one day they will come looking for me."

"Who?"

"The leaders of the Red Brigades. I told you on the boat how I had run away from the camp in Medicina. That was over a year ago and for over a year I have lived a lie far greater than the one I told you. They found me, and I was put on trial in the Red Court – they call it the Red Court of Revolutionary Justice. Sentences of death are not mere phrases, they are very real executions, as the world knows now.

"I had not been indoctrinated, yet knew the location of the camp and had witnessed the death of the boy. Most damaging, I had run away. I couldn't be trusted. Of course, I didn't matter compared to the objectives of the revolution; they said I had proved myself less than insignificant. A traitor.

"I saw what was coming, so I pleaded for my life. I claimed that I had been the student's lover, and that my reaction – although perhaps not admirable – was understandable. I stressed that I had said nothing to *anyone* let alone the police. I was as committed as any in that court to the revolution – more so than most, for I came from a truly poor family.

"In my own way, I was persuasive, but there was something else working for me. To understand you must know how such groups are organized. There is always a cadre of strong men, and one or two among these who vie for leadership, like male wolves in a pack – snarling, dominating, choosing their various mates at will, for that is part of the domination. A man such as this wanted me among the women. He was probably the most vicious of the pack; the others were frightened of him – and so was I.

"But he could save my life, and I made my choice. I lived with him for over a year, hating every day, despising the nights he took me, loathing myself as much as I loathed him.

"Still, I could do nothing. I lived in fear; in such a terrible fear that my slightest move would be mistaken, and my head blown away . . . their favourite method of execution." Antonia turned from the window. "You asked me why I did not run from you and the Russian. Perhaps you understand better now; the conditions of my survival were not new to me. To run away meant death; to run away from you means death now. I was a captive in Bologna, I became a captive in Porto Vecchio . . . and I am a captive now in Rome." She paused then spoke again. "I am tired of you all. I can't stand it much longer. The moment will come and I will run . . . and you will shoot." She held out the dress again. "Take your clothes, Signore Scofield. I am faster in a pair of trousers."

Bray did not move, nor did he object by gesture or voice. He almost smiled, but he could not do that, either. "I'm glad to hear that your sense of fatalism doesn't include intentional suicide. I mean, you *do* expect to give us a 'run'."

"You may count on it." She dropped the dress on the floor.

"I won't kill you, Antonia."

She laughed quietly, derisively. "Oh, yes, you will. You and the Russian are the worst kind. In Bologna, they kill with fire in their eyes, and mouthing slogans. You kill without anger . . . you need no inner urging."

I once did. You get over it. There's no compulsion, only necessity. Please don't talk about these things. The way you've lived is your stay of execution; that's all you need to know.

"I won't argue with you. I didn't say I couldn't – or wouldn't – I simply said I won't. I'm trying to tell you, you don't have to run."

The girl frowned. "Why?"

"Because I need you." Scofield knelt down and picked up the dress. He took her hand gently and gave it back to her. "All I've got to do is convince you that you need me."

"To save my life?"

"To give it back to you, at any rate. In what form, I'm not sure, but better than before. Without the fear, eventually."

" 'Eventually' is a long time. Why should I believe you?"

"I don't think you have a choice. I can't give you any other answer until I know more, but let's start with the fact that the *Brigatisti* aren't confined to Bologna. You said if you didn't go back, they'd come looking for you. Their . . . packs . . . roam all over Italy. How long can you keep hiding until they find you – if they want to find you badly enough?"

"I could have for years in Corsica. In Porto Vecchio. They would *never* find me."

"That's not possible now, and even if it were, is that the kind of existence you want? To spend your life as a recluse in those goddamn hills? Those men who killed that old woman are no different from the Brigades. One wants to keep its world – and its filthy little secret – and it will kill to do it. The other wants to change the world – with terror – and it kills every day to do *that*. Believe me, they're connected to each other. That's the connection Taleniekov and I are looking for. We'd better find it before the maniacs blow us all up. Your grandmother said it: it's happening *everywhere*. Stop hiding. Help us. Help *me*."

"There's no way I can help you."

"You don't know what I'm going to ask."

"Yes, I do. You want me to go back!"

"Later, perhaps. Not now."

"I won't! They're pigs. He's the pig of the world!"

"Then remove him from the world. Remove *them*. Don't let them grow, don't let them make you a prisoner – whether you're in Corsica or here or anywhere else. Don't you understand? They *will* find you if they think you're a threat to them. Do you want to go back that way? To an execution?"

Antonia broke away, stopped by the overstuffed sofa Bray had placed in front of the door. "How will they find me? Will you help them?"

"No," said Scofield, remaining motionless. "I won't have to."

"There are a hundred places I can go . . ."

"And there are a thousand ways they have of tracing you."

"That's a lie!" She turned and faced him. "They have no such methods."

"I think they do. Groups like the Brigades everywhere are being fed information, financed, given access to sophisticated equipment, and most of the time they don't know how or why. They're all pawns and that's the irony, but they'll find you."

"Pawns for what?"

"The Matarese."

"*Madness!*"

"I wish it were but I'm afraid it isn't. Too much has happened to be coincidence any longer. Men who believed in peace have been killed; a statesman respected by both sides went to others and spoke of it. He disappeared. It's in Washington, Moscow . . . in Italy and Corsica and God knows where. It's *there*, but we can't *see* it. I only know we've got to find it, and that old woman in the hills gave us the first concrete information to go on. She gave up what was left of her life to give it to us. She was blind but she saw it . . . because she was there when it began."

"Words!"

"Facts. Names."

A sound. Not part of the hum from the square below, but beyond the door blocked by the sofa. All sounds were part of a pattern, or distinctly their own; this was its own. A footstep, a shifting of weight, a scratch of leather against stone. Bray brought his index finger to his lips, then gestured for Antonia to move to the left end of the sofa while he walked quickly to the right. She was bewildered; she had heard nothing. He motioned for her to help him lift the sofa away from the door. Smoothly, silently.

It was done.

Scofield waved her back into the corner, took out his Browning and resumed a normal conversational tone as he inched his way to the door, his face turned away from it.

"It's not too crowded in the restaurants. Let's go down to *Tre Scalini* for some food. God knows I could use . . ."

He pulled the door open; there was no one in the hallway. Yet he had not been mistaken; he knew what he had heard; the years had taught him not to *make* mistakes about such things. And the years had also taught him when to be furious with himself over his own carelessness. Since Fiumicino he had been very careless, disregarding the probability of surveillance. Rome was a low-priority station; since the heavy traffic four years ago, CIA, *Cons Op* and KGB activity had been held to a minimum. It had been over eleven months since he had been in the city, and the scanner sheets then had shown no agents of status in operation there. If anything Rome had lessened in intelligence potential during the past year; who could be around?

Someone was and he had been spotted. Someone moments ago had been close to the door, listening, trying to confirm a sighting. The sudden break in conversation had served to warn whoever it was, but he was there, somewhere in the shadows of the squared-off hallway or on the staircase.

Goddamn it, thought Bray angrily as he walked silently around the landing, had he forgotten that alerts had been sent to every station in the world by now? He was a *fugitive* and he had been careless. Where had he been picked up? In the Via de Condotti? Crossing the Navona?

He heard a rush of air, and even as he heard it, his instinct told him he was too late to react. He stiffened his body as he spun to his right, lunging downward to lessen the impact of the blow.

A door behind him had suddenly been yanked open and a figure that was only a blur above his back rushed out, an arm held high, but only for an instant. It came crashing down, the sickening bolt of pain spreading from the base of his skull throughout his chest, surging downward into his kneecaps where it settled, bringing on the wind of collapse and darkness.

He blinked his eyes, tears of blunt hurt filling them, disorienting him, but somehow

182

providing a measure of relief. How many minutes had he been lying on the hallway floor? He could not tell, yet he sensed it was not long; his mouth was not filled with the dried spit which accompanied any lengthy period of breathing in pain. He rose slowly and looked at his watch, focusing on the dial in the dim light.

He had been out for roughly fifteen minutes; had he not twisted the instant before impact, the elapsed time would have been closer to an hour.

Why was he *there*? Alone? Where was his captor? It did not make sense! He had been taken, then left by himself. What was his capture *for*?

He heard a muted cry, quickly cut off, and turned towards the source, bewildered. Then the bewilderment left him. *He* was not the target; he never had been. It was *she*. Antonia. *She* was the one who had been spotted, not him.

Scofield got to his feet, braced himself against the railing and peered down at the floor around him. His Browning was gone, naturally, and he had no other weapon. But he had something else. Consciousness. His assailant would not expect that – the man had known precisely where to hammer the butt of his gun; in his mind his victim would be unconscious far longer than the few minutes involved. Drawing that man out was not a significant problem.

Bray walked noiselessly to the door of the single room and put his ear to the wood. The moans were more pronounced now. Sharp cries of pain, abruptly stilled. A strong hand clasped over a mouth, fingers pressed into flesh, choking off all but throated protests. And there were words, spoken harshly in Italian.

"*Whore! Pig!* It was to be *Marseilles*! Nine hundred thousand *lire!* Two or three weeks at most! We sent our people; you were not *there*. *He* was not there. No courier of drugs had ever heard of you! *Liar! Whore!* Where were you? What have you done!? *Traitor!*"

A scream was suddenly formed, more suddenly cut off, the guttural cry that followed searing in its torment. What in the name of God was *happening*? Scofield slammed his hand against the door, shouting as though only half-conscious, incoherent, his words slurred and barely comprehensible.

"Stop it! *Stop* it! What *is* this? I can't . . . can't . . . *Wait!* I'll run downstairs! There are police in the square. I'll bring the *police!*"

He pounded his feet on the stone floor as if running, his shouts trailing off until there was silence. He pressed his back into the wall and waited, listening to the commotion within. He heard cracks of slapping, gasps of pain as punches were delivered and hysterical cries aborted.

There was a sudden loud thud. A body – her body – was slammed into the door, and then the door was pulled open, Antonia propelled through it with such force she sprawled forward falling to her knees. What Bray saw of her caused him to suppress all reaction. There was no emotion, only movement . . . and the inevitable: he would inflict punishment.

The man rushed through the door, weapon first. Scofield shot out his right hand, catching the gun, pivoting as he did so, his left foot arcing up viciously into the attacker's groin. The man grimaced in shock and sudden agony; the gun fell to the floor, metal clattering against stone. Bray grabbed the man's throat, smashing his head into the wall, and twisting him by the neck into the open door frame. He held the Italian upright, and hammered his fist into the man's lower rib cage; he could hear the bone crack. He plunged his knee into the small of the man's back and with both hands acting as a battering ram, sent him plummeting through the door into the double room. The Italian collapsed over the obstructing sofa and fell senseless to the floor beyond it. Scofield turned and ran to Antonia.

Reaction was allowed now; he felt sick. Her face was bruised, spidery veins of red had spread from the swellings caused by repeated blows to the head. The corner of her left eye was so battered the skin had broken; a two-pronged rivulet of blood flowed down her cheek. The loose-fitting sweater had been removed by force, the white blouse torn to shreds, nothing left but ragged patches of fabric. Beneath, her brassiere had been pulled from its hasps, yanked off her breasts, hanging from a single shoulder strap.

It was the flesh of this exposed part of her body that made him swallow in revulsion. There were cigarette burns, ugly little circles of charred skin, progressing from her pelvic area across the flat of her stomach over the swell of her right breast to the small red nipple.

The man who had done this to her was no interrogator seeking information; that role was secondary. He was a sadist, indulging his sickness as brutally and as rapidly as possible. And Bray had not finished with that man.

Antonia moaned, shaking her head back and forth, pleading not to be hurt again. He picked her up and carried her back into the room, kicking the door shut, edging his way around the sofa, past the unconscious man on the floor, to the bed. He placed her gently down, sat beside her and drew her to him.

"It's all right. It's over, he can't touch you anymore." He felt her tears against his face, and then was aware that she had put her arms around him. She was suddenly holding him fiercely, her body trembling, the cries from her throat more than pleas for release from immediate pain. She was begging to be set free from a torment that had been deep within her for a very long time. But it was not the time now to probe; the extent of her wounds had to be examined and treated.

There was a doctor on the Viale Regina, and a man on the floor to be dealt with. Getting Antonia to the doctor might be difficult unless he could calm her down; disposing of the sadist on the floor would be simple. It might even accomplish something.

He would call the police from a booth somewhere in the city and direct them to the *pensione*. They would find a man and his weapon and a crude sign over his unconscious body.

Brigatisti.

184

19

The doctor closed the door of the examining room and spoke in English. He had been schooled in London and recruited by British intelligence. Scofield had found him during an operation involving *Cons Op* and MI6. The man was safe. He thought all clandestine services were slightly mad, but since the British had paid for his last two years in medical school, he accepted his part of the bargain. He was simply on-call to treat unbalanced people in a very foolish business. Bray liked him.

"She's sedated and my wife is with her. She'll come out of it in a few minutes and you can go."

"How is she?"

"In pain, but it won't last. I've treated the burns with an ointment that acts as a local anaesthetic for the skin areas. I've given her a jar." The doctor lit a cigarette; he had not finished. "An ice pack or two should be applied to the facial contusions; the swellings will go down overnight. The cuts are minor, no stitches required."

"Then she's all right," said Scofield, relieved.

"No, she's not, Bray." The doctor exhaled smoke. "Oh, medically she's sound and with a little makeup and dark glasses she'll no doubt be up and about by noon tomorrow. But she is not all right!"

"What do you mean?"

"How well do you know her?"

"Barely. I found her several days ago, it doesn't matter where . . ."

"I'm not interested," interrupted the doctor. "I never am. I just want you to know that tonight was not the first time this has happened to her. There is evidence of previous beatings, some quite severe."

"Good Lord . . ." Scofield thought immediately of the cries of anguish he had heard less than an hour ago. "What kind of evidence?"

"Scars from multiple lacerations and burns. All small and precisely placed to cause maximum pain."

"Recent?"

"Within the last year or so, I'd say. Some of the tissue is still soft, relatively new."

"Any ideas?"

"Yes. During severe trauma, people speak of things." The doctor stopped, inhaling on his cigarette. "I don't have to tell you that; you count on it."

"Go on," said Bray.

"I think she was systematically, psychologically broken. She kept repeating catchwords. Allegiances to this and that; loyalty beyond death and torture of self and comrades. That sort of garbage."

"The *Brigatisti* were busy little pricks," Bray said.

"What?"

"Forget it."

"Forgotten. She has a mass of confusion in that *lovely head* of hers."

"Not as much as you think. She got away."

"Intact and functioning?" asked the doctor.

"Mostly."

"Then she's remarkable."

"More to the point, she's exactly what I need," said Scofield.

"Is that, too, a required response?" The medical man's ire was apparent. "You people never cease to amaze me in a disappointing way. That woman's scars aren't only on her skin, Bray. She's been brutalized."

"She's alive. I'd like to be there when she comes out of sedation. May I?"

"So you can catch her while her mind is only *half* alive, extract your *own* responses?" The doctor paused again. "I'm sorry, it's not my business."

"I'd like her to be your business if she needs help. If you don't mind."

The doctor studied him. "My services are limited to medicine, you know that."

"I understand. She has no one else, she's not from Rome. Can she come to you . . . if any of those scars get torn away?"

The Italian nodded. "Tell her to come and see me if she needs medical attention. Or a friend."

"Thank you very much. And thanks for something else. You've fitted several pieces into a puzzle I couldn't figure out. I'll go in now, if it's all right."

"Go ahead. Send my wife out here."

Scofield touched Antonia's cheek. She lay still on the bed, but at the touch rolled her head to the side, her lips parted, a moan of protest escaping her throat. Things *were* clearer now, the puzzle that was Antonia Gravet coming more into focus. For it was the focus that had been lacking; he had not been able to see through the opaque glass wall she had erected between herself and the outside world. The commanding woman in the hills who displayed courage without essential strength; yet who could face a man she believed wanted her dead and tell him to fire away. And the childlike woman on the trawler drenched by the sea, given to sudden moments of infectious laughter. The laughter had confused him. But it was her way of grasping for small periods of relief and normality. The boat was her temporary sanctuary; she would not be hurt while at sea, and so she had made the most of it. An abused child – or a prisoner – allowed an hour of fresh air and sunshine. Take the moments and find joy in them. If only to forget. For those brief moments.

A scarred mind worked that way. Scofield had seen too many scarred minds not to recognize the syndrome once he understood the scars. The doctor had used the phrase "a mass of confusion" in her lovely head. What could anyone expect? Antonia Gravet had spent her own eternity in a maze of pain. That she had survived above a vegetable was not only remarkable . . . it was the sign of a professional.

Strange, thought Bray, but that conclusion was the highest compliment he could pay. In a way, it made him sick.

She opened her eyes, blinking in fear, her lips trembling. Then she seemed to recognize him; the fear receded and the trembling stopped. He touched her cheek again and her eyes reflected the comfort she felt at the touch.

"*Grazie*," she whispered. "Thank you, thank you, thank you . . ."

He bent over her. "I know most of it," he said quietly. "The doctor told me what they did to you. Now tell me the rest. What happened in Marseilles?"

Tears welled up in her eyes and the trembling began again. "No! No, you must not ask me!"

"*Please*. I have to know. They can't touch you; they'll never touch you again."

"You saw what they *do*! Oh, God, the *pain* . . ."

"It's over." He brushed away the tears with his fingers. "Listen to me. I understand now. I said stupid things to you because I didn't know. Of course you wanted to get away, stay away, isolate yourself – resign from the human race, for Christ's sake – I *understand* that. But don't you see? You *can't*. Help us stop them, help *me* stop them. They've put you through so much . . . make them pay for it, Antonia. Goddamn it, get *angry*. I look at you and I'm angry as hell!"

He was not sure what it was; perhaps the fact that he cared, for he did, and he did not try to conceal that care. It was in his eyes, in his words; he knew it. Whatever it was, the tears stopped, her brown eyes glistened, as they had glistened on the trawler. Anger and purpose were surfacing. She told the rest of her story.

"I was to be the drug whore," she said. "The woman who travelled with the courier, keeping her eyes open and her body available at all times. I was to sleep with men – or women, it made no difference – performing whatever services they wished." Antonia winced, the memories sickening to her. "The drug whore is valuable to the courier. She can do things he cannot do, being bribe and decoy and unsuspected watchdog. I was . . . trained. I let them think I had no resistance left. My courier was chosen, a foul-mouthed animal who could not wait to have me, for everyone knew he would, and I had been the favourite of the strongest; it gave him status. I was sick to my stomach at what was before me, but I counted the hours, knowing that each one brought me closer to what I had dreamed of for months. My filthy courier and I were taken to La Spezia where we were smuggled aboard a freighter, our destination Marseilles and the contact who would set up the drug runs.

"The courier could not wait, and I was ready for him. We were put into a storage room below deck. The ship was not scheduled to sail for over an hour, so I said to the pig that perhaps we should wait and not risk being intruded upon. But he would not and I knew he would not; if he had I would have provoked him, displaying one breast at a time, groping his soiled trousers if I had to. For each minute was precious to me. I knew I could not go out to sea; once at sea what remained of my life was over. I had made a promise to myself. I would leap into the water at night and drown in peace rather than face Marseilles where the horror would begin again. But I did not have to . . ."

Antonia stopped, the pain of the memory choking her. Bray took her hand and held it in his. "Go on," he said. She had to say it. It was the final moment she had to somehow face and exorcize; he felt it as surely as if it were his own.

"The pig pulled off my coat and tore the blouse from my chest. It did not matter that I was willing to remove them, he had to show his bull strength; he had to rape, for he was taking – not being given. He ripped the skirt off my waist until I stood naked before him. Like a maniac, he removed his own clothes and placed himself under the light, I suppose so that I might stand in awe of his nakedness.

"He grabbed me by the hair and forced me to my knees . . . to his waist . . . and

187

I was sick beyond sickness. But I knew the time was coming, and so I shut my eyes and played my part and thought about the beautiful hills in Porto Vecchio, where my grandmother lived ... where I would live for the rest of my life.

"It happened. The courier threw himself upon me, grunting like an animal, his sweat pouring over me, his stench filling my nostrils.

"I moved us both closer to the coil of rope, shouting in frenzied whispers the things my rapist wanted to hear, as I inched my hand towards the middle of the coil. My moment had come. I had carried a knife – a plain dinner knife I had sharpened on stone – and had shoved it into the coil of rope. I touched the handle and thought again about the beautiful hills in Porto Vecchio.

"And as that scum lay naked on top of me, I raised the knife behind him and plunged it into his back. He screamed and tried to raise himself, but the wound was too deep. I pulled it out and brought it down again, and again, and again ... and, *O mother of Christ*, again and *again*! I could not *stop killing*!"

She had said it, and now she cried uncontrollably, Scofield held her, stroking her hair, saying nothing for there was nothing he could say that would ease the pain. Finally, the terrible control she forced upon herself returned.

"It had to be done. You understand that, don't you?" Bray said.

She nodded, "Yes."

"He didn't deserve to live, that's clear to you, isn't it?"

"Yes."

"That's the first step, Antonia. You've got to accept it. We're not in a court of law where lawyers can argue philosophies. For us, it's cut and dried. It's a war and you kill because if you don't, someone will kill you."

She breathed deeply, her eyes roaming over his face, her hand still in his. "You are an odd man. You say the right words, but I have the feeling you don't like saying them."

I don't. I do not like what I am. I did not choose my life, it fell down upon me. I am in a tunnel deep in the earth and I cannot get out. The right words are a comfort. And most of the time I need them for my sanity.

Bray squeezed her hand. "What happened after ... ?"

"After I killed the courier?"

"After you killed the animal who raped you – who would have killed you."

"*Grazie ancora*," said Antonia. "I dressed in his clothes, rolled up the trousers, pushing my hair into the cap, and filling out the large jacket with what was left of my blouse and skirt. I made my way up to the deck. The sky was dark, but there was light on the pier. Dock workers were walking up and down the gangplank carrying boxes like an army of ants. It was simple. I got in line and walked off the ship."

"Very good," said Scofield, meaning it.

"It was not difficult. Except when I first put my foot on the ground."

"Why? What happened?"

"I wanted to scream. I wanted to shout and laugh and run off the pier yelling to everyone that I was free. *Free!* The rest was very easy. The courier had been given money; it was in his trousers' pocket. It was more than enough to get me to Genoa, where I bought clothes and a ticket on the plane to Corsica. I was in Bastia by noon the next day."

"And from there to Porto Vecchio?"

"Yes. Free!"

"Not exactly. God knows the prison was different, but you were still a prisoner. Those hills were your cell."

Antonia looked away. "I would have been happy there for the rest of my life. Since I was a child I loved the valley and the mountains."

"Keep the memories," said Bray. "Don't try to go back."

She turned her head towards him. "You said one day I could! Those men must pay for what they did! You, yourself, agreed to that!"

"I said I hoped they would. Maybe they will, but let others do the work, not you. Someone would blow your head off if you set foot in those hills." Scofield released her hand and brushed away the strands of dark hair that had fallen over her cheek when she turned so abruptly to him. Something disturbed him; he was not sure what it was. Something was missing, a quantum jump had been made, a step omitted. "I know it's not fair to ask you to talk about it, but I'm confused. These drug runs... how are they mounted? You say a courier is chosen, a woman assigned to travel with him, both to meet a contact at some given location?"

"Yes. A specific article of clothing is worn by the woman and the contact approaches her first. He pays for an hour of her time and they go off together, the courier following. If anything happens, anything like police interception, the courier claims he is the girl's *mezzano* . . . pimp."

"So the contact and the courier rendezvous through the woman. Is the narcotics delivery made then?"

"I don't think so. Remember, I never actually made a run, but I believe the contact only sets up the distribution schedules. Where the drugs are to be taken and who is to receive them. After that, he sends the courier to a source, again using the whore as his protection."

"So if there are any arrests, the . . . whore . . . takes the fall?"

"Yes. Drug authorities do not pay much attention to such women; they're let out quickly."

"But the source is now known, the schedules in hand and the courier protected . . ." What *was* it? Bray stared at the wall, trying to sort out the facts, trying to spot the omission that bothered him so. Was it in the pattern?

"Most of the risks are reduced to the minimum," said Antonia. "Even the delivery runs are made in such a way that the merchandise can be abandoned at a moment's notice. At least, that's what I gathered from the other girls."

" 'Most of the risks' . . ." repeated Scofield, " 'reduced to a minimum'?"

"Not all, of course, but a great many. It is very well organized. Each step has what is called a *covata evasione*. A way to escape."

"Organized? Escape . . . ?" *Organized!* That was *it*. Minimum risks, maximum returns! It *was* the pattern, the *entire* pattern. It went back to the beginning . . . to the concept *itself*. "Antonia, tell me, where did the contacts come from? How did they reach the Brigades in the first place?"

"The Brigades make a great deal of money from narcotics. The drug market is its main source of income."

"But how did it start? When?"

"A few years ago, when the Brigades began to expand."

"It didn't just *happen*. *How* did it happen?"

"I can only tell you what I heard. A man came to the leaders – several were in jail. He told them to find him when they got out on the streets again. He could lead them to large sources of money that could be made without the heavy risks involved in robbery and kidnapping."

"In other words," said Scofield, thinking rapidly as he spoke, "he offered to finance them in a major way with minor effort. Teams of two people going out for three or four weeks – and returning with something like nine hundred thousand lire. Seventy thousand dollars for a month's work. Minimum risk, maximum return. Very few personnel involved."

"Yes. In the beginning, the contacts came from him, that man. They in turn led to others. As you say, it does not take many people and they bring in large amounts of money."

"So the Brigades can concentrate on their true calling," completed Bray sardonically. "The disruption of the social order. In a single word, terrorism." He got up from the bed. "That man who came to see the leaders in jail. Did he stay in touch with them?"

She frowned. "Again, I can only tell you what I heard. He was never seen after the second meeting."

"I'll bet he wasn't. Every negotiation always five times removed from the source . . . A geometric progression, no single line to retrace. That's how they do it."

"Who?"

"The Matarese."

Antonia stared at him. "Why do you say that?"

"Because it's the only explanation. Serious dealers in narcotics wouldn't *touch* maniacs like the Brigades. It's a controlled situation, a charade mounted to finance terrorism, so the Matarese can continue to finance the guns and the killing. In Italy it's the Red Brigades; in Germany, Baader-Meinhof; in Lebanon, the PLO; in my country, the Minutemen and the Weathermen, the Ku-Klux-Klan and the JDL and all the goddamn fools who blew up banks and laboratories and embassies. Each financed differently, secretly. All pawns for the Matarese – maniacal pawns, and that's the scary thing. The longer they're fed the bigger they grow, and the bigger they grow the more damage they do." He reached for her hand, aware that he had done so only after they had touched. "What the hell is it all about?"

"You are convinced, aren't you? That it's happening."

"Now more than ever. You just showed me how one small part of the whole is manipulated. I knew – or thought I knew – it was *being* manipulated but I didn't know how. Now I do and it doesn't take much imagination to think of variations. It's a guerilla war with a thousand battlegrounds, none of them defined."

Antonia lifted his hand, as though reassuring herself it was there, freely given; and then her dark brown eyes shifted to his, suddenly questioning. "You talk as if it were new to you, this war. Surely that's not so. You're an intelligence agent . . ."

"I was," corrected Bray. "Not any more."

"That doesn't change what you know. You said to me only a moment ago that certain things must be accepted, that courts and *avvocati* had no place, that one killed in order not to be killed oneself. Is this war so different now?"

"More than I can explain," answered Scofield, glancing up at the white wall. "We were professionals and there were rules – most of them our own, most harsh, but there *were* rules and we abided by them. We knew what we were doing, nothing was pointless. I guess you could say we knew when to stop." He turned back to her. "These are wild animals, let loose in the streets. They have no rules. They don't know when to stop, and those who are financing them never want them to learn. Don't fool yourself; they're capable of paralysing governments."

Bray caught himself, his voice trailing off. He heard his own words and they astonished him. *He had said it.* In a single phrase he had said it! It was there all the time and neither he nor Taleniekov had seen it. They had approached it, circled it, used words that came close to defining it, but they had never clearly faced it.

. . . they're capable of paralysing governments . . .

When paralysis spreads, control is lost, all functions stop. A vacuum is created for a force *not* paralysed to move into the host and assume control.

You will inherit the earth. You will have your own again. Other words, spoken by a madman seventy years ago. Yet those words were not political; they were, in fact, *a-political.* Nor did they apply to given borders, no single nation rising to ascendancy. Instead, they were directed to a council, a group of men bound together by a common bond.

But those men were dead; who were they now? And what bound them together? *Now. Today.*

"What is it?" asked Antonia, seeing the strained expression on his face.

"There is a timetable," said Bray, his voice barely above a whisper. "It's being orchestrated. The terrorism escalates every month, as if on schedule. Blackburn, Yurievich . . . they *were* tests, probes for reaction at the highest level. Winthrop raised alarms in those circles; he had to be silenced. It all fits."

"And you're talking to yourself. You hold my hand, but you're talking to yourself."

Scofield looked at her, struck by another thought. He had heard two remarkable stories from two remarkable women, both tales rooted in violence as both women were tied to the violent world of Guillaume de Matarese. The dying *istrebitel* had said in Moscow that the answer might lie in Corsica. The answer did not, but the first clues to that answer did. Without Sophia Pastorine and Antonia Gravet, mistress and descendant, there was nothing; each in her own way had provided startling revelations. The enigma that was the Matarese remained still an enigma, but it was no longer inexplicable. It had form; it had purpose. Men bound together by some common cause, whose objective was to paralyse governments and assume control . . . *to inherit the earth.*

Therein lay the possibility of catastrophe: that same earth could be blown up in the process of inheriting it.

"I'm talking to myself," agreed Bray, "because I've changed my mind. I said I wanted you to help me, but you've gone through enough. There are others; I'll find them."

"I see." Antonia pressed her elbows into the bed, raising herself. "Just like that, I'm no longer needed?"

"No."

"Why was I considered at all?"

Scofield paused before replying; he wondered how she would accept the truth. "You were right before: it *was* one or the other. Enlisting you or killing you."

Antonia winced. "But that is no longer true. It's not necessary to kill me?"

"No. It'd be pointless. You won't say anything. You weren't lying, I know what you've lived through. You don't want to go back; you were going to kill yourself rather than land in Marseilles. I believe you would have."

"Then what's to become of me?"

"I found you in hiding, I'll send you back in hiding. I'll give you money, and in the morning get you papers and a flight out of Rome to some place very far away. I'll write a couple of letters; you'll give them to the people I tell you to. You'll be fine." Bray stopped for a moment. He could not help himself; he touched her swollen cheek and brushed aside a strand of hair. "You may even find another valley in a mountain, Antonia. As beautiful as the one you left, but with a difference. You won't be a prisoner there. No one from this life will ever bother you again."

"Including you, Brandon Scofield?"

"Yes."

"Then I think you had better kill me."

"What?"

"I will *not* leave! You cannot force me to, you cannot send me away because it is convenient . . . or *worse*, because you pity me!" Antonia's dark Corsican eyes glistened again. "What *right* have you? Where were you when the terrible things were done? To *me*, not to *you*. Don't make such decisions for me! Kill me first!"

"I don't want to kill you – I don't *have* to. You wanted to be free, Antonia. I'm offering you that freedom. Take it. Don't be a damn fool."

"*You're* the fool! I can help you in ways no one else could!"

"How? The courier's whore?"

"If need be, *yes*! Why not?"

"For Christ's sake, *why*?"

The girl was rigid; her answer was spoken quietly. "Because of things you said . . ."

"I know," interrupted Scofield. "I told you to get angry."

"There is something else. You said that all around the world, people who believe in causes – many not wisely, many with anger and defiance – are being manipulated by others, encouraged to violence and murder. Well, I've seen something of causes. Not all are unwise, and not all believers are animals. There are those of us who want to change this unfair world, and it is our right to try! And no one had the right to turn us into whores and killers. You call these manipulators the Matarese. I say they are richer, more powerful, but no better than the Brigades, who kill children and make liars and murderers out of people like me! I *will* help you. I will *not* be sent away!"

Bray studied her battered but still lovely face. "You're all alike," he said. "You can't stop making speeches."

Antonia smiled; it was a wry smile, engaging yet shy. "Most of the time, they're all we have." The smile disappeared, replaced by a sadness Scofield was not sure he understood. "There's another thing."

"What's that?"

"You. I've watched you. You are a man with so much sorrow. It's as clear on your face as the marks on my body. But I can remember when I was happy. Can you?"

"The question's not relevant."

"It is to me."

"Why?"

"I could say you saved my life and that would be enough, but that life wasn't worth much. You have given me something else: reason to leave the hills. I never thought anyone could ever do that for me. You offered me freedom just now but you're too late. I already have it, you gave it to me. I am breathing again. So you're important to me. I would like you to remember when you were happy."

"Is this the courier's . . . woman speaking?"

"She is not a whore. She never was."

"I'm sorry."

"Don't be. It is permitted. And if that is the gift you want, take it. I would like to think there are others."

Bray suddenly ached. The ingenuousness of her offer moved him, pained him. She was hurt and he had hurt her again and he knew why. He was afraid; he preferred whores; he did not want to go to bed with anyone he cared about – it was better not to remember a face or recall a voice. It was far better to remain deep within the earth; he had been there so long. And now this woman wanted to pull him out and he was afraid.

"You learn the things I teach you, that'll be gift enough."

"Then you'll let me stay?"

"You just said there wasn't anything I could do about it."

"I meant that."

"I know you did. If I thought otherwise I'd be on the telephone to one of the best counterfeiters in Rome."

"Why *are* we in Rome? Will you tell me now?"

Bray did not answer for a moment; then he nodded. "Why not? To find what's left of a family named Scozzi."

"Is it one of the names my grandmother gave you?"

"The first. They were from Rome."

"They're still from Rome," said Antonia, as if commenting on the weather. "At least a branch of the family, and not far outside Rome."

Amazed, Scofield looked at her. "How do you know?"

"The Red Brigades. They kidnapped a nephew of the Scozzi-Paravicinis from an estate near Tivoli. His index finger was cut off and sent to the family along with the ransom demand."

Scofield remembered the newspaper stories; the young man had been released, but Bray did not recall the name Scozzi, only Paravicini. However, he recalled something else: no ransom had ever been paid. The negotiations had been intense, a young life in balance. But there'd been a breakdown, a defection, the nephew released by a frightened kidnapper, several *Brigatisti* subsequently killed, led into an ambush by the defector.

Had the Red Brigades been taught a lesson by one of their unseen sponsors?

"Were you involved?" he asked. "In *any* way?"

"No. I was at the camp in Medicina."

"Did you overhear anything?"

"A great deal. The talk was mainly about traitors and how to kill them in brutal ways to make examples of them. The leaders always talked like that. With the Scozzi–Paravicini kidnapping it was very important to them. The traitor had been bribed by the Fascists."

"What do you mean by 'Fascists'?"

"A banker who represented the Scozzis years ago. The Paravicini interests authorized payment."

"How did he reach him?"

"With a large sum of money there are ways. Nobody really knows."

Bray got up from the bed. "I won't ask you how you're feeling, but are you up to getting out of here?"

"Of course," she replied, wincing as she swung her long legs over the side of the bed. The pain struck her; a sharp intake of breath followed. She remained still for a moment; Scofield held her shoulders.

Again he could not help himself; he touched her face. "The forty-eight hours are over," he said softly. "I'll cable Taleniekov in Helsinki."

"What does that mean?"

"It means you're alive and well and living in Rome. Come on, I'll help you dress."

She brought her fingers up to his hand. "If you had suggested that yesterday I am not sure what I'd have said."

"What do you say now?"

"Help me."

20

There was an expensive restaurant on the Via Frascati owned by the three Crispi brothers, the oldest of whom ran the establishment with the perceptions of an accomplished thief and the eyes of a hungry jackal, both masked by a cherubic face, and a sweeping ebullience. Most who inhabited the velvet lairs of Rome's *dolce vita* adored Crispi, for he was always understanding and discreet, the discretion more valuable than the sympathy. Messages left with him were passed between men and their mistresses, wives and their lovers, the makers and the made. He was a rock in the sea of frivolity, and the frivolous children of all ages loved him.

Scofield used him. Five years ago when NATO's problems had reached into Italy, Bray had put his clamp on Crispi. The restaurateur had been a willing drone.

Crispi was one of the men Bray had wanted to see before Antonia had told him about the Scozzi-Paravicinis; now it was imperative. If anyone in Rome could shed light on an aristocratic family like the Scozzi-Paravicinis, it was the effusive crown prince of foolishness that was Crispi. They would have lunch at the restaurant on the Via Frascati.

An early lunch for Rome, considered Scofield, putting down his coffee and looking at his watch. It was barely noon, the sun outside the window warming the sitting room of the hotel suite, the sounds of traffic floating up from the Via Veneto below. The doctor had called the Excelsior and made the arrangements shortly past midnight, explaining confidentially to the manager that a wealthy patient was in sudden need of quarters – confidentially. Bray and Antonia had been met at the delivery entrance and taken up the service elevator to a suite on the eighth floor.

He had ordered a bottle of brandy and poured three successive glasses for Antonia. The cumulative effects of the alcohol, the medication, the pain and the tension had brought about the state he knew was best: sleep. He had carried her into the bedroom, undressed her and put her to bed, covering her, touching her face, resisting the ache that would have placed him beside her.

On his way back to the couch in the sitting room he had remembered the clothes from the Via de Condotti, he had stuffed them in his duffelbag before leaving the *pensione*. The white hat was the worse for the packing, but the silk dress was less wrinkled than he had thought it would be. He had hung them up before sleeping himself.

He had got up at ten, gone down to the shops in the lobby to buy a flesh-coloured makeup base that would cover Antonia's bruises and a pair of Gucci sunglasses that looked remarkably like the eyes of a grasshopper. He had left them along with the clothes on the chair next to the bed.

She had found them an hour ago, the dress the first thing she had seen when she had opened her eyes.

"You are my personal *fanciulla*!" she had called out to him. "I am a princess in a fairy tale and my handmaidens wait upon me! What will my socialist comrades think?"

"That you know something they don't know," Bray had replied. "They'd hang Marx in effigy to change places with you. Have some coffee and then get dressed. We're having lunch with a disciple of the Medicis. You'll love his politics."

She was dressing now, humming fragments of an unfamiliar tune that sounded like a Corsican sea shanty. She had found part of her mind again and a semblance of freedom; he hoped she could keep both. There were no guarantees. The hunt would accelerate at the restaurant in the Via Frascati and she was part of it now.

The humming stopped, replaced by the sound of high-heeled shoes crossing a marble floor. She stood in the door and the ache returned to Scofield's chest. The sight of her moved him and he felt oddly helpless. Stranger still, for a moment he wanted only to hear her speak, listen to her voice, as if hearing it would somehow confirm her immediate presence. Yet she did not speak. She stood there, so lovely, so vulnerable, a grown-up child seeking approval, resentful that she felt the need to seek it. The silk dress was tinged with deep red, complementing her skin, bronzed by the Corsican sun; the large wide hat was angled, framing half her face in white, the other half bordered by her long dark brown hair. The strains of France and Italy had merged in Antonia Gravet; the results were striking.

"You look fine," said Bray, getting up from the chair.

"Does the makeup cover the marks on my face?"

"I forgot about them so I guess it does." In the ache he *had* forgotten. "How are you feeling?"

"I'm not sure. I think the brandy did as much damage as the *Brigatisti*."

"There's a remedy. A few glasses of wine."

"I think not, thank you."

"Whatever you say. I'll get your coat; it's in the closet." He started across the room, then stopped, seeing her wince. "You're not all right, are you? It hurts."

"No, please, really, I'm fine. The salve your doctor friend gave me is very good, very soothing. He's a nice man."

"I want you to go back and see him any time you need help," he said. "Whenever anything bothers you."

"You sound as though you won't be with me," she replied. I thought we settled that. I accepted your offer of employment, remember?"

Bray smiled. "It'd be hard to forget, but we haven't defined the job. We'll be together for a while in Rome, then depending on what we find, I'll be moving on. Your job will be to stay here and relay messages between Taleniekov and me."

"I am to be a *telegraph* service?" asked Antonia. "What kind of job is that?"

"A vital one. I'll explain as we go along. Come on, I'll get your coat." He saw her close her eyes again. Pain had jolted her. "Antonia, listen to me. When you hurt, don't try to hide it, that doesn't help anybody. How bad is it?"

"Not so bad. It will pass, I know. I've been through this before."

"Do you want to go back to the doctor?"

"No. But thank you for your concern."

The care was still there, but Scofield resisted it. "My only concern is that a person can't function well when he's hurt. Mistakes are made when he's in pain. You won't be allowed any mistakes."

"I may have that glass of wine after all."

"Please do," he said.

They stood in the foyer of the restaurant, Bray aware of the glances Antonia attracted. Beyond the delicate lattice work that was the entrance to the dining room, the oldest Crispi was all teeth and obsequiousness. When he saw Bray he was obviously startled; for a split second his eyes became clouded, serious, then he recovered and approached them.

"*Benvenuto, amico mio!*" he cried, the crown prince of frivolity.

"It's been over a year," said Scofield, returning the firm grip. "I'm here on business for only a day or so, and wanted my friend to try your *fettucine*."

These were the words that meant Bray wished to speak privately with Crispi at the table when the opportunity arose.

"They are the best in Rome, *signorina*!" Crispi snapped his fingers for an inferior brother to show the couple to their table. "I shall hear you say it yourself momentarily. But first, have some wine, in case the sauce is not perfect!" He winked broadly, giving Scofield's hand an additional clasp to signify he understood. Crispi never came to Bray's table unless summoned.

A waiter brought them a chilled bottle of Pouilly Fumé, compliments of the *fratelli*, but it was not until the *fettucine* had come and gone that Crispi came to the table. He sat in the third chair; introductions and the small talk that accompanied them were brief.

"Antonia's working with me," Scofield explained, "but she's never to be mentioned. To anyone, do you understand?"

"Of course."

"And neither am I. If anyone from the embassy – or anywhere else – asks about me, you haven't seen me. Is that clear?"

"Clear, but unusual."

"In fact, no one's to know I'm here. Or *was* here."

"Even your own people?"

"Especially my own people. My orders supersede embassy interests. That's as plainly as I can put it."

Crispi arched his brows, nodding slowly. "Defectors?"

"That'll do."

Crispi's eyes became serious. "Very well, I have not seen you, Brandon. Then why are you here? Will you be sending people to me?"

"Only Antonia. Whenever she needs help getting cables off to me . . . and to someone else."

"Why should she need my help to send cables?"

"I want them re-routed, different points of origin. Can you do it?"

"If the idiot *Communisti* do not strike the telephone service again, it is no problem. I call a cousin in Firenzi, he sends one; an exporter in Athens or Tunis or Tel Aviv, they do the same. Everybody does what Crispi wants and no one asks a single question. But you know that."

"What about your own phones? Are they clean?"

The prince of foolishness laughed. "With what is known to be said on my telephone, there is not an official in Rome who could permit such impertinence."

Scofield remembered Robert Winthrop in Washington. "Someone else said that to me not so long ago. He was wrong."

"No doubt he was," agreed Crispi, his eyes amused. "Forgive me, Brandon, but you people deal merely in matters of state. We on the Via Frascati deal in matters of the heart. Ours take precedence where confidentiality is concerned. They always have."

Bray returned the Italian's smile. "You know, you may be right." He lifted the glass of wine to his lips. "Let me throw a name at you. Scozzi-Paravicini." He drank.

Crispi nodded reflectively. "Blood seeks money, and money seeks blood. What else is there to say?"

"Say it plainly."

"The Scozzis are one of the noblest families in Rome. The venerable *contessa* to this day is chauffeured in her restored Bugatti up the Veneto, her children pretenders to thrones long since abandoned. Unfortunately, all they had were their pretensions, not a thousand lire between them. The Paravicinis had money, a great deal of money, but not a drop of decent blood in their veins. It was a marriage made in the heavenly courts of mutual convenience."

"Whose marriage?"

"The *contessa's* daughter to Signor Bernardo Paravicini. It was a long time ago, the dowry a number of millions and gainful employment for her son, the count. He assumed his father's title."

"What's his name?"

"Guillamo. Count Guillamo Scozzi."

"Where does he live?"

"Wherever his interests – financial and otherwise – take him. He has an estate near his sister's in Tivoli, but I don't think he's there very often. Why do you ask? Is he connected with defectors? It's hardly likely."

"He may not be aware of it. It could be he's being used by people who work for him."

"Even more unlikely. Beneath his charming personality, there's the mind of a Borgia. Take my word for it."

"How do you know that?"

"I know *him*," said Crispi, smiling. "He and I are not so different."

Bray leaned forward. "I want to meet him. Not as Scofield, of course. As someone else. Can you arrange it?"

"Perhaps. If he's in Italy, and I think he is. I read somewhere that his wife is a patron of the *Festa Villa d'Este*, being held tomorrow night. It is a charity affair for the gardens. He would not miss it; as they say, everyone in Rome will be there."

"Your Rome, I trust," interrupted Scofield. "Not mine."

He watched her across the hotel room as she lifted the skirt out of the box and folded it on her lap as though checking for imperfections. He understood that the pleasure he derived from buying her things was out of place. Clothes were a necessity; it was as simple as that, but his knowing it did not erase the warmth that spread through him watching her.

The prisoner was free, the decisions restored, and although she had commented about the exorbitant prices at the Excelsior she had not refused to let him buy clothes for her at the shops. It had been a game. She would look over at Bray; if he nodded, she would frown, feigning disapproval – invariably glancing at the price tag – then slowly re-evaluate, ultimately acknowledging his taste.

His wife used to do that in West Berlin. In West Berlin it had been one of *their* games. His Katrine was always worried about money. They were going to have children one day, money was important, and the government was not a generous corporation. No Grade Twelve foreign service officer was about to open a Swiss bank account.

Of course, by then Scofield had. In Bern. And in Paris and London and, naturally,

Berlin. He had not told her; his true professional life had never touched her. Until it touched her with finality. Had things been different, he might have given her one of those accounts. After he had transferred out of Consular Operations into a civilized branch of the State Department.

Goddamn it! He was *going* to! It had only been a matter of *weeks!*

"You are so far away."

"What?" Bray brought the glass to his lips; it was a reflex gesture for he had finished the drink. It occurred to him that he was drinking too much.

"You're looking at me, but I don't think you see me."

"I certainly do. I miss the hat. I liked the white hat."

She smiled. "You don't wear a hat inside. The waiter who brought us dinner would have thought me silly."

"You wore it at Crispi's place. That waiter didn't."

"A restaurant is different."

"Both inside." He got up and walked to the small table where the whisky was next to an ice bucket. He poured himself a drink.

"Thank you again for these." Antonia glanced at the boxes and shopping bags beside the chair. "It is like Christmas Eve, I don't know which to open next." She laughed. "But there was never a Christmas in Corsica like this! *Papa* would scowl for a month at the sight of such things. Yes, I *do* thank you."

"No need to." Scofield remained by the table, adding more whisky to his glass. "They're equipment. Like an office typewriter or an adding machine or file cabinets. They go with the job."

"I see." She replaced the skirt and the blouse into the box. "But you don't," she said.

"I beg your pardon?"

"*Niente.* Does the whisky help you relax?"

"You could say that. Would you like one?"

"No, thank you. I'm more relaxed than I have been in a very long time. It would be wasted."

"To each according to his needs. Or wants," said Scofield, lowering himself into the chair. "You can go to bed, if you like. Tomorrow's going to be a long day."

"Does my company bother you?"

"No, of course not."

"But you prefer to be alone."

"I hadn't thought about it."

She used to say that. In West Berlin, when there were problems and I would sit by myself trying to think as others might think. She would be talking and I would not hear her. She used to get angry — not angry, hurt — and say, "You'd rather be alone, wouldn't you?" And I would, but I could not explain. Perhaps if I had explained . . . Perhaps an explanation would have served as a warning.

"If something's troubling you, why not talk about it?"

Oh, God, her words! In West Berlin.

"Stop trying to be *somebody* else!" He heard the statement shouted in his own voice. It was the whisky, the goddamn *whisky!* "I'm sorry, I didn't mean that," he

199

added quickly, putting the glass down. "I'm tired and I've had too much to drink. I didn't mean it."

"Of course you did," said Antonia, getting up. "I think I understand now. But you should understand also. I am not somebody else. I have had to pretend to be someone who was not me and that is the surest way to know who you are. I am myself, and you helped me – find that person again." She turned and walked rapidly into the bedroom, closing the door behind her.

"Toni, I'm *sorry* . . ." Bray stood up, furious with himself. In an outburst, he had revealed far more than he cared to. He hated the loss of control.

There was a knock on the door, the hallway door; Scofield spun around. Instinctively felt the holster strapped to his chest under his jacket. He went to the side of the door and spoke.

"*Si? Chic'é?*"

"*Uno messaggio, Signor Pastorine. Da vostro amico, Crispi. Di Via Frascati.*"

Bray put his hand inside his jacket, checked the chain on the door and opened it. In the hallway stood the waiter from Crispi's who had served their table. He held up an envelope and handed it to Scofield through the open space. Crispi had taken no risks; his own man was the messenger.

"*Grazie. Uno momento,*" said Bray, reaching into his pocket for a lira note.

"*Prego,*" replied the waiter, accepting the tip.

Scofield closed the door, and tore open the envelope. Two gold-embossed tickets were attached to a note. He removed them and read Crispi's message, the hand-writing as well as the language florid.

> Word has reached Count Scozzi from the undersigned that an American named Pastor will introduce himself at Villa d'Este. The Count understands that this Pastor has extensive connections in the OPEC countries, acting frequently as a purchasing agent for oil-soaked sheiks. These are endeavours such men never discuss, so just smile and learn where the Arabian Gulf is located. The Count understands too that Pastor is merely on holiday and seeks pleasant diversions. All things considered, the Count may offer them.
>
> I kiss the hand of the *bella signorina*.
> Ciao,
> Crispi

Bray smiled. Crispi was right; no one who performed middleman services for the sheiks ever discussed those services. Profiles were kept excessively low because the stakes were excessively high. One simply did not talk about them – as he would not at Villa d'Este. Instead, he would talk of other things with Count Guillamo Scozzi.

He heard the latch turn on the bedroom door. There was a moment of hesitation before Antonia opened it. When she did, Bray realized why. She stood in the door frame in a black slip he had bought her downstairs. She had removed her brassiere, her breasts swelling against the sheer silk, her long legs outlined below in opaque darkness. She was barefoot, the bronzed skin of her calves and ankles in perfect concert with her arms and face. Her lovely face, striking yet gentle, with the dark eyes that held his without wavering, without judgement.

"You must have loved her very much," she said quietly.

"I did. It was a long time ago."

"Not long enough, apparently. You called me Toni. Was that her name?"

"No."

"I'm glad. I would not wish to be mistaken for someone else."

"You made that clear. It won't happen again."

Antonia was silent, remaining motionless in the doorway, her eyes still without judgement. When she spoke, it was a question. "Why do you refuse yourself?"

"I'm not an animal in the hold of a freighter."

"We both know that. I've seen you look at me, then look away as though it were not permitted. You're tense, but you seek no release."

"If I want that kind of . . . release . . . I know where to find it."

"I offer it to you."

"The offer will be taken under consideration."

"*Stop it!*" cried Antonia, stepping forward. "You want a whore? Then think of me as a courier's *whore!*"

"I can't do that."

"Then do not look at me the way you do! A part of you with me, another far away, what do you want?"

Please don't do this. Leave me where I was, deep in the earth, comfort in the darkness. Don't touch me, for if you do, you die. Can't you understand that? Men will call you across a barrier and they will kill you. Leave me with whores, professionals – as I am a professional. We know the rules. You don't.

She stood in front of him; he had not seen her come to him, she was simply there. He looked down at her, her face tilted up to his, her eyes close, her tears near, her lips parted.

Her whole body was trembling; she was gripped by fear, the scars had been torn away; he had ripped them because she had seen the ache in his eyes.

SHE could not erase HIS pain. What made her think he could erase hers?

And then, as if she were reading his thoughts, she whispered again.

"If you loved her so much, love me a little. It may help."

She reached up to him, her hands cupping his face, her lips inches from his, the trembling no less for the nearness. He put his arms around her; their lips touched and the ache was released. He was drawn into a wind; he felt his own tears well up in his eyes and roll down his cheeks, mingling with hers. He let his hands fall down her back, caressing her, pulling her to him, holding her, *holding* her. Please, *closer*, the moisture of her mouth arousing him, replacing the ache of pain with the ache of wanting her beside him. He swept his hand around to her breast; she pulled her own hand down and pressed it over his, pushing herself against him, revolving her body up to the rhythm that infused them both.

She pulled her mouth away. "Take me to bed. In the name of God, *take me*. And love me. Please, love me a little."

"I tried to warn you," he said, "I tried to warn us both."

He was coming out of the earth and there was sunlight above. Yet in the distance there was the darkness still. And fear; he felt it sharply. But for the moment, he chose to remain in the sunlight – if only for a while. With her.

21

The magnificence of the Villa d'Este was not lost in the chill of the evening. The floodlights had been turned on and the banks of fountains illuminated – thousands of cascading streams caught in the light as they arced in serrated ranks down the steep inclines. In the centres of the vast pools, the gushers surged up into the night, the umbrella sprays sparkling in the floodlights like diadems. And at each formation of rock constructed into a waterfall, screens of rushing silver fell in front of ancient statuary; saints and centaurs were drenched in splendour.

The gardens were officially closed to the public; only Rome's most beautiful people were invited to the *Festa Villa d'Este*. The purpose was ostensibly to raise funds for its maintenance, augmenting the dwindling government subsidies; but Scofield had the distinct impression that there was a secondary, no less desirable motive: to provide an evening when Villa d'Este could be enjoyed by its true inheritors, unencumbered by the tourist world. Crispi was right. Everyone in Rome was there.

Not his Rome, thought Bray, feeling the velvet lapels of his tuxedo. Their Rome.

The huge rooms of the villa itself had been transformed into palace courtyards, complete with banquet tables and gilded chairs lining the walls – resting spots for the courtiers and courtesans at play. Russian sable and mink, chinchilla and golden fox, draped shoulders dressed by Givenchy and Pucci; webs of diamonds and strings of pearls fell from elongated throats, and all too often from too many chins. Slender *cavalieri*, dashing in their scarlet cummerbunds and greying temples, co-existed with squat, bald men who had cigars, and more power than their appearances might signify. Music was provided by no fewer than four orchestras, ranging in size from six to twenty instruments, playing everything from the stately strains of Monteverdi to the frenzied beat of the disco. Villa d'Este belonged to the *belli Romani*.

Of all the beautiful people, one of the most striking was Antonia – Toni. (It was Toni now by dual decree arrived at in the comfort of the bed.) No jewels adorned her neck or wrists; somehow they would have been impediments to the smooth, bronzed skin set off by the simple gown of white and gold. The facial swellings had receded, as the doctor said they would. She wore no sunglasses now, her wide brown eyes reflecting the light. She was as lovely as any part of her surroundings, lovelier than most of her would-be equals, for her beauty was understated, and grew with each second of observation in the beholder's eyes.

For convenience, Toni was introduced quite simply as the rather mysterious Mr Pastor's friend from Lake Como. Certain parts of the lake were known to be retreats for the expensive children of the Mediterranean. Crispi had done his job well; he had provided just enough information to intrigue a number of guests. Those who might wish to learn the most about the quiet Mr Pastor were told the least, while others too engrossed with themselves to care about Pastor were told more, so they could relate what they had learned as gossip, which was their major industry.

Those men whose concerns were more directly – even exclusively – financial, were prone to take his elbow and inquire softly about the projected status of the dollar or the stability of investments in London, San Francisco and Buenos Aires. With such inquisitors, Scofield inclined his head briefly at some suggestions and shook it with a single motion at others. Eyebrows were raised – unobtrusively. Information had been imparted, although Bray had no idea what it was.

After one such encounter with a particularly insistent questioner he took Toni's arm and they walked through a massive archway into the next crowded "courtyard". Accepting two glasses of champagne from a waiter's tray, Bray handed one to Toni and looked around over the crystal rim as he drank.

Without having seen him before Scofield knew he had just found Count Guillamo Scozzi. The Italian was in a corner chatting with two long-legged young women, his eyes roaming from their attentive stares, glancing about the room with feigned casualness. He was a tall, slender man, a *cavaliero* complete with tails and greying hair that spread streaks from his temples throughout his perfectly groomed head. In his lapel were tiny colourful ribbons, around his waist a thin gold sash, bordered in dark red and knotted off-centre. If any missed the significance of the ribbons, they could not overlook the mark of distinction inherent in the sash; Scozzi wore his escutcheons prominently. In his late fifties the count was the embodiment of the *bello Romano*; no *Siciliano* had ever crept into the bed of his ancestors and *per Dio* the world had better know it.

"How will you find him?" asked Antonia, sipping the wine.

"I think I just have."

"Him? Over there?" she asked. Bray nodded. "You're right, I've seen his picture in the newspapers. He's a favourite subject of the *paparazzi*. Are you going to introduce yourself?"

"I don't think I'll have to. Unless I'm mistaken, he's looking for me." Scofield gestured towards a buffet table. "Let's walk over to the end table, by the pastries. He'll see us."

"But how would he know you?"

"Crispi. Our benevolent intermediary may not have bothered to describe me, but he sure as hell wouldn't overlook describing you. Not with someone like Scozzi."

"But I had those huge sunglasses on."

"You're very funny," said Bray.

It took less than a minute before they heard a mellifluous voice behind them at the buffet table.

"Signore Pastor, I believe."

They turned. "I beg your pardon? Have we met?" Scofield asked.

"We are about to, I think," said the count, extending his hand. "Scozzi. Guillamo Scozzi. It is a pleasure to make your acquaintance." The title was emphasized by its absence.

"Oh, of *course*. Count Scozzi. I told that delightful fellow Crispi I'd look you up. We arrived here less than an hour ago and it's been a little hectic. I would have recognized you, naturally, but I'm surprised you knew me."

Scozzi laughed, displaying teeth so white and so perfectly formed they could not possibly have come with the original machine. "Crispi is, indeed, delightful, but

I'm afraid a bit of a rascal. He was rapturous over *la bella signorina*." The count inclined his head to Antonia. "I see her, I find you. As always, Crispi's taste is impeccable."

"Excuse me." Scofield touched Toni's forearm. "Count Scozzi, my friend, Antonia . . . from Lake Como." The first name and the lake said it all; the count took her hand and raised it to his lips.

"An adorable creature. Rome must see more of you."

"You're too kind, Excellency," said Antonia, as if born to attend the *Festa Villa d'Este*.

"Truthfully, Mr Pastor," continued Scozzi, "I've been told that many of my more bothersome friends have been annoying you with questions. I apologize for them."

"No need to. I'm afraid Crispi's descriptions included more mundane matters." Bray smiled with disarming humility. "When people learn what I do, they ask questions. I'm used to it."

"You're very understanding."

"It's not hard to be. I just wish I were as knowledgeable as so many think I am. Usually I simply try to implement decisions taken before I got there."

"But in those decisions," said the count, "there is knowledge, is there not?"

"I hope so. Otherwise an awful lot of money's being thrown away."

"Blown away with the desert winds, as it were," clarified Scozzi. "Why do I think we actually *have* met before, Mr Pastor?"

The sudden question had been considered by Scofield; it was always a possibility and he was prepared for it. "If we had I think I'd remember; but it might have been the American embassy. Those parties were never as grand as this, but just as crowded."

"Then you are a fixture on Embassy Row?"

"Hardly a fixture, but sometimes a last-minute guest. Bray smiled, self-deprecatingly. "It seems there are times when my countrymen are as interested in asking me questions as your friends here in Tivoli."

Scozzi chuckled. "Information is often the road to heroic national stature, Mr Pastor. You are a reluctant hero."

"Not really. I have to make a living, that's all."

"I would not care to negotiate with you," said Scozzi. "I detect the mind of an experienced bargainer."

"That's too bad," replied Scofield, altering the tone of his voice just enough to signal to the Italian's inner antenna. "I thought we might talk for a bit."

"Oh?" The count glanced at Antonia. "But we bore the *bella signorina*."

"Not at all," said Toni pleasantly. "I've learned more about my friend during the last several minutes than for the past week. But I *am* famished . . ."

"Say no more," interrupted Scozzi, as if her hunger were a matter of corporate survival. He raised his hand. In a second a young, dark-haired man dressed in tails appeared beside him. "My aide will see to your needs, *signorina*. His name is Paolo and, incidentally, he is a charming dancer. I believe my wife taught him."

Paolo bowed, avoiding the count's eyes, and offered his arm to Antonia. She accepted it, stepping forward, her face turned to Scozzi and Bray.

"*Ciao*," she said, her eyes wishing Scofield good hunting.

"You are to be envied, Mr Pastor," remarked Count Guillamo Scozzi, watching the receding figure in white. "She is adorable. You bought her in Como?"

Bray glanced at the Italian. Scozzi meant exactly what he said. "To be honest with you, I'm not even sure she's ever been there," he answered, knowing the double lie was mandatory; the count could make inquiries too easily. "Actually, a friend in Ar-Riyād gave me a number to call at the lake. She joined me in Nice. From where I've never asked."

"Would you consider, however, asking her about her calendar? Tell her from me the sooner the better. She may reach me through the Paravicini offices in Torino."

"Turin?"

"Our plants in the north. Agnelli's Fiat gets far more attention, but I can assure you, Scozzi-Paravicini runs Turin – as well as a great deal of Europe."

"I never realized that."

"You didn't? I thought it was perhaps the basis for your wishing to . . . 'talk for a bit', I believe you said."

Scofield drank the last of his champagne, speaking as he took the glass from his lips. "Do you think we might go outside for a minute or two? I have a confidential message for you from a client on – let's say, the Arabian Gulf. It's why I'm here tonight."

Scozzi's eyes clouded. "A message for me? Naturally, as most of Rome and Torino, I've met casually with a number of gentlemen from the area, but none I can recall by name. But, of course, we'll take a stroll. You intrigue me." The count started forward, but Bray stopped him with a gesture.

"I'd rather we weren't seen going out together. Tell me where you'll be and I'll show up in twenty minutes."

"How extraordinary! Very well." The Italian paused. "Ippolito's Fountain, do you know it?"

"I'll find it."

"It's quite a distance. There shouldn't be anyone around."

"That's fine. Twenty minutes." Scofield nodded. Both turned and walked away, through the crowds, in opposite directions.

There were no floodlights at the fountain, nor sounds of disturbance as a man crawled around the rocks and walked silently through the foliage. Bray was taking no chances that Scozzi had stationed aides in the vicinity. If he had, Scofield would have sent a message to the Italian, naming a second, immediate rendezvous.

They were alone – or would be in a matter of minutes. The count was strolling down the path towards the fountain. Bray doubled back through a weed-filled garden, emerging on the path fifty feet behind Scozzi. He cleared his throat the moment Scozzi reached the waist-high wall of the fountain's pool. The count turned; there was just enough light from the terraces above for each to see the other. Scofield was bothered by the darkness. Scozzi could have chosen any number of places more convenient, less filled with shadows. Bray did not like shadows.

"Was it necessary to come down this far?" he asked. "I wanted to see you alone, but I hadn't figured on walking half-way back to Rome."

"Nor had I, Mr Pastor, until you made the statement that you did not care to have us seen leaving together. It brought to my mind the obvious. It is, perhaps, not to my advantage to be seen talking in private with you. You are a broker for the sheiks."

"Why should that bother you?"

"Why did you wish to leave separately?" Scozzi had a quick mind, bearing out Crispi's allusion to a Borgia mentality.

"A matter of being *too* obvious, I'd say. But if someone wandered down here and saw us, that would also be too obvious. There's a middle ground, a casual encounter in the gardens, for example."

"You have the encounter and no one will see us," said the count, fingering his thin gold sash in the shadows. "There is only one entrance to the fountain of Ippolito; it is forty metres behind us. I have an aide standing there. Guillamo Scozzi has been known to stroll with a companion of his choice down − if you will − a primrose path. At such times he does not care to be disturbed."

"Does my doing what I do call for those precautions?"

The count raised his head. "Remember, Mr Pastor. Scozzi-Paravicini deals throughout all Europe and both Americas. We look constantly for new markets, but we do not look for Arab capital. It is highly suspect; barriers are being erected everywhere to prevent its excessive infusion. We would not care to be so scrutinized. Jewish interests in Paris and New York alone could cost us dearly."

"What I have to say to you has nothing to do with Scozzi-Paravicini," said Scofield. "It concerns the Scozzi part, not the Paravicini."

"You allude to a sensitive area, Mr Pastor. Please be specific."

"You are the son of Count Alberto Scozzi, aren't you?"

"It is well known. As are my contributions to the growth of Paravicini Industries. The significance of the corporate conversion to the name of *Scozzi-Paravicini* is, I trust, not lost on you."

"It isn't, but even if it were, it doesn't matter. I'm only a go−between, supposedly the first of several contacts, each farther removed from the other. As far as I'm concerned, I ran into you casually at a charity affair in Tivoli. We never had this talk."

"Your message must, indeed, be dramatic. Who sends it?"

It was Bray's turn to raise his hand. "Please. As we understand the rules, identities are never specific at the first conference. Only a geographical area and a political equation that involves hypothetical antagonists."

Scozzi's eyes narrowed; the lids fell in concentration. "Go on," he said.

"You're a count, so I'll bend the rules a bit. Let's say there's a prince living in a sizable country, a sheikdom, really, on the Gulf. His uncle, the king, is from another era; he's old and senile but his word is law, just as it was when he led a Bedouin tribe in the desert. He's squandering millions with bad investments, depleting the sheikdom's resources, taking too much out of the ground too quickly. This hypo-thetical prince would like him removed. For everyone's good. He appeals to the council through the son of Alberto Scozzi, named for the Corsican *padrone*, Guillaume . . . That's the message. Now I'd like to speak for myself."

"Who *are* you?" interrupted the Italian, his eyes now wide. "Who sent you?"

206

"Let me finish," said Bray quickly. He had to get past the initial jolt, jump to a second plateau. "As an observer of this . . . hypothetical equation, I can tell you it's reached a crisis. There isn't a day to lose. The prince needs an answer and, frankly, if I bring it to him, I'll be a much richer man for it. You, of course, can name the council's price. And I can tell you that . . . fifty million, American, is not out of the question."

"Fifty *million*."

It worked; the second plateau was reached. Even for a man like Guillamo Scozzi, the amount was staggering. His arrogant lips were parted in amazement. It was the moment to complicate, to stun again.

"The sum is conditional, of course. It's a maximum figure that presumes an immediate answer, eliminating subsequent contacts, and delivery of the package within seven days. It won't be easy. The old man is guarded day and night by *fida'is* – they're a collection of mad dogs who . . ." Scofield paused. "But then, I don't have to tell you about anything related to Hasan ibn as-Sabbāh, do I? From what I gather the Corsican drew on him pretty extensively. At any rate, the prince suggests a programmed suicide."

"*Enough!*" whispered Scozzi. "Who *are* you, Pastor? Is the name intended to mean something to me? Pastor? *Priest?* Are you a high priest sent to *test* me?" The Italian's voice rose stridently. "You talk of things buried in the past. How *dare you?*"

"I'm talking about fifty million American dollars. And don't tell me – or my client – about things buried. His father was buried with his throat slit from chin to collar bone by a maniac sent by the council. Check your records, if you keep them; you'll find it. My client wants his own back again and he's willing to pay roughly fifty times what his father's brother paid." Bray stopped for a moment and shook his head in disapproval and sudden frustration. "This is crazy! I told him for less than half the amount I could buy him a legitimate revolution, sanctioned by the United Nations. But he wants it *this* way. With you. And I think I know why. He said something to me; I don't know if it's part of his message but I'll deliver it anyway. He said, 'The way of the Matarese is the only way. They'll see my faith.' He wants to join you."

Guillamo Scozzi recoiled; his legs were pressed against the wall of the fountain, his arms rigidly at his side. "What right have you to say these things to me? You are insane, a madman! I don't know what you're talking about."

"Really? Then we've got the wrong man. We'll find the right one; I'll find him. We were given the words; we know the response."

"What words?"

"*Perro nostro* . . ." Scofield let his voice trail off, his eyes riveted on Scozzi's lips in the dim light.

Involuntarily, the lips parted. The Italian was about to utter the third word, complete the phrase that had lived for seventy years in the remote hills of Porto Vecchio. Guillamo Scozzi was about to say . . . *circulo*.

He did not. Instead, he whispered again, shock replaced by a concern so deeply felt he could barely be heard. "My *God!* You cannot . . . you *must* not! Where have you *come* from? What have you been *told?*"

"Just enough to know I've found the right man. One of them, at any rate. Do we deal?"

"Do not presume, Mr Pastor! Or whatever your name is." There was fury now in the Italian's voice.

"Pastor'll do. All right, I've got my answer. You pass. I'll tell my client." Bray turned.

"*Fermator!*"

"*Perchè? Che causa?*" Scofield spoke over his shoulder without moving.

"Your Italian is very quick, very fluent."

"So are several other languages. It helps when you travel a lot. I travel a lot. What do you want?"

"You will stay here until I say you may leave."

"Really?" said Scofield, turning to face Scozzi again. "What's the point? I've got my answer."

"You'll do as I tell you. I have only to raise my voice and an aide will be beside you, blocking any departure you may consider."

Bray tried to understand. This powerful *consigliere* could deny everything – he had, after all, said nothing – and have a strange American followed. Or he could call for help; or he might simply walk away himself and send armed men to find him. He could do any of these things – he *was* part of the Matarese; the admission was in his eyes – but he chose to do none of them.

Then Scofield thought he did understand. Guillamo Scozzi, the quick-thinking industrial pirate with the Borgia mentality, was not sure what he should do. He was caught in a dilemma that had suddenly overwhelmed him. It had all happened too fast, he was not prepared to make a decision. So he made none.

Which meant that there was someone else – someone near-by, accessible – who *could*.

Someone at Villa d'Este that night.

"Does this mean that you're reconsidering?" asked Bray.

"It means *nothing!*"

"Then why should I stay? I don't think you should give orders to me; I'm not one of your Praetorians. We don't deal; it's as simple as that."

"It is *not* that simple!" Scozzi's voice rose again, fear more pronounced than anger now.

"I say it is, and I say the hell with it," said Scofield, turning again. It was important that the Italian summon his unseen guard. Very important.

Scozzi did so. "*Veni! Presto!*"

Bray heard racing feet on the dark path; in seconds a broad-shouldered, stocky man in evening clothes came running out of the shadows.

"*Esitare! Vicino!*"

The guard did not hesitate. He pulled out a short-barrelled revolver, levelling it at Bray. Scozzi spoke, as if imposing a control on himself, explaining the unnecessary.

"These are troubled times, Signore Pastor. All of us travel with these Praetorians you just mentioned. Terrorists are everywhere."

The moment was irresistible. It was the instant to insert the final, verbal blade.

"That's something you people should know about. Terrorists, I mean. Like the Brigades. Do the orders come from the shepherd boy?"

It was as though Scozzi had been struck by an unseen hammer. His upper body convulsed, fending off the blow, feeling its impact, trying to recover but not sure it was possible. In the dim light, Scofield could see perspiration forming at the Italian's hairline, matting the perfectly groomed grey temples. His eyes were the eyes of a terrified animal.

"*Rimanere*," he whispered to the guard, then rushed away up the dark path.

Scofield turned to the man, looking afraid and speaking in Italian. "I don't know what this is all about any more than *you* do! I offered your boss a lot of money from someone and he goes crazy. Christ, I'm just a salesman!" The guard said nothing, but Bray's obvious fear relieved him. "Do you mind if I have a cigarette? Guns scare the hell out of me."

"Go ahead," said the broad-shouldered man.

It was the last thing he would say for several hours. Scofield reached into his pocket with his left hand, his right at his side – in shadow, under the guard's elbow. As he pulled out a pack of cigarettes, he shot his right hand up, clasping his fingers around the short barrel of the guard's revolver, twisting hand and weapon violently in a counterclockwise motion. Dropping the cigarettes, he gripped the man's throat with his left hand, choking off all sound, propelling the guard off the path, over the bordering rocks into the dense foliage beyond. As the man fell, Bray ripped the gun away from the twisted wrist, and brought the handle down sharply on the man's skull. The guard went limp; Scofield pulled him farther into the weeds.

No second could be wasted. Guillamo Scozzi had raced away seeking counsel; it was the only explanation. Somewhere quiet, on a terrace or in a room, the *consigliere* was bringing his shocking information to another. Or others.

Bray ran up the path, keeping in the shadows as much as possible, slowing down to a rapid walk as he emerged on the plateau of terraces that fronted the final incline of steps into the villa itself. Somewhere just above, *somewhere* was the panicked Scozzi. To whom was he running? Who could make the decision this powerful, frightened man was incapable of making?

Scofield took the steps rapidly, the guard's revolver in his trouser pocket, his Browning strapped to his chest beneath his tuxedo. He walked through the French doors into a crowded room; it was the "courtyard" devoted anachronistically to the crashing sounds of the disco beat. Revolving mirrored globes of coloured lights hung from the ceiling, spinning crazily as dancers weaved and jolted their bodies, their faces set in rigid expressions, lost in the beat and grass and alcohol.

This was the nearest room to the most direct set of steps from the terrace closest to the path from Ippolito's Fountain. In Scozzi's state of mind it *had* to be the one he entered first; there were two entrances. Which had he taken?

There was a break in the movement on the dance floor, and Bray had his answer. There was a heavy door in the wall behind a long buffet table. Two men were rushing towards it; they had been summoned; an alarm had been raised.

Scofield made his way to the door, excusing himself around the rim of frenzied bodies, and slowly pushed it open, his hand on the Browning under his jacket.

Beyond was a narrow winding staircase of thick reddish stone; he could hear footsteps above.

There were other sounds as well. Men were shouting, two voices raised in counterpoint, one stronger, calmer, the other on the verge of hysteria. The latter voice was Count Guillamo Scozzi's.

Bray started up the steps, pressing his back against the wall, the Browning held at his side. Around the first curve was a door, but the voices did not come from within it; they were farther up, beyond a second door, diagonally above on a second landing. Scozzi was screaming now. Scofield was close enough to hear the words clearly.

"He spoke of the *Brigades*, and – oh, my *God*! – of the *shepherd*! Of the *Corsican*! He *knows*! Mother of Christ, he *knows*!"

"Silence! He probes, he does not know. We were told he might do so; the old man telephoned about him, and he had certain facts. More than we'd assumed, and that is troublesome, I grant you."

"*Troublesome?* It's *chaos*! A word, a hint, a breath, and I could be *ruined*! Everywhere!"

"You?" said the stronger voice contemptuously. "You are nothing, Guillamo! You are only what we tell you you are. Remember that . . . You walked away, of course. You gave him no inkling that there was a shred of credence to what he said."

There was a pause. "I called my guard, told the American to remain where he was. He is under the gun, still by the fountain."

"You *what*!? You left him with a *guard*? An *American*? Are you *mad*? That is impossible. He is no such thing!"

"He's American, of course he is! His English is American – *completely* American. He uses the name Pastor, I told you that!"

Another pause, this one ominous, the tension electric. "You were always the weakest link, Guillamo; we know that. But now you've caved in too far. You've left an open question where there can be *none*! That man is Vasili Taleniekov! He changes languages as a chameleon alters its colours, and he will kill a guard with no more effort than stepping on a maggot. We cannot afford you, Guillamo. There can be no link at all. None whatsoever."

Silence . . . brief, cut short by a gunshot and a guttural explosion of breath. Guillamo Scozzi was dead.

"Leave him!" commanded the unknown *consigliere* of the Matarese. "He'll be found in the morning, his car at the bottom of the gorge of Hadrian. Go find this 'Pastor', this elusive Taleniekov! He won't be taken alive, don't try. Find him. Kill him . . . And the girl in white. She, also. Kill them both."

Scofield lunged down the narrow staircase, around the curve. The last words he heard from beyond the door above, however, were so strange, so arresting, he nearly stopped, tempted to fire at the emerging killers and go back up to face the unknown man, who spoke them.

" . . . *Scozzi!* Mother of Christ! Reach Turin. Tell them to cable the eagles, the cat. The burials must be absolute . . ."

There was no time to think, he had to reach Antonia; he had to get them out of

210

Villa d'Este. He pulled back the door and rushed out into the pounding madness that was the disco scene. Suddenly, he was aware of the row of chairs lined up against the wall; most were empty, some draped with discarded capes and furs and stoles.

If he could eliminate one pursuer the advantage would be manifold. One man sending out an alarm would be far less effective than two. And there was something else. A trapped man convinced he was about to lose his life would more than likely reveal an identity to save it. He turned to the wall, his hands on the rim of a chair, a *cavaliero* with too much wine in him.

The heavy door burst open and the first of the two killers raced out, his companion close behind him, but still behind him. The first man headed for the French doors and the steps to the terrace below; the second started around the edge of the dance floor towards the far archway.

Scofield leaped forward, twisting his body in a series of contortions as though he were a lone dancer gone wild with the percussive sounds of the rock music; he was not the only picture of drunkenness; there were more than a few on the crowded dance floor. He reached the second man and threw his arm over a shoulder, clamping his hand on the holster beneath the jacket, immobilizing the weapon inside it by gripping the handle through the cloth, forcing the barrel into the man's chest. The Italian struggled; it was useless and in seconds he knew it. Bray surged his right hand along the edge of the man's waist and dug his fingers into the base of the rib cage, yanking back with such force that the man screamed.

The scream went unnoticed for there were screams everywhere, and deafening music and revolving lights that blinded one moment, leaving residues of white the next. Scofield pulled the man back to the row of chairs against the wall and spun him around, forcing him down into the one at the end nearest the heavy door. He plunged his fingers into the Italian's throat, his left hand now under the jacket, his fingers inching towards the trigger, the barrel still jammed into the man's flesh. He put his lips next to the killer's ear.

"The man upstairs! Who is *he*? Tell me, or your own gun will blow your lungs out! The shot won't even be heard in here! Who is he?"

"*No!*" The man tried to arch out of the chair; Bray sunk his kneecap into the rising groin, his fingers choking the windpipe. He pressed both; pain without release or relief.

"I warn you and it's final! *Who is he?*"

Saliva poured out of the man's mouth, his eyes two circles of red webs, his chest heaving in surrender. He abandoned his cause, and he expelled the name in a strained whisper.

"*Paravicini.*"

Bray viced a last clamp on the killer's windpipe; the air to the lungs and the head was suspended for slightly more than two seconds; the man fell limp. Scofield angled him down over the adjacent chair, one more *bello Romano* drunk.

He turned and threaded his way through the narrow path between the row of chairs and the jagged line of fever-pitched dancers. The first man had gone outside; Bray could roam freely for a minute or two; but no longer. He pressed his way through the crowd in the entranceway and walked into a less frenzied gathering in the next room.

He saw her in the corner, the dark-haired Paolo standing next to her, two other *cavalieri* in front, all vying for her attention. Paolo, however, seemed less insistent; he knew future possessions when he saw them, where his count was concerned. The first thought that came to Bray's mind was that Toni's dress had to be covered.

. . . the girl in white. She, also, kill them both . . .

He walked rapidly up to the foursome, knowing precisely what he would do. A diversion was needed, the more hysterical the better. He touched Paolo's arm, his eyes on Antonia, his look telling her to stay quiet.

"You *are* Paolo, aren't you?" he asked the dark-haired man in Italian.

"Yes, sir."

"Count Guillamo wants to see you right away. It's some kind of emergency, I think."

"Of course! Where is he, sir?"

"Go through the arch over there and turn right, past a row of chairs, to a door. There's a staircase . . ." The young Italian rushed away. Bray excused Toni and himself from the remaining two men. He held her arm and propelled her towards the arch that led into the disco.

"What's happening?" she asked.

"We're leaving," he answered. "Inside here, there are some coats and things on chairs. Grab the darkest and the largest one you can find. Quickly, we haven't much time."

She found a long black cape, as Bray stood between her and the jolting contortionists on the dance floor. She bunched it under her arm and they elbowed their way to the French doors and the steps outside.

"Here, put it on," ordered Scofield, draping it over her shoulders. "Let's go," he said, starting down the steps. "We'll cut through the terraces to the right and back inside through the hall to the parking . . ."

Screams erupted from inside. Men were shouting, women shrieking, and within seconds figures in various stages of drunkenness surged out of doors, colliding with each other. There was a sudden chaos inside and the panicked words were clear.

Omicidio!

Terroristi!

Fuggine!

The body of Count Guillamo Scozzi had been found.

Bray and Antonia raced down to the first level of terraces and began running by the wall filled with ornate boxes of plants. At the end of the enclosure there was a narrow opening into the next. Scofield held her hand and pulled her through.

"*Fermata!* You stay!"

The shout came from above; the first man, who had rushed out of the door only minutes before, stood on the stone steps, a weapon in his hand. Bray slammed his shoulder into Antonia, sending her crashing into the wall. He dived to his right on the concrete, rolled to his left, and yanked the Browning from his holster. The man's shots exploded the ancient stone above Scofield; Bray aimed from his back,

212

his shoulders off the pavement, his right hand steadied by his left. He fired twice; the killer fell forward, tumbling down the steps.

The gunshots accelerated the chaos; screams of terror filled the elegant terraces of the Villa d'Este as the panicked crowds of revellers raced everywhere. Bray reached Antonia; she was crouching by the wall.

"Are you all right?"

"I'm alive."

"Come on!"

They found a break in the wall where a trough carried a rushing stream of water to a pool below. They stepped through and ran down the side of the man-made rivulet to the first path, an alleyway, bordered on both sides by what appeared to be hundreds of stone statues spewing arcs of water in unison. The floodlights filtered through the trees; the scene was eerily peaceful, juxtaposed to but not affected by the stampeding chaos from the terraces above.

"Straight through!" said Scofield. "At the end there's a waterfall and another staircase. It'll get us back up there."

They started running through the tunnel of foliage, mist from the arcs of water joining the sweat on their faces.

"*Dannazione!*" Antonia fell, the long black cape torn from her shoulders by a branch of a sapling. Bray stopped and pulled her up.

"*Eccola!*"

"*La donna!*"

The shouts came from behind them; gunshots followed. Two men came racing through the water-filled alleyway; they were targets, silhouetted by the light from the fountain beyond. Scofield fired three rounds. One man fell, holding his thigh; the second grabbed his shoulder, his gun flying out of his hand as he dived for the protection of the nearest statue.

Bray and Antonia reached the staircase at the end of the path. An entrance of the villa. They ran up, taking the steps two at a time, until they joined the panicked crowds rushing out through the enclosed courtyard into the huge parking lot.

Chauffeurs were everywhere, standing by elegant automobiles, protecting them, waiting for sight of their employers – and as with all chauffeurs in Italy in these times, their guns were drawn, levelled; protection was everything. They had been schooled; they were prepared.

One, however, was not prepared enough. Bray approached him. "Is this Count Scozzi's car?" he asked breathlessly.

"No, it is not, *signore*! Stand back!"

"Sorry." Scofield took a step away from the man, sufficient to allay his fears, then lunged forward, hammering the barrel of his automatic into the side of the chauffeur's skull. The man collapsed. "Get in!" he yelled to Antonia. "Lock the doors and stay on the floor until we're out of here."

It took them nearly a quarter of an hour before they reached the highway out of Tivoli. They sped down the road for six miles, then took an offshoot to the right that was devoid of traffic. Bray pulled over to the side of the road, stopped, and for several moments let his head fall back against the seat and closed his eyes. The pounding lessened; he sat up, reached into his pocket for his cigarettes, and offered one to Antonia.

"Normally, I do not," she said. "But right now I will. What happened?"

He lighted both their cigarettes and told her, ending with the murder of Guillamo Scozzi, the enigmatic words that he had heard on the staircase, and the identity of the man who spoke them. Paravicini. The specifics were clear, the conclusions less so. He could only speculate.

"They thought I was Taleniekov; they'd been warned about him. But they knew nothing about *me*, my name was never mentioned. It doesn't make sense, Scozzi described an American. They should have known."

"Why?"

"Because Washington and Moscow both knew Taleniekov was coming after me. They tried to trap us; they failed, and so they had to presume we made contact . . ." Or did they? wondered Scofield. The only one who actually *knew* he and the Russian had made contact was Robert Winthrop, and if he was alive, his silence could be counted upon. The rest of the intelligence community had only circumstantial carnage to go on; no one had actually seen them together. Still, the presumption had to be made, unless . . . "They think I'm dead," he said out loud, staring through the cigarette smoke to the windshield. "It's the only explanation. Someone told them I was dead. That's what 'impossible' meant."

"Why would anyone do that?"

"I wish I knew. If it were purely an intelligence manoeuvre, it could be for a reason as basic as buying time, throwing the opposition off, your own trap to follow. But this isn't that kind of thing, it couldn't be. The Matarese has lines into Soviet and US operations – I don't doubt it for a minute – but not the other way round. I don't understand."

"Could whoever it was think you *are* dead?"

Bray looked at her, his mind racing. "I don't see how. Or why. It's a damn good idea but I didn't think of it. To pull off a burial without a corpse takes a lot of doing."

Burial . . . The burials must be absolute.

Reach Turin . . . Tell them to cable the eagles, the cat.

Turin. Paravicini.

"Have you thought of something?" asked Antonia.

"Something else," he replied. "This Paravicini. He runs the Scozzi–Paravicini companies in Turin?"

"He did once. And in Rome and Milan, New York and Paris, as well. All over. He married the Scozzi daughter and as time went on her brother, the count, assumed more and more control. The count's the one who ran the companies. At least, that's what the newspapers said."

"It's what Paravicini wanted them to say. It wasn't true. Scozzi was a well-put-together figurehead."

"Then he wasn't part of the Matarese?"

"Oh, he was part of it all right, in some ways the most important part. Unless I'm wrong, he brought it with him. He and his mother, the *contessa*, presented it to Paravicini along with his blue-blooded new wife. But now we come to the real

214

question. Why would a man like Paravicini even listen? Men like Paravicini need, above all things . . . political stability. They pour fortunes into governments that have it and candidates who promise it – because they lose fortunes when it isn't there. They look for strong authoritarian regimes, capable of stamping out a Red Brigade or a Baader-Meinhof no matter how indiscriminate the process, or how much legitimate dissent goes down with them."

"That government does not exist in Italy," interrupted Antonia.

"And in not many other places, either. That's what doesn't make sense. The Paravicinis of this world thrive on law and order. They have nothing to gain by, or nothing to substitute *for*, its breakdown. Yet the Matarese is against all that. It wants to *paralyse* governments; it feeds the terrorists, funnels money to them, spreads the paralysis as quickly as possible." Scofield drew on his cigarette. The clearer some things became, the more obscure did others.

"You're contradicting yourself, Bray." Antonia touched his arm; it had become a perfectly natural gesture during the past twenty-four hours. "You say Paravicini is the Matarese. Or part of it."

"He is. That's what's missing. The reason."

"Where do you look for it?"

"Not here any longer. I'll ask the doctor to pick up our things at the Excelsior. We're getting out."

"We?"

Scofield took her hand. "Tonight changed a lot of things. *La bella signorina* can't stay in Rome now."

"Then I can go with *you*."

"As far as Paris," said Bray hesitantly, the hesitation not born of doubt, only of how to arrange the avenues of communication in Paris. There were others. "You'll stay there. I'll work out the procedures and get you a place to stay."

"Where will you go?"

"London. We know about Paravicini now; he's the Scozzi factor. London's next."

"Why there?"

"Paravicini said Turin was to cable 'the eagles, the cat'. With what your grandmother told us in Corsica, that code isn't hard to figure out. One eagle is my country, the other Taleniekov's."

"It doesn't follow," disagreed Antonia. "Russia is the bear."

"Not in this case. The Russian bear is Bolshevik, the Russian eagle, Czarist. The third guest at Villa Matarese in April nineteen eleven was a man named Voroshin. Prince Andrei Voroshin. From St Petersburg. That's Leningrad now. Taleniekov's on his way there."

"And the 'cat'?"

"The British lion. The second guest, Sir John Waverly. A descendant, David Waverly, is England's Foreign Secretary."

"A very high position."

"Too high, too visible. It doesn't make sense for him to be involved, either. Any more than the man in Washington, a senator who will probably be President next year. And because it doesn't make sense, it scares the hell out of me." Scofield released her hand, and reached for the ignition. "We're getting closer. Whatever there is to be found under the two eagles and the cat may be harder to dig out, but it's there. Paravicini made that clear. He said the 'burials' had to be 'absolute'. He meant that all the connections had to be re-examined, put farther out of reach."

"You'll be in a great deal of danger." She touched his arm again.

"Nowhere near as much as Taleniekov. As far as the Matarese is concerned, I'm dead, remember? He's not. Which is why we're going to send our first cable. To Helsinki. We've got to warn him."

"About what?"

"That anyone prowling around Leningrad looking for information about an illustrious old St Petersburg family named Voroshin will probably get his head blown off." Bray started the car. "It's wild," he said. "We're going after the inheritors – or we think we are – because we've got their names. But there's someone else, and I don't think any of them means much without him."

"Who is that?"

"A shepherd boy. He's the one we've really got to find, and I don't have the vaguest idea of how to do it."

22

Taleniekov walked to the middle of the block on Helsinki's Itä Kaivopuisto, noting the lights of the American embassy down the street. The sight of the building was appropriate; he had been thinking of Beowulf Agate off and on for most of the day.

It had taken him most of the day to absorb the news in Scofield's cable. The words themselves were innocuous, a salesman's report to an executive of a home office regarding Italian imports of Finnish crystal, but the new information was startling and complex. Scofield had made extraordinary progress in a very short time.

He had found the first connection; it *was* a Scozzi – the first name on the guest list of Guillaume de Matarese and the man was dead, killed by those who controlled him. Therefore, the American's assumption in Corsica that the members of the Matarese council were not born but selected, proved accurate. The Matarese had been taken over, a mixture of descendants and usurpers, it was consistent with the dying words of Aleksie Krupsky in Moscow.

The Matarese was dormant for years. No one could make contact. Then it came back, but it was not the same. Killings ... without clients, senseless butchery without a pattern ... governments paralysed.

This was, indeed, a new Matarese and infinitely more deadly than a cult of fanatics dedicated to paid political assassination.

And Beowulf had added a warning to his cable. The Matarese now assumed that the guest list had been found; the stalking of the Voroshin family in Leningrad was infinitely more complicated than it might have been only days ago.

216

Men were waiting in Leningrad for someone to ask questions about the Voroshins. But not the men – or man – he would reach, thought Taleniekov, stamping his feet against the cold, looking for a sign of the automobile that was to meet him and drive him east along the coast past Hamina towards the Soviet border.

Scofield was on his way to Paris with the girl, the American to continue on to England after setting up procedures in Paris. The Corsican woman had passed whatever tests Beowulf Agate had created; she would live and be their conduit. But, as Vasili was beginning to learn, Scofield rarely operated on a simple line; there was a third party: the manager of the Tavastian Hotel in Helsinki.

Once in Leningrad, Taleniekov was to cable the manager with whatever particulars he could put into ciphers, and the man, in turn, would wait for direct telephone calls from Paris and relate the codes received from Leningrad. It was then up to the woman to reach Scofield in England. Vasili knew that monitoring cable traffic was a particular talent of the KGB; the only sure way to eliminate it was to use KGB equipment. Somehow, he would find a way to do that.

An automobile pulled up to the kerb, the headlights dimming once, the driver wearing a red muffler, one end draped over a dark leather jacket. Taleniekov crossed the pavement and got in the front seat beside the driver. He was on his way back to Russia.

The town of Vainikkala was on the north-west shore of the lake; across the water was the Soviet Union, the south-east banks patrolled by teams of soldiers and dogs plagued more often than not by *ennui* than by threats of penetration or escape. During the interminable winter months prolonged exposure to the freezing winds was simply too dangerous, and in summer the interminable flow of tourist visas in and out of Tallinn and Kiga, to say nothing of Leningrad itself, made those cities the easiest routes. As a result the north-west garrisons along the Finnish border were staffed by the least motivated military personnel, often a collection of misfits and drunks commanded by men being punished for errors of judgement. Checkpoint Vainikkala was a logical place to cross into Russia; even the dogs were third-rate.

The Finns, however, were not; nor had they ever lost their hatred of the Soviet invaders who had lunged into their country in '39. As they had been masters of the lakes and the forests then, repulsing whole divisions with brilliantly executed traps, so they were masters forty years later at avoiding others. It was not until Taleniekov had been escorted across an inlet of ice and brought up beyond the patrols above the snow-clogged banks that he realized Checkpoint Vainikkala had become an escape route of considerable magnitude. It was no longer minor.

"If ever," said the Finn who had taken him on his last leg of the journey, "any of you men from Washington wants to get beyond these Bolshevik bastards, remember us. Because we do not forget."

The irony was not lost on Vasili Vasilievich Taleniekov, former master strategist for the KGB. "You should be careful with such offers," he replied. "How do you know I'm not a Soviet plant?"

The Finn smiled. "We traced you to the Tavastian and made our own inquiries.

You were sent by the best there is. He has used us in a dozen different Baltic operations. Give the quiet one our regards." The man extended his hand. "Arrangements have been made to drive you south through Vyborg into Zelenogorsk," continued the escort.

"*What?*" Taleniekov had made no such request; he had made it clear that once inside the Soviet Union, he preferred to be on his own. "I didn't ask you to do that. I didn't pay for it."

The Finn smiled condescendingly. "We thought it best; it will be quicker for you. Walk two kilometres down this road. You'll find a car parked by the snowbank. Ask the man inside for the time, saying your car has broken down – but speak Russian; they say you can do so passably well. If the man answers, then begins winding his watch, that's your ride."

"I really don't think this is necessary," objected Vasili. "I expected to make my own arrangements – for both our sakes."

"Whatever you might arrange, this is better; it will be daybreak soon and the roads are watched. You have nothing to worry about. The man you're meeting has been on Washington's payroll for a long time." The Finn smiled again. "He is second-in-command, KGB-Vyborg."

Taleniekov returned the smile. Whatever annoyance he had felt evaporated. In one sentence his escort had provided the answers to several problems. If stealing from a thief was the safest form of larceny, a "defector" compromising a traitor was even safer.

"You're a remarkable people," he said to the Finn. "I'm sure we'll do business again."

"Why not? Geography keeps us occupied. We have scores to settle."

Taleniekov had to ask. "Still? After so many years?"

"It never ends. You are fortunate, my friend, you don't live with a wild, unpredictable bear in your backyard. Try it some time, it's depressing. Haven't you heard? We drink too much."

Vasili saw the car in the distance, a black shadow among other shadows surrounded by the snow on the road. It was dawn; in an hour the sun would throw its yellow shafts across the arctic mists and the mists would disappear. As a child, he had been warmed by that sun.

He was home. It had been so many years, but there was no sense of return, no joy at the prospect of seeing familiar sights, perhaps a familiar face . . . grown so much older, as he had grown older.

There was no elation at all, only purpose. Too much had happened; he was cold and the winter sun would bring no warmth on this trip. There was only a family named Voroshin. He approached the car, staying as far to the right as possible, in the blind spot, his Graz-Burya in his gloved right hand. He stepped through the shoulder of snow, keeping his body low, until he was parallel with the front window. He raised his head and looked at the man inside.

The glow of a cigarette partially illuminated the vaguely familiar face. Taleniekov had seen it before, in a dossier photograph, or perhaps during a brief interview in

Kiga too insignificant to be remembered. He even remembered the man's name, and that name triggered his memory of the facts.

Maletkin. Pyotr Maletkin. From Grodno, just east of the Polish border. He was in his early fifties – the face confirmed that – considered a sound if uninspired professional, someone who did his work quietly, by rote-efficiency, but with little else. Through seniority he had risen in the KGB, but his lack of initiative had delegated him to a post in Vyborg.

The Americans had made a perceptive choice in his recruitment. Here was a man doomed to insignificance by his own insignificance, yet privy to ciphers and schedules because of accumulated rank. A second-in-command at Vyborg knew the end of a rather inglorious road had been reached. Resentments could be played upon; promises of a richer life were powerful inducements. He could always be shot crossing the ice on a final trip to Vainikkala. No one would miss him, a minor success for the Americans, a minor embarrassment to the KGB. But all that was changed now. Pyotr Maletkin was about to become a very important person. He himself would know it the instant Vasili walked up to the window, for if the traitor's face was vaguely familiar to Taleniekov, the "defector's" would be completely known to Maletkin. Every KGB station in the world was after Vasili Vasilievich Taleniekov.

Sheltered by the bank of snow he crept back some twenty metres behind the automobile, then walked out on the road. Maletkin was either deep in thought or half asleep; he gave no indication that he saw anyone, no turn of the head, no crushing out of the cigarette. It was not until Vasili was within ten feet of the window that the traitor jerked his shoulders around, his face turned to the glass. Taleniekov angled his head away as if checking the road behind him as he walked; he did not want his face seen until the window was rolled down: it would interfere with what he had in mind. He stood directly by the door, his head hidden above the roof.

He heard the cranking of the handle, felt the brief swell of heat from inside the car. As he expected, the beam of a flashlight shot out from the seat; he bent over and showed his face, the Graz-Burya shoved through the open window.

"Good morning, Comrade Maletkin. It is Maletkin, isn't it?"

"My *God*! You!"

With his left hand, Taleniekov reached in and held the flashlight, turning it slowly away, no urgency in the act. "Don't upset yourself," he said. "We have something in common now, haven't we? Why don't you give me the keys?"

"What . . . *what*?" Maletkin was paralysed; he could not speak.

"Let me have the keys, please," continued Vasili. "I'll give them back to you as soon as I'm inside. You're nervous, comrade, and nervous people do nervous things. I don't want you driving away without me. The keys, please."

The ominous barrel of the Graz-Burya was inches from Maletkin's face, his eyes shifting alternately, rapidly, between the gun and Taleniekov; he fumbled for the ignition switch and removed the keys. "Here," he whispered.

"Thank you, comrade. And we are comrades, you know that, don't you? There'd be no point in either of us trying to take advantage of the other's predicament. We'd both lose."

Taleniekov walked around the front of the car, stepped through the snowbank, and climbed in the front seat beside the morose traitor.

"Come now, Colonel Maletkin – it is colonel by now, isn't it? – there's no reason for this hostility. I want to hear all the news."

"I'm a temporary colonel; the rank has not been made permanent."

"A shame. We never did appreciate you, did we? Well, we were certainly mistaken. Look what you've accomplished right under our noses. You must tell me how you did it. In Leningrad."

"*Leningrad?*"

"An hour's ride from Zelenogorsk. It's not so much, and I'm sure Vyborg's second-in-command can come up with a reasonable explanation for the trip. I'll help you. I'm very good at that sort of thing."

Maletkin swallowed, his eyes apprehensively on Vasili. "I am to be back in Vyborg tomorrow morning. To hold a briefing with the patrols."

"Delegate it, Colonel! Everyone loves to have responsibility delegated to them. It shows they're appreciated."

"It was delegated to me," said Maletkin.

"See what I mean? By the way, where are *your* bank accounts? Norway? Sweden? New York? Certainly not in Finland; that would be foolish."

"In the city of Atlanta. A bank owned by Arabs."

"Good thinking." Taleniekov handed him the keys. "Shall we get started, comrade?"

"This is *crazy*," said Maletkin. "We are dead men."

"Not for a while. We have business in Leningrad."

It was noon when they drove over the Kirov Bridge, past the summer gardens wrapped in burlap, and south to the enormous boulevard that was the Nevsky Prospekt. Taleniekov fell silent as he looked out the window at the monuments of grandeur that were Leningrad. The blood of millions had been sacrificed to turn the freezing mud and marshland of the Neva River into Peter's window-on-Europe.

They reached the end of the Prospekt under the gleaming spire of the Admiralty Building and turned into the Quay. There along the banks of the river stood the Winter Palace; its effect on Vasili was the same as it had always been. It made him think about the Russia that once had been and ended here when the cruiser *Aurora* steamed up the Neva and fired its cannons into the seat of the false provisional government of Kerensky, signifying the emergence of the new Soviet. The True Russia.

There was no time for such reflections, nor was this the Leningrad he would roam for the next several days—although, ironically, it was *this* Leningrad, *that* Russia, that brought him here. Prince Andrei Voroshin had been part of both.

"Drive over the Anichkov Bridge and turn left," he said. "Head into the old housing development district. I'll tell you where to stop."

"What's down there?" asked Maletkin, his apprehension growing with each block, each bridge they crossed, as they travelled into the heart of the city.

"I'm surprised you don't know; you should. A string of illegal boarding houses, and equally illegal cheap hotels that seem to have a collectively revisionist attitude regarding official papers."

"In *Leningrad?*"

"You *don't* know, do you?" said Taleniekov. "And no one ever told you. You *were* overlooked, comrade. When I was stationed in Riga, those of us who were area leaders frequently came up here and used the district for conferences we wished to keep secret, the ones that concerned our own people throughout the sector. It's where I first heard your name, I believe."

"*Me?* I was brought up?"

"Don't worry, I threw them off and protected you. You and the other man in Vyborg."

"*Vyborg?*" Maletkin lost his grip on the wheel; the car swerved, narrowly avoiding an oncoming truck.

"Control yourself!" Vasili shouted. "An accident would send us both to the black rooms of *Lubyanka!*"

"But Vyborg!" repeated the astonished traitor. "KGB-Vyborg? Do you know what you're *saying?*"

"Precisely," repeated Taleniekov. "Two informers from the same source, neither aware of the other. It's the most accurate way to verify information. But if one does learn about the other . . . well, he has the best of both worlds, wouldn't you say? In your case, the advantages would be incalculable."

"Who is he!?"

"Later, my friend, later. You co-operate fully with everything I ask and you'll have his name when I leave."

"Agreed," said Maletkin, his composure returning.

Taleniekov leaned back in the seat as they progressed down the traffic-laden Sadovaya into the crowded streets of the old housing district, the *dom-vashen*. The patina of clean pavements and sand-blasted buildings concealed the mounting tensions rampant within the area. Two and three families living in a single flat, four and five people sleeping in a room; it would all explode one day.

Vasili glanced at the traitor beside him; he despised the man. Maletkin thought he was going to be given an advantage undreamed-of only minutes before: the name of a high-ranking KGB intelligence officer from his own station, a traitor like himself, who could be manipulated unmercifully. He would do almost anything to get that name. It would be given to him – in three words, no other identification necessary. And, of course, it would be false. Pyotr Maletkin would not be shot by the Americans crossing the ice to Vainikkala, but instead in a barracks courtyard in Vyborg. So much for the politics of the insignificant man, thought Vasili, as he recognized the building he was looking for down the street.

"Stop at the next corner, comrade," he said. "Wait for me. If the person I want to see isn't there, I'll be right back. If he's home, I'll be an hour or so." Maletkin pulled to the right behind a cluster of bicycles chained to a post on the kerb. "Do remember," Taleniekov continued, "that you have two alternatives. You can race away to KGB headquarters – it's on the Ligovsky Prospekt, incidentally – and turn me in; that will lead to a chain of revelations which will result in your execution. Or you can wait for me, do as I ask you to do, and you will have bought yourself the identity of someone who can bring you present and future rewards. You'll have your hook in a very important man."

"Then I don't really have a choice, do I?" said Maletkin. "I'll be here." The traitor grinned; he perspired on his chin and his teeth were yellow.

Taleniekov approached the stone steps of the building; it was a three-storey structure with twenty to thirty flats, many crowded, but not hers. Lodzia Kronescha had her own apartment; that decision had been made by the KGB five years ago.

With the exception of a brief weekend conference fourteen months ago in Moscow, he had not seen her since Kiga. During the conference they had spent one night together – the first night – but had decided not to meet subsequently, for professional reasons. The "brilliant Taleniekov" had been showing signs of strain, his oddly intemperate behaviour annoying too many people – and too many people had been talking about it, whispering about it. Him. It was best they sever all associations outside the conference rooms. For in spite of total clearance, she was still being watched. He was not the sort of man she should be seen with; he had told her that, insisted upon it.

Five years ago Lodzia Kronescha had been in trouble; some said it was serious enough to remove her from her post in Leningrad. Others disagreed, claiming her lapses of judgement were due to a temporary siege of depression brought on by family problems. Besides, she was extremely effective in her work; whom would they get to replace her during those times of crisis? Lodzia was a highly qualified mathematician, a doctoral graduate from Moscow University, and trained in the Lenin Institute. She was among the most knowledgeable computer programmers in the field.

So she was kept on and given the proper warnings regarding her responsibility to the state – which had made her education possible. She was relegated to night operations, Computer Division, KGB-Leningrad, Ligovsky Prospekt. That was five years ago; she would remain there for at least another two.

Lodzia's "crimes" might have been dismissed as professional errors – a series of minor mathematical variations – had it not been for a disturbing occurrence thirteen hundred miles away in Vienna. Her brother had been a senior air defence officer and he had committed suicide, the reasons for the act unexplained. Nevertheless, the air defence plans for the entire south-west German border had been altered. And Lodzia Kronescha had been called in for questioning.

Taleniekov had been present, intrigued by the quiet, academic woman brought in under the KGB lamps. He had been fascinated by her slow, thoughtful responses that were as convincing as they were lacking in panic. She had readily admitted that she adored her brother and was distressed to the point of a breakdown over his death and the manner of it. No, she had known of nothing irregular about his life; yes, he had been a devoted member of the party; no, she had not kept his correspondence – it had never occurred to her to do so.

Taleniekov had kept silent, knowing what he knew by instinct and a thousand encounters with concealed truth. She had been lying. From the beginning. But her lies were not rooted in treason, or even for her own survival. It was something else.

When the daily KGB surveillance was called off, he had flown frequently to Leningrad from near-by Riga to institute his own.

Vasili's trailing of Lodzia had revealed what he then knew he would find. Extremely artful contacts in the parks of the Petrodvorets with an American agent out of Helsinki. The meetings were not sought, they had been forced upon her.

He had followed her to her flat one evening and had confronted her with his evidence. Instinct had told him to hold back official action. There was far less than treason in her activities.

"What I have done is *insignificant!*" she had cried, tears of exhaustion filling her eyes. "It is *nothing* compared to what they want! But if they have proof of my doing *something*, they will not do what they threaten to do!"

The Americans had shown her photographs, dozens of them, mostly of her brother, but also of other high-ranking Soviet officials in the Vienna sectors. They depicted the grossest obscenities, extremes of sexual behaviour – male with female, and male with male – all taken while the subjects were drunk, all showing a Vienna of excessive debauchery in which responsible Soviet figures were willingly corrupted by any who cared to corrupt them.

The threat was simple: these photographs would be spread across the world. Her brother – as well as those superior to him in rank and stature – would be held up to universal ridicule. As would the Soviet Union.

"What did you hope to gain by doing what you did?" he had asked.

"Wear them out!" she had replied. "They will keep me on a string, never knowing what I will do, can do . . . have *done*. Every now and then they get word of computer errors. They are minor, but it is enough. They will not carry out their threats."

"There is a better way," he had suggested. "I think you should leave it to me. There's a man in Washington who spent his fire in South-east Asia, a general named Blackburn. Mad Anthony Blackburn."

Vasili had returned to Riga and sent out word through his network in London. Washington got the information within hours: whatever exploitation American intelligence cared to make out of Vienna would be matched by equally devastating exposure – and photographs – of one of the most respected men in the American military establishment.

No one from Helsinki ever bothered Lodzia Kronescha again. And she and Taleniekov had become lovers.

As Vasili climbed the dark staircase to the second floor, memories came back to him. Theirs had been an affair of mutual need, without any feverish emotional attachment. They had been two insular people, dedicated to their professions almost to the exclusion of everything else; they had both required the release of mind and body. Neither had demanded more than that release from the other, and when he had been transferred to Sevastopol, their goodbyes were the painless parting of good friends who liked each other a great deal but who felt no dependence, grateful in fact for its absence. He wondered what she would say when she saw him, what she would feel . . . what he would feel.

He looked at his watch: ten minutes to one. If her schedule had not been altered, she would have been relieved from duty at eight in the morning, arrived home by nine, read the papers for a half hour and fallen asleep. Then a thought struck him.

Suppose she had a lover, as he had been her lover? If so, he would not put her in danger; he would leave quickly before any identification was made. But he hoped it was not the case; he needed Lodzia. The man he had to reach in Leningrad could not be approached directly; she could help him – if she would.

He knocked on her door. Within seconds he heard the footsteps beyond, the sharp cracks of leather heels against hard wood. Oddly, she had not been in bed. The door opened half-way and Lodzia Kronescha stood there fully clothed – strangely clothed – in a bright-coloured cotton dress, a *summer* dress, her light brown hair falling over her shoulders, her sharp, aquiline face set in a rigid expression, her hazel-green eyes staring at him – *staring* at him – as if his sudden appearance after so long were not so much unexpected as an intrusion.

"How nice of you to drop by, old friend," she said without a trace of an inflection.

She was telling him something. There was someone inside with her. Someone waiting for him.

"It's good to see you again, old friend," said Taleniekov, nodding in acknowledgement, studying the crack between the door. He could see the cloth of a jacket, the brown fabric of a pair of trousers. There was only one man, she was telling him that, too. He pulled out his Graz-Burya, holding up his left hand, three fingers extended, gesturing to his left. On the third nod of his head, she was to dive to her right; her eyes told him she understood. "It's been many months," he continued casually. "I was in the district, so I thought I would . . ."

He gave the third nod; she lunged to her right. Vasili crushed his shoulder into the door – into the left panel so the arc would be clean, the impact total – then battered it again, crushing the figure behind it into the wall.

He plunged inside, pivoting to the right, his shoulder smashing the door again. He ripped a gun out of the man's hand, peeling the body away from the wall, hammering his knee into the exposed neck, propelling his would-be assailant off his feet into a near-by armchair where he collapsed on the floor.

"You *understood*," cried Lodzia, crowding against the wall. "I was so worried that you wouldn't!"

Taleniekov shut the door. "It's not yet one o'clock," he said, reaching for her hand. "I thought you'd be asleep."

"I was hoping you'd realize that."

"Also it's freezing outside, hardly the season for a summer dress."

"I knew you'd notice that. Most men don't, but you would."

He held her shoulders, speaking rapidly. "I've brought you terrible trouble. I'm sorry. I'll leave immediately. Tear your clothes, say you tried to stop me. I'll break into a flat upstairs and . . ."

"Vasili, *listen* to me! That man's not one of us. He's not KGB."

Taleniekov turned towards the man on the floor. He was regaining consciousness slowly, trying to rise and orient himself at the same time. "Are you sure?"

"Very. To begin with he's an Englishman, his Russian shouts with it. When he mentioned your name I pretended to be shocked, angry that our people would think me capable of harbouring a fugitive . . . I said I wanted to telephone my superior. He refused to let me. He said, 'We have all we want from you.' Those were his exact words."

224

Vasili looked at her. "Would you have called your superior?"

"I'm not sure," replied Lodzia, her hazel-green eyes steady on his. "I suppose it would have depended on what he said. It's very difficult for me to believe you're what they say you are."

"I'm not. On the other hand, you must protect yourself."

"I was hoping it wouldn't come to that."

"Thank you . . . old friend." Taleniekov turned back to the man on the floor and started towards him.

He saw it. He was too late!

Vasili lunged, diving at the figure by the chair, his hands ripping at the man's mouth, pulling it apart, his knee hammering the stomach, jamming it up into the rib cage, trying to induce vomit.

The acrid odour of almonds. Potassium cyanide. A massive dose. Oblivion in seconds, death in minutes.

The cold blue English eyes beneath him were wide and clear with satisfaction. The Matarese had escaped.

23

"We have to go over it *again*," insisted Taleniekov, looking up from the naked corpse. They had stripped the body; Lodzia was sitting in a chair checking the articles of clothing meticulously for the second time. "Everything he said."

"I've left out nothing. He wasn't that talkative."

"You're a mathematician; we must fill in the missing numbers. The sums are clear."

"Sums?"

"Yes, sums," repeated Vasili, turning the corpse over. "He wanted me, but was willing to kill himself if the trap failed. That warrants two conclusions: first, he could not risk being taken alive because of what he knew. And second, he expected no assistance. If I thought otherwise, you and I would not be here now."

"But why did he think you would come here to begin with?"

"Not would," corrected Taleniekov. "*Might*. I'm sure it's in a file somewhere in Moscow that you and I saw a lot of each other. And the men who want me have access to those files, I know that. But they'll cover only the people here in Leningrad they think I *might* contact. They won't bother with the sector leaders or the Ligovsky staff. If any of them got wind of me they'd send out alarms heard in Siberia; those who want me would step in then. No, they'll only concern themselves with people they can't trust to turn me in. You're one of them."

"Are there others? Here in Leningrad?"

"Three or four, perhaps. A Jew at the university, a good friend I'd drink and argue with all night; he'll be watched. Another at the *Zhdanov*, a political theorist who teaches Marx but is more at home with Adam Smith. One or two others, I suppose. I never really worried about whom I was seen with."

"You didn't have to."

"I know. My post had its advantages; there were a dozen explanations for any single thing that I did, any person I saw." He paused. "How extensive is their coverage?"

"I don't understand."

"There's one man I do want to reach. They'd have to go back a great many years to find him, but they may have." Vasili paused again, his finger on the base of the spine of the naked body beneath him. He looked up at the strong yet curiously gentle face of the woman he had known so well. "What were the words again? 'We have all we want from you.' "

"Yes. At which point he grabbed the telephone away from my hand."

"He was convinced you were going to call Leningrad?"

"I was convincing. Had he told me to go ahead, I might have changed tactics, I don't know. Remember, I knew he was English. I didn't think he would let me call. But he did not deny being KGB."

"And later, when you put on the dress. He didn't object?"

"On the contrary. It convinced him you were actually coming here, that I was co-operating."

"What were his words, then? The precise words. You said he smiled and said something about women-being-all-alike; you don't recall what else."

"It was trivial."

"Nothing is. Try to remember. Something about 'whiling away the hours', that's what you mentioned."

"Yes. The language was ours but the phrase was very English, I remember that. He said he'd 'while away the hours pleasantly' . . . more so than others. That there were . . . 'no such sights on the Quay'. I told you, he insisted I change clothes in front of him."

"The 'Quay'. The Hermitage. Malachite Hall. There's a woman there," said Taleniekov, frowning. "They were thorough. One more missing number."

"My lover was unfaithful?"

"Frequently, but not with her. She was an unreconstructed Czarist put in charge of the architectural tours and perfectly delightful. She's also closer to seventy than sixty, although neither seems so far away to me now. I took her to tea quite often."

"That's touching."

"I enjoyed her company. She was a fine instructor in things I knew little about. Why would anyone have put her on a list in a file?"

"Speaking for Leningrad," said Lodzia, amused, "if we saw our competition from Riga meeting with such a person, we'd insert it."

"It's probably as stupid as that. What else did he say?"

"Nothing memorable. While I was in my underthings, he made a foolish remark to the effect that mathematicians had the advantage over academics and librarians. We studied figures . . ."

Taleniekov got to his feet. "That's it!" he said. "The missing number. They've found him."

"What are you talking about?"

"Our Englishman either couldn't resist the bad pun, or he was probing. The Quay – the Hermitage Museum. The academics – my drinking companions at the *Zhdanov*. The reference to a librarian – the Saltykov-Shchedrin Library. The man I want to reach is there."

"Who is he?"

Vasili hesitated. "An old man who years ago befriended a young university student and opened his eyes to things he knew nothing about."

"Who was he? Who is he?"

Taleniekov approached her, minor excitement returning with his memories. "I was a very confused young man," he said. "How was it possible for over three-quarters of the world to reject the teachings of the revolution? I could not accept the fact that so many millions were unenlightened. But that's what the textbooks said, what our professors told us. But *why*? I had to understand how our enemies thought the way they did."

"And this man was able to tell you?"

"He *showed* me. He let me find out for myself. I was sufficiently fluent in English and French then, reasonably so in Spanish. He opened the doors, literally *opened* the steel doors, of the forbidden books – thousands of volumes Moscow disapproved of – and left me free with them. I spent weeks, months poring over them, trying to understand. It was there that the . . . 'great Taleniekov' learned the most valuable lesson of all: how to see things as the enemy sees them, how to be able to *think* like him. That is the keystone of every success I've ever had. My old friend made it possible."

"And you must reach him now?"

"Yes. He's lived all his life here in Leningrad. When he was born it was St Petersburg; when a young man, Petrograd. He's seen it all happen and he's survived. If anyone can help me, he can."

"What are you looking for? I think I have a right to know."

"Of course you do, but it's a name you must forget. At least, never mention it. I need information about a family named Voroshin."

"A family? From Leningrad?"

"Yes."

Lodzia shook her head in exasperation. "Sometimes I think the great Taleniekov is a great fool! I can run the name through our computers!"

"The minute you did, you'd be marked – for all purposes, dead. That man on the floor has accomplices everywhere." He turned and walked back to the body, kneeling down to continue his examination of the corpse. "Besides, you'd find nothing; it's too many years ago, too many changes of regimes and emphases. If any entry, or entries, had ever been made, I doubt they'd be there now. The irony is that if there was something in the data banks, it would probably mean the Voroshin family is no longer involved."

"Involved with *what*, Vasili?"

He did not answer immediately, for he had turned the nude body over and saw it. A small discoloration of the skin on the lower mid-section of the chest, around the area of the heart, barely seen through the matted hair. It was tiny, no more than half an inch in diameter – and it *was* a diameter, for the bluish-purple mark was a circle. At first glance it appeared to be a birthmark, a perfectly natural phenomenon, in no way superimposed on the flesh. But it was not natural; it was placed there by a very experienced needle. Old Krupsky had said the words as he lay dying: *A man was caught, a blemish on his chest, a soldier of the Matarese.*

"With this." Taleniekov separated the black hair on the dead man's chest so the jagged circle could be seen clearly. "Come here."

Lodzia got up, walked to the corpse, and knelt down. "What? The birthmark?"

"*Perro nostro circulo,*" he said quietly. "It wasn't there when our Englishman was born. It had to be earned."

"I don't understand."

"You will. I'm going to tell you everything I know. I wasn't sure that I wanted to, but I don't think there's a choice now. They might easily kill me. If they do, there's someone you must reach. I'll tell you how. Describe this mark, fourth rib, border of the cage, near the heart. It was not meant to be found."

Lodzia was silent as she looked at the bluish mark on the flesh, and finally at Taleniekov. "Who is 'they'?"

"They go by the name of the Matarese . . ."

He told her. Everything. When he was finished, Lodzia did not speak for a long time, nor did he intrude on her thoughts. For she had heard shocking things, not the least of which was the incredible alliance between Vasili Vasilievich Taleniekov and a man known throughout the KGB world as Beowulf Agate. She sat up and walked to the window overlooking the dreary street in Leningrad's *dom-vashen*. She spoke, her face to the glass.

"I imagine you've asked this question of yourself a thousand times; I ask it again. Was it necessary to contact Scofield?"

"Yes," he said simply.

"Moscow *wouldn't* listen to you?"

"Moscow ordered my execution. Washington ordered his."

"Yes, but you say that neither Moscow nor Washington knows about this Matarese. The trap set for you and Beowulf was based on keeping you apart. I can understand that."

"*Official* Washington and *official* Moscow are blind to the Matarese. Otherwise, someone would have stepped forward on our behalf; we would have been summoned to present what we know – what I brought Scofield. Instead, we're branded traitors, ordered to be shot on sight, no provisions made to give us a hearing. The Matarese orchestrated it using the clandestine apparatuses of both countries."

"Then this Matarese is in Moscow, in Washington?"

"Absolutely. In, but not of. Capable of manipulating, but unseen."

"Not unseen, Vasili," objected Lodzia. "The men you spoke to in Moscow . . ."

"*Panicked old* men," interrupted Taleniekov. "Dying war horses put out to pasture, frightened by actions taken, contracts made, decades ago. Impotent."

"Then the man Scofield approached. The statesman, Winthrop. What of him?"

"Undoubtedly dead by now."

Lodzia walked away from the window and stood in front of him. "Then where do you go? You're cornered, stopped."

Vasili shook his head. "On the contrary, we're making progress. The first name on the list, Scozzi, was accurate. Now, we have our dead Englishman here. No papers, no proof of who he is or where he came from, but with a mark more telling than a wallet filled with false documents. He was part of their army, which means there's another soldier here in Leningrad watching an old man who's curator of literary archives at the Saltykov-Shchedrin Library. I want him almost as much as I want to reach my old friend; I want to break him, get answers. The Matarese are in Leningrad to protect the Voroshins, to conceal the truth. We're getting closer to that truth."

"But suppose you *find* it. Whom can you take it to? You cannot protect yourselves because you don't know who they are."

"We know who they are not, and that's enough. The Premier and the President to begin with."

"You won't get near them."

"We will if we have our proof. Beowulf was right about that; we need incontrovertible proof. Will you help us? Help *me*?"

Lodzia Kronescha looked into his eyes, her own softening. She reached up with both her hands and cupped his face. "Vasili Vasilievich. My life had become so uncomplicated, and now you return."

"I didn't know where else to go. I couldn't approach that old man directly. I testified on his behalf at a security hearing in nineteen fifty-four. I'm terribly sorry, Lodzia."

"Don't be. I've missed you. And, of course, I'll help you. Were it not for you, I might be teaching primary classes in our Tashkent sectors."

He touched her face, returning her gesture, staring into her hazel-green eyes. "That must not be the reason for your help."

"It isn't. What you've told me frightens me."

Under no condition was the traitor Maletkin to be aware of Lodzia. The Vyborg officer had remained in the automobile at the corner, but when more than an hour had passed Taleniekov could see him pacing nervously on the pavement below.

"He's not sure whether it's this building or the one next door," said Vasili, stepping back from the window. "The cellars still connect, don't they?"

"They did when I was last there."

"I'll go down and come out on the street several doors away. I'll meet him and tell him the man I'm with wants another half hour. That should give us enough time. Finish dressing the Englishman, will you?"

Lodzia was right, nothing had changed in the old buildings. All had merely grown older and dirtier and in greater disrepair. Each cellar connected with the one next door, the filthy, damp underground alleyway extending along most of the block. Taleniekov emerged on the street four buildings away from Lodzia's flat. He walked up to the unsuspecting Maletkin, startling him.

"I thought you went in there!" said the traitor from Vyborg, nodding his head at the staircase on his left.

"There?"

"Yes, I was sure of it."

"You're still too excited, comrade, it interferes with your observation. I don't

229

know anyone in that building. I came down to tell you that the man I'm meeting with needs more time. I suggest you wait in the car; it's not only extremely cold, but you'll draw less attention to yourself."

"You won't be any longer than that, will you?" asked Maletkin anxiously.

"Are you going somewhere? Without me?"

"No, no, of course not. I have to go to the toilet."

"Discipline your bladder," said Taleniekov, hurrying away.

Twenty minutes later he and Lodzia had worked out the details of his contact with the curator of archives at the Saltykov-Shchedrin Library on the Maiorov Prospekt. She would telephone the scholar at his office, speaking the truth without naming names. It was vital that a growing sense of fear be engendered – for everyone's sake. A student from many years ago, an exceptional student of languages and books as well as a friend – a man who had risen high in government office and who had testified for the old gentleman in 1954 – wanted to meet with him privately. That student, this friend, could not be seen in public; he was in trouble and needed help.

There was to be no doubt as to the identity of that student, nor of the danger in which he found himself. The old man had to be jolted, frightened, concern for a once-dear young friend brought to the surface. He had to communicate his alarms to any who might be watching him closely – the arrangements for the meeting just complicated enough to confuse an old man's mind. For in the scholar's confusion and fear would be found tentative movements, bewildered starts and stops, first in one direction, then in another, sudden turns and abrupt reversals, decisions made and instantly rejected. In these circumstances, whoever followed the old man would be revealed; for whatever moves the scholar made, the one following would have to make. They would not be natural.

Lodzia would instruct the old man to leave the enormous library complex by the south-west exit at ten minutes to six that evening; the streets would be dark and no snow was expected. He would be told to walk a number of blocks one way, then another. If no contact was made, he was to return to the library, and wait; if it were at all possible, his friend from long ago would try to get there. However, there were no guarantees.

Placed in this situation of stress, the numbers alone would serve to confuse the scholar, for Lodzia was to abruptly terminate the telephone call without repeating them. Vasili would take care of the rest, a traitor named Maletkin serving as an unknowing accomplice.

"What will you do after you see the old man?" asked Lodzia.

"That depends on what he tells me, or what I can learn from the man who follows him."

"Where will you stay? Will I see you?"

Vasili stood up. "It could be dangerous for you if I come back here."

"I'm willing to risk that."

"I'm not willing to let you. Besides, you work until morning."

"I can go in early and get off at midnight. Things are much more relaxed than when you were last in Leningrad. We trade hours frequently, and I am completely rehabilitated."

230

"Someone will ask you why."

"I'll tell them the truth. An old friend has arrived from Moscow."

"I don't think that's such a good idea."

"A party secretary from the Praesidium with a wife and several children. He wishes to remain anonymous."

"As I said, a splendid idea." Taleniekov smiled. "I'll be careful and go through the cellars."

"What will you do with him?" Lodzia nodded at the dead Englishman.

"Leave him in the farthest cellar I can find. Do you have a bottle of vodka?"

"Are you thirsty?"

"He is. One more unknown suicide in paradise. We don't publicize them. I'll need a razor blade."

Pyotr Maletkin stood next to Vasili in the shadows of an archway across from the south-west entrance to the Saltykov-Shchedrin Library. The floodlights in the rear courtyard of the complex shone down in wide circles from the high walls, giving the illusion of an enormous prison compound. But the arches that led to the street beyond were placed symmetrically every hundred feet in the wall; the prisoners could come and go at will. It was a busy evening at the library; streams of prisoners came and went.

"You say this old man is one of us?" asked Maletkin.

"Get your pronouns straight, comrade. The old fellow's KGB, the man following him – about to make contact – is one of *us*. We've got to reach him before he's trapped. The scholar is one of the most effective weapons Moscow's developed for counter-intelligence. His name is known to no more than five people in KGB; to be aware of him marks a person as an American informer. For God's sake, don't ever mention him."

"I've never heard of him," interrupted Maletkin. "But the Americans think he's *theirs?*"

"Yes. He's a plant. He reports everything directly to Moscow on a private line."

"Incredible," muttered the traitor. "An old man. Ingenious."

"My former associates are not fools," said Taleniekov, checking his watch. "Neither are your present ones. Forget you've ever heard of Comrade Mikovsky."

"That's his name?"

"Even I would rather not repeat it . . . There he is."

An old man bundled up in an overcoat and a black fur hat walked out of the entrance, vapour from his breath meeting the cold air. He stood for a moment on the steps, looking around as if trying to decide which archway to take into the street. His short beard was white, what could be seen of his face was filled with wrinkles and tired, pale flesh. He started down the marble stairs cautiously, holding on to the railing. He reached the concrete courtyard and walked towards the nearest arch on his right.

Taleniekov studied the stream of people that came out through the glass doors after the old curator. They seemed to be in groups of twos and threes; he looked for a single man whose eyes strayed to the courtyard below. None did and Vasili was disturbed. Had he been wrong? It did not seem likely, yet there was no single man Taleniekov could pick out of the crowds whose focus was on Mikovsky, now half-way across the courtyard. When the scholar reached the street, there was no point in waiting any longer; he *had* been wrong. The Matarese had not found his friend.

A woman. He was *not* wrong. It was a *woman*. A lone woman broke away from the crowd and hurried down the steps, her eyes on the old man. How plausible, thought Vasili. A single woman remaining for hours alone in a library would draw far less attention than a man. Among its élite soldiers, the Matarese trained women.

He was not sure why it surprised him — some of the best agents in the Soviet KGB and the American Consular Operations were women, but their duties rarely included violence. *That's* what startled him now. The woman following old Mikovsky was trailing the curator only to find *him*. Violence was intrinsic to that assignment.

"That woman," he said to Maletkin. "The one in the brown overcoat and the visored cap. She's the informer. We've got to stop her from making contact."

"A *woman?*"

"She is capable of a variety of things which you are not, comrade. Come along now, we must be careful. She won't approach him right away; she'll wait for the most opportune moment and so must we. We've got to separate her, take her when she's far enough away from him so he can't identify her if there's any noise."

"Noise?" interrupted the perplexed Maletkin. "Why would she make any noise?"

"Women are unpredictable, it's common knowledge. Let's go."

The next eighteen minutes were as disorganized and as painful to watch as Taleniekov had anticipated. Painful in that a concerned old man grew progressively bewildered as the moments passed, his agitation turning into panic when there was no sign of his young friend. He crossed the bitterly cold streets, automobiles and omnibuses blowing their horns as his walk was too slow, his legs unsteady. He kept checking his watch, the light too dim for his eyes; he was jostled by rushing pedestrians whenever he stopped. And he stopped incessantly, breath and strength diminishing. Twice he started for an omnibus shelter in the block beyond where he stood, momentarily convinced that he had made the wrong count of the streets; at the intersection where the Kirov Theatre stood, there were three shelters and his confusion mounted. He visited all three, more and more bewildered.

The strategy had the expected effect on the woman following Mikovsky. She interpreted the old man's actions as those of a subject aware that he might be under surveillance, a subject unschooled in methods of evasion but also old and frightened and capable of creating an uncontrollable situation. So the woman in the brown overcoat and visored cap kept her distance, staying in shadows, going from darkened shopfronts to dimly-lit alleyways, propelled into agitation herself by the unpredictability of her subject.

The old scholar started on his return pattern to the library. Vasili and Maletkin watched from a vantage point seventy-five metres away. Taleniekov studied the route directly across the wide avenue; there were two alleyways, both of which would be used by the woman as Mikovsky passed her on the way back.

"Come along," ordered Vasili, grabbing Maletkin's arm, pushing him forward. "We'll get behind him in the crowd on the other side. She'll turn away as he goes by, and when he passes that second alleyway, she'll use it."

"Why are you so sure?"

"Because she used it before; it's the natural thing to do. I'd use it. *We* will use it now."

"How?"

"I'll tell you when we're in position."

The moment was drawing near and Taleniekov could feel the drumlike beat in his chest. He had orchestrated the events of the past sixteen minutes, the next few would determine whether the orchestration had merit. He knew two indisputable facts: one, the woman would recognize him instantly; she would have been provided with photographs and a detailed physical description. Two, should the violence go against her, she would take her own life as quickly and as efficiently as the Englishman had done in Lodzia's flat.

Timing and shock were the only tools at his immediate disposal. He would provide the first, the traitor from Vyborg the second.

They crossed the square with a group of pedestrians and walked into the crowds in front of the Kirov Theatre.

Vasili glanced over his shoulder and saw Mikovsky weave his way awkwardly through the line forming for tickets, breathing with difficulty.

"Listen to me and do exactly as I say," said Taleniekov, holding Maletkin's arm. "Repeat the words I say to you . . ."

They entered the flow of pedestrians walking up the pavement, remaining behind a quartet of soldiers, their bulky overcoats serving as a wall.

Vasili could see beyond at will. The scholar up ahead approached the first alleyway; the woman briefly disappeared into it, then re-emerged as he passed.

Moments now. Only moments.

The second alleyway. Mikovsky was in front of it, the woman within.

"*Now!*" he ordered, rushing with Maletkin towards the entrance.

He heard the words Maletkin shouted so they would be unmistakable above the noise of the streets.

"Comrade, wait. Stop! *Circulo! Nostro circulo!*"

Silence. The shock was almost total.

"Who *are* you?" The question was asked in a cold, tense female voice.

"Stop everything! I have news from the shepherd!"

"What?"

The shock was now complete.

Taleniekov spun around the corner of the alley, rushing towards the woman, his hands two springs uncoiling as he lunged.

He grabbed her arms, his fingers sliding instantly down to her wrists, immobilizing her hands, one of which was in her overcoat pocket, gripped around a gun. She recoiled, spinning to her left, her weight dead, pulling him forward, then sprang to her right, her left foot lashing up into him, close to her body like an enraged cat's claw repelling another animal.

He countered, attacking directly, lifting her off her feet, crashing her twisting,

233

writhing body into the alleyway wall, pummelling her with his shoulder, crushing her into the brick.

It happened so fast he was only vaguely aware of what she was doing until he felt her teeth sinking into the flesh of his neck. She had thrust her face into his – a move so unexpected he could only twist away in pain. Her mouth was wide, her red lips parted grotesquely. The bite was vicious, her jaws two clamps vicing into the side of his neck. He could feel blood drenching his collar; she *would not let go*! The pain was excruciating; the harder he battered her into the wall, the deeper her teeth went into his flesh. He *could not stand it*. He released her arms, his hands clawing at her face, pulling her from him.

The explosion was loud, distinct, yet muffled by the heavy cloth of her overcoat, the echo carried on the wind throughout the alley; she fell away from him, limp against the stone.

He looked at her face; her eyes were wide and dead; she sank slowly to the pavement. She had done precisely what she had been programmed to do: she had appraised the odds – two men against herself – and fired the weapon in her pocket, blowing away her chest.

"She's *dead*! My God, she *killed* herself!" screamed Maletkin. "The *shot*, people will have heard it! We've got to run! The police!"

Several curious passersby stood motionless at the alley's entrance, peering in.

"Be quiet!" commanded Taleniekov. "If anyone comes in use your KGB card. This is official business, no one's permitted here. I want thirty seconds."

Vasili pulled a handkerchief from his pocket and pressed it against his neck, reducing the flow of blood. He knelt over the body of the dead woman. With his right hand he ripped the coat away, exposing a blouse stained everywhere with red. He tore the drenched fabric away from the skin; the hole below her left breast was massive, tissue and intestines clogging the opening. He probed the flesh around the wound; the light was too dim. He took out his cigarette lighter.

He snapped it, stretching the bloody skin beneath the breast, holding the light inches above it; the flame danced in the wind.

"For God's sake, *hurry*!" Maletkin stood several feet away, his voice a panicked whisper. "What are you doing?"

Taleniekov did not reply. Instead, he moved his fingers around the flesh, wiping away the blood to see more clearly.

He found it. In the crease beneath the left breast, angled towards the centre of the chest. A jagged circle of blue surrounded by white skin streaked with red. A blemish that was no blemish at all, but the mark of an incredible army.

The Matarese circle.

24

They walked rapidly out of the far end of the alley, melting into the crowds heading north. Maletkin was trembling, his face ashen. Vasili's right hand gripped the traitor's elbow, controlling the panic that might easily cause Maletkin to burst into a run, riveting attention on both of them. Taleniekov needed the man from Vyborg; a cable had to be sent that eluded KGB interception and Maletkin could send it. He realized that he had very little time to work out the cipher for Scofield. It would take old Mikovsky another ten minutes before he reached his office, but soon after that Vasili knew he should be there. A frightened old man could say the wrong things too.

Taleniekov held the handkerchief against the wound on his neck. The bleeding had ebbed to a trickle in the cold, it would stop sufficiently for a bandage soon; it occurred to Vasili that he should purchase a high-necked sweater to conceal it.

"Slow down!" he ordered, yanking Maletkin's elbow. "There's a café up ahead. We'll go inside for a few minutes, get a drink."

"I could *use* one," whispered Maletkin, his eyes glazed. "My God, she *killed* herself! Who *was* she?"

"Someone who made a mistake. Don't you make another."

The café was crowded; they shared a table with two middle-aged women, who objected to the intrusion and morosely kept to themselves; it was a splendid arrangement.

"Go up to the manager by the door," said Taleniekov. "Tell him your friend had too much to drink and cut himself. Ask for a bandage and some adhesive." Maletkin started to object; Vasili reached for his forearm. "Just do it. It's nothing unusual in a place like this."

The traitor got up and made his way to the man at the door. Taleniekov refolded the handkerchief, pressing the cleaner side against the torn skin, and dug into his pocket for a pencil. He moved the coarse paper napkin in front of him and began selecting the cipher for Beowulf Agate.

His mind closed out all noise, and he concentrated on an alphabet and progression of numbers. Even as Maletkin returned with a cotton bandage and a small roll of tape, Vasili wrote, crossing out errors as rapidly as he made them. Their drinks arrived; the traitor had ordered three apiece. Taleniekov kept writing.

Eight minutes later he was finished. He tore the napkin in two and copied the wording clearly in large unmistakable letters. He handed it to Maletkin. "I want this cable sent to Helsinki, to the name and hotel listed on top. I want it routed on a white line, commercial traffic, not subject to duplicate interception."

The traitor's eyes grew wide. "How do you expect *me* to do that?"

"The same way you get information to our friends in Washington. You know the unmonitored schedules; we all protect ourselves from ourselves. It's one of our more finely-honed talents."

"That's through Stockholm. We by-pass Helsinki!" Maletkin flushed; his state of agitation and the rapid infusion of alcohol had made him careless. He had not meant to reveal the Swedish connection. It wasn't done, even among fellow defectors.

Nor could Vasili use Stockholm. The cable would then be under American scrutiny, the manager of the Tavastian Hotel in Helsinki undoubtedly questioned by CIA personnel. There was another way.

"How often do you come down here to the Ligovsky headquarters for sector conferences?"

The traitor pursed his lips in embarrassment. "Not often. Perhaps three or four times during the past year."

"You're going over there now," said Taleniekov.

"I'm *what*? You've lost your head!"

"You'll lose yours if you don't. Don't worry, Colonel. Rank still has its privileges and its effect. You are sending an urgent cable to a Vyborg man in Helsinki. White line, non-duplicated traffic. However, you must bring me a verifying copy."

"Suppose they *check* with Vyborg?"

"Who on duty up there now would interfere with the second-in-command?"

Maletkin frowned nervously. "There will be questions later."

Vasili smiled, the promise of untold riches in his voice. "Take my word for it, Colonel. When you return to Vyborg there won't be anything you cannot have . . . or command."

The traitor grinned, the sweat on his chin glistening. "Where do I bring the verifying copy? Where will we meet? When?"

Taleniekov held the bandage in place over the wound on his neck and unrolled a strip of tape, the end in his teeth. "Tear it," he said to Maletkin. It was done and Vasili applied it, ripping off another strip as he spoke. "Stay the night at the Yevropeiskaya Hotel on Brodsky Street. I'll contact you there."

"They'll demand identification."

"By all means, give it to them. A colonel of the KGB will no doubt get a better room. A better woman, too, if you go down to the lounge."

"Both cost money."

"My treat," Taleniekov said.

It was the dinner hour. The huge reading rooms of the Saltykov-Shchedrin Library with their tapestried walls and the enormously high ceilings were nowhere near as crowded as usual. A scattering of students sat at the long tables, a few groups of tourists strolled about studying the tapestries and the oil paintings, speaking in hushed whispers, awed by the grandeur that was the Shchedrin.

As Vasili walked through the marble hallways towards the complex of offices in the west wing, he remembered the months he had spent in these rooms – that room – awakening his mind to a world he had known so little about. He had not exaggerated to Lodzia; it was here, through the enlightened courage of one man, that he had learned more about the enemy than in all the training he had later received in Moscow and Novograd.

The Saltykov-Shchedrin was his finest school, the man he was about to see after so many years his most accomplished teacher. He wondered whether the school or the teacher could help him now. If the Voroshin family was bound to the new Matarese there would be no revealing information in the intelligence data banks, of that he was certain. But was it here? Somewhere in the thousands of volumes that detailed the events of the revolution, of families and vast estates banished and carved up, all documented by historians of the time because they knew the time would never be seen again, the explosive beginnings of a new world. It had happened here in Leningrad – St Petersburg – and Prince Andrei Voroshin was a part of the cataclysm. The revolutionary archives at Saltykov-Shchedrin were the most extensive in all Russia; if there was a repository for any information about the Voroshins, it would be here. But being here was one thing, finding it something else again. Would his old teacher know where to look?

He turned left into the corridor lined with glass-panelled office doors, all dark except one at the end of the hallway. There was a dim light on inside, intermittently blocked by the silhouette of a figure passing back and forth in front of a desk lamp. It was Mikovsky's office, the same room he had occupied for over a quarter of a century, the slow-moving figure beyond the rippled glass unmistakably that of the scholar.

He walked up to the door and knocked softly; the dark figure loomed almost instantly behind the glass.

The door opened and Yanov Mikovsky stood there, his wrinkled face still flushed from the cold outside, his eyes beyond the thick lenses of his spectacles wide, questioning and afraid. He gestured for Vasili to come in quickly, shutting the door the instant Taleniekov was inside.

"Vasili Vasilievich!" The old man's voice was part whisper, part cry. He held out his arms, embracing his younger friend. "I never thought I'd see you again." He stepped back, his hands still on Taleniekov's overcoat, peering up at him, his wrinkled mouth tentatively forming words that did not emerge. The events of the past half hour were more than he could accept. Halting sounds emerged, but no meaning.

"Don't upset yourself," said Vasili as reassuringly as he could. "Everything's fine."

"But *why*? Why this secrecy? This running from place to place? Can it be called for? Of all men in the Soviet . . . *you*. The years you were in Riga you never came to see me, but I heard from others how respected you were, how you were in charge of so many things."

"It was better that we did not meet during those days. I told you that over the telephone."

"I never understood."

"They were merely precautions that seemed reasonable at the time." They had been more than reasonable, thought Taleniekov. He had learned that the scholar was drinking heavily, depressed over the death of his wife. If the head of KGB-Riga had been seen with the old man, people might have looked for other things. And found them.

"No matter, now," said Mikovsky. "It was a difficult period for me, as I'm

237

sure you were told. There are times when some men should be left to themselves, even by old friends. But this is now! What's *happened* to you?"

"It's a long story; I'll tell you everything I can. I must, for I need your help." Taleniekov glanced beyond the scholar; there was a kettle of water on the coils of an electric plate on the right side of the desk. Vasili could not be sure but he thought it was the same kettle, the same electric burner he remembered from so many years ago. "Your tea was always the best in Leningrad. Will you make some for us?"

The better part of a half hour passed as Taleniekov spoke, the old scholar sitting in his chair, listening in silence. When Vasili first mentioned the name, Prince Andrei Voroshin, he made no comment. But he did when his student had finished.

"The Voroshin estates were confiscated by the new revolutionary government. The family's wealth had been vastly reduced by the Romanovs and their industrial partners. Nicholas and his brother, Michael, loathed the Voroshins, claiming they were the thieves of all northern Russia and the sea routes. And, of course, the prince was marked by the Bolsheviks for execution. His only hope was Kerenski, who was too indecisive or corrupt to cut off the illustrious families so completely. That hope vanished with the collapse of the Winter Palace."

"What happened to Voroshin?"

"He was sentenced to death. I'm not positive, but I think his name was announced on the execution lists. Those who escaped were generally heard from during the succeeding years; I would have remembered had Voroshin been among them."

"Why would you? There were hundreds here in Leningrad alone. Why the Voroshins?"

"They were not easily forgotten for many reasons. It was not often that the czars of Russia called their own kind thieves and pirates and sought to destroy them. The Voroshin family was notorious. The prince's father and grandfather dealt in the Chinese and African slave trades, from the Indian Ocean to the American South; they manipulated the Imperial banks, forcing merchant fleets and companies into bankruptcies and absorbing them. It is said that when Nicholas secretly ordered Prince Andrei Voroshin from the palace court, he proclaimed: 'Should our Russia fall prey to maniacs, it will be because of men like you. You drive them to our throats.' That was a number of years before the revolution."

"You say 'secretly ordered' him. Why secretly?"

"It was not a time to expose dissent among the aristocrats. Their enemies would have used it to justify the cries of national crisis. The revolution was in foment decades before the event. Nicholas understood; he knew it was happening."

"Did Voroshin have sons?"

"I don't know, but I would presume so – one way or the other. He had many mistresses."

"What about the family itself?"

"Again I have no specific knowledge, but I assume they perished. As you're aware the tribunals were usually lenient where women and children were concerned. Thousands were allowed to flee; only the most frantic wanted that blood on their hands. But I don't believe the Voroshins were allowed to. Actually, I'm quite sure of it, but I don't know specifically."

238

"I need specific knowledge."

"I understand that, and in my judgement you have it. At least enough to refute any theory involving Voroshin and this incredible Matarese society."

"Why do you say that?"

"Because had the prince escaped, it would not have been to his advantage to keep silent. The Whites in exile were organizing everywhere. Those with legitimate titles were welcomed with open arms and excessive remuneration by the great companies and the international banks; it was good business. It was not in Voroshin's nature to reject such largesse and notoriety. No, Vasili. He was killed."

Taleniekov listened to the scholar's words, looking for an inconsistency. He got up from the chair and went to the pot of tea; he filled his cup and stared absently at the brown liquid. "Unless he was offered something of greater value to keep silent, to remain anonymous."

"This Matarese?" asked Mikovsky.

"Yes." Vasili looked down at the scholar. "Money had been made available. In Rome and in Genoa. It was their initial funding."

"But it was earmarked for just that, wasn't it?" Mikovsky leaned forward. "From what you've told me, it was to be used for the hiring of assassins, spreading the gospel of vengeance according to this Guillaume de Matarese, is that not so?"

"That's what the old woman implied," agreed Taleniekov.

"Then it was not to be spent recouping individual fortunes or financing new ones. You see, that's what I can't accept where Voroshin is concerned. If he had escaped he would not have turned his back on the opportunities offered him. Not to join an organization bent on political vengeance; he was far too pragmatic a man."

Vasili had started back to his chair; he stopped and turned, the cup suspended, motionless in his hand. "What did you just say?"

"That Voroshin was too pragmatic to reject . . ."

"No," interrupted Taleniekov. "Before that. The money was not to be used recouping fortunes or . . . ?"

"Financing new ones. You see, Vasili, large sums of capital *were* made available to the exiles."

Taleniekov held up his hand. "'Financing new ones,'" he repeated. "There are many ways to spread a gospel. Beggars and lunatics do it in the streets, priests from pulpits, politicians from rostrums. But how can you spread a gospel that cannot stand scrutiny? How do you *pay* for it?" Vasili put the cup down on the small table next to his chair. "You do both anonymously, using the complicated methods and procedures of an existing structure. One in which whole areas operate as separate entities, distinct from one another yet held together by a common identity. Where enormous sums of capital are transferred daily." Taleniekov walked back to the desk and leaned over, his hands on the edge. "You make the necessary *purchase*! You buy the seat of decision! The structure is yours for the using!"

The scholar studied Vasili's face, observing the words. "If I follow you – and I believe I do – the money left by Matarese was to be divided, and used to buy participation in giant, established enterprises."

"Exactly. I'm looking in the wrong *place* – sorry, the *right* place, but the wrong *country.* Voroshin *did* escape. He got out of Russia probably a long time before he had to because the Romanovs crippled him, stripped him, watched his every financial move. He was hamstrung here ... and later the sort of investments Guillaume de Matarese envisioned were prohibited in the Soviet. Don't you see, he had no reason to stay in Russia. His decision was made long *before* the revolution; it's why you never heard of him in exile. He became someone *else*."

"You're wrong, Vasili. His name was among those sentenced to death. I remember seeing it myself."

"But you're not sure you saw it later, in the announcements of those actually executed."

"There were so many."

"That's my point."

"There were his communications with the Kerensky provisional government; they're a matter of record."

"Easily dispatched and recorded." Taleniekov pushed himself away from the desk, his every instinct telling him he was near the truth. "What better way for a man like Voroshin to lose his identity but in the chaos of a revolution? The mobs out of control; the discipline did not come for weeks, and it was a miracle it came then. Absolute chaos. How easily it could be done."

"You're oversimplifying," said Mikovsky. "Although there was a period of rampage, teams of observers travelled throughout the cities and countryside writing down everything they saw and heard. Not only facts but impressions, opinions, interpretations of what they witnessed. The academicians insisted upon it, for it was a moment in history that would never be repeated and they wanted no instant lost, none unaccounted for. Everything was written down, no matter how harsh the observation. *That* was a form of discipline, Vasili."

Taleniekov nodded, holding the scholar's eyes with his own. "Why do you think I'm here?"

The old man sat forward. "The archives of the revolution?"

"I must see them."

"An easy request to make but most difficult to grant. The authority must come from Moscow."

"How is it relayed?"

"Through the Ministry of Cultural Affairs. A man is sent over from the Leningrad office with the key to the rooms below. There is no key here."

Vasili's eyes strayed to the mounds of papers on Mikovsky's desk. "Is that man an archivist? A scholar such as yourself?"

"No. He is merely a man with a key."

"How often are the authorizations granted?"

Mikovsky frowned. "Not very frequently. Perhaps twice a month."

"When was the last time?"

"About three weeks ago. An historian from the *Zhdanov* doing research."

"Where did he do his reading?"

"In the archive rooms. Nothing is permitted to be taken from them."

Taleniekov held up his hand. "Something was. It was sent to you. For everyone's sake it should be returned to the archives immediately. Your telephone call to the Leningrad office should be rather excited."

The man arrived in twenty-one minutes, his face burnt from the cold.

"The night duty officer said it was urgent, sir," said the young man breathlessly, opening his briefcase and removing the key, so intricately ridged it would take a precision-tooled instrument to duplicate it.

"Also highly irregular and without question a criminal offence," replied Mikovsky, getting up from his chair.

"But no harm done now that you're here." The scholar walked around the desk, a large envelope in his hand. "Shall we go below?"

"Is that the material?" asked the man with the key.

"Yes." The scholar lowered the envelope.

"*What* material?" Taleniekov's voice was sharp, the question an accusation.

The man was caught. He dropped the key and reached for his belt. Vasili lunged, grabbing the young man's hand, pulling it downward, throwing his shoulder into the man's chest, hurling him to the floor. "You said the wrong thing!" shouted Vasili. "No duty officer tells a messenger the particulars of an emergency. *Perro nostro circulo!* There'll be no pills this time! No guns. I've got you, *soldier*! And by your Corsican christ, you'll tell me what I want to know!"

"*Bei unserem Ring! Unsere Gottheit!*" whispered the young man, his mouth stretched, his lips bulging, his tongue . . . his *tongue*. His *teeth*. The bite came, the jaw clamped, the results irreversible.

Taleniekov watched in furious astonishment as the capsule's liquid entered the throat, paralysing the muscles. In seconds it happened; an expulsion of air, a final breath.

"Call the ministry!" he said to the shocked Mikovsky. "Tell the night duty officer that it will take several hours to re-insert the material."

"I don't *understand. Anything!*"

"They tapped the ministry's phone. This one intercepted the man with the key. He would have left it and fled after he had killed us both." Vasili ripped the dead man's overcoat apart and then the shirt beneath.

It was there. The blemish that was no blemish, the jagged blue circle of the Matarese.

The old scholar reached for the two ledgers on the top shelf of the metal racks and handed them to Taleniekov. They were the seventeenth and eighteenth volumes they had each gone through, searching for the name Voroshin.

"It would be far easier if we were in Moscow," said Mikovsky, descending the ladder cautiously, heading for the long table. "All this material has been transcribed and indexed. One volume would tell us exactly where to look."

"There'll be something; there *has* to be." Taleniekov handed one book to the scholar and opened the other record for himself. He began to scan the handwritten entries of ink, cautiously turning the brittle pages, yellowed with age.

Twelve minutes later Yanov Mikovsky spoke. "It's here."

"What?"

"The crimes of Prince Andrei Voroshin."

"His execution?"

"Not yet. His life, and the lives and criminal acts of his father and grandfather."

"Let me see."

It was all there, meticulously if superficially recorded by a steady, precise hand. The fathers Voroshin were described as enemies-of-the-masses, replete with the crimes of wanton murder of serfs and tenants, and the more rarefied manipulations of the Imperial banks, causing thousands to be unemployed, casting thousands more into the ranks of the starving. The prince had been sent to southern Europe for his higher education, a grand tour that lasted five years, solidifying his pursuance of imperialistic dominance and the suppression of the people.

"*Where?*" Taleniekov spoke out loud.

"Referring to what?" asked the scholar, reading the same page.

"Where was he *sent?*"

Mikovsky turned the page. "Krefeld. The University of Krefeld. Here it is."

"That bastard spoke *German. Bei unserem Ring! Unsere Gottheit!* It's in Germany!"

"What is?"

"Voroshin's new identity. It's *here*. Read further."

They read. The prince had spent three years at Krefeld, two in graduate studies at Düsseldorf, returning frequently in his adult years when he developed close personal ties with such German industrialists as Gustav von Bohlen-Halbach, Friedrich Schotte and Wilhelm Habernicht.

"Essen," said Vasili. "Düsseldorf led to Essen. It was territory Voroshin knew, a language he spoke. The timing was perfect; war in Europe, revolution in Russia, the world in chaos. The armaments companies in Essen, that's what he became a part of."

"*Krupp?*"

"Or Verachten. Krupp's competitor."

"You think he bought himself into one of them?"

"Through a rear door and a new identity. German industrial expansion then was as chaotic as the Kaiser's war, management personnel raided and shifted about like small armies. The circumstances were ideal for Voroshin."

"Here is the execution," interrupted Mikovsky, who had turned the pages. "The description starts here at the top. Your theory loses credence, I'm afraid."

Taleniekov leaned over, scanning the words. The entry detailed the deaths of Prince Andrei Voroshin, his wife, two sons and their wives, and one daughter, on the afternoon of 21 October 1917, at his estate in Tsarskoye Selo on the banks of the Slovyanka River. It described in bloody particulars the final minutes of fighting, the Voroshins trapped in the great house with their servants, repelling the attacking mob, firing weapons from the windows, hurling cans of flaming petrol from the sloping roofs – at the end, releasing their servants and, in a pact of death, using their own gunpowder to blow up themselves and the great house in a final conflagration. Nothing was left but the burning skeleton of a czarist estate, the remains of the Voroshins consumed in the flames.

Images came back to Vasili, memories from the hills at night high above Porto Vecchio. The ruins of Villa Matarese. There, too, was a final conflagration.

"I must disagree," he said softly to Mikovsky. "This was no execution at all."

"The tribunals' courts may have been absent," countered the scholar, "but I daresay the results were the same."

"There were no results, no evidence, no proof of death. There were only charred ruins. This entry is false."

"Vasili Vasilievich! These are the *archives*, every document was scrutinized and approved by the academicians! At the *time*."

"One was bought. I grant you a great estate was burned to the ground, but that is the limit of existing proof." Taleniekov turned several pages back. "Look. This report is very descriptive. Figures with guns at windows, men on roofs, servants streaming out, explosions starting in the kitchens, everything seemingly accounted for."

"Agreed," said Mikovsky, impressed with the minute details he read.

"Wrong. There's something missing. In every entry of this nature that we've seen – the storming of palaces and estates, the stopping of trains, the demon-strations – there are always such phrases as 'the advance column was led by Comrade So-and-So, the retreat under fire from the czarist guards commanded by provisional Captain Such-and-Such, the execution carried out under the authority of Comrade Blank. As you said before, these entries are all bulging with identities, everything recorded for future confirmation. Well, read this again." Vasili flipped the pages back and forth. "The detail *is* extraordinary, even to the temperature of the day and the colour of the afternoon sky and the fur overcoats worn by the men on the roof. But there's not one identity. Only the Voroshins are mentioned by name, no one else."

The scholar put his fingers on a yellowed page, his old eyes racing down the lines, his lips parted in astonishment. "You're right. The excessive detail obscures the absence of specific information."

"It always does," said Taleniekov. "The execution of the family Voroshin was a hoax. It never happened."

25

"That young man of yours was quite impossible," said Mikovsky into the telephone, words and tone harshly critical of the night duty officer at the Ministry of Cultural Affairs. "I made it quite clear – as I assume *you* made it clear – that he was to remain in the archives until the material was returned. *Now*, what do I find? The man gone and the key shoved under my door! Really, it's most irregular. I suggest you send someone over to pick it up."

The old scholar hung up quickly, terminating any chance for the duty officer to speak further. He glanced up at Taleniekov, his eyes filled with relief, but looking for approval.

"That performance would have merited you a certificate from Stanislavsky." Vasili smiled, as he continued to wipe his hands with paper towels taken from the near-by washroom. "We're covered — *you're* covered. Just remember, a body without papers will be found behind the furnaces. If you're questioned, you know nothing, you've never seen him before, your only reaction is one of shock and astonishment."

"But Cultural Affairs, surely *they'll* know him!"

"Surely they won't. He wasn't the man sent over with the key. The ministry will have its own problem, quite a serious one. It will have the key back in its possession, but it will have lost a messenger. If that phone is still tapped, the one listening will assume his man was successful. We've bought time."

"For what?"

"I've got to get to Essen."

"Essen. On an assumption, Vasili? On speculation?"

"It's more than speculation. Two of the names mentioned in the Voroshin report were significant. Schotte and Bohlen-Halbach. Friedrich Schotte was convicted by the German courts soon after the First World War for transferring sums of money out of the country; he was killed in prison the night he arrived. It was a highly publicized murder, the killers found. I think he made a mistake and the Matarese called for his silence. Gustav Bohlen-Halbach married the sole survivor of the Krupp family and assumed control of the Krupp Works. If these were Voroshin's friends more than half a century ago, they could have been extraordinarily helpful to him. It all fits."

Mikovsky shook his head. "You're looking for sixty-year-old ghosts."

"Only in the hope that they will lead to present substances. God knows they exist. Do you need further proof?"

"No. It's their existence that frightens me for you. An Englishman waits for you at someone's flat, a woman follows me, a young man arrives here with keys to the archives he steals from another . . . all from this Matarese. It seems they have you trapped."

"From their point of view, they do. They've studied my files and sent out their soldiers to cover my every conceivable course of action, the assumption being that if one fails another will not."

The scholar removed his spectacles, his watery eyes staring up at Taleniekov. "Where do they find such . . . soldiers, as you call them? Where are to be found these motivated men and women who give up their lives so readily?"

"The answer to that may be more frightening than either of us can imagine. Its roots go back centuries, to an Islamic prince named Hasan ibn as-Sabbāh. He formed cadres of political killers to keep him in power. They were called *fida'is*."

Mikovsky dropped his glasses on the desk; the sound was sharp. "The *fida'is?* The assassins? I'm familiar with what you're talking about, but the concept is preposterous. The *fida'is* — the assassins of Sabbāh — were based on the prohibitions of a stoic religion. They were Faustian; they exchanged their souls, their minds, their bodies

244

for the pleasures of a Valhalla while on this earth. Such incentives are not credible in these times."

"In these times?" asked Vasili. "These *are* the times. The larger house, the fattened bank account, or the use of a *dacha* for a longer period of time, supplied more luxuriously than one's comrades; a greater fleet of aircraft or a more powerful battleship; the ear of a superior or an invitation to an event others cannot attend. These are very much the times, Yanov. The world you and I live in – personally, professionally, even vicariously – is a global society bursting with greed, nine out of ten inhabitants a Faust. I think it was something Karl Marx never understood."

"A deliberate transitional omission, my friend. He understood fully; there were other issues to be attacked first."

Taleniekov smiled. "That sounds dangerously like an apology."

"Would you prefer words to the effect that the governing of a nation is too important to be left to the people?"

"A monarchist statement. Hardly applicable. It could have been made by the Czar."

"But it wasn't. It was made by America's Thomas Jefferson. Again, exercising a transitional omission. Both countries, you see, had just gone through their revolutions; each was a new, emerging nation. Words and decisions had to be practical."

"Your erudition does not change my judgement. I've seen too much, used too much."

"I don't want to change anything, least of all your talents of observation. I would like only for you to keep things in perspective, my old pupil. Perhaps we're all in a state of transition."

"To what?"

Mikovsky lifted his spectacles off the desk and put them on carefully. "To heaven or hell, Vasili. I haven't the vaguest idea which. My only consolation is that I will not be here to find out. How will you get to Essen?"

"Back through Helsinki."

"Will it be difficult?"

"No. There is a man from Vyborg who'll help."

"When will you leave?"

"In the morning."

"You're welcome to stay the night with me."

"No, it could be dangerous for you."

The scholar raised his head in surprise. "But I thought you said that my performance on the phone removed such concerns."

"I believe it. I don't think anything will be said for days. Eventually, of course, the police will be called; but by then the incident – as far as you're concerned – has faded into an unpleasant lapse in procedures."

"I understand that, so where is the immediate problem?"

"That I'm wrong. In which case I will have killed us both."

Mikovsky smiled. "There's a certain finality in that."

"I had to do what I did. There was no one else. I'm sorry."

"Don't be, my old pupil. And you are older, you know. In some ways older than me." The scholar rose from his chair and walked unsteadily around the desk. "You must go then, and I will not see you again. Embrace me, Vasili Vasilievich. Heaven or hell, which will it be? I think you know. It is the latter and you have reached it."

"I got there a long time ago," said Taleniekov, holding the gentle old man he would never see again.

"Colonel Maletkin?" asked Vasili, knowing that the hesitant voice on the other end of the line belonged indeed to the traitor from Vyborg.

"Where are you?"

"At a telephone in the street, not far away. Do you have something for me?"

"Yes."

"Good. And I have something for you."

"Also good," Maletkin said. "When?"

"Now. Walk out the front entrance of the hotel and turn right. Keep walking, I'll catch up with you."

There was a moment of silence. "It's almost midnight."

"I'm glad your watch is accurate. It must be expensive. It is one of those Swiss chronometers so popular with the Americans?"

"There's a woman here."

"Tell her to wait. *Order* her, Colonel. You're an officer of the KGB."

Seven minutes later Maletkin emerged ferret-like on the pavement in front of the entrance, looking smaller than life and glancing in several directions at once without seemingly turning his head. Although it was cold and dark, Vasili could almost see the sweat on the traitor's chin; in a day or so there would be no chin. It would be blown off in a courtyard in Vyborg.

Maletkin began walking north. There were not many pedestrians on Brodsky Street, a few couples linked arm in arm, the inevitable trio of young soldiers looking for warmth somewhere, anywhere, before returning to the sterility of their barracks.

Taleniekov waited, watched the scene in the street, looking for someone who did not belong.

There was no one. The traitor had not considered double-cross nor had any soldier of the Matarese picked him up. Vasili left the shadows of the doorway and hastened up the block; in sixty seconds he was directly across from Maletkin. He began whistling *Yankee Doodle Dandy*.

"There's your cable!" said the traitor, spitting out the words in the darkness of a recessed shopfront. "This is the only duplicate. Now tell me. Who is the informer in Vyborg?"

"The *other* informer, don't you mean?" Taleniekov spoke as he snapped his cigarette lighter and looked at the copy of the coded message to Helsinki. It was accurate. "You'll have the name in a matter of hours."

"I want it *now*! For all I know someone's already checked with Vyborg. I want my protection; you guaranteed it! I'm leaving here first thing in the morning."

"*We're* leaving," interrupted Vasili. "Before morning, actually."

"No!"

"Yes. It's a two-hour drive; you'll make that briefing after all."

"I don't want anything more to do with you. Your photograph's on every KGB bulletin board; there were *two* of them down at the Ligovsky headquarters! I found myself perspiring."

"I wouldn't have thought it! But, you see, you must drive me back to the lake and put me in contact with the Finns. My business here in Leningrad is finished."

"Why *me*? I've done enough!"

"Because if you don't, I will not be able to remember a name you should know in Vyborg." Taleniekov patted the traitor's cheek; Maletkin flinched. "Go back to your woman, comrade, and perform well. But finish with her before too long. I want you checked out of the hotel by three-thirty."

"Three-thirty?"

"Yes. Drive your car to the Anichkov Bridge; be there no later than four o'clock. Make two trips over the bridge and back. I'll meet you on one side or the other."

"The *militsianyeri*. They stop suspicious vehicles, and a car travelling back and forth over the Anichkov at four in the morning is not a normal sight."

"Exactly. If there are *militsianyeri* around, I want to know it."

"Suppose they stop me?"

"Must I keep reminding you that you are a colonel of the KGB? You're on official business. Very official and very secret." Vasili started to leave, then turned back. "It just struck me," he said. "It may have occurred to you to borrow a weapon and shoot me down at an opportune moment. On the one hand, you could take credit for bringing me in, and on the other, you could swear you tried to prevent my being killed at great risk to yourself. As long as you were willing to forgo the name of the man in Vyborg, such a strategy would appear to be sound. Very little risk, rewards from both camps. But you should know that every step I take in your presence here in Leningrad is being watched by another now."

Maletkin's immobile head did not prevent his eyes from sweeping about in an 180-degree arc. He spoke with mounting intensity. "I *swear* to you such a thing never occurred to me!"

You really are a damn fool, thought Taleniekov. "Four o'clock then, comrade."

The row of old buildings in the *dom-vashen* was a decaying black wall of stone mottled by an irregular pattern of dim lights in the windows. The night sounds were a muted cacophony that belonged to the district: voices raised in abrasive arguments alongside laughter that too often was too hysterical, too drunk.

Vasili approached the staircase of the building four doors down the block from Lodzia's flat. He had glanced up at her windows; her lights were on. She was home.

He climbed the steps slowly, as a tired man might, returning to an uninviting home after putting in unwanted, unpaid-for overtime behind a never-ending conveyor belt in the cause of some new economic plan no one understood. He opened the glass door and went inside the small vestibule.

Instantly, he straightened up, the brief performance over; there was no hesitation now. He opened the inner door, walked to the basement staircase, and descended into the dark, filthy environs of the connecting cellars. He passed the door behind which he had placed the dead Englishman, vodka poured down the throat, wrists slashed with a razor. He pulled out his lighter, ignited it and pushed the door back.

The Englishman was gone. Not only was he gone but there were no signs of blood; everything had been scrubbed clean.

Taleniekov's body went rigid, his thoughts suspended in shock. *Something terrible had happened. He had been wrong.*

So wrong!

Yet he had been so *sure*. The soldiers of the Matarese were expendable, but the last thing they would do would be to return to a scene of violence. The possibilities of a trap were too great; the Matarese would not, *could* not, take that risk!

But they had, the target worth the gamble. What had he *done*?

Lodzia!

He left the door ajar and started walking rapidly, through the connecting cellars, his Graz-Burya in his hand, his steps silent, his eyes and ears primed.

He reached Lodzia's building and started up the steps to the ground-level foyer. He pulled the door back slowly and listened; there was a burst of laughter from the staircase above. A high-pitched female voice, joined seconds later by the laughter of a man.

Vasili put the Graz-Burya in his pocket and stepped inside around the railing, and walked quickly, unsteadily up the steps after the couple. They approached the second-floor landing, diagonally across from Lodzia's door. Taleniekov spoke, a foolish grin on his face.

"Would you young people do a middle-aged lover a favour? I'm afraid I had that one vodka too many."

The couple turned, smiling as one.

"What's the problem, friend?" the young man asked.

"My friend is the problem," said Taleniekov, gesturing at Lodzia's door. "I was to meet her after the performance at the Kirov. I'm afraid I was delayed by an old army comrade. I think she's angry as hell. Please knock for me; if she hears my voice she probably won't let me in." Vasili grinned again, his thoughts in opposition to his smile. The possible sacrifice of the young and the attractive grew more painful as one got older.

"It's the least we can do for a soldier," said the girl, laughing brightly. "Go on, husband-mine, do your bit for the military."

"Why not?" The young man shrugged and walked to Lodzia's door. Taleniekov crossed beyond it, his back to the wall, his right hand again in his pocket. The youthful husband knocked.

There was no sound from within. He glanced over at Vasili, who nodded, indicating another try. The young man knocked again, now louder, more insistent, and again there was only silence from inside.

"Perhaps she's still waiting for you at the Kirov," said the girl.

"Then again," added the young man, smiling, "perhaps she found your old army comrade and they're both avoiding you."

Taleniekov tried to smile back but could not. He knew only too well what he might find behind the door. "I'll wait here," he said. "Thank you very much."

The husband seemed to realize he had been facetious at the wrong moment. "I'm sorry," he mumbled, taking his wife's arm.

"Good luck," said the girl, awkwardly. They both walked rapidly up the staircase.

Vasili waited until he heard the sound of a door closing two storeys above. He took his automatic from his pocket and reached for the knob in front of him, afraid to find out that it was not locked.

It was not and his fear mounted. He pushed the door open, stepped inside and closed it. What he saw sent a pain through his chest; he knew a greater pain would follow shortly. The room was a shambles, chairs, tables and lamps overturned; books and cushions were strewn on the floor, articles of clothing lying in scattered disarray. The scene was created to depict a violent struggle, but it was false, overdone, as such constructed scenes were usually overdone. There had been no struggle, but there had been something else. There had been an interrogation based in torture.

The bedroom door was open; he walked towards it, knowing the greater pain would come in seconds, sharp bolts of anguish. He went inside and looked at her. She was on the bed, her clothes torn from her body, the positioning of her legs indicating rape, the act, if it was done, done only for the purposes of an autopsy, undoubtedly performed after she had died. Her face was battered, lips and eyes swollen, teeth broken. Streaks of blood had flowed down her cheeks leaving abstract patterns of deep red on her light skin.

Taleniekov turned away, a terrible passivity sweeping over him. He had felt it many times before; he wanted only to kill. He would kill.

And then he was touched, so deeply that his eyes filled suddenly with tears and he could not breathe. Lodzia Kronescha had not broken; she had not revealed to the animal who had operated on her that her lover from the days of Riga was due after midnight. She had done more than keep the secret, far more. She had sent the animal off in another direction. What she must have *gone* through!

He had not loved in more than half a lifetime; he loved now and it was too late.

Too late? Oh, God!

... *where is the problem?*

... *that I'm wrong. In which case I will have killed us both.*

Yanov Mikovsky.

If a follow-up soldier had been sent by the Matarese to Lodzia Kronescha, another surely would have been sent to seek out the scholar.

Vasili raced into the sitting room, to the telephone that had carefully not been disturbed. It did not matter whether or not the line was tapped; he would learn what he had to learn in seconds, be away seconds later before anyone intercepting him could send men to the *dom-vashen*.

He dialled Mikovsky's number. The phone was picked up immediately ... too quickly for an old man.

"Yes?" The voice was muffled, unclear.

"Dr Mikovsky, please."

"Yes?" repeated the male voice. It was not the scholar's.

"I'm an associate of Comrade Mikovsky and it's urgent that I speak with him. I know he wasn't feeling well earlier; does he need medical attention? We'll send it right away, of course."

"No." The man spoke too swiftly. "Who is calling, please?"

Taleniekov forced a casual laugh. "It's only his office neighbour, Comrade Rydukov. Tell him I've found the book he was looking for . . . no, let me tell him myself."

Silence.

"Yes?" It was Mikovsky; they had let him get on the line.

"Are you all right? Are those men friends?"

"*Run, Vasili! Get away! They are . . .*"

A deafening explosion burst over the line. Taleniekov held the telephone in his hand, staring at it. He stood for a moment, allowing sharp bolts of pain to sear through his chest. He loved two people in Leningrad and he had killed them both.

No, that was not true. The Matarese had killed them. And now he would kill in return. Kill . . . and kill . . . and *kill.*

He went into a telephone booth on the Nevsky Prospekt and dialled the Yevropeis-kaya Hotel. There would be no small talk, no teasing indulgences that kept a puppet dancing on a string; there was no time to waste on insignificant men. He had to get across Lake Vainikkala, into Helsinki, reach the Corsican woman in Paris and send the word to Scofield. He was on his way to Essen, for the secret of the Voroshins was there and animals were loose, killing to prevent that secret from being revealed. He wanted them now . . . so badly . . . these élite soldiers of the Matarese. They were all dead men in his hands.

"Yes, yes what is it?" were the rushed, breathless words of the traitor from Vyborg.

"Get out of there at once," commanded Taleniekov. "Drive to the Moskva Station. I'll meet you at the kerb in front of the first entrance."

"*Now?* It is barely two o'clock! You said . . ."

"Forget what I said, do as I *say.* Did you make the arrangements with the Finns?"

"A simple telephone call."

"Did you *make* it?"

"It can be done in a minute."

"Do it. Be at the Moskva in fifteen."

The drive north was made in near-total silence, broken only by Maletkin's intermittent whining over the events of the past twenty-four hours. He was a man dealing in things so far beyond his depth that even his treachery had a rancid, shallow quality about it.

They drove through Vyborg, past Selzneva, towards the border. Vasili recognized the snow-bordered road he had walked down from the edge of the frozen lake; soon they would reach the fork in the road where he had first observed the traitor beside him. It had been dawn then; soon it would be dawn again. And so much had happened, so much learned. So tragically.

He was exhausted. He had had no sleep, and he needed it badly. He knew better than to try to function while his mind resisted thought; he would get to Helsinki and sleep for as long as his body and his faculties would permit, then make his arrangements. To Essen.

But there was a final arrangement to be made now, before he left his beloved Russia, *for* his Russia.

"In less than a minute we'll reach the rendezvous at the lake," Maletkin said. "You'll be met by a Finn along the path to the water's edge. Everything's arranged. Now, *comrade*, I've carried out my end of the bargain, you deliver yours. Who is the other informer at Vyborg?"

"You don't need his name. You just need his rank. He's the only man in your sector who can give you orders, your sole superior. First in command at Vyborg."

"*What?* He's a tyrant, a fanatic!"

"What better cover? Drop in to see him . . . privately. You'll know what to say."

"Yes," agreed Maletkin, his eyes on fire, slowing the car down as they approached a break in the snowbank. "Yes, I think I will know what to say . . . Here's the path."

"And here is your gun," said Taleniekov, handing the traitor his weapon, minus its firing pin.

"Oh? Yes, thank you," replied Maletkin, not listening, his thoughts on power unimagined only seconds ago.

Vasili got out of the car. "Goodbye," he said, closing the door.

As he rounded the back of the automobile towards the path, he heard the sound of Maletkin's window being rolled down.

"It's *incredible*," said the traitor, sheer gratitude in his voice. "*Thank* you."

"You're welcome."

The window was rolled up. The roar of the engine joined the screaming whine of the tyres as they spun on the snow. The car sped forward; Maletkin would waste no time getting back to Vyborg.

To his execution.

Taleniekov entered the path that would take him to an escort, to Helsinki, to Essen. He began whistling softly; the tune was *Yankee Doodle Dandy*.

26

The gentle-looking man in the rumpled clothes and the high-necked cotton sweater clamped a violin case between his knees and thanked the Finnair stewardess for the container of tea. If anyone on board was inclined to guess the musician's age, he'd probably say somewhere between fifty-five and sixty, possibly a little older. Those sitting farther away would start at sixty-plus and add that he was probably older than that.

Yet with the exception of streaks of white brushed into his hair he had used no cosmetics. Taleniekov had learned years ago that the muscles of the face and body conveyed age and infirmity far better than powders and liquid plastics.

The trick was to set the muscles in the desired position of abnormal stress, then go about one's business as normally as possible, overcoming the discomfort by fighting it, as older people fight the strain of age and cripples do the best they can with their deformities.

Essen. He had been to the "black jewel of the Ruhr" twice, neither trip recorded for they were sensitive assignments involving industrial espionage – operations Moscow did not care to have noted anywhere. Therefore, the Matarese had no information that could help it in Essen. No contacts to keep under surveillance, no friends to seek out and trap, nothing. No Yanov Mikovsky, no . . . Lodzia Kronescha.

Essen. Where could he begin? The scholar had been right: he was looking for a sixty-year-old ghost, a hidden absorption of one man and his family into a vast industrial complex during a period of world chaos. Legal documents going back more than half a century would be out of reach – if they had ever existed in the first place. And even if they had, and were available, they would be so obscured that it could take weeks to trace money and identities – in the tracing his own exposure guaranteed.

Too, the court records in Essen had to be among the most gargantuan and complicated anywhere. The practice of law in Essen the most lucrative of all professions. Where was the man who could make his way through such a maze? Where was the time to do it?

There *was* a man, a patent attorney, who would no doubt throw up his hands at the thought of trying to find the name of a single Russian entering Essen fifty years ago. But he *was* a lawyer; he was a place to start. If he was alive, and if he was willing to talk with a long-ago embarrassment. Vasili had not thought of the man in years. Heinrich Kassel had been a thirty-five-year-old junior partner in a firm that did legal work for many of Essen's prominent companies. The KGB dossier on him had depicted a man often at odds with his superiors, a man who championed extremely liberal causes – some so objectionable to his employers they had threatened to fire him. But he was too good; no superior cared to be responsible for his dismissal.

The conspiratorial asses in Moscow had decreed in their wisdom that Kassel was prime material for patent design espionage. In their better wisdom, the asses had sent their most persuasive negotiator, one Vasili Taleniekov, to enlist the attorney for a better world.

It took Vasili less than an hour over a trumped-up dinner to realize how absurd the assignment was. The realization came when Heinrich Kassel leaned back in his chair and exclaimed.

"Are you out of your *mind*? I do what I do to keep you bastards out!"

There had been nothing for it. The persuasive negotiator and the misguided attorney had got drunk, ending the evening at dawn, watching the sun come up over the gardens in Gruga Park. They had made a drunken pact: the lawyer would not report Moscow's attempt to the Bonn government – in so far as Moscow had conceived of it so badly – if Taleniekov would guarantee that the KGB dossier was substantially altered – in so far as such erroneous evaluations would do the attorney no good where a full partnership was concerned if they ever leaked out. The lawyer had kept silent, and Vasili had returned to Moscow, amending the German's file with the judgement that the "radical" attorney was probably a *provocateur* in the pay of the Americans. Kassel might help him, at least tell him where he could start.

If he was able to reach Heinrich Kassel. So many things might have happened to prevent it. Disease, death, relocation, accidents of living and livelihood; it had been twelve years since the abortive assignment in Essen.

There was something else he had to do in Essen, he mused. He had no gun; he would have to purchase one. The West German airport security was such these days that he could not chance the dismantling of his Graz-Burya and packing it in his carry-on travel bag.

There was so much to do, so little time. But a pattern was coming into focus. It was obscure, elusive, contradictory . . . but it was there. The Corsican fever was spreading, the infectors using massive sums of money and ingenious financing methods to create pockets of chaos everywhere, recruiting an army of élite soldiers who would give up their lives instantly to protect the cause. But again, *what* cause? To what purpose? What were the violent philosophical descendants of Guillaume de Matarese trying to achieve? Assassination, terrorism, indiscriminate bombings and riots, kidnapping and murder . . . all the things that men of wealth had to detest, for in the breakdown of order was their undoing. This was the giant contradiction. *Why?*

He felt the plane dip, the pilot was starting his descent into Essen.

Essen. Prince Andrei Voroshin. Who had he become?

"I don't believe it!" exclaimed Heinrich Kassel over the telephone, his voice conveying the same good-natured incredulity Taleniekov remembered from twelve years ago. "Every time I pass the gardens in the Gruga, I pause for a moment and laugh. My wife thinks it must be the memory of an old girl-friend."

"I trust you cleared that up."

Oh, yes. I tell her it was where I nearly became an international spy and she's *convinced* it's an old girl-friend."

"Meet me at the Gruga, please. It's urgent and has nothing to do with my former business."

"Are you sure? It would not do for one of Essen's more prominent attorneys to have a Russian connection. These are odd times. Rumours abound that the Baader-Meinhof are financed by Moscow, that our neighbours to the far north are up to some nasty old tricks."

Taleniekov paused for a moment, wincing at the coincidence. "You have the word of an old conspirator. I'm unemployed."

"Really? How interesting. Gruga Park then. It's almost noon. Shall we say one o'clock? Same place in the gardens, although there'll be no flowers this time of year."

The ice on the pond glistened in the sunlight, the shrubbery curled for the cold of winter, yet briefly alive in the noon-day's warmth from the sky. Vasili sat on the

253

bench; it was fifteen minutes past one and he felt the stirrings of concern. Without thinking, he touched the bulge in his right-hand pocket that was the small automatic he had purchased in Kopstadt Square, then took his hand away when he saw the hatless figure walking rapidly up the garden path.

Kassel had grown portly and nearly bald. In his large overcoat with the black fur lapels he was the image of a successful burgomaster, his obviously expensive attire at odds with Taleniekov's memory of the fiery young lawyer who had wanted to *keep you bastards out*! As he drew nearer, Taleniekov saw that the face was cherubic – a great deal of *Schlag* had gone down that throat, but the eyes were alive, still humorous . . . and sharp.

"I'm so sorry, my dear fellow," said the German as Taleniekov got up and accepted the outstretched hand. "A last-minute problem with an American contract."

"That has a certain symmetry to it," replied Vasili. "When I returned to Moscow twelve years ago, I wrote in your file that I thought you were on Washington's payroll."

"How perceptive. Actually, I'm paid out of New York, Detroit and Los Angeles, but why quibble over cities?"

"You look well, Heinrich. Quite prosperous. What happened to that very vocal champion of the underdog?"

"They made him an overdog." The lawyer chuckled. "It would never have happened if you people controlled the *Bundestag*. I'm an unprincipled capitalist who assuages his guilt with sizeable contributions to charity. My Reichsmarks do far more than my vocal cords ever did."

"A reasonable statement."

"I'm a reasonable man. And what appears somewhat unreasonable to me now is why you would look me up. Not that I don't enjoy your company, for I do. But why now? You say you're not employed in your former profession; what could I possibly have that you'd be interested in?"

"Advice."

"You have legal problems in *Essen*? Don't tell me a dedicated Communist has private investments in the Ruhr?"

"Only of time, and I have very little of that. I'm trying to trace a man, a family from Leningrad who came to Germany – to Essen, I'm convinced – between sixty and seventy years ago. I'm also convinced they entered illegally, and secretly bought into Ruhr industry."

Kassel frowned. "My dear fellow, you're mad. I'm trying to tick off the decades – I was never very good at figures – but if I'm not mistaken, you're referring to the period between 1910 and 1920. Is that correct?"

"Yes. They were turbulent times."

"You don't say. There was merely the great war to the south, the bloodiest revolution in history in the north, mass confusion in the eastern Slavic states, the Atlantic ports in chaos, and the ocean a graveyard. In essence, all Europe was – if I may be permitted – in flames and Essen itself experiencing an industrial expansion unseen before or since, including the Hitler years. Everything, naturally, was secret, fortunes made every day. Into this insanity comes one White Russian selling his

254

jewels – as hundreds did – to buy himself a piece of the pie in any of a dozen companies, and you expect me to *find* him?"

"I thought that might be your reaction."

"What other could I possibly have?" Kassel laughed again. "What is the name of this man?"

"For your own good, I'd rather not tell you."

"Then how can I help you?"

"By telling me where you would look first if you were me."

"In Russia."

"I did. The revolutionary archives. In Leningrad."

"You found nothing?"

"On the contrary. I found a detailed description of a mass family suicide so patently at odds with reality that it had to be false."

"How was this suicide described? Not the particulars, just in general."

"The family's estate was stormed by the mobs; they fought all day, but in the end used the remaining explosives and blew themselves up with the main house."

"One family holding off a rioting mob of Bolsheviks for an entire day? Hardly likely."

"Precisely. Yet the account was as detailed as a von Clausewitz exercise, even to the climate and the brightness of the sky. Every inch of the vast estate was described, but apart from the name of the family itself, not one other identity was entered. There were no witnesses listed to confirm the event."

The attorney frowned again. "Why did you just say that 'every inch of the vast estate was described'?"

"It was."

"But why?"

"To lend credibility to the false account, I assume. A profusion of detail."

"Too profuse, perhaps. Tell me, were the actions of this family on that day described in your usual enemies-of-the-people vitriol?"

Taleniekov thought back. "No, they weren't, actually. They could almost be termed individual acts of courage. Then he remembered specifically. "They released their servants before they took their own lives . . . they *released* them. That *wasn't* a normal thing."

"And the inclusion of such a generous act in a revolutionary's account would not really be all that acceptable, would it?"

"What are you driving at?"

"That account may have been written by the man himself, or a literate member of the family, and then passed on through corrupt channels to the archives."

"Entirely possible, but I still don't understand your point."

"The odds are long, I grant you, but bear with me. Over the years I've learned that when a client is asked to outline a deposition, he always shows himself in the best light; that's understandable. But he also invariably includes trivial particulars about things that mean a great deal to him. They slip out unconsciously: a lovely wife or a beautiful child, a profitable business or a . . . beautiful home. 'Every inch of the vast estate.' That was this family's passion, wasn't it? Land. Property."

"Yes." Vasili recalled Mikovsky's descriptions of the Voroshin estates. How the patriarchs were absolute rulers over the land, even to holding their own courts of law. "You could say they were excessively addicted to property."

"Might they have brought this addiction to Germany?"

"They might have. Why?"

The attorney's eyes turned cold. "Before I answer that, I must ask the old conspirator a very serious question. Is this search a Soviet reprisal of some sort? You say you're unemployed, that you're not working at your former occupation, but what proof do I have?"

Taleniekov breathed deeply, levelling his eyes with the German's. "I could say the word of a KGB strategist who altered an enemy s file twelve years ago, but I'll go farther than that. If you have connections with Bonn intelligence and can inquire discreetly, ask them about me. Moscow has sentenced me to death."

The coldness thawed in Kassel's eyes. "You wouldn't say such a thing if it weren't true. An attorney who deals every day with international business could check too easily. But you were a dedicated Communist."

"I still am."

"Then surely an enormous mistake has been made."

"A manipulated mistake," said Vasili.

"So this is not a Moscow operation, not in the Soviet interest?"

"No. It's in the interests of both sides, all sides, and that is all I'll say. Now, I've answered your serious question very seriously. Answer mine. What was your point regarding this family's preoccupation with the land?"

The lawyer pursed his thick lips, squinted at Taleniekov, then sighed as he spoke. "Tell me the name. I may be able to help you."

"How?"

"The Records of Property that are filed in the State House. There were rumours that several of the great estates in Rellinghausen and Stadtwald – those on the northern shores of Lake Baldeney – were bought by Russians decades ago."

"They would not have bought in their own name, I'm certain of that."

"Probably not. I said the odds were long, but the covert acquisition of property is not unlike depositions. Things slip out. Possession of land is very close to a man's view of himself; in some cultures he is the land."

"Why can't I look for myself? If the records are available, tell me where to find them."

"It wouldn't do you any good. Only certified attorneys are permitted to search the titles. Tell me the name."

"It could be dangerous for anyone who looks," said Taleniekov quietly.

"Oh, come now." Kassel laughed, his eyes amused again. "A seventy-year-old purchase of land."

"I believe there's a direct connection between that purchase and the extreme acts of violence that are occurring everywhere today."

"Extreme acts of . . ." The lawyer trailed off the phrase, his expression solemn. "An hour ago I mentioned Baader-Meinhof on the phone. Your silence was quite loud. Are you suggesting . . . ?"

"I'd rather not suggest anything," interrupted Vasili. "You're a prominent man,

256

a resourceful man. Give me a letter of certification and get me into the Records of Property."

The German shook his head. "No, I won't do that. You wouldn't know what to look for. But you may accompany me."

"You'd do this yourself? Why?"

"I despise extremists who deal in violence. I remember too vividly the screams and diatribes of the Third Reich. I shall, indeed, look for myself, and if we get lucky you can tell me what you wish." Kassel lightened his voice, but sadness was there. "Besides, anyone sentenced to death by Moscow cannot be all bad. Now, tell me the name."

Taleniekov stared at the attorney, seeing another sentence of death. "Voroshin," he said.

The uniformed clerk in the Essen Hall of Records, *Eigentum Abteilung*, treated the prominent Heinrich Kassel with extreme deference. Herr Kassel's firm was one of the most important in the city. He made it plain that the receptionist behind the desk would be delighted to make copies of anything Herr Kassel wished to have duplicated.

The steel filing cabinets in the enormous room that housed the Records of Property were like grey robots stacked one on top of the other, circling the room, staring down at the open cubicles where the certified lawyers did their research.

"Everything is recorded by date," said Kassel. "Year, month, day. Be as specific as you can. What was the earliest Voroshin might have reasonably bought property in the Essen districts?"

"Allowing for the slow methods of travel at the time, say late May or early June of 1911. But I told you, he wouldn't have bought under his own name."

"We won't be looking for his name, or even an assumed name. Not to begin with."

"Why not an assumed name? Why couldn't he arrive and buy what was available under another name if he had the funds?"

"Because of the times, and they haven't changed that much. A man does not simply enter a community with his family and proceed to assume ownership of a large estate without arousing curiosity. This Voroshin, as you've described him, would hardly have wanted that. He would establish a false identity very slowly, very carefully."

"Then what do we look for?"

"A purchase made by attorneys for owners *in absentia* or by a trust legation from a bank for an estate investment; or by officers of a company or a limited partnership for acquisition purposes. There are any number of ways to set up concealed ownership, but eventually the calendar runs out; the owners want to move in. It's always the pattern, whether you talk about a sweet shop or a conglomerate or a large estate. All the legal manoeuvres are no match for human nature." Kassel paused, looking at the grey cabinets. "Come. We'll start with the month of May 1911. If there's anything here it may not be that difficult to find. There were no more than

257

thirty or forty such estates in the whole of the Ruhr, perhaps ten to fifteen in the Rellinghausen-Stadtwald districts."

Taleniekov felt the same anticipation he had experienced with Yanov Mikovsky in the archives in Leningrad. The same feeling of peeling away layers of time, looking for a clue in documents recorded with precision decades ago. But now he was awed by the seeming irrelevancies that Heinrich Kassel spotted and extracted from the thick pages of legales. The attorney was like a child in that sweet shop he had referred to; a young expert whose eyes roamed over the jellybeans and the acid drops, picking out the flawed items for sale.

"Here. Learn something, my international spy. This tract of land in Bredeney, thirty-seven acres in the Baldeney valley – ideal for someone like Voroshin. It was purchased by the Staatsbank of Duisburg for the minors of a family in Remscheid."

"What's the name?"

"It's irrelevant. A device. We find out who moved in a year or so after, *that's* the name we want."

"You think it may be Voroshin. Under his new identity?"

"Don't jump. There are others like this." Kassel laughed.

"I had no idea my predecessors were so full of legal caprice; it's positively shocking. Look," he said, pulling out another sheaf of papers, his eyes automatically riveted on an indented clause on the first page. "Here's another. A cousin of the Krupps is transferring ownership of property in Rellinghausen to a woman in Düsseldorf in gratitude for her many years of service. Really!"

"It's possible, isn't it?"

"Of course not; the family would never permit it. A relative found a way to make a handsome profit by selling to someone who did not want his peers – or his creditors – to know he had the money. Someone who controlled the woman in Düsseldorf, if she ever existed. The Krupps probably congratulated their cousin."

And so it went: 1911, 1912, 1913, 1914 . . . 1915.

20 August 1915.

The name was there. It meant nothing to Heinrich Kassel, but it did to Taleniekov. It brought to mind another document two thousand miles away in the archives in Leningrad. The crimes of the family Voroshin, the intimate associates of Prince Andrei.

Friedrich Schotte.

"Wait a minute!" Vasili placed his hand over the pages. "Where's this?"

"Stadtwald. There's nothing irregular here. As a matter of fact, it's absolutely legal; very clean."

"Perhaps too legal, too clean. Just as the Voroshin massacre was too profuse with detail."

"What in God's name are you talking about?"

"What do you know of this Friedrich Schotte?"

The attorney grimaced in thought, trying to recall irrelevant history; this was not what he was looking for. "He worked for the Krupps, I think, in a very high position. It would have had to be for him to buy this. He got in trouble after the

258

First World War. I don't remember the circumstances – a prison sentence or something – but I can't see how it's relevant."

"I can," said Taleniekov. "He was convicted of manipulating money out of Germany. He was killed on the first night of that prison sentence in 1919. Was the estate sold then?"

"I would think so. It would appear by the map survey to be a rather expensive property for a prison widow to maintain."

"How can we find out?"

"Look through the year 1919. We'll get there . . ."

"Let's get there now. *Please*."

Kassel sighed. He got up and headed for the cabinets, returning a minute later with a bulging folder. "When a brief is interrupted continuity is lost," he muttered.

"Whatever we lose can be restored; we may gain time."

It took nearly thirty minutes before Kassel extracted a file within a file and placed it on the table. "I'm afraid we have just wasted half an hour."

"Why?"

"The estate was purchased by the Verachten family on 12 November 1919."

"The Verachten Works? Krupps' competitor?"

"Not then. More so now, perhaps. The Verachtens came to Essen from Munich soon after the turn of the century, sometime around nineteen six, or seven. It's common knowledge, the Verachtens were Munichers and they couldn't be more respectable. You have a *V*, but no Voroshin."

Vasili's mind raced back over the information already known. Guillaume de Matarese had summoned the heads of once-powerful families, stripped – nearly but not entirely – of their past riches and influences. According to old Mikovsky, the Romanovs had waged a long battle against the Voroshins, labelling them the thieves of Russia, provokers of revolution . . . It was clear! The *padrone* from the hills of Porto Vecchio had summoned a man – and by extension, his family – *already* in the *process* of a covert emigration, taking with them everything they could out of Russia!

"The imperial *V*, that's what we found," said Taleniekov. My God, what a strategy! Even to the prolonged use of truckloads of gold and silver sent out of Leningrad with the imperial *V*!" Vasili picked up the pages in front of the attorney. "You said it yourself, Heinrich. Voroshin would build a false identity very slowly, very carefully. That's exactly what he did; he simply began five or six years before I thought he had. I'm sure if such records were kept or memories could be activated, we'd find that Herr Verachten came first to Essen alone, until he was established. A man of wealth, testing new waters for investments and a future, bringing with him a carefully constructed history from faraway Munich, money flowing through the Austrian banks. So simple, and the times were so right!"

Suddenly Kassel frowned. "His wife," said the lawyer quietly.

"What about his wife?"

"She was not a Municher. She was Hungarian, from a wealthy family in Dèbrecen, it was said. Her German was never very good."

"Translated, she was from Leningrad and a poor linguist. What was Verachten's full name?"

"Ansel Verachten," said the attorney, his eyes now on Taleniekov. "*Ansel.*"

"*Andrei.*" Vasili let the pages fall. "It's incredible how the ego strives to be sublime, isn't it? Meet Prince Andrei Voroshin."

27

They strolled across the Gildenplatz, the Kaffee Hag building blazing with light, the Bosch insignia subdued but prominent below the enormous clock. It was eight in the evening now, the sky dark, the air cold. It was not a good night for walking, but Taleniekov and Kassel had spent nearly six hours in the Records of Property; the wind that blew across the square was refreshing.

"Nothing should shock a German from the Ruhr," said the lawyer, shaking his head. "After all, we are the Zürich of the north. But this is incredible. And I know only a *part* of the story. You won't reconsider and tell me the rest?"

"One day I may."

"That's too cryptic. Say what you mean."

"If I'm alive." Vasili looked at Kassel. "Tell me everything you can about the Verachtens."

"There isn't that much. The wife died in the mid-'thirties, I think. One son and a daughter-in-law were killed in a bombing raid during the war, I remember that. The bodies weren't found for several days, buried under the rubble as so many were. Ansel lived to a ripe old age, somehow avoiding the war-crimes penalties that caught the Krupps. He died in style, heart seizure while on horseback some time in the 'fifties."

"Who's left?"

"Walther Verachten, his wife and their daughter; she never married, but it didn't prevent her from enjoying connubial pleasures."

"What do you mean?"

"She cut a bold figure, as they say, and when she was younger, had one to match her reputation. The Americans have a term that fits: she was – in some ways, still is – a 'man-eater'." The attorney paused. "Strange how things turn out. It's Odile who really runs the companies now. Walther and his wife are in their late seventies and are rarely seen in public these days."

"Where do they live?"

"They're still in Stadtwald, but not at the original estate, of course. As we saw, it was one of those sold to post-war developers; it's why I didn't recognize it. They have a house farther out in the countryside now."

"What about the daughter, this Odile?"

"*That,*" replied Kassel, chuckling, "depends on the lady's whims. She keeps a penthouse on the Werden Strasse, and through those portals pass many a business adversary who wakes up the next morning too exhausted to best her at the conference table. When she's not in the city I understand she maintains a cottage in her parents' grounds."

"She sounds like quite a woman."

"In the forty-five-plus sweepstakes, few outclass her on the track." Kassel paused again, again not finished. "She has a flaw, however, and I'm told it's maddening. Although she runs Verachten firmly, when things aren't going well and swift decisions are called for, she often announces that she must confer with her father, thus postponing actions sometimes for days. At heart she's a woman, forced by circumstances to wear a man's hat, but the power still resides with old Walther."

"Do you know him?"

"We're acquaintances, that's all."

"What do you think of him?"

"Not much, never did. He always struck me as a rather pretentious autocrat without a great deal of talent."

"The Verachten Works thrive, however," said Vasili.

"I know, I know. That's what I'm told whenever I voice that opinion. My weak rejoinder is that it might do so much better without him; and it *is* weak. If Verachten did any better, it would own Europe. So, I assume it's a personal dislike on my part and I'm wrong."

Not necessarily, thought Taleniekov. *The Matarese make strange and effective arrangements. They need only the apparatus.*

"I want to meet him," said Vasili. "Alone. Have you ever been to his house?"

"Once, several years ago," replied Kassel. "The Verachten lawyers called us in on a patent problem. Odile was out of the country. I needed a Verachten signature on the affidavit of complaint – couldn't proceed without it, as a matter of fact – and so I called old Walther and drove out to get it. The dam broke when Odile got back to Essen. She shouted at me over the telephone: 'My father should not have been disturbed! You will never serve Verachten again!' Oh, she was impossible. I told her as courteously as I could that we never would have served her in the first place had *I* received the initial request."

Taleniekov watched the attorney's face as he spoke: the German was genuinely angry. "Why did you say that?"

"Because it's true. I don't like the company – companies. There is a meanness over there." Kassel laughed at himself. "My feeling's probably a hangover from that radical young lawyer you tried to recruit twelve years ago."

It is the perceptive instinct of a decent man, thought Vasili. *You sense the Matarese, yet you know nothing.*

"I have a last request to make of you, my old friendly enemy," said Taleniekov. "Two, actually. The first is not to say anything to anyone about our meeting today, or what we found. The second is to describe the location of the Verachten house and whatever you can remember about it."

The corner of the brick wall loomed into view in the glare of the headlights. Vasili pressed down on the accelerator of the rented Mercedes, his eyes glancing at the odometer, judging the distance between the start of the wall and the iron gate. Three-tenths of a mile, nearly 1,800 feet. The tall gate was closed; it was electronically operated, electronically protected.

He came to the end of the wall; this length was somewhat shorter than its counterpart on the other side of the gate. Beyond there was only the extension of the forest, in the middle of which had been built the Verachten compound. He depressed the pedal and looked for an opening off the road, somewhere he could conceal the Mercedes.

He found it between two trees, the shrubs dampened down by previous snows. He angled the coupé into the natural cave of greenery, plunging in as far off the road as possible. He turned off the engine, got out and retraced the car's path, pulling up the bushes until he reached the road fifteen feet away. He stood on the shoulder and examined the camouflage; in the darkness, it was sufficient. He started back towards the Verachten wall.

If he could get over it without setting off any alarms he knew he could reach the house. There was no way to scan a forest electronically; wires and cells were too easily tripped by animals and birds. It was the wall itself that had to be negotiated. He reached it and studied the brick in the flame of his cigarette lighter. There were no devices of any sort. It was an ordinary brick wall, its very ordinariness misleading, and Vasili knew it. There was a tall oak on his right, limbs curling up above the top of the wall, but not extending over it.

He leaped, his hands clawing the bark, his knees vicing the trunk; he scaled up to the first limb, swinging his leg over it, pulling himself up into a sitting position, his back against the tree. He leaned forward and downward, his hands balancing his body on the limb until he was prone, and studied the top of the wall in the dim light. He found what he knew had to be there.

Grooved into the flat surface of the concrete was a criss-crossing network of wire-coated plastic tubing through which air and current flowed. The electricity was of sufficient voltage to inhibit animals from gnawing at the plastic, and the air pressure was calibrated to set off alarms the instant a given amount of weight fell over the tube. The alarms were undoubtedly received in a scanning room in the compound, where instruments selected the point of penetration. Taleniekov knew the system was practically fail-safe; if one strand was shorted out, there were five or six others to back it up, and the pressure of a knife across the wire coating would be enough to set off the alarm.

But practically fail-safe was not totally fail-safe. Fire. Melting the plastic and releasing the air without the pressure of a blade. The only alarm set off in this was that of malfunction; the trace would begin where the system originated, which had to be much nearer the house.

He estimated the distance between the edge of the tree limb and the top of the wall. If he could loop his leg as close to the end as possible, swing underneath and brace himself with one hand against the ridge of the wall, his free hand could hold his lighter against the successive tubes of plastic.

He pulled out his cigarette lighter – his American lighter, he reflected with a certain chagrin – and pushed the tiny butane lever to its maximum. He tested it;

the flame shot out and held steady; he lowered it slightly, for the light was too bright. He took a deep breath, firmed the muscles of his right leg and dropped to his left, the left hand making contact with the edge of the wall as he arced downward. He steadied himself and began breathing slowly, orienting his vision to the upside-down view. The blood raced to his head; he revolved his neck briefly to lessen the pressure, then snapped on the lighter, holding the flame against the first tube.

There was a crackling of electricity, then an expulsion of air as the tube turned black and melted. He reached the second in the immediate series; this one exploded like a small, wet firecracker, the sound no more than a low-gauge air gun. The third grew into a thin outsized bubble. A *bubble*. Pressure! Weight! He pushed the flame into it and it burst; he held his breath, waiting for the sound of an alarm. It did not come; he had punctured the tube in time, before the heat and the expansion had reached the weight tolerance. It taught him something: hold the flame closer at first contact. He did so with the following two strands, each bursting on touch. There was a final tube.

Suddenly the flame receded, sinking back into its invisible source. He was out of fuel. He closed his eyes for a moment in frustration, and sheer anger. His leg ached furiously; the blood in his head made him dizzy. Then he thought of the obvious, annoyed with himself that he had not considered it immediately. The one remaining tube might well prevent a full malfunction-alarm; he was far better off leaving it intact. There were at least fifteen free inches on the surface of the concrete, more than enough to place a foot on and plunge over the wall to the other side.

He struggled back up to the limb and rested for a while, letting his head clear. Then slowly, carefully, he lowered his left foot to the wall, setting it securely on top of the burnt-out tubes. With equal caution he raised his leg over the limb, sliding down until the limb was in the small of his back. He took a deep breath, tensed his muscles and leaped forward, pressing his left foot into the stone, propelling himself over the wall. He fell to the ground, rolling to break his fall. He was inside the Verachten compound.

He got to his knees, listening for any sounds of an alert. There were none, so he rose to his feet and started threading his way through the dense woods towards what he presumed to be the central area of the property. The fact that he was half-walking, half-crawling in the right direction was confirmed in less than a minute. He could see the lights of the main house filtered through the trees, the beginning of a large expanse of lawn clearer with each step.

The glow of a cigarette! He dropped to the ground. Directly ahead, perhaps fifty feet away, stood a man at the edge of the lawn. Instantly, Taleniekov was aware of the forest breezes; he listened for the sounds of an animal.

Nothing. There were no dogs. Walther Verachten had confidence in his electronic gates and sophisticated alarm system; he needed only human patrols to make the darkness of his compound secure.

Vasili inched forward, his eyes on the guard ahead. The man was in uniform, visored hat and a heavy winter jacket pinched at the waist by a thick belt that held a holster gun. The guard checked his watch and stripped his cigarette, shaking the tobacco to the grass; he had been in the military, for it was a military custom. He walked several paces to his left, stretched, yawned, proceeded another twenty feet, then strolled aimlessly back towards where he had been standing. That short stretch of ground was his post, other guards were no doubt stationed every several hundred feet, ringing the main house like Caesar's Praetorian Guard. But these were neither Caesar's times nor Caesar's dangers; the duty was boring, relieved by openly smoked cigarettes and yawns and aimless wandering. The guard would not be a problem.

But getting across the stretch of lawn to the shadows of the drive on the right side of the house might well be. He would have to walk briefly in the glare of the floodlights that shot down from the roof.

A hatless man in a dark sweater and trousers doing such a thing would be ordered to stop, shot at if he did not. But a guard dressed in a visored cap and a heavy jacket with a holster at his side would not cause so much concern. And if reprimanded, that guard could always return to his post; it was important to bear that in mind.

Taleniekov crawled through the underbrush, elbows and knees working on the hard ground, pausing with every snap of a branch, blending what noise he made into the sounds of the night forest. He was within five feet, a spray of juniper between himself and the guard. The bored man reached into his jacket pocket and took out his pack of cigarettes. It was not the moment for the striking of a match; the juniper was too thin and a man bent his head in the cold to light a cigarette.

It was the moment to move. *Now.*

Vasili sprang up, his left hand clutching the guard's throat, his left heel dug into the earth to provide backward leverage. In one motion, he pulled the man off his feet, arcing him down into the juniper bush, crashing the guard's skull into the ground, his fingers clawing the windpipe, tightening around it. The shock of the assault combined with the blow to the head and the choking of air rendered the man unconscious. There was a time when Taleniekov would have finished the job, killing the guard because it was the most practical thing to do; that time was past. This was no soldier of the Matarese; there was no point in his death. He removed the man's jacket and visored hat, put them on quickly and buckled the holster around his waist. He dragged the guard farther into the woods, angled the head into the dirt, removed his own small weapon and smashed the handle down above the man's right ear. He would remain unconscious for hours; if the time was not sufficient, nothing was.

Vasili crept back to the edge of the lawn, stood up, breathed deeply and started across the grass. He had watched the guard walk – a slight casual swagger, the neck settled, the head angled back, and he imitated the memory. With each step he expected a loud rebuke or an order or an inquiry; if any were shouted he would shrug and return to the man's post. None came.

He reached the drive and the shadows. Fifty yards down the pavement there was a light streaming out of an open door and the figure of a woman opening a garbage can, two paper bags at her feet. Vasili walked faster, his decision made. He approached the woman; she was in the white uniform of a maid.

"Excuse me, the captain ordered me to bring a message to Herr Verachten."

"Who the hell are you?" asked the stocky woman.

"I'm new. Here, let me help you." Taleniekov picked up the bags.

"You *are* new. It's Helga this, Helga that. What do they care? What's the message? I'll take it to him."

"I wish I could give it to you. I've never met the old man and I don't want to, but that's what I was told to do."

"They're all farts down there. *Kommandos!* A bunch of beer-soaked ruffians, I say. But you're better-looking than most of them."

"Herr Verachten, please? I was told to hurry."

"Everything's hurry this and hurry that. It's ten o'clock. The old fool's wife is in her rooms and he's in his chapel, of course."

"Where . . . ?"

"Oh, all right. Come on in, I'll show you . . . You *are* better-looking, more polite, too. Stay that way."

Helga led him through a corridor that ended at a door opening into a large entrance hall. Here the walls were covered with numerous Renaissance oil paintings, the colours vivid and dramatic under pinpoint spotlights. They extended up a wide circular staircase, the steps of Italian marble. Branching off the hall were several larger rooms, and the brief glimpses Taleniekov had of them confirmed Heinrich Kassel's description of a house filled with priceless antiques. But the glimpses were brief; the maid turned the corner beyond the staircase and they approached a thick mahogany door filled with ornate biblical carvings. She opened it and they descended steps carpeted in scarlet until they reached some kind of ante-room, the floor marble like the staircase in the great hall, the walls here covered with tapestries depicting early Christian scenes. An ancient church pew was on the left, the bas-relief examples of an art long forgotten; it was a place of meditation, for the tapestry facing it was of the Stations of the Cross. At the end of the small room was an arched door, beyond it obviously Walther Verachten's chapel.

"You can interrupt, if you want to," said Helga without enthusiasm. "The head *Kommando* will be blamed for it, not you. But I'd wait a few minutes; the priest will be finished with his claptrap by then."

"A *priest?*" The word slipped out of Vasili's throat; the presence of such a man was the farthest thing in his mind. A *consigliere* of the Matarese with a priest?

"His fart-filled holiness, that's what I say." Helga turned and started back. "Do as you wish," she said, shrugging. "I don't tell anybody what to do."

Taleniekov waited for the heavy mahogany door above to open and close. Then he walked quietly to the door of the chapel, his ear against the wood, trying to pick up meaning from the sing-song chant he could hear from within.

Russian. The language being chanted was Russian!

He was not sure why he was so startled. After all, the congregation inside consisted of the sole surviving son of Prince Andrei Voroshin. It was the service itself that was so astonishing.

Vasili placed his hand on the knob, turned it silently and opened the door several inches. Two things struck him instantly: the sweet-sour odour of incense and the shimmering flames of outsized candles, which caused him to blink his eyes, adjusting to the chiaroscuro effect of bright fires against the moving black shadows on the grey concrete walls. Recessed in those walls everywhere were icons of the Russian Orthodox Church, those nearest the altar raising their saintly arms, reaching for the cross of gold in the centre.

In front of the cross was the priest, dressed in his cassock of white silk, trimmed with silver and gold. He had his eyes closed, his hands folded across his chest, and out of his barely moving mouth came words of a chant fashioned over a thousand years ago.

Then Taleniekov saw Walther Verachten – an old man with thinning white hair, strands of which fell over the back of a long, gaunt neck. He was prostrate on the three marble steps of the altar, at the feet of the high priest; his arms stretched out in supplication, his forehead pressed against the marble in absolute submission. The priest raised his voice, signifying the finish of the Orthodox *Kyrie Eleison*. The Litany of Forgiveness commenced; priestly statement followed by sinner's response, a choral exercise in self-indulgence and self-delusion. Vasili thought of the pain inflicted, demanded by the Matarese, and was revolted. He opened the door, stepped inside.

The priest opened his eyes, startled, his hands surging down from his chest in indignation. Verachten spun on the steps, his skeletal body trembling. Awkwardly, painfully, he struggled to his knees.

"How dare you interfere!" he shouted in German. "Who gave you permission to come in here?"

"An historian from Petrograd, Voroshin," said Taleniekov in Russian. "That's as good an answer as any, isn't it?"

Verachten fell back on the steps, gripping the edge of the stone with his hands. Steadying himself, he brought them up to his face, covering his eyes as if they had been clawed or burned. The priest dropped to his knees, grabbing the old man by the shoulders, embracing him. The cleric turned to Vasili, his voice harsh.

"Who *are* you? What *right* have you?"

"Don't talk to me of rights, *priest*! You turn my stomach. Parasite!"

The priest held his place, cradling the white-haired Verachten. "I was summoned years ago and I came. Like my predecessors in this house, I ask for nothing and I receive nothing."

The old man lowered his hands from his face, struggling to compose himself, nodding his trembling head; the priest released him. "So you've come at last," he said. "They always said you would. Vengeance is the Lord's, but then you people do not accept that, do you? You've taken God from the people and given so little in return. I have no quarrel with you on this earth. Take my life, Bolshevik. Carry out your orders, but let this good priest go. He's no Voroshin."

"You *are*, however."

"It is my burden." Verachten's voice grew firmer. "And our secret. I've borne both well, as God has given me the vision to do so."

"One talks of rights, the other of God!" spat out Taleniekov. "Hypocrites!" And then he shouted, "*Perro nostro circulo!*"

The old man blinked, no reaction in them whatsoever. "I beg your pardon?"

"You heard me! *Perro nostro circulo!*"

"I hear you, but I don't understand you."

"Corsica! Porto Vecchio! *Guillaume de Matarese!*"

Verachten looked up at the priest. "Am I senile, my father? What's he talking about?"

266

"Explain yourself," said the priest curtly. "Who are you? What do you want? What's the meaning of these words?"

"*He* knows!"

"I know *what*?" Verachten leaned forward. "We Voroshins have blood on our souls, I accept that. But I cannot accept what I don't know."

"The *shepherd* boy," said Taleniekov with quiet condemnation. "With a voice crueller than the wind. Do you need more than that? The shepherd boy!"

"The Lord is my shepherd . . ."

"Stop it, you sanctimonious *liar*!"

The priest stood up. "*You* stop it, whoever you are! This good and decent man has lived his life in atonement for sins that were never *his*! Since a child he wanted to be a man of God, but it was not permitted. Instead, he has become a man *with* God. Yes, *with God*."

"He is a Matarese!"

"I don't know what that is, but I know what *he* is. Millions dispensed every year to the starving, to the deprived. And he asks in return only our presence to see him through his devotions. It is all he has *ever* asked."

"You're a *fool*! Those funds are Matarese funds! They buy death!"

"They buy *hope*. You're the liar now!"

The door of the chapel burst open. Vasili spun around. A man in a dark business suit stood inside the frame, legs apart, arms outstretched, a gun in his right hand, steadied by his left. "Don't move!" The language was German.

Through the door came two women. One was tall and slender, dressed in an ankle-length velvet blue gown, a fur stole around her shoulders, her face very white, very angular, very beautiful. The woman at her side was short, in a cloth overcoat, her face puffy, her narrow eyes bewildered, yet filled with opportunity as she stared at Taleniekov. He had seen her only hours ago; a guard had said she would be accommodating should Heinrich Kassel need duplicates.

"That's the man," said the receptionist who had sat behind the desk at the Records of Property.

"Thank you," replied Odile Verachten. "You may go now, the chauffeur will drive you back into the city."

"Thank *you*, ma'am. Thank you *very* much."

"You're most welcome. The chauffeur's in the hallway. Good night."

"Good night, ma'am." The woman left.

"*Odile!*" cried her father, struggling to his feet. "This man came in . . ."

"I'm *sorry*, father," interrupted the daughter. "Putting off unpleasantries only compounds them; it's something you never understood. I'm sure this . . . man . . . said things you shouldn't have heard."

With those few words, Odile Verachten nodded at her escort. He shifted the weapon to his left and fired. The explosion was deafening; the old man fell. The killer raised his gun and fired again; the priest spun, the top of his head blown away.

Silence.

"That was one of the most brutal acts I've ever witnessed," said Taleniekov, the final decision of his life being made. He would kill . . . *somehow*.

"From Vasili Vasilievich Taleniekov, that's quite a statement," said the Verachten woman, taking a step forward. "Did you really believe that this ineffectual old man – this would-be priest – could be a part of *us?*"

"My error was in the man, not in the name. Voroshin is Matarese."

"Correction, Verachten. We are not merely born, we are chosen." Odile gestured at her dead father. "He never was. When his brother was killed during the war, Ansel chose me!" She glared at him. "We wondered what you had learned in Leningrad."

"Would you really like to know?"

"A name," answered the woman. "A name from a chaotic period in recent history. Voroshin. But it hardly matters that you know. There is nothing you could say, no accusation you could make, that the Verachtens could not deny."

"You don't *know* that."

"We know enough, don't we?" said Odile, glancing at the man with the gun.

"We know enough," repeated the killer. "I missed you in Leningrad. But I did not miss the woman, Kronescha, did I? If you know what I mean."

"*You!*" Taleniekov started forward; the man clicked the gun's hammer back with his thumb.

Vasili held his place, body and mind aching. He *would* kill; to do so control had to be found. And shock. *Lodzia my Lodzia! Help me.*

He stared at Odile Verachten, and spoke the words softly, slowly, giving each equal emphasis. "*Perro . . . nostro . . . circulo.*"

The smile faded from her lips, her white skin grew paler. "Again from the past. From a primitive people who don't know what they're saying. We should have known you might learn it."

"You believe that? You think they don't know what they're saying?"

"Yes."

It was now, or it was not, thought Taleniekov. He took a deliberate step towards the woman. The killer's gun inched out, only feet away, aimed directly at his skull. "Then why do they talk of the shepherd boy?"

He took another step; the killer breathed abruptly, audibly through his nostrils – prelude to fire – the trigger was being squeezed.

"Stop!" screamed the Verachten woman.

The explosion came as Vasili dropped to a crouch. Odile Verachten had thrust her arm out in a sudden command to prevent the gunshot, and in that instant, Taleniekov sprang, eye and mind and body on a single object. The gun, the *barrel* of the gun.

He reached it, his fingers gripping the warm steel, hand and wrist twisting counter-clockwise, pulling downward to inflict the greatest pain. He threw his right hand – fingers curled and rigid – into the man's stomach, tearing at the muscles, feeling the protrusion of the rib cage. He yanked up with all his strength; the killer screamed, and fell.

Vasili spun and lunged at the Verachten woman. In the brief moment of violence, she had hesitated; now she reacted with precision, her hand underneath her fur stole pulling out a gun. Taleniekov tore at that hand, that gun, throwing Odile to the chapel floor, his knee hammering into her chest. The handle of her own gun pressed across her throat.

"There'll be no mistake this time!" he said. "No capsules in the mouth."

"You'll be killed!" she whispered hoarsely.

"Probably," agreed Vasili. "But you'll go with me, and you don't want that. I was wrong. You're not one of your soldiers; the chosen don't take their own lives."

"I'm the only one who can save yours." She choked under the pressure of the steel, but went on. "The *shepherd* . . . Where? *How?*"

"You want information. Good! So do I." Taleniekov removed the gun from her throat, clamping his left hand where it had been, the fingers of his right hand entering her mouth, depressing the tongue, digging through the soft tissue downward. She coughed again, only mucus and spit rolling down her chin; there were no lethal pills in her mouth. He had been right; the chosen did not commit suicide. He then spread the stole and ran his hand over her body, pulling her off the floor, and reaching around her back, pushing her down again and plunging his hand between her legs, ankles to pelvis, feeling for the hard metal of a gun or a knife. There was nothing. "Get up!" he ordered.

She rose only partially, her knees pulled up under her, holding her neck. "*You must tell* me!" she whispered. "You know you can't get out. Don't be a fool, Russian! Save your life! What do you know of the shepherd?" Odile Verachten screamed. What am I offered to tell you?"

"What do you *want?*"

"What does the *Matarese* want!?"

The woman paused. "Order."

"Through *chaos?*"

"Yes! The shepherd? In the name of God, tell me!"

"I'll tell you when we're out of the compound."

"No! *Now.*"

"Do you think I'd trade that off?" He pulled her to her feet. "We're leaving now. Your friend here will wake up before too long; he'll know what to do, it's part of his job. If it wasn't I'd kill him. But you and I will be far away when he kills himself."

"No!"

"Then you'll die," said Taleniekov simply. "I got in, I'll get out."

"I gave orders! No one's to leave!"

"Who's leaving? A uniformed guard returns to his post. Those aren't Matarese out there. They're exactly what they're supposed to be: former *Kommandos* hired to protect a wealthy executive." Vasili jammed the gun into her throat. "Your choice? It doesn't matter to me."

She flinched; he grabbed the back of her neck, pulling it into the barrel. She nodded. "We will talk in my father's car, she whispered. "We're both civilized people. You have information I need, and I have a revelation for you. You have nowhere to turn but to us now. It could be far worse for you."

He sat next to her in the front seat of Walther Verachten's limousine. He had taken off the uniform and was now no more than another stud in Odile Verachten's stable. She was behind the wheel, his arm around her shoulders, his automatic again jammed into her, out of sight. As the guard at the gatehouse nodded and turned to press the release button, he leaned into her; one uncalled for move, one gesture, and she was dead. She knew it; none came.

She sped through the open gate, turning the wheel to the left. He grabbed it, his foot reaching across hers to the brake, and spun the wheel to the right. The car skidded into a half spin; he steadied it and slammed his foot over hers on the accelerator.

"What are you *doing?*" she cried.

"Avoiding any prearranged rendezvous."

It was in her eyes; another car had been waiting on the road to Essen. For the third time, Odile Verachten was genuinely frightened.

They sped down the country road; several hundred yards ahead he could see a fork clearly in the headlights. He waited; instinctively she bore to the right. The fork was reached, the turn began; he moved his hand swiftly to the rim of the wheel and pushed it up, sending them into the left road.

"You'll *kill* us!" screamed the Verachten woman.

"Then both of us will go," said Taleniekov. The surrounding woods diminished; there were open spaces ahead. "That field on the right. Pull over."

"*What?*"

He raised the gun and put it against her temple. "Stop the car," he repeated.

They got out. Vasili took the keys from the ignition and put them in his pocket. He pushed her forward, into the grass, and they walked towards the middle of the field. In the distance was a farmhouse, beyond it a barn. There were no lights; the farmers of Stadtwald were asleep. But the winter moon was brighter now than it was in the Gildenplatz.

"What are you going to do?" asked Odile.

"Find out if you have the courage you demand of your soldiers."

Taleniekov, *listen* to me! No matter what you do to me, you won't change anything. We're too far along. The world needs us too desperately!"

"This world needs killers?"

"To *save* it from killers! You talk of the shepherd. *He* knows. Can you *doubt* it? Join us. Come with us."

"Perhaps I will. But I have to know where you're going."

"Do we trade?"

"Again, perhaps."

"Where did you hear of the shepherd?"

Vasili shook his head. "Sorry, you first. Who are the Matarese? *What* are they? What are they doing?"

"Your first answer," said Odile, parting her stole, her hands on the neckline of her gown. She ripped it downward, the white buttons breaking from the threads, exposing her breasts. "It's one we know you've found," she added.

In the moonlight Taleniekov saw it. Larger than he had seen before, a jagged circle that was part of the breast, part of the body. The mark of the Matarese. "The grave in the hills of Corsica," he said quietly. "*Perro nostro circulo.*"

"It can be *yours,*" said Odile, reaching out to him. "How many lovers have lain across these breasts and admired my very distinctive birthmark. You are the *best,* Taleniekov. *Join* the best! Let me bring you over!"

270

"A little while ago, you said I had no choice. That you would reveal something to me, force me to turn to you. What is it?"

Odile pulled the top of her gown together. "The American is dead. You are alone."

"*What?*"

"Scofield was killed."

"*Where?*"

"In Washington . . ."

The sound of a powerful engine interrupted her words. Headlights pierced the darkness of the road that wound out of the woods from the south; a car came into view. Then suddenly, as if suspended in a black void, it stopped on the shoulder behind the limousine. Before the headlights could be extinguished, three men could be seen leaping out, the driver following. All were armed; two carried rifles. All were predators.

"They've found me!" cried Odile Verachten. "Your answer, Taleniekov! You really have no choice, you see that, don't you? Give me the gun. An order from me can change your life. Without it, you're dead."

Stunned, Vasili looked behind him; the fields stretched into pastures, the pastures into darkness. Escape was not a problem – perhaps not even the right decision. Scofield *dead*? In *Washington*? He had been on his way to England; what had sent him prematurely to Washington? But Odile Verachten was not lying; he would bank his life on it! She had spoken the truth as she knew the truth – just as her offer was made in truth. The Matarese would make good use of one Vasili Taleniekov.

Was it the *way*? The *only* way?

"Your *answer*!" Odile stood motionless, her hand outstretched.

"Before I give it, tell me. When was Scofield killed? How?"

"He was shot two weeks ago in a place called Rock Creek Park."

A *lie*. A *calculated* lie! She had been lied to! Someone *within* the Matarese was trying to *betray* the Matarese. They had an ally deep within the council! He had to reach that man. Vasili spun the automatic in his hand, offering it to Odile. "There's nowhere else to turn. I'm with you. Give your order."

She turned from him and shouted. "You men! Put up your guns! Hold your fire!"

A single flashlight beam shot out and Taleniekov saw what she did not see – and knew instantly what she did not know. The light was held by one man to free the other three; and although he was in the spill, the beam was not directed at him. It was directed at *her*. He dived to his left into the grass. A fusillade of bullets erupted from the rifles across the field.

Another order had been given. Odile Verachten screamed. She was blown off her feet, her body caved forward, then arched backward in mid-air under the force of the shells.

Other gunshots followed, digging up the earth to the right of Taleniekov as he lurched, scrambling through the grass away from the target ground. The shouts grew louder as the men attacked, converging on the site on which only seconds ago a living member of the Matarese council had stood – issuing an order that was not hers to give.

271

Vasili reached the relative safety of the woods. He rose and started running into the darkness, knowing that soon he would stop, and turn, and kill a man on his way back to the limousine. In other darkness.

But now he kept running.

The ageing musician sat in the last row of the plane, a shabby violin case between his knees. Absently, he thanked the stewardess for the cup of hot tea; his thoughts consumed him.

He would be in Paris in an hour, meet with the Corsican girl, and set up direct communications with Scofield. It was imperative they work in concert now; things were happening too rapidly. He had to join Beowulf Agate in England.

Two of the names on the guest list of Guillaume de Matarese seventy years ago were accounted for.

Scozzi. Dead.

Voroshin-Verachten. Dead.

Sacrificed.

The direct descendants were expendable, which meant they were not the true inheritors of the Corsican *padrone*. They had been merely messengers, bearing gifts for others far more powerful, far more capable of spreading the Corsican fever.

This world needs killers?

To save it from killers! Odile Verachten.

Enigma.

David Waverly, Foreign Secretary, Great Britain.

Joshua Appleton IV, Senator, United States Congress.

Were they, too, expendable messengers? Or were they something else? Did each carry the mark of the jagged blue circle on his chest? Had Scozzi? And if either did, or Scozzi had, was that unnatural blemish the mark of mystical distinction Odile Verachten had thought it was, or was it, too, something else? A symbol of expendability, perhaps. For it occurred to Vasili that wherever that mark appeared, death was a partner.

Scofield was searching in England now. The same Beowulf Agate that someone within the Matarese had reported killed in Rock Creek Park. Who was that someone, and why had the false report gone out? It was as though that person — or persons — wanted Scofield spared, beyond reach of the Matarese killers. But why?

You talk of the shepherd. He knows! Can you doubt it?

The shepherd. A shepherd boy.

Enigma.

Taleniekov put the tea down on the tray in front of him, his elbow jarred by his seat companion. The businessman from Essen had fallen asleep, his arm protruding over the divider. Vasili was about to remove it when his eyes fell on the folded newspaper spread out on the German's lap.

The photograph stared up at him and he stopped breathing, sharp bolts of pain returning to his chest – as they had in Leningrad.

The smiling, gentle face was that of Heinrich Kassel.

The bold print above the photograph screamed the information.

Advotat tot

Taleniekov reached over and picked up the paper, the pain accelerating as he read:

Heinrich Kassel, one of Essen's most prominent attorneys, was found murdered in his car outside his residence last evening. The authorities have called the killing bizarre and brutal. Kassel was found garrotted, with multiple head injuries and lacerations of the face and body. An odd aspect of the killing was the tearing of the victim's upper clothing, exposing the chest area on which was painted a circle of dark blue. The paint was still wet when the body was discovered shortly past midnight . . .

Perro nostro circulo.

Vasili closed his eyes. He had pronounced Kassel's sentence of death with the name *Voroshin*.

It had been carried out.

Book III

28

"*Scofield?*" The grey-faced man was astonished, the name uttered in shock.

Bray broke into a run through the crowds in the London Underground, towards the Charing Cross exit. It had happened; it was bound to happen sooner or later. No brim of a hat could conceal a face if trained eyes saw that face, and no unusual clothing dissuaded the professional once the face had been marked.

He had just been marked; the man making the identification – and without question now racing to a phone – was a veteran agent for the Central Intelligence Agency stationed at the American embassy on Grosvenor Square. Scofield knew him slightly; one or two lunches at The Guinea; two or three conferences, inevitably held prior to Consular Operations invading areas the Company considered possessively sacrosanct. Nothing close, only cold; the man was a fighter for CIA prerogatives and Beowulf Agate had transgressed too frequently.

Goddamn it! Within minutes the US network in London would be put on alert, within hours every available man, woman and paid informer would spread throughout the city looking for him. It was conceivable that even the British would be called in, but it was not likely. Those in Washington who wanted Brandon Alan Scofield wanted him dead, not questioned, and this was not the English style. No, the British would be avoided.

Bray counted on it. There was a man he had helped several years ago, in circumstances that had little to do with their allied professions, that had made it possible for the Englishman to remain in British Intelligence. Not only remain but advance to a position of considerable responsibility.

Roger Symonds had dropped £2,000 of MI6 funds at the tables of Les Ambassadeurs. Bray had replaced the sum from one of his accounts. He had never asked for repayment, but he would ask now.

The money had never been repaid – not by default, only because Scofield had not crossed Symonds' path. In their work, one did not leave a forwarding address.

A form of repayment would be asked for now. That it would be offered, Scofield did not question, but whether it could be delivered was something else again. Yet it would be neither if Roger Symonds learned that he was on Washington's terminal list. Debts aside, the Englishman took his work seriously; there'd be no Fuchs or Philby on his conscience. Much less a former killer from Consular Operations conceivably turned paid assassin.

Bray wanted Symonds to arrange a private, isolated meeting between himself and England's Foreign Secretary, David Waverly. The meeting, however, had to be negotiated without Scofield's name being used – the British agent would balk at that, refuse entirely if he learned of Washington's hunt for him. Scofield knew he had to come up with a credible motive; he had not thought of one yet.

He ran out of Charing Cross station and walked into the flow of pedestrians heading across the Strand. At Trafalgar Square, he crossed the wide intersection, joining the early-evening crowds. He looked at his watch. It was 6.15, 7.15 in Paris. In thirty minutes he was to start calling Toni at her flat in the rue du Bac; there was a telephone centre a few blocks away at Haymarket. He would make his way there by a roundabout route, stopping at one of the garishly lighted shops to buy a new hat and jacket. The CIA man would give a precise description of his clothing; changing it was imperative.

He was wearing the same windbreaker he had worn in Corsica, the same visored fishing cap. He left them in a curtained dressing room at a branch of Dunn's, buying a dark tweed jacket and an Irish walking hat, the soft brim falling around his head, a circle of narrow fabric throwing the shadows downward across his face. He walked again, more rapidly now, and cut through the winding back streets into Haymarket.

He chose a telephone box, went inside and closed the glass door, wishing it were solid. It was ten minutes to seven. Antonia would be waiting by the phone. They always allowed a variable of half an hour for cross-Channel telephone traffic; if he did not reach her by 8.15, Paris time, she could expect his next call between 11.45 and 12.15. The one condition Toni had insisted upon was for them to talk to each other every day. Bray had not objected; he had come out of the earth and found something very precious to him, something he had thought he had lost permanently. He could love again; the excitement of anticipation had come back. The sound of a voice stirred him, the touch of a hand was meaningful. He had found Antonia Gravet at the most inopportune time of his life, yet finding her gave a significance to his life he had not felt for a number of years. He wanted to live and grow old with her, it was as simple as that. And remarkable. He had never thought about growing old before; it was time he did.

If the Matarese allowed it.

The *Matarese*. An international power without a profile, its leaders faceless men trying to achieve *what*?

Chaos? *Why*?

Chaos. Scofield was suddenly struck by the root meaning of the word. The state of formless matter, of clashing bodies in space, before the creation. Before order was imposed on the universe.

He dialled the code. Antonia answered quickly.

"Vasili's here," she said. "This afternoon. He's hurt."

"How badly?"

"His neck. He should have stitches."

There was a brief hollow sound as the phone was being passed. Or taken.

"He should have sleep," said Taleniekov in English. "But I have things to tell you first, several warnings."

"What about Voroshin?"

276

"He kept the V for practical if foolish purposes. He became Essen's Verachten. Ansel Verachten."

"The *Verachten* Works?"

"Yes."

"Good Christ!"

"His son believed that."

"What?"

"It's irrelevant; there's too much to tell you. His granddaughter was the chosen one. She's dead, killed on Matarese orders."

"As Scozzi was," interrupted Scofield.

"Exactly," agreed the Soviet. "They were vessels; they carried the plans but were commandeered by others. It will be interesting to see what happens to the Verachten companies. They have no leadership now. We must watch and note who assumes control."

"We've reached the same conclusion then," said Bray. "The Matarese work through large corporations."

"It would appear so, but to what end I haven't the faintest idea. It's extremely contradictory."

"Chaos . . ." Scofield spoke the word softly.

"I beg your pardon."

"Nothing. You said you wanted to warn me."

"Yes. They've studied our files under microscopes. It seems they know every drone we've ever used, every past friend, every contact, every . . . teacher and lover. Be careful."

"They can't know what was never entered; they can't cover everyone."

"Don't bank on that. You received my cable about the body marks?"

"It's crazy! Squads of killers identifying themselves? I'm not sure I believe it."

"Believe it," said Taleniekov firmly. "But there's something I wasn't able to explain. They're suicidal; they won't be taken. Which leads me to believe they're not as extensive in numbers as the leaders would like us to think. They're some kind of élite soldiers sent out to the troubled areas, not to be confused with hired guns employed by second and third parties."

Bray paused, remembering. "You know what you're describing, don't you?"

"All too well," replied the Russian. "Hasan ibn as-Sabbāh. The *fida'is*."

"Cadres of assassins . . . till death us do part from our pleasures. How is it modernized?"

"I have a theory; it may be worthless. We'll discuss it when I see you."

"When will that be?"

"Tomorrow night – early the next morning probably. I can hire a pilot and a plane in the Cap Gris district; I've done it before. There's a private airfield between Hythe and Ashford. I should be in London by one o'clock or three at the latest. I know where you're staying, the girl told me."

"Taleniekov."

"Yes?"

"Her name's Antonia."

"I know that."

"Let me speak to her."

"Of course. Here she is."

He found the name in the London directory: *R. Symonds, Bradbry Lane, Chelsea*. He memorized the number and placed the first call at 7.30 from a booth in Piccadilly Circus. The woman who answered told him politely that Mr Symonds was on his way home from the office.

"He should be here any mo' now. Shall I tell him who called?"

"The name wouldn't mean anything. I'll call in a while, thank you."

"He's got a marvellous memory. You're sure you don't care to leave your name?"

"I'm sure, thank you."

"He's coming directly from the office."

"Yes, I understand that."

Scofield hung up, disturbed. He left the booth and walked down Piccadilly past Fortnum and Mason's to St James's Street and beyond. There was another booth at the entrance to Green Park; slightly more than ten minutes had passed. He wanted to hear the woman's voice again.

"Has your husband arrived?" he asked.

"He *just* called from the local, the Brace and Bit on Old Church Street. He's quite irritable. Must have had a *dreadful* day."

Bray hung up. He knew the number of MI6-London; it was one a member of the fraternity kept in mind. He dialled.

"Mr Symonds, please. Priority."

"Right away, sir."

Roger Symonds was not on his way home, nor was he in a pub called the Brace and Bit. Was he playing a domestic game?

"Symonds here," said the familiar English voice in the familiar casual tone Scofield remembered.

"Your wife just told me you were on your way home, but got detained at the Brace and Bit. Is that the best you could come up with?"

"I what? . . . Who's this?"

"An old friend."

"Not much of a one, I'm afraid. I'm not married. My friends know that."

Bray paused, then spoke urgently. "Quickly. Give me a sterile number, or one on a scrambler. *Quickly!*"

"Who is this?"

"Two thousand pounds."

It took Symonds less than a second to understand and adjust; he reeled off a number, repeated it once, then added. "The cellars. Twenty-five storeys high."

There was a click; the line went dead. Twenty-five storeys high to the cellars meant halving the figure, minus one. He was to call the number in exactly twelve minutes – within the one-minute span – when scrambling and jamming devices would be activated. He left the booth to find another as far away as time and rapid walking permitted. Telephone intercepts were potentially two-way traces; the booth at Green Park could be under observation in a matter of minutes.

He went up Old Bond Street into New until he reached Oxford Street, where he turned right and began running. At Wardour Street he slowed down, turned right again, and melted into the crowds of Soho.

Elapsed time: nine and a half minutes.

There was a booth at the corner of Shaftesbury Avenue; inside a callow young man wearing an electric-blue suit was screaming into the phone. Scofield waited by the door, looking at his watch.

Eleven minutes.

He could not take the chance. He took out a five-pound note and tapped on the glass. The young man turned; he saw the bill and held up his middle finger in a gesture that was not co-operative.

Bray opened the door, put his left hand on the electric-blue shoulder, tightened his grip, and as the offensive young man began screeching, pulled him out of the booth, tripping him with his left foot, dropping the fiver on top of him. It floated; the youth grabbed it and ran.

Eleven minutes, thirty seconds.

Scofield took several deep breaths, trying to slow the rapid pounding of his chest. Twelve minutes. He dialled.

"Don't go home," said Bray the instant Symonds was on the line.

"Don't *you* stay in London!" was the reply. "Grosvenor Square has an alert out for you."

"You *know*? Washington called you in?"

"Hardly. They won't say a word about you. You're terminated personnel, an off-limits subject. We probed several weeks ago when we first got word."

"Word from *where*?"

"Our sources in the Soviet. In KGB. They're after you, too, but then they always have been."

"What did Washington say when you probed?"

"Played it down. Failure to report whereabouts, something like that. They're too embarrassed to put an official stamp on the nonsense. Are you authoring something? There's a lot of that over there."

"How did you know about the alert?" interrupted Scofield. "The one out for me now?"

"Oh, come now, we do keep tabs, you know. A number of those Grosvenor Square has on its payroll quite rightly have first loyalties to us."

Bray paused briefly, bewildered. "Roger, why are you telling me this? I can't believe two thousand pounds would make you do it."

"That misappropriated sum has been sitting in a Chelsea bank drawing interest for you since the morning after you bailed me out."

"Then why?"

Symonds cleared his throat, a proper Englishman facing the necessity of showing emotion. "I have no idea what your quarrel is over there and I'm not sure I care to know you have such puritanical outbursts – but I was appalled to learn that our prime source in Washington confirmed that the State Department subscribes to the Soviet ploy. As I said, it's not only nonsense, I find it patently offensive."

"A ploy? What ploy?"

"That you joined forces with the Serpent."

"The 'Serpent'?"

"It's what we call Vasili Taleniekov, a name I'm sure you recall. To repeat, I don't know what your trouble is, but I *do* know a goddamned lie, a macabre lie at that, when I hear one." Symonds cleared his throat again. "Some of us remember East Berlin. And I was here when you came back from Prague. How dare they . . . after what you've *done*? Churlish bastards!"

Scofield took a long, deep breath. "Roger, don't go home."

"Yes, you said that before." Symonds was relieved they were back to practicality; it was in his voice. "You say someone's there, claiming to be my wife?"

"Probably not inside, but nearby, with a clear view. They've tapped into your phone and the equipment's good. No echoes, no static."

"*My* phone? They're trailing me? In *London*?"

"They're covering you; they're after me. They knew we were friends and thought I might try to reach you."

"Goddamned *cheek*! That embassy will get a bolt that'll char the gold feathers off that fucking ridiculous eagle! They go too *far*!"

"It's not the Americans."

"*Not* the? . . . Bray, what in God's name are you talking about?"

"That's just it. We have to talk. But it's got to be a very complicated route. Two networks are looking for me, and one of them has you under glass. They're good."

"We'll see about that," snapped Symonds, annoyed, challenged and curious. "I daresay several vehicles, one or two decoys, and a healthy bit of official lying can do the trick. Where are you?"

"Soho. Wardour and Shaftesbury."

"Good. Head over to Tottenham Court Road. In about twenty minutes, a grey Mini – rear licence plate askew – will come in from Oxford Street and stall at the kerb. The driver's black, a West Indian chap; he's your contact. Get in with him; the engine will make a remarkable recovery."

"Thank you, Roger."

"Not at all. But don't expect me to have the two thousand quid. The banks are closed, you know."

Scofield got in the front seat of the Mini, the black driver looking at him closely, courteously, his right hand out of sight. The man had obviously been given a photograph to study. Bray removed the Irish hat.

"Thank you," said the driver, his hand moving swiftly to his jacket pocket, then to the wheel. The engine caught instantly and they sped up Tottenham Court Road. "My name is Israel. You are Brandon Scofield – obviously. Good to make your acquaintance."

"Israel?" he asked.

"That's it, man," replied the driver, smiling, lending a pronounced West Indian lilt to his voice. "I don't think my parents had in mind the cohesiveness of minorities when they gave it to me, but they were avid readers of the Bible. Israel Isles."

"It's a nice name."

"My wife thinks they blew it, as you Americans say. She keeps telling me that if they had only used Ishmael instead, all my introductions would be memorable."

" 'My name is Ishmael' . . ." Bray laughed. "It's close enough."

"This banter covers a slight nervousness on my part, if I may say so," said Isles.

"Why?"

"We studied a number of your accomplishments in training; it wasn't that long ago. I'm chauffeuring a man we'd all like to emulate."

The trace of laughter vanished from Scofield's face. "That's very flattering. I'm sure you will if you want to." *And when you get to be my age, I hope you think it's been worth it.*

They drove south out of London on the Brighton road, branching west at Redhill and heading into the countryside. Israel Isles was sufficiently perceptive to curtail the banter. He apparently understood that he was driving either a very preoccupied or exhausted American. Bray was grateful for the silence; he had to reach a difficult decision. The risks were enormous no matter what he decided.

Yet part of that decision had already been forced upon him, which meant he had to tell Symonds that Washington wasn't the immediate issue. He could not permit Roger to vent his misplaced outrage on the American embassy; it was not the embassy that had placed the intercept on his telephone. It was the Matarese.

Yet to tell the whole truth meant involving Symonds, who would not remain silent. He would go to others and those others to their superiors. It was not the time to speak of conspiracy so massive and contradictory that it would be branded no more than the product of two terminated intelligence officers – both wanted for treason in their respective countries. The time *would* come, but it was not now. For the truth of the matter was that they did not possess a shred of hard evidence. Everything they knew to be true was so easily denied by powerful, faceless men of undoubted congeniality as the paranoid ramblings of lunatics and traitors. On the surface, the logic was with their enemies. Why would the leaders of mammoth corporations, conglomerates that depended on stability, finance chaos?

Chaos. Formless matter, clashing bodies in space.

"Another few minutes, we'll reach our first destination," said Israel Isles.

"First destination?"

"Yes, our trip's in two stages. We change vehicles up ahead; this one is driven back to London – the driver black, his passenger white – and we proceed in another, quite different car. The next leg is less than a quarter of an hour. Mr Symonds may be a little late, however. He had to make four changes of vehicles in city garages."

"I see," said Scofield, relieved. The West Indian had just provided Bray with his answer. As the rendezvous with Symonds was in stages, so, too, would be the explanations *to* Symonds. He would tell him part of the truth, but nothing that would implicate the Foreign Secretary, David Waverly. However, Waverly had to be given information on a most confidential basis; decisions of foreign policy could be affected by the news of massive shifts of capital being manipulated secretly. *This* was the information Scofield had come across and was tracing: massive shifts of capital. And although all clandestine economic manoeuvres were subjects for intelligence scrutiny, these went beyond MI5 and 6, just as they superseded the interests of the FBI and the CIA.

In Washington, there were those who wanted to prevent him from disclosing that which he knew, but could not prove. The surest way of doing so was to discredit him, kill him, if it came to that. Symonds would understand. Men killed facilely for money; no one knew it better than intelligence officers. So often it was the spine of their . . . accomplishments.

Isles slowed the Mini down and pulled to the side of the road. He made a U-turn, pointing the car in the direction from which they came.

Within thirty seconds another, larger automobile approached; it had picked them up along the way and had followed at a discreet distance. Bray knew what was expected; he got out, as did the West Indian. The Bentley came to a stop. A white driver opened the rear door for a black companion. No one spoke as the exchange was made, both cars now driven by blacks.

"May I ask you a question?" said Israel Isles hesitantly.

"Sure."

"I've gone through all the training, but I've never had to kill a man. I worry about that sometimes. What's it like?"

Scofield looked out the window at the shadows rushing past. *It's like walking through a door into a place you've never been before. I hope you do not have to go there, for it's filled with a thousand eyes – a few angry, more frightened, most pleading . . . all wondering. Why me now?* "There's not very much of that," said Bray. "You never take a life unless it's absolutely necessary, knowing that if you have to, you're saving a lot more. That's the justification, the only one there should ever be. You put it out of your mind, lock it away behind a door somewhere in your head."

"Yes, I think I understand. The justification is in the necessity. One has to accept that, doesn't one?"

"That's right. Necessity." *Until you grow older and the door opens more and more frequently. Finally it will not close and you stand there, staring inside.*

They drove into the deserted parking area of a picnic site in the Guildford countryside. Beyond the post-and-rail fence were swings and slides and seesaws, all silhouetted in the bright moonlight.

A car was waiting for them, but Roger Symonds was not in it; he was expected momentarily. Two men had arrived early to make certain there was no one else in the picnic ground, no intercepts placed on phones considered sterile.

"Hello, Brandon," said a short, stocky man in a bulky overcoat, extending his hand.

"Hi, how are you?" Scofield did not recall the agent's name, but remembered his face; he was one of the best men fielded by MI6. *Cons Op* had called him in – with British permission – when the Moscow-Paris-Cuba espionage ring was operating inside the Chamber of Deputies. Bray was impressed at seeing him now. Symonds was using a first team.

"It's been eight or ten years, hasn't it?"

"At least," agreed Scofield. "How've you been?"

"Still here. I'll be pensioned off before too long. Looking forward to that."

"Enjoy it."

The Englishman hesitated, then spoke with embarrassment. "Never did see you after that awful business in East Berlin. Not that we were such friends, but you know what I mean. Delayed condolences, old chap. Rotten thing. Fucking animals, I say."

"Thanks. It was a long time ago."

"Never that long," said the MI6 man. "It was my source in Moscow that brought us that garbage about you and the Serpent. Beowulf and the Serpent! My God, how could those pricks in D.C. swallow such rot?"

"It's complicated."

He saw the headlights first, then heard the engine. A London taxi drove into the picnic ground. The driver, however, was no London cabbie; it was Roger Symonds.

The middle-aged MI6 officer climbed out and for a second or two blinked and stretched, as if to get his bearings. Roger had not changed during the years since he and Bray had known each other. The Englishman was still given to an excess pound or two, and his thatch of rumpled brown hair was still unmanageable. There was an air of disorientation about the veteran operative that masked a first-rate analytical mind. He was not an easy man to fool – with part of the truth or none of it.

"Bray, how *are* you?" said Symonds, hand held out. "For God's sake, don't answer that, we'll get to it. Let me tell you, those are *not* easy cars to drive. I feel as though I've just limped through the worst rugger match in Liverpool. I'll be far more generous with cabbies in the future." Roger looked around, nodding to his men, then spotting the opening in the fence which led into the playground. "Let's take a stroll. If you're a good lad, I may even give you a push or two in one of the swings."

The Englishman listened in silence as Bray, sitting still on a swing, told his story of the massive shifting of funds. When Scofield had finished, Symonds walked behind him and shoved him between the shoulder blades.

"There's the push I promised you, although you don't deserve it. You haven't been a good lad."

"Why not?"

"You're not telling me what you should."

"I see. You don't understand why I'm asking you not to use my name with Waverly?"

"Oh, no, that's perfectly all right. He has to deal with Washington every day. Granting an *unofficial* meeting with a retired American intelligence officer is not something he'd care to have on the Foreign Office's record. I mean, we don't actually defect to one another, you know. Ill take that responsibility, if it's to be taken."

"Then what's bothering you?"

"The people after you. Not Grosvenor Square, of course, but the others. You haven't been candid; you said they were good, but you didn't tell me *how* good. Or the depth of their resources."

"What do you mean?"

"We pulled out your dossier and selected three names known to you, calling each, telling each that the man on the line was an intermediary from you, instructing each to go to a specific location. All three messages were intercepted; those called were followed."

"Why does that surprise you? I told you as much."

"What surprises me is that one of those names was known only to us. Not MI5, not Secret Service, not even the Admiralty. Only us."

"Who was it?"

"Grimes."

"Never heard of him," said Bray.

"You only met him once. In Prague. Under the name of Brazuk."

"KGB," said Scofield, astonished. "He defected in 'seventy-two. I gave him to you. He wouldn't have anything to do with us and there was no point in wasting him."

"But only you knew that. You said nothing to your people and, frankly, we at Six took credit for the purchase."

"You've got a leak, then."

"Quite impossible," replied Symonds. "At least regarding the present circumstances as you've described them to me."

"Why?"

"You say you ran across this global financial juggling act only a short while ago. Let's be generous and say several months, would you agree?"

"Yes."

"And since then, those who want to silence you have been active against you, also correct?" Bray nodded. The MI6 man leaned forward, his hand on the chain above Scofield's head. "From the day I took office two and a half years ago, Beowulf Agate's file has been in my private vault. It is removed only on dual signatures, one of which must be mine. It has not been removed, and it is the only file in England that contains any connection between you and the Grimes-Brazuk defection."

"What are you trying to say?"

"There's only one other place where that information might be found."

"Spell it out."

"Moscow." Symonds drew out the word softly.

Bray shook his head. "That assumes Moscow knows Grimes' identity."

"Entirely possible. Like a few you've purchased, Brazuk was a bust. We don't really want him, but we can't give him back. He's a chronic alcoholic, has been for years. His job at KGB was ornamental, a debt paid to a once-brave soldier. We suspect he blew his cover quite a while ago. Nobody cared, until you came along. Who are these people after you?"

"It seems I didn't do you any favours when I handed over Brazuk," said Scofield, avoiding the MI6 man's eyes.

"You didn't know that and neither did we. Who are these people, Bray?"

"Men who have contacts in Moscow. Obviously. Just as we do."

"Then I must ask you a question," continued Symonds. "One that would have been inconceivable several hours ago. Is it true what Washington thinks? Are you working with the Serpent?"

Scofield looked up at the Englishman. "Yes."

Calmly Symonds released the chain and rose to his full height. "I think I could kill you for that," he said. "For God's sake, *why?*"

"If it's a question of either your killing me or my telling you, I don't have a choice, do I?"

"There's a middle ground. I take you in and turn you over to Grosvenor Square."

"Don't do it, Roger. And don't ask me to tell you anything now. Later, yes. Not now."

"Why should I agree?"

"Because you know me; I can't think of any other reason."

Symonds turned away. Neither spoke for several moments. Finally, the Englishman turned again, facing Bray. "Such a simple phrase. 'You know me.' Do I?"

"I wouldn't have reached you if I didn't think you did. I don't ask strangers to risk their lives for me. I meant what I said before. Don't go home. You're marked . . . just as I'm marked. If you covered yourself, you'll be all right. If they find out you met with me, you're dead."

"I am at this moment logged in at an emergency meeting at the Admiralty. Phone calls were placed to my office and my flat demanding my presence."

"Good. I expected as much."

"Goddamn you, Scofield! It was always your gift. You pull a man in until he can't stand it. Yes, I *do* know you, and I'll do as you ask – for a little while. But not because of your melodramatics; they don't impress me. Something else does, however. I said I could kill you for working with Taleniekov. I think I could, but I suspect you kill yourself a little every time you look at him. That's reason enough for me."

29

Bray walked down the steps of the private hotel into the morning sunlight and the crowds of shoppers in Knightsbridge. It was an area of London compatible with staying out of sight; from nine A.M. on the streets were jammed with traffic, the pavements teeming with customers anxious to part with pounds, marks, yen, dollars and riyals. It was a concrete version of an ancient bazaar, anchored by the imposing monument that was Harrods.

Scofield stopped at a news-stand, shifted his attaché case to his left hand, picked up *The Times* and went in to a small restaurant. He slipped into a chair, satisfied that it provided a clear view of the entrance, more satisfied still that the pay telephone on the wall was only feet away. It was a quarter to ten; he was to call Roger Symonds at precisely 10.15 on the sterile number that could not be tapped.

He ordered breakfast from the laconic Cockney waitress and unfolded the newspaper. He found what he was looking for in a single column on the upper left section of the front page.

Verachten Heiress Dead

Essen. Odile Verachten, daughter of Walther, granddaughter of Ansel Verachten, founder of the Verachten Works, was found dead in her Werden Strasse penthouse last evening, an apparent victim of a massive coronary stroke according to a family physician. For nearly a decade, Fräulein Verachten had assumed the managerial reins of the diversified companies under the guidance of her father, who has receded from active participation during the past years. Both parents were in seclusion at their estate in Stadtwald, and were not available for comment. A private family burial will take place within the residential grounds. A corporate statement is expected shortly, but none from Walther Verachten who is reported to be seriously ill.

Odile Verachten was a dramatically attractive addition to the boardrooms of this city of coldly efficient executives. She was mercurial, and when younger, given to displays of exhibitionism often at odds with the behaviour of Essen's business leaders. But no one doubted her ability to run the vast Verachten Works . . .

Scofield's eyes quickly scanned the biographical hyperbole that was an obituary editor's way of describing a spoiled, headstrong bitch who undoubtedly slept around with the frequency if not the delicacy of a Soho whore.

There was a follow-up story directly beneath. Bray began reading and knew instantly, instinctively, that another fragment of the elusive truth was being revealed.

Verachten Death Concerns Trans-Comm

New York, N. Y. In a move that took Wall Street by surprise, it was learned today that a team of management consultants from Trans-Communications, Incorporated, was flying to Essen, Germany for conferences with executives of the Verachten Works. The untimely death of Fräulein Odile Verachten, 47, and the virtual seclusion of her father, Walther, aged 76, has left the Verachten companies without an authoritative voice at the top. What astonished supposedly well-informed sources here was the extent of Trans-Comm's holdings in Verachten. In the legal labyrinths of Essen, American investments are often beyond scrutiny, but rarely when those holdings exceed twenty per cent. Rumours persist that Trans-Comm's are in excess of fifty per cent, although denials labelling such figures as ridiculous have been issued by the Boston headquarters of the conglomerate . . .

The words sprang up from the page at Scofield, *the Boston headquarters* . . .

Were *two* fragments of that elusive truth being revealed? Joshua Appleton IV was the senator from Massachusetts, the Appleton family the most powerful political entity in the state. They were the Episcopal Kennedys, far more restrained in self-evocation, but every bit as influential on the national scene – which was intrinsic to the international financial scene.

Would a retrospective of the Appletons include connections – covert or otherwise – with Trans-Communications? It was something that would have to be learned.

The telephone on the wall behind him rang. It was eight minutes past ten; another seven and he would call Symonds at MI6 headquarters. He glanced at the phone, annoyed to see the waitress answer it. He stared at her lips. He hoped her conversation would not last long.

286

"Mister *Hagate*? Is there a Mister B. *Hagate* 'ere?" The question was shouted angrily by the irate waitress.

Bray froze. B. *Hagate 'ere?*

Agate, B.

Beowulf Agate.

Was Symonds playing some insane game of one-upmanship? Had the Englishman decided to prove the superior quality of British Intelligence's tracking techniques? Was the damn fool so egotistical he could not leave well enough alone?

God, what a fool!

Scofield rose as unobtrusively as possible, holding his attaché case. He went to the phone and spoke.

"What is it?"

"Good morning, Beowulf Agate," said a male voice with vowels so full and consonants so sharp they could have been formed at Oxford's Balliol College. "We trust you've rested since your arduous journey from Rome."

"Who's this?"

"My name's irrelevant; you don't know me. We merely wanted you to understand. We found you; we'll always be able to find you. But it's all so tedious. We feel that it would be far better for everyone concerned if we sat down and thrashed out the differences between us. You may discover they're not so great after all."

"I don't feel comfortable with people who've tried to kill me."

"I must correct you. *Some* have tried to kill you, others have tried to save you."

"For what? A session of chemical therapy? To find out what I've learned, what I've done?"

"What you've learned is meaningless, and you can't do anything. If your own people take you, you know what you can expect. There'll be no trial, no public hearing; you're far too dangerous to too many people. You've collaborated with the enemy, killed a young man your superiors believe was a fellow intelligence officer in Rock Creek Park, and fled the country. You're a traitor; you'll be executed at the first opportune moment. Can you doubt it after the events on Nebraska Avenue? We can execute you the instant you walk out of that restaurant. Or before you leave."

Bray looked around, studying the faces at the tables, looking for the inevitable pair of eyes, a glance behind a folded newspaper, or above the rim of a coffee cup. There were several candidates; he could not be sure. And without question, there were unseen killers in the crowds outside. He was trapped; his watch read eleven minutes past ten. Another four and he could dial Symonds on the sterile line. But he was dealing with professionals. If he hung up and dialled was there a man now at one of these tables – innocuously raising a fork to his mouth or sipping from a cup – who would pull out a weapon powerful enough to blow him into the wall? Or were those inside merely hired guns, unwilling to make the sacrifice the Matarese demanded of its élite? He had to buy time and take the risk, watching the tables every second as he did so, preparing himself for that instant when escape came with sudden movement and the conceivable – unfortunate – sacrifice of innocent people.

"You want to meet, I want a guarantee I'll get out here."

"You've got it."

"Your saying it isn't enough. Identify one of your employees in here."

"Let's put it this way, Beowulf. We can hold you there, call the American embassy, and within blinking time they'd have you cornered. Even should you get past them, we'd be waiting on the outer circle, as it were."

His watch read twelve past ten. *Three minutes.*

"Then obviously you're not that anxious to meet with me." Scofield listened, his concentration total. He was almost certain the man on the line was a messenger; someone above wanted Beowulf Agate taken, not killed. "I said we felt it would be better for everyone concerned . . ."

"Give me a face!" interrupted Bray. The voice *was* a messenger. "Otherwise call the goddamned embassy. I'll take my chances. *Now.*"

"Very well," came the reply, spoken rapidly. "There's a man with rather sunken cheeks, wearing a grey overcoat . . ."

"I see him." Bray did, five tables away.

"Leave the restaurant; he'll get up and follow you. He's your guarantee."

Thirteen past ten. Two minutes.

"What guarantee does he have? How do I know you won't take him out with me?"

"Oh, come now, Scofield . . ."

"I'm glad to hear you've got another name for me. What's your name?"

"I told you, it's irrelevant."

"Nothing's irrelevant." Bray paused. "I want to know your name."

"Smith. Accept it."

Ten-fourteen. One minute. Time to start.

"I'll have to think about it. I also want to finish my breakfast." Abruptly, he hung up the phone, shifted his attaché case to his right hand and walked over to the plain-looking man five tables away.

The man stiffened as Scofield approached; his hand reached under his overcoat.

"The alert's off," said Scofield, touching the concealed hand under the cloth of the coat. "I was told to tell you that; you're to take me out of here. But first, I'm to make a telephone call. He gave me the number; I hope I can remember it."

The hollow-cheeked killer remained immobile, speechless. Scofield walked back to the telephone on the wall.

Ten fourteen and fifty-one seconds. Nine seconds to go. He frowned, as if trying to recall a number, picked up the phone, and dialled. Three seconds past 10.15 he heard the echoing sound that followed the interruption of the bell; the electronic devices were activated. He inserted his coin.

"We have to talk fast," he said to Roger Symonds. "They found me. I've got a problem."

"Where are you? We'll help."

Scofield told him. "Just send in two sirens, regular police will do. Say it's an Irish incident, possible subjects inside. That's all I'll need."

"I'm writing it down, they're on their way."

"What about Waverly?"

"Tomorrow night. His house in Belgravia. I'm to escort you, of course."

"Not before then?"

"*Before* then? Good God, man, the only reason it's so soon is that I managed an open-end memorandum from the Admiralty. From that same mythical conference I was logged into last night." Bray was about to speak, but Symonds rushed on. "Incidentally, you were right. An inquiry was made to see if I was there."

"Were you covered?"

"The caller was told the conference could not be interrupted, that I would be given the message when it was over."

"Did you return the call?"

"Yes. From the Admiralty's cellars an hour and ten minutes after I left you. I woke up some poor chap in Kensington. An intercept, of course."

"Then if you got back there, they saw you leave? You didn't use my name with Waverly, did you?"

"I used a name, not yours. Unless your talk is extremely fruitful, I expect I'll take a lot of stick for that."

An obvious fact struck Bray. Roger Symonds' strategy had been successful. The Matarese had him trapped inside the Knightsbridge restaurant, yet Waverly had granted him a confidential interview thirty-six hours away. Therefore, no connection had been made between the interview in Belgravia and Beowulf Agate.

"Roger, what time tomorrow night?"

"Eightish. I'm to ring him first. I'll pick you up around seven. Have you any idea where you'll be?"

Scofield avoided the question. "I'll call you at this number at four-thirty. Is that convenient?"

"So far as I know. If I'm not here, leave an address two blocks north of where you'll be. I'll find you."

"You'll bring the photographs of all those following your decoys yesterday?"

"They should be on my desk by noon."

"Good. And one last thing. Think up a very good, very official reason why you can't bring me to Belgravia Square tomorrow night."

"*What?*"

"That's what you'll tell Waverly when you call him just before our meeting. It's an intelligence decision; you'll pick him up personally and drive back to MI6."

"*MI6?*"

"But you won't take him there; you'll bring him to the Connaught. I'll give you the room number at four-thirty. If you're not there, I'll leave a message. Subtract twenty-two from the number I give."

"See here, Brandon, you're asking *too* much!"

"You don't know that. I may be asking to save his life. And yours." In the distance, from somewhere outside, Bray could hear the piercing, two-note sound of a London siren; an instant later it was joined by a second. "Your help's arrived," said Scofield. "Thanks." He hung up and started back to the hollow-cheeked Matarese killer five tables away.

"Who were you talking to?" asked the man, his cold eyes nervous, his accent American. The sirens were drawing nearer; they were not lost on him.

"He didn't give me his name," replied Bray. "But he did give me instructions. We're to get out of here fast."

"Why?"

"Something happened. The police spotted a rifle in one of your cars; it's being held. There's been a lot of IRA activity in the stores around here. Let's go!"

The man got out of his chair, nodding to his right. Across the crowded restaurant, Scofield saw a stern-faced, middle-aged woman get up, acknowledge the command by slipping the wide strap of a large purse over her shoulder, and start for the door of the restaurant.

Bray reached the cashier's cage, timing his movements, fumbling his money and his bill, watching the scene beyond the glass window. Two black police cars converged, screeching simultaneously to a stop at the kerb. A crowd of noisy, curious pedestrians gathered, then dispersed, curiosity replaced by fear as four helmeted London police jumped out of the vehicles and headed for the restaurant.

Bray judged the distance, then moved quickly. He reached the glass door and yanked it open several seconds before the police had it blocked. The hollow-cheeked man and the middle-aged woman were at his heels, at the last moment side-stepping around him to avoid confronting the police.

Scofield turned suddenly and lurched to his right, clutching his attaché case under his arm, grabbing his would-be escorts by the shoulders and pulling them down.

"These are the ones!" he shouted. "Check them for guns! I heard them say they were going to bomb Scotch House!"

The police fell on the two Matarese, arms and hands and clubs thrashing the air. Bray dropped to his knees, releasing his double-grip and dived to his left out of the way. He scrambled to his feet, raced through the crowds to the corner and ran into the street, threading his way between the traffic. He kept up the frantic race for three blocks, stopping briefly, under canopies and at shop windows, to see if anyone followed him. None did, and two minutes later he slowed down and entered the enormous bronze-bordered portals of Harrods.

Once inside, he accelerated his pace as rapidly and as unobtrusively as possible, looking for a telephone. He had to reach Taleniekov at the flat in the rue du Bac before the Russian left for Cap Gris. He *had* to, for once Taleniekov reached England, he would head for London and a small hotel in Knightsbridge. If the KGB man did that he would be taken by the Matarese.

"Through the chemist's towards the south doorway," said an imperturbable clerk. "There's a bank of phones against the wall."

The late-morning telephone traffic was light; the call went through without delay.

"I was leaving in a few minutes," said Taleniekov, his voice oddly hesitant.

"Thank Christ you didn't. What's the matter with you?"

"Nothing. Why?"

"You sound strange. Where's Antonia? Why didn't she answer the phone?"

"She stepped out to the grocer's. She'll be back shortly. If I sounded strange, it's because I don't like answering this telephone." The Russian's voice was normal now, his explanation logical. "What is the matter with *you?* Why this unscheduled call?"

"I'll tell you when you get here, but forget Knightsbridge."

"Where will you be?"

Scofield was about to mention the Connaught, when Taleniekov interrupted.

"On second thoughts, when I get to London I'll phone tower-central. You recall that exchange, don't you?"

Tower-central? Bray hadn't heard the name in years, but he remembered. It was a code name for a KGB drop on the Victoria Embankment, abandoned when Consular Operations discovered it some time back in the late 'sixties. The tourist boats that travelled up and down the Thames, that was it. "I remember," said Scofield, bewildered. "I'll respond."

"Then I'll be going . . ."

"Wait a minute," interrupted Bray. "Tell Antonia I'll call in a while."

There was a brief silence before Taleniekov replied. "Actually, she said she might take in the Louvre; it's so close by. I can get to the Cap Gris district in an hour or so. There's nothing – I repeat – nothing to worry about." There was a click and the line to Paris went dead. The Russian had hung up.

There's nothing – I repeat – nothing to worry about. The words cracked with the explosive sounds of near-by thunder, his eyes blinded by bolts of lightning that carried the message into his brain. There *was* something to worry about and it concerned Antonia Gravet.

Actually, she said she might take in the Louvre . . . I can get to the Cap Gris district in an hour or so . . . Nothing to worry about.

Three disconnected statements, preceded by an interruption that prohibited disclosure of the contact point in London. Scofield tried to analyse the sequence; if there was meaning it was in the progression. The *Louvre* was only blocks away from rue du Bac – across the Seine, but near-by. The *Cap Gris district* could not be reached in an hour or so; two and a half or three were more logical. *Nothing – I repeat – nothing to worry about*; then why the interruption? Why the necessity of a third contact point, avoiding any mention of the second?

Sequence. Progression. Further *back?*

I do not like answering this telephone. Words spoken firmly, almost angrily. That was *it.* Suddenly Bray understood and the relief he felt was like cool water sprayed over a sweat-drenched body. Taleniekov had seen something wrong – a face in the street, a chance meeting with a former colleague, a car that remained too long on the rue du Bac – any number of unsettling incidents or observations. The Russian had decided to move Toni out of the Rive Gauche, across the river into another flat. *She* would be settled in an *hour or so* and he would not leave until she was; that was why there was nothing to worry about. Still, on the assumption that there could be substance to a disturbing incident or observation, the KGB man had operated with extreme caution – always caution, it was their truest shield – and the telephone was an instrument of revelation. Nothing revealing was to be said.

Sequence, progression . . . meaning. Or was it? The Serpent had killed his wife.

Was he finding comfort where none existed? The Russian had been the first to suggest eliminating the girl from the hills of Porto Vecchio – the love that had come into his life at the most inopportune time of his life. *Could* he? . . .

No! Things were different now! There was no Beowulf Agate to stretch to the breaking point, because that breaking point guaranteed the death of the Serpent, the end of the hunt for the Matarese. The best of professionals did not kill unnecessarily; the results were always geometric.

Still, he wondered, as he picked up the phone in Harrods' south entranceway, what was necessity but a man convinced of the need? He put the question out of his mind; he had to find sanctuary.

London's staid Connaught Hotel not only possessed one of the best kitchens in London but was an ideal choice for quick concealment, as long as one stayed out of the lobby and tested the kitchen from room service. Quite simply, it was impossible to get a room at the Connaught unless a reservation was made weeks in advance. The elegant hotel on Carlos Place was one of the last bastions of the Empire, catering in large measure to those who mourned its passing and had the wealth to do so gracefully. There were enough to keep it perpetually full; the Connaught rarely had an available room.

Scofield knew this, and years ago had decided that occasions might arise when the Connaught's particular exclusivity could be useful. He had reached and cultivated a director of the financial group that owned the hotel and made his appeal. As all theatres have "house seats", and most restaurants keep constantly "reserved" tables for those exalted patrons who have to be accommodated, so do hotels retain empty rooms for like purposes. Bray was convincing; his work was on the side of the angels, the Tory side. A room would be at his disposal whenever he needed it.

"Room six-twenty-six," were the director's first words when Scofield placed his second, confirming call. "Just go right up in the lift as usual. You can sign the registration in your room – as usual."

Bray thanked his accomplice, and turned his thoughts to another problem, an irritating one. He could not return to the small hotel several blocks away, and the only clothes except those on his back were there. In a duffelbag on the unmade bed. There was nothing else of consequence; his money as well as several dozen useful letterheads, identification cards, passports and bank books, were all in his attaché case. But apart from the rumpled trousers, the cheap tweed jacket and the Irish hat, he didn't have a damn thing to wear. And clothes were not merely coverings for the body, they were intrinsic to the work and had to match the work; they were tools, consistently more effective than weapons and the spoken word. He left the bank of telephones and walked back into the aisles of Harrods. The selections would take an hour; that was fine. It would take his mind off Paris. And the inopportune love of his life.

It was shortly past midnight when Scofield left his room at the Connaught, dressed in a dark raincoat and a narrow-brimmed black hat. He took the service elevator to the basement of the hotel and emerged on the street through the employees' entrance. He found a taxi and told the driver to take him to Waterloo Bridge. He settled back in the seat and smoked a cigarette, trying to control his swelling sense of concern. He wondered if Taleniekov understood the change that had taken place, a change so unreasonable, so illogical that he was not sure how he would react were he the Russian. The core of his excellence, his longevity in his work, had always been his ability to think as the enemy thought; he was incapable of doing so now.

I'm not your enemy!

Taleniekov had shouted that unreasonable, illogical statement over the telephone in Washington. Perhaps illogically – he was right. The Russian was no friend, but he was not *the* enemy. That enemy was the Matarese.

And crazily, *so* unreasonably, through the Matarese he had found Antonia Gravet. The love.

What had *happened*?

He forced the question out of his mind. He would learn soon enough, and what he learned would no doubt bring back the relief he had felt at Harrods, diminished by too much time on his hands and too little to do. The telephone call to Roger Symonds, made precisely at 4.30, had been routine. Roger was out of the office so he had given information to the security room operator. The unexplained number that was to be relayed was six-four-three . . . minus twenty-two . . . Room 621, Connaught.

The taxi swung out of Trafalgar Square, up the Strand, past Savoy Court, towards the entrance of Waterloo Bridge. Bray leaned forward; there was no point walking any farther than he had to. He would cut through side streets down to the Thames and the Victoria Embankment.

"This'll be fine," he said to the driver, holding out payment, annoyed to see that his hand shook.

He went down the cobbled lane by the angling structure of dark stone that was the Savoy Hotel, and reached the bottom of the hill. Across the wide, well-lighted boulevard was the concrete walk and the high brick wall that fronted the River Thames. Moored permanently as a pub was a huge refurbished barge named *Caledonia*, closed by the 11.00 curfew imposed on all England's drinking halls, the few lights beyond the thick windows signifying the labours of clean-up crews removing the stains and odours of the day. A quarter of a mile south on the tree-lined Embankment were the sturdy, wide-beamed, full-decked river boats that ploughed the Thames most of the year round, ferrying tourists up to the Tower of London and back to Lambeth Bridge before returning to the waters of Cleopatra's Needle.

Years ago these boats were known as tower-central, drops for Soviet couriers and KGB agents making contact with informers and deep-cover espionage personnel. Consular Operations had uncovered the drop; in time, the Russians knew it. Tower-central was taken out; a known drop was eliminated for some other that would take months to find.

Scofield cut through the garden paths of the park behind the Savoy; music from the ballroom floated down from above.

He reached a small band amphitheatre with its rows of slatted benches. A few couples were scattered around talking quietly. Bray looked for a single man, for he was within the vicinity of tower-central. The Russian would be somewhere in the area.

He was not. Scofield walked out of the amphitheatre into the widest path that led to the boulevard. He emerged on the pavement; the traffic in the street was constant, bright headlights flashing by in both directions, mottled by the winter mists that rolled off the water. It occurred to Bray that Taleniekov must have hired an automobile. He looked up and down the avenue to see if any were parked on either side; none was. Across the boulevard, in front of the Embankment wall, strollers walked casually in couples, threesomes and several larger groups; there was no man by himself. Scofield looked at his watch; it was five minutes to one. The Russian had said he might be as late as two or three o'clock in the morning. Bray swore at his impatience, at the anxiety in his chest whenever he thought about Paris. About Toni.

There was the sudden fire of a cigarette lighter, the flame steady, then extinguished, only to be relighted a second later. Diagonally across the wide avenue, to the right of the closed, chained gates of the pier that led to the tourist boats, a white-haired man was holding the flame under a blonde woman's cigarette; both leaned against the wall, looking at the water. Scofield studied the figure, what he could see of the face, and had to stop himself from breaking into a run. Taleniekov had arrived.

Bray turned right and walked until he was parallel with the Russian and the blonde decoy. He knew Taleniekov had seen him and wondered why the KGB man did not dismiss the woman, paying her whatever price they had agreed upon, and get her out of the way. It was foolish – conceivably dangerous – for a decoy to observe both parties at a contact point. Scofield waited at the kerb, seeing now that Taleniekov's head was fully turned, the Russian staring at him, his arm around the woman's waist. Bray gestured first to his left, then to his right, his meaning clear. Get her out! Walk south; we'll meet shortly.

Taleniekov did not move. What was the Soviet *doing*? It was no time for whores!

Whores? The whore that never was? The *courier's whore*? Oh, my *God*!

Scofield stepped off the kerb; an automobile horn bellowed, as a car swerved towards the centre of the road to avoid hitting him. Bray barely heard the sound, was barely aware of the sight; he could only stare at the woman beside Taleniekov.

The arm around the waist was no gesture of feigned affection, the Russian was holding her up. Taleniekov spoke in the woman's ear; she tried to spin around; her head fell back on her neck, her mouth open, a scream or a plea about to emerge, but nothing was heard.

The strained face was the face of his love. Under the blonde wig, it was *Toni*. All control left him; he raced across the wide avenue, speeding cars braking, spinning wheels, blowing horns. His thoughts converged like staccato shots of gunfire, one thought, one observation, more painful than all others.

Antonia looked more dead than alive.

30

"She's been *drugged*," said Taleniekov.

"Why the hell did you bring her *here*?" asked Bray angrily, taking his face away from Antonia's. "There are hundreds of places in France, dozens in Paris, where she'd be safe! Where she'd be cared for! You know them as well as I do!"

"If I could have been certain, I would have left her," replied Vasili, his voice calm. "Don't probe. I considered other alternatives."

Bray understood, his brief silence an expression of gratitude. Taleniekov could easily have killed Toni, probably would have killed her had it not been for East Berlin. Which meant that the Russian also understood. "A doctor?"

"Helpful in terms of time, but not essentially necessary."

"What was the chemical?"

"Scopolamine."

"When?"

"Early yesterday morning. Over eighteen hours."

"*Eighteen* . . . ?" It was no time for explanations. "Do you have a car?"

"I couldn't take the chance. A lone man with a woman who could not stand up under her own power; the trail would have been obvious. The pilot drove us up from Ashford."

"Can you trust him?"

"No, but he stopped for petrol ten minutes outside of London and went inside to relieve himself. I added a quart of oil to his fuel tank; it should be taking effect on the road back to Ashford."

"Find a taxi." Scofield's look conveyed the compliment he would not say.

"We have much to discuss," added Taleniekov, moving away from the wall.

"Then hurry," said Bray.

Antonia's breathing was steady, the muscles of her face relaxed in sleep. When she awoke she would be nauseous, but it would pass with the day. Scofield pulled the covers over her shoulders, leaned down and kissed her on her pale white lips, and got up from the bed.

He walked out of the bedroom, leaving the door ajar. Should Toni stir he wanted to hear her; hysterics were a by-product of scopolamine. They had to be controlled; it was why Taleniekov could not risk leaving her alone, even for the few minutes it would have taken to lease a car.

"What happened?" he asked the Russian, who sat in a chair, a glass of whisky in his hand.

"This morning – yesterday morning," said Taleniekov, correcting himself, his white-haired head angled back against the rim of the chair, his eyes closed; the man was clearly exhausted. "They say you're dead, did you know that?"

"Yes. What's that got to do with it?"

"It's how I got her back." The Russian opened his eyes and looked at Bray. "There's very little about Beowulf Agate I don't know."

"And?"

"I said I was you. There were several basic questions to answer; they were not difficult. I offered myself in exchange for her. They agreed."

"Start from the beginning."

"I wish I could, I wish I knew what it was. The Matarese, or someone within the Matarese, wants you alive. It's why certain people were told that you are not. They don't look for the American, only the Russian. I wish I understood." Taleniekov drank.

"What *happened*?"

"They found her. Don't ask me how, I don't know. Perhaps Helsinki, perhaps you were picked up in Rome, perhaps anything or anyone, I don't know."

"But they found her," said Scofield, sitting down. "Then what?"

"Early yesterday morning, four or five hours before you called, she went down to a bakery; it was only a few doors away. An hour later she had not returned. I knew then I had two choices. I could go out after her – but where to start, where to look? Or I could wait for someone to come to the flat. You see, *they* had no choice, I knew that. The telephone rang a number of times but I did not answer, knowing that each time I did not, it brought someone closer."

"You answered my call," interrupted Bray.

"That was later. By then we were negotiating."

"Then?"

"Finally two men came. It was one of the more testing moments of my life not to kill them both, especially one. He had that small, ugly little mark on his chest. When I ripped his clothes off and saw it, I went nearly mad."

"Why?"

"They killed in Leningrad. In Essen. Later you'll understand. It's part of what we must discuss."

"Go on." Scofield poured himself a drink.

"I'll tell it briefly, fill in the spaces yourself; you've been there. I kept the soldier and his hired gun bound and unconscious for over an hour. The phone rang and this time I answered, using the most pronounced American accent I could manage. You'd have thought the sky over Paris had fallen, so hysterical was the caller. 'An impostor in London!' he squeaked. Something about a 'gross error having been made by the embassy, the information they received completely erroneous'."

"I think you skipped something," interrupted Bray again. "I assume that was when you said you were me."

"Let's say I answered in the affirmative when the hysterical question was posed. It was a temptation I could not resist, since I had heard less than forty-eight hours previously that you had been killed." The Russian paused, then added, "Two weeks ago in Washington."

Scofield walked back to the chair, frowning. "But the man on the phone knew I was alive, just as those here in London knew I was alive. So you were right. Only certain people inside the Matarese were told I was dead."

"Does that tell you something?"

"The same thing it tells you. They make distinctions."

"Exactly. When either of us ever wanted a subordinate to do nothing, we told him the problem was solved. For such people you're no longer alive, no longer hunted."

"But why? I *am* hunted. They trapped me." Bray sat down, revolving the glass in his hand.

"One question with two answers, I think," said the Russian. "Like any diverse organization, the Matarese is imperfect. Among its ranks are the undisciplined, the violence-prone, men who kill for the score alone or because of fanatic beliefs. These were the people who were told you were dead. If they did not hunt you, they would not kill you."

"That's your first answer; what's the second? Why does someone want to keep me alive?"

"To make you a *consigliere* of the Matarese."

"*What?*"

"Think about it. Consider what you'd bring to such an organization."

Bray stared at the KGB man. "No more than you would."

"Oh, much more. There are no great shocks to come out of Moscow, I accept that. But there are astonishing revelations to be found in Washington. You could provide them; you'd be an enormous asset. The sanctimonious are always far more vulnerable."

"I accept that."

"Before Odile Verachten was killed, she made an offer to me. It was not an offer she was entitled to make; they don't want the Russian. They want you. If they can't have you, they'll kill you, but someone's giving you the option."

It would be far better for all concerned if we sat down and thrashed out the differences between us. You may discover they're not so great after all. Words from a faceless messenger.

"Let's get back to Paris," said Bray. "How did you get her?"

"It wasn't so difficult. The man on the phone was too anxious; he saw a generalship in his future, or his own execution. I discussed what might happen to the soldier with the ugly little mark on his chest; the fact that I knew about it was nearly enough in itself. I set up a series of moves, offering the soldier and Beowulf Agate for the girl. Beowulf was tired of running and was perfectly willing to listen to whatever anyone had to say. He – I – knew I was cornered, but professionalism demanded that he – you – extract certain guarantees. The girl had to go free. Were my reactions consistent with your well-known obstinacy?"

"Very plausible," replied Scofield. "Let's see if I can fill in a few spaces. You answered the questions: what was my mother's middle name? Or when did my father change jobs?"

"Nothing so ordinary," broke in the Russian. " 'Who was your fourth kill? Where?' "

"Lisbon," said Bray quietly. "An American beyond salvage. Yes, you'd know that . . . Then your moves were made by a sequence of telephone calls to the flat – my call from London was the intrusion – and with each call you gave new instructions, any deviation and the exchange was cancelled. The exchange ground itself was in traffic, preferably one-way traffic, with one vehicle, one man and Antonia. Everything to take place within a time span of sixty to a hundred seconds."

The Russian nodded. "Noon on the Champs Elysées, south of the Arch. Vehicle and girl taken, man and soldier bound at the elbows, thrown out at the intersection of the Place de la Concorde, and a swift, if roundabout, drive out of Paris." Bray put the whisky down and walked to the hotel window overlooking Carlos Place. "A little while ago you said you had two choices. To go out after her, or wait in the rue du Bac. It seems to me there was a third but you didn't take it. You could have got out of Paris yourself right away."

Taleniekov closed his eyes. "That was the one choice I didn't have. It was in her voice, in every reference she made to you. I thought I saw it in Corsica, that first night in the cave above Porto Vecchio when you looked at her. I thought then, how *insane*, how perfectly . . . " The Russian shook his head.

"Unreasonable?" asked Bray.

Taleniekov opened his eyes. "Yes. Unreasonable . . . as in unnecessary, uncalled for." The KGB man raised his glass and drank the remaining whisky in one swallow. "The slate from East Berlin is as clean as it will ever be; there'll be no more cleansing."

"None will be asked for. Or expected."

"Good. I presume you've seen the newspapers."

"Trans-Communications? Its holdings in Verachten?"

"Ownership would be more like it. I trust you noted the location of the corporate headquarters. Boston, Massachusetts. A city quite familiar to you, I think."

"What's more to the point, it's the city – and state – of Joshua Appleton the Fourth, patrician and senator, whose grandfather was the guest of Guillaume de Matarese. It'll be interesting to see what – if any – his connections are to Trans-Comm."

"Can you doubt they exist?"

"At this point I doubt everything," said Scofield. "Maybe I'll think differently after we've put together those facts you say we now have. Let's start with when we left Corsica."

Taleniekov nodded. "Rome came first. Tell me about Scozzi."

Bray did, taking the time to explain the role Antonia had been forced to play in the Red Brigades.

"That's why she was in Corsica, then?" asked Vasili. "Running from the Brigades?"

"Yes. Everything she told me about their financing spells Matarese . . . Scofield clarified his theories, moving swiftly on to the events at Villa d'Este and the murder of Guillamo Scozzi, ordered by a man named Paravicini. "It was the first time I heard that I was dead. They thought I was you . . . Now Leningrad. What happened there?"

Taleniekov breathed deeply, silently, before answering. "They killed in Leningrad, in Essen," he said, his voice barely audible. "Oh, how they kill, these twentieth-century *fida'is*, these contemporary mutants of Hasan ibn as-Sabbāh! I should tell you, the soldier I pushed from the car in the Place de la Concorde had

298

more than a blemish on his chest. His clothes were stained by a gunshot that left another mark. I told his associate it was for Leningrad, for Essen."

The Russian told his story quietly, the depth of his feelings apparent when he spoke of Lodzia Kronescha, the scholar Mikovsky and Heinrich Kassel. Especially Lodzia; it was necessary for him to stop for a while and replenish the whisky in his glass. Scofield remained silent; there was nothing he could say. The Russian finished with the field at night in Stadtwald and the death of Odile Verachten.

"Prince Andrei Voroshin became Ansel Verachten, founder of the Verachten Works, next to Krupp the largest company in Germany, now one of the most sprawling in all Europe. The granddaughter was his chosen successor in the Matarese."

"And Scozzi," said Bray, "joined Paravicini through a marriage of convenience. Blood-lines, a certain talent, and charm in exchange for a seat in the boardroom. But the chair was a prop; it's all it ever was. The count was expendable, killed because he made a mistake."

"As was Odile Verachten. Also expendable."

"And the name Scozzi-Paravicini is misleading. The control lies with Paravicini."

"Add to that Trans-Communication's ownership of Verachten. So two descendants of the *padrone's* guest list are accounted for, both a part of Matarese, yet neither is significant. What do we have?"

"What we suspected, what old Krupsky told you in Moscow. The Matarese was taken over, obviously in part, possibly in whole. Scozzi and Voroshin were useful for what they brought or what they knew or what they owned. They were tolerated – even made to feel important – as long as they were useful, eliminated the moment they were not."

"But useful for what? That's the question!" Taleniekov banged his glass down in frustration. "What does the Matarese want? They finance intimidation, and murder through huge corporate structures; they spread chaos, but *why*? This world is going mad with terror, bought and paid for by men who lose the most by it. Their investment is in total *disorder*! It makes no sense!"

Scofield heard the sound – the moan – and sprang out of the chair. He walked quickly to the bedroom door; Toni had changed her position, twisting to her left, the covers bunched around her shoulders. But she was still asleep; the cry had come from her unconscious. He went back to the chair and stood behind it.

"Total disorder," he said softly. "Chaos. The clashing of bodies in space. Creation."

"What are you talking about?" asked Taleniekov.

"I'm not sure," replied Scofield. "I keep going back to the word 'chaos' but I'm not sure why."

"We're not sure of *anything*. We have four names – but two didn't amount to much – and they're dead. We see an alignment of companies who are the superstructure – the *essential superstructure* – behind terrorism everywhere, but we cannot prove the alignment and don't know why they're sponsoring it. Scozzi-Paravicini finances the Red Brigades, Verachten no doubt Baader-Meinhof. God only knows what Trans-Communications pays for – and these may be only a few of the many involved. We have *found* the Matarese, but still we do not see them! Whatever charges we levelled against such conglomerates would be called the ravings of madmen, or worse."

"Much worse," said Bray, remembering the voice over the restaurant's telephone. "Traitors. We'd be shot."

"Your words have the ring of prophecy. I don't like them."

"Neither do I, but I like being executed less."

"A profound statement. Also a *non sequitur.*"

"Not when coupled with what you just said. 'We've found the Matarese, but still we don't see them,' wasn't that it?"

"Yes."

"Suppose we not only found one, but had him. In our hands."

"A *hostage?*"

"That's right."

"That's insane."

"Why? You had the Verachten woman."

"In a car. In a farmer's field. At night. I had no delusions of taking her into Essen and setting up a base of operations."

Scofield sat down. "The Red Brigades held Aldo Moro eight blocks away from a police headquarters in Rome. Although that's not exactly what I had in mind."

Taleniekov leaned forward. "Waverly?"

"Yes."

"*How?* The American network is after you, the Matarese nearly trapped you; what did *you* have in mind? Dropping into the Foreign Office and proffering an invitation for tea?"

"Waverly's to be brought here – to this room – at eight o'clock tonight."

The Russian whistled. "May I ask how you managed it?"

Bray told him about MI6's Roger Symonds. "He's doing it because he thinks whatever convinced me to work with you must be strong enough to get me an interview with Waverly."

"They have a name for me. Did he tell you?"

"Yes. The Serpent."

"I suppose I should be flattered, but I'm not. I find it ugly. Does Symonds have any idea that this meeting has a hostile basis? That you suspect Waverly of being something more than England's Foreign Secretary?"

"No; the reverse, in fact. When he objected, the last thing I said to him was that I might be trying to save Waverly's life."

"Very good," said Taleniekov. "Very frightening. Assassination, like acts of terror, is a spreading commodity. They'll be alone then?"

"Yes, I made a point of it. A room at the Connaught; there'd be no reason for Roger to think anything's wrong. And we know the Matarese haven't made the connection between me and the man Waverly is supposedly meeting at the MI6 offices."

"You're certain of that? It strikes me as the weakest part of the strategy. They've got you in London, they know you have the four names from Corsica. Suddenly, from nowhere, Waverly, the *consigliere*, is asked to meet secretly with a man at the office of a British intelligence agent known to have been a friend of Beowulf Agate.

The equation seems obvious to me; why should it elude the Matarese?"

"A very specific reason. They don't think I ever made contact with Symonds."

"They can't be sure you didn't."

"The odds are against it. Roger's an experienced field man; he covered himself. He was logged in at the Admiralty and later returned a blind inquiry. I wasn't picked up in the streets and we used a sterile phone. We met an hour outside of London, two changes of vehicle for me, at least four for him. No one followed."

"Impressive. Not conclusive."

"It's the best I can do. Except for a final qualification."

"Qualification?"

"Yes. There isn't going to be a meeting tonight. They'll never reach this room."

"No *meeting*? Then what's the purpose of their coming here?"

"So we can grab Waverly downstairs before Symonds knows what's happened. Roger'll be driving; when he gets here, he won't go through the lobby, he'll use a side entrance, I'll find out which one. In the event – and I agree it's possible – that Waverly is followed, you'll be down in the street. You'll know it; you'll see them. Take them out. I'll be right inside that entrance."

"Where they least expect you," broke in the Russian.

"That's right. I'm counting on it. I can take Roger by surprise, knock him out and force a pill down his throat. He won't wake up for hours."

"It's not enough," said Taleniekov, lowering his voice. "You'll have to kill him. Sacrifices inevitably must be made. Churchill understood that with Coventry and the Ultra; this is no less, Scofield. British Intelligence will mount the most extensive manhunt in England's history. We've got to get Waverly out of the country. If the death of one man can buy us time – a day perhaps – I submit it's worth it."

Bray looked at the Russian, studying him. "You submit too goddamn much."

"You know I'm right."

Silence. Suddenly Scofield hurled his glass across the room. It shattered against the wall. "*Goddamn* it!"

Taleniekov bolted forward, his right hand under his coat. "What is it?"

"You're right and I *do* know it. He trusts me and I've got to kill him. It'll be days before the British will know where to start. Neither MI6 nor the Foreign Office know anything about the Connaught."

The KGB man removed his hand, sliding it on to the arm of the chair. "We need the time, Scofield. I don't think there's any other way."

"If there is, I hope to God it comes to me." Bray shook his head. "I'm sick to death of necessity." He looked over at the bedroom door. "But then she told me that."

"The rest is detail," continued Taleniekov, rushing the moment. "I'll have an automobile on the street outside the entrances. The moment I'm finished – if indeed, there's anything for me to do – I'll come inside and help you. It will be necessary, of course, to take the dead man along with Waverly. Remove him."

"The dead man has no name," said Scofield quietly. He got out of the chair and walked to the window. "Has it occurred to you that the closer we get, the more like them we become?"

"What occurs to me," said the Russian, "is that your strategy is nothing short of extraordinary. Not only will we have a *consigliere* of the Matarese, but *what* a *consigliere!* The Foreign Secretary of England! Have you any idea what that means? We'll break that man wide open, and the world will listen. It will be *forced* to listen!" Taleniekov paused, then added softly, "What you've done lives up to the stories of Beowulf Agate."

"Bullshit," said Bray. "I hate that name."

The moan was sudden, bursting into a prolonged sob, followed by a cry of pain, muffled, uncertain, desperate. Scofield raced into the bedroom. Toni was writhing on the bed, her hands clawing her face, her legs kicking viciously at imaginary demons that surrounded her. Bray sat down and pulled her hands from her face, gently, firmly, bending each finger so that the nails would not puncture her skin. He pinned her arms and held her, cradling her as he had cradled her in Rome. Her cries subsided, replaced once more by sobs; she shivered, her breathing erratic, slowly returning to normal as her rigid body went limp. The first hysterics brought about by the dissipation of scopolamine had passed. Scofield heard footsteps in the doorway; he angled his head to signify that he was listening.

"It will keep up until morning, you know," said the KGB man. "It leaves the body slowly, with a great deal of pain. As much from the images in the mind as anything else. There's nothing you can do. Just hold her."

"I know. I will."

There was a moment of silence; Bray could feel the Russian's eyes on him, on Antonia. "I'll leave now," Taleniekov said. "I'll call you here at noon, come up later in the day. We can refine the details then, co-ordinate signals, that kind of thing."

"Sure. That kind of thing. Where'll you go? You can stay here, if you like."

"I think not. As in Paris, there are dozens of places here. I know them as well as you do. Besides, I must find a car, study the streets. Nothing takes the place of preparation, does it?"

"No, it doesn't."

"Good night. Take care of her."

"I'll try." Footsteps again; the Russian walked out of the room. Scofield spoke. "Taleniekov."

"Yes?"

"I'm sorry about Leningrad."

"Yes." Again there was silence; then the words were spoken quietly. "Thank you."

The outside door closed; he was alone with his love. He lowered her to the pillow and touched her face. So illogical, so unreasonable. *Why did I find you? Why did you find me? You should have left me where I was – deep in the earth. It isn't the time for either of us, can't you understand that? It's all so . . . uncalled for.*

It was as if his thoughts had been spoken out loud. Toni opened her eyes, the focus imperfect, the recognition slight, but she knew him. Her lips formed his name, the sound a whisper.

"Bray . . . ?"

"You'll be all right. They didn't hurt you. The pain you feel is from chemicals; it will pass, believe that."

"You came back."

302

"Yes."

"Don't go away again, *please*. Not without me."

"I won't."

Her eyes suddenly widened, the stare glazed, her white teeth bared like a young animal's caught in a snare that was breaking its back. A heartbreaking whimper came from deep inside her.

She collapsed in his arms.

Tomorrow, my love, my only love. Tomorrow comes with the sunlight, everyone knows that. And then the pain will pass, I promise you. And I promise you something else, my inopportune love so late in my life. Tomorrow, today, tonight . . . I will take the man who will bring this nightmare to a close. Taleniekov is right. We will break him – as no man has ever been broken – and the world will listen to us. When it does, my love, my only adorable love, you and I are free. We will go far away where the night brings sleep and love, not death, not fear and loathing of the darkness. We will be free because Beowulf Agate will be gone. He will disappear – for he hasn't done much good. But he has one more thing to do. Tonight.

Scofield touched Antonia's cheek. She held his hand briefly, moving it to her lips, smiling, reassuring him with her eyes.

"How's the head?" asked Bray.

"The ache is barely a numbness now," she said. "I'm fine, really."

Scofield released her hand and walked across the room where Taleniekov was bent over a table, studying a road map. Without having discussed it, both men were dressed nearly alike for their work. Sweaters and trousers of dark material, tightly strapped shoulder holsters with black leather belts laterally across the chest. Their shoes were also dark in colour, but light in weight, with thick rubber soles that had been scraped with knives until they were coarse.

Neither man had spoken with the other about the topic of clothing; it would have been foolish. The only subsequent remark was made by Vasili when he arrived at the hotel room and was about to remove his loose-fitting topcoat.

"I must commend your tailor," he had observed.

Taleniekov now glanced up as Bray approached the table. "After Great Dunmow, we'll head east towards Coggeshall on our way to Nayland. Incidentally, there's an airfield capable of handling small jets south of Hadleigh. Such a field might be of value to us in a few days."

"You may be right."

"Also," added the KGB man with obvious reluctance, "this route passes the Blackwater River; the forests are dense in that area. It would be a . . . good place to drop off the package."

"The dead man still hasn't got a name," said Scofield. "Give him his due. He's Roger Symonds, honourable man, and I hate this fucking world."

"At the risk of appearing fatuous, may I submit – forgive me, suggest – that what you do tonight will benefit that sad world we both have abused too well for too long."

"I'd just as soon you didn't submit or suggest anything." Bray looked at his watch. "He'll be calling soon. When he does, Toni will go down to the lobby and pay Mr Edmonton's bill – that's me. She'll come back up with a steward and take our bags and briefcase down to the car we've rented in Edmonton's name and drive directly to Colchester. She'll wait at a restaurant called Bonner's until 11.30. If there are any changes of plans or we need her, we'll reach her there. If she doesn't hear from us, she'll go on to Nayland, to the Double Crown Inn where she has a room reserved in the name of Vickery."

Taleniekov pushed himself up from the table. "My briefcase is not to be opened," he said. "It's tripped."

"So's mine," replied Scofield. "Any more questions?"

The telephone rang; all three looked at it – a moment suspended in time, for the bell meant the time had come. Bray walked over to the desk, let the phone ring a second time, then picked it up.

Whatever words he might have expected, whatever greetings, information, instructions or revelations that might have come, nothing on this earth could have prepared him for what he heard. Symonds' voice was a cry from some inner space of torment, a pain of such extremity that it was beyond belief.

"They're all *dead*. It's a *massacre*! Waverly, his wife, children, three servants . . . *dead*. What in *hell have you done*?"

"Oh, my *God*!" Scofield's mind raced, thoughts swiftly translated into carefully selected words. "Roger, listen to me. It's what I tried to *prevent*!" He cupped the phone, his eyes on Taleniekov. "Waverly's dead, everyone in the house killed."

"Method?" shouted the Russian. "Marks on the bodies. Weapons. Get it all!"

Bray shook his head. "We'll get it later." He took his hand from the mouthpiece; Symonds was talking rapidly, close to hysterics.

"It's *horrible*. Oh, God, the most terrible thing! They've been slaughtered . . . like animals!"

"*Roger!* Get hold of yourself! Now listen to me. It's part of a pattern. Waverly knew about it. He knew too much; it's why he was killed. I couldn't reach him in time."

"You couldn't? . . . For the love of God . . . why *didn't* you, *couldn't you . . . tell me*? He was the Foreign Secretary, England's *Foreign Secretary*! Have you any idea of the repercussions, the . . . oh, my *God*, a tragedy! *A catastrophe! Butchered!*" Symonds paused. When he spoke again it was obvious that the professional in him was struggling for control. "I want you down in my office as soon as you can get there. Consider yourself under detention by the British government."

"I can't do that. Don't ask me."

"I'm not asking, Scofield! I'm giving you a direct order backed up by the highest authorities in England. You will *not* leave that hotel! By the time you reached the lift, all the current would be shut off, every staircase, every exit under armed guard."

"All right, all right. I'll get to MI6," lied Bray.

"You'll be *escorted*. Remain in your room.

"Forget the room, Roger," said Scofield, grasping for whatever words he could find that might fit the crisis. "I've got to see you, but not at MI6."

"I don't think you *heard* me!"

"Put guards on the doors, shut off the goddamned elevators, do anything you like, but I've got to see you *here*. I'm going to walk out of this room and go down to the bar, to the darkest booth I can find. Meet me there."

"I *repeat* . . ."

"Repeat all you want to, but if you don't come over here and listen to me, there'll be other assassinations – *that's* what they are, Roger! *Assassinations*. And they won't stop at a Foreign Secretary, or a Secretary of State . . . or a President or a Prime Minister."

"Oh, my . . . *God*!" whispered Symonds.

"It's what I couldn't tell you last night. It's the reason you looked for when we talked. But I won't put it on-record, I can't work in-sanction. And that should tell you enough. Get over here, Roger." Bray closed his eyes, held his breath; it was now or it was not.

"I'll be there in ten minutes," said Symonds, his voice cracking.

Scofield hung up the phone, looking first at Antonia, then Taleniekov. "He's on his way."

"He'll take you in!" exclaimed the Russian.

"I don't think so. He knows me well enough to know I won't go on-record if I say I won't. And he doesn't want the rest of it on his head." Bray crossed to the chair where he had thrown his raincoat and travel bag. "I'm sure of one thing. He'll meet me downstairs, and give me a chance. If he accepts, I'll be back in an hour. If he doesn't . . . I'll kill him." Scofield unzipped his bag, reached into it and pulled out a sheathed, long-bladed hunting knife. It still had the Harrods' price tag on it. He looked at Toni; her eyes told him she understood. Both the necessity and his loathing of it.

Symonds sat across from Bray in the booth of the Connaught lounge. The subdued lighting could not conceal the pallor of the Englishman's face; he was a man forced to make decisions of such magnitude that the mere thought of them made him ill. Physically ill, mentally exhausted.

They had talked for nearly forty minutes. Scofield, as planned, had told him part of the truth – a great deal more of it than he cared to – but it was necessary. He was now about to make his final request of Roger, and both men knew it. Symonds felt the terrible weight of his decision; it was in his eyes. Bray felt the knife in his belt; his appalling decision to use it if necessary made it difficult for him to breathe.

"We don't know how extensive it is, or how many people in the various governments are involved, but we know it's being financed through large corporations," Scofield explained. "What happened in Belgrave Square tonight can be compared to what happened to Anthony Blackburn in New York, to the physicist Yurievich in Russia. We're closing in; we have names, covert alliances, knowledge that intelligence branches in Washington, Moscow and Bonn have been manipulated. But we have no proof; we'll get it, but we don't have it now. If you take me in, we'll never get it. The case against me is beyond salvage; I don't have to tell you what that means. I'll be executed at the first . . . opportune moment. For the wrong reason, by the wrong people, but the result will be the same. Give me *time*, Roger."

"What will you give me?"

"What more do you want?"

"Those names, the alliances."

"They're *meaningless* now. Worse than that, if they're recorded, they'll either go farther underground, cutting off all traces, or the killing, the terrorism, will accelerate. There'll be a series of bloodbaths . . . and you'll be dead."

"That's my condition. The names, the alliances. Or you will not leave here."

Bray stared at the man from MI6. "Will you stop me, Roger? I mean here, now, at this moment, will you? *Can* you?"

"Perhaps not. But those two men over there will." Symonds nodded to his left.

Scofield shifted his eyes. Across the room, at a table in the centre of the lounge, were two British agents, one of them the red-haired stocky man he had spoken with last night at the moonlit playground in Guildford. That same man now stared at him, no sympathy, only hostility in his look. "You covered yourself," said Scofield.

"Did you think I wouldn't? They're armed and have their instructions. The names, please." Symonds took out a notebook and a ballpoint pen; he placed them in front of Bray. "Don't write nonsense, I beg you. Be practical. If you and the Russian are killed, there's no one else. I may not be in a class with Beowulf Agate and the Serpent, but I'm not without certain talents."

"How much time will you give me?"

"One week. Not a day more."

Scofield picked up the pen, opened the small notebook and began to write.

4 April 1911
Porto Vecchio, Corsica
Scozzi
Vorostun
Waverly
Appleton

Current:
Guillamo Scozzi – Dead
Odile Verachten – Dead
John Waverly – Dead
Joshua Appleton – ?

Scozzi-*Paravicini*. Milan
Verachten Works. (Voroshin.) Essen
Trans-Communications. Boston.

Below the names and the companies, he then wrote one word:
Matarese

Bray walked out of the elevator, his mind on air routes, accessibilities and cover. Hours now took on the significance of days; there was so much to learn, so much to find, and so little time to do it all.

They had thought it might end in London with the breaking of David Waverly, *consigliere* of the Matarese, Foreign Secretary of the United Kingdom. They should have known better; the descendants were expendable.

Three were dead, three names removed from the guest list of Guillaume de Matarese for the date of 4 April 1911. Yet one was left. The golden politician of Boston, the man few doubted would win the summer primaries and without question the election in the fall. He would be President of the United States, Joshua Appleton IV seemed truly to be contemporary America's man-for-all-seasons. Many had cried out during the tragic, violent 'sixties and 'seventies that they could bind the country together; Appleton was never so presumptuous as to make the statement, but most of America thought he was perhaps the only man who could.

But bind it for what? For whom? That was the most frightening prospect of all. Was he the one descendant not expendable? Chosen by the council, by the shepherd boy, to do what the others could not do?

They would reach Appleton, thought Bray as he rounded the corner of the Connaught hallway towards his room, but not where Appleton expected to be reached – *if* he expected to be reached. They would not be drawn to Washington, where chance encounters with State, FBI and Company personnel were ten times greater than any other place in the hemisphere. There was no point in taking on two enemies simultaneously. Instead, they would go to Boston, to the conglomerate so aptly named Trans-Communications.

Somewhere, somehow, within the upper ranks of that vast company, they would find one man – one man with a blue circle on his chest or connections to Milan's Scozzi-Paravicini or Essen's Verachten, and that man would whisper an alarm sounding Joshua Appleton IV. They would trap him, take him in Boston. And when they were finished with him the secret of the Matarese would be exposed, told by a man whose impeccable credentials were matched only by his incredible deceit. It *had* to be Appleton; there was no one else. If they . . .

Scofield reached for the weapon in his holster. The door of his room twenty feet down the corridor was open. There were no circumstances imaginable that allowed it to be *conceivably* left open by choice! There had been an intruder – intruders.

He stopped, shook the paralysis from his mind, and ran to the side of the door, pivoting, pressing his back into the wall by the moulding. He lunged inside, crouching, levelling his gun in front of him, prepared to fire.

There was no one, no one at all. Nothing but silence and a very neat room. Too neat; the road map had been removed from the table, the glasses washed, returned to the silver tray on the bureau, the ashtrays wiped clean. There was no evidence that the room had been occupied. Then he saw it – them – and the paralysis returned.

On the floor by the table were his attaché case and travel bag, positioned – neatly – beside each other, the way a steward or a bellboy might position them. And folded – neatly – over the travel bag was his dark blue raincoat. A guest was prepared for departure.

Two visitors had already departed. Antonia was gone, Taleniekov was gone.

The bedroom door was open, the bed fully made up, the bedside table devoid of the water pitcher and the ashtray which an hour ago had been filled with half-smoked cigarettes – testimony to an anxious, pain-stricken night and day.

Silence. Nothing.

His eyes were suddenly drawn to the one thing – again on the floor – that was not in keeping with the neatness of the room, and he felt sick. On the rug by the left side of the table was a circle of blood – a jagged circle, still moist, still glistening. And then he looked up. A small pane of glass had been blown out of the window.

"*Toni!*" The scream was his; it broke the silence, but he could not help himself. He could not think, he could not move.

The glass shattered; a second window pane blew out of its wooden frame and he heard the spinning whine of a bullet as it embedded itself in the wall behind him. He dropped to the floor.

The telephone rang, its jangling, erratic bell somehow proof of insanity! He crawled to the desk below the sight-line of the window.

"Toni? . . . *Toni!*" He was screaming, crying, yet he had not reached the desk, had not touched the phone.

He raised his hand and pulled the instrument to the floor beside him. He picked up the receiver and held it to his ear.

"We can always find you, Beowulf," said the precise English voice on the other end of the line. "I told you that when we spoke before."

"What have you *done with her*!?" shouted Bray. "Where *is she*?"

"Yes, we thought that might be your reaction. Rather strange coming from you, isn't it? You don't even inquire about the Serpent."

"*Stop* it! Tell me!"

"I intend to. Incidentally, you had a grave lapse of judgement – again strange for one so experienced. We merely had to follow your friend Symonds from Belgravia. A quick perusal of the hotel register – as well as the time and the method of registering – gave us your room."

"What have you *done* with her? . . . *Them?*"

"The Russian's wounded, but he may survive. At least – sufficiently enough for our purposes."

"The *girl!*"

"She's on her way to an airfield, as is the Serpent."

"Where are you taking her?"

"We think you know. It was the last thing you wrote down before you named the Corsican. A city in the state of Massachusetts."

"Oh, *God* . . . Symonds?"

"Dead, Beowulf. We have the notebook. It was in his car. For all intents and purposes, Roger Symonds, MI6, has disappeared. In view of his schedule, he may even be tied in with the terrorists who massacred the Foreign Secretary of England and his family."

"You . . . *bastards.*"

"No. Merely professionals. I'd think you'd appreciate that. If you want the girl back you'll follow us. You see, there's someone who wants to meet with you."

"Who?"

"Don't be a fool," said the faceless messenger curtly.

"In Boston?"

"I'm afraid we can't help you get there, but we have every confidence in you.

Register at the Ritz-Carlton Hotel under the name of . . . Vickery. Yes, that's a good name, such a benign sound."

"Boston," said Bray, exhausted.

Again there was the sudden shattering of glass; a third window pane blew out of its frame.

"That shot," said the voice on the phone, "is a symbol of our good faith. We could have killed you with the first."

31

He reached the coast of France, the same way he had left it four days ago: by motor launch at night. The trip to Paris took longer than anticipated; the drone he had expected to use wanted no part of him. The word was out, the price for his dead body too high, the punishment for helping Beowulf Agate too severe. The man owed Bray; he preferred to walk away.

Scofield found an off-duty *gendarme* in a bar in Boulogne-sur-Mer; the negotiations were swift. He needed a fast ride to Paris, to Orly Airport. To the *gendarme*, the payment was staggering; Bray reached Orly by daybreak. By 9.00, a Mr Edmonton was on the first Air Canada flight to Montreal. The plane left the ground and he turned his thoughts to Antonia.

They would use her to trap him, but there was no way they would permit her to stay alive once the trap had closed. Any more than they would let Taleniekov live once they had learned everything he knew. Even the Serpent could not withstand injections of scopolamine or sodium amytal; no man could block his memory or prohibit the flow of information once the gates of recall were chemically pried open.

These were the things he had to accept, and having accepted them, base his every move on their reality. He would not grow old with Antonia Gravet; there would be no years of peace. Once he understood this, there was nothing left but to try to reverse the conclusion, knowing that the chances of doing so were remote. Simply put, since there was absolutely nothing to lose, conversely there was no risk not worth taking, no strategy too outlandish or outrageous to consider.

The key was Joshua Appleton; that remained constant. Was it possible that the senator was such a consummate actor that he had been able to deceive so many so well for so long? Apparently it was so; one trained from birth to achieve a single goal, with unlimited money and talent available to him, could possibly conceal anything. But the gap that Scofield needed filling was found in the stories of Josh Appleton, Marine combat officer, Korea. They were well known, publicized by campaign managers, emphasized by the candidate's reluctance to discuss them, other than to praise the men who had served with him.

Captain Joshua Appleton had been decorated for bravery under fire on five separate occasions, but the medals were only symbols, the tributes of his men paeans of genuine devotion. Josh Appleton was an officer dedicated to the proposition that no soldier should take a risk he would not take himself; and no infantryman, regardless of how badly he was wounded or how seemingly hopeless the situation, was to be left to the enemy if there was any chance at all to get him back. With such tenets, he was not always the best of officers, but he was the best of men. He continuously exposed himself to the severest punishment to save a private's life, or draw fire away from a corporal's squad. He had been wounded twice dragging men out of the hills of Panmunjom, and nearly lost his life at Ch'osan when he had crawled through enemy lines to direct a helicopter rescue.

After the war, and he was home, Appleton had faced another struggle as dangerous as any he had experienced in Korea. A near fatal accident on the Massachusetts Turnpike. His car had swerved over the divider, crashing into an onrushing truck, the injuries sustained from head to legs so punishing the doctors at Massachusetts General had about given him up for dead. When the bulletins were issued about this decorated son of a prominent family, men came from all over the country. Mechanics, bus drivers, farmhands and clerks; the soldiers who had served under "Captain Josh".

For two days and nights they had kept vigil, the more demonstrative praying openly, others simply sitting with their thoughts or reminiscing quietly with their former comrades. And when the crisis had passed and Appleton was taken off the critical list, these quiet men went home. They had come because they had wanted to come; they had left not knowing whether they had made any difference, but hoping that they had. Captain Joshua Appleton IV, USMCR, was deserving of that hope.

This was the gap that Bray could neither fill nor understand. The captain who had risked his life so frequently, so openly for the sake of other men; how could those risks be reconciled with a man programmed since birth to become the President of the United States? How could repeated exposures to death be justified to the Matarese?

Somehow they had been, for there was no longer any doubt where Senator Joshua Appleton stood. The man who would be elected President of the United States before the year was over was inextricably tied to a conspiracy as dangerous as any in American history.

At Orly, Scofield picked up the Paris edition of the *Herald-Tribune* to see if the news of the Waverly massacre had broken; it had not. But there was something else, on the second page. It was another follow-up story concerning Trans-Communications' holdings in Verachten, including a partial list of the Boston conglomerate's board of directors. The third name on the roster was the senator from Massachusetts.

Joshua Appleton was not only a *consigliere* of the Matarese, he was the sole descendant of that guest list seventy years ago in Porto Vecchio to become a true inheritor.

"*Mesdames et messieurs, s'il vous plait. A votre gauche, Les Îles de la Manche . . .*" The voice of the pilot droned from the aircraft's speaker. They were passing the Channel Islands; in six hours they would reach the coast of Nova Scotia, an hour later Montreal. And four hours after that, Bray would cross the US border south of Lacolle on the Richelieu River, into the waters of Lake Champlain.

In hours the final madness would begin. He would live or he would die. And if he could not live in peace with Toni, without the shadow of Beowulf Agate in front of him or behind him, he did not care to live any longer. He was filled with . . . emptiness. If the awful void could be erased, replaced with the simple delight of being with another human being, then whatever years he had left were most welcome.

If not, to hell with them.

Boston.

There's someone who wants to meet you.

Who? Why?

To make you a consigliere *of the Matarese . . . consider what you bring to such an organization.*

It was not hard to define. Taleniekov was right. Beowulf Agate knew where the bodies were, and how and why they no longer breathed. He could be invaluable.

They want you. If they can't have you, they'll kill you. So be it; he would be no prize for the Matarese.

Bray closed his eyes; he needed sleep. There would be little in the days ahead.

The rain splattered against the windshield in continuous sheets, streaking to the right under the force of the wind that blew off the Atlantic over the coastal highway. Scofield had rented the car in Portland, Maine with a driver's licence and credit card he had never used before. Soon he would be in Boston but not in the way the Matarese expected. He would not race half-way across the world and announce his arrival by registering at the Ritz-Carlton as Vickery, only to wait for the Matarese's next move. A man in panic would, a man who felt the only way to save the life of someone he deeply loved would – but he was beyond panic, he had accepted total loss, therefore he could hold back and conceive of his own strategy. It was the fundamental advantage of a man who had lost hope; there was nothing not worth trying.

He would be in Boston, in his enemy's den, but his enemy would not know it. The Ritz-Carlton would receive two telegrams spaced a day apart. The first would arrive tomorrow requesting a suite for Mr B. A. Vickery of Montreal, arriving the following day. The second would be sent the next afternoon, stating that Mr Vickery had been delayed, his arrival now anticipated two days later. There would be no address for Vickery, only telegraph offices on Montreal's King and Market Streets, and no request for confirmations, the assumption here being that someone in Boston would make sure rooms were available.

Only the two telegrams, sent from Montreal; the Matarese had little choice but to believe he was still in Canada. What they could not know – suspect surely, but not be certain – was that he had used a drone to send them. He had. He had contacted a man, a felony-prone *séparatiste* he had known before, and met him at the airport, giving him the two handwritten messages on telegraph forms along with a sum of money and instructions when and from where to send them. Should the Matarese

311

phone Montreal for immediate confirmation of origin, they would find the forms written in Bray's handwriting.

He had three days and one night to operate within Matarese territory, to learn everything he could about the conglomerate, Trans-Communications, and its hierarchy. To find another flaw, one significant enough to summon Senator Joshua Appleton IV, to Boston – on *his* terms. In panic.

So much to learn, so little time.

Scofield let his mind wander back to everyone he had ever known in Boston and Cambridge – both as student and professional. Among that crowd of fits and misfits there had to be someone who could help him.

He passed a road sign telling him he had left the town of Marblehead; he'd be in Boston in less than thirty minutes.

It was 5.35, the horns of impatient drivers blaring away on all sides as the taxi inched its way down Boylston Street's crowded shopping district. He had parked the rented car in the farthest reaches of the Prudential underground lot, available should he need it, but not subject to the vagaries of weather or vandalism. He was on his way to Cambridge; a name had come into focus. A man who had spent twenty-five years teaching corporate law at the Harvard School of Business. Bray had never met him; there was no way the Matarese could make him a target.

It was strange, thought Bray, as the cab clamoured over the ribs of the Longfellow Bridge, that both he and Taleniekov had been brought back – however briefly – to those places where it had begun for each of them. A lifetime ago . . . two students, one in Leningrad, one in Cambridge, Massachusetts, with a certain, not dissimilar talent for foreign languages.

He had begun a career in the State Department and been given such a fine title: Special Foreign Service Officer, Consular Operations. Neither the pay nor the grade was much, but the future was bright, productive . . . and, well, benevolent. Christ, the *irony*!

Had it happened that way with Taleniekov? Had the student from Leningrad pursued one course, veering into another, gradually, inexorably driven into waters he had not known were on any map? Until the pressures were so strong there was nothing left but to become the expert in order to survive? The questions were rhetorical; neither he nor the Russian would have become what they became unless the fundamentals had been there in the first place. Events shaped men, perhaps, but they did not remove alternatives of choice. It was not a pleasant thing to think about.

Was Taleniekov still alive? Or was he dead or dying somewhere in the city of Boston, Massachusetts?

Toni was alive; they'd keep her alive . . . for a while.

Don't think about them. Don't think about her now! There is no hope. Not really. Accept it, live with it. Then do the best you can . . .

The traffic congealed again at Harvard Square, the downpour causing havoc in the streets. People were crowded in storefronts, students in ponchos and jeans racing from kerb to kerb, slapping the hoods of cars, jumping over the flooded

312

gutters, crouching under the awning of the huge newspaper stand.

The newspaper stand. *Newspapers From All Over The World* was the legend printed across the white sign above the canopy. Bray peered out the window, through the rain and the collection of bodies. One name, one man, dominated the observable headlines.

Waverly! David Waverly! England's Foreign Secretary!

"Let me off here," he said to the driver, reaching for the soft travel bag and the hard-shelled briefcase at his feet.

He pushed his way through the crowd, grabbed two domestic papers off the row of twenty-odd different editions, left a dollar, and ran across the street at the first break in traffic. Half a block down Massachusetts Avenue was a German-style restaurant he vaguely remembered from his student days. The entrance was jammed; Scofield excused his way to the door, using his travel bag for interference, and went inside.

There was a line waiting for tables; he went to the bar, and ordered Scotch. The drink arrived; he unfolded the first newspaper. It was the Boston *Globe*; he started reading, his eyes racing over the words, picking out the salient points of the article. He finished and picked up the second paper; it was the Los Angeles *Times*, the story identical to the *Globe's* wire service report, and almost surely the official version put out by Whitehall, which was what Bray wanted to know.

The massacre of David Waverly, his wife, children and servants in Belgrave Square was held to be the work of terrorists, most likely a splinter group of fanatical Palestinians. It was pointed out, however, that no group had as yet come forth to claim responsibility, and the P.L.O. vehemently denied participation. Messages of shock and condolence were being sent by political leaders across the world; parliaments and praesidiums, congresses and royal courts, all interrupted their businesses at hand to express their fury and grief.

Bray re-read both articles and the related stories in each paper, looking for Roger Symonds' name. It was not to be found; it would not come for days, if ever. The speculations were too wild, the possibilities too improbable. A senior officer of British Intelligence somehow connected to the slaughter of Britain's Foreign Secretary. The Foreign Office would put a clamp on Symonds' death for any number of reasons. It was no time to . . .

Scofield's thoughts were interrupted. In the dim light of the bar he had missed the insert; it was a late bulletin in the *Globe*.

LONDON, March 3 – An odd and brutal aspect of the Waverly killings was revealed by the police only hours ago. After receiving a gunshot in the head, David Waverly apparently received a grotesque *coup de grâce* in the form of a shotgun blast directly into his chest, literally removing the left side of his upper abdomen and rib cage. The medical examiner was at a loss to explain the method of killing, for the administering of such a death wound – considering the caliber and the proximity of the weapon – is considered extremely dangerous to the one firing the gun. The London police speculate that the weapon might have been a primitive short-barreled, hand-held shotgun once favored by roaming gangs of bandits in the Mediterranean. The 1934 *Encyclopedia of Weaponry* refers to the gun as the Lupo, the Italian word for "wolf".

313

The medical examiner in London might have trouble finding a reason for the "method of killing", but Scofield did not. If England's Foreign Secretary had a jagged blue circle affixed to his chest in the form of a birthmark, it was gone.

And there was a message in the use of the Lupo. The Matarese wanted Beowulf Agate to understand clearly how far and how wide the Corsican fever had spread, into what rarefied circles of power it had reached.

He finished his drink, left his money on the bar with the two newspapers and looked around for a telephone. The name that had come into focus, the man he wanted to see, was Dr Theodore Goldman, a dean of the Harvard School of Business and a thorn in the side of the Justice Department. For he was an outspoken critic of the Anti-Trust Division, incessantly claiming that Justice prosecuted the minnows and let the sharks roam free. He was a middle-aged *enfant terrible* who enjoyed taking on the giants, for he was a giant himself, cloaking his genius behind a facade of good-humoured innocence that fooled no one.

If anyone could shed light on the conglomerate called Trans-Communications, it was Goldman.

Bray did not know the man, but he had met Goldman's son a year ago in The Hague – in circumstances that were potentially disastrous for a young pilot in the Air Force. Aaron Goldman had got drunk with the wrong people near the Groote Kerk, men known to be involved in a KGB infiltration of NATO. The son of a prominent American Jew was prime material for the Soviets.

An unknown intelligence officer had got the pilot away from the scene, slapped him into sobriety and told him to go back to his base. And after countless cups of coffee, Aaron Goldman had expressed his thanks.

"If you've got a kid who wants to go to Harvard, let me know, whoever you are. I'll talk to my dad, I swear it. What the hell's your name anyway?"

"Never mind," Scofield had said. "Just get out of here, and don't buy typing paper at the Co-op. It's cheaper down the block."

"What the . . ."

"Get out of here."

Bray saw the pay phone on the wall; he grabbed his luggage and walked over to it.

32

He picked up a small wet piece of newspaper on the rain-soaked sidewalk and walked to the MBTA subway station in Harvard Square. He went downstairs and checked his soft leather suitcase in a locker. If it was stolen that would tell him something, and there was nothing in it he could not replace. He slid the wet scrap of paper carefully under the far right corner of the bag. Later, if the fragile scrap was curled, or the surface broken, that would tell him something else: the bag had been searched and he was in the Matarese sights.

Ten minutes later he rang the bell of Theodore Goldman's house on Brattle Street. It was opened by a slender, middle-aged woman, her face pleasant, her eyes curious.

"Mrs Goldman?"

"Yes?"

"I telephoned your husband a few minutes ago . . ."

"Oh, yes, of course," she interrupted. "Well, for heaven's sake, get out of the rain! It's coming down like the forty-day flood. Come in, come in. I'm Anne Goldman."

She took his coat and hat; he held his attaché case.

"I apologize for disturbing you."

"Don't be foolish. Aaron told us all about that night in . . . The Hague. You know, I've never been able to figure out where that place *is*. Why would a city be called *the* anything?"

"It's confusing."

"I gather our son was very confused *that* night; which is a mother's way of saying he was plastered." She gestured towards a squared-off, double doorway so common to old New England houses. "Theo's on the telephone and trying to mix his stinger at the same time; it's making him frantic. He hates the telephone and loves his evening stinger."

Theodore Goldman was not much taller than his wife, but there was an expansiveness about him that made him appear much larger than he was. His intellect could not be concealed, so he took refuge in humour, putting guests – and, no doubt, associates – at ease.

They sat in three leather armchairs that faced the fire, the Goldmans with their stingers, Bray drinking Scotch. The rain outside was heavy, drumming on the windows. The recapping of their son's escapade in The Hague was over quickly, Scofield dismissing it as a minor night out on the town.

"With major consequences, I suspect," said Goldman, "if an unknown intelligence officer hadn't been in the vicinity."

"Your son's a good pilot."

"He'd better be; he's not much of a drinker." Goldman sat back in his chair. "But now, since we've met this unknown gentleman who's been kind enough to give us his name, what can we do for him?"

"To begin with, please don't tell anyone I came to see you."

"That sounds ominous, Mr Vickery. I'm not sure I approve of Washington's tactics in these areas."

"I'm no longer attached to the government; the request is personal. Frankly, the government doesn't approve of me any longer, because in my former capacity, I think I uncovered information Washington – especially the Department of Justice – doesn't want exposed. I believe it should be; that's as plain as I can put it."

Goldman, the legal nemesis of the Justice Department, rose to the occasion. "That's plain enough."

"In all honesty, I used my brief meeting with your son as an excuse to talk to you. It's not admirable, but it's the truth."

"I admire the truth. Why did you want to see me?"

Scofield put his glass down. "There's a company here in Boston, at least the corporate headquarters are here. It's a conglomerate called Trans-Communications."

"It certainly is." Goldman chuckled. "The Alabaster Bride of Boston. The Queen of Congress Street."

"Now I don't understand," said Bray.

"The Trans-Comm Tower," explained Anne Goldman. "It's a white stone building thirty or forty storeys high, with rows of tinted blue glass on every floor."

"The ivory tower with a thousand eyes staring down at you," added Goldman, still amused. "Depending on the angle of the sun, some seem to be open, some closed, while others appear to be winking."

"Winking? Closed?"

"*Eyes*," pressed Anne, blinking her own. "The horizontal lines of tinted glass are huge windows, rows and rows of large bluish circles."

Scofield caught his breath. *Perro nostro circulo.* "It sounds strange," he said without emphasis.

"Actually, it's quite imposing," replied Goldman. "A bit *outré* for my taste, but I gather that's the point. There's a kind of outraged purity about it, a white shaft set down in the middle of the dark concrete jungle of a financial district."

"That's interesting." Bray could not help himself; he found an obscure analogy in Goldman's words. The white shaft became a beam of light; the jungle was chaos. A beam of light shooting through a dark void filled with clashing bodies in space. Light piercing chaos. *Chaos.*

"So much for the Alabaster Bride," said the lawyer-professor. "What did you want to know about Trans-Comm?"

"Everything you can tell me," answered Scofield.

Goldman was mildly startled. "Everything? . . . I'm not sure I know that much. It's your classic multi-national conglomerate, I can tell you that. Extraordinarily diversified, brilliantly managed."

"I read the other day that a lot of financial people were stunned by the extent of its holdings in Verachten."

"Yes," agreed Goldman, nodding his head in that exaggerated way a man does when he hears a foolish point being repeated. "A lot of people *were* stunned, but I wasn't. Of course, Trans-Comm owns a great deal of Verachten. I daresay I could name four or five other countries where its holdings would stun these same people. The philosophy of a conglomerate is to buy as far and as wide as possible and diversify its markets. It both uses and refutes the Malthusian laws of economics. It creates aggressive competition within its own ranks, but does its best to remove all outside competitors. *That's* what multi-nationals are all about, and Trans-Comm's one of the most successful anywhere in the world."

Bray watched the lawyer as he spoke. Goldman was a born teacher – infectious in delivery, his voice rising with enthusiasm. "I understand what you're saying, but you lost me with one statement. You said you could name four or five other countries where Trans-Comm has heavy investments. How can you do that?"

"Not just me," objected Goldman. "Anybody can. All he has to do is read and

316

use a little imagination. The laws, Mr Scofield. The laws of the host country."

"The laws? Of a host country?"

"They're the only things that can't be avoided, the only protection buyers and sellers have. In the international financial community they take the place of armies. Every conglomerate must adhere to the laws of the country in which its divisions operate. Now, these same laws often ensure confidentiality; they're the frameworks within which the multi-nationals have to function – corrupting and altering them when they can, of course. And since they do, they must seek intermediaries to represent them. *Legally.* A Boston attorney practising before the Massachusetts bar would be of little value in Hong Kong. Or Essen."

"What are you driving at?" Bray asked.

"You study the *law firms.*" Goldman leaned forward again. "You match the firms and their locations with the general level of their clients and the services for which they're most recognized. When you find one that's known for negotiating stock purchases and exchanges, you look around to see what companies in the area might be ripe for invading." The legal academician was enjoying himself. "It's really quite simple," he continued, "and a hell of an amusing game to play. I've scared the be-jesus out of more than one corporate flunkie in those summer seminars by telling him where I thought his company's money men were heading. I've got a little index file – three by five cards – where I jot down my goodies."

Scofield spoke; he had to know. "What about Trans-Comm? Did you ever do a file card on it?"

"Oh, sure. That's what I meant about the other countries."

"What are they?"

Goldman stood up in front of the fire, frowning in recollection. "Let's start with the Verachten Works. Trans-Comm's overseas reports included sizable payments to the Gehmeinhoff-Salenger firm in Essen. Gehmeinhoff's a direct legal liaison to Verachten. And they're not interested in nickel-and-dime trans-actions; Trans-Comm had to be going after a big chunk of the complex. Although I admit, even I didn't think it was as much as the rumours indicate. Probably isn't."

"What about the others?"

"Let's see . . . Japan. Kyoto. T-C uses the firm of Aikawa-Onmura-and-some-thing. My guess would be Yakashubi Electronics."

"That's pretty substantial, isn't it?"

"Panasonic can't compare."

"What about Europe?"

"Well, we know about Verachten." Goldman pursed his lips. "Then, of course, there's Amsterdam; the law firm there is Hainaut and Sons, which leads me to think that Trans-Comm's bought into Netherlands Textiles, which is an umbrella for a score of companies ranging from Scandinavia to Lisbon. From here we can head over to Lyon . . ." The lawyer stopped and shook his head. "No, that's probably tied in with Turin."

"Turin?" Bray sat forward.

"Yes, they're so close together, the interests so compatible, there's no doubt prior ownership is buried in Turin."

"Who in Turin?"

"The law firm's Palladino–E–LaTona, which can only mean one company – or companies. Scozzi–Paravicini.'"

Scofield went rigid. "They're a cartel, aren't they?"

"My God, yes. They – *it* – certainly is. Agnelli and Fiat get all the publicity, but Scozzi–Paravicini runs the Colosseum and all the lions. When you combine it with Verachten and Netherlands Textiles, throw in Yakashubi, add Singapore, and Perth, and a dozen other names in England, Spain, and South Africa I haven't mentioned, the Alabaster Bride of Boston has put together a global federation."

"You sound as if you approve."

"No, actually, I don't. I don't think anyone can, when so much economic power is so centralized. It's a corruption of the Malthusian law; the competition is fake. But I respect the reality of genius when its accomplishments are so obviously staggering. Trans-Communications was an idea born and developed in the mind of one man. Nicholas Guiderone."

"I've heard of him. A modern-day Carnegie or Rockefeller, isn't he?"

"More. Much more. The Geneens, the Luces, the Bluhdorns, the wonderboys of Detroit and Wall Street, none of them can touch Guiderone. He's the last of the vanishing giants, a really benign monarch of industry and finance. He's been honoured by most of the major governments of the West, and not a few in the Eastern bloc, including Moscow."

"Moscow?"

"Certainly," said Goldman, nodding thanks to his wife, who was pouring a second stinger into his glass. "No one's done more to open up East-West trade than Nicholas Guiderone. As a matter of fact I can't think of anyone who's done more for world trade in general. He's over eighty now, but I understand he's still filled with as much pee and vinegar as he was the day he walked out of Boston Latin."

"He's from Boston?"

"Yes, a remarkable story. He came to this country as a boy. An immigrant boy of ten or eleven, without a mother, travelling with a barely literate father in the hold of a ship. I suppose you could call it the definitive story of the American dream."

Involuntarily, Scofield gripped the arm of the chair. He could feel the pressure on his chest, the tightening in his throat. "Where did that ship come from?"

"Italy," said Goldman, sipping his drink. "Southern part. Sicily, or one of the islands."

Bray was almost afraid to ask the question. "Would you by any chance know whether Nicholas Guiderone ever knew a member of the Appleton family?"

Goldman looked over the rim of his glass. "I know it, and so does most everyone in Boston. Guiderone's father worked for the Appletons. For the senator's grandfather at Appleton Hall. It was old Appleton who spotted the boy's promise, gave him the backing, and persuaded the schools to take him. It wasn't so easy in those days, the early nineteen hundreds. The two-toilet Irish had barely got their second john, and there weren't too many of them. An Italian kid – excuse me, *Eye*talian – was nowhere. Gutter meat."

Bray's words floated; he could hardly hear them himself.

"That was Joshua Appleton the second, wasn't it?"

"Yes."

"He did all that for this . . . child."

"Hell of a thing, wasn't it? And the Appletons had enough troubles then. They'd lost damn near everything in the market fluctuations. They were hanging on by the skin of their teeth. It was almost as if old Joshua had seen a message on some mystical wall."

"What do you mean?"

"Guiderone paid everything back several thousand fold. Before Appleton was in his grave he saw his companies back on top, making money in areas he'd never dreamed of, the capital flowing out of the banks owned by the Italian kid he'd found in his carriage house."

"Oh, my *God* . . . "

"I told you," said Goldman. "It's one hell of a story. It's all there to be read."

"If you know where to look. And why."

"I beg your pardon?"

"Guiderone . . . Scofield felt as though he were walking through swirling circles of mist towards some eerie light. He put his head back and stared at the ceiling, at the dancing shadows thrown up by the fire. "*Guiderone*. It's a derivative of the Italian '*guida*'. A guide."

"Or shepherd," said Goldman.

Bray snapped his head down, his eyes wide, riveted on the lawyer. "What did you say?"

Goldman was puzzled. "I didn't say it, he did. About seven or eight months ago at the UN."

"The United Nations?"

"Yes. Guiderone was invited to address the General Assembly; the invitation was unanimous, incidentally. Didn't you hear it? It was broadcast all over the world. He even taped it in French and Italian for Radio–International."

"I didn't hear it."

"The UN's perennial problem. Nobody listens."

"What did he say?"

"Pretty much what you just said. That his name had its roots in the word '*guida*', or guide. And that was the way he'd always thought of himself. As a simple shepherd, guiding his flocks, aware of the rocky slopes and uncrossable streams . . . that sort of thing. His plea was for international relationships based on the mutuality of material need, which he claimed would lead to the higher morality. It was a little strange philosophically, but it was damned effective. So effective, in fact, that there's a resolution on this session's agenda that'll make him a full-fledged member of the UN's Economic Council. That's not just a title, by the way. With his expertise and resources, there's not a government in the world which won't listen very hard when he talks. He'll be one damned powerful *amicus curiae*."

"Did you hear him give that speech?"

"Sure," laughed the lawyer. "It was mandatory in Boston; you were cut off the *Globe's* subscription list if you missed it. We saw the whole thing on Public Television."

"What did he sound like?"

Goldman creased the flesh around his deep-set eyes and looked at his wife. "Well, he's a very old man. Still vigorous, but nevertheless old. How would you describe him, darling?"

"Just as you do," said Anne. "An old man. Not large, but quite striking, with that look of a man who's so used to being listened to. I do remember one thing, though – about the voice. It was high-pitched and maybe a little breathless, but he spoke extremely clearly, every phrase very precise. You couldn't miss a word he said."

Scofield closed his eyes and thought of a blind woman in the mountains above Corsica's Porto Vecchio, twisting the dials of a radio, and hearing *a voice crueller than the wind.*

He had found the shepherd boy.

33

He had found him!

Toni, I've found him! Stay alive! Don't let them destroy you. They won't kill your body. Instead, they'll try to kill your mind. Don't let them do it. They will go after your thoughts and the way you think. They will try to change you, alter the processes that make you what you are. They have no choice, my darling. A hostage must be programmed even after the trap is closed; professionals understand that. No extremity is beyond consideration. Find something within yourself – for my sake. You see, my dearest love, I've found something. I've found him. The shepherd boy! It is a weapon. I need time to use it. Stay alive. Keep your mind!

Taleniekov, the enemy I can't bring myself to hate any more. If you're dead there's nothing I can do but turn away, knowing that I'm alone. If you're alive, keep breathing. I promise nothing; there is no hope, not really. But we have something we never had before. We have him. We know who the shepherd boy is. The web is defined now and it circles the world. Scozzi-Paravicini, Verachten, Trans-Communications . . . and a hundred different companies between each one. All put together by the shepherd boy, all run from an alabaster tower that look over the city with a thousand eyes . . . And yet there's something else. I know, I feel it! Something else that's in the middle of the web. We who've "abused this world so well for so long" develop instincts, don't we? Mine is so strong I can taste it. It's out there. I just need time. Keep breathing . . . my friend.

I can't think about them any longer. I've got to put them out of my mind; they intrude, they interfere, they are barriers. They do not exist; she does not exist and I have lost her. We will not grow old together; there is no hope . . . Now, move. For Christ's sake, move!

He had left the Goldmans quickly, thanking them, bewildering them by his abrupt departure. He had asked only a few more questions – about the Appleton family – questions any knowledgeable person in Boston could answer. Having the information was all he needed; there was no point in staying longer. He walked now in the rain, smoking a cigarette, his thoughts on the missing fragment his instinct told him was a greater weapon than the shepherd boy, yet somehow part of the shepherd boy, intrinsic to the deceits of Nicholas Guiderone. What *was* it? Where was the false note he heard so clearly?

He knew one thing, however, and it was more than instinct. He had enough to panic Senator Joshua Appleton IV. He would telephone the senator in Washington and quietly recite a bill-of-particulars that began over seventy years ago, on the date of 4 April 1911, in the hills of Porto Vecchio. Did the senator have anything to say? Could he shed any light on an organization known as the Matarese which began its activities in the second decade of the century – at Sarajevo, perhaps – by selling political murder? An organization the Appleton family had never left, for it could be traced to a white skyscraper in Boston, a company honoured by the senator's presence on its board of directors. The age of Aquarius had turned into the age of conspiracy. A man on his march to the White House would have to panic, and in panic mistakes were made.

But panic could be controlled. The Matarese would mount the senator's defences swiftly, the presidency too great a prize to lose. And charges levelled by a traitor were no charges at all; they were merely words spoken by a man who had betrayed his country.

Instinct. Look at the man – the *man* – more closely.

Joshua Appleton was *not* as he was perceived to be by the nation. The middle-aged paternal figure whose appeal ran across the spectrum. Then what about the day-to-day individual? Was that the smaller life, a dwarf with warts and blackheads and bloated appetites? Was it possible that the everyday man had weaknesses he'd find it infinitely more difficult to deny than a grand conspiracy levelled by a traitor? Was it conceivable – and the more Bray thought about it, the more logical it seemed – that the entire Korean experience had been a hoax? Had commanders been bought and medals paid for, a hundred men convinced by money to keep a vigil none gave a damn about? It would not have been the first time war had been used as a springboard for a celebrated civilian life. It was a natural, the perfect ploy, if the scenario could be executed with precision – and what scenario could not be with the resources controlled by the Matarese?

Look at the man. The *man.*

Goldman had brought the Appleton family up to date for Bray. The senator's official residence was a house in Concord where he and his family stayed only during the summer months. His father had died several years ago; Nicholas Guiderone had paid his last respects to the son of his mentor by purchasing the outsized Appleton Hall from the widow at a price far above the market, promising to keep the name in perpetuity. Old Mrs Appleton currently lived on Beacon Hill, in a brownstone on Louisburg Square.

The mother. What kind of a woman was she? In her middle seventies, Goldman had estimated. Could she tell him anything? Involuntarily perhaps a great deal. Mothers were much better sources of information than was generally believed, not for what they said, but for what they did not say, for subjects were changed abruptly.

It was twenty minutes past nine. Bray wondered if he could do it, reach

Appleton's mother and talk with her. The house might be watched, but not on a priority basis. A car parked in the Square with a view of the brownstone, one man, possibly two. If there were such men and he took them out, the Matarese would know he was in Boston; he was not ready for that. Still the mother might provide a short cut, a name, an incident, something he could trace quickly; there was so little time. Mr B. A. Vickery was expected at the Ritz-Carlton Hotel, but when he got there he had to bring leverage with him. At the optimum, he had to have his own hostage; he had to have Joshua Appleton IV.

There was no hope. There was nothing not worth trying. There was instinct.

The steep climb up Chestnut Street towards Louisburg Square was marked by progressively quieter blocks. It was as if one were leaving a profane world to enter a sacred one; garish neons were replaced by the muted flickering of gas lamps from another era, the cobblestone streets washed clean. He reached the Square, staying in the shadows of a brick building on the corner.

He took out a pair of small binoculars from his attaché case and raised them to his eyes. He focused the powerful Zeiss-Ikon lenses on each stationary car in the streets around the fenced-in park. It was the centre of Louisburg Square.

There was no one.

Bray put the binoculars back in his attaché case, left the shadows of the brick building and walked down the peaceful street towards the Appleton brownstone. The stately houses surrounding the small park with the wrought-iron fence and gate were quiet. The night air was bitterly cold now, the gas lamps flickering more rapidly with the intermittent gusts of winter wind; windows were closed, fires burning in the hearths of Louisburg Square. It *was* a different world, remote, almost isolated, certainly at peace with itself.

He climbed the white stone steps and rang the bell. The carriage lamps on either side of the door threw more light than he cared for.

He heard the sound of footsteps; a nurse opened the door and he knew instantly. The woman recognized him; it was in the short, involuntary gasp that escaped her lips, in the brief widening of her eyelids. It explained why no one was on the street: the guard was *inside* the house.

"Mrs Appleton, please?"

"I'm afraid she's retired."

The nurse started to close the door rapidly. Scofield jammed his left foot into the base, his shoulder against the heavy black panel, and forced it open.

"I'm afraid you know who I am," he said, stepping inside, dropping his attaché case.

The woman pivoted, her right hand plunging into the pocket of her uniform. Bray countered, pushing her farther into her own pivot, gripping her wrist, twisting it downward and away from her body. She screamed. Scofield yanked her to the floor, his knee crashing up into the base of her spine. With his left arm, he vised her neck from behind, forearm across her shoulder blades, and pulled up violently as she fell; ten more pounds of pressure and he would have broken her neck. But he did not want to do that. He wanted this woman alive; she collapsed to the floor unconscious.

He crouched in silence, removing the short-barrelled revolver from the nurse's pocket, waiting for sounds or signs of people. The scream must have been heard by anyone inside the house.

There was nothing – there was *something*, but it was so faint he could not channel a perception of what it was. He saw a telephone next to the staircase and crept over to pick it up. There was only the hum of a dial tone; no one was using the phone. Perhaps the woman had told the truth; it was entirely possible that Mrs Appleton had retired. He'd know shortly.

First, he had to know something else. He went back to the nurse, pulled her across the floor under the hallway light and ripped apart the front of her uniform. He tore the slip and brassiere beneath, pushed up her left breast, and studied the flesh.

There it was. The small, jagged blue circle as Taleniekov had described it. The birthmark that was no birthmark at all, but instead, the mark of the Matarese.

Suddenly, from above, there was the whirring sound of a motor, the vibration constant, bass-toned. Bray lunged across the unconscious body of the nurse, into the shadows of the stairs, and raised the revolver.

From around the curve of the first landing an old woman came into view. She was sitting in the ornate chair of an automatic lift, her frail hands holding the sculptured pole that shot up from the guard rail. She was encased in a high-collared dressing gown of dark grey, and her once-delicate face was ravaged, her voice strained.

"I imagine that's one way to leash the bitch-hound, or corner the wolf-in-season, but if your objective is sexual, young man, I question your taste."

Mrs Joshua Appleton III was drunk. From the looks of her, she had been drunk for years.

"My only objective, Mrs Appleton, is to see *you*. This woman tried to stop me; this is her gun, not mine. I'm an experienced intelligence officer employed by the United States government and fully prepared to show you my identification. In light of what happened I am checking for concealed weapons. I would do the same in like circumstances anywhere, anytime." With those words, he had begun; and with an equanimity born of prolonged alcohol-saturation, the old woman accepted his presence.

Scofield carried the nurse into a small drawing room, bound her hands and feet in slipknots made from the torn nylon of her hose, saving the elastic waistband for a gagging brace, pulled between her teeth, tied firmly to the back of her neck. He closed the door and returned to Mrs Appleton in the living room. She had poured herself a brandy; Bray looked at the odd-shaped glass and at the decanters that were placed on tables about the room. The glass was so thick that it could not be broken easily, and the crystal decanters were positioned so that a new drink was accessible every seven to ten feet in all directions. It was strange therapy for one so obviously an alcoholic.

"I'm afraid," said Scofield, pausing at the door, "that when your nurse regains consciousness I'm going to give her a lecture about the indiscriminate display of firearms. She has an odd way of protecting you, Mrs Appleton."

"Very odd, young man." The old woman raised her glass and cautiously sat down in an antimacassared armchair. "But since she tried and failed so miserably, why don't you tell me what she was protecting me from? Why did you come to see me?"

"May I sit down?"

"By all means."

Bray held her partially unfocused eyes. "As I mentioned, I'm an intelligence officer attached to the Department of State . . ." He began his ploy, the words spoken with restraint and sympathy. "A few days ago we received a report that implicates your son – through his father – to an organization in Europe known for years to be involved in international crime."

"In *what*?" Mrs Appleton giggled. "Really, you're very amusing."

"Forgive me, but there's nothing amusing about it."

"What are you talking about?"

Scofield described a group of men not unlike the Matarese council, watching the old woman closely for signs that she had made a connection. He was not even sure he had penetrated her clouded mind; he had to appeal to the mother, not the woman. "The information from Europe was sent and received under the highest security classification. To the best of my knowledge, I'm the only one in Washington that's read it, and further, I'm convinced I can contain it. You see, Mrs Appleton, I think it's very important for this country that none of this touch the senator."

"Young *man*," interrupted the old woman. "Nothing can touch the senator, don't you know that? My son will be the President of the United States. He'll be elected in the fall. Everybody says so. Everybody wants him."

"Then I haven't been clear, Mrs Appleton. The report from Europe is devastating and I need information. Before your son ran for office, how closely did he work with his father in the Appleton business ventures? Did he travel frequently to Europe with your husband? Who were his closest friends here in Boston? That's terribly important. People that only you might know, men and women who came to see him at Appleton Hall."

" 'Appleton Hall . . . way up on Appleton Hill,' " broke in the old woman in a strained, whispered sing-song of no discernible tune. " 'With the grandest view of Boston . . . and ever will be still.' Joshua the First wrote that over a hundred years ago. It's not very good, but they say he picked out the notes on a harpsichord. So like the Joshuas, a harpsichord. So like us all, really."

"Mrs Appleton? After your son came back from the Korean War . . ."

"We *never* discuss that war!" For an instant the old woman's eyes became focused, hostile. Then the clouds returned. "Of course, when my son is President they won't wheel me out like Rose or Miss Lillian. I'm kept for very special occasions." She paused and laughed a soft, eerie laugh that was self-mocking. "After very *special* sessions with the doctor." She paused again and raised her left forefinger to her lips. "You see, young man, sobriety isn't my strongest suit."

Scofield watched her closely, saddened by what he saw. Beneath the ravaged face there had been a lovely face, the eyes once clear and alive, not floating in dead sockets as they were now. "I'm sorry. It must be painful to know that."

"On the contrary," she replied whimsically. It was her turn to study him. "Do you think you're clever?"

"I've never thought about it one way or the other." *Instinct.* "How long have you been . . . ill, Mrs Appleton?"

"As long as I care to remember and that is quite long enough, thank you."

Bray looked again at the decanters. "Has the senator been here recently?"

"Why do you ask?" She seemed amused. Or was she on guard?

"Nothing, really," said Scofield casually; he could not alarm her. Not now. He was not sure why – or what – but something was happening. "I indicated to the nurse that the senator might have sent me here, that he might be on his way himself."

"Well, there you *are!*" cried the old woman, triumph in her strained, alcoholic voice. "No wonder she tried to stop you!"

"Because of all these?" asked Bray quietly, gesturing at the decanters. "Bottles filled – obviously every day – with booze. Perhaps your son might object."

"Oh, don't be a damn fool! She tried to stop you because you *lied.*"

"Lied?"

"Of course! The senator and I meet only on special occasions – after those *very* special treatments – when I'm trotted out so his adoring public can see his adoring mother. My son has never been to this house and he would never come here. The last time we were alone was over eight years ago. Even at his father's funeral, although we stood together. We barely spoke."

"May I ask why?"

"You may not. But I can tell you it has nothing to do with that gibberish – what I could make of it – you talked about."

"Why did you say you never discussed the Korean War?"

"Don't presume, young man!" Mrs Appleton raised the glass to her lips; her hand trembled and the glass fell, brandy spilling on her gown. "*Damn!*" Scofield started out of his chair. "Leave it alone," she commanded.

"I'll pick it up," he said, kneeling down in front of her. "No point stumbling over it."

"Then pick it up. And get me another, if you please."

"Certainly." He crossed to a near-by table and poured her a brandy in a fresh glass. "You say you don't like to discuss the war in Korea."

"I said," interrupted the old woman, "I *never* discussed it."

"You're very fortunate. I mean just to be able to say it and let it go at that. Some of us aren't so lucky." He remained in front of her, his shadow falling over her, the lie calculated. "I can't. I was there. So was your son."

The old woman drank several swallows without stopping, the way alcoholics do, needing the extra half ounce in their throats, abstractly convinced that it might not be there. She looked up at him, the brandy filling her head. "Wars kill so much more than the bodies they take. Terrible things happen. Did they happen to you, young man?"

"They've happened to me."

"Did they do those awful things to you?"

"What awful things, Mrs Appleton?"

"Starve you, beat you, bury you alive, your nostrils filled with dirt and mud, unable to breathe? Dying slowly, consciously, wide-awake and dying."

The old woman was describing tortures documented by men held captive in North Korean camps. What was the relevance? "No, those things didn't happen to me."

"They happened to him, you know. The doctors told me. It's what made him change. Inside. Change so much. But we must never talk about it."

"Talk about . . . ?" What was *she* talking about? "You mean the senator?"

"Shhh!" The old woman drank the remainder of the brandy. "We must never, *never* talk about it."

"I see," said Bray, but he did *not* see. Senator Joshua Appleton IV had never been held captive by the North Koreans. Captain Josh Appleton had *eluded* capture on numerous occasions, the very acts of doing so behind enemy lines a part of his commendations. Scofield remained in front of her chair and spoke again. "But I can't say I ever noticed any great changes in him, other than getting older. Of course, I didn't know him that well twenty years ago, but to me he's still one of the finest men I've ever known."

"*Inside!*" The old woman whispered harshly. "It's all inside! He's a *mask* . . . and people adore him so. Suddenly the tears were in her clouded eyes, and the words that followed a cry from deep within her memory. "They *should* adore him! He was such a beautiful boy, such a beautiful young man. There was no one ever like my Josh, no one more loving, more filled with kindness! . . . Until they did those terrible things to him." She wept. "And I was such a dreadful person. I was his mother and I couldn't understand. I wanted my Joshua back! I wanted him back so badly!"

Bray knelt down and took the glass from her. "What do you mean you wanted him back?"

"I couldn't understand. He was so cold, so distant. They'd taken the joy out of him. There was no *joy* in him! He came out of the hospital . . . and the pain had been too much and I *couldn't understand*. He looked at me and there was no joy, no love. Not inside!"

"The hospital? The accident after the war – just after the war?"

"He suffered so much . . . and I was drinking so much . . . so much. Every week he was in that awful war I drank more and more. I couldn't stand it! He was all I *had*. My husband was . . . in name only – as much my fault as his, I suppose. He was disgusted with me. But I loved my Josh so. The old woman reached for the glass. He got to it first and poured her a drink. She looked at him through her tears, her floating eyes filled with the sadness of knowing what she was. "I thank you very much," she said with simple dignity.

"You're welcome," he answered, feeling helpless, his mind pounding, but nevertheless helpless.

"In a way," she whispered, gripping the glass tightly, "I still have him but he doesn't know it. No one does."

"How is that?"

"When I moved out of Appleton Hall . . . on Appleton Hill. . . ." I kept his room just the way it was, the way it had been. You see, he never came back, not really. Only for an hour one night to pick up some things. So I took a room here and made it his. It will always be his, but he doesn't know it."

Bray knelt down in front of her again. "Mrs Appleton, may I see that room? *Please*, may I see it?"

"Oh, no, that wouldn't be right," she said. "It's very private. It's his, and I'm the only one he lets in. He lives there still, you see. My beautiful Joshua."

"I've got to see that room, Mrs Appleton. Where is it?" *Instinct.*

"Why do you have to see it?"

"I can help you. I can help your son. I know it."

She squinted, studying him from some inner place. "You're a kind man, aren't you? And you're not as young as I thought. Your face has lines, and there is grey at your temples. You have a strong mouth; did anyone ever tell you that?"

"No, I don't think anyone ever did. Please, Mrs Appleton, I *must* see that room. Allow me to."

"It's nice that you ask. People rarely ask me for anything any more; they just tell me. Very well, help me to my lift, and we'll go upstairs. You understand, of course, we'll have to knock first. If he says you can't come in, you'll have to stay outside."

Scofield guided her through the living room arch to the chair lift. He walked beside her up the staircase to the first-floor landing, where he helped her to her feet.

"This way," she said, gesturing towards a narrow, darkened corridor. "It's the last door on the right."

They reached it, stood in front of it for a moment, and then the old woman rapped lightly on the wood. "We'll know in a minute," she continued, bending her head as if listening for a command from within. "It's all right," she said, smiling. "He said you can come in, but you mustn't touch anything. He has everything arranged the way he likes it." She opened the door, and flipped a switch on the wall. Three separate lamps went on; still the light was dim. Shadows were thrown across the floor and up on the walls.

The room was a young man's room, mementoes of an expensive youth on display everywhere. The banners above the bed and the desk were those of Andover and Princeton, the trophies on the shelves for such sports as sailing, skiing, tennis and lacrosse. The room had been preserved – eerily preserved – as if it had once belonged to a Renaissance prince. A microscope sat alongside a chemistry set, a volume of *Britannica* lay open, most of the page underlined, handwritten notes in the margins. On the bedside table were novels of Dos Passos and Koestler, beside them the typewritten title page of an essay authored by the celebrated inhabitant of that room. It was called: *The Pleasures and Responsibilities of Sailing in Deep Waters. Submitted by Joshua Appleton, Senior. Andover Academy. March 1945.* Protruding from below the bed were three pairs of shoes: loafers, sneakers and black patent leathers worn with formal clothes. A life somehow covered in the display.

Bray winced in the dim light. He was in the tomb of a man very much alive, the artefacts of a life preserved, somehow meant to transport the dead safely on its journey through the darkness. It was a macabre experience when one thought of Joshua Appleton, the electric, mesmerizing senator from Massachusetts. Scofield glanced at the old woman. She was staring impassively at a cluster of photographs on the wall. Bray took a step forward and looked at them.

They were pictures of a younger Joshua Appleton and several friends – the same friends, apparently the crew of a sailboat – the occasion identified by the centre photograph. It showed a long banner being held by four men standing on the deck of a sloop. *Marblehead Regatta Championship – Summer 1949.*

Only the centre photograph and the three above it showed all four crew members. The three lower photographs were shots of only two of the four. Appleton and another young man, both stripped to the waist – slender, muscular, shaking hands above a tiller; smiling at the camera as they stood on either side of the mast, and sitting on the gunwhale, drinks held forward in a salute.

Scofield looked closely at the two men, then compared them to their associates. Appleton and his obviously closer friend had a strength about them absent in the other two, a sense of assurance, of conviction somehow. They were not alike except perhaps in height and breadth – athletic men comfortable in the company of each's peer – yet neither were they dissimilar. Both had sharp if distinctly different features – strong jaws, wide foreheads, large eyes and thatches of straight, dark hair – the kind of faces seen in scores of Ivy League yearbooks.

There was something disturbing about the photographs. Bray did not know what it was – but it was there. *Instinct.*

"They look as if they could be cousins," he said.

"For years they acted as though they were *brothers*," replied the old woman. "In peace, they would be *partners*, in war, *soldiers* together! But he was a coward, he betrayed my son. My beautiful Joshua went to war alone and terrible things were done to him. He ran away to Europe, to the safety of a château in France and Switzerland. But justice is odd; he died in Gstaad, from injuries on a slope. To the best of my knowledge, my son has never mentioned his name since."

"Since? . . . When was that?"

"Twenty-five years ago."

"Who was he?"

She told him.

Scofield could not breathe; there was no air in the room, only shadows in a vacuum. He had found the shepherd boy, but instinct told him to look for something else, a fragment as awesome as anything he had learned. He had found it. The most devastating piece of the puzzle was in place. He needed only proof, even the semblance of proof, for the truth was so extraordinary.

He was in a tomb; the dead had journeyed in darkness for twenty-five years.

34

He guided the old woman to her bedroom, poured her a final brandy and left her. As he closed the door she was sitting on the bed chanting that unsingable tune. *Appleton Hall . . . way up on Appleton Hill.*

Notes picked out on a harpsichord over a hundred years ago. Notes lost, as she was lost without ever knowing why.

He returned to the dimly-lit room that was the resting place of memories and went to the cluster of photographs on the wall. He removed one and pulled the small picture hook out of the plaster, smoothing the wallpaper around the hole; it might delay discovery, certainly not prevent it. He turned off the lights, closed the door, and went downstairs to the front hall.

The guard-nurse was still unconscious; he left her where she was. There was nothing to be gained by moving her or killing her. He turned off every light, including the carriage lamps above the front steps, opened the door and slipped out into Louisburg Square. On the pavement, he turned right and began walking rapidly to the corner where he would turn right again, descending Beacon Hill into Charles Street to find a taxi. He had to pick up his luggage in the subway locker in Cambridge. The walk down the hill gave him time to think, time to remove the photograph from its glass frame, folding it carefully into his pocket – folding it very carefully so that neither face was damaged.

He needed a place to stay. A place to sit and fill up pages of paper with facts, conjectures and probabilities, his bill-of-particulars. In the morning, he had several things to do, among which were visits to the Massachusetts General Hospital and the Boston Public Library.

The room was no different from any other room in a very cheap hotel in a very large city. The bed sagged, and the single window looked out on a filthy stone wall not ten feet from the cracked panes of glass. The advantages, however, were the same as everywhere in such places; nobody asked questions. Cheap hotels had a place in this world, usually for those who did not care to join it. Loneliness was a basic human right, not to be tampered with lightly.

Scofield was safe; he could concentrate on his bill-of-particulars.

By 4.35 in the morning, he had filled seventeen pages. Facts, conjectures, probabilities. He had written the words carefully, legibly, so they could be clearly reproduced. There was no room for interpretation: the indictment was specific even where the motives were not. He was gathering his weapons, storing his bandoliers of ammunition; they were all he had. He fell back on the sagging bed and closed his eyes. Two or three hours' sleep would be enough.

He heard his own whisper float up to the cracked ceiling.

"Taleniekov . . . keep breathing. Toni, my love, my dearest love. Stay alive . . . keep your mind."

*

The portly female clerk in the hospital's Department of Records and Billing seemed bewildered but she was not about to refuse Bray's request. It wasn't as if the medical information held there was that confidential, and a man who produced government identification certainly had to be given co-operation.

"Now, let me get this *cleah*," she said in her Boston accent, reading the labels on the front of the cabinets. "The senator wants the names of the doctors and the nurses who attended him during his stay here in 'fifty-three and 'fifty-four. From around November through March?"

"That's right. As I told you, next month's a sort of an anniversary for him. It'll be twenty-five years since he was given his 'reprieve', as he calls it. Confidentially, he's sending each of them a small medallion in the shape of the medical shield with their names and his thanks inscribed on them."

The clerk stopped. "Isn't that just like him, though? To *remembah*? Most people go through an experience like that and just want to forget the whole thing. They figure they beat the reaper so the hell with everybody. Until next time, of course. But not him; he's so . . . well, concerned, if you know what I mean."

"Yes, I do."

"The *votahs* know it too, let me tell you. The Bay State's going to have its first President since J.F.K. And there won't be any of that religious nonsense about the Pope and the *cahdnells* turning the White House, neither."

"No, there won't," agreed Bray. "I'd like to stress again the confidential nature of my being here. The senator doesn't want any publicity about his little gesture . . . " Scofield paused and smiled at the woman. "And as of now you're the only person in Boston who knows."

"Oh, don't you worry about that. As we used to say when we were kids, my lips are sealed. And I'd really treasure a note from Senator Appleton, with his signature and everything, I mean." The woman stopped and tapped a file cabinet. "Here we are," she said, opening the drawer. "Now, remember, all that's here are the names of the doctors — surgeons, anaesthesiologists, consultants — listed by floor and Operation Room desks; the staff nurses assigned, and a schedule of the equipment used. There are no psychiatric or medical evaluations; they can only be obtained directly through the physician. But then you're not interested in any of that; you'd think I was *tahkin'* to one of those damned insurance sneaks." She gave him the file. "There's a table at the end of the aisle. When you're finished, just leave the folder on my desk."

"That's OK," said Bray, knowing better. "I'll put it back; no sense bothering you. Thanks again."

"Thank *you*."

Scofield read through the pages rapidly to get a general impression. Medically, most of what he read was beyond his comprehension, but the conclusion was inescapable. Joshua Appleton had been more dead than alive when the ambulance had brought him to the hospital from the collision on the Turnpike. Lacerations, contusions, convulsions, fractures, along with severe head and neck wounds, painted the bloody picture of a mutilated human face and body. There were lists of drugs and serums used to prolong the life that was ebbing, detailed descriptions of the sophisticated machinery employed to stop deterioration. And ultimately, weeks later, the reversal began to take place. The incredibly more sophisticated machine that was the human body started to heal itself.

Bray wrote down the names of the doctors and the attending nurses listed in the floor and O.R. schedules. Two surgeons, one a skin-graft specialist, and a rotating team of eight nurses appeared consistently during the first weeks, then abruptly their names were no longer there, replaced by two different physicians and three private nurses, assigned to eight-hour shifts.

He had what he needed, a total of fifteen names, five primary, ten secondary. He would concentrate on the former, the last two physicians and the three nurses; the earlier names were removed from the time in question.

He replaced the folder and went back out to the clerk's desk. "All done," he said, then added as if the thought had just struck him. "Say, you could do me – the senator – one more favour, if you would."

"If I can, sure."

"I've got the names here, but I need a little updating. After all, it was twenty-five years ago. Some of them may not be around any longer. It would help if I got some current addresses."

"I can't help," said the clerk, reaching for the phone on her desk. "But I can send you upstairs. This is patient territory; they've got the personnel records. Lucky *bahstaads*, they're computerized."

"I'm still very concerned about keeping this confidential."

"Hey, don't you worry, you've got Peg Flannagan's word for it. My girl-friend runs that place."

Scofield sat next to a bearded black college student in front of a computer keyboard. The young man had been assigned to help by Peg Flannagan's girl-friend. He was annoyed that his office-temp job had suddenly required him to put down his textbooks.

"I'm sorry to bother you," said Bray, wanting a temporary friend.

"It's nothin', man," answered the student, punching the keys. "It's just that I got an exam tomorrow and any piss ant can run this barbarian hardware."

"What's the exam?"

"Tertiary kinetics."

Scofield looked at the student. "Someone once used the word 'tertiary' with me when I was in school around here. I didn't know what he meant."

"You probably went to Harvard, man. That's turkeytime. I'm at Tech."

Bray was glad the old school spirit was still alive in Cambridge. "What have you got?" he asked, looking at the screen above the keyboard. The black had keyed in the name of the first doctor.

"I've got an omniscient tape, and you've got nothin'."

"What do you mean?"

"The good doctor doesn't exist. Not as far as this institution is concerned. He's never so much as dispensed an aspirin in this joint."

"That's crazy. He was listed in the Appleton records."

"Speak to the lord-of-the-*phi's*, man. I punched the letters and up comes *No Rec.*"

"I know something about these machines. They're easily programmed."

The black nodded. "Which means they're easily de-programmed. Rectified, as it were. Your doctor was *dee*-leted. Maybe he stole from Medicare."

"Maybe. Let's try the next."

The student keyed in the name. "Well, we know what happened to this boy. *Ceb Hem*. He died right here on the third floor. Cerebral haemorrhage. Never even got a chance to get his tuition back."

"What do you mean?"

"Med school, man. He was only thirty-two. Hell of a way to go at thirty-two."

"Also unusual. What's the date?"

"21 March 1954."

"Appleton was discharged on the thirtieth," said Scofield as much to himself as to the student. These three names are nurses. Try them, please."

Katherine Connally. Deceased 3–26–54.

Alice Bonelli. Deceased 3–26–54.

Janet Drummond. Deceased 3–26–54.

The student sat back, he was not a fool. "Seems there was a real epidemic back then, wasn't there? March was a rough month, and the twenty-sixth was a *baad* day for three little girls in white."

"Any cause of death?"

"Nothin' listed. Which only means they didn't die on the premises."

"But all three on the same *day*? It's . . ."

"I dig," said the young man. "Crazy." He held up his hand. "Hey, there's an old cat who's been here for about six thousand years. He runs the supply room on the first floor. He might remember something; let me get him on the horn." The black wheeled his chair around and reached for a telephone on the counter. "Get on line two," he said to Bray, pointing to another phone on a near-by table.

"*Furst* floor supply," was the voice in a loud Irish brogue.

"Hey, Methuselah, this is Amos – as in Amos and Andy."

"You're a nutty boy-o, you are."

"Hey, Jimmy, I got this honky friend on the horn here. He's looking for information that goes back to when you were the terror of the angels' dorm. As a matter of fact, it concerns three of them. Jimmy, you recall a time in the middle 'fifties when three nurses all died on the same day?"

"Three . . ." The breathing over the line was that of a man remembering. "Oh, indeed I do. T'was a terrible thing. Little Katie Connally was one of 'em."

"What happened?" asked Bray.

"They drowned, sir. All three of the girls drowned. They was in a boat and the damn thing pitched over, throwin' 'em into a bad sea."

"In a boat? In *March*?"

"One of those crazy things, sir. You know how rich kids prowl around the nurses' dormitories. They figure the girls see naked bodies all the time, so maybe they wouldn't mind lookin' at theirs. Well, one night these punk-swells were throwin' a party at this fancy yacht club and asked the girls up. There was drinkin' and all kinds of nonsense, and some jackass got the bright idea to take out a boat. Damn fool thing, of course. As you say, it was in March."

"It happened at night?"

"Yes, indeed, sir. The bodies didn't wash up for a week, I believe."

"Was anyone else killed?"

"Of course not. It's never that way, is it? I mean, rich kids are always such good swimmers, aren't they now?"

"Where did it happen?" asked Scofield. "Can you remember?"

"Sure, I can, sir. It was up the coast. Marblehead."

Bray closed his eyes. "Thank you," he said quietly, replacing the phone.

"Thanks, Methuselah." The student hung up, his eyes on Scofield. "You got trouble, don't you?"

"I got trouble," agreed Bray, walking back to the keyboard. "I've also got ten more names. Two doctors and eight nurses. Can you run them through for me just as fast as you can?"

Of the eight nurses, exactly half were still alive. One had moved to San Francisco – address unknown; another lived with a daughter in Dallas, and the remaining two were in the St Agnes Retirement Home in Worcester. One of the doctors was still alive. The skin-graft specialist had died eighteen months ago at the age of seventy-three. The first surgeon, Nathaniel Crawford, had retired and was living in Quincy.

"May I use your phone?" asked Scofield. "I'll pay whatever charges there are."

"Last time I looked, none of these horns was in my name. Be my guest."

Bray had written down the number on the screen; he went to the telephone and dialled.

"Crawford here." The voice from Quincy was brusque but not discourteous.

"My name is Scofield, sir. We've never met and I'm not a physician, but I'm very interested in a case you were involved with a number of years ago at Massachusetts General. I'd like to discuss it briefly with you, if you wouldn't mind."

"Who was the patient? I had a few thousand."

"Senator Joshua Appleton, sir."

There was a slight pause on the line; when Crawford spoke, his brusque voice took on an added tone of weariness. "Those goddamned incidents have a way of following a man to his grave, don't they? Well, I haven't practised for over two years now, so whatever *you* say or *I* say, it won't make any goddamned difference . . . let's say I made a mistake."

"Mistake?"

"I didn't make many; I was head of surgery for damn near twelve years. My summary's in the Appleton medical file; the only reasonable conclusion is that the X-rays got fouled up, or the scanning equipment gave us the wrong data."

There was no summary from Nathaniel Crawford in the Appleton medical file.

"Are you referring to the fact that you were replaced as Appleton's surgeon?"

"Replaced, hell! Tommy Belford and I got our asses kicked four-square out of there by the family."

"Belford? Is that Belford the skin-graft specialist?"

"A *surgeon*. A plastic surgeon and a goddamned artist. Tommy put the man's face back on like he was Almighty God himself. That whiz-kid they brought in messed up Tommy's work, in my opinion. Sorry about him, though. The kid hardly finished when his head blew."

"Do you mean a cerebral haemorrhage, sir?"

"That's right. The Swiss was right there when it happened. He operated but it was too late."

"When you say 'the Swiss', do you mean the surgeon who replaced you?"

"You got it. The great *Herr Doktor* from Zurich. That *bahstaad* treated me like a retarded med. school drop-out."

"Do you know what happened to him?"

"Went back to Switzerland, I guess. Never was interested in looking him up, myself."

"Sir, you say you made a mistake. Or the X-rays did or the equipment. What kind of a mistake?"

"Simple; I gave up. We had run him on total support systems, and that's exactly what I figured they were. Total support; without them he wouldn't have lasted a day. And if he had, I thought it would be a waste; he'd live like a vegetable."

"You saw no hope of recovery?"

Crawford lowered his voice, strength in his humility. "I was a surgeon, I wasn't God. I was fallible. It was my opinion then that Appleton was not only beyond recovery, he was dying a little more with each minute . . . I was wrong."

"Thank you for talking to me, sir."

"As I said before, it can't make any difference now, and I don't mind. I had a hell of a lot of years with a knife in my hand; I didn't make many mistakes."

"I'm sure you didn't, sir. Goodbye." Scofield walked back to the keyboard; the black student was reading his textbook. "X-rays . . . ?" said Bray softly.

"What?" The black looked up. "What about X-rays?"

Bray sat down next to the young man. If he ever needed a temporary friend it was now; he hoped he had one. "How well do you know the hospital staff?"

"It's a big place, man."

"You knew enough to call Methuselah."

"Well, I've been working here off and on for three years. I get around."

"Is there a repository for X-rays going back a number of years?"

"Like maybe twenty-five?"

"Yes."

"There is. It's no big deal."

"Can you get me one?"

The student raised an eyebrow. "That's another matter, isn't it?"

"I'm willing to pay. Generously."

The black grimaced. "Oh, man! It's not that I look askance at bread, believe me. But I don't steal and I don't push and God knows I didn't inherit."

"What I'm asking you to do is the most legitimate – even moral, if you like – thing I could ask anyone to do. I'm not a liar."

The student looked into Bray's eyes. "If you are, you're a damned convincing one. And you've got troubles. I've seen that. What do you want?"

"An X-ray of Joshua Appleton's mouth."

"Mouth? His *mouth*?"

"His head injuries were extensive, dozens of pictures had to be taken. There had to be a lot of projected dental work. Can you do it?"

The young man nodded. "I think so."

"One more thing. I know it'll sound . . . outrageous to you, but take my word for it, nothing's outrageous. How much do you make a month here?"

"I average eighty, ninety a week. About three-fifty a month. It's not bad for a graduate student. Some of these interns make less. 'Course, they get room and board. Why?"

"Suppose I told you that I'd pay you ten thousand dollars to take a plane to Washington and bring me back another X-ray. Just an envelope with an X-ray in it."

The black tugged at his short beard, his eyes on Scofield as though he were observing a lunatic. "*Suppose?* I'd say 'feets, do your stuff!' Ten thousand *dollars?*"

"There'd be more time for those tertiary kinetics."

"And there's nothin' illegal? It's straight – I mean really straight?"

"For it to be considered remotely illegal as far as you're concerned, you'd have to know far more than anyone would tell you. That's straight."

"I'm just a messenger? I fly to Washington and bring back an envelope . . . with an X-ray in it?"

"Probably a number of small ones. That's all."

"What are they of?"

"Joshua Appleton's mouth."

It was 1.30 in the afternoon when Bray reached the library on Boylston Street. His new friend – Amos Lafollet – was taking the two P.M. shuttle to Washington and would return on the eight o'clock flight. Scofield would meet him at the airport.

Obtaining the X-rays had not been difficult; anyone who knew the bureaucratic ways of Washington could have got them. Bray made two calls, the first to the Congressional Liaison Office and the second to the dentist in question. The first call was made by a harried aide of a well-known Representative suffering from an abscessed tooth. Could Liaison please get this aide the name of Senator Appleton's dentist. The senator had mentioned the man's superior work to the congressman. Liaison gave out the dentist's name.

The call to the dentist was a routine spot check by the General Accounting Office, all bureaucratic form, no substance, forgotten tomorrow. GAO was collecting back-up evidence for dental work done on senators and some idiot on K Street had come up with X-rays. Would the receptionist please pull Appleton's and leave them at the front desk for a GAO messenger? They would be returned in twenty-four hours.

Washington operated at full speed; there simply was not enough time to do the work that had to be done and GAO spot checks were not legitimate work. They were irritants and complied with in irritation, but nevertheless obeyed. Appleton's X-rays would be left at the desk.

Scofield checked the library directory, took the elevator to the second floor, and walked down the hallway to the *Journalism Division – Current and Past Publications. Microfilm.*

He went to the counter at the far end of the room and spoke to the clerk behind it.

"March and April 1954, please. The *Globe* or the *Examiner*, whatever's available."

He was given eight boxes of film, and assigned a cubicle. He found it, sat down and inserted the first roll of film.

By March of '54 the bulletins detailing the condition of Joshua Appleton – "Captain Josh" – had been relegated to the back pages; he had been in the hospital over twenty weeks by then. But he was not ignored. The famous vigil was covered in detail. Bray wrote down the names of several of those interviewed; he would know by tomorrow whether there'd be any reason to get in touch with them.

21 March 1954
Young Doctor Dies of Cerebral Haemorrhage

The brief story was on page sixteen. No mention of the fact that the surgeon had attended Joshua Appleton.

26 March 1954
Three Mass. Gen'l Nurses
Killed in Freak Boating Accident

The story had made the lower left corner of the front page, but again, there was no mention of Joshua Appleton. Indeed, it would have been strange if there had been; the three were on a rotating twenty-four-hour schedule. If they were all in Marblehead that night, who was at the Appleton bedside?

10 April 1954
Bostonian Dies in Gstaad Skiing Tragedy

He had found it.

It was – naturally – on the front page, the headlines prominent, the copy written as much to evoke sympathy as to report the tragic death of a young man. Scofield studied the story, positive that he would come to certain lines.

He did.

Because of the victim's deep love of the Alps – and to spare family and friends further anguish – the family has announced that the burial will take place in Switzerland, in the village of Col du Pillon.

Bray wondered who was in that coffin in Col du Pillon. Or was it merely empty?

He returned to the cheap hotel, gathered his things together and took a cab to the Prudential Center Parking Lot, Gate A. He drove the rented car out of Boston, along Jamaica Way into Brookline. He found Appleton Hill, driving past the gates of Appleton Hall, absorbing every detail he could within the short space of time.

The huge estate was spread like a fortress across the crest of the hill, a high stone wall surrounding the inner structure, tall roofs that gave the illusion of parapets

336

seen above the distant wall. The roadway beyond the main gate wound up the hill around a huge brick carriage house, covered with ivy, housing no fewer than eight to ten complete apartments, five garages fronting an enormous concrete parking area below.

He drove around the hill. The ten-foot-high wrought-iron fence was continuous; every several hundred yards small lean-to shelters were built into the earth of the hill like miniature bunkers, and within a number of them he could see uniformed men sitting and standing, smoking cigarettes and on the telephone.

It was the seat of the Matarese, the home of the Shepherd Boy.

At 9.30 he drove out to Logan Airport. He had told Amos Lafollet to get off the plane and go directly to the dimly-lit bar across from the main news stand. The booths were so dark it was nearly impossible to see a face five feet in front of one, the only light a series of flashes from an enormous television screen on the wall.

Bray slid into the black plastic booth, adjusting his eyes to the lack of light. For an instant he thought of another booth in another dimly-lit room and another man. London, the Connaught Hotel, Roger Symonds. He pushed the memory from his mind; it was an obstacle. He could not handle obstacles right now.

He saw the student walk through the bar's entrance. Scofield stood up briefly; Amos saw him and came over. There was a manilla envelope in his hand and Bray felt a quick acceleration in his chest.

"I gather everything went all right," he said.

"I had to sign for it."

"You *what?*" Bray was sick; it was such a little thing, an obvious thing, and he had not thought of it.

"Take it easy. I wasn't brought up on 135th Street and Lennox Avenue for nothing."

"What name did you use?" asked Scofield, his pulse receding.

"R. M. Nixon. The receptionist was real nice. She thanked me."

"You'll go far, Amos."

"I intend to."

"I hope this'll help." Bray handed his envelope across the table.

The student held it between his fingers. "Hey, man, you know you don't really have to do this."

"Of course, I do. We had an agreement."

"I know that. But I've got an idea you've gone through a lot of sweat for a lot of people you don't know."

"And a number that I know very well. The money's incidental. Use it." Bray opened his attaché case and slipped the envelope inside – right above a file folder containing Joshua Appleton's X-ray from twenty-five years ago. "Remember, you never knew my name and you never went to Washington. If you're *ever* asked, you merely ran some forgotten names through a computer for a man who never identified himself. *Please.* Remember that."

"That's going to be tough."

"Why?" Scofield was alarmed.

"How am I going to dedicate my first textbook to you?"

Bray smiled. "You'll think of something. Goodbye," he said, getting out of the booth. "I've got an hour's drive and several more of sleep to catch up on."

"Stay well, man."

"Thanks, professor."

Scofield stood in the dentist's waiting room on Main Street in Andover, Massachusetts. The name of the dentist had been supplied – happily, even enthusiastically – by the Nurse's Office of Andover Academy. Anything for Andover's illustrious – and generous – alumnus, and by extension the senator's aide, of course. Naturally, the dentist was not the same name who had tended Senator Appleton when he was a student; that practice had been taken over by a nephew a number of years ago, but there was no question that the present doctor would co-operate. The Nurse's Office would call him and let him know the senator's aide was on the way over.

Bray had counted on a psychology as old as the dentist's drill. Two young boys who were close friends and away at prep school might not see eye-to-eye on every issue, but they would share the same dentist.

Yes, both boys had gone to the very same man in Andover.

The harried dentist came out of the door that led to a storeroom, half-glasses perched on the edge of his nose. In his hand were two sheets of cardboard, small negatives embedded in each. X-rays of two Andover students taken over thirty years ago.

"Here you are, Mr Vickery," said the dentist, holding out the X-rays. "*Damn*, will you look at the primitive way they used to mount these things! One of these days I've got to clean out that mess back there, but then you never know. Last year I had to identify an old patient of my uncle's who was burned to death in that fire over in Boxford."

"Thank you very much," said Scofield, accepting the X-ray sheets. "By the way, sir, I know you're rushed but I wonder if you'd mind one more favour? I've got two newer sets here of both men and I've got to match them with the ones you're lending us. Of course, I can get someone to do it, but if you've got a minute."

"Sure. Won't even take a minute. Let me have them." Bray removed the two sets of X-rays from their envelopes; one stolen from the Massachusetts General Hospital, the other obtained in Washington. He had placed white tape over the names. He gave them to the dentist, who carried them to a lamp and held them in sequence against the glare of the light bulb above the shade. "There you are," he said, holding the matching X-rays separately in each hand.

Scofield put each set in a different envelope. "Thanks again."

"Any time." The dentist walked rapidly back into his office. He was a man in a hurry.

Bray sat in the front seat of the car, his breathing erratic, perspiration on his forehead. He opened the envelopes and took out the X-ray sheets.

He pulled off the small strips of tape that covered the names.

He had been right. The awesome fragment was irrevocably in place, the proof in his hand.

338

The man who sat in the Senate, the man who unquestionably would be the next President of the United States, was not Joshua Appleton IV.

He was Julian Guiderone, son of the Shepherd Boy.

35

Scofield drove south-east to Salem. Delay was irrelevant now, previous schedules to be thrown away. He had everything to gain by moving as fast as he could, as long as every move was the right move, every decision the perceptive decision. He had his cannons and his nuclear bomb – his bill-of-particulars and the X-rays. It was a question now of mounting his weapons properly, *using* them, not only to blow the Matarese out of existence but first – above all, *first* – to find Antonia and force them to release her. And Taleniekov, if he was still alive.

Which meant he had to create a deception of his own. All deceptions were based on illusion, and the illusion he had to convey was that Beowulf Agate could be had, his cannons and his bomb defused, his assault stopped, the man himself destroyed. To do this he had to take the initial position of strength . . . the weakness to follow.

The hostage strategy would not wash any longer; he would not be able to get near Appleton. The Shepherd Boy would not permit it, the prize of the White House too great to place in jeopardy. Without the man there was no prize. So his position of strength lay in the X-rays. It was imperative he establish the fact that only a single set of X-rays existed, that duplicates were out of the question. Spectro-analysis would reveal any such duplicating process and Beowulf Agate was not a fool; he would expect an analysis to be made. He wanted the girl; he wanted the Russian; the X-rays could be had for them.

There would be a subtle omission in the mechanics of the exchange, a seeming weakness the enemy would pounce on; but it would be calculated, no weakness at all. The Matarese would be forced to go through with the exchange. A Corsican girl and a Soviet intelligence officer for X-rays that showed incontrovertibly that the man sitting in the Senate, on his way to the presidency, was not Joshua Appleton IV – legend of Korea, politician extraordinary – but instead, a man supposedly buried in 1954 in the Swiss village of Col du Pillon.

He drove down towards Salem harbour, drawn as he was always drawn towards the water, not precisely sure what he was looking for until he saw it: a shield-shaped sign on the lawn of a small hotel. *Efficiency Suites*. It made sense. Rooms with a refrigerator and cooking facilities. There'd be no stranger eating in restaurants; it was not the tourist season in Salem.

He parked the car in a lot covered with white gravel and bordered by a white picket fence, the grey water of the harbour across the way. He carried his attaché case and travel bag inside, registered under an innocuous name, and asked for a suite.

"Will payment be made by credit card, sir?" asked the young woman behind the counter.

"I beg your pardon?"

"You didn't check off the method of payment. If it's a credit card, our policy is to run the card through the machine."

"I see. No, actually, I'm one of those strange people who use real money. One man's fight against plastic. Why don't I pay you for a week in advance? I doubt I'll stay any longer." He gave her the money. "I assume there's a grocery store nearby."

"Yes, sir. Just up the street."

"What about other stores? I've a number of things to get."

"There's the Shopping Plaza about ten blocks west. I'm sure you'll find everything you need there."

Bray hoped so; he was counting on it.

He was taken to his "suite", which was in effect one large room with a pull-out bed and divider that concealed the smallest stove this side of a hot plate and a refrigerator. But the room looked out over the harbour; it was fine. He opened his attaché case, took out the photograph he had removed from the wall on Mrs Appleton's tomb for her son, and stared at it. Two young men, tall, muscular, neither to be mistaken for the other, but enough alike for an unknown surgeon somewhere in Switzerland to sculpt one into the other. A young American doctor paid to sign the medical authorization of discharge, then killed for security. A mother maintained as an alcoholic, kept at a distance, but paraded whenever it was convenient and fruitful to do so. Who knew a son better than his mother? Who in America would argue with, much less confront, Mrs Joshua Appleton III?

Scofield sat down and added a page to the seventeen in his bill-of-particulars. Doctors: *Nathaniel Crawford and Thomas Belford. A Swiss physician de-programmed from a computer; a young plastic surgeon dead suddenly of a cerebral haemorrhage. Three nurses drowned off Marblehead. Gstaad: a coffin in Col du Pillon; X-rays – one set from Boston, one set from Washington, two from Main Street, Andover, Massachusetts. Two different men merged into one, and the one was a lie. A fraud was about to become President of the United States.*

Bray finished writing, and walked to the window that looked out on the still, cold waters of Salem harbour. The dilemma was clearer than it had ever been: they had traced the Matarese from its roots in Corsica through a federation of multi-national corporations that encircled the globe; they knew it financed terror the world over, encouraged the chaos that resulted from assassinations and kidnappings, killing in the streets and aircraft blown out of the skies. They understood all this but they did not know why.

Why?

The reason would have to wait. Nothing mattered but the deception that was Senator Joshua Appleton IV. For once the son of the Shepherd Boy reached the presidency, the White House belonged to the Matarese.

What better residence for a consigliere.

Keep breathing, my old enemy.

Toni, my love. Stay alive. Keep your mind.

Scofield went back to his attaché case on the table, opened a side flap and took out a single-edge razor blade that was wedged down between the leather. He then took the two matted sheets of cardboard with the embedded X-ray slides of two Andover students thirty years ago and placed them on the table, one on top of the other. There were four rows of negatives, each with four slides, a total of sixteen on each card. Small red-bordered labels identifying the patients and the dates of the X-rays were affixed to the upper left-hand corners. He checked carefully to see that the borders of the cardboard sheets matched; they did. He pressed a manilla envelope down on the top sheet between the first and second rows of X-rays, took the razor blade and began to cut, slicing deeply so that the blade went through both sheets of X-rays. The top row fell clean, two strips of four X-ray negatives.

The names of the patients and dates of entry – typed on the small red-bordered labels over thirty-five years ago – were on the strips; the simplest chemical analysis would confirm their authenticity.

Bray doubted whether any such analysis would be made on the new labels he would purchase and stick on the remaining two sheets with twelve X-rays each; it would be a waste of time. The X-rays themselves would be compared with new X-rays of the man who called himself Joshua Appleton IV. Julian Guiderone. That was all the proof the Matarese would need.

He took the strips and the larger sheets of negatives, knelt down and carefully buffed the edges of the cuts across the rug. Within five minutes each of the edges was rubbed smooth, soiled just enough to match the age of the original borders.

He got up and put everything back in his attaché case. It was time to return to Andover, to put the plan in motion.

"Mr Vickery, is something wrong?" asked the dentist, coming out of his office, still harried, three afternoon patients reading magazines, glancing up in mild irritation.

"I'm afraid I forgot something. May I speak with you for a second?"

"Come on in here," said the dentist, ushering Scofield into a small workroom, the shelves lined with impressions of teeth mounted on movable clamps. He lit a cigarette from a pack on the counter. "I don't mind telling you it's been one hell of a day. What's the matter'?"

"The laws, actually." Bray smiled, opening his attaché case and taking out the two envelopes. "HR Seven-Four-Eight-Five."

"What the hell is that?"

"A new congressional regulation, part of the post-Watergate morality. Whenever a government employee borrows property from any source, for whatever purpose, a full description of said property must be accompanied by a signed authorization."

"Oh, for Christ's sake."

"I'm sorry, sir. The senator's a stickler for these things." Scofield took the X-rays from the envelopes. "If you'll re-examine these, call in your nurse and give her a description, she can type the authorization on your letterhead and I'll get out of here."

"I suppose anything for the next President of the United States," said the dentist, taking the shortened X-ray sheets and reaching for the telephone. "Tell Appleton to lower my taxes." He pressed the intercom button. "Bring in your pad, please."

"Do you mind?" Bray took out his cigarettes.

"Are you nuts? Carcinoma loves company." The nurse came through the door, shorthand pad and pencil in hand. "How do I start this?" asked the doctor, looking at Scofield.

" 'To Whom It May Concern' is fine."

"OK." The dentist glanced at his nurse. "We're keeping the government honest." He snapped on a scanning lamp and held both X-ray sheets against the glass. " 'To Whom It May Concern. Mr' . . ." The doctor stopped, looking at Bray again. "What's your first name?"

"B. A. will do."

" 'Mister B. A. Vickery of Senator Appleton's office in Washington, D.C. has requested and received from me two sets of X-rays dated 11 November 1943 for patients identified as Joshua Appleton and . . . Julian Guiderone. The dentist paused. "Anything else?"

"A description, Doctor. That's what HR Seven-Four-Eight-Five calls for."

The dentist sighed, the cigarette protruding from his lips. " 'Said identical sets include' . . . one, two, three, four across . . . 'twelve negatives.' " The dentist stopped, squinting through his half-glasses. "You know," he interjected. "My uncle wasn't only primitive, he was downright careless."

"What do you mean?" asked Scofield, watching the dentist closely.

"The right and left bicuspids are missing in both of these. I was so rushed I didn't notice before."

"They're the cards you gave me this morning."

"I'm sure they are; there are the labels. I think I matched the upper and lower incisors. He held out the X-rays for Scofield and turned to the nurse. "Put what I said into English and type it up, will you? I'll sign it outside." He crushed out his cigarette and extended his hand. "Nice to meet you, Mr Vickery. I've really got to get back in there."

"Just one more thing, sir. Would you mind initialling these sheets and dating them?" Bray separated the X-rays and placed them on the counter.

"Not at all," said the dentist.

Scofield drove back to Salem. A great deal was still to be clarified, new decisions to be made as events shaped them, but he had his overall plan; he had a place to begin. It was almost time for Mr B. A. Vickery to arrive at the Ritz-Carlton, but not yet.

He had stopped earlier at the Shopping Plaza in Salem where he had found small red-bordered labels almost identical to those used over thirty-five years ago, and a store selling typewriters where he had typed in the names and the dates, rubbing them lightly to give the labels an appearance of age. And while walking to his car he had looked briefly around at the shops, again seeing what he had hoped to see.

Copies Made While You Wait
Equipment Bought, Sold, Leased
Expert Service

342

It was conveniently two doors away from a liquor store, three from a supermarket. He would stop there now and have copies made of his bill-of-particulars, and afterwards pick up something to drink and eat. He would be in his room for a long time; he had phone calls to make. They would take five to seven hours to complete. They had to be routed on a very precise schedule through Lisbon.

Bray watched as the manager of the Plaza Duplicating Service extracted the collated sheets of his indictment from the levels of grey trays that protruded from the machine. He had chatted briefly with the balding man, remarking that he was doing a favour for a nephew; the young fellow was taking one of those creative writing courses at Emerson and had entered some sort of college competition.

"That kid's got some imagination," said the manager, clipping the stacks of copies together.

"Oh, did you read it?"

"Just parts. You stand over that machine with nothing to do but make sure there's no jamming; you look. But when people come in with personal things – like letters and wills, you know what I mean – I always try to keep my eyes on the dials. Sometimes it's hard."

Bray laughed. "I told my nephew he'd better win or he'd be put in gaol."

"Not any more. These kids today, they're great. They say anything. I know a lot of people don't like 'em for it, but I do."

"I think I do, too." Bray looked at the bill placed in front of him and took his money from his pocket. "Say, you wouldn't by any chance have an Alpha Twelve machine here, would you?"

"Alpha *Twelve*? That's an eighty-thousand-dollar piece of equipment. I do a good business, but I'm not in that class."

"I suppose I could find one in Boston."

"That insurance company over on Lafayette Street has one; you can bet your life the home office paid for it. It's the only one I know of *north* of Boston, and I mean right up to Montreal."

"An insurance company?"

"West Hartford Casualty. I trained the two girls who run the Alpha Twelve. Isn't that just like an insurance company? They buy a machine like that but they won't pay for a service contract. I'm probably a dollar and a half cheaper."

Scofield leaned on the counter, a weary man confiding. "Listen, I've been travelling for five days and I've got to get a report into the mails tonight. I need an Alpha Twelve. Now, I can drive into Boston and probably find one. But it's damn near four o'clock and I'd rather not do that. My company's a little crazy; it thinks my time is valuable and lets me have enough money to save it where I can. What do you say? Can you help me?" Bray removed a hundred-dollar bill from his clip.

"You work for one hell of a company."

"That I do."

"I'll make a call."

*

It was 5.45 when Bray returned to the hotel on Salem harbour. The Alpha Twelve had performed the service he had needed, and he had found a stationery store where he had purchased a stapler, seven manilla envelopes, two rolls of packaging tape and a Park-Sherman scale that measured weight in ounces and grammes. A final stop had been at the Salem Post Office where he had bought fifty dollars' worth of stamps.

A porterhouse steak and a bottle of Scotch completed his shopping list. He spread his purchases on the bed, removing some to the table, others to the Formica counter between the Lilliputian stove and refrigerator. He poured himself a drink and sat in the chair in front of the window overlooking the harbour. It was growing dark, the water barely seen except where it reflected the lights of the piers.

He drank the whisky in short swallows, letting the alcohol spread, suspending all thought. He had no more than ten minutes before the telephone calls would begin. His cannons were in place, his nuclear bomb in its rack. It was vital now that everything take place in sequence – always sequence – and that meant choosing the right words at the right time; there was no room for error. To do that, to avoid error, his mind had to be free, loose, unencumbered – capable of listening closely, picking up nuances.

Toni . . . ?

No!

He closed his eyes. The gulls in the distance were foraging the waters for their last meal before darkness was complete. He listened to their screeches, the dissonance somehow comforting; there was a kind of energy in every struggle to survive. He hoped he would have it.

He dozed, awakening with a start. He looked at his watch, annoyed. It was six minutes past six; his ten minutes had stretched nearer to fifteen. It was time for the first telephone call, the one he considered least likely to bring results. It would not have to be routed through Lisbon, the chances of a tap so remote as to be practically non-existent. But practically was not totally, therefore his conversation would last no longer than twenty seconds, the minimum amount of time needed for even the most sophisticated tracing equipment to function.

The twenty-second limit was the one he had instructed the French woman to use weeks ago when she had placed calls for him all through the night to a suite of rooms at the hotel on Nebraska Avenue. Twenty seconds was not much time, but a great deal could be said without interruptions. More so in French.

He rose from the chair and went to his attaché case, taking out notes he had written to himself. Notes with names and telephone numbers. He walked over to the bedside telephone, pulled the armchair next to the phone, and sat down. He thought for a moment, composing a verbal shorthand French for what he wanted to say, doubting, however, that it would make any difference. Ambassador Robert Winthrop had disappeared over a month ago; there was no reason to think he had survived. Winthrop had raised the names of the Matarese with the wrong men – or man – in Washington.

He picked up the phone and dialled; three rings followed before an operator got on the line and asked for his room number. He gave it and more distant rings continued.

"Hello?"

"Listen! There's no time. Do you understand?"

"Yes. Go ahead."

She knew him; she was with him. He spoke rapidly in French, his eyes on the sweep hand of his watch. "Ambassador Robert Winthrop. Georgetown. Take two Company men with you, no explanations. If Winthrop's there ask to see him alone, but say nothing out loud. Give him a note with the words: 'Beowulf wants to reach you'. Let him advise in writing. The contact must be sterile. I'll call you back."

Seventeen seconds.

"We *must* talk," was the strong, quick reply. "Call back."

He hung up; she'd be safe. Not only was it unlikely that the Matarese had found her and tapped her, but even if they had, they would not kill her. There was nothing to gain, more to learn by keeping the intermediary alive, and too much of a mess killing the Company men with her. Besides, there were limits to his liability under the circumstances; he was sorry, but there were.

It was time for Lisbon. He had known since Rome that he would use Lisbon when the moment came. A series of telephone calls could be placed through Lisbon only once, for once those receiving the calls were listed in the overnight data banks, red cards would fly out of computers into alarm slots, the coded source traced through other computers in Langley, and no further calls permitted by that source, all transmissions terminated. Access to Lisbon was restricted to those who dealt solely with high-level defections, men in the field who in times of emergency had to go directly to their superiors in Washington who in turn were authorized to make immediate decisions. No more than twenty intelligence officers in the country had the codes for Lisbon, and no man in Washington ever refused a call from Lisbon. One never knew whether a general, or a nuclear physicist, or a ranking member of the praesidium or the KGB might be the prize.

It was also understood that any abuse of the Lisbon access would result in the severest consequences for the abuser. Bray was amused – grimly – at the concept; the abuse he was about to inflict was beyond anything conceived by the men who made the rules. He looked at the five names and titles he was about to call. The names in themselves were not that unusual; they could probably be found in any telephone book. Their positions, however, could not.

The Secretary of State.

The Chairman of the National Security Council.

The Director of the Central Intelligence Agency.

The Chief Foreign Policy adviser to the President.

The Chairman of the Joint Chiefs of Staff.

The probability that one, possibly two of these men were *consiglieri* of the Matarese persuaded Bray not to try to send his indictment directly to the President. Taleniekov and he had believed that once the proof was in their hands the two leaders of both their countries could be reached and convinced. It was not true; Presidents and Premiers were too closely guarded, too protected; messages were filtered, words interpreted. The charges of "traitors" would be dismissed; time not to be wasted on them. Others had to reach Presidents and Premiers. Men whose positions of trust and responsibility were beyond reproach; such men had to bring them the news, not traitors.

The majority if not all of those he was about to call were committed to the well-being of the nation; any one of them could get the ear of the President. It was all he asked for, and none would refuse a call from Lisbon. He picked up the telephone and dialled the overseas operator.

Twenty minutes later the operator called back. Lisbon had, as always, cleared the traffic to Washington quickly; the Secretary of State was on the line.

"This is State One," said the Secretary. "Your codes are cleared, Lisbon. What is it?"

"Mr Secretary, within forty-eight hours you'll receive a manilla envelope in the mail; the name Agate will be printed in the upper left corner."

"Agate? *Beowulf Agate?*"

"Please, listen to me, sir. Have the envelope brought directly to you unopened. Inside there's a detailed report describing a series of events which have taken place – and are taking place right now – that amount to a conspiracy to assume control of the government . . ."

"Conspiracy? Please be specific. Communist?"

"I don't think so."

"You *must* be specific, Mr Scofield. You're a wanted man, and you're abusing the Lisbon connection! Self-seeking cries of alarm from you are not in your interest. Or in the interest of the country . . ."

"You'll find all the specifics you need in my report. Among them is proof – I repeat, *proof*, Mr Secretary that there's been a deception in the Senate that goes back twenty years. It's of such magnitude that I'm not at all sure the country can absorb the shock. It may not even be in its interest to expose it."

"Explain yourself!"

"The explanation's in the envelope. But not a recommendation. I haven't got any recommendations. That's your business. And the President's. Bring the information to him as soon as you get it."

"I order you to report to me immediately!"

"I'll come out in forty-eight hours, if I'm alive. When I do I want two things: vindication for me and asylum for a Soviet intelligence officer – if he's alive."

"Scofield, where *are you*?"

Bray hung up the phone.

He waited ten minutes and placed the second call to Lisbon. Thirty-five minutes later the Chairman of the National Security Council was on the line.

"Mr Chairman, within forty-eight hours you'll receive a manilla envelope in the mail; the name Agate will be printed in the upper left corner . . ."

It was exactly fourteen minutes past midnight when he completed the final call. Among the men he had reached were honourable men. Their voices would be heard by the President.

He had forty-eight hours. A lifetime.

It was time for a drink. Twice during the placement of calls he had looked at the bottle of Scotch, close to rationalizing the necessity of calming his anxieties, but both times rejected the method. Under pressure, he was the coldest man he knew; he might not always feel that way, but it was the way he functioned. He deserved a drink now; it would be a fitting salute to the call he was about to make to Senator Joshua Appleton IV, born Julian Guiderone, son of the Shepherd Boy.

The telephone rang, the shock of its sound causing Bray to grip the bottle in his hand, oblivious to the whisky he was pouring. Liquor spilled over the glass on to the counter. *It was impossible!* There was no way the calls to Lisbon could be traced so rapidly. The magnetic trunklines fluctuated hourly, insuring blind origins; the entire system would have to be shut down for a minimum of eight hours in order to trace a single call. Lisbon was an absolute; place a call through it and a man was safe, his location buried until it no longer mattered.

The phone rang again. Not to answer was not to know, the lack of knowledge infinitely more dangerous than any tracing. No matter what, he still had cards to play; or at least the conviction that those cards were playable. He would convey that. He lifted up the phone. "Yes?"

"Room Two-twelve?"

"What is it?"

"The manager, sir. It's nothing really, but the outside operator has – quite naturally – kept our switchboard informed of your overseas telephone calls. We noticed that you've chosen not to use a credit card, but rather have billed the calls to your room. We thought you'd appreciate knowing that the charges are currently in excess of three hundred dollars."

Scofield looked over at the depleted bottle of Scotch. Yankee scepticism would not change until the planet blew up; and then the New England bookkeepers would sue the universe.

"Why don't you come up personally and I'll give you the money for the calls. It'll be in cash."

"Oh, not necessary, not necessary at all, sir. Actually, I'm not at the hotel, I'm at home." There was the slightest, slightly embarrassed pause. "In Beverly. We'll just attach. . . ."

"Thank you for your concern," interrupted Bray, hanging up and heading back to the counter and the bottle of Scotch.

Five minutes later he was ready, ice-like calm spreading through him as he sat down next to the telephone. The words would be there because the outrage was there; he did not have to think about them, they would come easily. What he had thought about was the sequence. Extortion, compromise, weakness, exchange. Someone within the Matarese wanted to talk with him, recruit him for the most logical reasons in the world; he'd give that man – whoever he was – the chance to do both. It was part of the exchange, prelude to escape. But the first step on the tightrope would not be made by Beowulf Agate; it would be made by the son of the Shepherd Boy.

He picked up the phone; thirty seconds later he heard the famous voice laced with the pronounced Boston accent that reminded so many so often of a young President cut down in Dallas.

"Hello? *Hello?*" The senator had been roused from his sleep; it was in the clearing of his throat. "Who's there, for God's sake?"

"There is a grave in the Swiss village of Col du Pillon. If there's a body in the coffin below it's not the man whose name is on the stone."

The gasp on the line was electrifying, the silence that followed a scream suspended in the grip of fear. "Who . . . ?" The man was in shock, unable to form the question.

"There's no reason for you to say anything, Julian."

"*Stop it!*" The scream was released.

"All right, no names. You know who I am – if you don't, the Shepherd Boy hasn't kept his son informed."

"I won't *listen!*"

"Yes you will, Senator. Right now that phone is part of your hand; you won't let it go. You can't. So just listen. On 11 November 1943, you and a close friend of yours went to the same dentist on Main Street in Andover, Massachusetts. You had X-rays taken that day." Scofield paused for precisely one second. "I have them, Senator. Your office can confirm it in the morning. Your office also can confirm the fact that yesterday a messenger from the General Accounting Office picked up a set of more recent X-rays from your current dentist in Washington. And finally, if you're so inclined, your office might check the X-ray Depository of the Massachusetts General Hospital in Boston. They'll find that a single plate, frontal X-ray taken twenty-five years ago is missing from the Appleton file. As of an hour ago all are in my possession."

There was a quiet, plaintive cry on the line, a moan without words.

"Keep listening, Senator," continued Bray. "You've got a chance. If the girl's alive you've got a chance, if she's not you don't. Regarding the Russian, if he's going to die, I'll be the one who kills him. I think you know why. You see, accommodations can be made. What I know I don't *want* to know. What you do is no concern of mine, not any longer. What you want, you've already won, and men like me simply end up working for people like you, that's all that ever happens. Ultimately, there's not much difference between any of you. Anywhere." Scofield paused again, the bait was glaring; would he take it?

He did, the whisper hoarse, the statement tentative. "There are . . . people who want to talk with you."

"I'll listen. But only after the girl is free, the Russian turned over to me."

"The X-rays . . . ?" The words were rushed, cut off; a man was drowning.

"That's the exchange."

"*How?*"

"We'll negotiate it. You've got to understand, Senator, the only thing that matters to me now is me. The girl and I, we just want to get away."

"What . . . ?" Again the man was incapable of forming the question.

"Do I want?" completed Scofield. "Proof that she's alive, that she can still walk."

"I don't understand."

"You don't know much about exchanges, either. A package that's immobile isn't any package at all; it voids the exchange. I want proof and I've got a very powerful pair of binoculars."

"*Binoculars?*"

"Your people will understand. I want a telephone number and a sighting.

Obviously, I'm in the Boston vicinity. I'll call you in the morning. At this number."

"There's a debate on the Senate floor, a quorum . . ."

"You'll miss it," said Bray, hanging up.

The first move had been made; telephones would be in use all night between Washington and Boston. Move and counter-move, thrust and parry, press and check; the negotiations had begun. He looked at the manilla envelopes on the table. Between calls he had sealed all of them, weighed and stamped them; they were ready to go.

Except one, and there was no reason to believe he would mail it, the tragedy found in the disappearance of the man and what he might have done. It was time to call his old friend from Paris back.

"Bray, thank God! We've been waiting for hours!"

"We?"

"Ambassador Winthrop."

"He's *there*?"

"It's all right. It was handled extremely well. His man, Stanley, assured me that no one could possibly have followed them and for all purposes, the ambassador is in Alexandria."

"Stanley's good!" Scofield felt like yelling to the skies in sheer relief, sheer *joy*.

Winthrop was alive. The flanks were covered, the Matarese destroyed. He was free to negotiate as he had never negotiated in his life before, and he was the best there was. "Let me talk to Winthrop."

"Brandon, I'm on the line. I'm afraid I took the phone from your friend quite rudely. Forgive me, my dear."

"What *happened*? I tried calling you . . ."

"I was hurt – not seriously – but enough to require treatment. I went to a doctor I knew in Fredericksburg; he has a private clinic. It wouldn't do for the eldest of the so–called statesmen to show up at a Washington hospital with a bullet in his arm. I mean, can you imagine Harriman turning up in a Harlem emergency ward with a gunshot wound? . . . I couldn't involve you any further, Brandon."

"*Jesus*. I should have considered that."

"You had enough to consider. Where are you?"

"Outside of Boston. There's so much to tell you, but not on the phone. It's all in the envelope, along with four strips of X-rays. I've got to get it to you right away, and you've got to get it to the President."

"The Matarese?"

"More than either of us could ever imagine. I have the proof."

"Take the first plane to Washington. I'll reach the President now and get you full protection, a military escort, if need be. The search will be called off."

"I can't do that, sir."

"Why *not*?" The ambassador was incredulous.

"There are . . . hostages involved. I need time. They'll be killed unless I negotiate."

"Negotiate? You don't have to negotiate. If you have what you say you have, let the government do it."

349

"It takes roughly one pound of pressure and less than a fifth of a second to pull a trigger," said Scofield. "I've got to negotiate . . . But you see, I *can* now. I'll stay in touch, pinpoint the exchange ground. You can cover me."

"Those words again," said Winthrop. "They never leave your vocabulary, do they?"

"I've never been so grateful for them."

"How much time?"

"It depends; it's delicate. Twenty-four, possibly thirty hours. It has to be less than forty-eight; that's the deadline."

"Get the proof to me, Brandon. There's an attorney, his firm's in Boston but he lives in Waltham. He's a good friend. Do you have a car?"

"Yes. I can get to Waltham in about forty minutes."

"Good. I'll call him; he'll be on the first plane to Washington in the morning. His name is Bergeron; you'll have to get his address from the phone book."

"No problem."

It was 1.45 a.m. when Bray rang the bell of the fieldstone house in Waltham. The door was opened by Paul Bergeron, dressed in a bathrobe, creases of concern on his ageing, intelligent face.

"I know I'm not to ask you your name, but would you care to come in? From what I gather, I'm sure you can use a drink."

"Thanks just the same, but I still have work to do. Here's the envelope, and thanks again."

"Another time, perhaps." The attorney looked at the thick manilla envelope in his hand. "You know, I feel the way Jim St Clair must have felt when he got that last call from Al Haig. Is this some kind of smoking-gun?"

"It's on fire, Mr Bergeron."

"I called the airline an hour ago; I'm on the 7.55 to Washington. Winthrop will have this by ten in the morning."

"Thanks. Good night."

Scofield drove back towards Salem, scanning the roads instinctively for signs of anyone following him; there were none, nor did he expect to see any. He was also looking for an all-night supermarket. Their wares were rarely, if ever, restricted to foodstuffs.

He found one on the outskirts of Medford set back from the highway. He parked in front, walked inside, and saw what he was looking for in the second aisle. A display of inexpensive Big Ben alarm clocks. He bought ten of them.

It was 3.18 when he walked into his room. He took the alarm clocks from their boxes, lined them up on the table, and opened his attaché case, taking out a small leather case containing miniature hand tools. He would buy bell wire and the batteries first thing in the morning, the explosives later in the day. The charges might be a problem, but it was not insurmountable; he needed more show than power – and in all likelihood he would need nothing at all. The years, however, had taught him caution; an exchange was like the workings of a giant aircraft. Each system had a back-up system, each back-up an alternative.

He had six hours to prepare his alternatives. It was good he had something to do; sleep now was out of the question.

36

The shift from dawn to daybreak was barely discernible; winter rain was promised again. By 8.00 it had arrived. Bray stood, his hands on the window sill, looking out at the ocean, thinking about calmer, warmer seas, wondering if he and Toni would ever sail them. Yesterday there was no hope; today there was and he was primed to function as he had never functioned before. All that was Beowulf Agate would be seen and heard from this day. He had spent his life preparing for the few brief hours that would prolong it the only way that was acceptable to him. He would bring her out or he would die; that had not changed. The fact that he had effectively destroyed the Matarese was almost incidental now. That was a professional objective and he was the best . . . he and the Russian were the best.

He turned from the window and went to the table, surveying his work of the last few hours. It had taken less time than he had projected, so total was his concentration. Each clock was dismantled, every main wheel spring drilled at the spindle, new pinion screws inserted in the ratchet mechanisms, the miniature bolts balanced. Each was now prepared to accept the insertion of bell wires leading to battery terminals that would throw thirty seconds of sparks into exposed powder. These sparks would, in turn, burn and ignite explosives over a span of fifteen minutes. Each alarm had been set and reset a dozen times, infinitesimal grooves filed across the gears insuring sequence; all worked a dozen times in sequence. Professional tools, no particular significance attached to his knowing them. The designer was also a mechanic, the architect a builder, the critic a practitioner of the craft. It was essential.

Powder could be obtained at any gunsmith's with the purchase of shells. As for explosives, a simple visit to a demolition or excavation site, armed with the proper government identification, was all that it took for an on-the-spot inventory. The rest was a matter of having large pockets in a raincoat. He had done it all before; lay mentality was the same everywhere. Beware the man bearing a black plastic ID case and who spoke softly. He was dangerous. Co-operate; do not allow your name to get on a list.

He placed the clock mechanisms in a box given him by the supermarket clerk five hours ago, sealed the top and carried it downstairs, outside to his car. He opened the boot, wedged the box into the corner, closed the boot, and returned to the hotel lobby.

"I find that I'll be leaving shortly," he said to the young man behind the counter of the front desk. "I paid for a week, but my plans have changed."

"You also had a lot of phone calls billed to your room, mister."

"True," agreed Scofield, wondering how many people in Salem were also aware of it. Did witches still burn in Salem? "If you'd have the balance ready for me, I'll be down in about a half hour. Add these papers to my bill, please." He took two newspapers from the stacks on the counter, the morning *Examiner* and a local weekly. He walked back up the staircase to his room.

He made instant coffee, carried the cup to the table, and sat down with the newspapers and the Salem telephone book. It was 8.25. Paul Bergeron had been in the air thirty minutes, weather at Logan Airport permitting. It was something he would check when he moved to the telephone.

He opened the *Examiner*, turning to the classified section. There were two openings for construction workers, the first in Newton, the second in Braintree. He wrote down the addresses, hoping to find a third or a fourth nearer by.

He did. In the Salem weekly, there was a photograph taken five days ago showing Senator Joshua Appleton at a ground-breaking ceremony in Swampscott. It was a federal project co-ordinated with the state of Massachusetts, an enormous middle-income housing development being built on the rocky land north of Phillips Beach. The caption read, *Blasting and excavation to commence . . .*

The irony was splendid.

He opened the telephone book, and found a gunsmith in Salem; he had no reason to look further. He wrote down the address.

It was 8.37. Time to call the lie that went under the name of Joshua Appleton. He got up and went to the bed, deciding impulsively to phone Logan Airport first. He did, and the words he heard were the words he wanted to hear.

"Seven-fifty-five to Washington? That would be Eastern Flight Six-two. Let me check, sir . . . There was a twelve-minute delay, but the plane's airborne. No change in the E.T.A."

Paul Bergeron was on his way to Washington and Robert Winthrop. There would be no delays now, no crisis-conferences, no hastily summoned meetings between ranking arrogant men trying to decide how and when to proceed. Winthrop would call the Oval Office; an immediate audience would be granted and the full might of government would be pitted against the Matarese. And tomorrow morning the senator would be picked up by Secret Service and taken directly to Walter Reed Hospital where he would be subjected to intensive examinations. A twenty-five-year fraud would be exposed, the son destroyed with the Shepherd Boy.

Bray lit a cigarette, sipped his coffee and picked up the phone. He was in full command; he would concentrate totally on his negotiations, on the exchange that would be meaningless to the Matarese.

The senator's voice was tense, exhaustion in his tight delivery. "Nicholas Guiderone wants to see you."

"The Shepherd Boy himself," said Scofield. "You know my conditions. Does he? Is he prepared to meet them?"

"Yes," whispered the son. "A telephone number he agrees to. He's not sure what you mean by a 'sighting'."

"Then there's nothing further to talk about. I'll hang up."

"*Wait!*"

"Why? It's a simple word; I told you I had binoculars. What else is there to say? He's refused. Goodbye, Senator."

"No!" Appleton's breathing was audible. "All right, all right. You'll be told a time and a location when you call the number I give you."

"I'll be *what*? You're a dead man, Senator. If they want to sacrifice you, that's their business – and yours, I suppose, but not mine."

"What the hell are you talking about? What's wrong?"

"It's unacceptable. I'm not *told* a time and a location, I tell *you* and you tell them. Specifically, I give you a location and a time *span*, Senator. Between three and five o'clock this afternoon, at the north windows of Appleton Hall, the ones looking out over Jamaica Pond. Have you got that? Appleton Hall."

"That *is* the telephone number!"

"You don't say. Have the windows lighted, the woman in one room, the Russian in another. I want mobility, conversation; I want to see them walking, talking, reacting. Is that clear?"

"Yes. Walking . . . reacting."

"And, Senator, tell your people not to bother looking for me. I won't have the X-rays on me; they'll be with someone else who's been told to send them if I'm not back at a specific bus stop by five-thirty."

"A *bus* stop?"

"The north road below Appleton Hall is a public bus route. Those buses are always crowded and the long curve around Jamaica Pond makes them slow down. If the rain keeps up they'll be slower than usual, won't they? I'll have plenty of time to see what I want to see."

"Will you *see* Nicholas *Guiderone*?" The question was rushed, on the edge of hysteria.

"If I'm satisfied," said Scofield coldly. "I'll call you from a phone booth around five-thirty."

"He wants to talk with you *now*!"

"Mr Vickery doesn't talk to anyone until he checks with the Ritz-Carlton Hotel. I thought that was clear."

"He's concerned you may have duplicates made; he's very concerned about that."

"These are twenty-five- and thirty-six-year-old negatives. Any exposure to photographic light would show up on a spectrograph instantly. I won't get killed for that."

"He insisted you reach him *now*! He says it's vital!"

"Everything's vital."

"He says to tell you you're wrong. So very, *very* wrong."

"If I'm satisfied this afternoon he'll have a chance to prove it later. And you'll have the presidency. Or will he?" Bray hung up and crushed out his cigarette. As he had thought, Appleton Hall was the most logical place for Guiderone to hold his hostages. He had tried *not* to think about it when he had driven around the massive estate – the nearness of Toni was an obstruction he could barely surmount – but instinctively he had known it. And because he knew it, his eyes had reacted like the rapid shutters of a dozen cameras clicking off a hundred images. The grounds had

353

space; acres filled with dense trees and thick shrubbery and guards in lean-to shelters positioned around the hill. Such a fortress was a likely target for an invasion – indeed the possibility was obviously never far from Guiderone's mind – and Scofield intended to capitalize on that fear. He would mount an imaginary invasion, its roots in the sort of army the Shepherd Boy understood as well as anyone on earth.

He made a last call before leaving Salem; to Robert Winthrop in Washington. The ambassador might well be tied up for hours at the White House – his advice intrinsic to any decision made by the President – and Scofield wanted first line of protection. It was his only protection, really; imaginary invasions had no invaders.

"*Brandon?* I haven't slept all night."

"Neither did a lot of other people, sir. Is this line sterile?"

"I had it electronically checked early this morning. What's happening? Did you see Bergeron?"

"He's on his way. Eastern Flight Six-two. He's got the envelope and will be in Washington by ten."

"I'll send Stanley to meet him at the airport. I spoke to the President fifteen minutes ago. He's clearing his calendar and will see me at two o'clock this afternoon. I expect it will be a very long meeting. I'm sure he'll want to bring in others."

"That's why I'm calling now; I thought as much. I've got the exchange ground. Have you a pencil?"

"Yes, go ahead."

"It's a place called Appleton Hall in Brookline."

"Appleton? *Senator* Appleton?"

"You'll understand when you get the envelope from Bergeron."

"My *God!*"

"The estate's above Jamaica Pond, on a hill called Appleton Hill; it's well known. I'll set the meeting for eleven-thirty tonight; I'll time my arrival exactly. Tell whoever's in charge to start surrounding the hill at eleven-forty-five. Block off the roads a half-mile in all directions, using detour signs, and approach carefully. There are guards inside the fence every two or three hundred feet. Station the command post on the dirt road across from the front gate; there's a large white house there, if I remember correctly. Take it and sever the telephone wires; it may belong to the Matarese."

"Just a minute, Brandon," interrupted Winthrop. "I'm writing all this and my hands and eyes aren't what they once were."

"I'm sorry, I'll slow down."

"It's all right. 'Sever telephone wires.' Go on."

"My strategy's right out of the book. They may expect it, but they can't stop it. I'll say my deadline's fifteen minutes past midnight. That's when I'm to go out the front door with the hostages to my car and strike two matches one after the other; they'll recognize the pattern. I'll tell them a drone is outside the gate with an envelope containing the X-rays."

"Drone? *X-rays?*"

"The first is only a name for someone I hire. The second is the proof they expect me to deliver."

"But you *can't* deliver it!"

"It wouldn't make any difference if I did. You'll have enough in the envelope Bergeron's bringing you."

"Of course. What else?"

"When I strike the second match, tell the C.P. to give me corresponding signals."

"Corresponding . . . ?"

"Strike two matches."

"Of course. Sorry. Then?"

"Wait for me to drive down to the gate. I'll time everything as close to twelve-twenty as I can. As soon as the gate's opened, the troops move in. They'll be covered by diversionary static – tell them it's just that. Static."

"What? I don't understand."

"They will. I've got to leave now, Mr Ambassador. There's still a lot to do."

"Brandon!"

"Yes, sir?"

"There's one thing you do *not* have to do."

"What's that?"

"Worry about vindication. I promise you. You were always the best there was."

"Thank you, sir. Thank you for everything. I just want to be free."

The gunsmith on Salem's Hawthorne Boulevard was both amused and pleased that the stranger purchased two gross of *Ought-Four* shotgun shells during off-season. Tourists were damn fools anyway, but this one compounded the damn-foolery of paying good money not only for the shells, but for ten plastic display tubes that the manufacturers supplied for nothing. He spoke with one of those smooth, kinda' oily voices. Probably a New York lawyer who never had a gun in his hand. Damn fools.

The rain hammered down, forming pools in the mud as disgruntled crews of construction workers sat in cars waiting for a break in the weather so they could sign in; four hours meant a day's pay, but without signing in there was nothing.

Scofield approached the door of a pre-fabricated shack, stepping on a plank sinking into the mud in front of the rain-splashed window. Inside he could see the foreman sitting behind a desk talking into a telephone. Ten yards to the left was a concrete bunker, a heavy padlock on the steel door, the red-lettered sign stencilled across it explicit.

DANGER
AUTHORIZED PERSONNEL ONLY
SWAMPSCOTT DEV. CORP.

Bray rapped first on the window, distracting the man on the phone inside the shack, then stepped off the plank and opened the door.

"Yeah, what is it?" yelled the foreman.

"I'll wait till you're finished," said Scofield, closing the door. A sign on the table told the man's name. *A. Patelli.*

"That could be a while, pal! I got a thief on the phone. A fucking thief who says his fucking pansy drivers can't roll because it's wet out!"

"Don't make it too long, please." Bray removed his ID case. He flipped it open, holding it in front of the man. "You are Mr Patelli, aren't you?"

The foreman stared at the very official identification card.

"Yeah." He turned back to the phone. "I'll call you back, thief!" He got out of the chair. "You government?"

"Yes."

What the hell's the matter *now?*"

"Something we don't think you're aware of, Mr Patelli. My unit's working with the Federal Bureau of Investigation . . ."

"The FBI?"

"That's right. You've had several shipments of explosive materials delivered to the site here."

"Locked up tight and accounted for," interrupted the foreman. "Every fucking stick."

"We don't think so. That's why I'm here."

"*What?*"

"There was a bombing two days ago in New York, maybe you read about it. A bank in Wall Street. Oxidation raised several numbers on the serial imprint that blew with the detonating cap; we think it may be traced to one of your shipments."

"That's fuckin'-a-nuts!"

"Why don't we check?"

The explosives inside the concrete bunker were not sticks, they were solid blocks roughly five inches long, three inches high and two thick, packaged in cartons of twenty-four.

"Prepare a statement of consignment, please," said Scofield, studying the surface of a brick. "We were right. These are the ones."

"A statement of *what?*"

"I'm taking a carton for evidentiary analysis."

"*Who?*"

"Look, Mr Patelli, your ass may be in a very tight sling. You signed for these shipments and I don't think you counted. I'd advise you to co-operate fully. Any indication of resistance could be misinterpreted; after all, it's your responsibility. Frankly, I don't think you're involved, but I'm only the field investigator. On the other hand, my word counts."

"I'll sign any fucking thing you want. What do I write?"

At a hardware store, Bray bought ten dry-cell batteries, ten five-quart plastic containers, a roll of bell wire and a can of black spray-paint. He asked for a very large box to carry everything in through the rain.

*

356

He sat in the back seat of his rented car, placed the last of the clocks into its plastic container, pressing the explosive brick down beside the battery. He listened for the steady tick of the mechanism; it was there. Then he snapped the edges of the cover into place and sealed it with tape.

It was forty-two minutes past noon, the alarms set in sequence, the grooves in the gears locked by the teeth of the pinions, the sequence to begin in precisely eleven hours and twenty-six minutes.

As he had done with the previous nine, he sprayed the container with black paint. A great deal of it soiled the rear seat cushion; he would leave a hundred-dollar bill in the crease.

He inserted the coin in the pay phone; he was in West Roxbury, two minutes from the border of Brookline. He dialled, waited for the line to be answered and roared into the mouthpiece.

"Sanitation?"

"Yes, sir. What can we do for you?"

"Appleton Drive! Brookline! The sewer's packed up! It's all over my *goddamn* front lawn!"

"Where is that, sir?"

"I just told you. Appleton Drive and Beachnut Terrace! It's terrible."

"We'll dispatch a truck right away, sir."

"Please, hurry!"

The Sanitation Department van made its way haltingly up Beachnut Terrace towards the intersection of Appleton Drive, its driver obviously checking the sewer drains in the street. When he reached the corner, a man in a dark-blue raincoat flagged him down. It was impossible to go around the man; he moved back and forth in the middle of the street, waving his arms frantically. The driver opened his door and shouted through the rain.

"What's the *mattah?*"

It was the last thing he would say for several hours.

Within the Appleton Hall compound, a guard in a cedar lean-to picked up his wall telephone and told the operator on the switchboard to give him an outside line. He was calling the Sanitation Department in Brookline. One of their vans was on Appleton Drive, stopping every hundred feet or so.

"There are reports of a blockage in the vicinity of Beachnut and Appleton, sir. We have a truck checking it out."

"Thank you," said the guard, pushing a button that was the intercom for all stations. He relayed the information and returned to his chair.

What kind of idiot would check out sewers for a living?

*

Scofield wore the black rain slicker with the stencilled white letters across the back. *Sanitation Dept. Brookline.* It was 3.05. The sighting had started: Antonia and Taleniekov standing behind windows on the other side of the estate; the concentration in Appleton Hall would be on the road below. He drove the sanitation van slowly up Appleton Drive, staying close to the kerb, stopping at every sewer drain in the street. As the road was long, there were roughly twenty to thirty such drains. At each stop he got out carrying a six-foot extension snake and whatever other tools he could find in the van that seemed to fit a hastily imagined problem. This was at every stop; at ten, however, he added one other item. A five-quart plastic container that had been sprayed black. Seven of them he was able to wedge between the spikes of the wrought-iron fence beyond the sightlines of the lean-to's, pushing them into the foliage with the snake. With three he used what was left of the bell wire and suspended them beneath the grates of the sewers.

At 4.22 he was finished and drove back to Beachnut Terrace, where he began the embarrassing process of reviving the sanitation employee in the rear of the van. There was no time to be solicitous; he removed the rain slicker and slapped the man into consciousness.

"What the hell *happened?*" The man was frightened, recoiling at the sight of Bray above him.

"I made a mistake," said Scofield simply. "You can accept that or not, but nothing's missing, no harm's been done, and there is no problem with the sewers."

"You're crazy!"

Bray took out his money clip. "I'm sure it appears that way, so I'd like to pay you for the use of your truck. No one has to know about it. Here's five hundred dollars."

"Five . . . ?"

"For the past hour you've been checking the drains along Beachnut and Appleton, that's all anyone has to know. You were dispatched and did your job. That is, if you want the five hundred."

"You're *crazy!*"

"I haven't got time to argue with you. Do you want the money or not?"

The man's eyes bulged. He took the money.

It did not matter whether they saw him now; it only mattered what he saw. His watch read 4.57, three minutes remained before the sighting was terminated. He drove, stopped the car directly below the midpoint of Appleton Hall, rolled down his window and raised the Zeiss-Ikon binoculars to his eyes. He focused through the rain on the lighted windows three hundred yards above.

The first figure to come into view was Taleniekov, but it was not the Taleniekov he had last seen in London. The Russian stood motionless behind the window, the side of his head encased in a bandage, a bulge beneath the open collar of his shirt further evidence of wounds wrapped tightly with heavy gauze. Standing beside the Soviet was a dark-haired muscular man, his hand hidden behind Taleniekov's back. Scofield had the distinct impression that without that man's hand, Taleniekov would collapse. But he was alive, his eyes staring straight ahead, blinking every other second or so; the Russian was telling him he *was* alive.

Bray moved the glasses to the right; his breathing stopped, the pounding in his chest like a rapidly accelerating drum in an echo chamber. It was almost more than he could bear; the rain blurred the lenses; he was going out of his mind.

There she *was*! Standing erect behind the window, her head held up, angled first to her left, then to her right, her eyes levelled, responding to voices. *Responding*.

And then Scofield saw what he dared not hope to see. Relief swept over him and he wanted to shout through the rain in sheer exuberance. There was fear in Antonia's eyes, to be sure, but there was also something else. *Anger*.

The eyes of his love were filled with anger, and there was nothing on earth that took its place! An angry mind was a mind intact.

He put the binoculars down, rolled up the windows and started the engine. He had several telephone calls and a final arrangement to make. When these were done, it was time for Mr B. A. Vickery to arrive at the Ritz Carlton Hotel.

37

"Were you satisfied?" The senator's voice was more controlled than it had been that morning. The anxiety was still there but it was farther below the surface.

"How badly is the Russian hurt?"

"He's lost blood; he's weak."

"I could see that. Is he ambulatory?"

"Enough to put him into a car, if that's what you want to do."

"It's what I want to do. Both he and the woman in my car with me at the exact moment I say. I'll drive the car down to the gate and, on my signal, the gate will be opened. That's when you get the X-rays and we get out."

"I thought you wanted to kill him?"

"I want something else first. He has information that can make the rest of my life very pleasant, no matter who runs what."

"I see."

"I'm sure you do."

"You said you'd meet with Nicholas Guiderone, listen to what he has to say."

"I will. I'd be a liar if I didn't admit I had questions."

"He'll answer everything. When will you see him?"

"He'll know when I check into the Ritz-Carlton. Tell him to call me there. And let's get one thing clear, Senator. A telephone call, no troops. The X-rays won't be in the hotel."

"Where will they be?"

"That's my business." Scofield hung up and left the phone booth. He'd place his next call from a booth in the centre of Boston, to check in with Robert Winthrop, as much as to get the ambassador's reaction to the material in the envelope as anything else. And to make sure his protection was being mounted. If there were hitches he wanted to know about them.

"It's Stanley, Mr Scofield." As always, Winthrop's chauffeur spoke gruffly, not unpleasantly. "The ambassador's still at the White House; he asked me to come back here and wait for any calls from you. He told me to tell you that everything you asked for is being taken care of. He said I should repeat the times. Eleven-thirty, eleven forty-five and twelve-fifteen."

"That's what I wanted to hear. Thanks very much." Bray opened the door of the drugstore telephone booth, and walked over to a counter that sold construction paper and felt markers in varying colours. He chose bright yellow paper and a dark-blue marker.

He went back outside to his car and, using his attaché case for a desk, wrote his message in large, clear letters on the yellow paper. Satisfied, he opened the case, removed the five sealed manilla envelopes, stamped and addressed to five of the nation's most powerful men, and placed them on the seat next to him. It was time to mail them. Then he took out a sixth envelope and inserted the yellow page; he sealed it with tape and wrote on the front.

FOR THE BOSTON POLICE

He drove slowly up Newbury Street looking for the address he had found in the telephone booth. It was on the left side, four doors from the corner, a large painted sign in the window.

Phoenix Messenger Service
24 Hour Delivery – Medical, Academic, Industrial

He parked in a space vacated by a taxi, got out and went inside. A thin, prim-looking woman with an expression of serious efficiency rose from her desk and came to the counter.

"May I help you?"

"I hope so," said Scofield, efficiency in his voice as he opened his identification. "I'm with the BPD, attached to Inter-departmental Examinations."

"The police? Good heavens . . ."

"Nothing to be concerned about. We're running an exercise, checking up on precinct response to outside emergencies. We want this envelope delivered to the station on Boylston tonight. Can you handle it?"

"We certainly can."

"Fine. What's the charge?"

"Oh, I don't think that will be necessary, officer. We're all in this together."

"I couldn't accept that, thank you. Besides we need the outside record. And your name, of course."

"Of course. The charge for night deliveries is usually ten dollars."

"If you'll let me have a receipt, please." Scofield took the money from his pocket. "And if you wouldn't mind, please specify that delivery is to be made between eleven and eleven-fifteen, that's very important to us. You will make sure of it, won't you?"

"I'll do better than that, officer. I'll deliver it myself. I'm on until midnight, so I'll just leave one of the boys in charge and go right over there myself. I really admire the sort of thing you're doing. Crime is simply astronomical these days; we've all got to pitch in, I say."

"You're very kind, ma'am."

"You know, there're a lot of very strange people around the apartment house where I live. *Very* strange."

"What's the address? I'll have the patrol cars look a little more closely from here on."

"Why *thank* you."

"Thank *you*, ma'am."

It was 9.20 when he walked into the lobby of the Ritz-Carlton. He had driven down to the piers and eaten a fish dinner, the time spent thinking about what he and Toni would do after the night was over. Where would they go? How could they live? Finances did not concern him; Winthrop had promised vindication and the calculating head of Consular Operations, the would-be executioner named Daniel Congdon, had been generous in pension and unrecorded benefits that would come his way as long as his silence was maintained. Beowulf Agate was about to disappear from this world; where would Bray Scofield go? As long as Antonia was with him, it did not matter.

"There's a message for you, Mr Vickery," said the desk clerk, holding out a small envelope.

"Thank you," said Scofield, wondering if beneath the man's white shirt there was a small blue circle inked into his flesh.

The message was only a telephone number. He crumpled it in his hand and dropped it on the counter.

"Is something wrong?" asked the clerk.

Bray smiled. "Tell that son of a bitch I don't make calls to numbers. Only to names."

He let the telephone ring three times before he picked it up. "Yes?"

"You're an arrogant man, Beowulf." The voice was high-pitched, crueller-than-the-wind. It was the Shepherd Boy, Nicholas Guiderone.

"I was right, then," said Scofield. "That man downstairs doesn't work full-time for the Ritz-Carlton. And when he showers, he can't wash off a small blue circle on his chest."

"It's worn with enormous pride, sir. They are extraordinary men and women who have enlisted in our extraordinary cause."

"Where do you find them? People who'll blow themselves away and bite into cyanide?"

"Quite simply, in our companies. Men have been willing to make the ultimate sacrifice for causes since the dawn of time. It does not always have to be on a battlefield, or in a wartime underground, or even in the world of international espionage. There are many causes; I don't have to tell you that."

"Such as themselves? The *fida'is*, Guiderone? Hasan ibn as-Sabbāh's cadre of assassins?"

"You've studied the *padrone*, I see."

"Very closely."

"There are certain practical and philosophical similarities, I will not deny it. These men and women have everything they want on this earth, and when they leave it, their families – wives, children, husbands – will have more than they ever need. Isn't that the dream? With over five hundred companies, computers can select a handful of people willing and capable of entering into this arrangement. A simple extension of the dream, Mr Scofield."

"Pretty damned extended."

"Not really. Far more executives collapse from heart seizure than from violence. Read the daily obituaries. But I'm sure this is only one of many questions. May I send a car for you?"

"You may not."

"There's no cause for hostility."

"I'm not hostile, I'm cautious. Basically I'm a coward. I've set a schedule and I intend to stick with it. I'll get there at exactly eleven-thirty; you talk, I'll listen. At precisely twelve-fifteen, I'll walk out with the girl and the Russian. A signal will be given, we'll get into the car and drive to your main gate. That's when you'll get the X-rays and we get away. If there's the slightest deviation, the X-rays will disappear. They'll show up somewhere else."

"We have a right to examine them," protested Guiderone. "For accuracy and spectro-analysis; we want to make sure no duplicates were made. We must have time for that."

The Shepherd Boy bit; the omission of the examination was the weakness Guiderone quite naturally pounced upon. The huge electronic iron gate had to be opened and stay open. If it remained shut, all the troops and all the diversions that could be mounted, would not prevent a man firing a rifle into the car. Bray hesitated. "Fair enough. Have equipment and a technician down at the gatehouse. Verification will take two or three minutes, but the gate has to remain open while it's being done."

"Very well."

"By the way," added Scofield, "I meant what I said to your son . . ."

"You mean Senator Appleton, I believe."

"Believe it. You'll find the X-rays intact, no light-marks of duplication. I won't get killed for that."

"I'm convinced. But I find a weakness in these arrangements."

"A weakness . . . ?" Bray felt cold.

"Yes. Eleven-thirty to twelve-fifteen is only forty-five minutes. That's not much time for us to talk. For me to talk and you to listen."

Scofield breathed again. "If you're convincing, I'll know where to find you in the morning, won't I?"

Guiderone laughed softly in his eerily high-pitched voice. "Of course. So simple. You're a logical man."

"I try to be. Eleven-thirty, then." Bray hung up.

He had *done* it! Every system had a back-up system, every back-up an alternative. The exchange was covered on all flanks.

It was 11.29 when he drove through the gates of Appleton Hall and entered the drive that curved up past the carriage house to the walled mansion on the crest of the hill. As he drove by the cavernous garage of the carriage house, he was surprised to see a number of limousines. Between ten and twelve uniformed chauffeurs were talking; they were men who knew each other. They had been here before together.

The wall surrounding the enormous main house was more for effect than protection; it was barely eight feet high, designed to look far higher from below. Joshua Appleton, the first, had erected an expensive plaything. One-third castle, one-third fortress, one-third functional estate with an incredible view of Boston. The lights of the city flickered in the distance; the rain had stopped, leaving a chilly translucent mist in the air.

Bray saw two men in the glare of his headlights; the one on the right signalled him to stop in front of a separation in the eight-foot-high wall. He did so; the path beyond the wall was bordered by two heavy chains suspended from thick iron posts, the door at the end set in an archway. All that was missing was a portcullis, deadly spikes to come crashing down with the severing of a rope.

Bray got out of the car and was immediately shoved over the hood, every pocket, every area of his body searched for weapons. Flanked by the guards, he was escorted to the door in the archway and admitted.

At first full glance, Scofield understood why Nicholas Guiderone had to possess the Appleton estate. The staircase, the tapestries, the chandeliers . . . the sheer magnificence of the great hall was breathtaking. The nearest thing to it Bray could imagine was the burned-out skeleton in Porto Vecchio that once had been the Villa Matarese.

"Come this way, please," said the guard on his right, opening a door. "You have three minutes with the guests."

Antonia ran across the room into his arms, her tears moistening his cheeks, the strength of her embrace desperate. "My darling! You've come for us!"

"*Shhh . . .* " He held her. *Oh, God, he held her!* "We haven't time," he said softly. "In a little while we're going to walk out of here. Everything's going to be all right. We're going to be free."

"He wants to talk to you," she whispered. "Quickly."

"What?" Scofield opened his eyes and looked beyond Toni. Across the room Taleniekov sat rigidly in an armchair. The Russian's face was pale, so pale it was like chalk, the left side of his head taped; his ear and half his cheek had been blown away. His neck and shoulder blade were also bandaged, encased in a T-squared metal brace; he could barely move them. Bray held Antonia's hand and approached. Taleniekov was dying. "We're getting out of here," said Scofield. "We'll take you to a hospital. It'll be all right."

The Russian shook his head slowly, painfully, deliberately.

"He can't talk, darling." Toni touched Vasili's right cheek. "He has no voice."

"*Jesus!* What did they . . . ? Never mind, in forty-five minutes we're driving out of here."

Again Taleniekov shook his head; the Russian was trying to tell him something.

"When the guards were helping him down the staircase, he had a convulsion," said Antonia. "It was terrible, they were pulled down with him and were furious. They kept hitting him – and he's in such pain."

"They were pulled down . . . ?" asked Bray, wondering, looking at Taleniekov.

The Russian nodded, reaching under his shirt to the belt underneath. He pulled out a gun and shoved it across his legs towards Scofield.

"He fell all right," whispered Bray, smiling, kneeling down and taking the weapon. "You can't trust these Commie bastards." Then he shifted into Russian, putting his lips close to Taleniekov's right ear. "Everything's clean. We've got men outside. I've set explosive charges all around the hill. They want the proof I've got; we'll get out."

The KGB man once more shook his head. Then he stopped, his eyes wide, gesturing for Scofield to watch his lips.

The words were formed: *Pazhar . . . vsyegda pazhar.*

Bray translated into English. "Fire, always fire?"

Taleniekov nodded, then formed other words, a barely audible whisper now merging. "*Zazhiganiye . . . pazhar.*"

"Explosions? After the explosions, fire? Is that what you're saying?"

Again, Taleniekov nodded, his eyes staring, beseeching.

"You don't understand," said Bray. "We're covered."

The Russian once more shook his head, now violently. Then he raised his hand, two fingers across his lips.

"A cigarette?" asked Scofield. Vasili nodded. Bray took the pack out of his pocket along with a book of matches. Taleniekov waved away the cigarettes and grabbed the matches.

The door opened; the guard spoke sharply. "That's it. Mr Guiderone's waiting for you. They'll be here when you're finished."

"They'd better be." Scofield rose to his feet, hiding the gun in his belt beneath his raincoat. He gripped Antonia's hand and walked with her to the door. "I'll be back in a while. No one's going to stop us."

Nicholas Guiderone sat behind the desk in his library, his large head with the fringe of white hair supporting an old man's face, the pale skin taut, receding into the temples and stretched, sinking into the hollows that held his dark, shining eyes. There was a gnomelike quality about him; it was not hard to think of him as the Shepherd Boy.

"Would you care to reconsider your schedule, Mr Scofield?" asked Guiderone in

364

his high, somewhat breathless voice, not looking at Bray, but instead studying papers. "Forty minutes is really very little time, and I've got a great deal to tell you."

"You can tell me some other time, perhaps. Tonight the schedule stands."

"I see." The old man looked up, now staring at Scofield. "You think we've done terrible things, don't you?"

"I don't know what you've done."

"Certainly you do. We've had nearly four full days with the Russian. His monologues were not voluntary, but with chemical assistance, the words were there. You've uncovered the pattern of huge companies linked across the world; you've perceived that through these companies we have funnelled sums of money to terrorist groups everywhere. Incidentally, you're quite right. I doubt there's an effective group of fanatics anywhere that has not benefited from us. You perceive all this but you can't understand why. It's at your fingertips, but it eludes you."

"At my fingertips?"

"The words are yours. The Russian used them, but they were yours. Under chemical inducement, multi-lingual subjects speak the language of their sources . . . *Paralysis*, Mr Scofield. Governments must be paralysed. Nothing achieves this more rapidly or more completely than the rampant global chaos of what we call terrorism."

"Chaos . . ." Bray whispered; *that* was the word he kept coming back to, never sure why. *Chaos*. Clashing bodies in space . . .

"Yes. Chaos!" repeated Guiderone, his startling dark eyes wide, two shining black stones reflecting the light of the desk lamp. "When the chaos is complete, when civilian and military authorities are impotent, admitting they cannot destroy a thousand vanishing wolfpacks with tanks and warheads and tactical weapons, then men of reason will move in. The period of violence will at last be over and this world can go about the business of living productively."

"In a nuclear ash-heap?"

"There'll be no such consequences. We've tested the controls; we have men at them."

"What the hell are you talking about?"

"Governments, Mr Scofield!" shouted Guiderone, his eyes on fire. "Governments are obsolete! They can no longer be permitted to function as they have functioned throughout history. If they do, this planet will not see the next century. Governments as we have known them are no longer viable entities. They must be replaced."

"By whom? With what?"

The old man softened his voice; it became hollow, hypnotic. "By a new breed of philosopher-kings, if you like. Men who understand this world as it has truly emerged, who measure its potential in terms of resources, technology and productivity – who care not one whit about the colour of a man's skin, or the heritage of his ancestors, or what idols he may pray to. Who care only about his full productive potential as a human being. And his contribution to the market-place."

"My God!" said Bray quietly. "You're talking about conglomerates."

"Does it offend you?"

"Not if I owned one."

"Very good." Guiderone broke into a jackal-like laugh; it disappeared instantly. "But that's a limited point of view. There are those among us who thought you of all people would understand. You've seen the other futility; you've lived it."

"By choice."

"Very, very good. But that presumes there is no choice in our structure. Untrue. A man is free to develop his full potential; the greater his productivity – the greater his freedom and rewards."

"Suppose he doesn't want to be productive? As you define it."

"Then obviously there's a lesser reward for the lesser contribution."

"Who *does* define it?"

"Trained units of management personnel, using all the technology developed in modern industry."

"I guess it'd be a good idea to get to know them."

"Don't waste time with sarcasm. Such teams operate daily all over the world. The international companies are not in business to lose money or forfeit profits. The system *works*. We prove it every day. The new society will function within a competitive, non-violent structure. Governments can no longer guarantee that; they're on nuclear collision courses everywhere. But the Chrysler Corporation does not make war on Volkswagen; no planes fill the skies to wipe out factories and whole towns centred on one or the other company. The new world will be committed to the market-place, to the developing of resources and technology that insure the productive survival of mankind. There's no other way. The multi-national community is proof; it is aggressive, highly competitive, but it is non-violent. It bears no arms."

"Chaos," said Bray, his eyes locked with the Shepherd Boy's. "The clashing of bodies in space . . . destruction before the creation of order."

"Yes, Mr Scofield. The period of violence before the permanent era of tranquillity. But governments and their leaders do not relinquish their responsibilities easily. Alternatives must be given men whose backs are to the wall."

"Alternatives?"

"In Italy, we control nearly twenty per cent of the Parliament. In Bonn, twelve per cent of the *Bundestag*; in Japan, almost thirty-one per cent of the *Diet*. Could we have done this without the *Brigata Rossa* or Baader-Meinhof or the Red Army of Japan? We grow in authority every month. With each act of terrorism we are closer to our objective: the total absence of violence."

"That wasn't what Guillaume de Matarese had in mind seventy years ago."

"It's much closer than you think. The *padrone* wanted to destroy the corrupters in governments, which all too frequently meant entire governments themselves. He gave us the structure, the methods – hired assassins to pit political factions against adversaries everywhere. He provided the initial fortune to put it all in motion; he showed us the way to chaos. All that remained was to put something in its place. We have found it. We'll save the world from itself. There can be no greater cause."

"You're convincing," said Scofield. "I think we may have a basis for talking further."

"I'm glad you think so," answered Guiderone, his voice suddenly cold again. "It's gratifying to know one is convincing; but much more interesting to watch the reactions of a liar."

"Liar?"

"You could have been part of this!" Once more the old man shouted. "After that night in Rock Creek Park, I myself convened the council. I told it to re-assess, re-evaluate! Beowulf Agate could be of incalculable value. The Russian was useless, but not *you*. The information you possessed could make a mockery of Washington's moral positions. I myself would have made you director of all security! On my instructions, we tried for weeks to reach you, bring you in, make you one of us. It is, of course, no longer possible. You're relentless in your *deceptions*! In short words, you cannot be trusted. You can *never* be trusted!"

Bray sat forward. The Shepherd Boy was a maniac; it was in the maniacal eyes set in the hollows of his pale, gaunt skull. He was a man capable of quiet, seemingly logical discourse, but irrationality ruled him. He was a bomb; a bomb had to be controlled. "I wouldn't forget the purpose of my coming here, if I were you."

"Your *purpose*? By all means it will be achieved. You want the woman? You want Taleniekov? They're yours! You'll be together, I assure you. You will be taken from this house and driven far away, never to be heard from again, no loss to anyone."

"Let's deal, Guiderone. Don't make any foolish mistakes. You have a son who can be the next President of the United States – as long as he's Joshua Appleton. But he's not, and I have the X-rays to prove it."

"The X-rays!" roared Guiderone. "You *ass*!" He pressed a button on his desk console and spoke. "Bring him in," he said. "Bring in our esteemed guest." The Shepherd Boy sat back in his chair as the door behind Scofield opened.

Bray turned, mind and body suspended in pain at what he saw.

Seated in a wheelchair, his eyes glazed, his gentle face bruised, Robert Winthrop was brought through the door by his chauffeur of twenty years. Stanley smiled, his expression arrogant. Scofield sprang up; the chauffeur raised his hand from behind the wheelchair. In it was a gun.

"Years ago," said Guiderone, "a Marine combat sergeant was sentenced to spend the greater part of his life in prison. We found more productive work for a man of his skills. It was necessary that the benign elder statesman whom everyone in Washington sought out for comfort and advice be watched very thoroughly. We learned a great deal."

Bray looked away from the battered Winthrop and stared at Stanley. "Congratulations, you . . . *bastard*! What did you do? Pistol-whip him?"

"He didn't want to come," Stanley said, his smile vanishing. "He fell."

Scofield started forward; the chauffeur raised the gun higher, aiming at Bray's head. "I'm going to talk to him," said Scofield, disregarding the weapon, kneeling at Winthrop's feet. Stanley glanced at the Shepherd Boy; Bray could see Guiderone nod consent. "Mr Ambassador?"

"Brandon . . ." Winthrop's voice was weak, his tired eyes sad. "I'm afraid I wasn't much help. They told the President I was ill. There are no soldiers outside, no command post, no one waiting for you to strike a match and drive to the gate. I failed you."

"The envelope?"

"Bergeron thinks I have it; he knows Stanley, you see. He took the next plane back to Boston. I'm sorry, Brandon. I'm so very, very sorry. About so many things." The old man glanced up at the ex-marine he had befriended for so many years, then back at Scofield. "Do you know what they've done? My *God*, do you know what they've *done*?"

"They haven't done it yet," said Bray quietly.

"Next January they'll have the White House! The administration will be *their* administration."

"That won't happen."

"It *will* happen!" shouted Guiderone in his high-pitched voice. "And the world will be a better place. *Everywhere!* The period of violence will stop – a thousand years of productive tranquillity will take its place."

"A *thousand years* . . . ?' Scofield got to his feet. "Another maniac said that once. Is it going to be your own personal thousand-year Reich?"

"Parallels are meaningless, labels irrelevant! There's no connection." The Shepherd Boy rose behind his desk, his eyes again on fire. "In our world, nations can keep their leaders, people their identities. But governments will be controlled by the *companies. Everywhere.* The values of the market-place will link the peoples of the world!"

Bray caught the word and it revolted him. "*Identities?* In your world there *are* no identities! We're numbers and symbols on computers! Circles and squares."

"We must forget degrees of self for the continuity of peace."

"Then we are *robots*!"

"But alive. Functioning!"

"How? Tell me *how*? 'You, there! you're not a person any more; you're a *factor*. You're X or Y or Z, and whatever you do is measured and stored on wheels of tape by experts trained to evaluate *factors*. Go on *factor*! Be productive or the experts will take your loaf of bread away . . . or the shiny new car!'" Scofield paused in a fever. "You're wrong, Guiderone. *So* wrong. Give me an imperfect place where I know who I am."

"Find it in the next world, Beowulf-Agate!" screamed the Shepherd Boy. "You'll be there soon enough!"

Bray felt the weight in his belt under his raincoat – the gun supplied by the dying Taleniekov. The visitor to Appleton Hall had been searched thoroughly for weapons, none found, yet one provided by his old enemy. The decision to make a final gesture was clinical; there was no hope after all. But before he tried to kill and was killed, he would see Guiderone's face when he told him. "You said before that I was a liar, but you have no idea how extensive my lies were. You think you have the X-rays, don't you?"

"We know we have them."

"So do others."

"Really?"

"Yes, really. Have you ever heard of an Alpha Twelve duplicating machine? It's one of the finest pieces of equipment ever designed. It's the only copier made that can take an X-ray negative and turn out a positive print. A print so defined it's acceptable as evidence in court of law. I separated the four top X-rays off both the master sheets from Andover, made copies, and sent them to five different men in Washington! You're finished, you're through! They'll see to it."

"And this has gone on long enough." Guiderone came around his desk. "We're in the middle of a conference and you've taken up enough time."

"I think you'd better listen!"

"And I think you should walk over to that curtain, and pull the cord. You will see our conference room, but those inside will not see you . . . I'm sure I don't have to explain the technology. You've been so anxious to meet the Council of the Matarese, do so now. Not all are in attendance tonight, and not all are equal, but there's a fair gathering. Help yourself. Please."

Bray crossed to the drapery, felt the cord, and pulled it downward. The curtains parted, showing a huge room with a long oval conference table around which were seated twenty-odd men. There were decanters of brandy in front of each place setting, along with pads, pencils and pitchers of water. The lighting came from crystal chandeliers, swelled by a yellowish glow from the far end of the room where a fire was blazing. It could have been the enormous dining hall of the Villa Matarese, described in such detail by a blind woman in the mountains above Porto Vecchio. Scofield nearly found himself looking for a balcony and a frightened girl of seventeen hiding in the shadows.

But his eyes were drawn to the forty-foot wall behind the table. Between two enormous tapestries linked at the top border, was a map of the world. A man with a pointer in his hand was addressing the others from a small platform; all eyes were on him.

The man was in the uniform of the United States Army. He was the Chairman of the Joint Chiefs of Staff.

"I see you recognize the general in front of the map." The Shepherd Boy's voice once more lived up to the blind woman's words: crueller than the wind. "His presence I believe explains the death of Anthony Blackburn. Perhaps I should introduce you to a few of the others, *in absentia* . . . In the centre of the table, directly below the platform is the Secretary of State, next to him the Soviet ambassador. Across from the ambassador is the director of the Central Intelligence Agency; he seems to be having a side conversation with the Soviet Commissar for Planning and Development, Moscow. One man you might be interested in is missing. He didn't belong, you see, but he telephoned the CIA after receiving a very strange telephone call routed through Lisbon. The President's chief adviser on foreign affairs. He's had an accident; his mail is being intercepted, the last X-rays are no doubt in our hands by now . . . Need I go on?" Guiderone started to pull the cord, shutting out the window.

Scofield put up his hand; the curtain arced before closing. He was not looking at the men at the table; the message was clear. He was looking at a guard stationed at a small recessed door to the right of the fireplace. The man stood at attention, his eyes forward. In his hand was a .30 calibre, magazine-loaded sub-machine gun.

Taleniekov had known about these betrayals at the highest levels. He had heard the words spoken by others as they had inserted the needles that further drained his life away.

His enemy had tried to give him his last chance to live. *His last chance.* What were the words?

Pazhar . . . vsyegda pazhar! Zazhiganiye pazhar!

When the explosions begin, fire will follow.

He was not sure what his enemy meant, but he knew it was the path he had to follow. They were the best there were. One trusted the only professional on earth that was one's equal.

And that meant exercising the control his equal would demand. No false moves now. Stanley stood by Winthrop's wheelchair, his gun levelled at Bray. If somehow he could turn, twist, get the weapon from under his raincoat . . . He looked down at Winthrop, his attention caught by the old man's eyes. Winthrop was trying to tell him something, just as Taleniekov had tried to tell him something. It was in the eyes; the old man kept shifting them to his right. That was it! Stanley was *by* the wheelchair now, not *behind it*. In tiny, imperceptible movements, Winthrop was edging his chair around; he was going to go after Stanley's gun! His eyes were telling him that. They were also telling him to *keep talking*.

Scofield glanced unobtrusively at his watch. There were six minutes left before the sequence of explosions began. He needed three for preparation; that left three minutes to take out Stanley and bring in another. One-hundred-and-eighty seconds. *Keep talking!*

He turned to the monster at his side. "Do you remember when you killed him? When you pulled the trigger that night at Villa Matarese?"

Guiderone stared at him. "It was not a moment to be forgotten. It was my destiny. So the whore of Villa Matarese is alive."

"Not any longer."

"No? That was not in the pages you sent to Winthrop. She was killed then?"

"By the legend. *Perro nostro circulo.*"

The old man nodded. "Words that long ago meant one thing, now something else entirely. They guard the grave still."

"They still fear it. That grave's going to kill them all one of these days."

"The warning of Guillaume de Matarese." Guiderone started back to his desk.

Keep talking. Winthrop was pressing the wheels of the chair, each press an inch.

"Warning or prophecy?" asked Bray quickly.

"They're often interchangeable, aren't they?" said the old man over his shoulder.

"They called you the Shepherd Boy."

Guiderone turned. "Yes, I know. It was only partially true. As a child I took my turn herding the flocks, but the occasions diminished. The priests demanded it; they had other plans for me."

"The priests?"

Winthrop moved again.

"I had astonished them. By the time I was seven years of age I knew and understood the catechism better than they did. By eight years I could read and write in Latin; before I was ten I could debate the most complex issues of theology and dogma. The priests saw me as the first Corsican to be sent to the Vatican, to achieve high office . . . perhaps the highest. I would bring great honour to their parishes. Those simple priests in the hills of Porto Vecchio perceived my genius before I did.

They spoke to the *padrone*, petitioning him to sponsor my studies . . . Guillaume de Matarese did so in ways far beyond their comprehension."

Forty seconds, Winthrop was within two feet of the gun. Keep talking!

"Matarese made his arrangements with Appleton then? Joshua Appleton the Second."

"America's industrial expansion was extraordinary. It was the logical place for a gifted young man with a fortune at his disposal."

"You were married? You had a son."

"I bought a vessel, the most perfectly formed female through which to bear children. The design was always there."

"Including the death of young Joshua Appleton?"

"An accident of war and destiny. The decision was a result of the Captain's own exploits, not part of the original design. It was, instead, an unparalleled opportunity to be seized upon. I think we've said enough."

Now! Winthrop lunged out of the chair, his hands gripping Stanley's gun, pulling it to him, every ounce of his strength clawing at the weapon, refusing to let it go.

It fired, as Bray pulled out his own gun, aiming it at the chauffeur. Winthrop's body arched in the air, his throat blown away. Scofield squeezed the trigger once; it was all he needed. Stanley fell.

"Stay away from that desk!" yelled Bray.

"You were *searched*! It's not possible. Where . . . ?"

"From a better man than any computer of yours could ever find!" said Scofield, looking briefly in anguish at the dead Robert Winthrop. "Just as he was."

"You'll never get out."

Bray sprang forward, grabbing Nicholas Guiderone by the throat, pushing him against the desk. "You're going to do what I tell you to do or I'll blow your eyes out!" He shoved the pistol up into the hollow of Guiderone's right eye.

"Do *not* kill me!" commanded the overlord of the Matarese. "The value of my life is too extraordinary! My work is not *finished*; it must be finished before I die!"

"You're everything in this world I hate, Shepherd Boy," said Scofield, jamming the gun in sharp cracks into the old man's skull. "I don't have to tell you the odds. Every second you go on living means you might get another. Do as I say. I'm going to press the button – the same button you pressed before. You're going to give the following order. Say it right or you won't ever say anything more. You tell whoever answers: 'Send in the guard from the conference room, the one with the submachine gun.' Have you got that?" He shoved Guiderone's head down over the console and pressed the button.

"Send the guard in from the conference room." The words were rushed, but the fear was not audible. "The one with the sub-machine gun."

Scofield viced his left arm around Guiderone's neck, dragged him over to the curtains, and pulled them open. Through the glass, across the conference room, a man could be seen approaching the guard. The guard nodded, angled his weapon to the floor, and walked rapidly across the room towards the archway exit.

"*Perro nostro circulo*," whispered Bray. He yanked up with all his strength, the vice around Guiderone's throat clamping shut, crushing bone and cartilage. There was a snap, an expulsion of breath. The old man's eyes protruded from their sockets, his neck broken. The Shepherd Boy was dead.

Scofield ran across the room to the door, pressing his back against the wall by the hinges. The door opened; he saw the angled weapon first, the figure of the guard a split second later. Bray kicked the door closed, both his hands surging forward towards the man's throat.

The harassed desk sergeant at the precinct on Boylston Street looked down at the thin, prim-looking woman whose mouth was pursed, eyes narrowed in disapproval. He held the envelope in his hands.

"*OK*, lady, you've delivered it and I've got it. OK? The phones are a little busy tonight, OK? I'll get to it soon's I can, OK?"

"Not '*OK*', Sergeant . . . Witkowski," said the woman, reading the name on the desk sign. "The citizens of Boston will not stand idly by while their rights are being abridged by criminal elements. We are rising up in justifiable outrage, and our cries have not gone unheeded. You are being watched, Sergeant! There are those who understand our distress and they are testing you. I'd advise you not to be so cavalier . . ."

"*OK, OK.*" The sergeant tore open the envelope, and pulled out a sheet of yellow paper. He unfolded it and read the words printed in large blue letters. "Jesus Christ on a fuckin' *raft!*" he said quietly, his eyes suddenly widening in astonishment. He looked down at the disapproving woman as if he were seeing her for the first time. As he stared, he reached over to a button on the desk; he pressed it repeatedly.

"Sergeant, I strenuously object to your profanity . . ."

Above every visible door in the precinct house, red lights began flashing on and off; from deep within, the sound of an alarm bell echoed off the walls of unseen rooms and corridors. In seconds, doors began opening and helmeted men came out, hastily donned two-inch shields of canvas and steel strapped over their chests.

"*Grab her!*" shouted the sergeant. "Pin her arms! Throw her into the bomb room!"

Seven police officers converged on the woman. A precinct lieutenant came running out of his office. "What the hell is it, Sergeant?"

"Look at this!"

The lieutenant read the words on the yellow paper. "Oh, my *God!*"

To the Fascist Pigs of Boston, Protectors
of the Alabaster Bride.
Death to the Economic Tyrants! Death to Appleton Hall!
As Pigs Read This Our Bombs Will Do What
Our Pleas Cannot. Our Suicide Brigades Are
Positioned To Kill All Who Flee The Righteous
Holocaust. Death To Appleton Hill!
Signed:
The Third World Army of Liberation and Justice

The lieutenant issued his instructions. "Guiderone's got guards all around that place; reach the house! Then call Brookline, tell them what's going on, and raise every patrol car we've got in the vicinity of Jamaica Way; send them over." The officer paused, peering at the yellow page with the precise blue letters printed on it, then added harshly, "*Goddamn it!* Get Central Headquarters on the line. I want their best SWAT team dispatched to Appleton Hill." He started back to his office, pausing again to look in disgust at the woman being propelled through a door, arms pulled, stretched away from her sides, prodded by men with padded shields and helmets. "Third World Army of Liberation of Justice! Freaked-out bastards! *Book her*," he roared.

Scofield dragged the guard's body across the room, concealing it behind Guiderone's desk. He raced over to the dead Shepherd Boy, and for the briefest of moments, just stared at the arrogant face. If it were possible to kill beyond killing, Bray would do so now. He pulled Guiderone to the far corner, throwing his body in a crumpled heap. He then stopped at Winthrop's corpse, wishing there was time to somehow say goodbye. There was not.

He grabbed the guard's sub-machine gun off the floor and ran over to the curtains. He pulled them open and looked at his watch. Fifty seconds to go until the explosions would begin. He checked the weapon in his hands; all clips were full. He looked through the window into the conference room, seeing what he had not seen before because the man had not been there before.

The senator had arrived. All eyes were now on him, the magnetic presence mesmerizing the entire room; the easy grace, the worn, still-handsome face giving each man his attention, if only for an instant – telling that man he was special. And each man was seduced by the raw power of power; this was the next President of the United States and he was one of *them*.

For the first time in all the years Scofield had seen that face, he saw what a destroyed, alcoholic mother saw: it was a mask. A brilliantly conceived, ingeniously programmed mask . . . and mind.

Twelve seconds.

There was a burst of static from a speaker on the desk. A voice erupted. "Mr Guiderone, we must interrupt! We've had calls from the Boston and Brookline police! There are reports of an armed attack on Appleton Hall. Men calling themselves the Third World Army of Liberation and Justice. We have no such organization on any list, sir. Our patrols are alerted. The police want everyone to stay."

Two seconds.

The news had been relayed to the conference room. Men leaped up from chairs, gathering papers. Their own particular panic was breaking out: how could the presence of such men be explained? Who would explain it?

One second.

Bray heard the first explosion beyond the walls of Appleton Hall. It was in the distance, far down the hill, but unmistakable. The sound of rapid-fire weapons followed; men were shooting at the source of the first explosions.

Inside the conference room, the panic mounted. The *consiglieri* of the Matarese were rushing around, a single guard at the archway exit poised with his sub-machine gun levelled through the arch. Suddenly Scofield realized what the powerful men were doing: they were throwing papers and pads and maps into the fire at the end of the room.

It was his moment; the guard would be first, but merely the first.

Bray smashed the window with the barrel of his automatic weapon and opened fire. The guard span as the bullets caught him. His sub-machine gun was on rapid repeat; the death-pressure of his trigger finger caused the gun to erupt wildly, the spray of 30 calibre shells flying out of the ejector, the bullets fanning out in all directions, walls and chandeliers and men bursting, exploding, collapsing under their impacts. Screams of death and shrieks of horror filled the room.

Scofield knew his targets, his eye rehearsed over a lifetime of violence. He smashed the jagged fragments of glass and raised the weapon to his shoulder. He squeezed the trigger in rapidly defined, reasonably aimed sequences. One step – one death – at a time.

The bursts of gunfire exploded through the window frame. The general fell, the pointer in his hand lacerating his face as he collapsed. The Secretary of State cowered at the side of the table; Scofield blew his head off. The director of the Central Intelligence Agency raced his counterpart from the National Security Council towards the arch, leaping over bodies in their hysteria. Bray caught them both. The director's throat was a mass of blood; the NSC chairman raised his hands to a forehead that was no longer there.

Where was he? He of all men had to be found!

There he was!

The senator was crouched below the conference table in front of the roaring fire. Scofield took the aim of his life and squeezed the trigger. The spray of bullets exploded the wood, some *had* to penetrate. They did! The senator fell back, then rose to his feet. Bray fired another burst; the senator spun into the fireplace, then sprang back out, fire and blood covering his body. He raced blindly, forward, then to his left, grabbing the tapestry on the wall as he fell.

The tapestry caught fire; the senator in his collapse of death pulled it off the wall. The huge cloth arced down in flames over the conference table. The fire spread, flames leaping to every corner of the enormous room.

Fire!

After the explosions. *Fire!*

Taleniekov.

Scofield ran from the window. He had done what he had to do; it was the moment to do what he so desperately *wanted* to do. If it were possible; if there was any hope at *all*. He stopped in front of the door, checking the remaining ammunition; he had conserved it well. The third and fourth charges had detonated at the base of the hill. The fifth and sixth were timed to explode within seconds of each other.

The fifth came; he yanked the door back, lunging through, weapon levelled. He heard the sixth explosion. Two guards at the cathedral-like entrance doors sprang from the outside path into view. Bray fired two bursts; the guards of the Matarese fell.

He raced to the door of the room that held Antonia and Taleniekov. It was locked.

"Stand way back! It's me!" He fired five rounds into the wood around the lock casing; it splintered. He kicked the heavy door open; it crashed back against the wall. He ran in.

Taleniekov was out of the chair kneeling by the couch at the far end of the room, Toni beside him. Both were working furiously, tearing pillows out of slipcovers. Tearing . . . *pillows*? What were they *doing*? Antonia looked up and shouted.

"Quickly! Help us."

"What?" He raced over.

"*Pazhar!*" The Russian had to force the voice; it emerged now as a whispered roar.

Six pillows were free of their cases. Toni got to her feet, grabbing and throwing five of the pillows around the room.

"Now!" said Taleniekov, handing her the matches he had taken from Bray earlier. She ran to the farthest pillow, struck a match and held it to the soft fabric. It caught fire instantly. The Russian held out his hand for Scofield. "Help me . . . get *up*!"

Bray pulled him off the floor; Taleniekov clutched the last pillow to his chest. The seventh explosion was heard in the distance; staccato gunfire followed, piercing the screams of hysteria from within the house.

"Come on!" yelled Scofield, putting his arm around the Russian's waist. He looked over at Toni; she had set fire to the fourth pillow. Flames and smoke were filling the room. "Come on! We're getting out!"

"No!" whispered Taleniekov. "You! She! Get me to the *door*." The Russian held the pillow and lurched forward.

The great hall of the house was dense with smoke, flames from the inner conference room surging beneath doors and through archways, as men raced up the staircase to windows, vantage points – high ground – to aim their weapons at invaders.

A guard spotted them; he raised his sub-machine gun.

Scofield fired first; the man arched backwards, blown off his feet.

"Listen to me!" gasped Taleniekov. "Always *pazhar*! With you it is sequence, with me it is fire!" He held up the soft pillow. "Light this! I will have the race of my life!"

"Don't be a fool." Bray tried to take the pillow away; the Russian would not permit it.

"*Nyet!*" Taleniekov stared at Scofield; a final plea was in his eyes. "If I could, I would not care to live like this. Neither would you. Do this for me, Beowulf. I would do it for you."

Bray returned the Russian's look. "We've worked together," he said simply. "I'm proud of that."

"We were the best there were." Taleniekov smiled and raised his hand to Scofield's cheek. "Now, my friend. Do what I would do for you."

Bray nodded and turned to Antonia; there were tears in her eyes. He took the book of matches from her hand, struck one and held it beneath the pillow.

The flames leapt up. The Russian spun in place, clutching the fire to his chest. And with the roar of a wounded animal suddenly set free from the jaws of a lethal trap, Taleniekov lunged, propelling himself into a limping run, careening off the walls and chairs, pressing the flaming pillow and himself into everything he touched – and everything he touched caught fire. Two guards raced down the staircase, seeing the three of them; before they or Scofield could fire, the Russian was on them, hurling the flames and himself at them, throwing the fire into their faces.

"*Skaryei!*" screamed Taleniekov. "Run, Beowulf!" A burst of gunfire came upon the command, smothered by the flaming body of the Serpent; he fell, pulling both the Matarese guards with him down the staircase.

Bray grabbed Antonia by the arm and ran out to the stone path bordered by the lines of heavy, black chain. They raced through the opening in the wall into the concrete parking area; beams of floodlights shot down from the roof at Appleton Hall; men were at windows, weapons in their hands.

The eighth explosion came from below, at the base of the hill, the charge so filled with heat that the surrounding foliage burst into flames. Men at the windows smashed panes of glass and fired at the dancing light. Scofield saw that three of the other detonations had caused small brush fires. They were gifts he was grateful for; he and Taleniekov were both right. Sequence and fire, fire and sequence. Each was a diversion that could save one's life. There were no guarantees – ever – but there *was* hope.

The rented car was parked at the side of the wall about fifty yards to their right. It was in shadows, an isolated vehicle that was meant to stay there. Bray pulled Toni against the wall.

"The car over there. It's mine; it's our chance."

"They'll shoot at us!"

"The odds are better than running. There are patrols up and down the hill. On foot, they'd cut us down."

They raced along the wall. The ninth charge of dynamite lit up the sky at the north-west base of the hill. Automatic guns and single-shot weapons erupted. Suddenly, from within the growing fires of Appleton Hall, a massive explosion blew out a section of the front wall. Men fell from windows, fragments of stone and steel burst into the night as half the floodlights disappeared. Scofield understood. The seat of the Matarese had its arsenals; the fires had found one.

"Let's *go!*" he yelled, pushing Antonia towards the car. She threw herself inside as he ran around the back towards the driver's side.

The concrete exploded all around him; from somewhere on the remaining roof a man with a sub-machine gun had spotted them.

There *were* men; they had weapons and they were using them. The glass of the windshield shattered as a fusillade of bullets came from the open garage doors.

Antonia had rolled down the window; she now pushed the gun through the frame, held the trigger against its rim, and the explosions once again vibrated through the racing automobile. Bodies lurched as screams and the shattering of glass and the screeching ricochets of bullets filled the cavernous garage of the carriage house. The last clip of ammunition was exhausted as Scofield, his face cut from the windshield fragments, came to the final two hundred yards towards the gates of Appleton Hall. There were men below, armed men, uniformed men, but they were not soldiers of the Matarese. Bray thrust his hand down to the knob of the light switch and repeatedly pushed it in and pulled it out. The headlights flickered on and off – in sequence, *always* sequence. A sequence was a signal of a thousand possibilities; in this case it was survival.

The gates had been forced open; he slammed his foot on the brake. The automobile skidded to a stop, tyres screeching.

The police converged. Then more police; black-suited men in paramilitary gear, men trained for a specialized warfare, the battlegrounds defined by momentary bursts of armed fanaticism. Their commander approached the car.

"Take it *easy*," he said to Bray. "You're out. Who are you?"

"Vickery. B. A. Vickery. I had business with Nicholas Guiderone. As you say . . . we got out! When that hell broke loose, I grabbed my wife and we hid in a closet. They smashed into the house, in teams, I think. Our car was outside. It was the only chance we had."

"Now calmly, Mr Vickery, but quickly. What's happening up there?"

The tenth charge detonated from the other side of the hill, but its light was the flames that were spreading across the crest of the hill.

Appleton Hall was being consumed by fire, the explosions more frequent now as more arsenals were opened, more ignited. The Shepherd Boy was fulfilling his destiny. He had found his Villa Matarese, and like his *padrone* seventy years ago, his remains would perish in its skeleton.

"What's *happening*, Mr Vickery?"

"They're killers. They've killed everyone inside; they'll kill every one of you they can. You won't take them alive."

"Then we'll take them *dead*," said the commander, his voice filled with emotion. "They've come over here now, they've *really* come over. Italy, Germany, Mexico . . . Lebanon, Israel, Buenos Aires. Whatever made us think we were immune? . . . Pull your car out of here, Mr Vickery. Head down the road about a quarter of a mile. There are ambulances down there. We'll get your statements later."

"Yes, sir," said Scofield, starting the engine.

They passed the ambulances at the base of Appleton Drive and turned left into the road for Boston. Soon they would cross the Longfellow Bridge into Cambridge. There was a locker on the MBTA subway platform in Harvard Square; in that locker was his attaché case.

They were free. The Serpent had died at Appleton Hall, but they were free, their freedom his gift.

Beowulf Agate had disappeared at last.

Epilogue

Men and women were taken into custody swiftly, quietly, no charges processed through the courts, for their crimes were beyond the sanity of the courts, beyond the tolerance of the nation. Of all nations. Each dealt with the Matarese in its own way. Where it could find them.

Heads of state across the world conferred by telephone, the normal interpreters replaced by ranking government personnel fluent in the necessary languages. The leaders readily professed astonishment and shock, tacitly acknowledging both the inadequacy and the infiltration of their intelligence communities. They tested one another with subtle shades of accusation, knowing the attempts were futile; they were not idiots. They probed for vulnerabilities; they all had them. And with every word, each hoped for the reaction the other wanted to hear. Finally – tacitly – the single conclusion was universal. It was the only one that made sense in these insane times.

Silence.

Each to be responsible for his own deception, none to implicate the others beyond the normal levels of suspicion and hostility. For to admit the massive global conspiracy was to admit the existence of the fundamental proposition: governments were obsolete.

None cared for the theory to be analysed or given wide exposure; the analysis was never deep enough, the alternative too attractive in its simplicity.

They were not idiots. They were afraid.

In Washington, rapid decisions were made secretly by a handful of men.

Senator Joshua Appleton IV died as he had come into being. Burned to death in an automobile accident on a dark highway at night. There was a state funeral, the casket mounted in splendour in the Rotunda, where another vigil took place. The words intoned were befitting a man everyone knew would have occupied the White House but for the tragedy that had cut him down . . . on a dark highway at night.

A government-owned Lockheed Tristar was sacrificed in the Colorado Mountains north of Poudre Canyon, a dual engine malfunction causing the aircraft to lose altitude while crossing that dangerous range. The pilot and crew were mourned, full pensions granted their families regardless of their length of service. But the true mourning was accompanied by a tragic lesson never to be forgotten. For it was revealed that on board the plane were three of the nation's most distinguished men, killed in the service of their country while on an inspection tour of military installations relating to counter-strike preparedness. The Chairman of the Joint Chiefs of Staff had requested his counterparts at the Central Intelligence Agency and the National Security Council to accompany him on the tour. Along with a message of presidential sorrow, an executive order was issued from the Oval Office. Never again were such high-ranking government personnel permitted to fly together in a single aircraft; the nation could not sustain such a grievous loss again.

As the weeks went by upper-echelon employees of the State Department as well as numerous reporters who covered its day-to-day operations were gradually aware of an oddity. The Secretary of State had not been in evidence for a very long time. There was a growing concern as schedules were altered, trips abandoned, conferences postponed or cancelled. Rumours spread throughout the capital, some quarters insisting the secretary was involved with prolonged, secret negotiations in Peking, while others claimed he was in Moscow, close to a breakthrough with SALT. Then the rumours took on less attractive colorations; something was wrong; an explanation was required.

The President gave it on a warm afternoon in spring. He went on radio and television from a medical retreat in Moorefield, West Virginia, the mountains of the Shenandoah behind him in the distance.

"In this year of tragedy, it is my burden to bring you further sorrow. I have just said goodbye to a dear friend. A great and courageous man who understood the delicate balance required in our negotiations with our adversaries, who would not permit those adversaries to learn of his rapidly ebbing life. That extraordinary life ended only hours ago, succumbing at last to the ravages of disease. I have today ordered the flags of the capital . . ."

And so it went. All over the world.

The President sat back in his chair as Under-Secretary Daniel Congdon walked into the Oval Office. The commander-in-chief did not like Congdon; there was a ferret-like quality about him, his overly-sincere eyes concealing a dreadful ambition. But the man did his job well and that was all that mattered. Especially now, especially this job.

"What's the resolution?"

"As expected, Mr President. Beowulf Agate rarely did the normal thing."

"He didn't lead much of a normal life, did he? I mean you people didn't expect him to, did you?"

"No, sir. He was . . ."

"Tell me, Congdon," interrupted the President. "Did you really try to have him killed?"

"It was mandatory execution, sir. We considered him beyond salvage, working with the enemy, dangerous to our men everywhere. To a degree, I still believe that."

"You'd better. He is. So that's why he insisted on negotiating through you. I'd advise you – no, I *order* you – to push such mandatory actions out of your mind. Is that understood?"

"Yes, Mr President."

"I hope so. Because if it isn't, I might have to issue a mandatory sentence of my own. Now that I know how it's done."

"Understood, sir."

"Good. The resolution?"

"Beyond the initial demand, Scofield wants nothing further to do with us."

"But you know where he is."

"Yes, sir. The Caribbean. However, we don't know where the documents are."

"Don't bother to look for them; he's better than you. And leave him alone; never give him the slightest reason to think you have any interest in him. Because if you do, those documents will surface in a hundred different places at once. This government – this nation – cannot handle the repercussions. Not now. There are still too many questions, too many answers we don't have, too many men we can't find. Perhaps in a few years, but not now."

"I accept that judgement, Mr President."

"You damn well better. What did the resolution cost us and where is it buried?"

"One hundred and seventy-six thousand, four hundred and twelve dollars and eighteen cents. It was attached to a cost over-run for naval training equipment, the payment made by a CIA proprietary directly to the shipyard in Mystic, Connecticut."

The President looked out the window at the White House lawn; the blossoms on the cherry trees were dying, curling up and withering away. "He could have asked for the sky and we would have given it to him; he could have taken us for millions. Instead, all he wants is a boat and to be left alone."

March 198 –

The sixty-eight-foot charter yawl, *Serpent*, its mainsail luffing in the island breezes, glided into its slip, the woman jumping on to the pier, rope in hand. She looped it around the forward post, securing the bow. At the stern, the bearded skipper tied off the wheel, stepped up on the gunwhale and over to the dock, swinging the aft rope around the nearest post, pulling it taut, knotting it when all slack had vanished.

At midships, a pleasant-looking, middle-aged couple stepped cautiously on to the pier. It was obvious they had said their goodbyes, and those goodbyes had been just a little bit painful.

"Well, vacation's over," said the man, sighing, holding his wife's arm. "We'll be back next year, Captain Vickery. You're the best charter in the islands. And thank you again, Mrs Vickery. As always, the galley was terrific."

The couple walked up the dock.

"I'll take down the sails and stow the gear while you check on the supplies, OK?" said Scofield.

"All right, darling. We've got ten days before the couple from New Orleans arrive."

"Let's take a sail," said the captain, smiling, jumping back on board the *Serpent*.

An hour and twenty minutes passed; the supplies were loaded, the weather bulletins logged and the coastal charts studied. The *Serpent* was ready for departure.

"Let's get a drink," Bray said, taking Toni's hand, walking up the sandy path into the hot St Kitts' street. Across the way was a café, a shack with ancient wicker tables and chairs and a bar that had not changed in thirty years. It was a gathering place for charter boat skippers and their crews.

Antonia sat down, greeting several friends, laughing with her eyes and spontaneous voice; she was liked by the rough, capable runaways of the Caribbean. She was a lady and they knew it. Scofield watched her from the bar as he ordered their drinks, remembering another waterfront café in Corsica. It was only a few years ago – another lifetime, really – but she had not changed. There was still the easy grace, the sense of presence and gentle, open humour. She was liked because she was immensely likable; it was as simple as that.

He carried their drinks to the table and sat down. Antonia had reached over to an adjacent table, borrowing a week-old Barbados newspaper. An article had caught her attention.

"Darling, look at this," she said, turning the paper and pushing it towards him, her index finger marking the column.

TRANS-COMMUNICATIONS' LEGAL BATTLES OVER CONGLOMERATE REORGANIZES

Wash., D.C. – Combined Wire Services: After several years of ownership litigation in the federal courts, the way has been cleared for the executors of the Nicholas Guiderone estate to press ahead with re-organization plans which include significant mergers with European companies. It will be recalled that following the terrorist assault on the Guiderone mansion in Brookline, Massachusetts, when Guiderone and others holding large blocks of Trans-Comm stock were massacred, the conglomerate's line of ownership was thrown into a legal maze. It has been no secret that the Justice Department has been supportive of the executors, as, indeed, has been the Department of State. The feeling has been that, while the multi-national corporation has continued functioning, its lack of expansion due to unclear leadership has caused American prestige to suffer in the international market-place.

The President, upon learning of the final legal resolutions, sent the following wire to the executors:

"It seems fitting to me that during the week that marks my first year in office, the obstructions have been removed and, once again, a great American institution is in a position to export and expand American knowhow and technology across the world, joining the other great companies to give us a better world. I congratulate you."

Bray shoved the paper aside. "The subtlety gets less and less, doesn't it?"

They tacked into the wind out of Basseterre, the coast of St Kitts receding behind them. Antonia pulled the jib taut, tied off the sheet and climbed back to the wheel. She sat beside Scofield, running her fingers over the short, clipped beard that was more grey than dark. "Where are we going, darling?" she asked.

"I don't know," said Bray, meaning it. "With the wind for a while, if it's all right with you."

"It's all right with me." She leaned back, looking at his face, so pensive, so lost in thought. "What's going to happen?"

"It's happened. The mergers have taken over the earth," he answered, smiling. "Guiderone was right; nobody can stop it. Maybe nobody should. Let them have their day in the sun. It doesn't make any difference what I think. They'll leave me alone – leave us alone. They're still afraid."

"Of what?"

"Of people. Just people. Trim the jib, will you please? We're spilling too much. We can make better time."

"To where?"

"Damned if I know. Only that I want to be there."

The Parsifal Mosaic

For Dolores and Charles Ryducha.
Two of the finest people I've ever known.
From a grateful brother.

<u>Na Zdrowie!</u>

Book One

1

The cold rays of the moon streaked down from the night sky, bouncing off the rolling surf, which burst into suspended sprays of white where isolated waves crashed into the rocks of the shoreline. This stretch of beach between the towering boulders of the Costa Brava was the execution ground. It had to be.

He could see her now. And hear her through the sounds of the sea and the breaking surf. She was running wildly, screaming hysterically: *"Pro Boha Živetto! Proc! Co to Délás! Prestan! Proc! Proc!"*

Her blonde hair was caught in the moonlight, her racing silhouette given substance by the beam of a powerful light fifty yards behind her. She fell; the gap closed and a staccato burst of gunfire abruptly, insolently, split the night air, bullets exploding the sand and the wild grass all around her. She would be dead in a matter of seconds.

His love would be gone.

They were high on the hill overlooking the Moldau, the boats on the river ploughing the waters north and south, their wakes creating furrows. The curling smoke from the factories below diffused in the bright afternoon sky, obscuring the mountains in the distance; and Michael watched, wondering whether the wind above Prague would blow the smoke away so that he could see the mountains again. His head was on Jenna's lap, his long legs stretched out, touching the wicker basket she had packed with sandwiches and chilled wine. She sat on the grass, her back against the smooth bark of a birch tree, stroking his hair; then her fingers circled his face, gently outlining his lips and cheekbones.

"Mikhail, my darling, I was thinking. Those tweed jackets and dark trousers you wear, and that very proper English which must come from your very proper university, they will never remove the Havlicek from Havelock."

"I don't think they were meant to. One's a uniform of sorts, and the other you kind of learn in self-defence." He smiled, touching her hand. "Besides, that university was a long time ago."

"So much was a long time ago, wasn't it? Right down there."

"It happened."

"You were there, my poor darling."

"It's history. I survived."

"Many did not."

The blonde woman rose, spinning in the sand, pulling at the wild grass, plunging to her right, for several seconds eluding the beam of light. She headed towards the dirt road above the beach, staying in darkness, crouching, lunging, using the cover of night and the patches of tall grass to conceal her body.

It won't do her any good, thought the tall man in the black sweater at his post between two trees above the road, above the terrible violence that was taking place below. He had looked down at her once before, not so very long ago. She had not been panicked then; she had been magnificent.

In the dark office he folded the curtain back slowly, carefully, his back pressed against the wall, his face inching towards the window. He could see her crossing the floodlit courtyard below, the tattoo of her high heels on the cobblestones echoing martially between the surrounding buildings. The guards were recessed in shadows — rigid marionettes in their Soviet style uniforms. Heads turned, directing appreciative glances at the figure striding confidently towards the iron gate in the centre of the iron fence which enclosed the stone compound, the core of Prague's secret police. The thoughts behind the glances were clear: this was no mere secretary working overtime, this was a privileged kurva *who took dictation on a commissar's couch till all hours of the night.* Natsztrzency chlopak!

But others, too, were watching — from other darkened windows. One break in her confident stride, one instant of hesitation, and a phone would be picked up, detention orders issued to the gate. Embarrassments, of course, were to be avoided where commissars were concerned, but not if there appeared to be substance behind suspicions. Everything was appearance.

There was no break, no hesitation. She was carrying it off . . . carrying it out! They had done it! Suddenly he felt a jolt of pain in his chest, and he knew what it was: fear. Pure, raw, sickening fear. He was remembering memories within memories. As he watched her, his mind went back to a city of rubble, to the terrible sounds of mass execution. Lidice. And a child — one of many children scurrying through billowing grey, smoking debris, carrying messages, with pockets full of plastic explosives. One break, one hesitation then . . . history.

She reached the gate. An obsequious guard was permitted to leer. She was magnificent. God, he loved her!

She had reached the shoulder of the road, legs and arms working furiously, digging into the sand and dirt, clawing for survival. With no wild grass to conceal her, the beam of light would find her, and the end would come quickly.

He watched, suspending emotion, erasing pain, a human litmus paper accepting impressions without comment. He had to . . . professionally. He had learned the truth; the stretch of beach on the Costa Brava was confirmation of her guilt, proof of her crimes. The hysterical woman below was a killer, an agent for the infamous *Voennaya Kontr Razvedka*, the savage branch of the Soviet KGB that spawned terrorism everywhere. That was the undeniable truth. He had seen it all, talked to Washington from Madrid. The rendezvous that night had been ordered by Moscow; VKR Field Officer Jenna Karras was to deliver a schedule of assassination to a faction of the Baader-Meinhof at an isolated beach, called Montebello, north of the town of Blanes. That was the truth.

The truth bound him to another truth, an obligation of his profession. Those who betrayed the living and brokered death had to die. No matter who, no matter . . . Michael Havelock had made the decision, and it was irrevocable. He had set the last phase of the trap himself, for the death of the woman who briefly had given him more happiness than any other person on earth. His love was a killer; to permit her to live would mean the killing of hundreds, perhaps thousands. Irrevocable.

What Moscow did not know was that Langley had broken the VKR codes. He himself had sent the last transmission to a boat half a mile off the Costa Brava shoreline. *KGB confirmation. Officer contact compromised by US Intelligence. Schedules false. Eliminate.* The codes were virtually unbreakable; elimination was guaranteed.

She was rising now! It was going to *happen*! The woman about to die *was* his love. They had held each other and there had been quiet talk of a lifetime together, of children, of peace and the splendid comfort of being one . . . together. Once he had believed it all but it was not to be.

They were in bed, her head on his chest, her soft blonde hair falling across her face. He brushed it aside, lifting up the strands that concealed her eyes, and laughed.

"You're hiding," he said.

"It seems we're always hiding." She smiled sadly. "Except when we wish to be seen by people who should see us. We do nothing that we simply want to. Everything is calculated, Mikhail. Regimented. We live in a movable prison."

"It hasn't been that long, and it won't last for ever."

"I suppose not. One day they'll find they don't need us, don't want us any longer, perhaps. Will they let us go, do you think? Or will we disappear?"

"Washington's not Prague. Or Moscow. We'll walk out of our movable prison, me with a gold watch, you with some kind of silent decoration with your papers."

"Are you sure? We know a great deal. Too much, perhaps."

"Our protection lies in what we do know. What I know. They'll always wonder: Did he write it down somewhere? Take care, watch him, be good to him . . . It's not unusual, really. We'll walk out."

"Always protection," she said, tracing his eyebrows. "You never forget, do you? The early days, the terrible days."

"History. I've forgotten."

"What will we do?"

"Live. I love you."

"Do you think we'll have children? Watch them going off to school; hold them, scold them. Go to hockey ball games."

"Football . . . or baseball. Not hockey ball. Yes, I hope so."

"What will you do, Mikhail?"

"Teach, I suppose. At a college somewhere. I've a couple of starched degrees that say I'm qualified. We'll be happy, I know that. I'm counting on it."

"What will you teach?"

He looked at her, touching her face, then his eyes wandered up to the shabby ceiling in the run-down hotel room. "History," he said. And then he reached for her, taking her in his arms.

The beam of light swung across the darkness. It caught her, a bird on fire, trying to rise, trapped by the light that was her darkness. The gunshots followed – terrorists' gunfire for a terrorist. The woman arched backwards, the first bullets penetrating the base of her spine, her blonde hair cascading behind her. Three shots then came separately, with finality, a marksman's eye delivering a marksman's score; they entered the back of her neck and her skull, propelling her forward over the mound of dirt and sand, her fingers clawing the earth, her blood-streaked face mercifully concealed. A final spasm, and all movement stopped.

His love was dead – for some part of love was a part of whatever they were. He had done what he had to do, just as she had done the same. Each was right, each wrong, ultimately so terribly wrong. He closed his eyes, feeling the unwanted dampness.

What will you do, Mikhail?

Teach, I suppose. At a college somewhere.

What will you teach?

History.

It was all history now. Remembrances of things too painful. Let it be cold history, as the early days were history. They cannot be a part of me any longer. She cannot be a part of me, if she ever was, even in her pretence. Yet I will keep a promise, not to her now, but to myself. I am finished. I shall disappear into another life, a new life. I shall go somewhere, teach somewhere. Illuminate the lessons of futility.

He heard the voices and opened his eyes. Below, the Baader-Meinhof killers had reached the condemned woman, sprawled in death, clutching the ground that was her execution place . . . geopolitically preordained. Had she really been so magnificent a liar? Yes, she had been, for he had seen the truth. Even in her eyes, he had seen it.

The two executioners bent down to grab the corpse and drag it away, to consign her once-graceful body to fire or the deep. He would not interfere; the evidence would have to be reflected upon later when the trap was revealed, another lesson taught. Futility . . . geopolitically required.

A gust of wind suddenly whipped across the open beach; the killers braced themselves, their feet slipping in the sand. One of them raised a hand in an unsuccessful attempt to keep on his visored fishing cap; it blew away, rolling towards the dune that formed the shoulder of the road. He released his hold on the corpse and ran after it. Havelock watched as he came closer. There was something about him . . . about the face? No, it was the hair, seen clearly in the moonlight. It was wavy and dark, but not completely dark; there was a streak of white above his forehead, a sudden intrusion that could not be missed. He had seen that head of hair, seen that face somewhere before. But where? There were so many memories. Files analysed, photographs studied . . . contacts, sources, enemies. Where was this man from? *KGB?* The dreaded *Voennaya?* A splinter faction paid by Moscow when not drawing contingency funds from a CIA station chief in Lisbon?

It did not matter. The deadly puppets and the vulnerable pawns no longer concerned Michael Havelock . . . nor Mikhail Havlicek, for that matter. He would route a cable to Washington through the embassy in Madrid in the morning. He was finished, he had nothing more to give. Whatever his superiors wanted in the way of debriefing he would permit. Even going to a clinic; he simply did not care. But they would have no more of his life.

That was history. It had ended on an isolated beach called Montebello on the Costa Brava.

2

Time was the true narcotic for pain. Either the pain disappeared when it ran its course or a person learned to live with it. Havelock understood this, knowing that at this moment something of both applied. The pain had not disappeared, but there was less of it; there were periods when the memories were dulled, the scar tissue sensitive only when prodded. And travelling helped; he had forgotten what it was like to cope with the complexities facing the tourist.

"If you'll note, sir, it's printed here on your ticket. 'Subject to change without notice'."

"Where?"

"Down here."

"I can't read it."

"I can."

"You've memorized it."

"I'm familiar with it, sir."

And the immigration lines. Followed by customs inspections. The intolerable preceded by the impossible; men and women who countered their own boredom by slamming rubber stamps and savagely attacking defenceless zips planned for planned obsolescence.

There was no question about it, he was spoiled. His previous life had its difficulties and its risks, but they had not included the perils that confront the traveller at every turn. In his other life, on the other hand, whenever he got to where he was going, there was the movable prison. No, not exactly. There were appointments to keep, sources to contact, informers to pay. Too often at night, in shadows, far away from seeing or being seen. Now there was none of that. There hadn't been for nearly eight weeks. He walked in daylight, as he was walking now down the Damrak in Amsterdam towards the American Express office. He wondered whether the cable would be there. If it was, it would signify the beginning of something. A concrete beginning.

Employment. A job. Strange how the unexpected was so often connected to the routine. It had been three months since that night on the Costa Brava, two months and five days since the end of his debriefing and formal separation from the government. He had gone up to Washington from the clinic in Virginia where he had spent twelve days under therapy. (Whatever they had expected to find wasn't there; he could have told them that. He didn't care any more; couldn't they understand?) He had emerged from the doors of the State Department at four o'clock in the afternoon a free man ... also an unemployed, unpensioned citizen with resources hardly of a magnitude to be considered an annuity. It had occurred to him as he stood there on the pavement that some time in the future a job had to be found, a job where he could illuminate the lessons of ... the lessons. But not for a while; for a while he would do the minimum required of a functioning human being.

He would travel, revisit all those places he had never really visited ... in the sunlight. He would read ... reread, actually ... not codes and schedules and dossiers, but all those books he had not read since university. If he was going to illuminate anything for anybody, he had to relearn so much that he had forgotten.

But if there was one thing on his mind at four o'clock that afternoon, it was a fine dinner. After twelve days' treatment, with various chemicals and a restricted diet, he had ached at the thought of a good meal. He had been about to return to his hotel for a shower and a change of clothes when an accommodating taxi drove down C Street, the sun bouncing off its windows, obscuring any occupants. It stopped at the kerb in front of him – at the behest of his signal, Michael had assumed. Instead, a passenger carrying an attaché case stepped out quickly, a harried man late for an appointment, fumbling for his wallet. At first neither Havelock nor the passenger recognized each other; Michael's thoughts were on a restaurant, the other's on paying the driver.

"Havelock?" the passenger had inquired suddenly, adjusting his glasses. "It *is* you, isn't it, Michael?"

"Harry? Harry Lewis?"

"You've got it. How are you, M.H.?"

Lewis was one of the few people he ever saw – and he rarely saw Harry – who called him by his initials. It was a minor legacy from university – he and Lewis had both been at Princeton. Michael had gone into government, Lewis into academia. Dr Harry Lewis was chairman of the political science department at a small, prestigious university in New England, travelling down to DC now and then for consultation chores at State. They had run into each other several times when both were in Washington.

"Fine. Still picking up *per diems*, Harry?"

"A lot fewer than before. Someone taught you people how to read evaluation reports from our more esoteric graduate schools."

"Good Christ, I'm being replaced by a beard in blue jeans with funny cigarettes."

The bespectacled professor was stunned. "You're kidding. You're *out*? I thought you were in for life!"

"The opposite, Harry. Life began between five and seven minutes ago when I wrote my final signature. And in a couple of hours I'm going to be faced with the first dinner bill in years that I can't take out of contingency funds."

"What are you going to do, Michael?"

"No thoughts. Don't want any for a while."

The academician paused, taking his change from the taxi driver, then spoke rapidly. "Listen, I'm late for upstairs, but I'm in town overnight. Since I'm on *per diem*, let me pay for the dinner. Where are you staying? I may have an idea."

No government *per diem* in the civilized world could have paid for the dinner that night two months and five days ago, but Harry Lewis did have an idea. They had been friends once; they became friends again, and Havelock found it easier to talk with a person who was at least vaguely aware of the work he had done for the government rather than with someone who knew nothing about it. It was always difficult to explain that something could not be explained; Lewis understood. One thing led to another, which in turn led to Harry's idea.

"Have you ever given any thought to getting back to a campus?"

Michael smiled. "How would 'constantly' sound?"

"I know, I know," Lewis pressed, suspecting sarcasm. "You fellows – 'spooks', I assume, is the term – get all kinds of offers from the multinationals at damn good money; I'm aware of that. But, M.H., you were one of the best. Your dissertation was picked up by a dozen university presses; you even had your own seminars. Your academic record coupled with your years at State – most of which I realize you can't go into specifically – could make you very attractive to a university administration. We're always saying: 'Let's find someone who's been there, not just a theoretician.' Damn it, Michael, I think you're *it*. Now, I know the money's not."

"Harry, you misunderstood. I meant it. I *constantly* think about getting back."

It was Harry Lewis's turn to smile. "Then I've got another idea."

A week later Havelock had flown to Boston and driven from there to the brick-and-ivy-and-white-birch campus on the outskirts of Concord, New Hampshire. He spent four days with Harry Lewis and his wife, wandering around, attending various lectures and seminars, and meeting those of the faculty and administration whose support Harry thought likely to be helpful. Michael's opinions had been sought "casually" over coffee, drinks and dinners; men and women had looked at him as if they considered him a promising candidate. Lewis had done his missionary work well.

At the end of the fourth day Harry announced at lunch: "They like you!"

"Why not?" his wife had interrupted. "He's damned likeable."

"They're quite excited, actually. It's what I said the other day, M.H. You've *been there*. Sixteen years with the State Department kind of makes you special."

"And?"

"There's the annual administration-trustees conference coming up in eight weeks. That's when the supply-and-demand quotients are studied. Horseflesh. I think you'll be offered a job. Where can I reach you?"

"I'll be travelling. I'll call you."

He had called Harry from London two days ago. The conference was still in progress, but Lewis thought there would be an answer any moment.

"Cable me Am Ex, Amsterdam," Michael had said. "And thanks, Harry."

He saw the glass doors of the American Express office swing open just ahead. A couple emerged, the man awkwardly balancing the shoulder straps of two cameras while counting money. Havelock stopped, wondering for a moment whether he really wanted to go inside. If the cable was there it would contain either a rejection or an offer. If a rejection he would simply go on wandering – and there was a certain comfort in that; the floating passivity of not planning had become something of value to him. If an offer, what then? Was he ready for it? Was he prepared to make a decision? Not the kind of decision one made in the field, which had to be instinctive if one was to survive, but rather a decision to commit oneself. Was he capable of a commitment? Where were yesterday's commitments?

He took a deep breath, consciously putting one foot in front of the other, and approached the glass doors.

Position available Visiting Professor of Government for period of two years. Associate status pending mutual acceptance at the end of this time. Initial salary Twenty-seven. Will need your reply within ten days. Don't keep me holding my breath. Ever, Harry.

Michael folded the cable and put it in his jacket pocket; he did not go back to the counter to write out his own cable to Harry Lewis, Concord, New Hampshire, USA. It would come later. It was enough for the moment to be wanted, to know there was a beginning. It would take several days to absorb the knowledge of his own legitimacy, perhaps several days thereafter to come to grips with it. For in the legitimacy was the possibility of commitment; there was no real beginning without it.

He walked out onto the Damrak, breathing the cold air of Amsterdam, feeling the damp chill floating up from the canal. The sun was setting; briefly blocked by a low-flying cloud, it reemerged, an orange globe hurling its rays through the intercepting vapours. It reminded Havelock of an ocean dawn on the coast of Spain – on the Costa Brava. He had stayed there all night – that night, until the sun had forced itself up over the horizon, firing the mists above the water. He had gone down to the shoulder of the road, to the sand and the dirt . . .

Don't think about it. That was another life.

Two months and five days ago by sheer chance Harry Lewis had stepped out of a taxi and started to change the world for an old friend. Now, two months and five days later, that change was there to be taken. He would take it, Michael knew, but something was missing: change should be shared, and there was no one to share it with, no one to say, *What will you teach?*

The black-coated waiter at the *Dikker en Thijs* ground the lip of the flaming brandy glass into the silver receptacle of sugar; the ingredients would follow for the *café Jamique*. It was a ridiculous indulgence, and probably a waste of very good liqueur, but Harry Lewis had insisted they each have one that night in Washington. He would repeat the ritual in Amsterdam.

"Thank you, Harry," he said silently once the waiter had left, raising his glass to his invisible companion. It was better, after all, not to be completely alone.

He could both feel the approaching presence of a man and see an enlarging darkness in the corner of his eye. A figure dressed in a conservative, pin-striped suit was threading his way through the shadows and the candlelight towards his booth. Havelock angled the glass and raised his eyes to the face. The man's name was George; he was the CIA station chief in Amsterdam. They had worked together before, not always pleasantly, but professionally.

"That's one way to announce your arrival here," he said, glancing at the waiter's tray table, the silver sugar bowl still on it. "May I sit down?"

"My pleasure. How are you, George?"

"I've been better," said the CIA man, sliding across the seat opposite Michael.

"Sorry to hear that. Care for a drink?"

"That depends."

"On what?"

"Whether I'll stay long enough."

"Aren't we cryptic," said Havelock. "But then you're probably still working."

"I wasn't aware the hours were that clear cut."

"No, I guess they're not. Am I the reason, George?"

"At the moment maybe. I'm surprised to see you here. I heard you retired."

"You heard correctly."

"Then why are you here?"

"Why not? I'm travelling. I like Amsterdam. You could say I'm spending a lot of accumulated severance pay visiting all those places I rarely got to see in the daytime."

"You could *say* it, but that doesn't mean I believe it."

"Believe, George. It's the truth."

"No screen?" His curious eyes were levelled at Michael. "I can find out, you know."

"None at all. I'm out, finished, temporarily unemployed. If you check, that's what you'll learn, but I don't think you have to waste channel time to Langley. I'm sure the centrex codes have been altered where I was concerned, all sources and informers in Amsterdam alerted as to my status. I'm off-limits, George. Anyone dealing with me is asking for a short term payroll and quite possibly an obscure funeral."

"Those are the *surface* facts," agreed the CIA man.

"They're the only facts. Don't bother looking for anything else; you won't find it."

"All right, say I believe you. You're travelling, spending your severance pay." The agent paused as he leaned forward. "It's going to run out."

"What is?"

"The severance pay."

"Inevitably. At which time I expect I'll find gainful employment. As a matter of fact, this afternoon . . ."

"Why wait? I might be able to help you there."

"No, you can't, George. I haven't anything to sell."

"Sure you do. Expertise. A consultant's fee paid out of contingency. No name, no records, untraceable."

"If you're running a test, you're doing it badly."

"No test. I'm willing to pay in order to look better than I am. I wouldn't admit that if I were testing you."

"You might, but you'd be a damn fool. It's third-rate entrapment; it's so awkward you've probably done it for real. None of us wants those contingency funds scrutinized too carefully, do we?"

"I may not be in your league, but I'm not third-rate. I need help. We need help."

"That's better. You're appealing to my ego. Much better."

"How about it, Michael. The KGB's all over The Hague. We don't know who they've bought or how far up they go. NATO's compromised."

"We're all compromised, George, and I *can't* help. Because I don't think it makes any difference. We get to square five, pushing them back to four, so they jump over us to seven. Then we buy our way to eight; they block us at nine, and no one reaches square ten. Everyone nods pensively and starts all over again. In the meantime we lament our losses and extol the body count, never admitting that it doesn't make any difference."

"That's a crock of shit! We're not going to be buried by *anyone*."

"Yes, we are, George. All of us. By 'children yet unborn and unbegot'. Unless they're smarter than we are, which may very well be the case. Christ, I hope so."

"What the hell are you talking about?"

"'The purple atomic testament of bleeding war.'"

"*What!*"

"History, George. Let's have that drink."

"No, thanks." The CIA station chief slid back across the seat. "And I think you've had enough," he added, standing up.

"Not yet."

"Go to hell, Havelock." The intelligence officer started to turn away.

"George."

"What?"

"You missed. I was about to say something about this afternoon, but you didn't let me finish."

"So what?"

"So you knew what it was I was going to tell you. When did you intercept the cable? Around noon?"

"Go to hell."

Michael watched as the CIA man returned to his table across the room. He had been dining alone, but Havelock knew he was not alone. Within three minutes, the judgement was confirmed. George signed his bill – bad form – and walked rapidly through the entrance arch into the lobby. Forty-five seconds later a youngish man from a table on the right side of the room got up to leave, leading a bewildered lady by the elbow. A minute passed and two men who had been in a booth on the left side rose as one and started for the arch. Through the candlelight, Michael focused on the plates in the booth. Both were piled with food. Bad form.

They had been following him, watching him, employing intercepts. Why? Why couldn't they leave him alone?

So much for Amsterdam.

The noonday sun in Paris was a blinding yellow, its quivering rays bouncing off the

Seine below the bridge. Havelock reached the mid-point of the Pont Royal, his small hotel only blocks away on the rue du Bac, the route he followed being the most logical one from the Louvre. He knew it was important not to deviate, not to let whoever it was behind him think he suspected his or her presence. He had spotted the taxi, the same taxi, as it made two swift turns in traffic to keep him in sight. Whoever was directing the driver was good; the taxi had stopped for less than two or three seconds at a corner, and then had sped away in the opposite direction. Which meant that whoever was following him was now on foot on the crowded bridge. If contact was the objective, crowds were helpful, and a bridge even more so. People stopped on bridges over the Seine simply to stare absently down at the water; they had been doing so for centuries. Conversations could be had unobtrusively. If contact was the objective, and not surveillance alone.

Michael stopped, leaned against the chest-high stone wall that served as a railing, and lit a cigarette. If anyone were watching him, it would seem as if he were looking at the *bateau mouche* about to pass under the bridge, waving his hand casually at the passengers below. But he was not; pretending to shield his eyes from the sun, he concentrated on the tall figure approaching on his right.

He could distinguish the grey Homburg, the velvet collared overcoat and the glistening black patent leather shoes; they were enough. The man was the essence of Parisian wealth and elegance, his attendance coveted in the salons of the rich all over Europe. His name was Gravet. He was considered the most knowledgeable critic of classical art in Paris, which meant the Continent, and only those who had to knew that he also sold far more than his critical expertise.

He stopped at the railing seven feet to the right of Havelock and adjusted his velvet collar.

"I thought it was you. I've been following you since the rue Bernard." He spoke just loud enough to be heard.

"I know. What do you want?"

"The question is, What do *you* want? Why are you in Paris? We were given to understand you were no longer active. Quite frankly, you were to be avoided."

"And reported immediately if I made contact, right?"

"Naturally."

"But you're reversing the process. You've approached me. That's a little foolish, isn't it?"

"A minor risk worth taking," said Gravet, standing erect and glancing about. "We go back a long time, Michael. I don't for a moment believe you're in Paris for your cultural rebirth."

"Neither do I. Who said I was?"

"You were at the Louvre for exactly twenty-seven minutes. Too short a time to absorb anything, and too long to relieve yourself. But quite plausible for meeting someone inside a dark, crowded exhibition room, say at the far end of the third floor."

Havelock began to laugh. "Listen, Gravet – "

"Don't look at me, please! Keep your eyes on the water."

"I went to the Roman collection on the mezzanine. It was filled with a tour from Provence, so I left."

"You were always quick, I admired you for it. And now this ominous alarm. 'He's no longer active. Avoid him.'"

"It happens to be true."

"Whatever this new cover of yours," continued Gravet quickly, dusting the elbows of his coat, "for it to be so radical can only mean you are among very distinguished company. I'm also a broker with a wide range of information. The more distinguished my clients, the better I like it."

"Sorry, I'm not buying. Avoid me."

"Don't be preposterous. You don't know what I have to offer. Incredible things are happening everywhere. Allies become enemies, enemies allies. The Persian Gulf is on fire and all Africa moves in contradictory circles; the Warsaw block has lacerations you know nothing about, and Washington pursues a dozen counterproductive strategies matched only by the unbelievable stupidity of the Soviets. I could give you chapter and verse on *their* recent follies. Don't dismiss me, Michael. Pay me. You'll climb even higher."

"Why should I want to climb higher when I've climbed out?"

"Again preposterous. You're a relatively young man; they wouldn't let you go."

"They can watch me, but they can't hold me. All I had to do was give up a pension somewhere down the road."

"Too simple. You all have bank accounts in remote but accessible places, everyone knows that. Diverted contingency funds, covert payments made to non-existent sources, fees for sudden departures or suddenly required papers. You had your retirement covered by the time you were thirty-five."

"You're exaggerating both my talents and my financial security," said Havelock, smiling.

"Or perhaps a rather lengthy document," the Frenchman went on, as though Michael had not interrupted, "detailing certain covert procedures – solutions, you might say – that must, perforce, describe specific events and personnel. Placed beyond reach of those most interested."

Havelock stopped smiling, but Gravet persisted. "Naturally, that's not *financial* security, but it adds to a sense of well-being, doesn't it?"

"You're wasting your time, I'm not in the market. If you've got something of value, you'll get your price. You know whom to deal with."

"They're frightened second-raters. None of them has your direct avenues to the . . . centres of determination, shall we say."

"I don't have them any more."

"I don't believe you. You're the only man here in Europe who talks directly with Anthony Matthias."

"Leave him out of it. And for your information I haven't spoken with him in months." Suddenly Havelock stood up and turned openly to the Frenchman. "Let's find a taxi and go to the embassy. I know some people over there. I'll introduce you to a first-level attaché and tell him you're selling but I don't have either the resources or the interest to get involved. Okay?"

"You know I can't do that! And, *please* – " Gravet did not have to finish the request.

"All right, all right," Michael returned to the wall with the river below. "Then give me a number or a place of contact. I'll phone it in and you can listen."

"Why are you doing this? Why the charade?"

"Because it's not a charade. As you said, we go back a long time. I'll do you the favour and maybe you'll be convinced. Maybe you'll convince others, if they ask. Even if they don't ask. How about it?"

The Frenchman pivoted his head while leaning over the wall and stared at Havelock. "No, thank you, Michael. As with all manner of Satans, better a second-rater I've dealt with than one I haven't. For what it's worth, I think I believe you. You would not reveal a source like me, even to a first-level attaché. I'm down too deep, too respectable; you might need me. Yes, I do believe you."

"Make my life easier. Don't keep it a secret."

"What about your opposite numbers in the KGB? Will they be convinced?"

"I'm sure of it. Their moles probably got word to Dzerzhinsky Square before I signed the separation papers."

"They'll suspect a ploy."

"All the more reason to leave me alone. Why bite into poisoned bait?"

"They have chemicals. You all have chemicals."

"I can't tell them anything they don't know, and what I do know has already been changed. That's the funny thing: my enemies have nothing to fear from me. The few names they might learn aren't worth the price. There'd be reprisals."

"You've inflicted a great many wounds. There's pride, vengeance; it's the human condition."

"Not applicable. In those areas we're even, and again I'm not worth it because there's no practical result. Nobody kills unless there's a reason. None of us wants to be responsible for the fallout. Crazy, isn't it? Almost Victorian. When we're finished, we're out. Maybe we'll all get together in a large black strategy room in hell and have a few drinks, but while we're here, we're out. That's the irony, the futility, Gravet. When we're out we don't care any more. We don't have any reason to hate. Or to kill."

"Nicely phrased, my friend. You've obviously thought about these things."

"I've had a lot of time recently."

"And there are those who are extremely *interested* in your recent observations, your conclusions – your role in life, as it were. But then it's to be expected. They're such a manic-depressive people. Morose, then jubilant; one minute filled with violence, the next with songs of the earth and sadness. And often quite paranoid; the darker aspects of classicism, I think. The slashing diagonals of Delacroix in a multi-racial national psyche, so far-reaching, so contradictory. So suspicious . . . so Soviet."

Havelock stopped breathing; he returned Gravet's stare. "Why did you do it?"

"There was no harm. Had I learned otherwise, who knows what I should have told them? But since I do believe you, I explain why I had to test you."

"Moscow thinks I'm still in?"

"I shall render the judgement that you are not. Whether they accept it or not is another matter."

"Why won't they?" asked Havelock, his eyes on the water below.

"I have no idea. I shall miss you, Michael. You were always civilized. Difficult but civilized. Then again, you're not a native born American, are you? You're really European."

"I'm American," said Havelock quietly. "Really."

"You've done well by its cause, I'll say that. If you change your mind – or it's changed for you – get in touch with me. We can always do business."

"It's not likely, but thanks."

"That's not an outright rejection, either."

"I'm being polite."

"Civilized. *Au 'voir*, Mikhail . . . I prefer the name you were born with."

Havelock turned his head slowly and watched Gravet walk with studied grace down the pavement of the Pont Royal towards the entrance of the bridge. This elegant Frenchman had accepted a blind interrogation from people he found loathsome; he must have been paid very well. But why?

The CIA was in Amsterdam and the CIA did not believe him. The KGB was in Paris and the KGB did not believe him either. *Why?*

So much for Paris. How far would they go to keep him under a microscope?

The Arethusa Delphi was one of those small hotels near the Syntagma Square in Athens that never let the traveller forget he was in Greece. The rooms were white on white on shimmering white. Walls, furniture and space-dividing ornamental beads were relieved only by garish oil paintings framed in plastic, depicting the antiquities: temples, forums and oracles romanticized by postcard artists. Each room had a pair of narrow double doors that opened onto a miniature balcony – large enough for two small chairs and a Lilliputian table – on which guests could have black morning coffee. Throughout the lobby and in the lifts one never escaped the rhythmic pounding of Greek folk music, strings and cymbals predominant.

Havelock led the olive-skinned woman out of the lift, and as the doors closed, both stood for a moment in mock anticipation. The music was gone; they sighed in relief.

"Zorba took a break." Michael gestured to the left towards his room.

"The rest of the world must think we are nervous wrecks," said the woman, laughing, touching her dark hair and smoothing out the long white dress that complemented her skin and accentuated her breasts and tapered body. Her English was heavily accented, cultivated on those Mediterranean islands that were the playgrounds of the Mediterranean rich. She was a high-priced courtesan whose favours were sought after by the princes of commerce and inheritance, a good-natured whore with a decent wit and a quick laugh; a woman who knew her time of pleasure-giving was limited. "You rescued me," she said, squeezing Havelock's arm as they walked down the corridor.

"I kidnapped you."

"Often interchangeable terms," she replied, laughing again.

It had been a little of both. Michael had run across a man on the Marathonos with whom he had worked in the Thermaïkós sector five years ago. A dinner party was being held that night at a café in Syntagma Square; since it was convenient, Havelock accepted the invitation. The woman was there, escorted by a considerably older, boorish businessman. The ouzo and *bazouki* had done their damage. Havelock and the woman had been seated next to each other; legs and hands touched, they exchanged looks – comparisons were obvious. Michael and the island courtesan had slipped away.

"I think I'm going to face an angry Athenian tomorrow," said Havelock, opening the door of his room, leading the woman inside.

"Don't be silly," she protested. "He's not a gentleman. He's from Epidaurus; there are no gentlemen in Epidaurus. He's an ageing bull of a peasant who made money under the colonels. One of the nastier consequences of their regime."

"When in Athens," said Michael, going to the bureau where there was a bottle of prized Scotch and glasses, "stay away from Epidaurians." He poured drinks.

"Have you been to Athens often?"

"A few times."

"What did you do? What line of work?"

"I bought things. Sold things." Havelock carried the drinks back across the room. What he saw was what he wanted to see, although he had not expected to see it so quickly. The woman had removed her thin silk cape and draped it on a chair. She then proceeded to unbutton her gown from the top, the swelling of her breasts provocative, inviting.

"You didn't buy me," she said, taking the drink with her free hand. "I came of my own free will. *Efharistó*, Michael Havelock. Do I say your name right?"

"Very nicely."

She touched his glass with hers, the sound gentle as she stepped closer. She reached up and placed her fingers on his lips, then his cheek, and finally around the back of his neck, drawing his face to hers. They kissed, her lips parting, the soft swollen flesh and moisture of her mouth arousing him; she pressed her body against his, pulling his left hand to the breast beneath her open gown. She leaned back, breathing deeply.

"Where is your bathroom? I'll get into something – less."

"Over there."

"Why don't *you*? Get into something less, that is. We'll meet at the bed. I'm really rather anxious. You're very, *very* attractive, and I'm – very anxious."

She picked up her cape from the chair and walked casually, sensually towards the door beyond the bed. She went inside, glancing back over her shoulder, her eyes telling him things that probably were not true but were nevertheless exciting for the night. The practised whore, whatever her reasons were, would perform, and he wanted, needed, the release of that performance.

Michael stripped himself down to his pants, carried his drink to the bed and tore away the bedspread and the blanket. He climbed under the sheet and reached for a cigarette, turning his body away from the wall.

"*Dobriy vyecher, priyatyel.*"

At the sound of the deep male voice, Havelock spun around on the bed, instinctively reaching for a weapon – a weapon that was not there. Standing in the frame of the bathroom door was a balding man whose face Michael recognized from dozens of photographs going back years. He was from Moscow, one of the most powerful men in the Soviet KGB. In his hand was a gun, a large, black Graz–Burya automatic. There was a click; the hammer snapped into firing position.

3

"You may leave now," said the Russian to the woman concealed behind him. She slid past, glancing at Havelock, then rushed to the door and let herself out.

"You're Rostov. Pyotr Rostov. Director of External Strategies. KGB. Moscow."

"Your face and name are also known to me. And your dossier."

"You went to a lot of trouble, *priyatyel*," said Michael, using the Russian word for friend, its meaning, however, denied by his cold delivery. He shook his head, trying to clear it of a sickening mist, the effect of the ouzo and Scotch. "You could have stopped me on the street and invited me for a drink. You wouldn't have learned any more or any less, and very little that's valuable. Unless this is a *nyet gorya*."

"No execution, Havlicek."

"Havelock."

"Son of Havlicek."

"You'd do well not to remind me."

"The gun is in my hand, not yours." Rostov eased the hammer of his automatic back into its recess, the weapon still levelled at Michael's head. "But that's in the distant past and has no connection with me. Your recent activities, however, are very much my concern. Our concern, if you will."

"Then your moles aren't earning their money."

"They file reports with irritating frequency, if only to justify it. But are they accurate?"

"If they told you I was finished, they were accurate."

"'Finished'? A word with such finality, yet subject to interpretation, no? Finished with what? Finished with one phase, on to another?"

"Finished with anything that might concern you."

"Out of sanction?" asked the KGB officer, rounding the border of the door frame and leaning against the wall, his Graz–Burya steady, levelled now at Havelock's throat. "No longer employed by your government in any official capacity? It's difficult to accept. It must have been a blow to your dear friend Anthony Matthias."

Michael studied the Russian's face, lowering his eyes to the huge gun aimed at him. "A Frenchman mentioned Matthias the other day. I'll tell you what I told him, although I don't know why I should. You paid him to bring up Matthias's name."

"Gravet? He despises us. He's civil to us only when he's walking through the galleries of the Kremlin or the Hermitage in Leningrad. He might tell us anything."

"Why did you use him then?"

"Because he's fond of you. It's far easier to spot a lie when the liar is referring to someone he likes."

"Then you believed him."

"Or you convinced him and our people had no choice. Tell *me*. How did the brilliant and charismatic American Secretary of State react to his *krajan's* resignation?"

"I have no idea, but I assume he understood. It's exactly what I told Gravet. I haven't seen Matthias or spoken to him for months. He's got enough problems; there's no reason why those of an old student should be added."

"But you were far more than a student. His family knew your family in Prague. You became what you are – "

"*Were*," interrupted Havelock.

" – because of *Anton* Matthias," completed the Russian.

"It was a long time ago."

Rostov was silent; he lowered his weapon slightly, then spoke. "Very well, a long time ago. What about now? No one's irreplaceable, but you're a valuable man. Knowledgeable, productive."

"Value and productivity are generally associated with commitment. I don't have it any more. Let's say I lost it."

"Am I to infer you could be tempted?" The KGB man lowered the weapon farther. "In the direction of another commitment?"

"You know better than that. Apart from personal revulsions that go back a couple of decades, we've got a mole or two in the Dzerzhinsky. I've no intention of being marked beyond salvage."

"A hypocritical term. It implies compassion on the part of your executioners."

"It says it."

"Not well." Rostov raised his automatic, thrusting it forward slowly. "We have no such problems with verbal rationales. A traitor is a traitor. I could take you in, you know."

"Not easily." Michael remained still, his eyes locked with the Russian's. "There are corridors and lifts, lobbies to pass through and streets to cross; there's risk. You could lose. Everything. Because I have nothing to lose but a cell at the Lubyanka."

"A room, not a cell. We're not barbarians."

"Sorry. A room. The same kind of room we have reserved in Virginia for someone like you – and we're both wasting money. When people like you and me get out with our heads still on, everything's altered. The Amytals and the Pentothals are invitations to traps."

"There are still the moles."

"I don't know who they are any more than you did when you were in the field – for those same reasons, those same rooms. None of us do on either side. We only know the current codes, words that take us where we have to go. Whatever ones I had are meaningless now."

"In all sincerity, are you trying to persuade me a man of your experience is of no value to us?"

"I didn't say that," interrupted Havelock. "I'm simply suggesting that you weigh the risks. Also something else, which, frankly, you pulled off with reasonable success two years ago. We took a man of yours who was finished, ready for a farm in Grasnov. We got him out through Riga into Finland and flew him to a room in Fairfax, Virginia. He was injected with everything from scopolamine to triple Amytal, and we learned a lot. Strategies were aborted, whole networks restructured, confusion the order of the day. Then we learned something else: everything he told us was a lie. His head was programmed like a computer disc; valuable men became useless, time was lost. Supposing you got me to the Lubyanka – which I don't think you could – how do you know I'm not our answer to what you did to us?"

"Because you would not expose the possibility." Rostov pulled the gun back, but did not lower it.

"Really? It strikes me as a pretty good blanket. I mean, you'd never know, would you? On the other hand, we've developed a serum – which I know nothing about except that it's injected at the base of the skull – that voids the programming. Something to do with neutralizing the *lobus occipitalis*, whatever the hell that is. From now on we can make the distinction."

"Such an admission astonishes me."

"Why should it? Perhaps I'm just saving our respective directors a lot of aggravation; that could be my objective. Or maybe none of it's true; maybe there is no serum, no protection, and I'm making it all up. That's also a possibility."

The Russian smiled. "*Khvatit!* You *are* out! You amuse us both with logic that could serve you. You're on your way to that farm in your own Grasnov."

"That's what I've been trying to tell you. Am I worth the risk?"

"Let's find out." Suddenly the Russian flipped his automatic, barrel up; he slapped it back in the palm of his hand and threw it to Havelock on the bed. Michael's hand shot up, catching the weapon in mid air.

"What am I supposed to do with this?"

"What do you want to do with it?"

"Nothing. Assuming the first three shells are rubber capsules filled with dye, I'd only soil your clothes." Havelock pressed the magazine release; the clip dropped to the bed. "It's not a very good test anyway. Suppose the firing pin works and this thing makes any noise at all, twenty *chruscikis* could break in here and blow me out of the park."

"The firing pin works and there's no one outside in the hall. The Arethusa Delphi is very much in Washington's camp; it's watched and I'm not so foolish as to parade our personnel. I think you know that. It's why you're here."

"What are you trying to prove?"

The Russian smiled again and shrugged. "I'm not really sure. A brief something in the eyes, perhaps. When a man's under a hostile gun and that gun is suddenly his, there is an instant compulsion to eliminate the prior threat . . . assuming the hostility is returned. It's in the eyes; no amount of control can disguise it – if the enmity is active."

"What was in my eyes?"

"Absolute indifference. Weariness, if you will."

"I'm not sure you're right, but I admire your courage. It's more than I've got. The firing pin really works?"

"Yes."

404

"No capsules?"

The Russian shook his head, his expression conveying quiet amusement. "No bullets. That is to say, no power in the shells." Rostov raised his left hand, and with his right pulled back the sleeve of his overcoat. Strapped to the flat of his wrist, extending up towards his elbow, was a thin barrel, the trigger mechanism apparently activated by the bending of his arm. He touched the taut spring-like wires. "What you call narcotic darts. You would have slept peacefully for the better part of tomorrow, while a doctor insisted that your odd fever must be studied at the hospital. We'd have got you out, flown you up to Salonika and over the Dardanelles into Sevastopol." The Russian unsnapped a strap above his wrist and removed the weapon.

Havelock studied the KGB man, not a little perplexed. "You really could have taken me."

"Until the attempt is made, one never knows. I might have missed the first shot, and you're younger, stronger than me; you could have attacked, broken my neck. But the odds were on my side."

"I'd say completely. Why didn't you play them?"

"Because you're right. We *don't* want you. The risks *are* too great – not those you spoke of, but others. I simply had to know the truth and I'm now convinced. You are no longer in the service of your government."

"What risks?"

"They're unknown to us, but they are there. Anything you can't understand in this business is a risk, but I don't have to tell you that."

"Tell me *something*. I just got a pardon; I'd like to know why."

"Very well." The Soviet intelligence officer hesitated; he walked aimlessly towards the double doors that led to the miniature balcony and opened one several inches. Then he closed it and turned to Havelock. "I should tell you first that I'm not here on orders from Dzerzhinsky Square, or even with its blessings. To be frank, my ageing superiors in the KGB believe I'm in Athens on an unrelated matter. You can either accept that or not."

"Give me a reason to or not. Someone must know. You *people* don't do anything solo."

"Specifically, two others. A close associate in Moscow and a dedicated man – a mole, to be sure – out of Washington."

"You mean Langley?"

The Russian shook his head; he replied softly. "The White House."

"I'm impressed. So two ranking *Kantralyors* of the KGB and a Soviet mole within walking distance of the Oval Office decide they want to talk to me, but they don't want to take me. They can fly me into Sevastopol and from there to a room at the Lubyanka, where any talking we did would be far more productive – from their point of view – but they won't do that. Instead, the spokesman for these three – a man I know only from photographs and by reputation – tells me there are risks associated with me that he can't define but knows that they exist and because of them I'm given the option of talking or not – about what I haven't the vaguest idea. Is that a fair reading?"

"You have the Slavic propensity for going right to the core of a subject."

"I don't see any ancestral connection. It's common sense. You spoke, I listened; that's what you said – or what you're about to say. Basic logic."

Rostov stepped away from the balcony doors, his expression pensive. "I'm afraid that's the one factor that's missing. The logic."

"Now we're talking about something else."

"Yes, we are."

"What?"

"You. The Costa Brava."

Havelock paused. The anger was in his eyes, but it was controlled. "Go on."

"The woman. She's why you retired, isn't she?"

"This conversation is terminated," said Havelock abruptly. "Get out of here."

"Please." The Russian raised both hands, a gesture of truce, perhaps a plea. "I think you should listen to me."

"I don't think so. There's nothing you could say that would remotely interest me. The *Voennaya* is to be congratulated; it was a hell of a job. They won, she won. And then she lost. It's finished, and there's nothing further to say about it."

"There is."

"Not to me."

"The VKR are maniacs," said the Russian quietly, urgently. "I don't have to tell you that. You and I are enemies and neither would pretend otherwise, but we acknowledge certain rules between us. We're not salivating dogs, we're professionals. There's a fundamental respect each has for the other, perhaps grounded in fear, although not necessarily. Grant me that, *priyatyel*."

Their eyes were level, penetrating. Havelock nodded. "I know you from the files, just as you know me. You weren't part of it."

"Wasted death is still death, still a waste. Unnecessary and provocative death a very dangerous waste. It can be hurled back tenfold in fury at the instigator."

"Tell that to the *Voennaya*. There was no waste as far as they were concerned. Only necessity."

"Butchers!" snapped Rostov, his voice guttural. "Who can tell them anything? They're descendants of the old OGPU slaughter-houses, inheritors of the mad assassin Yagoda. They're also up to their throats in paranoid fantasies going back half a century, when Yagoda gunned down the quieter, more reasonable men, hating their lack of fanaticism, equating that lack with treason against the revolution. Do you *know* the VKR?"

"Enough to stand far back and hope to hell you can control it."

"I wish I could answer confidently in the affirmative. It's as if a band of your screaming right-wing zealots had been given official status as a subdivision of the Central Intelligence Agency."

"We have checks and balances – sometimes. If such subdivision came to be – and it could – it would be continuously scrutinized, openly criticized. Funds would be watched closely, methods studied, ultimately the group would be thrown out."

"You've had your lapses, your various un-American activities committees, your McCarthys, the Huston plans, purges in the irresponsible press. Careers have been destroyed, lives degraded. Yes, you've had your share of lapses."

"Always short-lived. We have no gulags, no 'rehabilitation' programmes in a

Lubyanka. And that irresponsible press has a way of becoming responsible now and then. It threw out a regime of arrogant hot shots. The Kremlin's wilder ones stay in place."

"We both have our lapses then. But we're so much younger; youth is allowed mistakes."

"And there's nothing," interrupted Michael, "to compare with the VKR's *paminyatchik* operation. That wouldn't be tolerated or funded by the worst Congress or administration in history."

"Another paranoid fantasy!" cried the KGB officer, adding derisively, "The *paminyatchik* travellers! A discredited strategy mounted decades ago! You can't honestly believe it still flourishes."

"Perhaps less than the *Voennaya* does. Obviously more than you do – if you're not lying."

"Oh, *come*, Havelock! Russian infants sent to the United States, growing up with old-line, no doubt pathetically senile Marxists so as to become entrenched Soviet agents? Insanity! Be reasonable. It's psychologically unsound – if not disastrous – to say nothing of certain inevitable comparisons. We'd lose the majority to blue jeans, rock music and fast cars. We'd be idiots."

"Now you're lying. They exist. You know it and we know it."

Rostov shrugged. "A question of numbers, then. And value, I might add. How many can be left? Fifty, a hundred, two hundred at the outside? Sad, amateurishly conspiratorial creatures wandering around a few cities, meeting in cellars to exchange nonsense, uncertain of their own values, the very reasons for being where they are. Very little credence is given these so-called 'travellers', take my word for it."

"But you haven't pulled them out."

"Where would we put them? Few even speak the Russian language; they're a large embarrassment. Attrition, *priyatyel*, that's the answer. And dismissing them with lip-service, as you Americans say."

"The *Voennaya* doesn't dismiss them."

"I told you, the men of the VKR pursue misguided fantasies."

"I wonder if you believe that," said Michael, studying the Russian. "Not all those families were pathetic and senile, not all the travellers amateurs."

"If there is currently – or in the recent past – any movement of consequence on the part of the *paminyatchiks*, we are not aware of it," said Rostov firmly.

"And if there is and you're not aware of it that would be something of consequence, wouldn't it?"

The Russian stood motionless; he spoke, his voice low and pensive. "The VKR is incredibly secretive. It would be something of consequence."

"Then maybe I've given you something to think about. Call it a parting gift from a retired enemy."

"I look for no such gifts," said Rostov coldly. "They're as gratuitous as your presence here in Athens."

"Since you don't approve, go back to Moscow and fight your own fights. Your infrastructure doesn't concern me any longer. And unless you've got another comic book weapon up your other sleeve, I suggest you leave."

"That's just it, *pyeshka*. Yes, *pyeshka*. *Pawn*. It is as you say . . . an infrastructure. Separate sections, indeed, but one entity. There is first the KGB; all else follows. A man – or a woman – may gravitate to the *Voennaya*, may even excel in its deepest operations, but first he – or she – must have sprung from the KGB. At the very minimum there *has* to be a Dzerzhinsky dossier *somewhere*. With foreign recruits it's, as you would say, a double imperative. Internal protection, of course."

Havelock sat forward on the bed, confusion joining the anger in his eyes. "Say what you're trying to say and say it quickly. There's a smell about you, *priyatyel*!"

"I suspect there is about all of us, Mikhail Havlicek. Our nostrils never quite adjust, do they? Perversely, they become sensitive – to variations of that basic odour. Like animals."

"Say it."

"There is no listing for a Jenna Karras at the KGB."

Havelock stared at the Russian, then suddenly spun off the bed, gripping the sheet and whipping it into the air, obscuring the Russian's vision. He lunged forward, hammering Rostov against the wall beyond the balcony doors. He twisted the KGB man clockwise by the wrist and smashed his head into the frame of a cheap oil painting as he whipped his right arm around Rostov's neck in a hammerlock. "I could kill you for that," he whispered, breathless, the muscles of his jaw pulsating against Rostov's bald head. "You said I might break your neck. I could do it right *now*!"

"You could," rejoined the Russian, choking. "And you'd be cut down. Either in this room or on the street outside."

"I thought you didn't have anyone in the hotel!"

"I lied. There are three men, two dressed as waiters in the hall by the lift, one inside the staircase. There's no final protection for you here in Athens. My people are out there – on the street as well – every doorway covered. My instructions are clear: I'm to emerge from a specific exit at a specific time. Any deviations from either will result in your death. The room will be stormed; the cordon around the Arethusa is unbreakable. I'm not an idiot."

"Maybe not, but as you said, you're an *animal*!" He released the Russian and hurled him across the room. "Go back to Moscow and tell them the bait's too obvious, the stench too *rotten*! I'm not taking it, *priyatyel*. Get out of here!"

"No bait," protested Rostov, regaining his balance and holding his throat. "Your own argument: what could you really tell us that would be worth the risks, or the reprisals, perhaps? *Or* the uncertainties? You're finished. Without programming you could lead us into a hundred traps – a theory that has crossed our minds, incidentally. You talk freely and we act on what you say, but what you tell us is no longer operative. Through you we go after strategies – not simple codes and ciphers, but supposedly long-term vital strategies – that Washington has aborted without telling *you*. In the process we reveal our personnel. Surely you're aware of this. You talk of *logic*? Heed your own words!"

Havelock stared at the Soviet officer, his breathing audible, anger and bewilderment compounding the emotional strain. Even the shadow of a possibility that an error had been made at Costa Brava was more than he could face. But there was no error. A Baader-Meinhof defector had set off the revealing chain of events. The evidence had been sent to Madrid, and he had pored over it, sifting every fragment for a shred to the contrary. There was nothing; there was everything. Even Anthony Matthias – *Anton* Matthias, friend, mentor, surrogate father – had demanded in-depth verification; it had been returned: positive.

"No! The proof was there! *She* was there! I saw for myself! I said I had to see for myself and they agreed!"

"'They'? Who is 'they'?"

"You know as well as I do! Men like you! The inside shell – strategists! You didn't look hard enough. You're *wrong*!"

The Russian moved his head slowly in circles, his left hand massaging his throat; he spoke softly. "I won't deny the possibility exists – as I said, the VKR is maniacally secretive, *especially* in Moscow – but that possibility is remote. We were astonished. An unusually productive decoy-conduit is led into a terrorist trap by her own people, who then proceed to hold the KGB responsible for her death by claiming she was one of us. The result of this manipulation is the neutering of the woman's constant companion, her lover, a deep-cover, multilingual field agent of exceptional talent. Disillusion and disgust overwhelm him; he takes himself out. We are amazed; we search the dossier vaults, including the most inaccessible. She is *nowhere*. Jenna Karras was never a part of us." Rostov paused, his eyes conveying his awareness: Michael Havelock was a dangerously provoked panther about to spring, about to strike. The Russian continued, his voice flat. "We are grateful; we profit by your elimination, but we ask ourselves why? Why was this done? Is it a trick? If so, for what purpose? Who gains? On the surface we do, but again, why? *How?*"

"Ask the VKR!" shouted Michael contemptuously. "They didn't plan it this way, but that's the way it happened. I'm the bonus! Ask *them*!"

"We did," said the Russian. "A section director saner than most, who, because of his relative sanity, is frightened of his peers. He told us that he personally was not familiar with the Karras woman or the details of Costa Brava, but since the field personnel raised no questions, he assumed no questions *should* be raised. As he pointed out, the results were favourable: two vultures shot down, both talented, one exceptional. The *Voennaya* was pleased to take credit."

"Why shouldn't they? I was out, and she could be justified. A sacrifice by any name is still the same. It's expendable for a purpose. He said it; he acknowledged it."

"He did not acknowledge it and he was saying something quite different. I told you, he's a frightened man. Only my rank persuaded him to go as far as he did."

"You're reaching."

"I listened. As you listened to me a few moments ago. He was telling us that he hadn't the vaguest idea what had happened or why."

"He *personally* didn't know," said Havelock angrily. "The people in the field knew. *She* knew!"

"A tenuous rationalization. His office is responsible for all activities in the south-west Mediterranean sector. The territory includes the Costa Brava. An emergency rendezvous – especially one ostensibly involving the Baader-Meinhof – would certainly be cleared by him." Rostov paused briefly, then added quietly, "Under normal circumstances."

"A not-so-tenuous rationalization?" asked Michael.

"I leave myself the narrowest margin for error. An extremely remote possibility."

"It's the one I accept!" Havelock shouted again, suddenly disturbed at his own outburst.

"You want to accept it. Perhaps you have to."

"The VKR more often than not gets its orders directly from the policy rooms of the Kremlin. It's no secret. If you're not lying, you were passed over."

"To be sure, and the thought frightens me more than I can tell you. But as much as I'm forced to acknowledge your professional accomplishments, *priyatyel*, I do not think the policy makers in the Kremlin are concerned with the likes of you and me. They have more weighty matters, global matters. And, to the point, they have no expertise where we're concerned."

"They do with Baader-Meinhof! *And* the PLO, *and* the Brigate Rosse, *and* a couple of dozen 'red armies' blowing things up all over the goddamn place! *That's* policy!"

"Only for maniacs."

"Which is exactly what we're talking about! Maniacs!" Michael paused, the obvious striking him. "We broke the VKR codes. They were authentic; I've seen too many variations not to know. *I* set up the contact. She *responded*. I sent the final transmission to the men in the boat offshore. *They* responded! Explain that!"

"I can't."

"Then get *out!*"

The KGB officer looked at his watch. "I must in any event. Time is up."

"Yes, it is."

"We're at an impasse," said the Russian.

"I'm not."

"No, I don't think you are, and that compounds the risk about you. You know what you know and I know what I know. Impasse, whether you like it or not."

"Your time's up, remember?"

"I'm not forgetting. I don't care to be caught in the crossfire. I'll leave now." Rostov went to the door and turned, his hand on the knob. "Several minutes ago you said the bait was too obvious, the stench too rotten. Tell that to Washington, *priyatyel*. We're not taking it either."

"Get *out!*"

The door closed and Havelock stood motionless for nearly a minute, picturing the Russian's eyes. They had held too much truth in them. Over the years Michael had learned to discern the truth, especially in his enemies. Rostov had not been lying; he had spoken the truth as he believed it to be. Which meant that this powerful strategist for the KGB was being manipulated by his own people in Moscow. Pyotr Rostov was a blind probe – an influential intelligence officer sent out with information he is convinced his superiors do not have in order to make contact with the enemy and turn an American agent, recruiting him for the Soviets. The higher up the officer, the more credible his story – as long as he spoke the truth as he saw it, truth that was perceived as such by his enemy.

Michael walked to the bedside table where he had left the glass of whisky a half hour ago. He picked it up, drained the Scotch and looked down at the bed. He smiled to himself, thinking how the evening had veered from where it had been heading thirty minutes ago. The whore had performed, but not in any way he might have expected. The sensuous courtesan from the playgrounds of the rich had been part of a well-planned set-up. When were the set-ups going to stop? Amsterdam. Paris. Athens.

Perhaps they would not stop until he did. Perhaps as long as he kept moving the would-be trappers would keep moving with him, watching him, cornering him, waiting for him to commit whatever crimes their imaginations led them to expect. It was in the movement itself that they found the ominous substance for their suspicions. No man wandered aimlessly after a lifetime of wandering under orders. If he kept it up, it must mean he was following other orders, different orders; otherwise he'd stay put. Somewhere.

Perhaps it was time he stopped. Maybe his odyssey of recovery had about run its course; there was a cable to be sent, a commitment to be made. A beginning. A nearly forgotten friend had become a friend again, and that man had offered him a new life, where the old life could be buried, where there were roots to cultivate, relationships to create, things to teach.

What will you teach, Mikhail?

Leave me alone! You are no part of me – you never were!

He would send the cable to Harry Lewis in the morning, then rent a car and drive north-west to catch the ferry for the Ionian port of Kerkira, where he would catch the boat to Brindisi in Italy. He had done it before under God knows what name or with what objective. He would do it now as Michael Havelock, Visiting Professor of Government. From Brindisi he would take the circuitous train routes across Italy into Rome, a city he enjoyed immensely. He would stay in Rome for a week or two; it would be the last stop on his odyssey, the place where he would put to rest all thoughts of a life that was over.

There were things to do in Concord, New Hampshire, USA. He would assume his duties as visiting professor in something less than three months; in the meantime there were practicalities to be dealt with: lectures to be sketched under the guidance of knowledgeable associates, curricula to study and evaluate, determining where his contributions might best be directed. A short stay, perhaps, with Matthias, who would certainly have insights to offer. No matter how pressed for time, Matthias would *make* the time, because, above all men, Anton would be happiest for him. His old student had returned to the campus. It was where it all began.

So many things to do. He needed a place to live: a house, furniture, pots and pans and books, a chair to sit in, a bed to sleep in. Choices. He had not thought about such things ever before. He thought about them now and felt the excitement growing inside him.

He went to the bureau, uncapped the Scotch and poured himself a drink. "*Priyatyel,*" he said softly, for no particular reason, as he looked at his face in the mirror. Suddenly he stared at his eyes and, in terror, slammed the glass down with such force that it shattered. Blood spread slowly over his hand. His eyes would not let him go! And he understood. Had they seen the truth that night on the Costa Brava?

411

"*Stop it!*" he screamed, whether silently or out loud he could not tell.

Dr Harry Lewis sat at his desk in his book-lined study, the cablegram in his hand. He listened for the sound of his wife's voice. It came.

"See you later, dear," she called from the hall beyond. The front door opened and closed. She was out of the house.

Lewis picked up his telephone and dialled the area code 202. Washington, DC. The seven digits that followed had been committed to memory, never written down. Nor would they be recorded on a bill, having bypassed the computers electronically.

"Yes?" asked the male voice on the other end of the line.

"Birchtree," said Harry.

"Go ahead, Birchtree. You're being taped."

"He's accepted. The cable came from Athens."

"Is there any change in dates?"

"No. He'll be here a month before the trimester starts."

"Did he say where he was going from Athens?"

"No."

"We'll watch the airports. Thank you, Birchtree."

The Rome Havelock had come to visit was not the Rome in which he cared to stay. Strikes were everywhere, the chaos compounded by volatile Italian tempers that erupted on every street corner, every picket line, in the parks and around the fountains. Mail had been strewn in gutters, adding to the uncollected rubbish; taxis were scarce, practically non-existent, and most of the restaurants had been closed for lack of deliveries. The *Poliziotti*, having taken sufficient abuse, had stopped work, snarling further the normal insanity of Rome's traffic; and since the telephones were part of the government's postal service, they functioned on a level below normal, which made them damn near impossible. The city was full of a kind of hysteria, aggravated by yet another stern papal decree – from a foreigner, a *Polacco*! – that was at odds with every progressive step since Vatican II. *Giovanni Ventitre! Dove sei?*

It was his second night, and Michael had left his *pensione* on the via Due Macelli more than two hours before, walking almost a mile to the via Flaminia in the hope of finding a favourite restaurant open. It was not, and no amount of patience brought forth a taxi to take him back to the Spanish Steps.

Reaching the north end of the via Veneto, he headed for the side street by which he could escape the crowds on the gaudy carnival of the busy shopping street, when he saw it: a poster in the lighted window of a travel agency proclaiming the glories of Venice.

Why not? Why the hell not? The floating passivity of not planning included sudden changes of plan. He looked at his watch; it was barely eight-thirty, probably too late to get out to the airport and chance a reservation on a plane, but if he remembered correctly – and he did – the trains kept running out of Rome until midnight. Why not a train? The lazy, circuitous trip by rail from Brindisi had been startlingly beautiful, passing through countryside that had not changed in centuries. He could pack his single suitcase in minutes, walk to the station in twenty. Surely the money he was willing to pay would buy him accommodation; if not, he could always return to the via Due Macelli. He had paid for a week in advance.

Forty-five minutes later Havelock passed through the huge portals of the massive Ostia Railway Station, built by Mussolini in the halcyon days of trumpets and drums and marching boots and trains that ran on time.

Italian was not Michael's best language, but he could read it well enough.

Biglietto per Venezia. Prima Classe.

The queue was short and his luck held. The famous *Venezia Ferrovia* was leaving in eight minutes, and if the *signore* wished to pay a premium, he could have the finest accommodation in the shape of his own compartment. He did wish, and, as the clerk stamped his ornate ticket, he was told that the *Ferrovia* was leaving from *Binario trentasei*, a double platform several football fields away.

"*Fate presto, signore! Non perdete tempo! Fate in fretta!*"

Michael walked rapidly into the mass of rushing humanity, threading his way as fast as possible towards platform 36. As usual – as he recalled from memories past – the giant dome was filled with crowds. Screeching arrivals and wailing departures were joined in counterpoint; screamed epithets punctuated the deafening roar because the porters, too, were obviously on strike. It took nearly five hectic minutes to shoulder a way through the huge stone arch and emerge on the double track platform. It was, if possible, more chaotic than the station itself. A crowded train had arrived from the north as the *Venezia Ferrovia* was about to depart. Freight dollies collided with hordes of embarking and disembarking passengers. It was a scene from a lower circle of Dante, screaming pandemonium.

Suddenly, across the platform, through the milling crowds, he caught sight of the back of a woman's head, the rim of a soft hat shadowing the side of her face. She was stepping out of the incoming train from the north, and had turned to talk to the guard. It had happened before: the same colour or cut of the hair, the shape of a neck. A scarf, or a hat or a raincoat, like those she had worn. It had happened before. Too often.

Then the woman turned, and sharp bolts of pain seared Havelock's eyes and temples, and surged downward – like hot knives into his chest. The face across the platform, seen sporadically through the weaving, colliding crowds, was no illusion. It was *she*.

Their eyes locked. Hers widened in raw fear; her face froze. Then she whipped her head away and plunged into the crowds in front of her.

Michael pressed his eyelids shut, then opened them, trying to rid himself of the pain and the shock and the sudden trembling that immobilized him. He dropped his suitcase. He had to *move*, run, race after this living corpse from the Costa Brava! She was alive! This woman he had loved, this apparition who had betrayed that love and had died for it was *alive*!

Like a crazed animal, he parted the bodies in his path screaming her name, ordering her to stop, commanding the crowds to stop her. He raced up the ramp and through the massive stone archway oblivious to the shrieking, furious

413

passengers he pummelled and left in his wake, unaware of the slaps and punches and body blocks hurled at him, unconscious of the hands that ripped his clothing.

She was nowhere to be seen in the station crowds.

4

With the terrifying impact of a bolt of lightning the sight of Jenna Karras had thrown him back in the shadow world he had left behind. She was alive! He had to keep moving; he had to find her. He ran blindly through the crowds, separating arms and gesturing hands and protesting shoulders. First one exit, then the other; and a third and a fourth. He stopped to question what few police he found, picking the words from a blurred Italian lexicon somewhere in his mind. He shouted her description, ending each distorted phrase with "*Soccorso!*" – only to be met with shrugs and looks of disapproval.

He kept running. A staircase – a door – a lift. He thrust 2000 lire on a woman heading into the ladies room; 5000 to a workman. He pleaded with three guards leaving the station, carrying satchels, on their way home.

Nothing. She was nowhere.

Havelock leaned over a litter bin, the sweat rolling down his face and neck, his hands scraped and bleeding. He thought for a moment that he would vomit into the rubbish; he had passed over the edge of hysteria. He had to pull himself back; he had to get hold of himself.

And the only way to do so was to keep moving, slower and slower, but to keep moving. Let the pounding in his chest decelerate, find a part of his mind so he could think. He vaguely remembered his suitcase; the possibility that it was still there was remote, but looking for it was something to do, somewhere to go at that moment. He started back through the crowds, body aching, perceptions numbed, buffeted by the gesticulating hordes around him as if he were in a dark tunnel filled with shadows and swirling winds. He had no idea how long it took for him to pass through the arch and walk down the ramp to the near-deserted platform. The *Ferrovia* had left, and the cleaners were invading the cars of the stationary train from the north . . . the train that had carried Jenna Karras.

There it was, crushed but still intact, straps broken, clothes protruding, yet oddly whole. His suitcase was wedged in the narrow space between the edge of the platform and the filthy, flat side of the third carriage. He knelt down and pulled it out of its jammed recess, sliding up first one side and then the other, hearing the abrasive squeaks of the leather, he lost his balance, falling to the concrete, still holding onto the half-destroyed handle. A man in overalls, pushing a wide broom, approached. Michael got to his feet, awkwardly, aware that the maintenance man had stopped, his broom motionless, his eyes conveying equal parts amusement and disgust. He thought Michael was drunk.

The handle broke; held by a single clasp, the suitcase abruptly tilted downward. Havelock yanked it up and clutched it in his arms; he started down the platform towards the ramp, knowing his walk was trance-like.

How many minutes later, or which particular exit he used, he would never know, but he was out on the street, the suitcase held against his chest, walking unsteadily past a row of lighted shops. He was conscious of the fact that people kept glancing at him, at his torn clothes and the crushed suitcase, its contents spilling out. The swirling mists were beginning to break up, the cold night air diffusing them. He had to find his sanity by concentrating on the little things: he would wash his face, change his clothes, have a cigarette, replace the suitcase.

Emporio Per Viaggiatori. The neon letters glowed impressively in deep red above the wide shop window filled with accessories for the traveller. It was one of those shops near the Ostia Station that catered to the wealthy foreigner and the self-indulgent Italian. The merchandise was expensive, replicas of ordinary objects turned into luxuries by way of sterling silver and polished brass.

Havelock stood for a moment, breathing deeply, holding onto the suitcase as if it were somehow an object that would carry him like a plank in a wild sea. He walked inside; mercifully, it was near closing time, and the shop was devoid of customers.

The manager emerged from behind the middle counter, his expression alarmed. He hesitated, then stepped back as if to retreat quickly. Havelock spoke rapidly in barely passable Italian. "I was caught in an insane crowd on the platform. I'm afraid I fell. I'll need to buy a few things . . . a number of things, actually. I'm expected at the Hassler fairly soon."

At the mention of Rome's most exclusive hotel, the manager at once turned sympathetic, even brotherly.

"*Animali!*" he exclaimed, gesturing to his God. "How perfectly dreadful for you, *signore*! Here, let me help you – "

"I'll need a new piece of luggage. Soft, very good leather, if you have it."

"*Naturalmente.*"

"I realize it's an imposition, but could I possibly wash somewhere? I'd hate to greet the *Contessa* the way I look now."

"This way, *signore*! A thousand apologies! I speak for all Rome! This way . . ."

While Michael washed and changed his clothes in the back room, he focused his thoughts – as they came to him on the brief visits he and Jenna Karras had made to Rome. There had been two. On the first they had passed through for a single night; the second was much longer, very official – three or four days, if he remembered correctly. They had been awaiting orders from Washington, having travelled as a Yugoslav couple through the Balkan countries in order to gather information on the sudden expansion in border defences. There had been a man, an army intelligence officer not easily forgotten; he had been Havelock's DC conduit. What made the man memorable was his cover; he was posing as the only first-level black attaché at the embassy.

Their first conference had not been without humour – black humour. Michael and Jenna were to meet the attaché at an out-of-the-way restaurant west of the Palatine. They had waited in the crowded stand-up bar, preferring to let the conduit select a table, oblivious of the tall black soldier ordering a vodka martini on their right. After several minutes the man smiled, and said,

"I'm jes' Rastus in the *pila di bosco*, Massa Havelock. Do you think we might sit down?"

His name was Lawrence Brown. Lieutenant-Colonel Lawrence B. Brown – the middle initial standing for his real name, Baylor.

"So help me God," the colonel had told them over after-dinner drinks that night, "the fellows in G-Two felt there was more 'concrete association' – that's what they called it – by using Brown in the cover. It went under the heading of 'psy-acceptance', can you believe it? Hell, I suppose it's better than Attaché Coffee-Face."

Baylor was a man he could talk to . . . if Baylor would agree to talk to him. And where? It would not be anywhere near the embassy; the United States government had several terrible things to explain to a retired field agent.

It took over twenty minutes on the manager's phone while the manager repacked Michael's clothing in an outrageously priced new suitcase – before Havelock reached the embassy switchboard. Senior Attaché Brown was currently attending a reception on the first floor.

"Tell him it's urgent," said Michael. "My name is . . . Baylor."

Lawrence Baylor was reluctant to the point of turning Havelock down. Anything a retired intelligence officer had to say would best be said at the embassy. For any number of reasons.

"Suppose I told you I just came out of retirement. I may not be on your payroll – or anyone else's – but I'm very much back in. I'd suggest you don't blow this, Colonel."

"There's a café on the via Pancrazio, *La Ruota del Pavone*. Do you know it?"

"I'll find it."

"Forty-five minutes."

"I'll be there. Waiting."

Havelock watched from a table in the darkest corner of the café as the army officer ordered a carafe of wine from the bar and began walking across the dimly-lit room. Baylor's mahogany face was taut; he was not comfortable, and when he reached the table, he did not offer his hand. He sat down opposite Michael, exhaled slowly and attempted a grim smile.

"Nice to see you," he said with little conviction.

"Thank you."

"And unless you've got something to say we want to hear, you're putting me in a pretty rough spot, buddy. I hope you know that."

"I've got something that'll blow your mind," said Havelock, his voice involuntarily a whisper. The trembling had returned; he gripped his wrist to control it. "It's blown mine."

The colonel studied Michael, his eyes dropping to Havelock's hands. "You're stretched, I can see that. What is it?"

"She's *alive*. I *saw* her!"

Baylor was silent, immobile. His eyes roamed Michael's face, noting the marks of recent scrapes and bruises on Havelock's skin. It was obvious that he had made the connection. "Are you referring to the Costa Brava?" he asked finally.

"You know damn well I am!" said Michael angrily. "My abrupt retirement and the circumstances thereof have been flashed to every goddamned station and post we've got. It's why you just said what you did. 'Beware the screwed-up talent,' Washington tells you. He might do anything, say anything, think he has scores to settle."

"It's happened."

"Not to me. I don't have any scores to think about because I'm not interested in the ballgame. I'm rational. I saw what I saw. And she saw *me*! She acknowledged *me*! She *ran*!"

"Emotional stress is the first cousin to hysteria," said the colonel quietly. "A man can see a lot of things that aren't there in that condition. And you had a jolt."

"Past tense, not currently applicable. I was out. I accepted the fact and the reasons – "

"Come *on*, buddy," insisted the soldier. "You don't throw away sixteen years of involvement."

"*I* did."

"You were here in Rome with her. Memories get activated, twisted. As I said, it happens."

"Again, negative. Nothing was activated, nothing twisted. I *saw* – "

"You even called me," interrupted Baylor sharply. "The three of us spent a couple of evenings together. A few drinks, a few laughs. Association; you reached me."

"There was no one else. My cover was D-squared. You were my only contact here in Rome! I can walk into the embassy now, I couldn't then."

"Then let's go," said the colonel quickly.

"No way! Besides, it's not the point. *You* are. You fielded orders to me from Washington seven months ago, and now you're going to send an emergency flag back to those same people. Tell them what I've told you, what I saw. You haven't got a choice."

"I've got an opinion. I'm relaying what a former talent said while in a state of extreme anxiety."

"Fine! Good! Then try this. Five days ago in Athens I nearly killed a man we both know from the Dzerzhinsky files for telling me Costa Brava wasn't a Soviet exercise. That she wasn't any part of the KGB, much less the VKR. I didn't kill him because I thought it was a probe, a *blind* probe – that man was telling the *truth*, as he knew the truth. I sent a message back to Moscow. The bait was too obvious, the smell too rotten."

"I suppose that was charitable of you considering your record."

"Oh, no, the charity started with *him*. You see, he could have taken me. I could have found myself in Sevastopol on my way to Dzerzhinsky Square without even knowing I'd left Athens."

"He was that good? That well connected?"

"So much so he was self-effacing. But he didn't take me. I wasn't booked on the Dardanelles airlift. He didn't want me."

417

"Why not?"

"Because he was convinced *I* was the bait. Pretty fair irony, isn't it? There was no room at the Lubyanka. I was turned out. Instead, he gave me his own message for Washington. Dzerzhinsky wouldn't touch me." Havelock paused. "And now *this*."

The colonel narrowed his eyes pensively, and, with both hands, turned his glass on the table. "I don't have your expertise, but say you actually did see what you say you saw . . ."

"I did. Accept it."

"No concessions, but say it's possible – it could still be a lure. They've got you under a glass, know your plans, your itinerary. Their computers pick up a woman reasonably similar in appearance, and with a little cosmetic surgery they've got a double good enough for short distances. 'Beware the screwed-up talent.' You never know when he thinks he has 'scores to settle'. Especially if he's given some time to stew, to get worked up."

"What I saw was in her *eyes!* But even if you won't accept that there's something else; it voids the strategy, and every point can be checked. Two hours ago I didn't know I'd be inside that station; ten minutes before I saw her I didn't know I'd be on that platform and neither could anyone else. I came here yesterday and took a room in a *pensione* on the Due Macelli for a week, paid in advance. At eight-thirty tonight I saw a poster in a window and decided to go to Venice. I didn't speak to anyone." Michael reached into his pocket, took out his ticket for the *Venezia Ferrovia* and laced it in front of Lawrence Baylor. "The *Ferrovia* was scheduled to leave at nine-thirty-five. The time of purchase is stamped across the top of this. Read it!"

"Twenty-one, twenty-seven," said Baylor, reading. "Twenty-seven past nine. Eight minutes before the train left."

"All verifiable. Now look at me and tell me I'm lying. And while you're at it, explain how that set-up could have been mounted given the time span *and* the fact that she was on an incoming train!"

"I can't. *If* she – "

"She was talking to a guard seconds before she got off. I'm sure I can find him."

Baylor was silent again; he stared at Havelock, then spoke softly. "Don't bother. I'll send the flag." He paused, adding, "Along with qualified support. Whatever you saw, you're not lying. Where can I reach you?"

"Sorry. I'll reach you."

"They'll want to talk to you, probably in a hurry."

"I'll be in touch."

"Why the static?"

"Something Rostov said in Athens."

"*Rostov?* Pyotr Rostov?" The colonel's eyes widened. "You don't go much higher in the Dzerzhinsky."

"There's higher."

"He'll do. What did he say? What did he tell you?"

"That our nostrils never quite adjust. Instead, they develop a kind of sensitivity – to variations of the basic rotten smell. Like animals."

"I expected something less abstract," said Baylor, annoyed.

"Really? From where I stand, it sounds concrete as hell. The Costa Brava trap was engineered in Washington, the evidence compiled by the inner shell in one of those white, sterile offices on the top floor of State."

"I understand you were in control," interrupted Baylor.

"The last phase. I insisted on it."

"Then you – "

"I acted on everything that was given to me. And now I want to know *why* it was given to me. Why I saw what I did tonight."

"*If* you saw – "

"She's *alive*. I want to know why! How!"

"I still don't understand."

"Costa Brava was meant for *me*. Someone wanted me out. Not dead, but out. Comfortably removed from those temptations that often afflict men like me."

"Scores to settle?" asked the colonel. "The Agee syndrome? The Snepp complex? I didn't know you were infected."

"I've had my quota of shocks, my share of questions. Someone wanted those questions buried and *she* went along. Why?"

"Two assumptions I'm not willing to concede are facts. And if you intended to bare a few shocks not in the national interest, I imagine – and I'm speaking hypothetically in the extreme, of course – there are other methods of . . . burying them."

"Dispatch? Call me dead?"

"I didn't say we'd kill you. We don't live in that kind of country." The colonel paused, then added, "On the other hand, why not?"

"For the same reason others haven't met with odd accidents that prearranged pathologists might label something else. Self-protection is ingrained in our job, brother. It's another syndrome; it's called the Nuremberg. Those shocks, instead of being buried, might surface. Sealed depositions to be opened by unnamed attorneys in the event of questionable et ceteras."

"*Jesus*, you said that? You went that far?"

"Strangely enough, I never did. Not seriously. I simply got angry. The rest was assumed."

"What kind of world do you people live in?"

"The same one you do – only we've been around a little longer, a little deeper. And that's why I won't tell you where you can reach me. My nostrils have picked up a sickening odour from the Potomac." Havelock leaned forward, his voice harsh, low, nearly a whisper again. "I know that girl. For her to do what she did, something must have been done to her, held over her. Something obscene. I want to know what it was and why."

"Assuming," Baylor began slowly, "assuming you're right, and I don't for an instant concede that you are, what makes you think they'll tell you?"

"It was all so sudden," said Michael, leaning back, his body rigid, his voice now floating as if in a painful dream. "It was a Tuesday and we were in Barcelona. We'd been there for a week; something was going to happen in the sector, that's all Washington told us. Then word came from Madrid: a Four Zero communication had been flown in by courier, contents restricted to the embassy, Eyes Only. Mine only. There's no Cons Op station in Madrid, no one cleared to relay the information, so I flew in on Wednesday morning, signed for that goddamned steel container, and opened it in a room guarded by three marines. Everything was there, everything she'd done, all the information she'd transmitted – information she could have got only from me. The trap was there, too, myself in control if I so wished – and I so wished. They knew it was the only way I'd be convinced. On Friday I was back in Barcelona, and by Saturday it was over . . . and I *was* convinced. Five days and the walls came tumbling down. No trumpets, just lights and screams and loud ugly noises intruding on the surf. Five days . . . so sudden, so swift, everything pitched at a crescendo. It was the only way it could have been done."

"You haven't answered my question," Baylor interrupted quietly. "If you're right, what makes you think they'll tell you?"

Havelock levelled his eyes at the soldier. "Because they're afraid. It comes down to the 'why'. The questions, the shocks; which one was it?"

"What are you talking about?"

"The decision to remove me wasn't made gradually, Colonel. Something triggered it. They don't force a man out the way I was forced out because of accumulated differences. Talent's expensive; proven field talent too difficult to replace. Accommodations can be made, explanations offered, agreements reached. All these are tried before they let the talent go. But no one tried with me."

"Can you be more specific?" the officer pressed, again annoyed.

"I wish I could be. It's something I know, or they *think* I know. Something I could have written down. And it's a bomb."

"Do you," Baylor asked, coldly, professionally, "have such a piece of information?"

"I'll find it," replied Havelock, suddenly moving his chair back, prepared to leave. "You tell them that. Just as I'll find her, tell them that, too. It won't be easy because she's not with them any more. She got away; she's gone under. I also saw that in her eyes. But I'll find her."

"Maybe – " Baylor said urgently, "maybe if everything you say proves out, they'd be willing to help."

"They'd better be," said Michael, getting to his feet and looking down at the soldier-conduit. "I'll need all the help I can get. In the meantime I want this whole goddamned thing spelled out – chapter and verse, to quote an old source of mine. Because if it isn't, I'm going to start telling tales out of school. When and from where none of you will know, but the words will be there loud and clear. And somewhere among them will be that bomb."

"Don't do anything stupid!"

"Don't mistake me, I don't want to. But what was done to her, to me – to *us* – just wasn't fair, Colonel. I'm back in. Solo. I'll be in touch."

Havelock turned and walked swiftly out of the café into the via Pancrazio.

He reached the via Galvani on his way back to the railway station where he had deposited his newly acquired suitcase in a locker. Suddenly, the painful irony struck him. It had been a suitcase in a locker at an airport in Barcelona that had condemned

Jenna Karras. The defector from the Baader-Meinhof had led them to it – in exchange for the quiet cancellation of a death sentence pronounced *in absentia*. The German terrorist had told Madrid that *die Fräulein Karras* kept secret, updated field records within her reach at all times. It was a *Voennaya* custom dictated by the strange relationship the violent and clandestine branch of Soviet intelligence had with the rest of the KGB. Certain field personnel on long-range deep cover operations had access to their own files in the event of their superiors in Moscow suddenly not being accessible. Self-protection sometimes assumed odd forms; no one had questioned it.

No one had questioned. Not even he.

Someone makes contact with her and gives her a key, stating a location. A room or a locker, even a bank. The material is there, including new objectives as they are developed.

A man had stopped her one afternoon two days before Michael left for Madrid. In a café on the Paseo Isabel. A drunk. He had shaken her hand, then kissed it. Three days later Michael had found a key in Jenna's purse. The next day she was dead.

There had been a key, but whose key was it? He had seen photocopies verified by Langley of every item in that suitcase. But whose suitcase was it? If not hers, how did three sets of fingerprints confirmed to be hers get inside? And if the prints were hers, why did she permit it?

What had they done to her? What had they done to a blonde woman on the Costa Brava who had screamed in Czech and whose spine and neck and head had been pierced with bullets? What kind of people were they who could put human beings on strings and blow them up as calmly as one might explode mannequins in a horror show. That woman had died; he had seen too much death to be mistaken. It was no charade, as the elegant Gravet might have put it.

Yet it was all a charade. They were all puppets. But on what stage and for whose benefit were they performing?

He hurried faster; the via Della Mamorata was in sight. He was only blocks now from the massive railway station; he would begin there. At least, he had an idea; whether it made sense or not the next half-hour would tell.

He passed a garishly lit news-stand where tabloids competed with glossy magazines. Capped teeth and outsized breasts battled for attention with mutilated bodies and graphic descriptions of rape and mayhem. And then he saw the famous face staring up at him from the cover of the international edition of *Time*. The clear eyes behind the horn-rimmed glasses shone as they always did, filled with high intelligence – cold at first glance, yet somehow warmer the longer one looked at them. Softened, perhaps by an understanding few on this earth possessed. There he was, the high cheekbones and the aquiline nose, the generous lips from which such extraordinary words poured forth.

"A Man for all seasons, all peoples." That was the simple caption beneath the photograph. No name, no title; none was necessary. The world knew the American Secretary of State, heard his reasoned, deliberate voice and understood. This *was* a man for all; he transcended borders and languages and national insanities. There were those who believed – and Michael was one of them – that either the world would listen to Anthony Matthias or it would be blown to hell in a mushroom cloud.

Anton Matthias. Friend, mentor, surrogate father. Where Costa Brava was concerned, he, too, had been a puppet.

As Havelock put several lire notes down on the counter and picked up the magazine, he remembered vividly the handwritten note Anton had insisted the strategists in Washington include with the Four Zero file flown to Madrid. From their few brief conversations with Havelock in Georgetown, Matthias had grasped the depth of his feelings for the woman assigned to him for the past eight months. At last, perhaps, he was ready to get out and find the peace that had eluded him all these years. The statesman had made gentle fun of the situation; when a fellow Czech past forty and in Michael's line of work decided to concentrate on one woman, Slav tradition and contemporary fiction suffered irreparable blows.

But there had been no such levity in Matthias's note.

Moje Rozmilý Syn
The attached pains my heart as it will yours. You who suffered so much in the early days, and have given of yourself so brilliantly and selflessly to our adopted country in these later ones, must again know pain. I have demanded and received a complete verification of these findings. If you wish to remove yourself from the scene, you may, of course, do so. Do not feel bound by the attached recommendations. There is only so much a nation can ask, and you have given with honour and more. Perhaps now the angers we spoke of years ago, the furies that propelled you into this terrible life, have subsided, permitting you to return to another world that needs the labours of your mind. I pray so.
                    Milovati, pritel,
                    Anton M.

Havelock forced the note from his mind; it served only to aggravate the incomprehensible. Verification: *Positive.* He opened the magazine to the article on Matthias. There was nothing new, merely a recap of his more recent accomplishments in the area of arms negotiations. It ended with the observation that the Secretary of State was off for a well-deserved vacation at an unnamed location. Michael smiled; he knew where it was. A cabin in the Shenandoah Valley. It was entirely possible that before the night was over he would use a dozen codes to reach that mountain cabin. But not until he found out what had happened. For Anton Matthias had been touched by it too.

The crowds inside the giant dome of the Ostia had thinned out, the last of the trains leaving Rome having departed or being just about to depart. Havelock pulled his suitcase from the locker and looked around for a sign; it had to be somewhere. It could well be a waste of time, but he did not think so; at least it was a place to start. He had told the intelligence officer-attaché in the café on the via Pancrazio: "She was talking to a guard seconds before she got off. I'm sure I can find him."

Surely someone running did not casually strike up a conversation with a guard for the sake of conviviality; too much was on that someone's mind. And in every city there were those sections where men and women who wished to disappear could do so, where cash was the only currency, mouths were kept shut, and hotel

422

registries rarely reflected accurate identities. Jenna Karras might know the names of districts, even streets, but she did not – had not known – Rome itself. A city on strike might just possibly persuade someone running that it was urgent to ask a question or a direction of someone who might have the answer.

There was the sign on the wall, an arrow pointing to the office complex: *Amministratore della Stazione.*

Thirty-five minutes later, having persuaded a night manager that it was imperative, and in both his and the guard's financial interest that the guard should be found, he had the address of the man assigned to cars *tre, quattro* and *cinque* for the incoming train on *Binario Trentasei* at eight-thirty that evening. As the rail system was a government service, a photograph was attached to the employment sheet. It was the man he had seen talking to Jenna Karras. Among his qualifications was a proficiency in English. *Livello Uno.*

He climbed the worn stone steps of the block of flats to the fifth floor, found the name "Mascolo" on the door and knocked. The red-faced guard was dressed in loose trousers held up by wide braces over a vest. His breath reeked of cheap wine and his eyes were not entirely focused. Havelock took a 10,000-lire note from his pocket.

"Who can remember one passenger among thousands?" protested the man, seated opposite Michael at the kitchen table.

"I'm sure *you* can," said Havelock, removing another bill. "*Think.* She was probably one of the last people you spoke to on that train. Slender, medium height, a wide-brimmed hat – you were standing at the door."

"*Sì! Naturalmente. Una bella ragazza!* I remember!" The guard took the money and drank some wine; he belched and continued. "She asked me if I knew where she could make connections for Civitavecchia."

"Civitavecchia? That's a town north of here, isn't it?"

"*Sì.* A port on the Tyrrhenian Sea."

"Did you know?"

"There are very few trains between Rome and Civitavecchia, *signore,* and certainly not at that hour. It is at best a stop for freight, not passengers."

"What did you tell her?"

"Just that. She appeared reasonably well dressed so I suggested she negotiate a taxi for a flat rate. If she could find one. Rome is a *manicomio di pazzi!*"

Havelock nodded thanks, placed another note on the table and went to the door. He glanced at his watch; it was twenty past one in the morning. Civitavecchia. A seaport on the Tyrrhenian. Ships heading out to sea on a given day invariably left with the early light. At dawn.

He had roughly three hours to reach Civitavecchia, search the waterfront, find a pier, find a ship – find an unlisted passenger.

5

He raced out of the marble lobby of the hotel in Bernini Circle, rushing blindly up through the winding streets until he reached the via Veneto. The desk clerk at the hotel had not been able to help him but not for lack of trying; spurred on by the thick folds of lire, he futilely punched the telephone bar and screamed numbers at the sleepy switchboard operator. The night clerk's contacts were limited; he could not raise a rented car.

Havelock stopped for breath, studying the lights on the Veneto. Several cafés and the Excelsior Hotel were still illuminated. Someone had to help him – he had to get to Civitavecchia! *He had to find her. He could not lose her.* Not again, not *ever* again! He had to reach her and hold her and tell her that terrible things had been done to them, tell her over and over again until she saw the truth in his eyes and heard that truth in his voice, and saw the love he felt so deeply, and understood the unendurable guilt that never left him – for he had killed that love.

He began running away, first into the Excelsior, where no amount of money interested an arrogant clerk.

"You've got to help me!"

"You are not even a guest, *signore*," said the man, glancing to his left.

Slowly Michael angled his head. Across the lobby two policemen were watching the scene. They conferred; obviously the night operation at the Excelsior was under open official scrutiny. Pedlars of capsules and pills, white powder and syringes, were working the world-famous street. One of the uniformed men stepped forward. Havelock turned and walked rapidly to the entrance, once again running into the half-deserted street, towards the nearest profusion of light.

The tired *maître d'hôtel* of the Café de Paris told him he was a *capo zuccone*. Who would rent a car to a stranger at this hour? The American manager of a third-rate saloon told him to "pound sand".

Again the winding streets, again the sweat drenching his hairline, rolling down his cheeks. The Hassler – the Villa Medici! He had used the name of the elegant hotel in the luggage shop near the station . . .

The night *concierge* at the Hassler's Villa Medici was accustomed to the vagaries of Rome's wealthiest hotel guests. Arrangements were made for Michael to hire a Fiat, one of the Hassler's staff vehicles. The price was exorbitant, but with it came a map of Rome and its environs, the most direct route to Civitavecchia marked in red.

He reached the port city at three-fifteen, and by three-forty-five he had driven up and down the waterfront, studying it until he had decided where to park.

It was a section common to most waterfronts, where the floodlights washing the piers remained on all night and activity never stopped; where groupings of dockworkers and deckhands mingled like slow-moving automatons, criss-crossing one another – men and machinery meshed in volatile conflict – loading the cargo holds and preparing the massive boilers and outdated engines of the larger vessels

424

soon to head out into deep water. Where cafés and coffee houses lined the mist-laden alleys, punctuated by the diffused light of the street lamps – places of refuge serving the harshest whisky and the most glutinous food.

To the north and south were the smaller piers, where halyards and masts swayed in silhouette against the moonlight; filthy harbours for the fishing boats and *controllori* trawlers that ventured no more than forty kilometres out to where decades of experience and tradition told the captains the catches were most plentiful. These piers did not begin to stir until early light was closer, when faint sprays of yellowish white inched their way over the south-east horizon, pushing the night sky up. Only then did groaning, dull-eyed men walk down the wooden planks towards oily gunwales and the interminable, blinding day ahead. Jenna Karras would not be here but somewhere in that complex of larger piers, where ships looked to the tides and charts and sailed to other ports, other countries.

She was somewhere in this stretch of the waterfront where swirling pockets of mist rolled off the sea and across the docks, through intersecting pools of floodlights and the hammering tattoo of nocturnal labours. She would be hidden from the *controllori* of the piers, who were paid by the state and the shipping companies to be on the lookout for material and human contraband. Keep her out of sight; the moment would come when she could be taken on board, after a *capo-operaio* had inspected a hold and signed the papers stating the ship in question was legally free to depart. Then she could walk swiftly out of the shadows and down a pier, *controllori* and *operai* themselves out of sight, their duties finished.

Which pier? Which ship? *Where are you, Jenna?* There were three freighters, all of medium tonnage, berthed alongside one another at three of the four major cargo docks. The fourth housed two smaller vessels barge class – with conveyor equipment and thick piping machinery transporting and pumping bulk cargo into the open holds. She would be taken aboard one of the freighters; the immediate thing to learn was the departure time of each.

He parked the Fiat on a side street that intersected the *viale* fronting the four piers. He walked across the wide avenue, dodging several vans and trucks, to the first pier on the left, to the gate manned by a uniformed guard, a civil servant of questionable civility. He was unpleasant, and the nuisance of having to piece together Havelock's barely fluent Italian added to his hostility.

"What do you want to know for?" asked the guard, filling the doorway of the gatehouse. "What's it to you?"

"I'm trying to find someone who may have booked passage," said Michael, hoping the words he used were close enough to his meaning.

"*Passaggio? Biglietto?* Who buys a ticket on a Portuguese freighter?"

Havelock saw his opening; he leaned closer, glancing about as he spoke. "This is the ship then. Forgive my poor use of your language, *Signor Controllore*. It's unforgivable. Actually, I'm with the Embassy of Portugal in Rome. In my way an . . . inspector, as you are. We were told there may be certain irregularities with this vessel. Any cooperation from you could be duly conveyed to your superiors."

The opportunistic human ego was not affected by the lowliness of a civil service rating. The hostile guard was abruptly pleasant, moving aside to admit the *straniero importante.*

"*Scusatemi, signore!* I did not understand. We who patrol these holes of corruption must cooperate with one another, no? And, in truth, a word to my superiors – in Rome, of course."

"Of course. Not here."

"Of course. Not here. They are brutes down here. Come in, come in. It must be chilly for you."

The *Miguel Cristobal* was scheduled to leave port at 5:00 A.M. Its captain was a man named Aliandro, who had been in the wheelhouse of the *Cristobal* for the past twelve years, a skipper who, it was said, knew every island, every shoal in the Western Mediterranean.

The two other freighters were of Italian registry. The guards at the gates were wearily co-operative, perfectly willing to give whatever information the oddly spoken foreigner requested. What he wished to know he could read in any newspaper under *Navi Informazione-Civitavecchia*, the pages of which were usually torn out and tacked to the walls of the various cafés around the waterfront. They helped when crewmen got drunk and forgot their schedules.

The *Isola d'Elba* was leaving at five-thirty, the *Santa Teresa* twenty minutes later at five-fifty.

Havelock started to walk away from the third gate. He looked at his watch, it was eight minutes past four. So little time.

Jenna! Where are you?

He heard the sound of a bell behind him. It was sudden, abrasive, echoing in its own vibrations, an outside bell meant to be heard above the shouts and machinery of the piers. Alarmed, he turned quickly. The guard had stepped inside the glass cubicle that was his gatehouse and was answering the telephone. The verbal flow of attentive *Sis* emphasized the fact that whoever was on the other end of the line was issuing orders that must be thoroughly understood.

Telephones and guards at checkpoints were sources of concern to Michael. For a moment he was not sure whether or not to run. The answer was given instantly. The guard hung up the phone and stuck his head out of the door.

"You! You want to know so much about this stinking tub, here's something else! The *Teresa* stays put. She doesn't sail until six godforsaken trucks get here from Torino, which could be eight hours from now. The unions will make those bastards pay, let me tell you! Then they'll fine the crew for being drunk! They're *all* bastards!"

The *Teresa* was out of the running, for a while at least. He could concentrate on the *Elba* and the *Cristobal*, and for them he still had only minutes. His approach had to be direct; there was no time for the subtleties of move and countermove, for circling the grounds of inquiry and selecting targets cautiously, being aware of whoever might be watching him. There was time only for money – if takers could be found. Or force.

Havelock walked quickly back to the second gate where the *Isola d'Elba* was berthed, altering his story only slightly for the weary guard. He wished to speak to a few of the vessel's crew, those who might be on shore awaiting the ship's call. Would the cooperative civil servant, having shaken a hand with several thousand

426

lire folded in the palm, know which of the waterfront cafés were favoured by the *Elba's* crew?

"They stick together, no, *signore*? When fights break out, seamen want their friends around, even those they hate on board. Try *Il Pinguino*. Or perhaps *La Carrozza Mare*. The whisky's cheaper at the first, but the food makes one vomit. It's better at *La Carrozza*."

The once hostile, now obsequious, guard at the gate of the *Cristobal* was more than co-operative; he was effusively friendly. "There is a café on the Via Maggio where it is said many things change hands."

"Would the *Cristobal's* men be there?"

"Some perhaps. The Portuguese do not mix well, of course. No one trusts them – Not *you*, signore! I refer only to the garbage of the sea. The same everywhere. Not *you*, may God forgive me!"

"The name please?"

"*Il Tritone*."

It took less than twelve minutes to disqualify *Il Tritone*. Michael walked through the heavy doors, beneath the crude *bas-relief* of a naked creature half-man and half-fish, into the raucous squalor of the waterfront bar. The smoke was thick, the stench of stale whisky thicker. Men shouted between the tables; others lurched about, and not a few were slumped at their tables, their heads resting on folded arms, small pools of alcohol surrounding hands and nostrils and bearded cheeks.

Havelock chose the oldest-looking man behind the bar and approached him first. "Are there any here from the *Cristobal*?"

"Portoghesi?"

"Sì."

"A few . . . over there, I think."

Michael looked through the smoke and the weaving bodies to a table across the room. There were four men. "What about the *Isola d'Elba*?" he asked, turning back to the bartender.

"*Maiali!*" replied the man. "Pigs! They come in here, I throw them out! Scum!"

"They must be something," said Havelock, scanning the *Tritone's* clientele, his throat trembling at the thought of Jenna among such men.

"You want crew from the *Elba*, go to *Il Pinguino*. Over there, they don't care."

Michael took out a ten thousand lire note and placed it in front of the barman. "Do you speak Portuguese? Enough to be understood?"

"Down here, if one cares to make a living one must be understood in half a dozen tongues." The man slipped the money into his apron pocket, adding, "They no doubt speak Italian, probably better than you, *signore*. So let us speak in English. What do you wish me to do?"

"There's an empty table back there," said Havelock, relieved, changing language, and gesturing with his head towards a rear corner of the café. "I'm going over to sit down. You go to those men and tell them I want to see them – one at a time. If you think they won't understand me, come over with each and be my interpreter."

"*Interprete?*"

"Sì."

"*Bene*."

One by one the four Portuguese sailors came to the table, each bewildered, two proficient in Italian, one in English, one needing the services of the *interprete*. To each, Michael said the same words.

"I'm looking for a woman. It's a minor matter, nothing to be concerned about; call it an affair of the heart. She's an impetuous woman; we've all known them, haven't we? But now she may have gone too far for her own good. I'm told she has a friend on the *Cristobal*. She may have been around the pier, asking questions, looking for transport. She's an attractive woman, average height, blonde hair, probably wearing a raincoat and a wide-brimmed hat. Have you seen anyone like that? If you have, there could be a lot more money in your pocket than there is now."

And to each man he gave an explanation for his summons that the sailor could take back to his companions, along with five thousand lire.

"Whatever you tell me remains between us. For my good more than yours. When you go back to your table you can say the same thing I'm telling everyone. I want rough sex with someone leaving Civitavecchia, but I'm not going to take it from any son of a bitch who won't leave his papers at a hotel desk. Got it?"

Only with the third man did the barman, who insisted on being present at each interview, caution Havelock firmly. "This one will leave his papers at a desk," he said.

"Then he's not my type."

"*Bene!*"

"*Grazie.*"

"*Prego.*"

Nothing. No such woman had been seen or heard of on the *Cristobal* pier. The four Portuguese crewmen resumed their drinking.

Havelock thanked the perplexed older man beside him and pressed another bill into his apron pocket. "Which way to *Il Pinguino*?" he asked.

"The *Elba* crew?"

"That's right."

"I'll go with you," said the barman, removing his apron and the money in its pocket.

"Why?"

"You sound like a decent man. Also stupid. You walk into *Il Pinguino* asking questions, your money's for everyone. All it takes is one sailor with a quiet knife."

"I can take care of myself."

"You are not only stupid, you are *very* stupid. I own *Il Tritone*; they respect me at *Pinguino*. You'll be safer with me. You pass money too quickly."

"I'm in a hurry."

"*Presto!* Let's get on with it. It's a bad morning here. Not like the old days when men knew that half a chestful was enough. You taste it in your throat, you know. These assholes mix up comfort with wanting no memory. *Vieni!*"

The café five blocks away brought back memories of a life he had thought was over. He had been in too many such places in that other life; it was a sewer, a place consigned to oblivion. If *Il Tritone* catered to the garbage of humanity, *Il Pinguino* took the dregs and considered it *prima clientela*. The smoke was thicker, the shouting louder; men did not lurch, they lunged at nothing and everything, intent only on the violence in their minds. These were men who found amusement in the sudden exposure of another's weakness – or a semblance of weakness – which they construed as an absence of manhood – and then attacked.

They had nothing else. They challenged the shadows of their own deepest fears.

The owner of *Il Tritone* was greeted by his counterpart within seconds of ushering Havelock through the door. The *Pinguino's proprietario* matched his establishment, having few teeth and arms that hung like huge, hairy cheeses. He was not as large as Michael's newfound friend, but there was a sense of violence about him reminiscent of a boar, that could be quickly stirred to anger.

The greetings between the two men were spoken rapidly, perfunctorily. But there was respect, as *Il Tritone's* owner said there would be, and the arrangements were made swiftly, with a minimum of explanation.

"The American looks for a woman. It is a *malinteso*, and not our business," said the owner of *Il Tritone*. "She may be sailing with the *Elba* and one of these thieves may have seen her. He's willing to pay."

"He'd better hurry," replied the sullen boar. "The oilers left an hour ago; they're sweating piss-green by now. The second mate will be here any minute to gather up the rest of the deck."

"How many are there?"

"Eight, ten, who knows? I count lire, not faces."

"Get one of your people to go round and ask quietly, find them, and tell me who they are. Clear a table for my companion. I'll bring each one to him."

Separately, warily, in varying phases of stupor, the remaining crew of the *Elba* sat down and listened to Havelock, whose Italian increasingly became more fluent as he repeated his question. And with each he studied the man's face, the eyes, looking for a reaction, a glint of recognition, a brief straying of glance that covered a lie. With the sixth man he thought he found it; it was in the lips – a sudden stretching unrelated to the sagging muscle tone induced by whisky, and in the clouded eyes, dulled by an instinctive desire not to listen. The man knew something.

"You've seen her, *haven't* you?" said Michael, losing control, speaking in English.

"*Ascolta*," broke in the owner of *Il Tritone*. "*In italiano, signore*."

"Sorry." Havelock repeated the question, which was more an accusation, in Italian.

The sailor responded with a shrug, shifted his position and started to get up. Michael reached over quickly, clamping his hand on the seaman's arm. The response was now ugly; the sailor squinted his rheumy, red-veined eyes, his mouth like that of an angry dog, lips parted, stained yellow teeth showing. In seconds he would lunge – drunkenly, to be sure – but nevertheless, attack was imminent.

"*Rilassati*," ordered the owner of *Il Tritone*; then spoke rapidly under his breath in English. "Show him money. Quickly! This pig will grab your throat, and they'll be all over us and you will learn nothing. You are right. He's seen her."

Havelock released the man's arm, reached into his pocket and took out the thick pack of awkwardly small lire notes. He separated two bills, placing them in front of the sailor; they totalled 40,000 lire, a day's pay on board ship.

"As you can see," he said in Italian, "there's more here. You can't take it from me, but I can give it to you. On the other hand, you can walk away and not tell me anything." Michael paused, leaned back in the chair, staring at the man, his expression hostile. "But I can make trouble for you. And I will."

"*In che modo?*" The crewman was as angry as he was bewildered, his eyes darting between Havelock's face, the money and the owner of *Il Tritone*, who sat impassively, his rigid posture showing that he was aware of the danger in Michael's tactic.

"How?" Havelock leaned forward, his fingers pulling the lire towards him, as though retrieving two vital cards in a game of *baccarat*. "I'll go over to the *Elba* and find your captain. Whatever I say to him about you he's not going to like."

"*Che cosa?* What? . . . What can you say to him *in riguardo a me* that he would *ascoltare?*" The sailor's sudden use of English words was unexpected. He turned to the owner of *Il Tritone*. "Perhaps this pig will grab *your* throat, old man. I need no help from others. For you or this *ricco americano*." The man unzipped his coarse wool jacket; the handle of a knife protruded from a scabbard strapped to his belt; his head swayed from the effects of the whisky. A very thin line was about to be crossed.

Abruptly, Michael settled back in his chair and laughed quietly. It was a genuine laugh, in no way hostile or challenging, further confusing the seaman. "*Bene!*" said Michael, suddenly leaning forward again, removing two more 5,000 lire notes from the loose packet of bills. "I wanted to find out if you had balls, and you told me. Good! A man without balls doesn't know what he sees. He makes things up because he's afraid, or because he sees money." Havelock gripped the man's hand at the wrist, forcing the palm open. It was a strong if friendly grip, indicating a strength the sailor had to acknowledge. "Here! Fifty thousand lire. There's no quarrel between us. Where did you see her?"

The abrupt changes of mood were beyond the man's comprehension. He was reluctant to forgo the challenge, but the combination of the money, the grip and the infectious laugh made him retreat. "Are you . . . go to my captain?" he asked in English, eyes swimming.

"What for? You just told me. It has nothing to do with him. Why bring that *farabutto* into it? Let him earn his own money. Where did you see her?"

"On the street. *Bionda. Bella. Largo cappello.*"

"Blonde, attractive . . . wide hat! *Where?* Who was she with? A mate, a ship's officer? Un *ufficiale?*"

"Not the *Elba*. The next ship. *Barca mercantile.*"

"There are only two. The *Cristobal* and the *Teresa*. Which one?"

The man glanced around, head bobbing, eyes only half focused. "She was talking to two men . . . one a *capitano*."

"Which *one?*"

"*A destra*," whispered the sailor, pulling the back of his hand across his wet lips.

"On the right?" asked Michael quickly. "The *Santa Teresa?*"

The seaman now rubbed his chin and blinked; he was afraid, his eyes suddenly focused to the left of the table. He shrugged, crushing the money in his right hand, as he pushed back his chair. "*Non conosco. Niente. Una prostituta di capitano.*"

"*Mercantile italiana?*" pressed Havelock. "The Italian freighter? The *Santa Teresa?*"

The sailor stood up, his face white. "*Sì . . . No! Destra . . . sinistra!*" The man's eyes were now riveted somewhere across the room; Michael angled his head unobtrusively. Three men at a table against the wall were watching the crewman from the *Elba.* "*Il capitano. Un marinaio superiore! Il migliore!*" cried the seaman hoarsely. "I know nothing else, *signore!*" He lurched away, shouldering a path through the bodies gathered at the bar towards the alley door.

"You play dangerously," commented the owner of *Il Tritone.* "It could have gone either way."

"With a mule – drunk or otherwise – nothing's ever replaced the carrot and the whip," said Havelock, his head still angled slightly, his concentration still on the three men at the table across the room.

"You could have had blood on your stomach and learned nothing at all."

"But I *did* learn something."

"Not a great deal. A freighter on the right, on the left. Which?"

"He said on the right first."

"Coming off the pier, or going onto it?"

"From his immediate point of view. Going on. *Destra.* The *Santa Teresa.* She'll be put on board the *Teresa,* which means I have time to find her before she's given the signal. She's somewhere within sight of the dock."

"I'm not so sure," said *Il Tritone's* owner, shaking his head. "Our mule was specific. The captain was *un marinaio superiore. Il migliore.* The best, a great seaman. The captain of the *Teresa* is a tired merchantman. He never sails past Marseilles."

"Who are those men at the table over there?" asked Michael, his question barely audible through the din. "Don't turn your head, just shift your eyes. Who are they?"

"I do not know them by name."

"What does that mean?"

"*Italiano,*" said the owner of *Il Tritone,* his voice flat.

"The *Santa Teresa,*" said Havelock, removing a number of bills and putting the rest of the money back into his pocket. "You've been a great help," he said. "I owe the *proprietario.* The rest is for you.

"*Grazie.*"

"*Prego.*

"I will see you down the alley to the waterfront. I still do not like it. We don't know those men are from the *Teresa.* Something is not *in equilibrio.*"

"The percentages say otherwise. It's the *Teresa.* Let's go."

Outside the loud café the narrow thoroughfare was comparatively silent; naked light bulbs shone weakly, enveloped in mist above intermittent doorways, and centuries-old smooth cobblestones muffled the sound of footsteps. At the end of the alley the wide avenue that fronted the piers could be seen in the glow of the street lamps; until one reached it the alley itself was a gauntlet of shadows. One walked cautiously, alert to the spaces of black silence.

"*Ecco!*" whispered the Italian. "Someone's in that doorway. On the left. Do you have a weapon?"

"No. I haven't had time . . ."

"Then *quickly!*" The owner of *Il Tritone* suddenly broke into a run, passing the

431

doorway as a figure lurched out – a stocky man with arms raised, hands poised for interception. But there was no gun in those hands, no weapon but the thick hands themselves.

Havelock took several rapid strides towards the prowler, then spun into the shadows on the opposite side of the alley. The man lunged; Michael spun around again and, grabbing his assailant's coat, hammered his right foot up into the man's midsection. He pivoted a third time, now yanking the intruder off the ground, and hurled him into the wall. As the man fell, Havelock sprang downwards, his left knee sinking into the man's stomach, his right hand gripping the face and clawing at the eyes.

"*Deter-se! Favor! Se Deus quizer!*" choked the prowler, holding his groin, saliva dribbling from his mouth.

The language was Portuguese, the man one of the crew of the *Cristobal*. Michael yanked him up against the wall, into the dim light; he was the seaman who had spoken a few words of English at the table in *Il Tritone*.

"If you're going into theft with assault and battery, you're not doing it very well!"

"No, *senhor!* I wish only to talk, but I cannot be seen! You pay me, I'll tell you things, but not where I can be seen with you!"

"Go on."

"You pay!"

Havelock clamped the sailor's neck against the brick with his forearm, reached into his pocket and took out his money. Shoving his knee into the man's chest and freeing his hand, he removed two notes. "Twenty thousand lire," he said. "Talk!"

"It's worth more. Much more, senhor! You will see."

"I can take it back if it's not . . . Thirty thousand, that's it. Go *on!*"

"The woman goes aboard the *Cristobal* . . . *sette* . . . seven *minutos* before we sail. It is arranged. She comes out of the east warehouse door. She is guarded now; you cannot reach her. But she must walk forty metres to the cargo boarding plank."

Michael released him and added another note to the three in the seaman's hand. "Get out of here," he said. "I never saw you."

"You must *swear* to it, senhor!" cried the man, scrambling to his feet.

"Sworn. Now get out."

Suddenly voices were heard at the end of the alley; two men came running out of the light.

"*Americano! Americano!*" It was the owner of *Il Tritone*; he had returned with help. As the Portuguese started to race away, they grabbed him.

"Let him go!" yelled Havelock. "It's all right! Let him go!"

Sixty seconds later Michael explained to the owner of *Il Tritone*. "It's not the *Teresa*. It's the *Cristobal*."

"It's what was missing!" cried the Italian. "The knowledgeable *capitano*, the great seaman. It was there and I did not see it. Aliandro. Juan Aliandro! The finest captain in the Mediterranean. He could work his ship into any dangerous coastline, dropping off cargo wherever he wished, wherever the rocks and shoals called for no observers on shore. You have found your woman, *signore*."

432

He crouched in the shadows of a stationary crane, the open spaces of the machinery allowing him unobstructed sight lines. The freighter's cargo had been loaded, the teams of stevedores dispersed, swearing as they went their various ways across the wide avenue and down the narrow alleys into the cafés. Except for the four-man cast-off crew the pier was deserted, and even they were barely visible, standing motionless by the huge piles, two men to a line, fore and aft.

A hundred yards behind him was the entrance gate, the obsequious guard inside his glass booth, his figure a grey silhouette in the rolling early-morning fog. Diagonally to the left in front of the crane some eighty-odd feet away was the ribbed, weather-beaten gangplank that went up to the *Cristobal's* forward deck. It was the last physical connection, to be hauled on board the ship before the giant hawsers were slipped off the pilings, freeing the behemoth for the open water.

On the right, no more than sixty feet from the crane, was the door to the pier's warehouse office; it was locked, and all lights were off inside. And beyond that door was Jenna Karras, a fugitive from her own and others' betrayal – his love, who had turned on that love for reasons only she could tell him.

A hundred and forty-odd feet was the span she had to cross in order to disappear. Again. Not in death, but in an enigma.

Michael looked at his watch; it was four-fifty-two, the second hand approaching the minute mark – seven minutes before the *Cristobal* was scheduled to blast its bass-toned departure signal, followed by sharper, higher sounds that warned all vessels of its imminent thrust out of its secure haven, the rules of the sea instantly in force. High up on the deck, fore and midships, a few men wandered aimlessly, pinpointed by the erratic glow of their cigarettes. Except for those on the rope winches and the gangplank detail, there was nothing for them to do but smoke and drink coffee and hope their heads would clear without excessive pain. From inside the massive black hull, the muffled roar of the turbines was heard; behind the fires the coarse, muted meshing of giant gear-wheels signified the approaching command to engage the mammoth screws in third-torque speed. Oily, dark waters churned around the curve of the *Cristobal's* stern.

The warehouse door opened and the hammering in Havelock's chest became intolerable, the pain in his eyes excruciating; he had to endure both for seconds longer. Once Jenna reached the midpoint of the pier, in sight of the gate and the guard and the alarms he could raise, Michael would intercept her. Not an instant sooner.

She was there! *Now.*

He lunged from behind the crane and raced forward, not caring about the sound of his footsteps, intent only on reaching her.

"Jenna! For God's sake, *Jenna!*"

He grabbed her shoulders; the woman spun around in terror.

His breath exploded from his throat. The face that was turned up to him was an old face, an ugly face, the pockmarked face of a waterfront whore. The eyes that stared at him were the wide, dark eyes of a rodent, outlined with thick, running borders of cheap mascara; the lips were blood-red and cracked, the teeth stained and chipped.

"*Who are you?*" His scream was the scream of a madman. "*Liar! Liar!* Why are you *lying?* Why are you *here?* Why *aren't* you here? *Liar!*"

Mists not of the sea filled his mind, cross-currents of blurred insanity: he was beyond reason, knowing only that his hands had become claws, then fists – scraping, hammering – *kill the rodent, kill the impostor! Kill, kill!*

Other screams, other shouts, commands and countercommands, filled the roaring caverns of his consciousness. There was no beginning, no end, only a furious core of frenzy.

Then he felt blows, but did not feel pain. Men were all around him, then above him; fists and heavy boots struck him. Repeatedly. Everywhere.

And then the darkness came. And silence.

Above the pier, on the second floor of the warehouse office, a figure stood at the window looking down at the scene of violence below. She breathed deeply, her fingers stretched across her lips, tears welling in her clear brown eyes. Absently Jenna Karras pulled her hand away from her face and pressed it against the side of her head, against the long blonde hair that fell beneath the wide-brimmed hat.

"Why did you do it, Mikhail?" she whispered softly to herself. "Why do you want to kill me?"

6

He opened his eyes, aware of the sickening stench of cheap whisky, feeling the dampness about his chest and throat – his shirt, jacket and trousers had been drenched. In front of him were gradations of darkness, shadows of grey and black interrupted by tiny, dancing specks of light that bobbed and weaved in the farthest darkness. There was dull pain everywhere, centred in his stomach, rising through his neck to his head, which felt swollen and numb. He had been beaten severely and dragged to the end of the pier – the far right end, beyond the warehouse, if his blurred orientation was anywhere near accurate – and left to regain consciousness, or conceivably, to roll over the edge into a watery death.

But he had not been killed; that told him something. Slowly, he moved his right hand to his left wrist; his watch was there. He stretched his legs and reached into his pocket; his money, too, was intact. He had not been robbed; that told him something else.

He had spoken with too many men, and too many others had seen him in those strange conversations. They had been his protection. Murder was murder, and regardless of what *Il Tritone's* owner had said, a "quiet knife" on the waterfront was a subject for investigation, as was assault and robbery when the victim was a wealthy foreigner. No one wanted too many questions asked on the piers; cool heads had

434

ordered him left as he was, which meant they had been paid to implement other orders, higher orders. Otherwise something would have been stolen – a watch, a few thousand lire; this was the waterfront.

Nothing. An inquisitive, wealthy foreigner had gone berserk, attacking a blonde whore on the pier, and men had protected her. No investigation was called for, as long as the *ricco americano maledetto* had his property intact, if not his senses.

A set-up. A professionally executed snare, the trappers exonerated once the trap had sprung shut. The whole night, the morning, had been a set-up! He rolled over to his left; the south-east ocean was a line of fire beyond the horizon. Dawn had come, and the *Cristobal* was but one of a dozen small silhouettes on the water.

Slowly Havelock got to his knees, pressing them against the wet planks beneath him, pushing himself up painfully with his hands. Once on his feet he turned around, again slowly, testing his legs and ankles, moving his shoulders, arching his neck, then his back. There was nothing broken, but the machine was badly bruised; it would not respond to quick commands, and he hoped he would not have to issue any.

The guard. Had the ego–stroked civil servant been part of the act? Had he been told to confront the foreigner with hostility at first, then turn to obsequiousness, pulling the mark in for the trap? It was effective strategy; he should have seen through it. Neither of the other two guards had been difficult, each perfectly willing to tell him whatever he wanted to know, the man at the gate of the *Teresa's* pier even going so far as to inform him of the freighter's delayed schedule.

The owner of *Il Tritone*? The sailor from the *Cristobal* in a narrow dark alley? Were they, too, part of it? Had the coincidence of logical progression led him to those men on the waterfront who had been waiting for him? Yet how could they have been waiting? Four hours ago Civitavecchia was a vaguely remembered name on a map; it had held no meaning for him. There had been no reason for him to come to Civitavecchia, no way for an unknown message to be telegraphed. Yet it had been; he had to accept that without knowing how or why. There was so much beyond his understanding, a maddening mosaic with too many pieces missing.

Anything you can't understand in this business is a risk, but I don't have to tell you that. Rostov. Athens.

A decoy had been paraded through the pre–dawn mist to pull him out and force him to act. But *why*? What had they expected him to do? He had made it plain what he intended to do. So what was learned, what clarified? What was the point? Was she trying to kill *him*? Was that what Costa Brava was all about?

Jenna, why are you doing this? What happened to you? To us?

He walked unsteadily, stopping occasionally to brace his legs and regain his balance. Reaching the edge of the warehouse, he propelled himself along the wall past darkened windows and the huge loading doors, until he came to the corner of the building. Beyond was the deserted pier, the wash of intersecting floodlights swollen with pockets of rolling fog. He peered around the steel moulding, squinting to focus on the glass cubicle of the guard's post. As before, the figure inside was barely visible, but he was there; Michael could see the stationary glow of a cigarette in the centre of the middle pane.

The glow moved to the right; the guard was sliding the door of the booth open.

A man was walking through the mist towards him, medium-sized, in an overcoat, wearing a hat, the brim angled as a stroller's might be on the Via Veneto. The clothes were not the clothes of the waterfront; they belonged in the city streets. The figure approached the glass booth, stopped by the door and spoke to the guard. Both then looked towards the end of the pier, at the warehouse; the guard gestured and Michael knew they were talking about him. The man nodded, turned and raised his hand; within seconds his summons was obeyed. Two other men came into view, both large, both wearing clothes more suited to the waterfront.

Havelock leaned his head against the edge of steel, a deep, despairing sense of futility mingling with his pain. Exhaustion overwhelmed him. He was no match for such men; he could barely raise his arms, nor his feet. He had no weapons at all.

Where was Jenna? Had she gone aboard the *Cristobal* after the decoy had succeeded? It was a logical – no, it wasn't! The commotion would have centred too much attention on the freighter and would have roused unfriendly or unpaid officials too easily. The ship itself had been a decoy. Jenna was boarding one of the other two!

Michael turned away from the wall and hobbled across the wet planks towards the edge of the pier. He wiped his eyes, staring through the heavy mist. Involuntarily, he gasped, the pain in his stomach acute. The *Elba* was gone. He had been pulled to the wrong pier, duped into an uncontrollable situation while Jenna went on board the *Elba*. Was the captain of the *Elba*, like the skipper of the *Cristobal*, a master navigator? Would he – could he – manoeuvre his awkward ship close enough to an unpatrolled shoreline for a small boat to ferry his contraband to a beach?

One man had the answer. A man in an overcoat and an angled hat, clothes worn on the waterfront by someone who did not haul and fork-lift but, instead, bought and sold. That man would know; he had negotiated Jenna's passage.

Havelock lurched back to the corner of the warehouse wall. He had to reach that man; he had to get by two others coming for him. If only he had a weapon, *any* kind of weapon. He looked around in the faintly lessening darkness. Nothing. Not even a loose board or a slat from a broken crate.

The water. The drop was long but he could manage it. If he could get to the far end of the pier before he was seen, it would be presumed he had plunged over while unconscious. How many seconds did he have? He peered around the moulding into the wash of the floodlights, prepared to push himself away and run.

But the two men were no longer walking towards him. They were standing motionless inside the fenced gate. Why? Why was he being left where he was without further interference?

Suddenly, from out of the impenetrable mist several piers away, came the ear-shattering screech of a ship's siren. Then another, followed by a prolonged, bass chord that vibrated throughout the harbour. It was the *Santa Teresa*! It was his answer! The two men had been summoned not to punish him further, but to restrict him to the first pier. There was no delayed schedule for the *Teresa*; that, too, was part of the set-up. She was sailing on time, and Jenna was *on board*. As the ship's clock ran down, there was only one thing left for the negotiator to do: keep the disabled hunter in place.

Fiercely he told himself he had to get to that pier, stop her, stop the freighter from casting off, for once the giant lines were slipped off the pilings there was nothing he could do, no way to reach her. She would disappear into one of a dozen countries, a hundred cities . . . nothing left, not for him, not any longer. Without her he didn't want to go on!

He wished he knew what the blaring signals meant, how much time he had. He could only estimate. There had been two high pitched blasts from the *Cristobal*; moments later the blonde decoy had emerged from the shadows of the warehouse door. Seven minutes. Did the bass-tone chord signify less or more time? He probed his memory, racing over scores of assignments that had taken him to waterfronts everywhere.

He remembered; more accurately, he *thought* he remembered, as a blurred recent memory tried to surface. The high-pitched shrieks were for ships in the distance, the vibrating lower tones for those nearer by – a rule of thumb for the sea – and the docks. And while he was being beaten, the outer vibrations of a low, grinding chord had fused with his own screams of protest and fury. The bass-toned whistle had followed shortly after the shrieks – prelude to imminent departure. Seven minutes – less one, more likely two, perhaps three.

He had only minutes. Six, five . . . four, no more than that. The *Teresa's* pier was several hundred yards away; in his condition it would take at least two minutes to get there, and that would happen only if he could get past the two jacketed men who had been called to stop him. Four minutes at the outside, two minimum. Jesus! *How?* He looked around again, trying to control his panic, aware that every second reduced his chances.

A stocky black object was silhouetted between two pilings ten yards away; he had not noticed it before because it was a stationary part of the dock. He studied it now. It was a barrel, an ordinary barrel, undoubtedly punctured during loading or unloading procedures, and now used as a receptacle for coffee cups, rubbish, pre-dawn fires; they were on piers everywhere. He ran to it, gripped it, rocked it. It swung free; he lowered it to its side and rolled it back towards the wall. Time elapsed: thirty, perhaps forty seconds. Time remaining; between one and a half and three-plus minutes. The tactic that came into focus was a desperate one . . . but it was the only one that was possible. He could not get past those men unless they came to him, unless the fog and the translucent, brightening darkness worked for him and against them. There was no time to think about the guard and the man in the overcoat.

He crouched in the shadows, against the wall, both hands on the sides of the filthy barrel. He took a deep breath and screamed as loud as he could, knowing the scream would echo throughout the deserted pier.

"*Soccorso! Presto! Sanguino! Muoio!*"

He stopped, listening. In the distance he heard the shouts; they were questions, then commands. He screamed again.

"*Assistenza! Soccorso!*"

Silence.

Then racing footsteps. Nearer . . . drawing nearer.

Now! He shoved the barrel with all the strength he could muster. It clanked as it rolled laterally over the planks, through the fog, towards the edge of the pier.

The two men rounded the corner of the warehouse in the misty light; the barrel reached the edge of the dock. It struck one of the pilings! Oh, *Christ!* Then it spun and plunged over. The sound of the splash below was loud; the two men shouted at each other and raced to the edge.

Now!

Havelock rose to his feet and ran out of the shadows, his hands extended, shoulders and arms like battering rams. He forced his unsteady legs to respond, each racing step painful, but calculated. He made contact. First the man on the right, pummelling him with both outstretched hands; then the Italian on his left, crashing his shoulder into the small of the man's back.

A deafening blast from the *Teresa's* funnels covered the screams of the two men as they plummeted into the water below. Michael swung to his left and hobbled back towards the corner of the warehouse; he would go out onto the deserted pier and face the once obsequious guard and the elegantly dressed man. Time elapsed: another minute. Less than three remained at most.

He ran unsteadily out into the vast expanse of the pier with its fog-laden pools of floodlights and immobile machinery. Pitching his voice at the edge of hysteria, he shouted in broken Italian: "Help me! Help *them*! It's *crazy*! I'm hurt. Two men came to help me. As they drew near there were gunshots! *Three gunshots!* From the next pier. I could hardly hear them because of the freighter but I did! *Gunshots!* Quickly! They're wounded. One dead, I think! Oh, *Christ*, hurry!"

The exchange between the two men was verbal chaos. As Havelock staggered erratically towards the gate he could see that the guard's automatic was drawn, but it was not the same guard; he was shorter, stockier, older. His broad face was full of angry resentment, in contrast to that of the civilian – in his mid-thirties, tanned, suave – which was cold and without expression. He was ordering the guard to investigate; but the guard was shouting that he would not leave his post, not for twenty thousand lire! The *capo-regime* could look after his own garbage; *he* was no frightened *bambino* of the docks. The *capo* could buy a few hours of his time, his disappearance, but no more!

A set-up. From the beginning, a charade.

"*Andate voi stesso!*" yelled the guard.

Swearing, the civilian started towards the warehouse and broke into a run, then abruptly slowed his pace. He cautiously approached the corner of the building.

The guard was now in front of the glass booth, his gun levelled at Michael. "You! Walk to the fence," he shouted in Italian. "Raise your hands above you and grab the wire as high as you can! Do not turn round! I'll fire into your head if you do!"

Barely two minutes left; if it was going to work, it would happen now.

"Oh, *Jesus*!" Havelock screamed as he gripped his chest and fell.

The guard rushed forward; Michael remained motionless in a foetal position, dead weight on the damp, hard surface. "Get up!" commanded the uniformed man. "Get to your feet!"

The guard reached down, grabbing Havelock's shoulder. It was the movement Michael had been waiting for. He spun off the ground, clasping the weapon above his head and gripped the wrist at his shoulder, wrenching it clockwise as he rose and hammered his knee into the falling guard's throat. The gun barrel was in his

438

hand; he swung it down, crashing it into the base of the Italian's skull. The man collapsed. Havelock dragged him into the shadows of the booth, then raced out of the open gate, jamming the weapon into his jacket pocket.

A prolonged, belching sound came from the distance, followed by four hysterically pitched screeches. The *Teresa* was about to slip away from its berth! Michael felt a sickening sense of futility sweeping over him as he ran breathlessly down the wide avenue, his legs barely able to carry him, his feet swerving, slapping the pavement. When he reached the *Teresa's* pier, the guard – the same guard – was inside his glass booth, once again on the telephone, nodding his outsized head, his dull eyes accepting other lies.

There was now a chain stretched across the open gate – only an official hindrance, not a prohibition. Havelock grabbed the hook and yanked it out of its cemented base; the chain curled snake-like into the air and clattered to the ground.

"Che cosa!? Fermati!"

Michael raced – his legs in agony – down the long stretch of the pier, through the circular pools of floodlights, past immobile machinery, towards the freighter outlined in the swirling mists at the end of the dock. His right leg collapsed; his hands broke the fall but not the impact, his right shoulder sliding across the moist surface. He grabbed his leg, forcing himself up, and propelled himself along the planks until he could work up the momentum to run again.

Gasping for air as he ran, he finally reached the end of the pier. The futility was complete: the freighter *Santa Teresa* was floating thirty feet beyond the pilings, the giant hawsers slithering over the dark waters, hauled in by men who looked down at him through the shadows.

"Jenna!" he screamed. "Jenna! *Jenna!*"

He fell to the wet wood of the pier, arms and legs throbbing, chest in spasms, his head splitting as if cracked open with an axe. He . . . had . . . lost her . . . A small boat could drop her off at any of a thousand unpatrolled stretches of coastline in the Mediterranean; she was gone. The only person on earth he cared about was gone for ever. Nothing was his, and he was nothing.

He heard the shouts behind him, then the hammering of racing feet. And as he heard the sounds he was reminded of other sounds, other feet . . . another pier. From where the *Cristobal* had sailed!

There was a man in an overcoat who had ordered other men to come after him; they, too, had run across a deserted pier through shimmering pools of floodlights and the mist. If he could find that man! If he found him, he would peel the suntanned flesh from the face until he was told what he had to know.

He got to his feet and began limping rapidly towards the guard who was running at him, weapon extended.

"Fermati! Mani in alto."

"Un errore!" Havelock shouted back, his voice both aggressive and apologetic; he had to get by the man, not be detained. He took several notes from his pocket, holding them in front of him so they could be seen in the spill of the floodlights. "What can I tell you?" he continued in Italian. "I made a mistake . . . which benefits *you*, doesn't it? You and I, we spoke before, remember?" He pressed the money into the guard's hand while slapping him on the back. "Come on, put that thing away.

I'm your friend, remember? What harm is there? Except I'm a little poorer and you're a little richer. Also, I've had too much wine."

"I thought it was you!" said the guard grudgingly, taking the bills and ramming them into his pocket, his eyes darting about. "You're crazy in the head! You could have been shot. For *what*?"

"You told me the *Teresa* wasn't sailing for hours."

"It's what *I* was told! They're bastards, *all* bastards! They're crazy too! They don't know what they're doing."

"They know exactly what they're doing," said Michael quietly. "I've got to get along now. Thanks for your help."

Before the angry guard could answer Havelock started forward rapidly, wincing in pain as he tried to control his throbbing legs and aching chest. *For God's sake, hurry!*

He reached the stretch of fence that enclosed the *Cristobal's* pier, his hand now in his pocket, grateful for the weapon. The unconscious guard was still on the ground in the lower shadows of the glass booth. He had neither moved nor been moved in the five minutes, perhaps six, that he had lain there. Was the man in the overcoat still on the pier? The odds favoured it; logic dictated that he would have looked for the guard because he did not see him in the booth and, when he found him, would have questioned the fallen man. In doing so, some part of the unconscious body would have been moved; it had not been.

But why would the *capo-regime* remain on the pier for so long? The answer came from the sea through the fog and the wind. Shouts, questions, followed by commands and further questions. The man in the overcoat was still on the pier, his gorillas screaming from the waters below.

Michael clenched his teeth, forcing the pain from his mind. He slid along the side wall of the warehouse, past the door from which the blonde decoy had emerged, to the corner of the building. The morning light was growing brighter, the mists rising, the absence of the freighter permitting the early rays of the sun to spread over the dock. In the distance, on the water, another ship was steaming slowly towards the harbour of Civitavecchia; it might well be heading for the berth recently vacated by the *Cristobal*. If so, there was very little time remaining before the landing crews arrived. He had to move swiftly, act effectively and he was not at all sure he was capable of doing either.

A stretch of unpatrolled coastline. Did the man only yards away from him now know which? He must find out. He had to be capable.

He rounded the corner, holding the weapon against the cloth of his jacket. He could not use it, he understood that; it would serve no purpose because it would only eliminate his source and draw attention to the pier. But the threat had to be conveyed as genuine; his anger had to seem desperate. He was capable of that.

He stared through the rising mist. The man in the overcoat was at the edge of the dock, excitedly barking instructions in a low voice; he, too, was obviously afraid of drawing attention from stray crewmen who might be loitering on the adjacent pier. The effect was comic. From what Michael could gather, one of the men below was hanging onto a piling strut, reluctant to let go because apparently he couldn't swim. The negotiator was ordering the second man to support his companion, but

440

he appeared to be refusing, concerned that he might be pulled under by his incompetent associate.

"Don't talk any more!" Havelock said sharply in Italian, his words clear if not precise, his voice commanding, not loud.

The startled man spun round, his right hand reaching under his overcoat.

"If I see a gun," continued Michael, moving closer, "you'll be dead and in the water before you can raise it. Move away from there. Walk towards me. Now to your left. Over to the wall. Move! Don't stop!"

The man lurched forward. "I could have had you killed, *signore*. I did not. Surely that is worth something to you."

"It is – obviously. I thank you."

"Nor was anything on your person taken, I assume you are aware of that. My orders were clear."

"I'm aware. Now tell me why. On both counts."

"I am neither a killer nor a thief, *signore*."

"Not good enough. Raise your hands! Lean against the wall and spread your legs!" The Italian complied; it was not the first time such orders had been given him. Havelock came up behind him, kicking the man's right calf as he whipped his hand around the *capo-regime's* waist, pulling the gun from the Italian's belt. He glanced at it, impressed. The weapon was a Spanish automatic, a Llama .38 calibre, with grip and manual safeties. A quality gun, undoubtedly less expensive on the waterfront. He shoved it into his own belt. "Tell me about the girl. Quickly!"

"I was paid. What more can I tell you?"

"A great deal." Michael reached up and grabbed the man's left hand; it was soft. The negotiator was not a violent man, the term *capo-regime* which the guard had used was misapplied. This Italian was no part of the Mafia; a Mafioso at his age would have come up through the ranks and would not have soft hands.

A sudden cacophony of ship's whistles erupted from the harbour. They were joined by panicked shouts from the lone man in the slapping waters below the pier. Taking advantage of the sounds, Michael rammed the pistol into the negotiator's kidney. The man screamed. Then Havelock crashed the handle into the side of the Italian's neck and there was another scream, followed by a gasping and a series of whimpering pleas.

"*Signore . . . signore!* You are American; we speak American! Do not do this to me! I saved your life – my word on it!"

"We'll get to that. The *girl*! Tell me about the girl! Quickly!"

"I do favours around the docks. Everyone knows that! She needed a favour. She paid!"

"To get out of Italy?"

"What else?"

"She paid for a lot more than that! How many did *you* pay? For the set-up."

"*Cosa dice?* Set . . . up?"

"That show you put on! The pig who walked out of that door over there!" Havelock gripped the Italian by the shoulder and spun him round, slamming him back into the wall. "Right around that corner," he added, gesturing. "What was that all about? Tell me! She paid for that, too. Why?"

"As you say, *signore*. She paid. *Spiegazzoni* ... explanations ... were not required."

Michael jammed the barrel of the pistol deep into the man's stomach. "Not good enough. *Tell* me!"

"She said she had to *know*," the negotiator spat out, doubling over.

"Know what?" Havelock slapped the man's hat off and, grabbing him by the hair, crashed his head into the wall. "Know *what*?"

"What you would do!"

"How did she know I'd follow her here?"

"She did not!"

"Then why?"

"She said you *might* do so! You were ... *ingegnoso*. A resourceful man. You've hunted other men; you have means at your disposal. Contacts, sources."

"That's too loose! *How*?" Michael bunched the Italian's hair in his fist, pulling it half out of its roots.

"*Signore* ... she said she spoke to three drivers on the *piattaforma* before she found a taxi to bring her to Civitavecchia! She was afraid!"

It made sense. It had not occurred to him to look for a taxi ramp at the station; taxis were not in abundant supply in Rome. In truth, he had simply not been thinking, only moving.

"*Perfavore! Soccorso! Mio Dio!*" The screams came from the water below.

The ships in the harbour filled the air with whistles and steam. There was so little time left; soon the crews would come, men and machinery crawling all over the pier. He had to learn exactly what the negotiator had sold; he gripped the man's throat with his left hand.

"She's on the *Teresa*, isn't she?"

"*Si!*"

Havelock recalled the words of *Il Tritone's* owner: the *Teresa* sailed to Marseilles. "How is she to be taken off the ship?"

The Italian did not answer; Michael plunged his fingers deeper into the man's throat, choking the windpipe. He went on: "Understand me, and understand me well. If you don't tell me, I'll kill you now. And if you lie, and she gets past me in Marseilles, I'll come back for you. She was right, I'm resourceful and I've hunted a great many men. I'll find you."

The negotiator went into a spasm, his mouth gaping as he tried to speak. Havelock reduced the pressure on his neck. The Italian coughed violently, grabbing his throat, and said, "What's it to me anyway, so I'll tell you. I don't want *afflizione* with the likes of you, *signore*! I should have known better. I should have listened better!"

"Go on."

"Not Marseilles. San Remo. The *Teresa* stops at San Remo. How or where she is to be brought on shore, I do not know – my word on it! She buys her way to Paris. She's to be taken across the border at Col des Moulinets. When, I do not know – my word! From there to Paris. I swear on the blood of Christ!"

The negotiator did not have to swear. It was clear he was telling the truth. He was being honest out of fear, extraordinary fear. What had Jenna told him? Why hadn't he ordered Michael killed? And why had nothing been stolen? Michael released his grip on the Italian's neck.

He spoke quietly. "You said you could have had me killed, but you didn't. Now tell me why."

"No, *signore*, I will not say it," whispered the man. "In the name of God, you'll never see me again! I say nothing, know nothing!"

Havelock raised the pistol slowly, resting the point of the barrel on the man's left eye. "Say it," he said.

"*Signore*, I have a small, profitable business here, but I have never once – *never* – involved myself with political activities! Or anything remotely connected to such things. I swear on the tears of the Madonna! I thought she was lying, appealing to me with lies! I never once believed her!"

"But I wasn't killed, nothing on my person taken, I think you said." Michael paused, then shouted, as he jammed the barrel into the Italian's eye. "*Why?*"

The man screamed, spitting out the words. "She said you were an American working with the *comunisti*! With the Soviets. I did not believe her! I know nothing of such things! But caution would naturally be called for . . . caution. In Civitavecchia we are outside such wars. They are too . . . *internazionali* . . . for people like us who make our few unimportant lire on the docks. These things mean nothing to us – my word on it! We wish no trouble from you, any of you! . . . *Signore*, you can *understand*. You attacked a woman – a *prostituta*, to be certain, but a woman – on the pier. Men stopped you, pulled you away, but when I saw, I stopped *them*! I told them we should be cautious. We had to think . . ."

The frightened man continued to babble, but Havelock was not listening. What he had heard stunned him beyond anything he imagined he might hear. *An American working with the Soviets.* Jenna had said this? It was insane!

Had she tried to appeal to the man with a lie, only to instil a very real fear in the small-time operator after the fact, *after* the trap? The Italian had not equivocated; he had repeated her story out of fear. He had not lied.

Did she believe it? Was that what he had seen in her eyes on the platform at the Ostia station? Did she really believe it – just as he had believed beyond any doubt in his mind that she was a deep cover officer for the *Voennaya*?

Oh, *Christ*! Each turned against the other with the same manoeuvre! Had the evidence against him been as airtight as the evidence against her? It must have been; that was also in her eyes. Fear, hurt . . . pain. There was no one she could trust, not now, not for a while, perhaps not ever. She could only run – as he had kept running. God! What had they *done*?

Why?

She was on her way to Paris. He would find her in Paris. Or fly to San Remo or Col des Moulinets, and intercept her at one or the other. He had the advantage of fast transport; she was on an old freighter plodding across the water and he would be flying. He had time.

He would use that time. There was an intelligence officer at the embassy in Rome who was about to know the depth of his anger. Lieutenant-Colonel Lawrence Baylor Brown was going to supply answers or all the exposés of Washington's clandestine activities would be mere footnotes compared with what he would reveal: the incompetences, the illegalities, the miscalculations and errors costing the lives of thousands the world over every year.

He would start with a black diplomat in Rome who funnelled secret orders to American agents throughout Italy and the western Mediterranean.

"*Capisce?* You *do* understand, *signore?*" The Italian was pleading, buying time, his eyes glancing furtively to the right. Over on the second pier three men were walking through the early light towards the far pile; two blasts of a ship's whistle told why. The freighter steaming into port was to be tied up at the *Elba*'s berth. In moments, additional crews would arrive. "We are cautious . . . *naturalmente*, but we know nothing of such things! We are *creature* of the docks, nothing more?"

"I understand," said Michael, touching the man's shoulder and turning him around. "Walk to the edge," he ordered quietly.

"*Signore*, please! I beg you!"

"Just do as I say. *Now.*"

"I swear on the patron saint of mercy Himself! On the blood of Christ, on the tears of the Holy Mother!" The Italian was weeping, his voice rising. "I am an insignificant merchant, *signore!* I know nothing! Say nothing!"

As they reached the edge of the pier, Havelock said, "Jump," and pushed the negotiator over the side.

"*Mio Dio! Assistenza!*" screamed the henchman below as his employer joined him in the water.

Michael turned and hobbled back to the corner of the warehouse wall. The dock was still deserted, but the guard was beginning to move, shaking his head, trying to pull himself up in the shadows of the booth. Havelock slapped open the cylinder of the pistol and shook the bullets out of their tracks; they clattered onto the dock. He hurried towards the gate, and when he reached the door of the glass booth, he threw the weapon inside. He ran as fast as he was capable of running through the gate, towards the rented car.

Rome. There would be answers in Rome.

7

The four men around the table in the white-walled room on the third floor of the State Department building were youngish men by upper-echelon Washington standards. Their ages ranged from the mid-thirties to the late forties, but their lined faces and hollow look made them old beyond their years. Their work entailed sleepless nights and prolonged periods of anxiety, exacerbated by their insular existence: none of them could discuss the crises they faced in that room with anyone outside it. These were the strategists of covert operations, the air traffic controllers of clandestine activities; roving vultures could be shot down on their slightest miscalculation. Others above them might request the broad objectives; others below might design the specific assignments. But only these men were aware of every conceivable variation, every likely consequence of a given operation; they were the clearing house. Each was a specialist, each an authority. Only they could give the final nod for the vultures to fly.

Yet they had no radar grids or circling antennae to aid them; they had only the projections of human behaviour to guide them. They had to examine actions and reactions, not simply those of the enemy but those of their own people in the field as well. Evaluation was a never-ending struggle, which was rarely resolved to everyone's satisfaction. The "what if" probabilities were geometrically compounded with each new twist of events, each human reaction to abruptly-altered circumstances. They were psychoanalysts in an endless labyrinth of abnormality, their patients the products of that disorder. They were specialists in a macabre way of life where the truth was usually a lie and lies too often were the only means of survival. Stress was the factor that frightened them most, for under maximum or prolonged stress both one's enemies and one's own people saw things and did things they might not do otherwise. The totally unpredictable added to the abnormal made dangerous territory.

This was the conclusion the four men had reached regarding the crisis late that night. Lt-Colonel Lawrence Baylor Brown in Rome had sent his cable on priority cipher; its contents required the opening of a dead file so that each strategist could study the facts.

They were beyond dispute. The events at that isolated beach on the Costa Brava had been verified by two on-site confirmations, one of them Foreign Service Officer Havelock himself, the other a man unknown to Havelock named Steven MacKenzie, one of the most experienced undercover operatives working in Europe for the Central Intelligence Agency. He had risked his life to bring back proof: torn garments stained with blood. Everything had been microscopically examined, the results positive: Jenna Karras. The reasons for a back-up confirmation had not been made explicit, nor was that necessary. The relationship between Havelock and the Karras woman was known to those who had to know; a man under maximum stress might fall apart, be incapable of carrying out what had to be done. Washington had to know. Agent MacKenzie had been positioned two hundred feet north of Havelock: his view was clear, his confirmation absolute, his proof incontrovertible. The Karras woman had been killed that night. The fact that Steven MacKenzie had died of a heart seizure while sailing in Chesapeake Bay three weeks after he returned from Barcelona, in no way diminished his contribution. The doctor who had been summoned by the Coast Guard patrol was a well-established physician on the Eastern Shore, a surgeon named Randolph with impeccable credentials. A thorough post-mortem was conclusive: MacKenzie's death was from natural causes.

Beyond Costa Brava itself, the evidence against Jenna Karras had been subjected to the most exhaustive scrutiny. Secretary of State Anthony Matthias had demanded it, and the strategists knew why. There was another relationship to take into consideration: one that had existed between Matthias and Michael Havelock for nearly twenty years since student had met teacher at Princeton University. Fellow Czechs by birth, one had established himself as perhaps the most brilliant geopolitical mind in the academic world, while the other, a young, haunted expatriate, was desperately searching for his own identity. The differences were considerable, but the friendship was strong.

Anton Matthias had come to America over forty years ago, the son of a prominent doctor from Prague who had hurried his family out of Czechoslovakia under the shadow of the Nazis and was welcomed by the medical community. Havelock's immigration, on the other hand, was managed covertly as a joint exercise of American and British intelligence; his origins were obscured, initially for the child's own safety. And whereas Matthias's meteoric rise in government followed from a succession of influential political figures who openly sought his counsel and publicly extolled his brilliance, the much younger man from Prague proceeded to establish his own worth through clandestine accomplishments that would never see the light of day. Yet in spite of the dissimilarities of age and reputation, intellect and temperament, there existed a bond between them, held firm by the elder, never taken advantage of by the younger.

Those who confirmed the evidence against the Karras woman understood that there was no room for error, just as the strategists understood now that the cable from Rome had to be studied carefully, handled delicately. Above all, for the time being, it must be kept from Anthony Matthias. For though the media had announced that the extraordinary Secretary of State was off on a well-deserved holiday, the truth was something else. Matthias was ill, some whispered gravely ill, and although through his subordinates he was in constant touch with State, he had not been in Washington for nearly five weeks. Even those perceptive men and women of the press corps who suspected the vacation ploy said nothing and printed nothing. No one really wanted to think about it; the world could not afford it.

And Rome could not become an additional burden for Anthony Matthias.

"He's hallucinating, of course," said the balding man named Miller, putting his copy of the cable down on the table in front of him. Paul Miller, MD, was a psychiatrist, an authority on diagnosing erratic behaviour.

"Is there anything in his record that might have warned us?" asked a red-haired, stocky man in a rumpled suit and an open collar, his tie unknotted. His name was Ogilvie, a former field agent.

"Nothing you would have read," replied Daniel Stern, the strategist on Miller's left. His title was Director of Consular Operations, which was a euphemism for the section chief of State's clandestine activities.

"Why not?" asked the fourth strategist, a conservatively dressed man who might have stepped out of an advertisement in the *Wall Street Journal* for IBM. He was seated next to Ogilvie. His name was Dawson, a specialist in international law. He pressed his point. "Are you saying there were – are – omissions in his service file?"

"Yes. A security hangover from years ago. No one ever bothered to reassess, so the file remained incomplete. But the answer to Ogilvie's question might be found there. The warning we missed."

"How so?" asked Miller, peering over his glasses, his fingers spread across his balding hairline.

"He could be finally burned out. Over the edge."

"What do you mean?" Ogilvie leaned forward, his expression none too pleasant. "Evaluation depends on available data, goddamn it."

446

"I don't think anyone thought it was necessary. His record's superior. Except for an outburst or two, he's been extremely productive, reasonable under very adverse conditions."

"Only, now he's seeing dead people in railroad stations," interrupted Dawson. "Why?"

"Do you know Havelock?" asked Stern.

"Only from a field personnel interview," answered the lawyer. "Eight or nine months ago; he flew back for it. He seemed efficient."

"He was," agreed the Director of Cons Op. "Efficient, productive, reasonable . . . very tough, very cold, very bright. But then he was trained at an early age under rather extraordinary circumstances. Maybe that's what we should have looked at." Stern paused, picked up a large manilla envelope, and removed a red bordered file folder, sliding it out carefully. "Here's the complete background dossier on Havelock. What we had before was basic and acceptable. A graduate from Princeton with a Ph.D. in European History and a lesser degree in Slavic languages. Home: Greenwich, Connecticut. A war orphan brought over from England and adopted by a couple named Webster, both cleared. What we all looked at, of course, was the recommendation from Matthias, someone even then to be reckoned with. And what the recruiters here at State saw sixteen years ago was fairly obvious. A highly intelligent graduate willing to work for bureaucratic spit, even willing to perfect his linguistic dialects and go into deep-cover work. But that wasn't necessary – the language part. Czech was his native tongue; he knew it better than we thought he did. That's what's here; it's the rest of his story and could be the reason for the breakdown we're witnessing now."

"That's a hell of a leap backward," said Ogilvie. "Can you sketch it for us? I don't like surprises; retired paranoids we don't need."

"Apparently we've got one," interjected Miller, picking up the cable. "If Brown's judgement means anything – "

"It does," Stern broke in. "He's one of the best we've got in Europe."

"Still, he's Pentagon," added Dawson. "Judgement's not a strong point."

"It is with him," corrected the Cons Op director. "He's black and had to be good."

"As I was about to say," Miller continued, "Baylor includes a strong recommendation that we take Havelock seriously. He saw what he saw."

"Which is impossible," said Ogilvie. "Which means we've got a whacko. What's in there, Dan?"

"An ugly early life," replied Stern, lifting the cover of the file and turning several pages. "We knew he was Czech, but that's all we knew. There were several thousand Czechoslovakian refugees in England during the war, and that was the explanation given for his being there. But it wasn't true. There were two stories, one real, the other a cover. He wasn't in England during the war, nor were his parents. He spent those years in and around Prague. It was a long nightmare and very real for him. It started when he was old enough to know it, see it. Unfortunately, we can't get inside his head, and that could be vital now." The director turned to Miller. "You'll have to advise us here, Paul. He could be extremely dangerous."

"Then you'd better clarify," said the doctor. "How far back do we go? And why?"

"Let's take the 'why' first," said Stern, removing a number of pages from the dossier. "He's lived with the spectre of betrayal since he was a child. There was a period during adolescence and early adulthood – at school and college – when the pressures were absent, but the memories must have been pretty horrible for him. Then for the next sixteen years – these past sixteen years – he's been back in that same kind of world. Perhaps he's seen too many ghosts."

"Be specific, Daniel," pressed the psychiatrist.

"To do that," said the director, his eyes scanning the top page in his hand, "we have to go back to June of 1942, the war in Czechoslovakia. You see, his name isn't Havelock, it's Havlicek. Mikhail Havlicek. He was born in Prague some time in the middle 'thirties, the exact date unknown. All the records were destroyed by the Gestapo."

"*Gestapo?*" The attorney, Dawson, leaned back in his chair; a recollection prodded. "June 1942 . . . there was something in the Nuremberg trials."

"It was a sizeable item on the Nuremberg agenda," agreed Stern. "On 27 May, Reinhard Heydrich, known as *der Henker* – the hangman of Prague – was killed by Czech partisans. They were led by a professor who'd been dismissed from the Karlova University and worked with British Intelligence. His name was Havlicek and he lived with his wife and son in a village roughly eight miles outside Prague where he organized the partisan cells. The village was Lidice."

"Oh, Christ," said Miller slowly, dropping the cable from Rome on the table.

"He wasn't noticeably in evidence," commented Stern dryly as he shifted the pages in his hand. "Afraid that he might have been seen at the site of Heydrich's assassination, Havlicek stayed away from his house for nearly two weeks, living in the cellars at the university. *He* hadn't been spotted, but someone else from Lidice had been; the price was set for Heydrich's death: execution for all adult males; for the women, conscription – slave labour for the factories, the more presentable to be sent to the officers' barracks to be *Feldhuren*. The children . . . they would simply 'disappear'. *Jugendmöglichkeiten*. The adaptable would be adopted, the rest gassed in mobile vans."

"Efficient bastards, weren't they?" said Ogilvie.

"The orders from Berlin were kept quiet until the morning of 10 June, the day of the mass executions," continued Stern, reading. "It was also the day Havlicek decided to go home. When the word went out – the proclamations were nailed to telephone poles and broadcast over the radio – the partisans stopped him. They locked him up, sedated him with drugs; they knew there was nothing he could do, and he was too valuable. Finally, he was told the worst. His wife had been sent to the whore camps – it was later learned that she killed herself the first night, taking a Wehrmacht officer with her – and his son was nowhere to be found."

"But he hadn't, obviously, been taken with the other children," said Dawson.

"No. He'd been trapping rabbits and came back in time to see the round-ups, the executions, the corpses thrown in ditches. He went into shock, fled into the woods and, for weeks, lived like an animal. The stories began spreading through the countryside: a child was seen running in the forest, footprints found near barns, leading back into the woods. The father heard them and knew; he had told his son that if the Germans ever came for him he was to escape into the forests. It took over a month, but Havlicek tracked the boy. He had been hiding in caves and trees, terrified to show himself, eating whatever he could steal and scratch from the ground, the nightmare of the massacre never leaving him."

"A lovely childhood," said the psychiatrist, making a note on a pad.

"It was only the beginning." The Director of Cons Op reached for another page in the dossier. "Havlicek and his son remained in the Prague-Boleslav sector and the underground war accelerated, with the father as the partisan leader. A few months later the boy became one of the youngest recruits in the *Děti Brigada*, the Children's Brigade. They were used as couriers, as often as not, carrying nitroglycerin and plastic explosives as messages. One mis-step, one search, one soldier hungry for a small boy, and it was over."

"His father *let* him?" asked Miller incredulously.

"He couldn't stop him. The boy found out what they'd done to his mother. For three years he lived that lovely childhood you described, Paul. It was uncanny, macabre. During those nights when his father was around, he was given lessons like any other school kid. Then during the days, in the woods and the fields, others taught him how to run and hide, how to lie. How to kill."

"That was the training you mentioned, wasn't it?" said Ogilvie quietly.

"Yes. He knew what it was like to take lives, see friends' lives taken, before he was ten years old. Grisly."

"Indelible," added the psychiatrist. "Explosives planted over thirty years ago."

"Could the Costa Brava trigger them thirty years later?" asked the lawyer, looking at the doctor.

"It could. There're a couple of dozen blood-red images floating around, some pretty grim symbols. I'd have to know a hell of a lot more." Miller turned to Stern, pencil poised above his pad. "What happened to him then?"

"To all of them," said Stern. "Peace finally came – I should say the formal war was over – but there was no peace in Prague. The Russians had their own plans, and another kind of madness took over. The elder Havlicek was visibly political, jealous of the freedom he and the partisans had fought for. He found himself in another war, as covert as before and just as brutal. With the Russians." The director turned to another page. "For him it ended on 10 March 1948, with the assassination of Jan Masaryk and the collapse of the Social Democrats."

"In what sense?"

"He disappeared. Shipped to a gulag in Siberia or to a nearer grave. His political friends were quick; the Czechs share a proverb with the Russians: 'The playful cub is tomorrow's wolf.' They hid young Havlicek and reached British MI6. Someone's conscience was stirred; the boy was smuggled out of the country, and taken to England."

"That proverb about the cub turning into tomorrow's wolf," interjected Ogilvie. "Proved to be true, didn't it?"

"In ways the Russians could never envision."

"How did the Websters fit in?" asked Miller. "They were his sponsors over here, obviously, but the boy was in England."

"It was chance, actually. Webster had been a reserve colonel in the war, attached to Supreme Command Central. In 'forty-eight he was in London on business, his wife with him, and one night at dinner with wartime friends they heard about the young Czech brought out of Prague, living at an orphanage in Kent. One thing led to another – the Websters had no children, and God knows the boy's story was intriguing, if not incredible – so the two of them drove down to Kent and interviewed him. That's the word here. 'Interviewed'. Cold, isn't it?"

"They obviously weren't."

"No, they weren't. Webster went to work. Papers were mocked up, laws bent and a very disturbed child flown over here with a new identity. Havlicek was fortunate; he went from an English orphanage to a comfortable home in a well-to-do American suburb, including one of the better prep schools and Princeton University."

"And a new name," said Dawson.

Daniel Stern smiled. "As long as a cover was deemed necessary, our reserve colonel and his lady apparently felt Anglicization was called for in Greenwich. We all have our foibles."

"Why not their name?"

"The boy wouldn't go that far. As I said before, the memories must be there. Indelibly, as Paul put it."

"Are the Websters still alive?"

"No. They'd be almost a hundred if they were. They both died in the early 'sixties when Havelock was at Princeton."

"Where he met Matthias?" asked Ogilvie, making a statement.

"Yes," answered the Director of Cons Op. "That softened the blow. Matthias took an interest in him, not only because of Havelock's work, but, perhaps more important, because his family had known the Havliceks in Prague. They were all part of the intellectual community until the Germans blew it apart and the Russians – for all intents and purposes – buried the survivors."

"Did Matthias know the full story?"

"All of it," replied Stern.

"That letter in the Costa Brava file makes more sense now," said the lawyer. "The note Matthias sent to Havelock."

"He wanted it included," explained Stern, "so there'd be no misunderstanding on our part. If Havelock opted for immediate withdrawal, we were to permit it."

"I know," continued Dawson. "But I assumed when Matthias made a reference to how much Havelock had suffered in . . . 'the early days', I think he wrote, he meant simply losing both parents in the war. Nothing like *this*."

"Now you know. We know." Stern again turned to the psychiatrist. "Any guidance, Paul?"

"The obvious," said Miller. "Bring him in. Promise him *anything*, but bring him in. And we can't afford any accidents. Get him here alive."

"I agree that's the optimum," interrupted the red-haired Ogilvie, "but I can't see it ruling out every option."

"You'd better," said the doctor. "You even said it yourself. Paranoid. Whacko. Costa Brava was intensely personal to Havelock. Witness to the execution. It could very well have set off those explosives planted thirty years ago. A part of him is back there protecting himself, building a web of defences against persecution, against attack. He's running through the woods after having witnessed the executions in

450

Lidice; he's with the Children's Brigade, nitroglycerin strapped to his body."

"It's what Baylor mentions in his cable." Dawson picked it up. "Here it is. 'Sealed depositions', 'tales out of school'. He could do it all."

"He could do anything," continued the psychiatrist. "There are no rules. Once he's hallucinated, he can slip back and forth between fantasy and reality, each phase serving the dual objective of at once convincing himself of the persecution and at the same time ridding himself of it."

"What about Rostov in Athens?" asked Stern.

"We don't know that there was any Rostov in Athens," Miller said. "It could be part of the fantasy, retroactively recalling a man in the street who looked like him. We *do* know the Karras woman was KGB. Why would a man like Rostov suddenly appear and deny it?"

Ogilvie leaned forward. "Baylor says Havelock called it a blind probe. Rostov could have taken him, got him out of Greece."

"Then why *didn't* he?" asked Miller. "Come on, Red, you were in the field for ten years. Blind probe or no blind probe, if you were Rostov and knew what was back at the Lubyanka, wouldn't you have taken Havelock under the circumstances described in that cable?"

Ogilvie paused, staring at the psychiatrist. "Yes," he said finally. "Because I could always let him go – if I wanted to – before anyone knew I'd taken him."

"Exactly. It's inconsistent. Was it Rostov in Athens, or anywhere else? Or was our patient fantasizing, building his own case for persecution and subsequent defence?"

"From what this Colonel Baylor says, he was damned convincing," interjected the lawyer Dawson.

"A hallucinating schizophrenic – if that's what he is – can be extraordinarily convincing because he believes totally what he's saying."

"But you can't be sure, Paul," insisted Daniel Stern.

"No, I can't be. But *we're* sure of one thing – two things, actually. The Karras woman *was* KGB and she was killed on that beach on the Costa Brava. The evidence was irrefutable for the first, and we have two on-site confirmations for the second, including one from Havelock himself." The psychiatrist looked at the faces of the three men. "That's all I can base a diagnosis on; that and this new information on one Mikhail Havlicek. I'm in no position to do anything else. You asked for guidance, not absolutes."

" 'Promise him anything . . .' " repeated Ogilvie. "Like that goddamned commercial."

"But bring him in," completed Miller. "And just as fast as you can. Get him into a clinic, under therapy, but find out what he's done and where he's left those defence mechanisms of his. The 'sealed depositions' and 'tales out of school'."

"I don't have to remind anyone here," interrupted Dawson quietly. "Havelock knows a great deal that could be extremely damaging if revealed. The damage would be as extensive to our own credibility – here and abroad – as in anything the Soviets might learn. Frankly, more so. Ciphers, informers, sources – all these can be changed, the networks warned. We can't go back and rewrite certain incidents

451

where intelligence treaties were violated, the laws of a host country broken by our people."

"To say nothing of the domestic restrictions placed on us over here," added Stern. "I know you included that, I just want to emphasize it. Havelock knows about them; he's negotiated a number of exchanges as a result of them."

"Whatever we've done was justified," said Ogilvie curtly. "If anyone wants proof, there's a couple of hundred files that show what we've accomplished."

"And a few thousand that don't," objected the lawyer. "Besides, there's also the Constitution. I'm playing devil's advocate, of course."

"Horseshit!" Ogilvie shot back. "By the time we get court orders and warrants, some poor son of a bitch over here has a wife or a father shipped to one of those gulags over there when someone like Havelock could have made a deal, *if* we could have placed a tap on time, assigned surveillance, and found out what was going on."

"It's a grey area, Red," explained Dawson, not unsympathetically. "When is homicide justified, *really* justified? On balance, there are those who would say our accomplishments don't justify our failures."

"One man crossing a checkpoint to our side justifies them." Ogilvie's eyes were rigid, cold. "One family taken out of a camp in Magya-Orszag or Krakow or Dannenwalde or Liberec justifies them. Because that's where they are, Counsellor, and they shouldn't *be* there. Who the hell gets hurt, *really* hurt? A few screaming freaks with political hatchets and outsize egos. They're not worth it."

"The law says they are. The Constitution says they are."

"Then fuck the law, and let's put a couple of holes in the Constitution. I'm sick to death of its being used by loud-mouthed, bushy-haired smart asses who mount any cause they can think of just to tie our hands and draw attention to themselves. I've seen those *rehabilitation* camps, Mr Lawyer. I've *been* there."

"Which is why you're valuable here," interceded Stern quickly, putting out the fire. "Each of us has a value, even when he renders judgements he'd rather avoid. I think the point Dawson's making is that this is no time for a Senate inquiry or the hanging judges of a congressional oversight committee. They could tie our hands far more effectively than any mob from the ageing radical-chic or the bran-and-wheatgerm crowd."

"Or," said Dawson, glancing at Ogilvie, his look conveying mutual understanding, "representatives of half a dozen governments showing up at our embassies and telling us to shut down certain operations. You've been there, too, Red. I don't think you want that."

"Our patient can make it happen," interjected Miller. "And very probably will unless we reach him in time. The longer his hallucinations are allowed to continue without medical attention, the farther he'll slip into fantasy, the rate of acceleration growing faster. The persecutions will multiply until they become unbearable to him and he thinks he has to strike out – strike back. With his own attacks. They're his defence mechanisms."

"What form might they take, Paul?" asked the director.

"Any of several," replied the psychiatrist. "The extreme would be his making contact with men he's known – or known of – in foreign intelligence circles and

452

offering to deliver classified information. That could be the root fantasy of the Rostov 'encounter'. Or he could write letters – with copies to us – or send cables – easily intercepted by us – that hint at past activities we can't afford to have scrutinized. Whatever he does, he'll be extremely cautious, secretive, the reality of his own expertise protecting his manipulative fantasies. You said it, Daniel; he could be dangerous. He *is* dangerous."

" '*Offering* to deliver'," said the lawyer, repeating Miller's phrase. "Hinting . . . not delivering, not giving outright?"

"Not at first. He'll try to force us – blackmail us – into telling him what he wants to hear. That the Karras woman is alive, that there was a conspiracy to retire him."

"Neither of which we can do convincingly because there's not a damn thing we can offer him as proof," said Ogilvie. "Nothing he'll accept. He's a field man. Whatever we send him, he'll filter, chew it around for accuracy and spit it back in the dungheap. So what do we tell him?"

"Don't *tell* him anything," answered Miller. "You *promise* to tell him. Put it any way you like. The information's too classified to send by courier, too dangerous to be permitted outside these rooms. Play his game, suck him in. Remember, he desperately wants – needs, if you like – his primary hallucination confirmed. He *saw* a dead woman; he has to believe that. And the confirmation's over here; it could be irresistible to him."

"Sorry, Headman." The red-haired former field agent raised the palms of his hands. "He won't buy it, not that way. His – what did you call it? His 'reality' part? – would reject it. That's buying a code in a box of crackers. It just doesn't happen. He'll want something stronger, much stronger."

"Matthias?" asked Dawson quietly.

"Optimum," agreed the psychiatrist.

"Not yet," said Stern. "Not until we have no other choice. The quiet word is that he's aware of his failing condition; he's conserving his strength for SALT 3. We can't lay this on him now."

"We may *have* to," insisted Dawson.

"We may, then again we may not." The director turned to Ogilvie. "Why does Havelock have to buy anything concrete, Red?"

"So we can get close enough to grab him."

"Couldn't a sequence be designed – say, one piece of information leading to another, each more vital than the last – to draw him in, suck him in, as Paul says? He can't get the last unless he shows up?"

"A treasure hunt?" asked Ogilvie, laughing.

"That's what he's on," said Miller quietly.

"The answer's no." The red-haired man leaned forward, his elbows on the table. "A sequence operation depends on credibility, the better the field man the firmer the credibility. It's also a very delicate exercise. The subject, if he's someone like Havelock, will use decoys, blind intermediaries. He'll reverse the process by programming his decoys with information of their own, give his intermediaries questions they want answered on the spot; he'll suck *you* in. He won't expect perfect answers; he'd be suspicious as hell if he got them, but he'll want what we used to call a 'stomach consensus'. It's not something you can write down on paper and analyse; it's a gut feeling for believability. There aren't that many good men who could fool Havelock in sequence. One substantial misstep and he closes the book and walks away."

"And sets off the explosions," said Miller.

"I see," said Stern.

And it was clear that the men around that table *did* see. It was one of those moments when the unkempt, irascible Ogilvie confirmed his value, as he did so frequently. He had been out in that labyrinth called the "field", and his conclusions had a peculiar eloquence and sagacity.

"There is a way, however," continued the former agent. "I'm not sure there's any other."

"What is it?" asked the Director of Cons Op.

"Me."

"Out of the question."

"Think about it," said Ogilvie quickly. "*I'm* the credibility. Havelock knows me – more important, he knows I sit at this table. To him I'm one of *them*, a half-assed strategist who may not know what he's asking for but sure as hell knows why. And with me there's a difference; a few of them out there might even count on it. I've been where they've been. None of the rest of you have. Apart from Matthias, if there's anyone he'll listen to, anyone he'll meet, it's me."

"I'm sorry, Red. Even if I agreed with you, and I think I do, I can't permit it. You know the rules. Once you step inside this room, you never go out in the field again."

"That rule was *made* in this room. It's not a holy writ."

"It was made for a very good reason," said the lawyer. "The same reason our houses are watched around the clock, our cars followed, our telephones tapped with our consent. If any of us was taken by interested parties, from Moscow to Peking to the Persian Gulf, the consequences would be beyond recall."

"No disrespect, Counsellor, but those safeguards were designed for people like you and the Headman here. Even Daniel. I'm a little different. They wouldn't try to take me because they know they'd wind up with nothing."

"No one doubts your capabilities," countered Dawson. "But I submit – "

"It hasn't anything to do with capabilities," interrupted Ogilvie, raising his hand to the lapel of his worn tweed jacket; he turned up the flap towards the lawyer next to him. "Look closely, Counsellor. There's a slight bulge an inch from the tip here."

Dawson's eyes dropped to the fabric, his expression noncommittal. "Cyanide?"

"That's right."

"Sometimes, Red, I find you hard to believe."

"Don't mistake me," said Ogilvie simply. "I don't ever want to use this – or the others I've got conveniently placed. I'm no macho freak trying to shock you. I don't hold my arm over a fire to show how brave I am any more than I want to kill someone or have him try to kill me. I've got these pills because I'm a coward, Mr Lawyer. You say we're being watched, guarded twenty-four hours a day. That's terrific, but I think you're overreacting to something that doesn't exist. I don't think there *is* a file on you in Dzerzhinsky Square; at least not on you or the doctor here.

I'm sure there's one on Stern, but grabbing him is like codes in crackers, or our going in and grabbing someone like Rostov. It doesn't happen. But there's a file on me – you can bet your legal ass on that – and I'm not retired. What I know is still very operative, more so than ever since I stepped inside this room. That's why I've got these little bastards. I know how I'd go in and how I'd come out, and they know I know. Strangely enough, these pills are my protection. They know I've got them and they know I'd use them. Because I'm a coward."

"And you've just spelled out the reasons why you can't go into the field," said the Director of Consular Operations.

"Have I? Then either you didn't listen or you should be fired for incompetence. For not taking into account what I *didn't* spell out. What do you want, teacher? A note from my doctor? Excusing me from all activity?"

The strategists glanced briefly at one another, looking uncomfortable. "Come on, Red, cut it out," said Stern. "That's not called for."

"Yes, it is, Dan. It's the sort of thing you consider when making a decision. We all know about it; we just don't talk about it, and I suppose that's another kind of consideration. How long have I got? Three months, maybe four? It's why I'm here, and *that* was an intelligent decision."

"It was hardly the sole reason," offered Dawson softly.

"If it didn't weigh heavily in my favour, it should have, Counsellor. You should always pick someone from the field whose longevity – or lack of it – can be counted on." Ogilvie turned to the balding Miller. "Our doctor knows, don't you, Paul?"

"I'm not your doctor, Red," said the psychiatrist quietly.

"You don't have to be; you've read the reports. In five weeks or so the pain will start getting worse . . . then worse after that. I won't feel it, of course, because by then I'll be moved to a hospital room where injections will keep it under control, and all those phoney cheerful voices will tell me I'm actually getting better. Until I can't focus, or hear them, and then they don't have to say anything." The former field man leaned back in his chair, looking now at Stern. "We've got here what our learned lawyer might call a confluence of beneficial prerogatives. Chances are that the Russians won't touch me, but if they tried, nothing's lost for me, you can be goddamned sure of that. And I'm the only one around who can pull Havelock out in the open, far enough so we can take him."

Stern's gaze was steady on the red-haired man who was dying. "You're persuasive," he said.

"I'm not only persuasive, I'm right." Suddenly Ogilvie pushed his chair back and stood up. "I'm so right I'm going home to pack and grab a cab to Andrews. Get me on a military transport to Italy; there's no point in advertising the trip on a commercial flight. Those KGB turkeys know every passport, every cover I've ever used and there's no time to be inventive. Route me through Brussels into the base at Palombara. Then cable Baylor to expect me . . . Call me Apache."

"Apache?" asked Dawson.

"Damn good trackers."

"Assuming Havelock will meet you," said the psychiatrist, "what'll you say to him?"

"Not a hell of a lot. Once he's an arm's length away he's mine."

"He's experienced, Red," said Stern, studying Ogilvie's face. "He may not be all there, but he's tough."

"I'll have equipment," replied the dying man, heading for the door. "And I'm experienced, too, which is why I'm a coward. I don't go near anything I can't walk away from. Mostly." Ogilvie opened the door and left without another word. The exit was clean, swift, the sound of the closing door final.

"We won't see him again," said Miller.

"I know," said Stern. "So does he."

"Do you think he'll reach Havelock?" asked Dawson.

"I'm sure of it," replied the director. "He'll take him, turn him over to Baylor and a couple of resident physicians we've got in Rome, then he'll disappear. He told us. He's not going into that hospital room with all those lying voices. He'll go his own way."

"He's entitled to that," said the psychiatrist.

"I suppose so," agreed the lawyer without conviction, turning to Stern. "As Red might say, 'No disrespect', but I wish to God we could be certain about Havelock. He's *got* to be immobilized. We could be hauled in by authorities all over Europe, fuel for the fanatics of every persuasion. Embassies could be burnt to the ground, networks scattered, time lost, hostages taken and – don't fool yourself – a great many people killed. All because one man fell off balance. We've seen it happen with far less provocation than Havelock could provide."

"That's why I'm so sure Ogilvie will bring him in," said Stern. "I'm not in Paul's line of work, but I think I know what's going through Red's mind. He's offended, deeply offended. He's watched friends die in the field – from Africa to Istanbul – unable to do anything because of his cover. He saw a wife and three children leave him because of his job; he hasn't seen his kids for five years. Now he's got to live with what he's got – die from what he's got. All things considered, if *he* stays on track, what gives Havelock the right, the privilege, to go over the edge? Our Apache's on his last hunt, setting his last trap. He'll see it through because he's angry."

"That and one other thing," said the psychiatrist. "There's nothing else left for him. It's his final justification."

"For what?" asked the lawyer.

"The pain," answered Miller. "His *and* Havelock's. You see, he respected him once. He can't forget that."

8

The unmarked jet swept down from the skies forty miles due north of the airport at Palombara Sabina. It had flown from Brussels, avoiding all military and commercial air routes, and, soaring over the Alps east of the Lepontine sector, its altitude was so great and its descent so rapid that the probability of observation was practically non-existent. Its blip on defence radar screens was prearranged: it would appear and disappear without comment, without investigation. And when it landed at Palombara, it would bring in a man who had been taken on board secretly at three o'clock in the morning, Brussels time. A man without a reasonable name, referred to only as the Apache. This man, as with many like him, could not risk the formalities of identification at immigration desks or border checkpoints. Appearances might be altered and names changed, but other men watched such places, knowing what to look for, their minds trained to react like memory banks; too often they were successful. For the Apache – as for many like him – the current means of travel was more the norm than otherwise.

The engines were cut back as the pilot – trained in carrier landings – guided his aircraft over the forests in the stretched-out, low approach to the field. It was a mile-long black strip cut out of the woods, with maintenance hangars and traffic towers set back and camouflaged, odd yet barely visible intrusions on the countryside. The plane touched down, and the young pilot turned in his seat as the reverse thrust of the jets echoed throughout the small cabin. He raised his voice to be heard, addressing the red-haired, middle-aged man behind him.

"Here we are, Indian. You can take out your bow and arrows."

"Funny boy," said Ogilvie, releasing the clamp that held the strap across his chest. He looked at his watch. "What's the time here? I'm still on a Washington clock."

"O-five-fifty-seven; you've lost six hours. You're working on midnight, but here it's morning. If you're expected at the office, I hope you got some sleep."

"Enough. Is transport arranged?"

"Right to the big chief's wigwam on the Via Vittorio."

"Very cute. The embassy?"

"That's right. You're a special package. Delivery guaranteed straight from Brussels."

"That's wrong. The embassy's out."

"We've got our orders."

"I'm issuing new ones."

Ogilvie walked into the small office reserved for men like himself in the maintenance building of the unmapped airfield. It was a room devoid of windows, with only basic furniture: there were two telephones, both routed perpetually through electronic scrambler systems. The outside corridor that led to the office was guarded by three men dressed innocuously in overalls. Under the bulging fabric, however, each carried a weapon and should any unidentified persons interfere with the incoming passenger or the presence of a camera even be suspected, the weapons would be bared, used instantly if necessary. These arrangements were the result of extraordinary conferences between unknown men of both governments whose concerns transcended the stated limits of covert co-operation; quite simply, they were necessary.

Ogilvie walked to the desk, sat down and picked up the telephone on his left; it was black, signifying domestic use. He dialled the number he had committed to memory, and twelve seconds later the sleepy voice of Lieutenant-Colonel Lawrence Brown was on the line.

"Brown. What is it?"

"Baylor Brown?"

"Apache?"

"Yes. I'm at Palombara. Have you heard anything?"

"Not a word. I've got tracers out all over Rome; there's not a line on him."

"You've got *what*?"

"Tracers. Every source we can pay or who owes us a favour – "

"Goddamn it, call them off! What the hell do you think you're doing?"

"Hey, easy, buddy. I don't think we're going to get along."

"And I don't give a duck's fuck whether we do or not! You're not dealing with a G-two crossword puzzle; he's a snake, *buddy*. You let him find out you're going after him, he figures you've broken the rules. And he *will* find out; that's when he bites. Jesus, you think he's never been traced before?"

"You think I don't know my tracers?" countered Baylor angrily, defensively.

"I think we'd better talk."

"Come on in, then," said the colonel.

"That's another thing," replied Ogilvie. "The embassy's out."

"Why?"

"Among other things, he could be in a window across the street."

"So?"

"He knows I'd never show up in-territory. KGB cameras operate around the clock, aimed at every entrance."

"He doesn't even know you're coming," protested Baylor. "Or who you are."

"He will when you tell him."

"A *name*, please?" said the army officer testily.

"Apache'll do for now."

"That'll mean something to him?"

"It will."

"It doesn't to me."

"It's not supposed to."

"We're definitely not going to get along."

"Sorry about that."

"Since you won't come in, where do we meet?"

"The Borghese. In the gardens. I'll find you."

"That'll be easier than my finding *you*."

"You're wrong, Baylor."

"About *that*?"

"No. I think we will get along." Ogilvie paused briefly.

"Make it two hours from now. Our target may try to reach you by then."

"Two hours."

"And, Baylor?"

"What?"

458

"Call off those duck-fucking tracers, *buddy*."

The month of March was not kind to the Borghese. The chill of the Roman winter, mild as the winter was, still lingered, inhibiting the budding of flowers and the full explosion of the gardens that in spring and summer formed rows and circles of dazzling colours. The myriad paths that led through the tall pines towards the great museum seemed just a little dirty, the green of the pine trees tired, dormant. Even the benches that lined the narrow footpaths were layered with dust. A transparent film had descended over the park that was the Villa Borghese; it would disappear with the April rains, but for now the lifelessness of March remained.

Ogilvie stood by the thick trunk of an oak tree on the border of the gardens behind the museum. It was too early for any but a few students and fewer tourists; a scattering of these strolled along the paths waiting for the guards to open the doors that led to the Casino Borghese's treasures. The former field man, now in the field again, looked at his watch, wrinkles of annoyance spreading across his deeply lined face. It was nearly twenty minutes to nine; the army intelligence officer was over half an hour late. Ogilvie's irritation was directed as much at himself as towards Baylor. In his haste to veto his going to the embassy as well as making it clear that he was the control he had chosen a poor rendezvous, and he knew it. So would the colonel, if he thought about it; perhaps he had, perhaps that was why he was late. The Borghese at this hour was too quiet, too remote, with far too many shadowed recesses from which either of them could be observed, visually and electronically. Ogilvie silently swore at himself; it was no way to initiate his authority. The attaché-conduit had probably taken a circuitous, change-of-vehicle route, employing frequency scanners in the hope of exposing and thus losing presumed surveillance. KGB cameras *were* trained on the embassy; the colonel had been put in a difficult situation, thanks to an abrasive source from Washington enigmatically called Apache, a cover from the back of a cereal box.

The enigma was there, but not the foolishness, not the cereal box. Seven years ago in Istanbul two undercover field men, code names Apache and Navajo, nearly lost their lives trying to prevent a KGB assassination on the Mesrutiyet. They had failed, and in the process Navajo had been cornered on the deserted Ataturk Boulevard at four o'clock in the morning, KGB killer teams at both ends. It was a total-loss situation until Apache sped across the bridge in a stolen car, screeching to a stop by the pedestrian alley, shouting at his associate to climb in or get his head blown off. Ogilvie had then raced through a fusillade of gunfire, receiving a graze-wound at his temple and two bullets in his right hand while breaking through the thunderous early-morning barricade. The man called Navajo seven years ago would not readily forget Apache. Without him Michael Havelock would have died in Istanbul. Ogilvie counted on that memory.

Snap. Behind him. He turned; a black hand was held up in front of him, the black face beyond the hand immobile, eyes wide and steady staring at him. Baylor shook his head sharply twice, bringing his index finger to his lips. Then slowly, moving closer and pulling both of them behind the tree trunk and the foliage, the army officer gestured towards the south garden, at the rear entrance of the stone museum.

About forty yards away a man in a dark suit was glancing about, his expression indecisive, as he moved first in one direction then in another, unable to choose a path. In the distance there were three rapid blasts of a high-pitched horn, followed by the gunning of an engine. The man stopped, then broke into a run towards the direction of the intruding sounds and disappeared beyond the east wall of the Borghese.

"This is a dumb location," said the colonel, checking his watch.

"That horn was yours?" asked Ogilvie.

"It's parked by the Veneto gates. It was near enough to be heard; that was all that mattered."

"Sorry," said the former field man quietly. "It's been a long time. I don't usually make mistakes like this. The Borghese was always crowded."

"No sweat. And I'm not sure it was a mistake."

"Let the needle out. Don't stick me with kindness."

"You're not reading me. Your feelings aren't any concern of mine. I've never been put under KGB surveillance before – not that I know of. Why now?"

Ogilvie smiled; he was the control after all. "You put out the tracers. I think I mentioned that."

The black officer was silent, his dark eyes aware. "Then I'm finished in Rome," he said finally.

"Maybe."

"No maybe. I'm finished, anyway. It's why I'm late."

"He reached you." The red-haired agent made the statement softly.

"With full artillery and I'm the first who'll be exposed. He picked up the Karras woman's trail and followed her to the port of Civitavecchia where she got out. He won't say how or on what ship. It was a trap; he waded through and reversed it, targeting the man responsible – a small-time operator on the docks. Havelock broke him, and what he learned – what he *thinks* he learned – has turned him into a stockpile of nitro."

"What is it?"

"Double programming. Same tactic supposedly employed with him. She was sandbagged against him by us."

"How?"

"By someone persuading her he'd gone over to the Soviets, that he was going to kill her."

"That's a crock of shit."

"I'm only repeating what he said – what he was told. All things considered, it's not without logic. It would explain a lot. The KGB's got some pretty fair actors; they could have put on a performance for her. It's sound strategy. He's out and she's running. A productive team neutralized."

"I mean the whole *thing's* a crock of shit," countered Ogilvie. "There is no Jenna Karras; she died on a beach called Montebello on the Costa Brava. And she *was* KGB – a deep-cover VKR field officer. No mistakes were made, but even that doesn't matter now. The main point is she's dead."

"He doesn't believe it; when you talk to him you may not, either. I'm not sure I do."

460

"Havelock believes what he wants to believe, what he has to believe. I've heard the medical terms and, reduced to our language, he's gone over the edge. He crosses back and forth between what is and what isn't, but fundamentally he's gone."

"He's damned convincing."

"Because he's not lying. That's part of it. He saw what he saw."

"That's what he says."

"But he couldn't have; that's also part of it. His vision's distorted. When he goes over, he doesn't see with his eyes, only his head, and that's damaged."

"You're convincing too."

"Because I'm not lying and my head's not damaged." Ogilvie reached into his pocket for a pack of cigarettes. He extracted one and lit it with an old, tarnished Zippo purchased a quarter of a century ago. "Those are the facts, Colonel. You can fill in the blank spaces, but the bottom line's firm. Havelock's got to be taken."

"That won't be so easy. He may be running around in his own foggy tunnels but he's not an amateur. He may not know where he's going but he's survived in the field for sixteen years. He's smart, defensive."

"We're aware of that. It's the reality part. You told him I was here, didn't you?"

"I told him a man named Apache was here." The army officer paused.

"Well?"

"He didn't like it. Why you?"

"Why not me?"

"I don't know. Maybe he doesn't like you."

"He owes me."

"Maybe that's your answer."

"What are you, a psychologist? Or a lawyer?"

"A little of both," said the colonel. "Constantly. Aren't you?"

"Right now I'm just annoyed. What the hell are you driving at?"

"Havelock's reaction to you was very quick, very vocal. 'So they sent the Gunslinger,' he said. Is that your other name?"

"Kid stuff. A bad joke."

"He didn't sound amused. He's going to call at noon with instructions for you."

"At the embassy?"

"No. I'm to take a room at the Excelsior. You're to be there with me; you're to get on the phone."

"Son of a bitch!" Ogilvie sucked breath through his teeth.

"That's a problem?"

"He knows where I am but I don't know where he is. He can watch me but I can't watch him."

"What difference does it make? He's obviously willing to meet you. In order to take him, you've got to meet him."

"You're the new boy on the block, Colonel, no offence intended. He's forcing my hand at the top."

"How so?"

"I'll need two men – Italians preferably, as inconspicuous as possible – to follow me when I leave the hotel."

"Why?"

"Because he could take *me*," said the former field man reflectively. "From behind. On any crowded pavement. There isn't a jump he doesn't know . . . A man collapses in the street, a friend helps him to a nearby car. Both Americans, nothing out of the ordinary."

"That presumes I won't be with you. Still, I'm the conduit. I could make a case for my being there."

"Definitely the new boy; he'd head for Cairo. And if you tried to keep me in sight, I have an idea he'd spot you. No – "

"Offence intended," completed the colonel. "There *are* drawbacks . . . I'll get you your cover." He paused again, then continued, "But not two men. I think a couple would be better."

"That's good. You've got possibilities, Colonel."

"I've also got a recommendation to make that I'll deny if it's ever ascribed to me. And considering that soubriquet, Gunslinger, I don't think I'd have any difficulty saying I heard it from you."

"I can't wait to hear it myself."

"I'm responsible for a large territory in this area of operations. The work I do for the Pentagon and State gets compounded; it's unavoidable. I need a favour, or someone needs one from us, so the circle quietly grows bigger, even if we've never met one another."

"I hate to repeat myself," interrupted Ogilvie, "but what the hell are you driving at now?"

"I have a lot of friends out there. Men and women who trust me, trust my office. If I have to go I'd like the office to remain intact, of course, but there's something more basic. I don't want those friends – known and unknown – to get hurt, and Havelock could hurt them. He's worked Italy, the Adriatic, the Ligurian – from Trieste across the borders, along the northern coast all the way to Gibraltar. He could provoke reprisals. I don't think one messed up retired field man is worth it."

"Neither do I."

"Then take him out. Don't just take him, take him out."

"You could have heard that from me."

"Do I hear it now?"

The man from Washington was silent for a moment, then he replied. "No."

"Why not?"

"Because the act could bring about the consequences you don't want."

"Impossible. He hasn't had time."

"You don't know that. If this thing's been growing since Costa Brava, there's no way to tell what deposits he's made or where he's made them. He could have left documents in half a dozen countries with specific instructions to release them if scheduled contacts were missed. During the last six weeks he's been in London, Amsterdam, Paris, Athens and Rome. Why? Why those places? With the whole world to choose from, and with money in his pocket, he returns to the cities where he operated extensively under cover. It could be a pattern."

"Or coincidence. He knew them. He was out; he felt safe."

"Maybe, maybe not."

462

"I don't follow the logic. If you simply take him, he still won't make those contacts."

"There are ways."

"The clinics, I assume. Laboratories where doctors inject drugs that loosen tongues and minds."

"That's right."

"And I think you're wrong. I don't know whether he saw the Karras woman or not, but whatever he saw – whatever happened – happened during the past twenty-four hours. He hasn't had time to do a *goddamned thing*. He may tell you he has, but he hasn't."

"Is that an opinion, or are you clairvoyant?"

"Neither. It's fact. I listened to a man in shock. A man who'd just gone through a mind-blowing experience – his phrase, incidentally. It wasn't the result of a festering mental aberration, it had just *happened*. When you talk about what he could have done, the deposits he could have made, you're using the words I gave you because they're the words he said to me. He was speculating on what he *might* do, not what he did. There's a hell of difference, Mr Strategist."

"And because of it you want him dead?"

"I want a lot of other people to live."

"So do we. That's why I'm here."

"So you can take him back alive," said Baylor sardonically. "Just like Frank Buck."

"That'll do."

"No, it won't. Suppose you miss? Suppose he gets away?"

"It won't happen."

"Opinion or clairvoyance?"

"Fact."

"No way. It's conjecture, a probability factor I don't want to count on."

"You don't have a choice, *soldier*. The chain of command has spoken."

"Then let me spell it out for you, *civilian*. Don't talk to me about chains of command. I worked my black ass off in this white man's army – white at the top, black at the bottom – until they had to make me a vital cog in the big white wheel. Now you come along with your secret agent act and a code name right out of – "

"The back of a cereal packet?" interjected Ogilvie.

"You got it. A cereal packet. No name I can point to, no identification I can bargain with to get me off the hook, just a balloon from a comic strip. And if you do miss, and Havelock does get away, I'm on the firing line – as the target. Coffee-Face blew it; his network's compromised. Take him out of the big white wheel."

"You hypocritical bastard," said the man from Washington in disgust. "The only thing you're interested in saving is your own skin."

"For a lot of reasons too benign for you to understand. There're going to be more like me, not less . . . Wherever you go in this town, I'm not far behind. You take him your way, that's fine with me. I'll get you back to Palombara and strap the two of you into a jet myself with a letter of recommendation written in classical Latin. But if you can't bring it off, and he breaks, he goes down my way."

"That doesn't sound like the man who believed his story, who pleaded his case."

463

"I didn't plead his case; I reported it. And it doesn't make any difference whether I believe him or not. He's an active, dangerous threat to me and my function here in Rome and a large part of the network I've cultivated on the orders of my government and at the expense of the American taxpayer." The colonel stopped; he smiled. "That's all I have to know to pull a trigger."

"You could go far."

"I intend to, I've got points to make."

Ogilvie stepped away from the tree; he looked past the bordering foliage at the dormant gardens beyond. He spoke quietly, his voice flat, noncommittal. "I could lose you, you know. Kill you, if I had to."

"Right on," agreed the officer. "So I'll forget about the Excelsior. You take a room in my name and when the call comes from Havelock, you pretend to be me. He expects me to be there, confirm your presence; he knows I've got a stake in this. And by the way, when you talk to him as me, don't make it too nigger. I'm a Rhodes Scholar. Oxford, seventy-one."

The agent turned. "You're also something else. I can bring you up on charges, a court martial guaranteed. Direct disobedience of a superior in the field."

"For a conversation that never took place? Or perhaps it did, and I exercised on-the-spot military judgement. The subject found the contact unacceptable; I wanted another man in Rome. How does that grab you, *Gunslinger?*"

Ogilvie did not answer for the better part of a minute. He threw his cigarette on the ground, crushing it underfoot, grinding his shoe into the dirt. "You're talented, Colonel," he said finally. "I need you."

"You really want him, don't you?"

"Yes."

"I thought so. It was in your voice on the phone. I wanted that confirmation, Mr Strategist. Just consider me an insurance policy you don't want to carry but your accountant says you must. If I have to pay off, nothing's lost. I can justify the act better than anyone around a DC conference table. I'm the only one who's spoken to him. I know what he's done and what he hasn't done."

"A very short time could prove you wrong."

"I'll chance it. That's how sure I am."

"You won't have to. There'll be no payoff from you because I won't miss, and he won't get away."

"Glad to hear it. Apart from the couple who'll pick you up when you leave the hotel, what else do you need?"

"Nothing. I brought my equipment with me."

"What are you going to tell him?"

"Whatever he wants to hear."

"What are you going to use?"

"Experience. Have you made arrangements for the room?"

"Forty-five minutes ago," said Baylor. "Only it's not a room, it's a suite. That way there're two phones. Just in case you're tempted to give me a wrong rendezvous, I'll be listening to everything he says."

"You're boxing me in, boy."

"I'll let that pass. Look at it this way. When today's over you'll be heading back to Washington either with him or without him, but with no hooks in you. If you've got him, fine. If not, I'll take the heat. My judgement's respected at the Pentagon; under the circumstances the solution will be 'last extremity', and acceptable."

"You know that book, don't you?"

"Right down to a hundred-odd contradictions. Go back to the good life, Mr Strategist. Be well and happy in the Georgetown circuit. Make your pronouncements from a distance and leave the field to us. You live better that way."

Ogilvie controlled the wince that was about to crease his face. He could feel the sharp pain shooting up through his rib cage, bolting and clawing at the base of his throat. It was spreading; every day it went a little farther, hurt a little more. Signals of the irreversible. "Thanks for the advice," he said.

9

The Palatine, one of the seven hills of Rome, rising beyond the Arch of Constantine, its sloping fields dotted with the alabaster ruins of antiquity. It was the rendezvous.

A quarter of a mile north-west of the Gregorio gate was an ancient arbour, with a bust of the Emperor Domitian resting upon a fluted pedestal at the end of a stone path bordered on both sides by the marble remnants of a jagged wall. Branches of wild olive cascaded over the chiselled rock, while vines of brown and green crept underneath, filling crevices and spreading a spidery latticework across the cracked yet ageless marble. At the end of the path, behind the blotched, stern face of Domitian, were the remains of a fountain built into the hill. The arbour abruptly stopped; there was no exit.

This sylvan fragment of another time was the contact ground. Time span: thirty minutes – between three o'clock and half past, when the sun was at midpoint in the western sky. Here two men would meet, each with different objectives, both aware that the differences might cause the death of one or the other, neither wanting that finality. Wariness was the order of the afternoon.

It was twenty minutes before three, the start of the span. Havelock had positioned himself behind a cluster of bushes on the nearest hill overlooking the arbour, several hundred feet above the bust of Domitian. He was concerned, angry, as his eyes roamed over the stone path and the untamed fields beyond the walls below. Half an hour ago from a pavement café across the Via Veneto from the Excelsior, he had seen what he was afraid he might see. Seconds after the red-haired Ogilvie had walked through the glass doors he had been picked up by a man and woman who had emerged casually – too casually, a bit too swiftly – from the jewellery shop next door. The shop had a wide-angled, display-case entrance, affording observers inside a decent range of vision. The man from Washington had veered briefly to his right and stopped before entering the stream of pedestrians heading left. It was a sighting back-up, an unobtrusive movement of a hand or a fleeting glance at the pavement, gestures that marked him in the crowds. There would be no taking the Apache unawares before he reached the Palatine. Ogilvie had anticipated that the attempt might be made and had protected himself. On the phone, the former field man, now a vaunted strategist, had offered only accommodation. He had reasonable – if highly classified – data to deliver; in them would be found the answers Michael sought.

Not to worry, Navajo. We'll talk.

But if the Apache had reasonable explanations to offer, he did not require protection. And why had Ogilvie agreed so readily to the out-of-the-way rendez-vous? Why hadn't he simply suggested meeting on the street, or at a café? A man confident of the news he bore did not set up defences, yet the strategist had done just that.

Instead of an explanation, had Washington sent another message?

Dispatch? Call me dead?

I didn't say we'd kill you. We don't live in that kind of country . . . On the other hand, why not? Lt-Colonel Baylor Brown, Intelligence conduit, US Embassy, Rome.

If Washington had reached that conclusion, the planners had sent a qualified assassin. Havelock respected Ogilvie's talents, but he did not admire the man. The former operative was one of those men who justified their violence too glibly, with self-serving scraps of philosophy that implied personal revulsion for committing even necessary acts of violence. Associates in the field knew better. Ogilvie was a killer, driven by some inner compulsion to avenge himself against his own personal furies, which he concealed from all but those who worked closely with him under maximum stress; and those who did know him tried their level best never to work with him again.

After Istanbul, Michael did something he had never thought he would do. He had reached Anthony Matthias and advised him to take Red Ogilvie out of the field. The man was dangerous. Michael had volunteered to appear before a closed hearing with the strategists, but, as always, Matthias had the better, less divisive method. Ogilvie was an expert; few men had his background in covert activities. The Secretary of State had ordered him up the ladder, making Ogilvie a strategist himself.

Matthias was out of Washington these days. It was not a comforting thought. Decisions were often arrived at without accountability for the simple reason that those who should be apprised in depth were not accessible. The urgency of a given crisis was frequently a green light for movement.

That was it, thought Havelock, as his eyes settled on a figure in the distance, in the sloping field beyond the right wall. It was the man who had accompanied the woman out of the jewellery store next to the Excelsior, the one who had picked up Ogilvie. Michael looked to his left; there was the woman. She was standing by the steps of an ancient bath, a sketch pad in her left hand. But there was no sketching pencil in her right which she held under the lapel of her gabardine coat. Havelock returned to the man in the field on the right. He was sitting on the ground now, legs stretched, a book open on his lap – a Roman finding an hour's peace, reading. And by no coincidence his hand, too, was held in place at the upper regions of his coarse tweed jacket. The two were in communication and Michael knew the language. Italian.

Italians. No subordinates from the embassy, no CIA stringers, no Baylor – no Americans in sight. When Ogilvie arrived, he'd be the only one. It fit; remove all US personnel, all avenues of record. Use only local back-ups, men or women themselves beyond salvage. Dispatch.

Why? Why was he a crisis? What had he done or what did he know that made men in Washington want him dead? First they wanted him out by way of Jenna Karras. Now dead. Christ in heaven, what was it?

Besides the couple, were there others? He strained his eyes against the sun, studying every patch of ground, separating the terrain into blocks – an awkward puzzle. The arbour of Domitian was not a prominent site on the Palatine Hill; it was a minor scrap of antiquity left to decay. The dismal month of March had further reduced the number of trespassers. In the distance, on a hill to the east, a group of children played under the watchful glances of two adults. Teachers, perhaps. Below, to the south, there was an uncut green lawn with marble columns of the early empire standing like upright, bloodless corpses of widely differing heights. Several tourists laden with camera equipment – straps over straps, and bulging cases – were taking photographs, posing one another in front of the fluted remains. But apart from the couple covering both sides of the arbour's entrance, there was no one in the immediate vicinity of Domitian's retreat. If they were competent marksmen, no additional back-ups were necessary. There was only one entrance, and a man climbing a wall was an easy target; it was a gauntlet with a single exit. That, too, fitted the policy of dispatch. Use as few locals as possible, remembering always that they can snap back with extortion.

The irony had come about unconsciously. Michael had wandered over the Palatine that morning, selecting the site for the very advantages that now could be used against him. He looked at his watch: fourteen minutes to three. He had to move quickly, but not until he saw Ogilvie. The Apache was smart; he knew the odds favoured his remaining out of sight as long as possible, riveting his adversary's concentration on his anticipated appearance. Michael understood, so he concentrated on his options: on the woman with a sketch pad in her hand, and the man reclining on the grass.

Suddenly, he was there. At one minute to three the red-haired agent came into view, his head and shoulders seen first as he walked up the path from the Gregorio gate, passing the man in the field without acknowledgement. Something was odd, thought Havelock, something about Ogilvie himself. Perhaps it was his clothes, as usual rumpled, ill-fitting . . . but too large for his stocky frame? Whatever it was, he seemed different; not the face – he was too far away for his face to be seen clearly. It was in his walk, the way he held his shoulders, as if the gentle slope of the hill was far steeper than it was. The Apache had changed since Istanbul; the two years had not been kind.

Ogilvie reached the remnants of the marble arch that was the arbour's entrance; he would remain inside. It was three o'clock; the time span had begun.

Michael crept away from his recess behind the cluster of wild bushes and crawled rapidly through the descending field of high grass, keeping his body close to the ground and making a wide arc north until he came to the base of the hill. He glanced at his watch; it had taken him nearly two minutes.

The woman was now above him, roughly a hundred yards away in the centre of the field below and to the right of Domitian's arbour. He could not see her, but he knew she had not moved. She had chosen her sight lines carefully, a back-up killer's habit. He started up the slope on his hands and knees, separating the blades of grass in front of him, listening for the sounds of unexpected voices. There were none.

He reached the crest. The woman was directly ahead, no more than sixty feet away, still standing on the first rung of curving white steps that led down to the ancient marble bath. She held the sketch pad in front of her, but her eyes were not on it. They were staring at the entrance of the arbour, her concentration absolute, her body primed to move instantly. Then Havelock saw what he had hoped he would see: the heavy-set woman's right hand was no longer on her lapel. It was now concealed under her gabardine coat, without question gripping an automatic she could remove quickly and aim accurately, unencumbered by the awkwardness of a pocket. Michael feared that weapon, but he feared the radio more. In moments it might be an ally; now it was his enemy, as deadly as any gun.

He looked at his watch again, annoyed at the sight of the seconds ticking off; he had to move swiftly. He did so, staying below the crest of the field working his way around towards the broken stone trench that led to the well of the Roman bath. Huge weeds sprang up from the sides and from the cracks in the trench, covering it and giving it the appearance of an ugly, giant centipede. Havelock parted the moist, filthy overgrowth, slid forward on his stomach and crawled along the jagged marble ditch. Thirty seconds later he emerged from the weeds into the ancient remains of the circular pool that centuries ago had held the oiled, pampered bodies of emperors and courtesans. Seven feet above him – eight decayed steps away – was the woman whose function was to kill him should her current employer be incapable of doing so. Her back was to him, her thick legs planted like those of a sergeant-major commanding a machine-gun squad.

He studied the remains of the marble staircase; it was fragile and was protected by a twelve-inch iron fence on the second rung to prevent onlookers from venturing farther down. The weight of a body on any single step could cause the stone to crack, and the sound would be his undoing. But what if the sound was accompanied by the impact of a severe physical blow? He knew he had to decide quickly, move quickly. Every minute that went by was adding to the growing alarm of the assassin in Domitian's arbour.

Silently he moved his hands about under the tangled weeds; his fingers struck a hard, rough-edged object. It was a fragment of marble, a chiselled part of an artisan's design two thousand years ago. He gripped it in his right hand and, with the other, removed from his belt the Llama automatic he had taken from the would-be mafioso in Civitavecchia. Long ago he had trained himself to fire with his left hand as well as with his right, a basic precaution. The skill would serve him now; it was his own particular back-up. If his tactic failed, he would kill the woman who had been hired to make certain he died on the Palatine Hill. But it was a back-up, merely an option to make sure he stayed alive. He wanted to keep his rendezvous in Domitian's arbour.

468

He brought his legs slowly into a crouch and, extending one knee, prepared to spring. The woman was less than four feet away, directly above him. He raised his right arm, the heavy, jagged fragment in his hand, and lunged as he hurled the heavy piece of marble at the wide expanse of gabardine between her shoulders, whipping his arm with all the force he could muster.

Sound and instinct. The woman started to turn, but the impact came. The jagged fragment crashed into her neck at the base of her skull, blood matting her dark hair instantly. Havelock rushed up the steps, and, grabbing her coat at the waist, pulled her down over the small iron fence while jamming his forearm against her mouth and choking off the scream. The two of them plunged down into the marble well, Michael twisting the woman's body as they fell. They hit the hard surface; he rammed his knee into her chest between her breasts and thrust the barrel of the Llama deep against her throat.

"You listen to me!" he whispered harshly, knowing that neither the embassy nor Ogilvie would employ a back-up who was not fluent in English and who might misinterpret orders. "Get on your radio and tell your friend to come over here as fast as he can! Say it's an emergency. Tell him to use the woods below the archway. You don't want the American to see him."

"*Cosa dici?*"

"You heard me and you understand me! Do as I say! Tell him you think you've both been betrayed. *Prudente! lo parlo Italiano! Capisci?*" added Havelock, applying further pressure both with his knee and the barrel of the gun. "*Presto!*"

The woman grimaced, sucking her breath between her clenched teeth, her broad, masculine face stretched like that of a striking cobra caught in a snake fork. Haltingly, as Michael removed his knee, she raised her right hand to her lapel and folded it back, revealing a transistorized microphone in the shape of a thick button attached to the cloth. In the centre was a small, flat transmission switch; she pressed it. There was a brief hum, the signal travelling three hundred feet due west on the Palatine Hill; she spoke.

"*Trifoglio, trifoglio,*" she said rapidly for identification. "*Ascolta! Abbiamo un'emergenza . . . . . .*" She carried out Michael's orders, the whispered urgency of her voice conveying the panic she felt as the Llama was shoved deeper into her throat. The response came in the sound of startled, metallic Italian.

"*Che avete? Quale?*"

"*I – retta!*"

"*Arrivo!*"

Havelock pulled the woman to her knees, ripping her coat apart as he did so. Held in place above her waist by a wide strap was an elongated holster, revealing the handle of a powerful Magnum automatic. The outsized leather case accommodated an appendage attached to the barrel: a perforated cylinder – a silencer, permanently secured and zeroed for accuracy. The woman was, indeed, a professional. Michael quickly removed the weapon and shoved it under his belt. He yanked the woman to her feet and pushed her violently into the curving stairs, forcing her up to the second step so that both of them could see – between the spikes of the small iron fence – over the top of the ancient bath. He was behind her, his body pressed into hers locking her in place, the Llama at her right temple, his left arm around her neck. In seconds he saw her companion, crouching as he raced through the foliage below the arbour; it was all he had to see. Without warning, he snapped his left arm back, choking the breath out of the woman's throat and forcing her head forward into the crushing vice. Her body went limp; she would remain unconscious until dark. He did not want to kill her; he wanted her to tell her story to the patriots who had hired her. He let her slide down the cracked marble to the weed-infested well below, and waited.

The man emerged cautiously on the sloping field, his hand beneath his tweed jacket. Too many minutes; time was passing too swiftly, the span half over. Much longer, and the assassin sent by Washington would become alarmed. If he walked outside the arbour he would know that his guards were not in place, that his control was lost; he would run. It must not happen! The answers Havelock sought were fifty yards away inside a remnant of antiquity. Once the control was shifted – *only* if it was shifted – could those answers be learned. *Make your move, employee*, thought Havelock, as the Italian approached.

"*Trifoglio, trifoglio!*" said Michael in a sharp whisper as he grabbed debris from the steps and threw it over the top of the marble casement to his right, at the opposite end of the circular enclosure.

The man broke into a run towards the sound of the voice repeating the code and the sight of flying dirt. Havelock moved to his left and crouched on the third step, his hand on a spoke of the fence, his feet constantly testing the stone beneath; it *had* to hold him.

It did. Michael lurched over the top as the Italian reached the marble rim, so startling the man that he gasped in shock, his panic immobilizing him. Havelock lunged, swinging the Llama into the Italian's face, shattering bone and teeth; blood burst from his mouth and splattered his shirt and jacket. The man started to collapse; Havelock rushed forward to grab him, then turned and propelled him over the side of the marble bath. The Italian plummeted, arms and legs flailing; at the bottom he lay motionless, sprawled over the body of the woman, his bloody head on her stomach. He, too, would have a story to tell, thought Michael. It was important that the strategists in Washington should hear it, for if the answers were not forthcoming during the next few minutes, the Palatine was only the beginning.

Havelock forced the Llama into the inside pocket of his jacket and felt the uncomfortable pressure of the out-sized Magnum automatic under his belt. He would keep both weapons; the Llama was a short piece and easily concealed, while the Magnum with its permanently attached silencer could be advantageous in other circumstances. Suddenly a cold wind of depression swept through him. Twenty-four hours ago he had thought that he would never again hold a gun in his hand for the rest of his life – his new life. In truth, he loathed weapons; feared and hated them, and for this reason he had learned to master them – so that he could go on living and use them to still other weapons – the guns of his childhood. The early days, the terrible days; in a way they were what his whole life had been about, the life he had thought he had put finally to rest. Root out the abusers, permit life to the living . . . destroy the killers of all Lidices in any form. He had left that life, but the killers were still there, in another form. He buttoned his jacket and started towards the entrance of the arbour, and the man who had come to kill him.

470

As he approached the decrepit marble archway his eyes instinctively scanned the ground, his feet avoiding stray branches that could snap underfoot, announcing his presence. He reached the jagged wall of the arch and silently sidestepped his way to the opening. Gently he pushed away the cascading vines and looked inside. Ogilvie was at the far end of the stone path by the pedestalled bust of Domitian. He was smoking a cigarette, studying the hill above the arbour to his right, the very hill – the same area with the cluster of wild bushes – where Michael had concealed himself nineteen minutes before. The Apache had made his own assessment, the accuracy of his analysis apparent.

There was a slight chill in the air and Havelock noted that Ogilvie's wrinkled, ill-fitting jacket was buttoned. But he also saw that this did not prevent swift access to a gun. Then Michael focused on the strategist's face; the change was startling. It was paler than Havelock remembered ever having seen it. The lines that had been there before were chiselled deeper now and drawn longer, like the ridges of decay in the faded marble of the ancient arbour. One did not have to be a doctor to know that Ogilvie was a sick man and that his illness was severe. If there was a great deal of strength left in him, it was as concealed as the weapons he carried.

Michael stepped inside, watching intently for any sudden movement on the part of the former field man. "Hello, Red?" he said.

Ogilvie's head turned only slightly, conveying the fact that he had seen Havelock out of the corner of his eye before the greeting. "Good to see you, Navajo."

"Drop the 'Navajo'. This isn't Istanbul."

"No, it isn't, but I saved your ass there, didn't I?"

"You saved it after you damn near got me killed. I told you the bridge was a trap, but you, my so-called superior – a label you overworked, incidentally – insisted otherwise. You came back for me because I told you it was a trap in front of our control in the Mesrutiyet. He would have racked you in his briefing report."

"Still, I came *back*," pressed Ogilvie quickly, angrily, colour spreading across his pallid face. Then he checked himself, smiled wanly and shrugged. "What the hell, it doesn't matter."

"No, it doesn't. I think you'd risk blowing yourself and all your kids apart to justify yourself, but as you say, you did come back. Thanks for that. It was quicker, if not necessarily safer, than jumping into the Bosporus."

"You never would have made it."

"Maybe, maybe not."

Ogilvie threw his cigarette on the ground, crushed it underfoot and stepped forward. "Not the kids, Havelock. Me, yes. Not the kids."

"All right, not the kids." At the reference to children – his unthinking reference – Michael felt momentary embarrassment. He recalled that Ogilvie's children had been taken away from him. This suddenly old man was alone in his shadow world with his personal furies.

"Let's talk," said the man from Washington, walking towards a marble bench on the border of the stone path. "Sit down . . . Michael. Or is it Mike? I don't remember."

"Whatever you like. I'll stand."

"I'll sit. I don't mind telling you, I'm beat. It's a long way from DC, a lot of flying time. I don't sleep well on planes."

"You look tired."

At the remark, Ogilvie stopped and glanced at Havelock. "Cute," he said, and then sat down. "Tell me something, Michael. Are *you* tired?"

"Yes," said Havelock. "Of the whole goddamned lie. Of everything that's happened. To her. To me. To all of you in your sterile white offices, with your filthy minds – God help me, I was part of you. What did you think you were doing? Why did you *do* it?"

"That's a large indictment, Navajo."

"I told you. Drop that fucking name."

"Like from a cereal packet, huh?"

"Worse. For your enlightenment, the Navajos were related to the Apaches; but unlike the Apaches, the tribe was essentially peaceful, defensive. The name didn't fit in Istanbul, and it doesn't fit now."

"That's interesting; I didn't know that. But then, I suppose it's the sort of thing someone not born in a country – brought over after a pretty harrowing childhood somewhere else – would find out about. I mean, studying that kind of history is a way of saying 'Thanks', isn't it?"

"I don't know what you're talking about."

"Sure you do. A kid lives through wholesale slaughter, sees friends and neighbours machine-gunned in a field and thrown into ditches, his own mother sent away to God knows what, knowing he'll never see her again. This kid is something. He hides in the woods with nothing to eat except what he can trap or steal, afraid to come out. Then he's found and spends the next few years running through the streets with explosives strapped to his back, the enemy everywhere, any one of them his potential executioner. All this before he's ten years old, and by the time he's twelve, his father's killed by the Soviets . . . Christ, a kid like that, when he finally gets to a safe harbour, he's going to learn everything he can about the place. He's really saying 'Thanks for letting me come here.' Wouldn't you agree . . . *Havlicek*?"

So the inviolate was not impenetrable. Of course the strategists knew, he should have realized that his own actions had brought it about. The sole guarantee he had been given was that his true file would be provided only on a need-to-know basis to the highest levels of personnel screening. Those below would be shown the British MI6 addendum. A Slovak orphan, parents killed in a Brighton bombing raid, cleared for adoption and immigration. It was all they had to know, all they should know. Before. Not now.

"It's not pertinent."

"Well, maybe it is," said the former field man, shifting his position on the bench, his hand casually moving towards his jacket pocket.

"Don't do that."

"What?"

"Your hand. Keep it out of there."

"Oh, sorry . . . As I was saying, all that early stuff *could* be pertinent. A man can take just so much over the years; it accumulates, you know what I mean? Then one day something snaps, and without his realizing it his head plays tricks on him. He

472

goes back – way back – to when things happened to him – terrible things – and the years and the motives of people he knew *then* get mixed up – with the years and the people he knows *now*. He begins to blame the present for all the lousy things that happened in the past. It happens a lot to men who live the way you and I have lived. It's not even unusual."

"Are you *finished*?" asked Havelock harshly. "Because if you *are* – "

"Come on back with me, Michael," interrupted the man from Washington. "You need help. We can help you."

"You travelled five thousand miles to tell me *that*?" shouted Havelock. "That's the *data*, your *explanation*?"

"Take it easy. Cool it."

"No, *you* take it easy! *You* cool it, because you are going to need every cold nerve you've got! All of you! I'll start here in Rome and work my way up and over, through Switzerland, Germany . . . Prague, Krakow, Warsaw . . . right up into Moscow, if I have to! And the more I talk, the more of a mess you'll be in, every one of you.

"Who the hell are you to explain what or where my head is? I saw that woman. She's *alive*! I followed her to Civitavecchia, where she faded, but I found out what you said to her, what you *did* to her! I'm going after her, but every day it takes will cost you! I'll start the minute I get out of here and you won't be able to stop me. Listen to the news tonight and read the morning papers. There's a conduit here in Rome, a respected first-level attaché, a member of a *minority* – one hell of a screen. Only he's going to lose his value *and* his network before the sun goes down! You *bastards*! Who do you think you *are*?"

"All right, all *right*!" pleaded Ogilvie, both hands in the air, nodding his head in a rapid gesture of conciliation. "You've got it all, but you can't blame me for trying. Those were the orders. 'Get him back so we can tell him over here,' that's what they said. 'Try anything, but don't *say* anything, not while he's out of the country.' I told them it wouldn't work, not with you. I made them give me the disclosure option; they didn't want to, but I hammered it out of them."

"Then *talk*!"

"Okay, okay, you've got it." The man from Washington expelled his breath, shaking his head slowly back and forth. "Jesus, things get screwed up."

"Unscrew them!"

Ogilvie looked up at Michael, raising his hand to the upper left area of his rumpled jacket. "A smoke, do you mind?"

"Pull it back."

The strategist peeled back his lapel, revealing a pack of cigarettes in his shirt pocket. Havelock nodded; Ogilvie took out the cigarettes and a book of matches behind the pack. He shook a cigarette into his right hand and flipped open the matchbook cover; the book was empty. "Shit," he muttered. "Have you got a light?"

Michael reached into his pocket, took out matches and handed them over. "What you've got to say had better make a great deal of sense – "

Oh, my God! Whether it was the slight movement of the head of red hair below him, or the odd position of Ogilvie's right hand, or the flash of sunlight reflecting off the cigarette pack's cellophane, he would never know, but in that confluence of unexpected factors he knew the trap had been sprung. He lashed out with his left foot, catching the strategist's right arm and reeling it back; the force of the blow threw Ogilvie off the bench. Suddenly the air was filled with a billowing cloud of mist. He dived to his right, beyond the path, holding his nostrils, closing his eyes, rolling on the ground until he slammed into the remains of the jagged wall, out of range of the gaseous cloud.

The collapsible vial had been concealed in the pack of cigarettes, and the acrid odour that permeated the arbour told him what the vial had contained. It was a nerve gas that inhibited all muscular control if a target was caught in the nucleus; its effect lasted no less than an hour, no more than three. It was used almost exclusively for abduction, rarely if ever as a prelude to dispatch.

Havelock opened his eyes and got to his knees, supporting himself on the wall. Beyond the marble bench the man from Washington was thrashing around on the overgrown grass, coughing, struggling to rise, his body in convulsions. He had been caught in the milder periphery of the burst, just enough to make him momentarily lose control.

Michael got to his feet, watching the bluish-grey cloud evaporate in the air above the Palatine, its centre holding until diffused by the breezes. He opened his jacket, feeling the pain of the scrapes and bruises made by the Magnum under his belt as a result of his violent movements. He took out the weapon with the ugly perforated cylinder on the barrel and walked unsteadily across the grass to Ogilvie. The red-haired man was breathing with difficulty, but his eyes were clear; he stopped struggling and stared up at Havelock and then at the weapon in Michael's hand.

"Go ahead, Navajo," he said, his voice barely above a whisper. "Save me the trouble."

"I thought so," replied Havelock, looking at the former field man's gaunt, lined face that had the chalk-white pallor of death about it.

"Don't think. Shoot."

"Why should I? Make it easier, I mean. Or harder, for that matter. You didn't come to kill me, you came to take me. And you don't have any answers at all."

"I gave them to you."

"When?"

"A couple of minutes ago . . . *Havlicek*. The war. Czechoslovakia, Prague. Your father and mother. Lidice. All those things that aren't pertinent."

"What the *hell* are you talking about?"

"Your head's damaged, Navajo. I'm not lying about that."

"*What?*"

"You didn't see the Karras woman. She's dead."

"She's *alive!*" shouted Michael, crouching beside the man from Washington, grabbing him by the lapel of his rumpled coat. "Goddamn you, she saw me! She ran from me!"

"No way," said Ogilvie, shaking his head. "You weren't the only one at Costa Brava; there was someone else. We have his sighting; he brought back proof . . . fragments of clothing, matching blood, the works. She died on that beach on the Costa Brava."

"That's a *lie!* I was there all night! I went down to the road, down to the beach.

474

There weren't any pieces of clothing; she was running, she wasn't touched until after she was dead, after the bullets hit her. Whoever she was, her body was carried away intact, nothing torn, nothing left on the beach! How *could* there be? *Why* would there be? That sighting's a lie!"

The strategist lay motionless, his eyes boring up into Havelock's, his breathing steadier now. It was obvious that his mind was racing, filtering truth where he could find the truth. "It was dark," he said in a monotone. "You couldn't tell."

"When I walked down to the beach, the sun was up."

Ogilvie winced, forcing his head into his left shoulder, his mouth stretched, a searing pain apparently shooting up through his chest and down his arm. "The man who made that sighting had a coronary three weeks later," said the strategist, his voice a strained whisper. "He died on a goddamned boat in the Chesapeake . . . If you're right, there's a problem back in DC neither you nor I know about. Help me. We've got to get out to Palombara."

"*You* get out to Palombara. I don't come in without answers. I told you that."

"You've got to! Because you're not getting out of here without me, and that's Holy Writ."

"You've lost your touch, Apache. I took this Magnum from that pretty face you hired. Incidentally, her *gumbar* is with her now, both resting at the bottom of a marble bath."

"Not them! *Him!*" The man from Washington was suddenly alarmed. He pushed himself up on his elbows, his neck craning, his eyes squinting into the sun, scanning the hill above the arbour.

"He's waiting, watching us," he whispered. "Put the gun down! Drop the advantage. Hurry up!"

"Who? Why? What for?"

"For Christ's sake, do as I say! Quickly!"

Michael shook his head and got to his feet. "You're full of little tricks, Red, but you've been away too long. You've got the same stench about you that I can smell all the way from the Potomac – "

"Don't! *No!*" screamed the former field man, his eyes wide, straining, focused on the high point of the hill. Then with an unreasonable reservoir of miraculous strength he lurched off the ground, clutching Havelock and pulling him away from the stone path.

Havelock raised the barrel with the heavy cylinder attached and was about to crash it into Ogilvie's skull, when the snaps came, two muted reports from above. Ogilvie gasped, then exhaled audibly, making a terrible sound like rushing water, and went limp, falling backwards on the grass. His throat was ripped open; he was dead, having stopped the bullet meant for Michael.

Havelock lunged to the wall; three more shots came, exploding marble and dirt all around him. He raced to the end of the jagged wall, the Magnum by his face, and peered between a V-shaped break in the stone.

Silence.

A forearm. A shoulder. Beyond a cluster of wild bushes. Now! He aimed carefully and fired four shots in rapid succession. A bloody hand whipped up in the air, followed by a pivoting shoulder. Then the wounded man lurched out of the foliage and limped rapidly over the crest of the hill. The hair on the hatless figure was close-cropped and black, the skin deep brown. Mahogany. The would-be assassin on the Palatine was Rome's conduit for covert activities in the northern sector of the Mediterranean. Had he squeezed the trigger in anger, or fear, or a combination of both, afraid and furious because his cover and his network would be exposed? Or had he coldly followed orders? Another question, one more shapeless fragment in the mosaic.

Havelock turned and leaned against the wall, exhausted, frightened, feeling as vulnerable as in the early days, the terrible days. He looked down at Red Ogilvie – John Philip Ogilvie, if he remembered correctly. Minutes ago he was a dying man; now he was a dead man. Killed saving the life of another he did not want to see die. The Apache had not come to dispatch the Navajo; he had come to save him. But safety was not found among the strategists in Washington; they had been programmed by liars. Liars were in control.

Why? For what purpose?

No time. He had to get out of Rome, out of Italy. To the border at Col des Moulinets, and if that failed, to Paris.

To Jenna. Always Jenna, now more than ever!

10

The two phone calls took forty-seven minutes to complete from two separate boxes in the crowded Leonardo da Vinci airport. The first was to the office of the *direttore* of Rome's *Amministrazione di Sicurezza*, Italy's watchdog over covert foreign activities. With short, succinct references to authentic clandestine operations going back several years, Havelock was put through without identification to the director's administrative assistant. He held the man on the line for less than a minute, hanging up after saying what he had to say. The second call, from a box at the opposite end of the hall, was placed to the *redattore* of *Il Progresso Giornale*, Rome's highly political, highly opinionated, largely anti-American newspaper. Considering the implied subject matter, the editor was a far less difficult man to reach. And when the journalist interrupted Michael for identification and clarification, Havelock countered with two suggestions: the first, to check with the administrative assistant to the *direttore* of the *Amministrazione di Sicurezza*; the second, to watch the United States embassy during the next seventy-two hours, with particular attention paid to the individual in question.

"*Mezzani!*" fumed the editor.

"*Addio,*" said Michael, replacing the receiver.

Lt-Colonel Lawrence Baylor Brown, diplomatic attaché and a prime example of America's recognition of minorities, was out of a job. The conduit was finished, his network rendered useless; it would take months, possibly a year, to rebuild. And regardless of how seriously he was wounded, the colonel would be flown out of Rome within hours to explain the death of the red-haired man on the Palatine.

The first floodgate had been opened. Others would follow. *Every day it takes will cost you.*

He meant it.

"I'm glad you got here," said Daniel Stern, closing the door of the white, windowless room on the fifth floor of the State Department. The two men he addressed were sitting at the conference table: the balding psychiatrist, Dr Paul Miller, going through his notes; the lawyer named Dawson gazing absently at the wall, his head resting on a yellow legal pad in front of him. "I've just come from Walter Reed hospital – the Baylor debriefing. It's all confirmed. I heard it myself, questioned him myself. He's one torn apart soldier, physically and emotionally. But he's reining tight; he's a good man."

"No deviations from the original report?" asked the lawyer.

"Nothing substantive; he was thorough the first time. The capsule was secreted in Ogilvie's cigarettes, a mild diphenylamine compound released through a CO_2 cartridge triggered by pressure."

"That's what Red meant when he told us he could take Havelock if he got him within arm's reach," interrupted Miller quietly.

"He nearly did," said Stern, walking into the room. There was a red telephone on a small table beside his chair; he flipped a switch on the sloping front of the instrument and sat down. "Hearing Baylor tell it is a lot more vivid than reading a dry report," said the Director of Consular Operations, and fell silent; the two strategists waited. Stern continued softly. "He's quiet, almost passive, but you look at his face and you know how deeply he feels. How responsible."

Dawson leaned forward. "Did you ask him what tipped Havelock off? It wasn't in the report."

"It wasn't there because he doesn't know. Until the last second, Havelock didn't appear to suspect anything. Just as the report says, the two of them were talking; Ogilvie took the cigarettes out of his pocket and apparently asked for a light. Havelock reached into his pocket for matches, brought them over to Red and then it happened. He suddenly kicked out, sending Ogilvie reeling off the bench, and the capsule exploded. When the smoke cleared, Red was on the ground and Havelock was standing over him with a gun in his hand."

"Why didn't Baylor shoot *then*? At that moment?" The lawyer was disturbed; it was in his voice.

"Because of us," replied Stern. "Our orders were firm. Havelock was to be brought in alive. Only a 'last extremity' judgement could intervene."

"He could have been," said Dawson quickly, almost questioningly. "I've read Brown's – Baylor's – service report. He's a qualified expert in weapons, special emphasis on side arms. There's very little he's not a 'qualified expert' in; he's a walking advertisement for the NAACP *and* the officer corps. Rhodes Scholar, Special Forces, tactical guerrilla warfare. You name it, he's got it in his file."

"He's black; he's had to be good. I told you that before. What's your point?"

"He could have wounded Havelock. Legs, shoulders, the pelvic area. Between them, he and Ogilvie *could* have taken him."

"That's asking for a lot of accuracy from seventy-five to a hundred feet."

"Twenty-five to thirty yards. Almost the equivalent of a handgun firing range, and Havelock was standing still. He wasn't a moving target. Did you question Baylor about that?"

"Frankly, I didn't see any reason to. He's got enough on his mind, including a shot-up hand that may take him out of the army. In my opinion, he acted correctly in a hairy situation. He waited until he saw Havelock point his gun at Ogilvie, until he was convinced Red didn't have a chance. He only fired then, at the precise moment Ogilvie lunged at Havelock, taking the bullet. Everything corresponds with the autopsy in Rome."

"The delay cost Red his life," said Dawson, not satisfied.

"Shortened it," corrected the doctor. "And not by much."

"That's also in the autopsy report," added Stern.

"This may sound pretty cold under the circumstances," said the lawyer. "But perhaps it's related. We overestimated him."

"No," disagreed the director. "We underestimated Havelock. What more do you need? It's been three days since the Palatine, and in those three days he's destroyed a conduit, frightened off the locals in Rome – no one wants to work for us now – and collapsed a network. In addition he routed a cable through Switzerland to the chairman of Congressional Oversight, alluding to CIA incompetence and corruption in Amsterdam. And this morning we get a call from the chief of White House security, who doesn't know whether to be panicked or outraged. He, too, received a cable, this one in sixteen-hundred cipher, implying that there was a Soviet mole close to the President."

"That comes from Havelock's so-called confrontation with Rostov in Athens," said Dawson, glancing at the yellow legal pad. "Baylor reported it."

"And Paul here doubts that it ever took place," said Stern, looking at Miller.

"Fantasy and reality," interjected the psychiatrist. "If all the information we've gathered is accurate, he slips back and forth unable to distinguish which. *If* our data is accurate. In all likelihood, there's a degree of incompetence, perhaps minor corruption, in Amsterdam. However, I'd think it's pretty unlikely that a Soviet mole could break into the presidential circle."

"We can and do make mistakes *here*," offered Stern, "as well as at the Pentagon, and, God knows, in Langley. But over there the chances of that type of error are minuscule. I don't say it can't happen or hasn't happened, but anyone close to the Oval Office has had every year, every month, every week of his life put under the microscope, even the President's closest friends. The bright recruits are studied as if they might be Stalin's heirs; it's been standard procedure since 'forty-seven." The director paused again, again not finished. His eyes strayed to the sheaf of loose notes in front of the doctor. He continued slowly, pensively. "Havelock knows which buttons to press, which people to reach, the right ciphers to use; even old ciphers have impact. He can create panic because he gives his information authenticity . . . How far will he go, Paul?"

"No absolutes, Daniel," said the psychiatrist, shaking his head. "Whatever I say is barely above guesswork."

"Trained guesswork," interrupted the lawyer.

"How would you like to assess a case without access to the client?" asked Miller.

"You've got depositions, statistics, a current on-site briefing and a detailed dossier. It's fair background."

"Bad analogy. Sorry I brought it up."

"If we can't find him, how far will he go?" pressed the Director of Cons Op. "How long have we got before he starts costing lives?"

"He already has," broke in Dawson.

"Not in a controlled sense," contradicted Miller. "It was a direct reaction to a violent attack on his own life. There's a difference."

"Spell out the difference, Paul."

"As *I* see it," said the psychiatrist, picking up his notes and adjusting his glasses. "And, to use a favourite phrase of Ogilvie's, I don't claim it's Holy Writ. But there are a couple of things that shed a little light, and I'll be honest with you, they disturb me. The key, of course, is in whatever was said between Havelock and Ogilvie; but since we can't know what it was, we can only go by Baylor's detailed description of the scene, the physical movements, the general tone. I've read it over and over again, and until the final moments – the eruption of violence – I was struck by a note I didn't expect to find. The absence of sustained hostility."

"Sustained hostility?" asked Stem. "I don't know what that implies in behavioural terms, but I hope it doesn't mean they didn't argue because they did. Baylor makes that clear."

"Of course they argued; it was a confrontation. There was a prolonged outburst on Havelock's part, restating the threats he's made before, but then the shouting stopped; it had to. Some kind of accommodation was reached. It couldn't have been otherwise in the light of what followed."

"In the light of what followed?" questioned Stern, bewildered. "What followed was Ogilvie's trap, the diphenylamine, the explosion."

"I'm sorry, you're wrong, Daniel. There was a retreat before then. Remember, from the moment Havelock showed himself until that instant at the bench when he kicked out, aborting the trap, there was no show of physical violence, no display of weapons. There was talk, *conversation*. Then the cigarettes, the matches. It's too damned reasonable."

"What do you mean?"

"Put yourself in Havelock's place. Your grievance is enormous, your anger at fever pitch, and a man you consider your enemy asks you for a light. What do you do?"

"It's only a match."

"That's right, only a match. But you're consumed, your head throbbing with anxiety, your state of mind actually vicious. The man in front of you represents betrayal at its worst, at its most personal, most deeply felt. These are the things a paranoid schizophrenic feels at a time like this, with a man like this. And that man, that enemy – even if he's promised to tell you everything you want to hear – asks you for a light. How do you react?"

"I'd give it to him."

"*How?*"

"Well, I'd – ," The section chief stopped, his eyes locked with Miller's. Then he completed the answer, speaking quietly. "I'd throw it to him."

"Or tell him to forget about it, or shove it, or just to keep on talking. But I don't think you'd take the matches from your pocket and walk over, handing them to that man as though it were a momentary pause in an argument rather than an interruption of a highly charged moment of extreme personal anxiety. No, I don't think you'd do that. I don't think any of us would."

"We don't know what Ogilvie said to him," objected Stern. "He could have – "

"It almost doesn't matter, don't you see?" interrupted the psychiatrist. "It's the pattern, the goddamned *pattern*."

"Discerned from a book of *matches?*"

"Yes, because it's symptomatic. Throughout the entire confrontation, with the exception of a single outburst, there was a remarkable absence of aggressiveness on Havelock's part. If Baylor is as accurate as you say and I suspect he is because under the circumstances he'd be prone to exaggerate any threatening movements or gestures – Havelock exercised extraordinary control . . . rational behaviour."

"What does that tell you?" asked Dawson, breaking his silence, watching Miller closely.

"I'm not sure," said the doctor, returning the lawyer's stare. "But I know it doesn't fit the portrait of the man we've persuaded ourselves we're dealing with. To twist a phrase, there's too much reason afoot, not enough madness."

"Even with his slipping in and out of reality?" continued Dawson.

"It's not relevant here. His reality is the product of his whole experience, his everyday living. Not his convictions; they're based largely on his emotions. Under the conditions of the rendezvous, they should have surfaced more, distorting his reality, forcing him into listening less, into a more aggressive posture . . . He listened too much."

"You know what you're saying, don't you, Paul?" said the lawyer.

"I know what I'm *implying*, based on the data we've all accepted as being totally accurate . . . from the beginning."

"That the man on the Palatine three days ago doesn't fit the portrait?" suggested Dawson.

"*Might* not fit it. No absolutes, only 'trained' guesswork. We don't know what was said, but there was too much rationality in what was described to suit me. Or the portrait."

"Which was predicated on information we've considered infallible," concluded the lawyer. "In your words, 'from the beginning'. From Costa Brava."

"Exactly. But suppose it wasn't? Suppose it *isn't?*"

"Impossible!" said the Director of Consular Operations. "That information was filtered through a dozen sieves, then filtered again through twenty more. There was *no* margin for error. The Karras woman *was* KGB; she *died* at Costa Brava."

"That's what we've accepted," agreed the psychiatrist. "And I hope to God it's accurate, and that my guesswork observations are worthless reactions to an inaccurately described scene. But if it's not and they're not, if there's the remotest possibility that we're not dealing with a psychopath but with a man who's telling the truth because it is the truth, then we're faced with something I don't even want to think about."

The three men fell silent, each grappling with the enormity of the implication. Finally Dawson spoke. "We have to think about it."

"It's appalling even to consider it," said Stern. "There was MacKenzie's confirmation, and it *was* a confirmation. The torn clothing, parts of a blouse, a skirt, they *belonged* to her, it was established. And the blood type, A-negative. *Hers.*"

"And Steven MacKenzie died of a coronary three weeks later," interrupted Miller. "We looked into it, but it just faded away."

"Come on, Paul," objected Stern. "That doctor in Maryland is one of the most respected on the Eastern Shore. What's his name? . . . Randolph. Matthew Randolph. Johns Hopkins, Mayo Clinic, on the boards of Massachusetts General and New York's Mount Sinai, and with his own medical centre. He was thoroughly interviewed."

"I'd like to talk to him again," the doctor said.

"And I remind you," pressed the director, "MacKenzie had just about the finest record that ever came out of the Central Intelligence Agency. What you're suggesting is inconceivable."

"So was the horse in Troy," said the lawyer. "When it was conceived." He turned to Miller, who had removed his glasses. "Trained guesswork, Paul. Let's take it all the way; we can always scratch it, but say there's substance. What do you think he'll do now?"

"I'll tell you what he won't do – if there's substance. He won't come in, and we can't trick him with ploys because he understands – rationally – that whatever's happened we're either a part of it, or ignorant of it, or it's beyond our control. The attack's been made on him; he'll mount every defence he's learned in the sixteen years he's been in the field. And from now on he'll be ruthless, because he *has* been betrayed. By men he can't see in places where they shouldn't be." The psychiatrist looked at Stern. "There's your answer, Daniel, if there's substance. Oddly enough, he's really back in his early days now – the machine-guns, Lidice, betrayal. He's running through the streets wondering who in the crowds might be his executioner."

A sharp, abrasive hum erupted from the red telephone on the small, low table next to Stern. The director reached down and picked it up, his eyes still on Miller. "Yes?"

Thirty seconds of silence followed, interrupted only by quiet acknowledgements on Stern's part as he listened, staring across at the psychiatrist's notes, absorbing the information being given him. "Stay on the line," he said finally, snapping the switch and looking up at both strategists. "This is Rome. They've found a man in Civitavecchia; the name of a ship. It may *be* the girl. Or a Soviet hoax; that's entirely possible. It was Baylor's theory and he still holds to it . . . The original order stands. Take Havelock, but not dispatch; he's not to be considered 'beyond salvage' . . . Now, I've got to ask you a question – primarily you, Paul, and I know I can t hold you to absolutes."

"That's the only absolute."

481

"We've acted on the assumption that we're dealing with an unbalanced man, with someone whose paranoia may compel him to place documents or statements exposing past operations with third parties, to be released on instructions. Is that right?"

"Basically, yes. It's the sort of manipulation a schizophrenic mentality would indulge in, the satisfaction derived as much from revenge as from the threat itself. Remember, the third parties in question would undoubtedly come from undesirable elements; respectable people would shun such a person, and underneath he knows that. It's a compulsive, involuntary game. He really can't win, only seek vengeance, and there's the danger."

"Would a sane man play that game?"

The psychiatrist paused, fingering his glasses. "Not the same way."

"How do you mean?"

"Would you?"

"*Please*, Paul."

"No, I'm serious. You'd be more concerned with the threat than with the revenge. You want something; revenge may be down the road, but it's not what's primarily on your mind now. You want answers. Threats might get them for you, but risking exposure of classified information by delivering it to highly suspect brokers defeats the purpose."

"What would a sane man do?"

"Probably get word to those he's threatening as to the kind of information he intends to reveal. Then he'd proceed to reach qualified third parties – publishers, perhaps, or men and women who head organizations that legitimately, openly, resist the kind of work we do here – and make arrangements with them. That's a sane man's approach, his attack, his ultimate threat."

"There's no evidence that Havelock's done any of these things."

"It's only been three days since the Palatine; he hasn't had time. These things take time."

"Lending credence to the matches. To his sanity."

"I think so, and I'm biting the bullet. I gave him the label – based on what we had – and now I'm wondering if it should be removed."

"And if we remove it, we accept the possibility of a sane man's attack. As you said, he'll be ruthless, far more dangerous than a schizophrenic."

"Yes," agreed the psychiatrist. "An unbalanced man can be repudiated, black-mailers dealt with . . . and it's important to realize that since Costa Brava no such extortionists have tried to reach us. But legitimate interests, no matter how misguided, could inflict extraordinary damage."

"Costing networks, informants, sources, years of work . . ." The director's hand reached down to the telephone, to the switch, "And lives."

"Yet if he's sane," interrupted Dawson sharply, once again breaking a silence, "if it *is* the girl, that presupposes a much deeper problem, doesn't it? Her guilt, her death, everything's in question. All that *infallible* information that was filtered through all those high-level sieves suddenly looks like a massive deception where deception shouldn't *be*. Those are the answers Havelock wants."

"We know the questions," replied Stern quietly, his hand still on the telephone switch, "and we can't *give* him the answers. We can only stop him from inflicting extraordinary damage." The Director of Cons Op fell silent for a moment, his eyes on the telephone. "When each of us entered this room, we understood. The only morality here is pragmatic morality, no philosophy but our own brand of utilitarianism. The greatest advantage for the many . . . over the few, over the individual."

"If you put him 'beyond salvage', Daniel," continued the lawyer softly, emphatically, "I can't support you. And not from an ethical point of view, but from a very practical one."

Stern looked up. "What is it?"

"We need him for tracing the second, deeper problem. If he's sane, there's an approach we haven't tried, an approach he may listen to. As you said, we've acted on the assumption that he was unbalanced; it was the only reasonable assumption we could make. But if he isn't, he may listen to the truth."

"What truth?"

"That we don't *know.* Let's grant him that he *did* see the Karras woman, that she is alive. Then tell him we want the answers as badly as he does. Perhaps more so."

"Assuming we can get that word to him, suppose he doesn't listen, suppose he demands only the answers we can't give, and considers everything else a trick to take him. Or take him out. What then? We've got the Costa Brava files; they contain the names of everyone involved. What help can he really be? On the other hand, we know the damage he can do, the panic he can create, the lives he can cost."

"The victim becomes the villain," said Miller wearily. "Jesus Christ."

"We take our problems in order of appearance and priority," said Stern, "and in my judgement these are two separate crises. Related but separate now. We go after the first. What else can we do?"

"We can admit we don't know!" answered Dawson urgently.

"Every effort will be made to comply with the original order, to take him alive. But they have to be given the option."

"By giving it you're telling them he's a traitor. They'll use it on the slightest provocation. They'll kill him. I repeat, I can't support you."

The director slowly looked up at the lawyer; there were deep creases around his tired eyes, which were filled with doubt. "If we're this far apart, then it's time," he said quietly, reluctantly.

"For what?" asked Miller.

"To give this to Matthias's office. They can reach the old man, or not, knowing that time's running out. I'll go up myself and summarize." Stern flipped the switch on the telephone. "Rome? Sorry to keep you hanging, and I'm afraid it's going to get worse. Keep the ship under air surveillance, and send your people to Col des Moulinets, their radio frequency on scrambler for instructions. If they don't get their orders by the time they land, they're to reach you every fifteen minutes. You stay by this line and close it down – for your use only. We'll get back to you as soon as we can, either myself or someone upstairs. If it's not me, the code will be . . . 'Ambiguity'. Have you got that? 'Ambiguity'. That's all for now, Rome." The director replaced the phone, snapped the switch, and got up from his chair. "I hate like hell doing this . . . at a time like this," he said. "We're supposed to be the shield with a thousand eyes, all-seeing, all knowing. Others can plan, others execute, but we're the ones who give the word. The lousy decisions are supposed to be made here, that's our *function*, goddamn it."

"We've needed help before," said the psychiatrist.

"Only on tactical questions that Ogilvie couldn't answer, never on matters of evaluation. Never for anything like this."

"Dan, we're not playing corporate chairs in the boardroom," added Dawson. "We inherited Costa Brava, we didn't initiate it."

"I know that," said Stern, going to the door. "I suppose it's a consolation."

"Do you want us to go with you?" asked Miller.

"No, I'll present it fairly."

"Never doubted it," interjected the lawyer.

"We're running against a clock in Rome," continued the director. "The fewer of us, the fewer questions. It's reduced to one anyway. Sane or insane. 'Beyond salvage' or not." Stern opened the door and left as the two strategists watched, an uneasy sense of relief apparent on both their faces.

"Do you realize," said Miller, turning in his chair. "That for the first time in three years the phrase 'I can't support you' was used? Not 'I don't think so' or 'I disagree', but 'I can't support you'."

"I couldn't," said Dawson. "Daniel's a statistician. He sees numbers – fractions, equations, totals – and they spell out the odds for him. God knows he's brilliant at it; he's saved the lives of hundreds with those statistics. But I'm a lawyer; I see complications, ramifications. Parties of the first part turning on parties of the second part. Prosecutors stymied because a point of law prohibits them from connecting one piece of evidence to another when it should be permitted. Criminals outraged over minor discrepancies of testimony when the only things outrageous were their crimes. I've seen it all, Paul, and there are times when the odds aren't found in numbers. They're found in things you can't perceive at the moment."

"Strange isn't it? The differences between us, I mean. Daniel sees numbers, you see complications, and I see – full-blown possibilities based on particles."

"A book of matches?"

"I guess so." The psychiatrist levelled his eyes at the lawyer. "I believe in those matches. I believe in what they stand for."

"So do I. At least in the possibility they represent. That's the complication, 'Headman' – as Ogilvie would have said. If there's a possibility that Havelock's sane, then everything he says is true. The girl – false guilt generated in our deepest laboratories – alive, running. Rostov in Athens – bait not taken to the Lubyanka for reasons unknown, a Soviet mole at Sixteen Hundred . . . Complications, Doctor. We need Michael Havelock to help us unravel a melted ball of wax. *If* it's happened – whatever it is – it's frightening." Dawson abruptly pushed his chair back and stood up. "I've got to get back to my office. I'll leave a message for Stem; he may want to come over and talk. How about you?"

"What? Oh, no, thanks," answered Miller, preoccupied. "I've got a five-thirty session at Bethesda, a marine from Teheran." He looked up. "It *is* frightening, isn't it?"

"Yes, Paul. Very."

"We did the right thing. No one in Matthias's section will put Mikhail Havlicek 'beyond salvage'."

"I know. I counted on it."

The Director of Consular Operations came out of the office on the fifth floor, L section, of State, closing the door quietly behind him – closing, too, a part of the problem from his mind. It was shared now, the responsibility spread. The man he had shared it with – the man who would reach Rome under the code name "Ambiguity" and render the judgement – was chosen carefully. He was one of Anthony Matthias's inner circle, someone the Secretary of State trusted implicitly. He would consider all the options before making the decision . . . undoubtedly not alone.

The issue was as clear as it could be. If Havelock was sane and telling the truth, he was capable of doing extraordinary damage because he had been betrayed. And if that was the case, there was treason here in Washington in inconceivable places. Related but separate crises. Should he then be placed immediately "beyond salvage", so that his death would prevent the great harm he could inflict on intelligence operations throughout all Europe? Or should the order for his execution be delayed, in the hope that something might happen which would reconcile a man who was an innocent victim to those who would *not* betray him?

The only way was to find the woman in Col des Moulinets, and if it *was* Jenna Karras to bring her to Havelock, let them join forces and together run down the second, potentially greater crisis here in Washington. But if it was *not* Jenna Karras, if it was a Soviet ploy, if she did not exist except as a deadly puppet-hoax to drive a man mad and into treason, what then? Or if she was alive and they could not find her, would Havelock listen? Would Mikhail Havlicek, victim, survivor of Lidice and Soviet Prague, listen? Or would he see betrayal where there was none, and in turn betray his own? Could the delay then be justified? God knew it could not be justified to dismantled networks or to undercover agents who found themselves in the Lubyanka. And if that was the answer there was the possibility – the probability – that a man had to die because he was right.

The only morality here is pragmatic reality, no philosophy but our own brand of utilitarianism: the greatest advantage for the many – over the few, over the individual.

That was the real answer, the statistics proved it. But this was the inner territory of Anthony Matthias's domain. Would they see it here? In all likelihood they would not, Stern realized. Fear would compel the man he had talked with to reach Matthias, and the revered Secretary of State would delay.

And a part of Daniel Stern – not the professional, but the person inside – did not object. A man should not die because he was right, because he was sane. Yet Stern had done his professional best to make the options clear, to justify that death if it came down to it. And he had been fortunate in one respect, he thought, as he approached the door to the outer reception room. He could not have brought the problem to a fairer, more level-headed man. Arthur Pierce's title – like that of so many other young middle-aged men in the Department – was Undersecretary of State, but he was head and shoulders above the many others. There had been about

485

twenty senior personnel still in L Section when Stern reached the fifth floor, but Pierce's name had stood out. To begin with, Pierce was not in Washington every day; he was assigned to the United Nations in New York as chief liaison officer between the ambassador and the State Department, a position decreed by Anthony Matthias who knew what he was doing. Given a respectable amount of time, Arthur Pierce would be made the UN ambassador, and a good man, a decent man, would be rewarded not only for his high intelligence, but for his decency.

And God knew decency was needed now . . . Or was it? wondered Stern, startling himself, his hand reaching for the knob of the reception room door. *The only morality here is pragmatic morality* . . . There was decency in that for hundreds of potential victims in the field.

No matter, it was out of his hands, Stern thought, as he opened the door. The decision to be made and transmitted under the code name Ambiguity was on Pierce's conscience now. Quiet, bright, understanding Arthur Pierce – apart from Mikhail Havlicek the closest to Matthias – would ponder all sides of the question, then bring in others. The decision would be made by committee, if it was to be made. *They* were Ambiguity now.

"Mr Stern?" the receptionist called out as he passed her, making for the lift.

"Yes?"

"Message for you, sir."

It said: "Daniel. I'll be at my office for a while. If you're of a mind, come over for a drink. I'll drive you home, chicken."

Dawson had not signed his name, nor was it necessary. The often aloof, circumspect lawyer always seemed to know when quiet talk was called for; it was his warmer side. The two cold, analytical men every now and then needed the solace of each other's rarely seen lighter traits. The humorous offer to drive him home was a reference to Stern's distaste for Washington traffic. He took taxis everywhere, to the annoyance of his personal surveillance. Well, whatever team was on now, it could take a break and pick him up later at home in Virginia; Dawson's guards could serve them both until then.

Ogilvie had been right, the whole business was foolish, a hangover from the Angleton days in Langley. Stern looked at his watch; it was twenty minutes past seven, but he knew the lawyer would still be at his office, still waiting for the quiet talk.

They talked for over an hour before going down to Dawson's car, analysing and reanalysing the events at Costa Brava, realizing there was no explanation, no answer within their grasp. Each had called his wife; both women were inured to the interminable hours demanded by the State Department, and claimed to understand. Each lied and both husbands understood; the clandestine regions of government placed too much strain on the marriage vows. It would all come to an end one day. There was a far healthier world beyond the Potomac than either man had known for too many years.

"Pierce will go to Matthias, and Matthias won't consider it, you know that, don't you?" said Dawson, turning off the crowded highway into the back country road in

Virginia, passing luminous signs that read *Construction Ahead.* "He'll demand a review."

"My conference with Pierce was one-to-one," said Stern, absently glancing at the rear-view mirror outside the window, knowing that a pair of headlights would be there in moments. The watchdogs stayed on their leashes. "I was balanced but firm; either decision has merit, both have drawbacks. When he talks to his committee they may decide to do without Matthias because of the time factor. I emphasized it. In less than three hours our people will be in Col des Moulinets; so will Havelock. They have to know how to proceed."

"Whatever comes down, they'll first try to take him alive."

"That's the priority; no one here wants it otherwise." Stern looked through the flashing shadows at his companion. "But I don't kid myself, you were right before. If it comes down 'beyond salvage', he's dead. It's a licence to kill someone who'll kill you if he can."

"Not necessarily. I may have overreacted. If the order's clear – dispatch the last resort – I could be wrong."

"You're wrong now, I'm afraid. Do you think Havelock will give them a choice? He survived the Palatine; he'll use every trick in his very thick book. No one'll get close enough to take him. But getting him in a rifle sight is another matter. That can be done and no doubt will be."

"I'm not sure I agree."

"That's better than not supporting me."

"It's easier," said Dawson, smiling briefly. "But Havelock doesn't know we found the man in Civitavecchia; he doesn't know we're on him in Col des Moulinets."

"He'll assume it. He told Baylor about the Karras woman getting out, how he's convinced she got out. He'll expect us to follow up. We'll concentrate on her, of course. If it is Jenna Karras, she's the answer to everything; we'd be home free without a shot. Then *with* Havelock we can go after the mess here. That's the optimum, and I hope to Christ it happens. But it may not."

"And then we're left with a man in the cross-hairs of a rifle scope," said Dawson with an edge to his voice, as he accelerated down the flat stretch of back country road. "If it is the Karras woman, we've *got* to find her. We *have* to."

"No matter who it is, we'll do our damnedest," said Stern, his eyes again straying to the mirror outside the window. There were no headlights. "That's odd. The watchdogs have strayed, or your foot's outracing them."

"There was a lot of traffic on the highway. If they got in a slow lane, they could crack their butts breaking out. It's Friday in Virginia, Martini time for the hunt country diplomats. On nights like this, I begin to understand why you don't drive."

"What team's on tonight, by the way?"

The question was never answered. Instead, an ear-shattering scream exploded from the attorney's throat as the deafening impact came, smashing the windshield into a thousand blades of flying glass, piercing flesh and eyes, severing veins and arteries. Metal shrieked against metal, twisting, breaking, curling, crushing against itself as the left side of the car rose off the ground throwing the bodies into the well of deep red rivulets below.

The steel behemoth of yellow and black, its colours glistening in the reflection of its single front floodlight, vibrated thunderously, the giant treads of its spiked cables rolled through the huge wheel casings, relentlessly pressing the monster forward. This enormous machine that moved earth from mountains and forests now crawled ahead, crushing the demolished vehicle as it sent it over and beyond the road. The lawyer's car plunged down the steep incline of a shallow ravine; the fuel tank exploded and fire spread everywhere, consuming the bodies within the car.

Then the brightly coloured machine, its curved implement of destruction hydraulically raised in triumph, jerked back and forth, its massive gears remeshing, the pitch of the sound higher – an animal proclaiming its kill. And with sporadic but deliberate movements it retreated across the road into its lair at the edge of the woods.

High in the darkness of the cab the unseen driver turned off the engine and raised a hand-held radio to his lips.

"Ambiguity terminated," he said.

"Get out of there," was the reply.

The long grey saloon roared off the highway into the small country road. The licence plates indicated that the vehicle was registered in the State of North Carolina, but a persistent investigator could learn that the individual in Raleigh listed as the owner was in reality one of twenty-four men stationed in Washington, DC. They were a unit, each having had extensive experience in military police and counter intelligence; they were assigned to the Department of State. The car now racing down the dark country road in Virginia, was one of a fleet of twelve; they, too, were assigned to State, Division of Consular Operations.

"File a report with the insurance company in Raleigh," said the man sitting next to the driver, speaking into a microphone attached to a large radio console beneath the dashboard. "Some clown side-swiped us and we ploughed into a guy from Jersey. There was no damage to us, of course, but he doesn't have much of a trunk left. We wanted to get out of there, so we told him – "

"*Graham!*"

"What?"

"Up ahead! The fire!"

"Jesus *Christ*! *Move!*"

The grey car leapt forward, the sound of its powerful engine echoing through the dark Virginia countryside. Nine seconds later it reached the steep incline that fronted the shallow ravine, and tyres screeched as the brakes were applied. Both men leaped out and raced to the edge, the heat of the flames directly below causing both to step back, with their hands shielding their eyes from the fire.

"Oh my *God*!" cried the driver. "It's Dawson's car! Maybe' we can – "

"*No!*" shouted the man named Graham, stopping his associate from crawling down the flank of the ravine. His eyes were drawn to the yellow-and-black bulldozer standing motionless in its recess on the side of the road. Then . . . "Miller!" he screamed. "Where's *Miller*?"

"The chart said Bethesda, I think."

"Find him!" ordered Graham, running across the road, crouching, reaching behind for the weapon in his hip holster. "Get Bethesda! *Raise* him!"

The head nurse at the reception counter on the sixth floor of the Bethesda Naval Hospital was adamant. Nor did she appreciate the aggressive tone of voice used by the man on the telephone; it was a poor connection to begin with and his shouting only made it worse.

"I repeat, Dr Miller is in psychiatric session and can't be disturbed."

"You get him on the line and you get him on *now*! This is a Four-Zero emergency, Department of State, Consular Operations. This is a direct order routed and coded through the State Department's switchboard. Confirm, please."

"Confirmed," said a third voice flatly. "This is operator one-seven, State, for your recheck."

"Very well, operator one-seven, and you may be sure we *will* check." The nurse jammed her forefinger on the hold button, cutting off further conversation as she got out of her chair and walked around the counter. It was hysterical men like the so-called special agent from Consular Operations that kept the psychiatric wards in full operation, she thought as she proceeded down the white corridor towards the row of therapy rooms. They screamed emergency for the flimsiest reason, more often than not trying to impress everyone with their so-called authority. It would serve special agent Consular-whatever right if the doctor refused to come to the phone. But he would not refuse; the head nurse knew that. Dr Miller's brilliance in no way thwarted his genuine kindness; if he had a fault, it was his excessive generosity. He had checked into T. R. Twenty; she approached it, noting that the red light at the side of the door was on, signifying occupancy. She pressed the intercom button.

"Dr Miller, I hate to interrupt but there's a man from the State Department on the telephone. He says it's an emergency."

There was no reply; perhaps the intercom was not working. The head nurse pressed the button again, applying more pressure, speaking louder. "Dr Miller? I realize this is highly irregular, but there's a man on the phone from State. He's most insistent and the operator *did* confirm the status of the call."

Nothing. Silence. No sound of the knob being turned, no acknowledgement whatsoever. The doctor obviously could not hear her; the intercom was not working. She rapped on the door.

"Dr Miller? Dr *Miller?*"

Really, the man was not deaf. What was he *doing?* His patient was a marine, one of the hostages from Teheran. Not violent; over passive, actually. Had there been a regression? The nurse turned the knob and opened the door of Therapy Room Twenty.

She screamed – again and again.

Crouched in the corner, trembling, was the young marine in his government issue bathrobe. He was staring through the light of the desk lamp, his gaze riveted on the figure sprawled back on the chair. Miller's eyes were open wide, glass-like – dead. In the centre of his forehead was a single bullet hole from which blood poured out, rolling down his face and onto the collar of his white shirt.

The man in Rome looked at his watch. It was a quarter past four in the morning, his men in position in Col des Moulinets, and still no word from Washington. The only other person in the code room was the radio operator. Bored with the inactivity, he was absently scanning his dials, picking up insignificant traffic signals, from ships mainly. Every now and then he would lean back and flip through the pages of an Italian magazine, mouthing the phrases that had become his third language – the radio was his second.

The light on the telephone preceded the hum. The man picked it up. "Rome," he said.

"This is Ambiguity, Rome." The voice was clear, deliberate. "That name gives me complete authority regarding all orders issued to your unit at Col des Moulinets. I assume Director Stem made that clear to you."

"Very clear, sir."

"Are we on total scrambler?"

"Total."

"We're not to be taped or logged. Is that understood?"

"Understood. No tape, no log. What's the word?"

"'Beyond salvage'. Complete."

"That's it, then."

"Not yet. There's more."

"What?"

"Clarification. There's been no contact with the freighter, has there?"

"Of course not. Small plane surveillance until it's too dark, then we shift to parallel coast sightings."

"Good. She'll be put ashore somewhere before San Remo, I'd guess."

"We're ready."

"Is the Corsican in charge up there?" asked the voice from Washington.

"The one who came on board three days ago?"

"Yes."

"He is. He put the unit together and I can tell you we owe him. Our drones over here have dwindled."

"Good."

"Speaking of clarification, I assume the colonel's order still holds. We bring the woman in."

"Inoperative. Whoever she is, she's *not* the Karras woman; she was killed at Costa Brava, we know that."

"Then what do we do?"

"Let Moscow have her back. This one's Soviet poison, a lure to drive the target out of his head. It worked; he's already talked. He's – "

"'Beyond salvage'," completed Rome.

"Just get her out of there. We don't want any trail that could lead back to us, no reopened speculations on Costa Brava. The Corsican will know what to do."

"I've got to say it, I'm not sure I understand."

490

"You don't have to. We just want proof of dispatch. His dispatch."

"You'll have it. Our man with the eyes is up there."

"Have a good day, Rome. A good day with no mistakes."

"No mistakes, no tape, no log."

"Out," said the voice known only as Ambiguity.

The man behind the desk was outlined in silhouette. He was in front of a window overlooking the grounds below the Department of State, the soft glow of faraway streetlamps the only light intruding on the dark office. The man had been facing the window, the telephone held close to his lips. He swivelled in his chair, his features in shadow and as he replaced the phone and leaned forward, resting his forehead on the extended fingers of both hands, the curious streak of white that shot through his dark hair gleamed even in the dim light.

Undersecretary of State Arthur Pierce, born Nicolai Petrovich Malyekov in the village of Ramenskoye, southeast of Moscow, and raised in the State of Iowa, breathed deeply, steadily, imposing calm over himself as he had learned to do throughout the years whenever a crisis called for swift, dangerous decisions; he knew full well the consequences of failure. That, of course, was the strength of men such as he: they were not afraid to fail. They understood that the great accomplishments in history demanded the greatest risks; that, indeed, history itself was shaped by the boldness not only of individual initiative but of collective action. Those who panicked at the thought of failure, who did not act with clarity and determination when the moments of crisis were upon them, deserved the limitations to which their fears committed them.

There had been another decision to make, a decision every bit as dangerous as the one he had transmitted to Rome; but there was no avoiding it. The strategists of Consular Operations had reopened the events of that night on the Costa Brava; they had been peeling away the layers of deceit, about which they knew *nothing*! It all had to be buried – *they* had to be buried. At all costs, at all risk. Costa Brava had to be submerged again, become an obscure deception in a convoluted world of lies. In a few hours word would be sent from Col des Moulinets: "*the order for beyond-salvage has been carried out. Authorization: Code Ambiguity – established and cleared by D. S. Stern, Director of Consular Operations.*"

But only the strategists knew whom Stern had come to with his ambiguous dilemma. In fact, Stern himself had not known whom he would approach until he had emerged on the fifth floor and studied the roster of senior personnel on the premises; he had made that clear. No matter, thought Arthur Pierce in the dark office as he glanced at the inscribed photograph of Anthony Matthias on the wall. All things considered, it would have been unthinkable for him not to have been consulted regarding the crisis. It was simply more convenient for him to have been in his office when Stern and the other strategists had made the decision to bring the insoluble problem upstairs. Had he not been on the floor, he would have been reached, his counsel sought. The result would have been the same: "beyond salvage". Only the method would have been different: an unacknowledged consensus by a faceless committee. Everything worked out for the best; the past two hours had been orchestrated properly. Failure had been considered, but not contemplated. Failure had been out of the question. The strategists were dead, all links to code-name Ambiguity severed.

They needed time. Days, a week, a month. They had to find the man who had accomplished the incredible – with *their help.* They would find him, for he was leaving a trail of fear – no, not fear, *terror* – and trails could be tracked. And when they found him, it would not be the meek who inherited the earth. It would be the *Voennaya.*

There were so few of them left on this side of the world. So few, but so strong, so right. They had seen it all, lived it all. The lies, the corruption, the essential rot at the cores of power; they had been part of it for a greater cause. They had not forgotten who they were, or what they were. Or *why* they were. They were the travellers, and there was no higher calling; its concept was based in reality, not in romantic illusions. They were the men and women of the new world, and the old one needed them desperately. They were not many in numbers – less than a hundred, committed beyond life – but they were finely tuned units, prepared to react instantly to any given opportunity or emergency. They had the positions, the right papers, the proper vehicles. The *Voennaya* was generous; they, in turn were loyal to the élite corps of the KGB.

The death of the strategists had been crucial. The resulting vacuum would paralyse the original architects of Costa Brava, stunning them into silence. They would say nothing: cover-up would be paramount. For the man in shadows behind the desk had not lied to Rome: there could be no reopened speculations on Costa Brava. For either side.

Darkness obscuring his movements, Arthur Pierce, the most powerful *paminyat-chik* in the Department of State, rose from the desk and walked silently to the armchair against the wall. He sat down and stretched his legs; he would remain there until morning, until the crowds of senior and subordinate personnel began to fill up the fifth floor. Then he would mingle with the others, signing a forgotten roster sheet; his morning presence would be temporary, for he was needed back in New York. He was, after all, Washington's senior aide to the ambassador of the American delegation at the United Nations. In essence, he was the State Department's major voice on the East River; soon he would be the ambassador. That had been Anthony Matthias's design; everyone knew it. It would be yet another significant step in his extraordinary career.

Suddenly Malyekov-Pierce bolted up in the chair. There was a last phone call to be placed to Rome, a last voice to be stilled: a man in a radio room who answered a sterile telephone and took an untaped, unlogged message.

492

11

"She's not on board, I *swear* it!" protested the harassed captain of the freighter *Santa Teresa*, seated at his desk in the small cabin aft of the wheelhouse. "Search, if you wish, *signore*. No one will interfere. We put her ashore three . . . three and a half hours ago. *Madre di Dio!* Such madness!"

"How? *Where?*" demanded Havelock.

"Same as you. A motor launch came out to meet us twelve kilometres south of Arma di Taggia. I swear to you, I knew *nothing*! I'll *kill* that pig in Civitavecchia! Just a political refugee from the Balkans, he said – a woman with a little money and friends in France. There are so many these days. Where is the sin in helping one more?"

Michael leaned over and picked up the outdated diplomatic identification card that gave his status as consular attaché, US Department of State, and said calmly, "No sin at all, if that's what you believed."

"It's true, *signore*! For nearly thirty years I've pushed my old cows through these waters. Soon I leave the sea with a little land, a little money. I grow grapes. Never *narcotici*! Never *contrabbandi*! But people – yes. Now and then *people*, and I am not ashamed. Those who flee places and men you and I know nothing about. I ask you again, where is the sin?"

"In making mistakes."

"I cannot believe this woman is a criminal."

"I didn't say that. I said we had to find her."

The captain nodded his head in resignation. "Badly enough to report me. I leave the sea for prison. *Graze, Signore Americano Grande.*"

"I didn't say that, either," said Michael quietly.

The captain's eyes widened as he looked up, his head motionless. "*Che cosa?*"

"I didn't expect you to be what you seem to be."

"*Quale?*"

"Never mind. There are times when embarrassment should be avoided. If you co-operate, nothing may have to be said. *If* you co-operate."

"In any way you wish! It's a gift I did not expect."

"Tell me everything she said to you. And do it quickly."

"There was much that was meaningless – "

"That's not what I want to hear."

"I understand. She was calm, obviously highly intelligent, but, beneath, a very frightened woman. She stayed in this cabin."

"Oh?"

"Not with me, I can assure you. I have daughters her age, *signore*. We had three meals together; there was no other place for her, and my crew is not what I would have my daughters eat with. Also, she carried a great deal of lire on her person. She had to; the transport she purchased did not come cheap . . . She looked forward to much trouble. Tonight."

493

"What do you mean?"

"She asked me if I had ever been to the village of Col des Moulinets in the Ligurian mountains."

"She told you about Col des Moulinets?"

"I think she assumed I knew, that I was merely one part of her journey, aware of the other parts. As it happened, I *have* been to Moulinets several times. The ships they give me are often in need of repair, here in San Remo, or Savona, or Marseilles, which, incidentally, is my farthest port of call. I am not what is known as a *capitano superiore* — "

"*Please*. Go on."

"We have been dry-docked here in San Remo a few times and I have gone up to the mountains, to Col des Moulinets. It's across the French border west of Monesi, a lovely town filled with mountain streams and . . . how do you say it? *Ruote a pale?*"

"Paddlewheels. *Moulinets* can also mean paddlewheels in French."

"*Sì*. It's a minor pass in the lower Alps, not used very much. It's difficult to reach, the facilities poor, the transport poorer. And the border guards are the most lax in the Ligurian or Maritime Alps; they barely take the Gauloises out of their mouths to glance at papers. I tried to assure my frightened refugee that she would have no trouble."

"You think they'll try to go through a checkpoint?"

"There's only one, a short bridge across a mountain river. Why not? I doubt if it would be necessary even to bribe a guard; one woman among a group of well-dressed people at night — what concern is it of theirs?"

"Men like me."

The captain paused; he leaned back in his chair appraising the American official, as if in a somewhat different light. "Then you would have to answer that yourself, *signore*. Who else knows?" Both men looked at each other, neither speaking. The captain nodded and continued. "But I tell you this; if they don't use the bridge, they will have to make their way through very dense forest with much steep rock, and don't forget the river."

"Thanks. That's the kind of information I need. Did she say why she was getting out this way?"

"The usual. The airports were watched; the train stations also, as well as the major roads that cross into France."

"Watched by whom?"

"Men like you, *signore*?"

"Is that what she said?"

"She did not have to say anything more than she did, and I did not inquire. That is the truth."

"I believe you."

"Will you answer the question then? Do others know?"

"I'm not sure," said Michael. "The truth."

"Because if they do, I am arrested. I leave the sea for prison."

"Would that mean it's public information?"

"Most certainly. Charges would be brought before a *commissione*."

494

"Then I don't think they'll touch you. I have an idea that this incident is the last thing on earth the men I'm involved with want known. If they haven't reached you by now – by radio, or a fast boat, or by helicopter – they either don't know about you, or they don't want to touch you."

Again the captain paused, looking carefully at Havelock. "Men you are involved with, *signore?*" he said, the words suspended. "*Avvolgere, non includere?*"

"I don't understand."

"Involved but not *of*, is that correct?"

"It's not important."

"You wish to help this woman, do you not? You are not after her to . . . penalize her."

"The answer to the first is yes. The second, no."

"Then I will tell you. She asked me if I knew the airfield near Col des Moulinets. I did not. I never heard of it."

"An airfield?" Michael understood. It was added information he would not have been given ten seconds ago. "A bridge over a mountain river, and an airfield. Tonight."

"That is all I can tell you."

The mountain road leading out of Monesi towards the French border was wide enough, but the profusion of rock and boulder and bordering overgrowth made it appear narrow, more suited to heavy-wheeled trucks and rugged jeeps than to any normal car. It was the excuse that Michael used to travel the last half mile on foot, to the relief of the taxi driver from Monesi.

He had learned there was a country inn just before the bridge, a watering spot for the Italian and French patrols, where both languages were sufficiently understood by the small garrisons on either side, as well as by the few nationals and fewer tourists who occasionally passed back and forth. From what little Havelock had seen and had been told, the captain of the *Santa Teresa* was right. The border checkpoint of Col des Moulinets was at a minor pass in the lower Alps, not easily accessible and poorly staffed, manned no doubt because it was there – had been for decades – and no bureaucratic legislation had bothered to remove it. The general flow of traffic between the two countries used either the wide coast roads of the Mediterranean fifteen miles south or the larger, more accommodating passes in the north, such as Col de Larche or Col du Mont Cenis, west of Turin.

The late afternoon sun was now a fan-shaped arc of deep orange and yellows, spraying up from behind the higher mountains, filling the sky above the Maritimes with receding echoes of light. The shadows on the primitive road were growing longer, sharper; in minutes their outlines would fade and they would become obscure grey shapes, indistinguishable within the dull darkness of early evening. Michael walked along the edge of the woods, prepared to spring into the undergrowth at the first sounds not part of the forest. He knew that every move he made must be prejudged on the assumption that Rome had learned about Col des Moulinets. He had not lied to the captain of the *Santa Teresa*; there could be any number of reasons why those working for the embassy would stay away from a ship in international waters. The slow freighter could be tracked and watched – very likely had been – but it was another matter to board her in a legitimate official capacity. It was a high-risk tactic, inquiries too easily raised with a *commissione*.

Had Rome found the man in Civitavecchia? He could only presume that others could do what he had done; no one was that unique or that lucky. He had in his anger – no, his outrage – shouted the name of the port city into the phone and Baylor Brown had repeated it. If the wounded intelligence officer was capable of functioning after the Palatine, he would order his people to prowl the Civitavecchia waterfront and find a broker of illegal passage.

Yet there were always gaps, spaces that could not be filled. Would the man in Civitavecchia name the specific ship, knowing that if he did so, he'd never again be trusted on the waterfront? Trusted, hell; he could be killed in any one of a dozen mist-filled back streets. Or might he plead ignorance to that phase of the escape – sold by others unknown to him – but reveal Col des Moulinets so as to curry favour with powerful Americans in Rome, who everyone knew could be inordinately generous. "One more refugee from the Balkans; where was the sin, *signori*?"

So many gaps, so little was concrete . . . so little time to think, so many inconsistencies. Who would have thought there'd be a tired, ageing captain opposed to trafficking in the profitable world of narcotics and contraband but perfectly willing to smuggle refugees out of Italy – no less a risk, no less a cause for imprisonment?

Or blunt Red Ogilvie, a violent man who never stopped trying to justify violence. There was ambivalence in that strange justification. What had driven John Philip Ogilvie? Why does a man strain all his life to break out of self-imposed chains? Who really was the Apache? The gunslinger. Whoever and whatever, he had died violently at the very moment he had understood a violent truth. The liars were in control in Washington.

Above all, Jenna. His love who had not betrayed that love but, instead, had been betrayed. How could she have believed the liars? What could they have said to her, what irrefutable proof could they have presented that she would accept? Most important of all, *who* were the liars? What were their names and where had they come from?

He was so close now that he could sense it, feel it with every step he took on the darkening mountain road. Before the disappearing sun came up on the other side of the world, he would have the answers, have his love back. If they *had* come from Rome, they were no match for him; he knew that. His belief in himself swelled within him; it was unjustified all too often, but it was necessary. One did not come out of the early days, the terrible days, and survive without it. Each step and he was nearer.

And when he had the answers, and his love, the call would be made to a cabin in another range of mountains thousands of miles away. To the Blue Ridge and the Shenandoah, USA. His mentor, his *pritel*, Anton Matthias would be presented with a conspiracy that reached into the bowels of clandestine operations, its existence incontrovertible, its purpose unknown.

Suddenly he saw a small circle of light up ahead, shining through the foliage on the left-hand side of the road. He crouched and studied it, trying to define it. It did not move; it was merely there, where no light had been before. He crept forward, mesmerized, frightened; what *was* it?

Then he stood up, relieved, breathing again. There was a bend in the road, and in its cradle were the outlines of a building; it was the country inn. Someone had just turned on an outside post lamp; other lights would follow shortly. The darkness had come abruptly, as if the sun had dropped into a chasm; the tall pines and the massive boulders blocked the shafts of orange and yellow that could still be seen in the sky. Light now appeared in windows, three on the nearest side, more in front – how many he could not tell, but at least six, judging from the spill that washed over the grass and gravelled entrance of the building.

Michael stepped into the woods to check the undergrowth and foliage. Both were manageable, so he made his way towards the three lighted windows. There was no point in staying on the road any longer; if there were surprises in store, he did not care to be on the receiving end.

He reached the border of the woods, where the thick trunk of a pine tree stood between him and a deeply rutted driveway of hard mud. The drive extended along the side of the inn and curved behind it into some kind of parking area next to what appeared to be a delivery entrance. The distance to the window directly across was about twenty-five feet; he stepped out from behind the tree.

Instantly he was blinded by headlights. The truck thundered out of the primitive road thirty yards to his right, careening into the narrow driveway of ridged mud. Havelock spun back into the foliage, behind the trunk of the pine, and reached for the Spanish automatic strapped to his chest. The truck bounced past, pitching and rolling over the hardened ruts of the drive like a small barge in choppy water. From inside the van could be heard the angry shouts of men objecting to the discomfort of their ride.

Havelock could not tell whether he had been seen or not; again he crouched for protective cover and watched. The truck lurched to a stop at the entrance of the wide, flat parking area; the driver opened his door and jumped to the ground. Prepared to race into the woods, Michael crept back several feet. It was not necessary; the driver stretched while swearing in Italian, his figure suddenly caught in the spill of a floodlight someone had switched on from inside the building. What the light revealed was bewildering: the driver was in the uniform of the Italian army, but the insignia was that of a border guard. He walked to the back of the truck and opened the large double doors.

"Get out, you bastards!" he shouted in Italian. "You've got about an hour to fill your kidneys before you go on duty. I'll walk up to the bridge and tell the others we're here."

"The way you drive, Sergeant," said a soldier, grimacing as he stepped out, "they heard you half-way back to Monesi."

"Up yours!"

Three other men got out in varying stages of contortions, stamping their feet and stretching; all were guards.

The sergeant continued, "Paolo you take the new man. Teach him the rules." As the non-commissioned officer lumbered up the driveway past Havelock, he scratched his groin and pulled down the underwear beneath his trousers – signs of a long, uncomfortable trip.

"You, Ricci!" shouted a soldier at the rear of the truck, looking up into the van. "Your name's Ricci, right?"

"Yes," said the voice from inside and a fifth figure emerged from the shadows.

"You've got the best duty you'll find in the army, *paesano*! The quarters are up at the bridge, but we have an arrangement: we damn near live *here*. We don't go up there until we go on. Once you walk in, you sign in, understand?"

"I understand," said the soldier named Ricci.

But his name was not Ricci, thought Michael, staring at the blond man slapping his barracks hat against his left hand. Havelock's mind raced back over a dozen photographs; his mind's eye selected one. The man was not a soldier in the Italian army – certainly no border guard. He was a Corsican, a very proficient drone with a rifle or a handgun, a string of wire or a knife. His real name was irrelevant; he used too many to count. He was a "specialist", used only in "extreme-prejudice" situations, a reliable executioner who knew his way around the western Mediterranean better than most such men, as much at home in the Balearic Islands as he was in the forests of Sicily. His photograph and a file of his known accomplishments had been provided for Michael several years ago by a CIA agent in a sealed-off room at Palombara. Havelock had tracked a *Brigate Rosse* unit and was moving in for a non-attributable kill; he had rejected the blond man now standing thirty feet away from him in the floodlit driveway. He had not cared to trust him then, but Rome did now.

Rome did now! The embassy had found a man in Civitavecchia, and Rome had sent an executioner – for a non-attributable kill. Something or someone had persuaded the liars in Washington that a former field officer was now a threat only if he lived; so they had put out the word that he was "beyond-salvage", his immediate dispatch the highest priority. Non-attributable, of course.

The liars could not let him reach Jenna Karras, for she was part of their lie, her mock death on the Spanish coast intrinsic to it. Yet Jenna was running too; somehow, some way after Costa Brava she had escaped. Was she now included in the execution order? It was inevitable; the bait could not be permitted to live, and therefore the blond assassin was not the only killer on the bridge at Col des Moulinets. On, or near it.

The four soldiers and the new recruit started towards the rear entrance of the country inn. The door beneath the floodlight was opened, and a heavy-set man spoke in a loud voice. "If you pigs spent all your money in Monesi, stay the hell out of here!"

"Ah, Gianni, then we'd have to close you up for selling French girls higher than ours!"

"*You* pay!" howled the obese man.

"Ricci, this is Gianni the thief. He owns this dung heap. Be careful what you eat."

"I want to use the bathroom," said the new recruit. He had just looked at his watch; it was an odd thing to do.

"Who doesn't?" shouted another soldier, as all five went inside.

498

The instant the door closed Havelock ran across the drive to the first window. It looked in on a dining-room. The tables were covered with red-checked cloths, with cheap silver and glassware in place, but there were no diners; either it was too early for the kitchen or there were no takers that evening. Beyond, separated only by a wide archway that extended the length of the wall, was the larger central bar. From what he could see there were a number of people seated at small round tables – between ten and fifteen would be his estimate – nearly all men. The two women in his sight lines were in their sixties, one fat, one gaunt, sitting at adjacent tables with mustachioed men: they were both talking and drinking beer. Early evening in the Ligurian Alps. He wondered if there were any other women in that room; he wondered – his chest aching – whether Jenna was huddled at a corner table he could not see. If that was the case, he must be able to watch a door from the rear quarters – from the kitchen, perhaps – from which the five soldiers would emerge into the bar. He *had* to be able to see. The next few minutes could tell him what he needed to know: who among the clientele in that bar would the blond killer recognize, if only with a glance, a twitch of his lips or an almost imperceptible nod?

Michael crouched and ran to the second window along the drive; the angle of vision was still too restricting. He raced to the third, appraised the view and rejected it, then rounded the corner of the building to the first window in front. He could see the door now – CUCINA the lettering said; the five soldiers would walk out of that door any second, but he could not see all the tables. There were two windows remaining that faced the stone path leading to the entrance. The second window was too close to the door for reasonable cover, but he held his breath and crawled swiftly to it, then stood up in the shadow of a spreading pine. He inched his face to the glass, and what he saw allowed him to let out the breath he had held. Jenna Karras was not an ambushed target sitting in a corner. The window was beyond the inside archway; he could see not only the kitchen entrance but every table, every person in the room. Jenna was not there. And then his eyes strayed to the far right wall; there was another door, a narrow door with two separate lines of letters. UOMINI and HOMMES, the men's room.

The door labelled CUCINA swung open and the five soldiers straggled in; Gianni the thief had his head on the shoulder of the blond man whose name was not Ricci. Havelock stared at the killer, stared at the eyes with all his concentration. The owner of the inn gestured to his left – Michael's right – and the assassin started across the room towards the men's room. The eyes. Watch the eyes!

It came! Barely a flicker of the lids, but it was there, the glance was there. Recognition. Havelock followed the blond man's line of sight. *Confirmed.* Two men were at a table in the centre of the room; one had lowered his eyes to his drink while talking, the other – bad form – had actually shifted his legs so as to turn his head away from the path of the killer's movement. Two more members of the unit – but only one of them was active. The other was an observer. The man who had shifted his legs was the agent of record who would confirm the dispatch but in no way participate. He was an American; his mistakes bore it out. His jacket was an expensive Swiss windbreaker, wrong for the scene and out of season; his shoes were soft black leather, and he wore a shiny digital chronometer on his wrist – all so impressive, so irresistible to a swollen paycheque overseas, so much in contrast to the shabby mountain garments of his companion. So American. The agent-of-record – but it was a file no more than six men alive would ever see.

Something else was inconsistent; it was in the numbers. A unit of three with only two active weapons was understaffed, considering the priority of the kill and the background of the foreign service officer who was the primary target. Michael began studying every face in the room, isolating each, watching eyes, seeing if any strayed to the oddly matched pair at the centre table. After the faces came the clothes, especially those belonging to the few faces angled away from him. Shoes, trousers and belts where they could be seen; shirts, jackets, hats and whatever jewellery was visible. He kept trying to spot another chronometer or an Alpine windbreaker or soft leather shoes. Inconsistencies. If they were there, he could not find them. With the exception of the two men at the centre table, the drinkers at the inn were a ramshackle collection of mountain people. Farmers, guides, shopkeepers – apparently French from across the bridge – and, of course, the border guards.

"*Ehi! Cosa avete?*" The words were hurled at him, a soldier's challenge. The sergeant from the truck stood, with his hand on his holster, in the semi darkness of the path that led to the entrance of the inn.

"*La mia sposa,*" said Havelock quickly, his voice low, urgent, properly respectful. "*Siamo molto disturbati, signor Maggiore. Ho avuto un affare con una ragazza francese. La mia sposa mi seguira!*"

The soldier grinned and removed his hand from the gun case. He admonished Havelock in barracks Italian: "So the men of Monesi still go across the border for French ass, eh? If your wife's not in there, she's probably back in your own bedroom being pumped by a Frenchman! Did you ever think of that?"

"The way of the world, Major," replied Michael obsequiously, shrugging, and wishing to Christ the loud-mouthed dolt would go inside and leave him alone. He had to get back to the window!

"You're not from Monesi," said the sergeant, suddenly alarmed. "You don't talk like a man from Monesi."

"The *Swiss* border, Major. I come from Lugano. I moved here two years ago."

The soldier was silent for a moment, his eyes squinting. Havelock slowly moved his hand in the shadows towards his waist, where, secured uncomfortably under his belt, was the heavy Magnum with the silencer attached. There could be no sound of gunfire, if it came to that.

Finally, the sergeant threw up his hands, shaking his head in disgust. "Swiss! Italian-Swiss, but more *Swiss* than Italian! All of you! Sneaky bastards. I won't serve in a battalion north of Milan, I swear it. I'll get out of the army first. Go back to your sneaking, *Swiss!*" He turned and stalked into the inn.

Inside, another door – the narrow door to the men's room – was opened. A man walked out, and Michael knew not only that he had found a third weapon in the unit from Rome but that there had to be a fourth. The man was part of a team – two demolition experts who worked together – veteran mercenaries who had spent several years in Africa blowing up everything from dams and airports to grand villas suddenly occupied by inept despots in comic opera regalia. The CIA had found them in Angola, on the wrong side, but the American dollar was healthier then, and persuasive. The two experts had been placed in a single black-bordered file deep in the cabinets of clandestine operations.

And their being at the bridge of Col des Moulinets gave Havelock a vital piece of information: a vehicle or vehicles were anticipated. One of these two demolition specialists could pause for ten seconds by a car and, ten minutes later, it would explode, killing everyone in the immediate vicinity. Jenna Karras was expected to cross the border by car; minutes later she would be dead, a successful, non-attributable kill.

The airfield. Rome had learned about the airfield from the man in Civitavecchia. Somewhere on the road out of Col des Moulinets whatever conveyance she was in would be blown into the night sky.

Michael dropped to the ground behind the pine tree. Through the window he could see the explosives expert walking directly to the front door of the inn; the man glanced at his watch, as the blond killer had done minutes ago. A schedule was in progress, but *what* schedule?

The man emerged; his swarthy face looked even darker in the dim light of the post lamp at the end of the path. He began walking faster, but the acceleration was barely perceptible; this was a professional who knew the value of control. Havelock rose cautiously, prepared to follow; he glanced at the window, then looked again, alarmed. Inside, by the bar, the sergeant was talking to the blond recruit he called Ricci, obviously delivering an unwanted order. The killer seemed to be protesting, raising his beer as if it were much needed medicine and thus an excuse for not obeying. Then he grimaced, drank his drink in several swallows, and started for the door.

The schedule was being adhered to. Through prearrangement, someone at the bridge had been instructed to call for the new recruit in advance of the duty hour; he was to be put on duty *before* the shift was over. Procedural methods would be the cover, and no one would argue; but it was not procedure, it was the schedule.

They knew. The unit from Rome knew that Jenna Karras was on her way to the bridge. A motor launch had been picked up in Arma di Taggia and the party had been followed; the vehicle in which she travelled into the Ligurian mountains had now been spotted within minutes of its arrival at the checkpoint of Col des Moulinets. It was so logical: what better time to cross a border than at the end of a shift, when the soldiers were tired, weary of the dull monotony, waiting for relief, more careless than usual?

The door opened, and Michael crouched again, peering to his right through the branches of the pine tree at the road beyond the post lamp. The mercenary had crossed diagonally to the shoulder on the other side, bearing left towards the bridge – an ordinary stroller, a Frenchman perhaps, returning to Col des Moulinets. But in moments he would fade into the woods, taking up a pre-determined position east of the bridge's entrance, from which he could crawl to a car briefly held up by the guards. The blond killer was now half-way to the post lamp; he paused, lighting a cigarette, which gave another reason for his delay. He heard the sound of the door being opened and was satisfied. The "soldier" continued on his way, as the two men from the centre table – the American agent-of-record and his roughly-dressed companion, the second weapon in the unit from Rome – came out.

Havelock understood now. The trap had been engineered with precision; in a matter of minutes it would be in place. Two expert marksmen would take out the intruder who tried to interfere with the car carrying Jenna Karras – take him out instantly, with a fusillade of bullets the second he came in sight; and two demolition specialists would guarantee that the car waved through would explode somewhere in the streets of Col des Moulinets, or on a road to an unmarked airfield.

Another assumption could be made, beyond the fact that there was a schedule in progress that included a car on its way to the bridge. The unit from Rome knew he was there, knew he would be close enough to the border patrols to observe all those in any vehicle offering passports to the guards. They would examine closely every male figure that came into view, their hands on their weapons as they did so. Their advantage was in their numbers, but he, too, had an advantage and it was considerable: he knew who they were.

The well-dressed American and his employee, the second gun, separated at the road, the agent-of-record turning right in order to remove himself from the execution ground, the killer going left to the bridge. Two small trucks clattered up the road from Monesi, one with only a single headlight, the other with both headlights but no windscreen. Neither the American nor his hired weapon paid any attention; they knew the vehicle they were waiting for, and it was neither of these.

If you know a strategy, you can counter a strategy – his father's words so many years ago. He could recall the tall, erudite man patiently explaining things to a cell of partisans, calming their fears, channelling their angers. Lidice was their cause, the death of Germans their objective. He remembered it all now as he crept back to the driveway and raced across into the woods.

He got his first glimpse of the bridge from three hundred yards, on the edge of the bend in the road that led to the country inn – the curve he had avoided by heading into the woods. From what he could see, it was narrow and not long, which was a blessing for drivers in that two cars crossing at the same time would doubtless have grazed fenders. A duel string of naked bulbs was now lighted; it arched over the central steel span, sagging between the struts; several of the bulbs had been burned out. The checkpoint itself consisted of two opposing structures that served as gatehouses, the windows high and wide, each with a ceiling light fixture; between the two small, square buildings, a hand-winched barrier painted with intense, light-reflecting orange fell across the road. To the right of the winch was a shoulder-high gate that opened onto the pedestrian walk.

Two soldiers in their brown uniforms with the red and green stripes were on either side of the second truck, talking wearily but animatedly with the driver. A third guard was at the rear, his attention not on the truck but on the woods beyond the bridge. He was studying the areas on both sides as a hunter might when stalking a wounded mountain cat: he stood motionless, his eyes roving, his head barely turning. He was the blond assassin. Who would suspect that a lowly soldier at a border checkpoint was a killer whose hunting-ground spanned the Mediterranean?

A fourth man had just been passed through the pedestrian gate. He was trudging slowly up the slight incline towards the midpoint of the bridge. But this man had no intention of crossing to the other side, no intention of greeting the French patrols in Ligurian *patois*, claiming as so many did that the air was different in *la belle France* and thank God for slender women. No, thought Michael, this crudely dressed peasant of the mountains with the drooping trousers and the large, heavy jacket would remain in the centre shadows and, if the light was dark enough, would check his weapon, probably a braced, repeating, rapid fire machine-gun, its stock a steel bar clamped to the shoulders, easily concealed beneath garments. He would release the safety catch and be prepared to race down to the checkpoint at the moment of execution, ready to kill the Italian guards if they interfered, intent on firing into the body of a man coming out of the darkness to reach a woman crossing the border. This man, last seen at a centre table in the country inn, was the back-up support for the blond-haired killer.

It was a gauntlet, at once simple and well-manned, using the natural procedure of roadblocks; once the target entered, he was trapped both within and without. Two men waited with explosives and weapons at the mouth of the trap, one at its core and a fourth at its outer rim. Well conceived, very professional.

12

The tiny glow of a cupped cigarette could be seen in the bushes diagonally across the dark road. Bad form. The agent-of-record was an indulgent man denying himself neither chronometers nor cigarettes during the early stages of a kill. He should be replaced; he would be replaced.

Havelock judged the angle of the cigarette, its distance to the ground; the man was crouched or sitting, not standing. Because of the density of the foliage it was impossible for the man to see the road clearly, which meant that he did not expect the car with Jenna Karras for some time yet; he was being too casual for a momentary sighting. The sergeant had said that the soldiers had an hour to fill their kidneys; twenty minutes had passed, leaving forty. Yet not really forty. The final ten minutes of the shift would be avoided because the changing of the guard would require an exchange of information, no matter how inconsequential or proforma. Michael had very little time to do what had to be done, to mount his own counter strategy. First, he had to learn all he could of Rome's.

He side-stepped his way back along the edge of the foliage until the distant spill of light from the bridge was virtually blocked by the trees. He ran across the road and into the undergrowth, turning left, testing every step to ensure the silence that was essential. For a brief, terrible moment he was back in the forests of Prague, the echoes of the guns of Lidice in his ears, the sight of screaming, writhing bodies before his eyes. Then he snapped back to the immediate present, remembering who and where he was. He was the mountain cat, the most meaningful lair of his life soiled, corrupted by liars who were no better than those who commanded the guns at Lidice . . . or others who ordered "suicides" and gulags when the guns were stilled. He was in his element, in the forest which had befriended him when he had no one to depend on, and no one better understood it.

The agent-of-record was sitting on a rock and, true to his indulgence, was playing with his watch, apparently pushing buttons, controlling time, master of the half-second. Havelock reached into his pocket and took out one of the items he had purchased in Monesi, a four-inch fish-scaling knife encased in a leather scabbard. He parted the branches in front of him, crouched low, then lunged.

"*You!* Jesus *Christ!* . . . *Don't!* What are you doing? Oh, my *God!*"

"You talk above a whisper, you won't have a face!" Michael's knee was rammed into the agent's throat, the razor-sharp, jagged blade pressed against the man's cheek below his left eye. "This knife cleans fish, you son of a bitch. I'll peel your skin off unless you tell me what I want to know. Right *now.*"

"You're a maniac!"

"And you're the loser, if you believe that. How long have you been here?"

"Twenty-six hours."

"Who gave the order?"

"How do I know?"

"Because even an asshole like you would cover yourself! It's the first thing we learn in dispatch, isn't it? The *order!* Who gave it?"

"*Ambiguity!* The code was Ambiguity," cried the agent-of-record, as the scaling edge of the blade dug into his face. "I swear to Christ, that's all I know! Whoever used it was cleared by Cons Op, DC. It can be traced back *there! Jesus*, I only know our orders came from the code! It was our clearance!"

"I'll accept it. Now, give me the step-schedule. *All* of it. You picked her up in Arma di Taggia, and she's been followed ever since. How?"

"Change of vehicles up from the coast."

"Where is she now? What's the car? When's it expected?"

"A Lancia. The ETA, as of a half-hour ago, barring – "

"Cut it out! *When?*"

"Seven-forty arrival. A bug was planted in the car; they'll be here at twenty to eight."

"I know you don't have a radio, a radio would be evidence in your case. How were you contacted?"

"The phone at the inn. *Jesus!* Get that thing away from me!"

"Not yet, sane man. The schedule, the steps? Who's on the car now?"

"Two men in a beat-up truck, a quarter of a mile behind. In case you intercept, they'll hear it and be on you."

"If I don't, then what?"

"We've made arrangements. Starting at seven-thirty everyone crossing the border gets out of his car or truck or whatever. Vehicles are searched – we spread lire – so one way or the other she'll have to show herself."

"That's when you figured I'd come out?"

"If we . . . *they* . . . don't find you first. They think they'll spot you before she gets here."

504

"And if they don't?"

"I don't know! It's *their* plan."

"It's *your* plan!" Havelock broke the skin on the agent's face; blood streaked down his cheek.

"Christ! Don't, *please!*"

"Tell me!"

"It's made to look as if you attacked. They know you've got a weapon, whether you show it or not. They nail you and pull it out if it's not in your hand. It doesn't matter; it's only for confusion. They'll run; the truck's got a good engine."

"And the car? What about the *car?*"

"It's shoved through. We just want it out of there. She's not Karras, she's a Soviet lure. We're to let Moscow have her back. The French won't argue, a guard was paid."

"Liar! Goddamned *liar!*" Michael slid the blade of the fishing knife across the agent's face to the other cheek. "Liars should be marked! You're going to be *marked, liar!*" He broke the skin with the point. "Those two nitro clowns, the ones who worked Africa – Tanzania, Mozambique, Angola – they're not here for the mountain air, *liar!*"

"Oh, *Jesus!* You're killing me!"

"Not yet, but it's entirely possible. What's their act?"

"They're just back-ups! Ricci brought them!"

"The Corsican?"

"I don't know . . . Corsican."

"The blond."

"*Yes!* Don't cut me! *Please*, don't *cut* me!"

"Back-ups? Like your friend at the table?"

"The *table?* Christ, what *are* you?"

"An observer, and you're stupid. For you, they're only guns?"

"Jesus, *yes!* That's what they *are!*"

So the liars in Washington lied even to their own in Rome. Jenna Karras did not exist. The woman in the car was to be dispatched beyond Rome's cognizance. Liars! Killers!

Why?

"Where are they?"

"I'm bleeding! I've got blood in my mouth!"

"You'll drown in it if you don't tell me. *Where?*"

"One on both sides! Twenty, thirty feet before the gate. *Christ*, I'm *dying!*"

"No, you're not dying, agent-of-record. You're just marked; you're finished. You're not worth surgery." Havelock switched the knife to his left hand and raised his right, his fingers straight out, taut, the muscles of the palm's underside rigid. He crashed the hand into the man's throat; he would be immobilized for no less than an hour. It would be long enough; it *had* to be.

He crawled through the undergrowth, sure of his footing, at home in the friendly forest.

He found him. The man was on his knees hunched over a canvas bag – a knapsack or small duffle bag; the light from the bridge was just bright enough to outline the figure but too dim to see clearly if one did not know what to look for. Suddenly there was the growing sound of an engine, accompanied by the clatter of a loose tailpipe or a bumper making contact with the rock-filled road. Michael spun around, holding his breath, his hand reaching towards his belt. A broken-down van came into view. A sickening feeling spread through him. Had the agent lied? he wondered. He looked back at the explosives specialist; the man crouched lower, making no other move at all, and Havelock slowly let out his breath.

The van rattled by and stopped at the bridge. The blond killer was standing by a guard; he had obviously been instructed to observe procedure, but instead his eyes were roaming the woods and the road below. Loud voices filled the gate area: a couple in the van was objecting to the unexpected demand to get out; apparently they made the trip daily across the border.

Michael knew the noise was his cover; he crept forward. He was within seven feet of the man when the rear door of the van was opened and the shouted obscenities rose to a crescendo. The door was slammed shut. Havelock lunged out of the undergrowth, arms extended, with fingers curved for the attack.

"*Di quale . . . ?*"

The specialist had no chance to experience further shock. His head was slammed into soft earth and rock, his neck viced by Michael's right hand; he coughed spastically and went limp. Havelock turned the unconscious body over and, whipping the man's belt out of his trousers, slipped it under the arms and yanked it taut beneath the shoulder-blades. He then looped it over, and knotted it. He removed the Llama from his chest holster, and brought the short barrel down on the man's head above the right temple – the expert would remain unconscious that much longer.

Michael tore into the canvas bag. It was a specialist's mobile laboratory, filled with compact blocks of dynamite and soft rolls of plastic explosive. The devices with wires extending from miniaturized clocks with radium dials were detonators, positive and negative poles plugged into one another across the lethal powder, set to emit charges at a given minute by a twist of the fingers. There was also another type of detonating device: small, flat, circular modules, no larger than the face of a man's watch; these were without wires, having only a bar with a luminous numerical read-out and a tiny button on the right with which to set the desired time. Designed specifically for the plastic charges, buried inside, they were accurate to five seconds over a time span of twenty-four hours. Havelock felt the casing of a single *plastique*. On the top surface was a self-sealing lip through which a module was inserted, while the bottom was marked by a flap which had to be peeled away several minutes before placement. The peeling process released an epoxy stronger than a weld; it would adhere to a second surface through earthquake and hurricane. He removed three charges and modules, and put them in his pockets. Then he crawled away, pulling the canvas bag behind him. Ten feet farther into the forest, he shoved it under a fallen pine branch. He looked at his watch. Twelve minutes to go.

The yelling at the bridge had stopped. The angry couple was back in the van, while the guards apologized for the crazy, temporary regulations. *Funzionari*

506

burocratici! The engine was started, a series of metallic groans preceding the full roar of an accelerator pressed to the floor. The headlights were turned back on and the orange barrier raised as the gears ground abrasively and the decrepit vehicle crept onto the bridge. The clatter was louder now, actually deafening as the van rumbled across the surface of the bridge ridged with narrow, open metal struts.

The noise echoed below and above, filling the air with an unrelenting staccato that made one of the guards wince and put both hands to his ears. The clatter, the headlights; the first was diversion, the second, distraction. If he could get into a decent line of sight, he might – just possibly – eliminate his back-up executioner; he would not make the attempt unless the odds were his.

The burly man in the heavy jacket would hug the rail, leaning over perhaps, to be as inconspicuous as possible in the glare of the headlights, a weary pedestrian with too much wine in him. No single shot could be counted on; no man was that accurate at eighty feet or more. But the Magnum was a powerful weapon, the permanently-attached silencer designed for zero sighting as much as any handgun could be. Therefore a marksman firing five or six rounds at a given target would have the probabilities on his side, but only if the bullets were fired in what amounted to a single burst; each instant of separation was a margin for error. It would require a steady arm supported by a solid object, a view undistorted by light and shadow. It would not hurt to get closer, either.

With his concentration split equally between the undergrowth in front of him and the blond assassin, whom he could see through the trees on his left, he made his way as swiftly, as silently as he could, to the edge of the river gorge.

A torch beam shot out behind him. He scrambled behind a huge boulder, sliding partially down the smooth surface and catching his foot on a protruding ridge. His sanctuary was the top of a jagged wall of rock and bush that led to the roiling waters several hundred feet below. His vision at the far side was clear; he stared at the end of the beam of light. Some part of the foliage he had raced through had snapped and the blond killer was standing motionless, the light in his hand. Gradually his attention waned: an animal or a night bird, he judged, there was no human being to be seen.

Above, the clattering truck neared the midpoint of the bridge. There he was! Less than seventy feet away, he leaned over the rail, his head huddled deep in the collar of his heavy jacket. The clanging was thunderous now, the echoes full as the back-up executioner was caught in the glare of the headlights. Havelock spun around on the boulder, steadying his feet on the flanking rocks. There would be no more than a second to make the decision, no more than two or three to fire the Magnum during the short space of time when the rear of the van would block the view from the booths at the entrance. Full of uncertainty, Michael pulled the heavy weapon from his belt and braced his arm against the boulder, his feet anchored by pressure, his left hand gripping his right wrist to steady the barrel that was aimed diagonally above. He had to be *sure*; he could not risk the night and everything the night stood for. But if the odds were his.

They *were*. As the bonnet of the van passed the man he stood up, now silhouetted in the back light, a large immobile target. Havelock fired four rounds in rapid succession in concert with the deafening clatter on the bridge. The support killer arched backwards, then sank down into the shadows of the solid steel barricade of the pedestrian walk.

The clanging receded as the van reached the far side of the bridge. There was no orange barrier across the entrance on the French side: francs had been paid; the two guards leaned against a gatehouse wall, smoking their cigarettes. However, another sound intruded; it came from behind, quite far behind, down the road from Monesi. Michael curved his spine into the surface of the rock and slid back into the edge of the woods, crouching instantly, shoving the warm Magnum under his belt. He glanced through the trees at the checkpoint; the two authentic soldiers in the nearest gatehouse on the right could be seen beyond the large glass windows, nodding as if counting something in their hands – lire had reached the second level. The blond impostor was outside, an outsider as far as the current transaction was concerned; he was staring down the road, squinting in the dim light.

He raised his hand to the midpoint of his chest and shook his wrist twice – an innocuous gesture, a man restoring circulation to a forearm strained by carrying too much weight too recently. It was a signal.

The killer brought his hand down to his right hip, and it took no imagination to realize he was releasing the snap on his holster while keeping his concentration on the road below. Havelock crept rapidly through the woods until he reached the unconscious figure of the explosives specialist. The sound of a motor grew louder, joined now by a faint, base-toned hum in the farther distance – a second vehicle steadily increasing its speed. Michael parted the thick branches of an overhanging pine and looked to his left. Several hundred yards down the road the glistening grille of a large car could be seen, reflecting the light from the bridge. It swung into the curve; it was a Lancia. Jenna! Havelock imposed a control over his mind and body he never thought possible. The next few minutes would bring into play everything he had learned – that no one should ever have to learn – since he was a child in Prague, every skill he had absorbed from the shadow world in which he had lived so long.

The Lancia drew nearer, and sharp bolts of pain shot through Michael's chest as he stared at the windscreen. Jenna was not there. Instead, two men could be seen in the wash of the dashboard, the driver smoking, his companion apparently talking garrulously, waving his hands for emphasis. Then the driver turned his head sideways, addressing a remark to someone in the back seat. The Lancia began to slow down; it was within two hundred feet of the checkpoint.

The blond impostor at the orange barrier turned and walked quickly to the gatehouse booth; he knocked on the window, then pointed to the approaching vehicle and then to himself. He was the eager recruit telling his veteran superiors that he could handle the immediate assignment. The two soldiers looked up, annoyed at the intrusion, perhaps wondering whether the intruder had seen money changing hands; they nodded, waving him away.

Instead of leaving immediately, the assassin employed by Rome reached into his pocket and took out an object, while moving unobtrusively towards the closed door of the booth. He reached down and inserted the object into the frame below the window, the movements of his shoulders indicating that he used considerable force. Havelock tried to imagine what it was, what the killer was doing. And then it was clear; the door of the booth was a sliding door, but it would not slide now. The man called Ricci had wedged a thin steel plate with small angled spikes into the space between frame and panel; the door was jammed. The more force that was used to open it, the deeper the tiny spikes would embed themselves until all movement would be impossible. The two soldiers were trapped inside, and as with checkpoints everywhere – no matter how minor – the booth was sturdily constructed with thick glass in the windows. Yet there was a fallacy: a simple call to the barracks somewhere on the other side would bring assistance. Michael peered through the dim light above the gatehouse and saw there was no fallacy. Dangling from the limb of a tree was a heavy-gauge telephone wire; it had been severed. The killers from Rome controlled the checkpoint.

The blond man strode to the metal plank that separated the road from the entrance to the bridge, assumed a military stance – the feet apart, the left hand at his waist, the right held up in the HALT position – and faced the oncoming sedan.

The Lancia came to a stop. The front windows were rolled down and passports were proffered by the two men in the front seat.

The killer walked to the driver's window and spoke quietly – too quietly for Havelock to hear the words – while looking past the driver into the rear seat.

The driver was explaining something and turned to his companion for confirmation. The second man leaned across the seat, nodding his head, then shaking it, as if in sorrow. The false guard stood back and spoke louder, with a soldier's authority.

"Regrets, *signori* and *signora*," he said in Italian. "Tonight's regulations require that all passengers step out of their cars while they are examined."

"But we were assured that we could proceed across into Col des Moulinets as rapidly as possible, *Caporale*," protested the driver, raising his voice. "The dear woman buried her husband less than two hours ago. She is distraught . . . Here are her papers, her passport. Ours also. Everything is in order, I can assure you. We are expected for an eight o'clock mass. She is from a fine family, a Franco-Italian marriage tragically ended by a dreadful accident. The mayors of both Monesi and Moulinets were at the funeral – "

"Regrets, *signore*," repeated the killer. "Please, step out. There is a truck behind you and it is not right that you should hold up the line."

Havelock turned his head, looking at the run-down truck with the powerful engine. There was no one inside. Instead, the two men were on opposite shoulders of the road, dressed in mountain clothes, their eyes scanning the country road and the woods, their hands in their pockets. Back-ups for back-ups, support for support. The border belonged to the unit from Rome, secure in its knowledge that no one could pass through without being seen; and if the target was seen, the target would die.

And if he was not seen? Would the secondary order hold? Would the secondary target – the bait – be eliminated in Col des Moulinets because she was no longer feasible bait? The answer was as painful for Michael to admit to himself as it was self-evident. She had to be. She did not exist, her existence was too dangerous for the liars who gave orders to strategists and embassies alike. The unit would return to Rome without its primary kill, the only loser an agent-of-record who had not been apprised of the secondary target.

The tall, slender figure in black climbed out of the car -- a woman in mourning, an opaque veil of black lace falling from her wide-brimmed hat and covering her face. Havelock stared; the pain in his chest was almost unbearable. She was no more than twenty feet away, yet the gulf was filled with death, her death to follow shortly whether his came or not.

"My regrets again, *signora*," said the killer in uniform. "It will be necessary for you to remove your hat."

"Good Lord, *why*?" asked Jenna Karras, her voice low, controlled, but with a trace of a throb, which could be a sign of grief, as well as of fear.

"Merely to match your face with the photograph on the passport, *signora*. Surely you know it's customary."

Jenna slowly lifted the veil from her face, and then the hat from her head. The skin that was so often bronzed by the sun was chalk white in the dim, eerie light of the bridge, her delicate features taut, the high cheekbones mask-like, chiselled in marble as if the owner belonged to the Palatine, her long blonde hair pulled back and knotted severely. Michael watched, breathing slowly, silently, a part of him wanting to cry out, another desperately, foolishly, placing them back in another time . . . lying together on the grass overlooking the Moldau, walking down the Ringstrasse, holding hands as children might, laughing at the irony of two deep cover agents behaving like human beings. In bed, holding each other, telling themselves they would somehow break out of their movable prison.

"The *signora* has lovely hair," said the blond killer, with a smile that denied his rank. "My mother would approve. We, too, are from the north."

"Thank you. May I replace my veil, *Caporale*? I am in mourning."

"In one moment, please," replied Ricci, holding up the passport but not looking at it. Instead, he was glancing everywhere at once without moving his head, his anger obviously mounting. Jenna's escorts stood motionless by the car, avoiding the soldier's looks.

Behind the Lancia, on either side of the run-down truck, the support assassins were tense, peering into the shadows, then repeatedly looking in the vicinity of the country inn, anticipation on their faces. It was as though they all expected him to materialize out of the darkness, to appear suddenly, walking either casually or resolutely up the path from the inn, or from behind the thick trunk of a pine tree on the edge of the road, calling out to the woman by the car. It was what they expected; these were the moments they had calculated as the crisis span -- the target would be found now if he had not been found before. And from their viewpoint, it had to happen. Everything was clean, nothing wrinkled. The target had not crossed over the bridge within the past twenty-six hours -- and it would have been stupid to have crossed over prior to minus-twenty-six. There was no way he could know which vehicle carried Jenna Karras or which road it would take through Col des Moulinets. Besides, there was no reason for the man marked for dispatch to know there was a unit from Rome at the checkpoint. It would happen now, or it would not happen.

The tension at the scene was stretched to breaking point. It was compounded by

510

the two soldiers inside the gatehouse booth, who were trying to open the door and shouting through the windows, their voices muted by the thick glass. Nothing was lost on Jenna Karras or her paid escorts; the driver had edged towards the door, his companion towards the border of the road and the woods. A trap was in the making, but for reasons they could not understand it was not a trap for them. If it had been, they would have been summarily taken.

Havelock knew that everything now was timing: the eternal wait until the moment came, and then that instant when instinct told him to move. He could not rearrange the odds to favour him, but he could reduce those against him. Against Jenna.

"*Finira in niente*," said the uniformed killer, just loud enough to be heard. He brought his hand to his waist and shook his wrist twice as he had done before, giving a signal as he had given it before.

Michael reached into his pocket and took out a packet of plastic explosive and a module. The luminous read-out was at *0000*; he pressed the timer button delicately until he had the figures he wanted, then inserted the module into the self-sealing lip. He had checked and rechecked his position in the darkness; he knew the path least obstructed and used it now. He snaked his way eight feet into the forest, observed the outlines of the branches against the night sky, and threw the packet into the air. The moment it was out of his hand, he scrambled back towards the road, arching to his left, now parallel to the run-down truck, ten feet from the back-up killer dressed in mountain clothes. He had two shells left in the Magnum, it was possible he would have to use both before he cared to, but the muted sounds were preferable to explosions from the Llama automatic. Seconds now.

"Regrets again for the delay, *signora* and *signori*," said the assassin sent by Rome, walking away from the Lancia towards the winch that operated the orange barrier. "Procedures must be followed. You may return to your vehicle now, all is in order." The blond man passed the windows of the booth, ignoring the angry shouts of the soldiers inside; he had no time to waste on minor players. A plan had failed, a finely tuned strategy became an exercise in futility; anger and frustration were second only to his professional instincts to get out of the area. There was only one chore left to finish, which an agent-of-record was to know nothing about. He raised the orange barrier and immediately stepped back out into the centre of the entrance, blocking passage. He removed a notebook and a pencil from his pocket – the border guard attending to his last procedure, the numbers of a vehicle's licence. It, too, was a signal.

Only seconds.

Jenna and her two escorts climbed back in the car, the faces of the two men betraying bewilderment and cautious relief. The doors slammed shut, and at the sound a short, stocky man came slowly out of the foliage across the road near the boot of the Lancia. He walked directly to the rear of the vehicle, but his attention was on the woods beyond the road. He raised his right hand to his waist and shook his wrist twice, perplexed at the lack of response to his signal. He stood for a moment, his frown conveying minor alarm but not panic. Men in his business understood the problems of equipment malfunction; they were sudden and deadly, which was why the two specialists travelled as a team. He turned his head quickly

511

towards the checkpoint; the blond assassin was impatient. The man knelt down, took an object out of his left hand, transferring it to his right. He reached under the car, the area directly beneath the fuel tank.

There were no seconds left. The target could not wait.

Havelock had the man in the sights of his Magnum. He fired; the specialist screamed as his body crashed up into the metal of the fender, the packet flying out of his hand as his arm whipped back; the bullet had lodged in his spine and his body arched in searing pain. Though in agony the killer turned towards the source of the explosive spit, pulled an automatic from his pocket and levelled it instantly. Frantically Michael rolled out of the area until the dense undergrowth stopped his movement. The gunshots echoed everywhere, bullets spraying the ground, as Havelock raised the Magnum and fired its last round. The muffled report was followed by a loud gasp from the man by the truck as his neck was blown away.

"*Di dove? Dove?*" shouted the blond assassin at the checkpoint, racing around the Lancia.

The explosion filled the air, the blinding light of the detonated *plastique* bathing the darkness of the woods, echoing throughout the mountains. The assassin lunged to the ground and, aiming at nothing, began shooting at everything. The Lancia's engine roared, its wheels spun and the car surged onto the bridge. Jenna was free.

Seconds more. He had to do it.

Michael got to his feet and raced out of the forest, the empty Magnum in his belt, the Llama in his hand. The assassin saw him in the light of the spreading flames in the woods; getting up on his knees, supporting his right arm with his left, he spun on the ground, pivoting up to his knees, aimed at Havelock. He fired rapidly, repeatedly; the bullets shrieked in ricochets and snapped the air above and to the right of Michael as he lurched for the cover of the truck. But it was no cover; he heard the scraping, then the footsteps behind him, and he whirled around, his back against the door. At the rear of the truck the killer-driver came out crouching – the movements of a professional cornering a quarry at close range – as he raised his weapon and fired. Havelock dropped to the ground at first sighting and returned two shots; feeling the ice-like pain in his shoulder, he knew he had been hit, but not how seriously. The driver rolled spastically off the edge of the road; if he was not gone, he would be soon.

Suddenly, the earth exploded in front of Michael; the blond assassin was free to resume firing now that his associate was finished. Havelock dived to his right, then plunged under the truck, crawling in panic to the other side. *Seconds. Only seconds left.* He sprang to his feet and sidestepped his way to the door. The crowd of frightened people down at the inn were shouting at one another, running in all directions. There was so little time; men would race out of barracks, perhaps were racing even now. He reached for the handle and yanked the door open; he saw what he wanted to see: the keys were in the ignition as he had dared to think they would be. The unit from Rome had been in control, and control meant being able to get away from the execution ground instantly.

He leaped up into the seat, his head low, his fingers working furiously. He turned the key; the powerful engine caught, and at the first sound, gunfire came from the road ahead and bullets embedded themselves in metal. There was a pause, and Michael understood; the assassin was reloading his gun. *These were the crucial seconds.* He switched on the headlights – like the motor, they were powerful, in themselves blinding. Up ahead, the blond man was crouched off the shoulder of the road, slamming a clip into the base of his automatic. Havelock jammed the clutch, pulled the gear lever and pressed the accelerator to the floor.

The heavy truck jolted forward, its tyres screeching over rock and earth. Michael spun the wheel to his right, and the engine roared with the gathering speed. Rapid gunshots; the windscreen was punctured and a web of cracks spread throughout the glass as bullets screamed into the cab. Havelock raised his head just high enough to see what he had to see; the killer was centred in the glare of the headlights. Michael kept his course until he felt and heard the impact, accompanied by a scream of fury which was abruptly cut short as the assassin lurched and twisted, but was held in place, his legs crushed under the heavy reinforced tyres of the truck. Havelock spun the wheel again, now to his left, back onto the road proper; he sped past the two gatehouses onto the bridge, noting as he raced by that the two guards were prone on the floor of the booth.

There was chaos on the French side, but no barrier to block his way. Soldiers were running to and from the checkpoint, shouting orders at no one and everyone; inside a lighted booth four guards were huddled together, one screaming into a telephone. The road into Col des Moulinets bore to the left off the bridge, then curved right, heading straight into a silhouetted patchwork of small wood-framed houses, set close together, with sloping roofs typical of a thousand villages in this part of the Alps. He entered a narrow cobblestoned street; several pedestrians jumped onto the narrow pavement, startled as much by the sound as by the sight of the heavy Italian truck.

He saw the red lights . . . the wide, rear lights of the Lancia. It was far in the distance; it turned into a street God only knew what street, there were so many. Col des Moulinets was one of those villages where every long-ago path and pasture bypass had been paved with stone; some had been converted into streets, others into merely quaint alleyways, barely wide enough for produce carts. But he would know it when he came to it; he *had* to.

The intersecting streets grew wider, the houses and shops set farther back; narrow pavements widened, and more and more villagers were seen strolling past the lighted shops. The Lancia was nowhere; it had disappeared!

"*S'il vous plait! Où est l'aéroport?*" he yelled out of the window to an elderly couple about to step off the pavement into the cobblestoned street.

"Airport?" said the old man in French, the word itself pronounced more with an Italian accent than Gallic. "There is no airport in Col des Moulinets, *monsieur.* You can take the southern road down to Cap Martin."

"There *is* an airport near the village, I'm sure of it," cried Havelock, trying to control his anxiety. "A friend, a very *good* friend, told me he was flying into Col des Moulinets. I'm to meet him. I'm late."

"Your friend meant Cap Martin, *monsieur.*"

"Perhaps not," called out a younger man, leaning against the doorway of a shop closed for the evening. "There is no real airport, *monsieur*, but there is an airfield fifteen, twenty kilometres north on the road to Tende. It's used by the rich who have estates in Roquebillière and Breil."

"That's it! What's the fastest way?"

"Take the next turning right, then right again back three streets to rue Maritimes. Turn left; it will lead you onto the mountain autoroute. Fifteen, eighteen kilometres north."

"Thank you."

Time was a racing montage of light and shadow, filled with peopled streets and leaping figures, small interfering cars and glaring headlights, gradually replaced by fewer buildings, fewer people, fewer streetlamps; he had reached the outskirts of the village. If the police had been alerted by the panicked border guards, he had eluded them by the odds of a small force versus a larger area. Minutes later – how many he would never know – he was tearing through the darkness of the Maritimes countryside, the rolling hills everywhere that were introductions to the mountains beyond, barricades to be negotiated with all the speed the powerful truck could manage. And as the grinding gears strained and the tyres under him screamed to a crescendo, he saw the silhouettes of paddlewheels – like the hills, they were everywhere – slowly turning, a certain majesty in their never-ending movements, alongside houses by mountain streams and rivulets, proof again that time and nature were constant whether attention was paid or not. In a strange way, Michael needed the reaffirmation; he was close to losing his mind.

There were no lights on the autoroute, no red specks in the darkness. The Lancia was nowhere to be seen. Was he even going in the right direction? Or had anxiety warped his senses? So close and yet so terribly far away, one gulf traversed, one more to breach. Traversed? Breach? We said it better in Prague. *Przheyest* said it better.

Milaji vas, maj sladky. We understand these words, Jenna. We do not need the language of liars. We never should have learned it. *Don't listen to the liars! They neutralized us; now they want to kill us. They have to because I know they're there. I know, and so will you.*

A searchlight! Its beam was sweeping the night sky. Beyond the nearest hills, diagonally ahead on the left. Somewhere the road would turn; somewhere minutes away was an airfield and a plane – and Jenna.

The second hill was steep, the other side of it steeper, with curves; he held the wheel with all his strength, careening into each turn. *Lights.* Wide white beams in front, two red dots behind. It was the Lancia! A mile, two miles ahead and below; it was impossible to tell, but the field was there. Parallel lines of yellow ground lights crossed each other at forty-plus degree points; the valley winds had been studied for maximum lift. The airfield was in a valley, sufficiently wide and long for small jets as well as prop aircraft . . . *used by the rich with estates in Roquebillière and Breil.*

Havelock kept the accelerator to the floor, his left foot grazing the brake for those instants when balance was in jeopardy. The road levelled out and became a flat track that circled the fenced-off airfield. Within the enormous compound were the vivid reflections of glistening wings and fuselages; perhaps a dozen stationary planes were moored to the ground in varying positions off the runways – the yachts of

514

yesterday had been replaced by silver tubes that sailed through the skies. The ten-foot high fence was strung with barbed wire across the top and angled an additional four feet inside. The rich of Roquebillière and Breil cared for their airborne possessions. Such a fence – a double mile in length – carried a price of several hundred thousand; and that being the case, would there be a security gate and guards somewhat more attentive than those at a remote French or Italian border post?

There were. He screeched into the entrance roadway. The heavy, ten-foot gate was closing three hundred feet in front of him. Inside, the Lancia was racing across the field. Suddenly, its lights were extinguished; somewhere within the expanse of grass and asphalt its driver had spotted a plane. Lights would reveal markings and markings were traces; if he could see the Lancia's headlights several miles away in the darkness of the valley, his, too, could be seen. There were only seconds and half-seconds now, each minuscule movement of a clock narrowing the final gulf or widening it.

While gripping the wheel, he jammed the palms of both hands on the rim of the truck's horn, hammering out the only alarm code that came to him. *Mayday, Mayday, Mayday!* He repeated it over and over again as he sped down the entrance drive towards the closing gate.

Two uniformed guards were inside the fence, one pushing the thick metal crossbar of the gate, the other standing by the latch, prepared to receive the sliding bar and insert the clamp. As the gate reached the three-quarter mark, both guards stared through the wire mesh at the powerful truck bearing down, the blaring series of shrieking notes not lost on them. Their terrified faces revealed no intention of staying in the path of the wild vehicle. The guard at the crossbar released it and ran to his left; the gate swung back partially – only partially – when he withdrew his grip. The man by the latch scrambled to his right, diving into the grass and the protection of the extended fence.

The impact came, the truck ripping the gate away, twisting it up off its hinges and smashing it into the small booth, shattering glass and severing an electrical wire that erupted in sparks and static. Michael raced onto the field, his wounded shoulder pitched in pain, the truck careening sharply, narrowly missing two adjacent planes parked in the shadows of a single wide hangar. He spun the wheel to his left, sending the truck in the direction the Lancia had been heading less than a minute ago.

Nothing. Absolutely *nothing!* Where was it? Where *was* it?

A flicker of light. Movement – at the far end of the field, beyond the glowing yellow lines of the north runway, slightly above the farthest row of grounded planes. The cabin of a plane had been opened, an interior light snapped briefly on, then instantly turned off. He whipped the wheel to the right – blood from his wrenched wounded shoulder spreading through his shirt – and raced diagonally across the enormous compound. Heavy, weatherproof bulbs exploded under the tyres as he sped towards the now darkened area where seconds ago there had been the dim flash of light.

There it was! Not a jet, but a twin-engine, single-wing, its propellers suddenly revving furiously, flames belching from its exhausts. It was not on the runway, but

515

instead beyond the glow of the parallel lines of yellow lights: the pilot was about to taxi into the take-off position. But he was not moving now; he was holding!

The Lancia. It was behind and to the right of the plane. Again, a light! Not from the aircraft now, but from the Lancia itself. Doors opened, figures leapt out, dashing for the plane. The cabin door, another light! For an instant Michael considered ramming the fuselage or crashing into the nearest wing, but it could be a tragic error. If he struck a fuel tank the aircraft would blow up in seconds. He swerved the heavy truck to the right, then to the left, screeching to a stop yards in front of the plane.

"Jenna! *Jenna! Poslouchat já! Stát! Listen to me!*"

She was climbing on board, pushed up the steps by the driver of the Lancia, who followed her inside and closed the door. He ran, oblivious to everything but her; he had to *stop* her! The plane spun in place like a grotesque, dark cormorant. Its path was free of the Lancia!

The blow came out of the shadows, muffled and at the same time magnified by the furious winds of the propeller's wash. His head snapped back as his legs buckled, blood matting the hair above his right temple. He was on his knees, supporting himself with his hands, staring up at the plane, at the window of the moving plane, and he could *not move!* The cabin lights remained on for several seconds and he saw her face in the glass, her eyes staring back at him. It was a sight he would remember for as long as he lived . . . if he lived. A second blow with a blunt instrument was delivered to the back of his neck.

He could not think about the terrible sight now, about *her* now! He could hear the sirens screaming across the field, see the glare of searchlights shooting over the runway, catching the glistening metal of the plane as it sped down between the yellow lights. The man who had struck him twice was running towards the Lancia; he had to *move!* He had to move *now*, or he would not be permitted to live, permitted ever to see her again. He struggled to his feet as he pulled the Llama automatic from under his jacket.

He fired twice above the roof of the car; the man leaping into the seat could have killed him moments ago; he would not kill that man now. His hands were too unsteady, the flashing, sweeping lights too bewildering to ensure inflicting only a wound. But he *had* to have the car. He fired again, the bullet ricocheting off the metal as he approached the window.

"Get out or you're dead!" he shouted, gripping the door handle. "You heard what I said! Get *out!*" Havelock yanked the man by the cloth of his coat and pulled him, propelling him onto the grass. There was no time for a dozen questions he wanted to ask. He had to escape! He slid behind the wheel and slammed the door shut; the engine was running.

For the next forty-five seconds he criss-crossed the airfield at enormous speeds, evading the airfield's security police by weaving in and out of searchlight beams. A dozen times he nearly crashed into stationary aircraft before reaching the demolished gate. He raced through, not seeing the road, functioning only on nerves and instinct.

He could not shut out the terrible sight of Jenna's face in the window of the moving plane. In Rome her face had shown raw fear and confusion. Moments ago there had been something else; it was in her eyes.

Cold, immaculate hatred.

13

He drove south-west to Provence, then due south towards the coast, to the small city of Cagnes-sur-Mer. He had worked the northern Mediterranean for years and knew a doctor between Cagnes and Antibes; he needed help. He had ripped the sleeve of his shirt and tied a knot around the wound in his shoulder, but it did not prevent the loss of blood. His entire chest was soaked, cloth sticking to skin and giving the sweet-acrid odour that he knew only too well. His neck was merely bruised – a paramedical opinion which in no way diminished the pain – but the blow to his head required stitches; the slightest graze would reopen the laceration that was sealed with coagulated blood.

He needed other help, too, and Dr Henri Salanne would provide it. He must reach Matthias; to delay any longer was asinine. Specific identities could be traced from orders, from a code name, Ambiguity; there was enough information. Surface evidence of the massive conspiracy was clear from Jenna's having survived Costa Brava – when she had been officially recorded as dead – and from his own condemnation as "beyond-salvage". The first Matthias would accept from his *pritel*, the second could be confirmed from sealed black-bordered directives in the files of Consular Operations. Granted the whys were beyond Havelock's reach, but not the facts – they existed, and Matthias could act on them. And while the Secretary of State acted, Michael had to get to Paris as quickly as possible. It would not be simple; every airport, main road and train station in Provence and the Maritimes would be watched, and Matthias could do nothing about it. Time and communications were on the side of the liars. Issuing covert orders was far easier than rescinding them; they spread like a darkening web of ink on soft paper as the recipients disappeared, each wanting credit for the kill.

Within an hour – if not already – Rome would be apprised of the events at Col des Moulinets. Telephones and little-used radio frequencies would be employed to send out the word: *the man "beyond salvage" is loose; he can cost us too much that's valuable, including time and our lives. All network personnel are on alert; use every source, every weapon available. Zero-area: Col des Moulinets. Radius: Maximum two hours' travel, reported to be wounded. Last known vehicles: a nondescript farm truck with a powerful engine, and a Lancia saloon. Find him. Kill him.*

No doubt the liars on the Potomac had already reached Salanne, but as with so many in the shadow world there were hidden confidences – things in and of his past – that those who cleared payrolls in Washington or Rome or Paris knew nothing about. Only certain men in the field who had been on a given scene at a given time knew drones such as Dr Henri Salanne; they stored away their names for future personal use should the necessity ever arise. There was even a vague morality about this practice, for more often than not the incriminating information or the events themselves were the result of a temporary crisis or a weakness that did not require that the man or the woman be destroyed . . . or killed.

With Salanne, Havelock had been there when it happened – to be precise, eleven hours after the act took place, time enough to alter the consequences. The doctor had sold out an American agent in Cannes who co-ordinated a small fleet of ocean-going pleasure craft for the purpose of monitoring Russian naval positions in the sector. Salanne had sold him for money to a KGB informant, and Michael had not understood; neither money nor betrayal was a motive that made sense where the doctor was concerned. It took only one, low-keyed confrontation to learn the truth, and it was a truth – or a juxtaposition of truths – as old as the grotesque world in which they all lived. The gentle if somewhat cynical middle-aged doctor was a compulsive gambler; it was the primary reason why years ago a brilliant young surgeon from the *L'Hôpital de Paris* had sought out a practice in the Monte Carlo triangle. His credentials and references were honoured in Monaco, which was a good thing, but his losses at the Casino were not.

Enter the American, whose cover was that of a yacht-owning jet-setter and who spent the taxpayers' money cautiously but obnoxiously at the tables. His obnoxiousness, however, did not end at Chemin de fer; he was a womanizer with a preference for young girls, an image, he rationalized, that did nothing to harm his cover. One of the girls he brought to his busy bed was Salanne's daughter, Claudie, an impressionable child who suffered a severe depression when nothing further came of the relationship.

The Russians were in the market; the doctor's losses could be covered, and a preying *violateur* removed from the scene. *Pourquoi pas?* The act had taken place.

Enter Havelock, who had traced the betrayal, got the American out before the boats were identified, and confronted Henri Salanne. He never reported his findings; there was no point, and the doctor understood the conditions of his "pardon". Never again . . . and an obligation was assumed.

Michael found a telephone box at a deserted corner in the centre of Cagnes-sur-Mer. He braced himself and got out of the car with difficulty, clutching his jacket around him as he stood up; he was cold, bleeding still. Inside the *cabine*, he pulled out the Llama from his holster, smashed the overhead light and studied the dial in the shadows. After what seemed like an interminable wait, he was given Salanne's number by Antibes information.

"*Votre fille Claudie, comment va-t-elle?*" he asked quietly.

There was dead silence. Finally the doctor spoke, his use of English deliberate. "I wondered if I'd hear from you. If it is you they say you may be hurt."

"I am."

"How badly?"

"I need cleaning up and a few stitches. That's all, I think."

"Nothing internal?"

"Not that I can tell."

"I hope you're right. A hospital would be in questionable taste right now. I suspect all emergency rooms in the area are being watched."

Michael was suddenly alarmed. "What about you?"

"There's only so much manpower. They won't waste it on someone they assume would rather see ten patients die on an operating table than be cut off from their generosity."

"Would you?"

"Let's halve it," said Salanne, laughing softly. "In spite of my habits, my conscience couldn't take more than five." The doctor paused but not long enough for Havelock to speak. "However, there could be a problem. They say you're driving a medium sized truck – "

"I'm not."

"Or possibly a dark grey Lancia," continued Salanne.

"I am."

"Get rid of it, or get away from it."

Michael looked at the large car outside the box. The engine had overheated; steam was escaping from the radiator, vapour rising and diffusing under the light of the street lamp. All this was calling attention to the car. "I'm not sure how far I can walk," he said to the doctor.

"Loss of blood?"

"Enough so I can feel it."

"*Merde!* Where are you?"

Havelock told him. "I've been here before, but I can't remember much."

"Disorientation or absence of impressions?"

"What difference does it make?"

"Blood."

"I feel dizzy, if that's what you mean."

"It is. I think I know the corner. Is there a *bijouterie* on the other side? Called something-and-son?"

Michael squinted through glass beyond the Lancia. "Ariale et Fils?" he said, reading the raised white letters of a sign above a dark shopfront across the street. "'Fine Jewellery, Watches, Diamonds'. Is that it?"

"Ariale, of course. I've had good nights, too, you know. They're much more reasonable than the thieves in the Spélugues. Now then, several shops north of Ariale's is an alley that leads to a small parking area behind. I'll get there as fast as I can, twenty minutes at the outside. I don't want to race through the streets under the circumstances."

"Please don't."

"Nor should you. Walk slowly, and if there are cars parked there, crawl under one and lie flat on your back. When you see me arrive, strike a match. As little movement as possible, is that understood?"

"Understood."

Havelock left the box, but before crossing the street he opened his jacket, pulled the blood-soaked shirt out of his belt and squeezed it until drops of dark red appeared on the pavement. Leaning over, he took a dozen rapid steps straight ahead, past the corner building into the shadows, scuffing the blood with the soles of his shoes, streaking it backwards; anyone studying the Lancia and the immediate area would assume he had run down the intersecting street. He then stopped, awkwardly removed both shoes, and sidestepped carefully to the kerb, pulling his jacket around him. He reversed direction and hobbled across the intersection to the side of the street that housed Ariale et Fils.

He lay on his back, matches in his hand, staring up at the black grease-laden underside of a Peugeot facing the car park wall, keeping his mind alert with an exercise in the improbable. Propositions: the owner returned with a companion, and both got into the car. What should Michael do and how would he do it without being seen? The answer to the first was to roll out – obviously – but on which side?

Twin headlight beams pierced the entrance of the parking area, cutting short his ruminations. The headlights were turned off ten feet inside the unmanned gate; the car stopped, the engine still running. It was Salanne, telling him he had arrived. Havelock crawled to the edge of the Peugeot's chassis and struck a match. Seconds later the doctor was above him, and within minutes they were driving south on the road towards Antibes, Michael in the back seat, angled in the corner, legs stretched, out of sight.

"If you recall," said Salanne, "there is a side entrance to my house, reached from the drive. It leads directly to my surgery."

"I remember. I've used it."

"I'll go inside first, just to make certain."

"What are you going to do if there are cars in front?"

"I'd rather not think about it."

"Maybe you should."

"Actually, I have. There's a colleague of mine in Villefranche, an elderly man, above reproach. I'd prefer not to involve him, of course."

"I appreciate what you're doing," said Havelock, looking at the back of the doctor's head in the coruscating light, noting that the hair touched with grey only a year or so ago was practically white now.

"I appreciate what you did for me," replied Salanne softly. "I assumed a debt. I never thought otherwise."

"I know. That's pretty cold, isn't it?"

"Not at all. You asked how Claudie was, so let me tell you. She is happy and with child and married to a young doctor at the hospital in Nice. Two years ago she nearly took her own life. How much is that worth to me, my friend?"

"I'm glad to hear it."

"Besides, what they say about you is preposterous."

"What do they say?"

"That you are insane, a dangerous psychopath who threatens us all with exposure – certain death from roving jackals of the KGB – if you are allowed to live."

"And that's preposterous to you?"

"Since an hour ago, *mon mauvais ami*. You remember the man in Cannes who was involved with my indiscretion?"

"The KGB informant?"

520

"Yes."

"Would you say he's knowledgeable?"

"As any in the sector," replied Havelock. "To the point where we left him alone and tried to feed him disinformation. What about him?"

"When the word came through about you, I rang him up – from a public box, of course. I wanted confirmation of this new, incredible judgement, so I asked him how soft the market was, how flexible in terms of price for the American consular attaché whose origins were in Prague. What he told me was both startling and specific."

"Which was?" asked Michael leaning forward in pain.

"There is no market for you, no price – high, low or otherwise. You are a leper and Moscow wants no part of your disease. You are not to be touched, even acknowledged. So who could you expose in this manner?" The doctor shook his head. "Rome lied, which means that someone in Washington lied to Rome. 'Beyond-salvage'? Beyond *belief*."

"Would you repeat those words to someone?"

"And by doing so, call for my own execution? There are limits to my gratitude."

"You won't be identified, my word on it."

"Who would believe you without naming a source he could check?"

"Anthony Matthias."

"*Matthias?*" cried Salanne, whipping his head to the side, gripping the wheel, his eyes straining to stay on the road. "Why would *he* . . . ?"

"Because you're with me. Again, my word on it."

"A man like Matthias is beyond one's well-intentioned word, my friend. He asks and you must tell him."

"Only if you cleared it."

"Why would he believe you? Believe me?"

"You just said it. The attaché whose origins were in Prague. So were his."

"I see," said the doctor pensively, his head turned forward again. "I never made the connection, never even thought about it."

"It's complicated, and I don't talk about it. We go back a long time; our families go back."

"I must think. To deal with such a man puts everything in another perspective, doesn't it? We are ordinary men doing our foolish things; he is not ordinary. He lives on another plane. The Americans have a phrase for what you ask."

"A different ballgame?"

"That's the one."

"It's not. It's the same game, and it's rigged against him. Against all of us."

There were no strange cars within a four-block radius of Salanne's house, no need to travel to Villefranche and an elderly physician above reproach. Inside the examining room Havelock's clothes were removed, his body sponged and the wounds sutured, the doctor's petite, somewhat uncommunicative wife assisting Salanne.

"You should rest for several days," said the Frenchman, after his wife had left, taking Michael's garments to wash out what she could and burn the irrecoverable.

"If there are no ruptures the dressing will last for five, perhaps six days, then it should be changed. But you should rest."

"I can't," answered Havelock, grimacing, raising himself into a sitting position on the table, his legs over the edge.

"It hurts to move even those few inches, doesn't it?"

"Only the shoulder, that's all."

"You've lost blood, you know that."

"I've lost more; I know that, too." Michael paused, studying Salanne. "Do you have a dictating machine in your office?"

"Of course. Letters and reports – medical reports – must be dealt with long after nurses and receptionists have gone home."

"I want you to show me how to use it, and I want you to listen. It won't take long, and you won't be identified on the tape. Then I want to place an overseas call to the United States."

"Matthias?"

"Yes. But the circumstances will determine how much I can tell him. Who's with him, how sterile the phone is; he'll know what to do. The point is, after you hear what I've got to say, listen to the tape in your machine, you can decide whether to speak to him or not – if it comes up."

"You place a burden on me."

"I'm sorry – there won't be many more. In the morning, I'll need clothes. Everything I had is back in Monesi."

"No problem. Mine would not fit, but my wife buys for me. Tomorrow, she will buy for you."

"Speaking of buying, I've got a fair amount of money but I'll need more. I have accounts in Paris; you'll get it back."

"Now you embarrass me."

"I don't mean to, but, you see, there's a catch. In order for you to get it back, I have to get to Paris."

"Surely Matthias can effect swift, safe transportation."

"I doubt it. You'll understand when you hear what I say in your office. Those who lied to Rome are very high in Washington. I don't know who or where they are, but I know they'll transmit only what they want. His orders will be sidetracked, because their orders have gone out and they don't want them voided. And if I say where I am, where I can be reached, they'll send in men after me. In any case, they might succeed, which is why I need the tape. May we do it now, please?"

Thirty-four minutes later, Havelock depressed the switch on the cassette microphone and placed it on the Frenchman's desk. He had told it all, from the screams at Costa Brava to the explosions at Col des Moulinets. He could not refrain from adding a last judgement. The civilized world might well survive the compromising of any sprawling, monolithic intelligence service – regardless of race, creed or national origin – but not when one of the victims was a man that the same civilized world depended on: Anthony Matthias, a statesman respected by geopolitical friends and adversaries everywhere. He had been systematically lied to on a matter to which he had addressed himself in depth. How many more lies had been fed to him?

Salanne sat across the office, deep in a soft leather armchair, his body motionless, his face rigid, his eyes staring at Havelock. He was stunned, speechless. After several moments he shook his head and broke his silence.

"Why?" he asked in a barely audible voice. "It's all so preposterous, as preposterous as what they say about you. *Why?*"

"I've asked myself that over and over again, and I keep going back to what I said to Baylor in Rome. They think I know something I shouldn't know, something that frightens them."

"Do you?"

"He asked me that."

"Who?"

"Baylor. And I was honest with him – perhaps too honest – but the shock of seeing her had blown my mind. I couldn't think straight. Especially after what Rostov had said in Athens."

"What did you say?"

"The truth. That if I *did* know something, I'd forgotten it, or it had never made much of an impression on me."

"That's not like you. They say you are a walking data bank, someone who recalls a name, a face, a minor event that took place years ago."

"Like most such opinions, it's a myth. I was a graduate student for a long time, so I developed certain disciplines, but I'm no computer."

"I'm aware of that," said the Frenchman quietly. "No computer would have done what you did for me." Salanne paused, leaning forward in the chair. "Have you gone over the months preceding Costa Brava?"

"Months, weeks, days – everything, every place we were . . . I was. Belgrade, Prague, Krakow, Vienna, Washington, Paris. There was nothing remotely startling, but I suppose that's a comparative term. With the exception of an exercise in Prague where we got some documents out of the *nachlazeni bezpečnost* – the secret police headquarters – everything was pretty routine. Gathering information which damn near any tourist could have done, that's all."

"Washington?"

"Less than nothing. I flew back for five days. It's an annual event for field men, an evaluation interview which is mostly a waste of time, but I suppose they catch a whack-o now and then."

"Whack-o?"

"Someone who's crossed over the mental line, thinks he's someone he's not, who's fantasized a basically routine job. Cloak-and-dagger flakes, I suppose you could call them. It comes with the stress, with too often pretending you are someone you're not."

"Interesting," said the doctor, nodding his head in some abstract recognition. "Did anything else happen while you were there?"

"Zero. I went to New York for a night to see a couple I knew when I was young. He owns a marina on Long Island, and if he ever had a political thought in his head I've never heard it. Then I spent two days with Matthias, a duty visit, really."

523

"You *were* close . . . *are* close."

"I told you, we go back a long time. He was there when I needed him; he understood."

"What about those two days?"

"Less than zero. I only saw him during the evenings when we had dinner together, two dinners, actually. Even then, although we were alone, he was constantly interrupted by phone calls and by harried people from State – suppliants, he called them – who insisted on bringing him reports." Havelock stopped, seeing a sudden tight expression on Salanne's face; he continued quickly. "No one saw me, if that's what you're thinking. He'd confer with them in his study, and the dining-room's on the other side of the house. Again, he understood; we agreed not to display our friendship. For my benefit, really. No one likes a great man's protégé."

"It's difficult for me to think of you that way."

"It'd be impossible if you'd had dinner with us," said Michael, laughing quietly. "All we did was rehash papers I'd written for him nearly twenty years ago; he could still punch holes in them. Talk about total recall, he has it." Havelock smiled, then the smile faded as he said, "It's time," and reached for the telephone.

The lodge in the Shenandoah Valley was reached by a sequence of telephone numbers, the first activating a remote mechanism at Matthias's residence in Georgetown, which in turn was electronically patched into a line a hundred and forty miles away in the Blue Ridge mountains, ringing the private telephone of the Secretary of State. If he was not on the premises, that phone was never answered; if he was, only he picked it up. The original number was known to perhaps a dozen people in the nation, among them the President and Vice-President, the Speaker of the House, the Chairman of the Joint Chiefs, the Secretary of Defense, the President of the Security Council of the United Nations, two senior aides at State, and Mikhail Havlicek. The last was a privilege that Matthias had insisted upon for his *krajan*, his *učenec* from the university, whose father in Prague had been a colleague in intellect and spirit, if not in good fortune. Michael had used it twice during the past six years. The first time when he was briefly in Washington for new instructions, Matthias had left word at his hotel that he should do so, and the call was merely social. The second was not pleasant for Havelock to recall. It had concerned a man named Ogilvie who Michael felt strongly should be removed from the field.

The Antibes operator offered to ring him back when the call to Washington, DC was put through, but experience had taught Havelock to stay on the line. Nothing so tested the concentration of an operator as an open circuit; calls were more swiftly completed by remaining connected. And while he listened to the series of high-pitched sounds that signified international transmission, Salanne spoke.

"Why haven't you called him before now?"

"Because nothing made sense, and I wanted it to. I wanted to give him something concrete. A name or names, a position, a title, some kind of identity."

"But from what I've heard you still can't do that."

"Yes I can. The authorization for dispatch had a source. Code name, Ambiguity. It could only come from one of three or four offices, the word itself cleared by someone very high at State who was in touch with Rome. Matthias reaches Rome, has the incoming logs checked, talks to the receiver and learns who gave Ambiguity its status. There's another name, too, but I don't know how much good it'll do. There was a second, so-called confirmation at Costa Brava, including torn pieces of blood-stained clothing. It's all a lie; there were no clothes left behind."

"Then find that man."

"He's dead. They say he died of a heart attack on a boat three weeks later. But there are things to look for, if they haven't been obscured. Where he came from, who assigned him to Costa Brava . . ."

"And if I may add," said the Frenchman, "the doctor who made out the death certificate."

"You're right." The sing-song tones disappeared from the line, replaced by two short, steady hums, then a break of silence, followed by a normal ring. The electronic remote control had done its work; the telephone in the Shenandoah lodge was ringing. Michael felt the pounding in his throat and the shortness of breath that came with anxiety. He had so much to say to *his pritel*; he hoped to Christ he could say it and so begin the ending of the nightmare. The ringing stopped, the phone was picked up. *Thank God!*

"Yes?" asked the voice over four thousand miles away in the Blue Ridge mountains, a male voice, but not the voice of Anton Matthias. Or was the sound distorted, the single word too short to identify the man?

"*Jak sè vam daŕé?*"

"What? Who's this?"

It was *not* Matthias. Had the rules been changed? If they had, it did not make sense. This was the emergency line, Matthias's personal phone, which was swept for intercepts daily; only he answered it. After five rings the caller was to hang up, dial the regular telephone number and leave his name and whatever message he cared to, aware that confidentiality was far less secure. Perhaps there was a simple explanation, an off-hand request by Matthias for a friend nearer to the ringing phone to pick it up.

"Secretary of State Matthias, please?" said Havelock.

"Who's calling?"

"The fact that I used this number relieves me of the need to answer that. The Secretary, if you please. This is an emergency and confidential."

"Mr Matthias is in conference at the moment and has asked for all calls to be held. If you'd give me your name – "

"Goddamn it, you're not listening! This is an emergency!"

"He has one, too, sir."

"You break into that conference and say the following words to him. *Krajan* . . . and *bouře*. Have you got that? Just two words! *Krajan* and *bouře*. Do it now! Because if you don't, he'll have your head and your job when I talk to him! Do it!"

"*Krajan*," said the male voice hesitantly. "*Bouře*."

The line went silent, the silence interrupted once by the low undercurrent of men talking in the distance. The waiting was agony, and Michael could hear the echoes of his own erratic breathing. Finally the voice came back.

"I'm afraid you'll have to be clearer, sir."

"What?"

"If you'd give me the details of the emergency and a telephone number where you can be reached – "

"Did you give him the message? The *words!* Did you say them?"

"The Secretary is extremely busy and requests that you clarify the nature of your call."

"Goddamn it, did you *say* them?"

"I'm repeating what the Secretary said, sir. He can't be disturbed now, but if you'll outline the details and leave a number, someone will be in contact with you."

"*Someone?* What the hell is this? Who *are* you? What's your name?"

There was a pause. "Smith," said the voice.

"Your name! I want your *name!*"

"I just gave it to you."

"You get Matthias on this phone – !" There was a click; the line went dead.

Havelock stared at the instrument in his hand, then closed his eyes. His mentor, his *krajan*, his *pritel*, had cut him off. What had happened?

He had to find out; it made no sense, no sense at all! There was another number in the Blue Ridge Mountains, the home of a man Matthias saw frequently when he was in the Shenandoah, an older man whose love of chess and fine old wine took Anton's mind off his monumental pressures. Michael had met Leon Zelienski a number of times and was always struck by the camaraderie between the two academics; he was happy for Matthias that such a person existed whose roots, though not in Prague, were not so far away, in Warsaw.

Zelienski had been a highly regarded professor of European history brought over to America years ago from the University of Warsaw to teach and lecture at Berkeley. Anton had met Leon during one of his early forays into the campus lecture circuit; additional funds were always welcome to Matthias. A friendship had developed – mostly by way of the mails and over chess – and upon retirement and the death of Zelienski's wife, Anton had persuaded the elderly scholar to come to the Shenandoah.

The Antibes operator took far longer with the second call, but finally Havelock heard the old man's voice.

"Good evening?"

"Leon? Is that you, Leon?"

"Who is this?"

"It's Michael Havelock. Do you remember me, Leon?"

"*Mikhail!* Do I *remember!* No, of course not, and I never touch *kielbasa*, either, you young *dupa!* How are you? Are you visiting our valley? You sound so far away."

"I'm very far away, Leon. I'm also very concerned . . ." Havelock explained his concern; he was unable to reach their beloved mutual friend, and was old Zelienski planning to see Anton while Matthias was in the Shenandoah?

"If he's here, Mikhail, I do not know it. Anton, of course, is a busy man. Sometimes I think the busiest man in this world . . . but he doesn't find time for me these days. I leave messages at the lodge, but I'm afraid he ignores them. Naturally, I understand. He moves with great figures . . . he is a great figure, and I am hardly one of them."

"I'm sorry to hear that . . . that he hasn't been in touch."

"Oh, men call me to express his regrets, saying that he rarely comes out to our valley these days, but I tell you, our chess games suffer. Incidentally, I must settle for another mutual friend of ours, Mikhail. He was out here frequently several months ago. That fine journalist Raymond Alexander. Alexander the Great, I call him, but as a player he's a far better writer."

"Raymond Alexander?" said Havelock, barely listening. "Give him my best. And thank you, Leon." Havelock replaced the phone and looked over at Salanne. "He hasn't time for us any more," he said, bewildered.

14

He had reached Paris by eight o'clock in the morning, made contact with Gravet by nine and, by a quarter past eleven, was walking south amid the crowds on the Boulevard Saint Germain. The fastidious art critic and broker of secrets would approach him somewhere between the rue de Pontoise and the Quai St Bernard. Gravet needed the two hours to seek out as many sources as possible relating to the information Havelock needed. Michael, on the other hand, used the time to move slowly, to rest – leaning upright against walls, never sitting – and to improve his immediate wardrobe.

There had been no time for Salanne's wife to buy him clothes in the morning, no thought but to get to Paris as quickly as he could, for every moment lost widened the distance between Jenna and himself. She had never been to Paris except with him and there were only so many options open to her; he must be there when she narrowed them down.

The doctor had driven for three and a half hours at very high speed to Avignon, where there had been a one o'clock produce train bound for Paris. Michael had caught it, dressed in what could be salvaged from his own clothes, in addition to a sweater and an ill-fitting gabardine topcoat furnished by Salanne. Now he looked at his reflection in a shop window; the jacket, trousers, open shirt and hat he had purchased off the racks in the Raspail forty-five minutes ago suited his purpose. They were loose and nondescript. A man wearing such clothes would not be singled out, and the brim of the soft hat fell just low enough over his forehead to cast a shadow across his face.

Beyond the window was a narrow pillar of clear glass, part of the merchandise display, a mirror. He was drawn to it, to the face in the shadow of the hat brim. *His* face. It was haggard, with black circles under his eyes and stubble of a dark beard. He had not thought of shaving. Even when shopping in Raspail – there had been mirrors in the store – he had looked only at the clothes, while concentrating his thoughts on the Paris he and Jenna Karras had known together: one or two embassy contacts; several colleagues-in-cover, as they were; a few French friends – government mainly, whose *ministères* brought them into his orbit; and three or four acquaintances they had made at late night cafés having nothing whatsoever to do with the world in which he made his living.

Now in the Boulevard Saint Germain the ashen face he saw reminded him of how tired and racked with pain he was, how much he just wanted to lie down and let his strength come back to him. As Salanne had said, he needed rest badly. He had tried to sleep on the train from Avignon, but the frequent stops at rural halts that were farmers' points of delivery had jolted him awake whenever he dozed. And when awake, his head had throbbed, his mind filled with a profound sense of loss, confusion and anger. The one man on earth to whom he had given his trust and love, the giant who had replaced his father and shaped his life, had cut him loose and he had no idea why. Throughout the years, during the most harrowing and isolated times, he was somehow never alone because the presence of Anton Matthias was always with him. Anton was the spur that drove him to be better than he was, his protection against the memories of the early terrible days, because his *pritel* had given them meaning, perspective. Certainly no justification, but a reason for doing what he was doing, for spending his life in an abnormal world until something inside him told him he could join the normal one. He had fought against the guns of Lidice and the arbiters of gulag termination in whatever form he had found them.

Those guns will always be with you, my pritel. *I wish to Almighty God you could walk away from them, but I don't think you can. So do what lessens the pain, what gives purpose for you, what removes the guilt of having survived. Absolution is not here among the books and argumentative theoreticians; you have no patience with their conceptualism. You have to see practical results . . . One day you will be free, your anger spent and you will return. I hope I am alive to witness it. I intend to be.*

He had come so close to being free, his anger reduced to an abstract sense of futility, his return to a normal world within his grasp and understanding. It had happened twice. Once with the woman he loved, who had given another breadth of meaning to his life . . . and then without her, loving neither her nor the memory of her, believing the lies of liars, betraying his innermost feelings – and her. Oh, *God*!

And now the one man who could fulfil the prophecy he had made years ago to his *krajan*, his student, his son, had thrown him out of his life. The giant was a mortal, after all. And now his enemy.

"*Mon Dieu*, you look like a graduate of Auschwitz!" whispered the tall Frenchman in the velvet-collared overcoat and gleaming black shoes standing several feet to the right of Havelock in front of the window. "What *happened* to you? . . . No, don't tell me! Not here."

"Where?"

"On the Quai Bernard, past the university, is a small park, a playground for children mostly," continued Gravet, admiring his own figure in the glass. "If the benches are occupied, find a place by the fence and I'll join you. On your way, purchase a bag of sweets and try to look like a father, not a sex deviate."

"Thanks for the confidence. Did you bring me anything?"

"Let's say you are heavily in my debt. Far more than your impecunious appearance would suggest you could pay."

528

"About *her?*"

"I'm still working on that. On her."

"Then *what?*"

"The Quai Bernard," said Gravet, adjusting his scarlet tie and tilting his grey Homburg in the reflection of the window. He turned with the grace of a ballet master and walked away.

The small park was chilled by the winds off the Seine, but they did not deter the nurses, nannies and young mothers from bringing their boisterous charges to the playground. Children were everywhere – on the swings, jungle-gyms, seesaws – it was bedlam. Fortunately for Michael's waning strength, there was a vacant bench against the far back wall, away from the more chaotic centre of the riverside part. He sat down, absently picking tiny coloured mints out of a white paper bag while looking at a particularly obnoxious child kicking a tricycle; he hoped that whoever might be observing him would think the youngster was his, reasoning that the small boy's real guardian would stay as far away as possible. The child stopped punishing the three wheels long enough to return his stare with an astonishing malevolence.

The elegant Gravet walked through the red-striped entrance and levitated his way around the outside aisle of the playground, nodding pleasantly, benignly to the screaming children in his path, an elder full of kindness towards the young. It was quite a performance, thought Havelock, knowing that the epicene critic loathed the surroundings. Finally he reached the bench and sat down, snapping a newspaper out in front of him.

"Should you see a doctor?" asked the critic, his eyes on the paper.

"I left one only hours ago," replied Michael, his lips by the edge of the white paper bag. "I'm all right, just tired."

"I'm relieved, but I suggest you clean yourself up, including a shave. The two of us in this particular park could bring on the *gendarmes*. The opposite poles of an obscene spectrum, would be the conclusion."

"I don't feel like being funny, Gravet. What have you got?"

The critic folded the paper, snapping it again, as he spoke. "A contradiction, if my sources are accurate, and I have every reason to believe they are. A somewhat incredible contradiction, in fact."

"What is it?"

"The KGB has no interest in you whatsoever. I could deliver you, a willing, garrulous defector snapped from the jaws of imperialists, to their Paris headquarters – an importing firm on the Beaumarchais, but I suspect you know that – and I wouldn't get a *sou*."

"Why is that a contradiction? I said the same thing to you several weeks ago on the Pont Royal."

"*That* isn't the contradiction."

"What is?"

"Someone else is looking for you. He flew in last night because he thinks you're either in Paris now or on your way here. The word is he'll pay a fortune for your corpse. He's not KGB in the usual sense, but make no mistake about it, he's Soviet."

"Not . . . in the usual sense?" asked Havelock, bewildered, yet sensing the approach of an ominous memory, a recent memory.

"I traced him through a source in the *Étrangers Militaires*. He's from a special branch of Soviet intelligence, an elite corps of . . ."

"*Voennaya Kontr Razvedka*," Michael broke in harshly.

"If the shortened form is VKR, that's it."

"It is."

"He wants you. He'll pay dearly."

"Maniacs."

"Mikhail, I should tell you. He flew in from Barcelona."

"*Costa Brava!*" Across the aisle, the ferocious child screamed. "Don't look at me! Move to the edge of the bench!"

"Do you know what you just *told* me?"

"You're upset. I must leave."

"No! . . . All right, all *right*!" Havelock lifted the white paper bag to his face; both his hands were trembling, and he could hardly breathe as the pain in his chest surged up to his temples. "You know what you've got to deliver now, don't you? You've got it, so give it to me."

"You're in no condition."

"I'll be the judge of that. *Tell* me!"

"I wonder if I should. Quite apart from the payment I may never see, there's a moral dilemma. You see, I like you, Mikhail. You're a civilized man, perhaps even a good man in a very unsavoury business. You took yourself out; have I the right to put you back in?"

"I *am* back in!"

"The Costa Brava?"

"Yes!"

"Go to your embassy."

"I *can't*! Don't you understand that?"

Gravet broke his own sacrosanct rule: he lowered the newspaper and looked at Havelock. "My God, they couldn't," he said quietly.

"Just tell me."

"You leave me no choice."

"*Tell* me! Where is he?"

The critic rose from the bench, folding the paper, as he spoke. "There's a rundown hotel on the rue Etienne. *La Couronne Nouvelle*. He's on the first floor, Room Twenty-three. It's at the front; he observes everyone who enters."

The bent-over figure of the tramp was like that of a derelict in any large city. His clothes were ragged but thick enough to ward off the cold in deserted alleyways at night, his shoes cast-off heavy-soled boots, the laces broken and tied in large, awkward knots. On his head was a woollen knitted cap set low on his brow; his eyes focused downward, avoiding the world in which he could not compete, and which in turn found his presence unnerving. But over the tramp's shoulder was his soiled canvas satchel, the oily straps held in a firm grip as if he were proclaiming the dignity of possession: *this is my all, what is left of me, and it is mine.* The man approaching *La Couronne Nouvelle* had no age; he measured time only by what he had lost. He stopped at a wire litter basket and dug through the contents with methodical patience – a pavement archaeologist.

Havelock separated a torn lampshade from a soggy bag of a half-eaten lunch and angled the small tinted mirror between them, his hands concealed by the filthy fabric of the shade. He could see the Russian directly above in the first floor window; the man was leaning against the sill, watching the street, studying the pedestrians, waiting. He would stay by that window for a simple reason: his strike force was deployed; had a counterstrike been mounted? Michael knew him – not by name or reputation, or even from a photograph in a file, but he knew him, knew the set of the face, the look in the eyes. Havelock had been where this man had been – where he was now. The process had been set in motion, the word cautiously put out; word was awaited back at the command post of one. The lethal compromisers had been reached, none having allegiance to anything or anybody except the dollar, the franc, the pound and the Deutschmark. A sliding scale of incentive payments had been circulated, bonuses matching the value of various contributions, the highest, of course, the kill with proof of the kill. Word and method of the target's arrival, sightings at specific locations, alone or with known or unknown associates, a hotel, a café, a *pension*, a rooming house – all had value in terms of immediate payment. A competition had been created among the qualified practitioners of violence, each professional enough to know that one did not lie to the command post. Today's loss was another day's kill.

Sooner or later the man in the window would start getting his responses. A few would be mere speculation based on second-hand information; others would be honest error, which would not be penalized but analysed for what it was, confirmation improbable. Then a single call would come, its authenticity established by a descriptive phrase or a certain reaction – unmistakably the target's – and the command post would have its first breakthrough. A street, a café, a bench perhaps in a children's park on the Seine – the practitioners would have spread out everywhere. The hunt was on, the prize many times a year's income. And when the hunt came to an end, the man in the window would come out of his movable prison. Yes, thought Michael, he had been there. The waiting was the worst part.

He looked at his watch, his hand buried in the refuse. There was a second wire litter basket down the block, on the other side of the hotel's entrance; he wondered if it would be necessary to go to it and continue foraging. He had gone past the hotel twice in a taxi – projecting his movements on foot, calculating his timing – before he had sought out the second-hand clothes shops in Séverin – those and an obscure shop beside the Somme where he had purchased ammunition for the Llama automatic and the Magnum. He had phoned Gravet seven minutes ago and told him the clock was on; the Frenchman would place his call from a booth in the Place Vendome; the crowds would guarantee his untraceable anonymity. What was holding him up? There were so many possibilities. Occupied booths, out-of-order phones, a talkative acquaintance who insisted on prolonging a street corner conversation, all were reasonable assumptions. But whatever the cause of delay, Havelock knew he could not stay where he was any longer. Awkwardly, like an old man in pain – and indeed he was a not-so-young man in pain – he began to push himself up. He would force a deliberately unfocused eye to see what it should not see.

The man in the window whipped his head round. An intrusion had interrupted his concentration on the street; he walked back into the shadows of the room. Gravet had made his call. *Now.*

Michael lifted the satchel off the ground, dropped it into the wire receptacle and rapidly walked diagonally across the pavement towards the short flight of steps that led to the hotel's entrance. With each stride he lessened his stooped posture to return gradually to normal height. As he climbed the concrete steps he placed his hand on the side of his face, his fingers gripping the edge of the woollen cap. No more than eight feet above was the window in which the Soviet VKR officer had been standing only seconds ago, and in seconds he would return. Gravet's call would be brief, professional, in no way could it be construed as a device. There was a possible sighting in the Montparnasse. Was the target injured? Did he walk with a pronounced limp? Whatever answers the Russian gave, the call would be terminated, probably in mid-sentence. If it *was* the target, he was heading for the *Métro*; the hunter would call back.

Inside the dark, musty lobby with the cracked tile floor and the cobwebs spanning the four corners of the ceiling, Havelock took off his cap, flattened the lapels of his dishevelled jacket and ripped the already torn cloth that hung from the bottom of his coat. It was not much of an improvement, but in the dim light and with erect bearing, it was not inappropriate to a hotel that catered for drifters and whores. It was not an establishment which scrutinized its clientele, only the legitimacy of their currency.

It had been Michael's intention to project the image of a man painfully coming out of a long drunk, seeking a bed in which to shake through the final ordeal. It was not necessary; an obese *concierge* behind the cracked marble counter was dozing in a chair, his soft, fat hands folded on his protruding stomach. There was one other person in the lobby: a gaunt old man seated on a bench, a cigarette dangling from his lips below an unkempt grey moustache, his head bent forward as he squinted at a newspaper in his hands. He did not look up.

Havelock dropped the cap on the floor, side-kicked it towards the wall and walked to his left, where there was a narrow staircase, the steps worn smooth from decades of use and neglect, the banister broken in several places. He started up the creaking steps and was relieved that the staircase was short. There were no turns, no mid-point landings; the steps led straight from one level to the next. He reached the first floor and stood motionless, listening. There was no sound other than the distant hum of traffic, punctuated by sporadic shrieks of impatient horns. He looked at the door ten feet away, at the faded painted number, 23. He could discern no vocal undercurrent of a one-sided telephone conversation; the call from Gravet was over and the Soviet VKR officer was back at his window, the elapsed time no more than forty-five seconds. Michael unbuttoned his ragged jacket, reached underneath and gripped the handle of the Magnum. As he pulled the gun out from under his belt, the perforated cylinder caught briefly on the leather; with his thumb he released the safety catch, and started down the dark, narrow hallway towards the door.

A creak in the floorboards, not his, not under him, *behind* him! He spun as the first door on the left beyond the staircase was pulled slowly open. Since it had been left ajar, there had been no sound of a turning knob; the open crack was a line of sight for someone inside. A short, heavy-set man emerged, shoulders and spine against the frame, a weapon in his hand at his side. He raised the gun. Havelock had no time for assessment or appraisal, he could only react. Under different circumstances he might have held up his hand and sharply whispered, a word, a signal, a note of warning to avert a terrible error; instead he fired. The man was blown off his feet, buckling back into the door frame. Michael looked at the gun still gripped in the man's hand. He had been right to shoot; the weapon was a Graz-Burya, the most powerful, accurate automatic produced in Russia. The VKR officer was not alone. And if there was one.

A knob was being turned; it was the door directly across from Room Twenty-three. Havelock lurched to the wall to the right of the frame; the door opened and he spun around, the Magnum raised chest high, prepared to fire or deliver a blow — or drop his arm if it should turn out to be an innocent hotel guest. The man was in a crouch, and held a gun. Havelock crashed the barrel of the Magnum on the man's head. The Russian fell back inside the room; Michael followed and gripped the door to prevent it from slamming shut. He held the crack open less than an inch, stood still and waited. There was silence in the hall, except for the far away sounds of traffic. He backed away from the door, the Magnum levelled at it, his eyes scanning the floor for the man's gun. It was several feet behind the prone, uncon-scious figure; he kicked it forward beside the body, kneeled down and picked it up. It, too, was a Graz-Burya; the detail sent to Paris was equipped with the best. He shoved it into his jacket pocket, reached over and pulled the Russian towards him; the man was limp and would not be conscious for hours.

He got to his feet and left the room. The violent movements had drained him; he leaned against the wall, breathing slowly, deeply, trying to put out of his mind the weakness and pain in his body. He could not stop now. There was the first man in the door beyond the staircase; the door was open. Someone walking past would look inside and have hysterics. Michael pushed himself away from the wall, and silently, on the balls of his thick-soled feet, made his way down the narrow corridor past the staircase. He pulled the door shut and started back towards Room Twenty-three.

He stood facing the barely legible numbers and knew he had to find the strength. There was nothing for it but to depend on the shock of the totally unexpected. He tensed his chest and stepped back from the door, then, leading with his unwounded shoulder, crashed the full weight of his body against the wood. The door splintered and broke open, as the VKR officer pivoted away from the window, his hand reaching for the exposed holster strapped to his belt. He stopped, swiftly thrusting both hands out in front of him, his eyes staring at the huge barrel of the Magnum pointed at his head.

"I believe you were looking for me," said Havelock.

"It appears I trusted the wrong people," answered the Russian quietly in well-accented English.

"But not your own people," interrupted Michael.

"You're special."

"You lost."

"I never ordered your death. They might have."

"Now you're lying, but it doesn't matter. As I said, you lost."

"You're to be commended," mumbled the VKR officer, his eyes straying above Havelock's shoulder to the broken door.

"You didn't hear me. You lost. There's a man in the room across the hall; he won't be attending you."

"I see."

"And another down the way, beyond the staircase. He's dead."

"*Nyet! Molniya!*" The Soviet agent blanched: his fingers were stretched, taut, six inches from his belt.

"I speak Russian, if you prefer."

"It's immaterial," said the startled man. "I'm a graduate of the Massachusetts Institute of Technology."

"Or of the American compound in Novgorod, KGB degree."

"Cambridge, Massachusetts, not Novgorod," objected the Russian, disdain in his voice.

"I forgot. The VKR is an élite corps. A degree from the parent organization might be considered an insult. The untutored and unskilled conferring honours upon its in-house superiors."

"There are no such divisions in the Soviet government."

"My ass."

"This is pointless."

"Yes, it is. What happened at the Costa Brava?"

"I have no idea what you mean."

"You're VKR, Barcelona! The Costa Brava is in your sector! What happened that night of 4 January?"

"Nothing that concerned us."

"*Move!*"

"What?"

"Against the wall!"

It was an outside wall, built of mortar and heavy brick, solid for decades, weight pressing against weight, impenetrable. The Russian moved slowly, haltingly in front of it. Havelock continued.

"I'm so special your sector chief in Moscow doesn't know the truth. But you do. It's why you're here in Paris, why you put out a premium call on me."

"You've been misinformed. It is a crime tantamount to treason to withhold information from our superiors. As to my coming from Barcelona, surely you understand that. It was your last assignment and I was your last counterpart. I had the most up-to-date information on you. Who better to send after you?"

"You're very good. You glide well."

"I've told you nothing you don't know, nothing you could not learn."

"You missed something. Why am I special? Your colleagues at KGB haven't the slightest interest in me. On the contrary, they won't touch me; they consider me a bad text. Yet you say I'm special. The *Voennaya* wants me."

"I won't deny there's a degree of inter-service rivalry, even departmental. Perhaps we learned it from you. You have an abundance of it."

"You haven't answered my question."

"We know certain things our comrades are not aware of."

"Such as?"

"You were placed 'beyond-salvage' by your own government."

"Do you know why?"

"The reasons at this juncture are secondary. We offer refuge."

"The reasons are never secondary," corrected Michael.

"Very well," agreed the Soviet officer reluctantly. "A judgement was made that you were unbalanced."

"On what basis?"

"Pronounced hostility, accompanied by threats, cables. Delusions, hallucinations."

"Because of Costa Brava?"

"Yes."

"Just like that? One day walking around sane, filing reports, honourably retired; the next a cuckoo bird whistling at the moon? Now you're not very good. You're not gliding well at all."

"I'm telling you what I know!" insisted the Russian. "I do not make these determinations, I follow instructions. The premium, as you call it, was to be paid for a meeting between us. Why should it be otherwise? If killing you was the objective, it would be far simpler to pay for your whereabouts and telephone your embassy on the Avenue Gabriel, asking for a specific extension; I can assure you we know it. The information would reach the proper personnel and we are not involved, no possibility of errors leading to future repercussions."

"But by offering me refuge and bringing me in, you take back a trophy your less talented comrades avoided because they thought I was a trap, programmed or otherwise."

"Basically, yes. May we talk?"

"We're talking." Havelock studied the man; he was convincing, quite possibly telling his version of the truth. Refuge or a bullet, which was it? Only the exposure of lies would tell. One had to look for the lies, not a subordinate's interpretation of the truth. In his peripheral vision Michael caught the reflection of a dull mirror above a shabby bureau against the wall; he spoke again. "You'd expect me to deliver information you know I've got."

"We'd be saving your life. The order for 'beyond-salvage' termination will not be rescinded, you know that."

"You're suggesting I defect."

"What choice do you have? How long do you think you can keep running? How many days or weeks will it be before their networks and their computers find you?"

"I'm experienced. I have resources. Perhaps I'm willing to take my chances. Men have been known to disappear not into gulags, but to other places – and live happily ever after. What else can you offer?"

"What are you looking for? Comfort, money, a good life? We offer these. You deserve them."

"Not in your country. I won't live in the Soviet Union."

"Oh?"

"Suppose I told you I've picked out a place. It's thousands of miles away in the Pacific, in the Solomon Islands. I've been there; it's civilized but remote, no one would ever find me. Given enough money, I could live well there."

"Arrangements can be made. I am empowered to guarantee that."

Lie number one. No defector ever left the Soviet Union and the VKR officer knew it.

"You flew into Paris last night. How did you know I was here?"

"Informants in Rome, how else?"

"How did they learn?"

"One doesn't question informants too closely."

"The hell one doesn't."

"*If* they are trusted."

"You ask for a source. You don't leave a station and fly to a city hundreds of miles away without being pretty damn sure the source can be confirmed."

"Very well," said the VKR officer, gliding confidently with the cross-currents again. "There was an investigation; a man was found in Civitavecchia. He said you were on your way to Paris."

"When did you get the word?"

"Yesterday, of course," replied the Russian impatiently.

"When yesterday?"

"Late afternoon. Five-thirty, I believe. Five-thirty-five, to be precise."

Lie number two, the falsehood found in the precision. The decision to head for Paris was forced on him after Col des Moulinets. Eight o'clock at night.

"You're convinced that what I can divulge about our European intelligence operations is of such value to you that you are willing to accept the retaliations that come with defection at my level?"

"Naturally."

"That opinion isn't shared by the directors' committee of the KGB."

"They're fools. Frightened, tired rabbits among the wolves. We'll replace them."

"You're not troubled that I may be programmed? That whatever I tell you could be poison, useless?"

"Not for a moment. It's why you're 'beyond-salvage'."

"Or that I'm paranoid?"

"Never. You're neither paranoid nor hallucinatory. You are what you have always been, a highly intelligent specialist in your field."

Lie number three. Word of his supposed psychotic condition had been spread. Washington believed it; the dead Ogilvie had confirmed it on the Palatine.

"I see," said Havelock, grimacing, feigning pain that needed very little pretence. "I'm so goddamned tired," he said, lowering the Magnum slightly, turning slightly to his left, his eyes millimetres from making contact with the mirror on the wall. "I was shot. I haven't had any sleep. As you said, I just keep running, trying to figure it out . . ."

"What more is there?" asked the Russian, his voice now gliding into compassion. "It's basically an economic, time-saving decision, you know that. Rather than altering codes, networks and sources, they've decided to eliminate the man who knows too much. Sixteen years of service in the field and this is your retirement bonus. 'Beyond-salvage'."

Michael lowered the gun further, his head bent down but his eyes now on the mirror. "I have to think," he whispered. "It's all so crazy, so impossible."

Lie number four – the most telling lie! The Russian went for his gun!

Havelock spun round and fired: the bullet snapped into the wall. The VKR officer grabbed his elbow as blood erupted through his shirt and dripped onto the floor.

"*Levobokec!*" he cried.

"We've only just begun!" said Michael, his voice a roar though still a whisper. He approached the Russian and pushed him against the wall, then removed the exposed weapon from the holster and threw it across the room. "You're too sure of yourself, comrade, too sure of your facts! Never state them so confidently; leave room for error because there *may* be one. You had several."

The Russian answered him with silence, his eyes full of both loathing and resignation. Havelock knew those eyes, knew the combination of hatred and the recognition of mortality; they were intrinsic to the nature of certain men, trained for years to hate and die. By any name they were recognizable: *Gestapo. Nippon Kai. Palestinian Liberationists. Voennaya* . . . And by lesser leagues whose amateur status stopped with arrogance and hate, death no part of their childish bargains, screeching fanatics who marched to the drums of sanctimonious loathing.

Michael returned silence for silence, look for look. And then he spoke.

"Don't waste the adrenalin," he said quietly. "I'm not going to kill you. You're prepared for that; you've been ready for it for years. Damned if I'm going to accommodate you. Instead, I'm going to blow off both your kneecaps – and then your hands. You're not trained to live with the results. No one is, really, especially not your kind. So many routine things'll be beyond you. Simple things. Walking to a door or a locked file cabinet, opening either. Dialling a phone or going to the toilet. Reaching for a gun and pulling a trigger."

The Russian's face went pale and his lower lip began to tremble. "*Nyet*," he whispered hoarsely.

"*Da*," said Havelock. "There's only one way you can stop me. Tell me what happened at the Costa Brava."

"I *told* you! *Nothing!*"

Michael lowered the Magnum and fired into the Soviet's thigh; blood splattered against the wall. The Russian started to scream, collapsing on the floor; Havelock gripped his mouth with his left hand.

"I missed the kneecap. I won't miss now. Either one." He stood up, levelling the weapon downward.

"*No!* Stop!" The VKR officer rolled over, clutching his leg. He was broken; he could accept death, but not what Michael promised him. "I'll tell you what I know."

"*I'll* know if you're lying. My finger's on the trigger, the gun pointed at your right hand. If you lie, you won't have it any more."

"What I told you *is* true. We were not at the Costa Brava that night."

"Your code was broken. Washington broke it. I saw it. I *sent* it!"

"Washington broke nothing. That code was abandoned seven days before the night of the fourth of January. Even if you sent it and we accepted it, we could not have responded. It would have been physically impossible."

"Why?"

"We were nowhere near the area, any of us. We were sent out of the sector." The Russian coughed in pain, his face twisted. "For the period of time in question, all activities were cancelled. We were prohibited from going within twenty miles of the Montebello beach on the Costa Brava."

"*Liar!*"

"No," said the VKR officer, his bleeding leg pulled up under him, his body taut, his eyes staring at Michael. "No, I am not lying. Those were the orders from Moscow."

Book Two

15

It was raining that night in Washington, angry, diagonal sheets of rain driven by erratic winds, making drivers and pedestrians alike mistrust their vision; headlights refracted, blinded in suddenly shifting angles. The chauffeur at the wheel of the limousine heading down 14th Street towards the East Gate of the White House was not immune to the problem. He slammed on his brakes and swerved to avoid an onrushing small car, whose high beams gave the illusion of a huge attacking insect. It was in fact well to his left, on its side of the line, so the manoeuvre proved unnecessary. The chauffeur wondered whether his very important passengers had noticed the error.

"Sorry, sirs," he said, his voice directed at the intercom, his eyes on the rear view mirror and the glass partition that separated him from them.

Neither man responded. It was as if neither had heard him, yet he knew both had; the blue intercom light was on, which meant that his voice was transmitted. The red light, of course, was dark; he could not hear anything being said in the rear seat. The red light was always off, except when instructions were being given, and twice every day the system was checked in the garage before he or any other driver left the premises. It was said that tiny circuit breakers had been installed that tripped at the slightest tampering with the intercom mechanism.

The men who rode in these limousines had been assigned to them by the President of the United States, and the chauffeurs who drove them were continuously subjected to the most stringent security checks. Each of them was unmarried and without children, and each was a combat veteran – proven under fire – with extensive experience in guerrilla warfare and diversionary tactics. The vehicles they drove were designed for maximum protection. The windows could withstand the impact of .45 calibre bullets, homing devices were implanted throughout the undersides, and small jets that released two separate types of gas with a flick of a switch were positioned at all points of the frame – one gas merely numbed and was used for riots and unruly protesters, while the other was a near-lethal dioxide compound, designed for terrorists. The chauffeurs' orders were to guard their passengers with their lives. For their charges held the secrets of the nation; they were the President's closest advisers in times of crisis.

The driver glanced at the dashboard clock. It was nine-twenty, nearly four hours since he had completed his previous assignment, waited for the electronics check back in the garage and left for the night. Thirty-five minutes later he had been having a drink at a restaurant on K Street and was about to order dinner when the jarring one-note signal of his bleeper erupted from its case on his belt. He had telephoned the unlisted number for Security Dispatch and been ordered to the garage immediately: *Aquarius One emergency, Scorpio descending*. Out of context and out of orbit, but the message was clear. The Oval Office had pushed a button; the senior drivers were now on duty, all previous schedules aborted.

Back in the garage he had been mildly surprised to see that only two vehicles had been prepared for transport. He had expected to find six or seven black-stretch Abrahams wheeled out of their docks and ready to roll; instead, there were just two – one ordered to an address in Berwyn Heights, Maryland, and the second – his – to Andrews Airfield to await the arrival of two men being flown in on Army jets from separate islands in the Caribbean. Times had been coordinated; the ETAs were within fifteen minutes of each other.

The younger of the two old men had arrived first, and the driver recognized him instantly; not everyone would have done so. His name was Halyard, like the line on a sailing boat, but his reputation had been made on land. Lt-General Malcolm Halyard: WWII, Korea, Vietnam. The bald soldier had started off commanding platoons and companies in France and across the Rhone, then battalions in Kaesong and Inchon, and, finally, armies in South-east Asia, where the driver had seen him more than once in Danang. He was something of an odd-ball in the upper ranks of the army; he was never known to have held a press conference, but he had been known to bar photographers – military and civilian alike – from wherever he happened to be. "Tightrope" Halyard was considered a brilliant tactician, one of the first to state for the *Congressional Record* that Vietnam was no-win idiocy. He avoided publicity with the same tenacity that he displayed on the battlefield, and his low profile, it was said, appealed to the President.

The retired general had been escorted to the limousine, and after greeting the driver, had waited in the back seat without another word.

The second man had arrived twelve minutes later. He was as far removed from "Tightrope" Halyard as the eagle is from the lion, but both were superb examples of their species. Addison Brooks had been a lawyer, an international banker, a consultant to statesmen, an ambassador and, finally, an elder statesman himself and adviser to presidents. He was the embodiment of the Eastern Establishment aristocracy, the last of the old-school-tie crowd, the ultimate WASP who tempered the image with a swift wit that could be as gentle and compassionate as it could be devastating. He had survived the political wars by exercising the same agility displayed by Halyard on the battlefield. In essence, both men would compromise with reality, but not with principle. This was not, of course, the driver's own judgement; he had read about it in the *Washington Post*, his interest having been drawn to a political column which had analysed the two advisers because he knew the ambassador and had seen the general in Danang. He had driven the ambassador on a number of occasions, and was always flattered that old Brooks remembered his name and had something a little personal to say to him: "Damn it, Jack, don't you ever put on weight? My wife makes me drink my gin with some Godawful diet fruit juice." Which had to be an exaggeration, for the ambassador was a tall, slender man, his silver hair, aquiline features and perfectly-groomed grey moustache making him look more English than American.

540

Tonight, however, there had been no personal greeting at Andrews Field, and no jokes. Instead, Brooks had nodded absently when the driver opened the rear door for him; then he had paused as his eyes made contact with the general inside. At that moment only one word was spoken.

"Parsifal," the ambassador said, his voice low, sombre; it was the sole greeting.

After Brooks had climbed in beside Halyard, they talked briefly, their faces set, glancing frequently at each other, as if asking questions neither could answer. Then they fell silent, or so it appeared, at least, whenever the driver's eyes strayed to the rear view mirror. The few times he had looked at them, as he was looking at them now, both the diplomat and the soldier had been staring straight ahead, neither speaking. Whatever crisis had brought them to the White House, each from an island in the Caribbean, it was obviously beyond discussion.

The driver's memories were stirred as he turned into the short drive that led to the East Gate guardhouse. Like many collegiate athletes whose ability was somewhat greater on the playing field than in the classroom or laboratory, he had had to take a course in musical appreciation at the instigation of his coaches. He had found much of it beyond him. Still, he remembered . . . Parsifal was an opera by Wagner.

The driver of Abraham Seven turned off the Kenilworth Road into the residential section of Berwyn Heights, Maryland. He had been to the house twice before, which was why he was selected for the route tonight despite his previous request not to be given Undersecretary of State Emory Bradford as an assignment again. When Security Dispatch had asked why, he could only answer that he did not like him.

"That doesn't really concern us, Yahoo," had been the reply. "Your likes and dislikes have yet to become policy around here. Just do your job."

Of course that was the point – the job. If part of the job included protecting Bradford's life at a risk to his own, he was not sure he could comply. Fifteen years ago the cold analytical Emory Bradford had been one of the best and the brightest, the new breed of young pragmatists who skewered adversaries right and left in the pursuit of power. And the tragedy at Dallas had done nothing to slow this pursuit; the mourning had been quickly replaced by adjustment to a changed situation. The nation was in peril and those endowed with the capacity to understand the aggressive nature of factionalized communism had to stand firm and rally the forces of strength. The tight-lipped, unemotional Bradford became an impassioned hawk. A game called dominoes was suddenly a theory on which the survival of freedom was based.

A strapping farm boy from Idaho was caught up in the fever. He answered the call; it was his personal statement against the long-haired freaks who burned flags and draft cards and spat on things that were decent and – *American*. Eight months later the farm boy was in the jungles watching friends getting blown away. He saw Arvin troops running from fire fights and their commanders selling rifles and jeeps and whole consignments of battalion rations. He came to understand what was so obvious to everyone but Washington and Command Saigon. The so-called victims of the so-called atheistic hordes didn't give a doodilly shit about anything except

541

their hides and their profits. They were the ones who were spitting and burning everything that could not be traded or sold, and laughing. *Jesus*, were they laughing! At their so-called saviours, the pink-faced, round-eyed suckers who took the fire and the land mines, and lost heads and faces and arms and legs.

And then it happened. The frenzied hawk that was Emory Bradford in Washington saw the light, a different light. In an extraordinary public display of *mea culpa* he appeared before a Senate committee and announced to the nation that something had gone wrong, the brilliant planners – himself included – had erred grievously. He advocated immediate withdrawal; the impassioned hawk became a passionate dove.

He was accorded a standing ovation. While heads and faces and arms and legs were scattered over the jungles, and a farm boy from Idaho was doing his damnedest not to want to die as a prisoner of war. A *standing ovation*, goddamn it!

No, Mr Emory Bradford, I will not risk my life for you. I will not die for you – again.

The large three-storeyed colonial house was set back beyond a manicured lawn that promised a pool and a tennis court hidden somewhere. The best and the brightest also frolicked; it was part of their life style, intrinsic to their worth and their image. The farm boy from Idaho wondered how Undersecretary of State Emory Bradford would behave in a river cage infested with water rats in the Mekong Delta. Probably very well, goddamn it.

The driver reached under the dashboard and pulled out the retractable microphone. He pressed the button and spoke.

"Abraham Seven to dispatch."

"Go ahead, Abraham Seven."

"Have reached location. Please raise cargo by phone."

"Will do, Seven. Good timing. You and Abraham Four should reach Aquarius at about the same time."

"Glad you approve. We try to please."

The three descended in the lift together, the two older men astonished that the conference was to take place in one of the underground strategy rooms and not in the Oval Office. The Undersecretary of State, briefcase in hand, seemed to understand why. The advantages, of course, were found in the equipment. There were computers and projectors that threw images and information on to a huge wall screen, communications devices that linked the White House to just about anybody anywhere in the world, and data processing machines that isolated facts from volumes of useless scholarship. Yet all the sophisticated equipment in Washington was in itself useless without a breakthrough. Had it happened? wondered the older advisers as each looked questioningly at the other. Had the breakthrough come? If it had, the summons from the President had given no indication of it. Instead, the opposite had been conveyed. "Scorpio descending" was akin to catastrophe, and each felt the tightening of his stomach muscles as the lower level was reached and the lift door opened onto the pristine white-walled corridor. They emerged and walked in unison down the hallway towards the assigned room and the President of the United States.

President Charles Berquist greeted each man curtly, and each understood. It was not the nature of the stocky Minnesotan to be cold – tough, yes, very tough – but not cold; he was frightened. He gestured impatiently at the raised U-shaped conference table at the end of the room; it faced the wall screen thirty feet away where images would be projected. The three men walked up the two steps with the President and took their places at the table; at each place was a small Tensor lamp angled down on a note pad. Addison Brooks sat on Berquist's right, General Halyard on his left, and the younger Emory Bradford beyond the statesman, one chair removed so that he could address the three. It was a pecking order rooted in logic; most of the questions would be directed at Bradford, as he in turn would ask most of the questions directed at anyone brought in for interrogation. Below the U-shaped table and facing it midway to the screen was another table, smaller, rectangular, with two swivel chairs that enabled whoever sat in them to turn and watch the images projected on the wall.

"You look tired, Mr President," said Brooks, once all were seated and the lamps adjusted.

"I'm tired," agreed Berquist. "I'm also sorry to bring you and Mal back to this rotten weather."

"Insofar as you saw fit to call us back," commented Halyard sincerely, "I'd say the weather is the least of our problems."

"You're right." The President pressed a button embedded in the table on his left. "The first slide, if you please." The overhead lights were extinguished and only the Tensors remained on; the photographs of four men appeared on a split screen at the end of the room. "Do you know any of these men?" asked Berquist, then added hastily. "The question's not for Emory. He does."

The ambassador and the general glanced at Bradford, then turned to the photographs. Addison Brooks spoke. "The fellow on the upper right is named Stern. David or Daniel Stern, I believe. He's over at State, isn't he? One of the European specialists, bright, analytical, a good man."

"Yes," confirmed Berquist quietly. "What about you, Mal? Recognize anybody up there?"

"I'm not sure," said the retired general, squinting at the screen. "The one below this Stern, lower right. I think I've seen him before."

"You have," said Bradford. "He spent time at the Pentagon."

"I can't picture the uniform, the rank."

"He didn't wear one, have one. He's a doctor; he testified before a number of panels on POW trauma. You were seated on two or three, I believe."

"Yes, of course, I remember now. He's a psychiatrist."

"One of the leading authorities on stress-behaviour," said Bradford, watching the two old men.

"What was that?" the ambassador asked urgently. "Stress-behaviour?"

The words had startled the advisers. The old soldier leaned forward. "Is there a connection?" he demanded of the Undersecretary.

"To Parsifal?"

"Who the hell else would I mean? *Is* there?"

"There is, but that's not it."

"What isn't?" asked Brooks apprehensively.

"Miller's specialization. That's his name. Dr Paul Miller. We don't think his link to Parsifal has anything to do with his studies of stress."

"Thank *God*," muttered the general.

"Then what is?" the elder diplomat pressed impatiently.

"May I, Mr President?" asked Bradford, his eyes on the Commander in Chief. Berquist nodded silently; the Undersecretary turned to the screen and the photographs. "The two men on the left, top and bottom, respectively, are John Philip Ogilvie, and Victor Alan Dawson."

"Dawson's a lawyer," interrupted Addison Brooks. "I've never met him but I've read a number of his briefs. He's brilliant on international treaty negotiations. He has a gut feeling for foreign legal systems and their nuances."

"Brilliant," agreed the President softly.

"The last man," continued Bradford rapidly, "was no less an expert in his line of work. He was an undercover agent for nearly twenty years, one of the most knowledgeable tacticians in the field of covert operations."

The Undersecretary's use of the past tense was not lost on the two advisers. They looked at each other, and then at President Berquist. The Minnesotan nodded.

"They're dead," said the President, bringing his right hand to his forehead, his fingers nervously massaging his brows. "All of them. Ogilvie died four days ago in Rome, a misplaced bullet, the circumstances acceptable. The others were not accidents; they were killed here. Dawson and Stern simultaneously, Miller twenty miles away at the same time."

The ambassador leaned forward, his eyes on the screen. "Four men," he said anxiously. "One an expert in European affairs and policies, another a lawyer whose work was almost exclusively in international law, the third a veteran undercover agent with broad tactical experience, and the fourth a psychiatrist acknowledged to be a leading specialist in stress-behaviour."

"An odd collection of targets," concluded the old soldier.

"They're connected, Mal," said Brooks. "To each other before Parsifal. Am I correct, Mr President?"

"Let Emory explain," replied Berquist. "He has to take the heat, so let him explain."

Bradford's glance conveyed the fact that the explanation might be his to give but responsibility should be shared. Nevertheless, his slow intake of breath and the quiet delivery of his voice also indicated that he expected the worst.

"These men were the strategists of Consular Operations."

"Costa Brava!" The name exploded in a whisper from the ambassador's lips.

"They peeled it away and found us," said Halyard, his eyes filled with a soldier's angry acceptance. "And they paid for it."

"Yes," agreed Bradford, "but we don't know how it happened."

"How they were *killed*?" asked the general incredulously.

"We know that," replied the Undersecretary. "Very professionally, the decision made quickly."

"Then what don't you understand?" Brooks was annoyed.

"The connection to Parsifal."

"But you said there *was* a connection," insisted the elder statesman. "Is there or isn't there?"

"There must be. We just can't follow it."

"I can't follow you," said the soldier.

"Start from the beginning, Emory," interrupted the President. "As you understand the beginning. From Rome."

Bradford nodded. "Five days ago the strategists received a priority cable from our conduit in Rome, a Lieutenant-Colonel Baylor – cover-name Brown. He oversees the clandestine activities network."

"Larry Baylor?"

"Yes, General."

"One hell of a fine officer. Give me twenty Negroes like him you can throw out the War College."

"Colonel Baylor's black, Mr Ambassador."

"Apparently, Mr Undersecretary."

"For Christ's sake, Emory," said Berquist.

"Yes, Mr President. To continue, Colonel Baylor's cable referred to a meeting he had with –" Bradford paused. He delivered the name reluctantly, "Michael Havelock."

"Costa Brava," muttered the soldier quietly.

"Parsifal," added Brooks, halting briefly, then continuing, his words a protest. "But Havelock was ruled out. After the clinic and his separation, he was watched, tested, his every move placed under what I believe is called a microscope. We were assured there was nothing, absolutely *nothing*."

"Less than nothing," agreed the man from State. "Under controlled circumstances he accepted a teaching position – an assistant professorship – at Concord University in New Hampshire. To all intents and purposes, he was completely out and we were back with the original scenario."

"What changed it?" asked the soldier. "What changed Havelock's status?"

Again Bradford paused, once more his delivery reluctant. "The Karras woman," he said quietly. "She surfaced; he saw her. In Rome."

The silence around the table conveyed the shock. The faces of the two old men hardened, both pairs of eyes boring into the Undersecretary, who accepted the looks with granite resignation. Finally, the ambassador spoke. "When did this happen?"

"Ten days ago."

"Why weren't we informed, Mr President?" continued Brooks, his eyes still on Bradford.

"Quite simply," replied the Undersecretary before the President could speak, his eyes locked with the statesman's, "because *I* wasn't informed."

"I find that unacceptable."

"Intolerable," added the old soldier sharply. "What the hell are you running over there?"

"An extremely efficient organization that responds to input. In this case, perhaps too efficient, too responsive."

"Explain that," ordered Halyard.

"These four men," said Bradford, gesturing at the projected photographs of the dead strategists, "were convinced beyond doubt that the Karras woman was killed at Costa Brava. How could they think otherwise? We played everything out – *carried* everything out – down to the smallest detail. Nothing was left to speculation; her death was witnessed by Havelock, later confirmed by bloodstained clothing. We wanted it accepted and no one questioned it, least of all Havelock himself."

"But she surfaced," insisted Halyard. "You say he *saw* her. I presume that information was in Colonel Baylor's cable."

"Yes."

"Then why wasn't it reported immediately?" demanded Brooks.

"Because they didn't believe it," answered Bradford. "They thought Havelock was crazy – hallucinating crazy, the real thing. They sent Ogilvie to Rome, which in itself was extraordinary, indicating how serious they considered the situation to be. Baylor confirmed it. He said Ogilvie told him Havelock had gone over the edge, seeing things that weren't there, the hallucinations brought on by deep, latent hostilities and years of pressure. He simply exploded; at least that's what Ogilvie implied."

"That'd be Miller's judgement," interrupted the President. "It's the only one he could have arrived at when you think of it."

"Havelock's behaviour deteriorated rapidly," continued the Undersecretary. "He threatened to expose past and present covert operations, which would have compromised us all over Europe, if he wasn't given answers, explanations. He even sent disrupting cables to show what he could do. The strategists took him very seriously. Ogilvie was in Rome either to bring Havelock back . . . or to kill him."

"Instead, he was killed himself," said the soldier. A statement.

"Tragically. Colonel Baylor was covering Ogilvie's meeting with Havelock on the Palatine Hill; it was an isolated area. There was an argument, a premature eruption of nerve gas triggered by Ogilvie and, when the device failed, Havelock went after him with a gun. As Baylor tells it, he waited until he couldn't wait any longer. He fired at the precise moment he believed Havelock was about to kill Ogilvie, and apparently he was right. Ogilvie must have felt the same thing; at that same moment he lunged up and caught the bullet. It's all in Baylor's report, available to you both, of course."

"Those were the acceptable circumstances, Mr President?" asked Brooks.

"Only in terms of explanation, Addison."

"Naturally," said Halyard, nodding, looking at Bradford. "If those are Larry Baylor's words, I don't need the report. How's he taking it? That buck doesn't like to lose or goof up."

"He was severely wounded in his right hand. It was shattered and may not come back. Naturally, it'll curtail his activities."

"Don't wash him out; it'd be a mistake. Put him behind a field desk."

"I'll recommend that to the Pentagon, General."

"Let's get back to the Cons Op strategists," said the statesman. "It's still not clear to me why they didn't report Colonel Baylor's information, especially the reasons behind Havelock's actions – those 'disrupting cables', I believe you called them. Incidentally, how disrupting were they?"

546

" 'Alarming' is a better word; 'false-alarming' better still. One message came here – in a recent sixteen-hundred priority cipher – stating that there was a deep-cover Soviet agent in the White House. Another was sent to Congressional Oversight; it claimed there was CIA corruption in Amsterdam. In both instances the use of the cipher and naming names in Amsterdam obviously lent authority to the data."

"Any substance?" asked the soldier.

"None whatsoever. But the reactions were volatile. The strategists knew they could get worse."

"All the more reason why they should have reported Havelock's motives," insisted Brooks.

"They may have," answered Bradford softly. "To someone. We'll get to that."

"Why they were killed? What their connection is to Parsifal?" The general lowered his voice. "To Costa Brava?"

"There was no 'Costa Brava' until we invented it, Mal," said the President. "But that, too, has to be told in sequence. It's the only way we can make sense out of it . . . if there *is* any sense."

"It never should have happened," interjected the silver-haired statesman. "We had no right."

"We had no *choice*, Mr Ambassador," said Bradford, leaning forward. "Secretary of State Matthias built the case against the Karras woman; we know that. His objective, as near as we can determine, was to remove Havelock from service, but we could never be certain. Their friendship was strong, going back years, their family ties stronger, reaching back to Prague. Was Havelock part of Matthias's plans or not? Was a willing player following orders, pretending to do what others would call perfectly understandable, or was he the unknowing victim of a terrible manipulation? We had to find out."

"We *did* find out," protested Addison Brooks quietly, indignantly. "At the clinic in Virginia. He was probed with everything doctors and laboratories can probe with; he knew absolutely nothing. As you said, we were back to the original scenario, completely in the dark ourselves. Why did Matthias want him out? It's the unanswered, perhaps now unanswerable, question. When we understood that, we should have told Havelock the truth."

"We couldn't." The Undersecretary leaned back in the chair. "Jenna Karras had disappeared; we had no idea whether she was alive or dead. Under the circumstances Havelock would have raised questions that cannot be raised outside the Oval Office – or a room like this."

"Questions," added the President of the United States, "which, if exposed, would plunge the world into a global nuclear war in a matter of hours. If the Soviet Union or the People's Republic of China knew this government was out of control, ICBMs would be launched from both hemispheres, a thousand submarines poised in both oceans for secondary tactical strikes – obliteration. And we *are* out of control."

Silence.

"There's someone I'd like you to meet," said Bradford finally. "I had him flown in from an Alpine pass called Col des Moulinets. He's from Rome."

"Nuclear war," whispered the President as he pressed the button on the huge, curved desk and the screen went dark.

16

Havelock drew two lines through the seventeenth and eighteenth names on the list, hung up the telephone on the wall and left the shabby café in Montmartre. Two calls per phone were all he permitted himself. Sophisticated electronic scanners could pick up a location in a matter of minutes and, should any of those he reached be patched into equipment at the American embassy, it would be no different from his calling the Paris conduit of Cons Op and setting the time for his own execution. Two calls per phone, each phone a minimum of six blocks from the previous one, no conversation lasting more than ninety seconds. He had worked through half the list, but now the rest of the names would have to wait. It was nearly nine o'clock, the gaudy lights of Montmartre were battering the streets with frenzied eruptions of colour that matched the frantic cacophony of the district's night-time revels. And he was to meet Gravet in an alley off the rue Norvins. The art critic had spent the afternoon tracking down anyone and everyone in his peculiar world who might have knowledge of Jenna Karras.

In a way, so had Michael, but his initial work had been cerebral. He had retrieved his clothes from a *Métro* locker, purchased basic toiletries, a note pad and a ballpoint pen, and taken a room at a cheap hotel around the corner from *La Couronne Nouvelle*. He reasoned that if the wounded VKR officer raised help, he would not think to send his killers down the street for the target. Havelock had shaved and bathed, and now lay on the decrepit bed, his body enjoying a respite but not his mind. He had gone back in time, disciplining his memory, recalling every moment he and Jenna had shared in Paris. He had approached the exercise academically, as a graduate student might doggedly follow a single development chronologically through a chaotic period in history. He and Jenna, Jenna and he; where they had gone, what they had seen, whom they had spoken with, all in order of sequence. Each place and scene had a location and a reason for their being there; finally, each face that had any meaning had a name, or if not a specific name, the identity of someone who knew him or her.

After two hours and forty minutes of probing, he had sat up, reached for the note pad and pen he had placed on a bedside chair and begun his list. A half hour later it was complete – as complete as his memory permitted – and he relaxed, back on the bed, knowing that much-needed sleep would come, knowing also that the clock in his mind would awaken him when daylight faded. It did. And minutes later he was out in the streets, going from one telephone box to another, one café with a *téléphone* sign in the window to the next, each instrument six blocks away from the last.

He began the conversations quickly but casually, and kept his ears primed to pick up any telltale signs of alarm in the responses. In each case his approach was the same; he was to have met Jenna that noon at the Meurice bar, each having flown into Paris from a different city, but his plane had been hours late. And since Jenna had mentioned the person's name frequently – fondness implied – Michael wondered if she had called him or her, perhaps looking for an afternoon companion in a city she barely knew.

Most were mildly surprised to hear from Havelock, especially so casually, and even more surprised that Jenna Karras would have remembered their names, much less having recalled them with affection; they were by and large only brief acquaintances. However, in no instance was there the slightest hesitation other than the normal caution required when confronted with the unexpected. Eighteen names. Nothing. Where had she gone? What was she doing? She could not go underground in Paris, not without his finding her; she had to know that. *Christ, where are you?*

He reached the rue Ravignan and began the steep ascent up the Montmartre hill, passing the dark, old houses that were once the homes of legends, emerged on the small square that was the Place Clément and started down the rue Norvins. The street was crowded, the revels of would-be Bohemians fuelled by the genuine residents who dressed their roles and later went home to count their profits. The alley Gravet had described was just before the narrow rue des Saules; he could see the break in the row of ancient buildings up ahead and walked faster.

The old brick alleyway was dark and empty. Havelock went in, his right hand instinctively edging towards the break in his jacket and belt where the Magnum was awkwardly in place. Gravet was late, a discourtesy the critic himself found abhorrent. What had happened?

Michael found a shadowed doorway in the dimly lit thoroughfare; he leaned against the brick frame, took out a cigarette and struck a match. As he cupped the flame his mind leaped back to the Palatine Hill, to a book of matches and a man who had tried to save his life, not take it. A dying man who had died only moments later, knowing there was betrayal at the highest levels of his government.

There was a sudden commotion out in the rue Norvins, a brief flare-up of tempers as two men collided. Then a tall, slender man stood momentarily erect, and let forth a stream of invective in French. His much younger, stockier adversary made a sullen comment about the man's ancestry and moved along. The injured party smoothed his lapels, turned to his left and entered the alley. Gravet had arrived, not without his customary *élan*.

"*Merde!*" the critic spat out, seeing Havelock walk out of the shadows into the dim light. "It's those filthy, ragged field jackets they wear! You just know they dribble when they eat and their teeth are yellow. God knows when they last bathed or spoke civilly. Sorry to be late."

"It's only a few minutes. I just got here."

"I'm late. I intended to be in the rue Norvins a half hour ago to make sure you weren't followed."

"I wasn't."

"Yes, you'd know that, wouldn't you?"

"I'd know. What kept you?"

"A young man I've cultivated who works in the catacombs of the Quai d'Orsay."

"You're honest."

"And you misinterpret." Gravet moved to the wall, turning his head back and forth, looking at both entrances of the alley; he was satisfied. He clasped his hands below his waist, arms extended, a balletic priest about to issue a priestly admonition. "Since you called after your business at the *Couronne Nouvelle* – a call, incidentally, I wasn't sure you'd ever make – I've been in touch with every conceivable contact who might know something about a lone woman in Paris looking for sanctuary, or papers, or secret transportation, and no one could help. It was really quite illogical; after all there are only so many sources of illegal machinations, and precious few I'm not aware of. I even checked the Italian districts, thinking her escorts from Col des Moulinets might have provided her with a name or two. Nothing . . . Then it occurred to me. *Illegal* efforts? Perhaps I was searching in the wrong areas. Perhaps, instead, such a woman might seek more legitimate assistance, without necessarily detailing her illegitimate reasons. After all, she was an experienced field operative. She had to know – or know of – certain personnel in allied governments if only through you."

"The Quai d'Orsay."

"*Naturellement*. But the undersides, the catacombs, where distinctly unpublicized conveniences had to exist for you."

"If they did, I'm not aware of them. I crossed paths with a number of people in the ministries but I never heard of the catacombs."

"London's Foreign Office calls them Clearing Centres. Your own State Department refers to them less subtly. Division of Diplomatic Transfers."

"Immunity," said Havelock. "Did you find something?"

"My young friend spent the last several hours tracing it down. I told him the timing was advantageously narrow. If anything happened, it could only have happened today. So he returned to his little cave after the dinner hour on some pretext or other and riffled through the day's security duplicates. He thinks he may have found it, but he can't be certain and neither can I. However, you might be able to make the connection."

"What is it?"

"At ten forty-five this morning there was a memorandum from the *Ministère des Affaires Etrangères* ordering an open identity. Subject: white female, early thirties, languages: Czech, Russian, Serbo-Croatian, cover name and statistics requested immediately. Now, I realize there are dozens . . ."

"What section at the ministry?" interrupted Havelock.

"Four. Section Four."

"Régine Broussac," said Havelock. "Madame Régine Broussac. First Assistant Deputy, Section Four."

"That's the connection. It's the name and signature on the request."

"She's twenty-ninth on my list, twenty-ninth out of thirty-one. We saw her – *I* saw her – for less than a minute on the street almost a year ago. I barely introduced Jenna. It doesn't make sense; she hardly knows her, *doesn't* know her."

"Were the circumstances of your seeing her a year ago notable?"

"I suppose so. One of their people was a double agent at the French embassy in

Bonn; he made periodic flights to the East by way of Luckenwalde. We found him on the wrong side of Berlin. At a meeting of the *Nachrichtgeheimdienst*."

"The Moscow puppet's offspring of the SS. I'd say quite notable." Gravet paused, unfolding his hands. "This Broussac. She's an older woman, isn't she? Years ago a heroine of the *Résistance?*"

"She and her husband, yes. He was taken by the Gestapo; what they found of him wasn't pleasant."

"But she carried on."

"Yes."

"Did you, perhaps, tell any of this to your friend?"

Havelock thought back as he drew on the cigarette, then dropped it, crushing it under foot. "Probably. Régine's not always easy to take; she can be abrupt, caustic, some call her a bitch, but she's not. She *had* to be tough."

"Then let me ask you another question, the answer to which I vaguely know, but it's based merely on rumour; nothing I've read that pretended to be official." The critic folded his hands again. "What prompted your friend to do what she did, to live the sort of life she led with you and, obviously, before you?"

"Nineteen-sixty-eight," replied Havelock flatly.

"The Warsaw bloc invasion?"

"The *černý den* of August. The black days. Her parents had died, and she was living in Ostrava with her two older brothers, one married. Both were Dubček activists, the younger a student, the older an engineer who was forbidden any meaningful work by the Novotny regime. When the tanks rolled in, the younger brother was killed in the streets, the older one rounded up by advance Soviet troops for 'interrogation'. He was crippled for life – arms and legs – almost helpless. He blew his brains out and his wife disappeared. Jenna travelled to Prague, where no one knew her, and went underground. She knew whom to reach, what she wanted to do."

Gravet nodded, his chiselled face drawn in the dim light, the lines deep. "The people who do what you do, quietly, so efficiently, you all have different stories, yet common themes run through them. Violence, pain . . . loss. And genuine revenge."

"What did you expect? Only ideologues can afford to shout; we've generally got other things on our minds. It's why we're sent in first. It doesn't take much to make us efficient."

"Or to recognize one another, I imagine."

"Under certain circumstances, yes. We don't make too much of it. What's your point?"

"The Broussac woman. Your friend from the Costa Brava would remember her. A husband, brothers, pain, loss . . . a woman alone. Such a woman would remember . . . another woman . . . who carried on."

"She obviously did, I just wouldn't have thought so." Havelock nodded silently. "You're right," he said quietly. "Thanks for giving it perspective. Of course she would."

"Be careful, Michael."

"Of what?"

"Genuine revenge. There must be a *sympathie* between them. She could turn you over to your own, trap you."

"I'll be careful; so will she. What else can you tell me about the memorandum? Was a destination mentioned?"

"No, she could be going anywhere. That will be fixed at *Etrangères* and kept quiet."

"What about her cover? A name?"

"That was processed and beyond my young friend's eyes, at least this evening. Perhaps tomorrow he can pry into files that are locked tonight."

"Too late. You said the memorandum asked for an immediate response. That passport's been mocked up and issued. She's on her way out of France. I have to move quickly."

"What's one day? Twelve hours from now perhaps we can find a name. You can call the airlines on an emergency basis and they'll check their manifests. You'll know where she's gone."

"But not how."

"*Je ne comprends pas.*"

"Broussac. If she's done this much for Jenna, she'll do more. She wouldn't leave her on her own at an airport somewhere. Arrangements were made. I have to know what they are."

"And you think she'll tell you?"

"She must." Havelock buttoned his loose-fitting jacket and pulled the lapels up around his neck. The alley was a tunnel for the damp breezes from below, and there was a chill. "One way or the other, she has to tell me. Thanks, Gravet, I owe you."

"Yes, you do."

"I'll see Broussac tonight and leave in the morning. one way or the other. But before I go, there's a bank here in Paris where I've got a safety deposit box; I'll clean it out and leave an envelope for you there. Call it part payment. It's the Banque Germaine on the Avenue Georges Cinq."

"You're most considerate, but is it wise? In all modesty, I'm something of a public figure and must be careful in my associations. Someone there might know you."

"Not by any name you've ever heard of."

"Then what name shall I use?"

"None. Just say the 'gentleman from Texas'; he's left an envelope for you. If it makes you feel any better, say you've never met me. I'm negotiating the purchase of a painting for an anonymous buyer in Houston."

"And if there are complications?"

"There won't be. You know where I'm going tonight, and by extension, tomorrow."

"At the last, we're professionals, aren't we, Michael?"

"I wouldn't have it any other way. It's cleaner." Havelock extended his hand. "Thanks again. You know the help you've been. I won't belabour it."

"You can forget about the envelope, if you like," said Gravet, shaking hands, studying Michael's face in the shadows. "You may need the money, and my expenses were minimal. I can always collect on your next trip to Paris."

"Don't change the rules, we've lived too long by them. But I appreciate the vote of confidence."

"You were always civilized, and I don't understand any of this business. Why her? Why you?"

"I wish to God I knew."

"That's the key, isn't it? Something you *do* know."

"If it is, I haven't the vaguest idea what it could be. Goodbye, Gravet."

"*Au 'voir*. I really don't want the envelope, *Mikhail*. Come back to Paris. You owe me." The distinguished critic turned and disappeared up the alley.

There was no point in being evasive with Régine Broussac; she would sense the evasion instantly, the coincidence of timing being too unbelievable. On the other hand, to give her the advantage of naming the rendezvous was equally foolish; she would stake out the area with personnel the Quai d'Orsay had no idea were on its payroll. Broussac was tough, knowing when and when not to involve her government, and depending upon what Jenna had told her, she might consider any dealings with an unbalanced retired American field officer more suited to treatment by unofficial methods. There were no checks and balances in those methods; they were dangerous because there was no line of responsibility, only diverted monies that no one cared to acknowledge. Drones by any other names or payments were first cousins to the practitioners of violence – whether employed by Rome in Col des Moulinets or by a VKR officer in a cheap hotel on the rue Etienne. All were essentially lethal, it was merely a question of degree, and all should be avoided unless one was the employer. Havelock understood; he had to get Broussac alone, and to do that, he had to persuade her he was not dangerous – to her – and might even have information that could be extraordinarily valuable.

An odd thought struck him as he descended the endless steps of Montmartre. He was talking to himself about the truth. He would tell her part of it, but not all of it. Liars twisted the truth and she might listen to their version of it, not his.

She was in the Paris telephone book. Rue Losserand.

" . . . I've never given you wrong information and I'm not going to start tonight. But it's out of sanction. Way out. To judge just how far, use someone else's name at the Quai d'Orsay and call the embassy. Ask about my status, directing the inquiry to the senior attaché of Consular Operations. Say I called you from somewhere in the south and wanted to set up a meeting. As an official of a friendly government, request instructions. I'll call you back in ten minutes, not on this phone, of course."

"Of course. Ten minutes."

"Régine?"

"Yes?"

"Remember Bonn."

"Ten minutes."

Havelock walked south to Berlioz Square, checking his watch frequently, knowing he would add an additional five to seven minutes beyond the stated ten. Stretching a call-back under tension often exposed more than the recipient intended to reveal.

There was a *cabine* on the corner, a young woman inside screaming into the phone, gesturing frantically. In a fit of temper, she slammed down the receiver and stalked out of the booth.

"*Vache!*" exclaimed the angry girl as she passed Havelock, furiously adjusting the shoulder strap of her large bag.

He opened the door and walked in; the extended stretch-time had reached nine minutes. He made the call and listened.

"Yes?" Broussac's voice broke off the first ring. She was anxious; she had reached the embassy.

"Did you speak to the attaché?"

"You're late. You said ten minutes."

"Did you speak to him?"

"Yes. I'll meet you. Come to my flat as soon as you can."

"Sorry. I'll call you back in a little while."

"*Havelock!*"

He hung up and walked out of the box, his eyes scanning the street for a vacant taxi.

Twenty-five minutes later he was in another *cabine*, the numbers indistinguishable in the shadows. He struck a match and dialled.

"*Yes!*"

"Take the *Métro* to the Bercy station and walk up into the street. Several blocks down on the right is a row of warehouses. I'll be in the area. Come alone, because I'll know if you don't. And if you don't, I won't show."

"This is *ridiculous*! A lone woman at night in Bercy!"

"If there's anyone around at this hour, I'll warn him about you."

"Preposterous! What are you *thinking* of?"

"A year ago in another street," said Michael. "Of Bonn." He lowered the phone into the cradle.

The area was deserted, the row of warehouses dark, the street lights dim, the wattage low by municipal decree. It was a favourable hour and location for a drop that entailed more than a pick up or an exchange of merchandise. A conversation could be held without the din of crowded streets or the jostling of impatient pedestrians, and unlike a café or a city park, there were few places where an unknown observer could conceal himself. The few residents who emerged from the lighted cavern of the *Métro* up the street could be watched, hesitation or sudden disappearance noted; a stray car could be seen blocks away. The complete advantage was found, of course, in being there at the rendezvous before it was established. He was; he left the box and started across the Boulevard de Bercy.

Two trucks were parked, one behind the other at the kerb in front of a loading platform. Their open planked carriers were empty, stationary symbols of an early morning call for the drivers. He would wait between the two vehicles, the sightlines in either direction clear. Régine Broussac would come; the agitated huntress, prodded and provoked, would be unable to resist the unexplained.

Eleven separate times he heard the muted rumble of the underground trains and felt the vibrations in the concrete and earth beneath him. Starting with the sixth, he concentrated on the *Métro's* entrance; she could not have arrived before it did. However, radio dispatch was commonplace and rapid; only minutes after his final call he had begun to study the street, the infrequent cars, the less frequent bicycles. He saw nothing that alarmed him, and the most insignificant intrusion would have done so.

The twelfth rumble stopped, the faint vibrations still echoing underfoot, and by the time the below-ground thunder commenced again he could see her climbing up out of the steps; her short, broad figure emerging from the brighter light into the dimly lit street. A couple preceded her; Michael watched them carefully. They were elderly, older than Broussac, their pace slow and deliberate; they would be of no value to her. They turned left, around the squared iron latticework of the entrance and away from the trucks and the warehouses; they were no part of a night unit. Régine continued forward, with the hesitant stride of an apprehensive older woman aware of her vulnerability, her head turning slowly, reluctantly, at each odd noise, real and imagined. She passed under a street light and Havelock remembered; her skin was as grey as her short-cropped hair, testimony to years of unacknowledged torments, yet her face was softened by wide blue eyes as often expressive as they were clouded. As she passed through the light into the shadows, Gravet's words came back to Havelock: "*Violence, pain, loss*". Régine Broussac had lived through it all and survived – quiet, wary, silently tough and in no way beaten. She revelled in the secret, unseen powers her government had given her; it helped her get even. Michael understood; after all, she was one of them. A survivor.

She came alongside him on the pavement. He called out softly from between the trucks. "Régine."

She stopped, standing motionless, her eyes straight ahead, not looking at him. She said, "Is it necessary to hold a weapon on me?"

"I have no gun aimed at you. I have a gun, but it's not in my hand."

"*Bien!*" Broussac spun around, her handbag raised. An explosion blew a hole through the fabric, and the concrete and stone shattered beneath Havelock's feet, fragments of rock and cement piercing his trousers, scraping his flesh. "For what you did to Jenna *Karras!*" shouted the woman, her grey face contorted. "Do not move! One step, one gesture, and I will put a hole in your throat!"

"What are you *doing?*"

"What have you *done?* Who do you work for *now?*"

"Myself, goddamn you! Myself and *Jenna!*" Havelock raised his hand, an instinctive move, but no less a plea. It was not accepted.

A second explosion came from the shattered bag, the bullet grazing his outer palm, ricocheting off the truck's metal, whining out into the night.

"*Arrêtez!* I'd as soon deliver a corpse as a breathing body. Perhaps more so in your case, *cochon.*"

"Deliver to whom?"

"You said you would call me 'in a little while' – were they not your words? Well, in a little while several colleagues of mine will be here, a time span I was willing to risk. In less than thirty minutes you would have felt secure; you would have shown yourself. When they arrive we'll drive to a house out in the countryside where we shall have a session with you. Then we'll give you to the Gabriel. They want you very badly. They called you dangerous, that's all I had to know . . . with what I knew."

"Not to *you*! I'm dangerous to *them*, not you!"

"What do you take me for? Take *us* for?"

"You saw Jenna. You helped her – "

"I saw her. I listened to her. I heard the truth."

"As she believes it, not as it *is*! Hear *me*! Listen to *me*!"

"You'll talk under the proper conditions. You know what they are as well as I do."

"I don't need chemicals, you bitch! You won't hear anything different!"

"We'll follow procedures," said Broussac, removing her hand and the gun from the ruptured bag. "Move out of there," she continued, gesturing with the weapon. "You're standing in the shadows. I don't like it."

Of course she didn't like it, thought Havelock, watching the old woman blink her eyes. As with many ageing people night was no friend to vision. It accounted for her constantly moving head as she walked away from the lighted entrance of the *Métro*; she had been as concerned with the unexpected shadows as with sounds. He had to keep her talking, direct some part of her concentration.

"You think the American embassy will tolerate what you're doing?" said Michael, stepping out of the patterned shadow created by the slats of the open truck and the spill of the street lamps.

"There'll be no international incident; we had no alternative but to sedate you. In their words, you're dangerous."

"They won't accept that and you know it."

"They'll have little choice. The Avenue Gabriel has been alerted that a situation of extreme abnormality exists in which a former American intelligence officer – a specialist in clandestine activities – may be attempting to compromise an official of the Quai d'Orsay. The anticipated confrontation will take place twenty miles from Paris, near Argenteuil, and the Americans are requested to have a vehicle with armed personnel in the vicinity. A radio frequency has been established. We shall turn over an American problem to the Americans once we learn the nature of the extortion. We protect the interests of our government. Perfectly acceptable, even generous."

"Christ, you're thorough."

"Very. I've known men like you. And women; we used to shave their heads. I despise you."

"Because of what she told you?"

"Like you, I know when I've heard the truth. She did not lie."

"I agree. Because she believes it all – just as I did. And I was wrong – *God*, was I wrong – just as she's wrong now. We were used, both of us *used*."

"By your own people? For what purpose?"

"I don't *know*!"

She was listening, her concentration beginning to split. She could not help herself, the unexplored was too compelling.

"Why do you think I reached you?" he asked. "For Christ's sake, if I had the

556

leverage to find you, I could have by-passed you! I don't need you, Régine. I could have learned what I wanted to learn without you. I called you because I trusted you!"

Broussac blinked, the grey flesh around her eyes wrinkling in thought. "You'll have your chance to talk . . . under the proper conditions."

"Don't do this!" cried Michael, taking a short step forward. She did not fire; she did not move her gun. "You've set it in motion; you'll have to turn me over! They know it's me and you'll be forced to. Your friends'll insist. They're not going to go down with you, no matter what you hear from me – under proper conditions!"

"Why should we go down?"

"Because the embassy is being lied to. By people way the hell up!"

The old woman's eyes now blinked rapidly as she flinched. She had not fired when he moved only seconds ago.

Now!

Havelock lunged forward, his right arm extended, rigid, as straight as an iron bar, his left hand under his wrist. He made contact with the gun, sweeping it aside as a third explosion broke the silence of the deserted street. With his left hand he grabbed the barrel and ripped it out of her grip, then slammed her against the wall of the warehouse.

"*Cochon! Traitre!*" screamed Broussac, her grey face twisted. "*Kill* me! You'll learn nothing from me!"

In agony from the wound in his shoulder he held his forearm across her throat, and pressed her head back into the brick, the weapon in his hand. "What I want can't be forced from you, Régine," he said, gasping for breath. "Don't you understand? It has to be given."

"*Nothing!* Which *terroristes* bought you? Meinhof cowards? Arab pigs? Israeli fanatics? *Brigate Rosse?* Who wants what you can sell? . . . She knew. She found out! And you must kill her! Kill me first, *betrayer!*"

Slowly Havelock released the pressure of his arm and, slower still, he moved his body away from hers. He knew the risk; he did not take it lightly. On the other hand, he knew Régine Broussac. After all, she was one of them; she had survived. He removed his arm and stood in front of her, his eyes steady, looking into hers.

"I've betrayed no one except myself," he began. "And through myself a person I love very much. I meant what I said. I can't force you to tell me what I have to know. Among other things, you could lie to me too easily, too successfully, and I'd be back where I was ten days ago. I won't do that. If I can't find her, if I can't have her back, perhaps it doesn't matter. I know what I did and it's killing me. I love her . . . I need her. I think we both need each other more than anything else in the world just now. We're all each other has left. But I've learned something about futility over the years." He raised the gun in his left hand, taking the barrel with his right. He held it out to her. "You've fired three times; there are four shells left."

Broussac stood still, staring at him, studying his face, his eyes. She took the weapon and levelled it at his head, her own eyes questioning, roaming his. Finally her grimacing features softened, astonishment replacing hostility. Slowly she lowered the gun.

"*Déraisonnable,*" she whispered. "This is the truth, then."

"The truth."

Régine looked at her watch. "*Vite!* We must leave. They'll be here in minutes; they'll search everywhere."

"Where to? There are no taxis — "

"The *Métro*. We'll take it to the Rochereau. There's a small park where we can talk."

"What about your team? What'll you tell them?"

"That I was testing their alertness," she said, taking his arm as they started up the pavement towards the lighted entrance leading to the underground trains. "That I wanted to see how they would react in a given situation. It's consistent: it's late, they're off duty and I'm a bitch."

"You've still got the embassy."

"I know, I was thorough. I'll have to think about that."

"Maybe I never showed up," said Havelock, rubbing his shoulder, grateful that the pain was receding.

"*Merci.*"

The pocket handkerchief park in Denfert Rochereau was a plot of grass dotted with stone benches, sculptured trees and a gravelled path circling a small pool with a fountain in its centre. The only source of light was a street lamp thirty feet away, its spill filtered by the branches of the trees. They sat beside each other on the cold bench. Michael told Broussac what he had seen – and what he had not seen – at the Costa Brava. He then had to ask the question. "Did she tell you what happened?"

"She was warned, told to follow instructions."

"By whom?"

"A high government official from Washington."

"How could she accept him?"

"He was brought to her by a man identified as the senior attaché from Madrid's Consular Operations."

"Consular . . . *Madrid*? Where was *I*?"

"Madrid."

"*Jesus*, right down to the hour!"

"What was?"

"The whole goddamned thing. What instructions was she given?"

"To meet a man that night and leave Barcelona with him."

"Did she?"

"No."

"Why not?"

"She panicked. In her words, everything had collapsed for her. She didn't feel she could trust *anyone*. She ran."

"Thank God. I don't know who was killed on that beach, but it was meant to be Jenna. In a way, it makes the whole thing even more obscene. Who was she? Someone who didn't know a damn thing? A woman brought there and told to chase a frisbee in the moonlight, suddenly shot at, knowing she was going to die. *Christ*, what kind of people *are* they?"

"Find out through Madrid. The attaché from Consular Operations."

"I can't. She was fed another lie. There's no Cons Op unit in Madrid; the climate's too rotten. It operates an hour away out of Lisbon."

Régine was silent, her eyes on him. "What's happening, Michael?"

Havelock watched the fountain in the dark pool. Its cascading spray was diminishing, folding, dying; somewhere a hand was turning a dial, shutting it off for the remainder of the night. "Liars are operating at very high places in my government. They've penetrated areas I used to think were impenetrable. They're controlling, killing – lying. And someone in Moscow is working with them."

"*Moscow?* Are you sure?"

"I'm sure. On the word of a man who wasn't afraid to die, but was afraid of living the way I promised him he'd be forced to live. Someone in Moscow, someone the controllers of the KGB know nothing about, is in contact with the liars."

"For what purpose. *You?* To destroy your credibility, then kill you? To void some recent accomplishment by maligning the record of a dead man?"

"It's not me; I'm only a part of it. I wasn't important before, but I am now." Havelock turned his head and looked at old Broussac, her grey face now soft and compassionate, yet still ashen-dark in the dim light. "Because I saw Jenna; because I found out she was alive. Now they have to kill me. They have to kill her, too."

"*Why?* You were the best!"

"I don't know. I only know that the Costa Brava is where I have to look for answers. It's where it started for Jenna and me . . . where it was supposed to end. One of us dead, the other dying inside, finished. Out."

"It is she who is dying inside now. It astonishes me that she can function as she does, move as she does. She's remarkable." Régine paused. The fountain's spray had collapsed and only trickles of water dripped over its saucerlike basin into the pool. "She loved you, you know."

"Past tense?"

"Oh, yes. We all learn to accept new realities, don't we? We're better at it than most people because sudden change is an old acquaintance as well as our enemy. We constantly seek out betrayal in others; we preach it. And all the while we're being tested ourselves, our adversaries intent on seducing our minds and our appetites. Sometimes we succeed, sometimes they do. That's the reality."

"The futility," said Havelock.

"You are too much the *philosophe* for this business."

"It's why I got out." Michael looked away. "I saw her face in the window of the plane in Col des Moulinets. Her eyes. Christ, it was awful."

"I'm certain it was. It happens. Hatred replaces love, doesn't it? It's the only defence in these cases . . . She'll kill you if she can."

"Oh, God . . ." Havelock leaned forward on the bench, his elbows on his knees, hands cupped under his chin, staring at the dead fountain. "I love her so. I loved her when I killed her that night, knowing a part of me would always be at that beach for the rest of my life, my eyes seeing her running, falling in the sand, my ears hearing her screams . . . wanting to race down and hold her, tell her the whole world was a *lie* and nothing mattered but us! Just us . . . Something inside me was trying to tell me that terrible things were being done to us, and I wouldn't listen . . . I was too hurt to listen to myself. I, I, *I*! *Me*! I couldn't get *me* out of the way and hear the truth she was screaming!"

"You were a professional in a professional crisis," said Régine softly, touching his arm. "According to everything you'd learned, everything you'd lived with for years, you were doing what you had to do. A professional."

Michael turned his head and looked at her. "Why wasn't I myself?" he asked simply. "Why didn't I listen to the other screams, the ones I couldn't get out of my throat?"

"We can't always trust what we call instinct, Michael. You know that."

"I know that I love her . . . loved her when I thought I hated her, when that professional in me expected to see her die because I'd closed the trap on an enemy. I didn't hate her, I loved her. Do you know why I know that?"

"Why, *mon cher?*"

"Because there was no satisfaction in winning, not the slightest. Only revulsion, only sadness . . . only wanting things to be the way they couldn't be."

"That's when you got out, isn't it? It's what we'd heard, what I found so difficult to believe. I understand now. You loved her very much. I *am* sorry, Michael."

Havelock shook his head, closing his eyes, the inner darkness comforting for a moment. "In Barcelona," he said, opening his eyes again, looking at the quiet pool in front of them, "what happened to her? Tell me what she told you."

"She can't understand what happened. Did the Russians actually buy you or did Washington order her execution? It's an enigma to her – a violent enigma. She got out of Spain and went to Italy, going from city to city, seeking out those few people she thought she could trust to help her, hide her. But always there were the questions: Where were *you*? Why was she alone and not with *you*? At first, she was afraid to say, and when she did no one believed her. Whenever she told the story and it was rejected, she felt she had to run again, convinced the few would reach you, and you would come after her. She lives with the nightmare that you're always there, following – hunting her down. And when she had settled briefly into a safe cover, a Russian appeared, someone you both knew in Prague, a KGB butcher. Coincidence? Who was to tell? She ran again, this time stealing a large sum of money from her employer."

"I wondered about that. How she could buy her way out of Italy, get across the border and up into Paris. Compared with some other routes, she travelled first class."

Broussac smiled, her blue eyes lively in the shadows, telling him that a brief moment of amusement was to follow. "She laughed about it – quietly to be sure – but the laughter was good; that she could laugh was good, Michael. Do you see what I mean? For a moment or two she was like a little girl remembering a prank."

"I hear her laughter in my sleep . . . when I don't hear her screams. Her laugh was always quiet, never loud, but somehow full . . . an echo from deep inside her. She loved to laugh; it was a release for her, something not usually permitted and therefore enjoyed so much more when it happened." He paused, his eyes again on the still fountain. "How did she steal the money? Where?"

"Milan."

"The Russians are crawling all over Milan. Whoever she saw, it was a migratory coincidence . . . Sorry, what happened?"

"She was working in that enormous shop in the Piazza del Duomo, the one that sells books and magazines and newspapers from all over the world. Do you know it?"

"I've seen it."

"Her languages got her the job, and she tinted her hair, wore glasses, all the usual things. But her figure also got her the undivided attention of the owner, a pig with a large wife he was terrified of and eight children. He was forever asking her into his office and mauling her and promising her the *Galleria Vittorio* for her favours. One day at noon the Russian came in; she recognized him and knew she had to run; she was afraid that he was connected to you, that you were scouring Europe for her . . . At the lunch hour, she literally assaulted the manager in his office, claiming that she could no longer wait for *his* favours, and that only a small loan stood between them and absolute ecstasy. By this time she had her blouse off and the poor man's wallet under a chair. In a state of utter apoplexy, the idiot opened the safe where several days' receipts were stored – it was a Friday, if you recall."

"Why should I?" interrupted Havelock.

"We'll get to that," said Régine, a partial smile on her lips.

"Anyway, when the ageing, perspiring Lothario had the safe open and our Jenna was removing her brassiere, he counted out a few thousand lire in his quivering hands and she struck him on the head with a clock. She then proceeded to empty the safe, positively stunned by the amounts of money filling the bank deposit pouches. That money was her passport and she knew it."

"It was also an invitation for a police hunt."

"A hunt that could be delayed, the delay permitting her to get out of Milan."

"How?"

"Fear, confusion and embarrassment," replied Broussac. "Jenna closed the safe, stripped the owner naked and marked him everywhere with streaks of lipstick. She then called his home and, speaking to a maid, said an urgent matter required the man's wife to come to the shop in an hour, not before and not later."

"Fear, confusion and embarrassment," agreed Michael, nodding. "She tapped him again, making sure he'd stay where he was, figuring he'd hardly rush to the safe in front of his wife, compounding the mess he was already in . . . And obviously, she took his clothes with her," added Havelock, smiling, remembering the woman who was Jenna Karras.

"Obviously. She used the next several hours to gather her things together and, realizing that a police warrant would be issued sooner or later, removed the dye from her hair. She then joined the crowds at the Milan railway station."

"The railway . . . ?" Michael sat back on the bench and looked at Régine. "The train. She took the train to Rome! That's where I saw her!"

"It's a moment she'll never forget. There you were, standing there, staring at her. The man who had forced her into hiding, into running, who'd caused her to alter her appearance and change the sequence of her languages. The one person on earth she was terrified might find her, kill her . . . and there *she* was, all her disguise gone, recognized by the one she most feared."

"If the shock hadn't been so paralysing, if only I'd been quicker . . . so much would have been so different." Michael arched his neck back and brought his hands to his face, covering his eyes. "Oh, *Christ*, we were so *close*! I yelled to her, I screamed and kept screaming, but she disappeared. I lost her in the crowds; she didn't hear me – she didn't *want* to hear me – and I lost her." Havelock lowered his hands and gripped the edge of the stone bench. "Civitavecchia came next. Did she tell you about that?"

"Yes. It was where she saw a crazed animal try to kill her on a pier – "

"It *wasn't* her! How could she think I thought it was? Jesus, a fucking whore from the docks!" Michael checked himself; it served no purpose to lose control.

"She saw what she saw," said old Broussac quietly. "She couldn't know what you were thinking."

"How did she know I'd go to Civitavecchia? A man there told me she thought I'd question the taxi drivers. I didn't. There's a strike, although a few are running, I suppose."

"There are, and you were the best of hunters. You yourself taught her that the surest way to get out of a country unseen is a busy waterfront in the early hours of the morning. There is always someone willing to broker space, if only in a cargo hold. She asked people on the train, pretending to be a Polish merchant seaman's wife, her husband on a freighter. People are not stupid; they understood; one more couple leaving the arms of the Bear. 'Civitavecchia,' they said. 'Try Civitavecchia!' She assumed you might reach the same conclusion – based on what you'd taught her – and so she made her preparations. She was right; you arrived."

"By a different route," said Havelock. "Because of a guard on the train who remembered a *bella ragazza*."

"In any case, she assumed the possibility and acted on it, placing herself in a position to observe. As I said, she's remarkable. The strain, the pressures. To do what she did without panic, to mount the strategy alone . . . remarkable. I think you were a splendid teacher, Michael."

"She had ten years of training before I met her. There was a lot she could teach me . . . and did. You gave her a cover and diplomatic clearance. Where did she go? What arrangements did you make?"

"How did you learn this?"

"Don't make me pay the price, I owe him. Instead, let me send him to you. Don't turn him in; use him for yourself. You won't regret it, but I need the guarantee."

"Fair enough. Talent should be shared, and I respect the sender. I remember Bonn."

"Where did she go?"

"Apart from a few remote islands in the Pacific, the safest place in the world for her now. The United States."

Havelock stared in astonishment at the old woman. "How did you deduce *that*?"

"I went back over the restricted cables from your State Department looking for any mention of Jenna Karras. Indeed, it was there. A single insertion dated 10 January, detailing briefly the events at the Costa Brava. She was described as an infiltrator caught in a reverse trap in which she had lost her life, her death confirmed by two separate sightings and forensic examination of bloodstained clothing. The file was closed to the satisfaction of Consular Operations."

"The rotes have it," said Michael. "Aye, aye, sir. Next case, please."

"The implausibility was glaring, of course. Sightings can be erroneous, but a forensic laboratory must work with materials. Yet they couldn't have, not with any legitimacy. Not only was Jenna Karras very much alive and sitting in my office, but she had never gone to that beach on the Costa Brava. The forensic confirmation was a lie, and someone must know it, someone who wanted the lie accepted as the truth." Broussac paused. "I assumed it was you. Termination carried out, execution as scheduled. If you had been bought by the Russians, what better proof could they have than the Department of State? If you had been carrying out Washington's instructions, you could not allow them to think you had failed."

"In the light of what she told you, I can understand."

"But I wasn't satisfied; the acceptance was too simple, so I looked farther. I went to the data-processing computers and placed her name in the security scanner relating to the past three months . . . It was extraordinary. She appeared no less than twelve times, but never on State Department communiqués. It was always on cables from the Central Intelligence Agency, and couched in very odd language. And always the same, cable after cable: the US government had an alert out for a woman matching her description who *might* be using the name of Karras – but it was third or fourth on a list of a half dozen *false* names. It was a highly classified search, but obviously an intense one, the widest co-operation sought. It was strange, almost amateurish. As though one branch of your intelligence community did not want the other to know what it was doing."

"That didn't exonerate me?"

"On the contrary. You had been found out, the lie had been exposed."

"Then why wasn't there an alert out for *me*?"

"There was, is. As of five days ago."

Five days, thought Havelock. The Palatine. "But you weren't aware of it."

"Those in the Quai d'Orsay who've listed you as an American liaison knew of it, and in time it would have crossed my desk as a matter of routine. However, neither you nor I have ever listed each other in our reports. That was the understanding between us."

"It served the purpose. Is the alert specific? Am I given a label?"

"No. Only that it is imperative that you should be located as a matter of internal security. Again, I presumed: you had been exposed, either as a defector or as someone who had lied to his superiors and disappeared. It really didn't matter which. Because of Jenna Karras, you were the enemy in either case. It was confirmed for me when I called the embassy."

"I forgot. I'm dangerous."

"You are. To someone. I checked with London, Brussels, Amsterdam and Bonn. Both alerts have been circulated, both highest priority, but not connected."

"You still haven't answered the question. Why did you send her to the States?"

"I just did answer you; you weren't listening. The search for her – and now you – is centred in Europe. Rome, the Mediterranean, Paris, London . . . Bonn. The curve is arching north, the destination presumed to be the Eastern bloc. This is the line of progress they're concentrating on, where their agents have fanned out, pulling in sources and contacts. They won't think to look in their own barnyard."

"Back yard," said Michael absently.

"*Qu'est-ce que c'est?*"

"*C'est américain. Peu importe.* When did she leave?"

"Three-thirty this afternoon . . . yesterday afternoon now. Air France to New York, diplomatic status, cover name drawn from a dead file – unblemished, of course."

"And unknown."

"Yes, it's not relevant. It will be changed."

"What are the arrangements?"

"She's to see a man; no doubt she's already seen him. *He* will make the arrangements, and it is our policy never to inquire what they are. You have the same sort of men over here – in Paris, London, Amsterdam, wherever. They do not speak with us directly."

"The landlords of the halfway houses," said Havelock, "guiding the people we send them into safe territory, providing identities, papers, families to live with, the towns and cities chosen carefully. We make our payments through blind conduits, and after contact we're not involved. We've never heard of them; ignorance is the order of the day. But there's another side, too, isn't there? We don't really know what happens to those people, do we?"

"With safe transfer, our obligations are fulfilled. They ask no more and we offer no more; that's always been the understanding between us. I, for one, have never been curious."

"I'm not *curious*, Régine, I'm going out of my mind! She's in sight now, I can find her! I *can find her*! For Christ's sake, help me! Who did you send her to?"

"You ask a great deal, Michael. You're asking me to violate a confidence I've sworn never to break. I could lose a valuable man."

"I could lose *her*! Look at me! Tell me I wouldn't do the same for you! If it was your husband and I was there and the Gestapo came for him, look at me and tell me I wouldn't *help* you!"

Broussac closed her eyes briefly, as if struck. "The reference is unkind but not without truth. You and he were much alike . . . Yes, you would have helped."

"Get me out of Paris. Right away. *Please!*"

Régine was silent for a moment, her eyes again roaming his face. "It would be better if you did so yourself. I know you can."

"It could take me days! I'd have to route myself through a back door in Mexico or Montreal. I can't lose the time. With every hour she's farther away. You know what can happen. She could get swallowed up, moving from one circle into the next, no one telling anyone anything. She could disappear and I'd never find her!"

"Very well. Tomorrow, the noon flight on Concorde. You'll be French, a member of the United Nations delegation. Flush the papers down a toilet the minute you're at Kennedy."

"Thanks. Now for the halfway man. Who is he?"

"I'll get word to him but he may choose to tell you nothing."

"Get word to him. Who is he?"

"A man named Handelman. Jacob Handelman. Columbia University."

17

The man with a single strip of surgical tape on each cheek sat at the small table below the curved dais in the underground strategy room of the White House. The flesh on his square face was taut, held in place by the sutures beneath the brown adhesive; the effect was robotlike, macabre. His replies in a subdued monotone to the questions put to him heightened the image of a man not totally whole, yet over-controlled. In truth, he was afraid; the agent-of-record from Col des Moulinets would have been more afraid thirty-five minutes before, when the panel of men facing him was complete. There had been four men then; now there were only three. The President had removed himself. He was observing the proceedings from an unseen cubicle behind the platform, through a pane of coated glass that was part of the inner wall and indistinguishable from it. Words were being said in that room which could not be said in his presence; he could not bear witness to orders of dispatch at an Alpine pass, and prior communications which included the phrase "beyond-salvage".

The interrogation was at midpoint, Undersecretary of State Emory Bradford probing the salient points while Ambassador Brooks and General Halyard made notes on their pads under the harsh glares of the Tensor lamps.

"Let me get this clear," said Bradford. "You were the field officer-of-record and the only one in contact with Rome. Is that correct?"

"Yes, sir."

"And you're absolutely certain no other member of the unit was in touch with the embassy?"

"Yes, sir. No, sir. I was the only channel. It's standard, not only for the security blackout, but to make sure there's no foul-up in the orders. One man transmits them, one man receives them."

"Yet you say Havelock referred to two of the unit's personnel as explosives specialists, a fact you were not aware of."

"I wasn't."

"But as the field officer-of-record . . ."

"Agent-of-record, sir."

"Sorry. As the agent-of-record shouldn't you have known?"

"Normally, I would have."

"But you didn't and the only explanation you can give us is that this new recruit, a Corsican named Ricci, hired the two men in question."

"It's the only reason I can think of. If Havelock was right; if he wasn't lying."

"The reports from Col des Moulinets stated that there were numerous explosions in the vicinity of the bridge's entrance at the time." Bradford scanned a typewritten page in front of him. "Including a massive detonation in the road which occurred approximately twelve minutes after the confrontation, killing three Italian soldiers and four civilians. Obviously Havelock knew what he was talking about; he wasn't lying to you."

"I wouldn't know, sir. I was unconscious . . . bleeding. The son of – Havelock cut me up."

"You're getting proper medical attention?" interrupted Ambassador Brooks, looking up from the yellow pad under the Tensor lamp.

"I guess so," replied the agent, his right hand slipping over his left wrist, his fingers massaging the glistening stainless steel case of his chronometer. "Except the doctors aren't sure the wounds'll require plastic surgery. I think I should have it."

"That's their province, of course," said the statesman.

"I'm . . . valuable, sir. Without that surgery I'm *marked*, sir."

"I'm sure Undersecretary Bradford will convey your feelings to Walter Reed," said the general, reading his notes.

"You say you never saw this man Ricci," continued Bradford, "prior to the briefing in Rome, just before the unit flew to Col des Moulinets. Is that correct?"

"Yes, sir. No, sir. I never saw him. He was new."

"And you didn't see him when you regained consciousness after the events at the bridge?"

"No, I didn't."

"You don't know where he went?"

"No, sir."

"Neither does Rome," added the Undersecretary quietly, pointedly.

"I learned that an Italian soldier was hit by a truck and was pretty badly mangled, screaming his head off. Someone said he had blond hair, so I figured it was Ricci."

"And?"

"A man came out of the woods – someone with a gash in his head – put the soldier in a car and drove him away."

"How did you learn this?"

"I asked questions, a lot of questions . . . after I got first aid. That was my job, sir. It was a madhouse up there, Italians and French yelling all over the place. But I didn't leave until I found out everything I could – without permitting anyone to ask *me* questions."

"You're to be commended," said the ambassador.

"Thank you, sir."

"Let's assume you're right." Bradford leaned forward. "The blond man *was* Ricci, and someone with a head wound got him out of there. Have you any idea who that someone might be?"

"I think so. One of the men he brought with him. The other was killed."

"So Ricci and this other man got away. But Rome hasn't heard from Ricci. Would you say that's normal?"

"No way, sir. It's not normal at all. Whenever any of those people are damaged, they bleed us for everything they can get, and they don't waste time about it. Our policy in black operations is clear. If we can't evacuate the wounded – "

566

"I think we understand," broke in Halyard, an old soldier's antenna picking up a signal couched in a soldier's vocabulary.

"Then it's your opinion that if Ricci and this demolitions expert got away intact, they'd have reached our embassy in Rome as quickly as they could."

"Yes, sir. With their hands out and shouting all the way. They would have expected attention pronto and threatened us with the kind we don't want if they didn't get it."

"What do you think happened?"

"I'd say it's pretty obvious. They didn't make it."

"What was that?" asked Brooks, raising his eyes from the yellow pad.

"There isn't any other explanation. I know those people, sir. They're garbage; they'd kill their mothers if the price was right. They would have been in touch with Rome, believe me."

" 'Didn't make it'?" repeated Halyard, staring at the man from Col des Moulinets. "What do you mean?"

"The roads, sir. They wind up and down those mountains like corkscrews, sometimes without lights for miles at a time. A wounded man driving, the other one banged up and screaming; that vehicle's a candidate for a long fall up there."

"Head wounds can be deceptive," Halyard commented. "A bloody nose looks a hell of a lot worse than it is."

"It strikes me," said Brooks, "that same man acted with considerable presence of mind amid the chaos. He functioned – "

"Forgive me, Mr Ambassador," interrupted Bradford, his voice rising slightly but deferentially. The intrusion was not a breach of manners but a signal. "I think the field officer's point is well taken. A thorough search of those roads will undoubtedly reveal a car somewhere at the bottom of a precipice."

Brooks exchanged looks with the man from State, the signal acknowledged. "Yes, of course. Realistically, there is no other explanation."

"Just one or two more points and we're finished," said Bradford, rearranging his papers. "As you know, whatever is said here is confidential. There are no hidden microphones, no recording devices; the words spoken are stored only in our memories. This is for the protection of all of us – not just you – so feel perfectly free to speak candidly. Don't try to soften the truth; we're in the same boat."

"I understand, sir."

"Your orders with regard to Havelock were unequivocal. He was officially classified 'beyond-salvage' and the word from Rome was to terminate with 'extreme prejudice'. Is that correct?"

"Yes, sir."

"In other words, he was to be executed. Killed at Col des Moulinets."

"That's what it meant."

"And you received those instructions from the senior attaché, Consular Operations, Rome. A man named Warren. Harry Warren."

"Yes, sir. I was in constant touch with him, waiting for the determination . . . waiting for Washington to give it to him."

"How could you be certain the man you spoke to was Harry Warren?"

The agent seemed perplexed as if the question were foolish, but the man who asked it was not foolish at all. "Among other things, I worked with Harry for over two years. I knew his voice."

"Just his voice?"

"And the number in Rome. It was a direct line to the embassy's radio room, unlisted and very classified. I knew that, too."

"Did it occur to you that when he gave you your final instructions he might have been doing so under duress? Against his will?"

"No, sir, not at all."

"It never crossed your mind?"

"If that had been the case, he would have told me."

"With a gun at his head?" said Halyard. "How?"

"The code had been established and he used it. He wouldn't have if there'd been anything wrong."

"Explain that, please," said Brooks. "What code?"

"A word or a couple of words that originate in Washington. They're referred to when decisions are transmitted; that way you know the authorization's there without naming names. If anything had been wrong, Harry wouldn't have used the code, and *I* would have known something wasn't right. I'd have asked for it and he would have given me a different one. He didn't and I didn't. He used the correct one at the beginning."

"What was the code for Col des Moulinets?" asked Emory Bradford.

"Ambiguity, sir. It came direct from Cons Op, Washington and will be listed in the embassy telephone logs, classified files."

"Which is proof of authorization," said Bradford, making a statement.

"Yes, sir. Dates, times and origins of clearance are in those logs."

Bradford held up an eight-by-ten-inch photograph of a man's face, adjusting the Tensor lamp so it could be seen clearly. "Is this Harry Warren?"

"Yes, sir. That's Harry."

"Thank you." The Undersecretary put down the photograph and made a check mark on the border of his notes. "Let me go back a bit; there's something I'm not sure is clear. Regarding the woman, she was to be sent across the border unharmed, if possible. Is that correct?"

"The operative words were 'if possible'. Nobody was going to risk anything for her. She was just a needle."

"A needle?"

"To stick into the Soviets. Let Moscow know we didn't buy the plant."

"Meaning she was a Russian device. A woman similar in appearance – perhaps someone who had undergone cosmetic surgery – whom the Russians produced repeatedly at selected locations for Havelock's benefit, letting him get close, but never close enough to take her. Is that what you mean?"

"Yes, sir."

"The purpose being to shock Havelock into a state of mental instability, to the point of defection?"

"To drive him nuts, yes, sir. I guess it worked; the 'beyond-salvage' came from Washington."

"From Ambiguity."

568

"Ambiguity, sir."

"Whose identity can be traced in the embassy's telephone logs."

"Yes, sir. The logs."

"So it was established beyond doubt that the woman at the bridge was *not* Jenna Karras."

"Beyond doubt. She was killed at the Costa Brava, everyone knew that. Havelock himself was the agent-of-record at that beach. He went crazy."

Ambassador Brooks slapped down his pencil and leaned forward, studying the man from Col des Moulinets. The sharp, echoing crack of the pencil, and the movement itself, were more than an interruption; they combined to indicate an objection. "This entire operation, didn't it strike you as . . . well, *bizarre*, to say the least? To be quite candid, was execution the only solution? Knowing what you all knew – presumed you knew – couldn't you have tried to take the man, spare his life, get him back here for treatment?"

"With respect, sir, that's a lot easier said than done. Jack Ogilvie tried in Rome and never left the Palatine. Havelock killed three men on that bridge that we know of; another two may be dead by now and probably are. He dug a knife into my face – he's a psycho." The agent paused, not finished. "Yes, sir. All things considered, we kill him. That's 'beyond-salvage', and has nothing to do with me. I follow orders."

"An all too familiar phrase, sir," said Brooks.

"But justified under the circumstances," Bradford broke in quickly, writing out the word *Ambiguity* on the page in front of him, continuing before anyone else could speak, or object. "What happened to Havelock? Did you learn?"

"They said an *uccisore pazzo* . . . crazy man, killer . . . drove the truck hell-bent across the bridge and out of sight. It had to be Havelock. There are alerts out all through the provinces – the towns and cities – and up and down the Mediterranean coast. He worked the coast; he'll get in touch with someone and they'll find him. They said he was wounded; he won't get far. My guess is a couple of days at the outside, and I wish I was there to take him myself."

"Again quite justified," said Bradford. "And we want to thank you for your co-operation this evening. You've been very concise and helpful. You may leave now, and good luck to you."

The man got out of the chair, nodded awkwardly and walked to the door. He stopped, touching his left cheek and the tape as he turned to face the powerful men on the dais. "I'm worth the surgery," he said.

"I'm sure you are," replied the Undersecretary.

The agent-of-record from Col des Moulinets opened the door and stepped out into the white-walled corridor. The instant the door was shut, Halyard turned to Bradford, and shouted, "Get hold of Rome! Get those logs and find this *Ambiguity*! It's what you were trying to tell us, isn't it? This is the link to Parsifal!"

"Yes, General," answered Bradford. "The Ambiguity code was established by the Director of Consular Operations, Daniel Stern, whose name appears in the embassy logs, entered by the Cons Op senior attaché Harry Warren. Warren was clear in his entry; the transcript was read to me. He wrote the following" – The

Undersecretary picked up a note on top of his papers – " 'Code: Ambiguity. Subject: M. Havelock. Decision pending.' "

" 'Pending'?" asked Brooks. "When was it *made*?"

"According to the embassy logs, it wasn't. There were no further entries that night making any reference whatsoever to Ambiguity, Havelock or the unit at Col des Moulinets."

"Impossible," protested the general. "You heard that man. The go-ahead was given, the authorization code was delivered. He didn't mince words. That call *must* have come through."

"It did."

"Are you saying that the entry was deleted?" asked Brooks.

"It was never made," said Bradford. "Warren never made it."

"Then get him," said Halyard. "Nail him. He knows who he talked to. Goddamn it, Emory, get on that phone. This is Parsifal!" He turned in his chair, addressing the wall. "Mr President?"

There was no reply.

The Undersecretary separated the papers in front of him and removed a thin manila envelope from the rest. He opened it, took out a second photograph and handed it to the former ambassador. Brooks studied it, a sharp intake of breath accompanying his first glance. Silently he passed it to Halyard.

"*Jesus* . . ." Halyard placed the photograph under the beam of the Tensor. The surface was grainy, the infinitesimal lines the result of a transmitting machine, but the image was clear. It was a photograph of a corpse stretched out on a white table, the clothes torn and bloody, the face bruised terribly but wiped clean for identification. The face of the dead man was the same as that in the first photograph Bradford had shown the agent from Moulinets only minutes before. It belonged to Harry Warren, Senior Attaché, Cons Op, Rome.

"That was telexed to us at one o'clock this afternoon. It's Warren. He was run down on the via Frascati in the early hours of the morning two days ago. There were witnesses, but they couldn't help much, except to tell our people the car was a large saloon with a powerful engine; it roared down the street, apparently gathering speed just before impact. Whoever drove it wasn't taking any chance of missing; he caught Warren stepping up onto the kerb and hammered him into the pole of a street light, doing considerable damage to the automobile. The police are searching for it, but there's not much hope. It's probably at the bottom of a river in the hills."

"So the link is gone." Halyard pushed the photograph towards Addison Brooks.

"I mourn the man," said the Undersecretary, "but I'm not sure how much of a link he was."

"Someone thought so," said the soldier.

"Or was covering a flank."

"What do you mean?" asked Brooks.

"Whoever made that final call authorizing 'beyond-salvage' couldn't know what Stern told Warren. All *we* know is that the decision hadn't been made."

"Please be clearer," the statesman insisted.

"Suppose the strategists of Consular Operations decided they couldn't *reach* a decision. On the surface, it wouldn't appear that difficult – a psychopath, a rogue

570

agent capable of causing extraordinary damage, a potential defector, a killer – the decision wasn't one that stretched their consciences. But suppose they learned something, or suspected something, that called everything into question."

"The Karras woman," said Halyard.

"Perhaps. Or maybe a communication, or a signal from Havelock that contradicted the assumption that he was a maniac. Implied that he was as sane as they were; a sane man caught in a terrible dilemma not of his own making."

"Which is, of course, the truth," interrupted Brooks quietly.

"The truth," agreed Bradford. "What would they do?"

"Get help," said Halyard. "Advice."

"Guidance," added the statesman.

"Or, practically speaking," said the Undersecretary, "especially if the facts weren't clear, to spread the responsibility for the decision. Hours later it was made, and they were dead . . . and we don't know who made it, who placed that final call. We only know it was someone sufficiently cleared, sufficiently trusted to be given the code Ambiguity. That man made the decision; he made the call to Rome."

"But Warren didn't log it," said Brooks. "Why didn't he? How could that happen?"

"The way it's happened before, Mr Ambassador. A routed line traceable only to a single telephone complex somewhere in Arlington is used, the authorization verified by code, and a request made on the basis of *internal* security: there is to be no log, no tape, no reference to the transmission; it's an order actually. The recipient is flattered; he's been chosen, deemed by men who make important decisions to be more reliable than those around him. And what difference does it make? The authorization can always be traced through the code – in this case through the Director of Cons Op, Daniel Stern. Only he's dead."

"It's appalling," said Brooks, looking down at his notes. "A man is to be executed because he's right, and when the attempt fails, he's held responsible for the death of those who try to kill him and labelled a killer himself. And we don't know who officially gave the order. We can't *find* him. What kind of people are we?"

"Men who keep secrets." The voice came from behind the dais. The President of the United States emerged from the white-panelled door set into the white wall. "Forgive me, I was watching you, listening. It's often helpful."

"Secrets, Mr President?"

"Yes, Mal," said Berquist, going to his chair. "The words are all there, aren't they? Top Secret, Eyes Only, Highly Classified, Maximum Clearance Required, Duplication Forbidden, Authorization to be Accompanied by Access Code . . . so many words. We sweep rooms and telephone lines with instruments that tell us whether bugs and intercepts have been placed, and then develop hardware that misdirects those same scanners when we implant our own devices. We jam radio broadcasts – including satellite transmissions – and override the jamming with laser beams that carry the words we want to send. We put a national security lid on information we don't want made public so we can leak selected sections at will, keeping the rest inviolate. We tell a certain agency or department one thing and another something else entirely, so as to conceal a third set of facts – the damaging truth. In history's most advanced age of communications, we're doing our damnedest to louse it up, to misuse it, really." The President sat down, looked at the photograph of the dead man in Rome and turned it over. "Keeping secrets and diverting the flow of accurate information have become prime objectives in our ever-expanding technology . . . of communications. Ironic, isn't it?"

"Unfortunately often vital, sir," said Bradford.

"Perhaps. If only we could be certain. I often wonder – late at night, watching the lights on the ceiling, trying to sleep – if we hadn't tried to keep a secret three months ago, whether we would be faced with what we're faced with now."

"Our options were extremely limited, Mr President," the Undersecretary said firmly. "We might have faced worse."

"*Worse*, Emory?"

"Earlier then. Time is the only thing on our side."

"And we have to use every goddamn minute," agreed Berquist, glancing first at the general and then at Brooks. "Now you're both aware of what's happened during the past seventy-two hours and why I had to call you back to Washington."

"Except the most relevant factor," said the statesman. "Parsifal's reaction."

"None," replied the President.

"Then he doesn't know," said Halyard rapidly, emphatically.

"If you'd get that written in stone, I could sleep at night," said Berquist.

"When did he last communicate with you?" asked Brooks.

"Sixteen days ago. There was no point in reaching you; it was another demand, as outrageous as the others and now as pointless."

"There's been no movement on the previous demands?" continued the statesman.

"Nothing. Fifteen days ago we funnelled eight hundred million dollars into banks throughout the Bahamas, the Caymans and Central America. We've set up every – " The President paused as he touched the photograph in front of him, folding a corner until part of a bloodied trouser leg could be seen. " – every code and counter code he's asked for, so that he could verify the deposits whenever he wished, have the monies sent to blind accounts in Zurich and Bern where they would be accessible to him. He hasn't moved a cent and, except for three verifications, he's made no contact at all with the other banks. He has no interest in the money; it's only a means of confirming our vulnerability. He knows we'll do anything he asks." Berquist paused again; when he spoke, his voice was barely audible. "God help us, we can't afford not to."

There was silence on the dais, an acknowledgement of the unthinkable. It was broken by the general's businesslike comment. "There are a couple of holes here," he said reading his notes, then looking at the Undersecretary. "Can you fill them in?"

"I can speculate," replied Bradford. "But to do even that we've got to go back to the very beginning. Before Rome."

"Costa Brava?" asked Brooks disdainfully.

"Before then, Mr Ambassador. To when we all agreed there had to *be* a Costa Brava."

"I stand rebuked," said the statesman icily. "Please go on."

572

"We go back to when we learned that it was Matthias himself who initiated the investigation of Jenna Karras. It was the great man himself, not his aides who relayed information from unnamed informants, sources so deep in Soviet intelligence that even to speculate on their identities was tantamount to exposing our own operations."

"Don't be modest, Emory," interrupted the President. "*We* didn't learn that it was Matthias. *You* did. You had the perspicacity to go round the 'great man', as you call him."

"Only with a sense of sadness, sir. It was you, Mr President, who demanded the truth from one of his aides in the Oval Office and he gave it to you. He said they *didn't* know where the information had come from, only that Matthias himself had brought it in. He never would have told me that."

"The room did it, I didn't," said Berquist. "You don't lie to a man sitting in that room . . . unless you're Anthony Matthias."

"In fairness, Mr President," said Brooks softly, "his intention was not to deceive you. He believed he was right."

"He believed he should have been sitting in my chair, my office! Good Christ, he still *believes* it. Even now! There's no end to his goddamned megalomania! Go on, Emory."

"Yes, sir." Bradford looked up. "We concluded that Matthias's objective was to force Havelock to retire, to get his old student and one of the best men we had out of Consular Operations. We've covered that before; we didn't know why then and we don't know why now."

"But we went along," said Berquist, "because we didn't know what we had. A broken foreign service officer who didn't want to go on, or a fraud – *worse* than a fraud, Matthias's lackey, willing to see a woman killed so that he could work for the *great* man on the outside. Oh, and the work he could have done! The international emissary for Saint Matthias. Or was it Emperor Matthias, ruler of all the states and territories of the republic?"

"Come on, Charley." Halyard touched the President's arm; no one else in that room would have risked such an intimate gesture. "It's over. It's not why we're here."

"If it wasn't for that son of a bitch Matthias we wouldn't *be* here! I find *that* hard to forget. And so could the world one day . . . if there's anyone left with a memory."

"Then may we return to that infinitely more ominous crisis, Mr President?" said Brooks gently.

Berquist leaned back; he looked at the aristocratic statesman, then at the old general. "When Bradford came to me and convinced me that there was a pattern of deception at the highest levels of state involving the great Anthony Matthias, I asked for you two – and only you two. At least, for now. I'd better be able to take your criticism, because you'll give it to me."

"Which I think is why you asked for us," said Halyard. "Sir."

"You're a ball-breaker, Mal." The President nodded towards the man from State. "Sorry. All right, we didn't know then, and we don't know now, why Matthias wanted Havelock out. But Emory brought us the scenario."

"An incredible scenario," agreed Bradford, his hands on top of the papers, no longer needing his notes. "The case that Matthias concocted against the Karras woman was a study in meticulous invention. A reformed terrorist from the Baader-Meinhof suddenly appears looking for absolution; he'll trade information for relocation and the cancellation of his death sentence. Bonn agrees – reluctantly – and we buy his story. The woman working with a Cons Op field officer then in Barcelona is actually a member of the KGB. A method of transferring orders is described, which entails the passing of a key, and a small overnight suitcase is located at an airport, *her* suitcase, filled with all the evidence needed to convict her – detailed analyses of the activities she and Havelock had been involved with during the past five weeks, summaries of in-depth, classified information Havelock had sent back to the State Department, and copies of the current codes and radio frequencies we used in the field. Also in that overnight bag were instructions from Moscow, including the KGB code that she was to employ should contact with KGB North-west Sector be required. We tested the code and got a response; it was authentic."

Brooks raised his left hand no more than a few inches, the gesture of a man used to commanding attention. "General Halyard and I are familiar with much of this, albeit not the specifics. I assume there's a reason for your restating it in such detail."

"There is, Mr Ambassador," agreed Bradford. "It concerns Daniel Stern. Please bear with me."

"Then while you're at it," said the general, "how did you verify that KGB code?"

"By using the three basic maritime frequencies for that area of the Mediterranean. It's standard procedure for the Soviets."

"That's pretty damn simple of them, isn't it?"

"I'm no expert, General, but I'd say it's pretty damn smart. I've studied the way we do it – I've had to – and I'm not sure ours is more effective. The frequencies we select are usually the weaker ones, not always clear and easily jammed if discovered. You don't tamper with maritime channels, and no matter how much traffic, the codes get through within a reasonable period of time."

"You're very impressive," said Brooks.

"I've had a series of crash courses during the past four months. Thanks to an executive order from the President, I've also had the benefit of the best brains in the intelligence community."

"The reason for that executive order was not explained," interrupted Berquist, glancing at the older men. Then he turned back to Bradford: "All right, you verified the KGB code to be authentic."

"It was the most incriminating document in that suitcase; it couldn't have been faked. So her name was put through the wheels at Central Intelligence – very deep wheels." Bradford paused. "As you may or may not know, General ... Mr Ambassador, it was at this point that I came on the scene. I didn't seek to be included; I was sought out by men I'd worked with during the Johnson administration ... and in south-east Asia."

"Remnants of the benevolent AID in Vientiane who stayed with the Agency?" asked Halyard sardonically.

"Yes," replied the Undersecretary; there was no apology in his answer. "Two men whose wide experience in undercover operations – favourable and unfavourable – led them to become what's called source-controls for informants deep within the Soviet apparatus. They phoned me at home one night, said they were at a local bar in Berwyn and why didn't I join them for a drink – old times' sake. When I said it was late, the one I was talking to pointed out that it was also late for them, and Berwyn Heights was a long drive from McLean and Langley. I understood and joined them."

"I've never heard this," interrupted the former ambassador. "Am I to infer that these men did not report back through normal channels but, instead, went directly to you?"

"Yes, sir. They were disturbed."

"Thank God for the communion of past sinners," said the President. "When they returned to those normal channels, they did it our way. It was beyond their scope, they reported. They pulled out and left it in Bradford's lap."

"The information requested about the Karras woman was a basic intelligence query," said Halyard. "Why were they disturbed?"

"Because it was a highly negative inquiry that presupposed the subject was too deep, too concealed for CIA detection. She was going to be found guilty no matter what the Agency came back with."

"Then it was the arrogance that angered them?" suggested Brooks.

"No, they're used to that from State. What *disturbed* them was that the supposition couldn't possibly be true. They reached five separate sources in Moscow, none aware of the others – moles who had access to every black file in the KGB. Each probe came back negative. She was clean, but someone at State wanted her dirty. When one of the men routinely called an aide of Matthias to get further background from Cons Op, he was told simply to send back a non-productive report – State had everything it needed. In other words, she was hanged no matter what the Agency returned, and the source control had the distinct impression that whatever was sent back to State would be buried. But Jenna Karras was no part of the KGB and never had been."

"How did your friends explain the KGB code?" asked the soldier.

"Someone in Moscow provided it," said Bradford. "Someone working with or for Matthias."

Again the silence on the dais suggested the unthinkable, and once again it was broken by the general. "We ruled that *out*!" he cried.

"I'd like to revive it," said Bradford quietly.

"We've explored the possibility to the point of exhaustion," said Brooks, staring at Bradford. "Practically and conceptually, there's no merit in the theory. Matthias is inexorably bound to Parsifal; one does not exist without the other. If the Soviet Union had any knowledge of Parsifal, ten thousand multiple warheads would be in position to destroy half our cities and all our military installations. The Russians would have no choice but to launch, posing their final questions after the first strike. We have intelligence penetration to alert us to any such missile deployment; there's been no such alert. In your words, Mr Bradford, time is the only thing on our side."

"I'll stay with that judgement, Mr Ambassador. Still the KGB code found its way into the manufactured evidence against the Karras woman even though she was clean. I can't believe it was for sale."

"Why not?" asked the general. "What isn't for sale?"

"Not a code like that. You don't *buy* a code that changes periodically, erratically, with no set schedule of change."

"What's your point?" Halyard interrupted.

"Someone in Moscow *had* to provide that code," said Bradford, raising his voice. "We may be closer to Parsifal than we think."

"What's your thesis, Mr Undersecretary?" Brooks leaned forward.

"There's someone trying to find Parsifal as frantically as we are – for the same reasons we are. Whoever he is, he's here in Washington – he may be someone we see every day, but we don't know who he is. I only know he's working for Moscow, and the difference between him and us right now is that he's been looking longer than we have. He knew about Parsifal *before* we did. And that means someone in Moscow knows." Bradford paused. "That's the reason for the most God-awful crisis this country has ever faced . . . the world has ever faced. There's a mole here in Washington who could tip the balance of power – of basic global recognition of our physical and moral superiority – which *is* power – if he reaches Parsifal first. And he may, because he knows who he is and we don't."

18

The man was wearing a dark overcoat and a low-brimmed hat that partially hid his face. As he climbed out of the two-toned coupé, he only just managed to avoid stepping into a puddle by the driver's door. The sounds of the night rain were everywhere, pinging off the bonnet and splattering against the glass of the windscreen, thumping into the vinyl roof and erupting in the myriad pools all over the deserted parking area on the banks of the Potomac River. The man reached into his pocket, took out a gold-plated butane lighter and ignited it. No sooner had the flame erupted than he extinguished it, replacing the lighter in his pocket. He kept his gloved hand there. He walked to the railing and looked down at the wet foliage and the border of thick mud that disappeared into the black flowing water. Raising his head, he scanned the opposite shoreline; the lights of Washington flickered in the downpour. Hearing the footsteps behind him, leather scraping over the soaked gravel, he turned.

A man approached, coming into view through blocks of darkness. He wore a canvas poncho printed with the erratic shapes of green and black that denoted military issue. On his head was a heavy wide-brimmed leather hat. The face beneath it was thirtyish, hard, with a stubble of a beard and dull eyes set far apart. He had

576

been drinking; the grin that followed recognition was as grotesque as the rest of him.

"Hey, how about it, *huh*!" cried the man in the poncho. "*Wham!* Splat! Boom . . . *Kaboom!* Like a fuckin' gook rickyshaw hit by a tank! *Wham!* You never seen nothin' like it!"

"Very fine work," said the man in the overcoat.

"You betch-er ass! I caught 'em at the pass, and *kaboom!* Hey, I can't hardly see you. It *is* you, ain't it?"

"Yes, but you disappoint me."

"Why! I did good!"

"You've been drinking. I thought we agreed you wouldn't."

"A couple of balls, that's all. In my room, not at no gin mill . . . no sir!"

"Did you talk to anyone?"

"Christ, *no!*"

"How did you get out here?"

"Like you said. On a bus . . . three buses . . . and I walked the last couple of miles."

"In the road?"

"*Off* it. Way off, like it was an S and D in Danang."

"Good. You've earned your R and R."

"Hey, Major . . . ? Sorry, I mean . . ."

"What is it?"

"How come there was nothin' in the papers? I mean it was one big blow! Musta' burned for hours, seen for a couple of miles. How come?"

"They weren't important, Sergeant. They were only what I told you they were. Bad men who betrayed people like you and me, who stayed over here and let us get killed."

"Yeah, well, I evened a few scores. I guess I should go back now, huh? To the hospital."

"You don't have to." The civilian who had been addressed as "major" calmly took his gloved hand out of his pocket. In it was a .22 calibre automatic, concealed by the darkness and the rain. He raised it at his side and fired once.

The man fell, his bleeding head sinking into the wet poncho. The civilian stepped forward, wiping the weapon against the cloth of his overcoat. He knelt down and spread the fingers of the dead man's right hand.

The two-toned coupé rounded the curve in the back country road, the headlights sweeping over a rock-strewn Maryland field, the high grass bending under the force of the wind and the night rain. The driver in the dark overcoat and low-brimmed hat saw what he expected to see and slowed down, switching off the lights before coming to a stop. On the shoulder of the road, standing motionless by a barbed wire fence, was a glistening white ambulance, the licence plates those of the federal government, the black lettering on the door proclaiming co-ownership with the taxpayer as well as the identification: *Bethesda Naval Hospital, Emergency Unit 14.*

The driver drew the coupé alongside the long white vehicle. He took out his lighter, flicked the top and held the flame briefly towards the opposite window. The door of the ambulance opened, and a man in his late twenties jumped out into the rain, his government issue raincoat parting to reveal the white uniform of a hospital attendant.

The driver lowered the right window by pressing a button above his armrest. "Get in!" he yelled through the sound of the downpour. "You'll get soaked out there!"

The man climbed in, slamming the door shut and wiping his face with his right hand. He was Hispanic, his large eyes two stones of shining hard coal, his hair jet black, matted to the dark skin of his forehead.

"You owe me, mama," said the Latin. "Oh, big mama owes me one big *lio grande*."

"You'll be paid, although I suppose I could say that you simply cancelled an old debt you owed me."

"No *dados*, mama Major!"

"You would have been executed in the field or still be pushing rocks around Leavenworth if it weren't for me. Don't you forget it, Corporal."

"I wasted that shrinker for you! You *pay*!"

"You wasted – as you put it – two MPs in Pleiku who caught you stealing narcotics from a Med-Evac truck. Weren't you lucky I was around? Two more MIAs in a river."

"Sure, mama, *real* lucky! Who was the *puerco* who *told* me about the truck? *You*, Major!"

"I knew you were enterprising. These past years I've kept my eye on you. You never saw me, but I saw you. I always knew where to find you, because debts should be paid."

"Yeah, well you're wrong, Major. I saw you the other night on the TV news. You were getting out of a big limousine in New York. You were at the United Nations place, wasn't it? It *was* you, wasn't it?"

"I doubt it."

"Sure, it was! I know big mama when I see her. You must be something! You pay, mama. You're going to pay a lot."

"My God, you're irritating."

"Just pay me."

"The gun first," said the man in the overcoat. "I gave it to you and I want it back. I protected you; no one could trace it ballistically."

The hospital attendant reached into his raincoat pocket and took out a small gun, identical in size and calibre to the weapon the driver of the coupé had used an hour ago in a parking area overlooking the Potomac.

"You won't find no bullets in it," said the Hispanic, holding out the automatic in the darkness. "Here, take it."

"Give it to me."

"*Take* it! For Christ's sake, I can't see nothin' in here! *Ouch! Shit!* What the hell . . . ?"

The driver's hand had slipped beyond the short barrel of the weapon, pushing the attendant's wide sleeve partially up his forearm. "Sorry," said the man in the overcoat. "My class ring is twisted. Did I scrape you?"

"Forget it, mama. The money. Give me the fuckin' *dinero*!"

"Certainly." The man took the gun and slipped it into his pocket. He picked up his lighter from his lap and ignited it; on the seat between them was a stack of money held together with an elastic band. "There it is. Fifty one-hundred-dollar bills – laundered, of course. Do you want to count it?"

"What for? I know where I can find you now," said the attendant, opening the door. "And you're going to see a lot of me, big mama."

"I look forward to it," replied the driver.

The wind again whipped the attendant's raincoat away from his white uniform as he slammed the door and started towards the ambulance. The man in the coupé leaned over in the shadows, watching through the opposite window with his fingers on the door latch beside him, prepared to leap out of the car the instant he saw what he expected to see.

The attendant began to stagger, rushing forward off balance, his arms stretched out, his hands clutching the side of the ambulance. He raised his head and screamed, the rain pounding his face; three seconds later he collapsed on the wet grass.

The man in the overcoat jumped out of the coupé and walked around the boot, removing a tubular glass object from his left pocket. He reached the attendant, knelt down and pushed the wide sleeve up the immobile arm. He then adjusted the glass vial in his left hand and, with his right, extracted a hypodermic needle. He plunged it into the soft flesh, depressed the shaft until the vial of white liquid was emptied into the arm, and let the long needle remain where it was, firmly embedded in the skin. Reaching across the attendant's body, he pulled the loose, lifeless hand towards the vial, he pressed the fingers around the glass tube, with the thumb firmly down on the plunger and then let the hand fall away.

The man stood up, seeing in the night light the scattered notes, many held in place by the weight of the attendant's body. He turned and opened the door of the ambulance; the inside was neat, the equipment in place, as befitted a trusted employee of the Bethesda Naval Hospital. He took out the small automatic from his pocket and threw it onto the seat. He then reached inside his overcoat for the contents of another pocket. Four additional glass vials, two filled, two empty. He checked the labels; each read the same:

Bethesda Naval Hospital
Security-Control-Supply
Contents: $C_{17}H_{19}NO_3H_2O$
Morphine

He held them out and dropped them on the floor of the ambulance.

Suddenly a gust of wind came swirling off the field, forcing the rain to fall in diagonal sheets. The man reached for his hat but it was too late. Caught in an updraught, the hat was lifted off his head and hurled against the side of the coupé. He walked across the grass to retrieve it. Even in the darkness the shock of white could be seen streaking from his forehead through his wavy black hair.

In truth, Nicolai Petrovich Malyekov was annoyed, and his dripping hair was only part of his irritation. Time was running short. In his identity as Undersecretary of State Arthur Pierce, he would have to change his clothes and make himself presentable. A man in his position in the United States government did not run around in the mud and the pouring rain; he would phone for his limousine the minute he reached home. He had agreed to have late night drinks with the British ambassador, as there was another OPEC problem and matters of state to be attended to.

It was not what his people in Moscow wanted, but knowledge of another Anglo-American oil strategy was not to be dismissed. All such information brought the *Voennaya* closer to the power they had been seeking since Yagoda set them on their path over a half century ago. Yet only the man who could not be found, the man who knew the secret of Anthony Matthias, could lead the *Voennaya* to its destiny – for the good of the world.

Arthur Pierce, raised as an Iowa farmboy but born in the Russian village of Ramenskoye, turned towards his car in the rain. There was no time to be tired for the charade never stopped. Not for him.

Ambassador Addison Brooks stared at Bradford across the dais. "You say this mole *knows* who Parsifal is, *knew* about him before *we* did!" he exclaimed. "On what basis do you make that extraordinary statement?"

"Costa Brava," said the Undersecretary. "And the past seventy-two hours."

"Take them in sequence," ordered the President.

"In the final hours of Costa Brava, Havelock was provided with a radio transmitter whose frequency calibrations had been altered by CIA technicians in Madrid. They were working under blind orders; they had no idea what the transmitter was for or who was going to use it. As you know, the entire Costa Brava assignment was controlled by a man named Steven MacKenzie, the most experienced black-operations officer in Central Intelligence; the security was guaranteed."

"Completely," interrupted Berquist. "MacKenzie died of a coronary three weeks after we pulled him out of Barcelona. There was nothing suspicious. The doctor's a respected, well-known physician and was thoroughly questioned. MacKenzie's death was from natural causes."

"Only *he* knew all the details," continued Bradford. "He'd hired a boat, two men and a blonde woman who spoke Czech and was to scream in the distance – in the dark – during the grisly scene they were performing on that beach. The three of them were the dregs – small-time narcotics dealers and a prostitute – picking up a sizeable fee. They didn't ask questions. Havelock sent out his transmission in KGB code to what he thought was a Baader-Meinhof unit in the boat off-shore. MacKenzie caught it on his scanner and signalled the boat to come in. A few minutes later Havelock saw what we wanted him to see – or he *thought* he saw it. The Costa Brava operation was over."

"Again," interrupted the ambassador impatiently, "General Halyard and I are aware of the essentials – "

"It was over, and except for the President and the three of us, no one else knew about it," said the Undersecretary, rushing ahead. "MacKenzie had structured it in fragments, no one group knowing what the other was doing. The only story we issued was the trapped double-agent version, no buried reports, no file within a file that contradicted it. And with MacKenzie's death, the last man on the outside who knew the truth was gone."

"The last man perhaps," said Halyard. "Not the last woman. Jenna Karras knew. She got away from you, but she knew."

"She knew only what she was told, and I was the one who spoke with her at the hotel in Barcelona. The story she was given had a dual purpose. One, to frighten her into doing exactly what we asked of her so we could ostensibly save her life; and two, to put her into a disturbed frame of mind that would startle Havelock, help convince him she *was* a KGB officer if he had any last doubts or emotional hurdles. If she'd followed my instructions she'd be safe. Or if we'd been able to find her, she wouldn't be running from the men who have to kill her now – and kill Havelock – so the truth about Costa Brava is kept secret. Because they *know* the truth."

Ambassador Brooks whistled softly; it was a low, swelling whistle, the sound made by a brilliant man genuinely astonished. "We've reached the last seventy-two hours," he said, "beginning with an untraceable call to Rome preceded by an authorization code established by Daniel Stern."

"Yes, sir. Col des Moulinets. I saw the outlines of the connection when I read the agent-of-record's report, but nothing was clear. Just shapes, shadows. Then it became clearer when he spoke to us here tonight."

"A man named Ricci he'd never seen before," said Brooks, "two demolitions experts he knew nothing about."

"And a massive explosion which detonated some twelve minutes *after* the gunfire at the bridge," added Bradford. "Then his description of the woman as a 'needle' for the Soviets, a Russian plant that Moscow could have back and be taught a lesson."

"Which was a lie," objected Halyard. "That bomb was meant for the car she was in. It killed how many? Seven people on the road to the bridge? Christ, it was powerful enough to blow that vehicle out of sight and everyone in it beyond recognition. And our own people weren't to know a goddamned thing about it."

"By way of a man named Ricci," said Bradford, "a Corsican no one knew and two so-called small arms backup personnel who were in reality explosives experts. They were sent by Rome, but the two who escaped never tried to get in touch with the embassy afterwards. In our agent's words, that's not normal. They didn't dare return to Rome."

"They were sent by our people," said Berquist. "But they didn't *come* from our people. They had a separate arrangement with the same person who made the last untraceable call from Washington to Rome. Ambiguity."

"That same person, Mr President, who was able to reach into Moscow and pull out an authentic KGB code – anything less would never have been accepted by Havelock. Someone who knew the truth about Costa Brava, and was as anxious, perhaps as desperate as we are to keep a blackout on it."

"Why?" asked the general.

"Because if we went back and examined every aspect of the operation we might find he was there."

The President and the general reacted as though each had been told of an unexpected death; only Brooks remained passive, watching Bradford carefully, a first-rate mind acknowledging the presence of another.

"That's a hell of a jump, son," said Halyard.

"I can't think of any other explanation," said Bradford. "Havelock's execution had been sanctioned; the sanction was understood even by those who respected his record. He'd turned; he was a 'psycho', a killer, dangerous to every man in the field. But why was the woman at Col des Moulinets to be sent across the border? Why was the point made that she was a 'needle', a plant? Why was her escape a lesson to the Russians, when all the while a bomb timed to explode minutes later would have blown her away beyond recognition?"

"To maintain the illusion that she had died at the Costa Brava," said Brooks. "If she remained alive, she'd ask for asylum and tell her story; she'd have nothing to lose."

"Forcing a re-examination of the events of that night on the beach," completed the President. "She had to be killed away from that bridge while still preserving the lie that she had died at the Costa Brava."

"And the person who made the call authorizing Havelock's execution," said Halyard, frowning, the uncertainty in his voice, "who used the Ambiguity code and put this Ricci and the two nitro men in Col des Moulinets by way of Rome . . . you say he was on the beach that night?"

"Everything points to it, yes, General."

"For Christ's sake, *why*?"

"Because he knows Jenna Karras is alive," replied Ambassador Brooks, still watching Bradford. "At least, he knows she wasn't killed at Costa Brava. No one else did."

"That's speculation. It may have been kept quiet, but we've been looking for her for nearly four months."

"Without ever acknowledging it *was* her," explained the Undersecretary, "without ever admitting she *was* alive. The alert was for a person, not a name. A woman whose expertise as a deep cover agent could lead her to people she'd worked with previously under multiple identities. The emphasis was on physical appearance and languages."

"What I can't accept is your jump." Halyard shook his head, the gesture of a military strategist who sees a practical gap in a plan for field manoeuvre. "MacKenzie put Costa Brava together in pieces, reporting only to you. The CIA in Langley didn't know about Madrid, and Barcelona was kept away from both. Under those conditions how could someone penetrate what wasn't there? Unless you believe MacKenzie sold you out or loused it up."

"I don't think either." The Undersecretary paused. "I think the man who took the Ambiguity code was already involved with Parsifal three months ago. He knew what to concentrate on and became alarmed when Havelock was ordered to Madrid under a Four-Zero security."

"Someone with maximum clearance right here in the State Department," the ambassador broke in. "Someone with access to confidential memoranda."

"Yes. He kept tabs on Havelock's activities and saw that something was happening. He flew to Spain, picked him up in Madrid and followed him back to Barcelona. *I* was there; so was MacKenzie. He'd almost certainly recognize me, and as I met MacKenzie twice, it's reasonable to assume we were seen together."

"And presuming you were, it's also reasonable to assume that Moscow had a file on MacKenzie thick enough to alarm Soviet Intelligence." Brooks leaned forward, once again locking his eyes with Bradford's. "A photograph wired to the KGB, and the man we're looking for, who saw you together in Barcelona, knew a black operation was in progress."

"It could have happened that way, yes."

"With a lot of conjecture on your part," said Halyard.

"I don't think the Undersecretary of State is finished, Mal." The ambassador nodded his head at the papers Bradford had just separated and was scanning. "I don't believe he'd permit his imagination to wander into such exotic regions unless something triggered it. Am I right?"

"Substantially, yes."

"How about just plain yes," said the President.

"Yes," said the man from State. "I suppose I could be prosecuted for what I did this afternoon, but I considered it essential. I had to get away from the phones and the interruptions; I had to reread some of this material and provoke whatever imagination I have. I went to the classified files of Cons Op, removed Havelock's summary of Costa Brava under chemical therapy and took it home. I've been studying it since three o'clock – and remembering MacKenzie's verbal report after he came back from Barcelona. There are discrepancies."

"In what way?" asked Brooks.

"In what MacKenzie planned and in what Havelock saw."

"He saw what we wanted him to see," said the President. "You made a point of it a few minutes ago."

"He may have seen more than we think, more than MacKenzie engineered."

"MacKenzie was *there*," protested Halyard. "What the hell are you talking about?"

"He was approximately seventy yards away from Havelock, with only a peripheral view of the beach. He was more concerned with watching Havelock's reactions than with what was taking place below. He'd rehearsed it a number of times with the two men and the blonde woman. According to those practice sessions everything was to take place near the water, the shots fired into the surf, the woman falling into the wet sand, her body rolling with the waves, the boat close by, within reach. The distance, the darkness – everything was for effect."

"Visually convincing," interrupted Brooks.

"Very," agreed Bradford. "But it wasn't what Havelock described. What he saw was infinitely *more* convincing. Under chemicals at the clinic in Virginia he literally re-lived the entire experience, including the emotional trauma that was part of it. He described bullets erupting in the sand, the woman running up to the road, not down by the water, and two men carrying the body away. *Two* men."

"Two men were hired," said Halyard, perplexed. "What's the problem?"

"*One* had to be in the boat; it was twenty feet off-shore, the engine running. The *second* man was to have fired the shots and pulled the woman into the water, throwing her 'dead body', into the boat. The distance, the darkness, a beam of light – these were part of MacKenzie's scene, what he'd rehearsed with the people he'd hired. But the light was the only constant between what MacKenzie planned and what Havelock saw. He didn't witness a performance; he saw a woman actually killed."

"*Jesus.*" The general sat back in his chair.

"MacKenzie never mentioned any of this?" said Brooks.

"I don't think he saw it. All he said to me was 'My employees must have put on a hell of a show'. He stayed where he was on that hill above the road for several hours watching Havelock. He left when it began to get light; he couldn't risk Havelock's spotting him."

Addison Brooks brought his right hand to his chin. "So the man we're looking for, the man who pulled the trigger at Costa Brava, who was given the Ambiguity code by Stern and put Havelock 'beyond-salvage', is a Soviet agent in the State Department."

"Yes," said the Undersecretary.

"And he wants to find Parsifal as desperately as we do," concluded the President.

"Yes, sir."

"Yet, if I follow you," said Brooks quickly. "There's an enormous inconsistency. He hasn't passed on his astonishing information to his normal KGB controls. We'd know it if he had. Good *God*, we'd know it!"

"Not only has he held it back, Mr Ambassador, he's purposely misled a senior director of the KGB." Bradford picked up the top page of his notes and slid it respectfully towards the silver-haired statesman on his right. "I've saved this for last. Not, incidentally, to startle you or shock you, but only because it didn't make any sense unless we looked at everything else in relationship to it. Frankly, I'm still not sure I understand. It's a cable from Pyotr Rostov in Moscow. He's Director of External Strategies, KGB."

"A cable from *Soviet Intelligence?*" said Brooks, astonished, picking up the paper.

"Contrary to what most people believe," added the Undersecretary, "strategists from opposing intelligence services often make contact with one another. They're practical men in a deadly practical business. They can't afford wrong signals . . . According to Rostov, the KGB had nothing to do with the Costa Brava and he wanted us to know it. Incidentally, Colonel Baylor, in his report said that Rostov trapped Havelock in Athens and, although he could have got him out of Greece and into Russia by way of the Dardanelles, he chose not to."

"When did you get this?" asked the statesman.

"Twenty-four hours ago," answered the President. "We've been studying it, trying to work it out. Obviously no response is called for."

"Read it, Addison," said Halyard.

"It was sent to D. S. Stern, Director of Consular Operations, United States

Department of – " Brooks looked up at Bradford. "Stern was killed *three days* ago. Wouldn't Rostov have *known* that?"

"He wouldn't have sent it if he did. He wouldn't have permitted the slightest speculation that the KGB was involved in Stern's death. He sent that cable because he *didn't* know Stern was dead – or the others."

"Only Miller's death was released," said Berquist. "We couldn't keep it quiet; it was all over Bethesda. We put a blackout on Stern and Dawson, at least for the time being, until we could learn what was happening. We moved their families to the Cheyenne security compound in Colorado Springs."

"Read it," said the general.

Brooks held the paper under the glare of the Tensor lamp. He spoke slowly, reading in a monotone:

"The betrayal at Costa Brava was not ours. Nor was the bait taken in Athens. The infamous Consular Operations continues its provocative actions and the Soviet Union continues to protest its disregard for human life as well as the crimes and terrorist acts it inflicts upon the innocent – peoples and nations alike. And should this notorious branch of the American Department of State believe it has collaborators within the walls of Dzerzhinsky, be assured such traitors will be rooted out and face the punishments demanded. I repeat, Costa Brava was not ours."

The statesman finished; the cable was over. He let his hand drop to the dais, the page still held between his thumb and forefinger. "*Good Lord,*" he whispered.

"I understand the words," said Halyard, "but not what he's trying to tell us."

" 'Better the denial you know'," replied Brooks. "There are no walls in Dzerzhinsky Square."

"That's *it*," said Bradford, turning to the President. "That's what we didn't see. The walls are in the *Kremlin*."

"Outside and inside," continued the former ambassador. "He's telling you that he knows Costa Brava could not have taken place without a collaborator or collaborators in Moscow – "

"We understood that," interrupted Berquist. "What about the walls? The Kremlin? How do you read that?"

"He's warning us. He's saying he doesn't know who they are and, since he doesn't, they're not controllable."

"Because they're outside the normal channels of communication?" asked the President.

"Even abnormal channels," said Brooks.

"A power struggle." Berquist turned to the Undersecretary of State. "Has there been anything of a serious nature about this from any of our intelligence departments?"

"Only the usual frictions. The old guard dying, the younger commissars anxious, ambitious."

"Where do the generals stand?" inquired the general.

"Half wanting to blow up Omaha, half wanting SALT 3."

"And Parsifal could unite them," said the statesman. "*All* their hands would be on the nuclear switches."

"But Rostov doesn't *know* about Parsifal," protested Bradford. "He has no *conception* — "

"He senses it," the ambassador broke in. "He knows Costa Brava was a Department of State operation somehow in conjunction with elements in Moscow. He's tried to trace them down and can't; that alarms him immensely. There's an imbalance, a shift from the norm at the highest levels."

"Why do you say that?" The President took the cable from Brooks, scrutinizing it as if trying to see what he had not seen before.

"It's not in there, sir," said Bradford, nodding at Brooks as he spoke. "Except for the word 'bait', which refers to Havelock. Remember, he didn't take Havelock in Athens. Rostov's aware of the very unusual relationship between Michael Havelock and Anthony Matthias. Czech and Czech, teacher and student, survivors really . . . in many ways father and son; where does one end and the other begin? Is one or both of them dealing with someone in Moscow? And for what purpose? Reasonable objectives can be ruled out; avoiding normal channels would indicate that. Not too many months ago we wondered the same thing: What had Matthias done, and where did Havelock stand? We created Costa Brava because of it."

"And then Parsifal reached us and it didn't make any difference," interrupted Berquist. "We were at the wall. We're still at the wall — only now it's grown larger, broken away from itself until there are two walls, our backs to each no matter which way we turn. The search for Parsifal is joined with another search for another man. Someone right here who's watching every move we make. A Soviet mole capable of pulling a buried code out of Moscow, and deep enough to change the face of Costa Brava . . . My *God*, we've got to blow him out of the ground! If he finds Parsifal before we do, he and the madmen he answers to in the Kremlin can dictate whatever terms they like to this country."

"You know where he is," said the general. "Go after him! He's at State. High up; with access to embassy cables and obviously goddamned close to Matthias. Because if *I* follow you now, he nailed the Karras woman. He supplied that code; he had it placed in her suitcase. He *nailed* her!"

"I think he supplied everything." Bradford shook his head slowly, arching his brows as if recalling the impossible. "Including the suitcase, the Baader-Meinhof informer, our own codes and the instructions from Moscow. Everything just appeared in Barcelona . . . out of nowhere. And no one really knows how."

"I imagine it's pointless to press Matthias further?" said Brooks, asking the question nevertheless.

"Pointless," replied Bradford. "He repeats what he's maintained from the beginning. 'The evidence was there. It was true. It was channelled to me'."

"The bells are heard by Saint Anthony!" exploded the President.

"The mole at *State*," Halyard persisted. "Good *Christ*, he can't be that hard to find. How many people would Stern talk to? What kind of time frame was involved? A few minutes? A few hours? Go back and trace every move he made."

"The Cons Op strategists operated in total secrecy," said Bradford. "There were no appointment calendars, no conference schedules. A call would come to a specific person upstairs, or over at the Agency, or the NSC, and the decks were cleared for whichever strategist it was, but no record of the meeting was ever written down. Internal security again; a great deal could be pieced together by informers with access to such records or memoranda."

"Misdirect the flow of accurate information at all costs," said the President softly.

"By our estimates, Stern could have spoken to any of sixty to seventy-five people," continued Bradford. "And we could be *underestimating* that figure. There are authorities within teams of specialists, specialists among those considered authorities. The lists are endless, and all those people have maximum clearance."

"But we're talking about the *State Department*," said the silver-haired Brooks emphatically. "Some time between Stern's last conversation with Rome and four hours later when the authorization was given to Col des Moulinets. That narrows down the possibilities considerably."

"And whoever it is knows that," said the Undersecretary. "It further obscures his movements. Even the check-ins and check-outs won't show him to be where he was."

"Didn't anyone *see* Stern?" persisted Brooks. "Surely you've asked."

"As quietly as we could. Not one of those we questioned admitted seeing him within twenty-four hours of the period in question, but then we didn't expect the one who did to say so."

"*Nobody* saw him?" asked the general, frowning in disbelief.

"Well, yes, someone did," said Bradford, nodding. "The outside receptionist on the fifth floor, L Section. Dawson had left a message for Stern; he picked it up on his way to the elevator. He could have been in any of seventy-five offices beyond the reception room door."

"Who was inside at the time?" The ambassador shook his head the instant he had asked the question, as if to say "sorry, never mind".

"Exactly," said Bradford, accepting the statesman's unspoken afterthought. "It wasn't any help. Twenty-three people were listed as not having checked out. There were conferences, secretaries taking notes and briefings by division personnel. Everything was substantiated. No one left a meeting long enough to place that call."

"But, damn it, you've got a floor!" cried the soldier. "Seventy-five offices, seventy-five people. That's not a hundred and fifty, or a thousand; it's seventy-five and one of them's your mole! Start with those closest to Matthias and pull them in. Put every goddamn one of them into a clinic if you have to!"

"There'd be panic; the entire State Department would be demoralized," said Brooks. "*Unless* . . . is there a clique, a particular group closest to Matthias?"

"You don't understand him." Bradford brought his folded hands to his chin, searching for words. "He's first, last and always *Doctor* Matthias, teacher, enlightener, provoker-of-thought. He's a hustling Socrates on the Potomac, gathering his worshippers wherever he can find them, extolling those who see the light, striking down the disbelievers with the cruellest humour I've ever heard. Cruel but always couched in brilliantly humble phrases. And like most self-appointed arbiters of an élite, his arrogance makes him fickle as hell. A section will catch his eye and they're his fair-haired boys and girls for a while, until another group comes along and flatters him at the right moment and there's suddenly a new court of supplicants he can lecture. Naturally, during the past year it's got worse – but it was always there." Bradford permitted himself the start of a strained smile. "Then, of course, I could be biased. I was never allowed into one of those charmed circles."

"Why do you think you were excluded?" asked the ambassador.

"I'm not sure. I had a certain reputation of my own once; perhaps he was uncomfortable with it. But I think it was because I used to watch him very closely, very hard. I was fascinated, and I know he was uncomfortable with that . . . You see, the 'best and the brightest' were led down a lot of strange paths by men like him. Some of us grew up and I don't think Matthias approved of that growth. Scepticism comes with it. The Thomistic leap isn't good enough any more; blind faith can ruin the eyesight – and the perspective." Bradford leaned forward, his eyes on Halyard. "I'm sorry, General. My answer to both you and Ambassador Brooks is that there is no one group I'd zero in on, no guarantee that our mole would be caught before he panicked and ran. And we can't let that happen. I know I'm right. If we can find him, he can lead us to the man we call Parsifal. He may have lost him temporarily, but he knows who Parsifal is."

The older men were silent; they gazed at each other, then turned back to Bradford. The general frowned, a questioning look in his clear eyes. The President nodded his head slowly, bringing his right hand to his cheek and staring at the man from State.

The ambassador spoke, his slender figure rigid in his chair. "I commend you, Mr Undersecretary. May I try to reconstruct the new scenario? . . . For reasons unknown, Matthias needed an incontrovertible case against the Karras woman, which would lead to Havelock's retirement. By now, because of what he's done, Matthias is Parsifal's puppet – his prisoner, really – but Parsifal knows it's in his interest to carry out Matthias's obsession. He goes to a well-entrenched Soviet agent in the upper regions of the State Department and the incriminating evidence against the Karras woman is provided, studied and accepted. Except that two source controls from the CIA come to you and tell you it can't be true – any of it – and you, Emory Bradford, enter the picture. In fact, the President, alarmed by what appears to be a conspiracy at State, brings us *all* into the picture – and we in turn recruit a black-operations officer to mount the Costa Brava exercise. That exercise – that scene – is turned into murder and at this juncture, it's your thesis that the mole lost sight of Parsifal."

"Yes. Parsifal, whoever he is, got what he wanted from the mole, then dropped him. The mole is stunned, possibly frantic. He's undoubtedly made promises to Moscow based on assurances from Parsifal – that projected a major setback for American foreign policy, conceivably, its collapse."

"Either," interjected the President in a quiet monotone, "would be benevolent alternatives."

"And whoever has the information contained in Parsifal's documents will assume control of the Kremlin." Brooks remained rigid, his aristocratic face pale, drawn. "We're at war," he added softly.

"I repeat," said Halyard. "Go after those seventy-five offices at State. Mount a sweep, call it a medical quarantine; it's simple but effective, even acceptable. Do it in the early evening after they've left work. Round them up in their homes, restaurants; pull them in and get them down to your laboratories. Find your mole!" The general's forceful rendering of the tactic impressed the civilians, who remained silent. Halyard lowered his voice. "I know it smells, but I don't think you've got a choice."

"We'd need two hundred men posing as medical technicians and drivers," said Bradford. "Between thirty and forty government vehicles. No one knowing anything."

"We'd also be dealing with families and neighbours with 'technicians' knocking on doors at night," countered Berquist. "*Christ*, that son of a bitch! That *man* for all *seasons*!" The President stopped; he took a deep breath, then continued. "We'd never get away with it; the rumours would spread like a Mesabi brush fire in a dry July. The press would break it open and call us everything in the book, everything we deserve. Mass arrests without explanation – there's none we could give – interrogations without due process, storm troopers . . . chemicals. We'd be crucified on every editorial page in the country, hanged in effigy on every campus, denounced from every pulpit and soap box, to say nothing of the acid from our legislative brethren. I'd be impeached."

"More important, Mr President," said the ambassador, "and I'm sorry to say I mean that, the action itself would undoubtedly throw Parsifal into panic. He'd see what we were doing, know whom we were trying to unearth in order to find him. He could carry out his threats, carry out the inconceivable."

"Yes, I know. We're damned if we move, helpless if we don't."

"It could *work*," persisted the general.

"Handled correctly, it might, Mr President," added Bradford.

"For God's sake how?"

"Anyone who objected strenuously, to the point of refusal or evasion, would probably be our man," replied Bradford.

"Or someone with something else to hide," said Brooks gently. "We're in the age of anxiety, Mr Undersecretary, and this is a city with a low threshold for privacy. You might very well corner a person who has nothing more to conceal than an unopened closet. The loathing of a superior, or an unpopular viewpoint, or an office affair. Parsifal will see only what his insanity compels him to see."

Bradford listened, reluctantly accepting the statesman's judgement. "There's another approach we haven't had time to implement. An itinerary check. Tracing the whereabouts of every person on that floor during the week of Costa Brava. If we're right . . . if I'm not wrong . . . he wasn't here. He was in Madrid, in Barcelona."

"He'd cover himself," objected Halyard.

"Even so, General, he'd have to account for being away from Washington. How many such absences can there be?"

"When can you start?" asked Berquist.

"First thing in the morning – "

"Why not tonight?" the general interrupted.

"If those records were accessible, I could. They're not, and to call someone in to open them at this hour would cause talk. We can't afford that."

"Even in the morning," said the ambassador, "how can you suppress curiosity, keep it quiet?"

Bradford paused before speaking, his eyes cast downward, seeking an answer. "Time study," he replied, looking up, the phrase bordering on a question. "I'll tell whoever controls those records that it's a routine time study. Someone's always doing something like that."

"Acceptable," agreed Brooks. "Banal and acceptable."

"Nothing's acceptable," said the President of the United States quietly, staring at the white wall where an hour ago the faces of four dead men had been projected. " 'A man for all seasons', they call him. The original was a scholar, a statesman, the creator of Utopia . . . *and* a burner of heretics – they conveniently forget that, don't they? 'Condemn the nonbelievers; they don't see what I see, and I'm – inviolate' . . . Goddamn it, if I had my way, I'd do what fat Henry did with Thomas More. I'd cut off Matthias's head, and jam it on top of the Washington Monument as a reminder. Heretics, too, are citizens of the Republic, and as such, *holy* man, there is no heresy! *Goddamn him!*"

"You know what would happen, don't you, Mr President?"

"Yes, Mr Ambassador, I do. The people would look up at that bleeding neck, at that ever-benign face – no doubt with those tortoiseshell glasses still intact – and in their infinite wisdom they'd say he was right, had been right all along. Citizens – heretics included – would canonize him, and that's the lousy irony."

"He could still do it, I think," Brooks mused. "He could walk out and the cries would start again. They'd offer him the crown and he'd refuse and they'd persist – until it became inevitable. Another irony. Hail not Caesar but Anthony – a coronation. A constitutional amendment would be rammed through the House and the Senate and President Matthias would sit in the Oval Office. As incredible as it might seem, he could probably still do it. Even now."

"Maybe we should let him," said Berquist softly, bitterly. "Maybe the people – in their *infinite* wisdom – are right after all. Maybe *he's* been right all along. Sometimes I don't know any more. Perhaps he really does see things others don't see. Even now."

The aristocratic statesman and the plainspoken general left the underground room. The four would meet again at noon the next day, each arriving separately at the south portico entrance, away from the inquisitive eyes of the White House press corps. If, in the morning, there were any startling developments in Bradford's research at State, the time would be moved forward, the President's calendar erased. The mole took all precedence. He could lead them to a madman the President and his advisers called Parsifal.

" 'I commend you, Mr Undersecretary'," said Berquist, lowering his voice in an amateur's imitation of the ambassador's fluid and graceful speech. It was an imitation with only a trace of rancour; respect was also there. "He's the last of the originals, isn't he?"

"Yes, sir. There aren't many left, and none that I know of who care that much.

Taxes and the great democratization have removed them – or alienated them. They feel uncomfortable and I think it's the country's loss."

"Don't be sepulchral, Emory, it doesn't suit you. We need him; the power brokers on the Hill are still in awe of him. If there was ever an answer to Matthias, it's Addison Brooks. *The Mayflower* and Plymouth Rock, New York's Four Hundred and fortunes built on the backs of immigrants – leading to the guilt feelings of the inheritors: benevolent liberals who weep at the sight of swollen black bellies in the Mississippi Delta. But for Christ's sake, don't take away the *Château d'Yquem*."

"Yes, Mr President."

"You mean 'No, Mr President'. It's in your eyes, Emory; it's always in the eyes. Don't mistake me, I admire old elegant-ass, respect what's in that head of his. Just as I think Tightrope Halyard's one of the few military relics who've actually read the Constitution and understand what civilian authority really means. It's not that war's too important to leave to the generals; that's horseshit. We'd both be rotten pincering up the Rhine. It's the *ending* of wars, the aftermath. The generals are reluctant to accept the first and have no concept of the second. Halyard's different, and the Pentagon knows it. The Joint Chiefs listen to him because he's better than they are. We need him, too."

"I agree."

"That's what this office is all about. Need. Not likes or dislikes, only need. If I ever get back to Mountain Iron, Minnesota, alive and in one piece, I can think about whether I like someone or not. But I can't do that now. It's only what I need. And what I need right now is to stop Parsifal, stop what he's done, what he did to Anthony Matthias." The President paused, then continued, "I meant what I said – *he* said. I *do* commend you. It was a hell of a job."

"Thank you, sir."

"Especially what you didn't say. Havelock. Where is he?"

"Almost certainly in Paris; it's where Jenna Karras was heading. Between pages this afternoon I placed a number of calls to people I know in the Assembly, the Senate, several ministries, the Quai d'Orsay and our own embassy. I applied pressure, hinting that my orders came from the White House, but without mentioning you by name."

"You could have."

"Not yet, Mr President. Perhaps never, but certainly not now."

"Then we understand each other," said Berquist.

"Yes, sir. Necessity."

"Halyard might have understood; he's a practical soldier. Brooks wouldn't; underneath that diplomatic exterior he's a thorough moralist."

"That was my assessment, why I didn't clarify Havelock's status."

"It remains what it was at Col des Moulinets. If he exposed Costa Brava, it would panic Parsifal more quickly than anything we might do in the State Department. Havelock was at the centre – from the beginning."

"I understand, sir."

Berquist's eyes strayed to the blank white screen at the far end of the room. "In World War Two, Churchill had to make a decision that tore him apart. The German code machine Enigma had been broken by Allied Intelligence, a feat which meant that military strategies issued from Berlin could be intercepted and hundreds of thousands – ultimately perhaps millions – of lives could be saved. Word came that a massive air strike had been called against Coventry. It was a single transmission, coded through Enigma. But to acknowledge it, to evacuate the city or even to mount sudden, abnormal defences, would reveal that the riddle of Enigma had been solved . . . Coventry had to be bombed half out of existence so the secret could be kept. The secret of Costa Brava cannot be exposed for the same reason – millions of lives are in the balance. Find Havelock, Mr Undersecretary. Find him and have him killed. Reinstate the order for his execution."

19

Havelock knew he had been spotted. A newspaper was abruptly lowered as he walked between the roped stanchions of Air France's disembarkation lounge at Kennedy into the corridor that led to Immigration. He had been pre-cleared on diplomatic status, the papers Broussac had provided guaranteeing a rapid exit through US Customs, and because of this accommodation he understood that he must destroy those papers as quickly as possible. He carried his small suitcase – officially lock-taped and stamped *Diplomatique* in Paris – and once through the corridor he would be admitted through the heavy metal doors that led into the terminal by simply showing his United Nations credentials and declaring that he had no other luggage. A dead-file name would be checked against a dead-file name on the manifest and he would be free to search or be killed in the United States of America. It was all so simple.

However, for Régine Broussac's protection – and ultimately his own – he had to get rid of the false papers that made all this possible. Also, he had to find out who had lowered the newspaper. The grey-faced man had risen slowly from his seat, folded the newspaper under his arm and started for the outer, crowded hallway that paralleled the inner corridor that led to questionable freedom. Who was that man?

If he could not find out, it was entirely possible that he would be killed before he could search, before he reached a halfway broker named Jacob Handelman. And that was not acceptable.

The uniformed immigration officer was astute, polite. He asked the proper questions while looking Havelock directly in the eyes.

"You have no luggage, sir?"

"*Non, monsieur.* Only the one piece here."

"Then you don't expect to be on First Avenue very long?"

"A day, forty-eight hours," replied Michael, with a Gallic shrug. "*One conference.*"

"I'm sure your government has made arrangements for transportation into the city. Wouldn't you care to wait for the rest of your party?"

The official was *very* good. "Forgive me, *monsieur*, you force me to be candid." Michael smiled awkwardly, as though his dignity had been somewhat compromised. "There is a lady waiting for me; we see each other so seldom. Perhaps it is noted on your information, I was posted at . . . First Avenue for several months last year. Haste, *mon ami*, haste is on my mind."

Slowly the official returned the smile as he checked off the name and reached for a button. "Have a good day, sir," he said.

"Many thanks," said Havelock, walking rapidly through the parting steel checkpoint. *Vive les amours des gentilshommes français*, he thought.

The grey-faced man was standing by a short row of telephones, each occupied; he was second in line behind the third. The newspaper, which had been folded under the arm, was instantly removed and snapped open. He had not been able to make his call, and under the circumstances that was the best sight Michael could hope to see.

He started walking in the man's direction, passing him quickly and looking straight ahead. He took the first turning left, into an intersecting wide corridor crowded with streams of departing passengers heading for their gates. He swung right into a narrower hallway, this one with far fewer people and the majority of these in the uniforms of the various airlines.

Left again, the corridor longer, still narrow, even fewer people, mostly men in white overalls and shirtsleeves; he had entered some kind of freight complex, the office section. There were no passengers, no business suits, no briefcases or carry-on bags.

There were no public telephones. The walls were stark, broken up by widely spaced glass doors. The nearest phones were far behind, around the corner in the first, main hallway. Out of sight.

He found the men's room; it said, *Airport Employees Only*. Michael pushed the door open and walked inside. It was a large tiled room, two air vents whirring on the far wall, no windows. A row of toilet booths was on the left, basins and urinals on the right. A man in overalls with the words *Excelsior Airline Caterers* was positioned in front of the fourth urinal; a flush came from one of the booths. Havelock went to a sink, placing his suitcase under it.

The man at the urinal stepped back and zipped up his overalls; he glanced at Michael, his eyes taking in an expensive dark suit purchased that morning in Paris. Then, as if to say, all right Mr Executive, I'll wash my hands, he ambled to the nearest basin and turned on the water.

A second man emerged from a booth; he pulled his belt taut and started for the door, swearing under his breath, the plastic ID tag pinned to his shirt indicating a harried supervisor.

The man in overalls ripped a paper towel out of a stainless steel machine, cursorily wiped his hands and threw the harsh brown paper into a receptacle. He opened the door, and stepped out. As the door swung back Havelock ran to catch it, holding it open no more than an inch, and peered outside.

The unknown surveillance was fifty-odd feet up the corridor, casually leaning against the wall next to an office door, reading the folded newspaper. He looked at his watch, then glanced at the frosted glass panel; he was the image of a visitor waiting for a friend to come out and join him for a late lunch or drinks, or a drive to a motel near the airport. There was nothing menacing about him, but in that control Michael knew there was menace, professionalism.

Still, two could have control, two could wait, be professional. The advantage belonged to the one behind a door; he knew what was inside. The one outside did not, and could not afford to move away – to a telephone, perhaps – because once out of sight the quarry could escape.

Wait. Keep your control. And get rid of the false papers that could lead the pursuers to Régine Broussac and a halfway man named Jacob Handelman. A dead-file name on an aircraft's manifest was meaningless, inserted by mindless computers that could not say who punched the keys, but the papers could be traced to their origin. Havelock tore the documents into shreds, which he flushed down a toilet. With a penknife he sliced the ribbed *Diplomatique* tape which guaranteed the absence of official inspection, and opened his suitcase in a booth at the end of the row. He removed the short-barrelled Llama automatic from beneath his folded clothes, and a passport case containing his own very authentic papers. Presented properly, the papers were essentially harmless. The objective, however, was not to have to present them at all, and it was rarely required in the streets of his adopted country, one of the benefits for which he was profoundly thankful.

During the time he destroyed the mocked-up papers and inserted his passport case and weapon in their proper places, the employees' men's room had two more visitors. They came in together – an Air France pilot and his First Officer to judge from their conversation: Michael remained in the stall. They argued, urinated, swore at pre-flight red tape and wondered how much their Havana *Monte Cristos* would fetch at the bar of *L'Auberge au Coin*, a restaurant apparently in mid-town Manhattan. They continued talking about their profits on the way out.

Havelock took off the jacket of his suit, rolled it up and waited in the stall. He held the door open no more than a quarter of an inch and looked at his watch. He had been inside the lavatory nearly fifteen minutes. It would happen soon, he thought.

It did. The white metal door swung slowly back, and Havelock saw part of a shoulder first, then the edge of a folded newspaper. The unknown surveillance *was* professional: no folded jacket or coat concealed a gun – no draped cloth that could be grabbed and twisted, to be used against the holder – just a loose newspaper that could be easily discarded and the weapon fired cleanly.

The man whipped around the door, his back against the metal panel, his eyes scanning the walls, the vents, the row of stalls. Satisfied, he bent his knees, lowering himself, but apparently not for the purpose of checking the open spaces under the doors of the first several stalls. His body was turned away from Michael. His eyes darted back and forth. What was he doing?

And then he did it, and the image of another professional on the bridge at Col des Moulinets came to Michael, a blond professional in the uniform of an Italian guard. But the killer "Ricci" had come prepared, knowing what his landscape was, knowing there was a gatehouse door to be jammed. This grey-faced professional had improvised, the test of on-site ingenuity. He had broken off a piece of wood, a small strip of cheap industrial moulding – found in a dozen places in any airport

594

corridor – and was now wedging it under the door. He stood up, placed his foot against the strip, and pulled on the metal knob. The door was jammed; they were alone. The man turned.

Peering from inside the stall, Havelock studied him. The menace was not at first glance in the man's physical equipment. He was perhaps in his mid-fifties, with thinning hair above a flat grey face with thick eyebrows and high cheekbones. He was no taller than five feet, eight inches, and his shoulders were narrow, compact. But then Michael saw the left hand – the right was concealed beneath the newspaper; it was huge, a peasant's powerful hand, formed by years of working with heavy objects and equipment.

The man started down the row of stalls, the sides of each about two inches above the tiled floor, which made it necessary for him to be within three feet of a front panel to ascertain whether it was occupied. Wearing shoes with thick rubber soles, he moved in total silence. Suddenly he spun his right hand in a circle, flipping off the newspaper. Havelock stared at the gun, as the intruder approached the final three stalls. He was angry but bewildered – the weapon was a Graz-Burya. The Russian bent over. . .

Now. Michael threw his rolled-up suit jacket over the side of the booth on his right. The sound made the Russian leap up, spinning to his left, his gun raised.

Havelock grabbed the handle of his suitcase and simultaneously yanked the door open, then swung the heavy case at the man, body and extended arms following, his eyes on the Graz-Burya, his left hand reaching it, gripping it, tearing it upwards. The Russian spun away, his powerful arms blocking Havelock; Michael used them. He locked the man's left arm under his right, wrenched it forward until the Russian's face was stretched in pain; then he prised the weapon loose, crashing the barrel into the man's head. The Russian started to fall and Havelock crouched and jammed his shoulder into the man's kidney, propelling him back into the row of urinals.

The grey-faced man fell to his knees, supporting himself on his right hand and holding his left arm across his chest in pain. He gasped for breath, shaking his head. "*Nyet, nyet,*" he choked. "Talk only! Only *talk.*"

"With the door as good as locked and a gun in your hand?"

"Would you have agreed to a conversation if I had come up and introduced myself? In Russian, perhaps?"

"You should have tried me."

"You did not stay still long enough . . . May I?" The Russian leaned back on his knees, holding his arm and raising one leg as he requested permission to stand.

"Go ahead," said Havelock, the Graz-Burya steady in his hand. "You were trying to make a phone call."

"Certainly. To relay word that you had been found. What would you have done? I don't know, or perhaps I should not ask."

"What *do* you know? How did you find me?" Michael raised the gun, aiming it at the man's head. "I'd advise you to tell me the truth. I haven't got a thing to lose with your corpse in here."

The Russian stared at the barrel and then at Havelock's eyes. "No, you have nothing to lose; you would not hesitate. A younger man should have been sent out here."

"How did you know I'd be on that plane?"

"I didn't. No one knows anywhere . . . A VKR officer was shot in Paris; he had nowhere to turn but to us."

"An importing firm on the Beaumarchais?" interrupted Michael. "KGB headquarters, Paris?"

The Russian overlooked the interruption. "We knew you had connections throughout the French government. Military intelligence, the Quai d'Orsay, the Deputies. If it was your intention to leave France there was only one way you could do it. Diplomatic cover. All Air France flights listing diplomatic personnel are being watched. Everywhere. London, Rome, Bonn, Athens, the Netherlands, all of South America – everywhere. It's my misfortune that you chose to come back here; it was not expected. You're 'beyond-salvage'."

"That seems to be a well-publicized piece of information."

"It has been circulated in certain quarters."

"Is that what you wanted to talk about? Because if it is, Moscow's wasting a lot of man hours in all those airports."

"I bring you a message from Pyotr Rostov. He believes that after Rome, you might listen."

"*Rome?* What about Rome?"

"The Palatine. It would seem it was conclusive for you. You were meant to die on the Palatine Hill."

"I was?" Havelock watched the man's eyes, the set of his lips. So Rostov knew about the Palatine; it was to be expected. Bodies had been found there: the corpse of a former American agent known for jugular operations and his two wounded Italian drones who had nothing to lose and something to bargain with by telling the truth. Certainly Moscow knew. But Rostov did not know about Jenna Karras or Col des Moulinets or he would have included them in his opening lure. Under different circumstances, it might have been necessary to shout the words quickly: *Jenna Karras is alive! Col des Moulinets!* Both were far more conclusive. "What's the message?"

"He says to tell you the bait's been reconsidered. He'll take it now and thinks you should agree. He says he's not your enemy any longer, but others are who may be his as well."

"What does that mean?"

"I can't answer you," said the man, his thick eyebrows motionless above his deep-set peasant eyes. "I'm merely the messenger. The substance is for you to know, not me."

"You knew about the Palatine."

"The death of a maniac travels fast, especially if he's your adversary – most especially if he's killed a number of your friends . . . What was the name his own people gave him? The 'Gunslinger', I believe. A romantic figure from your Western films, which, incidentally, I enjoy immensely. But in history such a fellow was invariably a filthy, unprincipled pig, devoid of morals or ideology, motivated solely by profit or pathological brutality. In these times he might be the president of an enormous corporation, no?"

"Spare me. Save it for the state schools."

"Rostov would like a reply, but you don't have to give it at once. I can reach you. A day, two days – a few hours from now. You may name the drop. We can get you out. To safety."

Again Michael studied the Russian's face. Like Rostov in Athens before him, the man was relaying the truth – as he knew the truth, and as he knew the word of his superior in Moscow. "What does Rostov offer?"

"I told you. Safety. You know what's ahead of you here. The Palatine Hill."

"Safety in exchange for what?"

"That's between you and Rostov. Why should I invent conditions? You would not believe them."

"Tell Rostov he's wrong."

"About Rome? The Palatine?"

"The Palatine," said Havelock, wondering briefly whether a KGB director ten thousand miles away would perceive the essential truth within the larger lie. "I don't need the safety of the Lubyanka."

"You refuse his offer then?"

"I refuse the bait."

There was a sudden thud against the men's-room door, followed by a muffled voice swearing, then repeated banging against the metal panel. The strip of wood wedged under the door scraped the tile; it gave less than an inch, which was enough to make the intruder shout, while continuing to pound the door, "Hey, what the hell is this! Open up!"

The Russian glanced at the door; Havelock did not. The man spoke rapidly: "Should you change your mind, there is a row of trash cans in Bryant Park, behind the Public Library. Place a red mark on the front of one of them – I suggest a felt marker or, better still, a spot of woman's nail polish. Then, starting at ten o'clock that same night, walk north and south on Broadway, between Forty-second and Fifty-third Streets, staying on the east side. Someone will reach you, giving you the address of the contact. It will be outside, naturally. No traps."

"What's going *on* in there? Fa' *Christ's sake*, open this goddamned *door!*"

"I thought you said I could pick the drop."

"You may. Simply tell the man who reaches you where you want to meet. Just give us three hours."

"To sweep it?"

"Son of a bitch! *Open up!*" The metal door was smashed back several inches, the strip of wood scratching against the tiles.

A second, authoritative voice joined that of the angry intruder. "All right, what's this all about?"

"The door's jammed! I can't get in, but I hear 'em talkin'! They jammed the fuckin' door!" Another crash, another screech, another inch.

"We take precautions, just as you do," said the Russian. "What's between you and Rostov . . . is between you and Moscow. We are not in Moscow, *I* am not in Moscow. I do not call for the police when I'm in trouble in New York City."

"All *right* in there!" shouted the second voice in lower-register officiousness. "Fair warning, you punks! Obstruction of normal operating procedures at an international airport constitutes a felony, and that includes the toilets! I'm calling Airport Security!" The stern-toned one addressed the angry intruder. "If I were you, I'd find another men's room. These kids use needles; they can get hopped up and pretty violent."

"I've gotta' take one pisser of a leak, man! And they don't *sound* like no kids — There's a cop! Hey, *Fuzz!*"

"He can't hear you. He's walking past. I'll get to a phone."

"*Shit!*"

"Let's go," said Havelock, reaching down for his jacket. He slipped it on, switching the gun back and forth as he did so.

"My life, then?" asked the Russian. "No corpse in a men's room?"

"I want my reply delivered. Forget the nail polish on those trash cans."

"Then, if I may, my weapon, please?"

"I'm not that charitable. You see, you *are* my enemy. You have been for a long time."

"It's difficult to explain a missing weapon. *You* understand."

"Tell them you sold it on the open market; it's the first step in capitalism. Buy cheap — or get it for nothing and sell high. The Burya's a good gun; it'd bring a large profit."

"*Please!*"

"You don't understand, *Comrade.* You'd be surprised how many hustlers in Moscow would respect you. Come *on!*" Havelock grabbed the grey-faced man by the shoulder, propelling him towards the door. "Kick out the wood," he ordered, shoving the weapon into his belt and picking up his suitcase.

The Russian did as he was told. He pressed the side of his shoe on the protruding wedge, moving it back and forth as he pushed the door shut. The wedge came loose; he swept it away with his foot, and pulled the door open.

"Jesus *Christ!*" exclaimed an obese man in sky-blue overalls. "A couple of fuckin' fairies!"

"They're *coming!*" yelled a shirtsleeved man, running out of an office door across the corridor.

"I think you're too late, Mr Supervisor," said the wide-eyed freight employee, staring at Havelock and the Russian. "Here're your fuckin' punks. Two old queens who figured the parking lot was too cold."

"Let's *go!*" whispered Havelock, grabbing the Russian's elbow.

"Disgusting! Revolting!" shouted the supervisor. "At your age! Have you no *shame?* Perverts *everywhere!*"

"You won't change your mind about the weapon?" asked the Russian, walking breathlessly up the corridor, wincing as Michael gripped his damaged left arm. "I'll be severely disciplined. I haven't used it for years; it's really a form of dress, you know."

"*Perverts!* You should all be in jail, not in public toilets! You're a menace!"

"I'm telling you, you'll get a promotion if the right people think you made a bundle."

"*Faggots!*"

"Let go of my arm. That idiot's marking us."

"Why? You're adorable."

They reached the second hallway, turning left towards the centre of the terminal. There were, as before, men in overalls and shirtsleeves milling about, watching an occasional secretary emerge from an office door. Up ahead was the main corridor, crowds surging in both directions, towards departing gates and luggage areas.

In seconds they were swept into the flow of arrivals. Seconds later a trio of uniformed police could be seen breaking through the stream of departing passengers, pushing aside shoulders and small suitcases and plastic clothes bags. Havelock switched sides with the Russian, yanking him to the left, and as the police came parallel in the opposite aisle Michael crashed his shoulder into his companion, pummelling him into a blue uniform.

"*Nyet! Kishki!*" yelled the Russian.

"*Goddamn* it!" shouted the police officer as he plunged off balance to his right, tripping one of his associates, who in turn fell on top of an elderly blue-haired woman.

Havelock accelerated his pace, threading his way past startled passengers who were rushing towards an escalator on the right that led to the baggage area, where they could retrieve their belongings. On the left was someone's idea of a celestial arch which led into the central terminal; he headed towards it, walking faster still as the path became less congested. In the terminal the bright afternoon sunlight streamed through the huge floor-to-ceiling windows. He looked around as he went towards the exit door marked *Taxis*. There were rows of counters beneath panoplies of white-lettered schedules, isolated slots constantly in motion; circular booths selling knick-knacks and gewgaws were dotted about in the middle of the dome-like building. Along the walls were banks of telephones and indented racks of telephone books. He veered towards the nearest one.

Thirty seconds later he found it: *Handelman, J.* The address was in upper Manhattan, on 116th Street, Morningside Heights.

Jacob Handelman, halfway man, broker of sanctuary for the pursued and the dispossessed. The man who would conceal Jenna Karras.

"Stop over there," said Havelock, leaning forward in the seat and pointing to a blue canopy emblazoned with a small gold crown and the name *The King's Arms Hotel* across the scalloped valance. He hoped he would not have to spend the night – each hour put greater distance between Jenna and himself – but on the other hand, he could not walk around Columbia University carrying even a small suitcase while tracking down Jacob Handelman. He had told the cab driver to take the Triborough Bridge, head west towards the Hudson and south into Morningside Heights; he wanted to pass the address on 116th, then find a secure place to leave his luggage. It was mid-afternoon and the halfway man could be anywhere within the sprawling urban campus.

Michael had been to Columbia twice while a graduate student at Princeton, once for a lecture on Europe after Napoleon delivered by a visiting bore from Oxford, and the second time for an inter-graduate-school seminar on university placement. Neither occasion was memorable, both were brief, and as a result he really knew nothing about the place. That was probably irrelevant, but the fact that he knew absolutely nothing about Jacob Handelman was not.

The King's Arms was around the corner from Handelman's apartment. It was one of those small hotels that somehow managed to survive tastefully within the environs of a city university, upper Manhattan's answer to the old Taft in New Haven or, stretching a point, the Inn at Princeton. In essence, a campus fixture, temporary quarters for visiting lecturers rather than an undergraduate drinking spot. It had the appearance of dark-leather English comfort and the smell of Academe. It was only an outside possibility, but since the hotel was so close to Handelman's residence, there was a chance someone might know him.

"Certainly, Mr Hereford," said the clerk, reading the registration card. "Dr Handelman calls in now and then – a little wine or dinner with friends. A delightful gentleman, a most charming sense of humour. We here, like almost everyone else, call him the Rabbi."

"I didn't know that. His being a rabbi, I mean."

"I'm not sure he is formally, although I doubt anyone would question his credentials. He's Jarmaine Professor of Philosophy and I understand he lectures frequently at Jewish Theological. You'll enjoy your interview."

"I'm sure I will. Thank you."

"Front," said the clerk, tapping a bell.

Handelman's apartment was between Broadway and Riverside Drive. The sloping street overlooked Riverside Park and the Hudson. It was a solid structure of heavy white stone – once a monument to New York's exploding upward mobility – which had been permitted to age gently, and to pass through periods of brief renaissance, only to recede into that graveyard of tall, awkwardly ornate edifices too cumbersome for efficient economics. Once there had been a doorman standing in front of the glass-and-ironwork façade; now there were double locks on the inner door and a functioning communications system between visitor and resident.

Havelock pressed the bell, intending merely to make sure Handelman was home; there was no reply from the speaker. He rang again. Nothing.

He went back outside, crossing the street to an opposite doorway, and considered his options. He had telephoned the university's information centre and been given the location and number of Handelman's office. A second call – placed anonymously by an administrations clerk requesting a Thursday *Stat sheet* – revealed the fact that Handelman had doctoral appointments until after four P.M. It was now nearly five o'clock, and Michael's frustration was growing. Where *was* Handelman? There was, of course, no guarantee that he would come directly home from his office, but a broker of sanctuary who had just placed – or was placing – a woman fugitive from Paris had certain obligations. Havelock had considered going to Handelman's office, or intercepting him on the street; he considered both again. Perhaps an appointment had run late, or dinner been proffered; someone could still be there who might know, who might help him. Coping with the tension of waiting – a practice he was normally superb at – was causing him pain, actual physical pain in his stomach. He breathed deeply; he could not confront the halfway man in an office or on the street or in any public place and he knew it. The meeting must take place where there were names and numbers, maps and codes; these were the tools of a halfway man. They would only be kept where he could store them safely, reach them quickly. Under a floorboard, or deep in a wall, or microscopically reduced and in the toe of a shoe or implanted in shirt buttons.

He had not seen a photograph of Handelman, but he knew what he looked like. The florid-faced bartender at The King's Arms Hotel – himself apparently a fixture, with the flair and verbosity of a fifth-rate poet from Dublin – had described "the Rabbi". Jacob Handelman was a medium-tall man with long white hair and a short grey beard, slightly given to overweight and more than slightly to a paunch. His walk was "slow and stately", the bartender said, "as if he was the Judaic blood-royal, sir, forever partin' the waters, or mountin' the ark to discourse with the animals. Ah, but he has a gleam in his eye and a lovely heart, sir."

Havelock had listened to the man and ordered a double scotch.

Three minutes past five. *Breathe deep. Really breathe and think of Jenna, think what you're going to say to her. It could be an hour or two, or longer, perhaps half the night. Half the night for the halfway man. Don't dwell on it.*

Dusk lingered, the orange sun inflaming the New Jersey skyline beyond the Hudson River. The West Side Highway was jammed, and Riverside Drive, parallel to it, was barely less so. The temperature was dropping and grey clouds joined the darkening sky; a March snow was in the air.

And across the street a medium-tall man, wide at the girth, in a full black overcoat, walked slowly down the pavement. His bearing was indeed stately, matching the distinguished image created by his pure white hair, which fell several inches below the brim of his black hat. In the light of a street lamp, Michael could see the grey beard; it was the halfway man.

Jacob Handelman approached the outer glass doors of his apartment building and was now in the stronger light of the large entrance lamps. Havelock stared, at once mesmerized and disturbed; did he know the halfway man? Had "the Rabbi" been part of an operation eight . . . ten years ago? Perhaps in the Middle East, Tel Aviv, Lebanon? Michael had the distinct feeling that he *did* know him. Was it the walk? The deliberate pace that seemed almost anachronistic, as if the figure should be strolling in mediaeval robes? Or was it the thin steel-rimmed glasses, set so firmly in the centre of the large face?

The moment passed; it was, of course, possible that the halfway man might have crossed his path in any number of situations. They could have been in the same sector at one time or another, a respected professor supposedly on holiday but in reality meeting someone like Régine Broussac. Entirely possible.

Handelman went inside the enclosed entrance way, climbed the inner steps and stopped at the row of mailboxes. It was all Michael could do to restrain himself; the desire to race across the street and confront the halfway man was nearly overpowering.

He may choose to tell you nothing. Broussac.

And old man who did not care to negotiate could scream on a staircase and yell for help. And the one who *needed* help did not know what was behind a door across the street, what devices a group of intelligent city dwellers had mounted to defend themselves from hallway thugs. Security-alarms had flooded the market; he had to wait until Jacob Handelman was safely in his flat. And then a knock on the door and the words "Quai d'Orsay" would be enough; there was respect for a man who could elude alarms, an inherent threat in someone outside a door who knew that the one inside was a halfway man. Handelman would see him; he could not afford to refuse.

The old man disappeared through the inner door, the heavy panel of ironwork and glass swinging slowly shut behind him. Havelock waited three minutes; the lights went on in several front windows on the fourth floor. It was logical that Handelman's apartment number was 4-A. A halfway man had certain things in common with deep-cover field personnel and the Soviet VKR; he had to be able to watch the streets.

He was not watching now; there was no figure behind the curtains. Michael stepped out of the doorway and crossed the street. Inside the ornate entrance way he struck a match and held it waist-high as he looked down the row of names above the buttons.

R. Charles, Superintendent ID

He pressed the button and put his lips close to the webbed speaker.

"Yes, what is it?" asked the male voice in clear, well-spoken English.

"Mr Charles?" said Havelock, not knowing why the man's voice struck him as odd.

"Yes, it's Charles. Who's this?"

"United States Government, Department of State – "

"*What?*"

"Nothing to be alarmed about, Mr Charles. If you'll come to the door, you can check my identification through the glass, and either admit me or I can give you a number to call."

R. Charles paused, then answered slowly. "Fair enough."

Thirty seconds later a huge, muscular young man appeared in the hallway beyond the door. He was wearing track shorts and a sweatshirt marked with a large number 20. It was either a proclamation of age or the gridiron identity of one of Columbia's larger football players. This, then, was the protection the apartment dwellers on Morningside Heights had chosen. Again, logical; take care of your own to take care of you. Free lodgings for an imposing presence. Michael held up his old ID card in its black plastic case; the dates, of course, were blurred.

R. Charles squinted through the glass, shrugged and opened the door. "What the hell is this?" he asked, more curiosity than hostility in his voice. A man his size did not have to be aggressive; his thick legs and neck and muscular arms were sufficiently intimidating. Also his youth.

"There's a man here I'd like to see on official State Department business, but he's not in. I rang, of course; he's a friend."

"Who is it?"

"Dr Jacob Handelman. He's a consultant for us but he doesn't advertise it."

602

"Nice old guy, Handelman."

"The best, Mr Charles. However, I think he'd be alarmed if he thought I might be recognized." Havelock grinned. "Also, it's damned cold out there."

"I can't let you in his apartment. I *won't* let you in."

"And I wouldn't allow you to. I'll just wait here, if it's all right."

R. Charles hesitated, his eyes dropping to the open ID case still in Michael's hand. "Yeah, well, okay. I'd ask you into my place but my roommate and I are busting our humps for a mid-term exam tomorrow."

"Please, I wouldn't think of it . . ."

Havelock was interrupted by the appearance of an even larger young man in a doorway at the end of the hall. He was in a full sweatsuit, a book gripped in one hand, a pair of glasses in the other. "Hey, man, what is it?"

"Nothing. Someone looking for the Rabbi."

"Another one? Come on, we're wasting time. You're the brain, I just want to get through tomorrow."

"Your roommate on the team?" asked Michael, trying to appear contemporary.

"No. He wrestles. That is, he does when they don't throw him out for dirty holds. Okay, Mastiff, coming." The roommate went inside.

"Thanks again."

"Sure. You even sound official. The Rabbi ought to show up any minute."

"Pretty punctual, huh?"

"Like a Swiss clock." Number *Twenty* turned, then looked back at Havelock. "You know, I figured something like this. Like you, I mean."

"How so?"

"I don't know . . . the people who come to see him, I guess. Late at night sometimes; not exactly campus types."

There was nothing to lose in asking, thought Michael. The young man himself had provided the opening. "We're most concerned about the woman, I don't mind telling you that. For . . . the Rabbi's sake we hope she got here. Did you by any chance see her? A blonde woman, about five feet five, probably in a raincoat, maybe a hat. Yesterday? Today?"

"Last night," said the young man. "I didn't, but Mastiff did. Foxy lady, he told me. But nervous; she rang the wrong bell and got old Weinberg – he's in Four-B and even more nervous."

"We're relieved she's here. What time last night?"

"About now, I guess. I was on the phone when Weinberg buzzed us on the intercom."

"Thank you." *Twenty-four hours. A halfway man upstairs. She was within reach – he could feel it, sense it!* "Incidentally, by sheer coincidence, you've been given privileged information. Please respect it."

"Man, you *are* official. I never saw you, Mr Havalatch. But if they institute that draft I may look you up."

"Do that. Thanks again."

"Take care." The huge student walked down the hallway to the open door.

The instant it was closed, Havelock moved quickly to the wide stone staircase in the centre of the foyer, the steps worn smooth, indented from decades of use. He could not use the lift beyond; its sound might well alarm a trusting, muscular student who could suddenly reject the concept of privileged information in favour of less esoteric responsibilities.

In Paris Michael had had the presence of mind to have the expensive black shoes he had purchased to match his suit resoled with hard rubber. They served him well on the staircase; he went up swiftly, silently, taking the steps two and three at a time, rounding the landings without a sound. In less than half a minute he reached the fourth floor; Apartment 4A was at the end of the tiled, dimly lit hallway. He stood for several moments catching his breath, then approached the door and pressed the small button embedded in the moulding. From beyond he heard the bell chime softly and seconds later the sound of footsteps.

"Yes?" said the curiously high-pitched voice, in a rolling European accent.

"Dr Jacob Handelman?"

"Who is this, please?" The speech was Hebrew-rooted German.

"I have news from the Quai d'Orsay. May we talk?"

"Vos?" The silence was brief, the words that followed rushed. "You are mistaken. I have no idea what you're talking about? I know no one in . . . what you say, the Quai d'Orsay?"

"In that case, I'll have to get in touch with Paris, and tell my contact she's made a dreadful error. Naturally, Jacob Handelman will be removed from the catacomb's computer terminal."

"Just one minute, please. I must jog this old man's memory."

Havelock could hear the moving footsteps again, faster now, receding, then returning long before the stated minute was up. The metallic sounds of several locks were heard behind the thick wood; the door opened and the halfway man stared at him, then gestured with his head for Michael to come inside.

What was it? Why was he so certain he knew this man, this old man with the grey beard and the long white hair? The large face was soft but the eyes in the creased flesh behind the heavy-lensed glasses were . . . he was not sure, he could not tell.

"You are in my house, sir," said Handelman, closing the door and manipulating the locks. "I've travelled widely, of course, not always by my own wishes, like so many thousands in my situation. Perhaps we have a mutual friend I cannot at the moment recall. At the Quai d'Orsay. Naturally, I know a number of professors at the Sorbonne."

Was it the high-pitched, sing-song voice? Or the questioning tilt of the head? Or the way the old man stood, feet planted firmly, the posture soft, yet somehow rigid? No, it was not any single thing; it was all of them . . . somehow.

" 'A mutual friend' isn't quite accurate. You know a name. Broussac. Ministry of Foreign Affairs, Section Four. She was to have reached you today; she's a person of her word. I think she did."

"Ah, but my office is filled with scores of messages only my secretary is aware of, Mister . . . Mister . . . ?"

"Havelock."

"Yes, Mr Havellacht. Come in, come in. I knew a Habernicht in Berlin in the old days. Friedrich Habernicht. Quite similar, no?"

"Close, I guess." *Was it the walk?* The same deliberate stride that he had seen outside. The stately . . . arrogant steps that should be cloaked in mediaeval robes or a high priest's cassock. He had to ask. "We've met before, haven't we?"

"*We?*" The halfway man's eyebrows arched; he adjusted his steel-rimmed glasses and peered through them at Michael. "I cannot imagine where. Unless you were a student in a large class of mine, but that would have to be a number of years ago, I would think. In such a case, you would remember me, I would not necessarily remember you. Age and the sheer mass of numbers, you understand."

"Never mind." *A number of years ago. How many years?* "Are you telling me you haven't heard from Broussac?"

"I'm telling you nothing . . . Sit down, do sit down . . . I am merely saying that I do not know. You say this person Broussac sent me a message today, and *I* am saying I receive dozens of messages *every* day that I frequently do not get to for *many* days. Again, age and the sheer mass of numbers."

"I heard you before," interrupted Havelock; he remained standing, his eyes scanning the room. There were bookshelves everywhere, old furniture – overstuffed chairs, fringed lamps, hassocks – nothing Spartan. Once more the smell of Academe. "Jenna Karras!" said Michael suddenly, raising his voice.

"Another message?" asked Handelman ingenuously, an old man bemused by a younger antagonist. "So many messages – I must have a talk with my secretary. She overprotects me."

"Jenna Karras came to see you last night, I know that!"

"Three . . . no, *four* people came to see me last night, each a student of mine. I even have their names over here, and the outlines of two graduate papers." Handelman walked to a cluttered desk against the wall.

"Cut it out!" shouted Havelock. "You packaged her and I've got to *find* her! That was Broussac's message."

"So many messages," intoned the halfway man, as if chanting a Talmudic response. "Ahh, here are the names, the graduate outlines," continued Handelman, bending over the disorganized pile of papers. "So many visitors . . . so many messages. Who can keep track?"

"*Listen* to me! Broussac wouldn't have given me your name or told me where to find you if I weren't telling you the truth. I have to *reach* her! A terrible thing was done to her – to *us* – and she doesn't understand!"

" 'The Filioque Denials in the Councils of Arius'," chanted Handelman, standing erect and holding a sheaf of papers under the light of a floor lamp. "Those would be the Nicene rejections of the Eastern Church around the fifth century. Very little understood – speaking of understanding."

He may choose to tell you nothing. "Goddamn you, where did you *send* her?! Stop *playing* with me! Because – if I have to – I'll – "

"Yes?" Jacob Handelman turned his head in the spill of the floor lamp and peered once again through the steel-rimmed glasses. He took several steps to his left and replaced the papers on the desk.

It was there, at that moment. It was all there. The eyes behind the thin rims of silver, the rigid posture of the soft body . . . the walk. Not the strolling of a high-prelate in the church or a mediaeval baron entering a great hall . . . but the strutting of a man in uniform. A black uniform!

Sheets of lightning filled Havelock's eyes. His mind exploded . . . *then and now, now and then!* Not eight or ten years ago, but the early years, the terrible years! He was one of *them!* The images of his memory confirmed it; he saw the man in front of him now as he was then. The large face – without a beard, the hair straight and long, not white but *Aryan yellow.* Walking . . . *strutting* . . . down to rows of ditches. *Machine-gun fire. Screams.*

Lidice!

As if in a trance, Michael started towards the halfway man, his hands taut and hard, his fingers curving into claws, tensed for combat with another animal – a lower form of animal.

"*Vos?*" Handelman drew out the sibilant *s* in his high-pitched whine. "What is the matter with you? Are you crazy, perhaps? Look at you . . . are you sick? Stay away from me!"

"The *Rabbi* . . . ? Oh, Christ, you son of a bitch. You *incredible son of a bitch!* What were you – *Oberstleutnant? Major?* . . . No, it was *Reichsführer!* It was *you! Lidice!*"

The old man's eyes widened, magnified by the thick lenses, they looked monstrous. "You are mad, completely, utterly *mad!* Leave my house! You are not welcome here. With the pain I've suffered, I will not listen to the ravings of a madman!"

The intense sing-song chant of the words covered the halfway man's movement. His right hand slipped down to the desk, to the clutter of papers. Havelock lunged as a gun emerged in Handelman's hand, placed there minutes ago by a *Reichsführer* who could never afford to forget his origins. The halfway man was a killer of Czechs and Poles and Jews, a man who had taken the identity of a ragged inmate he had sent into a shower of gas or a cave of fire.

Havelock grabbed the hand with the gun, jammed his third finger behind the trigger and slammed it repeatedly against the edge of the desk. It would not come loose! The halfway man was arched beneath him, pinning his right arm, the face grotesque, the mouth stretched like a rabid dog's, the soft body suddenly hard, writhing in spasms. Handelman's left hand surged up and clapped on Michael's face, the fingers digging into his eyes.

Havelock twisted violently back and forth and the halfway man slipped out from under him. They were at the edge of the desk, immobilized by each other's arms bent to the breaking point. Suddenly Michael freed his right hand; he clenched it into a fist and brought it crashing down like a hammer into where he could see the blur of Handelman's face.

The steel-rimmed glasses shattered. The German screamed and the gun clattered to the floor as he brought both his hands to his face.

Havelock leaped backward, yanking the German to his feet, and clamped his hand across the ugly mouth. His eyes burned; tears and specks of blood clouded his vision – but he could see and the Nazi could not.

"You raise your voice, old man, I'll kill you the instant you do. Now sit down!"

He pulled the German away from the desk and pushed him into the nearest chair with such force that the halfway man's neck snapped back. The shattered glasses, however, remained secure on Handelman's face; they were a part of that face, part of the ugliness.

"You have blinded me!" whined the soldier from Lidice. "A madman comes into my house – "

"Forget it!" said Michael. "I was *there*!"

"Madness!" Gasping through his stretched open mouth, Handelman raised his hands to remove his glasses.

"Leave them alone!" ordered Havelock. "Let them stay right where they are."

"Young man, you are – "

"Don't talk! Listen. I can put out a trace on a man named Jacob Handelman going back fifty years. Everything about him – old pictures, Germans still alive who knew him – if he ever existed. Then circulate a photograph of you, minus the beard, of course, in certain sections of Prague. You were there; I saw you later and wanted to kill you. A boy of nine or ten wanted to put a knife in your back in the street. And someone still living in Prague or Rudna or Kladno would want to do the same even now. That's the bottom line, you *bastard*! So don't talk to me about people who weren't here last night, tell me about the one who was. Where *is* she?"

"I am a very valuable man – "

"I'll bet you are. Who'd know more about finding safe territories than someone who did it so well. And who could protect himself better than someone who could expose the whereabouts of so many. You've covered yourself, *Totschläger*. But not with me, do you understand that? Because I don't care. Now, where is *Jenna Karras*?"

"While not addressing myself to the preposterous accusations you make," whined the German, "there are considerations of exchange."

"You have your life," said Havelock. "I'm not interested in it. It's enough that you know I'm out there and can end it any time I like. That's your exchange. Where is she?"

"The top drawer of the desk." The halfway man gestured with his trembling hand, his eyes unseeing behind the shattered glasses. "Lift up the pencil rack. There's a folded green paper."

Michael went to the desk, opened the drawer and pulled out the concave receptacle for pens and pencils. There was the light green paper; he picked it up and unfolded it. It was a page of memorandum stationery from the Columbia University Graduate Faculty of Philosophy. In precise, handwritten block letters was the information Havelock would have killed for; it was everything.

Broussac. Applicant for Doctoral Candidate.

Name: Arvidas Corescu. c/o Kohoutek

RFD 3, Mason Falls, Penna.

"Is Corescu the name she's using?" asked Havelock sharply.

"Temporarily. The papers are only temporary; they had to be manufactured in a few hours. Others will follow . . . if they are to follow."

"Which means?"

"They must be paid for. Nothing is for nothing."

"Naturally; the hook's sunk in and the line keeps reeling out. You must have some very impressive fish out there."

"You could say I have powerful – friends. In many places."

"Who's this Kohoutek?"

"A Slav," said the halfway man, shrugging derisively. "He has farm land."

"When did she leave?"

"She was picked up this morning."

"What's her cover?"

"Another destitute refugee – a niece, perhaps – got out of the Balkans, or wherever. Away from the Bear, as they say. Kohoutek will get her work; he has friends in the textile unions."

"From which she pays him *and* you, or the papers don't follow."

"One needs papers," whined Handelman, "to drive a car, or use a bank – "

"Or to be left alone by Immigration," interrupted Michael. "That threat's always there, isn't it?"

"We are a nation of laws, sir."

"You make me *sick*," said Havelock, approaching the chair. "I could kill you now, feeling nothing but joy," he added quietly. "Can you understand that, philosopher? But I won't, because I want you to know what it's like to realize it can happen any moment, any day, any night. With a knock on your door. You live with that, you snake. *Heil Hitler.*"

He turned and started for the door.

The *crack* came from behind him! He spun around to see the long blade of a knife streaking towards him, directly at his chest. The halfway man had torn the shattered glasses off his face and seized the weapon concealed in the overstuffed chair; the musty smell of Academe was suddenly the putrid odour of a no-man's land in a far away battlefield. Havelock jumped back, but not before the blade had ripped through the jacket of his suit, the razor-sharp edge slitting his flesh and marking his white shirt with a line of blood.

His right hand whipped under his coat for the Llama automatic. He kicked wildly in front of him, hoping to make contact with any part of the German's body. As the blade came arching back, he spun away from its trajectory and raised his gun, aiming at the face.

He fired twice; the halfway man fell to the floor, his head soaked in blood, one eye blown away.

A gun had stilled another gun from Lidice. But there was no joy; it had ceased to matter.

There was only Jenna. He had found her! She could not stop him from reaching her now. She might kill him, but first she would have to look into his eyes. That *did* matter.

He shoved the Llama into his belt, the page of green paper into his pocket, and raced out of the apartment.

20

"The name's Broussac, Mr President," said Emory Bradford into the phone at his desk in the State Department. "Madame Régine Broussac. The Quai d'Orsay, Foreign Ministry, Section Four. She contacted the embassy the night before last, instructing a radio-car unit to be in the vicinity of Argenteuil for the purpose of picking up a former American intelligence officer who was to meet her there. Under highly unorthodox circumstances, she said."

"Havelock?"

"She's admitted that much, yes."

"And?"

The car drove up and down the streets of Argenteuil all night. It was never contacted."

"What did this Broussac say? I assume she's been questioned."

"Angrily. She claims he never showed up."

"Well?"

"Our people think she's lying."

"Why?"

"One of our men went round to her flat and asked some questions. He learned that she had returned home by one o'clock in the morning. If that was the case and apparently it was; two neighbours confirmed it – why didn't she phone the embassy and call off the car?"

"Has she been asked about this?"

"No, sir. Our people are waiting for instructions. It's not customary for embassy personnel to go around asking surreptitious questions about ministers of the Quai d'Orsay."

Charles Berquist paused, then spoke firmly. "Ask Ambassador Richardson to call Madame Broussac and respectfully request her to accept an invitation to come to the embassy as soon as it's convenient, preferably within the hour. A car will be sent for her, of course. The President of the United States wishes to speak to her on a confidential basis."

"Mr *President* – "

"Just do as I say, Mr Undersecretary."

"Yes, sir."

"And, Emory?"

"Sir?"

"How's the other task? The seventy-odd diplomats who may have been out of town during the Spanish problem?"

Bradford paused before answering. When he spoke, it was apparent he was trying to control his voice. "As of this moment, five are missing."

"*What?*"

"I didn't want to say anything until noon, until I have all the information, but the last report indicates that nineteen personnel were off the premises. Fourteen are accounted for, five aren't."

"Get it! Get *all* your information!"

"I'm trying."

"By noon! Get it!"

The cold rain of the night before had lingered with diminishing strength, and the sky outside the Oval Office was dark. A drop of only a degree or two in temperature and there would be thin, erratic patches of snow on the White House lawn. Berquist stood by the window, briefly wondering how deep the drifts were in Mountain Iron, Minnesota. And how he wished to Christ he were back there now! There was a buzzing from his telephone console. He glanced at his watch as he walked to the desk; it was eleven-fifteen.

"Yes?"

"Your call from Paris, sir."

"Thank you." Berquist pushed the appropriate red button. "Madame Broussac?"

"*Oui, Monsieur le Président.* It is an honour, sir. I am flattered to have been summoned to speak with you." The old woman's voice was strong, but not without astonishment. And a measure of fear.

"And I'm most grateful, Madame. As I instructed, are we alone?"

"Yes, *Monsieur le Président.* Ambassador Richardson most courteously permitted me the use of his office. Quite honestly, I am, as you might say, bewildered."

"You have the word of the President of the United States that we *are* alone, Madame Broussac. There is no interference on this telephone, no third parties or mechanical devices to record our conversation. Will you accept that word?"

"Assuredly. Why would such an august figure deceive a mere minister of the Quai d'Orsay?"

"For a lot of reasons. But I'm not."

"*Mais oui.* Then I am convinced."

"Good. I need your co-operation in a matter of the utmost importance *and* delicacy. It in no way affects the government of France, but any help you might give us could only be in its ultimate interests. Again, you have my word on it, the word of this office."

"It is sufficient, *Monsieur le Président.*"

"It's imperative we reach a retired foreign service officer recently separated from the Department of State. His name is Michael Havelock."

"*Mais, Monsieur le . . .*"

"No, please," interrupted Berquist. "Let me finish. This office has too many staggering concerns to be involved with the work you do, or with the activities Mr Havelock was engaged in. I only ask you to help us locate him. A destination, a routing, a name he might be using. Whatever you tell me will be held in the strictest confidence; no detail will be compromised, or ever used against you or your operations. I promise you that."

"*Monsieur –*"

"Lastly," continued the President, overriding her voice, "no matter what he may have told you, his government has never meant him harm. We have too much respect for his service record, too much gratitude for his contributions. The tragedy he thinks is his alone is all of ours, and that is all I can tell you, but I hope you consider the source – the office from which it comes. Will you help us, help *me*, Madame Broussac?"

Berquist could hear the breathing over the line from Paris, as well as the pounding tattoo in his own chest. He looked out of the window; fine flecks of white were intermingling with the mottled drizzle. The virgin drifts in the fields of Mountain Iron were at their most beautiful at sundown; one caressed them with the eyes, touched the colours from a distance, never wanting them to change.

"As you are trying to find him," began Broussac. "He is looking for someone else."

"We know that. We've been looking for her, too. To save her life. To save his." The President closed his eyes; it was a lie he would remember back in the hills of the Mesabi country. But then he would remember, too, Churchill and Coventry. The Enigma . . . Costa Brava.

"There is a man in New York."

"New *York*?" Berquist sat forward, startled. "He's *here*? She's – ?"

"It surprises you, *Monsieur le Président*?"

"Very much."

"It was intended to. It was I who sent her. Sent him."

"This man in New York?"

"He must be approached with a great deal of – as you mentioned – delicacy. He cannot be compromised. You have the same such people in Europe; we all need them, *Monsieur le Président*. Even when we know of those who belong to other – companies, we leave them alone."

"I understand perfectly." Berquist did; the warning was clear. "This man can tell us where he is?"

"He can tell you where *she* is. That's what you need to know. But he must be convinced he is not compromised."

"I'll send only one man and only he will know. My word."

"*J'y compte*. I must tell you, I do not know him, except through his dossier. He is a great man with much compassion, a survivor, *monsieur*. In April of 1945 he was taken out of the Bergen-Belsen camp in Germany."

"He will be accorded all the respect this office can summon, as well as the confidentiality I promised you. His name, please."

"Jacob Handelman. Columbia University."

The three men listened intently as Emory Bradford slowly, methodically delivered his findings in the strategy room of the underground complex of the White House. Speaking in a deliberate monotone, he described the confirmed whereabouts of all nineteen State Department personnel from the fifth floor L Section who were not in Washington during the week of Costa Brava. When he had finished, each man's expression conveyed both pain and frustration, none more so than the President's.

He leaned forward on the dais, his heavy Scandinavian face worn and lined, his intelligent eyes angry.

"You were so *sure* this morning," he said. "You told me five were missing, five not accounted for. What happened?"

"I was wrong, Mr President."

"*Goddamn it*, I didn't want to hear that! . . . But go on, who were the five?"

"The woman in hospital. It was an abortion. Her husband's a lawyer and has been in protracted litigation at The Hague for several months. They've been apart. The picture was pretty clear."

"How could you even consider a woman?" demanded Halyard. "No double standard implied, but a woman would leave her mark somewhere."

"Not if she – through Moscow-controlled men. Actually, I was quite excited when her name surfaced. I thought, 'Good God, it's perfect.' It wasn't."

"Keep it surgery, and tell that to whomever you spoke to. Who were the others?"

"The two attachés at our embassy in Mexico. They'd been recalled for change-of-policy briefings, then didn't return to Mexico City until the fifth."

"Explanation?" asked the President.

"Holidays. They went their separate ways and their families joined them. One to ski lodge in Vermont, the other to the Caribbean. Credit-card charges confirmed everything."

"Who else?" pressed Berquist.

"Arthur Pierce."

"Pierce?" interrupted the general, startled. "The fellow at the UN now?"

"Yes, General."

"I could have straightened you out there. So could have Addison here."

"So would Matthias," agreed Bradford. "If there was anyone at State who maintained clear access to Matthias for a longer period of time, I don't know who it is. He appointed Pierce to the UN with the obvious intention of submitting him for the ambassadorship."

"If you'll permit me the correction," said Berquist, "*I* appointed him after Matthias gave him to us and then took him away. He worked over here with the National Security Council for a couple of months last year before the great man said he was needed in New York."

"And he was one fella *I* told the Pentagon to bribe the hell out of," exclaimed the general. "I wanted to keep him in the army; he was too good to lose. He didn't like that mess in South-east Asia any more than I did, but his record was as good as mine . . . Let's face it; it was a damn sight better."

The ambassador leaned back in his chair. "I know Pierce. He was brought to my attention by an old style career foreign officer. I suppose I was as responsible as anyone for bringing him into the State Department. He was one of the few in this day and age who really went from rags to riches – well, influential if not literally rich, but he could have been – Iowa farmboy, rather humble beginnings, I believe, and then a brilliant academic record, everything on scholarship. A dozen or so of the country's largest corporations were after him, not to mention Rand and the Brookings Institute. I was persuasive and quite practical. Patriotism aside, I pointed out that a tour of duty with the Department of State could only enhance his value in the market place. Of course, he's still a relatively young man; with his accomplishments, if he leaves government, he'll be able to name his own price anywhere. He's a typical American success story – how could you possibly conceive of a Moscow connection?"

"I didn't *preconceive* anything, especially not in this case," said Bradford. "Arthur Pierce is a friend – and I don't have many. I consider him one of the best men we have at State. But in spite of our friendship, I went by the reports given me. Only me, incidentally. Not to my secretary or any assistant. Only to me."

"What did you get that made you think Pierce could possibly have anything to do with Soviet Intelligence? Christ, he's mother, God, apple pie and the flag."

"An error in the UN message logs. The initial report showed that during the last days of December and the first three days of January – the week of Costa Brava – Pierce hadn't responded to four separate queries from the Middle East Section. Then, of course, they showed up – four replies that could be entered in a diplomatic analyst's handbook. They were as penetrating as anything I've read on that area and dovetailed with the specific proceedings in the Security Council. As a matter of fact, they were used to block a particularly aggressive Soviet proposal."

"The error in the logs was the explanation?" said Brooks.

"That's the maddening thing. There's always an explanation, then a confirmation of an explanation. Message traffic's so heavy, twenty per cent of it gets misplaced. Pierce's responses had been there all along."

"Who's the last man?" Berquist was not going to give up. It was clear from his eyes that he could not readily accept the altered findings, desperation his electric prod.

"A man I was so convinced might be the mole, I nearly had a White House secret service detail pick him up. Thank God I didn't; he's volatile, a screamer."

"Who?"

"Nikolai Sitmarin. Born and raised in Leningrad, parents dissident immigrants over a dozen years ago. He's the State Department's most accomplished analyst of Soviet internal affairs, accurate about seventy per cent. He's a prize, and in his case I thought, What better way for Moscow to put a mole into the ground? An eighteen-year-old son of immigrants, dissidents permitted a family visa when they were damned hard to come by."

"Is Sitmarin Jewish?" asked the general.

"No, but I expect most people think he is; in my view it added to his cover. Soviet dissidency isn't the exclusive province of Russian Jews, although that seems to be the general impression. Also, he's received a fair amount of media exposure – the thirty-year-old *wunderkind* carrying out a personal vendetta. It all seemed so logically convoluted; so right."

"What were the circumstances?" The President's words were clipped.

"Again, an unexplained absence. He was gone from his office from mid Christmas week until the eighth of January. He just wasn't in Washington and there was no assignment listed for his not being here. I asked a time-stat man to call the section head; the explanation was given."

"Which was?" pressed Berquist.

"A personal leave was granted. Sitmarin's mother was gravely ill in Chicago."

"Pretty damned convenient illness, wasn't it?"

"So much so she nearly died. The Cook County General Hospital confirmed it."

"But she didn't die," interrupted Brooks.

"I spoke personally to the physician-of-record and he had a very clear idea of the gravity of my inquiry. He quoted from his files."

"Have them sent to you," ordered the President. "There are too damned many explanations; one of them's a lie."

"I agree, but which one?" added Bradford. "Not just these five, but the entire nineteen. Someone who thinks he's – or she's – doing a superior a harmless favour is concealing Ambiguity from us, hiding the mole. What's going down as a few extra days' skiing or going to the Caribbean or shacking up . . . excuse me."

"Oh, for Christ's sake. Go back and dig into every explanation given you. Find one that won't hold up."

"One that has a discrepancy in it," added the ambassador. "Meetings that didn't take place, a conference that was postponed, credit-card charges where the signatures are questionable . . . a gravely ill woman who just may have been given an assumed name."

"It'll take time," said the Undersecretary.

"You've accomplished a great deal in something over twelve hours," continued Brooks sympathetically. "Again, I commend you."

"And you have the authority of this office to get you what you need, anything you need. Use it! Find the mole!" Berquist shook his head in exasperation. "He and we are in a race after a madman we call Parsifal. If the Russians reach him first, this country has no viable foreign policy. And if Parsifal panics, it won't make a damn bit of difference." The President put his hands on the desk. "Is there anything else? I'm keeping two curious senators waiting and it's no time to do it. They're on the Foreign Relations Committee and I've a gut feeling they've got wind of Matthias." Berquist stopped; he got up and looked at Bradford. "Reassure me again – that *every man* at Poole's Island is secure?"

"Yes, sir. Each was screened down to his fingernails, and no one leaves that island for the duration."

"That, too, will run its course," said Brooks. "What is the duration? It's an unnatural condition."

"These are unnatural circumstances," broke in General Halyard. "The patrols are armed, the place a fortress."

"Armed?" the President spoke softly, in his own personal anguish. "Of course, they're armed. Insane!"

"What about Havelock?" asked the statesman. "Has there been anything?"

"No," replied the commander-in-chief, leaving the dais and heading for the door. "Call me later, Mr Undersecretary," he said without explanation. "Call me at three o'clock."

The snow, though not heavy, was a whipping snow. Tiny white flakes careened off the windscreen, bouncing silently away like thousands of miniature asteroids.

Havelock in his rented car had driven past the sign several minutes before, the letters reflected in the headlights: MASON FALLS 3 MILES.

He had checked out of The King's Arms Hotel, relieved to see a different clerk on duty, and had taken a cab to LaGuardia Airport. A hastily purchased map pinpointed Mason Falls, Pennsylvania; his only choice was a domestic flight to Pittsburgh. He was not at the time concerned with further Soviet surveillance. The Russian he had trapped had undoubtedly reported his arrival, but even if he had not, LaGuardia was not an international terminal. No diplomatic personnel came through its gates on overseas flights.

He had been issued a last-moment seat on US Air's 7:56 P.M. plane, reached Pittsburgh by 9:15 and hired a car, the signed credit slip permitting him to drop it off at any Hertz location. By 9:45 he was driving south through the long stretches of dark countryside on Route 51.

MASON FALLS
ESTABLISHED 1858

Through the swirling pockets of snow – thicker now, fuller – Michael could see the glow of a red neon sign ahead on the right. He approached, slowed down and read the letters; a touch of the absurd had intruded: HARRY'S BAR. Either someone along the banks of the Monongahela had a sense of humour, or there was a man named Harry who did not know how far away he was from Venice or Paris. Or perhaps he did.

He obviously did. Inside there were enlarged World War II photographs on the walls depicting Parisian scenes, several showing a soldier standing outside the door of Paris's Harry's Bar on the Left Bank. The place was rustic – thick wood dulled by use and totally untouched by furniture polish – heavy glasses and high-backed bar stools. A juke box in the corner was bleating out country music to the bored half dozen or so patrons at the bar. They were in keeping with their surroundings: everyone male, a profusion of red-checked flannel shirts, wide-ribbed corduroy trousers and ankle-length boots worn in the fields and in barns. These were farmers and farmhands; he might have assumed as much from the pick-up trucks outside, but the biting wind had distracted him – that and the fact that he was in Mason Falls, Pennsylvania.

He looked around for a wall telephone; it was inappropriately placed six feet from the juke box. That did not concern him, but the absence of a telephone book did; he needed an address. There had been no time at LaGuardia to find the correct book for Mason Falls, and as Pittsburgh was an international airport he wanted to get out of the terminal as fast as possible. He walked to the bar, stood between two empty stools and waited for an ageing, morose-looking Harry to serve him.

"Yeah, what'll it be?"

"Scotch-on-the-rocks, and a telephone book, if you've got one, please."

The owner studied Havelock briefly. "I don't get much call for Scotch. It ain't the best."

"I probably wouldn't know the best."

"It's your throat." Harry reached under the bar to his right, but instead of coming up with a glass and ice, he put a thin telephone book in front of Michael. He then walked to his left, to a row of bottles on a lighted shelf.

Havelock leafed through the pages rapidly, his index finger descending the row of K's.

Kohoutek, Janos RFD 3 Box 12

Goddamn it!

Rural Free Delivery, routing number *3* could be anywhere in Mason Falls, which although small in population was large in square mileage. Acres and acres of farmland, winding roads that threaded through the countryside. And to call the number was to give an alarm; if there were special words he did not know them and, all things considered, there undoubtedly *were* special words. To mention Jacob Handelman over the phone was asking for a confirmation call to be made to New York. There would be no answer on the dead halfway man's phone until he was found, possibly in the morning, possibly not for several days.

"Here y'are," said Harry, placing the drink on the bar. "Would you know a man named Kohoutek?" asked Havelock softly. "Janos Kohoutek?"

The owner squinted in minor thought. "Know the name, not him, though. He's one of them foreigners with some land over in the west end."

"Would you know where in the west end."

"No. Doesn't it tell you there?" Harry gestured at the telephone book.

"It only gives an RFD and a box number."

"Call him, for Christ's sake."

"I'd rather not. As you say, he's a foreigner; he might not understand over the phone."

"Hey!" yelled Harry over the sounds of the country music. "Any you assholes know a guy named Kohoutek?"

"Foreigner," said one red-checked flannel shirt.

"He's got more'n forty acres over west," added a hunting cap farther down. "Fuckin' refugees with their government handouts can afford it. We can't."

"Would you know where?" asked Havelock.

"It's either on Chamberlain or Youngfield, maybe Fourforks, I don't know which. Don't it say in the book?"

"No, just RFD-three, that's all. And a box number."

"Route three," said another patron, this one with a growth of beard and bleary eyes. "That's Davey Hooker's route. He's a carrier, and that son of a bitch soaks 'em. Got the job through his uncle, the fuckin' grafter."

"Would you know where the route is?"

"Sure. Fourforks Pike. Heads due west from the depot a mile down fifty-one."

"Thanks very much." Michael raised the glass to his lips and drank. It was not very good; it was not even Scotch. He reached into his pocket, pulled out his money and left two dollars on the bar. "Thanks again," he said to the owner.

"It's sixty cents," said Harry.

"For old times' sake," replied Havelock. "For the other place in Paris."

"Hey, you *been* there?"

"Once or twice."

"You shoulda told me! You woulda got decent whisky! Let me tell you, in 'forty-five me and – "

"I'm really sorry, I don't have time."

Michael pressed himself away from the bar and started for the door. He did not see a man at the far end of the room get off his stool and walk to the telephone.

Fourforks Pike became a slowly curving, interminable back country road less than a mile west of the old railway depot. The first post office box, marked 5, prominently anchored in the ground on his right, was clearly visible through the snow in the glare of the headlights. The next, however, Havelock would have missed had he not suddenly become aware of a break in the foliage; it was a narrow track on his left, and the box could not be seen from the pike. It was number 7, negating the theory that odd and even numbers meant different sides of a delivery route. He would have to drive more slowly and keep his eyes more alert.

The next three boxes were all within a half mile, each in sequence, the last number 10. Two hundred yards beyond, the road split – the first of, presumably, four forks on the pike. He took the straighter line, the fork on the right. Number 11 did not appear until he had driven nearly a mile and a half; when he saw it he briefly closed his eyes in relief. For several agonizing moments he had been convinced he had taken the wrong road. He pressed his foot on the accelerator, his mouth dry, the muscles of his face rigid, his eyes straining.

If the road was interminable – made worse by the spiralling snow against the windscreen – the wait for the final sighting was torturously so. He entered a long, seemingly endless stretch of flat, straight ground, which, as near as he could determine, was bordered by fields or pastures; but there were no houses, no lights anywhere. Had he passed it? Was his vision so distorted by the silent pounding of the snow that the post office box had gone by without his spotting it? Was there an unseen road on his right or his left, a metal receptacle off the shoulder, covered perhaps? It was not logical; the snow was heavier, but not yet heavy, and the wind was too strong for the snow to settle.

It was *there!* On the right. A large black mailbox, shaped like a miniature Quonset hut, the covered opening wide enough to receive small packages. The number 12 was stencilled in white – thick white enamel that threw back the light as though challenging the darkness. Havelock slowed down and peered through the window; again there were no lights beyond, no signs of life whatsoever. There was only what appeared to be a long road that disappeared into a wall of trees and further darkness.

He drove on, eyes straining, looking for something else, something he could not miss if and when he came across it. He only hoped it would be soon, and several hundred yards beyond box number 12, he found a reasonable facsimile. Not ideal but, with the snow, acceptable. It was a bank of wild foliage that had crept towards the edge of the road, the end of a property line, or a demarcation signifying no responsibility. Whatever it was, it would do.

He drove the hired car off the shoulder and into the cluster of bushes and high grass. He extinguished the headlights and opened his suitcase on the front seat. He removed all identification and shoved it into the elasticized rear pocket, then took out a heavy leaded plastic bag impervious to X-rays, the kind often used for transporting exposed film. He peeled it open and removed the Llama automatic;

the magazine was full. Lastly, he reached into the suitcase for the scaling knife he had used at Col des Moulinets; it was sheathed in a thin leather scabbard with a clip. Awkwardly he pulled up the sides of his overcoat and shoved it behind his trousers into the small of his back, clipping it to his belt at the base of his spine. He hoped neither weapon would be called for; words were infinitely preferable, frequently more effective.

He got out of the car, locked it, pushed the snow-swept foliage up around the sides, obliterated the tracks and started down the Fourforks Pike towards PO Box 12, RFD 3, Mason Falls, Pennsylvania.

He had walked no more than thirty feet off the highway into the long narrow road that seemed to disappear into a wall of darkness when he stopped. Whether it was the years he had spent instinctively studying alien ground – aware that an unknown path at night might hold lethal surprises – or the wind off the fields that caused him to angle his head downward against it, he could not tell. He was merely grateful that he saw it: a tiny greenish dot of light on his right about two feet above the snow-patched earth. It appeared to be suspended but he knew it wasn't. Instead, it was wired to the end of a thin black metal tube that was sunk at least another two feet into the ground for stability. It was a photoelectric cell, its counterpart across the road, an invisible beam of light crossing the darkness, connecting both terminals. Anything breaking that beam for more than a second or with a weight-density of more than fifty pounds would trigger an alarm somewhere. Small animals could not do it; cars and human beings could not fail to do it.

Michael side-stepped cautiously to his right through the cold, wet overgrowth, to pass beyond the device. He stopped again at the edge of the tangled bushes, aware of a line of flickering white parallel with his shoulders, knowing suddenly that there was another obstacle. It was a barbed wire fence bordering an adjacent field, flakes of snow clinging briefly to the barbs before being whipped away. He had not seen it when he entered the side road marked by post office box number 12; he looked back and understood. The fence did not begin until the foliage was high enough to conceal it. And that meant he understood something else; again, weight-density. Sufficient pressure against the thinly-spaced wires would set off further alarms. Janos Kohoutek was very security-conscious. Considering his location he had paid for the best he could get.

This, then, was the path, thought Havelock. Between the green trip-light and the shoulder-high barbed wire fence. For if there was one photo-electric alarm, there would be others along the way – the expectation of malfunction was an innate part of protection technology. He wondered how long "the way" was; he could see virtually nothing but foliage and darkness and swirling snow in front of him. He started literally to push ahead, bending the tangled brushwood and webbed branches with his hands and arms as he kept his eyes riveted on the ground for dots of eerie green light.

He passed three, then four, spaced roughly two hundred and fifty to three hundred feet apart. He reached the wall of tall trees, the fence growing higher as if commanded by nature. He was soaked now, his face cold, his brows iced, but movement was easier through the thick-trunked trees that seemingly had been planted at random but nevertheless formed a visual wall. Suddenly he realized he

618

was heading downwards, descending. He looked over at the road; the decline there was sharper, the mottled surface of earth and snow no longer in sight. There was a break in the trees; the narrow, sloping path he had to take was still overgrown, the high grass and untamed bushes bending in the wind and glazed with white.

And then spread below him was a sight that both hypnotized and disturbed him, in the same way he had reacted to the first sight of Jacob Handelman. He plunged down through the thickets of brush, falling twice into the cold, prickly bushes, his eyes on the bewildering view below.

At first glance it was like any farm buried in the deeper countryside, protected in front by sloping fields, endless woods beyond. There was a group of buildings, solid, simple, constructed of heavy wood for severe winters, the lights in various windows flickering in the snowfall: a main house and several barns, a silo, tool sheds and shelters for tractors and ploughs and harvesting equipment. They were indeed what they seemed to be, Havelock was sure, but he knew they were more. Much more.

It began with the gate at the end of the sloping road. It was framed unpretentiously with iron piping; the mesh was ordinary mesh; but it was higher than it had to be, higher than it should be for the entrance to a farm, as if the builder had made a slight error in the height specification and had decided to live with the mistake. Then there was the fence that spanned out from both sides of the unprepossessing gate; it, too, was strange, somehow askew, also higher than it had to be for the purpose of containing animals in the ascending grazing fields before it. Was it just the height? It was no more than seven feet, Michael judged as he drew closer; it had appeared much shorter from above – again nothing strange . . . but somehow wrong. And then he realized what it was, why the word "askew" had come to mind. The top of the barbed wire fence was angled *inwards*. That fence was not meant to keep animals from breaking in, it was designed to keep people from breaking out!

Suddenly the blinding beam of a searchlight shot out from the upper regions of the silo; it was sweeping round – towards *him*!

This was the 1980s, but he was standing in front of a symbol of human carnage that went back forty years. It was a concentration camp!

"We wondered how long it would take you," said a voice behind him.

He spun around, reaching for his weapon. It was too late.

Powerful arms gripped him around the neck, arching him backwards as a pair of hands plunged a soft, wet, acrid-smelling cloth into his face.

The beam of the searchlight zeroed in on him. He could see it, feel it, as his nostrils began to burn. Then the darkness came, and he could neither see nor feel.

21

He felt the warmth first; he found it not particularly pleasant but different from the cold. When he opened his eyes, his vision blurred and came into focus slowly; simultaneously he became aware of the nausea in his throat and the stinging sensation on his face. The pungent odour lingered in his nostrils; he had been anaesthetized with pure ethyl ether.

He saw flames, logs burning behind a black-bordered screen, in a large brick fireplace. He was on the floor in front of the slate hearth; his overcoat had been removed, and his wet clothes were heating up uncomfortably. But part of the discomfort was in the small of his back; the scaling knife was still in place, the leather scabbard irritating his skin. He was grateful for the pain.

He rolled over slowly, inch by inch, his eyes half closed, observing what he could by the light of the fire and several table lamps. He heard the sound of muffled voices; two men were standing together in a hallway, talking quietly. They had not noticed his movement. The room itself was in concert with the rustic structures outside – solid, functional furniture, thick plaited rag tugs scattered about over a wide-beamed floor, windows bordered by red-checked curtains that might have come from a Sears-Roebuck catalogue. It was a simple living-room in a country farmhouse, nothing more or less, and nothing suggesting it might be something else – or some place else – to disturb a visitor's eye. If anything, the room was Spartan, lacking a woman's touch, entirely male.

Michael slid his watch slowly into view. It was one o'clock in the morning; he had been unconscious for nearly forty-five minutes.

"Hey, he's awake!" cried one of the men.

"Get Mr Kohoutek," said the other, walking across the room towards Havelock. He rounded the sofa and reached under his leather jacket to pull out a gun. He smiled; the weapon was the Spanish Llama automatic that had travelled from a mist-laden pier in Civitavecchia, over the Palatine Hill and Col des Moulinets, to Mason Falls, Pennsylvania. "This is good hardware, Mr No-Name. I haven't seen one like it in years. Thanks a lot."

Michael was about to answer, but was interrupted by the rapid, heavy-footed entrance of a man who walked out of the hallway carrying a glass of steaming liquid in his hand.

"You are very free with odds and ends," thundered Janos Kohoutek. "Be careful or you'll walk barefoot in the snow."

Hocs ne sniegu bez buttow.

Kohoutek's accent was the dialect of the Carpathian Mountains south of Otrokovice. The words alluding to bare feet in the snow were part of the Czech-Moravian admonition to wastrels who did not earn their keep or their clothes. *To understand the cold, walk barefoot in the snow.*

Kohoutek came round the guard and was now fully in view. He was a bull of a man, his open shirt emphasizing the thickness of his neck and chest, the stretched

620

cloth marking the breadth of his heavy shoulders; age had not touched his physique. He was not tall, but he was large, and the only indication of his years was in his face – more jowl than face – deeply lined, eyes deeply set, the flesh worn by well over sixty years of driven living. The hot, dark brown liquid in the glass was tea – black Carpathian tea. The man holding it was Czech by birth, Moravian by conviction.

"So here is our invader!" he roared, staring down at Havelock. "A man with a gun but no identification – not even a driver's licence or credit card, or a wallet to carry such things in – attacks my farm like a commando! Who is this stalker in the night? What is his business? His name?"

"Havlicek," said Michael in a low, sullen voice, pronouncing the name in an accent close to Moravian. "Mikhail Havlicek."

"*Český?*"

"*Ano.*"

"*Obchodní?*" shouted Kohoutek, asking Havelock his business.

"*Mi žena,*" replied Michael, answering "the woman".

"*Co žena?*" demanded the ageing bull.

"The one who was brought here this morning," said Havelock, continuing in Czech.

"Two were brought in this morning! Which?"

"Blonde hair . . . when we last saw her."

Kohoutek grinned, but not with amusement. "*Chlipný,*" he said leering. "*Ďobrý těleso!*"

"Her body doesn't interest me, the information she has does." Michael raised himself. "May I get up?"

"*Zadnyne supsobem!*" The mountain bull roared again as he rushed forward, lashing his right foot out, the boot catching Havelock in the throat, making him reel back on the slate hearth.

"*Prokili!*" shouted Havelock, grabbing his neck. It was the moment to react in anger, the beginning of the words that mattered. "I *paid*!" he yelled in Czech. "What do you think you're doing?"

"You paid what? To ask about me on the highway? To sneak up on my house in the middle of the night? To carry a gun into my farm? I'll pay *you*!"

"I did what I was told!"

"By whom?"

"Jacob Handelman."

"Handelman?" Kohoutek's full, battered face was stretched into an expression of bewilderment. "You paid Handelman? *He* sent you?"

"He told me he would phone you, get in touch with you," said Michael quickly, using a truth from Paris that the halfway man had denied in New York; denied for profit. "I was not to call you under any circumstances, I was to leave my car on the road past your mailbox and walk down the track to your farm."

"The highway? You asked questions about me in a café on the highway!"

"I didn't know where the Fourforks Pike was. How could I? Did you have a man there? Did he call you?"

The Czech-Moravian shook his head. "It doesn't matter. An Italian with a truck. He drives produce for me sometimes." Kohoutek stopped; the menace returned to his eyes. "But you did not walk down my road. You came in like a thief, an armed thief!"

"I'm no fool, *pritel*. I know what you have here and I looked for trip–alarms. I was with the *Podzemni*. I found them and so I was cautious; I wanted no dogs on me or men shooting at me. Why do you think it took me so long to get here from that café on the highway?"

"You *paid* Handelman?"

"Very handsomely. May I get up?"

"Get up! Sit, *sit!*" ordered the mountain bull, pointing to a short bench to the left of the fireplace, his expression more bewildered than seconds before. "You gave him money?"

"A great deal. He said I'd reach a point in the road when I could see the farm below. Someone would be waiting for me by the gate, wave me down with a light. There was nobody I could see, no one at the gate. But then the weather's rotten so I came down."

Gripping his steaming glass of tea, Kohoutek turned and walked across the room to a table against the wall. There was a telephone on it; he put down the glass, picked up the phone and dialled.

"If you're calling Handelman . . ."

"I do not call Handelman," the Czech-Moravian broke in. "I never call Handelman. I call a man who calls another; he phones the German."

"You mean the Rabbi?"

Kohoutek raised his head and looked at Havelock. "Yes, the Rabbi," he said without comment.

"Well, whoever . . . there won't be any answer at his apartment. That's all I wanted to tell you."

"Why not?"

"He told me he was on his way to Boston. He's lecturing at some place called Brandese or Brandeis."

"Jew school," said the bull, then talked into the phone. "This is Janos. Call New York. The name you will give is Havlicek, have you got that? *Havlicek*. I want an explanation." He hung up, grabbed his tea and started back towards the fireplace. "Put that away!" he commanded the guard in the leather jacket who was rubbing the Llama against his sleeve. "Stand in the hall." The man walked away as Kohoutek approached the fire, sitting down opposite Michael in a rustic-looking rocking chair. "Now we wait, Mikhail Havlicek. It won't be long, a few minutes, ten . . . fifteen perhaps."

"I can't be responsible if he's not at home," said Havelock, shrugging. "I wouldn't be here if we didn't have an agreement. I wouldn't know your name or where to find you if he hadn't told me. How could I?"

"We'll see."

"Where's the woman?"

"Here. We have several buildings," answered the man from the Carpathians as he sipped his tea and rocked slowly back and forth. "She's upset, of course. It is not quite what she expected, but she will understand; they all do. We are their only hope."

622

"How upset?"

Kohoutek squinted. "You are interested?"

"Only professionally. I've got to take her out and I don't want trouble."

"We shall see."

"Is she all right?" asked Michael, controlling his anxiety.

"Like some others – the educated ones – she lost her reason for a while." Kohoutek grinned, then coughed an ugly laugh, as he drank his tea. "We explained the regulations and she told us they were not acceptable. Can you imagine? Not *acceptable*!" The bull roared, then his voice dropped. "She will be watched carefully, and before she is sent outside she will understand. As they all understand."

"You don't have to worry. I'm taking her."

"You say that."

"I paid."

Kohoutek leaned forward, stopping the motion of the chair. "How much?"

It was the question the Czech-Moravian had wanted to ask several minutes ago, but Carpathian progress was serpentine. Michael knew he was on a tightrope; there would be no answer in New York. He was about to negotiate and both men knew it.

"Wouldn't you rather hear it from Handelman? If he's at home."

"Perhaps I would rather hear it from you, *pritel*."

"How do you know you can trust me?"

"How do I know I can trust the Rabbi? How do you know *you* can trust him?"

"Why shouldn't I? I found you, found this place. Not in the way I would have preferred, but I'm here."

"You must represent influential interests," said Kohoutek, veering quickly, as was the custom of mountain men in negotiations.

"So influential I don't carry identification. But then you know that."

The ageing lion began rocking again. "Such influence, however, always carries money."

"Enough."

"How much did you pay Handelman?" All movement stopped as the question was asked.

"Twenty thousand dollars American."

"*Twenty* . . . ?" Kohoutek's weathered face lost some of its colour and his deep-set eyes squinted through the slits of flesh. "A considerable sum, *pritel*."

"He said it was reasonable." Havelock crossed his legs, his damp trousers warmed by the fire. "We were prepared for it."

"Are you prepared to learn why he did not reach me?"

"With the complicated arrangements you have for contacting one another, I'm not surprised. He was on his way to Boston, and if someone was not by a phone . . ."

"Someone is always by a phone; he is a cripple. And you were on your way to a trap that would have cost you your life."

Michael uncrossed his legs, his eyes riveted on Kohoutek. "The trip lights?"

"You spoke of dogs; we have dogs. They only attack on command, but an intruder does not know that. They circle him, barking viciously. What would you have done?"

"Used my gun, of course."

"And for that you would have been shot."

Both men were silent. Finally, Havelock spoke. "And the Rabbi has twenty thousand dollars you don't know about and I can't tell you because I'm dead."

"Now you see."

"He'd *do* that to you – for twenty thousand dollars?" The mountain bull again started to rock his chair. "There could be other considerations. I've had minor troubles here – nothing we cannot control – but this is a depressed area. Certain jealousies arise when you have a successful farm. Handelman might care to replace me, have a reason to replace me."

"I don't understand."

"I would have a corpse on my hands, a corpse who might have made a telephone call while he was alive. He could have told someone where he was going."

"You shot an intruder, a man with a gun, who probably used his gun. You were defending your property, no one would blame you."

"No one," agreed Kohoutek, still rocking. "But it would be enough. The Moravian is a troublemaker, we cannot afford him. Cut him off."

"From what?"

The mountain man sipped his tea. "You spent twenty thousand dollars. Are you prepared to pay more?"

"I might be persuaded. We want the woman; she's worked with our enemies."

"Who is 'we'?"

"That I won't tell you. It wouldn't mean anything to you if I did . . . Cut you off from what?"

Kohoutek shrugged his heavy shoulders. "This is only the first step for these people . . . like the Corescu woman."

"That's not her name."

"I'm certain it's not, but that's no concern of mine. Like the others, she'll be pacified, work from here for a month or two, then be sent elsewhere. The south, south-west, the northern midwest, wherever we place her." The bull grinned. "The papers are always about to arrive – just another month, one more congressman to pay, a senator to reach. After a while, they're like goats."

"Even goats can rebel."

"To what end? Their own? To be sent back to the place where they came from? To a firing squad, or a gulag, or garrotte in an alleyway? You must understand, these are panicked people. It's a *fantastic* business!"

"Do the papers ever arrive?"

"Oh, yes, frequently. Especially for the talented, the productive. The payments go on for years."

"I'd think there'd be risks. Someone who refuses, someone who threatens you with exposure."

"Then we provide another paper, *pritel*. A death certificate."

"My turn to ask. Who is 'we'?"

"My turn to answer. I will not tell you."

"But the Rabbi wants to cut you out of this fantastic business."

"It's possible." The telephone rang, its bell abrasive. Kohoutek got out of the

624

rocking chair and walked rapidly across the room. "Perhaps we shall learn now," he said, placing his tea on the table and picking up the phone in the middle of the second bell. "Yes?"

Havelock involuntarily held his breath; there were so many probabilities. A curious university athlete whose responsibility was the well-being of his tenants, who might have walked out into the hallway. A graduate student with an appointment. So many accidents.

"Keep trying," said the Carpathian.

Michael breathed again.

Kohoutek came back to the chair, leaving his tea on the table. "There is no answer on Handelman's phone."

"He's in Boston."

"How much could you be persuaded to pay?"

"I don't carry large sums with me," replied Havelock, estimating the amount of cash in his suitcase. It was close to six thousand dollars – money he had taken out of Paris.

"You had twenty large sums for the Rabbi."

"It was prearranged. I could give you a down payment. Five thousand."

"Down payment on what?"

"I'll be frank," said Michael, leaning forward on the bench. "The woman's worth thirty-five thousand to us; that was the sum allocated. I've spent twenty."

"With five, that leaves ten," said the bull.

"It's in New York. You can have it tomorrow, but I've got to see the woman tonight. I've got to take her tonight."

"And be on a plane with my ten thousand dollars?"

"Why should I do that? It's a budget item and I don't concern myself with finances. Also, I suspect you can collect a fair amount from Handelman. A thief caught stealing from a thief. You've got him now; you could cut *him* out."

Kohoutek laughed his bull of a laugh. "You are from the mountains, *Český*! But what guarantees do I have?"

"Send your best man with us. I have no gun; tell him to keep his at my head."

"Through an airport? I am not a goat!"

"We'll drive."

"Why tonight?"

"They expect her in the early morning. I'm to bring her to a man at the corner of Sixty-second Street and York Avenue, at the entrance of the East River Drive. He has the remaining money. He's to take her to Kennedy Airport, where arrangements have been made on an Aeroflot flight. Your man can make sure; she doesn't get into the car until the money is paid. What more do you want?"

Kohoutek rocked, his squint returning. "The Rabbi is a thief. Is the *Český* as well?"

"Where's the hole? Can't you trust your best man?"

"I am the best. Suppose it was me?"

"Why not?"

"*Done!* We shall travel together, the woman in the back seat with me. One gun at her head, the other at yours. Two guns, *přítel*! Where is the five thousand dollars?"

"In my car up on the road. Send someone with me, but I get it myself; he stays outside. That's the condition or we have no negotiation."

"You Communists are all so suspicious."

"We learned it in the mountains."

"*Český!*"

"Where's the woman?"

"In a back building. She refused to eat, threw the tray at our Cuban. But then, she's educated; it is not always a favourable thing, although it brings a higher price later. First, she must be broken; perhaps the Cuban has already begun. He's a hot tempered *macho* with balls that clank on the floor. Her type of women are his favourites."

Michael smiled; it was the most difficult smile he had rendered in his life. "Are the rooms wired?"

"What for? Where are they going? What plans can they hatch alone? Besides, to install and service such items could raise gossip. The alarms on the road are enough trouble; a man comes from Cleveland to look after them."

"I want to see her. Then I want to get out of here."

"Why not? When I see five thousand dollars." Kohoutek stopped rocking and turned to his left, shouting in English. "*You!* Take our guest up to his car. Make him drive and keep your gun on his head!"

Sixteen minutes later, Havelock counted out the money into the Moravian's hands.

"Go to the woman, *pritel,*" said Kohoutek.

He walked across the fenced-in compound to the left of the silo, the man with the Spanish Llama behind him.

"Over there, to your right," said the guard.

There was a barn at the edge of the woods, but it was more than a barn. There were lights in several windows above the ground level; there was a second floor. And silhouetted in those lights were straight black lines; they were bars. Whoever was inside those windows could not get out. It was a *Kaserne. Ein Konzentrationslager.*

Michael could feel the welcome pressure of the leather scabbard at the base of his spine; the scaling knife was still in place. He knew he could take the guard *and* the Llama – a slip in the snow, a skid over iced grass and the man in the leather jacket was a dead man – but not yet. It would come later, when Jenna understood, when – and if – he could convince her. And if he could not, both of them would die. One losing his life, the other in a hell that would kill her.

Listen to me! Listen to me, for we are all that's left of sanity! What happened to us? What did they do to us?

"Knock on the door," said the man behind.

Havelock rapped on the wood. A voice with a Latin accent answered.

"Yes? What is it?"

"Open up, Mr K's orders. This is Ryan. Hurry!"

The door was opened two or three inches by a stocky man in a tee-shirt and dungarees. He stared first at Michael, then saw the guard and opened the door completely.

"Nobody called," he said.

"We thought you might be busy," said the man behind Havelock, a snide laugh in his voice.

"With what? Two pigs and a crazy woman?"

"She's the one we want to see. *He* wants to see."

"He better have a *palo* made like rock, I tell you no lie! I looked in ten minutes ago; she's asleep. I don't think she slept for a couple of days maybe."

"Then he can jump her," said the guard, pushing Michael through the door.

They climbed the stairs and entered a narrow corridor with doors on both sides. Steel doors with slits in the centre, sliding panels for peering inside.

We are in our movable prison. Where was it? Prague? Trieste? . . . Barcelona?

"She's in this room," said the Latin, stopping at the third door. "You want to look?"

"Just open the door," said Havelock. "And wait downstairs."

"*Esperare* – "

"Mr K's orders," broke in the leather-jacketed guard. "Do what the man says."

The Cuban took a key from his belt, unlocked the cell door and stood aside.

"Get out of here," said Michael.

The two men walked up the corridor.

Havelock opened the door.

The small room was dark, and the dark light of night grudgingly spilled through the window, the white flakes bouncing off the glass and the bars. He could see her on the bed, more cot than bed. Fully dressed, she was lying face down, her blonde hair cascading over her shoulders, one arm hanging down limply, the hand touching the floor. She lay on top of the covers, her clothes dishevelled, the position of her body and the sound of her deep breathing proof of exhaustion. Watching her, he ached, pain pressing his chest for the pain she had endured, so much of it because of him. Trust had fled, instincts rejected, love repulsed; he had been no less an animal than the animals who had done this to her . . . he was ashamed. And filled with love.

He could see the outline of a floor lamp next to the bed; lighted, it would shine down on her. A cold fear went through him and his throat tightened. He had faced risks before, but never a danger like this, never a moment that meant so much to him. If he lost it – lost her, the bond between them shattered irremediably – nothing mattered except the death of liars. He was profoundly aware that he would willingly give up years of life for the moment to be frozen, not to have to turn on the light – simply to call out her name softly, as he had called it a hundred times a hundred, and have her hand fall into his, her face come against his. But the waiting, too, was self-inflicted torture; what were the words? *Between the acting of a dreadful thing and the first motion, all the interim is like a phantasma, or a hideous dream.* It would end or it would begin when he turned on the lamp. He walked silently to the bed.

An arm shot up in the darkness. Pale skin flashing in the dim light, a hand plunged into his abdomen. He felt the impact of a sharp pointed object – not a knife, something else. He leaped back and grabbed the hand, twisting yet not twisting – to cause her further pain was not in him. He could not hurt her.

She'll kill you if she can. Broussac.

Jenna rolled off the bed, her left leg bent, her knee crashing into his kidney, her sharp fingernails clawing his neck, digging into his skin. He could not strike her, he could not do it. She grabbed his hair, pulling his face down, and her right knee smashed into the bridge of his nose. The darkness was splintered into fragments of white light.

"*Prasátko!*" she cried in a low, muted scream, made guttural by her fury.

He understood; he had taught her well. *Use an enemy. Kill him only if you must. But use him first.* Escape was her intent; it accounted for the dishevelled clothes, the skirt pulled up to expose her thigh. He had attributed it all to exhaustion but he had been wrong; it was a sight for a *prasátko* peering through a slot in the cell door.

"*Stát!*" he whispered harshly, as he held her, twisting nothing, damaging nothing. "*Těží já!*" He freed his left hand and pulled her writhing body across the small room to the lamp. He reached over and found the switch; he snapped it on, her face in front of his.

She stared at him, her wide brown eyes bursting from their sockets with that strange admixture of fear and loathing he had seen in the window of the small plane in Col des Moulinets. The cry that was wrenched from her throat came also from the centre of her life; the scream that grew from it was prolonged and horrible – a child in a cellar of terror, a woman who faced the return of infinite pain. She kicked wildly and spun away, breaking his grip, threw herself across the bed and against the wall. She whipped her hand back and forth, slashing crazily, a wide-eyed animal cornered, with nothing left but to end its life screaming, clawing, thrashing as the trap snapped shut. In her hand she grasped the instrument that had been her only hope for freedom; it was a fork, its tines tinted with his blood.

"*Listen* to me!" he whispered sharply again. "It was done to both of us! It's what I've come to tell you, what I tried to tell you at Col des Moulinets!"

"It was done to *me!* You tried to *kill* me . . . how many times? If I'm to die, then you – "

He lunged and pinned her hand against the wall, forcing her to stop writhing.

"Broussac *believed* you . . . but then she believed *me!* Try to understand. She knew I told her the truth!"

"You don't know the truth! Liar, *liar!*" She spat in his face, kicking out, twisting digging the nails of her trapped hand into his back.

"They wanted me out and you were the way! I don't know why, but I know men have been killed . . . a woman, too, who was meant to be you! They want to kill us both now, they *have* to!"

"*Liar!*"

"There are liars, yes, but I'm not one of them!"

"You are, you *are!* You sold yourself to the *zvířata! Kurva!*"

"No!" He twisted her hand, the bloodied fork protruding from her clenched fist. She winced in pain as he pulled her wrist down. Then she slowly reduced the counter-pressure, her eyes frightened still, hating still, but wide, too, with confusion. He placed the fork against his throat and whispered. "You know what to do," he said carefully, clearly. "The windpipe. Once punctured there's no way out for me here . . . But there is for you. Pretend to go along with them; be passive, but watch the guard – as you know, he's a goat. The sooner you're co-operative, the sooner they'll find you work on the outside. Remember, all you want are your papers; they're everything to you. But when they let you out, somehow get to a phone and reach Broussac in Paris – you can do it. She'll help you because she knows the truth." He stopped and took his hand away, leaving hers free. "Now, do it. Either kill me or believe me."

Her stare was to him a scream, echoing in the dark regions of his mind, and hurling him into the horror of a thousand memories. Her lips trembled, and slowly it happened. Fear and bewilderment remained in her eyes, but the hatred was receding. Then the tears came, welling up slowly; they were the balm that meant the healing could begin.

Jenna dropped her hand and he took it, holding it in his own. The fork fell from her unclenched hand, and her body went limp, as the deep, terrible sobs came.

He held her. It was all he could do, all he wanted to do.

The sobs subsided and the minutes went by in silence. All they could hear was their own breathing, all they felt was each other as they clung together. Finally he whispered, "We're getting out, but it won't be clean. Did you meet Kohoutek?"

"Yes, a horrible man."

"He's going with us, supposedly to pick up a final payment for you."

"But there isn't any," said Jenna, pulling her face back, studying his, her eyes absorbing him, enveloping him. "Let me look at you, just look at you."

"There isn't time – "

"*Shhh.*" She placed her fingers on his lips. "There must be time, because there's nothing else."

"I thought the same when I was walking over here, and when I was looking down at you." He smiled, stroking her hair, his hand gently caressing her lovely face. "You played well, *překrásný.*"

"I've hurt you."

"A minor cut and a few major scratches. Don't be insulted."

"You're bleeding . . . your neck."

"And my back, and a fork-scrape – I guess you'd call it – on my stomach," said Michael. "You can nurse me later and I'll be grateful, but right now it fits the picture they have. I'm taking you back on Aeroflot."

"Do I continue fighting?"

"No, just be hostile. You're resigned; you know you can't win. It'll go harder for you if you struggle."

"And Kohoutek?"

"He says you're to stay in the back seat with him. He'll have us both under a gun."

"Then I shall smoke a great deal. His hand will drop."

"Something like that. It's a long trip, a lot can happen. A gas station, a breakdown, no lights. He may be a mountain bull but he's close to seventy." Havelock held her shoulders. "He may decide to drug you. If he does I'll try to stop him."

"He won't give me anything dangerous; he wants his money. I'm not concerned, *odvážný*. I'll know you're there and I know what you can do."

"Come on."

"*Mikhail*." She gripped his hands. "What *happened*? To me . . . to *you*? They said such dreadful things, such *terrible* things! I couldn't believe them, yet I had to believe. It was *there*!"

"It was all there. Down to my watching you die."

"I've been running away ever since, until that night in Rome. Then I started running in a different direction. After you, after them – after the liars who did this to us."

"How did they do it?"

"There's no time now. I'll tell you everything I can later, and then I want to hear *you*. Everything. You have the names, you know the people. Later."

They stood up and embraced, holding each other briefly, feeling the warmth and the hope each gave the other. Michael pulled a handkerchief from his breast pocket and held it against his neck. Jenna took his hand away and blotted the deep scratches herself; she touched the bridge of his nose where she had struck him with her knee, then smoothed his hair at the temples.

"Remember, my darling," she whispered. "Treat me sternly. Push me and shove me and grab my arm firmly as you do it. A man who's been scratched by a woman, whether she's his enemy or not, is an angry man. Especially among other men; his masculinity suffers more than the wounds."

"Thank you, Sigmund Freud. Let's go."

The guard in the black leather jacket smiled at the sight of Havelock's bleeding neck while the Cuban nodded his head, his expression confirming a previous judgement. As instructed, Michael held Jenna's arm in a vice-like grip, propelling her forward at his side, his mouth set, his eyes controlled but furious.

"I want to go back to Kohoutek and get out of here!" he said angrily. "And I don't care for any discussion, is that understood?"

"Did the great big man get hurt by the little bitty girl?" said the guard, grinning.

"Shut up, you goddamned idiot!"

"Come to think of it, she's not that little."

Janos Kohoutek was dressed in a heavy waterproof jacket, a fur-lined cap on his head. He too, smiled at the handkerchief held in place on Havelock's neck. "Perhaps this one's a witch from the Carpathians," he said, speaking English, his stained teeth showing. "The old wives' tales say they have the strength of mountain cats and the cunning of demons."

"Spell it with their *w*, *pritel*. She's a *bitch*." Michael pressed Jenna towards the door. "I want to get started; the snow will make for a longer trip."

"It's not so bad, more wind than anything," said the bull, taking a roll of thick cord out of his pocket and walking towards Jenna. "They keep the turnpike clear."

"What's that?" asked Havelock, gesturing at the cord.

"Hold out her hands," ordered Kohoutek, addressing the guard.

"You may care to put up with this cat, but I do not."

"I smoke," protested Jenna. "Let me smoke, I'm very nervous. What can I *do*?"

"Perhaps you would prefer a needle? Then there will be no thought of smoking."

630

"My people won't accept drugs," interrupted Michael firmly. "The airports are watched, especially our departure gates. No narcotics."

"Then she'll be tied. Come, take her hand." The guard in the leather jacket approached Jenna; haltingly she put out her hands, so as not to be touched more than necessary. Kohoutek stopped. "Has she been to the toilet?" he asked harshly of no one, and no one answered. "Tell me, woman, have you been to the toilet?"

"I'm all right," said Jenna.

"For a number of hours? There'll be no stops, you understand? Even to sit on the side of the road with a gun at your head, there'll be no stops. *Rozumět?*"

"I said I'm all right."

"Tie her, and let's go." Havelock took several impatient steps towards the door, passing the Moravian and glancing at Jenna. Her eyes were impersonal glass; she was magnificent. "I assume this refugee from a *žalár* will take us up in the truck."

The guard looked angry as Kohoutek grinned. "You are not far wrong, Havlicek. He's been put away for aggravated assault several times. Yes, he'll take us." The bull pulled the cord tight around Jenna's hands, then turned and shouted, *"Axel!"*

"He has my weapon," said Michael, gesturing at the man in the leather jacket. "I'd like it back."

"You shall have it. At a street corner in New York."

The second guard entered the room from the hallway, the same man who had first seen Havelock awake on the floor.

"Yes, Mr Kohoutek?"

"You're handling the schedules tomorrow, no?"

"Yes, sir."

"Stay in radio contact with the northbound trucks and have one pick me up in Monongahela after my plane arrives tomorrow. I will phone from the airport and give you the time of the flight."

"Right."

"We go," said the mountain bull, heading for the door.

Michael took Jenna's arm, the guard in the leather jacket following. Outside, the wind was stronger than before, the snow angrier, whipping in circles and stinging the face. With Kohoutek leading, they ran down the farmhouse path to the vehicle on the drive. A third guard, wearing a white parka, stood by the gate fifty yards away; he saw them and walked to the centre latch.

It was an enclosed van, with facing wooden benches to take five or six people on each side, and with coiled ropes on the walls. At the sight of the covered, windowless quarters Jenna was visibly shaken, and Havelock understood. Her country – his native country – had seen too many such vehicles over the years, heard too many stories told in whispers of convoys carrying away men and women and children who were never seen again. This was Mason Falls, Pennsylvania, USA, but the owners and drivers of these vehicles were no different from their brothers in Prague and Warsaw, late of Moscow – before then Berlin.

"Get in, get *in!*" shouted Kohoutek, now waving a large .45 automatic, as the guard held the handle of the rear door.

"I'm not your prisoner!" yelled Havelock. "We negotiated! We have an agreement!"

"And part of that agreement, *pritel*, is that you are my guest as well as my hostage until we reach New York. After delivery – both deliveries – I shall be happy to put away the gun and buy you dinner."

The mountain bull roared with laughter as Jenna and Michael climbed into the van. They sat next to each other, but this was not to Kohoutek's liking.

"The woman sits with me," he said. "You move across. *Quickly.*"

"You're paranoid," said Havelock, moving to the other side, seeking out the shadows.

The door was closed, the latch and lock manipulated by the guard. A dim light came through the windscreen. In seconds, thought Michael, the headlights would be turned on, the reflected spill partially illuminating the van. In the darkness he pulled up his coat and reached behind him with his right hand, inching towards the knife clipped to his belt in the small of his back. If he did not remove it now, it would be infinitely more difficult later when he was behind the wheel of his car.

"What's *that*?" shouted the bull, raising his gun in the shadows, pointing it at Havelock's head. "What are you doing?"

"The bitch–cat clawed my back; the blood's sticking to my shirt," said Michael in a normal voice. Then he yelled, "Do you want to see it, *feel* it!?"

Kohoutek grinned, glancing at Jenna. "A Carpathian *čarodĕka*. The moon's probably full but we can't see it." He laughed his crude mountain laugh once more. "I trust the Lubyanka is as tight as it ever was. She'll eat your guards up!"

At the word "Lubyanka' Jenna gasped, shuddering, drawing out the words. "Oh, God! Oh, my *God*!"

Kohoutek looked at her again, and again Havelock understood – she was covering for him. He quickly pulled the knife out of the scabbard and palmed it in his right hand. It had all taken less than twelve seconds.

The driver's door opened; the guard climbed in and switched on the lights. He looked behind; the old bull nodded and he turned the ignition key. The vehicle had a powerful engine, and a minute later they had passed through the gate and were climbing the steep hill, the heavy-treaded tyres crunching the snow and the soft earth beneath them, lurching, vibrating, rolling with the uneven pitch of the ground. They reached the wall of trees where the road flattened out; there was perhaps three-eighths of a winding mile to go before the Fourforks Pike. The guard-driver gathered speed, then suddenly stepped on the brake, stopping the truck instantly. A red light was flashing on the dashboard. He reached over for a switch, then a second, and snapped both. There was a prolonged burst of static over the radio as an excited voice shouted through the eruptions: "Mr Kohoutek! Mr *Kohoutek*!"

"What is it?" asked the guard, grabbing a microphone from the dashboard and depressing a button. "You're on the emergency channel."

"The sparrow in New York . . . he's on the phone! Handelman's dead! He heard it on the radio! He was shot in his apartment, and the police are looking for a man . . ."

Havelock lunged, twisting the handle of the knife into his clenched fist, the blade protruding downward, his left hand reaching for the barrel of the .45 automatic. Jenna sprang away; he gripped the long, flat steel as Kohoutek rose, then slamming the gun back down on the wooden bench, he plunged the knife through the mountain bull's hand, embedding the point through flesh and bone into the wood.

Kohoutek screamed; the guard in the front seat spun around as Jenna threw herself at him, crashing her roped hands down on his neck, and pulled the microphone out of his grip, cutting off the transmission. Havelock swung the gun up into the old bull's head; Kohoutek lurched back into the wall and fell forward on the floor of the van, his arm stretched out, his hand still nailed to the wooden bench.

"*Mikhail!*"

The guard had recovered from Jenna's blows and was pulling the Llama out of his leather jacket. Michael sprang forward and jammed the heavy barrel of the .45 into the man's temple; reaching over his shoulder, he pressed down, holding the Llama in place.

"Mr Kohoutek? Have you *got* it?" yelled the voice through the radio static. "What should the sparrow do? He wants to know!"

"Tell him you've got it," ordered Havelock, breathing hard, thumbing back the hammer of the gun. "Say the sparrow should do nothing. You'll be in touch."

"We've got it." The guard's voice was a whisper. "Tell the sparrow not to do anything. We'll be in touch."

Michael yanked the microphone away and pointed to the Llama. "Now just hand it to me slowly," he said. "Use your fingers, just *two* fingers," he continued. "After all, it's mine, isn't it?"

"I was going to give it back," said the frightened guard, his lips trembling.

"How many years can you give back to the people you drove in this thing?"

"That hasn't anything to do with me, I swear it! I just work for a living. I do what I'm told."

"You all do." Havelock took the Llama and moved the automatic around the man's head, pressing it into the base of his skull. "Now drive us out of here," he said.

22

The slender, middle-aged man with the straight dark hair opened the door of the telephone booth at the corner of 116th Street and Riverside Drive. The wet city snow was clinging to the glass, blurring the rotating red lights of the police cars up the block. He inserted the coin, dialled O, then five additional digits; he heard the second tone and dialled again. In moments a private phone was ringing in the living quarters of the White House.

"Yes?"

"Mr President?"

"Emory? How did it go?"

"It didn't. He's dead. He was shot."

The silence from Washington was interrupted only by the sound of Berquist's breathing. "Tell me what happened," said the President.

"It was Havelock, but the name wasn't reported correctly. We can deny the existence of any such person at State."

"*Havelock?* At . . . ? Oh my God!"

"I don't know all the details, but enough. The shuttle was delayed by the snow and we circled LaGuardia for nearly an hour. By the time I got here there were crowds, police cars, a few press and an ambulance."

"The *press?*"

"Yes, sir. Handelman's prominent here. Not only because he was a Jew who survived Bergen-Belsen, but because of his standing at the university. He was respected, even revered."

"Oh, Christ . . . What did you learn? *How* did you learn it? Your name won't surface, will it?"

"No, sir. I used my rank at State and reached the precinct up here; the detective was co-operative. Apparently Handelman had an appointment with a female graduate student who came back to the building twice before ringing the superintendent. They went up to Handelman's apartment, saw the door was unlocked, went inside and found him. The superintendent called the police and, when they got here, he admitted having let in a man who had State Department credentials. He said his name was Havilitch; he didn't recall the first name, but insisted the ID was in order. The police are still in Handelman's apartment getting fingerprints, cloth and blood scrapings."

"Have the details been made public?"

"In this town they can't wait. It was all released twenty minutes ago. There was no way I could stop it, if I wanted to. But State doesn't have to clarify; we *can* deny."

The President was silent, then he spoke. "When the time is right, the Department of State will co-operate fully with the authorities. Until then I want a file built and circulated on a restricted basis – around Havelock's activities since his separation from the government. It must reflect the government's alarm over his mental state, his apparent homicidal tendencies . . . his loyalty. However, in the interests of national security, that file will remain under restricted classification. It will not be made public."

"I'm not sure I understand."

"The facts will be revealed when Havelock is no longer a threat to this country's interests."

"Sir?"

"One man is insignificant," said the President softly. "Coventry, Mr Under-secretary. Enigma . . . Parsifal."

"I accept the reasoning, sir, not the assumption. How can we be sure we'll find him?"

"He'll find us; he'll find *you*. If everything we've learned about Havelock is as accurate as we believe, he wouldn't have killed Jacob Handelman unless he had an extraordinary reason. And he would never have killed him if he hadn't learned where Handelman sent the Karras woman. When he reaches her, he'll know about you."

Bradford paused, his breath visible, the vapour briefly interrupted. "Yes, of course, Mr President."

"Get back here as fast as you can. We must be ready . . . *you* must be ready. I'll have two men flown up from Poole's Island. They'll meet you at National; stay in airport security until they arrive."

"Yes, sir."

"Now, listen to me, Emory. My instructions will be direct, the explanation clear. By presidential order you are to be given round-the-clock protection; your life is in their hands. You are being hunted by a killer who's sold his government's secrets to the enemy. Those will be the words *I* use; *yours* will be different. You will use the language of Consular Operations: Havelock is 'beyond-salvage'. Every additional hour he lives is a danger to our men in the field."

"I understand."

"Emory?"

"Sir?"

"Before this all happened I never really knew you, not personally," said Berquist softly. "What's your situation at home?"

"Home?"

"It's where he'll come for you. Are there children at home?"

"Children? No, no there are no children. My older son's in college, my younger boy away at boarding school."

"I thought I heard somewhere that you had daughters."

"Two. They're with their mother. In Wisconsin."

"I see. I didn't know. Is there another wife?"

"There were. Again, two. They didn't last."

"Then there are no women living in your house?"

"There are frequently, but not at the minute. Very few during the past four months."

"I see."

"I live alone. The circumstances are optimum, Mr President."

"Yes, I guess they are."

Using the coiled ropes on the wall of the van, they tied the guard to the steering wheel, Kohoutek to the bench.

"Find whatever you can and bind his hand," said Michael. "I want him alive. I want someone to ask him questions."

Jenna found a farmer's kerchief in the glove compartment. She removed the scaling knife from the old mountain bull's huge hand, ripped the cloth in two and expertly bound the wound, stemming the blood at both the gash and the wrist.

"It will hold for three, perhaps four hours," she said. "After that, I don't know. If he wakes and tears it, he could bleed to death . . . Knowing what I know, I have no use for prayers."

"Someone'll find him. Them. This truck. It'll be light in an hour or so, and the

Fourforks Pike's a county route. Sit down for a minute." Havelock started the engine and, reaching his foot over the guard's leg, depressed the clutch and shoved the truck in gear. Wrenching the man back and forth over the steering wheel, he manoeuvred the vehicle so that it was broadside across the road. "Okay, let's get out."

"You can't leave me here!" whined the guard. "*Jesus!*"

"Have you been to the toilet?"

"*What?*"

"I hope so, for your sake."

"Mikhail?"

"Yes?"

"The radio. He'd use it. Someone might come along and free him. We need every minute."

Havelock picked up the .45 from the seat and smashed the thick, blunt handle repeatedly into the dials and switches until there was nothing but shattered glass and plastic. Finally, he ripped the microphone out of its receptacle, severing the wires; he opened the door and turned to Jenna. "We'll leave the lights on so no one smashes into it," he said, stepping out and pulling the seat forward for her. "One more thing to do. Come on."

Because of the wind, the Fourforks Pike had less than an inch of snow on the surface except for the intermittent drifts that had been pummelled into the bordering grass. Michael handed the .45 to Jenna and switched the Llama to his right hand. "That makes too much noise," he continued. "The wind might carry it down to the farmhouse. Stay here."

He ran to the back of the van and fired twice, blowing out both rear tyres. He raced up the other side and fired into the front tyres. The van rocked back and forth as the tyres deflated and settled into the road. To clear the highway, it could be driven into the grass, but it would go no farther than that. He put the Llama into his pocket.

"Let me have the forty-five," he said to Jenna, pulling his shirt out of his trousers. She gave it to him. "What are you going to do?"

"Wipe it clean. Not that it'll do much good, our prints are all over the inside. But they may not brush there; they will this."

"So?"

"I'm gambling that our driver in his own self interest will yell like hell that it's not his, that it belongs to his employer, your host, Kohoutek."

"Ballistics," said Jenna, nodding. "Killings on file."

"Maybe something else. That farm will be torn apart and when it is they may start digging around those acres. There could be killings not on file." He held the automatic with his shirt-tail, opened the door of the truck and arched the weapon over the front seat into the covered van.

"Hey, come *on*, for Christ's sake!" shouted the driver, twisting and turning against the ropes. "Let me out of here, will ya? I didn't do nothing to you! They'll send me back for ten years!"

"They're a lot easier on people who turn state's evidence. Think about it." Havelock slammed the door and walked rapidly back to Jenna. "The car's about a quarter of a mile down on the other side of Kohoutek's road. Are you all right?"

She looked at him; particles of snow stuck to her blonde hair swirling in the wind and her face was drenched, but her eyes were alive. "Yes, my darling, I'm all right . . . Wherever we are at this moment, I'm home."

He took her hand and they started down the road. "Walk in the centre, so our footsteps will be covered."

She sat close to him, touching him, her arm through his, her head intermittently resting on his shoulder as he drove.

The words between them were few, the silences comforting; they were too tired, too afraid, to talk sensibly, at least for a while. They had been there before; they knew a fraction of peace would come with the quiet – and being with each other.

Remembering Kohoutek's words, Havelock headed north to the Pennsylvania Turnpike, then east towards Harrisburg. The old Moravian had been right; the low-flying winds virtually swept the wide expanse of highway, and the sub-freezing temperature kept the snow dry and buoyant. Although the visibility was poor, the travelling was fast.

"Is this the main autoroute?" asked Jenna.

"It's the state turnpike, yes."

"Is it wise to be on it? If Kohoutek's found before daybreak, might not men be watching this 'turnpike', as they do the *dráhas?*"

"We're the last people on earth he wants the police to find. We know what that farm is. He'll stall, use the intruder story, say *he* was the hostage, the victim. And the guard won't say anything until he hasn't got a choice, or until they find his record, and then he'll bargain. We're all right."

"That's the police, darling," said Jenna, her hand gently touching his forearm. "Suppose it is not the police? You want it to be the police, so you persuade yourself. But suppose it is someone else? A farmer or a driver of a milk truck. I think Kohoutek would pay a great deal of money to get safely back to his home."

Michael looked at her in the dim light of the dashboard. Her eyes were tired, with dark circles under them; fear was still in the centre of her stare. Yet in spite of the exhaustion and the dread, she was thinking better than he was. But then she had been hunted far more often than he, and more recently. Above all, she would not panic; she knew the value of control even when the pain and the fear were overwhelming. He leaned over and brushed his lips on her face.

"You're magnificent," he said.

"I'm frightened," she replied.

"And you're also right. There's a childish song that says 'wishing will make it so'. It's a lie, and only for children, but I was counting on it, hoping for it. The odds of the police finding Kohoutek, or a citizen reporting what he found to the police, are no better than seventy-thirty. Against. We'll get off at the next exit and head south."

"To where? Where are we going?"

"First, where we can be alone, and not moving. Not running."

*

She sat in a chair by the motel window, the early light spreading up and over the Allegheny Mountains outside in the distance. The yellow rays heightened the gold in the long blonde hair that fell across her shoulders. Alternately she would look at him, then turn her face away and close her eyes, his words too painful to hear in the light.

When he had finished, he was still caught in the anguish that came with the admission: he had been her executioner. He had killed his love and there had been no love left in him.

Jenna rose from the chair and stood silently by the window. "What did they *do* to us?" she whispered.

Havelock stood across the room watching her; he could not look away. And then, he was drifting back through indeterminate time, through the rolling mists of a haunting, obsessive dream that never left him. The images were there, the moments remembered, but they had been pushed out of his life only to rise up and attack him, inflaming him whenever the memories refused to stay buried. *What's left when your memory's gone, Mr Smith?* Nothing, of course, yet how often had he wished for oblivion, with no images or remembered moments – trading nothingness for the absence of pain. But now he had passed through the nightmare of interrupted sleep and had come to life just as the tears had come to Jenna's eyes, washing away the hatred. But the reality was fragile; its fragments had to be pieced together.

"We must find out why," said Michael. "Broussac told me what happened to you, but there were gaps I couldn't understand."

"I didn't tell her everything," said Jenna, gazing at the snow outside. "I didn't lie to her, but I didn't tell her everything. I was afraid she wouldn't help me."

"What did you leave out?"

"The name of the man who came to see me. He's been with your government for a number of years. He was once quite controversial, but still respected, I think. At least, I'd heard of him."

"Who was it?"

"A man named Bradford, Emory Bradford."

"Good *God* . . ." Havelock was stunned. Bradford was a name from the past, a disquieting past. He had been one of the political comets born under Kennedy and had won dubious spurs with Johnson. When the comets had faded from the Washington firmament, heading for the international banks and the foundations, the prestigious law offices and the corporate boardrooms, Bradford had remained – less celebrated, to be sure, less influential, certainly – where the political wars had been fought. It was never understood why. A degree of personal wealth aside, he could have done a thousand other things, but he had chosen not to. *Bradford*, thought Havelock, the name echoing in his head. All these years, had Emory Bradford merely been marking time, waiting for another version of Camelot to carry him into another tune of self-professed glory? It had to be. If he had reached Jenna in Barcelona, he was at the core of the deception at Costa Brava, a deception that went far beyond himself and Jenna, two lovers turned against each other. It linked unseen men in Moscow with powerful men in the United States government.

"Do you know him?" asked Jenna, still staring out of the window.

"Not personally. I've never met him. But you're right, he *was* controversial, and almost everyone knows him. The last I heard he was an Undersecretary of State with a low profile but pretty highly regarded – buried but valuable, you could say. He told you he was with Cons Op out of Madrid?"

"He said he was on special assignment with Consular Operations, an emergency involving internal security."

"Me?"

"Yes. He showed me copies of documents found in a bank vault on the Ramblas." Jenna turned from the window. "Do you recall telling me you had to go to the Ramblas on several occasions?"

"It was a drop for Lisbon, I also told you that. Never mind, it was orchestrated."

"But you can understand. The Ramblas stayed in my mind."

"They made sure of it. What were the documents?"

"Instructions from Moscow that could only have been meant for you. There were dates, itineraries; everything corresponded to where we'd been, where we were going. And there were codes; if they weren't authentic, then I'd never seen a Russian cipher."

"The same materials *I* was given," said Havelock, his anger surfacing.

"Yes, I knew it when you told me what they gave you in Madrid. Not all, of course, but many of the same documents and much of the information they showed you, they showed me. Even down to the radio in the hotel room."

"The maritime frequency? I thought you'd been careless; we never listened to the radio."

"When I saw it, a great part of me died," said Jenna.

"When I found the key in your bag and it matched the one the evidence in Madrid stated that you would have – a key to an airport locker – I couldn't stay in the same room with you."

"That was it, wasn't it? The final confirmation for both of us. I had changed, I couldn't help it. And when you came back from Madrid, *you* were different. It was as if you were being pulled violently in several directions, but with only one true commitment, and it was not to me, not to us. You had sold yourself to the Russians for reasons I couldn't understand . . . I even tried to rationalize; perhaps after thirty years there was news of your father – stranger things have happened. Or you were going into deep cover without me; a defector in the process of becoming a double agent. I simply knew that the transition – whatever it was – did not include me." Jenna turned back to the window. She continued, her voice barely audible, "Then Bradford reached me again; this time he was panicking, nearly out of control. He said the word had just been intercepted – Moscow had ordered my execution. You were to lead me into a trap, and you were going to do it that night."

"At the Costa Brava?"

"No, he never mentioned the Costa Brava. He said a man would call around six o'clock while you were out, using a phrase or description I'd recognize as coming only from you. He would say that you could not get to a telephone, but I was to take the car and drive down the coast to Villanueva, that you would meet me by the fountains in the plaza. But you wouldn't, because I'd never get there. I'd be taken on the road."

"I *told* you I was going to Villanueva," said Michael. "It was part of the Cons Op strategy. With me supposedly twenty miles south on business, you had time to get up to the Montebello beach on the Costa Brava. It was the final proof against you. I was to witness it – I demanded that, hoping to Christ you'd never show up."

"It all fitted, it was *made* to fit!" cried Jenna. "Bradford said if that call came I was to run. Another American would be in the lobby with him, watching for the KGB. They'd take me to the consulate."

"But you didn't leave with them. The woman I saw die wasn't you."

"I couldn't. I suddenly couldn't trust anyone . . . Do you remember the incident that night at the café in the Paseo Isabel just before you went to Madrid?"

"The drunk," said Havelock, remembering all too well. "He bumped into you – fell into you, actually – then insisted on shaking your hand and kissing it. He was all over you."

"We laughed about it. You more than I."

"I didn't a couple of days later. I was convinced that was when you were given the key to the airport locker."

"Which I never knew about."

"And which I found in your bag because Bradford put it there while he was in the hotel room and I was in Madrid. I assume you excused yourself for a moment or two."

"I was in shock; I was ill. I'm sure I did."

"It explains the radio, the maritime frequency . . . What about the drunk?"

"He was the other American in the lobby of the hotel. Why was he there? Who *was* he? I went back up as fast as I could."

"He didn't see you?"

"No, I used the staircase. His face frightened me, I can't tell you why. Perhaps because he had pretended to be someone else before, someone so different, I don't know. I *do* know his eyes disturbed me; they were angry, but they did not look round. He *wasn't* watching the lobby for the KGB; he only kept glancing at his watch. By then I was in a panic myself . . . confused, hurt more than I'd ever been hurt in my life. *You* were going to let me die, and suddenly I couldn't trust *them*."

"You went back to the room?"

"God, no, I'd have been cornered. I went up to the floor, stayed in the stairwell and tried to think things through. I thought perhaps I was being hysterical, too frightened to act reasonably. Why *didn't* I trust the Americans? I'd just about made up my mind to go back down when I heard noises from the corridor. I opened the door a bit . . . and knew that I was right to do what I did."

"They came after you?"

"The lift. Bradford knocked on the door several times, and while he was knocking, the other man – the drunk from the café – took out a gun. When there was no answer, they waited until they were sure there was no one in the hallway. Then, with one kick, the man with the gun broke down the door and rushed inside. It was not the action of men who'd come to save someone. I ran."

Havelock, watching her, tried to think. There were so many ambiguities . . . *ambiguity.* Where were the outlines of the man who had used the code Ambiguity?

"How did they get your suitcase?" he asked.

"As you described it, it was an old one of mine. The last I recall I simply left it in the basement of the flat I leased in Prague. You may have carried it down, in fact."

"The KGB would find it."

"The *KGB*?"

"Someone in the KGB."

"Yes, you said that, didn't you? . . . There has to be someone."

"What was the phrase or description the man gave you over the phone? The words you were to think came from me."

"Again Prague. He said there was 'a cobblestone courtyard in the centre of the city'."

"*Veřejná mistnostmi*," said Michael, nodding. "Prague's Soviet police. They'd know about that. In a report I sent to Washington I described how you got out of that place, how great you were. And how I damn near died watching you from a window three storeys above."

"Thank you for the commendation."

"We were putting all our points together, remember? We were going to break out of our movable prison."

"And you were going to teach."

"History."

"And we were going to have children – "

"And send them off to school – "

"And love them and scold them."

"And go to hockey games."

"You said there were no such things – "

"I love you . . ."

"*Mikhail?*"

The first steps were tentative, but the pavane was suddenly finished. They ran to each other, and held each other, pushing time away, and hurt, and a thousand moments of anguish. Her tears came, washing away the final barricades mounted by liars and men who served the liars. Their arms grew stronger around each other, the straining of their bodies an exertion each understood; their lips met, swollen, probing, searching for the release they held for each other. They were trapped as never before in their movable prison – they understood that, too – but for the moment they were also free.

The dream had come fully to life, the reality no longer fragile. She was beside him; her face touching his shoulder, her lips parted, the breath of her deep, steady breathing warming his skin. As so often in the past, strands of her hair fell across his chest, somehow a reminder that even in sleep she was a part of him. He turned carefully so as not to awaken her, and looked down at her. The dark shadows beneath her eyes were still there, but they were fading fast as a hint of colour returned to her pale flesh. It would take days, weeks perhaps, for the fear in her wide eyes to disappear, yet in spite of it, her strength was there; it had carried her through unbearable tensions.

She moved, stretching, and her face was bathed in the sunlight that streamed through the windows. As he watched her he thought of what she had been through, what resources she must have had to summon in order to survive. Where had she been? Who were the people who had helped her, hurt her? There were so many questions, so many things he wanted to know. A part of him was a callow adolescent, jealous of the images he did not wish to imagine, while another part of him was a survivor who knew only too well the prices one had to pay to remain alive in their disorderly, so frequently violent world. The answers would come with time, revealed slowly or in eruptions of memory or resentment, but they would not be provoked by him. The healing process could not be forced; it would be too easy for Jenna to sink back and relive the terrors and, by reliving them, prolong them.

She moved again, her face returning to him, her breath warm. And then the absurdity of his thoughts struck him. Where did he think he was . . . *they* were? What did he think would be permitted them? How could he dare to think in terms of any time at all?

Jacob Handelman was dead, his killer as good as identified – certainly known by now to the liars in Washington. The manhunt would be given respectability; he could see the story in the newspapers: a beloved scholar brutally slaughtered by a deranged former foreign service officer wanted by his government for all manner of crimes. Who could possibly believe the truth? That a kindly old Jew who had suffered the horrors of the camps was in reality a strutting man-monster who had ordered up the guns of Lidice? *Insane!*

Broussac would turn; anyone he might have counted on would not touch him now, touch *them* now. There was no time for healing, they needed every hour; the swiftness of their strikes – *his* strikes – was essential. He looked at his watch; it was 2:45, the day three-quarters gone. There were strategies to consider, rapid plans to make . . . liars to reach at night.

Yet there had to be *something*. For them, only themselves; to ease the ache, erase the vestiges of fragility. If there was not, there was nothing.

He did what he had often dreamt of, waking up in sweat whenever the dream recurred, knowing it could never be. It could be now. He whispered her name, calling out to her across the chasms of sleep, and, as if the moments away from each other had vanished, her hand reached for his. She opened her eyes and they roamed his face; then, without speaking, she raised the covers and came to him. She pressed her naked body against his, her arms enveloping him, her lips against his.

They were silent as their excitement grew, except for their throated-cries of need and anxiety. The need was each for the other, and the anxiety was not to be feared.

They made love twice more, but the third time was more successful in the attempt than in the completion. The rays of the sun no longer streaked through the window; instead an orange glow reflected a country sundown. They sat up in bed, Michael lighting her cigarette, both laughing softly at their misguided energies, their temporary exhaustion.

"You're going to throw me out for a hot-blooded stag from Ankara."

"You have nothing at all to apologize for, my darling, my Mikhail. Besides, I really don't like their coffee."

642

"I'm relieved."

"You're a love," she said, touching the bandage on his shoulder.

"I'm *in* love. There's so much to make up for."

"Both of us, not you alone. You must not think that way. I accepted the lies, just as you did. Incredible lies, incredibly presented. And we don't know why."

"But we know the purpose, which gives us part of the why. To get me out but keep me under control, under a microscope."

"With *my* defection, *my* death? There are other ways of terminating a man you no longer want."

"Killing him?" said Havelock, nodding, then he paused and shook his head. "It's one way, yes. But then there's no way to control whatever damaging evidence he may have left behind. The possibility that such a man has left that information often keeps him alive."

"But they want to kill you *now*. You're 'beyond-salvage'."

"Someone changed his mind."

"This person called 'Ambiguity'," said Jenna.

"Yes. Whatever I know – or they think I know – has been supplanted by a larger threat much more dangerous to them. Again, me. What I found, what I learned."

"I don't understand."

"You," said Havelock. "The Costa Brava. It has to be buried."

"The Soviet connection?"

"I don't know. Who was the woman on the beach? What did she think she was doing there? Why wasn't it you – thank Christ, it wasn't – but *why* wasn't it? Where were they taking you?"

"To my grave, I think."

"If that was the case, why weren't you sent to that beach? Why weren't you killed then?"

"Perhaps they felt I wouldn't go. I didn't leave the hotel with them."

"They couldn't have known that then. They thought they had you – frightened, in shock, wanting protection. The point is, they never mentioned the Costa Brava; they didn't even try to *prime* you."

"I would have driven there that night – all you had to do was call me. I would have come. They could have had their execution; you would have seen what they wanted you to see."

"It doesn't make sense." Michael struck a match and lit a cigarette for himself. "And that's the basic inconsistency, because whoever put Costa Brava together was a hell of a technician, an expert in black operations. It was brilliantly structured, down to split-second timing . . . It doesn't make sense!"

Jenna broke the long silence. "Mikhail," she said quietly, sitting forward, her eyes clouded, focused inward. "*Two* operations," she whispered.

"What?"

"Suppose there were two operations, not one?" She turned to him, her eyes alive now. "The first set in motion in Madrid – the evidence against *me* – then carried forward to Barcelona – the evidence against *you*."

"Still one blanket," said Havelock.

"But then it was *torn*," insisted Jenna. "It became *two*."

"How?"

"The original operation is intercepted," she said. "By someone not part of it."

"Then altered," he said, beginning to understand. "The cloth is the same but the stitches are twisted, ending up being something else. A *different* blanket."

"Still, for what purpose?" she asked.

"Control," he answered. "Then you got away and the control was lost. Broussac told me there's been a coded alert out for you ever since Costa Brava."

"Very coded," agreed Jenna, crushing out her cigarette. "Which could mean whoever intercepted the operation and altered it might not have known that I *had* got out of Barcelona alive."

"Until I saw you and let *everyone* know – everyone who counted. At which point we both had to die; one by the black-operations book – that was me. The other out of strategy – no one in sanction aware – a bomb blowing up a car outside Col des Moulinets. You. Everything buried."

"Again Ambiguity?"

"No one else could have done it. No one but a man with the clearance code could have infiltrated the strategy at that bridge."

Jenna looked at him, then across at the windows; the orange glow was fading. "There are still too many omissions. Too many gaps."

"We'll fill some of them in, maybe all."

"Emory Bradford, of course."

"And someone else," said Havelock. "Matthias. Four days ago I tried to reach him from Cagnes-sur-Mer on his private line – very few people have the number. I couldn't understand it, but he wouldn't talk to me. You can't know how crazy it was, in a way unbelievable. But he wouldn't and I thought the worst: the man closest to me had cut me off. Then you tell me about Bradford, and I'm beginning to think I was wrong."

"How do you mean?"

"Suppose Anton wasn't there? Suppose others had taken over that private place, that very private line?"

"*Bradford?*"

"And whatever's left of his tribe. The return of the political comets, looking for a way to get their fires back. According to *Time* magazine, Matthias is off on an extended holiday, but what if he's not? What if the most celebrated Secretary of State in history is being held incommunicado. In a clinic somewhere, unable to get word out."

"But that's incredible, Mikhail. A man like that would have to stay in touch with his office. There are daily briefings, decisions – "

"It could be done through second and third parties, aides known to State personnel."

"It's too preposterous."

"Maybe it's not. When they told me Anton wouldn't talk to me, I couldn't accept it. I made another call – to an old man, a neighbour of Matthias's whom he saw whenever he went to his lodge in the Shenandoah. His name's Zelienski and he was good for Anton – a retired professor brought over from Warsaw a number of years ago. They used to sit around playing chess, talking about the old days. He was a tonic for Matthias and both of them knew it, especially Anton; but when I spoke to Zelienski he said Anton didn't have time for him these days. Didn't have time."

"It's entirely possible, Mikhail."

"But not consistent. Matthias would *make* the time; he wouldn't cut off an old friend without at least some kind of explanation, any more than he would me. It is not like him."

"How do you mean?"

"I remember Zelienski's words. He said he'd leave messages for Anton and men would call him back expressing Matthias's regrets, saying he rarely drove out to the valley any more. But he did; he was there in the valley when I called. Or he was *supposed* to be. My point is he may not have been."

"Now *you're* not consistent," broke in Jenna. "If what you say is true, why didn't they simply say he wasn't there?"

"They couldn't. I used the private line and it's to be answered only if he's on the premises, and only by him. Someone picked up the phone by mistake and tried to cover it."

"Someone working for Bradford?"

"Someone who's part of a conspiracy against Matthias, at any rate, and I wouldn't exclude Bradford. Men in Washington are dealing secretly with men in Moscow. Together they built Costa Brava convincing Matthias you're a Soviet agent – his note to me made that clear. We don't know whether everything went off the track or not, but we do know Matthias had nothing to do with it and Bradford did. Anton didn't trust Emory Bradford and his crowd; he considered them the worst sort of opportunists. He kept them away from extremely sensitive negotiations because he believed they'd use them for their own ends. He had a point; they did it before, letting the country know only what they wanted people to hear, using the classification stamp so that it became their signature." Michael paused, inhaling on his cigarette as Jenna looked at him. "He may be doing it again, God knows for what purpose. It'll be dark soon and we can drive. We'll head across into Maryland, then down to Washington."

"To Bradford?"

Havelock nodded. Jenna touched his arm. "They'll connect you with Handelman," she said, "and assume you reached me. They'll know the first name I'd give you is Bradford's. They'll guard him."

"I know that," said Michael. "Let's get dressed. We've got to eat and find a newspaper, one that carries the wire services. We'll talk in the car." He began walking towards his suitcase, then stopped. "My God, your clothes. I didn't think; you don't have your clothes."

"Kohoutek's people took them, took everything. They said foreign labels, European luggage, mementoes – anything like that – had to be confiscated for our own good. There could be no traces of where we came from. They would supply me with something suitable later."

"Suitable for what?"

"I was too frightened to think."

"Take all your possessions, and leave you alone in a cell." *So much to make up for.* "Let's go," he said.

"We should stop somewhere and pick up a First Aid kit," added Jenna. "That dressing on your shoulder should be changed. I can do it."

So much to make up for!

23

At a diner on the outskirts of Hagerstown, they saw a dispenser for newspapers reflected in the light of the entrance. There were two papers left, both afternoon editions of the Baltimore *Sun*. They took both, to see whether any photographs had been released that might alert someone inside the roadside restaurant. Shaving the negative odds was instinct.

They sat across from each other in a corner booth. They turned the pages rapidly, and when they had gone through them all they breathed easier. There were no photographs. They would go back and study the article in a moment; it was on page three.

"You must be starved," said Havelock.

"To tell you the truth, I'd like a drink, if they serve one here."

"They do. I'll order." He glanced at the counter and held up his hand.

"I haven't even thought about eating."

"That's strange. Kohoutek said you wouldn't eat last night, that you threw the tray at his Cuban."

"A tray full of scraps. I ate; you always told me never to leave food when you're in a bad situation. That you never know when you'll get another meal."

"Listen to mother."

"I listened to a child running for his life through the woods."

"History. Why did you throw the tray? To keep him away from you?"

"To get the fork. There was no knife."

"You're something, lady."

"I was desperate. Stop complimenting me."

A plump, over-made up waitress approached the table, her eyes appraising Jenna with a mixture of sadness and envy. Michael understood, neither with satisfaction nor in condescension; he merely understood. Jenna Karras was that often-forgotten person, whether she was forced to kill in order to survive or be seduced so she might live. She was a lady. Havelock ordered their drinks.

"Let's get to the bad news," said Michael, opening the newspaper.

"It's on the third page."

"I know. Did you read it?"

"Only the bottom line where it said 'continued on page eleven'. I thought they might have included a photograph there."

"So did I." Havelock began reading as Jenna watched him. The waitress placed their drinks on the table. "We'll order food in a minute," said Michael, his eyes riveted to the paper. The waitress left as Havelock quickly flipped the pages, snapping the paper in place. As he read on, he experienced relief, then concern, and finally alarm. He finished and leaned back in the booth, staring at Jenna.

"What is it? What does it say?"

"They're covering it up," he said softly.

"*What?*"

"They're protecting me . . . actually protecting me."

"You couldn't have read it properly."

"I'm afraid I did." He leaned forward, his fingers scanning the lines in the column of the paper. "Listen to this:

"According to the State Department, no such individual matching the name, the description or the fingerprints is currently or has ever been in the employ of the Department of State. Further, a spokesman for State said that to speculate on the similarity of the reported name of the killer with that of any present or past employee would be grossly unfair and inaccurate. A thorough computer check was made upon receipt of the Manhattan police report and the results were negative. However, the State Department's report revealed that the slain Professor Handelman had acted as a consultant to the Department in the area of European refugee displacement, with emphasis on those persons who had survived the Nazi period. According to a spokesman, the Manhattan police believe that the killer may be a member of a terrorist organization violently hostile to the Jewish community. The State Department pointed out that it is not uncommon for terrorists in all countries to assume the identities of government personnel."

Havelock stopped and looked up at Jenna. "That's it," he said. "They've thrown everybody off."

"Could they believe it?"

"Not possible. To begin with, there are a hundred people in and out of State who know I was with Consular Operations. They'd put the names together and come up with mine. Second, my fingerprints must have been all over Handelman's apartment; they're on file. Lastly, Handelman had nothing whatsoever to do with any part of the government; that was his strength. He was a halfway man for the Quai d'Orsay, and they never would have used him if they thought he'd ever be under government scrutiny. It isn't done; we're all off-limits."

"What do you make of it?"

Michael sank back in the booth, reached for his whisky and drank. "It's too blatant," he mused, holding the glass in front of his lips.

"A trap, then," said Jenna. "They want you to come in – presumably after Bradford – and take you."

"To a point 'beyond-salvage', to coin a phrase. And once I'm dead, I can't talk, but they can explain they trapped a killer. Reaching Bradford would be easy, coming out with him impossible . . . Unless I could draw *him* out, make him come to *me*."

"They'd never permit it. He'd be flanked by guards and they'd be watching for you. They'd kill you on sight."

Havelock drank again, a thought stirring at the bottom of his mind but unclear as yet. "Watching for me," he repeated, putting the glass down. "*Looking* for me . . .

But no one's *looking* for me except the men who did this to us."

"The liars, as you call them," said Jenna.

"Yes. We need help, but I assumed we couldn't get it, that anyone I might want to reach wouldn't touch us. That's not the case now; they called *off* the hunt."

"Don't be foolish, Mikhail," interrupted Jenna. "It's part of the trap. There's an alert out for you as well as for me, and yours isn't coded; there's nothing ambiguous about it. You're you, and every agency that might be of value has you on its list. Who in your government do you think you could trust?"

"No one," agreed Havelock. "And no one who could survive a 'beyond-salvage' association, if I did trust him."

"Then what are you saying?"

"Cagnes-sur-Mer," said Michael, squinting. "At Salanne's house when I couldn't reach Anton, I called old Zelienski – I told you, remember? He mentioned him. 'Alexander the Great', he called him. Raymond Alexander. Not just a mutual friend, but a pretty damned good friend – of mine as well as Matthias. He could do it."

"How?"

"Because he's *outside* the government. Outside but in a way very much a part of it; Washington needs him and he needs Washington. He's a writer for the *Potomac Review*, and knows as much about the government as anyone I've ever met. But he relies on his contacts; he'd never let me get near him if I'd been identified in the newspapers, but I wasn't."

"How could he help us?"

"I'm not sure. Maybe draw out Bradford for me. He does in-depth interviews, and to be interviewed by him is a plus for anyone in the government. He's above suspicion. They might drive Bradford out in a tank, but they'd let him go inside the house by himself. I could hint at something unexpected, a substantive change in the State Department with Bradford at the centre. Then suggest an interview – with me in the house to listen, to verify."

"The house?"

"He works at home; it's part of his mystique. Like James Reston at the *Times*; if a politician or a bureaucrat says he was at Fiery Run, everyone knows what he means; there'll be a story by Scotty Reston. If he says he was out at Fox Hollow, the same people know he was interviewed by Raymond Alexander. Fox Hollow's in Virginia just west of Washington. We could be there in an hour and a half, two hours at the most."

"Would he do it?"

"He might. I won't tell him why, but he might. We're friends."

"The university?"

"No, but there's a connection. I met him through Matthias. When I first started at State, Matthias would come down to Washington on one thing or another, building his contacts, charming the asses off influential asses, and I'd frequently get a hurry-up call from Anton, asking me to join them both for dinner. I never refused, not only because of the company, but the restaurants were way beyond my income."

"That was gracious of your *pritel*."

"And not very bright for a brilliant man, considering the nature of my training.

He was the *učitel* extolling his not-too-gifted student from Praha, when the last thing I needed was any sort of notice. I explained this quietly to Alexander. We both laughed and, as a result, had dinner now and then when Anton was safely back in his tower at Princeton, tending his academic gardens and not trying to grow arbours in Washington. Make no mistake, the great Matthias was not above fertilizing the seeds he'd sown."

"You'd have dinner at Alexander's home?"

"Always. He understood that he also wasn't someone I wanted to be seen with in public."

"Then you *are* good friends."

"Reasonably so."

"And he's influential?"

"Of course."

Jenna reached over and touched his arm. "Mikhail, why not tell him *everything*?"

Havelock frowned and put his hand over hers. "I don't think he'd want to hear it. It's the sort of thing he runs from."

"He's a writer. In *Washington*. How can you say that?"

"He's an analyst, a commentator. Not an investigative reporter; not a muck raker. He doesn't like stepping on toes, only on opinions."

"But what you have to tell him is extraordinary."

"He'd tell me to go straight to the State Department security bureau in the belief that I'd get a fair hearing. I wouldn't. I'd get a bullet in my head. Alexander's a sixty-five-year-old curmudgeon who's heard it all – from Dallas to Watergate – and he thinks a hundred and ten per cent of it is a conspiracy of horseshit. And if he found out what I'd done – Handelman excluded – he'd call security himself."

"He's not much of a friend."

"By his lights he is; just don't transgress." Michael paused, turning her hand over. "But beyond the possibility that he'd bring Bradford out to Fox Hollow, there's something he might clear up. My *přítel*. I'll ask him to find out where Matthias is, say that I don't want to call myself because I may not have time to see him and Anton would be upset. He'd do it; with his connections he *could* do it."

"Suppose he can't?"

"Then that'll tell us something, won't it? In which case, I'll force him to get Bradford out there, if I have to put a gun to his head. But if he does reach Matthias at a lodge in the Shenandoah . . . we'll know something else, and it frightens the hell out of me. It will mean that the Secretary of State has a Moscow connection in the KGB."

The village of Fox Hollow was small. The streets were lit by gas lamps and the architecture was colonial by township decree; the stores were called shops, their clientele among the wealthiest in the Washington-New York orbit. The village's charm was not only apparent, it was proclaimed, but it was not for the benefit of outsiders – tourists were discouraged, if not harassed. The minimum police force had maximum arms and a communications system that, proportionately, rivalled that of the Pentagon, where it was probably designed. Fox Hollow was an island in a landlocked area of Virginia as surely as if its square-mileage were surrounded by an impassable sea.

The air had been warmed up by the Potomac River, the snow had receded on the outskirts of Harper's Ferry. It had turned into a cold drizzle at Leesburg, by which time Havelock had prepared his scenario for Raymond Alexander. Its bureaucratic plausibility lent it conviction, plausibility based on genuine anxiety where present or past covert operations were concerned. There had been a killing in New York – if Alexander had not heard of it, he would by morning; he was a voracious reader of newspapers – and the killer had mocked up an impersonation, including an ID and an appearance uncomfortably close to Michael's own. The State Department had flown him back from London on military transport; any assistance the retired foreign service officer could give Consular Operations would be appreciated; also, he *had been* in London, hadn't he?

The Bradford ploy would be refined as their conversation progressed, but the basic thrust would be that the once-controversial Undersecretary of State was about to be rehabilitated and put back in the limelight. In London, Havelock would say, he had been given a detailed report of Bradford's extensive but secret negotiations on the touchy matter of NATO missile deployment; it was a major shift in policy. It was also sufficiently explosive to get Alexander's juices running. It was the sort of advance leak he thrived on, giving him time to put together an exhaustive analysis of the pros and cons. But if the old warhorse wished to interview Emory Bradford – with on-site but unseen verification, possibly confrontation – he must persuade the Undersecretary to come out to Fox Hollow in the morning. Havelock had a reservation on the afternoon flight back to London – and, of course, time and schedules permitting, he wanted to drop in on his old mentor Anthony Matthias, if only for a few minutes. If Alexander knew where he could find him.

As for Bradford, he had no choice. If summoned by the redoubtable journalist, he would comply. Other things – such as Costa Brava – being paramount, he had to maintain his low-profile at all costs, and one way to lose it was to refuse to be interviewed by Raymond Alexander. And when he came into the house in Fox Hollow, with his guards remaining outside in a limousine, Michael would take him. His disappearance would baffle the liars and the guards hired by the liars. The journalist's large, rambling house was surrounded by miles of dense woods, overgrown fields and steep ravines. No one knew the forests the way Mikhail Havlicek knew them; he would take Bradford through them until they came to a back country road somewhere, and a car, and the woman that Bradford had used in Barcelona. After his meeting with Alexander, they would have all night to study the map and travel the roads, watching for the Fox Hollow police, explanations at the ready if they were stopped. They could do it. They *had* to do it.

"It's lovely!" cried Jenna, charmed by the gas-lit streets and the small alabaster columns of the store fronts.

"It's wired," said Michael, spotting a blue-and-white patrol car at the kerb in the middle of the block.

"Get down!" he ordered. "Stay out of sight."

"What?"

"*Please.*"

Jenna did as she was told, curling up on the floor.

He slowed down, pulling alongside the police car; he saw the officer in the window, then eased to his right and parked directly in front.

"What are you doing?" whispered Jenna, bewildered.

"Showing my credentials before anyone asks for them."

"That's very good, Mikhail."

Havelock got out of the coupé and walked back to the patrol car. The police officer rolled down the window, first studying the licence plate on Michael's hired car. It was precisely what Michael wanted him to see; it could be of value later that night if a "suspicious vehicle" were reported.

"Officer, could you tell me where there's a pay phone around here? I thought there was one on the corner, but then I haven't been back here in a couple of years."

"You've been here before?" asked the policeman, his voice friendly, his eyes not.

"Oh, sure. Used to spend weekends out here a lot."

"You have business in Fox Hollow, sir?"

"Well . . ." Havelock paused, as if the question bordered on impertinence. Then he shrugged as if to say, After all the police have a job to do. He spoke in a slightly lower tone. "All right, I understand. My business is with an old friend, Raymond Alexander. I want to call and tell him I'm here . . . Just in case someone's dropped in on him he'd prefer I don't meet. It's standard procedure with Mr Alexander, Officer, but you probably know that. I could drive around for a while. I'll probably have to later on anyway."

The policeman's posture had visibly improved at the mention of Alexander's name. Limousines and military staff cars were common sights on the road to the venerated political commentator's retreat. There was no such vehicle in front of him now, but the operative phrases were printed in the officer's eyes. "An old friend. Used to spend weekends . . ."

"Yes, sir. Of course, sir. There's a restaurant five blocks up with a phone in the lobby."

"The Lamplighter?" said Havelock, remembering.

"That's it."

"I don't think so, Officer. It could be a busy night. Isn't there a booth on the street?"

"There's one over on Acacia."

"If you'll tell me how to get there, both RA and I would appreciate it."

"You can follow me, sir."

"Thanks very much." Michael started for his car, then stopped and returned to the window. "I know this sounds silly, but I was usually driven out here. I think I know the way to his home. I take a left on Webster to Underhill Road, then straight out for two or three miles, isn't that it?"

"It's nearer six miles, sir."

"Oh? Thanks."

"After you make your call, I could lead you out, sir. It's quiet in town tonight."

"That's *very* kind of you. But really, I couldn't ask you."

"No problem. That's what we're here for."

"Well, thanks, again. I appreciate it."

The call to Raymond Alexander brought forth the response Havelock expected. Nothing would do but that he should drop in and see the journalist if only for a drink. Michael said he was glad Raymond was free, not only to renew an old friendship but because he had learned something in London that Alexander might want to know about. It might even make up partially for a great many expensive dinners Havelock had enjoyed at Raymond's expense.

On the way back to his car Michael stopped at the police officer's window. "Mr Alexander wanted me to get your name. He's very grateful to you."

"It's nothing, sir. My name's Lewis. Officer Lewis; there's only one."

Lewis, he thought. *Harry Lewis*, Professor of Political Science, Concord University. He could not think about Harry now, but he would have to think about him soon. Lewis must be convinced he had dropped out of civilization. He had and, to re-enter it, liars would have to be found and exposed.

"Is something the matter, sir?"

"No, nothing at all. I know a man named Lewis. I remembered I was to call him. Thanks once again. I'll follow you."

Havelock climbed behind the wheel of the rented car and looked at Jenna. "How are you doing?"

"Uncomfortable and frightened out of my mind! Suppose that man had come over?"

"I would have stopped him, called to him from the booth, but I didn't think it was likely. The police in Fox Hollow stay close to their radios. I just don't want you seen, if we can help it. Not around here, not with me."

The drive out to Alexander's house took less than twelve minutes. The white post-and-rail fence marking the journalist's property shone in the glare of the headlights of both cars. The home itself was set far back from the road. It was a tasteful combination of stone and wood, with floodlights shining down on the circular drive in front of wide, slate steps that led to the heavy oak entrance door. The grounds were cleared in the front and on the sides of the house; thick, tall trees shot up at random about the close-cropped lawn. But where the lawn ended on either side the dense woods abruptly began. From memory, Michael pictured the rear of the house; the woods were no farther away from the large back patio than they were from the sides of the building. He would use those woods; and Bradford would enter them with him.

"When you hear the police car leave," he said to Jenna, "get up and stretch, but don't get out. I don't know what kind of alarms Alexander has around here."

"It's been a strange introduction to this free country of yours, Mikhail."

"Also, don't smoke."

"*Děkuji.*"

"You're welcome."

Havelock purposely touched the rim of the horn as he got out of the car; the sound was abrupt and short, easily explained. There were no dogs. He walked towards the patrol car in front, hoping the horn would serve its function before he

652

reached the window. It did; the front door opened and a uniformed maid stood in the frame, looking out.

"Hello, Margaret!" yelled Michael over the bonnet of the police car. "Be right there." He looked down at the police officer, who had glanced at the door, the scene not lost on him. "Thanks again, Mr Lewis," he said, taking a note from his pocket. "I'd like to – "

"Oh, no, sir, thanks just the same. Have a good evening, sir." The officer nodded with a smile, pulled the gear in place and drove off.

Havelock waved; no police, no dogs, only unseen alarms. As long as Jenna stayed in the car, she was safe. He walked up the slate steps to the door and the maid.

"Good evening, sir," said the woman in a distinct Irish brogue. "My name is Enid, not Margaret."

"I'm terribly sorry."

"Mr Alexander is expecting you. I never heard of a Margaret; the girl before me was Gretchen. She lasted four years, may the Lord rest her soul."

Raymond Alexander got up from the soft easy chair in his book-lined, wood-panelled library and walked towards Michael, his hand outstretched. His gait was more lively than one might have expected from his portly figure; his cherubic face with the clear green eyes was topped by a mass of dishevelled hair that managed to stay darker than the years normally permitted. In keeping with his anachronistic life-style, he wore a deep red velvet smoking jacket, something Havelock had not seen since his adolescent days in Greenwich, Connecticut.

"Michael, how *are* you? My God, it's been four, five years now!" cried the journalist in his clipped, high-pitched voice.

"They've served you well, Raymond. You look great."

"*You* don't! Forgive me, young man, but you look like something one of my cats would have left outside. I don't think retirement agrees with you." Alexander released Havelock's hand and quickly raised both of his own. "Yes, I know all about it. I keep track when friends answer questions. Pour yourself a drink; you know the rules here and you look like you need one."

"I will, thanks," said Michael, heading for the familiar copper bar against the wall.

"I suppose you'd look better with some sleep . . ."

It was the opportune opening. Havelock sat down opposite the journalist and told him the story of the killing in New York and State's flying him back from London at four A.M. UK time.

"I read about that this morning," said Alexander, shaking his head. "Naturally, I thought of you – the name of course – but knew right away it was ridiculous. You, of all people, with *your* background? Did someone steal an old identification of yours?"

"No, it was mocked, that's what we think. At any rate, it's been a long two days. For a while I thought I was a prisoner."

"Well, they never would have brought you over this way if Anton had been apprised, I can tell you that."

Only Matthias's closest friends called him by his Czech first name, and because Michael knew it, the statement alarmed him. By necessity, it reversed the sequence that Havelock had intended, but it would have been unnatural not to inquire. The Bradford ploy would come last; Matthias now.

"I wondered about that," said Havelock, revolving the glass in his hand, his voice casual. "I simply thought he was too damned busy. As a matter of fact, I was going to ask you if he was in Washington. I'd like to drop in and see him, but my time's limited. I have to get back to London, and if I call him myself . . . well, you know Anton. He'd insist I spend a couple of days."

Alexander leaned forward in the heavily cushioned chair, his intelligent face expressing concern. "You don't know, then?"

"Know what?"

"Damn it, that's when government paranoia goes too far! He's the closest thing you have to a father and you're the closest thing he has to a son! You who've kept the secrets of a thousand operations and they haven't told you."

"Told me what?"

"Anton's ill. I'm sorry you have to hear it from me, Michael."

"How ill?"

"The rumours range from serious to fatal. Apparently he's aware of whichever it is, and, true to form, thinks of himself last. When State learned that I'd found out, he sent me a personal note swearing me to secrecy."

"How did you learn of it?"

"One of those odd things you don't really think about . . . until you think about it. I was inveigled into going to a party in Arlington several weeks ago – you know how I detest those exhausting exercises in verbal endurance, but the hostess was a close friend of my late wife."

"I'm sorry," interrupted Havelock, only vaguely remembering the journalist's wife, a willowy thing who had opted for gardens and flower arrangements. "I didn't know."

"It's all right. It's been over two years now."

"The party in Arlington?"

"Yes, well, to my embarrassment a youngish woman who was quite drunk virtually assaulted me. Now, if she'd been a predatory female intent on a sexual liaison, I could have understood her being drawn to the most desirable man on the premises, but I'm afraid it wasn't the case. Apparently she had marital difficulties of a most unusual nature. Her husband was an army officer absent from the household – read 'connubial bed' – for nearly three months and no one at the Pentagon would tell her where he was. She feigned illness, which I doubt took a great deal of self-persuasion, and he was brought back on emergency leave. When she got him in her net she demanded to know where he'd been, what he was doing – read 'other woman'. He refused to tell her, so when soldier-boy was asleep she went through his clothes and found a security pass for a post she'd never heard of; I hadn't either, as a matter of fact. I gather she battered him awake and confronted him, and this time in self-defence he blurted out that it was the highest-priority classification. It was where a very important man was being treated, and he couldn't say any more."

"Anton?" broke in Michael.

"I didn't piece it together until the next morning. The last thing she said to me –

before some charitable or over-sexed guest drove her home – was that the country should be told about such things, that the government was behaving like Mother Russia. That morning she phoned me, quite sober and in serious panic. She apologized for what she described as her 'ghastly behaviour' and pleaded with me to forget everything she'd told me. I was entirely sympathetic, but added that perhaps her instincts were right, although I wasn't the person she should appeal to; there were others who would serve her better. She replied something to the effect that her husband could be ruined, a brilliant military career destroyed. So that was that."

"That was *what*? How did you find out it was Matthias?"

"Because that same morning I read in the *Washington Post* that Anton was prolonging a brief vacation and would not appear before the Senate Foreign Relations Committee. I kept thinking about the woman and what she'd said . . . and the fact that Anton rarely gave up a chance to perform for the Senate newsreels. And then I thought, Why not? Like you, I know where he spends every free moment he has . . ."

"The Shenandoah lodge," interrupted Havelock, feeling a sense of *déjà vu*.

"Exactly. I reasoned that if the story were true and he was taking an extra few days, we might get together for some valley fishing, or his beloved chess. Like you, again, I have the telephone number so I called him."

"He wasn't there," said Michael.

"They didn't say that," corrected the journalist. "They said he couldn't come to the phone."

"*That* phone?"

"Yes . . . *that* phone. It was the private line."

"The one that goes unanswered unless he's there."

"Yes." Alexander raised his brandy glass and drank.

Havelock was close to screaming. He wanted to rush over to the portly writer and shake him. *Go on! Go on, tell me!* Instead, he said quietly, "That must have been a shock."

"Wouldn't it have been to you?"

"Certainly." *It was. Can't you see it in my eyes?* "What did you do?"

"The first thing was to call Zelienski. You remember old Leon, don't you? Whenever Matthias drove or flew out to the lodge it was standard procedure for Zelienski to be summoned for dinner – has been standard for years now."

"Did you reach him?"

"Yes, and he told me a very odd thing. He said he hadn't seen Anton in months, that Matthias never answered his calls any more – not personally – and that he didn't think our great man had time for the Valley these days."

The *déjà vu* was complete for Michael. Then he remembered. "You're a friend of Zelienski's, aren't you?"

"Through Anton, mainly. Very much the way we met. He comes up now and then for lunch and chess. Never for dinner, though; he won't drive at night. But my point is that the one place where Matthias should have been for a holiday he wasn't. I really can't imagine his not seeing old Leon, can you? After all, Zelienski lets him win."

"I can't imagine your letting the issue drop, either."

"You're quite right, I didn't. I called Anton's office and asked to speak with his first assistant. I emphasized that I expected someone who represented the Secretary of State in his absence, as I considered my inquiry to be that substantive. Of *all* people, guess who was put on to me."

"Who?"

"Emory Bradford. Do you remember him? Bradford the 'boomerang', scourge of the warlords where once he'd been their spokesman. I was fascinated because actually I admire him for having had the courage to reverse himself, but I always thought Matthias detested the whole flock. If anything, he was more sympathetic to those who went down in flames because they didn't change their spots."

"What did Bradford tell you?" Michael gripped the glass in his hand, suddenly terrified that he might break it.

"You mean, what did he tell me after I told him what I thought had happened? Naturally, I never mentioned the woman and, God knows, it wasn't necessary. Bradford was in shock. He begged me not to say anything or write anything, that Matthias himself would be in touch with me. I agreed, and by mid-afternoon, I received Anton's note by messenger. I've abided by his request – until now. I can't for a minute believe he'd want you excluded."

"I don't know what to say." Havelock lessened the pressure on the glass, breathing deeply, the moment to be interpreted in any way the journalist wished. But for Michael it was the prelude to perhaps the most important question he had ever asked in his life. "Do you remember the name of the post where the woman's husband was stationed? The one you'd never heard of before."

"Yes," said Alexander, studying Havelock. "But no one knows I know. Or my source."

"Will you tell me? No one will ever know *my* source; you have my word on it."

"For what purpose, Michael?"

Havelock paused, then smiled. "Send a basket of fruit probably. A letter, of course."

The journalist nodded his head, smiled and answered, "It's a place called Poole's Island, somewhere off the coast of Georgia."

"Thank you."

Alexander noted his empty glass. "Come now, we're both out. Freshen yours and do mine while you're at it. That's also part of the rules, remember?"

Michael got out of the chair, shaking his head, smiling still despite the tension he felt. "Be happy to pour yours, but I really have to get going." He picked up the journalist's glass. "I was expected in Maclean an hour ago."

"You're *leaving*?" exclaimed the old warhorse, his eyebrows arched, turning in the chair. "What about this piece of information from London you claimed would make up for some of the best meals you ever had, young man?"

Havelock stood at the copper bar, pouring brandy. "I was thinking about that as I drove out here," he said pensively. "I may have been impetuous."

"Spoilsport," said Alexander, chuckling.

"Well, it's up to you. It concerns a very complicated, deep cover intelligence operation, which in my judgement will take us nowhere. Do you want to hear it?"

"Stop there, dear boy! You've got the wrong scribbler. I wouldn't touch it. I subscribe to Anton's maxim. Eighty per cent of all intelligence is a chess game played by idiots for the benefit of paranoid morons!"

Michael climbed into the car; there was the faint odour of cigarettes. "You've been smoking," he said.

"Feeling like a little boy in a graveyard," replied Jenna, curled up on the floor. "What about Bradford? Will your friend bring him out here?"

Havelock started the engine, engaged the gear and swung rapidly around the circular drive towards the entrance. "You can get up now."

"What about *Bradford?*"

"We're going to let him sweat for a while, stretch him out."

Jenna crawled up on the seat, staring at him. "What are you saying, Mikhail?"

"We're going to drive all night, rest for a while in the morning, then keep going. I want to get there late tomorrow."

"My God, *where?*"

"A place called Poole's Island, wherever it is."

24

The island was off the coast, east of Savannah; five years ago it had been a sparsely populated island of less than two square miles, before it was taken over by the government for oceanic research. Several times a week, said the fishermen, helicopters from Hunter Air Force Base could be seen skimming above the water towards an unseen pad somewhere beyond the tall pines that bordered the rocky shoreline.

They had reached Savannah by three-thirty in the afternoon and by four had found a nondescript motel on the ocean highway. At four-twenty they walked onto the piers of a commercial marina across the way in time to watch a dozen or so fishing boats come in with the day's catch. By a quarter past five they had talked to various fishermen, and at five-thirty Havelock had a quiet conversation with the manager of the marina. By ten to six two hundred dollars had exchanged hands, and a fifteen foot skiff with a twelve horsepower outboard had been made available to him, with the hours at his discretion and the night watchman of the marina informed.

They drove back along the highway to a shopping centre in Fort Pulaski where Michael found a sports shop and purchased the items he needed. These included a woollen hat, tight sweater, trousers and thick, rubber-soled ankle boots – all black. In addition to the clothes he bought the following: a waterproof torch and an oilcloth packet, a hunting knife and five packages of seventy-two-inch rawhide shoelaces.

"A sweater, a hat, a torch, a knife," Jenna said rapidly, angrily. "You buy one of each. Buy two. I'm going with you."

"No, you're not."

"Do you forget Prague and Warsaw? Trieste or the Balkans?"

"No, but you do. In each place – everywhere we went – there was always a secondary we could fall back on, if only to buy time. Someone at an embassy or a consulate who was given the words that constituted a counter-threat."

"We never used such people."

"We were never caught."

She looked at him, her eyes reluctantly accepting his logic. "What words do *I* have?"

"I'll write them out for you. There's a stationery store across the mall. I want to get a yellow legal pad and carbon paper. Let's go."

Jenna sat in an armchair next to the motel desk where Havelock wrote. Taking the carbon copies from him as he tore them off the yellow pad, she checked the blue impressions for legibility. He had filled up nine pages, each line in precise block letters, each item numbered, every detail specific, every name accurate. It was a compendium of selected top secret intelligence operations and penetrations perpetuated by the United States government throughout Europe during the past eighteen months. It included sources, informants, deep-cover and double agents, as well as a list of diplomats and attachés in three embassies who in reality were controls for the Central Intelligence Agency. On the tenth page he gave an account of Costa Brava, naming Emory Bradford and the men he had spoken with who had confirmed evidence that could only have been obtained with the co-operation of the KGB and of a VKR officer in Paris who admitted Soviet knowledge of the deception. On the eleventh page he wrote of the fatal meeting on the Palatine Hill, and of an American intelligence officer who had died saving his life and, moments before his death, had exclaimed that there were lies being told by powerful men in Washington. On the twelfth he briefly described the events at Col des Moulinets and the order for execution issued by the codename Ambiguity. On the thirteenth and last page he told the truth about a killer from Lidice who had called himself Jacob Handelman, and the purpose of a farm in Mason Falls, Pennsylvania which sold the services of slaves as efficiently as any camp that provided labour for Albert Speer. The final line was concise: *Secretary of State Anthony Matthias is being held against his will at a government installation called Poole's Island in Georgia.*

"There are your words," he said, handing Jenna the last page and getting up to stretch. His body ached; he had written furiously for nearly two hours. While Jenna read, he lit a cigarette and walked to the window overlooking the highway and the ocean beyond. It was dark, the moon intermittently shining through a night sky streaked with clouds. The weather was fair, the seas normal; he hoped both would stay that way.

"They're strong words, Mikhail," said Jenna, placing the last carbon on the desk.

"It's the truth."

"Forgive me for not approving. You could cost the lives of many people, many friends, with this."

"Not the last four pages. There're no friends there . . . except the Apache, and he's gone."

"Then use only the last four pages, said Jenna. Havelock turned from the window. "No, I have to go all the way or not at all. There's no middle ground now; they've got to believe I'll do it. More important, they've got to believe *you'll* do it. If there's the slightest doubt, I'm dead and you might as well be. The threat's got to be real, not hollow."

"You're assuming you'll be caught."

"If I find what I think I'm going to find, I intend to be."

"That's insane!" cried Jenna, quickly getting to her feet.

"No, it isn't. You're not usually wrong, but you are now. That island's the shortcut we've been looking for." He walked towards the chair where he had dropped the purchases from the sports shop. "I'll get dressed and we'll work out a telephone relay."

"You mean this, don't you?"

"I mean it."

"Booths, then," she said reluctantly. "No call over twelve seconds."

"But only one number." Michael changed direction and went to the desk. He picked up a pencil, wrote on the pad, tore off the page and gave it to Jenna. "Here it is; it's the Cons Op emergency reception. Dial direct – I'll show you how – and have a pocket full of change."

"I have no pocket."

"And no money, and no clothes," added Havelock, taking her by the shoulders, pulling her to him. "Remedy that, will you? It'll take your mind off things for a while. Go shopping."

"You're mad."

"No, I mean it. You won't have much time, but most of the shops in that centre stay open until ten-thirty. Then there's a bowling alley, a couple of restaurants and an all-night supermarket."

"I don't *believe* you," she exclaimed, pulling her face back and looking at him.

"Believe," he said. "It's safer than telephone booths on the highway." He glanced at his watch. "It's ten to nine now and Poole's Island is only a mile and a half offshore. It shouldn't take me more than twenty minutes to reach it – say, by ten. At eleven, I want you to start calling that number and say the words 'billiards or pool'. Got it?"

"Certainly. 'Billiards or pool'."

"Good. If you don't get an immediate response, hang up and get to another phone. Call every fifteen minutes."

"You say a response. What will it be?"

Havelock frowned. ' "We prefer pool'."

' "We prefer pool'. Then what?"

"A last call, again fifteen minutes later. Someone else other than the operator will be slotted into the emergency line. He won't use a name but he'll give the response. The second he does, read him the first two lines on the first page. I'll take the carbons with me so that the words match. Do it fast and hang up."

"And then the waiting begins," said Jenna, holding him, her cheek against his. "Now, our immovable prison."

"Very immovable, stationary, in fact. Pick up food at the supermarket and stay here. Don't go out. I'll reach you."

"How long will it be, do you think?"

Havelock gently pulled his cheek away from hers and looked at her. "It could be as long as a day, two days. I hope not but it may be."

"And if . . ." Jenna could not finish the sentence, and tears came to her eyes. Her pale, striking face looked drawn.

"After three days call Alexander in Fox Hollow and tell him I've been killed or taken, that Anton Matthias is being held prisoner. Say you've got the proof in my own handwriting, plus my voice on the tape I made at Salanne's house in Cagnes-sur-Mer. Under the circumstances, he can't walk away from you. He won't. His beloved republic is being poisoned." Michael paused. "Just the last four pages," he said quietly. "Burn the first nine. You're right, they don't deserve to die."

Jenna closed her eyes. "I cannot promise you that," she said. "I love you so. If I lose you, none of them matter. None."

The water was choppy, as it often was when coastal currents were interrupted by sudden offshore land masses. He was about a quarter of a mile from the island's rocky coastline, approaching from the leeward side, the wind carrying the minimal sound of the engine out to sea. He would cut it off soon and use the oars, rowing forward towards the darkest section of the surrounding pines, guided by the soft glow of light beyond the tree tops.

He had made his own separate arrangements with the marina's night watchman, tenuous arrangements any experienced field man would attempt to make if he hired a boat knowing he might have to abandon it. One never gave up means of escape unless it was absolutely necessary, but one obscured those means as best one could, if only to buy time; five minutes of confusion was often the difference between capture and escape. So far, however, the trip had been clean. He could propel the skiff into the blackest inlet and beach it.

Now was the moment. He pushed in the throttle; the engine coughed quietly and died. He jumped to the mid-seat, body forward, and lifted the oars into their locks. The outgoing current was stronger than he expected; he pressed against the seaward tide, hoping it would alter before his arms and shoulders weakened. The wound from Col des Moulinets was beginning to pain him; he had to be careful and use the weight of his body.

Sound. Not his, not the abrasive creaking of oarlocks or the lapping waves against the bow. A muffled sound . . . an *engine.*

A light, a searchlight, sweeping the water about half a mile to his right. It was a patrol boat rounding the far point of the island, veering starboard, directly at him. Did the island's security system include sonar? Sonic beams shooting over the water, rising and falling with the tides, capable of picking up small craft approaching the shore? Or was the boat on a routine patrol? It was not the moment to speculate. Keeping his body low, Havelock swiftly lifted the oars out of their locks, shoving both under the slatted seats so that they rested on the floor of the hull. He reached forward for the mooring line, throwing it over the bow, and then slipped over the side into the ocean, breathing deeply and tensing his muscles to ward off the cold. He slid back and held onto the propeller shaft, splashing water over the outboard motor, cooling the top surface. He had travelled at very low throttle; in minutes only a sensitive hand would be able to determine whether the engine had been running – if anyone thought to check.

The searchlight suddenly blinded him; the skiff had been spotted. The far-away engine roared through the wind, joined by the wobbling wail of a siren. The patrol boat accelerated, bearing down on him. He dived under the water, swimming out, away from the island, the current propelling him. The skiff was still nearly a quarter-mile from the shoreline, too far for a swimmer to attempt comfortably in these waters; it was a fact that might weigh in his favour when the boat was found.

By the time the large patrol boat had side-slipped in to the skiff and cut its motors, Michael was twenty yards behind its stern, breaking the surface, pulling the wet woollen hat down over his head. The searchlight was crisscrossing the water everywhere; he went under twice, his eyes open, re-emerging when the beam had passed. It continued scanning the area, but no longer behind, only in the front and to the sides. Two men with grappling hooks had the skiff in tow; the one at the bow shouted.

"Leo's Marina, Lieutenant! Out of Savannah! Marker number GA-zero-eight-two!"

"Tell base to raise Leo's Marina in Savannah and cut us in!" yelled the officer to an unseen radio operator in the open cabin. "The number's GA-zero-eight-two! Get a reading!"

"Yes, sir!" came the reply.

"And inform base of our location. Have a security check run on sector four."

"This thing couldn't have got in there, Lieutenant," said the man with the stern hook. "It'd be tripped by the flat nets. Everywhere there ain't no rocks we got flat nets."

"Then what the hell's it doing here? Are there any clothes, any equipment? Anything?"

"Nothin', sir!" yelled the first man, climbing down into the skiff. "Stinks of fish, that's all."

Havelock watched while treading and bobbing in the water. He was struck by an odd thing: the men on the patrol boat were in khaki fatigues, the officer in a field jacket. They were army, not navy. Yet the boat had a naval registration.

"Lieutenant!" The voice came from within the cabin as a face with a headset framing it appeared in the open archway. "The watchman at Leo's said a couple of drunks had that skiff out and brought it in late. He figured they didn't tie it up proper and it went out with the tide. He'd appreciate it if we towed it in; it'd be his ass. The boat's shit, but the outboard's worth money."

"I don't like it," said the officer.

"Hey, come on, sir. Who's gonna swim a half mile in these waters? The fishermen've seen sharks around here."

"Suppose it's *been* in?"

"With the flat nets?" asked the man with the stern hook. "No place else to park, Lieutenant."

"Fuck it! Throw up the line and let's circle around nearer the nets and rocks. This Leo owes us."

And Havelock knew he owed a night watchman far more than the hundred dollars he had given him. The patrol boat's engines roared as the first man climbed aboard and another tied the skiff's mooring line to a stern cleat. In seconds the surface prowler was heading towards the shoreline, crisscrossing the waters as its powerful searchlight roamed the darkness.

Flat nets. Fields of lightweight fabric, stretched and held afloat just below the surface by buoyant cork or styrofoam, woven together with strands of piano wire. Fish could not break the wire but propellers could, and would activate alarms accordingly. *Rocks.* Stretches of the island's coastline that were prohibitive to vessels of any size. He had to keep the patrol boat in sight; it was approaching the rocks.

Sharks. He did not care to think about them; there simply was no point.

What he must concentrate on was reaching land. The current was almost intolerable, but by breast-stroking between the waves and the undertow beneath he made slow progress, and when he could see the beams of a dozen torches shining through the pines he knew he was getting closer. Time was irrelevant, its passage reflected only in the straining pain in his arms and legs, but his concentration was complete. He had to reach a net or a rock, or some other obstruction beneath him that told him he could stand.

A net came first. He worked himself to the right, hand over hand, slipping on the thick nylon cord, until he felt a huge floating styrofoam barrel shaped like an ocean buoy. He rounded it and pulled himself in on the border of cord until his knees struck two sharp objects that told him he had reached the rocks. He held onto the net, his body battered by the incoming surf, and waited, gasping for air. The torch beams were receding into the pines; the security check in sector four had proved fruitless. When the last beam disappeared between the trunks, he inched his way towards the shore, holding on to the wire net with all his strength as the waves crashed over him. He must stay away from the rocks! They loomed above him – sharp white, jagged points of stone made razor sharp by millennia of rushing waters. One enormous wave and he would be impaled.

He lurched to his left, spreading himself over the net, when suddenly it was gone. It was gone! He could feel the sand under him. He had crossed the manmade barrier reef and was on land.

He crawled out of the water, barely able to lift his arms, while his legs kept collapsing into the wet softness beneath him. The moon made one of its sporadic appearances, illuminating a dune of wild grass twenty yards ahead; he crept forward, each foot bringing him nearer a resting place. He reached the dune and climbed up onto its dry sand; he rolled over on his back and stared at the dark sky.

He remained motionless for the better part of half an hour, until he could feel the blood filling his arms again, the weight returning to his legs. Ten years ago, even five, he reflected, the gauntlet he had struggled through would have taken him fifteen minutes, at most, from which to recover. Now, he would appreciate several hours', if not a night's, sleep and a hot bath.

He lifted his hand and looked at the dial of his watch. It was 10:43. In seventeen minutes Jenna would place her first call to Cons Op emergency reception. He had wanted an hour on the island – to explore, to make decisions before that first call, but it was not to be. He was forty-three minutes behind schedule. On the other hand, there would have been no schedule at all to adhere to if he had failed to cross the island's barrier reef.

He got to his feet, tested his legs, shook his arms and twisted his torso back and forth, barely noticing the discomfort of his soaked clothing and the abrasive scraping of sand over his entire body. It was enough that he could function, that signals from brain to muscle still filtered through the proper motor controls. He could move – swiftly if he had to – and his mind was clear; he needed nothing else.

He checked his gear. The waterproof torch was hooked into a strap around his waist next to the oilcloth packet on his left; the hunting knife in its scabbard was on the right. He removed the packet, unzipped the waterproof flap and felt the contents. The thirteen folded pages were dry. So was the small Spanish automatic. He took out the weapon, shoved it under his belt, and replaced the packet on the strap. He then checked his trouser pockets; the rawhide shoelaces were soaked but intact – each lace separate, rolled into a ball – five in his right hand pocket, five in the left. If more than ten were needed, then none would be needed. They would all be worthless. He was ready.

Footsteps . . . Were there *footsteps*? If so, the sound was incongruous with the sand and the soft earth that must lie beneath the ocean pines. It was a slow tattoo of sharp cracks – leather heels beating a hard surface. Havelock crouched, then raced towards the cover of the tall trees and peered diagonally to his right in the direction of the sound.

A second tattoo, now on his left, farther away, but coming closer. It was similar to the first – slow, deliberate. He crawled deeper into the pines until he came within several feet of the edge, where he dived to the ground and immediately raised his head to take advantage of the sudden new light. What he saw explained the sound of the footsteps, but nothing else. Directly ahead was a wide, smoothly surfaced concrete road, with just beyond it a stockade fence at least twelve feet high extending as far as the eye could see in both directions. The light came from behind it; a roof of light hung everywhere. It was the glow he had seen from the water, now much brighter, but still oddly soft, lacking intensity.

The first soldier appeared on the right, walking slowly. Like the crew on the patrol boat, he wore army fatigues, but strapped to his waist was a government-issue Colt .45 automatic. He was a young foot soldier on guard duty, his bored face reflecting the waste of time and motion. His counterpart emerged from the shadows on the left, perhaps fifty yards away; his walk, if anything, was slower than that of his comrade. They approached each other like two robots on a treadmill, meeting no more than thirty feet from Havelock.

"Did anyone fill you in?" asked the soldier on the right.

"Yeah, some rowboat with a motor drifted out from Savannah with the tide, that's all. No one in it."

"Anybody check the engine?"

"What do you mean?"

"The oil. The oil stays warm if it's been running. Like any motor."

"Hey, come on. Who the hell could get in here anyway?"

"I didn't say they could. I just said it was one way to tell."

"Forget it. They're still doing a three-sixty search — in case somebody's got wings, I guess. The whips around here are all swacked in the head."

"Wouldn't you be?"

The guard on the left looked at his watch. "You've got a point. See you inside."

"If Jackson shows up you will. Last night he was half an hour late. Can you believe it? He said he had to see the end of a lousy TV movie."

"He pulls that a lot. Willis told him the other night that someday someone's going to just walk off and say he took over. Let him hang."

"He'd talk his way out of it."

Each man turned and began trudging back on his familiar, useless course. Michael pieced together the essentials of their conversation. A search party was combing the island and the guards' watch was almost over — a watch that was apparently loose, if a midnight relief could be half an hour late. It was an inconsistency; the island was a security fortress, yet guard duty was treated as though it were a futile if necessary performance. Why?

The answer, he surmised, might be found in an old observation. The ordinary soldier is the first to perceive an unnecessary duty. Which could only mean the shoreline alarms were matched by interior sensors. Michael studied the high stockade fence. It was new, the wood a pale tan, and it took little imagination to picture the trips wired behind it — dual beams set off by mass, weight and body heat, impossible to tunnel under or vault over or cut through. And then he saw what he had not concentrated on: the fence curved — as the concrete road curved — on both sides. Gates must be beyond the sightlines, entrances manned by personnel at the only points of penetration. Not casual at all.

A three-sixty search.

Soldiers with torches treading through the pines and over the beaches, looking for the shadow of a possibility. They had begun directly behind him, on a stretch of the coastline called sector four, moving quickly — a dozen men, or maybe thirteen, in a squad. Wherever they had come from, they would undoubtedly return to the same place once they had completed the circle . . . and the night was dark, the moonlight increasingly infrequent. Using the search party as part of his strategy was an outside possibility — the only one he could think of — but for the tactic to work, he had to move. *Now.*

The soldier on the right not only was closest but was the most logical to deal with first. He was nearly out of sight, rounding the bend in the road, disappearing beyond the angle of the fence. Havelock got up and ran across the road, then started racing down the sandy shoulder, furious at the sound of his waterlogged boots. He reached the bend; there were gate lights up ahead, perhaps six hundred feet away. He ran faster, closing the gap between himself and the slow-moving guard, hoping the wind rustling through the trees muffled the sponge-like crunching beneath him.

He was within twelve feet when the man stopped, alarmed, his head whipping to the side. Havelock sprang, covering the final six feet in mid-air; his right hand

664

clamped onto the soldier's mouth and his left grabbed the base of the man's skull, controlling both their falls to the ground. He held the soldier firmly, his knee under the young man's back, arching the body over it.

"Don't try to shout!" he whispered. "This is only a security exercise – like war games, you understand? Half the garrison here knows about it, half doesn't. Now, I'm going to take you across the road and tie you up and gag you, but nothing'll be too tight. You're simply out on manoeuvres. Okay?"

The young guard was too shocked to respond except with his large, frightened eyes, which blinked repeatedly. Michael could not trust him – more accurately, he could not trust him not to panic. He reached for the fallen barracks cap and rose with the soldier, pulling the young man up, his hand still clamped on his mouth; they both dashed across the road, turning right, heading for the pines. Once in the darkness under the branches, Havelock stopped and tripped the soldier to the ground; they were far enough into sector four.

"Now, I'm going to take my hand away," said Michael, kneeling, "but if you make a sound, I'll have to chop you out, you got that? If I didn't I'd lose points. Okay?"

The young man nodded and Havelock slowly removed his hand, prepared to clamp it back at the first loud utterance. The guard rubbed his cheeks and said quietly, "You scared the shit out of me. What the hell's going on?"

"Just what I told you," said Michael, unstrapping the soldier's weapons belt and yanking off his field jacket. "It's a security exercise," he added, reaching into his own pocket for a rawhide lace and pulling the guard's arms behind him. "We're going to get inside." He tied the guard's wrists and forearms together, lacing the rawhide up to the elbows.

"Into the compound?"

"That's right."

"No way, man. You lose!"

"The alarm system?"

"It's seven ways to Memphis and back. A pelican got burned on the fence the other night; it sizzled for a goddamn half an hour. Son of a bitch if we didn't have chicken the next day."

"What about inside?"

"What about it?"

"Are there alarms inside?"

"Only in Georgetown."

"What? What's Georgetown?"

"Hey, I know the rules. All I've got to give you is my name, rank and serial number!"

"The gate," said Havelock menacingly. "Who's on the gate?"

"The gate detail, who else? What goes out comes in."

"Now, you *tell* me – "

A faint glow of light caught Michael's eye; it was far away, through the trees, the distant beam of a torch. The search party was rounding the island. There was no more time for conversation. He tore off part of the soldier's shirt, rolled it up and stuffed it into the protesting mouth, then strung another rawhide lace around the young man's face and tied it at the back of his neck, holding the gag in place. A third lace bound his ankles.

Havelock put on the field jacket, strapped the weapons belt around his waist, removed his knitted hat and shoved it into a pocket. He put the barracks cap on his head, pulling it down as far as he could, then reached under his soaked sweater and unhooked the waterproof torch. He judged the angles of passage through the trees, the distance of the emerging beams of light, and started running diagonally to his right through the pines – towards an edge of rock or beach, he had no idea which.

He clung to the rock, the crashing sea beneath him, the wind strong, and waited until the last soldier passed above. The instant he did, Michael pulled himself up and raced towards the receding figure; with the experience born of a hundred such encounters, he grabbed the man around the neck, choking off all sound as he yanked him to the ground. Thirty seconds later the unconscious soldier was bound – arms, legs and mouth. Havelock ran to catch up with the others.

"All right, you guys!" shouted an authoritative voice. "Screw-off time is over! Back to your kennels!"

"Shit, Captain," yelled a soldier. "We thought you were bringing in a boatload of broads and this was a treasure hunt!"

"Call it a trial run, *gumbar*. Next time you may score."

"He can't even score at pinball!" shouted another. "What's he gonna do with a broad?"

Havelock followed the beams of light through the pines. The road appeared – the light-coloured smooth concrete reflecting the harsh glare of the gate lights. The squad crossed the road in a formless group, Michael jostling himself ahead so there would be soldiers behind him. They passed through the steel structure, a guard shouting off the numbers as each man went past.

"*One, two, three, four . . .*"

He was number eight; he put his head down, rubbing his eyes.

"*Seven, eight, nine . . .*"

He was inside. He took his hands away from his eyes as he moved with the squad across an oddly smooth surface, and looked up.

His breathing stopped, his legs froze. He was barely able to move forward, for he was in another time, another place. What he saw in front of him and around him was surreal. Abstract images, isolated fragments of an unearthly scene.

He was not inside a compound on a small land mass off the Georgia coast called Poole's Island. He was in Washington, DC.

25

It was something out of a macabre dream, reality twisted, abstracted, deformed to fulfil a demonic fantasy. Scaled-down models of familiar sights were alongside six-foot-high photographic blow-ups of places he knew only too well. There were small, narrow tree-lined streets, abruptly starting, suddenly ending, falling off into dirt, and street signs and street lamps – all in miniature. The soft glow of light that came from the lamps washed over massive, life-size doorways and on buildings – which were not buildings but only the façades of buildings.

There were the glass doors of the Department of State. And over there, the stone entrance of the new FBI building, and across the way, beyond a tiny park dotted with small white benches, the brown steps leading to the main doors of the Pentagon. Far to his left he could see a tall black wrought-iron fence, with an opening in the centre to accommodate a drive flanked by two tiny glass-enclosed guardhouses. It was the South Portico entrance to the White House.

Incredible!

And cars of normal size, glistening. A taxi, two army staff cars, two outsized limousines, all parked separately, stationary symbols of another place. And there were the unmistakable symbols, seen in the distance to his right beyond the miniature park: small alabaster models – no more than four feet in size – of the Jefferson Memorial, the Washington Monument and small compact duplicates of the Reflecting Pools on the mall.

It was all there, all *insane*! It was a spread-out film set, filled with outlandish grainy photographs, miniaturized models, partial structures. The whole scene could have been the product of a mad imagination, a film maker intent on exploring a white-light nightmare that was his warped, personal statement about Washington, DC.

Uncanny.

A bizarre, false world had been created to duplicate a distorted version of the real one hundreds of miles away!

It was more than Havelock could absorb. He had to break away and find a few moments of sanity, to try to piece together the meaning of the macabre spectacle. To find Anton Matthias.

The squad began to separate, several to the left, others to the right. Beyond the false façade of State was a receding lawn and low-hanging willows, then darkness. Suddenly a prolonged burst of cursing came from behind, from the entrance gate, and Michael tensed.

"Goddamned son-of-a-bitch-fuck-off, where *is* he!"

"Who, Sergeant?"

"Jackson, Lieutenant! He's late again?"

"He goes on report, Sergeant. This duty's become far too lax. I want it tightened up."

There were amused rumblings from the search party squad, a number looking behind, laughing quietly. Havelock took advantage of the moment to slip down the street and around the corner into the shadows of the lawn.

He leaned against a wall; it was solid. It enclosed something within and was not part of the false façade in front. He crouched in the darkness, trying to think, trying to understand. And that was the problem: it was beyond his understanding. He knew, of course, about the Soviet training centre in Novgorod called the American Compound, a vast complex where everything was "Americanized", where there were stores and supermarkets and motels and gas stations, where everyone used US currency and spoke American-English, slang and different dialects. And he had heard about further Soviet experiments in the Urals, where entire US Army camps had been built, American military customs and regulations followed with extraordinary accuracy, and where, again, only American-English was spoken, barracks language encouraged, everything authentic down to the most minute detail. Then, of course, there were the *paminyatchiks* – the so-called Travellers – a deep-cover operation scorned as a paranoid fantasy by Rostov in Athens, but still alive, still functioning. These were men and women who had been brought over as infants and placed in homes as sons and daughters, growing up entirely within the total American experience, but whose mission as adults was to serve the Soviet Union. It was said – and confirmed by Rostov – that the *paminyatchik* apparatus had been absorbed by the *Voennaya*, that maniacally secretive cult of fanatics which even the KGB found difficult to control. It was further rumoured that some of these fanatics had reached positions of power and influence. Where did rumour stop and reality begin? What was the reality here?

Was it possible? Was it even conceivable that Poole's Island was peopled by graduates of Novgorod and the Urals, whose lower ranks were filled by *paminyatchiks* coming of age, and whose highest ranks were run by still other *paminyatchiks* who had risen to positions of power at State, who were capable of abducting Anton Matthias? Emory Bradford . . . was *he* . . . ?

Perhaps it was all rumour. Men in Washington were working with men in Moscow; there was madness enough in that acknowledged connection.

He was not going to learn anything crouched in the shadows of a wall; he must move, explore – above all, not be caught. He edged his way to the corner of the building and peered around it at the softly lit tree-lined streets and the tiny structures that surrounded it. Beyond the guard detail at the gate a trio of officers strolled through the miniature park in the direction of the alabaster monuments in the distance, and four enlisted men hurried towards a large Quonset hut set back on a lawn between two unfamiliar brick structures that looked like the ground floor of some tasteful apartment complex. Then, to Havelock's surprise, a civilian emerged from the doorway of the brick building on the left, followed by another in a white laboratory coat, who seemed to be speaking quietly but emphatically. Michael wondered briefly whether the language were Russian. The two men walked down the path and turned right to a set-piece "intersection", whose simulated traffic lights, however, were not operating. They turned right again, continuing their conversation, the first civilian now upbraiding his white-coated companion, but not obstreperously. Nothing was loud; the scene was still, with only the penetrating cacophony of the crickets breaking the stillness. Whatever secrets

Poole's Island held, they were buried beneath a peaceful exterior . . . itself a lie created by liars.

As the two civilians walked down the allée and out of sight, Havelock noticed the metal sign affixed to a post on the other side of the street. Had he seen it before? Of course he had! Every time he had driven or taken a cab out to Matthias's house in Georgetown. There was a blue arrow preceded by the words: CHESAPEAKE AND OHIO CANAL. It was the picturesque waterway that separated the stridency of Washington from the tranquillity of the residential enclaves in Georgetown, whose quiet streets housed the wealthiest and most powerful men in the nation's capital.

Georgetown.

Are there alarms inside?

Only in Georgetown.

Anton Matthias was somewhere down that street, somewhere over a bridge, with or without water, in a house that was a lie. My *God*! Had they simulated his house so as to rehearse his abduction? It was entirely possible; Anton's residence was protected by presidential order, guards were on duty around the clock, as befitted the nation's most valuable living asset. It was not only possible, it was the only way it could have been done. Matthias *must* have been taken at home, the alarms circumvented, the guards pulled away and replaced by State Department orders – orders issued by liars. A mission had been rehearsed and executed.

He moved out into the street, walking casually – an enlisted man getting some air or getting away from his fellow soldiers. He reached the brick building on the left and crossed over the lawn to the sidewalk; the receding street was dark, no lamps shone above the line of short trees. He walked faster, feeling more comfortable in the shadows, and noted the paths that turned to the right, leading to a row of three Quonset huts – there were lights in several windows and the glow of a few television sets. He assumed these were the living quarters of whatever officers there were and their civilian counterparts. Graduates of Novgorod and the Urals?

Suddenly, civilization stopped. The street and the sidewalk ended, and there was nothing ahead but a dirt road bordered by high foliage and darkness. But it was a road; it led somewhere. Havelock began a slow lope; jogging would be his excuse if stopped – before he took out his interrogator. He thought of Jenna, going from telephone to telephone five miles away on the mainland, reaching a bewildered Cons Op emergency operator and saying words that brought no response: there might never be a response. Michael understood that, and, strangely, it only served to infuriate him. One accepted the risks in his profession and treated them with respect, for they induced fear and caution – a valuable protection – but one could not accept betrayal by one's own. It was the final circle of futility, proof of the ultimate sham – of a wasted life.

A glow of light. Far down the road, to the left. He broke into a run, and as he came nearer, he knew what it was: the outlines of a house, part of a house that stopped at the first floor. It was, unmistakably, the façade of Anton's home in Georgetown, the area of the street accurate in every detail. He approached the end of the dirt road and halted where the tarred surface began on the left. He stared in disbelief.

The brick steps were the same brick steps that led up to the porticoed entrance with the white door and the carriage lamps and the brass hardware. Everything was identical to its original hundreds of miles away, even to the lace curtains in the windows; he could picture the rooms inside and knew that they, too, were the same. The lessons of Novgorod had been learned well, their fruits transplanted to a small island minutes away from the coast of the United States, *seconds* by air. *My God, what's happened?*

"Stay right where you are, soldier!" the command came from behind. "What the *hell* do you think you're doing out here!"

Havelock turned, covering the .45 as best he could. A guard stepped out of the foliage, with a gun in his hand, but he was not military; he was dressed in civilian clothes. Havelock said, "What's wrong with you? A guy can't take a walk?"

"You weren't walking, you were running."

"Jogging, pal. Ever heard of it?"

"Every morning, *pal*, when I don't pull this late night crap. But on the island road with everybody else, not down here. You know the rules. No one goes past sector six; you don't go off the macadam."

"Hey, come on, man," said Havelock. "Don't be a hard nose – "

A sudden swelling of music burst from the house, filling the night and drowning out the crickets. Michael knew it well; it was one of Matthias's favourites. Handel's Water Music. His *pritel* was there!

"Every night, a goddamn concert," said the civilian. "How come?"

"How the hell do I know? He goes into the garden and plays that stuff for an hour or more."

Music is for thought, Mikhail. The better the music the better the thinking. There's a causal relationship, you know.

"Nice of you people to let him have it."

"Why not? What else has he got, and where's he going to go? But *you're* going to get your GI ass in a sling if you don't get out of here." The guard holstered his gun inside his jacket. "You're lucky I don't – Hey, wait a minute! You've got a weapon!"

Havelock lunged, gripped the man's throat and hurled him to the ground over his left leg. He fell on the guard and rammed his knee into the man's chest as he ripped the field jacket open and pulled out the hunting knife. "You're not lucky at all!" he whispered. "Where are you from, *zapanka*? Novgorod? The Urals? A *paminyatchik*?" Michael held the point of the knife's blade between the guard's nostrils and lips. "I'm going to cut your face off unless you tell me what I want to know. First, how many men are up there? *Easy!*" He released the pressure on the man's throat; the guard coughed.

"You'll . . . never get off here," he choked.

Havelock drew blood, the trickle covering the man's lips. "Don't push me, butcher! I have a lot of memories, *ponimayu*. How many *men*?"

"One."

"*Liar!*"

"No, *one*! The two of us are on till four. One outside, one inside!"

"Alarms. Where are they? *What* are they?"

"Crossbeams, shoulder to knee. In the door."

670

"That's *all?*"

"It's all that's on. To keep him in."

"The garden?"

"Wall. Too high. For Christ's sake, where's he going to *go?* Where are *you* going to go?"

"We'll see." Michael pulled the guard's head up by his hair, then dropped the knife and struck him, a sharp, hard blow behind the right ear; the man collapsed. Havelock took out a rawhide lace, cut it in two with the knife and bound his hands and feet. Finally, he gagged the man with his own handkerchief, tying the cloth in place with one of the three remaining laces. He dragged the unconscious body into the foliage and started for the "house".

The Water Music soared into its thematic march, horns and strings intermingling, reverberating above and behind the half-house. Havelock climbed the short hill that bordered the brick steps until he was within ten feet of the first lace-curtained window. He crouched and crept to it, his head below the sill, then stepped to the side and stood up. He inched his face to the glass. The room was exactly as he remembered it from another time and place. The worn, fine oriental rugs, the heavy, comfortable arm chairs, the brass lamps – it was Matthias's sitting-room – his parlour, as he called it – a place to greet visitors. Michael had spent many pleasant hours in that room, yet this was not that room.

He crouched and made his way to the edge of the strange structure, rounded the corner and started towards the rear – towards a wall he could picture in his mind, a wall that enclosed a garden – hundreds of miles away. There were three windows to pass, to duck under, to check, and the second window told him what he had to know. Inside, a heavy-set man sat on a couch, smoking a cigarette, his feet on a coffee table, watching television. The volume was high, apparently to counteract the stereophonic sound of the music.

Havelock ran to the wall and jumped; he clung to the top with both hands and then, his chest aching and the wound close to tearing apart, he pulled himself up. He lay prone, catching his breath, letting the pain subside.

Below, the eerily lit garden was as he remembered it. Soft light coming from the house, a single lamp on the all-important chess table between two brown wicker chairs, other white wicker furniture, and a slate path roaming in circles around the beds of flowers.

There he was, his beloved *pritel*, sitting in a chair at the end of the garden, his eyes closed, seeing images the music evoked in his mind. The tortoiseshell glasses were still in place, the silver hair waved back over his strong head.

Silently Havelock swung his legs over the side, rolled on his stomach and dropped to the ground. He stayed in the shadows for several moments; the music had dropped to pianissimo and the sound of the television could be heard distinctly. The guard would remain inside; that was to say, he would remain inside until Michael wanted him. And when he had taken the hired gun of liars, he would use him or kill him. Somehow.

Havelock came away slowly from the wall and walked down the circular path towards Matthias.

For no apparent reason the statesman suddenly opened his eyes. Michael rushed forward, holding up both hands, the gesture a command for silence – but it was ignored. Matthias spoke, his deep voice rising with the music. "*Dobré Srovnani, Mikhail.* So good of you to come round. I was thinking about you the other day, about that paper you wrote several weeks ago. What was it? The 'Effects of Hegelian Revisionism' or some such immodest and inappropriate title. After all, my *darebak akademik*, Hegel is his own best revisionist, no? The *revisionist maximus!* How do you like that?"

"Anton . . . ?"

Again suddenly, without warning or indication, Matthias rose from his chair, eyes wide, face contorted. He began backing away unsteadily, his arms crossed in front of his chest, his voice now a horrible whisper: "*No!* You *cannot . . . you must not . . .* come near me! You don't understand, you can never understand! *Get away from me!*"

Havelock stared; the shock was as unbearable as the truth.

Anthony Matthias was insane.

Book Three

26

"Raise your hands! Walk to the wall and spread your legs! *Move! . . . Now!* Lean into the brick, palms straight out!"

As if in a trance, his eyes still on Matthias, who was crouching like a child on one knee by a rosebush, Havelock did as the guard ordered. He was in shock, his impressions a blur, his thoughts suspended. His *pritel*, his mentor . . . his father . . . was mad. The shell of the man who had astonished the world with his brilliance, with his perceptions, was cowering by the flowers, his head trembling, the frightened eyes behind the glasses filled with a terror no one knew but himself.

Havelock had heard the guard's footsteps on the slate and had known the blow was coming. Somehow it had not mattered. Nothing mattered.

A spreading web of pain shuddered through his head, and the darkness came.

He was on a parlour tug, circles of bright white light spinning in front of his eyes, his temples throbbing, his drenched, sand-filled trousers pressing against his skin. He could hear men rushing up the steps outside, barking orders in panic. As they came through the door he felt his jacket, his waist; his gun had been taken, but he had not been searched. That process and the interrogation would presumably be left to the guard's superiors.

Two men approached: one in uniform, a major; the other, a civilian. He knew the latter; he was from State, an agent from Cons Op with whom he had worked in London or Beirut, or Paris or . . . he could not recall.

"That's him," said the civilian. "Bradford told me it might be – he didn't know how – but it is. He gave me the details; you're not involved."

"Just get him out of here," replied the soldier. "What you do is your business."

"Hello, Havelock." The man from State looked down with contempt. "You've been busy. It must have been fun killing that old guy in New York. What were you doing? Setting him up for contingency funds, with a little more of the same down here? Get on your feet, you bastard!"

Body and head racked, Michael slowly rolled onto his knees and pushed himself up. "What happened to him? What *happened?*"

"I don't answer questions."

"Somebody has to . . . for Christ's sake, *somebody* has to!"

"And give you a free ticket? No way, you son of a bitch." The civilian addressed the guard who was standing across the room. "Did you search him?"

"No, sir. I just removed his weapon and punched the alarm. There's a flashlight on his belt and some kind of pouch."

"Let me help you, Charley," said Havelock, spreading the field jacket and reaching for the oilcloth packet. "It is Charley, isn't it? Charley Loring . . . was it Beirut?"

"It was, and keep your goddamned hands still!"

"What you want's in there. Go on, take it. It won't detonate."

The man from State nodded at the major; the soldier stepped forward and grabbed Michael's hands as Charles Loring ripped the packet off the webbed belt.

"Open it," continued Havelock. "It's from me to you. All of you."

The Cons Op agent unzipped the packet and took out the folded yellow pages. The major released his grip as the civilian walked to a floor lamp and began reading. He stopped, looked over at Michael, then spoke to the soldier. "Wait outside, Major. And you," he added, glancing at the guard. "In the other room, please."

"Are you sure?" asked the officer.

"Very," said Charley. "He's not going anywhere, and I'll shout if I need you." The two men left, the soldier by the front door, the guard into the next room. "You're the lowest piece of garbage I've ever known," said the man from State.

"It's a carbon, Charley."

"I can see that."

"Call Cons Op emergency. Every fifteen minutes since eleven o'clock they've got a message. It's in the form of a question. 'Billiards or pool?' The response is 'We prefer pool'. Tell them to give it."

"Then what?"

"Patch yourself into the next call, give the response and listen."

"So some other piece of garbage can read this to me."

"Oh, no, just twelve seconds' worth. No way to trace. And don't bother to think about giving me a needle. I've been in therapy before, so I took precautions. I have no idea where the calls are coming from, take my word."

"I wouldn't take your word for a goddamn thing, *garbage!*"

"You'd better right now, because if you don't, copies of those pages will be sent to appropriate addresses all over Europe. From Moscow to Athens, from London to Prague – from Paris to Berlin. Get on the phone."

Twenty-one minutes later the man from State stared at the wall as he gave the response to Jenna Karras. Eleven seconds after that he hung up and looked over at Havelock. "You're everything they said you were. You're below filth."

"And 'beyond-salvage'?"

"That's right."

"Then so are you, because you're programmed, Charley. You're useless. You forgot how to ask questions."

"*What?*"

"You just accepted the verdict on me. You knew me – knew my record – but it didn't make any difference. The word came down and the good little sheep said 'Why not?' "

"I could *kill* you."

"And live with the consequences? Don't do that. Call the White House."

He could hear the deafening roar of the giant helicopter's rotating blades and knew that the President of the United States had arrived at Poole's Island. It was mid-morning, and the Georgia sun was burning the pavements outside the open window. He was in a room and there was no question that it was a cell even though there were no bars in the single window. He was two storeys off the ground; there were four soldiers beneath, and the eerie façades and photographs of familiar buildings could be seen beyond. A world of lies, of artifice, of transplanted, warped reality.

Havelock walked back to the bed – more cot than bed and sat down. He thought of Jenna, what she must be going through – again what resources she must summon to survive the unbearable tension. And of Matthias – good *God*, what had *happened?* Michael relived the horrible scene in the garden, trying to find a thread of sense.

You must not come near me. You don't understand. You can never understand!
Understand *what?*

He had no idea how long he sat there thinking; he only knew that his thoughts were interrupted by the crack of the glass panel in the centre of the door. A face appeared; it was under the gold braid of a visor cap, another military liar. The door opened and a broad-shouldered, middle-aged colonel walked in, gripping a pair of handcuffs.

"Turn around," he ordered. "Extend your arms."

Havelock did as he was told, and the cuffs were clamped on his wrists. "What about my feet?" asked Michael curtly. "Aren't they considered weapons?"

"I'll have a much more effective one in my hand," said the officer, "and I'll be watching you every second. You pull one thing I could even misinterpret, I'm inside, and you're dead."

"A one-to-one conference. I'm flattered."

The colonel spun Havelock around. "I don't know who you are, or what you're doing, or what you've done, but you remember this, cowboy. That man is my responsibility and there's no way I wouldn't blow you out of this room and ask questions later."

"Who's the cowboy?"

As if to punctuate his threat, the officer shoved Michael back into the wall. "Stay there," he commanded, and left the room.

Thirty seconds later the door opened again, and President Charles Berquist walked in. In his hand were the thirteen carbons of Havelock's indictment. The President stopped and looked at Michael. He raised the yellow pages.

"This is an extraordinary document, Mr Havelock."

"It's the truth."

"I believe you. I find a great part of it beneath contempt, of course, but then I tell myself that a man with your record would not cavalierly cause the exposure and death of so many. That, basically, this is a threat – an irresistible threat – to get yourself heard."

"Then you'd be telling yourself another lie," said Michael, motionless against

675

the wall. "I was placed 'beyond-salvage'. Why should I concern myself with anyone?"

"Because you're an intelligent man who knows there must be explanations."

"Lies, you mean?"

"Some are lies and they will remain lies for the good of this country."

Havelock paused, studying the hard Scandinavian face of the President, the steady eyes that were somehow a hunter's eyes. "Matthias?"

"Yes."

"How long do you think you can bury him here?"

"For as long as we possibly can."

"He needs help."

"So do we. He had to be stopped."

"What have you done to him?"

"I was only part of it, Mr Havelock. So were you. We all were. We made him an emperor when there were no personal empires to be allocated by divine right, much less ours. We made him a god when we didn't own the heavens. There's only so much the mind can absorb and act upon when elevated to such heights in these very complicated times. He was forced to exist in the perpetual illusion of being unique, above all other men. We asked too much. He went mad. His mind – that extraordinary instrument – snapped, and when it could no longer control itself, it sought control elsewhere. To compensate, perhaps, to convince himself that he was what we said he was, although a part of him told him he wasn't. Not any longer."

"What do you mean 'sought control elsewhere'? How could he do that?"

"By committing this nation to a series of obligations that were, to say the least, unacceptable. Try to understand, he had feet of quicksilver, not of clay like you and me. Yes, even I, the President of the United States, some say the most powerful man in the world. It's not true. I'm bound by the body politic, subject to the goddamn polls, guided by the so-called principles of a political ideology, with my head on a congressional chopping block. Checks and balances, Mr Havelock. But not him. We made him a superstar; he was bound to nothing, accountable to no one. His word was law, all other judgements subordinate to his brilliance. And then there was his charm, I might add."

"Generalities," said Michael. "Abstractions."

"Lies?" asked Berquist.

"I don't know. What are the specifics?"

"I'm going to show you. And if after what you've seen you still feel compelled to carry out your threat, let it be on your head, not mine."

"I don't have a head. I'm 'beyond-salvage'."

"I told you, I've read these pages. All of them. The order's been rescinded. You have the word of the President of the United States."

"Why should I accept it?"

"If I were you I probably wouldn't. I'm simply telling you. There are many lies and there will continue to be lies, but that's not one of them . . . I'll have the handcuffs removed."

*

676

The scene in the large, dark windowless room was an unearthly depiction of a science-fiction nightmare. There were a dozen television screens mounted in a row on the wall, monitors that recorded and taped the activities seen by the various cameras. Below the screens was an enormous console manned by four technicians, several white-jacketed doctors entered, watching a scene or scanning tapes, writing notes, leaving quickly or conferring with colleagues. And the object of the whole sophisticated operation was to record and analyse every movement made and every word spoken by Anthony Matthias.

His face and body were projected on seven screens at once, and under each monitor was a green digital read-out showing the exact hour and minute of the filming; the screen on the far left was marked "Current". The day was an illusion for Matthias, starting with morning coffee in the garden identical to his own in Georgetown.

"Before he wakes he's given two injections," said the President, sitting next to Havelock at a second, smaller console at the rear wall. "One's a muscle-relaxant that reduces physical and mental tensions, the other a stimulant that accelerates the heart, pumping blood without interfering with the first narcotic. Don't ask me the medical terms, I don't know them, I just know it works. He's free to associate with a degree of simulated confidence . . . in a way, a replica of his former self."

"Then his day begins? His . . . simulated day?"

"Exactly. Read the monitors from right to left. His day starts with breakfast in the garden. He's brought intelligence reports and newspapers corresponding to the dates of whatever issue is being probed. Then in the next screen you see him walking out of *his* home and down *his* steps with an aide who's talking to him, refining the options of the problem, building up the case, whatever it is. Everything, by the way, is taken from his logs; that remains constant throughout 'the day'." Berquist paused, and gestured at the third monitor from the right. "There you see him in his limousine, the aide still talking, bringing his focus back. He's driven around for a while, then gradually brought in sight of places that are familiar to him, the Jefferson Memorial, the monument, certain streets, past the South Portico . . . the sequence is irrelevant."

"But they're not *whole*," insisted Michael. "They're fragments!"

"He doesn't see that; he sees only the impression. But even if he did see that they were fragments, as you call them, or miniatures of the existing places, the doctors tell me his mind would reject them and accept the reality of the impressions. Just as he refused to accept his own deterioration, and kept pressing for wider and wider responsibilities, until he simply reached out and took them . . . Watch the fourth screen. He's getting out at the State Department, going inside and telling his aide something; it will be studied. In the fifth, you can see him walking into his office – the same in every respect as his own on the eighth floor – and immediately scanning the cables and reading the day's appointments, again identical to those that were there at the time. The sixth shows him taking a series of phone calls, the same calls he has taken before. Often his responses are meaningless, a part of him rejecting a voice or a lack of authentic repartee, but at other times what we learn is mind-blowing . . . He's been here nearly six weeks and there are times when we think we've only scratched the surface. We're only beginning to learn the extent of his massive excesses."

"You mean the things he's done?" asked Havelock, recoiling from the frightening turn of events.

Berquist looked at Michael in the glow of the console and the flickering light emanating from the screens across the room. "Yes, Mr Havelock, the – 'things' – he's done. If ever a man in the history of representative government exceeded the authority of his office, Anthony Matthias is that man. There were no limits to what he promised – what he *guaranteed* – in the name of the United States government. Take today. A policy was set and in the process of being implemented, but it did not suit the Secretary of State at this particular moment of irrationality, so he altered it . . . Watch the seventh screen, the one marked 'Current'. Listen. He's at his desk and in his mind he's back about five months, when a bipartisan decision was made to close an embassy in a new African country slaughtering its citizens with mass hangings and death squads, revolting the civilized world. The aide is explaining."

Mr Secretary. The President and the Joint Chiefs as well as the Senate have gone on record as opposing any further contact at this time . . .

Then we won't tell them, will we? Antediluvian reactions cannot be a keystone of a coherent foreign policy. I shall make contact myself and present a cohesive and judicious plan. Arms and well-sweetened butter are international lubricants, and we shall provide them.

Michael was stunned. "He said that? He *did* that?"

"He's reliving it now," replied Berquist. "In a few minutes he'll place a call to the mission in Geneva, and another unbelievable commitment will be made . . . This, however, is only a minor example, one they're working on this morning. Actually, as outrageous as it is, it's insignificant compared to so many others. So many . . . so dangerous . . . so incredible."

"Dangerous?"

"One voice overriding all others, entering unthinkable negotiations, processing agreements contrary to everything this nation supposedly stands for, agreements which an outraged Congress would impeach me for even considering. But even that fact – and it *is* a fact – is insignificant. We can't let the world know what he's done. We'd be humiliated, a giant on its knees, begging forgiveness and, if it was not forthcoming, answered with guns and bombs. You see, he's put it all in writing."

"Could he *do* that?"

"Not constitutionally, no. But he was the superstar. The uncrowned king of the republic had spoken, a god had given his word. Who questions kings or gods? The mere existence of such documents is the most fertile grounds on earth for international extortion. If we can't quietly invalidate those negotiations – diplomatically void them by anticipated congressional rejection – they *will* be exposed. If they are, every treaty, every agreement we've concluded during the past decade – all the sensitive alliances we're currently negotiating everywhere in the world – will be called into question. This country's foreign policy will collapse; we'd never be trusted again. And when a nation such as ours has no foreign policy, Mr Havelock, it has war."

Michael leaned over the console, staring at the "Current" screen, and brought

678

his hand to his forehead; he felt the beads of perspiration. "He's gone this far?"

"Beyond. Remember, he's been Secretary of State for nearly six years, and before he took office his influence was significant, perhaps too much so, in the two previous administrations. He was nothing short of an ambassador-plenipotentiary for both, roaming the globe, cementing his power bases."

"But they were for *good*, not this!"

"They were, and no one knew it better than I did. I'm the one who persuaded him to chuck the consulting business and take over. I said the world needed his imprimatur, the time was right. You see, I appealed to his ego; all great men have outrageous egos. De Gaulle was right: the man of destiny knows it before anybody else. What he doesn't know is the limit of his capabilities. God knows Matthias didn't."

"You said it a few minutes ago, Mr President. We made him a god. We asked too much of him." Havelock shook his head slowly, overwhelmed.

"Just hold it there," answered Berquist, his voice cold, his eyes penetrating in the incandescent reflections of light. "I said it by way of an oversimplified explanation. No one makes a man a god unless that man wants to *be* one. And, Christ-on-a-raft, Matthias has been looking for that divine appointment all his life! He's been tasting the holy water for years – in his mind *bathing* in it . . . You know what someone called him the other day? A hustling Socrates on the Potomac, and that's exactly what he was. A hustler, Mr Havelock. A grade A, high-I-Q'd, brilliant opportunist. A man with extraordinarily persuasive words, capable of first-rate global diplomacy – the best we could field – so long as *he* was the eye of the world-wide hurricane. He could be magnificent and, as I also said, no one knew it better than I did, and I used him. But for all that, he was a hustler. He never stopped pushing, the omniscient Anthony Matthias."

"And knowing this," said Michael, refusing to permit Berquist's stare to cower him, "you still used him. *You* pushed him as much as he pushed himself. You appealed to a 'man of destiny', wasn't that it?"

The President lowered his eyes to the dials on the console. "Yes," he said softly. "Until he blew apart. Because I was watching a performance, not the man, and I was blinded. I didn't see what was really happening."

"*Jesus!*" exclaimed Havelock, his whisper a cry. "It's all so hard to believe!"

"On that assumption," interrupted Berquist, regaining his composure, I've had several tapes prepared for you. They're re-enactments of actual conversations that took place during his final months in office. The psychiatrists tell me they're valid, and the papers we've unearthed bear them out. Put on the earphones and I'll press the appropriate buttons . . . The images will appear on the last monitor on the right."

What took place on that screen during the next twelve minutes was a portrait of a man Havelock did not know. The tapes showed Matthias at emotional extremes, as he was psychologically stimulated by the combined effects of the chemicals and the visual trappings, and prodded by aides using his own words. He was screaming one moment, weeping the next, cajoling a diplomat over the phone with charm and flattery – and brilliant humility – then condemning the man as a fool and a moron once the conversation was finished. Above all were the lies where once there had been essential truth. The telephone was his instrument, his resonant voice with its European cadence the organ.

"This first," said Berquist, angrily stabbing a button, "is his response to me when I had just told him I wanted a reassessment of foreign aid in San Miguel."

Your policy is firm, Mr President, a clear call for decency and human rights. I applaud you, sir. Goodbye . . . Idiot! Imbecile! One does not have to endorse a brother, one must merely accept geopolitical realities! Get me General Sandoza on the line. Set up a very private appointment with his ambassador. The colonels will understand we back them!

"This little number followed a joint House and Senate resolution, which I thoroughly endorsed, to withhold diplomatic recognition."

You understand, Mr Prime Minister, that our existing accords in your part of the world prohibit what you suggest, but you should know that I am in agreement with you. I'm meeting with the President . . . no, no, I assure you he will have an open mind . . . and I have already convinced the chairman of the Senate Foreign Relations Committee. A treaty between our two countries is desirable progress, and should it be in contradistinction to prior agreements . . . well, enlightened self-interest was the essence of Bismarck's reign.

"I can't believe this," said Havelock, mesmerized.

"Neither did I, but it's true." The President pushed a third button. "We're now in the Persian Gulf."

You are, of course, speaking unofficially, not as your country's Minister of Finance but as a friend, and what you are seeking are additional guarantees of eight hundred and fifty million for your current-fiscal year, and one billion two hundred million for the next . . . Contrary to what you may believe, my good friend, they are entirely plausible figures. I say this confidentially, but our territorial strategies are not what they appear. I shall prepare, again on a confidential basis, a memorandum-of-intent.

"Now we're in the Balkans, a Soviet satellite, loyal to Moscow, and at our throats . . . Insanity!"

Mr Premier, the restrictions on arms sales to your nation, if they cannot be lifted outright, will be overlooked. I find specific and considerable advantages in our co-operating with you. "Equipment" can and will be funnelled through certain North African regimes considered to be in our adversary's camp but with whom I've met – shall we say ex-et non officio – recently and frequently. Confidentially, a new geopolitical axis is being formed.

"Being formed!" exploded Berquist. "Suicide! Here's a *coup* in the Yemen. Headlong instability, wholesale bloodshed guaranteed!"

The emerging of a great new independent nation, Sirach Bal Shazar, though slow to gain the recognition you deserve, will have the quiet support of this administration. We recognize the necessity of dealing firmly and realistically with internal subversion. You may be assured that the funds you ask for will be allocated. Three hundred million, once transferred, will indicate to the legislative branch of our government the faith we place in you.

"Finally," said the President, touching a last button, his whisper strained, his lined face looking exhausted. "The new madman of Africa."

To speak frankly and in the utmost confidence, Major-General Halafi, we approve of your proposed incursion north into the Straits. Our so-called allies there have been weak and ineffectual, but, naturally, our disassociation must, because of the current treaties, be gradual. The educating process is always difficult, the re-educating of the entrenched unfortunately a maddening chess game, fortunately played by those of us who understand. You shall have your weapons. Salaam, my warrior friend.

The scenes were paralysing. Alliances not in the interests of the United States had been tacitly formed or half-formed, treaties proposed or negotiated that were in violation of existing agreements; guarantees of billions had been made that Congress would never authorize, nor the American taxpayer tolerate; military obligations had been assumed that were immoral in concept, crossed the bounds of national honour, and were irrationally provocative to boot. It was a portrait of a brilliant mind that had fragmented itself into a profusion of global commitments, each a lethal missile.

Michael slowly recovered from his state of shock. Suddenly, the gap came into focus; it must be filled, explained. Havelock took off the earphones and turned to the President. "Costa Brava," he whispered harshly. "*Why?* Why 'beyond-salvage'?"

"I was part of the first, but I did not call for the second. As near as we can determine, it was not officially sanctioned."

"Ambiguity?"

"Yes. We don't know who he is. However, I should tell you, I personally confirmed the salvage order later."

"*Why?*"

"Because I accepted one aspect of the oath you signed when you entered the service of your government."

"Which was?"

"To lay down your life for your country, should your country need it desperately enough to ask for it. Any of us would, you know that as well as I do. Nor do I have to remind you that untold thousands have done so even when the needs were questionable."

"Meaning the need for my life – my death – was not questionable?"

"When I gave the order, no it was not."

Michael held his breath. "And the Czechoslovakian woman? Jenna Karras?"

"Her death was never sought."

"It *was!*"

"Not by us."

"Ambiguity?"

"Apparently."

"And you don't know . . . Oh, my *God*. But my execution was sanctioned. By *you*."

The President nodded, his Nordic face less hard than before, his eyes still level, still steady, but no longer a hunter's eyes.

"May the condemned man ask why?"

"Come with me," said Berquist, rising from the console in the dim, flickering light. "It's time for the last phase of your education, Mr Havelock. I hope to God you're ready for it."

They left the monitor room and entered what appeared to be a short, white corridor, guarded by a huge master sergeant whose face and display of ribbons indicated many tours and many battles. He cracked to attention the instant he saw the President; his commander-in-chief nodded and proceeded towards a wide black door at the end of the enclosure. However, it was not a door, Michael realized as he drew nearer behind Berquist. It was a vault, its wheel-of-entry in the centre, a small hand-sensor plate to the right of the frame. The President pressed his right palm against it; a tiny row of coloured lights raced back and forth above the plate, settling on green and white. He then reached over with his left hand and gripped the wheel; the lights were tripped again, a combination of three greens this time.

"I'm sure you know more about these devices than I do," said Berquist, "so I'll only add that it can be released solely by myself . . . and one other person in the event of my death."

The significance was obvious and required no comment. The President swung the heavy door back, reached up and pressed an unseen plate on the inner frame; somewhere cross-beam trips were deactivated. Once again he nodded at the soldier, gesturing for Havelock to enter. They stepped inside as the master sergeant approached the steel panel and closed it, then spun the wheel into its locked position.

It was a room, but not an ordinary room, for there were no windows, no prints on the walls, no extraneous furniture, no amenities, only the quiet whir of ventilating machines. There was an oblong conference table in the centre with five chairs around it, note pads, pencils and ashtrays in place, a paper shredder in the far left corner; it was a table in a room pre-set for immediate consultation and instant destruction of whatever came from a given meeting. Whereas the room they had just left had twelve television monitors across the wall, this had a single large reflector screen, an odd-shaped projector bracketed into the far wall next to a panel of circular switches.

Without speaking, Charles Berquist went directly to the panel, dimmed the overhead lights and snapped on the projector. The screen across the dark room was instantly filled with a double image, a straight black line dividing the two photographs. Each was a single page of two separate documents, both obviously related, the forms nearly identical. Havelock stared at them in growing terror.

"This is the essence of what we call 'Parsifal'," said the President quietly. "Do you recall Wagner's last opera?"

"Not well," replied Havelock, barely able to speak.

"No matter. Just bear in mind that whenever Parsifal took up the spear used at Christ's crucifixion and held it against wounds, he had the power to heal. Conversely, whoever holds these has the power to rip them open. All over the world."

"I . . . don't . . . *believe* this," whispered Havelock.

"I wish to God I didn't have to," said Berquist, raising his hand and pointing to the projected document on the left. "This first agreement calls for a nuclear strike against the People's Republic of China, executed by the combined forces of the United States of America and the Soviet Union. Objective: the destruction of all military installations, government centres, hydro-electric plants, communications systems and seven major cities ranging from the Manchurian border to the China Sea." The President paused and gestured at the document on the right. "This second agreement calls for a nearly identical strike against the Union of Soviet Socialist Republics carried out by the combined forces of the United States and the People's Republic of China. The differences are minor, vital only to a few million people who will be burnt to death in the nuclear fires. There are an additional five cities, including Moscow, Leningrad and Kiev. Total destruction: twelve cities obliterated from the face of the earth . . . This nation has entered into two separate agreements, one with the Soviet Union, the other with the People's Republic of China. In each instance, we have committed the full range of our nuclear weapons to a combined strike with a partner to destroy the mutual enemy. Two diametrically opposed commitments, and the United States is the whore serving two studs gone berserk. Mass annihilation. The world has its nuclear war, Mr Havelock, engineered with brilliant precision by Anthony Matthias, superstar."

27

"These are . . . *insane!*" whispered Havelock, his eyes riveted on the screen. "And we're a partner to *each*? Each commits us to a nuclear strike – a *first* strike?"

"A second also, and a third, if necessary, from submarines ringing the coasts first of China then of Russia. Two insane agreements, Mr Havelock, and we are, indeed, a party to each. There it is in writing."

"My *God* . . . " Michael scanned the lines of both documents as if studying the deformed appendages of an obscene, horrible thing. "If these are ever exposed, there's nothing left."

"Now you understand," said Berquist, his gaze, too, fixed on the agreements that filled both sides of the screen, his face drawn, his eyes hollow. "That's the unendurable threat we're living with. Unless we follow to the letter the instructions delivered to my office, we face global catastrophe in the truest sense. The threat is simple: the nuclear pact with Russia will be shown to the leaders of the People's Republic of China, and our agreement with the PRC will be given to Moscow. Each will know they've been betrayed – by the richest whore in history. That's what they'll believe, and the world will go up in a thousand nuclear explosions. The last words heard will be: 'This is not an exercise, this is *it*!' And that is the truth, Mr Havelock."

Michael felt the trembling in his hands, the throbbing at his temples. Something Berquist had just said triggered a sudden uneasiness but he could not concentrate to identify its source. He could only stare at the two documents projected on the screen.

"There's nothing here about dates," he said, almost pointlessly.

"It's on a separate page – these are memoranda-of-intent. Conferences are to be held during the months of April and May, at which the precise dates of the strikes will be determined. The Russians are scheduled for April, May is for China. Next month and the month after. The strikes are to occur within forty-five days of each conference."

"It's . . . beyond belief." Overwhelmed, Havelock suddenly felt the paralysis again. He stared at Berquist. "You connected me with *this? These?*"

"You were connected. God knows not through your own doing, but dangerously connected. We know how; we don't know why. But the how was enough to place you 'beyond-salvage'."

"For Christ's sake, *how?*"

"To begin with, Matthias built the case against your friend Jenna Karras."

"*Matthias?*"

"It was he who wanted you out. But we couldn't be sure. Were you out, or were you simply changing jobs? From the government of the United States to the holy empire of Matthias the Great."

"Which is why I was watched. London, Amsterdam, Paris . . . God knows where else."

"Everywhere you went. But you gave us nothing."

"And that was grounds for 'beyond-salvage'?"

"I told you, I had nothing to do with the original order."

"All right, it was this Ambiguity. But later it was *you*. You reconfirmed it."

"Later, much later; when we learned what he had learned. Both orders were given, one in sanction, one not, for the same reason. You were penetrating the manipulation – the structure – behind these documents, the link between men in Washington and their unknown counterparts in the KGB. We're in a race. One miscalculation on your part, one exposure of the flaw in that structure, and we have every reason to believe that these agreements, these invitations to Armageddon, would be shown to the leaders in Moscow and Peking."

"*Wait* a minute!" cried Havelock, bewildered, angry. "That's what you said before! Goddamn it, these were *negotiated* with Moscow and Peking!"

The President of the United States did not reply. Instead, he walked to the nearest chair at the table and sat down, the back of his large head and his thinning blond hair reflected in the shaft of light. And then he spoke. "No, they were not, Mr Havelock," he said, looking at the screen. "These are the detailed fantasies of a brilliant but mad mind, the words of a superb negotiator."

"Good *God*, then *deny* them! They aren't real!"

Berquist shook his head. "Read the language!" he said sharply. "It's literally *beyond* deniability. There are detailed references to the most secret weapons in our arsenals. Locations, activating codes, specifications, logistics – information that men would be labelled traitors for revealing, their lives ended in prison, none sentenced to less than thirty years for their acts. In Moscow or Peking those even remotely associated with the armaments data in these documents would be shot without a hearing on the mere possibility they had divulged, knowingly or unknowingly, even a part of it." The President paused, turning his head slightly to the left, his eyes still on the screen. "What you must understand is that should the leaders in either Moscow or Peking be shown the adversary document, they would be convinced beyond doubt of its authenticity. Every strategic position, each missile capability, every area of destructive responsibility has been hammered out down to the last

684

detail, nothing left to debate . . . even to the hours of vehicular robot-controlled occupation of territories."

"Hammered out?" asked Michael, the phrase a glaring intrusion.

Berquist turned around, his eyes once again the hunter's, but wary, afraid. "Yes, Mr Havelock, hammered out. Now you've reached the core of Parsifal. These agreements were negotiated by two extraordinary – and extraordinarily informed – minds. *Two* men *hammering out* every detail, each step, each point as though his stature in history depended on the task. A nuclear chess game, the universe to the winner . . . what's left of it."

"How do you know that?"

"Language again. It's the product of two minds. It doesn't take a psychiatrist, or a pathologist, to spot the different inputs. More to the point, Matthias couldn't have created these by himself, he didn't have the in-depth information so readily available. But with another – a Russian, as knowledgeable about Chinese capabilities as we are – together they could do it. *Did* it. Two men."

His gaze fixed on the President, Havelock spoke in a monotone. "Parsifal is that other man, isn't he?" he asked quietly. "The one who could rip open wounds . . . all over the world."

"Yes. He has the original set of these agreements, the only other set that exists, he claims. We must believe him. He's got a nuclear gun to our heads – my head."

"Then he's been in touch with you," said Michael, his eyes shifting to the screen. "You got these from *him*, not Anton."

"Yes. His demands at first were financial, growing with each contact, until they were beyond being outrageous; they were astronomical. Millions upon millions . . . and millions after that. We assumed his motive was political. He had the resources to buy lesser governments, to finance revolutions throughout the Third World, to promote terrorism. We kept dozens of unstable countries under the closest intelligence scrutiny, penetrating their most entrenched elements with our best people, telling them only to look for the slightest substantive change. We thought we might trace him, trap him. And then we learned that Parsifal had not gone near the money; it was merely the means that told him we would do as he ordered. He's not interested in money; he never was. He wants control, power. He wants to dictate to the strongest nation on earth."

"He *has* dictated. That's where you made your first mistake."

"We were buying time. We're still buying it."

"At the risk of annihilation?"

"In the all-consuming hope of preventing it. You still don't understand, Mr Havelock. We can and probably will parade Anthony Matthias before the world as a madman, destroying the credibility of ten years of treaties and negotiations, but it will not answer the fundamental question. How in the name of *God* did the information in these agreements get there? Was it given to a man certifiably insane? If it was, whom else has he divulged it to? And do we willingly deliver to potential enemies the innermost secrets of our offence and defence capabilities? Or let them know how deeply we've penetrated their own weapons systems? . . . We have no monopoly on nuclear maniacs. There are men in Moscow and Peking who at the first perusal of these would reach for the buttons and launch. Do you know why?"

"I'm not sure . . . I'm not sure of anything."

"Welcome to a very élite club . . . Let me tell you why. Because it's taken all of us forty years and uncountable billions to get where we are today. Atomic knives at each other's throats. There's no time and not enough money left to begin again. In short, Mr Havelock, in the desperate attempt to avert a global nuclear holocaust, we might start one."

Michael swallowed, conscious of doing so, the blood draining from his throat. "Simplistic assumptions are out," he said.

"They're not even fashionable," replied Berquist.

"Who is Parsifal?"

"We don't know. Any more than we know who Ambiguity is."

"You don't *know*?"

"Except that they're connected. We can assume that."

"*Wait* a minute!"

"You keep saying that."

"You've got *Matthias*! You're running him through a computerized charade here. Tear into his head! You've got a hundred therapies! Use them. Find out!"

"You think we haven't tried? There's nothing in the annals of therapy that hasn't been used . . . isn't *being* used. He's erased reality from his mind; he's convinced himself he negotiated with the militarists in Peking and Moscow. He can't allow it to be otherwise; his fantasies have to be real to him. They protect him."

"But Parsifal's *alive*, he's not a fantasy! He has a face, eyes, features! Anton's got to be able to give you *something*!"

"Nothing. Instead, he describes – accurately to be sure – known extremists in the Soviet Presidium and China's Central Commission. Those are the people he sees when these agreements are mentioned . . . with or without chemicals. That mind of his – that incredible instrument – is as creative in protecting him now as it was when he was instructing the world of lesser mortals before."

"*Abstractions!*" cried Havelock.

"You've said that, too."

"This Parsifal's *real*! He exists! He's got you under a *gun*!"

"My words, I believe."

Michael ran to the table and pounded it with his clenched fist. "I can't *believe* this!"

"Believe or not," said the President, "but don't do that again. There's some kind of sonic thing that registers solid decibels, not conversations. If I don't speak immediately, the vault is opened and you could lose your life."

"Oh, my *God*!"

"I don't need your vote. There's no third term any longer – if there is an any longer – and I wouldn't seek it anyway."

"Are you trying to be funny, Mr President?"

"Possibly. In times like these, and if circumstances permit you to grow older, you may find a certain comfort in the rare attempt. But I'm not sure . . . of anything any longer. Millions to build this place, secrecy unparalleled, the finest psychiatrists in the country. Am I being sold an illusion? I don't know. I just know I have nowhere else to go."

686

Havelock sank into the chair at the end of the table, vaguely uncomfortable at sitting down in Berquist's presence without having been instructed to do so. "Oh," he said meaninglessly, his voice trailing off, looking abjectly at Berquist.

"Forget it," said the President. "I ordered up your own personal firing squad, remember?"

"I still don't understand why. You say I penetrated something, a flaw in some structure or other. That if I kept going, these – " Michael looked up at the screen, wincing – "would be given to Moscow or Peking."

"Not would, *might*. We couldn't take the slightest chance that Parsifal might panic. If he did, he'd undoubtedly head for Moscow. I think you know why."

"He has a Soviet connection. The evidence against Jenna, everything that happened in Barcelona; none of it could have taken place without Russian intelligence."

"The KGB denies it; that is, a man denies it on an official basis. According to the Cons Op records and a Lieutenant Colonel Lawrence Baylor, that man met you in Athens."

"Rostov?"

"Yes. He didn't know what he was denying, of course, but he as much as told us that if there was a connection it wasn't sanctioned. We think he's a worried man; he has no idea how justified he is."

"He may," said Havelock. "He's telling you it could be the VKR."

"What the hell is that? I'm no expert in your field."

"*Voennaya Kontr Razvedka.* A branch of the KGB, an élite corps that frightens anyone possessing a scrap of sanity. Is that what I penetrated?" Michael stopped and shook his head. "No, it couldn't be. I broke it in Paris, after Col des Moulinets. A VKR officer from Barcelona who came after me. I was placed 'beyond-salvage' in Rome, not Paris."

"That was Ambiguity's decision," said Berquist. "Not mine."

"But for the same reason. Your words . . . sir."

"Yes." The President leaned forward. "It was the Costa Brava. That night on the Costa Brava."

The frustration and the anger returned; it was all Michael could do to control himself. "The Costa Brava was a sham! A fraud! I was *used*, and for that you pinned the label on me! You knew about it. You said you were a *part* of it!"

"You saw a woman killed on that beach."

Havelock got up swiftly and gripped the back of the chair. "Is this another attempt to be funny . . . Mr *President*!"

"I don't remotely feel like being amusing. No one was to be killed that night on the Costa Brava."

"No one . . . *Christ!* You *did* it! You and Bradford and those bastards in Langley I spoke with from Madrid! Don't tell me about Costa Brava, I was *there*! And you were responsible, all of you!"

"We initiated it, we set it in motion, but we didn't finish it. And that, Mr Havelock, is the truth."

Michael wanted to rush to the screen and smash his hands against the terrible images. Instead, the words, Jenna's words, came back to him. *Not one operation, but two.* Then his own. *Intercepted. Altered.*

"Wait a minute," he said.

"Find another expression."

"No, please. You started it, and without your knowing it the scenario was read, then taken over, the threads altered, going into another weave."

"Those phrases aren't in my lexicon."

"They're very clear. You're making a rug and the birds in the pattern are swans; suddenly they turn into vultures."

"I stand corrected. That's what happened."

"*Shit!* Excuse me."

"I'm from Minnesota. I've shovelled more than you've ever seen, most of it in Washington." Berquist leaned back in his chair. "Do you understand now?"

"I think so. It's the flaw that could trap him. Parsifal was at Costa Brava."

"*Or his Soviet connection,*" amended the President. "When you saw the Karras woman three months later you began probing that night. If you exposed it, you might have alarmed Parsifal. We don't *know* that you would have, but as long as the possibility existed, we couldn't risk the consequences."

"Why didn't anyone tell me? Why didn't anyone reach me and spell it out?"

"You wouldn't come in. The strategists at Consular Operations went to extreme lengths to bring you in. You eluded them."

"Not because of – " Havelock gestured helplessly, angrily at the screen – "*these*. You could have *told* me, not tried to kill me!"

"There was no time, nor could we send couriers with any part of this information or with the slightest intimations as to Matthias's mental condition. We didn't know what you'd do at any given moment, what you might say about that night, or whom you might say it to. In our judgement – in my judgement – if the man we call Parsifal *was* at Costa Brava, or was part of the altered strategy, and he thought he was being identified with that night, he could well have been provoked into doing the unthinkable. We could not permit even the possibility of that."

"So many questions . . ." Michael blinked in the harsh glare of light. "So much I can't fit together."

"You may when and if the decision is made on both our parts to bring you all the way in."

"The Apache," said Havelock, avoiding Berquist's comment. "The Palatine Hill . . . Jack Ogilvie. Was it an accident? Was that shot meant for me, or was it really meant for him because he knew about something back here? He mentioned a man who died of a heart attack on the Chesapeake."

"Ogilvie's death was exactly what it appeared to be. A mistake. The bullet was meant for you . . . The others, however, were not accidents."

"What others?"

"The remaining three strategists at Consular Operations were murdered in Washington."

Havelock stood motionless, absorbing the information in silence.

"Because of me?" he asked finally.

"Indirectly. But then you're at the core of everything because of the single, imponderable question. Why did Matthias do what he did to you?"

"Tell me about the strategists, please."

"They knew who Parsifal's Soviet connection was," said the President. "Or they would have known the next night if you had been killed at Col des Moulinets."

"Code name. Ambiguity. He's here?"

"Yes. Stern gave him the clearance code. We know where he is, not who he is."

"Where?"

"You may or may not be given that information."

"For *God's sake*! In all due respect, Mr President, hasn't it occurred to you even now to *use* me? Not kill me, but *use* me!"

"Why should I? Could you help me? Help us?"

"I've spent sixteen years in the field, hunting and being hunted. I speak five languages fluently, three marginally and more dialects than I can count. I know one side of Anthony Matthias better than anyone else alive; I know his *feelings*. More to the immediate point, I've uncovered as many double entries – agents – as any other man in Europe. Yes, I think I can help."

"Then you must give me your answer. Do you intend to carry out your threat? These thirteen pages that could . . ."

"Burn them," interrupted Havelock; he was watching the President's eyes, believing him.

"They're carbons," said Berquist.

"I'll reach her. She's a couple of miles away in Savannah."

"Very well. Code name Ambiguity is on the fifth floor of the State Department. One of sixty-five, maybe seventy, men and women. The word, I believe, is 'mole'."

"You've narrowed it down that *far*?" asked Michael, sitting down.

"Emory Bradford did. He's a better man than you think. He never wanted to harm the Karras woman."

"Then he was incompetent."

"He'd be the first to agree with that. Still, if she'd followed his instructions, she'd eventually have been told the truth; the two of you would have been brought in."

"Instead, I was put 'beyond-salvage'."

"Tell me something, Mr Havelock," said the President, once again leaning forward in the chair. "If you were I, knowing what you know now, what would you have done?"

Michael looked at the screen, the astonishing words burning into his mind. "The same thing you did. I was expendable."

"Thank you." The President rose. "Incidentally, no one here on Poole's Island knows anything about these. Not the doctors, the technicians or the military. Only five other men are aware of them. Or of Parsifal. One of them is a psychiatrist from Bethesda, a specialist in hallucinatory disorders who flies down once a week to work with Matthias only in this room."

"I understand."

"Now, let's get out of here while we're still sane," said Berquist as he walked to the projector; he snapped it off, then turned on the overhead lights. "Arrangements will be made to fly the two of you to Andrews Air Force Base this afternoon. We'll find you a place somewhere in the country, not in Washington. We can't risk your being seen."

"If I'm going to be effective, I must have access to records, logs, files. They can't be moved to the country, Mr President."

"If they can't be, we'll bring you in under very controlled circumstances ... There'll be two more chairs placed at the table. You'll be given clearance for everything under another name. And Bradford will brief you as soon as possible."

"Before I leave here, I want to talk to the doctors. I'd also like to see Anton, but I understand; it'll be brief, only a few minutes."

"I'm not sure they'll permit it."

"Then overrule them. I want to talk to him in Czech, his own language. I've got to dig around something he said to me. He said, 'You don't understand. You can never understand.' It's deep inside him, something between himself and me. Maybe I'm the only one who can get it out. It could be everything, why he did what he did, not only to me but to himself. Somewhere in my head there's a bomb, I've known it from the beginning."

"The doctors are overruled. But I remind you, you spent twelve days at a clinic, a total of eighty-five hours in chemical therapy, and you couldn't help us."

"You didn't know where to look. God help me, neither do I."

The three doctors were not able to tell him anything he could not have guessed from Berquist's descriptions, and in fact the psychiatric terminology tended to obscure the picture for him. The President's characterization of a delicate, remarkable instrument exploding under the inhuman pressures of responsibilities was far more graphic than the dry explanation of the limits of stress-tolerance. Then one of the analysts interrupted – the youngest, as it happened.

"There is no reality for him in the accepted sense of the word. He filters his impressions, permitting only those that support what he wants to see and hear. These are his reality – more real to him, perhaps, than anything was before – because they're his fantasies and they've got to protect him now. He has nothing else, only fragmented memories."

President Charles Berquist was not only adept at description, thought Michael. He also listened.

"The deterioration can't be reversed?" asked Havelock.

"No," said another psychiatrist. "The cellular structure has degenerated. It's irreversible."

"He's too old," said the younger man.

"I want to see him. I'll be brief."

"We've registered our objections," said the third doctor, "but the President feels differently. Please understand, we're working here under virtually impossible conditions, with a patient who's failing – how rapidly is difficult to tell. He has to be both artificially repressed and stimulated for us to achieve any results at all. It's extremely delicate, and a prolonged trauma could set us back days. We haven't the time, Mr Havelock."

"I'll be quick. Ten minutes."

"Make it five. *Please.*"

"All right. Five minutes."

"I'll take you over," said the younger psychiatrist. "It's where you saw him last night. The garden."

Outside on the street, the white-jacketed doctor directed Michael to an army jeep behind the red brick building. "You were getting pissed off in there," he said. "You shouldn't have. They're two of the best men in the country and nobody was exaggerating. Sometimes this place seems like Futilityville."

"Futility – what?"

"The results don't come fast enough. We'll never catch up."

"With what?"

"With what he's done."

"I see. You can't be too much of a slouch yourself," said Havelock as they drove down the tree-lined street towards the track that approached Matthias's mocked-up house.

"I've written a couple of papers, and I'm good with stats, but I'm happy to fetch and carry for these guys."

"Where'd they find you?"

"I worked with Dr Schramm at Menninger's – he's the one who insisted on the five minutes, and the finest neuropsychiatrist in the business. I operated machines for him – brain scanners, electrospectrographs, that sort of thing. I still do."

"There's a lot of machinery around here, isn't there?"

"No expense spared."

"I can't get over it," exclaimed Michael, glancing around at the receding scenery, the macabre façades and alabaster models, and the miniature streets and street lamps and odd-shaped blow-ups placed on manicured lawns. "It's incredible. It's something out of a movie – a *weird movie*! Who the hell built it and how were they persuaded not to say anything? The rumours must be flying all over south Georgia."

"Not because of them – the people who built it, I mean."

"How could you stop them?"

"They're nowhere near here. They're hundreds of miles away working on a half-dozen other projects."

"*What?*"

"You just said it," explained the young doctor, grinning. "A movie. This whole complex was built by a Canadian film company that thinks it was hired by a cost-conscious producer on the West Coast. They started the scenic construction twenty-four hours after the Corps of Engineers threw up the stockade and converted the existing buildings for our use."

"What about the helicopters that fly in from Savannah?"

"They're routed on a path and into a threshold beyond the stockade; they can't see anything. And anyway, except for the President and one or two others, they're all from Quartermaster, bringing in supplies. They've been told it's an oceanic research centre and have no reason to think otherwise."

"What about the personnel?"

"We doctors, the technicians who can handle just about everything, a few aides," the guards and a platoon of enlisted men and five officers. These last are all army, even the ones who man the patrol boat."

"What have they been told?"

"As little as possible. Apart from us, the technicians and the aides know more than anyone else, but they were screened as if they were being sent to Moscow. Also the guards, but I guess you know that. I gather you're acquainted."

"With one anyway." The jeep entered the rutted dirt road, the island dust billowing behind them. "I can't understand the army. How do they keep it quiet?"

"To begin with, they don't go anywhere. None of us do, that's the official word. And even if they did they wouldn't worry about the officers. They're all from the Pentagon Rolladex and each one sees himself as a future Chairman of the Joint Chiefs. They wouldn't say anything; silence is their guarantee of quick promotion."

"And the enlisted men? They must be a boiling pot."

"That's stereotypical thinking, isn't it? Young guys like that took a lot of beaches once, fought in a lot of jungles."

"I only meant there's got to be gossip, wild tales all over the place. How are they contained?"

"For a start, they don't see that much, not of anything that counts. They're told Poole's Island is a simulated exercise in survival, everything top secret, ten years in a stockade if the secrecy's broken. They're also screened, and they're all regular army; they've got a home here. Why louse it up?"

"It still sounds loose."

"Well, there's always the bottom line. I mean, before too long it's not going to make a hell of a lot of difference, is it?"

Havelock whipped his head around and stared at the psychiatrist. *Incidentally, no one here on Poole's Island knows anything about these. Neither the doctors, the technicians* . . . Berquist's words. Had that vault, that very odd room, been entered? "What do you mean?"

"One of these days Matthias will quietly slip away. When he's gone the rumours won't make any difference. All great men and women have post-mortem stories told about them; it's part of the ball game."

If there is a ball game, Doctor.

"*Dobrý odpoledne, pritel,*" said Michael softly as he walked out of the house into the sun-drenched garden. Matthias was sitting in the same chair at the end of the winding slate path where he had been seated the night before, protected from the sun by the shade of a palm tree that fanned out in front of the wall. Havelock continued speaking, quickly, ever so gently, in Czech. "I know you're upset with me, my dear friend, and I wish only to put to rest the difficulty between us. After all, you are my beloved teacher, the only father I have left, and it isn't right for fathers and sons to be estranged."

At first Matthias recoiled in the chair, pulling himself farther into the shadows of the palm, the intermittent streaks of light crossing his frightened contorted face. But a mist began to cover the wide eyes behind the tortoiseshell glasses, a film of uncertainty; perhaps he was remembering words from long ago – perhaps a father's words in Prague, or a child's plea. It did not matter. The language, the soft, deliberate cadence – they were having their effect. It was crucial now to touch. The touch was vital, a symbol of so much that was of another language, of another country – of remembered trust. Michael approached, the words flowing softly, the cadence rhythmic, evoking another time, another land.

"There are the hills above Moldau, our great Vltava with its beautiful bridges and the Wenceslas when the snow falls . . . the Striba Lake in summer. And the valleys of the Váh and the Nitra, sailing with the currents towards the mountains."

They touched, the student's hand on the teacher's arm. Matthias trembled, breathing deeply, his own hand rising haltingly from his lap and covering Havelock's.

"You told me I didn't understand, that I could never understand. It's not so, my teacher . . . my father . . . I *can* understand. Above all, I *must* understand. There should be nothing between us . . . ever. I owe everything to you."

The mist in Matthias's eyes began to clear, the focus returning and in that focus there was something suddenly wild – something mad.

"No, *please*, Anton," said Michael quickly. "Tell me what it is. Help me, help me to understand."

The hollow whisper began as it had in the darkness of the garden before. Only now there was blinding sunlight and the language was different, the words different.

"The most dreadful agreements on earth are the ultimate *solutions*. That is what you could never understand . . . But you saw them all . . . all coming and going, the negotiators of the world! Coming to me! Pleading with me! The world knew I could do it and it came to me!" Matthias stopped and then, as suddenly as it had the night before, the deep whisper was replaced by a scream that seemed to block out the sunlight, a nightmare in the middle of the afternoon. "*Get away from me!* You will betray me! You will betray us *all*."

"How can I?"

"Because you *know*!"

"I *don't* know!"

"Betrayer! Betrayer of your countrymen! Your father! Betrayer of the world!"

"Then why not *kill me*!" roared Michael, knowing there was nothing left, nowhere else to go with Anton Matthias. "Why didn't you have me *killed*?"

"Havelock, cut it out!" shouted the young doctor from the doorway.

"Not now!" yelled Michael in English.

"*Yes*, goddamn it!"

"*Slyšet ja!*" screamed Havelock into Matthias's face, returning to Czech. "You could have killed me but you didn't! Why not? I'm nothing compared to the world, to *your solutions* for the world! What *stopped* you?"

"That's it, mister!"

"Let me alone! He's got to tell me!"

"Tell you *what*?"

"*Ted'*, *starý pán*." Michael gripped the arms of Matthias's chair, locking him into it. "What *stopped* you?"

The hollow whisper returned, the wild eyes now clear of uncertainty. "You left the conference and we did not see you, we could not find you. We had to know what you had done, whom you had told."

Madness.

"You're finished here, Havelock!" said the psychiatrist, gripping Michael's arm and pulling him away from the chair. "What were you two talking about? I know it's Czech, but that's *all* I know. What did he tell you? I want it verbatim!"

Havelock tried to shake the numbness from his mind, the utter sense of futility. He looked at the doctor, remembering his use of the word; he would not corrupt it as the young man had. "It wouldn't do you any good. He was back in his childhood; it was meaningless rambling . . . an angry, frightened child. I thought he was going to tell me something. He didn't."

The doctor nodded, his eyes those of a learned, older man. "He does that a lot," said the psychiatrist, voice and face relaxing. "It's a degenerative syndrome in old people born in another country, with a different language. It doesn't make much difference whether they're sane or insane; they go back. And why not? They're entitled to the comfort . . . Sorry. Nice try. Come on, I have to get you out of here. There's a chopper waiting for you at the pad."

"Thanks." Michael backed away on the slate path and looked, he knew, for the last time at Anton Matthias . . . *pritel*, mentor, father. The once great man was cowering again, seeking sanctuary in the shadows of the palm tree.

Madness. Or was it?

Was it *possible*? Did he – Mikhail Havlicek – know the answer? *Did he know Parsifal?*

28

It was called Sterile House Five – Sterile Five for short – and was ten miles south of Alexandria in the Fairfax countryside. Once the estate of a horse breeder, it had been purchased by an elderly, apparently wealthy, retired couple who were in fact buyers-of-record for the United States government. They were appropriate "owners" because they had spent their adult lives in the Foreign Service; they had been attached to various embassies and given various titles, but in reality they were two of the most proficient cryptoanalysts in US Intelligence. Their cover was simple; he had been an investment banker living in Europe for several decades. It was eminently acceptable to the distant, affluent neighbours and accounted for the frequent sight of limousines turning off the country road into the half-mile drive that led to the house. Once a visitor arrived, the "owners" were rarely visible – unless visibility was pre-arranged – for their quarters were in the north wing, a separate section of the house, with a separate entrance and independent facilities.

Sterile Five was another form of halfway house, serving clients who had far more to offer the United States government than the castaway inmates of Mason Falls, Pennsylvania. Over the years it had seen a procession of high-level defectors pass through its doors for a period of interrogation and debriefing. Scientists, diplomats, espionage agents, military men – all had been residents at one time or another. Sterile Five was reserved for those people Washington felt were vital to the immediate interests of the country at given moments of crisis. Havelock and Jenna Karras arrived in an unmarked government vehicle at twenty minutes past four. Undersecretary of State Emory Bradford was waiting for them.

The recriminations were brief; there was no point in going over past errors. Bradford had spoken with the President and understood that there would be "two new chairs". At Sterile Five, however, they sat in the "owner's study", a small room outfitted for a country squire: a couch and thick armchairs; leather, brass, and expensive wood in harmony; mementoes signifying little of substance on the walls. There was a heavy pine table behind the single couch, with a silver tray bearing bottles, glasses and ice. Havelock made himself and Jenna drinks; Bradford declined.

"What have you told Miss Karras?" asked the Undersecretary.

"Everything I learned at Poole's Island."

"It's difficult to know what to say . . . what to think," said Jenna. "I suppose I'm awe-struck and terrified at the same time."

"It's a good combination," agreed Bradford.

"What I want from you," Havelock said to Bradford as he went around the couch with the drinks and sat down beside Jenna, "is everything you have, the names of everyone involved – no matter how remotely – from the beginning. I don't care how long it takes; we can be here all night. As you go along I'll ask questions, make notes, and when you're finished I'll give you a list of what I need."

It took less than four minutes for Michael's first question: "MacKenzie? CIA? Black operations. One of the best out of Langley."

"I was told *the* best," Bradford said.

"He set up Costa Brava, then?"

"Yes."

"He was the second sighting, the one who brought back the bloodstained clothing for forensic?"

"I was about to – "

"Tell me," interrupted Havelock. "Did he die of a stroke – a coronary – on the Chesapeake?"

"In his boat, yes."

"Was there an inquest? An autopsy?"

"Not formally, but, again, the answer is yes."

"What does that mean?"

"With a man like that you don't promote speculation. The doctor was co-operative and thoroughly questioned; he's a highly respected physician. X-rays were examined by him and our own people, the conclusion was unanimous. A massive aortal haemorrhage." Bradford lowered his voice. "It was the first thought we had when we heard the news. We didn't overlook a thing."

"Thanks," said Havelock, writing a note to himself. "Go on."

Jenna placed her drink on the coffee table. "Was he the man with you in the lobby of the hotel in Barcelona?"

"Yes, it was his operation."

"He was an angry man. His eyes were angry, not concerned, just angry."

"He was in an angry occupation."

"He crashed my door in; he had a gun in his hand."

"He was worried; we both were. Miss Karras, if you'd come downstairs or even stayed in your room – "

"Please, go on," Michael broke in.

The Undersecretary continued as Havelock and Jenna listened intently, interrupting whenever either had a question or felt details should be clarified. Within the hour it was apparent to Bradford that Jenna Karras had a mind to contend with and the experience to match. She asked nearly as many questions as Michael, frequently pursuing specifics until possibilities not previously considered were suddenly brought to light.

Bradford reached the night when the three strategists were killed, when the unknown Ambiguity routed the call to Rome placing Havelock "beyond-salvage". The Undersecretary of State was thorough, detailing the checks he had made on the personnel in the L Section of the fifth floor during the hours in question. None, he was certain, could be Ambiguity.

"Because the conferences and briefings they held were . . . how do you say it?" Jenna looked at Michael. "*Potvrdit?*"

"Confirmed," said Havelock, watching her. "Logged in the official records."

"Yes, official." She turned back to Bradford. "Is this the reason you rule out these people?"

"None left their meetings long enough to have reached Rome on a code circuit."

"Forgive me," continued Jenna, "but do you exclude the possibility that this Ambiguity might have associates? Persons who would lie for him?"

"I don't even want to think about it," said the Undersecretary. "But considering the diversity of those who were there, I *do* think it's mathematically impossible. I know too many of those people, have known them for years, some for nearly two decades."

"Still . . ."

"*Paminyatchiks?*" asked Havelock, his eyes on Jenna.

"*Pročne? Jestli mužete.*"

"*Či slos.*"

"*Jest malý.*"

"What are you talking about?" asked Bradford.

"We're being rude," said Jenna. "Sorry. I thought – "

"She thought it was something to think about," interrupted Michael. "I explained that the numbers didn't add up. Go on, please."

Jenna looked at Havelock and reached for her drink.

The Undersecretary of State spoke for nearly four hours, half the time answering questions and refining countless details, until the elegant den came to seem like a quietly-charged courtroom. Bradford was the reluctant hostile witness facing two agile and relentless prosecuting lawyers.

"How are you handling Jacob Handelman?"

"Unsolved. The President read me what you wrote over the phone. It's incredible . . . about Handelman, I mean. Are you sure you weren't mistaken?"

"It was his gun, his knife. There was no mistake."

"Berquist said you must have had extraordinary reason to kill him."

"Oddly enough, I didn't. I wanted him to sweat – for years, if I could. He came after me. Are you going to tell the truth about him?"

"The President says no. What purpose would it serve? He says the Jews have been through enough; let it be."

"Another necessary lie?"

"Not necessary, but compassionate, I think."

"Kohoutek? That farm in Mason Falls?"

"He's being taken now."

"His clients?"

"Each case will be studied individually and decisions made, again compassionately."

Havelock leafed through the pages of his notebook, then put it down on the coffee table and reached for his empty glass. He glanced at Jenna; she shook her head. He got up and walked round the couch to pour himself a drink. "Let me try to put this together," he began quietly. "Ambiguity's somewhere on the fifth floor of the State Department, and he's probably been there for years, feeding Moscow everything he gets his hands on." Michael paused and walked aimlessly to the thick-paned window; outside the floodlights illuminated the landscaped grounds. "Matthias meets this Parsifal and together they create these incredible – no, not incredible – *unthinkable* agreements." Havelock stopped, turning suddenly from the window and looking hard at Bradford. "How could it have happened? For Christ's sake, where *were* all of you? You saw him every day, talked to him, watched him! Couldn't you see what was happening to him?"

"We never knew what role he was playing," said the Undersecretary of State, returning the stare, slow anger finally surfacing. "Charisma has many facets, like a diamond seen in different lights, different turns. Was he Dean Matthias sitting in academic judgement, or Dr Matthias at a lectern, holding forth for an enraptured convocation? Or was he simply Mr Chips, over sherry, with Handel in the background, enlightening his favourite idolators of the moment? He did that very well. Then there was the *bon vivant*, the darling of Georgetown, Chevy Chase and the Eastern Shore. My God, what a coup for a hostess! And how magnificently he performed . . . what charm! What wit! The sheer force of his personality, a paunchy little man who suddenly emanated power! If he'd been capable, he could have had any woman he wanted. Then, of course, there was the office tyrant. Demanding, petulant, self-seeking, jealous . . . so conscious of his image he scoured the papers for the most minor mention, swelling up with the headlines, furious at the slightest criticism. And speaking of criticism, what did he do last year when a lowly senator questioned his motives at the Geneva conference? He went on television, voice choking, close to tears, and said he would remove himself from public life. *Jesus*, what an uproar! That senator's a pariah today!" Bradford paused, shaking his head, embarrassed at his outburst. He continued, lowering his voice. "Then there was

Anthony Matthias, the most brilliant Secretary of State in this nation's history . . . No, Mr Havelock, we saw him but we didn't see him. We didn't know him because he was too many people."

"You're nit-picking at a man's vanity," said Michael, walking towards the couch. "Those're called shortcomings; you may not have any, the rest of us do. He *was* many people; he had to be. Your problem is that you hated him."

"No, you're wrong." Again Bradford shook his head. "You don't hate a man like Matthias," he continued, glancing at Jenna. "You may be awe-struck, or frightened, or mesmerized – but you don't hate."

"Let's get back to Parsifal," said Havelock, sitting on the arm of the couch. "Where do you think he came from?"

"He came from nowhere and he disappeared into nowhere."

"The second he may have done, the first he couldn't have. He came from somewhere. He met Matthias time after time, certainly for weeks, possibly months."

"We've checked Matthias's diaries over and over again. Also his logs, his telephone records, his classified appointments, his every travel itinerary – where he went, whom he met, from diplomats to doormen. There were no consistent repeats. Nothing."

"I'll want them all. Can you arrange it?"

"It's arranged."

"Anything on a time span?"

"Yes, spectroanalysis of the copy page type indicates recent impressions. Within six months."

"Very good."

"We could have assumed it."

"Do me a favour," said Michael, sitting down and reaching for his notebook.

"What's that?" asked the Undersecretary.

"Never assume." Havelock wrote on the pad and added, "Which is exactly what I'm going to do right now. Parsifal's a Russian. Most likely an untouched, unlisted defector."

"We've . . . assumed that. Somebody with extraordinary knowledge of the Soviet Union's strategic arms capabilities."

"Why do you say that?" asked Jenna Karras.

"The agreements. They contain offensive and defensive nuclear-strike data that matches our deepest and most accurate penetrations of their systems."

Michael wrote another note for himself. "Just as important," he said. "Parsifal knew where to find 'Ambiguity'. The connection is made, the mole reaches Moscow, and the evidence against you is provided – for my benefit. Then 'Ambiguity' moves into Costa Brava, rewriting the scenario on the beach." Michael turned back to the Undersecretary of State. "It's here you think the break came, isn't it?"

"I do, and I agree with you. I think it was 'Ambiguity' on that beach, not Parsifal. I believe further that 'Ambiguity' returned to Washington and found he'd lost Parsifal. He'd been used, then discarded, a situation that must have panicked him."

"Because in order to get the KGB to co-operate he obviously had to promise something extraordinary?" asked Havelock.

"Yes, but then there's Rostov's cable and it's a snag. He as much as told us that if there was a connection it wasn't sanctioned, or even controllable."

"He was right. I explained it to Berquist, and it fits . . . from the beginning. It's the answer to Athens. Rostov was referring to a *branch* of the KGB, a descendant of the old OGPU slaughterhouse maniacs, a pack of wolves."

"*Voennaya Kontr Razvedka*," said Jenna, adding quietly, "VKR."

" 'Ambiguity' isn't just a major or a colonel in the KGB, he's a member of the wolf pack. Those are the men he's dealing with, and that, Mr Bradford, is about the worst news you could hear. The KGB with all its paranoia is a stable intelligence-gathering organization compared to the fanatics of the *Voennaya*."

"Fanatics and anything nuclear are a combination this world can't afford."

"If the *Voennaya* reach Parsifal first, that's precisely the combination the world is stuck with." Michael drank, swallowing more than he intended to, fear enveloping him. He picked up the notebook. "So we have a mole called Ambiguity who co-operated with a fellow Russian we've labelled Parsifal, Matthias's partner in creating these insane agreements that could blow up the globe. Matthias virtually collapses, is taken into custody – and therapy – at Poole's Island, and Parsifal goes on alone. But now really alone because he's dropped the mole."

"You agree with me then," said Bradford.

Havelock looked up from the pad. "If you were wrong, we'd know it. Or maybe we wouldn't; maybe we'd be a pile of ashes . . . Or, from a less melodramatic though hardly less tragic point of view in my judgement, the Soviet Union would be running this country with the blessings of the rest of the world. 'The giant ran amok; for God's sake, chain him.' Moscow might even get a vote of confidence from our own citizens. 'Better dead than Red' is not a euphemism I care to test. When push comes to shove, people opt for living."

"But you and I know what that living is, Mikhail," broke in Jenna. "Would you opt for it?"

"Of course," said the Undersecretary of State, mildly surprising the other two. "You can't change anything by dying – unless you're a martyr – or by taking yourself out. Especially when you've seen the worst."

Havelock looked again at Bradford, now studying him. "I think the jury just came back in for you, Mr Undersecretary. That's why you stayed in this city, isn't it? You saw the worst."

"I'm not the issue."

"You were for us for a while. It's nice to know the terrain's firmer. Call me Havelock, or Michael, or whatever you like, but why not drop the mister?"

"Thanks. I'm Emory – or whatever you like."   ●

"I'm Jenna, and I'm starved."

"There's a fully stocked kitchen with a cook in residence. He's also one of the guards. When we're finished, I'll introduce you."

"Just a few more minutes." Havelock tore off a page from his notebook. "You said you were checking the whereabouts of everyone on the fifth floor at the time of Costa Brava."

"Re-checking," interrupted Bradford. "The first check was negative all the way. Everyone was accounted for."

"But we know someone wasn't," said Michael. "He was at Costa Brava. One of those checks of yours ran into a smokescreen, the man inside leaving and returning while supposedly in place."

"Oh?" It was the Undersecretary's turn to write a note, which he did on the back of one of his countless pages. "I hadn't thought of it that way. I was looking for an absence where the explanation might not hold up. You're saying something quite different."

"Yes, I am. Our man's better than that; there won't be any explanation. Don't look for someone missing; look for someone who wasn't there, who wasn't where he was supposed to be."

"Someone on assignment, then."

"It's a place to start," agreed Havelock, tearing off a second page. "The higher the profile the better, incidentally. Remember we're looking for a man who's got maximum clearance, and the more prominent the man the better the smokescreens work. Don't forget Kissinger's diarrhoea in Tokyo; he was really in Peking."

"I'm beginning to understand your accomplishments."

"Considering the mistakes I've made," replied Michael, writing on the page he had just torn out of the notebook, "I wouldn't qualify for a code ring on the back of a cereal box." He got up, stepped around the coffee table to Bradford, and held out the two pages. "This is the list. Do you want to look it over and see if there are any problems?"

"Sure." The Undersecretary of State took the papers and settled back into the chair. "By the way, I'll have that drink now, if you don't mind. Bourbon on the rocks, please."

"I thought you'd never ask." Havelock looked at Jenna; she nodded. He took her glass from the coffee table and walked round the couch as Bradford spoke.

"There are a couple of surprises here," he said, glancing up and frowning. "There's no problem with the Matthias material – the appointments, logs, itineraries – but why do you need all this stuff on the doctor in Maryland? Background, financial statements, employees, laboratories. We *were* thorough, believe me."

"I do believe you. Call it a throwback. I know a doctor in the south of France and he's one hell of a surgeon. But he gets brain fever when he's near the gaming tables; he's crashed a couple of times and had to be bailed out."

"There's no parallel here. Randolph hasn't had to work since his mother first saw him in the hospital. His family owns half the Eastern Shore, the richer half."

"But not the people who work for him," said Michael, pouring drinks. "They may not even own a boat."

Bradford's gaze again dropped to the page. "I see," he said, more bewilderment in his voice than conviction. "I'm not sure I understand this. You want the names of people in the Pentagon who form the Nuclear Contingency Committees."

"I read somewhere that there were three," added Havelock, carrying the drinks back. "They play war games, changing sides and cross-checking their strategies." He handed Bradford his bourbon, then sat down next to Jenna; she took her drink, her eyes on Michael.

"You think Matthias used them?" asked the Undersecretary.

"I don't know. He must have used somebody."

"For what purpose? There's nothing in our arsenals he didn't know about, had on file somewhere. He *had* to know; he negotiated."

"I just want to be thorough."

Bradford nodded with an embarrassed smile. "I've heard that before. Okay." He went back to the page, reading aloud. " 'List of negative-possibles going back ten years. Follow-ups on each. Sources: CIA, Cons Op, Army Intelligence.' I don't know what this means."

"They will. There'll be dozens of them."

"What are 'they'?"

"Men and women who were priority targets for defection but never came over."

"Well, if they didn't come over – "

"Moscow doesn't announce those who got out themselves," interrupted Havelock. "The computer follow-ups will clarify current statuses."

Bradford paused, then nodded again, reading silently.

Jenna touched Michael's arm; he looked at her. She spoke softly, her eyes questioning. "*Proč ne paminyatchik?*"

"*Ne Ted'.*"

"I beg your pardon?" The Undersecretary glanced up as he shifted the pages in his hands.

"Nothing," said Havelock. "She's hungry."

"I'll be finished in a minute, get back to Washington and leave you alone; the rest of this is routine. The DC psychiatrists' reports on Matthias will have to be signed over by the President and additional security put on here, but it can be done. I'm seeing him when I get back tonight."

"Why don't you just take me over to Bethesda?"

"Those records aren't there. They're down at Poole's Island locked away with the other psychiatric probings and very special. They're in a steel container and can't be removed without presidential clearance. I'll have to get them. I'll fly down tomorrow." Bradford stopped reading and looked up, startled. "This last item . . . are you sure? What can they tell you? They couldn't tell *us* anything."

"Put it down as my own personal Freedom of Information Act."

"It could be very painful for you."

"What is it?" asked Jenna.

"He wants the results of his own twelve days in therapy," Bradford said.

They ate by candlelight in the country-elegant dining-room, the scene somehow shifting from the deadly sublime to the faintly ridiculous. Adding to the contrast was a large, reticent man who was a surprisingly accomplished cook; but the bulge of a weapon beneath his white jacket did little to emphasize his talents in the kitchen. There was, however, nothing humorous about his eyes; he was a military guard and as accomplished with a gun as he was at preparing Beef Wellington. Yet whenever he left the room after serving and clearing, Jenna and Michael looked across the table at each other, trying unsuccessfully not to laugh. Although even these brief minutes of laughter did not last; the unthinkable never left them.

"You trust Bradford," said Jenna, over coffee. "I know you do. I can tell when you trust a person."

"You're right, I do. He has a conscience and I think he's paid for it. You can trust a man like that."

"Then why did you stop me from bringing up the *paminyatchiks* – the travellers?"

"Because he couldn't handle it and it can't help him. You heard him; he's the methodical man, one step at a time, each step exhaustingly analysed. That's his value. With the *paminyatchiks* he's suddenly asked to question everything geometrically."

"I don't understand. Geometrically?"

"In a dozen different directions at once. Everyone's immediately suspect; he wouldn't be looking for one man, he'd be studying whole groups. I want him to concentrate on smokescreens, bore into every assignment on the fifth floor, whether eight blocks or eight hundred miles away from the State Department, until he finds someone who might not have been where he was supposed to be."

"You explained it very well."

"Thanks."

"You might have added the use of a puppet, however."

Havelock looked at her through the glow of the candles, a half smile coming to his lips. She levelled her eyes with his, smiling also. "Damn it, you know you're absolutely right," he said, laughing softly.

"I wasn't making a list, you were. You can't be expected to think of everything."

"Thanks for the kindness, I'll bring it up in the morning. Incidentally, why didn't you? You weren't shy in there."

"That was asking questions, not giving orders or advice. There's a difference. I wouldn't care to give orders or advice to Bradford until he accepted me. And if I were forced to, it would be in the form of questions, leading to a suggestion."

"That's an odd thing to say. You're accepted; Bradford heard it from Berquist. There's no higher authority."

"I don't mean in that sense. I mean him. He's uncomfortable with women, impatient, perhaps. I don't envy his wife or his women; he's a deeply troubled man."

"He couldn't have more to be troubled about."

"Long before this, Mikhail. He reminds me of a brilliant talented man whose brilliance and talent don't mix very well. I think he feels impotent, and that touches his women . . . all women, really."

"Am I with Sigmund again?"

"*Limburský syr!*" Jenna laughed. "I watch people, you know I do. Do you remember the jeweller in Trieste, the bald-headed man whose shop was an MI Six drop? You said he was – what's the peculiar word you have? Like *houkacka?*"

"Horny. I said he was horny, that he walked round the women in his store with a spike in the middle of his trousers."

"And I said he was gay."

"And you were right, because you unbuttoned your blouse a few inches and the son of a bitch kept following me."

They both laughed, the laughter echoing off the veloured walls. Jenna reached over and touched his hand.

"It's good to laugh again, Mikhail."

"It's good to laugh with you. I don't know how often we'll be able to."

"We must make time for it. I think it's terribly important."

"I love you, Jenna."

"Then why don't we ask our gun-bearing Escoffier where we sleep? I don't want to appear *doslat*, my darling, but I love you, too. I want to be close to you, not with a table between us."

"You figured I wasn't gay."

"Latent, perhaps. I'll take what I can get."

"Direct. I always said you were direct."

The gun-bearing Escoffier walked in. "More coffee?" he asked.

"No thank you," said Havelock.

"Some brandy?"

"I think not," said Jenna.

"How about television?"

"How about the sleeping quarters?"

"The reception's lousy up there."

"We'll manage," said Michael.

He sat on the antique bench in front of the dying fire in the bedroom, stretching his neck and moving his shoulder in circles. He was sitting there under orders, Jenna's favours to be withheld for seven years or some such nonsense if he disobeyed. She had gone downstairs to find bandages, antiseptic, and no doubt whatever else she could lay her hands on in pursuit of her immediate medical aims.

Ten minutes ago they had walked into the room together, hands clasped, bodies touching, both laughing softly. When she leaned into him, Michael suddenly winced from the pain in his shoulder, and she had looked into his eyes. She had then unbuttoned his shirt and studied the dressing underneath on his shoulder in the light of a table lamp. An accommodating guard had started the fire over an hour before; it was nearly out, but the coals were glowing, the stone hearth throwing off heat.

"Sit down here and stay warm," Jenna had said, leading him to the bench. "We never did pick up a Red Cross kit. They must have something downstairs."

"You'd better call it first aid or they'll think you're taking up a collection."

"Just be still, my darling. That shoulder's raw."

"I haven't thought about it, I haven't felt it," said Havelock, watching her go to the door and let herself out.

It was true, he had neither thought about the wound from Col des Moulinets nor, except for mild spasms, been aware of the pain. There had been no time. It hadn't been important enough to think about. Too much had been too overwhelming too quickly. He looked over at the large bedroom window, a window with the same thick, bevelled glass as the one below in the study. He could see the wash of floodlights beyond – distorted by the glass – and wondered briefly how many men prowled the grounds protecting the sanctity of Sterile Five. Then his eyes wandered back to the burning coals that were the end of the fire. So much . . . so overwhelming . . . so quickly. The mind had to catch up before it was drowned in the on-rushing revelations released by floodgates no longer holding back unthinkable – unbearable – truths. If he was going to keep his sanity, he had to find time to think.

It's good to laugh with you. I don't know how often we'll be able to.

We must make the time for it. I think it's terribly important.

Jenna was right. Laughter was not inconsequential. *Her* laugh was not; he suddenly wanted so desperately to hear it. Where was she? How long did it take to find a roll of elastoplast and a couple of bandages? Every sterile house was fully equipped with all manner of medical supplies, they went with the territory. Where *was* she?

He got up from the antique bench, suddenly alarmed. Perhaps other men – men not assigned to Sterile Five – were prowling the grounds outside. He had a certain expertise in such matters. Infiltration was made easier by a profusion of woods and underbrush, and Sterile Five was a country house, surrounded by trees and foliage – natural cover for unnatural experts bent on penetration. He could intrude, invade, undoubtedly take out opposition silently, and if he could, others could. Where *was* she?

Havelock walked rapidly to the window, realizing as he approached it that the thick glass which was impervious to bullets would also distort any movement outside. It did; he turned swiftly for the door. Then he realized something else: he had no weapon!

The door opened before he reached it. He stopped, his breath cut short, relief sweeping through him as Jenna stood there with one hand on the knob and the other holding a plastic tray filled with bandages, scissors, tape and antiseptic.

"Mikhail, what is it? What's the matter?"

"Nothing. I . . . I felt like getting up."

"Darling, you're perspiring," said Jenna, closing the door and coming to him, touching his forehead, then his right temple. "What is it?"

"I'm sorry. My imagination went a little off the track. I . . . I thought you were gone longer than . . . I expected. I'm sorry."

"I was gone longer than *I* expected." Jenna took his arm and led him to the bench. "Let's get the shirt off," she said, placing the tray down and helping him.

"Just that?" asked Havelock, sitting down and looking at her, removing his arms from his sleeves. "Just longer than you expected? That's it?"

"Well, apart from two brief affairs under the staircase and a mild flirtation with the cook, I'd say it was sufficient . . . Now, stay still while I take this off." Jenna carefully, expertly, sliced through the borders of the dressing on his shoulder, peeled it back and removed the bandage. "Actually, it's healing quite well, considering what you've put it through," she said, as she stripped off the tape and reached for the spirit and cotton wool. "More irritation than anything else. The salt water probably prevented infection . . . This will sting a bit."

"It *does*," said Michael, wincing as Jenna swabbed the flesh around the wound, then stroked the remains of the elastoplast away. "Apart from that activity under the staircase, what the hell were you doing?" he asked while she placed squares of gauze over his skin.

"Concentrating on the mild flirtation," she replied, reeling out the surgical tape and strapping the clean dressing in place. "There. You won't feel any better, but you look better."

"And you're avoiding me."

"Don't you like surprises?"

"Never did."

"*Koláče!*" she said, drawing out the word, while laughing, and pouring alcohol over his exposed skin. "In the morning we'll have *koláče*," she added, massaging his back.

"Sweet rolls? . . . You're crazy. You're positively out of your mind! We've spent twenty-four hours in a goddamned hell and you're talking about hot cross buns!"

"We must live, Mikhail," said Jenna, her voice suddenly soft beside him, the movement of her hands slowing to a halt. "I did speak with our armed-to-the-teeth cook, and I'm sure I flirted. In the morning he'll make sure we have apricots and dry yeast; nutmeg he has . . . and ground mace. He'll order it all tonight. In the morning, *koláče*."

"I don't believe you – "

"Try and you'll see." She laughed again, and held his face in her hands. "In Prague you found a bakery that made *koláče*. You loved it and asked me to bake some for you."

"In Prague, there was another set of problems, not what's facing us now."

"But it is *us*, Mikhail. *Us* once more, and we must have our moments. I lost you once, and now you're here, with me again. Let me have these moments, let *us* have them . . . even knowing what we know."

He reached for her, pulling her to him. "You have them. We have them."

"Thank you, my darling."

"I love to hear you laugh, have I told you that?"

"A number of times. You said I laughed like a small child watching a marionette show. Do you remember saying that?"

"I do, and I was right." Michael tilted her head back. "It fits, a child and sudden laughter . . . a nervous child sometimes. Broussac saw it too. She told me what happened in Milan, how you stripped that poor bastard, coloured him red, and stole his clothes."

"As well as an enormous sum of money!" interrupted Jenna. "He was a dreadful man."

"Régine said you laughed about it like a small child remembering a joke or a prank or something like that."

"I suppose I did." Jenna glanced at the fire. "I was so frightened, hoping so much that she would help me, thinking she might not. I think I was holding on to a memory that amused me, that might calm me down. I don't know, but it's happened before."

"What do you mean?" asked Michael.

Jenna turned back to him, her wide eyes inches from his but not looking at him – instead, looking beyond, seeing images from the past. "When I ran away from

Ostrava, when my brothers were killed, and I was marked by the anti-Dubičeks – when my life there was finished – I came into the world of Prague. It was a world filled with hatred, a world so violent that I thought at times I couldn't stand it any more. But I knew what I had to do, I couldn't turn back to a life that wasn't mine any longer . . . So I used to remember things, relive the memories as if I were actually *there*, not in Prague, not in that world of fear. I was back in Ostrava, my adoring brothers taking me for rides, telling their sister outrageous stories to make me laugh. During those moments I was free, I wasn't afraid." She looked at him. "Those memories were hardly like Milan, were they? But I could laugh, I *did* laugh . . . Enough! I'm not making sense."

"You're making sense," said Michael, pulling her to him again, his face against hers. "Thank you for that. Not much sense is being made these days. Anywhere."

"You're tired, my darling. More than tired, you're exhausted. Come on, let's go to bed."

"I always obey my doctors."

"You need rest, Mikhail."

"I always obey my doctors up to a point."

"*Zlomený*," said Jenna, laughing softly against his ear.

Strands of her blonde hair were layered over his face, her arm across his chest, but neither was asleep. The splendid, warm comfort of their love-making did not bring sleep; the unthinkable was too much with them. A soft shaft of light came from the partially closed bathroom door.

"You didn't tell me everything that happened to you on Poole's Island, did you?" said Jenna, her head next to his on the pillow. "You told Bradford that you did, but you didn't."

"Almost everything," replied Havelock, staring at the ceiling. "I'm still trying to figure it out."

Jenna took her arm away and, supporting herself on her elbow, faced him. "Can I help you?" she asked.

"I don't think anybody can. It's the bomb in my head."

"What is, my darling?"

"I know Parsifal."

"You *what* . . . ?"

"That's what Matthias said. He said I saw them all coming and going, the 'negotiators of the world', he called them. But there was only one and I must have seen him. I must know him."

"That was the reason he did what he did to you? To us? Why he wanted you out?"

"He said I could never understand . . . the deadliest treaties were the only solution."

"And I was the sacrifice."

"Yes. What can I say? He's not sane; he wasn't when he ordered the case against you. You were to die and I was to live, live and be watched." Michael shook his head in frustration. "*That's* what I can't understand."

706

"My death?"

"No, my *living*."

"Even in his insanity, he loved you."

"Not *him*. Parsifal. If I was a threat why didn't Parsifal kill me? Why was it left to the mole to put out the order three months later?"

"Bradford explained that," said Jenna. "You'd seen me; you were reopening Costa Brava, and it could have led you back to the mole."

"It still doesn't explain Parsifal. He could have had me taken out twenty times over. He didn't. That's the gap. What kind of a man are we dealing with?"

"Certainly not rational. It's what's so terrifying."

Havelock turned his head and looked at her. "I wonder," he said.

The ringing was harsh, unexpected, reverberating throughout the room. He bolted up from a deep sleep, his hand reaching for a non-existent weapon. It was the telephone, and Michael stared at it before picking it up from the bedside table. He glanced at his watch as he spoke. It was 4:45 in the morning.

"Yes?"

"Havelock, it's Bradford."

"What's the matter? Where are you?"

"In my office. I've been here since eleven. Incidentally, I've had people working through the night. Everything you wanted will be at Sterile Five by eight o'clock, except the records at Poole's Island. There'll be a few hours' delay with those."

"You called at this hour to tell me that?"

"Of course not." Bradford paused, an intake of breath filling the moment. "I may have found him," he said rapidly. "I did as you suggested. I looked for someone who might not have been where he was supposed to be. I won't know for certain until late this morning; that's the delay with Poole's Island. If it's true, it's incredible; his record is as clean as they come, his military service – "

"Don't say any more," ordered Michael.

"Your phone is as sterile as that house."

"Mine may be. Yours may not be. Or your office. Just listen to me."

"What is it?"

"Look for a puppet. He could be alive or dead."

"A what?"

"Someone filling in, the strings leading back to your man. Do you understand that?"

"Yes, I think so. As a matter of fact, I do. It's part of what I've found already."

"Call me when you know. From the street, from a booth. But don't close in, don't do anything." Havelock hung up and looked at Jenna. "Bradford may have found 'Ambiguity'. If he has, you were right."

"*Paminyatchik?*"

"A traveller."

It was a morning such as Sterile Five had never experienced and would probably never see again. A persuasive inmate had taken over the sombre asylum. In spite of the tension, despite the anticipated call from Bradford, by 8:30 Jenna had commandeered the kitchen, the gun-bearing Escoffier relegated to the position of assistant. Ingredients were measured and mixed to the accompaniment of glances of approval and the gradual breaking down of culinary barriers; the armed cook began to smile. Pans were selected and the outsized oven turned on; then two additional guards emerged on the scene as if their nostrils belonged to hounds and the kitchen had become a meat market.

"Please call me Jenna," said Jenna to the others, as Havelock was demoted to a corner table and dismissed with a newspaper.

First names were exchanged, wide grins appeared, and before long there was conversation interspersed with laughter. Home towns were compared – bakeries the basis of comparison – and a kind of frivolity took over the kitchen at Sterile Five. It was as though no one had ever before dared lighten the oppressive atmosphere of the security-conscious compound. It was lightened now and Jenna was the bearer of that light. To say that the men – these professionals familiar with the deadly arts – were taken with her was too modest an observation. They were actually having fun, and fun was not normal at Sterile Five. The world was going to hell in a galactic basket and Jenna Karras was baking *koláče*.

At 9:55, however, after quantities of sweet rolls had been eaten in the kitchen and dispensed throughout the grounds, the serious air of the sterile house returned. Static on a dozen radios erupted as inside bells and television monitors became operational. An armoured van from the Department of State had entered the long, guarded drive from the highway. It was expected.

By 10:30 Havelock and Jenna were back in the ornate study to examine the papers and photographs, which were separated by classification. There were six stacks, some thicker than others: four on the desk in front of Michael; two on the coffee table, where Jenna sat reading on the couch. Bradford had been thorough, and if more-was-more his only error was in duplication. An hour and twenty minutes passed, the near-noon sun filling the windows, refracted in the bullet-proof glass, the rays scattered across the walls. There was silence, except for the turning of pages.

The approach they used was standard when dealing with such a mass of diverse information. They read everything rapidly, concentrating on the totality, not on specifics, trying first to get a feel of the landscape; they would get to the details later and relentlessly scrutinize them. Despite the concentration on reading, a comment was inevitable now and then.

"Ambassador Addison Brooks and General Malcolm Halyard," said Michael, reading a page that contained the names of all those involved – however remotely, with or without knowledge – with the Parsifal mosaic. "They're the President's back-ups if he's forced to expose Matthias."

"In what sense?" asked Jenna.

"After Anton, they're among the most respected men in the country. Berquist will need them."

Several minutes later Jenna spoke. "You're listed here."

"Where."

"An entry in an early Matthias calendar."

"How early?"

"Eight – no, nine months ago. You were a house guest of his. It was when you were flown over for the Cons Op personnel-evaluation, I think. We hadn't known each other very long."

"Long enough for me to want to get back to Prague as fast as I could. Those sessions were usually a monumental waste of time."

"You told me once they served a purpose, that the field often had strange effects on certain men and they should be periodically checked."

"I wasn't one of them. Anyway, I said usually, not always. On occasions they'd pick out a . . . a gunslinger."

Jenna put the page down on her lap. "Mikhail, could it have been then? That visit to Matthias? Could you have seen Parsifal then?"

"Anton was himself nine months ago. There was no Parsifal."

"You said he was tired – 'terribly tired' were the words you used. You were worried about him."

"His health, not his sanity. He was sane."

"Still – "

"You think I haven't gone over every minute in my mind?" interrupted Havelock. "It was in Georgetown, and I was there two days, two nights, the length of the evaluation. We had dinner twice, both times alone. I didn't see anybody."

"Certainly people came to the house."

"They certainly did; they never gave him a moment's peace, day or night."

"Then you saw them."

"I'm afraid I didn't. You'd have to know that old place; it's a maze of small rooms in the front. There's a parlour to the right in the hallway, a library on the left that one goes through to get to his office. I think Anton liked it; he could keep people waiting who probably wouldn't see each other. Petitioners in stages, moved from one area to the next. He'd greet them in the parlour, then they'd be taken to the library and, finally, to the *sanctum-sanctorum*, his office."

"And you were never in those rooms."

"Not with anybody else. When he was interrupted at dinner, I remained in the dining-room in the back. I even used a separate side entrance when coming or going from the house, never the front door. We had an understanding."

"Yes, I remember. You didn't care to be seen with him."

"I'd put it differently. I'd have been honoured – I mean that, honoured – to have been seen with him. It just wasn't a very good idea, for either of us."

"But if it wasn't during those two days, when was it? When *could* you have seen Parsifal?"

Michael looked at her, feeling helpless. "I'd have to go back over half a lifetime, that's part of the madness. In his fantasy he sees me leaving a conference; that could be anything from a classroom to a seminar to a lecture hall. How many were there? Fifty, a hundred, a thousand? Post-graduate degrees take time. How many have I forgotten? Was it there, in one of those? Was Parsifal somewhere in the past?"

"If he was, you could hardly be considered a threat to him now." Jenna sat forward, recognition suddenly in her eyes. " 'He could have taken me out twenty times over but he didn't,' " she repeated. "Parsifal *didn't* try to kill you."

"Exactly."

"Then he could be someone you knew years ago."

"Or there's another possibility. I said he could have taken me out, and he would have, but regardless of how careful or how removed a person is, there's always a risk in killing someone, or contracting for a gun, no matter how slight. Maybe he can't tolerate even the hint of a risk. Maybe he's in a crowd of faces right in front of me and I can't pick him out. But if I knew who he was, or what he looked like, I'd know where to find him. *I'd* know, but not necessarily many others, probably no one in our line of work."

"The mole could supply you with both, an identity and a description."

"Good hunting, Mr Undersecretary," said Havelock. "And I wish to hell he'd *call*! . . . Anything else in there?" he added, going back to the material on a Maryland physician.

"I haven't got that far with the diaries. But there's something in the itineraries and it's repeated frequently. I'm not sure I understand. Why is the Shenandoah mentioned so often, Mikhail?"

Havelock looked up from the page as a dissonant chord echoed in the recesses of his brain.

Emory Bradford struggled to keep his eyes open. Except for brief catnaps, taken when he could no longer function, he had not slept in nearly thirty-six hours. Yet he *had* to stay awake; it was past noon. The newsreel tapes and photographs from New York would be arriving any minute, rushed down by an accommodating television station that accepted an innocuous explanation in exchange for a new and confidential source at the Department of State. The Undersecretary had ordered up the proper equipment; he could run the tapes within minutes of receiving them. And then he would know.

Incredible. Arthur Pierce! *Was* it Pierce, after all? The senior State Department official at the United Nations delegation, chief aide to the ambassador, a career officer with a service record to be envied by just about anyone working in the upper regions of the government, a record that fairly screamed "advancement"! And prior to his arrival in Washington there was a superb military record. Had he stayed in the army he would have been on his way to the Joint Chiefs of Staff. Pierce had arrived in South-east Asia as a second-lieutenant from the University of Michigan, his Master's degree *summa cum laude* and an experienced officer cadet. Thereafter during five voluntarily uninterrupted tours of duty he had risen to the rank of major, replete with decorations for bravery, citations for leadership and recommendations for further strategic studies. And before *that*, before Vietnam, there was a dossier that exemplified the young American achievement of a farm boy: church acolyte, Eagle Scout, high school valedictorian, college scholarship with academic honours – even membership of the most envied student clubs. As General Halyard had put it, Arthur Pierce was flag, mother, apple pie and God. *Where* was the connection with Moscow?

Yet there was one if there was validity in Havelock's use of the term "smokescreen" and especially in his next phrase "the puppet who might be dead or alive". It was the initial suggestion, however, that had first caught Bradford's attention: *Look for a man who wasn't there, who wasn't where he was supposed to be.*

He had been studying routinely – too routinely for the thought seemed too farfetched – the recommendations and positions taken by the American delegation at the Security Council's meetings during the week of Costa Brava. These included the confidential discussions within the delegation, as summarized by an attaché named Carpenter. His superior, Pierce, the man second only to the ambassador, was mentioned frequently, his suggestions concise, astute, very much in character. Then Bradford came upon a parenthetical abbreviated phrase deep in the text of that Thursday's meeting: "*(Del./F. C.)*".

It followed a strong and lengthy recommendation presented to the ambassador by Pierce. Bradford had not picked it up before, probably because of the unnecessarily complicated diplomatic verbiage, but seven hours ago he had looked hard at it. "(Del./F.C.) *Delivered by Franklyn Carpenter.*"

Translation: not offered by the ambassador's senior aide, Arthur Pierce, whose words they were, but, instead, relayed by a subordinate. Meaning: Pierce was not there, not where he was supposed to be.

Bradford had then studied every subsequent line in the delegation report. He'd found two additional bracketed *F.C.s* for Thursday and three more for Friday. *Friday.* Then he had remembered the obvious and gone back to the beginning of the week. It had been the end of the year; the operation at Costa Brava had taken place on the night of 4 January. Sunday. *A weekend.*

There had been no Security Council meeting that Wednesday because the majority of the delegations who were still on speaking terms were holding diplomatic receptions for New Year's Eve. On Thursday, the first day of the New Year, as if to show the world the UN meant to greet it seriously, the Council had resumed, then again on Friday . . . but not Saturday or Sunday.

Therefore, if Arthur Pierce was not where he was supposed to be, and had instructed a subordinate to deliver his words, he could have left the country on Tuesday evening, allowing five days for the Costa Brava. If, if . . . if. *Ambiguity?*

He had called Havelock, who told him what to look for next. The puppet.

The lateness of the hour was irrelevant. Bradford had raised an operator on the all-night tracing switchboard and told him to reach one Franklyn Carpenter, wherever he might be. Eight minutes later the operator had called back; Franklyn Carpenter had resigned from the Department of State a little over three months ago. The number on file was useless; the telephone had been disconnected. Bradford had then given the name of the only other person listed as at the American desk during that Thursday meeting of the Security Council, a lower level attaché no doubt still in New York.

The tracing operator had called back at 5:15 A.M., the UN attaché on the line.

"This is Undersecretary of State Bradford . . ."

The man's initial response had been one of astonishment mixed with the fuzziness of sleep, and more than a touch of fear. Bradford had to spend several minutes reassuring him, trying to bring him back to those few days nearly four months ago.

"Can you remember them?"

"Reasonably, I suppose."

"Did anything strike you as unusual during the end of that week?"

"Nothing that comes to mind, no, sir."

"The American team for those sessions – and I'm mainly concerned with Thursday and Friday – consisted of the ambassador, the senior State Department official, Arthur Pierce, yourself and a man named Carpenter, is that right?"

"I'd reverse the last two. I was low man on the totem pole then."

"Were all four of you there every day?"

"Well . . . I think so. It's hard to recall every day four months ago. The attendance rolls would tell you."

"Thursday was New Year's Day, does that help you?"

There was a pause before the attaché answered. When he did so, Bradford closed his eyes. "Yes," the aide said. "I *do* remember. I may have been listed at the desk, but I wasn't there. The White Flash had – Excuse me, I'm sorry, sir."

"I know what you mean. What did Undersecretary Pierce do?"

"He asked me to fly down to Washington to compile an analysis of the entire Middle East position. I spent damn near the whole weekend on it. Then, wouldn't you know, he didn't use it. Never has to this day."

"I have a last question," Bradford said quietly, trying to control his voice. "When a team member's recommendations are given to the ambassador by someone else at the desk, what exactly does it signify?"

"That's easy. The senior members try to anticipate adversary proposals and write up strategies or counterproposals to block them. In the event he's out of the council room when a controversial proposal is brought up, his advice is there for the ambassador."

"Isn't that dangerous? Couldn't someone simply write up something under an official title and hand it to a member?"

"Oh, no, it doesn't work that way. You don't just drop those deliveries and disappear. You've got to be on the premises, that's a must. Suppose the ambassador likes an argument, uses it, and gets hit with a reply that he can't handle. He wants the man responsible back in session to get him away from the fan."

"Undersecretary Pierce gave a number of deliveries, as you call them, during the Thursday and Friday meetings."

"That's standard. He's out of that room as much as he's in it. He's terrific in the Diplomats' Lounge, I've got to say it. He's there a lot, button-holing God knows who, but it works. I think he's as effective as anyone up here; I mean he's really impressive. Even the Soviets like him."

Yes, they do, Mr Attaché. So much so that controversial proposals could be avoided by pre-arrangement, Bradford said to himself.

"I know I said a last question; may I have one more?"

"I'm not going to argue, sir."

"What happened to Carpenter?"

"I wish to hell I knew. I wish I could find him. I guess he just fell apart."

"What do you mean?"

"I guess you didn't know. His wife and kids were killed in an automobile accident a couple of days before Christmas. How'd you like to have three coffins in front of a Christmas tree with the presents unopened?"

"I'm sorry."

"He showed a lot of guts coming back as soon as he did. Of course, we all agreed it'd be the best thing for him. To be with people who cared; not alone."

"I imagine that Undersecretary Pierce concurred."

"Yes, sir. He was the one who persuaded him to come back."

"I see."

"Then one morning he just didn't show up. The next day a telegram arrived; it was his resignation, effective immediately."

"That was unusual, wasn't it? Actually improper, I believe."

"After what he'd been through, I don't think anyone wanted to pursue formalities."

"And again the Undersecretary concurred."

"Yes, sir. It was Pierce's idea, Carpenter just disappeared. I hope he's all right."

He's dead, Mr Attaché. The puppet is dead.

Bradford had continued until the sun was up, until his eyes ached from the strain. The next items he examined were the time sheets for the night the Ambiguity code had been stolen, the "beyond-salvage" sent to Rome. He saw what he expected to see: Arthur Pierce had been not in New York but in Washington, at his office on the fifth floor – and, naturally, he had checked out shortly after five o'clock in the evening, the time corresponding to half a dozen others. How simple it must have been to walk out in a crowd, sign the security sheet and go right back inside. He could have stayed there all night, signed in in the morning and no one would have known the difference. Just as he, Undersecretary Emory Bradford, could do the same thing *this* morning.

He had gone back to the military transcripts – *a nonpareil* army record – to the State Department dossier – an inventory of achievement – to an early life that read like an officially documented tribute to Jack Armstrong, All-American Boy. Where in God's name was the connection with Moscow?

By eight o'clock it had become impossible to concentrate so he leaned back in his chair and slept. At eight thirty-five he was stirred awake by the hum of life beyond his office door. The day had begun for the Department of State. Coffee was made and poured, appointments checked, schedules set up as secretaries awaited the arrival of their crisp, starched superiors. There was an unwritten but understood dress code at State these days; frizzled hair, loud ties and unkempt beards were out. He had got up, walked outside and greeted his own middle-aged secretary, startling her by his appearance. At that moment he realized what an impression he must have made – tieless, in shirtsleeves, dark circles under his eyes, his hair rumpled and the black stubble of a beard on his face.

He had asked for coffee and headed for the men's room to relieve himself, wash and straighten up as best he could. And as he walked through the large office, past desks and secretaries and arriving executives, he felt the stares levelled at him. If they only knew, he thought to himself.

By ten o'clock, remembering Havelock's admonition, he went out to a public phone and made arrangements for the tapes and the photographs to be flown down from New York. He was tempted to call the President. He did not; he spoke to no one.

Now he glanced at his watch. It was twenty-two minutes past twelve, three minutes later than it was when he last checked. The shuttle flights were every hour from New York; which one was the shipment on?

His thoughts were interrupted by a quiet rapping on his door and a corresponding acceleration in his heartbeat. "Come in!"

It was his secretary, and she looked at him the way she had looked at him early in the morning, concern in her deep-set eyes. "I'm off to lunch, okay?"

"Sure, Liz."

"Can I get you anything?"

"No, thanks."

The woman stood awkwardly in the door frame, pausing before she continued. "Are you feeling all right, Mr Bradford?" she asked.

"Yes, I'm fine."

"Is there anything I can do?"

"Stop worrying about me and go to lunch," he said, attempting a smile; it was not successful.

"See you later then."

If she only knew, he thought.

His telephone rang. It was lobby security; the unmarked delivery from New York had arrived. "Sign for it and send it up with a guard, please."

Seven minutes later the tape was inserted into the video recorder and an interior view of the Security Council of the United Nations appeared on the screen. On the bottom of the picture a date was flashed: *Tues. December* 30 2:56 *P.* The occasion was an address by the Saudi Arabian ambassador. A few minutes into the speech there was a pan shot for reaction, first the Israeli delegation, then the Egyptian, followed by the American team. Bradford stopped the tape with the remote control and studied the picture. The four men were in place; the ambassador and his senior aide, Arthur Pierce, in front, two men seated behind. There was no point in listening or watching further for Tuesday the 30th; Bradford resumed the movement, pulling the remote mechanism up in front of him to locate the forward button. He pressed it and a rushing blur appeared on the screen. He released the button; the Saudi was still speaking. He was about to resume the forward motion when a quick-cut shot revealed the American delegation again. Arthur Pierce was not there.

Bradford pressed the reverse several times until he found the action that he was looking for, that he knew would be there. An official from State did not walk out on a friendly speech without at least some explanation. There it was. Pierce was looking at his watch as he rose, leaning first towards the ambassador and whispering, then to the man behind him, presumably the lower-level attaché, who nodded. A female announcer's voice came from the speaker. "We understand that a telephone call has been received by the United States delegation, quite possibly from the Secretary of State, who may care to register his comments on Ibn Kashani's most laudatory speech."

Bradford pressed the forward button again, and again, and once again. The address was over; many delegations rose in an ovation. Arthur Pierce had not returned to his chair.

Thurs. Jan. 1 10:43 A. The welcoming of the New Year by the President of the Security Council. Pierce was not at the American desk. In his place was the man – presumably Franklyn Carpenter – who had been seated behind the ambassador; he was beside him now, a sheaf of papers in his hands.

Fri. Jan. 2 4:10 P. A provocative speech by the P.C.R. delegate, necessitating the use of translation earphones. Pierce was not at the American desk.

Mon. Jan. 5 11:43 A. Arthur Pierce was absent.

Mon. Jan. 5 2:16 P. Arthur Pierce was absent.

Mon. Jan. 5 4:45 P. Arthur Pierce was in his chair, shaking his head in response to comments by the ambassador from Yemen.

Bradford turned off the video tape and looked at the manila envelope containing photographs of the New Year's Eve receptions. He did not really need them; he knew the Undersecretary of the American delegation would appear in none.

He had been at the Costa Brava.

There was a final check, and with computer scanners it would take less than a minute. Bradford reached for his phone; he asked for transport backlog information, made his request and waited, rubbing his eyes, aware that a tremble had developed in his breathing. Forty-seven seconds later the reply came: "On Tuesday, 30 December there were five flights out of New York to Madrid. Ten o'clock, twelve, one-fifteen, two-thirty and five-ten. On Monday, 4 January, Spanish time, there were four flights from Barcelona routed through Madrid, starting at seven-thirty, A.M., arrival Kennedy Airport, E.S.T., twelve-twenty-one; nine-fifteen, A.M., arrival Kennedy, E.S.T., three o'clock . . ."

"Thank you," said Bradford, interrupting. "I have what I need."

He did. Pierce had taken the 5:10 Tuesday flight to Madrid and had returned on the 9:15 Monday flight from Barcelona, permitting him to appear at the United Nations by 4:45, Eastern Standard Time. Somewhere in the passenger manifests there would be a single traveller whose name on a passport would in no way correspond to that of the Undersecretary of the delegation.

Bradford pivoted in his chair, breathing deeply, staring out of the large window at the tree-lined streets of Washington below. It was time to go out into one of those streets and find another telephone. Havelock had to know. He got up and walked around his desk towards his jacket and overcoat, both draped carelessly over a straight-backed chair against the wall.

The door opened without a knock, and the Undersecretary of State froze, his every muscle paralysed. Standing there, closing the door and leaning against the frame, was another Undersecretary of State, a shock of white streaking through his dark hair. It was Pierce. He stood erect, his eyes level, cold, somehow weary, his voice flat as he said, "You look exhausted, Emory. You're also inexperienced. Exhaustion and inexperience are a bad combination; together they cause lapses. When you ask questions of subordinates, you should remember to demand confidentiality. That young man, the one who took Carpenter's place, was really quite excited this morning."

"You killed Carpenter," whispered Bradford, finding a part of his voice. "He didn't resign, you killed him."

"He was in great emotional pain."

"Oh, *Christ* . . . His wife and children, you did that, too!"

"You have to plan, create circumstances, foster need . . . dependence. You can accept that, can't you? Good Lord, in the old days you never gave it a thought. And how many did *you* kill? Before your celebrated conversion, that is. I was out there, Emory. I saw what you did."

"But you *were* there . . ."

"Hating every minute of it. Sickened by the waste, the body counts – on both sides – and the lies. Always the lies, from Saigon and Washington. It was the slaughter of children, yours and theirs."

"Why *you*? There's nothing anywhere to *explain*! Why *you*?"

"Because it's what I was meant to do. We're on different sides, Emory, and I believe in mine far more than you believe in yours. That's understandable; you've seen what it's like here, and you can't do anything about it. I can and I will. There's a better way for this world than yours. We'll bring it about."

"*How?* By blowing it *up*? By plunging us all into a nuclear war that was never meant to *be*?!"

Pierce stood motionless, his eyes boring into Bradford's. "It's true then," he said quietly. "They did it."

"You didn't *know* . . . Oh, my *God*!"

"Don't blame yourself, we were close. We were told – I was told – that he was going mad, that he was creating a strategy so intolerable the world would be revolted, the United States would never be trusted again. When it was completed, and the documents were in our hands we would have the ammunition to dictate or destroy, the option would be ours, in either case your system would be finished, wiped from the face of the earth you've raped."

"You're so *wrong* . . . so misguided." Bradford's voice was a whisper. "Great mistakes, yes! Massive errors of judgement, *yes!* . . . But we face them. In the end we always face them!"

"Only when you're caught. Because you haven't the courage to fail, and without that you can't win."

"You think suppression's the answer? You think because you silence people they won't be heard?"

"Not where it matters; that's the practical answer. You've never understood us, anyway. You read our books but you don't grasp their meaning; you even choose to overlook specific points. Marx said it, Lenin reconfirmed it, but you didn't listen. Our system is in constant transition, phases to be passed through until change isn't needed any longer. One day our freedom will be complete, not like yours. Not hollow."

"You're spoonfed! No change? People have to change. Every day! According to the weather, to birth, to death . . . to needs! You can't turn them into automatons; they won't stand for it! That's what you can't understand. You're the ones who are afraid of failure. You won't let anybody argue with you!"

"Not those who would undo more than sixty years of hope, of progress. Our great scientists, the doctors, the engineers . . . the vast majority of their parents weren't able to read."

"So you taught the children and banned the books."

"I thought you were better than that." Pierce took several steps forward away from the door. "You can't find him, can you? He delivered his nuclear blueprints, then went underground. You don't know who he's shown them to, or sold them to. You're in panic."

"You can't find him either. You lost him."

"But we know who he is. We've studied his habits, his needs, his talents. Like all men with outstanding minds, he's complicated but predictable. We'll find him. We know what to look for; you don't."

"He defected from you, didn't he?"

"A temporary condition. His quarrel was with the bureaucracy, with unimaginative superiors, not the objectives of the state. When he came to me, I could have taken him, but I chose not to; he offered me too high a price. You see, he believes in us not you – certainly not you, *never* you. His father was a tenant serf on the lands of Prince Voroshin. He was hanged by that grand nobleman for stealing a wild pig in winter to feed his family. He won't turn on us."

"Who's 'us'? Moscow doesn't acknowledge you, we've learned that much through Costa Brava. The KGB had nothing to do with Costa Brava; it was never sanctioned."

"Not by anyone you deal with. They're old and tired; they accommodate. They've lost sight of our promise, our destiny, if you like. We haven't." Pierce looked at the television set and the video recorder beneath it; then at the box on Bradford's desk. "A network film library – or is it archives? Images recorded so they can be studied to settle disputes or investigate death. Very good, Emory." The mole glanced up. "Or we could add a third *d*. Disappearance. Yes, those would tell you; that feeble excuse for a diplomat we call an ambassador certainly couldn't. He'd check his records, find that I'd given him the best arguments for those sessions and swear I was there. It might amuse you to know that I frequently talk with my true associates in the lounge and tell them to go easy on him, let him win a few. He was heaven-sent for me."

"It doesn't amuse me."

Pierce approached Bradford, standing directly in front of him. "Havlicek's come back, hasn't he?"

"Who?"

"We prefer his real name. Mikhail Havlicek, son of Vaclav, an enemy of the state and named for a grandfather from Rovno, across the Carpathians. Mikhail is a Russian name, you know. Not Czech. On the other hand, you probably *don't* know that; you put such little emphasis on heritage. Under different circumstances, he might be standing where I am at this moment. He's a talented man; I'm sorry he was so misguided. He's here, isn't he?"

"I don't know what you're talking about."

"Oh, come on, Emory. That outrageous newspaper story, that very opaque whitewash done so very badly by State in response to the killing on Morningside Heights. That old Jew knew something, didn't he? And the pathological Havlicek shot his head off finding out what it was. Then you covered for him because he'd found *you* out, and no doubt found the girl as well. You need him now; he could blow you apart. You made your accommodation with him. You told him the truth, you had to. It all goes back to the Costa Brava doesn't it?"

"*You* go back to the Costa Brava!"

"Certainly. We were on our way to the total compromise of one of the most powerful men in the Western world. We wanted to make sure it was done right. You didn't have the stomachs for it. We did."

"But you didn't know why. You still don't!"

"It never mattered, can't you see that? He was going insane. You, with your extraordinary expectations, were driving him insane; he was a gifted man doing the work of twenty. The Georgian syndrome, Emory. Stalin was a babbling idiot when he was killed. All we had to do with Matthias was fuel his fantasies, gratify his every whim, grievance and suspicion . . . encourage his madness. Because that madness compromised this country into its own madness."

"There's no compromise now. Only annihilation. Extinction."

Pierce nodded his head slowly. "There's the risk, of course, but one can't be afraid to fail."

"Now *you're* the one who's insane!"

"Not at all. The extinction would be yours, the annihilation yours. That court of world opinion you whiningly appeal to so frequently would see to it. And right now all that matters is that we find the man who single handedly ushered Anton Matthias into his disintegration, those documents given to us. Don't worry about Havlicek; you were going to put him 'beyond-salvage', we weren't."

"You did. *You* did!"

"At the time it was right. It isn't now. Now he'll help us. I wasn't joking before; he's one of the most talented men you've ever fielded, a very accomplished hunter. With his expertise and what we know, we'll find the man who'll bring this government to its knees."

"I've told people who you are!" whispered Bradford. "What you are!"

"I'd have been followed at the airport – especially the airport – and I wasn't. You didn't tell anyone because you didn't know until a few minutes ago. I'm far too important a figure for such speculations from a man like you. You've made too many mistakes; you can't afford any more. This city doesn't like you, Mr Undersecretary."

"Havelock will kill you on sight."

"I'm sure he would if he could see us, but that's his problem, isn't it. We *know* Havlicek; he doesn't know us; he doesn't know me. That puts him at quite a disadvantage. We'll just watch him; it's all we have to do."

718

"You'll never find him!" Bradford lurched to his left, instantly blocked by Pierce, who shoved him against the wall.

"Don't, Emory. You're tired and very weak. Before you could raise your voice you'd be dead. As for finding him, how many safe houses are there? Steriles one to seventeen? And who wouldn't tell a man like me – a man involved with numerous diplomatic 'defections' – which ones are available? I've brought in several enviable catches – or presumed catches." Pierce took several steps, once again standing in front of Bradford. "Now, don't die. Tell me. Where is this catastrophic document? I assume it's a photostat. The original is held over your head, a nuclear sword on a very thin thread."

"Where you could never find it."

"I believe you," said the traveller. "But you could."

"There's no way . . . could or would."

"Unfortunately, I believe that, too."

There was a brief snapping sound as Pierce suddenly thrust out his right hand, gripping Bradford's bare arm, pressing his palm into the flesh. With his left, the mole simultaneously reached up and clamped his fingers over Bradford's mouth, twisting the Undersecretary's body, arching him to the side. In seconds, Bradford's eyes widened, then closed as the choking sounds from his throat were muted. He collapsed to the floor, as Pierce withdrew the palmed needle. The mole raced behind the desk and picked up the tape container; beneath it was a note on headed stationery. He reached for the telephone, pressed the outside-line button and dialled.

"Federal Bureau of Investigation, New York Office," a voice answered.

"Internal Security, please. Field Agent Abrams."

"Abrams," said a male voice seconds later.

"Your travels went well, I hope."

"A smooth flight," was the reply. "Go ahead."

"There's a network executive," continued Pierce, reading the note, "an R. B. Denning at the Trans American News Division. He supplied library footage to the wrong man at State, an unbalanced man named Bradford whose motives were offensive to the interests of the United States government. The tapes were destroyed by Bradford in a rage, but for the good of Trans Am's news department – the entire company as well, of course – Denning's officially advised to say nothing. The Department of State feels its mandatory to contain the embarrassment, et cetera, et cetera. This is a very green light."

"I'll reach him right away even if he's into his second martini."

"You could add that State might be reluctant to deal with Trans Am in the future, insofar as they delivered company materials without checking the source of the request through proper channels. However, if everyone co-operates for the good of the country."

"The picture will be clear," interrupted the *paminyatchik* from New York. "I'll get on to it."

Pierce hung up, walked to the television set and carefully moved it back against the wall. He would have the video-recorder taken away, sent to another office. There would be no hint of the news reel tapes or any way to trace them.

There was no prolonged, agonized scream, no cry of protest against offending gods or mortals – only the sound of shattering of glass in the huge window as a body plummeted downward from the seventh floor of the State Department.

It was said by those who had seen him that morning that it was the way he had to go – in a moment of frenzy, of total despair, wanting it over with, not wanting to think any longer. The pressures had become overpowering; he had never really recovered from those soul-searching days of the late 'sixties, everyone knew that. He was a man whose time had come and gone, and he had never reasoned out the role he had played in its arrival and departure. Substance had eluded him; at the end he was a voice in the shadows, a voice disturbing to many, but dismissed by many others because he couldn't *do* anything.

The press printed it all in the evening editions, the obituaries ranging from kind to cool, depending on their editorial stripe. But it should be noted that none were very long; no one really cared. Inconsistency was not compatible with that most desirable of political sins: type-casting. To change was to be weak. We want Jesus or the strong-jawed cowboy. Who the hell can be both?

Undersecretary of State Emory Bradford, committed hawk turned passionate dove, was dead. By his own hand, of course.

And there was no odd piece of equipment such as a video recorder in the stand beneath the television set. It had been delivered to the wrong office, a G-12 on the third floor confirming his original request. The set was pushed back against the wall. Apparently unused.

30

"You couldn't have prevented it," said Jenna firmly, standing in front of Havelock at the desk. "You're not permitted to go to the State Department and it's a condition you accept. If the mole saw you he'd either kill you quietly and remain where he was, or bolt and run to Moscow. You want him, and your being seen isn't the way to find him."

"Maybe I couldn't have prevented it but I might have let his death – his life – mean more than it did. He wanted to tell me and I told him not to say any more. He said this phone was as sterile as the house and I wouldn't accept that."

"That's not what you said. You told him *his* phone, *his* office, might not be sterile. From everything you've learned over the years, everything you've seen, you made the logical decision. And I still believe there are *paminyatchiks* in your State Department who would lie for this man, tap an office for him."

"You know, a paranoid named McCarthy said things like that and tore this country apart thirty years ago. Tore it apart with fear and frenzy."

"Perhaps he was one himself. Who could have done it better?"

"It's possible. The *paminyatchik* is the total patriot. He'll call for a loyalty oath every time because he has no compunction about signing one."

"That's what you must look for now, Mikhail. A total patriot, a man with an unblemished record. He will be the mole."

"If I could find out what it was Bradford was waiting for yesterday, I think I'd have both. He said he wouldn't know until 'late morning'. That means he expected something that would tell him where a man wasn't, proof someone on the fifth floor wasn't where he was supposed to be. The security desk said Bradford received a package at 12:25, but no one knows what it was, and naturally it wasn't there later."

"There was no return address or company name?"

"If there was, nobody noticed. It was delivered by messenger."

"Check the firms who provide those services. Certainly someone can recall the colour of the uniform; that would narrow it down."

"She wasn't that kind of messenger. She wore a fur-collared tweed coat and the only thing security remembers is that she was pretty high-toned for delivering packages."

"High-toned?"

"Attractive, well-spoken, direct. I think that covers it."

"Someone's secretary."

"Yes, but whose? What sort of person would Bradford go to, what kind of proof?"

"What was the size of the package?"

"The guard who took it up said it was a large, padded envelope with a bulge in the bottom, and thick throughout. Papers and something else."

"Papers?" said Jenna. "Newspapers? Could he have gone to a newspaper?"

"He might have. Four-month-old clippings that would describe an event or events during that time. Or he could have pulled in data from the CIA; he had friends there: something from the files that pertained to the evidence against you, or perhaps Costa Brava . . . something we've overlooked. Or he could have been checking hospitals, or ski lodges, or home towns, small town neighbourhoods or divorce court dockets – representation *in absentia*, or Caribbean resort reservations – signatures on meal and bar checks, a *maître d'hôtel* or a beach boy who makes his money by remembering. It's all possible because everything I've said pertains to someone in these records." Michael touched the sheaf of pages on the desk, running his thumb along the edge. "And a dozen other possibilities I haven't even thought about." Havelock leaned back in the chair, folding his hands under his chin. "Our man's good, Jenna. He'll cover himself with a layer of invisible paint."

"Then go on to something else."

"I am. A doctor in Maryland. Talbot County's most revered physician."

"Mikhail?"

"Yes?"

"Before . . . you were reading the reports of your own therapy at the clinic. After the Costa Brava."

"How did you know?"

"Every now and then you'd close your eyes. Those pages weren't easy for you."

"They weren't easy."

"Did they tell you anything?"

"No. Other than describing your execution and my reactions to it, nothing."

"May I see them."

"I wish to Christ I could think of a reason to stop you. I can't."

"Your not wanting me to is reason enough."

"No, it's not. You were the one being killed; you have to know." He opened the drawer on his right, reached in and pulled out a thick, black-bordered manila envelope. He gave it to her, their eyes briefly locking. "I'm not proud of it," he said. "And I'll have to live with it for the rest of my life. I know what that means now."

"We'll help each other . . . for the rest of both our lives. I believed them too."

She carried the envelope to the couch, sat down and opened it removing the file folders inside. They were in sequence; she picked up the first and leaned slowly back, looking at the object in her hands as though it were some horrible yet holy thing. She opened the cover and began reading.

Havelock could not move, could not concentrate. He sat rigid in the chair, the papers in front of him blurred, dark lines without meaning. While Jenna read, he relived that terrible night; images flashed across his inner vision and exploded inside his head. Just as he had watched her die, she was now witnessing the naked thoughts of a mind in chemical therapy – *his* mind, his deepest emotions – and was watching him die also.

The phrases – the screams – came back to him; she was hearing them too. She had to be, for it was she who now closed her eyes and held her breath, a tremor developing in her hands as she went on . . . and on. She finished the third folder and he could feel her staring at him. It was a look he could not return. The screams were pounding in his ears, thunderbolts of intolerable violence unforgivable errors. Betrayal.

Go quickly! Die quickly! Leave me quickly! You were never mine. You were a lie and I loved a lie but you were never part of me! . . . How can you be what you are, yet so much that you are not? Why did you do this to us? To me? You were the only thing I had and now you're my personal hell . . . Die now, go now! . . . No! For God's sake, let me die with you! I want to die . . . but I won't die for you! . . . Only for myself, against myself! Never for you. You gave yourself to me but you gave me a whore and I took a whore! . . . and I believed in the whore. A rotten slut of a whore! Oh, Christ, she's hit! She's hit again. Go to her! For God's sake, go to her! Hold her! . . . No, never to her! It's over! It's all over and it's history and I won't listen to the lies any longer. Oh, Jesus, she's crawling, crawling in the sand like a cut up, bleeding animal. She's alive! Go to her! Hold her! Lessen the final pain – with a bullet if you have to! No! . . . She's gone. There's no movement now, only blood on her hands and streaked through her hair. She's dead and a part of me is dead, too. Still, it's got to be history, as the early days are history . . . Oh, my God, they're dragging her away, dragging the lanced, dead animal away. Who? Who are they? Have I seen . . . photographs, files . . . It doesn't matter. Do they know what they've done? Did she? Killer, slut, whore! . . . My once, my only love. It's history now, it has to be history. A killer is gone . . . love gone. A fool survives.

She had finished. She placed the last file on the coffee table in front of her and turned to him; she was crying, silently. "So much love and so much hatred. Hatred and self-hatred. I wasn't forced to go through what you did; perhaps it was easier, if more bewildering, to be the victim. But when the bewilderment was replaced by anger, I *felt* the way you did. Hating you so very much, yet loathing myself for the hatred, never forgetting the love that I knew – I *knew* – had been there. It couldn't have been false, not so much, not all of it. The anger took over at the border and later at the airfield in Col des Moulinets when I thought you had come to finally kill me. Kill me with the violence you had shown that woman on the pier at Civitavecchia. I saw your face through the window of the plane and – if there's a God may He forgive me – you were my enemy. My love was my enemy."

"I remember," said Michael. "I saw your eyes and I remember the cold, immaculate hatred. I tried to shout, tried to tell you, but you couldn't hear me; I couldn't hear myself through the sound of the engines. But your eyes were weapons that night, more frightening than any I'd ever faced. I wouldn't have the courage to see them again, but I suppose in a way I always will."

"Only in your memory, Mikhail."

The telephone rang; Havelock let it ring again. He could not take his gaze off Jenna. Then he picked it up.

"Yes?"

"Havelock?"

"Mr President."

"Did you get the information on Emory?" asked Berquist, the Minnesotan's voice laced with sadness and exhaustion, yet forcing an illusion of strength.

"Nowhere near what I need."

"What you need is a liaison. I'll pick someone here at the White House, someone with authority and a man I can trust. I'll have to bring him on board, but that can't be helped. Bradford's gone and you do need a funnel."

"Not yet, sir. And not anyone at the White House."

There was a pause from Washington. "Because of what Rostov told you in Athens?"

"Possibly. The percentages are minor but I'd rather not test them. Not now."

"You *believed* him?"

"With all due respect, Mr President, he was the only one who told me the truth. From the beginning."

"Why would he tell you a truth like that?"

"I'm not sure. On the other hand, why did he send Cons Op that cable? In both instances the information was sufficiently startling to force us all to pay attention. That's the first step in sending a signal."

"Addison Brooks said very much the same thing."

"He was talking diplomatically, and he was right. The *Voennaya* doesn't speak for Moscow."

"I understand. Bradford – " Berquist paused, as if he suddenly remembered he was referring to a dead man. "Bradford explained it to me last night. So you really believe there's a Soviet agent operating inside the White House?"

"As I said, I'm not sure. But there may be – or more than likely, may have been. I don't think Rostov would have brought it up unless he could have substantiated the reality, present or past. He was probing, looking for responses. The truth provokes the most genuine answers in this business; he learned that when he brought up Costa Brava. In this case, I don't want to take the risk."

"All right, but then, how can you function? You can't be seen walking around questioning people."

"No, but I can question them without being seen. I can use the phone if it's set up properly. I know what I want to ask and I'll know what to listen for. From these conversations I'll refine whom I want to see and set up contacts . . . I'm experienced in this, Mr President."

"I don't have to take your word for it. How is it set up . . . properly?"

"Give me a name, and call me an assistant counsel to the President, or something like that. It's not unusual for the Oval Office to make its own discreet inquiries into certain matters, is it?"

"Hell, no, I've got a staff for that, and it's not necessarily discreet. Hundreds of reports are sent to the White House every week. They have to be checked out, experts questioned, figures substantiated. Without it all, responsible decisions can't be made. In Lincoln's time he had two young men and they took care of everything including the drafting of letters. Now we have scores of aides and assistants to aides and secretaries to assistants and they can't handle half the volume. The answer is yes."

"What happens if someone is called by an aide or an assistant aide and that someone doubts the authority of the person questioning him."

"It happens a lot, especially at the Pentagon; there's a simple solution. He's told to call the White House switchboard and ask to be connected to the aide's or the assistant's office. It works."

"It *will* work," said Michael. "Along with the lines already on this phone can you add another one, listing me in the White House index, the extension routed here?"

"Havelock, one of the more exotic pleasures in being President, or close to a President, is the trunk full of electronic gimmickry available on short notice. You'll be indexed and patched into the switchboard within the hour. What name do you want to use?"

"You'll have to choose one, sir. I might duplicate someone already there."

"I'll call you back."

"Mr President, before you hang up."

"What is it?"

"I'll need another one of those things that may not be in your lexicon. A context back-up."

"It sure as hell isn't. What is it?"

"In the event someone calls the White House index and wants to know exactly what I do, there should be someone else there who can tell him."

Again there was the pause from Washington. "You were right down on Poole's Island," said Berquist pensively.

"The words say exactly what they mean, don't they? You need someone to back you up in the context of what you're presuming to do, or be."

"That's right, sir."

"Call you back."

"May I suggest something?" said Michael quickly.

"What?"

"Within the next few days – if we have a few days someone is going to come up to that someone else in the White House and ask where my office is. When he or she does, hold him – or her – because whoever it is will bring us a step closer."

"If that happens," said Berquist angrily, "whoever-it-is may be strangled by a Minnesota farm boy before you get a chance to talk to him. Or her."

"I'm sure you don't mean that, Mr President."

"I'm not going to throw a nuclear warhead on Leningrad either. Call you back."

Havelock replaced the phone and looked over at Jenna. "We can begin narrowing down the names. We'll start calling in an hour."

"Your name is Cross. Robert Cross. Your title is special assistant to the President, and all inquiries as to your status and functions are to be directed to Mrs Howell, she's counsel to White House internal affairs. She's been told what to do."

"What about my office?"

"You've got one."

"What?"

"You've even got an assistant. In the security area of the east office block. You need a key to get in the main corridor over there, and your man is instructed to take into custody anyone who comes around looking for Mr Cross. He's a member of the secret service detail and if anyone does show up asking for you he'll alert you and bring that person down to Fairfax under guard. I assumed that's what you wanted."

"It is. What about the other offices in that area? Will the people in them be curious?"

"Unlikely. By and large those assignments are temporary, everyone working on his own quiet project. Curiosity's discouraged. And if it surfaces, you've got your man in place."

"It sounds tight."

"I think so. Where are you going to start? . . . Emory showed me the list of the items you wanted and assured me you'd have it all in the morning. Did you get everything?"

"Everything. Bradford's secretary is first, then the doctor in Maryland. MacKenzie's death."

"We were extremely thorough with him," said Berquist. "Under the circumstances we were able to bring in the Central Intelligence Agency and those people were aggressive. What are you looking for?"

"I'm not sure. Someone who's not around any more, perhaps. A puppet."

"I won't try to follow that."

"I may need your direct intervention in one area, however. You said before that the Pentagon frequently balks at being questioned by White House personnel."

"It goes with the uniforms; they're not worn over here. I expect you're referring to the Nuclear Contingency Committees. I saw them on your list."

"I am."

"They're touchy. Rightly so, I'd say."

"I have to talk to every member of those three teams; that's fifteen senior officers. Can you get word to the chairman that you expect them all to co-operate with Mr Cross? Not in the area of maximum restricted information, but in terms of . . . progress evaluation."

"One of those phrases again."

"It says it Mr President. It would help if you could work Matthias in."

"All right," said Berquist, slowly. "I'll lay it on the great man. It's not in character, but he can hardly deny it. I'll have my military aide convey the word: the Secretary of State wants those committees to provide an in-depth progress report for the Oval Office. A simple memorandum ordering co-operation within the limits of maximum classification should do it . . . They'll say there's a cross-over, of course. You can't have one without violating the other."

"Then tell them to err on the side of classification. The final report's for your eyes only anyway."

"Anything else?"

"The psychiatric file on Matthias. Bradford was to have got it for me."

"I'm going to Camp David tomorrow. I'll take a detour by Poole's Island and bring it back with me."

"One thing more. This Mrs Howell; apart from calling in the secret service if anyone approaches her about me, what has she been told to say? About me, my functions?"

"Only that you're on a special assignment for the President."

"Can you change it?"

"To what?"

"Routine assignment. Researching old agendas so that White House files can be completed on various matters."

"We have people doing that. It's basically political – how is this position defended, or why did that senator buck us and how do we stop him from doing it again?"

"Put me in with the crowd."

"You're in it. Good luck . . . but then you'll need a great deal more than luck. This world needs more than luck. Sometimes I think we need a miracle to last another week . . . Keep me informed; my orders are that whenever Mr Cross calls, I'm to be interrupted."

Bradford's secretary, one Elizabeth Andrews, was at home, the sensational death of her superior having had its emotional impact. A number of newspaper people had telephoned her and she had relayed the events of the morning calmly, sadly, but clearly, until a gossip-oriented reporter, noting Bradford's marital track record, hinted at a sexual entanglement.

"You sick bitch," Elizabeth had said, slamming down the phone.

Havelock's call came twenty minutes later and Elizabeth Andrews was not eager to recount the tale again. He suggested she call him back at the White House when she felt better; the ploy worked. The phone in the study in Fairfax rang six minutes after Michael had hung up.

"I'm sorry, Mr Cross. It's been a very trying time and some very trying reporters."

"I'll be as brief as possible."

She described the morning, beginning with Bradford's sudden and unexpected emergence from his office shortly after she had arrived.

"He looked dreadful. He'd obviously been up all night and was exhausted, but there was something else. A kind of manic energy; he was excited about something. I've seen him like that lots of times, of course, but somehow yesterday it was different. He spoke louder than he usually did."

"That could have been the exhaustion," said Havelock. "It often works that way. A person compensates because he feels weak."

"Perhaps, but I don't think so, not with him, not yesterday morning. I know it sounds ghastly, but I think he'd made up his mind . . . that's a horrible thing to say, but I believe it. It was as though he were exhilarated, actually looking forward to the moment when it was going to happen. It's ghoulish, but he left the office shortly before ten, said he was going out for a few minutes, and I have this terrible picture of him out on the street, looking up at the window . . . and thinking to himself, Yes, this is it."

"Could there be another explanation? Could he have been going to see someone?"

"No, I don't think so. I asked him if he'd be in another office in case a call came for him and he said no, he was going out for some air."

"He never mentioned why he'd been there all night?"

"Only that he'd been working on a project that he'd fallen behind on. He'd been doing a fair amount of travelling recently – "

"Did you set up the transportation arrangements for him?" interrupted Havelock.

"No, he usually did that himself. As you probably know, he often . . . took someone with him. He was divorced, several times actually. He was a very private person, Mr Cross. And so very unhappy."

"Why do you say that?"

Ms Andrews paused, then spoke firmly. "Emory Bradford was a brilliant man, and they didn't pay attention to him. He was once very influential in this city until he told the truth – as he saw the truth – and as soon as the applause died down, they all ran away from him."

"You've been with him a long time."

"A long time. I saw it all happen."

"Could you give me examples of this running away from him?"

"Sure. To begin with he was consistently overlooked when his experience, his expertise could have been of value. Then he'd frequently write position papers, correcting powerful men and women – senators, congressmen, secretaries of this and that – who had made stupid mistakes in interviews and press conferences; but if one out of ten ever responded or thanked him, I never knew about it, and I would have. He'd monitor the early morning television programmes, where the worst gaffs are made – just as he was doing yesterday, right up to the end – and dictate what he called clarifications. They were always gentle, even kind, never offensive, and sure enough 'clarifications' were usually issued, but never any thanks."

"He was watching television yesterday morning?"

"For a while . . . before it happened. At least the set was rolled out to the front of his desk. He moved it back . . . before it happened. Right up until the end he couldn't break the habit. He wanted people to be better than they were; he wanted the government to be better."

"Were there any notes on his desk that could have told you whom he was watching?"

"No, nothing. It was like his final gesture, leaving this world tidier than he'd found it. I've never seen his desk so neat, so clean."

"I'm sure you didn't."

"I beg your pardon?"

"Nothing. I was agreeing with you . . . I know you were at lunch, but were there any people in the vicinity of his office door who might have seen someone go in or out?"

"The police covered that, Mr Cross. There are always people milling around; we all have different lunch breaks depending on what's happening in what time zone, but no one saw anything unusual. Actually, our section was pretty much cleared out. We had a secretarial pool meeting at one-thirty, so most of us – "

"Who called that meeting, Miss Andrews?"

"This month's chairman; then, of course, he said he didn't, so we sat around drinking coffee."

"Didn't you get a memo about the meeting?"

"No, the word was just passed around this morning. It frequently is; that's standard."

"Thank you very much. You've been most helpful."

"It's all such a waste, Mr Cross. Such a goddamned terrible waste."

"I know. Goodbye." Havelock hung up and spoke, his eyes still on the phone. "Our man *is* good," he said. "Invisible paint."

"She couldn't tell you anything?"

"Yes, she did. Bradford listened to me. He went outside to a phone and called for whatever it was he wanted. The number we need won't be found charged to his office; it's among a couple of million lost in the underground trunk lines."

"Nothing else?"

"Maybe something." Michael looked over at Jenna, a frown on his face, his eyes clouded. "See if you can find a copy of yesterday's paper around here, will you? I want to know the name of every senior official at State who was interviewed on the morning television programmes. It's crazy. The last thing on Bradford's mind was television."

Jenna found the newspaper. No one from the Department of State had been on television that morning.

31

If Talbot County, Maryland, had an esteemed physician in Dr Matthew Randolph, it also had an extremely unpleasant man. Born to Eastern Shore money, raised in the tradition of privilege which included the finest schools and clubs, and possessing what amounted to unlimited funds, he nevertheless abused everyone and everything within these rarefied circles in the pursuit of medicine.

When he was thirty, having graduated *magna cum laude* from Johns Hopkins and completed pathological and surgical residencies at Massachusetts General and New York, he decided he could not function at his talented best within the stultifying, politicized confines of a normal hospital. The answer for him was simple: he bullied and extorted monies from the legions of the Chesapeake privileged, threw in an initial two million dollars himself and opened his own fifty-bed medical centre.

It was run his way, which amounted to a none too benevolent dictatorship. There was no exclusivity with regard to admission but there was a rule-of-thumb policy: the rich were soaked outrageously for services rendered, and the poor given financial consideration only after having endured the ignominy of disclosing overwhelming proof of poverty and listening to a lecture on the sins of indolence. Rich and poor alike, however, continued in growing numbers to put up with these insults for, over the years, the Randolph Medical Center had established a reputation that was second to none. Its laboratory equipment was the finest money could buy; its generously paid staff physicians were the brightest graduates from the best schools and toughest residencies; the visiting surgical and pathological specialists were flown in from all over the globe, and the talents of the overpaid technicians and nursing corps far in excess of normal hospital standards. In essence, treatment at Randolph was both medically superb and personally gratifying. The only way it might be improved upon, some said, was to remove the abrasive personality of the now sixty-eight-year-old Matthew Randolph. However, others pointed out that one way to cripple a smoothly running craft in rough waters was to tear out the throttle because the engine pitch was grating to the ears. And in Randolph's case, short of his own death – which seemed unlikely for several centuries – physically tearing him out was the only way to remove him.

Besides, who else could look down at a nephew of Emile du Pont just before an operation and ask: "how much is your life worth to you?"

In the du Pont case, it was a million-dollar-plus tie-in computer with four of the nation's leading research centres.

Havelock learned these details from CIA files as he researched the death of a black operations officer named Steven MacKenzie, the "engineer" of Costa Brava. In Cagnes sur Mer, Henri Salanne had by implication questioned the veracity of the doctor who signed MacKenzie's death certificate. In his own mind Michael had gone further; he had considered altered laboratory reports, autopsy findings not consistent with the state of the corpse and, after the President had mentioned X-rays, the obvious switching of photographic plates. However, in the light of the information on Randolph and his Medical Center, it was difficult to credit these possibilities. Everything connected to and with the official cause of death was processed under Randolph's personal on-site attendance and his own laboratories. The abrasive doctor might well be dictatorial, certainly petulant, most definitely opinionated and unpleasant, but if ever there was a person who deserved to be called a man of integrity it was Matthew Randolph. The same was true of his Medical Center. All things considered – *all* things – there was no reason on earth for either to be otherwise.

And for Havelock, that was the flaw. It was simply too symmetrical. Pieces rarely, if ever, fell in place – even negatively – so precisely. There were always caves to explore that might lead to hidden pools – whether they did or not was irrelevant, the caves were *there*. Here, there were none.

The first indication Michael had that there might be substance to his doubts was the fact that Matthew Randolph did not return his first call. In every other instance, including calls to eight senior officers of the Pentagon's Nuclear Contingency Committees, Bradford's secretary, CIA and NSC personnel, the phone in Fairfax had rung minutes after he had placed the contact call. One did not dismiss lightly a request to reach a presidential aide at the White House.

Dr Matthew Randolph apparently felt no such compulsion. And so Havelock had phoned a second time only to be told: "The doctor is extremely busy today. He said to say he'll get back to you, Mr Cross, when he has the free time."

"Did you explain that I'm to be reached at the White House?"

"Yes, sir." The secretary had paused, embarrassment in her brief silence. "He said to tell you the Center's painted white, too," she added in a very soft voice. "*He* said that, Mr Cross, *I* didn't."

"Then tell Genghis Khan from me that I'll either hear from him within the hour or he may find the sheriff of Talbot County escorting him to the DC-Maryland border, where a White House detail will pick him up and bring him down here."

Matthew Randolph returned the call, in fifty-eight minutes.

"Who the *hell* do you think you are, Cross?"

"An extremely overworked nonentity, Dr Randolph."

"You threatened me! I don't like threats, whether they come from the White House or a blue house or an outhouse! I trust you get my meaning."

"I'll convey your feelings to the President."

"Do that. He's not the worst, but I could think of better."

"You might even get along."

"I doubt it. Sincere politicians bore me. Sincerity and politics are diametrically opposed. What do you want? If it's any kind of endorsement, you can start with a healthy government research grant."

"I have an idea President Berquist might entertain that idea only if you openly opposed him."

Randolph paused. "Not bad," he said. "What do you want? We're busy here."

"I want to ask you several questions about a man – a dead man – named Steven MacKenzie."

Again the doctor paused, but it was a different silence. And when he resumed speaking, it was in a different tone. Previously his hostility was genuine; now it was forced.

"Damn it, how many times do we have to go over that? MacKenzie died of stroke – a massive aortal haemorrhage to be precise. I turned over the pathology report and conferred with your spook doctors till hell froze over. They've got it all."

"*Spook* doctors?"

"They sure as hell weren't from Mary-General or Baltimore's Mother of Mercy, I can tell you. Nor did they claim to be." Randolph paused again; Michael did not fill the moment. He was listening with a trained ear, silences and audible breathing being a part of the abstract tonal picture he was trying to define. The doctor continued, his phrases too rushed, the edge of his voice too sharp; his previous confidence was waning, replaced by volume alone. "You want any information on MacKenzie, you get it from them. We all concurred; there was never any doubt. Aortal haemorrhage, plain and simple, and I don't have the time to rehash this sort of thing. Do I make myself clear?"

"More than you know, Dr Randolph." It was Havelock's turn to pause. He did so until he could see in his mind's eye a mouth that had dropped open, and hear the aggressive breathing of a man with something to hide. "I'd find the time, if I were you. The file isn't closed here, Doctor, and for reasons of specific external pressures we can't shut it – much as we'd like to. You see, we *want* to conclude it precisely the way you determined, but we have to co-operate with each other. Do *I* make myself clear?"

"The pathology was unequivocal, you all agree with that?"

"We *want* to. Please understand that. Be convinced of it."

"What do you mean 'external pressures'?" The doctor's confidence was returning, the question asked sincerely.

"Let's say in-house intelligence trouble makers. We'd like to shut them up."

Costa Brava was never far away. Even in deceit.

Randolph's final pause was brief. "Come up tomorrow, he said. "Be here at noon."

Havelock sat in the back seat of the nondescript, armour-plated car; three secret service men were his companions. Conversation was at a minimum. The two men in front and the pleasant but quiet agent beside Michael had obviously been ordered to make no direct inquiries.

The Randolph Medical Center was indeed painted white. It was a glistening complex of three buildings connected by enclosed walkways set down in the middle of a generous acreage of lawns, paths and a central winding driveway. They parked in the nearest available space to the entrance labelled Admissions and Administration. Michael got out of the car, walked up the smooth concrete path that led to the glass double doors and went inside; he was expected.

"Dr Randolph's in his office, Mr Cross," said a uniformed nurse behind the marble counter. "Take the first corridor to your right; his is the last door at the end of the hall. I'll tell his secretary you're on your way."

"Thank you."

As he walked down the spotless white corridor towards Randolph's office, Havelock considered the options available to him. How much he told the doctor depended upon how much Randolph already knew about Steven MacKenzie. If what he knew was little, Michael's words would be laced with security – conscious innuendo. If a great deal, there was no harm in corroborating parts of the truth. However, what primarily concerned Havelock was the reason behind the doctor's extraordinary behaviour. The man as much as admitted having twisted or concealed *some* aspect of MacKenzie's death and, regardless of whether he considered it minor or not, it was a dangerous act. Tampering with cause-of-death or withholding pertinent information was a criminal act. What had the physician done and why had he done it? Even to consider Matthew Randolph as part of an intelligence conspiracy was absurd, irrational. What had he done?

A stern-visaged secretary with disciplined angry hair pulled back and lashed into a bun rose from her chair, but her voice contradicted her appearance; it was the same voice that had relayed the doctor's comment about his medical centre being the same colour as the White House. It was obvious that she had thrown up a wall to protect herself from the Randolph hurricane.

"He's very upset today, Mr Cross," she said in that frail, intense tone. "You'll do better getting straight to your business. He hates to waste time."

"So do I," replied Michael, as the woman escorted him to an ornate, panelled door. She rapped twice – not once or three times, but precisely twice, standing motionless with splendid posture as though she were about to refuse a blindfold.

The cause of her stoicism was soon apparent. The door opened, revealing a tall, slender, angular man with a fringe of light grey hair circling a bald head, the eyes behind the steel-rimmed glasses alive and impatient. Dr Matthew Randolph was rich American Gothic, with not a little of Savonarola thrown in, his long graceful hands somehow appropriate for holding a pitchfork, a torch or a scalpel. He looked past his secretary and barked; he did not speak.

"You Cross?"

"Yes."

"You're eight minutes late."

"Your watch is fast."

"Maybe. Come on in." He now looked at his secretary, who had stepped aside. "No interruptions," he instructed.

"Yes, Dr Randolph."

The physician closed the door and nodded at the chair in front of his large, cluttered desk. "Sit down," he said, "but before you do, I want to make sure you don't have one of those recording machines on you."

"You have my word."

"Is it any good?"

"Is yours?"

"You called me. I didn't call you."

Havelock shook his head. "I have no taping device on me for the simple reason that our conversation could be far more harmful to us than to you."

"Maybe," muttered Randolph, going behind the desk as Michael sat down. "Maybe not. We'll see."

"That's a promising beginning."

"Don't get smart ass, young fella'."

"I apologize if I sounded that way. I meant it. We have a problem and you could put it to rest."

"Meaning I didn't before."

"Let's say there are new questions and, frankly, they may be valid. Certainly they could be embarrassing, not only politically, but in terms of morale in certain areas of the intelligence community. Someone might even care to go into print. That's our problem."

"That's what I want to hear." The physician nodded, adjusting his glasses so as to look over the steel rims. "Your problem. Spell it out."

Havelock understood. Randolph wanted an admission of guilt from the White House before he would implicate himself in any conceivable wrong-doing. Therefore, it was reasonable to assume that the more serious Havelock's first admission, the more latitude Randolph would permit himself regarding his own possible duplicity. Thieves in concert and conversation; who could go screaming to a judge?

"Do you know the kind of work MacKenzie was involved in?"

"I've known Mac and his family for over forty years. His parents were close friends of mine and his three children were born right here at the Center. I delivered them myself – probably delivered his wife, Midge, too."

"That doesn't answer my question."

"It should. I've been caring for the MacKenzies most of their lives and that included young Steve, as well as the adult Steve – as far as you permitted him to live as an adult. Actually, to be more accurate, these past years I more or less double-checked whatever the doctors did at Walter Reed; by and large they were damned good. You could hardly tell from the scars that four of them were bullet wounds."

"Then you did know," said Michael, nodding.

"I told him to get out. My God, I told him that over and over again for the last five, six years now. The strain on him was something fierce – worse, I think, for Midge. Him flying all over the world, she never knowing whether he'd come back; not that he ever told her a hell of a lot, he wouldn't do that . . . Yes, Mr Cross, I knew what Steve did – not the specifics or his title or anything like that, but I knew it wasn't your everyday desk job."

"It's strange," mused Havelock, indeed sensing the strangeness. "I never thought of MacKenzie as having a wife and children, coming from a relatively normal background." *He was not a survivor. Why did he do it?*

"Maybe that's why he was so good. You looked at him and saw a pretty average successful executive . . . something like you, in fact. But underneath he had a fever because you bastards poisoned him."

The suddenness of the charge, its harshness, and the fact that it was delivered in a conversational tone was unnerving. "That's quite a statement," said Michael, his eyes roaming over the doctor's face. "Would you care to explain it? To the best of my knowledge, no one held a gun to MacKenzie's head and told him to do whatever it was he was doing."

"You didn't have to, and you're damn right I care to explain it. I figure it's your blueprint for *narcotizing* a man so that he turns away from a normal, productive, reasonably happy life to one where he wakes up in a cold sweat in the middle of the night because he probably hasn't had the luxury of sleeping for the past several weeks. Or, if he does sleep, the first sharp sound sends him lunging for protection. Or a gun."

"You're very dramatic."

"It's what you did."

"How?"

"You fed him a diet of tension, excitement – even frenzy – with fair doses of blood to go with it."

"Now you're melodramatic."

"You know where it started for him?" Randolph went on, as if Havelock had not spoken. "Thirteen, fourteen years ago Mac was one of the best sailors on the Eastern Shore, probably the Atlantic coast and the Caribbean, too. He could sense a new wind and smell the currents. He could look at the stars in a dark sky and helm a craft – engine or sail – all through the night and take you within sight of where he said you'd be by dawn. It was a gift . . . Then came the war in Vietnam and he was a naval officer. Well, it didn't take those brass boys long to spot a good thing. Before you could pronounce one of those unpronounceable places, he was ferrying men and supplies up the coast and the inland waterways. That's where it started. He was the best there was; he could read gook maps and get anybody anywhere."

"I'm not sure I understand."

"Then you're thick. He was taking assassination and sabotage teams behind enemy lines. Fleets of small craft were under his command; he was a secret navy all by himself. Then it happened."

"What?"

"One day he didn't just ferry those people, he became one of them."

"I see."

"I wonder if you do. It's where the fever first touched him. Men who were nothing more than cargo became friends he made plans with, fought beside, who died in front of his eyes. He did that for twenty-eight months until he was wounded and sent home. Midge was waiting for him; they got married and he went back to finish law school. Only, he couldn't stand it. Before a year was up, he left, and began talking with people in Washington. A part of him missed that crazy – Christ, I don't know what you call it."

"It doesn't make any difference," said Havelock quietly. "I know what you mean."

The doctor looked hard at Michael. "Maybe you do. Maybe that's why you're here . . . Like a lot of men, Mac came back from that war a different person; not on the surface, but underneath. There was an anger in him I'd never seen before, a need to compete – angrily – for the highest stakes he could find. He couldn't sit still for twenty minutes at a time much less absorb the finer points of law. He had to keep moving."

"Yes, I know," interrupted Michael involuntarily.

"And you bastards in Washington knew just what to feed him. Get him back into the excitement, the tension. Promise him the best – or worst – competition *you* could find, and make the stakes so high no normal man would consider them. And all the while keep telling him he was the best, the best, the *best*! He thrived on it . . . and at the same time it was tearing him apart."

Havelock brought his hands together, gripping them, moved both to anger and understanding. It was no time, however, to betray either; he wanted information. "What should we . . . bastards in Washington . . . have done then?" he asked calmly.

"That's such a stupid question only one of you sons of bitches would ask it."

"Would you mind answering?"

"Get him medical attention! Psychiatric care!"

"Why didn't you? You were his doctor."

"Damn it, I *tried*! I even tried to *stop* you!"

"I beg your pardon?"

"Somewhere in a number of old files there are letters from me to the Central Intelligence Agency describing—goddamn it, *diagnosing* – a troubled man, a disturbed man. Mac would come home and for a few weeks he'd cover it, driving back and forth to Langley like a regular commuter. Then you could see it happening; he'd go into a kind of depression, wouldn't talk very much and, when he did, he sure as hell wasn't listening. Then he became restless, impatient . . . his mind always somewhere else. You see, he was *waiting*, waiting for his next *fix*!"

"And we gave it to him," said Michael.

"Right on, as the youngsters say! You knew exactly how long he could take it. You were priming him, honing his machine until he'd either blow apart or get back into – whatever the hell you call it."

"The field," said Havelock.

"That's it, the goddamned *field*! Midge would come to me and tell me Mac was going to pieces, couldn't sleep, wouldn't communicate, and I'd write another letter. You know what I'd get back? A 'thank-you-for-your-interest', as though I'd suggested you bastards change your laundry service! Midge and those kids were going through hell, and you people thought your shirts had just the right amount of starch in 'em!"

Michael's eyes strayed to bare white wall behind Randolph. *How many buried letters were there in how many unopened files? How many MacKenzies . . . and Ogilvies . . . and Havelocks? What was the Gunslinger count these days? Men primed, machines honed in the cause of futility. Deadly talents kept in the field because somewhere it was written they could do the job regardless of the mind and body count . . . their own and others. Who profited?*

"I'm sorry," said Havelock. "With your permission, I'll report this conversation where it won't be overlooked."

"So far you've got my permission. Up to now."

"Up to now," agreed Michael.

The physician leaned back in his chair. "I've drawn a picture for you. It's not pretty, but I've got my reasons. Now, you draw one for me and we'll see where we stand."

"All right." Havelock crossed his legs, then spoke, choosing his words cautiously. "As I'm sure you're aware, most intelligence work is dull, pedestrian. It's routine digging for facts, reading newspapers, reports, scientific journals, and gathering information from a wide variety of other sources, the majority of which are reasonable people, perfectly amenable to imparting what they know because they see no reason to conceal it. Then, of course, there are others who are in the business of making a profit by selling the facts they've bought; buy low, sell higher, a time-honoured principle. These people generally deal with a different kind of intelligence officer, one trained to distinguish between fact and fiction; the buy-low, sell-highers can be pretty imaginative." Michael paused, knowing that the timing of his delivery was vital. "Normally," he continued, "the combination of these sources and the sheer volume of – is sufficient for specialists to put together an accurate pattern of facts and events, like fitting the pieces of a puzzle together. That's an abused expression, but it says it." Again Havelock paused. What Randolph wanted – needed – to hear called for a silent introduction. Three seconds were enough. "Finally, there's a last category of potential information. It's the most difficult to obtain because it has to be extorted from sources that know they possess secrets that could cost them their lives if their superiors knew they had revealed them. These require an entirely different sort of intelligence officer, a specialist himself. He's trained to manipulate, to engineer situations in which individuals are convinced they have no choice but to take a specific course of action, in the end revealing secrets – or doing something – they would not previously have considered. Steven MacKenzie was that kind of specialist, and he *was* one of the best; no one had to convince him. But on his last, his final assignment, someone intercepted and altered the situation MacKenzie had created. And in order for that original situation to remain the accepted one, he was marked for take-out."

"What the hell is that, a plate of spaghetti?"

"He was killed."

Randolph shot forward in his chair. "He was *what?*"

"Murdered. We might have prevented it if we'd taken the proper precautions. That's our problem, Doctor, and a growing number of people know it. 'Mac', as you call him, didn't die of a stroke on his boat, he was killed. We're aware of it, but we don't want to acknowledge it . . . Now, you can understand why I don't have any taping device concealed anywhere. The picture I just painted is uglier than yours."

"It sure as hell is – if it were true. But I'm afraid it isn't. We'll stick to the aortal haemorrhage because it works. You bastards couldn't be farther off base. You blew it."

"What does that mean?"

"Steven MacKenzie committed suicide."

32

"That's impossible!" cried Havelock, rising to his feet. "You're *wrong*!"

"Am I? Are you a doctor, too, Mr Cross?"

"I don't have to be. I know men like MacKenzie. *I* am one!"

"I figured as much, and that statement is about on a par with my assessment of the lot of you."

"No, don't mistake me," said Michael quickly, shaking his head emphatically. "It's no adolescent generalization. I'm the first to admit that the thought of packing it in can become a recurrent fixation, obsessive, but not *this* way. Not alone on a boat. That doesn't work!"

"Sorry. The pathology – the evidence – is against you. I wish to almighty God it wasn't, but it is."

Havelock could not help himself; he leaned over Randolph's desk and shouted, "There was evidence against a woman very close to me and that evidence was a lie!"

"I don't know what that's got to do with the price of perfume in Alaska, but it doesn't change anything."

"In this case, it does. There's a connection!"

"You're downright incoherent, young fella'."

"*Please.* Listen to me. I'm not a 'young fella'' and I'm not a raving idiot. Whatever you found you were *meant* to find."

"You don't even know what it was."

"I don't *have* to! Try to understand me, Doctor. A black operations officer like MacKenzie . . ."

"A *what*? Mac was white!"

"Oh, Jesus! An engineer, a manipulator . . . a man in sanction, with the authority to bring about events in which people might be killed, usually *are* killed – because it has to be done. More often than I can tell you, men like this have very painful doubts, enormous feelings of guilt, feelings of . . . goddamn it, *futility*! Certainly, depression sets in, sure they've considered blowing their brains out, but not *this* way! There are other ways that make sense, because if there's one thing ingrained in such men it's function, function, *function*! For Christ's sake; *take* yourself out, but *accomplish* something when you do it! And do it *right*."

"That's sub–kindergarten psychobabble," protested Randolph.

"Call it whatever you like but it's true. It's the first thing, the most *important* thing recruiters look for in a candidate. It's the single overriding factor . . . You said it yourself. You said MacKenzie had to compete – angrily compete – for the highest stakes he could find."

"Ultimately, he did. Himself."

"No, that's waste! That's not even making a statement . . . Look, I'm *not* a doctor, not a psychiatrist, and I probably can't convince you, but I know I'm right, so let it pass. Just tell me what you found, what you did."

"Mac gave himself a needle and let it all drift away. "

"*Never.*"

"Sorry. He was damned smart about it too. He used a steroid compound of digoxin combined with enough alcohol to float an elephant. The alcohol blood-count overshadowed everything else, but the digoxin blew the heart. It's one hell of a combination."

"Then the X-ray was valid?"

Randolph did not reply at first. Instead, he pursed his thin lips and fingered his glasses. Then he spoke. "No."

"You *did* switch the plates."

"Yes."

"Why?"

"To carry out what Mac intended. To make sure."

"Go back."

The doctor leaned forward. "He knew what he'd put Midge and the kids through all these years and it was his way of trying to make up for it, make peace with himself. Midge had had about all she could take; she was finished with pleading. She told him he had to get out of the Agency or get out of the house." Randolph stopped briefly, shaking his head. "Mac knew he couldn't do either so he just decided to get out, period."

"You've skipped something."

"He had a whale of an insurance policy and, considering the work he did work the insurance company didn't know a damned thing about – it was understandable. Those kinds of policies don't pay on suicide. I was going to be damned before Midge and those kids were cheated out of what they deserved . . . That's the story, Mr Cross. You made him what he was and, together, he and I made him better."

Havelock stared at the physician, then turned and sat down in the chair, his eyes still on Randolph. "Even if you were right," he began wearily, "and believe me you weren't then – you're not now – you could have spelled it out for the Agency and they'd have gone along with you; the last thing they want is for this sort of killing to get into print. Instead, you put everyone off, wasted valuable time and the damage you've done is incalculable."

"What in *hell*! Twenty minutes ago you said you *wanted* it my way! Yesterday on the phone you said you wanted to shut up some troublemakers!"

"I lied. Just as you lied. But at least I knew what I was doing; you didn't. If you'd told the truth – if only to one person – every minute of MacKenzie's day would have been examined; something might have turned up, somewhere a connection . . . No one even bothered to go over the boat. Oh, *Christ*!"

"Maybe you didn't *hear* me!" shouted the physician, his eyes wild, his face apoplectic. "Midge MacKenzie had given her last ultimatum! He was between a rock and a hard place. He couldn't, as you put it, *function* any more! He fell apart!"

"That accounted for the alcohol, I don't doubt it."

"And when he was plastered he made his final decision. It's all there!"

"It's not there," said Michael, feeling far older than the elderly doctor in front of him. "I don't expect you to accept this, but the last thing a man like MacKenzie would do is make a decision when he's drunk."

"Hogwash!"

"Let me ask you something. I assume you take a drink now and then, and when you do, you know when you've had a few."

"Certainly."

"Would you ever operate when you knew you were high?"

"Certainly not, but there's no parallel!"

"Yes, there is, Dr Randolph. Because when men like MacKenzie or myself – twenty or thirty more I could mention – are in the field, *we're* surgeons. They even call most of the jobs we do 'operations'. It's hammered into us from our first day of training that every reflex, every observation, every reaction has to be as accurate and as fast and as clear as we can make them. We're primed – our machines are honed."

"You're playing with words – yours *and* mine! Mac wasn't in the field."

"If what you believe is true, he was. The highest stakes. Himself."

"*Goddamn* it, you're twisting everything I said!"

"No, I'm not. Because a lot of what you said was as perceptive as I've ever heard it expressed. I respect it . . . Don't you *understand*? MacKenzie wouldn't have killed himself this way because – everything else aside – the digoxin might not have *worked*! And that he *couldn't* accept. It was too much a part of him, had been for far too many years. If it was going to be his final decision, the one thing he couldn't afford was a mistake! Can't you *see* that?"

It was as though Matthew Randolph had been struck. His eyes were wide and fixed, the muscles of his face taut, his mouth rigid. When he spoke, it was a whisper. "God *almighty* . . ." he said, his voice drifting off into silence. Then softly, unexpectedly, he rose from his chair and stood motionless, a helpless old man struggling with a massive error he did not want to confront. "Oh, my God," he added, taking off his glasses, breathing deeply.

Havelock watched him, moved to make things easier. "You did the right thing by your lights. Mine, too, if I'd been you. But at the wrong time, the wrong way. Still, we can go back over everything. We might find something."

"Shut up!"

It was the last thing Michael expected to hear. "What?"

"I said shut *up*!"

"You're full of surprises."

"I may have a real one for you."

"MacKenzie?"

Randolph did not answer. Instead, he walked rapidly to a filing cabinet against the wall, taking out a small chain of keys; he selected one and literally jammed it into the upper lock. "These are my private files, *very* private. A lot of broken marriages and altered wills could result if they were read. Mac's in here."

"What about him?"

"Not *him*. The staff pathologist who put it all together, who worked with me to convince those fellas from Langley it was a haemorrhage, pure and simple."

"A question," interrupted Havelock. "The CIA report says everything was processed here. Your laboratories, your equipment . . . your staff. Why didn't they remove the body to Bethesda or Walter Reed?"

The physician turned, his hands in an open file drawer, his long fingers inserted between the folders. "Some pretty strong language on my part with the promise of a lot stronger from Midge MacKenzie if they tried. I told them she'd kick up a mess of feathers such as they haven't seen since the Bay of Pigs, that she hated their guts, figured the strain killed Mac and the least they could do was leave him in peace."

"Did they talk to her?"

"They tried to. She gave them five minutes, answered their questions, and told them to go to hell. They got the picture; they didn't want any loud trouble from her."

"I'll bet they didn't."

"Also," said Randolph, turning back to the files, "we've got a hell of a reputation here, treat some of the most important people in the country. Who's going to call us liars?"

"You counted on that, didn't you?"

"You're damn right . . . Here it is."

"What did your pathologist find that you think might help?"

"It's not what he found. Like I said, it's *him*. He was a temporary."

"A what?" Michael could feel a sudden, hollow suspension of breath in his chest.

"You heard me," went on Randolph, carrying the file back to his desk and sitting down. "He was a temporary replacement, took over for our regular man who was out with a case of mono . . ."

"Mononucleosis?"

"Infectious glandular fever. Easy thing to transmit, if you've a mind to."

"You're losing me."

"Catch up," said the surgeon, turning the pages in the folder. "Several days before Mac's death our pathologist comes down with mono. Then, thank-you-very-much, a highly qualified man shows up; he's in the middle of a transfer, has a month or so free, and is staying with a sister in Easton. Jesus, I grabbed him."

"And?"

"Mac's body's brought in; he does the initial work, and asks to see me in my office. I'll never forget it; the first thing he says to me is, 'How well did you know this MacKenzie?' "

Havelock nodded. "One thing led to another and the bottom line was that MacKenzie's body couldn't stand an independent autopsy."

"He'd found minute traces of digoxin," said Randolph.

"And a puncture wound, the position and angle indicating that it was probably self-inflicted," Havelock added.

"You've got it."

"I'm sure he also inquired about MacKenzie's work, his mental state, his family . . . and somewhere along the line brought up the subject of insurance."

"He did. Oh, *Christ!*"

"Don't cut your throat, Doctor. These people do their homework like no one else on earth."

"What people?"

"If I'm right, they're called *paminyatchiks*."

"Who?"

"Never mind. And don't bother looking for holes in there. He covered himself; he didn't tell you a single lie, that's his blanket. He simply knew it all in advance. You couldn't touch him without incriminating yourself and ruining your centre."

"I'm not looking for holes," replied the doctor, rapidly scanning pages.

"A sister in Easton? Forget it. She never was, and he's gone, and you won't find him."

"That's just it. I know where he is."

Michael bolted forward in the chair. "You *what?*"

"His name came up several weeks ago. I was talking to a salesman from a surgical supply house and he mentioned that he had to check our purchase orders because a pathologist wanted to duplicate a piece of equipment we had. I recognized the name, of course, but not the place. It wasn't where I thought he'd transferred to." Randolph stopped and looked up from the file. "I did an odd thing," he continued. "Childish, I suppose. It was as though I didn't want to acknowledge him, or think about what he and I had done . . . just wanted to keep tabs on him. I didn't tell my secretary – as I usually do – to list his current position in our personnel records. Instead, I came in here and wrote it in Mac's file. Somewhere." The doctor went back to the pages.

Stunned, Havelock sat rigidly on the edge of the chair. Over the years in his shadow world, he had learned that the most incredible turns of circumstance generally had the most credible reasons for happening. He barely found his voice as he explained. "Your pathologist kept the name because he knew that you of all people could never come after him. Conversely, he had his hooks into you *with* the name, not without it. Believe me, Doctor, sooner or later he would have pulled you in, viciously and effectively."

"I've got it," said Randolph, raising his eyes and staring at Michael. "He still could, you know. Pull me in, I mean."

"So could I, but I won't unless you destroy the information on that page. It's not likely because I wouldn't give you the chance. On the other hand, he'll never come near you because I won't give *him* the chance. He's made the one mistake he can't afford to make in his very strange life. It's fatal. The name, please."

"Colin Shippers. Chief Pathologist, The Regency Foundation. It's a private research centre."

It's far more than that, Doctor. It's where a paminyatchik *can be found. The first concrete step towards Ambiguity. Towards Parsifal.*

"This is what I want you to do," said Havelock. "And I'm afraid you'll have to do it."

It was vital to operate not only once removed but almost blindly, and that was the most difficult thing in the world for Michael to do. The highly concentrated surveillance had to be left to others, something Havelock hated because his team was operating totally in the dark, told only to follow instructions, given no clear reason for the job they were doing. There were always built-in risks in such methods; responsibility without knowledge or authority led to resentments, and resentment was the first cousin to carelessness. That could *not* be permitted. Nor, unfortunately, could inquiries be made regarding routine habits, friends, medical associates, places frequented . . . all the *minutiae* that might help them was denied.

For if MacKenzie's death linked Dr Colin Shippers back to the initial cover-up of Costa Brava – a cover-up that was no part of the White House strategy – he was at the medical centre under orders from the mole at State, a *paminyatchik* who had assumed the Ambiguity code. And a *paminyatchik* in that position would never entrust an assignment as sensitive as the killing of a CIA black-operations officer to any but one of his own. Therefore, they had to operate on the assumption that Shippers himself was a traveller, and that even the hint of an alarm would send him underground, severing the connection to Ambiguity and, with it, any possibility of tracing the mole through the link. Sources of information were continuously covered by the travellers; personnel offices, bank and credit references, professional records . . . even FBI checks . . . all were assiduously scrutinized by informants – willing and unwilling, Russian plants and blackmailed clerks – who alerted the thoroughly Americanized Soviet agents that someone was interested in them. This practice, in concert with Amendments IV, V and VI of the Bill of Rights, made it virtually impossible to trap the *paminyatchik*; he was a citizen and entitled to the protection of the Constitution of the United States. By the time probable cause eliminated unreasonable search, or a grand jury returned a presentment or an indictment and the accused was informed of the nature and cause of his possible crime the traveller had long since departed, only to surface in weeks or months with another identity, a wholly original *curriculum vitae* and, not infrequently, a new face, courtesy of surgeons in Moscow.

However, as Rostov had pointed out in Athens, the irony of this long-range Soviet penetration was found in the practical results. Far too often the American experience' served to undermine the Soviet commitment. During his rare but necessary trips to Moscow's Dzerzhinsky Square, the *paminyatchik* was made aware of the inevitable comparisons between the two countries. In the final analysis, the travellers were far less productive than the KGB felt it had a right to expect in the light of the money and effort it had expended. Yet to threaten one was to court exposure of the whole programme.

Futility was not always the province of those with a god on their side, thought Havelock.

Yet again, there were the exceptions, and exposure would never come from them. A mole called Ambiguity who roamed the sacrosanct corridors of the State Department, and a bright, persuasive pathologist named Colin Shippers who could grasshop from laboratory to laboratory – how often were these laboratories branches of United States intelligence – ? These justified the expense and whatever manpower Moscow allotted to the *paminyatchik* operation. Ambiguity was obviously Shippers's superior, the on-site control, and without doubt a respected satellite in the KGB firmament – but he was not keeping his normal KGB channels informed of the present crisis. Costa Brava, and all the madness it represented was not only disavowed by Dzerzhinsky Square, but what little they did know about it alarmed men like Pyotr Rostov.

It must do; events had taken place which could *not* have taken place without complicity in Moscow. A VKR officer had been trapped and wounded in Paris by the central figure at Costa Brava, and it took little imagination to know that the orders the officer followed were obfuscated so as to be untraceable within the complex machinery of Russian intelligence. Of course Rostov was alarmed; the spectre of the fanatical VKR was enough to frighten the most dedicated Marxist, just as it frightened Havelock. For the unknown Ambiguity obviously sent routine dispatches to his controls in the KGB, but he reserved his most explosive information for his masters in the *Voennaya*.

Rostov sensed it, but he could not pin it down, much less expose it. It was the reason for his offer to a former counterpart in Consular Operations. *He says he's not your enemy any longer, but others are who may be his as well.*

If Rostov had any idea how valid his instincts were, he would risk a firing squad to make contact, thought Michael. But Rostov was wrong; the Russian *was* his enemy. Essentially neither could trust the other because neither Washington nor Moscow would permit such trust, and not even the horror of Parsifal could change that.

Futility in a world gone mad . . . as mad as its former saviour, Anthony Matthias. Superstar.

"How long do you think it will take?" asked Jenna, sitting across from Havelock in the small, sunlit alcove off the kitchen where they had their morning coffee.

"It's difficult to tell. It'll depend on how convincing Randolph is and how quickly Shippers suspects that an insurance company may be something else, something that alarms him. It could be today, tonight, tomorrow . . . the day after."

"I'd think you'd want Randolph to force him to react immediately. Can you afford the time?"

"I can't afford to lose him; he's the only link we've got. His name didn't appear in the laboratory report – which was easy for him to insist on in the light of Randolph's decision to cover up what he thought was a suicide. Shippers knows the only way he could surface would be for Randolph to incriminate himself, which he'd never do. Apart from practical considerations his ego wouldn't permit it."

"But swiftness is everything, Mikhail," objected Jenna. "I'm not sure I understand your strategy."

Havelock looked into her eyes, his own eyes questioning. "I'm not sure I do, either. I've always known that to make things work in this business – this so-called profession of ours – was to think as your enemy thinks, to *be* him, then do what you're convinced he doesn't expect. Now, I'm asked to think like someone I can't possibly relate to, a man who literally has to be *two people*." Michael sipped his coffee, staring now at the rim of the cup. "Think about it. An American childhood, adolescence . . . baseball, hockey, books and music . . . friends at school and college; going out with girls, talking about yourself, confiding in people you really like. These are the years when secrets are for telling; it's against human nature to keep them to yourself . . . part of growing up to reveal yourself. So explain it to me. How does a man like this, a *paminyatchik*, keep the one secret he can never reveal so deep inside him."

"I don't know, but you've just described someone I do know very well."

"Who?"

"You, my darling."

"That's crazy." Havelock put his cup down. He was anxious to leave the table; that, too, was in his eyes.

"Is it?" Jenna reached over, putting her hand briefly over his. "How many friends at school and in college, how many girls and people you really liked did you tell about Mikhail Havlicek, and Lidice? How many know about the agonies of Prague and a child who hid in the forests and carried secret messages and explosives strapped to his person? Tell me, how many?"

"It was pointless. It was history."

"I would never have known – *we* would never have known – except that our leaders insisted on a thorough background check. Your intelligence services have not always sent the best people into our part of Europe and we paid for the mistakes. But when the dossier of Havlicek and the Havlicek family was brought to us – all easily verified – it came sealed with a man from the highest office of your State Department who took it away with him. It was apparent that your immediate superiors – our normal contacts – were not aware of your early days. For some reason they were concealed; for some reason . . . you were two people. Why, Mikhail?"

"I just told you. Matthias and I agreed; it was history."

"You didn't want to live with it, then. You wanted that part of your life to remain hidden, out of sight."

"That'll do."

"I was with you so many times when older people spoke of those days and you never said anything, never let on that you were there. Because if you had, it could have led to your secret, the years you didn't care to talk about."

"That's consistent."

"Like this Shippers, you'd been there and you were staying out of sight. You *were* there but your signature didn't appear anywhere."

"It's a far-fetched parallel."

"Different, perhaps; not far-fetched," insisted Jenna. "You can't make even the usual inquiries about Shippers because informants might alert him and he'd disappear, protecting his secret. You're waiting for him to consider Randolph's call, finally perhaps – you hope – he'll decide that he should find out whether or not this insurance company is really . . . how do you say it?"

"Balking," offered Michael. "Asking last questions before agreeing to the final settlement on MacKenzie's policy. It's standard; they hate like hell paying money."

"Yes, you believe he'll do this. And when he discovers there *are* no questions, he'll be alarmed, then make his move to contact his control: again you hope, Ambiguity."

"I think that's the way he *will* behave. It's the best and safest way I can come up with. Anything else would send him underground."

"And each hour he . . ." Jenna shook her head, searching for words.

"Thinks about it," said Havelock. "Concentrates."

"Yes, concentrates. Every moment is a lost moment, giving him time to spot his surveillance, the men who worry you because you don't know them and you can't give them the true background material on their subject."

"I don't like it, but it's been done before."

"Hardly under these conditions, never with such terrible consequences for error. Swiftness *is* everything, Mikhail."

"You're trying to tell me something and I don't know what it is."

744

"You're afraid of alarming Shippers, afraid he might disappear."

" 'Terrified' is a better word."

"Then don't go after *him*. Go after the man who was silent, who was at the medical centre when MacKenzie died but whose signature did not appear. Just as you were two men in Prague, he is two men here. Go after the one you *see* because you have no reason to believe he *is* two men, or has a secret to conceal."

Havelock touched his cup, his eyes fixed on Jenna's eyes. "Go after a laboratory pathologist," he said quietly. "On the assumption that someone had to be there with Randolph . . . Corroboration. The insurance company insists on a corroborating physician."

"In my country five signatures are barely adequate for any one document."

"He'll refuse, of course."

"Can he? He *was there*."

"He'll tell Randolph he can't support him, can't agree openly to the diagnosis of aortal haemorrhage."

"Then I think the doctor should be quite firm. If that's Shippers's medical position, why didn't he take it before?"

Michael smiled, the realization clear. "That's very good. Blackmail an extortionist with his own material."

"Why not? Randolph has . . . how do you say it? . . . the leverage. Age, reputation, wealth; who is this Shippers to oppose him?"

"And none of it makes a damn bit of difference anyway. We're simply forcing him to move quickly. For his own protection – not even as a traveller, but as a doctor – he'll have to determine how serious the insurance people are. Whether it's a routine measure or whether they mean it. Then he finds out there's nothing: he's got to move again."

"What's today's schedule?" asked Jenna.

"Initial surveillance will pick up Shippers when he leaves his apartment this morning. Secondary will take over inside the Regency buildings."

"How? . . . I'm sorry, I wasn't listening last night when you were on the phone."

"I know you weren't, I was watching you. Are you going to have something for me?"

"Later, perhaps. How did you get them inside the buildings?"

"The Regency Foundation's a private firm with its share of classified government contracts. That's obviously the reason Shippers went there; a lot of those contracts are defence orientated. Regency was the company that first projected the radius burn level of napalm . . . It's common for government technocrats and General Accounting Office personnel to be around there, shuffling papers and looking official. From this morning there are two more."

"I hope no one asks them questions."

"They wouldn't answer if anyone did; that's standard. Also they've got briefcases and plastic IDs on their lapels to identify them. They're covered if anyone checks." Havelock looked at his watch as he got up from the table. "Randolph's making his call between ten and ten-thirty. Let's go. I'll reach him and give him the new words."

"If Shippers reacts," said Jenna, following Michael down the hall towards the panelled study, "he won't use his office phone."

"There are three mobile units in the streets, separated by blocks, everyone in radio contact, wrist cameras activated by arm movements. They can move out on foot or by car — cars alternating in traffic. If they're any good, they won't lose him."

"They *do* worry you, don't they?"

"They worry me." Havelock opened the door of the study, holding it for Jenna. "They'd worry me more if it wasn't for a fellow named Charley who wanted to put a bullet in my head down on Poole's Island."

"The one from Consular Operations?"

Michael nodded, going to the desk. "He flew up last night; my personal request, which didn't exactly thrill him. But he's good, he's thorough, and he knows that Shippers is involved with the Matthias crisis. That's enough to make him better than he ever was. He's in charge, and if he doesn't choke on the mobile phone he'll keep me posted, let me know if anything breaks."

Jenna had gone to her own desk — the couch; on the coffee table in front of it there were neat, narrow stacks of papers and several pages of handwritten notes. She sat down and picked up a bound typewritten report from the pile on the left. She spoke while reading, her voice indefinite, her concentration split. "Have you got in touch with the insurance company?"

"No, that's a risk I don't want to take," replied Havelock, sitting down at the desk and watching Jenna, but his interest diverted. "MacKenzie's policy might be flagged."

"You're probably right."

"What have you got there? It's the same thing you were looking at last night."

"It's the report from your Central Intelligence Agency. The list of potential Soviet defectors over the past ten years, none of whom materialized."

"Look for a nuclear scientist or an armaments strategist who disappeared."

"Others disappeared too, Mikhail," said Jenna, reading and reaching for a pencil.

Havelock kept his eyes on her for several moments, then looked down at a sheet of paper on which were scribbled various telephone numbers. He checked one, picked up the phone, and dialled.

"He's a cold son of a bitch, I can tell you," snapped Dr Matthew Randolph. "When I put it to him he clammed up, asked a couple of questions like a mortician settling with a family lawyer and said he'd get back to me."

"How did you put out, and what were his questions?" asked Michael, putting down the page of Pentagon stationery on which were written the identities of the senior officers on the Nuclear Contingency Committees. He had circled a name. "Try to be as accurate as possible."

"I'll be completely accurate," objected the surgeon testily.

"I only meant in terms of the words, the phrases he used."

"It won't be hard; they were damned few and damned short. As you suggested, he said I had no right to involve him, that was our understanding. He simply brought me his findings and how I altered them was my responsibility, not his. So I said I wasn't a goddamned lawyer but if my memory for trivia served me, he was an accessory and there was no way round it and I was going to be fried in hell before Midge MacKenzie and those kids got screwed out of what was coming to them."

746

"So far very good. What was his response?"

"He didn't have any, so I blasted along. I told him he was a damned fool if he thought he was invisible around here four months ago and a bigger fool if he thought anyone on the staff would believe I'd spend hours in a pathology laboratory over the body of a friend all by myself."

"*Very* good."

"He had an answer to that. Like a talking piece of dry ice, he asked who specifically knew."

Havelock felt a sudden spasm in his chest, the spectre of unnecessary execution rising. "What did you say? Did you mention anybody?"

"Hell, I said probably *everybody*!"

Michael relaxed. "You can come on the payroll, Doctor."

"You couldn't afford me, son."

"Please, go on."

"I backed down a bit, told him he was getting all worked up over nothing. I said the fellow who came to see me from the insurance company said it was just a formality, that they required a second signature on the path-report before sending the cheque. I even suggested he call Ben Jackson over at Talbot Insurance if he was worried, that Ben was an old friend –"

"You gave him a *name?*"

"Sure. Ben *is* an old friend; he set up Mac's policy. I figured if anyone phoned Ben he'd call me and ask what the hell was going on."

"And what were *you* going to say?"

"That whoever it was got it backwards. *I* was the one who wanted the second signature for our own records."

"What did *Shippers* say?"

"Just a few words, spoken like a frozen computer. He asked whether I had told either Ben or the man from the insurance company who he was."

"And?"

"I said no I didn't. Fair was fair, and I guessed the best way was to handle it quietly. For him to get over here and sign the damned report without any fan fare."

"His response here?"

"Again, damned short and bloodless." Randolph paused and, spacing his words apart in a monotone, continued, " 'Have you told me everything?' he wanted to know. I tell you he was a zombie."

"What did you say?"

"I said of course I had, what else was there? That's when he told me he'd call me back. Just like that, 'I'll call you back', in that God-awful voice."

Havelock breathed deeply, his eyes dropping to the names on the Pentagon stationery, to one name in particular. "Doctor, either you've done a remarkable job or I'm going to have your inflated head."

"What the hell are you *talking* about?"

"If you'd done it my way, just using the insurance company alone, without any other name, Shippers would have assumed MacKenzie's death was being re-examined by a third party without telling you. Now, if he calls this Jackson he'll know you're lying."

"So what? Same result, isn't it?"

"Not for you, Doctor, and we can't bring in your friend; we can't take the risk. For your sake I hope he's gone fishing. And I mean it – if you've given me another complication, I'll see your head rolling down the street."

"Well, now, young fellow, I've been doing some thinking about that. There could be a *couple* of heads rolling down a *two-way* street, couldn't there? Here you are, a mucka-muck from the White House telling me the executive branch of our government is trying to cover up the brutal killing of a heroic veteran, an employee of the CIA, and I'm just a country doctor trying to protect the interests of his bereaved widow and fatherless orphans because they've suffered more than anyone had a right to ask them to suffer. You want to tangle with me, you bastard?"

"Please call me if you hear anything further, Dr Randolph."

Special Detachment Officer Charles Loring, Consular Operations, late of Poole's Island, rubbed his eyes and raised the thermos of black coffee to his lips as he sat in the front seat of the grey car. The driver was for all intents and purposes a stranger; that was to say, Loring had not seen him before ten o'clock last night, when he had met the entire unit selected by Havelock from thirty odd service records submitted by the Federal Bureau of Investigation at the Justice Department's request. The unit was now his responsibility, the assignment of continuity-surveillance understood, the reasons behind it withheld – which was not the smartest thing to do when dealing with superior talent.

And despite Havelock's minor – very minor – attempt to flatter him, Charley Loring knew that the former Cons Op field man was getting some of his own back by claiming privilege. The only clue Havelock gave him was that this Shippers was tied in with Poole's Island, and it was – with reluctance – enough for Charley. Havelock was a low-blow-dealing prick, and he had made fools of Savannah, but if he was running some part of the Matthias show in Washington he had more problems than they did. Loring would do what he could to help. There were times when likes and dislikes just did not mean very much, the catastrophe – the tragedy – of Poole's Island was such a time.

The unit had met at ten o'clock at Sterile Eleven down in Quantico, and had stayed up until four o'clock in the morning covering the variables of total surveillance. without knowing a damn thing about the subject. They had a photograph but, apart from an inadequate description furnished by Randolph, that was about all they had, and it too was inadequate. It was a blow-up made at Sterile Eleven from a 1971 Jefferson Medical School Yearbook that had been located by the FBI office in Philadelphia. No reason was given to the agents who found it, only that they should observe complete secrecy. Actually, it had been stolen out of the university's library by an agent who had concealed it under his coat. Examining the grainy blow-up the unit had to imagine a face considerably older than that in the photograph and, since no one they could speak to had seen Shippers in four months, the possibility of a beard or a moustache could not be discounted. And they could speak to no one about Dr Colin Shippers, no one at all. Havelock's orders.

Initial surveillance had disposed of the conjecture about any hirsute additions to the subject's face; tinted glasses and a heavier frame were the essential differences between his appearance now and the yearbook photograph. The men inside the Regency Foundation had radioed out twice; they had picked up Shippers. One man was down the hall from the laboratory where the pathologist worked; the other covered his office on the floor below. The waiting had begun, thought Loring. But waiting for what?

The hours or the days would tell. All Charles Loring knew was that he had done everything he could to position the unit effectively: spaced apart and in contact to ensure maximum concealment. The cars were at one-way intersections, his own down the street and across from the research centre with a full view of the entrance and the adjacent garage used for personnel parking.

A sharp, high-pitched hum came from the dashboard console; it was a signal from one of the men inside. Loring reached for the microphone, depressed the switch, and spoke. "S–Five. What is it?"

"S–Three. He just left the lab, seems in a hurry."

"Any clues?"

"I heard a telephone ring in there a few minutes ago. He's alone so he could have talked, but that's spec. I wasn't able to overhear any conversation."

"It's good enough. Stay where you are and stay out of sight."

Loring replaced the microphone, only to hear a second jarring signal before he could lean back in the seat.

"S–Five."

"S–Two. Subject went into his office. From the way he walked – his general demeanour – he's agitated."

"Good description; it fits upstairs. We may be moving faster than any of us –"

"Hold it! Stay on the line," instructed Surveillance-Two as static filled the speaker. The man had concealed his radio under his clothing without breaking the open circuit. In seconds his voice was back. "Sorry. Subject came right back out and I had to spin. He chucked the white coat and is in his street clothes. Same tan raincoat, same soft, floppy hat. I guess he's yours."

"I guess he is. Out." Loring held the microphone in his hand and turned to the driver. "Get ready, the package is coming our way. If I have to go on foot take over. I'll stay in touch." He reached under his jacket and took out the small compact hand-held radio, checking by habit the battery charge. He then pulled back his left sleeve, revealing the flat miniaturized high-speed camera attached to the under-side of his wrist. He twisted his hand and heard the muted click; he was ready. "I wonder who this Shippers is," he said, watching the entrance of the Regency Foundation.

The telephone rang, breaking Havelock's concentration on his Pentagon notes. He picked it up.

"Yes?"

"Cross?"

Michael blinked, recognizing Randolph's strident voice. "Yes, Doctor?"

Maybe we can both keep our heads. Ben Jackson just called, angrier than a Point Judith squall."

"What about?"

"Seems this lawyer phoned him asking why the final payment on MacKenzie's policy was being held up."

"Shippers," said Havelock.

"You got it, and Ben was madder'n hell. There *was* no final payment. The entire settlement was mailed to Midge's lawyer about eight weeks ago."

"Why did Jackson call you and not Mrs MacKenzie's attorney?"

"Because Shippers – I figure it was Shippers or someone calling for him – got shook up and said there was some confusion over signatures on a medical report and did Ben know anything about it. Naturally, Ben said he didn't; the money was paid – processed through his agency – and that was that. He also added that he didn't appreciate his reputation –"

"Listen to me," interrupted Havelock. "I won't lose *my* head but you may have blown yours away. I want you to stay in your office, and don't see anybody until I can get a couple of men up there. If anyone tries to reach you, ask the desk to say you're operating."

"Forget it!" shot back Randolph. "A mealy-mouthed snot like Shippers doesn't worry me. He comes near here I'll have one of the guards throw him into a padded cell."

"If he did and you could, I'd kiss your feet at this point, but it won't *be* Shippers. He may call you; that's as near as he'll come and it'd be the best thing that could happen to you. If he does, say you're sorry for the white lie, but after long consideration, you wanted to cover yourself on that report."

"He wouldn't believe it."

"Neither would I, but it's a stall. I'll have men up there within the hour."

"I don't want them!"

"You have no choice, Dr Randolph," said Michael, hanging up and immediately drawing his page of telephone numbers in front of him.

"Do you really think Shippers will go after him?" asked Jenna, standing by the window with the CIA report in her hand.

"*He* won't, but others'll be sent up there, not at first to kill him, but to take him. Take him and get him alone where they can press his head until they find out who he's dealing with, who he's lying for. Killing could be nicer." Havelock reached for the phone, his eyes on the page below.

"On the other hand," observed Jenna, "knowing Randolph lied, knowing he was involved, made Shippers move faster than we thought possible. How long ago was Loring's last call?"

"Over an hour. Shippers took a taxi downtown; they're with him on foot by now. We should be hearing soon. Michael dialled; the line answered quickly. "This is Sterile Five, Fairfax. Under that code name I was taken under escort up to the Randolph Medical Center yesterday. Talbot County, Maryland, Eastern Shore. Will you confirm, please?" While waiting, Havelock covered the phone and said to Jenna, "I just thought of something. With any luck we might turn a liability into an asset," then returned to the phone: " . . . Yes, that's right. Three man team; departure was eleven hundred hours. Are you ready for instructions? . . . Return two men up there immediately on a priority basis. Subject is Dr Matthew Randolph; he's to be given protection, maximum visual contact, but there's a hook. I want the men to be part of the local scenery, orderlies or staff or whatever I can work out with Randolph. Tell them to get en route and call me on the mobile phone in twenty minutes; patch it through." Michael paused again, looking again at Jenna as the Secret Service dispatcher checked schedules. "Randolph may have done us another favour at a risk to himself he'll never understand."

"*If* he co-operates."

"He hasn't got a choice, I meant that." The dispatcher returned; Havelock listened, then spoke. "No, that's fine. Actually, I prefer men who weren't up there yesterday. By the way, the code will be –' Michael stopped, his thoughts going back to the Palatine Hill, to a dead man whose words had sent him to Maryland's Eastern Shore. "Apache," he said. "They were hunters. Tell Apache to call me in twenty minutes."

Dr Matthew Randolph roared his objections to no avail. He would either co-operate, Havelock told him, or they could all take their chances *and* the fallout 'tangling' with each other. 'Mr Cross' was prepared to press his suit to the limit even if it meant admitting the murder of a CIA operations officer named Steven MacKenzie. And Randolph, understanding that he was now between a rock and a hard place, entered into the dangerous charade with a fair degree of inventiveness. The Apache team would be two visiting cardiologists from California, complete with white jackets and stethoscopes.

Havelock's orders were explicit, no room for error. Whoever came for Matthew Randolph – and someone was bound to come – he or they were to be taken alive. Wounds were permitted, but only in the legs, the feet, nothing above the waist.

It was a four-zero order, none more sacrosanct in the clandestine services.

"Havelock, it's Loring."

"How goes it?"

"My driver said he wasn't able to raise you."

"I was talking with an irascible doctor, but if there was an emergency, your man could have broken in. He knows that."

"It wasn't and it isn't. It's just weird." Loring stopped. The pause was uncomfortable.

"What's going on, Charley?"

"That's just it. Nothing. Shippers' taxi let him off in front of Garfinckle's Department Store. He went inside, made a call from one of the phones on the ground floor, and for the past hour or so he's been wandering around the men's shop on the fifth. I'm calling from there; I've got him in sight."

"He's waiting for someone."

"If he is, it's an odd way of doing it quietly."

"What do you mean?"

"He's buying clothes like he was going on a cruise, trying on things and laughing with the clerks. He's a one-man gross for the day."

"It's not usual, but be patient. The main point is he made the call, made his first outside move. You're doing fine."

"Who the hell is he, Havelock?"

Michael reflected. Loring deserved to be told more than he had; it was the moment to bring him nearer to the truth. So much depended on the sharp, plainspoken Cons Op officer.

"A deep cover entry who's going to meet a man who could blow Poole's Island out of Savannah harbour. I'm glad you're there, Charley. We *have* to know who that man is."

"Good enough, and thanks. All the floors and exits here are covered, we're in contact and our cameras are ready"

If it's a question of choice, do we drop Shippers and stay with his contact?"

"You may not have to. You may recognize him. The others probably wouldn't, but you might."

"Jesus, from *State?*"

"That's right. My guess is fairly high-level, forty-five to middle fifties, and some kind of specialist. If you *do* recognize him, stay far back until they separate, then pick up Shippers and bring him down here. But when you close in, be very fast and very careful and check for capsules."

"Shippers is that deep? Christ, how do they do it?"

"Past tense, Charley. Did. A long time ago."

The waiting would have been intolerable had it not been for Havelock's growing fascination with a Lieutenant-Commander Thomas Decker, Annapolis '61, former skipper of the submarine *Starfire* and a member of the Pentagon's Nuclear Contingency Committees. Decker was a liar with no apparent reason for lying.

Michael had spoken to all fifteen NCC senior officers, calling several twice, a few three times, ostensibly to put together a clear picture of the committees' working methods for updated presidential comprehension. In most of the conversations, the initial remarks were guarded – each, of course, demanding White House switchboard verification – but as the words flowed and the officers realized Havelock knew what he was talking about, they grew less wary and more specific within the bounds of maximum security. Hypothetical events were matched with theoretical responses, and beyond his fundamental reason for speaking to each man, Havelock was impressed. If the laws of physics determined that for every action there was an equal and opposite reaction, the NCC Teams had come up with a better equation. For any nuclear action on the part of an enemy the reaction was anything but equal; it was devastatingly superior. Even Lieutenant-Commander Decker's contributions were electric in this sense. He made it clear that a ring-perimeter of undersea nuclear marauders could demolish all major enemy installations from the north Atlantic to the Black Sea and most points in between in a matter of minutes. In this area he did not lie; he did in another. He said he had never met Secretary of State Anthony Matthias.

His name had appeared on three separate telephone logs from Matthias's office, all within the past six months.

It was, of course, possible that Decker's statement *was* true, that he had not actually *met* Matthias, merely spoken with him on the phone. But if that was the case, why had he not volunteered the information? A man who was asked whether or not he knew a statesman of Matthias's stature did not deny it readily without quickly offering the qualification that he *did* know him by way of the telephone. It was not natural, actually contradictory for an obviously ambitious naval officer rising fast in the Pentagon, who could be expected to clutch ferociously at the coat-tails of Anthony Matthias.

Thomas Decker, USN, had lied. He did know Matthias and, for obscure reasons, did not care to admit it.

It was time for the fourth call to Lieutenant-Commander Decker.

"You know, Mr Cross, I've given you about all I can or should in these matters. I'm sure you re aware that there are restrictions placed on me that can only be countered by the President himself – in his presence, I might add."

"I'm aware of that, Commander, but I'm confused by one of my notes. It probably has nothing to do with anything we've talked about, but the Secretary of State didn't understand it, either. You said you didn't know him, never met him."

Decker's pause was as electric as his data on undersea nuclear warfare. "That's the way he wanted it," he said quietly. "That's the way he said it had to be."

"Thank you, Commander. Incidentally, Secretary of State Matthias was trying to pin-point it this morning. He couldn't recall where you and he last talked with each other."

"The lodge, of course. Sometime in August or September, I think."

"Of course. The lodge. The Shenandoah."

"That's where it was, where it always was. No one knew anything. It was just ourselves. How is it possible he can't remember?"

"Thank you, Commander. Goodbye."

The *Shenandoah*.

The bell was piercing, the ring unbroken; it was the switchboard's way of signalling emergency! Havelock had been pacing, thinking; he rushed across the room and grabbed the phone. It was Loring.

"You've got my tail on a plate and I'll start carving it for you! Jesus, I'm *sorry!*"

"You lost him," said Michael, drained, his throat dry.

"*Christ*. I'll turn in my cards! Every fucking one of them!"

"Calm down, Charley. What happened?"

"A switch. A *goddamned switch!* I . . . I just wasn't *looking* for it! I *should* have, but I *wasn't!*"

"Tell me what happened," repeated Michael, sitting down as Jenna got up from the couch and started towards the desk.

"Shippers paid for the stuff he bought, arranging for most of it to be delivered except for a couple of boxes he took with him. He went into the fitting room and came out dressed for the street, same raincoat, same soft hat, carrying the boxes."

"Held high," Havelock broke in, wearily, again the sense of futility spreading through him.

"Naturally," agreed Loring. "I followed him to the elevator, staying several aisles away — frankly looking at every son of a bitch in the men's department, figuring one of them might be your man. One lousy son of a bitch who might have brushed up against Shippers and got something from him . . . The lift door closed, and I raised the men on each floor, every stop covered, each man to head below and join the others at the outside exits the second that lift passed his floor . . . My S-Nine picked him up at the 14th Street entrance and followed him, radioing the rest of us his position; we spread out in cars and on foot. *Jesus!*"

"When did it happen?" asked Michael.

"On the corner of 11th Street, four minutes after I left the store, and I was the last one out. The man hailed a cab, threw the boxes inside and, just before he got in, took off his hat. It wasn't Shippers at all. It was some guy ten, fifteen years older and mostly bald."

"What did your Nine do?"

"The best he could. He tried to stop the cab but he couldn't; it shot right in a break in traffic. He called us, spelling everything out, giving the cab's number and description. Five of us ran back to the store, covering what exits we could, but we all knew we'd lost him. S-Eleven and Twelve went after the cab; I told them to stay with it if they had to break every traffic law on the books — since we'd lost the subject, we could still grab the plant. They picked it up six blocks west and there was no one inside. Only the raincoat, the hat and the two boxes lying on the floor."

"The driver?"

"He said some nut got in, took off his coat, gave him five dollars, and jumped out at the next light. The men are taking the boxes in for possible prints."

"They won't find any matching anything in the Bureau's computers."

"I'm *sorry*. Havelock, I'm really sorry. Shippers' whole act was a diversion, and I bought it. Of all the goddamned times to lose an instinct, I had to pick this one."

Michael shook his head, as he spoke. "You didn't lose it, Charley, I pushed it out of your head. At least you sensed a break in the pattern and I told you to forget it. I told you to be patient and concentrate on a man who never intended to be there."

"You don't have to do this," said Loring. "I wouldn't if I were you."

"You don't know that. Besides, I need you. You're not off the hook, Charley, I want those instincts of yours. There's a naval officer at the Pentagon, a Lieutenant-Commander Thomas Decker. Under a very thick screen find out everything you can about him. Everything."

"An entry?"

"No. A liar."

Jenna Karras supported herself on the desk at Michael's side, looking over his shoulder as he studied the names and brief summaries of the men she had selected from the CIA, Cons Op and Army Intelligence reports. Out of a hundred and thirty-five potential Soviet defectors who neither came over to the West nor whose current whereabouts were known she had chosen eight for priority consideration.

Michael looked at the list, put it down and slowly turned to her. "This has been a rotten day. It's no time for jokes."

"I'm not joking, Mikhail," said Jenna.

"There's not an armaments expert, or a high-ranking military man, or even an atomic scientist here. These are doctors, specialists – old men now, none of whom was remotely connected with any sort of strategic planning or nuclear strike capabilities."

"Parsifal needs no such connections."

"Then perhaps I wasn't clear about what those documents *say*. They spell out a series of nuclear moves – first and second strikes, interceptor counterstrikes, territorial neutralization and automated reclamation – detailed strategies that could only be conceived and negotiated by experts."

"Matthias didn't carry around such details in his head, you've said as much."

"Of course not, which is why I'm going after the men on the contingency committees – one in particular. But Parsifal *did*. He must have had those projections available to him. They were chips, his bargaining points in their insane game."

"Then someone is missing," insisted Jenna, walking round the desk, then suddenly turning to face Havelock. "Who spoke for the People's Republic? Who bargained China's position? Who gave *its* projections, *its* strategic details? According to your theory, there has to be a *third* negotiator."

"No, there doesn't. Their combined sources would be enough to build a totally convincing case for a China strategy. It's common knowledge in intelligence circles that if US and Soviet penetration of the PRC arsenals were linked up, we'd know more about China's nuclear capabilities than anyone in Peking."

"A convincing *case*?"

"Totally."

"*Combined* sources, Mikhail? Why?"

Havelock studied Jenna's face, gradually understanding what she was trying to say. "*One* source," he said quietly. "Why not?"

The telephone rang, its strident signal producing an abrupt tightness in Michael's throat. He reached for it; the President of the United States was on the line, his first words as ominous as Havelock had ever heard.

"The Russians know about Matthias. There's no way to tell their next move."

"Parsifal?" asked Michael, with no breath in him.

"They can smell him, and what they smell is flaring their nostrils. They're close to panic."

"How did you find out?"

"They reached one of our high diplomatic personnel. They told him that they were prepared to expose Matthias. Our only hope now is that the man they contacted is one of the best we've got. They respect him; he could be our single hope for containment. I'm bringing him on board; he's taking Bradford's place. He's got to be told everything, understand everything."

"Who is he?"

"A man named Pierce. Arthur Pierce."

33

The *paminyatchik* sat in the underground strategy room of the White House as the President of the United States and two of the nation's most influential men briefed him. The conference had taken precedence over all Charles Berquist's prior appointments and obligations. It had so far lasted nearly three hours, the incredulous Undersecretary of State for the UN delegation rapidly taking brief notes, his intelligent grey eyes conveying a deep awareness of impending catastrophe, while at the same time his mind remained in complete control, seeking answers, avoiding panic.

The tension was electric, intermittently broken by expressions of courtesy and respect. Arthur Pierce could not be called a friend of either the President or of Addison Brooks, but nor was he a stranger. He was a professional with whom both men had worked, and in whom both had confidence. They remembered with gratitude his penetrating analyses in previous crises. As for General Malcolm Halyard, "Tightrope" had met Major Pierce in Saigon years ago, and was so impressed with his performance that he had cabled the Pentagon recommending that the War College make a serious appraisal of the major's potential for permanent, as opposed to reserve, status.

Yet despite these extremely favourable appraisals, the outstanding citizen-soldier had chosen civilian status, albeit government orientated. And since, to its dismay, the military establishment was frequently part of the government, the word had gone out: an exceptional man was available and looking for challenging work; someone should come up with something before the commercial headhunters descended on him. Washington needed all the genuine talent it could find.

It had happened so easily, so logically in its arithmetic: one plus one plus one. People became steps and the steps led to a high place. An elderly career officer at State said he just happened to be at a dinner party in Alexandria where his military host mentioned Pierce to him. Naturally the career officer felt compelled to mention Pierce's name at a conference attended by Addison Brooks. State was perpetually scouting for that rare man with proven abilities who also had a potential for further intellectual growth. Arthur Pierce was summoned for an interview, which evolved into a lengthy lunch with the aristocratic statesman. This, in turn, led to an offer of employment, an entirely feasible decision in the light of the record.

The mole was in place. There had in fact been no dinner party in Alexandria, no host who had discussed in uniquely flattering terms an outstanding soldier from Saigon. It did not matter; others were discussing him; Brooks had verified that. A dozen corporations were about to make offers to the brilliant young man, so Addison Brooks spoke first.

As the years went by, the decision to recruit Arthur Pierce could only be applauded. He *was* outstanding, with an increasingly apparent ability to comprehend and counter Soviet manoeuvres, especially in face-to-face confrontations. There were, of course, specialists who studied *Tass* and the various Russian journals

756

and communiqués to interpret often obscure Soviet positions, but where Pierce was most effective was at the conference table, whether in Helsinki, Vienna or Geneva. At times his perceptions were uncanny; he frequently seemed to be ten steps ahead of the spokesmen sent by Moscow, preparing counter-proposals before the Soviet position had even been made clear, thus giving the US team the advantage of an immediate response. His presence was increasingly sought by upper-level diplomats until the inevitable took place: he was brought into Matthias's orbit, and the Secretary of State lost little time making Arthur Pierce an upper-level diplomat himself.

The *paminyatchik* had arrived. An infant, genetically selected in Moscow and sent covertly into the heartland of America, was in place after a lifetime of preparation, and at this moment was being addressed by the President of the United States.

"You now have the whole ungodly picture, Mr Undersecretary." Berquist stopped as a painful memory flooded his mind. "It's strange using that title," he continued softly. "Only days ago another Undersecretary sat on this same dais."

"I hope I can contribute even a fraction of what he did," said Pierce, studying his notes. "The fact that he was killed is appalling. Emory was a friend of mine . . . he didn't have many friends."

"He said the same thing about himself," observed Addison Brooks. "And about you."

"Me?"

"That you were his friend."

"I'm flattered."

"You might not have been at the time," said General Halyard. "You were one of nineteen people he was looking into."

"In what way?"

"He was trying to find someone on the fifth floor of State who might have been out of the country, who might have been at the Costa Brava," explained the President.

"The man who later used the Ambiguity code?" asked Pierce, frowning.

"That's right."

"How did my name come up? Emory never told me, never called me."

"Under the circumstances," said the ambassador, "he couldn't. Several query-responses between you and Washington during that week had been misplaced. I don't have to tell you what a shock it was to him at first. They were found, of course."

"Those misfilings are a constant irritant," said Pierce, going back to his notes, checking off items with his gold-plated ballpoint pen. "I don't even know that there's a solution. The volume of traffic is simply too great and there are too few people cleared for the material at that level." The Undersecretary circled a note, adding as an afterthought, "On the other hand, I'd rather put up with the irritation than take the chance that some of those confidential memoranda ever got out."

"How much of what you've learned here in this room do you think the Russians know?" Berquist's Nordic face was set, his eyes hard and level, the muscles in his jaws pulsating.

"Less than I've learned here in this room but probably more than we suspect. The Russians are so damned elliptical. What's more, they're also working themselves up into a frenzy. I can't form a judgement until I've had a chance to study those – incredible documents."

"*False* documents," said Halyard emphatically. "Agreements between two madmen, that's what they are."

"I'm not sure either Moscow or Peking would believe that, General," said Pierce, shaking his head. "One of those madmen is Anthony Matthias, and the world isn't ready to accept him as insane."

"Because it doesn't want to," interrupted Brooks. "It's afraid to."

"That's right, sir," agreed the Undersecretary of State. "But apart from Matthias, these so-called nuclear aggression pacts, as the President has described them, contain extraordinary classified information: locations, megatonnage, detailed delivery capabilities, launching codes . . . even abort systems. From what I can gather, the gates of the arsenals of the two superpowers and their runner-up in China have been opened, the most secret hardware in each camp there for anyone who reads the agreements to see." Pierce turned to the soldier. "What would be the Pentagon's recommendation if a similar Sino-Soviet pact against *us* were brought in by clandestine services, General?"

"Launch," answered Halyard flatly. "There'd be no alternative."

"Only if you were convinced it was authentic," interjected Brooks.

"I'd be convinced," said the general. "So would you be. Who else but men with access to that information could include it? Also, there are the projected dates. I'd be *damned* convinced."

"When you say the Russians are elliptical," said the statesman, "I concur wholeheartedly, but how do you mean it in the current sense?"

"They threw phrases at me – disjointed *non-sequiturs* – watching me to see if I'd follow up on any of them. We've been confronting each other for a number of years now, whether in Vienna or Bern or New York; you get to spot even concealed reactions."

"But first they told you they knew Matthias was insane," said Berquist. "That was their opening, wasn't it?"

"Yes, sir. I don't think I used the exact words before. I will now. I was in the Russian ambassador's office at his request – summons, really – along with his senior aide. Frankly, I thought he'd asked to see me so we might work out a compromise on the Pan-Arab resolution, but instead he greeted me with a statement that could only refer to Matthias: 'We understand from a most reliable source that a holiday has been extended because the mental condition of the vacationer has deteriorated to a point beyond recovery.' "

"What was your reply?" asked Brooks. "The exact words, please."

" 'The Russian compulsion for brooding, self-serving fantasy is no different now from what it was when Dostoevski described it.' Those were my exact words."

"Provocative yet insouciant," said the statesman. "Very good."

"That's when the fireworks started. 'He's mad!' shouted the ambassador. 'Matthias is mad! He's done insane things, undermined what's left of *detente*.' Then his aide joined in, demanding to know where the next meetings were being held, which

758

unstable governments Matthias had been in contact with and whether they knew he was insane, or was a madman sending out secret communications, concealing his insanity from the people he was reaching? What frightens me, Mr President, Mr Ambassador, General Halyard, is that *they* described what you've described to *me*. If I understood correctly, Matthias has been doing just that for the past six months. Reaching unstable regimes, instant prime ministers, revolutionary juntas we shouldn't be touching."

"That's where the Russians got their information, of course," said Berquist. "They think a demented Matthias is implementing a number of his well-known 'geopolitical realities'. Moving in on them."

"They think far more than that, sir," corrected Pierce. "They believe he may have funnelled nuclear materials to extremist regimes and fanatic camps – Islamic, for example, or Afghan, or anti-Soviet Arab factions – that we've all agreed shouldn't have them. They're paranoid about it. We can protect ourselves from each other by the sheer magnitude of our arsenals; but neither of us can protect ourselves from an irrational partisan junta or sect that possesses launch and nuclear capability. Actually, we're far safer; we're separated by oceans. Strategic Russia is part of the Euro-Asian land mass; its borders are vulnerable if only by proximity to potential enemies. If I read them correctly, it's these concerns that are pushing them towards the panic button."

"But not Parsifal," said Brooks. "In your judgement, the man we call Parsifal has *not* made contact with Moscow."

"I can't rule *anything* out," said Pierce. "There were so many phrases, threats, implications – as I said, elliptical references. For instance, they mentioned 'next meetings', 'unstable governments', 'nuclear materials'. All of these – again if I understood correctly – are actually a part of these agreements. If I could study them I'd be able to spot parallels with the original texts." The Undersecretary paused, then spoke quietly, firmly. "I think it's possible this Parsifal *has* made contact, delivering provocative hints, perhaps nothing more. And I think it's urgent that we know even this."

"He wants to blow us all up," said the President. "My God, that's all he wants to do."

"The sooner I can get to Poole's Island, Mr –' Pierce was interrupted by the humming of the white telephone on the white dais, a red light flashing on its miniaturized console. Berquist picked it up. "Yes?"

The President listened in silence for nearly thirty seconds, then answered, nodding. "I understand. Let me know what happens as soon as it happens." He replaced the phone and turned to the others. "That was Havelock. He won't get here this afternoon."

"What is happening?" asked the soldier.

"Too many things for him to leave the phone."

"I'm sorry," said Arthur Pierce. "I wanted to meet him. I think it's vital we stay in touch. I can tell him what's going on with the Soviets and he can keep me up to date. I have to know when to press forward, when to back off."

"You'll be kept informed; he has his orders from me . . . They lost the pathologist."

"*Damn!*" exploded the general.

"He either picked up the surveillance or, knowing things were out of control, decided to disappear."

"Or was ordered to disappear," added the statesman.

"That's what I can't understand," said Berquist, turning to the silent Undersecretary of State. "The Russians gave you no indication that they were *aware* of any Soviet involvement in this whole damn thing? They didn't mention the Costa Brava or Rostov's cable to us?"

"No, sir. That may be the one advantage we have. We know, but they don't."

"*Rostov* knows," insisted the President.

"Then he's too frightened to act," replied Pierce. "It's often the case with entrenched KGB personnel; they're never sure whose toes they may be stepping on. Or if he is searching, he's not getting anywhere."

"You're talking as though we were speaking about two different Moscows," objected Halyard.

"I agree with Havelock," said the mole. "We are. And until the Moscow that wants to get its hands on Matthias's documents succeeds, the one I'm dealing with speaks for the Kremlin. Otherwise, that won't be the case. It's all the more reason why I've *got* to be kept current. If Havelock caught even one man we could trace to that other Moscow, it would be leverage. I could use it."

"He's already told us," interrupted Brooks. "A branch of Soviet intelligence known as the VKR. Rostov as much as admitted it."

Pierce looked bewildered. "I didn't hear that mentioned."

"Perhaps I overlooked it," said Berquist.

"In any event, it's too general. The VKR is a consolidation of many units. I'd need specifics. Which unit? Which directors?"

"You may get them."

"I beg your pardon, sir?" Pierce's gold-plated pen was suspended above his notes.

"It's one of the things that's keeping Havelock at Sterile Five."

"Sterile Five . . ."

"They may have lost this Shippers but Havelock expects that whoever gave him orders will send men up to Maryland to find out who Matthew Randolph's been working with. He's got his own people in place with orders to wound and take. As I told you, the doctor lied about MacKenzie's death but for the wrong reasons."

"Yes, I know." Pierce looked down at his notes as he replaced the pen inside the coat of his dark, pin-stripe suit. "It helps me to write things out; I didn't expect to take these with me."

"I'm glad," said the President. "I wouldn't have let you . . . You've got a lot to think about, Mr Undersecretary, and not much time. How do you plan to handle the Russians?"

"Cautiously," replied the mole. "With your permission, I'd like to substantiate a part of what they told me."

"You're out of your *mind*," said the general.

"Please, General, only a very minor part. They obviously have a fairly accurate source, so to deny the whole would only make them more suspicious, more hostile. We can't afford that now. In the President's words, we must contain them as much as possible for as long as possible."

"How do you think you can do it?" asked Berquist, his eyes squinting, wary.

"By admitting that Matthias collapsed from exhaustion. Everything else has been exaggerated way out of proportion to the medical diagnosis, which is of minor consequence. He's been ordered to rest for several weeks; that's all. The rest is rumour and wild gossip, the sort of thing that goes with a man like Matthias. Don't forget, they have their memories of Stalin; they can't dismiss them. By the time Stalin was dead most of Moscow believed he was certifiably insane."

"Excellent," interjected Ambassador Brooks.

"They can't dismiss the other sources," said Halyard, obviously wanting to agree but the strategist in him prohibiting it. "The leaks from unstable regimes – instant prime ministers or whatever you called them. Matthias *reached* them."

"Then they must be more specific with *me*. I think I can handle them case by case. At the least, they'd have to confer with Moscow, double check the origins. Every case could buy us time." Pierce stopped, turning to Berquist. "And time, Mr President, is what's on my mind now. I think the sooner I get back to New York and ask – no, demand – a meeting with the Soviet ambassador, the better chance I have of pushing their hands away from the buttons. I *do* believe they'll listen to me. I can't guarantee how long, but for a while – a few days, a week – they will."

"Which prompts the obvious question," said the statesman, his well-tailored elbows on the table, his slender hands folded beneath his chin. "Why do you think they contacted you and not the more direct, crisis-oriented channels in Washington?"

"I'd like to know that too," added Berquist. "There's a phone never more than fifty feet away from me for such contingencies."

Arthur Pierce did not at first reply, his eyes shifting back and forth between the President and the ambassador. "It's difficult for me to answer that without appearing arrogant or overly ambitious, and I don't believe I'm either."

"We'll accept that," said Berquist. "Just give us your opinion."

"With all due respect to our ambassador in New York – and I'm sincere; he has an extremely likeable presence, which is terribly important, and he's had an outstanding career in government –"

"*Had*," the President broke in. "He's a soft bush in a high wind, but the roots are deep. He's there because of his *lovable* presence, and the fact that he doesn't make a goddamn decision. We'll accept that, too. Go on."

"The Soviets know you appointed me – at Matthias's request – to be the State Department's spokesman. To be *your* spokesman, sir."

"And the spokesman for Anthony Matthias," said Brooks, nodding his head. "Which assumes a close relationship with our Secretary of State."

"I enjoyed such a relationship until a number of months ago – when apparently all relationships were terminated by his illness."

"But they think you still have it," observed Halyard. "And why the hell not? You're the closest thing we could have there *except* Matthias."

"Thank you, General. Basically, I think they came to me because they thought

I'd know if there was any substance to the Matthias rumours. The madness."

"And if they thought you knew but were lying, what would be their response?"

"They'd disregard the hot-line, Mr President. They'd put the world on nuclear alert."

"Get back to New York and do what you can. I'll make the security arrangements for you to get down to Poole's Island. Study those agreements until you know them word by word."

The *paminyatchik* rose from the dais, leaving his unnecessary notes behind.

The limousine passed through the White House gates as Arthur Pierce shot forward in the seat, his hand gripping the strap and, in a harsh voice, spoke to the driver assigned to him by the Department of State. "Get me to a phone booth as fast as you can."

"The mobile phone's in working order, sir. It's in the case in the centre of the floor." The driver removed his right hand from the wheel and gestured at the black leather receptacle behind him. "Just pull up on the latch."

"I don't care to use this phone! A booth, please."

"Sorry, sir, just trying to be helpful."

The Undersecretary checked himself. "I apologize. It's those mobile operators; they can take for ever and I'm in a great hurry."

"Yeah, I've heard that complaint before." The driver accelerated briefly, only to apply the brakes seconds later. "There's one, sir. On the corner."

Pierce got out of the car and walked rapidly to the glass box, coins in his hand. Inside, he pulled the door shut, inserted a quarter and dialled. "Your trip?" he asked curtly.

"Smooth flight. Go ahead."

"Has the detail left for Maryland?"

"About fifteen minutes ago."

"*Stop* them!"

"How?"

The *paminyatchik* bit his lip. There could be no mobile phones for them, no system where numbers could be recorded. He had only one question left before issuing the order. "Is there any way you can reach them once they're on the premises? Any way at all?"

The initial silence was his answer. "Not the way it's orchestrated," was the quiet reply.

"Send a second detail immediately. Police vehicle, automatic weapons, silencers. Kill them; kill them all. No one must be left alive."

"You *sent* them!"

"It's a trap."

"Oh, *Christ* . . . Are you sure?"

"I've just left the White House."

A low whistle was the astonished response. "It really paid off, didn't it?"

"They had no choice. As we say over here, I had all the marbles and I was shooting from the top of the circle. I'm inside. There's also something else."

"What?"

"Reach Mother. Rostov's centred in on Victor. Find out how deep; elimination must be considered."

Loring walked down the steps of the Pentagon thinking about Lieutenant-Commander Thomas Decker. He was not sure what Havelock was looking for, but he was fairly certain he had not got it. After having read Decker's complete service record, including endless evaluation and fitness reports over at the Department of the Navy, Charley had decided to pull in a few debts owed him at the Pentagon. On the pretext that the officer was being considered for a sensitive embassy position that required tact and a fair degree of personality, he called on several friends in Army Intelligence and said he needed a few confidential interviews. Could they help and did they remember when he had helped them? They did and they could.

Five people, each held accountable for confidentiality, were brought separately to him for informal, very off-the-record conversations. There were three fellow naval officers who had served with Decker aboard the submarine, *Starfire*, a secretary who had worked in his office for six months and a marine who was on his Nuclear Committee team.

Havelock had said Decker was a liar. If he was, Loring had found no evidence to support it. He was, if anything, something of a moralizer, who had run a taut ship on the basis of strict Judeo-Christian principles to the point where he read the Lessons at each weekly interdenominational religious service he insisted should be part of the *Starfire's* schedule. His reputation was that of a firm but fair skipper; like Solomon, he weighed all sides of an issue before rendering his decision, which he then proceeded to justify on the basis of what he had heard. As a fellow officer put it, one might disagree with a given course of action on Decker's part, but one understood how he had arrived at it. His "engineer's mind", said another, grasped the "blocks and tackles" of a complicated argument quicker than most and he was adept at spotting fallacies. Yet he never, according to the third officer, used another man's honest error to assert his own superiority; he accepted others' mistakes compassionately, so long as a man had given his best. This, thought Loring, was not a liar's approach. Liars jumped on the failings of others when they were gratuitously provided.

It was the secretary, however, who shed light on another side of Thomas Decker not readily perceived from his service record and the statements of his fellow naval officers. The Lieutenant Commander apparently went to great lengths to please and support his own superiors.

He was always so tactful, so generous in his appraisals of other people's work even when you knew he thought it wasn't very good. There was this admiral . . . Then the White House put out a directive that choked him, but still he . . . And he gave his full endorsement to a Joint Chiefs of Staff position which he told me was really counter productive . . . You talk about tact – well, the commander is about the most diplomatic man I've ever known.

The last person to talk with Charley Loring was the marine, a major and a member of Decker's Nuclear Contingency Committee. He put his own assessment of his colleague somewhat more succinctly.

He kisses ass something fierce, but what the hell, he's damned good. Also, that's not exactly an unknown exercise around here. Tact? . . . Christ, yes, he's got tact, but he's not going to hang himself over something really important. I mean, he'll find ways of greasing an issue so the oil's all over the table.

Translation: spread the responsibility for disagreement, preferably as high as it will flow, but if this attitude made for a dangerous liar, there were few truthful men at the Pentagon – or anywhere else, for that matter.

Loring reached his car in the side parking area, settled back in the seat and pulled out the microphone from its cradle beneath the dashboard. He flipped to power switch and pressed the transmission button, making contact with the White House mobile operator.

"Patch me through to Sterile Five, please," he instructed. While everything was fresh in his mind he would relay it all to Havelock. For all the good it might do.

The Apache unit roamed the corridors of the medical centre, one or other of the two men keeping Dr Matthew Randolph in sight wherever he went. Neither man approved of the arrangements and let Sterile Five know it; they were inadequate for this particular subject. Randolph was an ageing jack rabbit who darted in and out of doors and hallways and outside exits with determined alacrity. Whatever had prompted the doctor to co-operate initially had evaporated as his contrariness reasserted itself. It was as though he were consciously trying to draw attention to himself, to *make* something happen, to challenge any one who might be waiting for him in an empty room or darkened corner to show himself. Beyond the intrinsic difficulty of protecting such a person, the two men found it senselessly unsafe to be forced to show *themselves*. Professionals were, by training and nature, cautious, and Randolph was making them behave otherwise. Neither man relished the thought of being picked off by a sharpshooter a hundred-odd yards away as he followed the cantankerous doctor down a driveway or across a lawn. There was nothing amusing about the situation. Two men were not enough. Even one other man covering the outside would relieve the pressure; more than one, they understood, might defeat the purpose of the strategy by making the whole operation too obvious. One more, however, was mandatory.

Sterile Five accommodated. The emergency call from Apache had interrupted Loring's report to Havelock on Decker. Since Loring was free, he would be flown up by a Pentagon helicopter to within a few miles of the medical centre, where a car would be waiting for him. He would be there in thirty-five to forty minutes.

"How will we know when he gets here?"

"Check the desk by an intercom phone. He'll come inside and ask directions to – Easton. Then he'll drive out and return on foot."

"Thank you, Sterile Five."

*

764

The sun was at the tree-top mark in the western sky, bathing the Virginia country-side in soft bursts of yellow and gold. Havelock wearily got up from the desk, his hand still warm from clutching the ever-present telephone.

"The Agency will dig all night, cross-checking with Cons Op and G-Two. They've located two photographs; six are still missing."

"I'd think photographs would be the first consideration in these files," said Jenna, standing by the silver tray, pouring Michael a drink. "You can't bring over such people if you don't know what they look like."

He watched her as she repeated the words he had heard over the phone.

"The men you chose were never considered that important," Havelock said. "They were marginal, to begin with, their value limited."

"They were specialists."

"Psychiatrists, psychologists and a couple of professors of philosophy. Old men who were permitted the privilege of expressing their views – some vaguely offensive, none earthshaking to the Kremlin."

"But they all questioned theories promoted by Soviet strategists. Their questions were relevant to everything you've learned about Anton Matthias."

"Yes, I know. We'll keep looking."

Jenna carried the short glass of straight whisky to the desk. "Here, you need this."

"Thanks." Havelock took the glass and walked slowly towards the window. "I want to pull in Decker," he said. "I've got to bring him down here. He'll never tell me over the phone. Not everything."

"You're convinced he's your man, then?"

"No question about it. I just had to understand why."

"Loring told you. He fawns on superiors, says he agrees with them even when he doesn't. Such a man would do Matthias's bidding."

"Strangely enough, that's only part of it," said Michael, shaking his head, then sipping his drink. "That description fits most ambitious men everywhere; the exceptions are rare. Too rare."

"Then what?"

Havelock stared out of the window. "He makes a point of justifying everything he does," began Michael slowly. "He reads the Lessons at services instituted at his command; he plays at being Solomon. Underneath that tactful, unctuous exterior there has to be a zealot. And only a zealot in his position would commit a crime for which – as Berquist says – he'd be summarily executed in most countries, and even here he would spend thirty years in prison . . . It wouldn't surprise me if Lieuten-ant-Commander Thomas Decker did it all. If I had my way, he'd be taken out and shot. For all the good it would do."

The sun had dropped below the trees, mottled orange rays filtered by branches, spreading across the lawns and bouncing off the alabaster walls of the Randolph Medical Center. Charles Loring crouched by the trunk of a tall oak at the far end of the parking area, the front entrance and rear emergency ramp in clear view, his radio in his hand. An ambulance had just brought in the victim of a traffic accident and his wife from *US50*; the injured man was being examined by Dr Randolph and the Apache unit was in place in the corridor outside the examining room.

The Cons Op agent looked at his watch. He'd been at his post for nearly three-quarters of an hour – after a hastily arranged flight from the Pentagon helicopter pad to a car waiting for him at a private field on the outskirts of Denton, eight minutes away. He understood the Apache team's concerns. The man they were assigned to protect was making things difficult, but Charley would have handled it differently. He would have sat on this Randolph and told the doctor he didn't give a good goddamn whether he was chopped down or not, that the primary objective of the stake-out was to take even one of those coming after him, that *that* man's life was far more important than his. Such an explanation might have made Randolph more co-operative. And Loring might have been having a decent dinner somewhere, instead of waiting for God knew what on a cold, wet lawn in Maryland.

Charley looked up towards the intruding sound. A black and white patrol car swerved into the rear parking area, turned abruptly and came to a sudden stop at the side of the emergency ramp. Two police officers got out quickly and raced up towards the doors, one leaping onto the platform, both awkwardly holding their sides. Loring lifted the radio to his lips.

"Apache, this is Outside. A police car just drove up to the emergency dock in a hurry. Two cops are entering."

"We see them," came the reply, accompanied by static. "We'll let you know."

Charley looked again at the patrol car, and what he saw struck him as odd. Both doors were left open, something the police rarely did unless they intended to stay close to their vehicle. There was always the possibility that a radio might be tampered with, or a signal book stolen, or even concealed weapons.

The static erupted, words following. "Interesting, but no sweat," said an Apache as yet unseen by the Cons Op agent. "Seems the wreck on Highway Fifty was traced to a prominent member of a Baltimore family. Mafia all the way, wanted on a dozen counts. They've just been admitted for identification and any possible last statements."

"Okay. Out." Loring lowered the radio and considered a cigarette, deciding against it for fear the light would give him away. His eyes strayed again to the stationary patrol car, his mind wandering. Suddenly, there was something to think about, something immediate.

He had passed a police station on the road to the medical centre, not five minutes away. He had recognized it not at first from the sign but by the cluster of three or four patrol cars in the side lot – not black-and-whites, but red-and-whites, the kind of bright colour scheme often adopted by shore resort areas. And if a sought-after, major league Mafioso had been taken minutes ago to a local hospital after a collision, there certainly would be more than one patrol car covering the action.

Open doors, men racing, arms at their sides – concealed weapons. Oh, my *God*!

"Apache! Apache, come in!"

"What is it, Outside?"

"Are those police still in there?"

"They just *went* in."

"Go in after them! *Now!*"

"What?"

"Don't argue, just *do* it! With weapons!"

By the time the radio was in his pocket and the .38 in his hand, Charley was halfway across the parking area, racing as fast as he could towards the emergency dock. He reached the platform and sprang up with one hand, legs scrambling, body lunging for the wide metal doors. He crashed them open and dashed past a startled nurse behind a glass-partitioned reception counter, his head turning in all directions, his eyes choosing the corridor straight ahead; it conformed to the Apaches' position, their immediate sighting of the policemen. He ran down to an intersecting hallway, staring first to his left, then his right. There it was, ten feet away! *EXAMINING ROOM.* The door was shut; it did not make sense.

Loring approached swiftly, silently, taking long cautious steps, his back pressed against the wall. Suddenly he heard two muted spits and the start of a terrible, throated scream from behind the heavy steel door, and he knew his instincts had been as right as he now wished they had been wrong. He spun around the frame, so as to give his left hand free access to the metal handle, then jammed the handle down and threw his shoulder against the panel, crashing the door open, then turned back for the protection of the frame.

The shots came, exploding into the wall in front of him; they were high, the spits from deep inside the room, not close by. Charley crouched and dived, rolling as he hit the floor, and fired into a blue uniform. He fired low, bullets ricocheting off obstructing steel. *Legs, ankles, feet! Arms, if you have to, but not the chest, not the head! Keep him alive!*

The second blue uniform lunged over an examining table – a rushing blur of dark colour – and Loring had no choice. He fired directly at the attacking man who held a pipe-stock repeating weapon in his arms. The killer spun off the padded table, plummeting to the floor, his throat ripped open. Dead.

Keep the other alive, keep the other alive! The order kept screaming in his head as Charley kicked the door shut and lurched, rolling, firing at the ceiling and blowing out the bright overhead fluorescent tubes, leaving only the harsh glow of a small high-intensity lamp on a faraway table.

Three spits erupted from the shadows, the bullets embedding themselves into the plaster and wood above him. He rolled furiously to his left and collided with two lifeless bodies – were they Apaches? He could not tell; he only knew he could not let the man who was alive escape. And there were only two alive in that room, blood, shattered flesh and corpses everywhere.

It had been a massacre.

A spitting burst of gunfire staccatoed across the floor and he could feel the searing heat of the bullet that had punctured his stomach. But the pain did an odd thing to him, which he had no time to think about. He could only experience the reaction. His mind exploded in anger, but the anger was controlled, the fury directed. He had lost before. He could not lose again. He simply *could not!*

He sprang diagonally to his right, crashing into a stretcher table and sending it rolling towards the shadows from which the staccato burst had come; he heard the impact and rose swiftly, held his gun in both hands and aimed at another hand in the shadows. He fired as the screams swelled in the corridors beyond the closed door.

He had one last thing to do. And then he would not have lost.

34

Lieutenant-Commander Thomas Decker walked into the study of Sterile Five, escorted by two men from the White House Secret Service. His angular face was set, and he looked both purposeful and a trifle anxious. The broad-shouldered frame under the well-tailored blue uniform was that of a man who kept in shape not from enjoyment but from compulsion; the body was too rigid, with too little fluidity in its movement. But it was the face that fascinated Havelock. It was a hard-shelled mask about to crack, and once that process started, it would shatter. Strength, purpose and anxiety aside, Decker was petrified, and try as he might he could not conceal his inner terror.

Michael spoke, addressing the Secret Service detail. "Thanks very much, gentlemen. The kitchen is outside to the right, at the end of the hallway. The cook will find you something to eat – beer, coffee, whatever you want. I'm sure I've interrupted your dinner break and I don't know when we'll be finished here. Make any phone calls you like, of course."

"Thank you, sir," said the man on Decker's left, nodding to his companion as they both turned and started for the door.

"You've also interrupted *my* dinner, and I expect – "

"Shut up, Commander," broke in Havelock quietly.

The door closed, and Decker took several angry steps towards the desk but the anger was too contrived, too forced. It had been summoned to replace the fear. "I have an engagement this evening with Admiral James at the Fifth Naval District!"

"He's been informed that pressing naval business precludes your being there."

"This is outrageous! I *demand* an explanation!"

"You're entitled to a firing squad." Havelock rose as Decker gasped. "I think you know why."

" *You!*" The officer's eyes grew wide; he swallowed as the colour left his mask of a face. "You're the one who's been calling me, asking me those questions! Telling me . . . a very *great man* . . . doesn't remember! It's a *lie!*"

"It's the truth," said Michael simply. "But you can't understand and it's been driving you up the wall. It's all you've been thinking about since I told you – because you know what you've done."

Decker became rigid again, brows arched, eyes clouded, a military man having given his serial number but refusing any subsequent interrogation despite impending torture. "I have nothing to say to you. Mr Cross. It *is* Cross, isn't it?"

"It'll do," said Havelock, nodding once. "But you've got a great deal to say, and you *are* going to say it. Because if you don't, a presidential order will send you to the deepest cell in Leavenworth and the key will be thrown away. To put you on trial would be far too dangerous to the security of this country."

"No! . . . You *can't*! I did nothing wrong! I was right, *we* were right!"

"The Joint Chiefs and key members of the House and Senate will agree," continued Michael. "It'll be one of the few times when the umbrella of national security will be completely valid."

The mask cracked; the face shattered. Fear turned to desperation as Decker whispered, "What do they say I've done?"

"In violation of your oath as an officer and the codes of secrecy you've sworn to uphold, you reproduced dozens of the most sensitive documents in this country's military history and removed them from the Pentagon."

"And to *whom* did I deliver them? Answer me that."

"It doesn't matter."

"It *does*! It's everything!"

"You had no authorization."

"*That* man has all the authority he needs!" Decker's voice trembled as he tried to regain control. "I demand that you get Secretary of State Matthias on the phone."

Havelock walked away from the desk, away from the telephone. The movement was not lost on the naval officer. It was the moment to retreat slightly.

"I've been given *my* orders, Commander," said Michael, permitting a degree of uncertainty in his own voice. "By the President and several of his closest advisers. The Secretary of State is not to be consulted in this matter under any circumstances whatsoever. He's not to be informed. I don't know why, but those are my orders."

Decker took a halting step, then another, zeal joining the desperation in his stretched, frantic eyes. He began barely above a whisper, the words growing louder with a zealot's conviction. "The *President*? His *advisers* . . . ? For God's sake, can't you *see*? Of course they don't want him informed because he's right and they're *wrong*. They're afraid and he isn't! Do you think for a moment if I disappeared he wouldn't know what had happened? Do you think he wouldn't confront the President and his advisers and force a showdown? You talk about the Joint Chiefs, members of the House and the Senate. My God, do you think he couldn't call them together and show what a weak, ineffective, *immoral* administration this really *is*? There'd *be* no administration! It would be repudiated, crippled, thrown out!"

"By whom, Commander?"

Decker straightened his broad-shouldered body, a condemned man knowing that ultimate justice would bring a pardon. "The people, Mr Cross. The people of this nation recognize a giant. They won't turn their backs on him because a hack politician and his weak-kneed advisers say so. They won't stand for it! The world has lamented the loss of great leadership these past few decades. Well, we produced a great leader and the world knows it. And my advice to you is to get Anthony Matthias on the telephone. You don't have to say anything, I'll speak to him."

Havelock stood motionless, something more than uncertainty now in his voice. "You believe there could be a showdown? The President – impeached?"

"Look at Matthias. Can you doubt it? Where in the last thirty years has there been a man like him?"

Michael slowly walked back to the desk and lowered himself into the chair, glancing up at Decker. "Sit down, Commander," he said.

Decker quickly sat in the chair that Havelock had purposely placed in front of the desk. "We've used some harsh words with each other, and for my part I apologize. But you *must* understand. We *are* right."

"I need more than that," said Havelock. "We know you removed copies of detailed strategies developed by the Nuclear Contingency Committees, documents that spelled out everything in our own arsenals as well as the results of our deepest penetrations of both the Soviet and the Chinese systems. You delivered these to Matthias over a period of months, but we've never understood why. If you could tell me, give me a reason. *Why?*"

"For the most obvious reason in the world! It goes back to the key word in the title of those committees. Contingency. *Contingency*, Mr Cross, always contingency! *Reaction* – reaction to *this*, reaction to *that*! Always replying, never *initiating*! We don't need contingencies. We can't let our enemies think we'll only *respond*. We need a master plan, to let them know we have a master plan that will ensure their total destruction should they transgress. Our strength, our survival, can no longer be based on defence, Mr Cross, it must be based on *offence*! Anthony Matthias understands this. The others are afraid to face it."

"And you helped him develop this – master plan?"

"I'm proud to say I contributed," said the officer, his words rushed – the pardon was in sight. "I sat with him hour after hour going over every conceivable nuclear option, every possible Soviet and Chinese response, not a single capability overlooked."

"When did you meet?"

"Every Sunday, for weeks on end." Decker lowered his voice, confidentiality joined now with zeal and desperation. "He impressed on me the highly classified nature of our relationship, so I used to drive out in a rented car to his lodge in West Virginia, to a cabin on the secondary road where we'd meet alone."

"The 'Woodshed'," said Michael, the word escaping from him.

"You know it, then?"

"I've been there." Havelock briefly closed his eyes; he knew the "Woodshed" only too well: a small cabin retreat where Anton went to work on his projected memoirs – to talk out his thoughts, every phrase picked up by a voice-activated tape recorder. "Is there anything else? I want you to know I'm listening, Commander. You're very impressive – and I'm listening."

"He's such a truly *brilliant* man," continued Decker, his tone close to an awestruck whisper, his eyes gazing on some unseen holy light. "That probing mind, the depth of his every observation, his grasp of global realities – all *truly* remarkable. A statesman like Anthony Matthias can take this nation to its zenith, bring us to where we were meant to be in the eyes of man and God. Yes, I did what I did and I'd do it again, because I'm a patriot. I love this country as I love the scriptures, and I would lay down my life for it, knowing that I would retain my honour ... There really is no choice, Mr Cross. We *are* right. Pick up the phone and call Matthias, tell him I'm here. And *I'll* tell him the truth. Small men who worship graven images have crawled out of the ground and are trying to destroy him. He'll stamp them out – with our help."

Michael leaned back in the chair, the weariness, the futility, as complete as they had ever been. " 'With our help'," he repeated in a voice so low he was barely aware he had spoken.

"Yes, of course!"

Havelock shook his head slowly back and forth. "You sanctimonious son of a bitch," he said.

"What?"

"You heard me. *You sanctimonious son of a bitch!*" Michael roared. Then he breathed deeply and continued quietly, rapidly, "You want me to call Matthias? I wish to hell I could, just to watch your goddamn face, to see your steely, self-righteous eyes grow wild when you learned the truth."

"What are you talking about?" whispered Decker.

"Matthias wouldn't know who you *are!* Any more than he knows who the President is, or his aides, or the undersecretaries, or the diplomats he works with every day – or me, who's known him for over twenty years, closer to him than any other person alive."

"No . . . no, you're wrong. No!"

"*Yes*, Commander! He broke. More precisely, *we broke him.* That mind is gone! It's shattered. He's insane. He couldn't take it any longer. And, by Christ, you did your part. You gave him his ultimate authority, his final responsibility. You stole the world's – yes, the *world's* secrets – and told him his genius could handle them. You took a thousand facts and a hundred theoretical strategies, mixed them up and turned them into the most terrifying weapon this earth has ever known. A blueprint for global annihilation."

"That's *not* what I did!"

"Granted, not all by yourself, but you provided the – what the hell's that God-awful Pentagonese? – support-structure, that's it. You provided the support structure for a fiction that's so real there's not a nuclear expert alive who wouldn't accept it as truth. *Gospel* truth, if you like, Commander."

"We only discussed, analysed, tore apart options! The final plan was to be his; you can't *understand*. His grasp was brilliant! There was nothing he couldn't comprehend; it was incredible!"

"It was the act of a mind dying, on the edge of becoming its own convoluted vegetable. He wanted you to believe, and he was still good enough to make you believe. He had to, and you wanted to."

"I did! So would *you!*"

"That's what I've been told by a better man than you'll ever be."

"I don't deserve that. He appealed to a truth I *do* believe in. We *must* be strong!"

"I don't know any sane person who would argue with that, but there are different kinds and degrees of strength. Some work – usually quietly; others don't, because they're swollen with bellicosity. The savage explodes from his own tension; he can't contain himself, he's got to flex. And somewhere along the line he blows up, setting in motion a dozen responses that are explosions in themselves."

"Who *are* you? *What* are you?"

"A student of history who went astray. But I'm not the issue. You are. Everything you gave Matthias is within arm's reach of the Russians, Commander. That master plan, which you're so convinced we must let the world know we have, may in all its details be on its way to Moscow. Because the man you gave it to is insane, was on his way to becoming insane when you delivered the materials to him."

Decker rose slowly from the chair. "I don't believe you," he said, his voice hollow, the words spoken in dread.

"Then why am I here? Why would I say it? Personal considerations aside, do you think anyone with the brains to get out of the rain wants to make that statement? Have you any idea what it means to this country to know that the mind of its Secretary of State has been destroyed? I'd like to remind you, Commander, that you don't have an exclusive claim to patriotism. None of you do."

Decker stared down at Havelock until he could no longer bear the contact. He turned away, the broad-shouldered body somehow shrinking beneath the tunic. "You tricked me. You made me say things I never would have said."

"It's my job."

"Everything's over for me. I'm finished."

"Maybe not. As of this moment, I'd guess you were the least likely candidate for a security risk in the Pentagon. You've been burned by a legend and it's a pain you'll never forget. Nobody knows better than I do how persuasive Matthias could be . . . We need help, not prison sentences. Packing you off to Leavenworth would only raise questions no one wants raised. We're in a blind race; maybe you can help."

Decker turned, swallowing, his face ashen. "In any way I can. How?"

Michael got out of the chair and came round the desk to face the officer. "For starters, nothing I've told you can be repeated."

"My God, of *course* not."

"No, of course not. You'd be hanging yourself."

"I'd be hanging the country. I have no exclusivity on patriotism, but I am a patriot, Mr Cross."

Havelock walked past the coffee table and the couch, and was reminded of Jenna's absence. Since they had agreed her presence would be inhibiting, she was upstairs; more accurately, she had insisted on not being there. He reached the wall, aimlessly studied a brass plaque, and spoke. "I'm going to guess again, Commander. There came a time when Matthias wouldn't see you any more. Am I right?"

"Yes. I phoned repeatedly – not at State, of course – but he never returned my calls."

"Not at State?" asked Michael, turning. "But you *did* call there. It's how I found you."

"Only three times. Twice to say there were Sunday conferences at the Pentagon, and once to tell him I was going into hospital for minor surgery on a Friday and expected to be there until Tuesday or Wednesday. He was very solicitous, but that was when he told me never again to contact him at the State Department."

"You called the lodge, then?"

"And his house in Georgetown."

"This is later?"

"Yes. I called night after night, but he wouldn't come to the phone. Try to understand, Mr Cross. I was aware of what I'd done, of the enormity of the violation I'd committed. Mind you, until a few minutes ago I've never regretted it. I can't change my beliefs; they're ingrained in me. But back then – five or six months ago – I was bewildered, frightened perhaps, I'm not sure. I'd been left stranded – "

"You were in withdrawal," interrupted Havelock. "You'd been on a high, on one of the most potent narcotics in the world: Anthony Matthias. Suddenly he wasn't there any longer."

"Yes, that's it. Those were heady days, magnificent memories. Then without knowing why my connection to greatness was severed. I thought perhaps it was something I'd done that displeased him, or information I'd brought him that was deficient, incomplete. I didn't know, I just knew that I'd been cut off, with no explanation."

"I understand," said Michael, remembering so clearly the night in Cagnes-sur-Mer when his *pritel* did not come to the telephone five thousand miles away. "I'm surprised you didn't force the issue, confront him somehow, somewhere. You were entitled to that explanation."

"I didn't have to. It was finally given to me."

"*What?*"

"One evening, after I'd tried to reach him again, to no avail again, a man called me back. A very strange man – "

The prolonged outburst of the phone shattered the moment, blowing apart the taut line of concentration. Havelock ran to it, to the sustained ring that signalled *Emergency.*

"It's Loring," said the strained voice in a half-whisper. "I'm hit. I'm okay, but I'm hit."

"Where are you?"

"A motel on Highway Three-seventeen, near Harrington. The Pheasant Run Motel. Cabin Twelve."

"I'll send a doctor."

"A very *special* doctor, Havelock. Use the field in Denton."

"What do you mean?"

"I had to get out of there. I grabbed a police car – "

"A police . . . ? *Why?*"

"I'll tell you later. Everything . . . Special doctor with a bag full of needles."

"For Christ's sake, spell it out, Charley!"

"I've got one of those sons of bitches. He's strapped naked on the bed – no capsules, no razors. I've got one!"

Havelock stabbed the buttons on the Sterile Five telephone one after another, issuing orders one after another as Lieutenant-Commander Decker stood rigidly across the room, watching, listening, a helpless shell of a crusader whose cause had collapsed. The President was informed, and a very special doctor was being tracked down, to be sent to Maryland by helicopter, a Secret Service detail accompanying him. A second helicopter was prepared for take off, waiting for Michael at the field in Quantico six miles away; he would be driven there by the Secret Service escorts who had brought Decker to Sterile Five. The final call placed by Havelock was within the house itself. Upstairs. To Jenna Karras.

"I have to leave. It's Loring in Maryland. He's wounded, but he may have picked up a traveller – don't ask me how. And you were right. One source. He's here and has more to say; please come down and take it. I have to go . . . Thanks."

Michael got up from the desk and addressed the frightened naval officer. "A lady's on her way here, and I'm ordering you – ordering you, Commander – to tell her everything you were going to tell me, and answer fully any questions she may ask. Your escort will be back in twenty minutes or so. When you're finished, and only if she agrees, you may go. But once you reach your house you're not to leave it for any reason whatsoever. You'll be watched."

"Yes, Mr Cross."

Havelock grabbed his jacket off the back of the chair and started towards the door. He stopped and turned to Decker, his hand on the knob. "Incidentally, her name is Mrs Cross."

All low-flying traffic was diverted as the two helicopters roared into the small private field in Denton, Maryland, the aircraft from the Bethesda Naval Hospital arriving eleven minutes before the chopper from Quantico. Havelock raced across the tarmac to the staff car sent over from Annapolis, the driver an ensign reputed to know the roads on the Eastern Shore of Chesapeake Bay. The ensign knew nothing else; no one did; not even the doctor whose orders were to take care of Charles Loring first and not to administer anything to Loring's prisoner until Sterile Five was on the scene. Two state police patrol cars had been sent to the Pheasant Run Motel; they would be given their instructions by the Secret Service.

If the name Pheasant Run gave rise to images of squiredom and hunt country, it was misapplied to the sleazy motel's row of run-down cabins just off the main road. Apparently, the motel's primary function was to serve as a meeting place for assignations lasting an hour or so; cars were parked in small unpaved areas at the rear, out of sight of the main road. The management catered to its clientele's idiosyncrasies if not their comforts, and Loring had used his head. A man in pain, concealing wounds, without luggage but with a prisoner he wanted to rush surreptitiously into hiding, could hardly hope to register at a brightly lit Howard Johnson's Motor Lodge.

Havelock thanked the ensign and told him to return to Annapolis, reminding him that the present emergency called for the utmost secrecy. Washington had his name, and his co-operation would not be overlooked. The young man, obviously impressed by the sight of searchlights and military helicopters at night, as well as by his own participation, replied in a monotone, "You may be assured of my silence, sir."

"Just say you went out for a beer, that's good enough. Better, maybe."

A government man, holding up an encased silver badge in his palm, intercepted Michael as he ran along the row of cabins looking for number 12.

"Sterile Five," said Havelock, noticing for the first time the two state police cars parked in the shadows twenty feet apart to his left. Number 12 was nearby.

"This way," said the man, pocketing his badge as he led Michael between two cabins towards the rear of the motel's grounds. Beyond was a shorter row of cabins, which were not visible from the front. Loring had spent precious moments of pain and anxiety studying the motel's layout – again an indication that he was in control.

In the distance, behind the cabin on the left, the bonnet of a stationary car could be seen, but it was not an ordinary car. A streak of white ending in an arrowhead was stencilled over the black chassis at midpoint. It was the patrol car Loring had stolen, the only indication that perhaps he had lost a part of the control that had served them all so well. Someone in Washington would have to reach a panicked police headquarters and call off the hunt.

"This is it," said the federal agent, pointing to the door of a cabin which opened onto a verandah three steps above ground level. "I'll be out here," added the man. "Watch those steps; they're loose."

"Thanks," said Havelock, going cautiously up to the door. He tried the knob; it was locked. In answer to his knock, someone inside asked, "Who is it?"

"Sterile Five," replied Michael.

The door was opened by a stocky, red-haired man in his middle thirties, his Celtic face freckled, his eyes wary, his sleeves rolled up. "Havelock?"

"That's right."

"Name's Taylor. Come on in, we've got to talk fast."

Michael walked inside the room with the soiled wallpaper; the doctor closed the door. On the bed was a naked man, spread-eagled, bloody hands and feet tied to the frame, belts around the wrists, torn sheets lashed to his ankles. His mouth was pulled taut by a striped blue tie to inhibit any loud sound and his eyes were wide with anger and fear.

"Where's . . . ?"

Taylor gestured towards the far corner of the room. There on the floor, his head on a pillow and a blanket over him, was Charles Loring, his eyes only partially open; he was dazed or in shock. Havelock started across the filthy grey carpet but was stopped by the doctor's grip on his arm.

"That's what we have to talk about. I don't know what's going on here, but I do know I can't be responsible for that man s life unless we got him to a hospital an hour ago. Do I make myself clear?"

"As soon as we can, not right now," said Michael, shaking his head. "I've got to question him. He's the only person who can give me the information I need. Everyone else is dead."

"Maybe you didn't hear me. I said an hour ago."

"I heard you, but I know what I have to do. I'm sorry."

"I don't *like* you," said Taylor, staring at Havelock, removing his hand as if he had touched something loathsome.

"I wish that could concern me, Doctor, because I like *him*. I'll be as brief and as quiet as I can. He'd want it this way, take my word for it."

"I have to. I couldn't persuade him to get out of here ten minutes ago."

Michael walked over to Loring and knelt down, putting his face close to the wounded man's. "Charley, it's Havelock. Can you hear me?"

Loring opened his eyes wider, his lips trembling, struggling to form the words. Finally the whisper came. "Yes. Hear . . . you . . . fine."

"I'll tell you what I've learned, which is damned little. Nod your head if I'm on the track, shake it if I'm not. Don't waste words or breath. Okay?" The Cons Op agent nodded and Michael continued, "I spoke with police who are trying to put it together. As they tell it, an ambulance brought in a traffic accident with his wife, and Randolph, a staff doctor and a nurse were cleaning him up, checking the extent of injuries." Loring shook his head, but Havelock went on, "Let me finish, then we'll go back. They weren't in there five minutes when two state troopers came running in and spoke with our cardiologists. No one knows what was said, but they were admitted into the examining room. Again the Cons Op agent shook his head. "A couple of minutes later a third man – I assume that was you – crashed through emergency doors, and that's when everything went down." Loring nodded; Havelock took a breath and continued softly, rapidly.

"The staff heard gunshots, perhaps five or six, no one's sure. Most of them ran out of the building. The rest hid in the corridors and patients' rooms behind locked doors, everyone trying to reach a phone. When the gunfire stopped, someone outside saw you and one of the state police come running down the ramp – you were bent over with a gun in your hand, the officer was bleeding, limping and holding his arm. You forced him into the patrol car and got out of there. The police are trying to find out who the other trooper was, but identifications were taken off some of the bodies, not all." Loring shook his head violently. Michael touched his shoulder. "Take it easy; we'll go back. I don't have to tell you the body count was full. Randolph, the staff doctor, the nurse, the accident victim and his wife and our Apache unit. Two automatic weapons equipped with silencers were found; they're still counting the shells. Yours was the gunfire that was heard; they're tracing the weapons, matching prints. Beyond what I've told you, no one knows what happened . . . Now, let's go back." Havelock squinted, remembering. "The traffic accident."

Loring shook his head, whispering. "No accident."

"Why not?"

"They *weren't* troopers."

Michael looked up at the naked man strapped to the bed, and at the uniform rumpled on the floor. "Of course they weren't. And the patrol car was a mock-up; they've got the money for that kind of thing. I should have known; you wouldn't have taken it otherwise."

The wounded agent nodded, his hand emerging from under the blanket, gesturing for Havelock to lean closer. "The man and the woman . . . from the ambulance. the accident. Any IDs?"

"No."

"Same with the troopers . . . right?"

"Right."

"The accident," whispered Loring, stopping for breath. "Too easy. Man hurt . . . a woman who won't leave his side. They get in . . . to a room . . . doctor, nurse . . . Randolph. They got him."

"How could they know Randolph would be there?"

"Doesn't matter. They'd tell the doctor . . . or the nurse to call for him . . . under a gun. Probably did. They *got* him. Too easy."

"And the troopers?"

"In a hurry . . . running like hell. They were sent to break it up, break it *all* up . . . in a hurry."

"How did you figure that?"

"They left the doors open, ran funny . . . heavy weapons under their coats. The pattern wasn't normal, wasn't right . . . Apache said the accident was a big-balled Mafioso the cops came to question. If he was, there'd be ten vehicles there, not one." Loring expelled his breath, coughing; blood trickled out of the corners of his mouth. He gasped, and resumed breathing. The doctor was now behind Havelock.

"For Christ's sake," said Taylor quietly but with angry intensity. "Why don't you just put a bullet in his head?"

"Why don't I put one in yours?" Michael leaned back towards Loring. "*Why,* Charley? Why do you think they were sent in to break it up?"

"I'm not sure. Maybe I was spotted . . . maybe I blew it again."

"I don't believe that."

"Don't be so goddamn nice, I can't stand it . . . I probably did blow it . . . I'm getting old."

"Then just pass on your instincts, Methuselah, we need them. You didn't blow anything. You brought us one, you *brought* us one, Charley."

Loring tried to raise his shoulders, Michael gently holding him down. "Tell me something, Havelock. You said this morning . . . about Shippers. 'A long time ago'. You said he was programmed a long time ago. Tell me. Is that son of a bitch over there a . . . a traveller?"

"I think he is."

"Goddamn . . . maybe I'm not so old."

Michael got to his feet and turned to the doctor behind him. "All right, Taylor, he's yours. Get him over to the field and have him taken to the best facilities at Bethesda. And get on the phone and tell those mothers the White House wants the finest team of surgeons you've got ready and waiting for this man."

"Yes, *sir,*" said the doctor sardonically. "Anything else, *sir?*"

"Oh, yes, physician. Prepare your bag of magic. You're about to go to work."

Loring was carried out on a stretcher by two male nurses who had been standing by; they were given firm instructions by the doctor as they took away the wounded Cons Op agent. Taylor turned to Havelock.

"Do we start now?"

"What about the wounds?" asked Michael, looking down at the naked man's bandaged but blood-streaked right arm and left foot.

"Your friend put tourniquets where they were needed, and I added dressings; the bleeding's arrested. Also, he was damned accurate. Bone was shattered, but apart from the pain, nothing'll drain him. Naturally, I gave him a couple of locals to ease him, keep his head clearer."

"Will they interfere with the chemicals?"

"I wouldn't have administered them if they did."

"Then shoot him up, Doctor. I can't waste time."

Taylor went to his large black leather case which was open and on a table near the window under the glow of a lamp. He studied the contents for several moments, took out three vials and three cased syringes and placed them on the edge of the bed next to the naked man's thigh. The prisoner raised his head, his features contorted, his eyes glazed, frenzied; he was close to hysterics. Suddenly he began to writhe furiously, and muffled animal-like howls came from his throat. He stopped, overwhelmed, by the pain in his right arm, and, gasping for breath, he stared at the ceiling. Then abruptly he held the air in his lungs, his face becoming redder by the second, eyes now bulging.

"What the hell is he – "

"Get out of my *way*!" shouted Havelock, pushing the doctor aside and crashing his clenched fist down on the killer's bare stomach. The breath exploded out of the traveller's bound mouth, and the eyes and flesh tone began returning to normal.

"*Jesus*," said Taylor, rushing forward to steady the vials which were about to roll off the edge of the bed. "What was *that*?"

"You're dealing with something you may never have dealt with before, Doctor. They're programmed like robots, killing whomever they're told to kill – without any feeling at all, without the slightest concern. Not even for themselves."

"Then he won't negotiate. I thought maybe if he saw these things, he might."

"No way. He'd stall us, throw us off with every plausible lie in the books, and they know them all. They're masters of the craft. Let's go, Doctor."

"How do you want to progress? In stages, which will bring him back one step at a time, or do you want to chance a maximum? It's the fastest, but there's a risk."

"What's the worst with it?"

"Incoherence. Disjointed rambling, no logical pattern."

"No logical . . . ? That's it. I'll chance the incoherence, just get him away from any patterns that might trigger programmed responses."

"It doesn't work quite that way. The flow becomes formless; dissociation is the first reaction. The key is to hit certain words – "

"You're saying everything I want to hear, Doctor, and you're also wasting time."

"You think so?" With the swiftness of a surgeon stemming a sudden internal eruption, Taylor broke off a vial's tiny glass casing, inserted the syringe, withdrew it and plunged it into the traveller's thigh before the bound man knew it was happening. The killer writhed violently, yanking at the belts and the torn sheets in an effort to break them, rolling from side to side as muffled cries filled the room. "The more he does that, the quicker it'll take effect," added Taylor, pressing his hand on the side of the stretched, whipping neck. "Only a minute or so."

Michael watched, fascinated and revolted, as he always was when observing the effect of these chemicals on a human being. He had to remind himself that this killer had brutally taken the lives of men and women less than three hours ago – his own people and others, the guilty and the totally innocent. How many would mourn for them and never understand? And how many were laid at the feet of one Michael Havelock, courtesy of Anton Matthias? Two career officers, a young doctor, a younger nurse, a man named Randolph, whose only crime was to try to right a terrible wrong.

Futility.

"He's about ready now," said Taylor, studying the filmy, partially closed eyes of the prisoner, whose movements had contracted into slow, weaving motions accompanied by moans.

"You must be happy in your work, Doctor."

"I was always a nosy kid," answered the red-haired man, gently removing the striped tie from the traveller's mouth. "Besides, someone's got to do it and big uncle paid for my medical degree. My old man couldn't pay for a bucket of suds in Paddy O'Rourke's saloon. I'll pay my debt and get out."

Havelock leaned over the bed as Taylor backed away. "May I begin?" he asked.

"Talk, he's your crossword puzzle."

"*Orders*," began Michael, his hand on the headboard, his lips near the traveller's ear, his voice firm, steady, low. "Orders, orders, *orders*. None of us can move without our *orders*! But we have to be certain, we can't make a mistake. Who can clear our *orders*, clear our orders *now*?"

The prisoner's head moved back and forth, his mouth alternately opening and closing, stretching the bruised flesh. But no sound came.

"It's an emergency," continued Havelock. "Everybody *knows* it's an emergency . . . an *emergency*. We've got to hurry, hurry . . . hurry up."

"Hurry . . . hurry *up*." The whisper emerged, tentative, uncertain.

"But how can we be *sure*?" Michael raced on. "We have to be *certain*."

"The flight . . . the flight was *smooth*. We heard it twice. That's all we have to know. The flight . . . *smooth*."

"Of course. A *smooth flight*. We're all right now. We can hurry . . . Now, let's float back . . . before the emergency. Relax. Sleep."

"Very good," said the doctor from across the dimly lit, squalid room. "You centred him as quickly as I've ever seen it done. That was a response."

"It wasn't difficult," replied Havelock, rising from the bed and studying the traveller. "Since he's been given his orders he's had three things on his mind. Emergency, speed and clearance. His instructions were to kill – an extreme order, also a dangerous one – so clearance was vital. You heard him, he had to hear it twice."

"The code was a 'smooth flight'. He gave it to you, and now you'll give it back to him. You're closer."

"And you're no amateur, Doctor. Get me a chair, will you? I've also got speed and emergency on my mind. Things may get rough." Taylor brought a straight-backed chair over to the bed; Michael sat down; the chair was unsteady but serviceable. He leaned forward, arms on the edge of the bed, and spoke again to the bound man. "We have a smooth flight . . . a smooth flight . . . a *very smooth flight*! Now, kill your partner!"

The traveller whipped his head to the right, his clouded eyes blinking, lips moving – protest without sound.

"You heard me!" shouted Havelock. "We have a smooth flight, so *kill him*!"

"What . . . ? *Why?*" The whispered words were guttural.

"Are you married? Tell me, since we're on a smooth flight, are you *married*?"

"Yes . . . yes, married."

"Kill your *wife*!"

"Why?"

"We're on a *smooth flight*! How can you *refuse*?"

"Why . . . *why*?"

"Kill your partner! Kill your wife! Do you have children?"

"*No!*" The traveller's eyes widened, the glaze within on fire. "You could never ask . . . *never*!"

"I do! A smooth flight! What more do you need?"

"*Clearance*. I demand clearance! I . . . must have it!"

"From where? From whom? I've already told you. We're on a *smooth flight*! That's *it*"!

"*Please* . . . *!* Me, kill *me*. I'm . . . confused!"

"Why are you confused? You heard my orders, just as you heard the orders for today. Did I give you those orders?"

"No."

"No? You don't remember? If not me, *who*?"

"The trip . . . the smooth flight. The . . . control."

"The *control*?"

"The source."

"The source-control! *Your* source-control. I *am* your source-control! Kill your partner! Kill your wife! *Kill the children! All* the children!"

"I . . . *I*. You can't ask me . . . please don't ask me."

"I don't ask. I demand, I give orders! Do you want to sleep?"

"Yes."

"You *can't* sleep!" Michael turned his head and spoke to Taylor, his voice soft, barely audible. "How long will the dose last?"

"The way you're eating it up, half the normal time. Another ten minutes, tops."

"Prepare another. I'm taking him up."

"It'll blow him into space."

"He'll come down."

"You're the doctor," said the doctor.

"*I* am your source-control!" shouted Havelock, getting out of the chair, leaning over the traveller's face. "You have no one else, *paminyatchik*! You will do as I tell you and only what I tell you! Now, your *partner*, your *wife*, the *children*."

"*Ahhhh* . . . *!*" The scream was prolonged, a cry beyond helplessness.

"I've only *begun* . . ."

The bound, drugged killer, strained against the leather and the cloth, body and features twisted, his mind in a labyrinth of terror, with sacrifice demanded upon sacrifice, pain upon pain, no way out of the impossible maze.

"*Now*," said Havelock to the doctor beside him.

Taylor plunged the hypodermic needle into the traveller's arm; the reaction was there in moments, drug accelerating drug. The screams turned into animal screeches, saliva flowing from the killer's mouth – violence the only answer to violence.

"*Give* it to me!" yelled Michael. "*Prove* it to me! Or be killed with everyone else!

Partner, wife, children . . . you all die unless you can prove yourself to me. Right now, this moment! . . . *What is the code for your source-control?*"

"*Hammer-zero-two!* You *know* it!"

"Yes, I know it. Now tell me, where can I be reached – don't *lie!*"

"Don't know . . . don't know! I'm called . . . We're all called."

"When you want clearance! When you have information to deliver. How do you reach me when you want clearance, when you have information that has to be relayed."

"Tell them . . . need it. We all do. Everyone."

"Who?"

"Orphan. Reach . . . Orphan."

"*Orphan?*"

"Ninety-six."

"Orphan-ninety-six? Where is he? *Where?*"

"*O . . . r . . . p . . . h . . .* " The final scream was shattering. The traveller thrashed his full strength and weight against the belts and broke one, releasing his left arm. He lunged upwards, then arched his back in a spasm and fell unconscious over the far side of the bed.

"He's had it," said Taylor, reaching across Havelock and holding the prisoner's wrist in his fingers. "His pulse is a jackhammer; it'll be eight hours before he can sustain another jolt. Sorry – Doctor."

"It's all right, Doctor," said Michael, walking away from the bed and reaching into his pocket for cigarettes. "We could have done worse. You're a hell of a good chemist."

"I don't consider it my life's work."

"If it weren't right now, you might not have – " Havelock stopped to light a cigarette.

"What?"

"Nothing. I meant you might not have time for a drink, but I do."

"Sure, I do. I'll get Boris here down to a clinic."

"Boris? . . . You know?"

"Enough to know he's not a Boy Scout."

"That's the funny thing. He probably was."

"Tell me," asked the red-haired doctor, "would a source-control order him to do that? Kill his wife and kids, people that close to him?"

"Never. Moscow wouldn't risk it. These people are like robots, but it's blood inside, not oil. They're monitored continuously, and if the KGB wants taken out, an execution squad is sent in to do it. A normal family is part of the cover; it's also a powerful secondary hook. If a man's ever tempted, he knows what will happen."

"You used it the same way, didn't you? Only in reverse."

"I'm not wildly proud of the accomplishment, but yes."

"Jesus, Mary and Paddy O'Rourke," muttered the doctor.

Michael watched as Taylor reached for the bedside phone to issue his instructions through Bethesda Central. The *telephone. Orphan-96.* "Wait a minute!" Michael cried suddenly.

"What's the matter?"

"Let me use that phone!" Havelock rushed to the table, picked up the telephone and dialled, talking out loud as he did so.

"O, r, p, h, a, n . . . *nine-six.*"

"Operator," said the female voice on the line.

"What?"

"Is this a collect call, billed to a credit card, or to another number?"

"Credit card." Michael stared at the wall to remember his untraceable, State-assigned number. He gave it to the operator and heard the subsequent ringing.

"Good evening and thank you for calling the Voyagers Emporium, luggage for the sophisticated globe-trotter. If you'll state the numbered item or items from our catalogue you wish to purchase, you will be connected to the proper representative in our twenty-four-hour service department."

Havelock replaced the phone. He needed another code; it would be found in a clinic. It *had* to be found. . . . *We all do. Everyone* . . . Ambiguity was at the end of that code.

"Anything?" asked the bewildered Taylor.

"That'll be up to you, Doctor. Ever heard of the Voyagers Emporium? I don't know it, but then for years I've bought my stuff in Europe."

"The Voyagers? Sure. They've got branches all over the place. They're the Tiffany of the luggage business. My wife bought one of those carry-on bags and I swear to God when I got the bill I thought she'd picked up a car. They're first class."

"They're also trade marked KGB. That's what you're going to work on. Whatever your schedule is, scratch it. I want you down at the clinic with our globe-trotter here. We need another series of numbers. Just one more set."

There was a sound of heavy footsteps outside the cabin, followed by a harsh rapping on the door.

"What is it?" asked Havelock, loud enough to be heard outside.

"Sterile Five, you're wanted. Urgent call over the state police vehicles. You're to be taken to the airfield pronto."

"On my way. Havelock turned to Taylor. "Make your arrangements. Stay with it – with *him.* I'll be in touch. Sorry about the drink."

"So's Paddy O'Rourke."

"Who the hell is Paddy O'Rourke?"

"A little man who sits on my shoulder and tells me not to think too much."

Michael climbed into the marine helicopter, the giant overhead blades thundering, the pilot beckoning him forward to the flight deck.

"There's a patch-phone back there!" shouted the pilot. "It'll be quieter when the hatch is closed. We'll put your call through."

"Who is it?"

"We'll never know!" yelled the radio-man, turning from his console against the bulkhead. "Our link is filtered. We're bypassed."

The heavy metal door was electronically swung into place, shutting out the spill of the airfield's searchlights and reducing the thunder of the rotors to a muffled roar. Havelock crouched in the flashing darkness and gripped the phone, holding it to his right ear, his free hand covering the other. The voice that came last on the line was that of the President of the United States.

"You're being flown directly to Andrews Air Force Base to meet with Arthur Pierce."

"What's happened, sir?"

"He's on his way to Poole's Island with the vault specialist, but wants to talk with you first. He's a frightened man, and I don't think he frightens easily."

"The Russians?"

"Yes. He can't tell whether they accepted his story or not. They listened to him in silence, nodded and showed him the door. He has an idea that during the past eighteen hours they've learned something major, something they won't talk about – something that could blow everything apart. He warned them not to make any precipitous moves without communication at the highest levels."

"What was their response?"

"Deadly. 'Look to yourselves', they said."

"They've got something. Pierce knows his enemy."

"In the last extremity, we'll be forced to parade Matthias . . . hoping to deter a launch, no guarantee that it will. I don't have to tell you what it will mean – we'll be a government of lepers, never trusted again. If we're on the map."

"What can I do? What does Pierce want?"

"All you've got, everything you've learned. He's trying to find something, *anything*, he can use as a lever. Every hour he can present a counter change and prevent escalation, every day he can buy us, is a day for you. You *are* making progress?"

"Yes. We know the Ambiguity connection now, where he sends and receives. By mid-morning we should learn just how he does it, through whom. When we do we'll find him."

"Then you *could* be a step away from Parsifal."

"I think so."

"I don't want to hear that! I want to hear *yes*."

"Yes, Mr President." Havelock paused, thinking about the few, brief words they needed to break the Voyagers code. They would be heard and recorded in a clinic. "I believe it."

"You wouldn't say it otherwise, thank *God*. Get down to Pierce. Give him everything you've got. *Help* him!"

35

The intersecting runways were lined with amber airstrip lamps. Searchlight beams crisscrossed and penetrated the dense cloud cover as routine patrols and check-out flights soared off into the night sky and swooped down from the darkness onto the floodlit open field. Andrews was a vast, guarded military city unto itself. The activity was intense, both on the field and off. As headquarters of the US Air Force Systems Command, its responsibilities were as far-ranging as they were endless. For thousands there was no such thing as day or night – merely duty hours and assignments. Banks of computers in a dozen buildings coexisted with the constant flow of expertise from the human interpreters, all forming judgements that affected NORAD, CONAD, the DEW line stations and SAC. The base occupied some 4,400 acres east of the Potomac and west of Chesapeake Bay, but its interests circled the globe, its purpose being the defence of the North American continent.

The marine helicopter was given clearance to enter a low-altitude pattern and set down on a pad north of the main field. Searchlights caught them a quarter of a mile away from ground-zero as radar, radio and a pilot's sharp eyes eased them into the threshold from which they could make the vertical descent. Among the instructions radioed from the control tower was a message for Sterile Five. A jeep would be standing by to take Havelock to a runway on the south perimeter. It would wait there until his business was concluded and return him to the helicopter.

Havelock climbed out of the hatch and jumped to the ground. The damp chill of the air was accentuated by the rushing wash of the decelerating rotors, and as he walked rapidly away from it he pulled the lapels of his overcoat around his throat, wishing he had worn a hat – but then he remembered that the only hat he owned at the moment was a ragged knit cap that he'd left somewhere down on Poole's Island.

"Sir! *Sir!*" The shout came from Michael's left, beyond the tail assembly of the helicopter. It was the driver of the jeep, the vehicle itself barely visible in the shadows between the blinding arc lights of the pad.

Havelock ran over as the sergeant behind the wheel started to get out as a gesture of courtesy. "Forget it," said Michael, approaching the side panel, his hand on the windscreen frame. "I didn't see you, he added, stepping over and lowering himself into the seat."

"Those were my instructions," explained the air force non-com. "Stay out of sight as much as possible."

"Why?"

"You'll have to ask the man who gives the orders, sir. I'd say he's careful, and since nobody's got a name I don't ask questions."

The jeep shot forward, expertly manoeuvred by the driver onto a narrow asphalt road fifty yards east of the helicopter pad. He turned left and accelerated, the road virtually circled the massive field, passing lighted buildings and enormous parking lots – flickering black structures and dark, spacious blurs – interspersed with the glare of onrushing headlights; everything at Andrews was apparently always at triple time. The wind whipped through the open vehicle, the slapping damp air penetrating Michael's coat, making him tense his muscles against the cold.

"I don't care if he calls himself Little Bo Beep," said Havelock, as much for conversation as for anything else. "So long as there's heat wherever we're going."

The sergeant glanced briefly at Michael. "Sorry again," he replied, "but the man doesn't have it that way. My instructions are to take you to a runway on the south perimeter. I'm afraid that's it. A runway."

Havelock folded his arms and kept his eyes on the road ahead, wondering why the Undersecretary of State was being so cautious within a military compound. Then his thoughts dwelt briefly on the man himself and he found part of the answer – the blind part, but nevertheless intrinsic: there had to *be* a reason. From what he had read about Arthur Pierce in the State Department dossier, coupled with what he had known from a distance, the Undersecretary was a bright, persuasive spokesman for American interests at the United Nations, as well as around the international conference tables, with an avowed and profound mistrust of the Russians. This mistrust, however, was couched in a swift, aggressive wit and woven in deceptively pleasant frontal assaults that drove the stolid Russians wild for they had no matching counterattacks, except for bluster and defiance. Perhaps Pierce's outstanding credential was that he had been hand-picked by Matthias himself when Anton was at the height of his intellectual powers. But the characteristic that stood out in Havelock's mind while racing down the dark airfield road was the highly regarded self-discipline attributed to Arthur Pierce by just about everybody who had contributed to his service dossier. He was never known to say anything unless he had something to say. By extension, thought Michael, he would not do something unless there was a reason for doing it.

And he had chosen to meet on a runway.

The driver swung left into an intersecting road that ran the distance of a huge maintenance hangar, then turned right onto the border of a deserted airstrip. In the distance, silhouetted in the glare of the headlights, was the figure of a man standing alone. Behind him, perhaps five hundred feet beyond and off the strip, was a small prop-jet with interior and exterior lights on and a fuel truck alongside it.

"There's the man," said the sergeant, slowing down. "I'll drop you off and wait back by the junk shop."

"The what?"

"The maintenance hangar. Just shout when you want me."

The jeep came to a stop thirty feet from Arthur Pierce. Havelock got out and saw the Undersecretary of State starting towards him, a tall, slender man in a dark overcoat and hat, his stride long and energetic. Protocol was obviously unimportant to Pierce; there were too many with his title in the State Department who, regardless of the crisis, would expect a mere foreign service officer to approach *them*. Michael began walking, noticing that Pierce was removing the glove from his right hand.

"Mr Havelock?" said the diplomat, hand extended, as the jeep sped away.

"Mr Undersecretary?"

"But of course it's you," continued Pierce, his grip firm and genuine. "I've seen your photograph. Frankly, I've read everything I could get my hands on about you. Now, I suppose I should get this over with."

"What?"

"Well, I guess I'm a little awe-struck, which is a pretty silly thing for a grown man to say. But your accomplishments in a world I don't claim to understand are very impressive." The Undersecretary paused, looking embarrassed. "I imagine the exotic nature of your work evokes this kind of reaction quite a lot."

"I wish it would; you make me feel terrific. Especially considering the mistakes I've made – particularly during the last few months."

"The mistakes weren't yours."

"I should also tell you," Michael went on, overlooking the comment, "I've read a great deal about you, too. There aren't many people in your league at State. Anthony Matthias knew what he was doing – when he knew what he was doing – when he pulled you out of the pack and put you where you are."

"That's one thing we have in common, isn't it? Anthony Matthias. You far more than me in depth, and I'd never pretend otherwise. But the privilege, the goddamn *privilege* – there's no other way I can put it – of having known him the way I knew him makes the years, the tensions, the sweat worthwhile. It was a time of my life when everything jelled for me; he made it come together."

"I think we both feel the same way."

"When I read the material on you, you have no idea how I envied you. I was close to him but I could never be what you were to him. What an extraordinary experience those years must have been."

"It was – they were. But nothing's there for either of us any longer."

"I know. It's unbelievable."

"Believe. I saw him."

"I wonder if they'll let me see him. I'm on my way to Poole's Island, you know."

"Do yourself a favour. Don't. It sounds trite, but remember him – especially him – the way he was, not the way he is."

"Which brings us to now." Pierce shook his head while staring at Havelock in the chiaroscuro light of the runway. "It's not good. I don't think I really described to the President how close we are to the edge."

"He understood. He told me what they said to you when you warned them. 'Look to yourselves', wasn't that it?"

"Yes. When they get that simple, that direct, I shake. They'll strike out at shadows; one violent shove and we're over. I'm a fair debater and not bad at negotiations, but you know the Russians better than I do. How do you read it?"

"The same as you. Understatement isn't their way, bombast is. When they don't bother to threaten, they're threatening. Moves will take the place of words."

"That's what frightens me. The only thing I cling to is that I really don't believe they've brought in the men who push the buttons. Not yet. They know they have to be absolutely accurate. If they have concrete proof, not just hints, that Matthias entered into nuclear aggression pacts against the USSR and if they even smell China, they won't hesitate to push the decision up where it won't be theirs any longer. That's when we can all start digging into the ground."

"Nuclear aggression . . . ?" Havelock paused, alarmed more than he thought possible. "You think they've assumed *that* much?"

"They're close to it. It's what's been working them into a frenzy. Pacts negotiated by a maniac . . . with other maniacs."

"And now the frenzy's gone. They keep quiet and show you the door. You warn them and they tell you we should look to ourselves. I'm frightened, too, Mr Undersecretary."

"You know what I'm thinking, then?"

"Parsifal."

"Yes."

"Berquist said you thought the Soviets had learned something during the past eighteen hours. Is this it?"

"I'm not sure," said Pierce. "I'm not even sure I'm working the right side of the street, but *something's* happened. It's why I wanted to see you. You're the only one who knows what's going on hour by hour. If I could pick something out, piece it together with something they said or reacted to, I might find a connection. What I'm looking for is a person or an event, anything that I can use to interdict them, to bring up before they do and deflect them. *Anything* to keep them from alarming the warlords in the Presidium."

"They're not fools; they know those men. They'd know what they were delivering."

"I don't think that would stop them." Pierce hesitated, as if debating with himself whether or not to cite an example, then decided to speak. "You know General Halyard?"

"I've never met him. Or Ambassador Brooks. I was supposed to meet them both this afternoon. What about him?"

"I consider him one of the most thoughtful, *sceptical* military men in this country."

"Agreed. Not only from his reputation but I was given his dossier. And?"

"I asked him this afternoon what he thought the reaction would be – his included – if our clandestine services unearthed a Sino–Soviet pact against us, one that projected attack dates within forty-five days and contained the kind of information found in those documents on Poole's Island. His reply was one word: 'Launch.' If he can say that, what about lesser, far more insecure men?"

Arthur Pierce did not dramatize the question but asked it calmly, and the chill Michael felt was now only partially due to the damp, cold air. Forces were closing in; time was running out. "The President said to help you," he began. "I don't know if I can, but I'll try. You say you're looking for something to deflect them; I may have it. There's a long-standing KGB operation that goes back to the days of the NKVD – to the nineteen-thirties. It's called *Aspiratsiya Paminyatchik* – "

"Sorry," interrupted the man from State. "My Russian's not very good without an interpreter."

"It doesn't matter, it's just a name. It stands for a strategy that calls for young children, even infants, to be selected by doctors and brought over here. They're placed with specific families – deep-cover Marxists – and grow up as Americans, in every superficial way normal, the more successful the better. But all through the years they're being trained – programmed, if you like – for their adult assignments, which are dependent on their given skills and developments. It comes down to infiltration – again, the higher the better."

"Good *Lord*," said Pierce quietly. "I'd think there'd be enormous risks in such a strategy. Such people have to be instilled with extraordinary belief."

"Oh, they believe, it's the essential part of their programming. They're also monitored; the slightest deviation and they're either eliminated or brought back to Mother Russia where they're re-educated while training others at the American compounds in the Urals and in Novgorod. The main point is that we've never really been able to crack the operation, the few we've taken have been the least competent and so low on the ladder they haven't been able to shed any light. But we may have cracked it now. We've got ourselves an honest-to-God *paminyatchik* who's sanctioned for killing, as part of an execution unit. His kind has access – must have access – to clearance centres and source-controls. There's too much risk in killing, too many possibilities for overreaction, to say nothing of being caught. Orders have to be rechecked, authorization confirmed."

"You've *got* such a man? My God, where?"

"He's being flown now to Bethesda – he's wounded – and later tonight will be transferred to a clinic in Virginia."

"Don't *lose* him! Is there a doctor with him? A good one."

"I think so. He's a clinic specialist named Taylor; he'll stay with him."

"Then by morning you think you'll be able to give me something I can use with the Russians? This could be the deflection I need. I counter their attack with an attack of my own. I accuse – "

"I can give it to you now," interrupted Havelock, "but you can't use it until I tell you. Tomorrow night at the earliest. Can you stall that long?"

"I think so. What is it?"

"We put him under chemicals an hour ago. I don't know how the right people are reached, but I know the cover identity of their clearing centre. Also the code name for the *paminyatchik* source-control for this area – which I have to assume includes the Washington operation, the most vital in the US."

Arthur Pierce shook his head in astonishment and admiration. "You floor me," he said, with respect in his quiet voice. "I told you I was a little awe-struck. Well, I take it back, I'm *a lot* awe-struck. What can I use?"

"Whatever you have to. After tomorrow I'll trade the whole *Aspiratsiya Paminyatchik* for another few days."

"The President told me a few minutes ago . . . he called after speaking to you. You think you're that close to Parsifal?"

"We'll be closer still when we get Taylor's patient down to the clinic. With a few words he can put us within arm's reach of the man we call Ambiguity. And unless everything that we've projected – that Bradford projected – is wrong and I don't think it is, it *can't be*—once we have Ambiguity we'll know who Parsifal is. *I'll* know."

"Christ, *how*?"

"Matthias as good as told me I knew him. Are you familiar with a company, a chain of stores, called the Voyagers Emporium?"

"Most of my luggage is, I regret to say. At least, my bank account regrets it."

"Somewhere inside, in a department or a section, is the KGB clearing centre. Ambiguity has to stay in touch; it's where he gets his orders, transmits information. We'll break it quietly – *very* quietly – tear it apart and find him. We don't need much; we know where he's located."

"Right where you see him every day," said Pierce, nodding. "What about the code name for the source-control?"

"Hammer-zero-two. It doesn't mean anything to us, and it can be changed by the network overnight; but the fact that we broke it, broke the *paminyatchik* circle so decisively, has got to make someone sweat inside the Kremlin." Michael paused, then added, "When I give you the go-ahead, use what you need, all of it or any part. It's basically a diversion, what you call deflection, but I think it's a strong one. Create a diplomatic rhubarb, cause a storm of cables between Moscow and New York. Just buy us time."

"You're sure?"

"I'm sure we don't have a choice. We *need* time."

"You could lose the source-control."

"Then we'll lose him. We can live with a source-control – we've all got them in more than sixty countries. We can't live with Parsifal. Any of us."

"I'll wait for your call." The Undersecretary of State glanced at his watch, squinting in the dim light to read the radium dial. "I still have a few minutes before we leave. The vault specialist had to be flown in from Los Alamos; he's meeting with one of the men from his company who brought him the internal diagrams . . . There're so many things I want to ask, so much I need to know."

"I'm here as long as you are; when you leave, I leave. I heard it from the President."

"I like him. I haven't always liked presidents."

"Because you know he doesn't give a damn whether you do or not – not while he's in the Oval Office. That's the way I read him. I like him too, and I have every reason in the book not to."

"Costa Brava? They told me everything."

"It's history. Let's deal with the present. What else can I tell you that may help?"

"The obvious," said Pierce, his voice descending to a reluctant hollow sound. "If Parsifal *has* reached the Russians what can I say – if I'm given the chance to say it? If he's hinted at the China factor, or at the vulnerabilities in their own counter-strike capabilities, how can I explain it? Where did he *get* it all? Exposing Matthias is only part of the answer. Frankly, it's not enough, and I think you know that."

"I know it." Havelock tried to collect his thoughts, to be as clear and concise as possible. "What's in those so-called agreements is a mix of a thousand moves in a triple-sided chess game, the anchor player being us. Our penetration of the Russian and Chinese systems is far deeper than we've ever hinted at, and there are strategy committees set up to study and evaluate every conceivable Option in the event some goddamn fool – on *any* side – gives the order to launch."

"Such committees, I'm sure, exist in Moscow and Peking."

"But neither Moscow nor Peking could produce an Anthony Matthias, the man with geopolitical panaceas, respected, even worshipped – there is no one on either side of the world like him."

Pierce nodded. "The Soviets treat him as a valued go-between, not as an adversary. The Chinese throw banquets for him and call him a visionary."

"And when he began to fall apart, he still had the imagination to conceive of the ultimate nuclear chess game."

"But *how*?"

"He found a zealot. A naval officer on one of the Pentagon committees who's up to his eyeballs in overkill theories. He gave Matthias everything. He made copies of all the strategies and counter-strategies the three committees exchanged with one another. They contained authentic data – they *had* to contain it; those war games are very real on paper. Everything can be checked by computers – the extent of megaton damage inflicted, damage sustained, the limits of punishment before the ground is useless. It was all there, and Matthias put it together. Matthias and the man who's got us by the throat. Parsifal."

"I'd say that naval officer is scheduled to begin a long period of confinement."

"I'm not sure what that would accomplish. At any rate, I'm not finished with him; he's still got more to give – may have given it by now."

"Just a minute," said the Undersecretary of State, his face suddenly alive. "Could *he* be Parsifal?"

"No, not possible."

"Why not?"

"Because in his own misguided way he believed in what he was doing. He has a permanent love affair with his uniform and his country; he'd neither allow the possibility of compromise nor give the Russians an ounce of ammunition. Decker's not an original, but he's genuine. I doubt the Lubyanka could break him."

"Decker . . . You've got him put away, haven't you?"

"He's not going anywhere. He's at home with an escort unit outside."

Pierce shook his head while reaching into his pocket. "It's all so insane!" he said as he pulled out a packet of cigarettes and matches. "Care for one?" he asked, proffering the pack.

"No, thanks. I've had my quota of five hundred for the day."

The man from State struck a match, holding the flame under the cigarette. Without the protection of a second hand, the wind extinguished it. He struck another, left palm up, and inhaled, the smoke from his mouth mingling with the vapour of his breath. "At the meeting this afternoon, Ambassador Brooks brought up something I didn't understand. He said an intelligence officer from the KGB had made contact with you and speculated on the identity of the faction in Moscow who'd worked with Matthias at the Costa Brava."

"He meant with Parsifal; Matthias was being led by then. And Rostov – his name's Rostov – didn't speculate. He knew. They're a collection of fanatics in a branch called the VKR, the *Voennaya*. They make even our Deckers look like flower children. He's trying to break it open and I wish him luck. It's crazy, but a dedicated enemy may be one of our hopes."

"What do you mean, 'break it open'?"

"Get names, find out who did what and let the saner people deal with them.

Rostov's good; he may do it and, if he does, he'll somehow get word to me."

"He *will?*"

"He's already offered me a white contact. It happened at Kennedy Airport when I flew in from Paris."

There was the sound of a gunning engine in the distance. Pierce threw down his cigarette and crushed it under his foot as he spoke. "What more do you think this Decker can give you?"

"He may have spoken to Parsifal but doesn't know it, or someone speaking for Parsifal. In either case, he was reached at home, which means that somewhere in a couple of hundred thousand long distance records is a specific call made to a specific number at a specific time."

"Why not a couple of million records?"

"Not if we've got a general location."

"Do you?"

"I'll know more by tomorrow. When you get back – "

"Mr Undersecretary! Mr *Undersecretary!*" The shouting was accompanied by the roar of the jeep's motor and the screeching of its tyres as it came to a stop only a few feet from them. "Undersecretary Pierce?" said the driver.

"Who gave you my name?" asked Pierce, icily.

"There's an urgent telephone call for you, sir. They said it was your office at the United Nations and they must speak to you."

"The Russians," said Pierce under his breath to Havelock; his alarm was apparent. "Please, wait for me."

The Undersecretary of State swung himself rapidly into the Air Force jeep and nodded to the driver; his eyes were on the lights of the maintenance hangar. Michael pulled his coat around him, his attention drawn to the small prop-jet aircraft several hundred feet away in the opposite direction. The left engine had been started and the pilot was revving it. The right coughed into operation seconds later. Then Havelock saw another jeep; it had taken the place of the fuel truck next to the plane. The vault specialist had arrived; the departure for Poole's Island was imminent.

Arthur Pierce returned six minutes later, climbed out of the open vehicle and dismissed the driver. "It *was* the Russians," he said, approaching Michael. "They wanted an unrecorded, unlogged meeting tomorrow morning; that means an emergency. I reached the senior aide of the delegation and told him I had called my own emergency conference tomorrow on the strength of their reactions late this afternoon. I also suggested I might have information for them that would necessitate a storm of cables – I used your phrase – between New York, their embassy in Washington and Moscow. I hinted that perhaps the pounding shoe was in another hand." The Undersecretary stopped, hearing the preliminary warm-up of the jets from the plane in the distance; the second jeep was leaving the area. That's my signal; the vault specialist's here. You know, it's going to take at least three hours to break into that room. Walk over with me, will you?"

"Sure. What was the Russians' reaction?"

"Very negative, of course. They know me; they sense a deflection, a diversion –

to use your word. We agreed to meet tomorrow evening." Pierce paused and turned to Havelock. "For God's sake, give me the green light, then. I'll need every argument, every weapon I can have. Among them a medical report diagnosing exhaustion for Matthias ... God knows, not the psychiatric file I'm bringing back to you."

"I forgot. The President was to have got it to me yesterday – today."

"I'm bringing it up." Pierce started walking again as Michael kept pace. "I can see how it happens."

"What happens?"

"The days blending into one another. Yesterday, today ... tomorrow, if there is a tomorrow. One long, unending sleepless night."

"Yes," said Havelock, feeling no need to amplify.

"How many weeks have you been living it?"

"More than a few."

"*Jesus.*" The roar of the combined engines grew louder as they drew nearer to the plane. "I suppose this is actually the safest place to talk," said Pierce, raising his voice to be heard. "No device could filter that noise."

"Is that why you wanted to meet on the runway?" asked Michael.

"You probably think I'm paranoid, but yes it is. I wouldn't care if we were in the control room of a NORAD base, I'd want the walls swept before having a conversation like the one we just had. You probably *do* think I'm paranoid. After all, this is Andrews – "

"I don't think you're paranoid at all," interrupted Havelock. "I think I should have thought of it."

The door of the small aircraft was open, the metal steps in place. The pilot signalled from his lighted window; Pierce waved back, nodding agreement. Michael walked with the Undersecretary to within ten feet of the door where the wash of the propellers was strong and growing stronger.

"You said something about having a general location in mind regarding that call to Decker," shouted Pierce. "Where is it?"

"Somewhere in the Shenandoah," yelled Havelock. "It's only speculation, but Decker delivered the materials there."

"I see."

. The engines roared a sudden crescendo and the wind from the propeller blades reached gale force, whipping the hat from Arthur Pierce's head. Michael crouched, scrambling after it through the powerful wash. He stopped it with his foot and carried it back to the Undersecretary of State.

"Thanks very much!" shouted Pierce.

Havelock stared at the face in front of him, at the streak of white that sprang up from the forehead and shot through the mass of wavy dark hair.

36

It was an hour and forty-five minutes before he saw the floodlights that marked the entrance to the drive at Sterile Five. The flight from Andrews to Quantico and the trip by car to Fairfax had been oddly disturbing, and he did not know why. It was as though a part of his mind were refusing to function; he was conscious of a gap in his own thought process but was blocked by a compulsion not to probe. It was like a drunk's refusal to face the gross embarrassments of the night before: something not remembered did not exist. And he was incapable of doing anything about it; he did not know what it was, only that it was not, and therefore, it was.

One long, unending, sleepless night. Perhaps that was it. He needed sleep . . . he needed Jenna. But there was no time for sleep, no time for them to be together in the way they wanted to be together. No time for anything or anyone but Parsifal.

What was it? Why had a part of him suddenly died?

The marine car pulled up in front of the ornate entrance of the estate. He got out, thanked the driver and the armed guard, and walked up to the door. He thought as he stood there, with a finger on the bell, that like so many other doors in so many other houses he had entered he had no key with which to open it. Would he ever have a key to a house that was his – theirs – and be able to open it as so many millions opened theirs every day? It was a silly thought, foolishly pondered. Where was the significance of a house and a key? Still, the thought – the need, perhaps – persisted.

The door opened abruptly, and Jenna Karras, her striking, lovely face so taut, brought him back to the urgent present, her eyes burning into his.

"Thank *God*!" she cried, reaching for him, clutching him and pulling him inside. "You're *back*! I was going out of my mind!"

"What is it?"

"Mikhail, come with me. Quickly!" She gripped his hand as they walked rapidly down the foyer past the staircase to the study, which she had left open. Going to the desk, she picked up a note and said, "You must call the Bethesda Hospital. Extension six-seven-one. But first you have to know what happened!"

"What – "

"The *paminyatchik* is dead."

"Oh, *Christ*!" Michael grabbed the phone that Jenna held out for him. He dialled, his hand trembling. "When?" he shouted. "*How?*"

"An execution," she replied as he waited for Bethesda to answer. "Less than an hour ago. Two men. They took out the guard with a knife, got into the room and killed the traveller while he was sedated. Four shots in the head. The doctor's beside himself."

"Six-seven-one! *Hurry*, please!"

"I couldn't stand it," whispered Jenna staring at him, touching his face. "I thought you were there . . . outside somewhere . . . seen, perhaps. They said you weren't, but I didn't know whether to believe them or not."

"*Taylor?* How did it *happen?*"

As Havelock listened to the doctor, a numbing pain spread through him, stealing his breath. Taylor was still in shock and spoke disjointedly. Jenna's brief description had been clearer. There was nothing further to learn. Two killers in the uniforms of naval officers had come to the sixth floor, found Taylor's patient and proceeded professionally with the execution, killing a marine guard in the process.

"We've lost Ambiguity," said Michael, hanging up, his hand so heavy the phone fell into the cradle, clapping into place. "*How?* That's what I can't understand! . . . We had maximum security, military transport, every precaution!" He looked helplessly at Jenna.

"Was it all highly visible?" she asked. "Could the precautions and the transport have drawn attention."

Havelock nodded wearily. "Yes. Yes, of course. We commandeered an airfield, flew in and out of there like a commando raid, diverting the other traffic."

"And not that far from the medical centre," completed Jenna. "Someone alerted to the disturbance would be drawn to the scene. He would see what you didn't want him to see. In this case, a stretcher would be enough."

Michael slipped off his overcoat and listlessly dropped it on a chair. "But that doesn't explain what happened at the medical centre itself. An execution team was sent in to abort a trap, to kill their own people, no chance that anyone would be taken alive."

"*Paminyatchiks,*" said Jenna. "It's happened before."

"But how did their controls *know* it was a trap? I spoke only to the Apache unit and to Loring. *No one* else! How *could* they? How could they have been so sure that they sent in sanctioned killers? The risk is enormous!" Havelock walked round the desk, looking at the scattered papers, hating them, hating the terror they evoked. "Loring told me that he was probably spotted, that it was his fault; but I don't believe it. That mocked-up patrol car didn't just emerge from round the block, it was sent from somewhere by someone in authority who had made the most dangerous decision he could make. He wouldn't have made it on the strength of one man seen in a parking lot – that man, incidentally, was too damned experienced to show himself so obviously."

"It doesn't seem logical," agreed Jenna. "Unless the others were spotted earlier."

"Even if the cardiologist cover was blown, at best they'd be considered protection. No, the control *knew* it was a trap, knew that the primary objective – let's face it, the sole objective – was to take even one of them alive . . . Goddamn it, *how?*" Michael leaned over the desk, his hands gripping the edge, his head pounding. He pushed himself away and walked towards the wide, dark windows with the thick, bevelled glass. And then he heard the words, spoken softly by Jenna Karras.

"Mikhail, you did speak to someone else. You spoke to the President."

"Of *course,* but . . ." He stopped, staring at the distorted image of his face in the window, but slowly *not* seeing his face . . . seeing, instead, the formless outline of another. Then the night mist that had rolled in through the trees and over the lawns outside became another mist, from another time. The crashing of waves suddenly filled his ears, thundering, deafening, unbearable. Lightning shattered across the luminous, unseen screen in his mind, and then the sharp cracks came, one after another until they grew into ear-splitting explosions, blowing him into a frenzied galaxy of flashing lights . . . and *dread*.

Costa Brava. He was *back* at the *Costa Brava*!

And the face in the mirror took on form . . . distant form . . . unmistakable form. And the shock of white hair sprang up from that face, surrounded by waves of black, framed, isolated . . . an image unto itself.

"No . . . no!" He heard himself screaming; he could feel Jenna's hands on his arms, then his face . . . but not his face! The face in the window! The face with the sharp path of white in the hair . . . his hair, but *not* his hair, his face but *not* his face! Yet both were the faces of *killers*, his and the one he had seen that night on the Costa Brava!

A fisherman's cap had suddenly been blown away in the ocean wind; a hat had been whipped off the head of a man by the sudden wash of propellers. On a runway . . . in a shadowed light . . . two hours ago!

The same man? Was it *possible*? Even *conceivable*?

"Mikhail!" Jenna held his face in her hands. "Mikhail, what *is* it? What's wrong?"

"It's *not* possible!" he screamed. "It can't be!"

"What, my darling? *What* can't be?"

"*Jesus*. I'm losing my mind!"

"Darling, *stop it*!" shouted Jenna, shaking him, holding him.

"No . . . no, I'll be all right. Let me alone. Let me *alone*!" He spun away from her and raced to the desk. "Where is it. Where the *hell is it*?"

"Where is what?" asked Jenna calmly, now beside him.

"The file."

"What file?"

"My file!" He yanked the top right-hand drawer open, rummaging furiously among the papers until he found the black-bordered folder. He pulled it out, slammed it on the desk and opened it; breathing with difficulty, he leafed through the pages, eyes and fingers working maniacally.

"What's troubling you, Mikhail? Tell me. Let me help you. What started this? What's making you go back? . . . We agreed not to punish each other!"

"Not me! *Him!*"

"Who?"

"I can't make a mistake! I *can't*!" Havelock found the page he was looking for. He scanned the lines using his index finger, his eyes riveted on the page. He read in a flat voice: " 'They're killing her. Oh, my God, he's killed her and I can't bear the screams. Go to her, stop them . . . stop them. No, not me, never me. Oh, Christ, they're pulling her away . . . she's bleeding so, but not in pain now. She's gone. Oh, my God, she's gone, my love is gone . . . The wind is strong, it's blown his cap away . . . The face? Do I know the face? A photograph somewhere? A dossier? The dossier of a killer . . . No, it's the hair. The streak of white in the hair.' " Michael stood up and looked at Jenna, he was perspiring. "A streak . . . of . . . white," he said slowly, desperately trying to enunciate the words clearly. "It *could be him*!"

Jenna leaned into him and held his shoulders. "You must take hold of yourself, my darling. You're not being rational; you're in some kind of shock. Can you understand me?"

"No time," he said, removing her hands and reaching for the phone. "I'm okay, and you're right. I am in shock, but only because it's so incredible. *Incredible!*" He dialled, breathed deeply, and spoke. "I want to be connected to the main switchboard of Andrews Air Force Base, and I want you to give instructions to the duty officer to comply with any requests I make with regard to information."

Jenna watched him, then backed away to the table with the decanters. She poured him some brandy and handed it to him. "You're pale," she said. "I've never seen you so pale."

Havelock waited, listening as the head of the White House Secret Service gave his instructions to Andrews and, conversely, the electronic verification check was made by the colonel in charge of field communications. The incredible was always rooted in the credible, he thought. For the most credible reasons on earth he had been on that beach at the Costa Brava that night, observing the extraordinary; and the simple phenomenon of a gust of wind had blown a man's cap away. Now he must know whether there was substance in the observation. *Both* observations.

"There are calls from New York constantly," said the colonel in answer to his question.

"I'm talking about those five to ten minutes," countered Michael. "Transferred to a maintenance hangar on the south perimeter. It was less than two hours ago; someone must remember. Check every operator on the boards. Now!"

"Christ, take it easy."

"You take it fast!"

No operator at Andrews Air Force base had transferred a call to a maintenance hangar on the south perimeter.

"There was a sergeant driving a jeep, ordered to pick up cargo labelled Sterile Five, Marine equipment. Are you with me?"

"I'm aware of the Sterile classification and of the flight. Helicopter, north pad."

"What's his name?"

"The driver?"

"Yes."

The colonel paused, obviously concerned as he answered. "We understand the original driver was replaced. Another relieved him on verbal orders."

"Whose?"

"We haven't traced it."

"What was the second driver's name?"

"We don't know."

"Thank you, Colonel."

Paminyatchik!

"Find me the dossier on Pierce," said Havelock, looking up at Jenna, his hand on the telephone button.

"*Arthur Pierce?*" asked Jenna, astonished.

"As quickly as you can. Michael dialled again. "I can't make a mistake, I *can't make a mistake*. Not here, not *now*. Then "Mr President? It's Havelock. I've been with Pierce and tried to help him . . . Yes, sir, he's bright, very bright and very good. We'd like a point clarified; it's minor but it would clear something up for both of us. He had a lot on his mind, a lot to absorb. At the meeting this afternoon, after I called you, did you bring up the Apache operation at the Randolph Medical Center? . . . Then everyone's current. Thank you, Mr President." Michael replaced the phone as Jenna handed him a dark brown file folder.

"Here's Pierce's dossier."

Havelock opened it and immediately turned to the synopsis of personal characteristics.

The subject drinks moderately at social occasions, and has never been known to abuse alcohol. He does not use any form of tobacco

The match, the open flame unprotected, extinguished by the wind . . . A second flame, the flare of light prolonged, unmistakable. The sequence as odd and unmistakable as the cigarette smoke emerging solely from the mouth and mingling with the curling vapour of breath, a nonsmoker's exhalation. A *signal*. Followed moments later by an unknown driver delivering an urgent message, using a name he was not supposed to know, angering the man he was addressing. Every sequence had been detailed, timed, reactions considered. Arthur Pierce had not been called to the phone, he had been *making* a call.

Or had he? There could be *no* mistake, not now. Had an operator transferring rapidly incoming calls throughout the vast expanse of an Air Force base forgotten one among so many? And how often did soldiers take over innocuous assignments for friends without informing their superiors? How frequently did highly visible men appear to be on the side of the avenging medical angels by never smoking in public but in a crisis pulling out a concealed pack of cigarettes, a habit they were sincerely trying to break, the act of smoking actually awkward? . . . How many men had streaks of premature white in their hair?

No mistakes. Once the accusation was made it could not be taken back and if it could not be sustained, trust at the highest level would be eroded, possibly destroyed, the very people who *had* to communicate would become guarded, wary, commanders in silent conflict. Where was the ultimate proof?

Moscow?

There is first the KGB; all else follows. A man may gravitate to the VKR, but first he must have sprung from the KGB. Rostov. Athens.

He says he is not your enemy . . . but others are who may be his as well. A Soviet agent. Kennedy Airport.

"I can see it in your eyes, Mikhail." Jenna touched his shoulder, forcing him to look at her. "Call the President."

"I must be absolutely certain. Pierce said it would take at least three hours for the vault to be opened, another two to sort out the documents. I've got some time. If he's Ambiguity, he's trapped."

"How can you be absolutely certain about a *paminyatchik*?"

"At the source. Moscow."

"Rostov?"

"I can try. He may be as desperate as I am, but if he isn't, I'll tell him he should

797

be. We've got our maniacs, and he's got his." Havelock picked up the phone and dialled the three digits for the White House switchboard. "Please get me the Russian consulate in New York. I'm afraid I don't know the number . . . No, I'll hold on." Michael covered the mouthpiece, speaking to Jenna. "Go over Pierce's file. Look for something we can trace. Parents, if they're alive."

"A wife," said Jenna."

"He's not married."

"Convenient. Lovers, then."

"He's discreet."

"Naturally." Jenna picked up the file from the desk.

"*Dobriy vyecher*," said Havelock into the phone, his hand removed. "I need to speak to the director of street security." Every operator at every Soviet embassy and consulate understood when a caller asked to be connected to the street security director. A deep male voice got on the line, acknowledging merely that he had picked up the phone. Michael continued in Russian: "My name is Havelock and I have to assume I'm speaking to the right person, the one who can put me in touch with the man I'm trying to reach."

"Who might that be, sir?"

"I'm afraid I didn't get his name, but he knows mine. As I'm quite sure you do."

"That's not much help, Mr Havelock."

"I think it's enough. The man met me at Kennedy Airport and we had a lengthy conversation, including the means I might employ to reach him again; a forty-eight-hour time span and the New York Public Library figured prominently among them. There was also some discussion about a missing Graz-Burya automatic, a splendid weapon, I think you'll agree. It's urgent I speak with that man – as urgent as his message was for me."

"Perhaps if you could recall the message, it might be more helpful, sir."

"An offer of sanctuary from the Director of External Strategies, Pyotr Rostov, KGB, Moscow. And I wouldn't say those words if I were taping this. *You* can, but I can't afford it."

"There is always the possibility of a reverse order of events."

"Take the chance, comrade. You can't afford not to."

"Then why not talk with me . . . comrade?"

"Because I don't know you." Michael looked down at the list of the direct, unlisted numbers he had been assigned; he repeated one to the Russian. "I'll be here for the next five minutes." He hung up and reached for the brandy.

"Will he call back, do you think?" asked Jenna, sitting in the chair in front of the desk, the Pierce file in her hand.

"Why not? He need not say anything, just listen. Anything there we can use?"

"The mother died in nineteen-sixty-eight. The father disappeared eight months later and has never been seen since. He wrote to his son in Vietnam saying that he 'didn't care to go on without his wife, that he'd join her with God'."

"Naturally. But no suicide, no body. Just a Christian fade out."

"Naturally. *Paminyatchik*. He had too much to offer in Novgorod."

The telephone rang, the lighted button corresponding to the number he had given the Soviet consulate in New York.

"You understand, Mr Havelock," began the sing-song voice, the English unmistakably that of the Soviet agent from Kennedy Airport, "that the message delivered to you was offered in the spirit of compassion for the great injustice done by those in your government who called for the execution of a man of peace – "

"If you're doing this," interrupted Havelock, "for the benefit of any recording on this end, forget it. And if you're auditioning for the consulate, do it later. I haven't got time. I'm accepting a part of Rostov's offer."

"I was not aware that it was divided into parts."

"I'm assuming prior communication."

"I assume that's reasonable," said the Russian. "Under extremely limited circumstances."

"Any circumstances you like, just use this telephone number and get him back to me within the hour." Michael looked at his watch. "It's not quite seven o'clock in the morning in Moscow. Reach him."

"I don't believe those circumstances are acceptable."

"They've got to be. Tell him I may have found the enemy. *Our* enemy, the word's temporary, of course – assuming again there's a future for either of us."

"I really don't think – "

"*Don't* think. Reach him. Because if you don't, I'll try myself and that could be acutely embarrassing – to you, comrade, not to me. I don't care any more. I'm the *prize*." Havelock replaced the phone, aware of the beads of perspiration that had broken out on his forehead.

"What can Rostov actually tell you?" Jenna got up from the chair and placed Pierce's dossier on the desk. "There's nothing here, incidentally. Just a brilliant, modest hero of the republic."

"Naturally." Michael wiped his forehead with the back of his hand and leaned forward, supporting himself on his elbows. "Rostov told me in Athens that one of his sources for Costa Brava was a mole operating from the White House. I didn't believe him; it's the kind of shock treatment that makes you listen harder. But suppose he was telling me the truth – a past truth – because he knew the mole was out and untraceable. The perfect traveller."

Jenna raised her hand, pointing to the dossier on the desk.

"Pierce was assigned to the National Security Council. He had an office in the White House for several months."

"Yes. And Rostov meant what he said; he couldn't understand, and what you can't understand in this business is cause for alarm. Everything he had learned about Costa Brava – which I confirmed – told him it couldn't have taken place without the cooperation of someone in Moscow. But *who*? These operations are under his direct control, but he didn't have anything to do with it, knew nothing about it. So he tested me, thinking I could tell him something, bringing in the mole for credibility, knowing that we both accepted a mole's information as being reliable. The truth – as he was told the truth – except it was a lie."

"Told by a KGB officer, a *paminyatchik* mole, who had transferred his allegiance from the KGB to the *Voennaya*, said Jenna. "He throws off his former superiors for his new ones."

"Then proceeds to intercept and take over Costa Brava. If he was at Costa Brava. If . . . *if.*"

"How will you handle Rostov? He'll be taped; he'll be monitored."

"It'll be light. He is, after all, Director of External Strategies. I'll play on the power struggle. KGB versus VKR. He'll understand."

"He won't talk about the *paminyatchik* operation over the telephone. You know that. He can't."

"I won't ask him to. I'll name the name and listen. He'll tell me somehow. We've both been around a long time – too long – and the words we use have never been written to mean what we say they mean, the silences we use never understood except by people like us. He wants what I have – if I have it – as much as I want what he can confirm. It'll work. Somehow. He'll tell me whether Arthur Pierce is the mole . . . if he's convinced the mole has gone behind his back and joined the maniacs."

Jenna walked to the coffee table, picked up a note pad, then sat down in the leather armchair. "While you're waiting, do you want to talk about Commander Decker?"

"*Christ!*" Havelock's right hand shot out for the phone, his left stabbing the list of numbers in front of him. He dialled as he spoke, his voice strained. "I mentioned him to Pierce. Oh, *God*, did I mention him! . . . Raise the Decker escort, please. *Hurry.*"

"Naval escort. In position."

The words over the radio phone were clear, and the sudden throbbing in Michael's temples began to subside. "This is Sterile Five. We have reason to believe there could be hostile activity in your area."

"No signs of it," was the reply. "Everything's quiet and the street's well lighted."

"Nevertheless, I'd like additional personnel."

"We're stretched pretty thin at Sixteen Hundred, Sterile Five. Why not call in the locals? They don't have to know any more than we do, and we don't know a damn thing."

"Can you do it?"

"Sure. We'll label it diplomatic and they'll get overtime. By the way, how do you read the activity?"

"Abduction. Neutering you first, then taking Decker."

"Thanks for the warning. We'll get right on it. Out."

Havelock leaned back in the chair, his neck stretched over the rim, and stared at the ceiling. "Now that we know there still *is* a Commander Decker, what did he tell you?"

"Where did you leave off? I went back over everything."

Michael closed his eyes, remembering. "A phone call," he said slowly. "It was later, after their Sunday meetings at the lodge. He tried for days, weeks, to get in touch with Matthias, but Anton wouldn't talk to him. Then someone called him . . . with an explanation. That was it, he said it was an explanation."

Jenna flipped through her notes, stopping at a page, then going back two. "A man with a strange voice, an odd accent – 'clipped and rushed' was the way Decker described it. I asked him to recall as thoroughly as possible every word the man said. Fortunately, that call was very important to him; he remembered nearly everything, I think. I wrote it down." ·

"Read it, will you?"

Jenna rolled the page over. "The man identified himself as a colleague of the Secretary of State, and asked Decker several questions about his naval career, obviously to make sure it *was* Decker . . . Then here it begins – I tried to write it down as though I'd heard it myself . . . 'Secretary Matthias appreciates everything you've done, and wants you to know that you will be mentioned prominently and frequently in his memoirs. But you must understand the rules, the rules can't be broken. For the Secretary's global strategy to be effective, it must be developed in total secrecy, the element of surprise paramount, no one *in* or out of government –' " Jenna paused. "The emphases were Decker's," she added." ' . . . *in* or *out* of government aware that a master plan has been created.' " Again Jenna stopped and looked up. "Here Decker wasn't precise, the man's reasons for excluding people in government were apparently based on the assumption that there were too many who couldn't be trusted, who might divulge secrets regardless of their clearance."

"Of course he wasn't precise. He was talking about himself and it was a painful reference."

"I agree . . . This last part I'm sure was accurate, probably word-for-word. 'The Secretary of State wants you to know that when the time comes you will be summoned and made his chief executive officer, all controls in your hands. But because of your superb reputation in the field of nuclear tactics, there can't be even a hint of any association between you. If anyone ever asks you if you know the Secretary of State, you must say you do not. That's also part of the rules.' " Jenna put the note pad down on her lap. "That's it. Decker's ego was thoroughly flattered, and by his lights his place in history was assured."

"Nothing else was needed," said Havelock, straightening himself up in the chair. "Did you write that out, so I can read it?"

"I write more clearly in English than I do in Czech. Why?"

"Because I want to study it – over and over and over again. The man who spoke those words is Parsifal, and somewhere in the past I've heard that man speak before."

"Go back over the years, Mikhail," said Jenna, sitting forward, raising the note pad and flipping the pages. "I'll go back with you. *Now!* It's not impossible. A Russian who speaks English rapidly, clipping his words. It's *there*. That's what Decker said. 'Clipped and rushed.' Those were his words. How many such men can you have known?"

"Let's do it." Havelock got up from the desk as Jenna tore off the two pages that contained her notes on the call to Thomas Decker. Michael came round and took them from her. "Men I *know* who've met Matthias. We'll start with this year and work backwards. Write down every name I come up with."

"Why not do it geographically? City by city. You can eliminate some quickly, concentrate on the others."

"Association," he added. "We scratch Barcelona and Madrid; we never touched the Soviets . . . Belgrade . . . a river warehouse on the Sava, the attaché from the Russian consulate, Vasili Yankovitch. He was with Anton in Paris."

"Yankovitch," said Jenna, writing.

"And Ilitch Borin, visiting professor at the University of Belgrade; we had drinks, dinner. He knew Matthias from the cultural exchange conferences."

"Borin."

"No one else in Belgrade . . . Prague. There must be at least a dozen men in Prague. The Russians are crawling all over Prague."

"Their names? Start alphabetically."

The names came, some rapidly, others slowly, some striking chords of possibility, others completely improbable. Nevertheless, Jenna wrote them all down, prodding Michael, forcing him to jolt his memories, one name leading to another.

Krakow. Vienna. Paris. London. New York. Washington.

The months became a year, then two, and finally three. The list grew as Havelock probed, pushing his conscious, permitting the free association of his subconscious, digging, straining, forcing his mind to function as if it were a finely-tuned instrument. And again the sweat broke out on his forehead, his pulse oddly quickening as he reached the end of his energies.

"God, I'm tired," said Michael quietly, staring at the bevelled windowpane where over an hour ago two faces had appeared, one replacing the other, both killers, both from the Costa Brava. Or were they?

"You have thirty-nine names," said Jenna, coming to him, touching the back of his neck, massaging it gently. "Sit down and study them, study the telephone conversation. Find Parsifal, Mikhail."

"Do any match the names on your list? I thought of that when I mentioned Ilitch Borin; he's a doctor of philosophy. Is there anyone?"

"No."

"I'm sorry."

"So am I."

"He hasn't called. Rostov hasn't called."

"I know."

"I said an hour, the deadline was an hour." Havelock looked at his watch. "It's thirty-four minutes past the deadline."

"There could be mechanical troubles in Moscow. It would be nothing new."

"Not for him. He's pulled in the white contact; he doesn't want to acknowledge."

"How often have you stretched a deadline? Waiting until the one who expected your call was filled with anxiety, his defences eroded."

"He knows my dossier too well for that." Michael turned to her. "I must make a decision. If I'm right Pierce can't be allowed off that island. If I'm wrong they'll think I've crashed, gone over the edge. Berquist won't have any choice, he'll have to remove me."

"Not necessarily."

"Of course necessarily. I'm seeing monsters in dark closets, wasting valuable hours on delusions. That's not a man you want giving orders. My God, Arthur Pierce! The most valuable asset we have – if we have him."

"Only you know what you *did* see."

"It was night, a night that was racking me. Look through that clinic file. Is that a rational man talking or thinking? What *was* he seeing? . . . I need one word, one silence from Rostov."

"Wait, Mikhail," said Jenna, touching his arm and urging him back to the armchair. "You still have time. Study the list of names, the words spoken to Decker. It may happen for you. A name, a voice, a phrase. It could happen . . ."

Scholars. Soldiers. Lawyers. Doctors. Attachés. Diplomats . . . Defectors. All Russians who at one time or another had direct contact with Anthony Matthias. Havelock pictured each man, each face, his inner ear hearing dozens of voices speaking in English, matching the voices with the faces, listening for phrases that were spoken rapidly, words that were clipped, consonants harsh. It was maddening, faces and voices intermingling, lips moving, suddenly no sound followed by shouts. *You will be mentioned prominently and frequently.* Did *he* say that, *would* he say that? You *will be summoned* . . . how many times had that phrase been used. So many. But who used it? Who?

An hour passed, then most of another and a second packet of cigarettes with it. The expired deadline for Moscow was approaching the final deadline for Poole's Island. A decision – *the* decision – would have to be made. Nothing was forgotten, only submerged, eyes straying to watches as the inner search for Parsifal reached a frightening level of intensity.

"I can't find him!" cried Michael, pounding his hand on the coffee table. "He's here, the *words* are here, but I can't find him!"

The telephone rang. *Rostov?* Havelock shot up from the chair, staring at it, motionless. He was drained, and the thought of finding the resources to fence verbally with the Soviet intelligence officer eight thousand miles away drained him further. The abrasive bell sounded again. He went to the phone and picked it up, Jenna watching him.

"Yes?" he said quietly, marshalling his thoughts for the opening moves on both sides.

"It is your friend from Kennedy Airport, who no longer has his weapon – "

"Where's Rostov? I gave you a deadline."

"It was met. Listen to me carefully. I'm calling from a phone booth on Eighth Avenue and must keep my eyes on the street. The call came through half an hour ago. Fortunately, I took it, as my superior had an engagement for the evening. He will expect to find me when he returns."

"What are you driving at?"

"Rostov is dead. He was found at nine-thirty in the morning, Moscow time, after repeated calls failed to rouse him."

"How did he *die?*"

"Four bullets in the head."

"Oh, *Christ!* Have they any idea who killed him?"

"The rumour is *Voennaya Kontr Razvedka*, and I, for one, believe it. There have been many such rumours lately, and if a man like Rostov can be taken out, then I am too old, and must call from a phone booth. You are fools here, but it's better to live with fools than lie among jackals who will rip your throat open if they don't care for the way you laugh or drink."

At the meeting this afternoon . . . something I didn't understand . . . An intelligence officer from the KGB made contact . . . speculated on the identity . . . Arthur Pierce, while awkwardly smoking a cigarette on a deserted runway.

"*Rostov didn't speculate. He knew. A collection of fanatics in a branch called the VKR, the Voennaya. He'll break it open . . .*" A fellow killer from the Costa Brava.

Had Pierce's call encompassed more than the death of a *paminyatchik*? Had he demanded the execution of a man in Moscow? Four bullets in the head. It had cost Rostov's life, but it could be the proof he needed. Was it conclusive? Could anything be conclusive?

"Code name Hammer-zero-two," said Michael, thinking, reaching. "Does it mean anything to you?"

"A part of it possibly, not all of it."

"What *part*?"

"The 'hammer'. It was used years ago, and very restricted. Then it was abandoned, I believe. Hammarskjöld, Dag Hammarskjöld. The United Nations."

"*Jesus!* . . . Zero, zero . . . two. A zero is a circle. a circle. A council! Two . . . double, twice, *second*. The second voice in the delegation! That's it!"

"As you gather," interrupted the Soviet, "I must cross over."

"Call the New York office of the FBI. Go there. I'll get word to them."

"That is one place I will *not* go. It is one of the things I can tell you."

"Then keep moving and call me back in thirty minutes. I have to move quickly."

"Fools or jackals. Where is the choice?"

Havelock pressed the adjacent button on the phone, disconnecting the line. He looked up at Jenna. "It's Pierce. Hammer-zero-two. I told him – we all told him – about Rostov closing in on the *Voennaya*. He had Rostov killed. It's *him*."

"He's trapped," said Jenna. "You've got him."

"I've got him. I've got Ambiguity, the man who called us dead at Col des Moulinets . . . And when I get him to a clinic I'll shoot him into space. Whatever he knows I'll know." Michael dialled quickly. "The President, please. Mr Cross calling."

"You must be very quiet, Mikhail," said Jenna, approaching the desk. "Very quiet and precise. Remember, it will be an extraordinary shock to him and, above all, he must believe you."

Havelock nodded. "That's the hardest part. Thanks. I was about to plunge in with conclusions first. You're right. Take him up slowly . . . Mr President?"

"What is it?" asked Berquist anxiously. "What's happened?"

"I have something to tell you, sir. It will take a few minutes, and I want you to listen very closely to what I've got to say."

"All right. Let me get on another phone; there are people in the next room . . . By the way, did Pierce reach you?"

"What?"

"Arthur. Pierce. Did he call you?"

"What *about* Pierce?"

"He telephoned about an hour ago; he needed a second clearance. I told him about your call to me, that you both wanted to know whether I'd brought up the Randolph Medical Center business – lousy goddamned mess – and I said I had, that we all knew about it."

"*Please*, Mr President! Go back. What *exactly* did you say?"

"What's the matter with you?"

"What did he say to you?"

"About what?"

"Just *tell* me! First, what you said to him!"

"Now, just a minute, Havelock – "

"*Tell* me! You don't have time, *none* of us has time! What did you *say*?"

The urgency was telegraphed. Berquist paused, then answered calmly, a leader aware of a subordinate's alarm, not understanding it but willing to respect its source. "I said that you'd phoned me and specifically asked if I had brought up the Randolph Medical Center at the meeting this afternoon. I said that I had, and that you seemed relieved that everyone knew about it."

"What did *he* say?"

"He seemed confused, frankly. I think he said 'I see', then asked me if you'd given any reason for wanting to know."

"Know *what*?"

"About the Medical – What *is* wrong with you?"

"What did you *say*?"

"That I understood you were both concerned, although I wasn't sure why."

"What was his reply?"

"I don't think he had one . . . Oh, yes. He asked if you'd made any progress with the man you've got at Bethesda."

"Which wasn't until tomorrow and he knew it!"

"What?"

"Mr President, I don't have time to explain and you can't lose a moment. Has Pierce got into that vault, that room?"

"I don't know."

"Stop him! He's the mole!"

"You're *insane*!"

"Goddamn it, Berquist, you can have me shot, but right now I'm *telling* you! He's got cameras you don't know about! In rings, watches, cuff-links! Stop him! Take him! Strip him and check for capsules, *cyanide*! I can't give that order but you can! You *have* to! *Now!*"

"Stay by the phone," said the President of the United States. "I *may* have you shot."

Havelock got out of the chair, if for no other reason than the need to move, to keep in motion. The dark mists were closing in again; he had to get out from under them. He looked at Jenna, and her eyes told him she understood.

"Pierce found me. I found him, and he found me."

"He's trapped."

"I could have killed him at Costa Brava. I wanted to kill him, but I wouldn't listen. I wouldn't listen to myself."

"Don't go back. You've got him. You're within the time span."

Michael walked away from the desk, away from the dark mists that pursued him. "I don't pray," he whispered. "I don't believe. I'm praying now, to what I don't know."

The telephone rang and he lunged for it. "Yes?"

"He's gone. He ordered the patrol boat to take him back to Savannah."

"Did he get into that *room*?"

"No."

"Thank Christ!"

"He's got something else," said the President in a voice that was barely audible.

"What?"

"The complete psychiatric file on Matthias. It says everything."

37

The police swept through the streets of Savannah, patrol cars roaring out to the airport and screeching into bus and train stations. Car-rental agencies were checked throughout the city and road blocks set up on the major highways and back country routes – north to Augusta, south to Saint Marys, west to Macon and Valdosta. The man's description was radioed to all units – municipal, county, state – and the word spread down through the ranks from the highest levels of authority: *Find him. Find the man with the streak of white in his hair. If seen, approach with extreme caution, weapons drawn. If movements are unexpected, shoot. Shoot to kill.*

The manhunt was unparalleled in numbers and intensity, the federal government assuring the state, the cities and townships that all costs would be borne by Washington. Men off duty were called in by precincts and station houses; vehicles in for minor repairs were put back on the streets, and private cars belonging to police personnel were issued magnetic, circling roof lamps and sent out to prowl the dark country roads. Everywhere cars and pedestrians were stopped; anyone even vaguely approaching the man s description was politely requested to remove hats where they were worn, and torches roamed over faces and hairlines, searching for a hastily, imperfectly dyed streak of white hair rising above a forehead. Hotels, motels and rural inns were descended upon, registers were checked for late arrivals, desk clerks questioned, the interrogators alerted to the possibility of evasion or deception. Farmhouses where lights remained on were entered – courteously to be sure but the intruders were aware that the inhabitants could be hostages, that an unseen child or wife might be held somewhere on the premises by the man with the streak of white in his hair. Rooms and barns and silos were searched, nothing left to speculation.

Morning came and weary thousands reported back to points of dispatch, angry, frustrated, bewildered by the government's ineffectual methods. For no photographs or sketches were issued; the only name given was that of an elusive "Mr Smith". The alarm was still out, but the *blitzkrieg* search was essentially over, and the professionals knew it. The man with the streak in his hair had slipped through the net. He could be blond or bald or grey by now, limping with a cane or a crutch and dressed in tattered clothes, or in the uniform of the police or the army, without a vestige of his former appearance.

The newspapers carrying early-morning stories of the strange, massive hunt abruptly called off their reporters. Owners and editors had been reached by respected men in government who claimed no special knowledge of the situation but had profound trust in those higher up who had appealed to them. *Play it down, let the story die.* In second editions the search was relegated to a few lines near the back pages, and those papers with third editions carried no mention of it at all.

And an odd thing happened at a telephone exchange beginning with the digits *0–7 7 4 2* . . . Since midnight, it had not functioned, and by eight A.M., when service was suddenly, inexplicably, resumed, telephone "repairmen" were in the building of the Voyagers Emporium annex, where orders were received, and every incoming call monitored and taped, all tapes *under* fifteen seconds in length played instantly over the phone to Sterile Five. The brevity reduced the number to a very few.

International airports were infiltrated by federal agents using sophisticated X-ray equipment that scanned briefcases and hand luggage to look for a two-inch thick metal case with a combination lock on the side. There were two assumptions: one, the devastating file would not be entrusted to a cargo hold and, two, it would remain in its original government container for authenticity. Even so, in case container and file were separated, either shape was sufficient cause for examination. By eleven-thirty A.M. over 2,700 attaché cases had been opened and searched, from Kennedy to Atlanta to Miami International.

"Thanks very much," said Havelock into the phone, forcing energy into his voice, feeling the effects of the sleepless night. He hung up and looked over at Jenna, who was pouring coffee. "They can't understand and I can't tell them. Pierce wouldn't call Orphan-ninety-six unless he thought he could get his message across with a very few words, spoken quickly. He knows I've got the place wired and manned by now."

"You've done everything you can," said Jenna, carrying the coffee to the desk. "All the airports are covered – "

"Not for him," Michael broke in. "He wouldn't risk it, and besides, he doesn't want to leave. He wants what I want. Parsifal . . . It's that *file*! One small single-engined plane crossing the Mexican border or a fishing boat meeting another between here and Cuba, or out of Galveston towards Matamoros, and that file's on its way to Moscow, into the hands of the overkill specialists in the *Voennaya*. And there's not a damn thing I can do about it."

"The Mexican border is being patrolled, the agents doubled. The piers and marinas are watched both here and in the Gulf, all boats tracked, stopped if directions are in question. You insisted on these things and the President issued the orders."

"It's a long border and those are large bodies of water."

"Get some rest, Mikhail. You can't function if you're exhausted; it's one of your rules, remember."

"One of the rules . . . ?" Havelock brought both hands to the sides of his head, massaging his temples with his fingers. "Yes, that's one of the rules, part of the rules."

"Lie down on the couch and close your eyes. I can take the calls, let you know what they are. I slept for a while, you didn't."

"When did you sleep?" asked Michael, looking up, doubting.

"I rested before the sun was up. You were talking to your Coast Guards."

"They don't belong to me," said Havelock wearily, pushing himself up. "Maybe I will lie down . . . just for a few minutes. It's part of the rules." He walked round the desk, then stopped; his eyes roamed the elegant study strewn with papers, notebooks and file folders. "God, I hate this room!" he said, heading for the couch. "Thanks for the coffee, but no thanks."

The telephone rang, and Michael steeled himself, wondering whether the bell would stop before a second ring, or whether it would remain unbroken, the signal of an *emergency*. It stopped, then resumed ringing. Havelock lowered himself down on the couch as Jenna answered, speaking calmly.

"This is Sterile Five . . . Who's calling?" She listened, then covered the phone and looked over at Michael. "It's the State Department, New York City, Division of Security. Your man's come in from the Soviet consulate."

Havelock rose unsteadily, briefly finding it necessary to centre his balance. "I must talk to him," he said, walking towards the desk. "I thought he'd be there hours ago." He took the phone from Jenna and, after peremptory identifications, made his request. "Let me have the candidate, please." The Russian came on the line. "Where the hell have you been?"

"Apparently it is considered in poor taste over here to defect except during business hours," began the Russian in a weary, sing-song voice. "I arrived down here at the Federal Plaza at four o'clock this morning, after having survived an attempted mugging on the subway, only to be told by one of the night guards that there was nothing he could do until the *office* opened! I explained my somewhat precarious position and the kind, vacuous idiot offered to buy me a cup of coffee – in a public restaurant. Finally getting into the building by myself – your security is ludicrous – I waited in a dark, draughty hallway until nine o'clock when your militia arrived. I then presented myself and the imbeciles, they wanted to call the *police*! They wanted to have me *arrested* for breaking and entering and the possible destruction of government property!"

"All right, you're there now – "

"I haven't *fin-nished*!" yelled the Russian. "Since that auspicious beginning I have been filling out uncountable forms – with Russian nursery rhymes, incidentally – and have repeatedly given your number, asking to be put in touch with you. What *is* the matter with you people? Do you limit *toll calls*?"

"We're in touch now – "

"Not *fin-nished*! This past hour I have been sitting alone in a room so poorly wired I was tempted to lower my trousers and fart into the microphones. And I have *just* been given additional forms to fill out, including one inquiring about my hobbies and favourite recreational pastimes! Are you sending me to *camp*, perhaps?"

Michael smiled, grateful beyond words for a momentary break in the tension.

"Only where you'll be safe," he said. "Consider the source. We're fools, remember, not jackals. You made the right choice."

The Russian sighed audibly. "Why do I work myself up? The *frukti galavas* are no better in the Dzerzhinsky . . . why not admit it? They're worse. Your Albert Einstein would be on his way to Siberia, assigned to lead mules in a gulag. Where is the sense in it all?"

"There's very little," said Havelock softly. "Except to survive. All of us."

"A premise I subscribe to."

"So did Rostov."

"I remember the words he sent you. 'He's not my enemy any longer, but others are who may be mine as well.' They are ominous words, Havelock."

"The *Voennaya*."

"Maniacs!" was the guttural reply. "In their heads they march with the Third Reich."

"How operational are they here?"

"Who knows? They have their own councils, their own methods of recruitment. They touch too many you can't see."

"The *paminyatchiks*? You can't see them."

"Believe me when I tell you I was trusted but never that trusted. However, one can speculate . . . on rumours. There are always rumours, aren't there? You might say the speculation has persuaded me to take the action I have." The Russian paused. "I will be treated as a valuable asset, will I not?"

"Guarded and housed as a treasure. What's the speculation?"

"In recent months certain men have left our ranks unexpected retirements to well-earned dachas, untimely illnesses . . . disappearances. None so crudely as Rostov, but perhaps there was no time to be clever. Nevertheless, it seems there is a disturbing sameness about the departed. They were generally categorized as quiet realists, men who sought solutions and knew when to pull back from confrontation. Pyotr Rostov exemplified this group; he was in fact their spokesman in a way. Make no mistake, you were his enemy, he despised your system – too much for the few, too little for the many – but he understood there was a point where enemies could no longer push forward. Or there was nothing. He knew time was on our side, not bombs."

"Are you saying those who replaced the Rostovs think otherwise?"

"That is the rumour."

"The *Voennaya*?"

"That is the speculation. And should they take over the power centres of the KGB, can leadership of the Kremlin be far behind? This cannot happen. If it does . . ." The Russian did not finish the statement.

"There'll be nothing?" offered Havelock.

"That is the judgement. You see, they think *you'll* do nothing. They believe they can chew you up, first in one area, then in another."

"That's nothing new."

"With tactical nuclear weapons?"

"That's very new."

"It's insane," said the man from the KGB. "You'll have to react; the world will demand it."

"How can we stop the VKR?"

"By giving them little or no ammunition."

"What do you mean, 'ammunition'."

"Knowledge of provocative or inflammatory actions that they can use to threaten the tired old men in the Presidium. It is the same as over here; you have your jackals, beribboned generals and wild-eyed colonels closeting themselves with overweight, over-aged senators and congressmen, making pronouncements of disaster if you don't strike first. The wisest men do not always prevail; actually, you're better at that than we are. Your controls are better."

"I hope so," said Michael, thinking fleetingly of men like Lieutenant-Commander Thomas Decker. "But you say the *Voennaya* has filtered into your ranks, into the KGB."

"Speculation."

"If it's true it means that at least several of them could be walking around the embassy here or the consulate in New York."

"I'm not even sure of my own superior."

"And a *paminyatchik* outside would know them, could reach them, make a delivery."

"You assume I know something. I don't. What delivery?"

Havelock paused, trying to still the throbbing in his temples. "Suppose I were to tell you that just such ammunition as you describe was stolen last night by a mole so deep and entrenched he had access to information released only by executive order. He disappeared."

"Willing to give up his entrenched position?"

"He was found out. You were instrumental; you told me about Rostov's death and the VKR. He is a *Voennaya*. He's the enemy."

"Then look for the sudden diplomatic departure of a low-level attaché, a street security man or a communications officer. If there is a VKR recruit, he would be among these. Intercept, if you can, hold up the plane, if you have to. Claim stolen property, espionage, go to the limit. Don't let them have that ammunition."

"If we're too late."

"What can I tell you without knowing the nature of the delivery?"

"The worst."

"Can you deny?"

"It's beyond deniability. Part of it's false – the worst part but it will be accepted as the truth . . . by the beribboned generals and the wild-eyed colonels."

The Russian was silent, then replied quietly, "You must speak with others much higher, much wiser. We have, as you say here, a rule-of-thumb when dealing with such matters. Go to substantial men in the Party between the ages of fifty and seventy who went through Operation Barbarossa and Stalingrad. Their memories are acute; they may help you. I'm afraid I can't."

"You have. We know what to watch for at the embassy and the consulate . . . You'll be brought down here for debriefing, you understand that."

"I understand. Will I be permitted to see American films on the television, perhaps. After the interrogation sessions, of course."

"I'm sure something can be arranged."

"I do so like the Westerns . . . Havelock, stop the delivery to Moscow. You don't know the *Voennaya*."

"I'm afraid I do know it," said Michael, rounding the desk and sinking once again into the chair. "And I'm afraid," he added, hanging up.

There was no rest for the next three hours, coffee, aspirin and cold water compresses serving to keep him awake and numb the piercing ache that pounded through his head. Every department in every intelligence and investigatory agency that had information on or access to the Soviet embassy or the consulate in New York was contacted and ordered to divulge whatever Sterile Five requested. The schedules for Aeroflot, LOT Airlines, Czechoslovak CSA and all the carriers to the Eastern bloc were studied, their manifests checked for diplomatic passengers. The cameras were doubled on both Soviet buildings in Washington and New York, personnel leaving the premises placed under surveillance, the units told to keep their subjects in sight even at the risk of being seen themselves. Everything was designed to inhibit contact, to cut off the delivery on its way to Moscow, and nothing could achieve this more effectively than a VKR agent knowing he might expose the fugitive if he kept a rendezvous, or Pierce realizing he might be caught if he made one.

Helicopters criss-crossed along the Mexican border by the score, following small aircraft; radio checks were constant, and those planes making unsatisfactory replies were ordered to return to be searched. Off the coasts of Florida, Georgia and the Carolinas navy jets soared low over the water, tracking boats that veered too far south-east; radios were used here, too; either explanations were satisfactory or directions were altered. Out of Corpus Christi, other jets and Coast Guard patrols spotted and intercepted fishing and pleasure craft on their way towards Mexican waters; fortunately, inclement weather in the western Gulf had reduced their numbers. None made contact with other boats; none went beyond Port Isabel or Brazos Island.

It was a quarter to four when an exhausted Havelock returned to the couch. "We're holding," he said. "Unless we've missed something, we're holding. But we may have . . ." He fell onto the pillows. "I've got to go back to the names. He's there. Parsifal's *there* and I must find him! Berquist says we can't go beyond tonight, he can't take the chance. The *world* can't take the chance."

"But Pierce never got into that room," protested Jenna. "He never saw the agreements."

"The psychiatric file on Matthias spells them out – in all their insanity. In some ways, it's worse. A diagnosed madman running the foreign policy of the most powerful, most feared country on earth. We're lepers . . . Berquist said we'll be lepers. If we're alive."

The telephone rang; Michael expelled his breath and buried his head. The mists were closing in again, now enveloping him, suffocating him.

"Yes, thank you very much," said Jenna into the phone across the room.

"What is it?" asked Havelock, Opening his eyes, staring at the floor.

"The Central Intelligence Agency unearthed five more photographs. That leaves only one, and that man they're quite sure is dead. Others may be also, of course."

"Photographs? Of what, whom?"

"The old men on *my* list."

"Oh?" Michael turned over; his eyes, fixed on the ceiling, were closing. "Old men," he whispered. "Why?"

"Sleep, Mikhail. You *must* sleep. You're no good to yourself or anyone else this way." Jenna walked to the couch and knelt beside him. She pressed her lips lightly against his cheek. "Sleep, my darling."

Jenna sat at the desk, and each time the phone began to ring she pounced on it like a breathless blonde cat protecting its lair from predators. The calls came from everywhere – progress reports issued by men who were following orders blindly.

They were holding.

The handsome couple in riding breeches, boots and emblazoned red jackets galloped across the field on their hunters, the horses straining, nostrils flared, long legs pounding the hard earth and plunging through the tall grass. In the distance to their right, was a split-rail fence signifying the property line of an adjacent estate, beyond it another field that disappeared into a wall of giant maples and oaks. The man gestured at the fence, laughing and nodding his head. The woman at first feigned surprise and maidenly reluctance, then suddenly whipped her mount to the right and raced ahead of her companion, high in the saddle as she approached the fence. She soared over it, followed by the man only yards behind and to her left; they rode swiftly towards the edge of the woods, where both reined in their horses. The woman grimaced as she came to a stop.

"*Damn!*" she shouted. "I pulled the muscle in my calf! It's screaming!"

"Get off and walk around. Don't sit on it."

The woman dismounted as the man reached over for the reins of her horse. His companion walked in circles, her limp pronounced, swearing under her breath.

"Good God, where are we?" she asked, half shouting.

"I think it's the Heffernans' place. How's the leg?"

"Murder, absolute murder! *Christ!*"

"You can't ride on it."

"I can hardly walk on it, you damn fool."

"Temper, temper. Come on, let's find a phone." The man and woman started through the edge of trees, the man leading both horses, threading them past several thick trunks. "Here," he said, reaching for a low branch on a thick bush. "I can tie them up here and come back for them; they won't go anywhere."

"Then you can help me. This really is excruciating."

The horses tied and grazing, the couple began to walk. Through the trees they could see the outlines of the wide semicircular drive at the front entrance of the large house. They also saw the figure of a man who seemed to emerge from nowhere.

He was in a gabardine overcoat, with both hands in his pockets. They met and the man in the overcoat spoke.

"May I help you? This is private property."

"I trust we *all* have private property, old man," replied the sportsman supporting the woman. "My wife pulled a muscle over our last jump. She can't ride."

"What?"

"Horses, sport. Our horses are tied up back there. We were doing a little pre-hunt work over the course before Saturday's meet and I'm afraid we came a cropper, as they say. Take us to a phone, please."

"Well, I . . . I . . ."

"This *is* the Heffernans' house, isn't it?" demanded the husband.

"Yes, but neither Mr or Mrs Heffernan is here, sir. Our orders are not to allow anyone inside."

"Oh, shit!" exploded the wife. "How tacky can you be? My leg hurts, you ass! I need a ride back to the club."

"One of the men will be happy to drive you, ma'am."

"And my chauffeur can bloody well come and pick me up! Really, just who *are* these Heffernans? Are they members, darling?"

"I don't think so, Buff. Look, the man has his orders, and tacky as they are, it's not his fault. You go along and I'll take the horses back."

"They'd better not try to *become* members," said the wife as the two men helped her across the drive to a car.

The man walked back through the woods to the horses, untied them and led them across the field, where he removed the rails and prodded them through into the tall grass. He replaced the rails, mounted his hunter and, with the woman's horse in tow, trotted south over the course of Saturday's hunt – as he understood the course to be from his first and only study of the charts as a guest of the club.

He reached under his saddle and pulled out a powerful hand-held radio; he pressed a switch and raised the instrument to his lips.

"There are two cars," he said into the radio. "A black Lincoln, licence plate seven-four-zero, MRL; and a dark green Buick, licence one-three-seven, GMJ. The place is ringed with guards, and there are no rear exit roads. The windows are thick; you'd need a cannon to blow through them, and we were picked up by density infrareds."

"Got it," was the reply, amplified over the tiny speaker. "We're mainly interested in the vehicles . . . By the way, I can see the Buick now."

The man with various saws clipped to and dangling from his wide leather belt was high up in the tall pine tree bordering the road, his safety strap around it and clamped to his harness. He shoved the hand-held radio into its holster and adjusted the binoculars to his eyes, looking diagonally down through the branches, focusing on the car coming out of the tree-lined drive.

The view was clean, all angles covered. No cars could enter or leave the premises of Sterile Five without being seen – even at night; the capabilities of infrared applied to lenses as well as trip lights.

The man whistled; the door of the truck far below opened, and on its panel were the words HIGH TOP TREE SURGEONS. A second man stepped out and looked up.

"Take off," said the man above, loud enough to be heard. "Relieve me in two hours."

The driver of the truck headed north for a mile and a half to the first intersection. There was a garage on the right; the doors of its repair shop were open, and a car was inside on a hydraulic lift, facing the front. The driver reached for the switch and snapped his headlights on and off. Instantly, within the garage's shop the headlights of the car on the lift flashed on and off – the signal had been acknowledged, the vehicle was in position. The station's owner believed he was co-operating – confidentially – with the Narcotics Division of the State Police. It was the least a citizen could do.

The driver swung to his right, then immediately to the left, making a U-turn between the converging roads; he headed south. Three minutes later he passed the pine tree that concealed his companion beyond the branches near the top. Under different circumstances he might have touched his horn; he couldn't now. There could be no sound, no sight that marked in any way that area of the road. Instead, he accelerated, and in fifty seconds came to another intersection, the first south of Sterile Five.

Diagonally across on the left was a small old country inn, Southern style, like a large doll house built to bring back memories of an old plantation. Behind was a black asphalt parking area, where perhaps a dozen cars were lined up like large brightly-coloured toys. Except for one, the fourth from the end, which had a clear view of the intersection and swift access to the exit. Facing the front, it was layered with dirt, and dark, a poor relation in the company of its shiny, expensive cousins.

Again the driver leaned forward and flicked his headlights on and off. The dirty, worn-looking car – with an engine more powerful than any other in the lot – did the same. Another signal was acknowledged. Whatever emerged from Sterile Five could be picked up in either direction.

Arthur Pierce studied his face in the mirror of the rundown motel on the outskirts of Falls Church, Virginia; he was satisfied with what he saw. The fringe of grey circling his shaved head was in concert with the rimless glasses and the shabby brown cardigan worn over the soiled white shirt with the frayed collar. He was the image of the loser, whose minor talents and lack of illusion kept him securely, if barely, above the poverty level. Nothing was ventured because it was useless. Why bother? No one stopped such men on the street; they walked too slowly; they were inconsequential.

Pierce turned from the mirror and walked across the room to the road map spread out under the light of a plastic lamp on the cheap, stained desk against the wall. On the right, holding the map in place, was a grey metal container with the emblem of the United States Navy stamped on the top, the medical insignia below it and a brass, built-in combination lock on the side. In it was a document as lethal as any in history. The psychiatric diagnosis of a statesman the world revered, a diagnosis proving that man insane – to have *been* insane while functioning as the international voice of one of the two most powerful nations on earth. And the nation that permitted this intolerable condition to exist could no longer serve as the leader of the cause it espoused. A madman had betrayed not only his own government but the world; lying, deceiving, misleading forging alliances with enemies, scheming against supposed allies. No matter that he was insane, it had happened. It was all there.

The contents of the grey metal container was an incredible weapon, but for it to be used with devastating effect it had to reach the proper hands in Moscow. Not the tired old compromisers, but the visionaries with the strength and the will to move swiftly to bring the corrupt, incompetent giant to its knees. The possibilities that the Matthias file might fall into soft, wrinkled hands in Moscow was insufferable; it would be bartered, *negotiated*, finally thrown away by weak men frightened of the very people they controlled. No, thought Arthur Pierce, this metal container belonged to the VKR. Only the *Voennaya*.

He could not risk otherwise, and several phone calls had convinced him that there *was* risk in channelling it out with the few he could trust. As expected, embassy and consulate personnel were under heavy surveillance; all international flights were being monitored, and hand and cargo luggage X-rayed. Too much risk.

He would take it out himself, along with the ultimate weapon, the terminal weapon, documents that called for successive nuclear strikes against Soviet Russia and the People's Republic of China, agreements signed by the great American Secretary of State. They were nuclear fantasies conceived by an insane genius, working with one of the most brilliant minds ever produced by the Soviet Union. Fantasies so real that the tired old men in the Kremlin would run for their dachas and their vodka, leaving decisions to those who could cope, to the men of the *Voennaya*.

Where *was* the brilliant mind that had made it all possible? The man who had turned on his homeland only to learn the truth – that he had been wrong. So *wrong*! Where was Parsifal? Where was Alexi Kalyazin?

With these thoughts Pierce turned to the map again. The inept – and not so inept – Havelock had mentioned the Shenandoah – that the man they called Parsifal was somewhere in the Shenandoah area, by implication within a reasonable distance of Matthias's country home. The implied reasonable distance, however, was the variable quotient. The Shenandoah Valley was more than a hundred miles long, over twenty wide, from the Allegheny to the Blue Ridge Mountains. What might be considered reasonable? There was no reasonable answer, so the solution must be found in the opposite direction: in the plodding mind of Michael Havelock – Mikhail Havlicek, son of Vaclav, named for a Russian grandfather from Rovno – a man whose talents lay in persistence and a degree of imagination, not brilliance. Havelock would reduce the arc, put in use a hundred computers to trace a single telephone call made at a specific time to a specific place to a man he called a zealot. Havelock would do the work and a *paminyatchik* would reap the benefits.

Lieutenant-Commander Decker would be left alone; he was a key that might well unlock a door.

Pierce bent over the map, his index finger shifting from one line to another. The arc, the semi-circle that blanketed the Shenandoah from Sterile Five, was covered, with men and vehicles in position. From Harper's Ferry to the Valley Pike, Highways 11 and 66, Routes 7, 50, 15, 17, 29 and 33, all were manned, waiting for word that a specific car was approaching at a specific time heading for a specific place. That place was to be determined and reported; nothing else was required of the men in those vehicles. They were hirelings, not participants, their time paid for in money, not purpose or destiny.

Arthur Pierce, born Nicolai Petrovich Malyekov in the village of Ramenskoye, Union of Soviet Socialist Republics, suddenly thought about that destiny, and the years that had led to his own electrifying part in it. He had never wavered, never forgotten who he was or why he had been given the supreme opportunity to serve the ultimate cause, a cause so meaningful and so necessary for a world where the relative few tyrannized the many, where millions upon millions lived on the edge of despair or in hopeless poverty so that the capitalist manipulators could laugh over global balance sheets while their armies burned pyjama-clad children in far away lands. These were not the blatant, provocative conclusions of banal propagandists, they were truths. He had seen it all for himself – from the burning villages in South-east Asia to the corporate dining-rooms where offers of employment were accompanied by grins and winks and promises of stock options that were the first steps towards wealth to the inner corridors of government power where hypocrites and incompetents encouraged yet more hypocrisy and incompetence. How he hated it all! Hated the corruption and the greed and the sanctimonious liars who deceived the masses to whom they were responsible, abusing the powers given them, lining their pockets and the pockets of their own . . . There *was* a better way. There was *commitment*. There was the *Voennaya*.

He had been thirteen years old when he was told by the loving couple he called "Mother" and "Father". They explained while holding him and gazing into his eyes to let him see their love. He was theirs, they said, but he was also not theirs. He had been born to a chosen couple thousands of miles away who loved him so much they gave him to the State, to a cause that would make a better world for generations to come. And as his "mother" and "father" spoke, so many things in Arthur Pierce's young memory began to fall into place. All the discussions – not only with his "mother" and "father", but with the scores of visitors who came so frequently to the farm house – discussions that told of suffering and oppression and of a despotic form of government that would be replaced by a government dedicated to the people – *all* the people.

He was to be a part of that change. Over the early years certain other visitors had come and had given him games to play, puzzles to work, exercises to read – tests that graded his capabilities. And one day when he was thirteen he was pronounced extraordinary; on that same day he was told his real name. He was ready to join the cause.

It would not be easy, his "mother" and "father" had said, but he was to remember when pressures seemed overwhelming that *they* were there, *always* there. And should anything happen to them, others would take their place to help him, encourage him ... guide him, knowing that still others were watching. He was to be the best in all things; he was to be *American* – kind, generous and above all, seemingly fair; he was to use his gifts to rise as far as he was capable of rising. But he was never to forget who and what he was, or the cause that gave him the gift of life and the opportunity to help make the world better than it was.

Things after that auspicious day were not as difficult as his "mother" and "father" had predicted. Through his high school years and college, his secret served to prod him – because it was *his* secret and he *was* extraordinary. They were years of exhilaration: each new prize and award was proof of his superiority. He found it easy to be liked, as though in a never-ending popularity contest, the crown was always his. Yet there were self-denials, too, and they served to remind him of his commitment. He had many friends but no deep friendships, no relationships. Men liked him but accepted his basic distance, ascribing it usually to his having to find jobs to pay his way through school. Women he used only for sexual release; he formed no attachments whatsoever.

During his post-graduate studies at Michigan he was contacted by Moscow and told his new life was about to begin. The meeting was not without amusement, the contact a recruitment executive from a large conservative corporation who had supposedly read the graduate student files and wanted to meet one Arthur Pierce. But there was nothing amusing in his news; it was deadly serious – and exhilarating.

He was to join the army, where certain opportunities would lead to advancement, further advancement and contact with civilian and military authorities. He would serve an appropriate amount of time and return not to the mid-west but to Washington, where word of his record and talents would be spread. Companies would be lined up, anxious to employ him, but the government would step in. He was to accept.

But first the army – and he was to give it everything he had, he was to continue to be the *best*. His "father" and "mother" had thrown him a farewell party on the farm inviting all his friends, including most of the old Boy Scout Troop 37. And it *was* a farewell party in more than one sense. His "father" and "mother" told him at the end of the night that they would not see him again. They were getting old and they had done their job: him. And he would make them proud. Besides, their talents were needed elsewhere. He understood; the cause was everything.

For the first time since he was thirteen, he had cried that night. But it was permitted – and, besides, they were tears of joy.

All those years, thought Arthur Pierce, glancing in the cheap motel mirror at the fringe of grey and the frayed collar around his neck. They had been worth it; the proof would be found in the next few hours.

The waiting had begun. The reward would be a place in history.

Michael opened his eyes, a sea of dark brown leather confronting him, moisture everywhere, the heat oppressive. He turned over and raised his head, suddenly aware that it was not sunlight but the glow of a distant lamp that washed the room.

817

He was drenched with sweat. It was night, and he was not ready for night. What had *happened*?

"*Dobriy den.*" The greeting floated over to him.

"What time is it?" he asked, sitting up on the couch.

"Ten past seven," said Jenna, at the desk. "You slept a little over three hours. How do you feel?"

"I don't know. Left out, I think. What's going on?"

"Not a great deal. As you said, we're holding. Did you know that the lights on these buttons actually go on before the telephone rings? Only a split half-second, but they do."

"It's not comforting. Who called?"

"Very serious, bewildered men reporting nothing, reporting that they had nothing to report. Several asked how long they were to keep up what they referred to as their 'reconnaissance'. I said until they were told otherwise."

"That says it."

"The photographs arrived."

"What . . . ? Oh, your list."

"They're on the coffee table. Look at them."

Havelock focused on the row of five grainy faces staring at him. He rubbed his eyes and wiped the perspiration from his hairline, blinking repeatedly as he tried to concentrate. He began with the face on the far left; it meant nothing to him. Then the next, and the next, and the . . . next.

"Him," he said, not knowing why he said it.

"Who?"

"The fourth one. Who is he?"

Jenna glanced down at a paper in front of her. "It's a very old picture, taken in nineteen-forty-eight. The only one they could find. It's over thirty years old."

"Who is he? Who was he?"

"A man named Kalyazin. Alexi Kalyazin. Do you recognize him?" Jenna got up from the desk.

"Yes . . . no. I don't know."

"It's an *old* photograph, Mikhail. *Look* at it. *Study* it. The eyes, the chin, the shape of the mouth. Where? Who?"

"I don't know. It's there . . . and it's not there. What did he do?"

"He was a clinical psychotherapist," said Jenna, reading. "He wrote definitive studies evaluating the effects on men of the stress of combat or prolonged periods of enduring unnatural conditions. His expertise was used by the KGB; he became what you call here a strategist, but with a difference. He screened information sent in to the KGB by people in the field, looking for deviations that might reveal either double agents or men no longer capable of functioning in their jobs."

"An evaluator. A fake with a penchant for overlooking the obvious."

"I don't understand you."

"Gunslingers. They never spot the gunslingers."

"I still don't know what you're talking about."

"I don't know him. It's a face like so many other faces, so many dossiers. God, the *faces*!"

818

"But there's *something!*"

"Maybe, I'm not sure."

"Keep looking at it. *Concentrate.*"

"Coffee. Is there any coffee?"

"I forgot," said Jenna. "The first rule upon waking is coffee. Black and too strong. You *are* Czech, Mikhail." She went to the table behind the couch, where an accommodating guard had plugged in the silver pot.

"The first rule," repeated Havelock, suddenly disturbed. "The first *rule?*"

"What?"

"Where are your notes on Decker's telephone call?"

"You had them."

"Where *are* they?"

"Down there. On the table."

"*Where?*"

"Under the last photograph. On the right."

Get yourself a drink. You know the rules.

Michael threw the photograph of an unknown face off the table and gripped the two notebook pages in his hand. He stared at them, shifting them back and forth.

"Oh, my God! The rules, the goddamned *rules!*"

Havelock got up and lurched towards the desk, his legs unsteady, his balance fragile.

"What is it?" asked Jenna, alarmed, the cup in her hand.

"*Decker!*" shouted Michael. "Where are the notes on Decker?"

"Right there. On the left. The pad."

Havelock riffled through the pages, his hand trembling again, his eyes seeing and not seeing, looking for the words. He found them.

" 'An odd accent'," he whispered. " 'An *odd* accent', but *what* accent?"

He grabbed the phone, barely able to control his finger as he dialled. "Get me Lieutenant–Commander Decker, you've got his number on your index."

"Mikhail, get hold of yourself."

"Shut up!" The elongated buzz signified the ring, the wait intolerable.

"Hello?" said the tentative voice of a woman.

"Commander Decker, please."

"I'm . . . terribly sorry, he's not here."

"He's there to *me!* This is Mr Cross calling. Get him on the phone."

Twenty seconds elapsed, and Michael thought his head would explode.

"What is it, Mr Cross?" Decker asked.

"You said an 'odd accent'. What did you mean?"

"I beg your pardon?"

"The call! The call you got from Matthias, from the one who said he was speaking for Matthias! When you said he had an odd accent, did you mean foreign, Russian?"

"No, not at all. It was high pitched and very Anglicized. Almost British, but not British."

"Good night, Commander," said Michael, hanging up.

Pour yourself a drink . . . you know the rules here. Come now, we re both out. Freshen yours and do mine while you're at it. That's also part of the rules, remember?

Havelock picked up the phone again, pulling the list of numbers in front of him. He dialled. The waiting was almost a pleasure, but it was too short; he needed time to adjust. Poole's Island!

"This is Mr Cross. Let me have Security, please."

Two short hums were heard, and a voice answered. "Check-point," said the officer on duty.

"This is Cross. Executive order, priority-zero. Please confirm."

"Start counting," said the voice.

"One, two, three, four, five, six – "

"Okay. Scanners match. What is it, Mr Cross?"

"Who was the officer who took emergency leave approximately six weeks ago?"

The silence was interminable; when the reply came, it was a matter-of-fact response by a knowledgeable man. "Your information's incorrect, Mr Cross. There's been no request for emergency leave from the officer corps or anyone else. No one's left the island."

"Thank you, Security."

Alexander the Great . . . *Raymond Alexander!*

Fox Hollow!

38

"It's him," said Michael, leaning over the desk, his hand still gripping the phone. "He's Parsifal. Raymond Alexander."

"*Alexander?*" Jenna took several steps away from the table and stared at Havelock, shaking her head slowly.

"It *must* be! It's in the words – 'the rules'. 'One of the rules, part of the rules.' Always rules; his life is a series of unbreakable rules! The odd accent wasn't foreign, *wasn't* Russian. It was 'thirties-Harvard with Alexander's pretentious emphasis. He's used it in a thousand lecture halls, hundreds of debates. Points made quickly, retorts thrown in unexpectedly, thrust and parry. That's Alexander!"

"As you've described him," said Jenna calmly but firmly, "there's an enormous contradiction I don't think you can explain. Are you prepared to accuse him of knowing the identity of a Soviet mole and doing nothing about it? Especially one so dangerous as an Undersecretary of State?"

"No, I *can't* explain it, but he can. He will. He sent me to Poole's Island, telling me a bullshit story about an army officer on emergency leave who let it slip to his wife. There wasn't any such person; no emergency leaves were taken."

"Perhaps he was protecting another source."

"Then why the elaborate lie? Why not a simple refusal to disclose? No, he wanted me to believe it, put me on my word to protect him – knowing I would protect him!"

"For what *purpose*?" said Jenna, coming to the desk. "Why did he tell you in the first place? To have you *killed*?"

"Let him answer that." Havelock picked up the phone, pressing the house intercom button. "I want a car and an escort to follow me. It's about an hour's drive from here. Right away." He replaced the phone and, for a moment, looked at it, then shook his head. "No," he said.

"The President?" asked Jenna.

"I'm not going to call him. Not yet. The state he's in he'd send in a battalion of commandos. We won't learn the truth that way. Cornered like that, Alexander might blow his brains out."

"If you're right, what more is there to learn?"

"*Why!*" said Michael furiously, opening the top drawer and taking out the Llama automatic. "And how," he added, checking the magazine and cracking it back in place. "That large contradiction you mentioned. His beloved republic."

"I'm going with you."

"No."

"*Yes!* This time you have no right to refuse me. My life is in this room – my death as well. I have a right to *be* there."

"You may have a right but you're not going. That son of a bitch set you up, he marked you for extinction."

"I have to know why."

"I'll tell you." Michael started to leave.

"Suppose you can't!" cried Jenna, blocking him. "Yes, Mikhail, look at me! Suppose you do not come back it's possible, you know. Would you finally rob me of my sanity?"

"We've been out there. There are no alarms, no dogs or guards. Besides, he doesn't expect me. I'll come back – with him! . . . What the hell do you mean, your 'sanity'?"

"I lost you once – I loved you and lost you! Do you think I can take even the risk of losing you again and never knowing why? How much do you *want* from me?"

"I want you to live."

"I can't live, I *won't* live unless you're with me! I've tried it – it simply doesn't appeal to me. Whatever's out there is for both of us, not you alone. It's not fair, Mikhail, and you know it."

"I don't give a damn about being fair!" He reached for her and pulled her into his arms; aware of the gun in his hand, wishing they were somewhere else where there were no guns – *ever*. "I only care about you. I know what you've been through, what I *did* to you. I want you here, where I'll know you're all right. I can't risk you, don't you understand?"

"Because you love me?"

"So much . . . so very much."

"Then respect me!" cried Jenna, whipping her head back, her blond hair swirling over her shoulders. "Damn you, Mikhail, *respect* me!"

Havelock looked at her, at the anger and the pleading in her eyes. So *much to make up for.* "Come on," he said. "Let's get our coats. Let's go."

Jenna turned and went to the coffee table, where she picked up the photographs, including the one on the floor. "All right," she said.

"Why?" asked Michael, gesturing at the pictures.

"Why not?" she replied.

The man concealed high up in the darkness of the tall pine, drove his spikes deeper into the trunk, adjusting his harness to relax the pressure of the straps. Suddenly, in the distance far below, he saw the beams of headlights streaking out of the tree-lined drive at Sterile Five. He raised the infrared binoculars to his eyes with his right hand as his left pulled out the radio from its holder. He brought it to his lips and pressed the switch.

"Activity," he said. "Stay alert. Respond."

"North in touch," came the first reply.

"South also," was the second.

Pushing the open-channel radio into the leather collar around his throat, the man focused the binoculars on the car emerging from the drive. It was the Buick; he refined the focus, and the images beyond the windshield sharpened.

"It's our man and the woman," he said. "Turning north. It's yours, North."

"We're ready."

"South, take off and assume your alternate position."

"Leaving now. North keep us posted. Let us know when you want relief."

"Will do."

"*Hold* it! There's a second car . . . It's the Lincoln, two federals in the front; I can't see in the back . . . Now I can. No one else."

"It's an escort," said one of the two men in the car a mile and a half north. "We'll wait till he passes."

"Give him plenty of room," ordered the man in the tree. "They're curious people."

"Don't worry."

The Buick reached the intersection and turned left, the Lincoln Continental several hundred feet behind and following, a prowling behemoth protecting its young. Both vehicles headed west.

Inside the dark repair shop of the gas station, a hissing sound accompanied the lowering of the hydraulic lift; the engine of the descending car was turned on and gunned. The driver raised his radio and spoke.

"South, they've taken the B route. Head west on the parallel road and pick us up six miles down."

"Heading across into west parallel," was the reply.

"Hurry," said North. "They are."

The white fence that marked the start of Alexander's property shone in the glare of the headlights. Seconds later the floodlights beaming on the trees scattered throughout the immense front acreage could be seen on the left, the wood and stone house beyond. Havelock then saw what he hoped he would see. There were no cars in the circular drive, very few lights in the windows. He slowed down and pulled the microphone from its dashboard recess.

"Escort, this is it," he said, depressing the transmission switch. "Stay up here on the road. There are no visitors and I want the man we're seeing to think we're alone."

"Suppose you need us?" asked Escort

"I won't."

"That's not good enough. Sorry, sir."

"All right, you'll hear me. I'm not shy; I'll fire a couple of shots."

"That's good enough, as long as we're down there at the house."

"I want you up here on the road."

"Sorry, again. We'll leave the Abraham up here, but we'll be down there, right outside. On foot."

Michael shrugged, replacing the microphone; it was pointless to argue. He snapped off the headlights and turned into the drive, idled the engine and let the Buick glide to within thirty feet of the entrance. The car came to a stop and he looked at Jenna. "Ready?"

"I think more than my life. Or death. He wanted both." She slipped the photographs under her coat. "Ready," she said.

They got out, closed the doors quietly and walked up the broad steps to the huge panelled oak door. Havelock rang the bell; again the waiting was unbearable. The door opened and the uniformed maid stood there, startled.

"Good evening. It's Enid, isn't it?"

"Yes, sir. Good evening, sir. I didn't know Mr Alexander was expecting guests."

"We're old friends," said Michael, his hand on Jenna's arm, as both stepped inside. "Invitations aren't required. It's part of the rules."

"I've never heard that one."

"It's fairly new. Is Mr Alexander where he usually is at this hour? In his library?"

"Yes, sir. I'll tell him you're here. The name, please?"

There was a sudden hollow echo preceding the voice that filled the large hall. "It won't be necessary, Enid." It was the clipped, high-pitched voice of Raymond Alexander pouring out of an unseen speaker. "And I *have* been expecting Mr Havelock."

Michael's eyes darted about the walls, his hand now gripping Jenna's arm. "Is this another rule, Raymond? Make sure the guest is who he says he is?"

"It's fairly new," replied the voice.

Havelock walked with Jenna through the elegant living-room filled with antiques from the far corners of the earth to the hand-carved door of the library. He guided her to his left, beyond the frame; she understood. He reached under his jacket for the Llama automatic and held it at his side before turning the heavy brass knob. He shoved the door open, his back pressed against the wall, his weapon ready.

"Is that really necessary, Michael?"

Havelock moved slowly into the frame, quickly adjusting his eyes to the shadowy, indirect lighting of the library. The source was two lamps: one fringed and on the large desk at the far end of the room; the other a floor lamp above the soft, leather armchair, shining down on the wild, unkempt head of Raymond Alexander. The old warhorse sat motionless, and in his bloated, pale white hands was a brandy glass held in front of his deep red velvet smoking jacket.

"Come in," he said, turning to a small box-like device on the side table. He pressed a button, and somewhere overhead, on the wall above the door, the dim glow of a television monitor faded away. "Miss Karras is a handsome woman. Very lovely . . . Come in, my dear."

Jenna appeared, standing next to Michael. "You're a monster," she said simply.

"Far worse."

"You wanted to kill us both," she continued. "Why?"

"Not him, never him. Not . . . *Mikhail*." Alexander raised his glass and drank. "Your life – or death – was never really considered one way or the other. It was out of our hands."

"I could kill you for that," said Havelock.

"I repeat. Out of our hands. Frankly, we thought she'd be retired, returned to Prague and eventually cleared. Don't you see, Michael, she wasn't important. Only you; you were the only one that mattered. You had to go and we knew they'd never let you, you were too valuable. You had to do it yourself, insist on it yourself. Your revulsion had to be so deep, so painful that there was no other way for you. It worked. You left. It was necessary."

"Because I knew you," said Havelock. "I knew the man who led a sick, disintegrating friend down the road of insanity, turning him into some kind of grotesque thing – Belial with his finger on the nuclear switch. I knew the man who did this to Anton Matthias. I knew Parsifal."

"Is that the name they've given me? Parsifal? Exquisite irony. No healing wounds with this fellow, only tearing them apart. Everywhere."

"It's why you did what you did, isn't it? *I* knew who you were."

Alexander shook his head, the unkempt hair a thousand coiled springs in motion, his green eyes under the full, arched brows, briefly closing. "I wasn't important, either. Anton insisted; you became an obsession with him. You were what was left of his failing integrity, his decaying conscience."

"But you knew how to *do* it. You knew a Soviet double agent so high in the government he could have been made Secretary of State. Would have been if he hadn't been there on that beach at the Costa Brava. You knew where he was, you knew his name, you *reached* him!"

"We had no part of the Costa Brava! I learned of it only after inquiring about you. We couldn't understand, we were shocked."

"Not Matthias. He was beyond being shocked."

"It was when we knew everything was out of control."

"Not we! *You!*"

The old journalist again stopped all movement, his hands gripping the glass. He locked his eyes with Michael's and answered. "Yes. Me. I knew."

"So you sent me to Poole's Island, expecting me to be killed, and once dead I was guilty by reason of silence."

"No!" Alexander shook his head, now violently. "I never thought you'd go there, never thought you'd be *permitted* to go there."

"That very convincing story about a soldier's wife you met and how she told you. It was all a lie. There've been no emergency leaves, no one's left that island. But I believed you, gave you my word I'd protect the source. Protect you. I never said anything, not even to Bradford."

"Yes, yes, I wanted to convince you, but not *that* way. I wanted you to go ɔ the ladder, using your regular channels, confront them, make them tell you the truth . . . And once you learned the truth, the *entire* truth, you might see, you might understand. You might be able to stop it . . . Without me."

"How? For Christ's sake, how?"

"I think I know, Mikhail," said Jenna, touching Havelock's arm as she stared down at Alexander. "He did mean we. Not 'I'. This man is not Parsifal. His servant, perhaps, but not Parsifal."

"Is that true?" asked Havelock.

"Pour yourself and Miss Karras a drink, Michael. You know the rules. I have a story to tell you."

"No drinks. Your rules don't apply any longer."

"At least sit down, and put that gun away. You have nothing to fear here. Not from me. Not any longer."

Havelock looked at Jenna; he nodded, leading them both to adjacent chairs across from Alexander. They sat down, Jenna removing the photographs from her coat and placing them beside her. Michael shoved the weapon into his pocket. "Go on," he said curtly.

"A number of years ago, began the journalist, staring at the glass in his hands, "Anton and I committed a crime. In our minds it was far more serious than any punishment might indicate, and the punishment would have been severe in the extreme. We were fooled . . . 'gulled' is the innocuous word, 'deceived' more appropriate, 'betrayed' more appropriate still. But the fact that it could have happened to us – two pragmatic intellectuals, as we believed we were – was intolerable to us. Still, it had happened." Alexander drained his glass and placed it on the table next to his chair. He folded his puffed, delicate hands and continued. "Whether it was because of my friendship with Matthias, or for whatever standing I might have had in this city, a man called me from Toronto saying he had obtained a false passport and was flying to Washington. He was a Soviet citizen, an educated man in his early sixties, and an employee in a reasonably high position in the Soviet government. His intention was to defect and could I put him in touch with Anthony Matthias." The journalist paused and leaned forward, gripping the arms of the chair. "You see, in those days everyone knew Anton was about to be tapped for extraordinary things; his influence was growing with every article he wrote, every trip to Washington. I arranged a meeting; it took place in this room." Alexander leaned back and kept his eyes on the floor. "That man had remarkable insights to offer, a wide knowledge of internal Soviet affairs. A month later he was working for the State Department. Three years after that Matthias was special assistant to the President, two years later Secretary of State. The man from Russia, by way of Toronto, was still in the Department, his talents so appreciated that by then he was

825

processing highly classified information as the director of Eastern Bloc debriefings and reports."

"When did you find out?" asked Havelock.

The journalist looked up. "Four years ago, he said quietly. "Again, in this room. The defector asked to meet us both; he said that what he had to say was urgent and our schedules for that very night must be cleared – there could be no delays. He sat where Miss Karras is sitting now and told us the truth. He was a Soviet agent and had been continuously funnelling the most sensitive information to Moscow for the past six years. But something had happened and he could no longer function in his role. He felt old and worn out, the pressures were too great. He wanted to disappear.

"And since you and Anton – the pragmatic intellectuals had been responsible for six years of infiltration, he had you exactly where he wanted you." Michael spoke sharply, revolted by the ineptitude and essential corruption that Alexander was describing. "God forbid that great men should be tarnished."

"That was part of it, surely, but then there was a certain justification. Anthony Matthias was at his zenith, reshaping global policies, reaching secure accommodations and *détente*, making the world somewhat safer than it was before him. Such a revelation would have been politically disastrous; it would have destroyed him . . . and the good he was doing. I myself presented this argument strongly."

"I'm sure it didn't take long to convince him," said Havelock.

"Longer than perhaps you think," replied Alexander, a trace of weary anger in his voice. "You seem to have forgotten what he was."

"Perhaps I never really knew."

"You say this was part of it," interrupted Jenna. "What was the other part?"

The journalist shifted his gaze to rest on Jenna before he spoke. "That man was given an order with which he could not – would not – comply. He was told to be prepared for a series of shocking Eastern Bloc reports and to shape them in such a way that would force Anton to request a naval blockade of Cuba along with a presidential Red Alert."

"Nuclear?"

"Yes, Miss Karras. A replay of the 'sixty-two missile crisis, but far more provocative. These startling reports would corroborate photographic 'evidence' purporting to show the jungles and southern coastal regions of Cuba ringed with offensive nuclear weapons, the first bridge of an imminent attack."

"For what *purpose*?" asked Jenna.

"A geopolitical trap," said Michael. "He walks into it, he's finished."

"Precisely," agreed Alexander. "Anton brings the full military might of the United States to the brink of war, and suddenly the gates of Cuba are opened and inspection teams from the world over invited to see for themselves. There is nothing, and Anthony Matthias is humiliated, portrayed as an hysterical alarmist – the one thing he never was – all his brilliant negotiations thrown away. The healing with them, I might add."

"But this Soviet agent," said Jenna, bewildered, "this man who had for six years fed Moscow secrets, was a professional, if nothing else; he refused. Did he say why?"

826

"Quite movingly, I thought. He said Anton Matthias was too valuable to be sacrificed to a cabal of hotheads in Moscow."

"The *Voennaya*," said Havelock.

"Those shocking reports came in and they were ignored. No crisis ever took place."

"Would Matthias have accepted them as authentic even if he hadn't known?" asked Michael.

"Somebody would have forced him to. Perfectly conscientious men and women in the section would have become alarmed, would possibly have come to someone like me – if they hadn't been told in advance what to expect, what the intemperate strategy was. Anton called in the Soviet ambassador for a long confidential talk. Men were replaced in Moscow."

"They've come back," said Havelock.

The journalist blinked; he did not understand, nor did he pretend to. He continued. "The man who had deceived us, but who ultimately would not betray some voice inside himself, disappeared. Anton made it possible. He was given a new identity, a new life, beyond those who would have had him killed."

"He came back, too," said Michael.

"He never really went away. But yes, he came back. A little over a year ago, without calling, without warning, he came to see me and said we had to talk. But not in this room; he wouldn't talk in here and I think I appreciated that. I remembered too well that night when he told us what we'd done. It was late afternoon and we walked along the ridge above the ravine – two old men making their way slowly, cautiously over the ground, one profoundly frightened, the other curiously intense . . . in a quiet way, possessed." Alexander paused. "I'd like some more brandy; this isn't easy for me."

"I'm not interested," said Michael.

"Where is it?" asked Jenna, getting up and going to the table, reaching for the glass.

"The copper bar," said the old man, looking up at her. "Against the wall, my dear."

"Go on," said Havelock impatiently. "She can hear you; we can both hear you."

"I meant what I said. I *need* the brandy . . . You don't look well, Michael. You look tired; you're unshaven and there are dark circles under your eyes. You should take better care of yourself."

"I'll make a note of it."

Jenna returned. "Here you are," she said, handing Alexander his drink and going to her chair.

It was the first time Havelock noticed that Raymond's hand shook. It was why he held the glass in both hands, gripping it to reduce the tremble. " 'In a quiet way, possessed.' That's where you were."

"Yes, I remember." Alexander drank, then looked again at Jenna. "Thank you," he said.

She nodded. "Please, go on."

"Yes, of course . . . We walked along the ridge, we two old men that late afternoon, when suddenly he stopped and said to me, 'You must do as I ask, for we have an opportunity that will never be presented to the world again.' I replied that I was not in the habit of acceding to such requests without knowing what was being asked of me. He said it was not a request but a demand, that if I refused he would reveal the roles Matthias and I had played in his espionage activities. He would expose us both, destroy us both. It was what I feared most – for both of us, Anton more than myself, of course. But still myself, I can't say otherwise."

"What did he want you to do?" asked Havelock.

"I was to be the Boswell; my journals would record the deterioration and collapse of a man with such power that he could plunge the world into the insanity that was down the road for him. My Samuel Johnson was, of course, Anthony Matthias, and the message to mankind was to be a sobering one: 'This must not be allowed to happen again; no one man should ever again be elevated to such heights.' "

" 'We made him a god'," said Michael, recalling Berquist's words, " 'when we didn't own the heavens.' "

"Well put." The journalist nodded his head. "I wish I'd written it. But then, to borrow from Wilde, I probably will, if I ever get the chance."

"This man, this Russian," said Jenna, "told you that afternoon what was happening to Matthias?"

"Yes. He'd seen him, been with him, knew the signs. Sudden tirades followed by weeping, constant self-justification, false humility that only served to point up his accomplishments . . . growing suspicions about everyone around him, yet in public there was always the façade of normality. Then there were the lapses of memory – mainly concerning failures and, when prodded, the need to blame others for those failures . . . I came to see it all, write it all. I'd drive to the Shenandoah every week or so – "

"On Sundays?" broke in Havelock.

"Sundays, yes."

"Decker?"

"Oh, yes, Commander Decker. By then, you see, the man you call Parsifal had persuaded a deteriorating Anton that all his policies, all his visions, would find their ultimate justification in total strength. The Master Plan they called it . . . and they found the man who could provide them with what they needed."

"For the ultimate chess game," said Michael.

"Yes. Decker would use the back road and meet Matthias in the cabin he used when he wanted to be alone."

"The Woodshed," said Havelock. "A voice-activated tape system."

"It never failed," agreed Alexander in a voice barely above a whisper. "Never. Even afterwards, when Matthias and . . . Parsifal played their dreadful game, all the more terrifying because Matthias was one of the players. It was frightening in another aspect, too, for Anton would become the warlord statesman, the brilliant negotiator, not seeing the man you call Parsifal but seeing others, addressing others. Russian generals and scientists who weren't there, Chinese army commanders and commissars half way across the globe. During those moments he *saw* them, they were *there*. It was a running pattern of self-induced seances, therapy of the most destructive kind. And each time he came out of it he was a little bit worse, his eyes guarded by those tortoiseshell glasses a little less focused. He was a man who'd been on some sort of drug trip, his mind a touch less clear for it. Yet he could still function in both worlds . . . I saw it all, wrote it all."

"When did I come up?" asked Havelock. "Why me?"

"You were there all the time, photographs of you were on his desk, his bureau . . . in the Woodshed. An album of the two of you on a camping trip through the Canadian far west."

"I'd forgotten," said Michael. "It was so long ago. I was in graduate school, Anton was my adviser."

"Far more than that. You were the son he never had, speaking to him in his native language, recalling another place, another time." Alexander raised his head from the cradle of his chest, riveting his eyes on Havelock. "Above all you were the son who refused to believe that his visions, his solutions for the world, were the right ones. He couldn't convince you. Your voice kept telling him he was wrong, and he couldn't stand that. He couldn't stand being told he was wrong, especially by you."

"He was. He knew I'd tell him."

"His eyes would stray to your pictures, and suddenly he would see you and be talking to you, tormented by your arguments, your anger. He was afraid of you really . . . and the work would stop."

"So I had to be put out of reach."

"Where you could no longer judge him, I think. You were part of his everyday reality, the Department of State. You had to be separated from that reality. It began to consume him; he couldn't tolerate your interference. You had to go; he wouldn't have it any other way."

"And Parsifal knew how to do it," said Michael bitterly. "He knew the mole at State. He reached him and told him what to do."

"I had no part of that. I knew it was being done but I didn't know how . . . You had spoken to Anton about Miss Karras. About your devotion to her and how, after the long years of your own inner turmoil – going back to your childhood – you were ready to come out. With her. Getting out was very important to you. Your decision had been made."

"You thought I'd come out *without* her? Why?"

"Because Parsifal was experienced in such matters," said Jenna. She selected one of the photographs and handed it to Michael. "A clinical psychologist attached to the KGB. A man named Alexi Kalyazin – the face that struck a chord with you."

"I don't *know* him!" shouted Havelock, getting out of the chair and turning on Raymond Alexander. "Who is he?"

"Don't ask me to say the name," whispered the journalist, shaking his head, shrinking back into the chair. "Don't ask me. I can't be involved."

"Goddamn you, you *are* involved!" yelled Michael, throwing the photograph on Alexander's lap. "You're the *Boswell*! . . . Wait a minute!" Michael looked at Jenna. "He was a defector. Forget the fact that he was a plant, he was a *defector*. He must have been listed!"

"All references to the defection of Alexi Kalyazin were expurgated," said Alexander quietly. "All files were removed; a man with another name simply disappeared."

"Naturally. So the great man couldn't possibly be tarnished!" Havelock approached Alexander's chair; he reached down and gripped the lapels of the journalist's jacket, yanked him up. "Who *is* he? *Tell* me!"

"Look at the photograph." Alexander's body was trembling. "Look at it. Remove much of the hair, the eyebrows as well. Give him many lines around his face, his eyes . . . . a small white beard, speckled with grey."

Michael grabbed the photograph and stared at it. "Zelienski . . . Leon *Zelienski*!"

"I thought you'd see, I thought you'd understand. Without me. The ultimate chess game . . . the finest chess player Anton knew."

"He isn't Russian, he's a Pole! A retired professor of history from Berkeley . . . brought over here years ago from the University of Warsaw!"

"A new identity, a new life, papers in place and locations obscured. Living on a back country road less than two miles from Matthias. Anton always knew where he was."

Havelock brought his hands to his temples, trying to contain the racking pain in his head. "You . . . you and Zelienski. Two *demented old men*! Do you know what you've *done*?"

"It's out of control. Everything's out of control."

"You never had it in control! The instant Zelienski reached the mole you lost! We all lost! Couldn't you see what was happening? Did you think it would end with a goddamn *message*? Couldn't you *stop* him? You knew Matthias was at Poole's Island . . . *how* did you know?"

"A source. One of the doctors – he's frightened."

"Then you knew he'd been diagnosed insane! How could you let it go on?"

"You just said it. I couldn't stop him. He wouldn't listen to me – he *won't* listen to me. I *can't stop him*! He's as crazed as Anton now. He has a Christ complex – his is the only light, the only way."

"And you traded your holy name in print so he could have it! What the *hell* are you made of?"

"Leave me something, Michael. He had me caged. Zelienski told me that if I went to anyone, if anyone came for him, a telephone call which he made daily from various phones would *not* be made, and those so–called nuclear agreements – *signed* by Anthony Matthias – would be on their way to Moscow and Peking."

Havelock watched the uneasy green eyes of the old journalist and looked at the bloated hands gripping the arms of the chair. "No, Raymond, that's only part of it. You couldn't stand being exposed, being wrong. You're like Anton, frightened by the truth of your own mistakes. The blind but omniscient Tiresias, seeing things others can't see, the myth to be sustained whatever the cost."

"*Look* at me!" shouted Alexander suddenly, his whole body shaking. "I've lived with this – *through* this – for nearly a year! What would *you* have done?"

"God help me, I don't know, I can only hope better than you . . . but I don't know. Pour yourself a lot of brandy, Raymond. Maintain the myth; keep saying to yourself over and over again that you're infallible. It may help. It also may not make any difference any more. Go out with a grin on that pompous face of yours. Just go." Michael turned to Jenna. "Let's get out of here," he said. "We've got a long drive."

"South to North, come in."

"North in touch. What is it?"

"Get to a phone and call Victor. There's movement. Our people came out fast and spoke with the escort; they were on the grounds. Both cars raced out of here a few moments ago, heading west, pedals to the floor."

"Don't lose them."

"No chance. The escort left the Lincoln up on the road and we placed a directional homer under the chassis. An earthquake couldn't move it. We've got them tracked up to twenty miles and down to a hundred yards. We've got them."

39

The night sky was oddly divided – clear moonlight behind, a ceiling of darkness ahead. The two cars raced along the country roads, the men in the Lincoln committed to protection without understanding, and Michael and Jenna understanding too well and afraid.

"There are no rules now," said Michael. "The book hasn't been written."

"He's capable of change, that's all you really know. He was sent here for one purpose and walked over to the other side."

"Or did he stumble? Alexander said Zelienski – Kalyazin – told them he felt old and worn out, the pressures too great. Maybe he just gave up and walked into sanctuary."

"Until he found another commitment and accepted an entirely different set of pressures," said Jenna. "Exhilarating pressures for a man of his age, I imagine. He's over seventy, isn't he?"

"About that, I'd guess."

"Think of it. The end may not come for a long time but, still, it's in sight. And as you approach it you suddenly find you've discovered an extraordinary solution you believe the world needs desperately, a lesson it must be taught. What do you do?"

Havelock glanced at her. "That's what frightens me. Why should you move off centre? How can I make him move?"

"I wish I could answer that." Jenna looked up at the windscreen, at the myriad tiny globules of water forming over the glass. "We're heading into the rain," she said.

"Unless there's another solution," said Michael quietly, switching on the wipers. "Exchange one lesson for another."

"What?"

"I'm not sure, I don't know. There aren't any rules." Havelock reached for the microphone and pulled it to his lips. "Escort, are you with me?"

"About four hundred feet behind, Sterile Five."

"Slow down and make it at least a mile and a half. We're getting into the area and to a lot of people you're an obvious government vehicle. I don't want any connection between us or any startled eyes. If the man I'm making contact with gets even a hint of you, I don't want to think about the consequences."

"We don't like the distance," said the escort.

"Sorry to offend, but it's an order. Stay out of sight. You know the destination; just take the mountain road as I described it. Seneca something-or-other. Go up about half a mile. We'll be there."

"Would you mind repeating the order, sir?"

Michael did so. "Is that clear?"

"Yes, Sterile Five. It's also on tape."

The dirt-layered car met the blanket of rain, dust and mud dissolving under the downpour. The driver swung into a long curve as the red signal light on the powerful radio amplifier suddenly glowed.

"We're on a different frequency," said the man in the passenger seat as he reached for the microphone. He pressed the scanner for contact. "Yes?" he said.

"South?"

"We're here."

"It's Victor. I'm approaching Warrenton on Sixty-six. Where are you?"

The man with the microphone studied the map on his lap with a pencil light. "North on Seventeen, heading into Marshall. You can pick it up in Warrenton."

"Status?"

"Normal. We reckon once they reach Marshall, they'll either continue north on Seventeen or head west on the Front Royal Road. The turns are getting hairy; we're going into the mountains."

"We've got men covering both routes up there. I want to know which road they take and the distance between Sterile Five and his escort. Use this channel. I should catch up with you in ten to fifteen minutes."

"What flight plan?"

"My own."

The blond man sitting in the brown saloon in front of the Blue Ridge Diner slumped back in the seat, the microphone in his hand, his eyes on the road. He depressed the button and spoke.

"It's the Front Royal Road," he said as the Buick coupé rushed by in the rain. "Right on time and in a hurry."

"How far behind is the Lincoln?" asked the voice from the speaker.

"No sign of it yet."

"You're sure?"

"No headlights, and anyone damn fool enough to drive up here in this mess isn't going to roll in the dark."

"It's not normal. I'll be right back."

"It's your equipment."

The blond man lowered the microphone and reached for the cigarettes on the seat beside him. He jerked one out of the pack, put it to his lips and snapped his butane lighter. Thirty seconds went by and still the Lincoln Continental had not come into view; nothing was in view but sheets of rain. Forty-five seconds. Nothing. A minute, and the voice accompanied by static, burst out of the speaker. "Front Royal, where are you?"

"Here and waiting. You said you'd be right back, remember?"

"The escort. Has it gone by?"

"Nope. If it had I would have rung you up, pal . . . Wait. Stay there. We may have it." A stream of light came out of the curve and seconds later the long, dark car roared by in the downpour. "He just went by, old buddy. I'll roll now. The blond man sat up and eased the car out into the road."

"I'll be right back," said the voice.

"You keep repeating yourself, pal," said the blond man, stepping on the accelerator. Gathering speed while watching the rain-soaked road closely, he saw the red tail-lights of the Lincoln flickering in the distance through the downpour. He breathed easier.

"Front Royal," erupted the voice from the speaker.

"Right here, li'l darlin'."

"Scan to seventeen-twenty megahertz for separate instructions."

"Scanning now." The blond man reached down and pressed the metal button; the digital read-outs appeared on the narrow horizontal strip above the radio's dials. "Front Royal in position," he said.

"This is the man you don't know, Front Royal."

"Nice not to know you, old buddy."

"How much are you being paid for tonight?" asked the new voice.

"Since you're the man I don't know, I figure you ought to know how much."

"How good are you?"

"Very. How good's your money?"

"You've been paid."

"Not for what you want now."

"You're perceptive."

"You're kind of obvious."

"That big fellow up ahead. He knows where the little fellow's going, wouldn't you agree?"

"Sure would. There's a lot of space between them, 'specially for a night like this."

"Do you think you could get between them?"

"Can do. Then what?"

"A bonus."

"For what?"

"The little fellow's going to stop somewhere. After he does, I don't want the big fellow around him any longer."

"You're talking about a pretty big bonus, Mr No-name. That car's an Abraham."

"Six figures," said the voice. "A reckless driver. Very reckless and very accurate."

"You're on, li'l darlin'."

Arthur Pierce nodded through the window and the rain as he passed the old car four miles down the Front Royal Road. He lifted the microphone and spoke on the 1720 frequency.

"All right, South, here's the manual. You stay with me, everyone else is dismissed. Thank them all for their time and say we'll be in touch."

"What about North? They travel."

"I want them back with the naval contingent. It's theirs now; they can alternate. Sooner or later – tonight, tomorrow, the next day – they'll let him out. When they do, terminate. We don't want to hear his voice."

Havelock stopped the car and lowered the window; he peered through the rain at the sign nailed to the tree, feeling certain it was the one. It was:

SENECA'S NOTCH
Dead End

He had driven Leon Zelienski home twice, once in the afternoon when the old man's car would not start, and then several years later on a night like tonight, when Matthias was worried that Leon might get stuck in the mud. Zelienski had not got stuck, but Michael had; it had been a long, wet walk back to Anton's house. He remembered the roads.

He had taken Leon Zelienski home; he was coming after Alexi Kalyazin. Parsifal.

"Here we go," said Havelock, turning up into the rocky road with only remnants of long-eroded tar on its surface. "If we stay in the centre we should make it."

"Stay in the centre," said Jenna.

They lurched and skidded up the narrow road, drenched darkness all around them, tyres spinning, hurling loose stones behind and up into the metal fenders. The jarring ride did nothing to steady their nerves or set the tone for awesome negotiations. Michael had been brutal with Raymond Alexander, knowing he was right, but only partly right. He began to understand the other aspect of the journalist's profound fear, fear that was driving him to the edge of hysteria. Zelienski's threat was clear and terrifying. Should Alexander betray the Russian or interfere in any way, the daily telephone call that Zelienski placed from various phones would not be made. The silence would be the signal for the nuclear agreements to be sent to Moscow and Peking.

And chemicals could not be used to force Zelienski to reveal the number that he was calling. There was too great a risk with a man of his age. One cubic-centimetre of excess dosage and his heart could blow apart, the number lost with the internal explosion. There were only words. What were the words one found for a man who would save the world with a blueprint for its annihilation? There was no reason in such a mind, nothing but its own distorted vision.

The small house came into view above them on the right; it was hardly larger than a cabin, square in design and made of heavy stone. A sloping stony driveway ended in a carport, where a nondescript vehicle stood motionless, protected from the downpour. A single light shone through a bay window, which was oddly out of place in the small dwelling.

Havelock switched off the headlights and turned to Jenna. "It all began here," he said. "In the mind of the man up there. All of it. From the Costa Brava to Poole's Island, from Col des Moulinets to Sterile Five; it started here."

"Can we end it here, Mikhail?"

"Let's try. Let's go."

They got out of the car and walked through the rain up the wet, soft mud of the driveway, rivulets of water racing down around their feet. They reached the carport; there was a door centred under the attached roof with a concrete step below. Havelock walked to the door; he looked briefly at Jenna and then knocked.

Moments later the door opened, and a slight, stooped old man with only a few strands of hair and a small white beard peppered with grey stood in the open space. As he stared at Havelock his eyes grew wide and his mouth parted, lips trembling.

"*Mikhail*," he whispered.

"Hello, Leon. I bring you Anton's affection."

The blond man had seen the sign, the only part with any meaning to him were the words "Dead End". It was all he needed to know. With his headlights still extinguished, he manoeuvred the brown saloon several hundred feet down the smooth wet road, and stopped on the far right, the engine idling. He turned the headlights back on and reached under his coat to remove a large automatic with a silencer attached. He understood Mr No-name's instructions; they were in sequence. The Lincoln would be along any moment now.

There it was! Two hundred yards away at the mouth of the road that branched off the highway. The blond man released the brake and began coasting, spinning the wheel back and forth, weaving, the unmistakable sign of a drunken, reckless driver. Cautiously, the limousine slowed down, pulling as far to the right as possible. The blond man accelerated, and the weaving became more violent as the Lincoln's horn roared through the torrents of rain. When he was within thirty feet, the blond man suddenly pressed the accelerator to the floor and swung to the right before making a sharp turn to the left.

The impact came, the saloon's radiator grill ramming the left rear door of the Lincoln. The car skidded and crashed into the other car, pinning the driver's door.

"Goddamn you sons of *bitches*!" screamed the blond man through the open window, slurring his words, his head swaying back and forth. "Holy *Christ*, I'm bleeding! My whole stomach's *bleeding*!"

The two men lurched out of the limousine from the other side. As they came running around the bonnet in the blinding glare of the headlights, the blond man leaned out the window and fired twice. Accurately.

"Do I call you Leon or Alexi?"

"I can't *believe* you!" cried the old Russian, sitting in front of the fire, his eyes rheumy and blinking, riveted on Havelock. "It was degenerative, irreversible. There was *no hope*."

"There are very few minds, very few wills, like Anton's. Whether he'll ever regain his full capacities no one can tell, but he's come back a long way. Drugs helped, electro-therapy as well; he's cognizant now . . . And appalled at what he did." Havelock sat down in the straight-backed chair opposite Zelienski-Kalyazin. Jenna remained standing by the door that led to the small kitchen.

"It's never *happened*!"

"There's never been a man like Matthias, either. He asked for me; they sent me to Poole's Island and he told me everything. Only me."

"Poole's Island?"

"It's where he's being treated. Is it Leon or Alexi, old friend?"

Kalyazin shook his head. "Not Leon, it's never been Leon. Always Alexi."

"You had good years as Leon Zelienski."

"Enforced sanctuary, Mikhail. I am a Russian, nothing else. Sanctuary."

Havelock and Jenna exchanged glances, her eyes telling him that she approved – approved with enormous admiration – the course he had suddenly chosen.

"You came over to us . . . Alexi."

"I did not come over to you. I fled others. Men who would corrupt the soul of my homeland, who went beyond the bounds of our convictions, who killed needlessly, wantonly, seeking only power for its own sake. I believe in our system, Mikhail, not yours. But these men did not; they would have changed words into weapons and then no one would have been proved right. We'd all be gone."

"Jackals," said Havelock, repeating the word he had heard only hours ago, "fanatics who in their heads marched with the Third Reich, who didn't believe time was on your side, only bombs."

"That will suffice."

"The *Voennaya*."

Kalyazin's head snapped up. "I never told Matthias that!"

"I never told him, either. I've been in the field for sixteen years. Do you think I don't know the VKR?"

"They do not speak for Russia, not our Russia . . . Anton and I would argue until the early hours of the morning. He couldn't understand; he came from a background of brilliance and respectability, money and a full table. Over here none of you will ever understand, except the black people, perhaps. We had nothing and were told to expect nothing, not in this world. Books, schools, simple reading – these were not for us, the millions of us. We were placed on this earth as the earth's cattle, worked and disposed of by our 'betters' – decreed by God . . . My father was hanged by a Voroshin prince for stealing game. Stealing *game*! All that was changed – by the millions of us, led by prophets who had no use for a God who decreed human cattle." An odd smile appeared on Kalyazin's thin, white lips. "They call us atheistic communists. What would they wish us to be? We *knew* what it was like under the Holy *Church*! A God who threatens eternal fires if one rises up against a living hell is no God for nine-tenths of mankind. He can and should be replaced, dismissed for incompetence and unwarranted partiality."

"That argument is hardly restricted to pre-revolutionary Russia," said Michael.

836

"Certainly not, but it's symptomatic . . . and we were *there!* It's why you'll lose one day. Not in this decade or the next – perhaps not for many, many years, but you'll lose. Too many tables are bare, too many stomachs swollen and you care too little."

"If that proves to be true then we deserve to lose. I don't think it is." Havelock leaned forward, elbows on knees and looked into the old Russian's eyes. "Are you telling me you were given sanctuary but you gave nothing in return?"

"Not of my country's secrets, nor did Anton ever ask me a second time. I think he considered the work I did – the work you did before you resigned – to be in the main quite pointless. Our decisions counted for very little, our accomplishments were not important at the summits. I did, however, give you a gift that served us both, served the world as well. I gave you Anthony Matthias. I saved him from the Cuban trap; it would have driven him from office. I did so because I believed in him, and not in the madmen who temporarily had far too much control of my government."

"Yes, he told me. He would have been destroyed, his influence finished . . . It's on that basis . . . your belief in him – that he asked me to come and see you. It's got to stop, Leon – excuse me Alexi. He knows why you did what you did, but it's got to *stop.*"

Kalyazin's gaze strayed to Jenna. "Where is the hatred in your eyes, young lady? Surely, it must be there."

"I won't lie to you, it's close to my thoughts. I'm trying to understand."

"It had to be done; there was no other way. Anton had to be rid of the spectre of Mikhail. He had to know he was far away from the government, with other interests, other pursuits. He was so afraid his . . . his son . . . would learn of his work and come to stop him." Kalyazin turned to Havelock. "He couldn't get you out of his mind."

"He approved of what you did?" asked Michael.

"He looked away, I think, a part of him revolted by himself, another part crying to survive. He was failing rapidly by then, his sanity pleading to be left intact whatever the cost. Miss Karras became the price."

"He never asked you how you did it? How you reached men in Moscow to provide what you needed?"

"Never. That, too, was part of the price. Remember, the world you and I lived in was very unimportant to him. Then, of course, everything became chaos."

"Out of control?" suggested Jenna.

"Yes, young lady. The things we heard were so unbelievable, so horrible. A woman killed on a beach."

"What did you expect?" asked Havelock, controlling himself and not finding it easy. *Two . . . three demented old men . . .*

"Not that. We weren't killers. Anton had given orders that she was to be sent back to Prague and watched, her contacts observed and eventually, her innocence was to be established."

"Those orders were intercepted, changed."

"By then he could do nothing. You had disappeared and he finally went completely, totally mad."

"Disappeared? *I* disappeared?"

"That's what he was told. And when they told him he collapsed, his mind went. He thought he'd killed you, too. It was the final pressure he could not withstand."

"How do you know this?" pressed Michael.

Kalyazin balked, his rheumy eyes blinking. "There was someone else. He had sources, a doctor. He found out."

"Raymond Alexander," said Havelock.

"Anton told you, then?"

"Boswell."

"Yes, our Boswell."

"You mentioned him when I called you from Europe."

"I was frightened. I thought you might speak to someone who had seen him at Anton's house; he was there so often. I wanted to give you a perfectly acceptable reason for his visits, to keep you away from him."

"Why?"

"Because Alexander the Great has become Alexander the Diseased. You've been away, you don't know. He rarely writes any more. He drinks all day and most of the night; he can't stand the strain. Fortunately, for his public, there's the death of his wife to blame it on."

"Matthias told me you had a wife," said Michael, his ear picking up something in Kalyazin's voice. "In California. She died and he persuaded you to come here to the Shenandoah."

"I had a wife, Mikhail. In Moscow. And she was killed by the soldiers of Stalin. A man I helped destroy, a man who came from the *Voennaya*."

"I'm sorry."

A brief rattling somewhere in the small house was louder than the pounding rain outside. Jenna looked at Havelock.

"It's nothing," said Kalyazin. "There's a piece of wood, a wedge, I place in that old door on windy nights. The sight of you made me forget." The old man leaned back in his chair and brought his thin, veined hands to his chin. "You must be very clear with me, Mikhail, and you must give me time to think. It's why I did not answer you a few moments ago."

"About Anton?"

"Yes. Does he really know why I did what I did? Why I took him through those terrible nights? Auto and external suggestion, swelling him up until he performed like the genius he was, debating with men who weren't there. Does he *really* understand?"

"Yes, he does," replied Havelock, feeling a thousand pounds on the back of his neck. He was so close, but a wrong response would send this Parsifal back into self-imposed, unbreakable silence. Alexander was right after all; Kalyazin had a Christ complex. Beneath the old Russian's mild speech was a commitment forged in steel. He knew he was right. "No single man," said Michael, "should be given such power, and the strains of that power, ever again. He begs you, pleads with you on the strength of all the talks you and he had before his illness, to give me those incredible agreements you both created and whatever copies exist. Let me burn them."

"He understands then, but is it enough? Do the others? Have *they* learned?"

"Who?"

"The men who allocate such power, who permit the canonization of would-be saints only to find that their heroes are simple mortals, broken by swollen egos and by the demands made on them."

"They're terrified. What more do you want?"

"I want them to know what they've done, how this world can be set on fire by a single brilliant mind caught in the vortex of unbearable pressures. The madness is contagious; it does not stop with a broken saint."

"They understand. Above all, the one man most people consider the most powerful on earth, he understands. He told me they had created an emperor, a god, and they had no right to do either. They took him up too high; he was blinded."

"And Icarus fell to the sea," said Kalyazin. "Berquist is a decent man, hard but decent. He's also in an impossible job, but he handles it better than most."

"There's no one I'd rather see there now."

"I'm inclined to agree."

"You're killing him," said Havelock. "Let him go. Free him. The lesson's been taught, and it won't be forgotten. Let him get back to that impossible job and do the best he can."

Kalyazin looked at the glowing embers of the fire. "Twenty-seven pages, each document, each agreement. I typed them myself, using the form employed by Bismarck in the treaties of Schleswig-Holstein. It so appealed to Anton . . . I was never interested in the money, they know that, don't they?"

"They know that. He knows it."

"Only the lesson."

"Yes."

The old man turned back to Michael. "There are no copies except the one I sent to President Berquist in an envelope from the State Department, from Matthias's office, with the word *Restricted* stamped across the front. It was marked, of course, for his eyes only."

Havelock tensed, recalling so clearly Raymond Alexander's statement that Kalyazin had "caged" him, that if a telephone call was not made the documents would be sent to Moscow and Peking. The numbers added up to four, not two. "No other copies at all, Alexi?"

"None."

"I would think," remarked Jenna unexpectedly, taking two hesitant steps towards the frail, old Russian, "that Raymond Alexander, your Boswell, would have insisted on one. It's the core of his writing."

"It's the core of his fear, young lady. I control him by telling him that if he divulges anything to anyone copies will be sent to your enemies. That was never my intention, on the contrary, the thought farthest from my mind. It would bring about the very cataclysm I pray will be avoided."

"Pray, Alexi?"

"Not to any god you know, Mikhail. Only to a collective conscience. Not to. a Holy Church with a biased Almighty."

"May I have the documents?"

Kalyazin nodded. "Yes," he said, drawing out the word. "But not in the sense of possession. We will burn them together."

"Why?"

"You know the reason; we were both in the same profession. The men who allow the Matthiases of this world to soar so high they're blinded by the sun, those men will never know. Did an old man lie? I deceived them before. Am I deceiving them again? *Are* there copies?"

"Are there?"

"No, but they won't know that." Kalyazin struggled out of the chair; he stood up and breathed deeply, planting his feet firmly on the floor. "Come with me, Mikhail. They're buried in the woods along the path to the Notch. I pass them every afternoon, seventy-three steps to a dogwood tree, the only one in Seneca's burial ground. I often wonder how it got there . . . Come, let's get it over with. We will dig in the rain and get terribly wet and return with the weapons of Armageddon. Perhaps Miss Karras might make us some tea. Also, glasses of vodka . . . with buffalo grass, always buffalo grass. Then we shall burn the evidence and rekindle the fire."

The door to the kitchen crashed open like a sudden explosion of thunder, and a tall man with a fringe of grey around his bald head stood there, a gun in his hand.

"They lie to you, Alexi. They *always* lie and you never know it. *Don't move*, Havelock!" Arthur Pierce reached out, gripped Jenna's elbow and yanked her to him, lashing his left arm around her neck, the automatic pressed against her head. "I'm going to count to five," he said to Michael. "By which time you will have removed your weapon with two fingers and thrown it on the floor or you will see this woman's skull blown into the wall. One, *two, three –* "

Havelock unbuttoned his coat, spreading it open, and using two fingers like pincers, took the Llama from its holster. He dropped it on the floor.

"Kick it over!" yelled the traveller.

Michael did so. "I don't know how you got here, but you can't get out," he said quietly.

"Really?" Pierce released Jenna, shoving her towards the astonished old Russian. "Then I should tell you that your Abraham was cut down by an ungrateful Ishmael. You can't get out."

"Others know where we are."

"I doubt that. There'd be a hidden army out there on that road if they did. Oh, no, you went in solo – "

"*You?*" cried Kalyazin, shaking, then nodding his trembling head. "It *is* you!"

"Glad you're with us, Alexi. You're slowing down in your old age. You don't hear lies when you're told them."

"What lies? How did you find me?"

"By following a persistent man. Let's talk about the lies."

"What *lies?*"

"Matthias recovering. That's the biggest lie of all. There's a metal case in my car the contents of which will make remarkable reading all over the world. It shows Anthony Matthias for what he is. A screaming, hollow shell, a maniac, violent and paranoid, who has no working concept of reality. He builds delusions out of images, fantasies out of abstractions – he can be programmed like a deranged robot, re-enacting his crimes and offences. He's insane and getting worse."

"That can't be true!" Kalyazin looked at Michael. "The things he told me . . . only Anton would know them, recall them."

"Another lie. Your convincing friend failed to mention that he's just driven down from the village of Fox Hollow, the residence and dateline of a well-known commentator. One Raymond Alexander . . . what did Miss Karras just call him? Your Boswell, I think. I'll visit him. He can add to our collection."

"*Mikhail?* Why? Why did you say these things? Why did you lie to me?"

"I had to. I was afraid you wouldn't listen to me. And because I believe that the Anton we both knew once would have wanted me to."

"Still another lie," said Pierce, lowering himself cautiously, his gun extended as he picked up the Llama from the floor and shoved it into his belt. "All they want are those papers so business can go on as usual. So their nuclear committees can go on designing new ways to blow the godless out of existence. That's what they call us, Alexi. Godless. Perhaps they'll make Commander Decker the next Secretary of State. His type is very much in vogue, ambitious zealots are the order of the day."

"That couldn't happen and you know it, Traveller."

Pierce looked at Havelock, studying him. "Yes, a traveller. How did you do it? How did you find me?"

"You'll never know that. Or how deeply we've penetrated the *paminyatchik* operation. That's right. Penetrated."

The traveller stared at Michael. "I don't believe you."

"That doesn't matter."

"It won't make any difference. We'll have the documents. All the options will be ours, nothing left to you. *Nothing.* Except burning cities if you make a wrong turn, a wrong judgement. The world won't tolerate you any longer." Pierce stabbed the air with his gun. "Let's go, all of you. You're going to dig them up for me, Havelock. 'Seventy-three steps to a dogwood tree'."

"There are a dozen paths up to the Notch," said Michael quickly. "You don't know which one."

"Alexi will show me. When it comes down to it he chooses us, not you. Never you. Not business as usual, conducted by liars. He'll tell me."

"Don't do it, Kalyazin."

"You lied to me, Mikhail. If there must be ultimate weapons – even on paper – they can't be yours."

"I told you why I lied, but there's a final reason. Him. You came over to us not because you believed in us but because you couldn't believe in *them.* They've come back. He was the man at the Costa Brava – he killed at the Costa Brava."

"I carried out what you only pretended! You had the stomachs only for pretence. It had to be *done*, not faked!"

"No, it didn't. But where there's a choice, you kill. You killed the man who set up the operation, an operation where *no* one's death was called for."

"I did exactly what you would have done but with far more finesse and inventive-ness. His death had to be credible, accepted for what it appeared to be. MacKenzie was the only one who could retrace the events of that night, who knew his personnel."

"Also killed!"

"Inevitable."

"And Bradford? Inevitable, too?"

"Of course. He'd found me."

"You see the pattern, Kalyazin?" shouted Havelock, his eyes on Pierce. "Kill, kill, *kill*! . . . Do you remember Rostov, Alexi?"

"Yes, I remember him."

"He was my enemy, but he was a decent man. They killed him, too. Only hours ago. They've come back and they're marching."

"Who?" asked the old Russian haltingly, memories stirred.

"The *Voennaya*. The maniacs of the VKR!"

"*Not* maniacs," said Pierce firmly, quietly. "Dedicated men who understand the nature of your hatred, your mendacity. Men who will not compromise the principles of the Soviet Union only to watch you spread your sanctimonious lies, turning the world against us . . . Our time has come, Alexi. You'll be with us."

Kalyazin blinked, his watery eyes staring at Arthur Pierce. Slowly he shook his head, his words whispered. "No . . . no I will never be a part of you."

"What?"

"You do not speak for Russia," said the old man, his voice growing until it filled the room. "You kill too easily . . . you killed someone very dear to me. Your words are measured and there's truth in what you say . . . but not in what you *do* or the way you *do it*! You are *animals*!" Without the slightest warning, Kalyazin lunged at Pierce, hurling his frail body at the traveller, his gaunt hands gripping the weapon. "*Mikhail*, run! Run, Mikhail!" There was a muffled roar as the gun exploded into the old man's stomach. Still he would not let go. "*Run . . . !*" The whisper was a shout, a final command.

Havelock spun around and propelled Jenna towards the open kitchen door. He turned, prepared to throw himself on Pierce, but stopped, holding himself in check, for what he saw caused him to make an instantaneous decision. The dying Kalyazin held on fiercely, but the bloody gun was coming free; in an instant it would be aimed at him, fired into his head.

He lurched for the kitchen door and slammed it shut as he raced inside, colliding with Jenna. She held two kitchen knives in her hand; Michael grabbed the shorter blade, and they ran for the outside door.

"The woods!" he shouted in the carport. "Kalyazin can't hold him. Hurry *up*! You go to the right, I'll head left!" They ran across the drenched grass in the downpour. "We'll converge a couple of hundred yards inside!"

"Where is the path? Which *is* it?"

"I don't know!"

"He'll be looking for it!"

"I know."

Five gunshots exploded, but not from a single gun; there were two. They separated, Michael zig-zagging towards the darkness of the trees on his left, spinning quickly to look behind him. Three men. Pierce was shouting orders to two others who had raced up the muddy drive. They ran from the carport, fanning out, torches on, weapons ready.

He reached the edge of the tall grass and plunged into the protective cover of the woods; he removed his coat and scrambled to his right, diving for the thickest underbrush. He crawled forward, his eyes on the field, on the beam of the middle light, and worked his way back towards the edge. His body was soaked, mud and wet foliage were everywhere. The border of the grass was his battle line; the downpour was loud enough to drown out the sound of quick movements. The man would come swiftly, then be stopped both by the undergrowth and by his own caution.

As the beam approached, Havelock inched towards the last bank of tangled bush; he waited, crouching. The man slowed down, sweeping the area with light. Then he entered the woods quickly, the beam moving up and down as he used his arm to open a path through the thick brush.

Now. Michael rolled out on the grass and rushed ahead; he was directly behind the traveller. He sprang, the knife gripped in his hand. As he plunged the blade into the killer's back, his left hand yanked back the man's neck and clamped over his mouth. Both fell into mud and brush, Michael working the blade brutally until there was no movement beneath him. He yanked the head up as he ripped the gun from the lifeless hand; It was not Arthur Pierce. He lunged for the torch and snapped it off.

Jenna raced into the dark, narrow alleyway cut through the trees and foliage. Was this *it*? she wondered. Was it the path to Seneca's Notch . . . "seventy-three steps to a dogwood tree". If it was, it was her responsibility. No one could be allowed to pass through, and the surest way of preventing it was as distasteful as it was frightening.

Yet she had done it before, always terrified by the prospect, sickened with the results, but there was no time to think of such things. She looked behind her; the torch beam was veering to its left, towards the path! She let out a short cry loud enough to be heard through the pounding rain. The light halted and was briefly immobile before shifting, now focusing directly on the entrance of the path. The man rushed into it.

Jenna lurched into the tangled branches on the border and crouched, holding the long blade of the kitchen knife rigid, diagonally up from her knees. The oscillating beam of light drew nearer, the figure behind it running hard, slipping on the mud, his concentration up ahead on the path, a killer racing after the remembered cry of an unarmed woman.

Ten feet, five . . . now!

Jenna lunged up through the brush with her eyes and blade centred on the body directly behind the light. The contact was sickening. A rush of blood erupted as the long blade sank into the flesh, impaling the body that had raced into it.

The man screamed, a terrible scream that filled the woods, drowning the downpour for a long moment.

Jenna lay gasping for air beside the dead man, rubbing her blood-soaked hand in the soft mud. She grabbed the torch and switched it off. Then she rolled to the border of the path and vomited.

Havelock heard the sudden scream and closed his eyes – then opened them, grateful beyond life itself to realize it was a man's scream. Jenna had done it; she had taken out the man whose orders were to kill her. And that man was not Pierce. He knew it. He had seen the positions in the carport. Pierce had been on the left, closest to the door, the angles consistent when the chase had begun.

Arthur Pierce was somewhere between the middle ground and the road beyond Kalyazin's house, an acre of drenched forest, rain surging downward, dripping everywhere from the imperfect roof of the trees.

Where was the last beam of light? It was not there of course it wasn't there! Light was a target and Pierce was no fool. They were two animals now, two predators stalking each other in the waterlogged darkness. But one had the advantage, and Michael knew it instinctively, felt it strongly: The forests had been good to Mikhail Havlíček; they were his friend and sanctuary. He did not fear the webbed darkness, for it had saved him too often, protected him from uniformed hunters who would shoot a child because of his father.

He crawled swiftly through undergrowth, eyes straining, ears alert, trying to pick up sounds that were not part of the rain and the creaking weight of drenched limbs above. He semicircled the area, noting among a thousand other intuitively-gathered bits of information that there were no paths, no breaks in the forest leading to Seneca's Notch. Inside the house he had said there were a dozen such paths to confuse Pierce, not knowing whether there were any, never having been beyond Zelienski-Kalyazin's front door.

He swept the arc again, closing it, snaking through the overgrowth; the trunks of trees were his intermittent fortress walls – he used them like parapets, as he peered around them.

Movement! The sound of suction, not weight. A foot or a knee pressing into and rising from the mud.

Light was a target . . . light *was* a target.

He crawled out of the arc, fifteen, twenty, thirty, forty feet beyond the perimeter, knowing what he was looking for, feeling for – a branch. He found it.

A sapling – strong, supple, no more than four feet high, its roots deep, clawing the earth beneath.

Havelock reached into his belt and pulled out the torch he had taken from the dead traveller. He placed it on the ground and removed his shirt, spreading it in front of him, moving the torch to the centre of the cloth.

Thirty seconds later the torch was securely tied, wrapped in the shirt, the sleeves wound around it, sufficient cloth remaining for the final attachment. He knelt next to the small tree and lashed the package laterally against the thin shaft of the trunk; he crisscrossed what remained of the sleeves so it was held firmly in place. He pulled the trunk back and let it go, testing it.

He snapped on the light and pulled the trunk back for the last time, then raced into the woods to his right. He spun around a thick tree and waited, watching the beam of light as it eerily swept back and forth over the ground. He levelled the traveller's gun, steadying it against the bark.

His ears picked up the sound of suction again, footsteps coming through the rain. Then the figure emerged, looming grotesquely through the webbed branches.

Pierce crouched, trying to avoid the light, and fired his automatic; the ear-shattering explosions echoed throughout the dripping forest.

"You lose," said Michael as he pulled the trigger and watched the killer of Costa Brava reel backwards, screaming. He fired again, and the man from the *Voennaya* fell to the ground motionless, silent. Dead. "You didn't know the woods," said Michael. "I learned them from people like you."

"Jenna! *Jenna!*" he yelled, lurching through the trees towards the open grass. "It's *over*! The field, the *field*!"

"Mikhail? *Mikhail!*"

He saw her walking slowly, unsteadily, in the distance through the sheets of the downpour. Seeing him, she quickened her pace and broke into a run. He, too, raced over the wet grass, wanting – needing – the distance between them to vanish.

They held each other; the world for a few brief moments was no part of them. The cold rain on his bare skin was only cool water, warmed by her embrace, her face against his face.

"Were there other paths?" she asked, breathless.

"None."

"Then I found it. Come, Mikhail. *Hurry!*"

They stood in Kalyazin's house. The old Russian's body was covered with a blanket, his tortured face mercifully hidden. Havelock walked to the telephone. "It's time," he said, dialling.

"What's *happened*?" asked the President of the United States, his voice tense. "I've been trying to reach you all night!"

"It's over," said Michael. "Parsifal's dead. We've got the documents. I'll write a report telling you what I think you'll have to know."

There was a stunned silence on the line, then Berquist whispered simply, "I know you wouldn't lie."

"I would, but not about this."

"What *you* think *I* have to know?" said Berquist, finding a part of his voice.

"Yes. I'll leave out nothing that's essential to you, for that impossible job you're in."

"Where are you? I'll send an army for you – just get those documents here."

"No, Mr President. We have a last stop to make, to a man they called Boswell. But before we leave I'm going to burn them. There's only one set and I'm burning it. The psychiatric file as well."

"*You've . . . ?*"

"It'll be in the report . . . There's a practical reason for my doing what I'm doing.

I don't know what's out there – I think I know, but I can't be certain. It started here and it's going to end here."

"I see." Berquist paused. "I can't change your mind and I can't stop you."

"That's true."

"Very well, I won't try. I like to think I'm a judge of men. You have to be to sit in this office. At least, you should be . . . What can a grateful nation, a very grateful President do for you?"

"Leave me alone, sir. Leave us alone."

"Havelock?"

"Yes?"

"How can I be certain? The burning?"

"Parsifal didn't want you to be. You see, he never wanted it to happen again. No more Matthiases. Superstars are out. He never wanted you to be absolutely sure."

"I'll have to think about that, won't I?"

"It'd be a good idea."

"Matthias died this evening. It's why I tried to call you."

"He died a long time ago, Mr President."

Epilogue

Autumn. New Hampshire alternately chilled into grey submission by the gathering arctic winds and then warmed by the vibrant colours of fall, the persistent sun giving life to the fields and refusing to submit to the slow approach of winter.

Havelock hung up the phone in the enclosed porch that Jenna had insisted be his study . . . She had seen him, had watched his eyes, as he had walked through the living-room door of the old house and had stood there, mesmerized by the expanse of glass and the framed countryside beyond. A desk, bookshelves against the inner brick wall, and an odd assortment of comfortable furniture had transformed the bare porch into an airy room, protected by transparent walls that allowed a wide view of the fields and the woods that meant so much to him. She had understood, and he loved her for understanding. What he could see from that very unusual place was not what others would see, not simply the tall grass and vastly taller trees in the distance, but an ever-changing landscape of sanctuary.

And memories of tension and survival, they were there, too, suddenly welling up until he had to move – physically move to overcome them . . . to suppress them. It would take time; normality was not to be found in a matter of weeks, even months.

Underneath he had a fever because you bastards poisoned him. You fed him a diet of . . . frenzy. He needed his fix! Dr Matthew Randolph, dead man, talking about another dead man . . . and so many others.

They had discussed it, Jenna and he, had defined the fever that gripped him every now and then, and she was the only doctor he needed. They would take long walks; sudden bursts of running frequently became necessary for him, until the sweat came and his chest pounded. But the fever would pass, the explosions in his head dissolve – the guns would be stilled.

Sleep came easier these days, and his fits of restlessness caused him to reach only for her and not for a weapon. There were no weapons in the house. There never would be in any house they would ever live in.

"*Mikhail?*" The cheerful shout was accompanied by the opening and closing of the door beyond the living-room.

"In here!" He turned in the leather swivel chair that was her last addition to his study.

Jenna walked into the sun-drenched room, the light catching her long blond hair that fell from beneath a dark wool cap, her tweed coat buttoned to ward off the autumn chill outside. She lowered a canvas bag to the floor and kissed him lightly on the lips. "There are the books you wanted. Anybody call?" she asked, taking off her coat. "They put me on the student foreign exchange committee and I think I'm supposed to be at a meeting tonight."

"You are. Eight o'clock, Dean Crane's place."

"Good."

"You enjoy it, don't you?"

"I can help, I *do* help. Not only because of the languages, but mainly with the government papers. All those years falsifying documents does give one an advantage. At times I find it terribly difficult to be so honest. As if I'm doing something wrong."

They both laughed. Havelock reached for her hand. "Someone else called."

"Who?"

"Berquist."

Jenna stiffened. "He hasn't tried to reach you since you sent in your report."

"He honoured my request. I told him to leave us alone."

"Then why call you now? What does he want?"

"He doesn't want anything. He thought I should be brought up to date."

"About what?"

"Loring's all right, but he'll never get back in the field again."

"I'm glad. On both counts."

"I hope he can handle it."

"He will. They'll make him a strategist."

"That's what I suggested."

"I thought you would."

Michael released her hand. "Decker didn't make it."

"What?"

"It happened months ago, but they covered it up. It was the most generous thing they could do. He walked out of his house the morning after Seneca's Notch and was caught in the cross-hairs. The guards moved in on the killer's car – the one sent by Pierce – and so did Decker. He just kept walking into the fire, so help me God, singing 'The Battle Hymn of the Republic'. He wanted to die."

"The death of a zealot."

"Futility. He'd learned; in his twisted way he had a lot to offer."

"It's history, Mikhail."

"History," agreed Havelock.

Jenna walked back to the canvas bag and took out the books. "I had coffee with Harry Lewis. I think he's working up the courage to tell you."

" 'Birchtree'?" Michael smiled. "It'll be something he can tell his grandchildren. Professor Harry Lewis, undercover man, complete with a code name."

"I don't think he's terribly proud of it."

"Why not? He didn't do anything wrong and he did it better than most. Besides, he got me a job I happen to like very much . . . Let's have Harry and his wife to dinner, and when the phone rings – believe me, it'll ring – I'll say it's for 'Birchtree'."

"You're outrageous," said Jenna, laughing.

Havelock stopped smiling. "I'm restless," he said.

"It was the call."

"I get so goddamned . . . *restless*." He looked at her.

"Let's take a walk."

848

They climbed the steep hill several miles west of the house, the high grass bending with the breezes, the hard earth sunbaked, the sky an eloquent blue, speckled with the tassels of wind-swept clouds. Below to the north was a winding stream, the waters curling gently around the bends, flirting with the low-hanging branches and heading south with a purpose on the other side of the hill.

"We had a picnic in Prague," said Michael, looking down. "Remember? The Moldau was below then."

"We'll have a picnic here," said Jenna, watching him closely. "Chilled wine, salad – those dreadful sandwiches you like so much."

"Ham and cheese, with celery, onions and mustard."

"Yes," she said, smiling. "Unfortunately I remember."

"If I were famous, they'd name it after me. It'd sweep the country, be on every menu."

"Then keep a low profile, my darling."

His smile waned. "You're stronger than I am, Jenna."

"If you want to believe that, fine, but it isn't true."

"It keeps coming back . . . the restlessness."

"Depression, Mikhail. And less and less, we both know that."

"Still, it comes back and I turn to you. You don't have to turn to me."

"But I do."

"Not this way."

"I never went through what you did for the length of time you did. And there's something else. It was always your responsibility, not mine. Every decision you made had to cost you a part of yourself. It was yours, you were there. I could hide – behind you. I couldn't have done what you did. Quite simply, I don't have the strength."

"That's not true."

"Stamina, then, and that is true. All those weeks I was running, every now and then I had to stop, stay where I was and do nothing, think of nothing. I couldn't go on, not during those times, and I didn't question myself. I just knew I couldn't. You did; you could. As a child and as a man, and a price has to be paid for what you did . . . what was done to you. It will pass; it is passing."

"A child," said Havelock, glancing down at the stream below. "I see him, I feel him, but I don't really know him. But I remember him. When he was frightened or awfully hungry or tired and afraid to sleep, he'd climb a tree at daybreak and check for patrols. If there were none, he'd climb down and run through the fields as fast as he could, faster and faster and *faster*. After a while he felt good again, somehow – confident. Then he'd find a trench in a ravine or a deserted bombed-out barn and sleep. A six-year-old getting a shot of whisky, all that oxygen in his lungs. It worked, and that was the only thing that mattered. The fever went down."

Jenna touched his arm, studying his face and began to smile. "Run *now*, Mikhail. Run down the hill and wait for me, but run by yourself. Go on, you lazy thing! Run!"

He ran, his legs scissoring the air, his feet pounding the earth, the wind whipping his face and cooling his body, taking the breath from him, replacing it with new breath. He reached the bottom of the hill far below, his chest expanding with each gasp, quiet laughter coming from his throat. The fever was passing, soon it would be gone. Again.

He looked up at Jenna, the sun behind her, the blue sky above. He shouted between swallows of air. "Come *on*, you lazy *thing*! I'll race you back to the house. Our house!"

"I'll trip you at the last moment!" yelled Jenna, coming down the hill rapidly, but not running. "You know I can do it!"

"It won't do you any good!" Michael took out a bright metal object from his pocket. "I've got the key to the door. *Our* door!"

"Silly!" Jenna shouted, breaking into a run. "You didn't lock it! We've *never* locked it!"

She came to him and they held each other.

"We don't have to," he said. "Not any longer."